THE DOORS OF MIDNIGHT

ALSO BY R.R. VIRDI

TALES OF TREMAINE

The First Binding

THE DOORS OF MIDNIGHT

TALES *of* TREMAINE

R.R. VIRDI

TOR PUBLISHING GROUP
NEW YORK

This is a work of fiction. All of the characters, organizations, and events portrayed in this novel are either products of the author's imagination or are used fictitiously.

THE DOORS OF MIDNIGHT

Map by Priscilla Spencer

A Tor Book
Published by Tom Doherty Associates / Tor Publishing Group
120 Broadway
New York, NY 10271

www.torpublishinggroup.com

The Library of Congress Cataloging-in-Publication Data is available upon request.

ISBN 978-1-250-79618-9 (hardcover)
ISBN 978-1-250-79935-7 (ebook)

Our books may be purchased in bulk for promotional, educational, or business use. Please contact your local bookseller or the Macmillan Corporate and Premium Sales Department at 1-800-221-7945, extension 5442, or by email at MacmillanSpecialMarkets@macmillan.com.

First Edition: 2024

Printed in the United States of America

0 9 8 7 6 5 4 3 2 1

To Jim Hurd

For being another influential and inspiring Jim in my life. For teaching me a valuable lesson about life, and people: that all a marble needs is a little push, just some help, and it can journey around a very large table. And, that even if people try to knock it off its path, there are usually enough kind people out there who will help that marble get back on the road and give it another push just for good measure. Thank you for giving me that push, and always being there with the reminder that kind people exist.

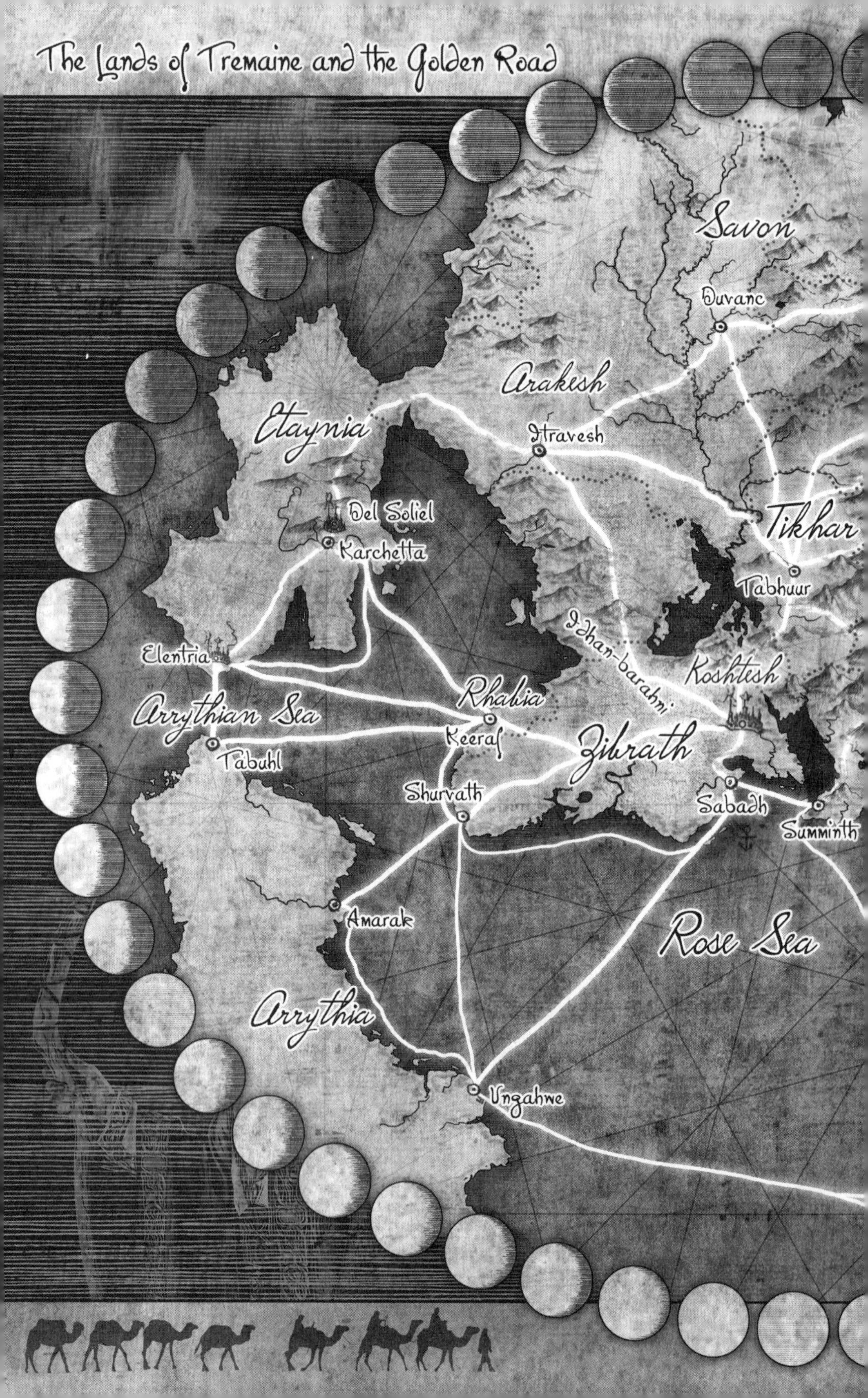
The Lands of Tremaine and the Golden Road
Savon
Duvanc
Arakesh
Etaynia
Itravesh
Del Soliel
Karchetta
Tikhar
Tabhuur
Idhan-barahni
Koshtesh
Elentria
Rhahia
Arrythian Sea
Keeraf
Zibrath
Tabuhl
Shurvath
Sabadh
Summinth
Amarak
Rose Sea
Arrythia
Ungahwe

To Jim Hurd

For being another influential and inspiring Jim in my life. For teaching me a valuable lesson about life, and people: that all a marble needs is a little push, just some help, and it can journey around a very large table. And, that even if people try to knock it off its path, there are usually enough kind people out there who will help that marble get back on the road and give it another push just for good measure. Thank you for giving me that push, and always being there with the reminder that kind people exist.

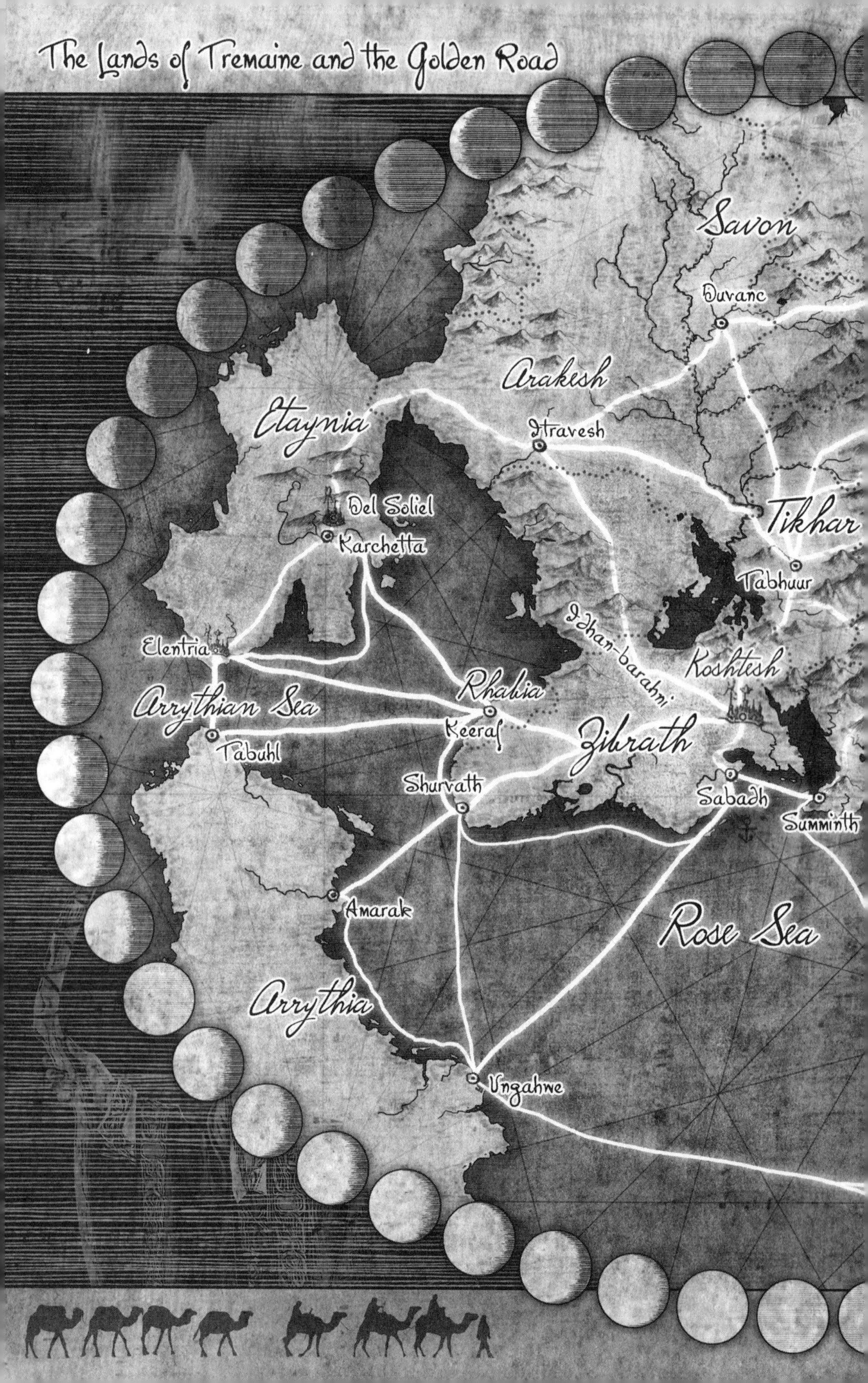
The Lands of Tremaine and the Golden Road
Savon
Duvanc
Arakesh
Etaynia
Itravesh
Del Soliel
Karchetta
Tikhar
Tabhuur
Idhan-barahmi
Koshtesh
Elentria
Rhakia
Arrythian Sea
Keeraf
Zikrath
Tabuhl
Shurvath
Sabadh
Summinth
Amarak
Rose Sea
Arrythia
Ungahwe

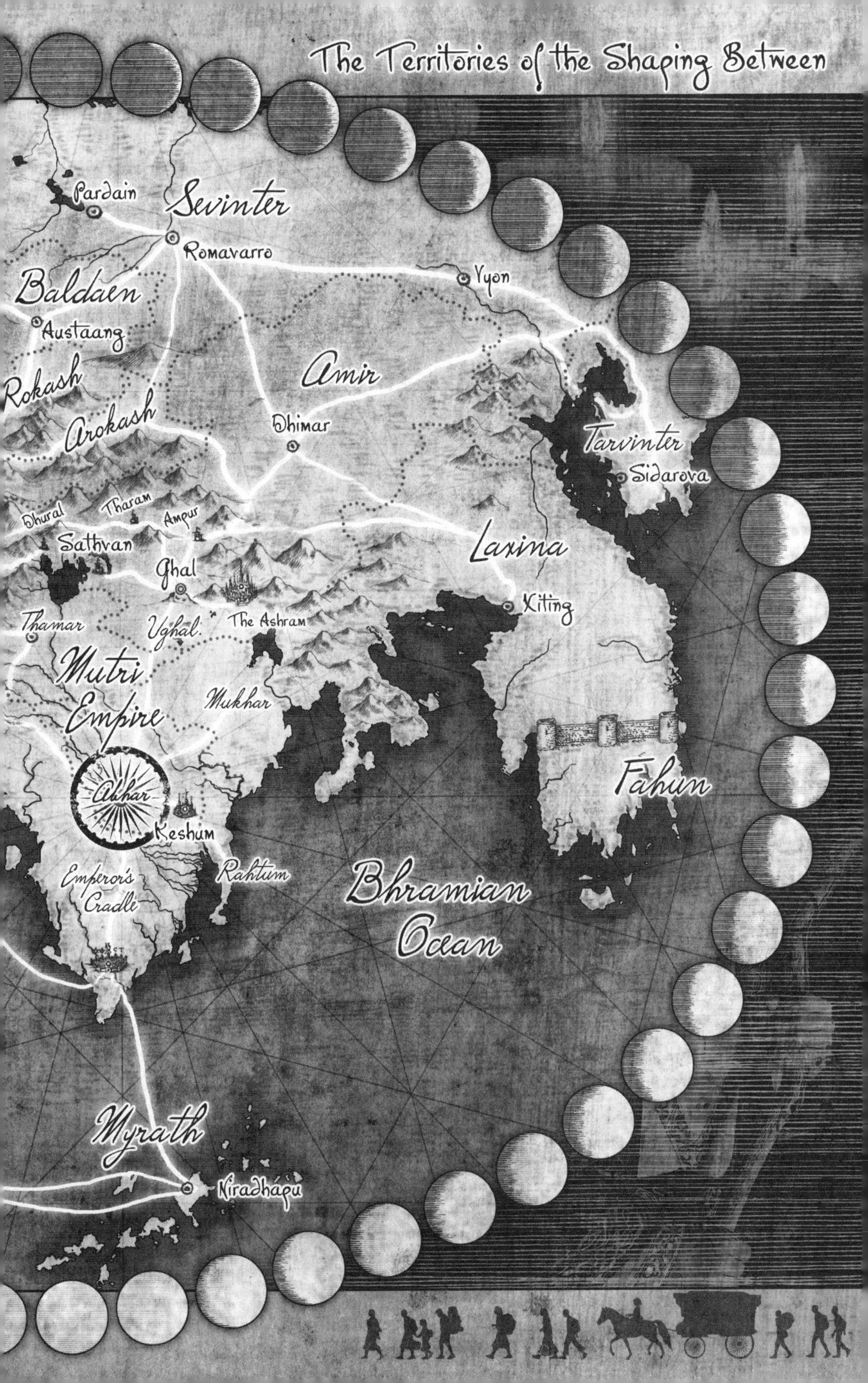

The Territories of the Shaping Between
Pardain
Sevinter
Romavarro
Yvon
Baldaen
Austaang
Rokash
Arokash
Amir
Dhimar
Tarvinter
Sidarova
Dhural
Tharam
Ampur
Sathvan
Ghal
Laxina
Xiting
Thamar
Vghal
The Ashram
Mutri
Empire
Mukhar
Abhar
Keshum
Fahun
Emperor's
Cradle
Rahtum
Bhramian
Ocean
Myrath
Niradhapu

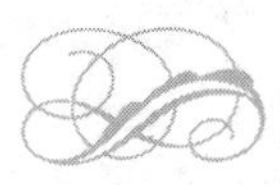

ONE

Stories in Stillness

I came to Etaynia in search of the most important thing in the world.

A story.

A secret—the sort best held and better kept from the world.

But I met with a prince instead.

The second the stories will say I've killed.

And I did not find the story I came looking for.

I wound up in the most dangerous one of all.

⁂

The prison was blanketed with the weight of stone, and its stillness. A silent-heavy assurance of what we would find in this place. It was the unmoving noiselessness of a place so deep down it has forgotten the sounds of the world above—knowing only the echoing quiet of things buried to be lost to memory. This was the soft-sullen silence of the weary who see no point bothering with speech as it has failed them all before.

It was a stillness found in the iron bars that knew nothing but the keeping of things inside. Long-rusted, as if to make their promise clear: The way would not open, no matter the protests of those within—no matter their efforts.

This was the unspoken prayer, muttered in thought only, full-apparent in the fingernail scratches along the rough stone of the cell floor.

And all the soundlessness of a man whose story might be coming to an end.

As once before, the stillness sat before me, waiting for me to do what I do and have done best.

Break it.

And so I did.

Because it was mine to break.

"My name is Ari, and I killed a prince of Etaynia." The words hung quivering in the air as if they themselves did not have the heart to disturb the quiet that had persisted in this place.

The other prisoners traded a look—the only one they had left to themselves. The long-hollow stare of men who have forgotten all the shapes the world has to offer. They knew only the cold and unblinking regard of stone. One of them traced lines through the air with his gaze—first over the bars of my cell, then over my cloak and cowl.

He was a man who had been hobbled by hard life well before his time, and the years in prison had done no favors to his body. Frail, knotted, and bent in a way that came just as much from pain in back as from the broken pieces inside. His cheeks had a pointed gauntness to them that spoke of little to eat and much less to live for. And the brown of his eyes had long lost whatever spark they once held. He raked fingers through his long hair as he spoke.

"Ari." His mouth moved as if chewing over the name—tasting something foreign. He spoke it again. Then a third time.

And the stillness returned in the space between words.

I said nothing, adding another layer to it as I used what little strength I could muster to pull my cloak around me. A steady band of torchlight filtered through a slit in the wall above, coming from the halls I'd been dragged through. It washed over the incarnadine fabric obscuring most of my body, painting it a brighter red. A color found fresh in blood.

The man who'd spoken now settled his gaze on my garment, his lips pressing tight. The hollow of his throat tensed visibly. "He wears a blood-red cloak." The words had no weight—whisper soft and short-lived.

Another man found the strength to throw his weight against the bars of his cell, using them more for support than anything else. "The one that killed a Shaen princess?"

The words brought an unseen fire to my heart and banded it with a heat none of the prison's cold stone could leach out of me.

"No," said a third man. He sat with his legs folded, hair hanging so low as to hide his face as he slumped. "He's the one called that storm down off the Rose Sea. A fury that laid low a fleet of ships, they say. Not a one survived." The man's stare weighed heavier as he regarded me.

The first of the trio took advantage of the pause to add his own piece to my legends. "Heard said he killed the emperor of Mutri . . . or was it a prince?" The man's lips pursed and eyes fluttered as if losing himself in thought. "They say he rescued Enshae from some Shaen lords, and for it, he earned their wrath."

I nodded. "They say that." I turned my attention to the lance of light coming through the wall. It resembled a rod—like something I could reach out and take hold of. The thought brought a crooked smile to my mouth that faded as a piece of memory came with it.

The second man rubbed his chin. "Been said he had some swords, no? Three." The man held up just as many fingers. "Magic. The sorts out of stories."

I said nothing.

"How's it go?" He knuckled his forehead and his gaze fell far away. "*He took a piece of morning light, then turned it into a sword burning bright? Then he blew a breath, light and thin, to shape a sword that held the wind within.*"

"No, no." The third man waved a hand and faced the second of the prisoners. "That's half wrong and only two. It goes like this: *With a word that no one heard, he pinched a piece of Solus' light, to make a sword that burned true bright. Then came the breath, whisper thin, to shape the sword with the wind within. Then there is the final sword. The one of brass and blood and jade. The one all cursed and wrong-made.*"

The trio turned on each other then. They bickered over the lay of the lines, though none found the proper wording.

I cleared my throat, then spoke for all to hear.

"With just a word,
one gone unheard,
he bound a blade // of pale morn light
without edge,
that burned full-bright
to cast back shadows,
far from sight.

With a second word then,
came the gossamer breath,
blown whisper thin,
to shape the sword // full-formless,
the wind within

And lastly there is the sword of jade
of brass, and stone, and blood it's made
twisted, tainted, cursed,
and still waiting for its price // to be paid."

The third speaker licked his lips, regarding his fellow inmates as if seeking approval to speak to me. "So, you don't happen to have any of them magic swords with you, then? Something to cut our way out of here, hm?"

"No, I suppose I don't." I raised upturned hands to show the utter lack of anything left to me.

No candle. No cane. Just the blood-red cloak, and my name.

"But you are him?" said the third man.

I inclined my head.

"All that. Princesses, magic swords, sinking ships, walking the Shaen lands. Heard some say he's kin to gods. Others that he's demon spawn. Heard him called Godsgrief once."

"I've heard that too." I brushed my cloak with my hands, seeking something to do with myself as I sat without my books and staff. Having traveled so long with those items now left me with an uneasy lightness in their absence.

"Fire and lightning. Doorways in the sky. So many stories." The third man exhaled and looked to the ground, tracing his finger against the tiles. "So, can you conjure a way out?"

I blinked. "What?"

"Break down these walls. Shatter the stones. Bend these bars."

Stone and steel were foreign to me, but fire was not. So I chose to show them what I knew.

I cupped my hands together, eyeing the empty space above my palms, envisioning where to set the ball of fire. The ring of fire at the heart of me came to mind and I fell into the folds. Just a small performance then. I could do that much, couldn't I?

"Start with whent, then—"

The third man burst into laughter and the folds slipped from me before I could even shape them. He slumped against one of the walls, his amusement growing louder. The others stared at him before getting the joke I didn't and joining in his merriment.

After a moment to take in the strangeness of those sounds in this place, I added a chuckle of my own. What else was there to do? And, if I could give these men even that little reprieve—at the expense of myself—well, why not?

The third man ground both palms against his eyes. "Solus, I haven't had a laugh like that in a long time. We lot haven't heard our own voices in . . ." He trailed off, frowning at the thought.

"Years, Matio. Years," said the second man. "They took our voices when they took our freedom. Took everything else too."

And the silence returned, and with it, the weary resignation the men had grown so accustomed to. Hopelessness serves as a better set of shackles than any metal.

But for a moment, I'd roused them out of it. And I would again, making them think it was their idea all along.

Because after losing our voices to whims of others, the most rebellious thing we can do is take them back. And every voice has something worth saying—hearing.

"What else have you heard?" The simple question would draw more out of them now that they'd begun.

The first man didn't hesitate. "Heard his name, for what it's worth to you, *sengero,* wasn't Ari. Been said it's Araiyo. Or was it Ariyo?" His face lost whatever clarity it had moments earlier. "Sorry to say, but he weren't one of you off-foreign folks. Stories say he's one of ours. I think."

The second man waggled a finger toward the first. "No, no. His name was Aram, or so I heard."

Stones filled my gut at mention of that name. They churned and ground against the core of me.

"Or was it Athwun? No, no, it *was* Ari, much like our friend here. Though I'm thinking you're more a storyteller whose tales grew a bit too tall for the crowd above, eh?"

I gave him a practiced smile. Thin as a razor and just as cold.

The second prisoner went on. "I know it for fact because I was there to see him, once."

"You what, Satbien?" Matio crawled closer to the bars that divided their cells. "You what? God's honest truth, tell me now, when and where were you anywhere near that man? I call you a liar."

The man named Satbien shrank a little. "Was close enough, wasn't I? Heard it from a friend who heard it from a friend of his who talked to a sailor who shared that man's ship. I swear it, I do." He gestured in front of his body in the same manner I'd seen others do when making silent prayer to Solus.

Matio waved him off and Satbien readopted the hollow sunkenness the man had kept to before.

My one chance then—a moment to be even a shadow of the storyteller I thought myself to be, and rouse them.

All I needed was a few simple words. "I believe you. What did you hear? Tell me."

It was enough.

And the prison soon carried the sounds of stories.

❧

"Ari stood on the deck of the large Zibrathi ship and knew a storm was a-comin'. But that weren't the worst of it, as much as a storm's a bad thing to face at sea. He'd been strung up on account of seducing the captain's daughter."

I smiled at the detail and wondered where it could have come from.

Voices echoed along the stone stairs above. Heavy thuds that meant boots clomping closer. Guards. We would have visitors soon enough, and I had an idea who they were keenest on seeing.

"On account of old sailor's law, the guilty gets one thing to say and the captain has to give 'em an honest hear of it. So, Ari says, 'If you drown me, you'll drown yourselves. I can see the way ahead as clear as I can see you now. A storm will come, and a ship will sail before it. A ship of ill omens. Red as the waters of the Rose Sea can be said to run.'"

"God above, what a lie, Satbien. Everyone knows the waters out there are as blue and green as ours. Maybe gray on some cold bad days. No such thing as red waters." Matio crossed his arms and legs, winding himself so tight I feared his old joints would lock in place like a knot wound too far in on itself.

"Go back to when you forgot you could speak, Matio. Can't bother with that? Then swallow your tongue. Let me say my piece." Satbien scooted closer to the front of his cell, now directing his performance at me and the other member of their trio.

"Now, a red ship ain't much of an omen. Any crew can paint their ship so, right?" The question lingered in the air and I realized he wanted an answer.

I gave him the simple pleasure and leaned forward, hands on knees. "What happened then?"

That did the trick and Satbien sat back, smug satisfaction plain across his face. A snap of his fingers punctuated the next line of the story. "They all took one look at the ship and realized it weren't painted red at all. It was what was coming off the ship. Smoke. Like there'd been a fire, and all aboard could see some embers still alight. Red, red as blood."

"*When the chimney smoke goes red as blood.*" Matio's words left him in a whisper. "*And comes the storm that brings the flood.*" Satbien nodded as Matio went on, and the third man watched in silence. "*Nuevellos*—the Nine."

Satbien gestured with a finger. "That's right. Ari and the crew had come across a ship with the *Nuevellos* on it. Now, the sailors of the crew weren't smart enough nor well-learned of the world to know what they looked at. But Ari knew. And seeing as he was the only one who knew what was happening—"

The footsteps loudened. Approaching men—the sort you didn't want visiting your quiet little cell on account they would likely ruin what little peace you had to yourself.

Satbien cast a look to the prison's entry, eyes wide and tongue peeking between his lips. He sucked in a breath and quickened the story. "Ari knew a great many things, and he knew that the men and women aboard the ship had no hope to survive the *Nuevellos* without him. So he took charge, didn't he? Commanded 'em with just a word, loud as thunder, and called down the same against the *Nuevellos.* Solus strike me down if it ain't true. He called fire and lightning on that ship and—"

Metal groaned, almost more in protest against the story than from its own age and neglected state. The door to the prison opened and the guards of Del Soliel entered.

Satbien gave us one last look—the stare of a desperate man uttering a final secret before the chance is taken from him once again. "And heard it told that no one survived but for him." He shut his mouth, and the other men followed his lead.

All of them turned away from me.

And the silence returned again, now waiting for someone else to break it. But it wouldn't be me.

Heavy boots beat against the stone of the prison floor, drawing a splash where water had worn down the ground and formed a puddle. Matio and the others adopted the looks of dogs long beaten into submissiveness. Their gazes fell low, not even taking in the feet of those walking by.

I never did learn to keep a supple spine. So I straightened and looked up, eyeing each of the approaching men.

Two guards, dressed unlike those who'd first tried to bar my way into Del Soliel. If they had armor, I wagered it to be linked mail hidden beneath their padded plum-colored jackets. They had matching pants the same shade and were cut from cloth too similar, and I didn't mean their clothing.

Twins?

The pair had trimmed their hair in identical fashion, short-cropped and tight in the manner of career soldiers. Lean, angular, and cold of face. But what took my attention the most was the long knife each wore at their side.

Odd choice of weapon for a guard. I reassessed the thought as soon as I'd finished it. *No, not guards. Something else.*

The man between them was the greatest oddity. A figure so thin I wondered if he only ate every third day, and then kept to just one meal. Just enough to stay alive. Were he not dressed as he was, I'd have thought him the lowest of paupers. A rake of a man in the clothes of the gentry.

He ran a thin finger under the length of his equally narrow mustache. It didn't suit him, especially under the crook of his long and curved nose. "Storyteller." The word left him as more accusation than greeting.

I gave him a lopsided smile. "I was, and then I never got to be, mostly on account of being locked in here before I had a chance to perform."

The slender man glowered, but his face couldn't lend any real menace to the stare. His brows looked more like scant lines traced in charcoal than real hair grown. Nothing about him spoke of severity. "I think you've performed enough, haven't you." It wasn't a question.

I kept silent, knowing it to be bait, and that nothing good would come of replying.

The man was set in his opinion before he'd stepped in to see me. And I knew on what his mind dwelt. After all, there could be only one thought.

But before he could speak, a smattering of whispers broke out in the cells behind them.

"The storyteller?" Satbien's gaze rose from where it had been fixed before. He didn't have eyes for the men in front of me, however. His look was for me alone.

Matio mirrored him, as did the last man. "*The* Storyteller? The red cloak. Of course. You're the Storyteller. That's why you started with all that talk of *him*." Matio rubbed the palm of a hand against his forehead, face nearly cracking into the smile of someone just catching a joke's meaning. "Solus. I swear. You had us going for a moment and I—"

"Quiet." The starved bird of a man turned on a heel and stared at the prisoners. "If you haven't forgotten how to still your tongues after all this time, then perhaps it's best I help you remember." He whirled and reached for one of the long knives on the belts of the twins. The sound of metal sliding out of a sheath filled the air, and then all eyes went to the length of silver catching what little light the prison held.

"Tongues"—the man waggled the blade—"do not grow back. Or so I'm told." He took a step toward Matio.

My mind tumbled into the folds. I saw and felt my voice bound to the very air around me—my atham, the space that I occupied greater than my own physical being. First two folds, then four. I saw a fishing-line-fine length of imaginary cord flow from the core of me and pass through my lips. It flowed outward, fraying into countless threads to spread through the room. Eight folds now, more than enough. "Start with Whent, then go to Ern."

Someone shuffled but I barely had ears for it, shutting the sound from my thoughts.

I stood straight, lunging and clasping my hands to the bars of my cell. "I am!" The two words cracked with the force of thunder in a cave, resonating through the prison with almost enough force to shake free stone and rattle iron.

Almost. But the performance had done the job.

The three men who'd come into the prison yelped and leapt back. The whole of their collective attention now fell on me, leaving none for the poor men who'd only just found their voices after far too long a time without them. Their chests heaved in unison and their eyes went wide as a child's caught in the act of making mischief.

The echoes of my voice died and a new stillness spread through the place. This one tremulous—shaking, and one we all knew could not last. In fact, it meant not to. It *wanted* to be broken. And the man who broke it would control the conversation to come.

So I seized it and spoke the words again. "I am." This time a whisper, just soft enough they couldn't be sure they'd heard me clearly. "I am the Storyteller. I've made lords and ladies cry with tales of daring heroes and tragic romances. I've set taverns and inns shaking with applause so loud heaven itself has heard the noise. I've been the guest of kings and princes and emperors alike. And I've held them, hearts and mind, all enraptured till the end of my tales. I've learned every story there is to know and told them back to men like you as if it's your first time hearing them.

"That's who I am. And that is why I came here." The last line was only half the truth, but it would have to do for now. For the whole of it would surely see me hanged even faster.

The thin man licked his lips, looking to the men at his side for support. It never came, and the knife shook in his hands.

"If you need someone to brandish that at"—I nodded to the blade in hand—"you can try me. It's not the first time a group of men have pointed blades my way. And I don't believe it will be the last." I found a candle flame's worth of heat in my heart and drew on it, willing it into my eyes as I glared at the men just beyond my bars.

The man with the dagger took the challenge and stepped close enough that his nose nearly touched the metal separating us. "I can assure you, murderer, it *will not* be the last. You killed a prince of Etaynia. An *efante. My efante.*" Each word came as quiet as a breath blown into the wind, yet fell with all the weight of lead hitting stone.

His *efante*. His prince. Brahm's blood and ashes, he must have served Prince Arturo. Voted for him in the election, and dreamed of seeing him king. A dream that had now died with the *efante*'s passing. "I'm sorry." I knew the words wouldn't do anything but spur the man into greater fury, but they were the truth, and a piece of him needed to hear it no matter how he'd take it.

He quivered in place. The knuckles of one hand going white as he squeezed the handle of the knife with more strength than a man of his build should have been able to manage. "You're sorry? You killed a prince of this country in cold blood, over tea, after he welcomed you into his company . . . and you're *sorry*?" His arm snapped out, thrusting the knife as far as he could into my cell. The point of the blade stopped just short of the hollow of my throat.

I did not move.

"No. You are not. But I swear it, by Solus, Etaynia, and Prince Arturo's rest, you will be." His lips trembled long after he'd finished speaking.

Then he took a slow breath, shutting his eyes until he'd regained his composure.

Most of it.

"I could kill you now. No one would know." He fixed me with a knowing look that told me it was more than mere temptation. A piece of him had already committed to the act and all that stood in the way was a set of iron bars.

"I would know." I kept from adding that the imprisoned men would know as well, lest it bring his ire back upon them. I had nothing to do with them being here, but a storyteller's job is to offer reprieve and escape to those who need it most. I could offer them a poor form of that in the moment, but I would do that much at least.

The man with the knife clenched and unclenched his free fist as if the muscles in his hand were in the throes of a bad spasm. "You think you're terribly clever, don't you?"

I gave him a thin curved smile—sharper than the edge of his knife, but with none of the malice in it. "I know I am. Clever, and terrible, in all the ways that can be. That has been my problem all my life." I lost focus for a moment and failed to see the men, the bars, and all the stone of the prison.

The man in front of me spoke, but I did not hear him. Nothing could reach me in that moment.

When clarity returned, it came with one last thought—a kindness I felt obliged to offer the well-dressed rake. "A piece of advice, friend. Don't swear promises on the name of a dead man. They never go well. They're rarely fulfilled. And they don't bring the dead back . . . or any satisfaction."

My words reached the wrong part of the man, for he threw his open hand against the bars, taking one in his grip and wrenching at it. If he had the strength, I'm sure he would have torn the metal free and sunk his knife through my ribs. But the iron held firm and his grip slackened. Some of the color waned from his face and his collar darkened with sweat seeping into the fabric.

"My name is Ernesto Vengenza. Remember it. Keep it in your mind, now and until the end. I want you to know there is a knife to haunt your dreams. That this knife is waiting to find your heart. And I want you to know the name of the man who will put it there." Ernesto didn't return the blade to the man he'd taken it from and turned to leave. The pair at his side gave me one last look before following suit.

You're in line behind a great many others. I hope you're content to wait your turn.

The door to the prison shut.

The silence returned.

And this time, no one tried to break it.

TWO

Things Best Left Forgotten

It would have disappointed Ernesto Vengenza to know that I slept like a rolling stone that had finally come to a heavy rest.

A shame it wasn't meant to last.

Something clacked at the edge of my hearing—slow, rhythmic—a pattern. I blinked half-awake and tried to shut the sound out.

It loudened, then took on a metallic edge, like stone against the flat of a blade.

"Hsst." The sharp whisper just reached me. "Hsst."

I groaned, my body protesting against the unforgiving prison floor. "It is a terrible thing to wake a man from his sleep before he's decided to rouse himself."

Something clattered near me, eliciting sharp cracks as it bounced closer before stopping.

The stone looked as large as one of my knuckles, and all its irregularity let me know its story. A longer look told me the rest. It had been a piece of the floor of Matio's cell. Once.

Once it had been laid flat—a piece of a larger piece and meant to remain solid-still. It had been set with care. It had been shaped and given purpose. To sit. To hold. To be silent. It wasn't supposed to make noise. It wasn't meant to know motion.

Now it did. And it grew restless from it—for it.

I picked it up, bouncing it once in my palm before tossing it underhand toward Matio's cell. It arced overhead in a manner I'd once grown familiar with, then long-forgotten.

Matio clapped his hands together over the stone—the sound reverberating through the prison with much needed noise. He looked like a child that had just done something he'd been expressly warned not to and expected punishment quick to come. But it never came, so Matio grinned and tossed the stone back to me.

My mind went to the folds. To the Athir and the atham. I recalled stones soaring over my skull, promising to crack into it if my will—my faith—wasn't strong enough. Every image showed the rock sailing harmlessly by. My mouth moved, remembering old words and giving them voice. "There are ten bindings all men must know. One for Tak. Another for Roh." I caught myself in the moment and let my thoughts go.

The focus and clarity left, as did my hold on the folds. One of my hands blurred and snatched the stone out of the air.

"What was that you were muttering then?" Matio tilted his head toward me.

I looked to the stone, turning my hand sideways so it rolled out of my palm and onto the floor. "Nothing. Just something better left forgotten." I cleared my throat and looked back at Matio.

He held my stare for a count of ten before finally shying away, but I'd seen the thoughts behind his eyes. He wanted to ask something more. Another passing moment of quiet before he found a question to give voice to. "He called you the Storyteller."

I nodded. "He did. I am. You heard it all right."

Matio grunted and looked to Satbien. The two shared the glance and came to some silent conclusion between themselves. Whatever they traded was enough to prompt Matio to speak again. "So, do you know any tales of *him*? You took his name and place earlier, but what do you know of him?"

Matio didn't need to elaborate. There was only one "him" worth telling tales about. And that Ari lived a life far beyond what many could believe. Certainly more than they could believe I had.

I inclined my head. "I do. But the three of you seem to have some of your own about Ari. How about we trade? I'll tell you a tale for a tale. Give me your best story about Ari—demon spawn, god-kin, or Godsgrief, and whatever else you may have heard."

And they did.

❧

"Heard this bit long ago. Longer before the years I got to doing things best left undone—the sort of things that get a man in a bind like this." Matio touched the prison bars. "Clean away the fluff of what Satbien told you about Ari. He didn't sail no seas nor call any storms over 'em. I'll tell you the truth of it now. He was a man who lit the fire some say still burns to this day." Matio let a pause hang in the air before continuing.

"Happens out there—far, far as can be from this place Solus blessed to be our home. A place of golden sands and not a drop o' water. No rains. A place where man goes days without slaking a thirst that needs tending to. And he'll die there. Burning hot in the morning. Freezing cold at night. A place any good god would have forgotten, and only fools live. But they do live there. Veiled riders—murderers and thieves out in the sands of Zibrath. They butcher their own as they do anyone else.

"A place of hard stone, and not much in the way of eating. And ain't nothing growing there. Nothing." Matio cut through the air with a hand that signaled finality. "And, they ain't ever will be. Not after *he* got done with the place."

I straightened now, lending a sharper ear to what Matio had to say.

"Ari went out to the sands for a debt needing paid. Some say it was to win the hand of the daughter of one of those savage chiefs that wander the desert. And those who know more than most men"—Matio stopped short and tapped a knowing finger to his nose—"say he went out there looking for a secret.

"Ari ventured out deep into the sands, the place run by a band of cutthroats, bad as any, called the Wolves. And, if this weren't bad enough, Ari was on the run from another group of thieves he'd run afoul of earlier. The Hundred Thieves. Set on from two sides, man didn't have much else to do but hope to lose them in the desert. Or so he thought, but he ran into even worse trouble there."

"What?" The interruption came from third man.

"I'm getting to that, aren't I, Jencarlo?" Matio cleared his throat and looked to all of us with a sweeping stare. "He ran into the band of one of them desert kings. All in black, riders of death, don't you doubt me. Men who hunt with birds and bows, but it's not game they're after. No. It's a different sort of meat." Matio narrowed his eyes and gave us another long look.

Jencarlo swallowed. "You don't mean . . . ?"

Matio nodded, somber and silent as old dark stone. "I do. See, not much out there for them to eat. So what's them to do but hunt for folk like me and you? But Ari was a clever man. He struck a bargain with their leader. See, Ari knew all the stories of the world, and he offered them in trade for the desert king's tired men. A tale a night. And every night he told a tale worth telling was another he was spared from being sent off to hell. So Ari went on for a hundred days and a hundred nights. Giving himself what time he could.

"First, he spent it looking for a way to escape. But their desert's a wide and treacherous thing. And so are the people. Ari knew this, and as the sets passed, he knew that they had no mind for letting him go. So he went to working on getting their trust. He learned to hunt and hawk with them. He learned to ride, to cross their sands near as well as the folk born there. He learned how to use their bows and walk by starlight. And he learned how to fight their enemies."

Jencarlo broke into the gap between words. "I recall something 'bout that Ari. You was wrong earlier, Satbien, 'bout his cloak, that is. It weren't no blood-red thing—all grim and mighty macabre. S'truth of it is this: He wore a cloak of all pure white. Of scales and stars and old moonlight. Something shining a silver all noble bright. S'truth. Blood-red—atch!" Jencarlo spat.

Matio crossed his arms and shot both his prison mates a long heated glare. "When you two are done trying to trip me up in telling this, let me know, *sieta*? Otherwise, I'm fit to find myself down here for another bout of years on account of knocking all your teeth out."

No one spoke, and Matio continued.

"Now, Ari had earned himself a proper spot in this desert king's followers. Some'd say he was as close to this man as his own right hand. And it proved no truer than the day the wolves of that desert came looking to make trouble. The sort that don't end too well for those on the other end of it . . . if you take my meaning.

"Now, the leader of this band of wolves was something more terrible than any of those wandering sand-folk. Trust me on that. Said he was half mortal. A beast in the shape of a man—as far as a thing could be from Solus and his good grace. And Ari knew this. So he rallied the desert king's army and led them into battle. A fierce thing it was. Shattered spears and splintered shafts. Arrows staking already fallen men. And that weren't the worst of it. See, Ari and this desert wolf bandit got to fighting the way only the stories can speak of. With magic." Matio sucked in a breath and held it, like he was trying hold any noise from us with the action.

Content that he'd dragged the quiet out long *enough,* he exhaled. "The bandit let loose a cry that shook the world. S'truth. He tore up sand and earth. Called down a terrible storm. But it didn't stop Ari. He met him and called back just as much and worse still. He called fire. Something so hot it burned under a storm not even God Himself would put on this world. A fire so hot they say it could have come from only one place: hell."

It was now Satbien's turn to suck in a breath and hold it. He gave Matio a look that said he didn't believe him. Not entirely, at least. A piece of him wanted to. And that much shone clear in his eyes. "Then what?"

Matio grinned. "Then the fire took root. It burned, so heavy and hot it turned the sands to glass. Glass they say is still there—just like the fire. Still burning. A door to hell. And the foul things that call it home. See, when Ari did that magic, he opened something best left shut. And Solus cursed him from that day to the end of his days."

Did he now? I fought to keep a small smile from spreading across my face.

"And what Ari had done was a horrible scar on the world, and so the world tried to punish him for it. Even the sun couldn't bear to look on what he'd done. So then came the moon, blocking the view. She came and put a shadow on the world that day, and masked the horror from the sun himself. But bad things happen on days cast in the shadow of the moon."

"What bad things?" Jencarlo pressed himself up against the bars of his cell almost like he had half a mind to force himself through them. "What happened, Matio?"

The man telling the story shrugged. "Don't know, do I? I look like someone stupid enough to be venturing out so far from home? Dabbling in things best left undabbled? No." He brushed his hands against his chest. "Not for me. Not ever. And I've got no shame in telling you this: I don't want to know. Whatever happens to men like that and on days even the sun can't shine on our world? Those things are best left forgotten. Never known. Hard enough to sleep when you're stuck here." Matio gestured to our surroundings. "You know what it'd be like to sleep with those kinds of thoughts in your head?"

I do. I kept the answer to myself, however.

"Besides, it don't matter too much, does it? Ari got swept up that day to a place hung between the sun and the moon's shadow. Some say he still came back after, but it weren't all him. Something came back inside of him. Something foul. Fouler than whatever he'd been before. And that now, if he's still alive, he's more a monster in a man, than a man with a sliver of a monster inside of him."

A thousand words crossed my mind, all fighting to come out in response. Then a thousand more. And all of them were wrong. I clapped instead, slow, steady, and forced the smile from earlier across my face now. "I've heard the same. That he's a monster, I mean." A little laugh punctuated the end of what I'd said.

"Man would have to be, no? You don't hear much good about Ari, when you do at all. Though, suppose he's not the only one out there with stories like that. Half a dozen men have done just as bad, or worse." Matio shrugged.

"Or better. But people don't remember those stories. Not often." I thought I'd kept my words low enough to go unheard.

"What was that?" Matio leaned toward me, cupping a hand to one ear.

I shook my head. "Nothing. Just talking to myself."

Matio inclined his head and pursed his lips in an almost sage-like manner. "Places like this, still and silent, with enough time, send a man to doing that. Solus knows the lot of us have done it ourselves—"

"Once we couldn't talk to each other anymore, that is." Jencarlo rubbed a hand against his mouth. "Eventually, though, we forgot how to talk altogether. Or so I thought."

The trio of men exchanged a long, silent look, and, for a moment, I thought the weight of the prison and its memories had silenced them once again.

But there is always a price for memories. And they can break a man.

I cleared my throat and spoke. "Thank you for that story, Matio. I don't often get to play the part of audience in my line of work. I appreciated it."

The Etaynian prisoner opened his mouth, then froze—searching for words that wouldn't come. He pressed his lips tight together and nodded instead.

It wasn't a stretch to guess that it had been many years since someone thanked him for something in earnest.

More footsteps sounded against the stone, and anything anyone else might have wanted to say now died with the promise of new visitors. Old ghosts revisited the trio of men. Their faces sank—stares going long and hollow. But not for long. The three men remembered the freshly given gift of their own sounds. And they sat straighter, heads held high. And while they did not speak, no longer were they cowed—broken as before.

I might have let myself smile at that.

No story is without magic. Even if it is a small one.

The door to the prison opened with a low moan, as if the hinges protested so many visitors passing through in one day.

Faint firelight caught along the brightest threads of the newcomer's overcoat. Every strand of gold flickered better to life under the glow, and the red lion embroidered on his clothing seemed to carry a shine of its own. A mask, fashioned from what looked like silvery ivy, obscured part of the man's face. Some of his dark hair clung to the side of his scalp with a wetness that could have been from rain, or sweat. And he held a leather satchel in one of his hands.

I'd met him the night before Eloine had come to my rooms in Del Soliel. I stood and offered him the customary greeting due someone of his position. A full bow from the waist. "Prince Artenyo."

The prince's mouth worked in silence, like he hadn't quite decided what to say. He found the words the next moment. "Storyteller. It seems perusing our library wasn't enough for you."

I gave him a hapless smile. "Would you believe that it was better than I'd hoped for? It's been quite the while since I've had access to a library like that."

His lips pressed tight again—a gash in stone. Prince Artenyo drew out the pause between us, and none of the other prisoners dared look at the man. He took a deep breath, some of the stiffness leaving his shoulders. "I wanted to see you before the others came."

The others. So many things that could mean, and he didn't bother to elaborate. So I settled the simple question then. "Why?"

"To know." Prince Artenyo took a half step toward me, placing himself just before the bars. That took confidence, or foolishness. All it would take was one quick step and I could reach through the gaps of my cell to grab hold of the man. That line of thought led me to realize there was a third option behind the prince's action.

I crossed the distance between us best I could, putting myself just on the other side of him. A few lengths of iron separated us now.

Prince Artenyo's eyes remained steady as he stared at me from behind the mask. "Did you do it? Did you kill my brother?"

Had I killed a prince of Etaynia? I had certainly wanted to. Only, the wrong one had died. I'd come to the country for a story, and in hopes of finding one of the Tainted. A person so far twisted and turned that they were as close to monsters as a person could become. A shadow deep in them that steered them toward wrongdoing, even when they believed they were right.

Few things are as dangerous as man doing evil that he believes is for the best good.

I met his gaze, and hoped mine held as much steel as his. "No."

He watched me for a moment, then exhaled.

And I knew I'd been right. "You didn't think I did either, did you?" I motioned to the door barring my way. "You wouldn't have put yourself within arm's reach of a killer if you had." I sent a hand between the bars slowly until it rested before the man's heart.

He looked down at it, then me. "I wouldn't say that, Storyteller." Prince Artenyo brushed aside a part of his coat to reveal a long knife that rested there. "It would have been an easy thing to have pulled that and ended the affair that's still to come." He reached out with his other hand, taking mine in a firm grip before I had a chance to respond. "But, no, I don't think you did. Where did the poison come from? You didn't have it on you."

I arched a brow but the prince went on.

"Your belongings were searched whenever you ventured from your room. You're surprised to hear this? You were a guest in our home, but a stranger—a foreigner. And we are hosting a great many nobles at this time. You can't fault us for our curiosity or security."

I couldn't.

Prince Artenyo raised the bag he'd come in with. He opened it, drawing out a book. One I knew all too well. Because it belonged to me. Much like the one my mentor Mahrab had given to me all those years ago. "What is this, Storyteller?"

"It's a book—a story."

The prince pursed his lips, clearly not used to receiving dismissive answers like that. "*Whose* story is in there?"

"Someone better left forgotten. A painful story. Someone whose story deserves to be locked away." Every word I spoke was true. This was not a story to be shared with just anyone. One to be freely opened and given away. This was a story meant for locking away, and keeping from the world. I turned my gaze away from him and onto Matio. The man watched us with quiet interest, no longer bent, or broken.

Good.

The prince frowned, and placed the book back inside the bag. "Well, I'd like to think I can take decent measure of a man when I meet him. I think a few things about you, yes. But I don't count murderer among them. And that should matter, since a trial is to come. One in which I, among others, will be judging you for the murder of my brother."

Of which, I noted, he didn't seem that heartbroken over. I kept that thought to myself, however.

We all grieve in our own ways, even if we don't always show it.

"I would spend what free time you have on the task of proving your innocence, Storyteller. We do not treat murderers well in Etaynia. Even worse, those who spill royal blood."

Curiosity took the better of me and my tongue. "And what do you do to those who do that?"

The smile Prince Artenyo had been holding back finally broke through, pulling his mouth to one side at a sharp angle. His teeth showed when he spoke, and I noticed his canines. "You know, I can't recall. It's been so long since we've caught someone behind an *efante*'s murder. I confess a part of me is intrigued to see what would be done to you."

And like that, my curiosity was sated. A shame the answer brought no satisfaction.

"Farewell, Storyteller. We'll be seeing each other again." And then he left.

Once gone, the prisoners broke into a low clamor, all asking for me to honor our earlier bargain.

"Hoy, come on, Storyteller," urged Matio.

Satbien chimed in with a hooting cry of support.

And Jencarlo slapped a hand to one of his thighs.

I had given them the gift of sound—of story. Now they ached for it—for more. They could not wholly return to the shadows of themselves that they had been.

And while I had promised them a tale of my own, there were no more stories that day. They, like many other things, were things best left forgotten.

THREE

Exchanges

I lost track of all time in the dark, letting my mind wander until it had no place to go but for the candle and the flame. The old practice took hold of me. A flicker of flame blossomed to life within my thoughts, and I fed it everything: my fears, doubts, the lingering questions of what was to come. And it steadied me.

I reached deeper then, to the folds of my mind. I had nothing to fill them with but longed for their old familiarity, and hoped they would help me figure out what to do next.

But they never came.

Then came the sound of heavy boots, and the promise of more visitors.

Again . . .

I opened my eyes to find an array of guardsmen. All of them with their backs turned to me.

One of the men pulled free a ring of keys, thumbing through them until he found the one he'd been looking for. He slipped it into the lock of Matio's cell, then opened the door. No words were exchanged as some of the men went in to hoist the prisoner to his feet and drag him out. The guards repeated the process, taking Satbien next, and finally Jencarlo. Once they might have accepted the rough treatment without protest. Now each man voiced incoherent cries, a few curses about the parentage of the guards, and made feeble attempts to shake free.

So I spoke for them. "What are you doing? Where are you taking them?"

The guard who held the ring of keys turned to face me. He had a face hewn from rough stone. Large, solid, and with no flattering lines to it. His hair had been shaved close to his skull, leaving nothing but dark stubble behind. And a heavy, serious brow made his eyes appear darker and more menacing than they were in truth. "To be questioned."

"About what? From what I gather, no one's spoken to them about anything in years, except for bringing them their food. What could you possibly have to ask them about now?"

"You." He said nothing else, leaving with the three men I'd barely come to know.

Then, nothing. The door to the prison shut. And I sank to my knees.

For a while, I did nothing but stare at the empty cells. It did nothing to soothe the storm brewing inside me. So I did the only thing I could.

I grabbed hold of the bars and wrenched. The thunder that had built inside me finally asked to be let out, and I obliged. I screamed. Pulled on the bars as if I could tear them free. The curses that left my mouth would have offended every god and goddess across the world, had they the ears and desire to hear me.

But they didn't.

Finally, strength left me, and I felt like a water skin wrung dry.

I slumped against the cold iron, wanting to reach back inside myself and find a piece of the Ari that knew what to do.

Low and steady humming filled the air and I opened my eyes to spot the source. It came from just beyond the door into the prison, but what brought me pause was that I knew that voice.

The door opened and Eloine walked through . . . accompanied by two armed men.

They didn't cross the prison's threshold. Eloine motioned with a hand and said something I couldn't catch. The guards exchanged frowns, but didn't argue, remaining in place like they were fixtures of the prison itself.

Eloine saw me and smiled.

Even in this place, that look brought a spot of warmth to me.

She wore a dress as dark as night from head to toe. It lacked any of the vibrancy and trimmings of the clothes she'd worn before, but even still, she looked nothing short of breathtaking. We locked eyes, and I noticed the green of hers looked faded—closer to gray tinged with sage.

"Well, this is a far cry from where we last spent time together." Her smile vanished and she looked at me like someone coming across a starved kitten. "How are you?"

"Well, they haven't killed me . . . yet. So there is that."

"And they won't." Something hardened in Eloine's gaze. Her eyes reminded me of pine boughs then, and they held a heat that would have been appreciated down in the cold of the prison. "You won't rot in here."

"This isn't the first time I've been locked away."

Her glare intensified, and something told me facing the trial would be less an ordeal than pushing Eloine further.

So I stopped. Never let it be said I cannot learn.

She reached through the bars of my cell with one hand, moving it toward my face.

One of the guards stepped through the doorway—fist going tight against the hilt of a sword. "Lady—"

Eloine whipped her head toward the man. "Do not speak. Do not worry. Step back where you came from. He won't hurt me." She turned back to me, her face a mask but for her eyes. They glimmered with a light of mischief. "Will you?" Her hand drew closer.

I bared my teeth. "I have been known to bite." That did nothing to stop her as her hand came to rest on my cheek. I winced as her fingers took hold of one corner of my mouth and she tugged lightly. "Ow."

She didn't pull her hand away, massaging my cheek in an attempt to assuage some of the pain. "When I want you to lighten your heart, you're dour. When you should be serious, you make jokes. Has anyone ever taught you how to behave appropriately for the moment?"

I opened my mouth to speak, but she clamped her hand over my lips, pressing tight.

"I didn't think so."

I glared.

Eloine let out a breath and pulled her hand away. "Ari, what are you going to do?" She cast a quick look at the two men standing outside the doorway. "Word has spread well past the palace. The town knows Prince Arturo is dead, and soon the whole of the country. They'll think you did it whether it's true or not."

Which made me wonder one thing. "And what do you think, Eloine?"

Her eyes widened and she looked at me like I'd slapped her. Eloine leaned close and stared at me with an intensity that could have scoured the prison stone clean. "You have a lot of nerve to ask me that. Especially after . . ." She trailed off, one corner of her mouth folding under her teeth as she chewed on it for a second.

I waited for her to say it—our kiss. But she never did.

"If I had thought you'd done it, I wouldn't be here. I'd be gone—far as anyone could be from this place. No matter what I—" She caught herself and stopped short of saying whatever had been there at the tip of her tongue.

"What you . . . what?" I kept all expectation and want free from my face, slipping back behind an old mask I'd learned long ago. Perfect placidness. The surface of an undisturbed lake, betraying nothing about its depths.

"Nothing." Eloine looked away from me, adopting a stare I'd grown too familiar with of late. The same one the prisoners had used when looking somewhere but at nothing as well. The one I'd been using just moments ago.

I watched her, hoping to find a way to bring the conversation back to where it had been. A part of me wished for more. To speak as we'd done at the masquerade. Anything but the dancing around without words we were doing now.

Eloine finally turned her gaze back on me. Her mouth opened, then closed. Finally, she spoke. "What's your plan?"

I arched a brow.

She ran one of her hands against an iron bar, trailing its length. "To get free?"

"I don't have one? What do you want me to do?"

Her look was answer enough. It held expectation. The demand for me to live up to all I had been—that the world thought me to be, from the tales I'd spread myself.

I laughed. "Shall I bend the bars to my cell and walk free? No—better. Shatter stone and command the very tops of this palace to fall, much like a mountain long ago and far away, yes?"

Eloine's eyes narrowed. "Don't. Don't do that to me. I've seen what you can do. I remember the night the clergos came."

I sighed. "So do I. And that very nearly brought us a host of trouble we can't afford now."

A hint of the old smile returned to the curves of her mouth. But just a hint. "'We' now? I suppose I could leave. After all, I'm not the one bound by bars."

"I suppose you could. So why don't you then?"

Eloine stiffened. "For a moment I almost believed you wanted me gone."

A part of me thinks it'd be for the best. And the rest of me hates even the thought of it. The temptation took me then to tell her so. That it would be better for us both if she left. But another look at her face swept the idea from me.

Her anger fled, and she reached through the bars again. This time taking my hand within hers. "If I did that, where else would I get the story I've been promised?"

I couldn't help but let a breath out through my nose in lieu of a proper laugh. "Still after that? Why?" I didn't give her a chance to answer, however. "It's not so much a story, and maybe I'm not so much as I've claimed." A silence filled the space between us until I spoke again. "I told them, you know?" I motioned to the empty cells across from me. "The three men imprisoned here. Told them my name. Who I was. You know what they did?"

Eloine shook her head.

"They laughed. It . . . was a good sound to hear in this place. I know they needed to hear themselves do that—remember that they could. But, all the same, they laughed at me when I told them." I gave her a thin smile—porcelain smooth and practiced, and just as brittle-hollow. "They asked to see a small piece of magic, and I failed to show them that."

"The price for your art. Telling stories as well as you have—spreading them and passing your legends off. If not for this—losing the real Ari to a host of other names and stories, then what? Wasn't this the point, to lose your true self and walk hidden among others? To be so great a myth that the real man vanishes—a thing unbelievable?" Eloine's voice held no reproach, nor the soothing tones you'd expect in the moment. Just matter-of-fact.

I gave her a weak nod. "And I've done that well enough that most moments I believe it too. Maybe it's better that way."

Eloine exhaled and squeezed my hand hard enough to build a dull pressure through the small bones of my limb. "I'm sure you've thought that for a long time. Long enough. But there was a time things were different—you were. Tell me of it."

I looked at her, then the guards. "I think maybe people have heard enough about me today. Besides, I wonder what they'll do if they overhear even a piece of my true story. They'll skip my trial and go straight to execution."

Eloine pulled her hand from mine and turned without missing a beat. She went over to the guards, speaking so low I couldn't make out even a whisper. The guards frowned—one took a step closer to her, raising a hand in protest. She met him unmoving as stone before waves. He broke first, relenting and stepping back, head bowed a shade in what could have been a silent apology.

A piece of me wished terribly to know what she'd told them to have both men obey her like that.

Eloine moved toward the prison door where the guards lingered, shutting it behind her. "There. A piece of privacy for us. And for that, I do believe a fair exchange is continuing your story."

I couldn't help it. My mouth pulled to one side in a lopsided smirk. "Are we trading favors, then? What am I getting out of this?"

"A chance to spend more time with me. Time to think of a way out of this, maybe a chance to remember the Ari who could. And I'd very much like to see more of that Ari."

Something stirred inside me when she said my name. It was like the first true steady breath given to a flickering flame that had nearly lost hope at fanning into something larger. The bit of wind to keep it burning so that it may grow.

I nodded, not trusting myself to reply. She had a point, of course. But the Ari who could do those things was not someone to be taken lightly. And I told her this. "You want me to remember a person I've convinced the world it's better off forgetting. There are reasons why. And if you ask me to remember, you might not like what you find."

She gave me a look as hard and resolute as stone. "Why don't you let me be the judge of that? Just tell your story. Tell me."

I exhaled in resignation. "I suppose I don't have anything better to do. Where did we leave off?"

Eloine seized the opening left in my breath. "You'd bound fire, burned Nitham, and nearly been set for execution by the Ashram's laws."

I cocked a brow and tilted my head at one side of the prison. "Not much has changed." A small smile played across my face, but she had no eyes for it, going on as if I hadn't spoken.

"You'd celebrated your promotion in rank with your friends, as well as avoiding punishment by personally training under the Master Binder. And the season was coming to an end."

"The end of one part of a story is how you get to the beginning of another. So maybe that's the best place to begin. Past the *mostly* quiet sets of time I spent lingering somewhere between what had happened and what was to come. To the beginning of learning more of the secrets behind the ten bindings. To debts being called due. To walking paths best left forgotten and calling things best left uncalled. To my once-white shining cloak.

"Yes. That is the place to start. The Ashram. A place of learning the wonders of the world, and more than that—magic. The sort found in storybooks. I had a home, though I didn't give it nearly the love and respect it deserved then. I'd made friends.

"And enemies. I'd always been gifted in stealing and quickness of tongue, and with those gifts, stole more trouble and attention than any young boy ever should have. I can't say I'd have done things differently knowing what I know now. I was proud, clever, and, in many ways, hurt. Not a safe combination for a child who'd learned the things I had by then. Or made the promise I had. This is the time when one of the many oaths I've sworn over my life would be tested, and called in full.

"It is the story behind The Ghost of Ghal. And his many myths. Unstruck, Unharmed, Unfallen. It is a story of doors best left unwalked through, and how I lived up to the mantle of Unburned once again. And it is a story of the first time I would earn the name 'devil.' Do you still want me to continue?"

Eloine didn't have to say the word, but she spoke it all the same.

And I might have loved her more for it.

"Yes."

FOUR

Troubles Made

Winter's full weight had come over Ghal. My first season at the Ashram had ended, and I enjoyed a peaceful break in the sets before the next.

A rarity for me. Especially since Nitham gave me a wide berth. At least, for a while.

Whispers had spread quickly through the Ashram, like a fire through a straw field. And if you listened carefully, you'd hear just the edges of new stories taking shape.

Stories about me. Of battling a monstrous serpent, God Himself, high atop the mountains of Ampur. Burying the village and the beast in my wrath.

Of the boy who'd bound fire and let it loose on Nitham, burning him, as well as parts of the Ashram's stone. Some even said they caught sight of me sending a roaring wave of bright flame to swallow another figure. A man. Possibly one of the rishis. But the festival had people deep in their drink, and eyes fixed to the wild and wonderful whimsy made with fireworks, merriment, performers, and more. My spectacle hadn't lasted long, however.

After all, a violent storm had broken out and doused the flames. But people remembered enough. They remembered the boy who'd called fire.

And they remembered that I was Sullied. Born as low as one could be.

Nitham would remind me he hadn't forgotten, and that he would make me pay for the troubles I'd given him.

I left the Rookery early that morning, having fed Shola—making sure my flame-colored kitten had his royal needs met. My stomach, however, made clear it needed tending to as well. So I rushed toward Clanks, the Ashram's food hall.

But I stopped in the main courtyard when I caught sight of a figure shambling my way.

Their hood had been turned up against the cold breeze, and they moved with the gingerness of someone who'd injured a leg, wishing not to further aggravate their body with each step.

A chance gust of wind rolled through, throwing back their hood to reveal a young man just a few years older than me. His hair was long-tousled-midnight—

waves falling past his shoulders. Sallow-cheeked and hard-jawed, with deep-set eyes of powdered jade. A color not commonly found in Mutri people.

The makings of a bruise showed on one side of his face, its purpling just visible against the color of his face. A shade of ochre darkened by a brush of rich red clay.

"Valhum?" I moved closer to the student.

He whipped his head toward me with all the skittishness of an alley cat freshly come upon by a threat. "W-what?" He recoiled a step, eyes going wide.

"Brahm's blood, man, it's me, Ari."

That did not help calm him. . . .

He backpedaled. "I don't want any more trouble." Valhum raised his hands as if trying to ward off a threat.

I stopped in place, repeating what he'd said to myself. *Any more?* "What happened to you? You look like you were beaten?"

He gave me a thin, sorrowful smile. It was then I realized my guess might have been truer than I'd first thought. One corner of his lip had swollen, and I might have just spotted the fresh touch of blood still lingering in his mouth.

Brahm's tits.

Valhum rubbed the back of a hand against his lips, wincing as he did.

I reached toward him. "We should get you to the Mendery. Come on."

He waved me off. "N-no. I'll take myself. I don't want to make a scene." Each word came clipped, and with the rough-drawn hoarseness in throat that made it clear he was close to losing his voice.

Valhum swallowed then told me what happened. "The kuthri grabbed me as soon as I left my room today. They said there've been a string of burglaries targeting some nobles. Being Sullied, I was a suspect because who else would they think of when they don't have any other proof."

I gnashed my teeth at that. Members of the Sullied were always the first to blame when it came to any kind of problem or discomfort that didn't have an easy solution. So the *better-blooded* members of polite society chose to make us their scapegoats.

When it comes to justice, the innocence of the poor, and lesser thought of, is rarely considered.

"Why did they single you out, though? I'm Sullied too." I hooked a thumb to my chest.

Valhum sighed. "I don't know, but I overheard the kuthri talking when they had me locked up. Prince Nitham's name was mentioned. I think he started the rumor and convinced some of his friends to spread it. What could the kuthri do after that? They had to take *some* action."

I filled in the gaps myself after that. "And Nitham's been avoiding me since last season after . . ." I trailed off, and Valhum didn't need further explanation.

He nodded. "The kuthri said I'd be a lesson to any thieving Sullied in the city."

What they'd really meant was: Valhum would be a lesson to me, from Nitham.

I looked the student over again and realized the severity of all he'd been hiding.

"They beat you in prison?"

He nodded.

"How bad is it?"

Valhum gave me a broken smile. "It only hurts when I breathe . . . or think." He winced again, then shuffled by me.

"Wait, Valhum. I . . ." The apology formed in my mouth, but never left it. What did I have to say? What could make things better after he'd just caught a beating simply because Nitham wanted to send a message. And if he couldn't get to me, he'd go after someone like me.

But Valhum didn't wait to hear my sympathies. Instead, he gave me his own, and a warning. "Be careful, Ari. I don't think I'll be the only Sullied he'll make trouble for."

Me either, Valhum.

Me either . . .

By the time I reached Clanks, the place had already seen one group of students pass through it, evident by the stack of trays piled haphazardly before the long narrow stone channel used to wash them.

I gazed at the crowd as they broke into their various cliques and circles, searching for my friends. Radi spotted me as my eyes fell on him.

He'd bound his long dark hair into a tail with a ribbon as vibrant red as a rose from stories. A series of burnished copper clasps sat below, splitting his hair into further tails, all threaded with beads of the same metal. You would think the look silly, but somehow, Radi made it seem as natural a thing as breathing. And it suited him.

He smiled and rushed over to me. His mandolin, strapped to his back, bounced as he closed the distance. My friend wasted no time in embracing me in a single-armed hug. "Brahm's blood, Ari, I thought you'd have the sense to stay in your rooms for another set before coming down here." Radi jostled me before.

A weight, like a length of cord resting along your throat, fell on me: the distinct feeling of being watched. And the ever-most edge of words just touched my ears. I turned toward the source of it all.

Five students stood in a close circle—all of them shooting me furtive glances that died as my attention fell on them. They turned their heads and adopted the poorly practiced stares of those who'd been caught gawking at someone.

Radi grunted. "Ten chips says they're talking about you."

I frowned. "Not much of a fair bet. People have been talking about me since I came here. Twice as much after that night. Besides"—I let a smile creep across my face—"I want them talking about me."

Radi found and wore the frown I'd let go of. "It'd be better if they weren't. It's the first day of the new season. You should have taken my advice and lodged somewhere down in the city proper. This drama won't be good for you."

I arched a brow as way of asking the question without speaking.

"You're the only student that I can think of to be banned from studies for a whole year, Ari. And everyone else knows that too. What they don't know is how the year will go for you. Any more problems, too much noise—the sort only you seem able to drum up—and then what? They skip the probation and . . ." He trailed off, dragging an index finger along his throat. "Better if you were out of sight for a while and let things calm down."

I stared at him and opened my mouth but he spoke before I could.

"Right, what was I thinking?" He threw his hands to the air with an unnecessary dramatic flair. "'Subtlety' and 'calm' are words you're well acquainted with."

"Conspiring to cause more trouble?" The new voice fell over us, and we turned to find Aram coming to Radi's side. Her features were delicate and pointed—sharp in a manner that suited her, and one could almost say she had a certain Shaen quality to her looks. But she never bothered with appearances the way Radi seemed to. She'd cut her brown hair to a length where now only a few rogue strands fell halfway over her eyes. Short and out of the way.

I groused under my breath before filling both my friends in on what had just happened with the kuthri, and Nitham's hand behind it.

Aram brushed some of her hair aside. "All the more reason to step carefully, Ari. You're under probation by the masters. You could die, or be locked in the Crow's Nest. If you avoid all of that, and Brahm's blood, I hope you do, Nitham can still make trouble for you in other ways." She rubbed her fingers to mimic dealing with coins.

Still, it dropped cold stones into my gut. She had a point. If things with Nitham worsened, he could see me beggared out of the Ashram through fees. He had that power, and that privilege. Even Aram, a merchant's daughter, had a better measure of safety here than me when it came to finances.

And then there was what he'd just done to Valhum.

I tried to change the subject to better thoughts. "What are they serving today?"

My friends answered in unison, not that it mattered. They'd already eaten, and I had missed their company because of Nitham. I'd caught them on their way out, and couldn't keep them for much longer.

I cursed the noble-blooded sprat in a tone only my friends could hear.

Radi unslung his mandolin, fingers blurring idly for the space of a breath, and a few notes rang out. Together, they made a harmony that said: *There's still trouble to come.*

I had a feeling the strings and Radi were right.

Aram pursed her lips. "Maybe this season will go smoother for you if you stop being a prodigy."

I waved a dismissive hand as I dug into my pudding. "I'm not a prodigy. I did well enough last season in classes."

Radi and Aram traded a long look before my friend plucked a series of notes from the mandolin. They cried out in discord—no harmony in their jarring awkward twangs. "He actually thinks we're talking about his performance in classes."

I scowled.

"We mean your aptitude for stirring up trouble unbeknownst to the Ashram for a time since . . . ever. Not to mention how many whispers there are about you. I swear, it's like there's half a dozen more every set." Radi's fingers stopped mid-strum, leaving a pair of strings to quaver in a low and moaning thrum.

I shouldn't have smiled, but I did. A part of me wished I could catch some of these new whispers as they were spread—offer my storyteller's touch on them. Perhaps fan and spread a few more of my own. After all, they'd been as much a boon to me as a bother. They did attract attention to me that made it easier for Nitham to draw me into trouble, of course. But they offered me just as much in protection.

And sometimes that's better. A lesson from my time with the sparrows. A good reputation can serve as a shield.

Sometimes a noose . . .

Another thing I'd learned as a sparrow when I walked into a trap set by a merchant king who'd heard all about the things I'd gotten up to.

My meeting with my friends had run its course, however. They did me the courtesy of letting me know the masters had opened the Admittance Hall, so I had to make all haste to see them and deal with the fallout of what had happened the previous season.

Not something I looked forward to.

A small part of me ached to attend classes with Aram and Radi, but my actions had cost me that. And now I had one year to apprentice myself under Rishi Ibrahm to prove I had some level of control in the major bindings, otherwise, I'd pay a steep price.

The sort that would cut all whispers about me painfully short.

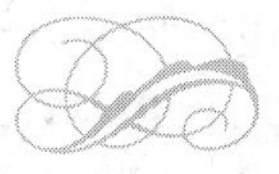

FIVE

NECESSITIES

I traded goodbyes with my friends and rushed through the main courtyard to where the rishis gathered in the Admittance Hall.

In truth, the place was more a giant cavern with a ceiling that stretched up so far you could barely see it. It better resembled a deep mine shaft than anything else. And that led to its nickname as Mines.

Candles burned throughout. All brighter than any flame should ever be, bringing an odd light to the chamber. Every flickering mote of fire served to accentuate just how dark the stone walls of Mines truly were, because no amount of shine could penetrate the black of those rocks.

Eight men and women sat behind a curved desk of the same stone. There had been another member of the masters in the previous season. Master Philosopher, Rishi Vruk. Or, as I had known him, Vathin.

My friend. A mentor. And one of the Ashura. The demons who'd killed my family, laid waste to the village of Ampur, and riled an old god in the process. And of course, utterly fictional as far as most of the world was concerned.

His absence from the Ashram had been greeted with nothing other than relief, at least among the other masters. He'd been an annoyance to many of them. And attendees cared little as one of Master Philosopher's students took his place as a rishi, though not elevated to master.

Many teachers left after a time in the Ashram. After all, there were many places along the empire, and the Golden Road, that were in want of educated folk.

I took a deep breath and approached the table, stopping short by a dozen paces. "Masters." I inclined my head in what I hoped looked respectful. My gaze drifted to a man who refused to sit behind the desk like the other rishis, choosing to rest atop it in a cross-legged position.

He didn't wear a robe like the rest of the masters. His had the sleeves torn away, and looked to be stitched from various fabrics of every color imaginable. A jarring patchwork that sent my head spinning. The man's face had no sign of beard or stubble—clean. A wild shock of black hair atop his head made it look like dark dandelion's fluff. And, he was remarkably younger than the rest of the rishis seated near him. The only person who looked to be somewhere in his middle twenties.

Rishi Ibrahm, Master Binder, flashed me a smile that burned twice as bright in his eyes. His stare held something close to excitement, but also mania, and it brought an uncomfortable coldness to my spine.

I shied away from his look and addressed the man at the center of the masters. The only one to be dressed in a robe of pure white. Master Spiritualist looked his age. Somewhere in the middle years of his life, with threads of steel gray for his hair and beard. And just as many iron-hard lines framing his face. "Headmaster, I'm here to discuss my continuance at the Ashram. . . ." I let the words hang in the air before adding the necessary amendment. "For lodgings and dedicating myself to Rishi Ibrahm's tutelage in learning control of the bindings. To make sure I don't repeat what happened last season."

Rishi Ibrahm let out a bark of laughter that nearly set him toppling backward off the desk. Several of the masters turned to stare as he righted himself. "You say that like it's a horrible thing. Brahm's blood, with the weather as cold as it is now, maybe we could use a bit more fire, eh?" He waggled his brows and his earlier smiled widened. "Maybe you ought to set a building or two aflame." Rishi Ibrahm flung his hands into the air, mimicking tendrils of fire climbing. "Whoosh!"

The headmaster's gaze fell somewhere between exasperation and contempt for the Master Binder. He shook his head instead and turned his attention back on me. "Kaethar Ari, you're in a peculiar place that the Ashram hasn't had to deal with in quite some time. Usually a student shows less . . . explosive talent in the bindings than what you demonstrated. And for that, they find themselves able to pursue more complex classes. A few pose a small danger to others or their own selves, leaving it incumbent upon us to confine them to the Crow's Nest."

A quick glance at Rishi Ibrahm showed me he'd sobered at that comment—almost growing sullen.

"Some students' minds deteriorate under the strain of the bindings. You've not fallen into that state, which leaves us here. You are barred from attending the Ashram in any official capacity. However, you are permitted to continue lodging here so long as you abide by the agreement we laid the previous season." It wasn't a question.

I nodded as the headmaster continued.

"You will apprentice yourself to Rishi Ibrahm in whatever fashion he deems best suited to help you control your bindings. And I will remind you that you have the time of one year to prove to us that you can safely engage in the ten bindings all men must know. Failure to do so will leave us with one of two options: Kaether Ari, you will either be confined to the Crow's Nest for the safety of all those in the Ashram, or if we determine you to be a greater threat . . . you will be executed."

The last word fell with leaden weight and the edge of a blade. My hearing failed me for a moment as the headmaster continued like he hadn't spoken of ending my life as casually as one would debate the weather.

"You are free to take meals along with other students, and to take up work with any of the masters that have it for you. You will not be compensated for that time." Master Spiritualist stressed this last point.

"Given these circumstances, you will not be asked for a regular donation. Instead, you will pay the cost of lodging and meals for the season in accordance with what you can afford." The headmaster gave me a look that said the sum would still be something I'd notice the absence of.

I'd made a spectacle with my first donation, then with paying grievances and for damages to part of the Ashram. All I could do was nod in silent acceptance. They could have hit me harder than that, and everyone in the room knew it. A spot of mercy in my favor to be getting off lightly.

The headmaster leaned in close with the other rishis and they spoke in low murmurs. After a moment, he addressed me. "Kaethar Ari, you will be required to donate the sum of one silver dole and six tin chips."

I kept the frown from showing on my face. That sum was still a great deal more than what lodgings in the Rookery and meals from Clanks should amount to.

Most students' entire donations were counted all in copper rounds. A few who had progressed far enough in rank could be asked for iron bunts. But no one short of nobility was asked to part with silver or gold.

And as Nitham's first move against me had shown, I was no noble.

I flashed Rishi Ibrahm a stare and he returned it with a crooked grin and a waggle of his eyebrows. The look said I'd deserved as much as I'd gotten. That I'd have just as many chances to get myself in as much trouble again. And that he would certainly play his part in making it happen.

Not the look you want to see from the man whose judgment determined whether you went free, or were carted off to the Crow's Nest for the foreseeable future. Never mind the possibility of execution.

If you're going to be spoiled for options, I'd advise making sure they don't end with your incarceration or your death. Both can be rather final.

The longer Rishi Ibrahm and I held our look, the more I saw something else behind his gaze. Something that spoke of a joke you can't explain, but sets you rocking with uncontrollable laughter. A piece of mischief that any sane person would want no part in. And, lastly, a sliver of something utterly mad. The sort of thing you find in people who no longer see the world as normal folks do. The ones who speak to thin air, imagine themselves to be things out of fiction, and the ones who might push someone off a tower top simply because they could.

I broke the exchange, looking anywhere else but at Master Binder.

"You're dismissed, Kaethar Ari. Make sure you head to the bursary to pay your donation, and not the Financiary." The headmaster gestured to usher me off.

I gave a short, curt bow before turning on a heel and rushing from Mines. A few students headed past me toward the Admittance Hall. Each shot me a glance that quickly fell away when I returned it.

I swallowed a sigh as I moved by them and reached the bursary. Sethi look up at me, opening his mouth, but I reached into my purse to draw what I owed before he could speak. One silver dole and six tin chips. That left me with four doles, twenty-two iron bunts, six copper rounds, and twenty-two chips. More than enough for a comfortable season in the Ashram, even if I chose to apprentice myself in the Artisanry to continue my tinkering.

A small luxury.

Sethi palmed the sum and made a neat note in a ledger book by his side. "Thought they'd hit you harder than that."

I offered Sethi a thin, satisfied smile. "In my defense, I only burned a small portion of the Ashram grounds. Most of it stone, which copes with fire rather well." I'd hoped the comment would draw an easy grin out of him, but his eyes widened by a fraction, and his mouth pressed into a line.

Whatever he was going to say next was lost as he turned his attention away from me. I followed his stare to find someone else standing a dozen feet away.

Nitham. I glared at him with a heat that could set flesh ablaze. My gaze fell to his arm, and I noticed it bound with bandages . . . on the outsides of his robes in a sling. One wholly unnecessary for the burns I'd given him as his clothing had taken the brunt of the fire.

I knew Master Mender had tended to Nitham and that the injuries would heal in a few sets, which had long since passed. He likely didn't even have scars from them.

No, the bandages were just a quiet reminder to everyone of what I'd done to him. Though, he wouldn't be keeping those whispers alive with intent of bolstering my reputation. He had a reason, and whatever it was beyond garnering him sympathy must have included something particularly foul befalling me.

Nitham locked eyes with me. His lips twisted to one side as the beginnings of a snarl appeared on his face. But he had better self-control than I'd credited him for. One glance at Sethi—a witness, and the look vanished, now replaced by the placidness of still water. Nitham placed a hand on the sling, emphasizing it.

Sethi stared at the pair of us, managing to shrink inside his robe.

Nitham and I held our stares, and I spoke. "You set Valhum up, and it was a message to me, wasn't it?"

He smirked, and said nothing else. Then he turned, and left.

For a moment, a silence lingered in the bursary. Then Sethi broke it.

"No offense, Ari, but I hope I don't see you much at all this season. Or the next."

I kept my face as flat and emotionless as the wood of Sethi's desk. The comment pricked me in a way I hadn't expected, but I should have. Nothing I'd done since arriving at the Ashram had led me to making many friends.

I'd been focused on survival after those years of hardship in Keshum. But friendship isn't one of life's little luxuries.

It's a necessity.

To go through the world without the closest of friends is like walking it with a missing leg, with no crutch to be found when you need that support.

Friends are the breath left to us when we run out of our own. They're the mirrors we need when we cannot see ourselves clearly. They point out our little flaws and, in times, the larger ones we must tend to. And, of course, they help us out of trouble as much as they help us into it. They are the truest form of reciprocation.

You may think me callow for describing friendship in this way. That I demean friendship—make it seem like an exchange. But you are wrong. Friends are the ones willing and most able to give anything—everything when they can. And you do the same. It is never said. But it is the unspoken agreement in friendship. A reciprocation of feelings—actions. Of time.

Which, I have learned over the course of my life, is an alternate way of spelling the word "love." People want time given to them—for them. For it's a kind of love the world is in all too short supply of. And for that, they will love you back.

That is friendship.

And beyond Aram and Radi, I found myself in serious lack of it. Something that made me value them all the more.

I walked away from Sethi, deciding that maybe I'd be better served by showing the students of the Ashram I could do more than cause trouble. So I left with other kinds of necessities on my mind.

The ones I could create myself.

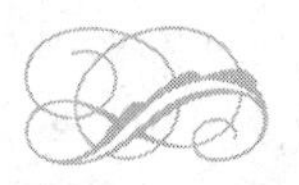

SIX

MESSAGES

While I may have been barred from classes, I was still allowed access to other parts of the Ashram. So I made my way to Holds, the place where the Artisanry kept all its materials and innovations. For a fee, students could rent tools and buy supplies needed to craft all manner of wonders. Doubly so if they had a good grasp of the minor bindings.

I'd been brought up on grievances last season for cheating when I'd entered the Athrayaan kite-fighting festival. My entry had been inked and engraved with a series of minor bindings that allowed it to outlast all other contestants until I'd won. I'd hidden my work well enough, I'd thought, but Nitham had me brought before the masters and my wrongdoing had been discovered. My winnings were taken, and my prize kite confiscated. But the time to myself over the break had given me a new idea.

My minor bindings had worked, so I could fashion something else inspired by my old work. Something that would serve me a great deal better in my other pursuits outside of the Ashram.

Like confronting the Ashura.

My list of materials didn't amount to much. A set of engraving tools, and a steel band—particularly a kardan. The metal bracelets worn by members of a young religion that had been introduced into the empire years ago. One that shunned Brahm and other deities for a single god—one nameless and faceless. I myself had no interest in gods so long as they kept their interest away from me. But the steel circlet would serve my purpose.

I also purchased a bundle of suthin—flashsteel. A thin, hair-like strand of metal that burned on contact with sufficient moisture and salt. A candle would have served for my practicing with binding fire, but they continued to burn once lit. I needed something that snuffed out in an instant, lest I risk burning down the whole damnable Rookery should I lose control.

All in all, my spending spree cost one bunt, two rounds, and three chips. Not much when considering what I had to my name, but if the expenses continued, and Nitham found a way to stir up trouble . . . I'd lose more.

And I had no way of replacing what coin left my pockets.

I returned to my room to find that my blankets had been thrown unceremoniously from my bed to the floor. But that wasn't enough—no. They'd been pulled and trampled into something approximating a lumpen cushion, which just so happened to be nearly the perfect size for one kitten. "Merciful gods, Shola. Why?"

My cat lacked the grace to appear ashamed, looking at me straight on with a lazy, self-satisfied grin. It told me that he had quite enjoyed his nap, my frustration was unwarranted, and any inconveniences on my part weren't worth the consideration on his.

I glared for a moment before realizing the futility of it. "Well, glad someone's season is off to a decent start at least."

Shola yawned, mouth spreading into a larger smile that told me he was in fact relishing his time.

I shook my head and put my materials and sack down on my bare bed. Content that Shola would soon return to his nap and not try to rearrange my recently acquired goods, I pulled free the metal band I'd bought from Holds, and an engraving tool.

A kardan consisted of mostly soft steel—flexible, but strong enough to keep its shape and endure a decent amount of external pressure before caving. Just what I needed. My kite project had focused on taking incoming forces, dispersing them along the length of the string, and then storing as much of them as possible in the bulk of the wooden spool.

I saw no reason why I couldn't alter that and apply it to a band of something stronger than wood and string. The surface of the metal bracelet didn't offer much space to engrave the traditional symbols and scripts used by artisans, but I had an answer for that as well.

My trip to Ampur the previous season had me riding with one of the traveling folk. And I'd used the time to grasp the basics of their silent language. A series of complex dots and dashes displayed on the sides of their wagon homes. They could tell an entire story with a few lines of their metal knobs and strips.

I thought back on how I'd constructed my kite, then how I would be better off retooling the minor bindings for my personal needs. If I encountered the Ashura, I'd need to be able to fight them. At least survive.

And I'd barely managed that in Ampur.

I couldn't rely on calling on the ten bindings. That power remained a far cry from my control.

For now.

But I could craft something that would let me punch above my weight, so to speak.

I fell into my work, slowly moving through the language structure and exact phrasings needed to imbue the kardan with the set of bindings to take it from a piece of religious jewelry to a weapon hidden in plain sight. Resting on my wrist meant it would be privy to every bit of motion from my arm. Motion that was energy. And that could always be stored.

I'd have to take into account the bracelet's natural composition, and that meant the limits of steel. But flexible steel could hold a great deal more energy than most people credited it for. The experiment pivoted on finding out just how much.

I went through the process taught by Rishi Bharia, reaching the inscription stage. Slow, steady, my hand worked with painstaking control that brought an ache to the small bones of my fingers. But soon I'd finished etching in the string of bindings I'd desired. Then, a thought came to me. The idea of trying my hand at more than one system of bindings.

After all, the bindings were rooted in Athir—the binder's will and faith in their ability to imagine and impress their unshaking belief on the world around them.

Why couldn't I push that belief? Especially when working on something as safe as a trinket with the minor bindings. I bit my tongue and set to inscribing again, now altering my will and thoughts to impress a second set of bindings. The idea was rooted in accounting for more than one set of script to accomplish the same thing, but making sure both sets were recognized by the kardan. A duplication of effort, but hopefully doubling the results. But it meant more than simply rewriting the same set of bindings. I had to weave them together to work in concert. Otherwise, two sets of the same commands were no different as telling Shola something twice.

A fruitless thing.

I completed the process and wrote the final piece. A script that allowed me to release the stored energy from the bracelet upon pressure from my thumb and palm. Only under those circumstances would the pent-up momentum be released. A safeguard of sorts.

Satisfied with my progress, I slipped the kardan over my wrist and repacked my bag. Shola remained sound asleep and I knew he'd stay that way for most of the day. It left me free to wander a bit and clear my mind. Classes wouldn't have started as students would still be finalizing the last of their schedules, and some still needed to pay donations. The Ashram would also be taking in refugees from Ampur who'd decided to trek out of the province of Sathvan and find temporary shelter here. Some would take up residence, intent on becoming monks.

It wasn't a great life, but it was a way to ensure a secure roof over your head and hot meals. And having been a sparrow for a handful of years made me realize just how important it was to have the basic necessities met. And once reached, a person could be tempted to give up much to keep that comfort. Even their freedom. In a way, I'd given up the same.

Those years in Keshum had come at the cost of me burying my dreams, and with them, a piece of myself. I'd come too close to forging a life I wouldn't have been able to leave. A trap of another sort, I suppose.

I shook the thoughts from my head, opening my door to leave. A smell struck me that I didn't have the breadth of experience yet to properly identify. What I could make out reminded me of orange peels, lavender, and something of fresh-cut tree boughs.

No one stood before my doorway, but the smell lingered regardless, like someone had passed by with an odd and strong perfume. I noticed something sitting at my feet.

A parcel, wrapped in paper with a single binding of twine.

I reached down and inspected it. It was no larger than one of my boots in length, but had the weight of a brick. I frowned and plucked at the wrapping, letting the scraps of paper and twine fall away.

Shola, who must have had an extra sense solely created for the intention of detecting newfound debris in my room, roused from his sleep with vigor. He bounced across the floor before I could turn and took up the length of twine. A low burble left his throat as a piece of the string caught in his claws. He batted at empty air, trying to shake the twine free, but it wouldn't let go.

Determined to best his self-made foe, he scampered to a corner of my room to continue his fight far from me.

I sighed and examined the wooden box. It lacked any adornment or carvings that could have served as a clue to who'd sent it. I lifted the lid and wished I hadn't. My hands never shook, but all the same, the blood ran cold enough through my fingers that I almost lost my grip.

A color shone within the box I'd only seen once in my life. Gold. A bed of coins filled most of the wooden container, atop which rested the body of a small bird. One that I'd grown familiar with.

A sparrow.

And it was most certainly dead.

The lump that formed in my throat threatened to choke me. I stepped back into my room, shutting the door behind me. A bit of my meal rose from my stomach until I tasted bile.

Shola had managed to free himself of his predicament and turned his attention on me, somehow aware of my discomfort. He sauntered toward me and bumped his head into my leg, letting out a low *mrowl*, almost serving as a question.

I set the box on the ground, letting him inspect it.

He gave the sparrow a look and a sniff. His back arched and he turned to retch. Thankfully, he had nothing to spit up over my floors.

Merciful gods.

I sank to my haunches, looking at the box's contents again, trying to take the meaning of it all. The gold called to me, but something in its color bothered me. I pinched a coin between a thumb and forefinger. It looked the same size and shape as a proper rupai, but the weight was off. Lighter, and its surface had a roughness to it that wouldn't be found in true gold.

I rubbed at it and something brushed back against my thumb. An inspection showed me flecks of gold powder clinging to my skin, and a duller surface below. I picked harder at the coin with a fingernail, abrading more of it away until I found something that resembled iron below. But it wasn't that metal in truth. Not gold. Not anything I knew of.

Every other coin was the same.

The sparrow, then. The only thing I hadn't examined beyond a cursory look.

I took it in my hands with more care than the dead bird warranted. Maybe it came from my years sharing the same name as the little creature. Maybe it was that I had come but a breath from the doors of death myself. Or maybe simply because it was something small, forgotten, and alone. And I have always had a tender spot in my heart for those things.

I glanced at Shola before placing the sparrow to rest on my floor. Something fell from between the bird's beak as soon as it came into contact with the wooden boards. A seed. I reached for it, my hand placing more pressure on the bird's chest by mistake. Another seed slipped from its mouth. Then another.

Shola watched with feigned disinterest, but he crept closer, sniffing at the air.

I picked up all three seeds, inspecting them. Nothing remarkable about them, but I'd seen something like this before. Pips were used in parts of the underworld or where secrets were concerned. A pip marked a point of time. Three of them served the same purpose. But how long?

Three days? Sets? Months? Or years?

I rubbed my mouth with the sleeve of my robe as I thought.

Regardless, this was a message. One with singular meaning and a nod to my past.

Someone wanted me dead.

SEVEN

Jealous Secrets

My heart beat hard as hailstorm on glass. I felt like a young sparrow again who'd just clutched his first purse, manic that a kuthri had seen me in the act, and that the iron sharp-swift judgment of a sword would follow.

I placed the bird back in the box and shut the lid, pushing it away.

Shola tilted his head, asking a silent question.

"I think someone wants to kill me."

He let out a little purr that said he occasionally nursed similar thoughts, but reconsidered on account of lacking a manservant should he follow through with that.

I dismissed him and gave the box a longer look. No one had reason to kill me. No one save for Nitham.

I'd made no enemies at the Ashram other than him. And the false gold was nothing more than a sign. A symbol of what he could afford to pay to have the deed done. Not to mention the fact that even Aram had reminded me of just how much wealth the prince had to spend. Even so, the box itself didn't amount to much in proof.

No.

Too many excuses could be conjured in his defense. I'd made it myself. Anyone could have sent it. Nothing overtly pointed to Nitham besides the obvious fact he was the only one out for me. The rishis could dismiss that as paranoia on my part, especially since Nitham and I had given each other a wide berth since the festival.

And I couldn't take any action against him lest I push my already tenuous position in the Ashram further. One mistake and I'd go from probationary suspension to execution. Something Nitham knew of.

So, that was his game, then. First harassing Valhum with the kuthri, now this. Subtle moves that didn't overtly lead back to him.

I fetched the length of twine Shola had since discarded, using it to fasten the box lid before stowing the container under my bed. There was little point in keeping such a macabre thing around, but it was the only proof I had of Nitham's threat. It might come in handy later.

If you live that long.

A sparrow's old fear crept back into me and I closed my eyes, falling back into an old exercise. The candle and the flame. It came to me, slower than before, but not too long later I'd centered my mind. I fed all the doubts and apprehension I could into that single flickering flame. Soon, clarity remained. Just me. Myself.

I took a breath and returned to my feet, deciding that threat or no, I couldn't let it keep me barred inside. I'd made a prison for myself before.

Never again.

And if I couldn't attend classes, I could do something else. Continue my search for the Ashura.

I shut my door behind me, hoisting my sack over a shoulder, and headed downstairs.

The snowfall had intensified outside, now threatening to cake my hair with clumps of frost. I ignored it, focusing instead on the Scriptory.

It would at least offer me a place to pursue something I hadn't given enough due to since arriving at the Ashram.

Stories about the Ashura.

I knocked on the heavy wooden doors to the building.

No answer.

I banged the base of my fist against them again, this time taking a moment to rub my skin against one of the brass studs, clearing it free of building frost.

The lone slit in the doors opened and a pair of eyes stared back at me. "Oh, you." The opening closed just as fast.

"Oi—hey!" I banged harder now, rattling wood and some of the metal pieces fixed there as well.

The slit slid open, smacking hard within its frame. The chill of the student's gray eyes had now taken on a color closer to cold morning clouds. "Don't bang the doors like that. Don't make noise like that." Each word left her lips clipped, harsh as full winter wind's bite, and sharp as ice.

I pulled my clenched fist back from where it had stopped mid-swing. "Sorry. But what's with not letting me in? I'm a student here and I'm—"

"No, you're not. Not technically this season. Everyone's heard."

I glowered, matching her stare with as much flame and fury as I could for every bit of coldness she showed me. "And, what, that's enough to bar me from here? I donated a full silver dole—Brahm's blood and ashes."

"No. It's what you did. You bound fire . . . and let it spill onto the Ashram grounds—the walls. *Fire.*" The word left her as a curse, like there was nothing more horrible in this world.

The heat of my stare left me for honest confusion, and I just stared, hoping she'd clarify.

"What happens if I let you in here and you lose control again? If you whip up another storm of fire here—*here.*" She leaned closer until her brow rested against the lip of the slit. "Do you know how hard lorists in training work to keep the temperature in here perfect? Everything: The light, the humidity, especially in summer, and the dryness in winter, must be absolutely within the margins given to us by Master Lorist."

I swallowed. "Right, and a fire can make your jobs too hot to handle, I suppose?" I flashed her a grin and hoped the little jest would lighten her mood just a fraction.

I was wrong.

Her eyes narrowed and she shot me a looker hotter than anything I could dare to conjure in fire. "Not funny."

I raised my hands in a gesture of placation, then placed one to the hollow of my throat. "I swear I won't be any trouble. Please?" I worked my face into the most pitiful mask I could, thinking back to my days in the theater, and then when I performed on the streets of Keshum begging for tin chips. "I don't have anywhere else to spend this season." It wasn't wholly true, but close enough to the mark. "I won't be a trouble. I won't make noise. I won't—"

"All right, all right." She shut the slit and I heard the unmistakable sound of metal latches being undone. The doors opened to reveal the same student who I'd met my first trip here. She couldn't have been more than two years older than me at best. Heart-shaped in face with some fat in her cheeks that was likely a holdover from childhood. Her hair was a warm brown that once tempered the cold of her eyes, but not much today. "Brahm above, you look like someone kicked your kitten."

I tensed at that, then relaxed realizing she'd just said that as an offhand comment, and nothing to do with Shola himself. People had watched the incident with Nitham and me, but I had no idea how many had taken note of the flame-colored kitten involved. None besides Master Binder who'd promised to keep my furry friend a secret.

I hoped . . .

"Well, are you going to come inside, or stand there and let all the snow in?"

I didn't need her to say another word. She shut the doors behind me as I slid inside, shaking myself clean of every bit of snow and water that held to my robes.

"Go wait in the dry room until you're absolutely sure you're not carrying a drop on you, *ji-ah*?" Her tone brooked no argument.

I nodded. "*Ji.*" The room she'd pointed me to lived up to its name. Solid stone on all sides without a hint of warmth to them, except from the fireplace at the far end. No other students occupied the small and narrow place, which felt more like an oversized closet than anything else. Carvings ran along every inch of the room and I realized they were minor bindings.

A longer look at them gave me an idea to their purpose. I held out my hand toward the fire, then slowly backed away until I'd left the room. It felt as if the fire had never been there at all. Every bit of warmth vanished as if by magic. That was part of how the Scriptory managed to keep the temperatures so constant, and stopped students from bringing in extra moisture that risked ruining the more fragile documents stored here. I returned to the dry room and waited until I was sure I was properly dry.

My eyes lingered on the script running along the walls, committing it to memory. A similar minor binding lined the rooms of all students to help improve the temperatures within. But they weren't perfect, and they could do so much more. And I wanted to see just how far they could be taken. I filed that away for a later time as I set about the shelves, looking for anything that could point me to stories about the Ashura.

My last trip had proven less than fruitful. Nothing but a childish rumor of the Ashura hiding in the mountains. Their appearance in Ampur had nothing to do with that, and they'd left just as quickly, leaving behind nothing but ruins and an angry old god.

Another student walked by, opening one of the glass panels that held the bound scrolls and leather-bound tomes. A lorist in training.

I signaled to him, keeping to my promise of making as little noise as possible.

He noticed me and came over. The student could have been more than five years older than me, somewhere in his early twenties. Slender of face and build.

A hawkish nose drawn far enough down it made it seem like he was looking down at me. Eyes nearly as deep a dark brown to be a match for the black of his short-cropped hair. "Yes?"

"I'm looking for any scripts or works about the Ashura." I saw his face shape into the beginnings of a frown, but I headed him off before he could say something. "I'm working on a project tracing the evolution of stories, you see. How tales travel and change through folklore. I took a trip up to Ampur, and even in parts of Sathvan, they tell stories of the Ashura. They've spread through all of Mutri, and I wonder if they've gone farther."

I'd practiced the lie and used it before when trying to mollify Master Lorist when she made it clear how disappointing an Ashram student's interest in the Ashura was.

"They're just children's stories, though?" His look told me he mirrored Rishi Saira's opinion on the matter.

I tried not to let my frustration show on my face. "That's what makes them perfect. What spreads easier than children's tales? Everyone sings their songs, talks about them, even when their parents tell them not to."

"Have you already looked into this?"

I nodded and rattled off the list of stories and histories I'd perused before, hoping he knew of something better to direct me toward.

"Mm. There's not much outside of those works." He gave me a look that said I should have expected as much.

This time I didn't bother hiding the sigh that'd bubbled inside me. "Nothing?"

He cradled his chin, rubbing the spot as he thought. "Stories about them are kind of scattered. Few people ever bothered to write a detailed tome solely on the Ashura. It's usually how they fit into other works, history, and folktales."

It was better than nothing. "Do you know of a good place to start from there?"

The lorist in training fetched a leather-bound tome for me, passing it my way. The title had been sewn into the thick cover with gold thread that had long ago lost its luster.

I gave it a look. *The Asir: A Study on the Heretical Son and His Agents.* The name pulled a frown out of me I hadn't expected, and it must have caught the apprentice lorist's eyes.

"What's wrong?" He glanced at the book, then me again.

"Bit of a strong title."

"It's fitting, given the material."

I stared, making it clear I needed more in the way of an answer.

"Radhivahn isn't accepted by most Mutri temples. You know that." His tone carried enough acid in it that he should have been barred from the Scriptory on that account alone. It let me know he was of a similar school of thought himself. "Why would Brahm birth a Son of Himself when he'd already birthed the other gods and the Sirathrae? It's just human arrogance. Some storyteller spouting lies, and it caught a long time ago. But, there are some stories about the Ashura in this. I wouldn't put much academic stock into them, though, given the overall subject." He gave the book a look I wouldn't have thought any apprentice lorist would have thrown toward a text.

Realizing any further conversation with him was a lost cause, I inclined my head in silent thanks and headed off to find a small table to read by. A long wooden lip ran along the length of windows at one end of the Scriptory. Countless orbs fashioned of glass rested along the surface. More dotted the desks and little nooks throughout the building, and all of them gave off the winter-pale glow of a sun before gray skies.

I grabbed one of the binder's lights, tucking it into the crook of my arm as I made my way to an empty desk in a far corner. The book began with a summation of the scholar's thesis about Radhivahn, Son of Himself, and why the following material would be enough to disprove he ever existed at all.

I cared little for that argument, flipping through the pages until the academic prattling ceased, and the storytelling began.

The Ashura were created by the Shaen, who'd first spurned Brahm and his love, turning away from him behind the darkened doors of the realm. Something made to show what imperfections rested within Brahm's makings, and what evil lingered within the hearts of men and their shapings.

Nonsense. But I read on.

Brahm, realizing what was happening in his world, was not content to sit idly by. So he decided to come to the aid of mortal men in the only way he could, as something closer to mortal himself but still not truly removed from all he was—divine and above all things. So, he made an avatar for himself: Radhivahn, and through this, brought to life those to equal the Ashura—to hound them night and day. Give them chase and keep them far from man's affairs. Far, far away.

Another lie.

If that were true, they wouldn't have been in Keshum all those years ago. They wouldn't have come into the life of a young boy dreaming to be on stage. And they wouldn't have made the walls run red with blood and set a fire that burned my whole world down.

Where were the Asir then, though?

I thought back to the story I'd once heard long ago. The Asir had risen out of the first men and women who'd spurned Radhivahn as a child, ignoring his pleas and needs. For it, he chastised them when he'd grown to a man full, and then offered them a path to redemption. A path to him.

For the first that chose it, he offered to remake them. And they had taken his hand and been reborn.

Their purpose? To rid mankind of their own demons—the darkest shadows that could be taken, twisted, tempted, and tainted. The first victims of this? The Ashura. Or so the scholar said.

The Asir were warriors shaped by Radhivahn's own hands to match the Ashura in their abilities of combat and magic. What those were, he failed to elaborate on as well.

I flipped through the book, looking for anything of substance pertaining to Radhivahn's risen knights, but I found little.

A few accounts where people had, and still continued to, pray to the Asir in moments of crisis. And just as many notable miracles people attributed to the Asir's hands, for those that believed, of course. Others dismissed them as deeds done by the Sithre, Brahm's handmade angels, who existed solely for that cause.

One line in particular caught my interest. "It is said that the Asir can be found to linger in the aftermath of the Ashura's destruction, offering aid to those in need. Sometimes they've been said to lead the way to where the Ashura will be—their ears kept ever keen for these demons' activities and whereabouts.

"But no eye-witness accounts exist of ever having seen an Asir, even though some of their signs are known. As is their service to the goddess Naathiya, who serves as Brahm's wise council, and his eyes and ears to mortal affairs. The only one to know all the Asir's mysteries, and they guard those jealously. And since we cannot question the goddess . . ."

The piece ended without a hint as to what those signs were.

Of course.

Naathiya. I'd once heard something about the goddess, but what I could recall came muddled. She looked out for the lost, the orphaned, the clever, and those who felt more at home in the night. Owls were her symbol, a sign of her favor. None of that spoke to what this book claimed about her position within Brahm's pantheon. Maybe I had misremembered?

I thumbed through the rest of the book, but nothing of note remained. More carefully curated pieces of history, logical fallacies, and testimonies clearly catered to dismiss the notion of Radhivahn himself.

With a heavy sigh, I shut the book.

"—Be there around the start of seventh candle, maybe earlier."

I frowned as their conversation carried through the Scriptory, loud enough that an apprentice lorist should have fallen on the student.

"Not like there's much else to do up in Ghal in winter. Brahm's tits, it's bleak here. Nothing like down south. At least there's performers still out, and the girls aren't wearing so much that they're—"

Someone hissed at them—a cue for them to shut up.

They didn't take it.

"A good storyteller's worth a few chips, even if we have to walk all the way down into the city proper for it."

I paused, now leaning in the direction of the noise. They had to be a row or two away from me.

"My father sat in on his stories once. Said he was a dab hand at them. Name's Maashi." Silence. "No, that's not right."

The other speaker chimed in. "Meethi? Mithu? I heard of him before, too. Maathi?"

I bolted from my seat, rounding the nearest corner to catch up to them. "Where, who?" My voice carried through the Scriptory, but I didn't care.

Both of them turned to face me. Their eyes wide, mouths agape.

The closest, a boy who looked just shy of his twentieth year, let out nothing but half-uttered words. He finally found a thought he could string together and pass through his lips. "You're him."

I blinked, quickly regaining my composure. "Last I checked I'm certainly a him, but I don't know if I'm the he that's him you're thinking I am. You were saying about a storyteller?"

The other student, who'd been gawking in silence, found something just as useless to say. "You set the Ashram on fire?" It sounded more a question than a statement.

"A small one, yes. Brahm's ashes, man, are you dumb or deaf?" I took hold of his collar and pulled him close. "The storyteller. His name is Maathi?"

He nodded.

"Where?"

He blinked.

"*Where?*" The single word echoed through the Scriptory like a thunderclap through a cavern.

"Uh . . . a tavern. The Fireside, I think."

I bit my lip, resisting the urge to shake the student. "You think? You were just talking about it."

Someone cleared their throat behind me.

I released the other student and turned to face the young woman who'd admitted me into the Scriptory.

To say her eyes were cold would be to utterly underserve just how much ice and winter's hateful bite a glare could carry. The look spoke of being left on the highest peaks of Ampur's mountains . . . and all without a stitch to spare you from the snow. It held all the sharpness of a cold glass edge, and enough frost to chill you to the bone.

I hoped my eyes carried just as much apology as hers did murder. "Sorry, I—"

"Out." The word left her like the cracking of an ice sheet underfoot.

I nodded, turning and leaving without a word. A small hint of shame warmed my walk toward the door, but my trip to the Scriptory had been worth it. I may not have gotten what I needed from the tomes, but I'd left with a hint.

And something more.

The chance for a story.

Those had always carried some truth for me to rely on. And just as many secrets. Maybe the sort that would help me with my search for the Ashura. Maathi had certainly helped me before in that regard. A story about the first Ashura. A push to come to the Ashram, which led me to Koli. I just had to believe he could do the same again.

Either way, it was time to go see Maathi.

EIGHT

Like Things

Brahm's blood, seventh candle. I didn't have long to reach The Fireside tavern and find a seat. A storyteller this far north in the empire, and during the heart of winter, no less, would draw a crowd.

There is little else better than a good story in the deepest cold. And all by the comfort of a fire, with good food, around even better people. It is one of life's greatest pleasures. And, sadly, one of the least indulged.

Everyone should hear a good story performed by a proper teller of tales at least once. Aloud. With passion. With something warm in their mug that has the right kind of bite. A meal that makes them remember what it's like to be a child, and forget the woes of being an adult and the world around them.

Just once.

But more than that, stories hold the shape of the world within them.

And there is no better way to explore parts of the world than with the stories that travel its roads.

I crossed through the snow-laden paths of the main courtyard, bustling toward the Rookery. A particularly hard pocket of ice, nestled within the frost, caught against my foot and refused to budge. I stumbled and bit off a curse. One of my hands clenched against empty air and I found myself missing my staff terribly. The thought prompted me to tighten my fist.

Nitham and his friends had broken it, leaving me without the tool old binders of legend carried with them. All the memory did was remind me to find myself a new one . . . and renew some of my anger toward the spoiled prat who'd taken it from me.

Our feud had cooled over the break, but all snows thaw eventually. And there was no way of knowing when and where his next move would come.

I made my way up the tower of the Rookery and reached my room. Shola lay sprawled on my bed, wriggling halfway over to regard me through lazy slits that told me I'd roused him from an enjoyable sleep. A low inquisitive *mrow* left his mouth and he flexed his toes.

"We're going out," I answered him as I rested my sack, emptying it of nearly everything but for the suthin, which I moved to a pocket in my robes. My clothing had enough material and folds to comfortably shield the volatile metallic strands from any snow or salt.

I hoped.

"Come on—*tch-tch*." I motioned at the mouth of my pack for Shola to climb inside. He gave me a look that said he was rather content where he was. And to drive home the notion, he scrambled in a circle, kicking up my blankets and bedding until they folded over him. I glowered and he had the grace to meet my eyes with a self-indulgent smile. "Brahm's blood, I swear, Shola. Fine. Stay here." I shouldered my sack again, choosing to keep it with me in case I came along something worth taking back on my trip.

Shola managed a sound close to a chirp that I pretended was a distressed and caring farewell—that he would miss me and of course await my quick return.

The little lies we tell ourselves.

I left my room and all but raced toward the thousands of steps leading down and away from the Ashram into the city of Ghal. The cold found new ways to bite at me despite my layers, and only my cussedness toward too many things to count kept me warm enough in thought until I reached my destination.

The Agni-thaan—The Fireside—lived up to its name. Wood a shade of orange pulled from smoldering coals made up the building's sides. A warmth sat in that color as if it held to the promise of a comforting fire. The roof was shaped like every other, blue tiles arranged in a cone to break up the ice. But something new had been done to it. A few plumes of thin-worked steel ringed its lip. They'd been cut and styled into swirling bands that almost reminded me of fire's tendrils. Yet, they were still in the process of being painted the appropriate tones, holding now mostly to the cold gray of metal.

I shook the would-be crown of fire from my head and entered the establishment.

My earlier guess had been right. The Fireside had attracted no end of patrons, packing the place until some customers sat elbow to elbow. One of the wooden bench seats flexed under the weight of the people crammed along it. Finding a place for myself would have been easier had I come several hours earlier, and my only option now rested in forcibly relieving another customer of their seat through the persuasive power of fists.

Not an option I wanted to pursue.

I moved toward one of the thick wooden beams that supported the rafters, resting my back against the sturdy pole. My gaze flickered to the black stone hearth nestled within the far wall. Its once-fire now existed only as smoldering coals. But something else filled the dark of those glowing rocks.

The promise of what those embers could be again were they fanned full with just a breath of air. A piece of the right fuel and they would grow—find new life, and consume and spread to fill the space with a better brightness and warmth.

That is what fire does. Or so it told me.

Once.

"Story!" The cry rattled me like the clapper of a bell struck against its bow.

I turned toward the source of the call, but couldn't spot it through the throng of people. My eyes caught on a flash of silver, holding warm light along its edge. A knife. The man held it tight to the outside of his hip, but still under the folds of his robe. Only the barest hint of metal had been betrayed by the slip of his clothing.

There was only one reason to hold a knife like that. He meant to use it. And my next look told me on whom.

I traded stares with the knifeman, eyes locking while something flickered behind his. Recognition? Realization? I couldn't tell, but for a moment, his hand moved under his heavy robes.

What could I do in this crowded place?

Just as my thoughts turned to a solution, someone clapped a hand on the knifeman's shoulder. He turned to face the newcomer and produced the blade, turning it over in his grip to pass it to the other man. The stranger inclined his head and offered a barely audible thanks.

Both men looked relieved.

I realized the exchange could have been any number of things. The passing of a knife to someone who was without one for their meal, or perhaps a commissioned piece now given over. Nothing so sinister as murdering me in a packed tavern.

My paranoia had grown since the package with the dead sparrow. And that is not the mindset fit for a binder. I exhaled, blowing the breath out slowly through my nostrils. My gaze returned to the low-burning coals, envisioning something else entirely.

Just when I had found the candle and the flame, forming them within the folds of my mind, something jostled my side. I blinked, falling from the lucidity of the mental state, and glowered at the passerby.

The man looked like he hadn't quite reached his thirtieth year. Youthful in face with the sharp lines of bottle glass and all the hardness of stone. Looks women would find beautiful and handsome at the same time. His hair fell to his shoulders in waving curls as dark as The Fireside's hearth. Even in the frozen climate of Ghal, he'd chosen not to dress for the unforgiving weather. A few lengths of red cord were braided and wrapped around his biceps, while black dots had been pricked deep into his skin to form a shape like an owl. And I spotted something pinned to his sleeveless shirt. It resembled pressed flame, flattened and shaped from shining metal with all the colors of fire itself. Something close to the token I'd once bought for Immi.

"Maathi!" I grinned, taking a step forward and extending both my hands.

He returned the expression and offered me an arm that I clasped hard to. We shook and he broke from my grasp, taking my shoulders in his grip next. "Good to see you found your path, Ari." Maathi gave me a little shake. "I see you're making stories of your own up here, ah?"

I opened my mouth to speak, but he didn't give me a chance.

"I'm a storyteller, *yaara,* and I'm a good one. I've heard tell of a few tales concerning you." His smile widened and he reached out to take one of my earlobes between his fingers, giving it a gentle tug. "There've been whispers through other parts of the empire about a young man who's called down a mountain. Some said he battled a serpent of white ice and scales like stone. He killed it. He buried the village beneath it all. Some said the fires burned bright red. Red as blood and the smoke just the same."

Maathi leaned forward, his voice dropping to a conspiratorial whisper. "Some say the Ashura were there."

The word sent a cord of ice through my spine and chest. I stiffened and almost opened my mouth to ask him what he knew of them, but no. I couldn't. No one else took me seriously, so why would he? After all, storytellers know one thing above all.

And that is stories keep to themselves. They are not real.

So long as they tell that lie, they can hope to believe it. For the betterment of all, I suppose.

It doesn't do for your audience to think your tales real. Fantasy is best kept behind the doors of imagination. Because few can cope with the truth that monsters *are* real. And that if we're not careful, they will come for us.

I swallowed the moisture in my throat, turning the conversation back to my deeds. "I went to Ampur looking for something . . . and I think I found it. Everything else that happened . . ." I trailed off, unable to give voice to the words.

Maathi nodded as if understanding. "Life has a way of doing that, Ari. Live long enough and you'll see many other stories come to pass—some quite unbelievable."

I could believe a lot after being through what I had been, but I kept that to myself as well.

"I'm sure you'll find yourself in the midst of many more. Grander. Greater. If you keep following your path."

"And what's that? The last time we met you knew what I wanted—"

"Hoya!" Someone in the tavern banged a mug. "Hoya, storyteller. Stop running your mouth with talk that's not filling this place with tales, *ji-ah*?"

Maathi's eyes narrowed but the expression faded just as fast as it had come. I recognized the mask forming over his face. Something performers adopted when slipping into a role outside their normal selves. He was no longer my friend, or a simple patron. He'd become the storyteller, here to entertain. Maathi flashed me a quick wink before moving toward the black stone hearth.

He stood there—patient, waiting—as much of stone as the wall behind him.

Some of the customers took note of him and began to quiet, but they hadn't adopted the necessary silence and stillness. The ones Maathi expected. But he had a trick for that.

A miniature thunderclap rang through the taproom and it cut through some of the clamor. But not all. Then another clap.

Another.

People still moved through The Fireside. Men and women bustling by with serving trays and pitchers. A few lingered by the supporting beams and wherever else a light shone from.

Soon Maathi fell into slow and rhythmic clapping that overtook the conversations. He beat his feet, adding a deep percussion that quelled the remaining noise. He stopped as the place hushed. Now, the silence, the stillness, belonged to him.

And he decided when to break it.

Everyone's breath sat full-formed in their mouths, but none dared exhale or make a sound.

Maathi opened his mouth but didn't speak. His arms rose at his sides.

Then.

Clap.

The single smack of flesh echoed through The Fireside and all the light within died. We sat there, half-swallowed gasps resting in a place between our throats and just above our hearts. Something crackled. Then hissed.

The coals were the only source of light in the dark. Maathi's silhouette moved and a flash of flame sparked to life to wash away the black.

The crowd let loose with a torrent of noise—yet all kept to just above a whisper. Choked breaths, hushed sounds of excitement, and curses just loud enough to catch the ears of their neighbors, but not so loud as to carry through the whole of the tavern.

I had no mind left for words. I sat there looking for the trick of it. Every candlewick within the building had been snuffed clean as if he'd plucked the flame from them with just a word—a snap of his fingers. Almost like magic.

Like a binding. But, no. Maathi wasn't a binder. At least not that I knew of. So, how then? Just as I started to form a reasonable hypothesis, he spoke. And when he did, I felt another sort of magic. Something that I'd spend my later life searching for.

"People of Ghal!" His words hung in the air like fine cobwebs, too thin to be seen unless caught in the right light. But I felt them tie us—bind us all within the tavern, and we waited for his next breath, anything to shake and shiver the bonds that held us in listening. "The nights are long . . . and they are dark. Mornings are cold and there must always be a fire to warm your bones and your flesh. Your breath. And your blood. But what is there left to warm your hearts—your souls?

"That is why I am here. For there is something more you still desire. Another piece you're missing. But, not to worry, for I've brought it with me. It is here. I'm holding it. And I will share it." But he did not say what that was. His words hung there, once again, like quivering strings. None of us wanted to reach out and grab hold of them—rattle them in hopes of drawing loose whatever secret he held tight-pressed between his lips.

Breath built in my chest in a wish to speak, but I couldn't find voice to break the quiet that Maathi had blanketed us with.

Finally, the storyteller gave us reprieve. "A story." The two words were like the release of breath, deeply held, that we didn't even know rested at the core of us. "Stories were the first gifts Brahm gave to us. Blown from his own lips to ours. Everything made by his hand has a story as well. Every one of you, and everything there is. Stories. They make us—shape us. And they help us remember. Tonight is a night to remember things. But what? What story?"

Another quiet fell and I began to see the shape of what Maathi wove. The little tricks—manipulations to make the audience dance and move to his tune. Like a puppeteer.

Like an actor, I realized. This was stagecraft. I smiled when I noticed the similarities and felt rather clever for having figured that out. If I had known then just how much more went into Maathi's storytelling, I never would have thought myself quick at all.

Stories, like hearts, work best when some things are kept secret—left behind only for those worthy enough to take note and speak to them. Of them.

And Maathi knew this.

Someone stood from their table, thighs bumping the edge and setting several drinks rattling in place. A clamor rose but died as soon as the man opened his mouth. "Hoya, tell me of Sithre and Brahm's first war against the dark. Against Saithaan."

Hush. Silence. The stillness of a room after an unwanted gust of wind passes through.

A deep tale. A dark one. One that left some uncomfortable. Even though everyone knew the shape of it and its ending, it was the sort of story that would have some looking over their shoulders as they walked home across night roads—all without the safety of candlelight.

"I wanna hear about Bodhi and his travels east. Off to Laxina where they have halls of jade and they eat from bowls made of moonstone and pearls!" I couldn't spot who'd asked for that story.

"No. Give us one about the pirates off of Zibrath's waters. Wait—no. I want to hear about Sakhan of the seas!"

"Hoya! Athwun, the Heir of Sunlight!"

The suggestions came in. One after another. Each as loud as hammer striking brass, but only one idea came to my mind. A chance to get answers about what I'd read in the Scriptory.

"The Asir!" My words should have been drowned out by the arguing voices, but they cut through them all instead. Several turned their heads to regard me while raising their hands to the hollows of their throats. A few touched three fingers to their foreheads before raising them to the sky—a gesture of shock and warding off something ungodly.

Maybe it was. But just as there was no proof of Radhivahn's birth, I'd seen nothing to disprove it either.

Hubris. Heresy. Those were the words resting on their tongues, but who knew what another man believed in a place as packed as this. And saying the wrong thing could provoke a fight. No one wanted that.

"The Asir?" Maathi's voice held all the uncertainty of a man hearing a word for the first time. "Hm. There's a story to tell. The kind that people don't want me sharing. The sort that gets some folk into trouble." He waved a dismissive hand. "But, no. You lot aren't the kind with ears for that . . . are you?" Maathi turned halfway, casting a long and questioning look over his shoulder to the crowd.

They bristled, nearly tripping over their own voices to speak. He'd done it now. Held the story hostage. Promised them something forbidden.

And there are few things people want more than that which they're denied.

"I'm a godly man," said one. "But that don't mean I'm afraid of a tale like that. I walk in Brahm's light—that I do. So he strike me down if I don't. I'm not one to shy away from story that ain't right by the temples. Just a story, isn't it?"

That spurred the rest.

"Asir!"

"I'm not afraid." The call came with thumping fists, drawing more from the crowd. Soon a storm broke out within The Fireside, complete with drumming thunder and cracking voices.

Maathi turned back around and added his own clap. "So be it!"

The noise died.

"The Asir. A story of one of their best, their brightest, and among their most lost. This is a story of Hahnbadh, son of Hahn himself. For if Brahm could birth a son of Himself, why couldn't another do the same? The god of strength, strongmen and wrestlers, champion of the brave, decided to walk in his father's path, and make a son of his own making. And so came about a man born for greatness, but who found himself lost along the way. A man who had to make the journey westward to find all that he could be. An Asir. A rebuke to the Ashura. A thorn to evil. So long as he overcame his own."

The Fireside fell still—silent. Not even the hearth's fire cracked against the quiet.

And then Maathi told us of one of the Asir.

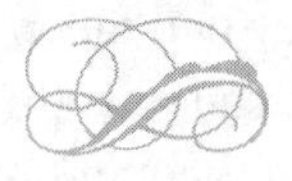

NINE

Westward Bound

Hahnbadh was born not of breath and flame like Brahm or his makings. He was shaped from clay and stone. Metal and bone. A child of strength with the wind within him. Strong and hardy as a young man could be. He had the swiftness of a river in his step, and all the crashing strength of the tide in his blows.

Maathi motioned for one of the serving girls to bring him an unlit torch. She did and he quickly buried its head in the hearth, bringing it to life. With its flame he cast a shadow of himself against the walls, flexing one of his biceps much like Hahnbadh might have done.

But he'd come too quickly into this world and was without guide. So while he grew strong of arm, he fell short in temper and could never find his father's calm and patient stride. Rash. Prone to mischief making and pleasure taking, the son of Hahn fell far from his father's grace. And soon was cursed to bear a cursed face.

But once, he was too proud of himself. Hahnbadh challenged a mortal student of his father's to a wrestling bout. But it would not do to simply win. That was expected of him. He must defeat them so soundly as not to put a shred of his prowess within doubt. So he turned to guile and snuck into his opponent's chambers that night to fill their water skin with herbs to make them weak and weary come the morning.

And at first light, he ventured to his father's field and readied himself for the fight. His opponent, Savarthi, waited for him there. Clay-rich of skin, and coal-dark of hair.

"You can't hope to best me here. I'm my father's son, born of Hahn himself, and every fight I've taken is a fight I've won." He took a swig from his own wine-skin, self-assured and surely certain.

Savarthi said nothing, tying her braid tightly wound, and pinning it to her collar, fasten-bound. She kicked off her shoes and beckoned the son of Hahn to meet over fresh dirt and grass. Neither gave an inch of ground as they locked and broke free over another's holds. Rolling-pitching until Hahnbadh's world began to tilt and tumble.

"You're bested." There was no joy or triumph in Savarthi's voice. Only measured truth as she pressed Hahnbadh's back to the ground.

The son of Hahn's eyes swam with the murkiness of cloudy water. His muscles felt faint and distant, like they had fallen far from his mind's control. His words slurred and promised to catch in his throat. "What's happening to me?"

Savarthi pushed herself off him then and rose to her feet. Her look spoke of anger held deep in keeping, but it shone in her eyes bright as any flame could be. "The trickery you had planned for me. Last night when you stole into my room to taint my water, I returned to yours hours later to repay you in kind. Your wine was honey-sweet and sharp as ever, perfect to mask your own foul tricks."

Maathi stood straight, a hand on his hip as if in victory, before pointing a finger in accusation toward the audience.

Hahnbadh's eyes went wide with fury and he fought to right himself, but his body would not obey. "Cheater. Charlatan! Arrogant, mortal trickster." He cursed her then, spitting every thought he could dare to think.

"It is you who cheated, son of myself." And so came Hahn himself, who had been there all along, watching the bout take place. The shame and tiredness wearing mask-clear on his face.

Maathi brought the torch below his chin, casting the light across his visage, and drew his mouth down low and eyes just as much in sorrow.

"You were born blessed—better made than many a man could hope to be, yet you've only ever been complacent—lazy. Gifted with my strength of arm and back, you've chosen to rely on guile and trickery." *Maathi looked down and shook his head much like old Hahn would have, I imagined.*

"Where you failed though you had every chance to win, Savarthi succeeded by turning your own mischief against you. You are the maker of your own undoing. No champion of myself or others. No guide to the honorable or the brave. And now I see the wisdom in my father's choice of what he did to my brother.

And I now know his ache. For this choice I must make will leave my heart to break."

Maathi's face twisted as if caught in the grip of unseen hands all pulling on it at once. His eyelids quivered and moisture rolled down one cheek. His chest shook, and for a moment, the flames wavered as if threatening to wink out from the torch.

"Brahm above cast down Saithaan, and now I cast you out as well. To find your own way across this world, only to return when you've found a path to being a better man—more a hero and a champion. For your treachery and tricksome ways, I curse you to no longer wear this face of mine, but of a beast just as wilesome to fit your crime."

And so his son's face soon turned to be one of his father, but somewhere between man and an animal. A tail sprouted from his rear, curling crooked as his sense of honor. And fur did grow along his limbs.

Hahnbadh's legs shook at this and he protested then. "But father, where am I to go? What am I to do? Please don't send me away." *Maathi fell to his knees, clutching both hands to the shaft of the torch as if in prayer or pleading.*

But Hahn would not hear another word, and so, like once before, a banished son fell from grace, and was left to wander the world to find his place.

Hahnbadh did not tire, nor did he thirst, but he did come to feel the pain of those come before him. The lonely ache and emptiness of his grandsire.

The pain of Brahm.

Maathi shuffled before the hearth, drawing a long shadow across the wall that moved with head hung, shoulders slumped.

And he sought to remedy this. So he wandered west, far from home.

First he turned to villages along his way as he moved across the land before the Mutri as it is now. He asked for shelter—for the company and warmth of conversation as well as a fire's.

Villagers rejected him upon sight, declaring him ill-made, monstrous, and a blight. Turned away from reprieve and respite, Hahnbadh was left with no place to grieve, or to rest at night. Lonely. Lost. Without aid. Finally learning the first of many lessons for the mischievous games he had played.

Until one day he came across a village that welcomed him with open arms and did not see him as monster-born or made.

He sat around their flames one night, concerned by the sullen silence spread across the circle of people who were once more prone to telling stories and dancing in the dark. "What is wrong?"

One of the villagers, a young woman named Ashu, spoke up then. "Some of the young men from our village have gone missing. Every time another goes to look for the lost, he too fails to return. The last one to . . ." Her voice stopped and she fell to sobbing.

Now Hahnbadh saw a pain beyond his own and something inside him stirred. Something hot as freshly fanned flames: compassion and the anger to match. He came to her side and offered her comfort. "What can I do? How can I help? You've offered me food, company, and a place to rest along my wanderings. Please let me do something in kind."

Ashu brushed the tears from her face, taking Hahnbadh's hands within hers. "Find them. Bring them back, if you can?"

"I promise." And Hahnbadh leapt to the task. *Maathi bounded once, waving the torch to cast an arc of light before the front row of the crowd.*

They gasped and reeled as he jumped onto the nearest table, putting a hand to his forehead, searching for a scene only he could see.

But the son of Hahn found no signs—no clues to his quarry. And so he journeyed on, coming to the forest outside the village boundary. At its edge rested a man brought low by years and the world itself.

Gnarled in body, long and lanky limbed, he looked to be carved of old wood just like his walking stick. Dark as bark and threaded with wild hair and beard as silver bright as distant stars and moonlight. The old traveler regarded Hahnbadh and rubbed his eyes in disbelief. "What are you, then, hm? Look more a monkey than a man to me. Or maybe I've been too long in my drink." The old man pulled a gourd from his side, unstoppering it and turning it over. Nary a drop fell from its mouth. "Or maybe I'm sober as a sailor who's never set to sea much less even a boat."

Hahnbadh bristled at this disrespect. He'd grown used to the quiet shunning most folks showed at his cursed appearance, more so the outward fear, but never had someone shown him the sharper side of their tongue like this old man. Lonely, hurt, but never without his pride, Hahnbadh hadn't learned quiet yet, and set to show this old man who truly stood before him.

Maathi mounted the nearest table, taking care not to upset a single dish as he stood atop—chest puffed, an arm raised overhead with clenched fist. A triumphant pose.

"I am the son of Hahn, god of champions, the strong and the brave. He with the fist of iron and the wind within him. I am grandson to Brahm, first of all things, and I have mastered his bindings." *Maathi leapt down from the table, spinning once as he waved the torch in a circle, trailing a dizzying blur of faint orange light.*

The crowd gasped, a few laughed.

But the truth Hahnbadh spoke wasn't the truth in whole—no. For he hadn't come close to learning all of Brahm's gifts. How could he, when he hadn't given himself fully to his own father's teachings? But the old man did not know this, and gave our hero-to-be a longer look and warier eye.

"*Hrmph.* That so? All that and you can't fix your face, can you? Must not be much in those bindings of yours, hm?" The old man's face never changed, but a light danced in his eyes. One that Hahnbadh should have noticed. But before he could speak, the elderly traveler opened his mouth to begin again. "That's good you've got those bindings, though. You'll need them for traveling these woods." He rapped the end of his walking stick against the nearest tree trunk. "There's something foul within.

"Something's taking young men, much like you, and made it so they're never heard from again. Terrible thing, that. Imagine losing a son. Don't know the pain that brings a mother—a father." The old man looked down to his bare feet.

Hahnbadh forgot the traveler's slights and moved closer. "That's what I'm here to see to. To find the missing men and stop whatever is behind this. Do you know?"

The old man looked at him, eyes wide. "Of course I know. Any man with two wits to rub together knows. It's a demon."

Maathi moved to the nearest beam, slipping the torch into a sconce. Its light cast his shadow large against the wall. He spread his arms, making himself appear all the greater then. His head turned to one side and he bared his teeth, and I'm still not sure of how he did it, but in the moment, the shadow of his teeth was as large as a wolf's fangs.

Hahnbadh didn't know what to make of this. He'd never seen a demon before, but he knew that some of Brahm's older makings went wrong—things turned, twisted . . . tainted. They took the hearts and minds of men and, sometimes, greater things, and set them askew. Hahnbadh knew there was little else for him to do. He'd been shown compassion unknown to him for time uncounted and he meant to pay the villagers back in kind. "I worry not for what resides within these woods. I'll face it, and bring those men back."

The old man nodded, accepting the monkey-warrior's resolution. "Then may you be as hard of heart as you seem to be in determination. You will need that as well."

Hahnbadh meant to ask the old man what he meant, but the elderly traveler rose to his feet and slipped into the forest. "Follow me, monkey-man, and maybe you'll find what you're looking for. Though, I daresay, mayhaps it would be better if you didn't, hm?"

Hahnbadh followed the man through the overarching trees, their trunks almost a row of teeth of some old beast closing in around him. Tighter—tighter still they grew together as if promising to swallow him should he go any farther down the path.

Maathi sank to his feet, curling his fingers and bringing both his hands up along the wall to emulate the mouth of what could have been a large serpent.

The old man hobbled along, bent in back, and crooked in knee, yet without a hint of hesitation in his step. Hahnbadh, born of the brave, had little by way of that in his heart then. His legs felt cold and distant. Ice water coursed through his veins and settled in his fingers, making them feel just as far away as his courage.

The branches creaked. Trunks groaned, almost as if the forest had held in ages of discontent it finally felt free to let loose. And the wind moaned through the woods.

Hahnbadh tried to turn his mind from his fear. "How long have you known the missing men, traveler?"

"I don't. Just of them. I don't know the woods any better."

"Then how do you know where to take us, old man?"

"Don't know that either, monkey-man. Just know this: We're two men walking through this forest, and there's a demon in it. It'll find us, I wager. Sooner. Later. Doesn't matter. It'll find us."

Hahnbadh wished terribly that he had a weapon to his name. He'd left with nothing but the strength in his arms, and the sack on his back. Just enough to carry him through the world as a wanderer. He didn't know the three things all travelers must bring: A cane on which to lean, when your feet are weary and back's in pain. The cloak, the cape, to keep the biting wind from your chest and your nape. And lastly, the candle, with which to cast your own light, for when you wander, you are bound to come across the monsters lurking in the night.

And he had none of them then on which to call.

Then came the cry of an owl. Its hoot almost a warning to turn away.

But Hahnbadh refused to heed it, no matter how much he wished to.

"Wise creatures, owls." The old traveler cast the bird a short look. "They know a great deal of things worth knowing, and have the wit with which to warn others of trouble coming. Maybe we should listen, eh?"

Hahnbadh shook his head. "I confess that for the first time, yes, I feel the weight of a challenge that I do not think I can meet. But . . ."

As they wandered deeper into the forest, they heard the distant thrum of thunder.

Thrum. Thrum. Thump. Thump.

Maathi beat the heel of one of his boots against a nearby beam that could take the blows, adding his own thunder to the performance.

Closer then they ventured to the heart of the woods, but the storm never came. Hahnbadh's chest heaved with every step he took. Only then did he realize where the storm had taken root—within himself.

His heart had set to beating like a drum deep-kept within his skull.

Tharump. Tharump. Thatter-rump. It skipped just once—a stutter in the rhythm.

And when he looked ahead, he knew why.

Her hair held all the color of freshly tilled earth and just as much the night sky, which rested too in her eyes, alight with flecks of diamond bright taken from the stars. She wore a shift, thin and form-fit so perfectly to her frame you would have thunk it breath-blown thread spun and woven solely for her body. She held the moon's own glow in her skin and its curve in the shape of her mouth.

The woman placed a hand to her heart. "Who are you, stranger?" She had eyes for only Hahnbadh.

"I am called—"

The old man hissed, smacking the head of his traveler's cane against Hahnbadh's chest. "No, fool. No trading of names here."

"I am Adurah. Speak it freely. If you are afraid of sharing yours, may I then hear the sound of mine from your lips?" She smiled then, bright and full. Whether or not she knew her words would rile our young hero-to-be, that cannot be said, but still she spoke.

And Hahnbadh reacted.

He bristled, taking it as a challenge. Hand over heart, he spoke. "My name is Hahnbadh. First born to and of Hahn himself. I'm not afraid."

Though, nothing could have been further from the truth.

Maathi put a hand to his heart and slowly tapped the spot. Thump-thump. Thump-thump.

Hahnbadh's heart beat louder until he heard his own blood between his ears.

Adurah spoke his name. "Hahnbadh." She ran a hand down her throat—slowly, trailing the shape of her until she reached her heart, beating the spot like a drum.

Ta-dum. Ta-dum.

As Adurah did, she pulled her other hand along the curve of her thigh, striking her flesh just as above.

Thap-thap. Thap-thap. Each beat a drum. The drumbeat a heart.

The storm within Hahnbadh grew—louder. Louder still. It thrummed into a percussion that would not stop and promised to thunder until he shook apart.

"What's wrong, Hahnbadh?"

His head and heart quaked at the sound of his name on her lips.

Maathi beat his chest faster than before.

Our hero rested his hands on his knees—head and heart growing heavy. "I don't understand." The vision of the woman swam before him.

"Fool of a man." The old traveler thumped Hahnbadh once—twice, then again, striking him with the head of his cane. "Look at what sits behind her feet."

And Hahnbadh did.

Resting just behind the pale woman were the bodies of men, no older than him, wearing clothing he'd grown all too familiar with.

"The men from the village." Wroth at his findings, Hahnbadh found his strength reinvigorated, and used it to close in on the woman.

But Adurah fled before he could reach her. And with a word, she split the ground between them. With another breath she sang a word then that fanned a fire in the fresh opening. Flames licked their way up and formed a barrier to the pursuit.

But Hahnbadh would not be deterred. He leapt, born with a strength unrivaled but for his father's, and cleared the gap but not unscathed.

The fire seared his feet, but like men and women once before in story, he bore the pain and crossed the flames.

He set after her. "I'll hound you till the ends of the world." And he was as good as his word.

Hahnbadh chased her westward across the lands. He walked until his feet cracked and bled. Until the brambles and thorns along the paths tore his back and the red ichor fell down his muscles in the shapes of wings.

And all along the way, Hahnbadh did what he could to spare the common folk from her wrath. His story spread. His name carried. As did his reputation for kindness. No longer was he the trickster layabout.

The elderly traveler made sure of this, staying on his heels all the while, and never once losing his pace.

Until Hahnbadh could chase Adurah no longer. Lost, weary, and so far from home, he collapsed.

Maathi sank to his knees.

"What is wrong, son of Hahn?" The old traveler stood more steady-sure and straight in back than ever before. Than even Hahnbadh himself could have managed.

"I cannot go on any longer. My body is failing me. My mind is in knots. And my heart has not once ceased its painful beating since I first set eyes on her."

"So go home. Surely you've done enough."

Hahnbadh took offense to this, used what little strength he had left to get to his feet.

Maathi shot up and jabbed a finger in accusation toward one side of The Fireside tavern.

"Enough? What is enough?" His voice shook the very air. "She is still free. Still set to harm and take others from this world—this life. The strong, the champions, all have their shepherd in my father. What of the ones who are not warriors, born or made? What of them? The common. The lowborn. Who will care and watch over them?"

The old man raised his brows at this and smiled. "Who indeed? There are already the Asir, raised of Radhivahn's own hands—Son of Himself that he is. What need is there of you, then, hm?"

"Then where are they?"

The question was met by another smile from the old man. "Why, I'm looking at one before me, if he only has the will to continue his quest. Do you?"

Hahnbadh blinked, then for the first time saw who truly stood before him.

The form of the old man rippled like a reflection in water struck with stone. And soon no other than Naathiya, goddess of night, the ne'er-do-wells, rogues, and the Asir themselves, looked down at her nephew.

Maathi mimed two figures, shaped from his hands, taking the roles of Hahnbadh and Naathiya.

"You've traveled far, blood of my blood, and grown ever so much. I am proud of you. You journeyed as a wounded man, hurt in pride, and only thinking of yourself. And now you are a man, perhaps not in shape and in face, but in heart. You can return now to your father if you wish. I will tell him of what I've seen, but if you can find it in you, you can journey with me, ever westward, to tend to the needs of the forgotten folk of the world."

Hahnbadh took Naathiya's hand and agreed.

And he who would become the greatest of the Asir rose and set out again.

Westward bound.

For the journey to the west was not over.

Not yet.

Maathi's shadow figures vanished.

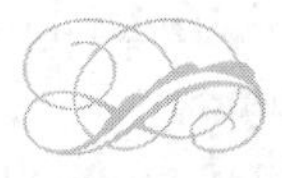

TEN

Knives in the Dark, Fire in Hand

There was a single breath, drawn by all, within The Fireside. It sat held in all of us as if no one dared to be the first to let it loose. Maathi retrieved his torch from the sconce, holding it up like a sword. He bowed at the waist.

And the performance truly ended.

The tavern erupted into thunder. Mugs rattled and cutlery clattered as clenched fists pounded the tables. People stomped their feet. And all through it, cheers and whistles peppered the percussive beats.

I caught Maathi's eye as he took in the applause, and he flashed me a knowing wink. While I wanted to rush over and offer to stand him a drink, I knew enough to leave him be and enjoy the moment. And the nearest of the crowd already had him sorted.

Some clapped hands to his sides and arms. A few offers of drinks were made. One man offered to cover the cost of his meal.

And all that for a story that many would rather not have heard, much less asked for, given the taboo subject.

But that is one of the truths of stories.

We admire them more for how they're told than the things told within. When old tales are spun anew with fresh breath by the right person, we will laud them as if it's the first time we've heard them.

Maathi had done just that. Taken a story the temples would wish forgotten, and he'd told it in a way that even the divided Fireside could come together to celebrate.

He finally shuffled through the crowd, making his way over to me. Maathi reached out with a thumb and forefinger, tugging one of my earlobes in his grip. "Ears open during all of that, hm? Learn anything?"

I laughed and swatted away his hand. "That you're a damnable show-off? I didn't need to see you tell this story to know that." I grinned while grinding a palm against my ear, rubbing the spot he'd pulled. "Are you going to tell the rest of the story? There's more, isn't there?"

"Maybe in a set or two. There can be too much of a thing, you know. A good storyteller doesn't just perform. He manipulates. He lets certain tastes sit with an audience—rest with them. Lets a tale hold them as much as they hold on to it—the memory of the thing. And just when it becomes too long in longing for them, you give them the next piece. Understand?"

I didn't, at least then, but I nodded.

He then led me to a table that had an opening for us, and drinks were soon brought as thanks for his performance.

The joyful outburst at the conclusion of Maathi's story had now dimmed as people returned to their prior conversations, finding familiar comfort in old complaints and keeping to their own business.

I opened my mouth to break the quiet but Maathi beat me to it. "So, Ari, why the Asir, huh? Children don't ask for things like that. First the Ashura, then the Asir. You're supposed to ask about Sakhan, pirate princes and the like. Athwun, a warrior of sunlight after Brahm's own fashion."

I said nothing at first, bristling at the comment about being a child. While it was true, I certainly didn't see myself as one. Not after everything I'd gone through. Normal children didn't have their families killed by story-tale demons. And they didn't make vows of vengeance against those monsters. They didn't kill men, sword in hand, and then take over a gang of thieves. And they didn't bind fire.

But I couldn't tell Maathi all of those things. I never knew how much I could tell anyone, even my friends. So I chose the easy answer—the cheap one.

"I've been studying them, but most of the things I've found don't add up. What little there is, I mean." I frowned.

Maathi mirrored my expression. "Mm. That much is true. You won't find many stories about them. Half the Mutri doesn't even believe in them, you know?" He cast a slow look around the tavern. "Then again, suppose you do, huh? You could have made a real problem here, Ari, asking for that. . . ." Maathi's face didn't change but a sharp light filled his eyes. "If I wasn't such a good teller of tales, ah? Had this lot eating almonds out of my palms." He polished off the statement with a long drink from his cup, releasing a satisfied sigh.

His comment brought another question to my lips before I realized I'd had it, much less spoken it. "But if people don't believe in Radhivahn, how come the days of a set are named after the story?" I rattled some off. "Wanting, Pleaing, Singing, Judgment—each one set to the day of him waiting before judging."

Maathi gave me a thin, curving smile. "People don't have to believe a thing to take from it. Them not believing in it doesn't make it any less real."

I knew that to be true, but it led me into another question. The one perhaps better kept inside. "Do you . . . believe that Radhivahn was real?" I paused, punctuating the short silence with a sip from my own drink. "That the Asir are?"

Maathi brought his mug to his mouth, eyeing me over its rim, brows arched. "*Are,* Ari?"

I swallowed whatever reply came to me and waited for Maathi to answer.

He took another long sip, letting out an even longer sigh afterward. "Real, Ari. That's a hard thing—*real.*" Maathi set the mug down and its thunk sounded like the drub of distant thunder—louder than it should have by any right. "There are a great many things in stories, Ari. But real? All stories are real, after one fashion or another."

He didn't answer my question, and he knew it. I fixed him with a look.

Maathi relented. "I believe that there are most certainly monsters out there in the world, and those who would chase them down—try to right their wrongs and be what salve they can to those harmed. Not the answer you want to hear, I know. But it's the one you'll get. Life, you'll find, is seldom as clear-cut and clean as simple yeses and nos, Ari."

I nodded.

We finished what remained of our drinks in another silence then, a count of ten breaths before I found something else to say. "Maathi . . ."

"Mhm?"

I chose my next words carefully. "You once spoke about *our* blood."

"I did."

"What did you mean about that? You never said. You just vanished."

He grinned at that. "It was a good trick. A very good trick, that." Maathi inhaled and turned in his seat to look at me. "The old blood sings in us both, *yaara.* We're storytellers, born true to it like a bird to the wind."

I shook my head at that. "I'm Sullied, Maathi." I took care to keep my voice as low as possible lest someone nearby pick up on it. "There's no blood in me worth tallying for anyone . . . or anything."

"How sure are you about that, your blood, I mean? Your parents . . ."

I shook my head. "Didn't know them. I can't remember my mother. Not even her face. Sometimes I remember her voice, or I think it's hers. Memories of voices—stories. But I'm not sure if there's any truth to them, or it's just me grasping at things not there."

Maathi nodded as if he understood. "Sometimes the memories of things are too hard to bear going over. There's a cost to them. And we can't always pay that toll, so we bury them in a place where only the whispers of them can reach us. A place of stillness and silence within ourselves. And whispers are easily ignored."

Mahrab, my first true mentor, had promised me answers of a sort. But they rested within a book I couldn't open, no matter how hard I tried. So I looked for another answer from Maathi.

"How did you know I wanted to come up here? That I had to." He didn't need any more clarification than that.

"Ah." Maathi tapped a finger to the side of his nose. "Now that, Ari, would be telling." His smile finally matched the one shining in his eyes, a look better suited to a cat that had found itself in the peak of self-satisfaction. "If you want answers like that, you'll have to go looking, and not here." He punctuated his words by waving a hand at our table. "You're asking me this because you want to know what's next. Where to go? What to do?"

There was no point in denying it, so I nodded.

"You're going to have to leave again." Maathi didn't wait for me to ask the obvious question. "Out there, Ari. Out in the world." He gestured with a wider wave of his hand. "That's the only way to get more answers."

Leave the Ashram? The place had become something of a home to me. I'd made friends here. I could learn about the Ashura.

Maathi went on. "You stay here long enough, you'll start to think you're one of them."

I cocked a brow and repeated his last words back to him.

"The students. Them that go about prancing from study to study, ending up as gurus—wise ones, sages, and all that. Some go on to become bankers and scribes, tallying sums. Others take in history. Some serve in political appointments. But what of you, hm? You asked for stories of the Ashura, now the Asir. You're here to become a binder, no? And you've been cobbling up stories of your own."

I shook my head. "I suppose I'm not really like the other students, am I?"

Maathi hoisted his empty cup. "Up to you to choose. Every man gets that much a say in his own story. And you've written a piece of your story here. But is this how yours ends? There's a whole world out there, all with a gentle flow of all things in it. Does a man good to see it—live it."

How much of my life would I let slip away again as I had once before? I needed to know more about how to deal with the Ashura for the next time I encountered them—the next time I saw Koli.

It would happen. I would make sure of it.

But I didn't know where best to learn that. Out there in the world, or here at the Ashram.

"The Asir fight the Ashura," I said aloud.

Maathi tilted his head a bit. "That's up for some debate, but yes, I suppose they do in the stories."

I licked my lips, knowing I was getting closer. "How?"

Maathi raised his hands, palms up, at that. "With bindings. Swords and staves. Words of power. It changes with the story and the storyteller."

I didn't wait for him to go on. I needed to know more, so I cut in. "How do you find them, what are they like?"

A few of the patrons had stopped talking and turned to look at us. My voice had carried and caught ears better left untouched.

Maathi clapped a hand to my shoulder and let out a well-practiced laugh. As soon as some of the heads turned back, he dropped to a whisper. "Brahm's blood, Ari. You're talking about them like they're real, and a bit too loudly at that. Wrong kind of talk in the wrong tavern gets a man knifed, *ji-ah*?"

"*Ji.*"

"It's all fine when someone's spinning pretty threads pulling on ears. But when the theater's done, a good storyteller learns to keep silent and still. Remember that."

I nodded.

"Good man." He pulled away, but still kept his voice to hushed tones. "Now, for all you asked . . ."

I sat straighter, waiting for him to answer.

"The stories vary, and across most of the Golden Road I've traveled, at that. But, there are some consistencies about *them*." His inflection made it clear who we were speaking of. "They all seem to have walked through fire, much like in Radhivahn's story. Healed by his hands afterward, and it's said that they can never again be burned by walking through fires. Some say their cloaks are white because they're fashioned from moonbeams and old pearls, all sewn tight and hard as diamonds. No knife can pierce them. Some say they ride the winds on eagles' wings and can open the doors to hell to cast down the Ashura.

"They all carry three things that all binders must have. And, yes, they hound the Ashura." Maathi shrugged.

I didn't know how much stock to put into most of what he'd said, but it was more than I had moments ago. So I thanked him for that.

Maathi brushed off the kindness. "We're just trading stories, *yaara*. You want to thank me, you know how to pay a storyteller."

I did, and I smiled, getting up to hail one of the serving girls. The Fireside probably didn't serve Maathi's favorite drink, but I could order more of what we had.

The nearest server was a few tables down, but packed as the place was, she wouldn't hear me unless I moved closer.

I did so, not looking back at Maathi as he addressed me.

"Just remember this: To make yours, learn yours, you have to venture out. No man learns the truth of who he is hidden in comfort. Behind big safe walls where everyone knows your face and there's a place to rest your head. *Ji-ah?*"

"*Ji-ji!*" My tone was better kept for consoling a nagging father. I reached the woman and placed a gentle hand on her shoulder, getting her attention. "Two more of the same, please." I motioned back at the table where Maathi sat.

Only he'd gone. Our mugs remained, and no sight of Maathi anywhere.

Someone quickly noted the open spaces and claimed our seats, leaving me to stand there dumbfounded.

The woman recited my order back to me but I dismissed it, heading toward The Fireside's entrance.

A few patrons crowded together in a staggering line, each person resting against the next for support. They teetered one way, then the other, somehow managing to keep hold of their mugs. Dark beer sloshed over the rims as the patrons broke into a drunken song.

I forced my way through the throng, not bothering with apologies, rushing toward the doorway. I reached it only to find no Maathi.

No sign of the storyteller. Nothing.

A look at the ground showed me impressions in the snow from too many boots to count. So no way of knowing which way he'd taken off to.

I bit off a curse and pulled my robes tighter around myself, stepping out into the cold.

What little light there had been when I entered The Fireside had now vanished behind the cloak of night. Deep dark that held deeper still in the alleys of Ghal, barely alleviated by torches or braziers on the paths I walked. I had little desire to return to the Ashram immediately, deciding to cool my frustrations over Maathi's vanishing.

A weight hung around the back of my neck—a pressure I hadn't felt much since my life as a sparrow. The familiar tightness along my upper back, which made its way into the base of my skull. I looked behind myself as best I could without turning.

Someone followed me down the alley.

Their face remained hidden by the high drawn cowl, and the bulk of their robes obscured most of their figure. But they kept a good distance between us.

All the same, I turned at the next split in the road, moving onto a new path. Snow crunched underfoot as I sped up. My thumb ran along the edge of the kardan I wore, the motion soon developing into a nervous one as I traced the metal lip. But another look over my shoulder showed me the way behind me remained clear.

When I returned my gaze ahead, I saw someone else approaching me. Something about them struck me as familiar. A moment's thought brought nothing to mind, however.

I moved to one side to give them a wider berth as we passed one another.

The stranger staggered as if they'd been deep in their drink, tilting closer to me. Their hands moved and a lance of ice shot through my spine as they lurched closer. They crashed against me and their hands found purchase within my robes, clenching tight.

I shook hard, trying to break their hold. I opened my mouth to curse but their own cry drove the thought from my mind.

"Sorry—sorry." The man lowered his cowl, revealing someone in his early thirties. Lighter skinned than me with curly hair just as dark as that of his beard. A few deep lines had been etched into his face, telling me he'd lived a hard life. He ran his hands over me, smoothing my robes by way of apology. "Sorry again, boy. Tipped one too many back tonight." He gave me a smile that showed a single missing front tooth. "What about you? Got the look of a boy who found some drink of his own, *ji-ah*?" He reached out and tugged one of my earlobes in an act that could have passed for affectionate if not for how hard he'd pulled.

I winced and managed a weak laugh. "Something like that." My smile vanished when I realized he hadn't let go of my ear. I raised a hand to his but he spoke before I could take hold of him.

"Ari?"

My eyes widened at that and, while I'd relished the enjoyment of people beginning to recognize my name, this was not one of those moments. My years on the streets of Keshum had taught me that much, and to spot the sharp look in some men's eyes. The wrong sort—hunter's eyes.

It's a hint of recognition. It sparks within them and you can see it like the first flickering of flame. It's a narrowing of the gaze as someone knows they have prey in hand.

"N-no." My throat seized as I spoke the single word. "No." I spoke it clearer then, hoping my adamancy would convince the man.

"You're him from the Ashram, yes? Boy who went up to Ampur and brought down the mountain?"

That gave me a different pause. But I said nothing.

The man released my ear and put his hands on my shoulders, giving me a squeeze that could have been reassuring in any other situation. "Had family up that way. Said you saved them. You killed some great ole beast up there."

I nodded, not trusting myself to speak. My hands broke into a sweat and some beaded along the nape of my neck despite the cold. I reached into my pockets, taking hold of what sat there.

"Arrey." The man motioned with a nod of his head and I followed the gesture to spot the stranger who'd been following me earlier. They now crossed the way toward us, closing by the second. "I think this is the boy we've been looking for. *Yaara* who saved Ampur."

I breathed a sigh of relief.

But the other man now lowered his cowl and my reprieve was short-lived. I recognized him. The patron from earlier who'd passed a knife to someone else.

My attention went back to the man holding me and my heart quickened.

"You're the one who called the fire, *ah*? The one that burned that boy?" The man asking the question came closer now. One of his hands went into the folds of his robes and silver flashed in the night.

"Get off me!" I tried to break free of the man gripping me tight, but I failed. He had strength and size that I couldn't work against. So I relied on something else.

Something I'd held on to, even if my time at the Ashram had dulled its edge.

Savagery.

I grabbed onto one of his hands and brought my mouth to it, sinking my teeth into the flesh of his palm just under his thumb.

He yowled and tried to pull away, but I kept biting until salt and copper sparked against my tongue. His palm crashed against the ridge of my brow.

I reeled back, blinking from the blow. My feet slipped and I tried to break into a run but fell to one knee. I scrabbled, pulling some of the suthin free from my pocket. The fine strands bent and rolled in my sweaty grip.

I scooped a mound of snow with my other hand, mixing it with the fine metal.

"Oi." A hand gripped my shoulder, wrenching me up and around.

I screamed a single word with more force than I thought I had the wherewithal for. "Burn!" The suthin had taken in the salt from my sweat, and now took in more moisture than it would have ever needed to do what I'd purchased it for.

The man brought his knife overhead. Its edge held the silver-pale promise of moonlight, and that it would soon run red instead.

The suthin flew free from my hand, bursting into an arc of flame between the man's face and me.

He screamed, letting go of his hold.

I collapsed as the man stumbled sideways, swatting at the air out of fear.

"*Aagh, jadhu, aagh!*" He fell to the ground, kicking his legs away from me. *Fire, magic, fire,* went his cry.

I took a hint from and tried to find my own footing. Once I had, I broke into a sprint. Only it didn't last.

A hand closed around the back of my robes and yanked me back. I turned, swinging a blind strike at the other man while his friend still lay on the ground.

He batted it aside. "No, no, little *jadhu* one. None of your tricks." Another piece of silver steel flashed in the night.

The metal kardan bumped against the knuckle of my thumb, and I decided it was time to test my experiment. I gripped it tight, aligning my fingers to trigger the bindings. A part of the metal band hung over my fingers almost like the guard of a sword. I pivoted, snapping my arm out.

My fist crashed into him and thunder roared back through me just as much as through my attacker. A force like falling stones struck me and my arm wrenched backward while my assailant sailed several feet away.

We both hit the ground—hard. The snow did little to cushion me as my head whipped onto a patch of firm ice. My world shook and my stomach found itself deciding whether it was best to lodge itself in my throat or my skull. I struggled to my feet, watching the ground spin beneath me.

"Saithaan. Saithaan!" I couldn't tell which one of the two men called out or if both of them did. Naming me a devil through the night.

Good.

I managed to finally stand straight, but the ground hadn't stopped spinning. A hand in my pocket revealed that I had some suthin left. It was enough for another quick flash of fire to scare the men, but after that? I had nothing.

No more tricks. And there was another problem.

The arm I'd used to punch the man hung at my side and felt distant. Clearly not broken, but well sprained, and the cold seeped into me. The kardan hung from my wrist—its metal warped like I'd put it in a vise and hammered it from every end.

My calculations had been off somehow, and it had stored more momentum than I had accounted for. And I'd paid a price for it.

A groan sounded behind me and I turned halfway.

The man I'd punched lay there, rolling side to side. His hands pressed to his stomach and blood pooled over his lips. "My stomach . . . shit." He coughed. More blood fell and turned the white of Ghal red. "I don't care how much the rich bastard is willing to pay. I'm not knifing this one for all the gold in Ghal." His friend quickly slipped an arm under the fallen man and helped him to his feet. "Up. Move. Before he does more devilry. Move!"

Both men lurched the other way, leaving me alone in the alley.

Alone in the dark.

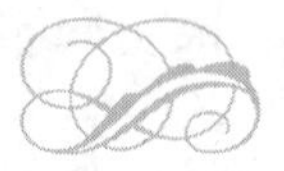

ELEVEN

Gleanings and Gossip

I staggered through the night, leaning with my good shoulder against the nearest wall for support. Finding the closest main road wouldn't be difficult, but if I came out holding my arm and looking like I'd been thrashed, questions would be raised.

Ones I had few answers for.

Except the obvious: Nitham had sent cutters after me.

Trying anything within the Ashram would be foolish, especially with our shared animosity being well-known to anyone with eyes and ears. But out on the open streets? Well, cutthroats weren't so rare a thing, even with all the kuthri patrolling.

Accidents happen, after all. And the wealthy seem to be quite immune to suffering those misfortunes. It's the poor that often bear the fall. And the hurt.

A cold and wary paranoia gripped me as I shuffled my way back to the Ashram, entering the main courtyard as some late-night students and monks moved through the place. Some stared at me, noting that I still held my aching arm. I let go of the limb and averted my gaze.

This wasn't a time for people to spot a weakness in me. Not after so carefully building a reputation to try to protect myself with.

I drew up my hood and made my way toward the Rookery.

"Ari?" Aram stood there, a pack over her shoulder and a book in her hands. "Brahm's ashes. What happened? You look like you've been—"

I gave her a look that told her the truth without any words. She swallowed and nodded.

"Come on, then. Let's get you back to your rooms. I'll have a look at you."

I arched a brow.

Aram let out a short breath and motioned for me to take the lead up to the Rookery. "I just came from the Mendery. I've been working under Master Mender, seeking apprenticeship." The stare she gave me made it clear I should have known that.

In truth, it was something I'd either forgotten or overlooked altogether. I nodded and trundled up to my rooms, Aram right in tow. We made it inside to find a disgruntled Shola rising from my bed. He gave the pair of us a narrow-eyed glare that fell between wanting to return to sleep, and displeasure at my long absence.

A moment's consideration later, he decided he'd find better rest off in the corner of my room. He took one of my blankets in his mouth as extra padding.

Of course.

"All right, sit. Robes and shirt off." She spoke with the cold authority of a kuthri, or someone of noble parentage, not of a student in the Mendery.

I eyed her, pausing halfway through undoing my robes. "What?"

Aram simply held the look of someone unaccustomed to being kept waiting.

I swallowed what I'd been about to say next and removed the cumbersome garment, stripping out of my shirt next.

Aram sat by my side, pulling something from her sack. "You're bruised. Blood and ashes, Ari, what happened?" She put a hand on my hurt shoulder, drawing a sharp wince from me. "This is deep. It's like someone beat you with a rod and tried to pull your arm from your socket."

"That's about how it feels." I gave her a thin and crooked smile, but her stare wiped it clean from my face. I'd never seen this side of Aram before.

Hard. Resolute. Sharply focused. A steel knife's edge if ever she could be one. "What happened?"

So I told her all of it.

"Brahm's breath, Ari. That was remarkably stupid, even for you." She kneaded the muscles of my arm, drawing a series of grunts from me. "It's sprained, not so bad you won't be able to use it, but I'd keep from putting a lot of weight on it for at least a good set. The smaller muscles inside, especially around your wrist and elbow, they're more fragile. And they've been wrenched hard." To make her point, she squeezed the areas around the joints.

I found a new place between the folds of my mind to bury my thoughts . . . and the pain. When that place failed me, I returned to the candle and the flame, finding no real light within my room on which to focus.

Aram continued examining. "Where'd you get the cut?"

That pulled me back. "What?"

She gestured with a thrust of her chin, and I followed her look to the broad side of my bicep. A long, shallow cut ran along the muscle, and I'd never felt it happen. The blood had dried along the robes and the skin had grown purple around it. "Must have been the cold and whatever you did with the binding. Sharp knife and the excitement made it so you didn't know it happened. And there was probably more pain in your joints and muscles." Aram now spoke more to herself than me.

I simply nodded. "When'd you learn all this? Why?"

"The cut doesn't need stitches. Salve and bandages will do. I have some.

There'll be swelling around your wrist and shoulder, though. I don't have anything for that with me—sorry."

I waved off her apology and reiterated my earlier question.

"Father was hurt once when I was a child. The menders said he was lucky not to lose his leg, but after a while, they had him properly walking again. I took an interest in the studies after that, though Father always said I needn't bother. Not necessary learning . . ." She trailed off.

"For a merchant's daughter?" I guessed.

She blinked and realized I'd spoken, then nodded a moment later.

"Well, I'm glad you did." I flashed her a smile that conveyed my thanks better than words could.

Aram returned it and worked the salve between her palms. Once sure that it had reached a consistency she desired, she spread it over my long cut, then rubbed until a good portion of the concoction had been absorbed.

A renewed coolness spread through my arm that had nothing to do with a lingering chill from outdoors. The mixture Aram treated me with brought a breath of gray morning ice through my flesh. A small comfort now that the excitement of the night began to leave me, and my senses just registered the promise of pain sitting within the wound.

The rest of my arm, however, ached like I had decided to let a hundred students walk over it.

Aram picked up on that. Her hands moved with the quiet steady motions that come from long practice and familiarity. Fingers kneaded my bruised and beaten flesh. "This won't stop all of the hurt, but it should help get some blood flowing to stop the worst of it. You'll be stiff though, and anything you can do to move your arm, even a little, will really help."

I nodded, not trusting myself to speak in the moment. My mind drifted through extremes of all that had happened.

Maathi's story, and what he'd said about Radhivahn and the Asir. The way he'd vanished as clean as if he'd never been there at all. I'd seen stranger things, of course, and it could just as easily have been that he had snuck out when I wasn't looking. I couldn't begrudge a performer their theatricality.

Then the two men who had followed me into the alley. Men who spoke of only two things. My name. And a boy who'd been burned.

The one who'd likely hired them.

Nitham, who it seemed was quicker to make good on a threat than I'd thought. First the dead sparrow and show of coins he could spend to have me done in. Soon after that, an attempt on my life.

My stillness and silence spoke for me, and Aram picked up on them.

"What's wrong?"

I pursed my lips before telling her what rested on my mind.

"You sure it was him?" She didn't meet my gaze, her tight frown making it clear enough that she too believed Nitham to be behind the attack.

"Who else? Who has the money to spend on cutters like that? Brahm's tits, who's comfortable sending a pair of men to kill another student?"

Aram still refused to meet my eyes, but I could almost see the thoughts racing through her mind. "I suppose you have a point. But this is too far—"

I waved her off. "Don't. Don't say 'too far even for him,' because it's not. You know he'd do it if he could get away with it."

"And he has . . . in a way." Aram fixed me with a knowing look that told me not to interrupt again. "You can't prove it, Ari. And that's what you'll need to do if you want to take it before the masters."

Who said anything about bringing it to them? I kept the thought to myself, however.

Aram passed me my shirt and robes. "You shouldn't push this."

I stopped halfway through slipping into a sleeve. "What?" My brows rose and some of the shock from earlier returned, now settling in the space between my ears. "You want me to leave this alone? Aram, he sent two men to try to kill me. If I hadn't made this"—I raised the mangled piece of metal and minor bindings—"they would have done the deed. And none of you would have been the wiser about it until someone brought news up to the Ashram. Then what? Two cutters killing someone on the streets? It happens. The kuthri would look into it . . . for a while. But when they found out I was Sullied—no family, no caste?" I then told her what had happened to Valhum.

Aram shied away from my stare. "I know, Ari. The kuthri aren't really here for the protection of the lower castes. They're really for listening to the grievances of blooded ones." She gave me a shrug that could have passed for an apology at any other time, but her words brought out a heat in me that would've been better left resting in the hearth of The Fireside.

"*Lower. Castes?*" Each word left my mouth with the sharp-edged hardness of the knife that'd cut me. "What the hell do you know about lower castes? What do you know about what it means to be Sullied?" My good arm moved and I jabbed a finger at her in accusation. "Caste? I don't get a caste, Aram. *I. Don't. Count.* I'm not a person to most people. For me, my blood doesn't just mean I don't get to pick the trade I want, or that someone of middling caste won't bow or speak honorifics at me.

"Being Sullied means I have to step ten times as carefully as most, because if anyone learns what I am, I can be told to get out of their establishment. Or, maybe their patrons will feel they don't want to share their rarified air and meals around someone like me. So they'll leave."

Aram had packed her sack and took to clutching it tight to her chest, eyes wide. "Ari, the Ashram's not like that, though." Her words might as well have been smoke in the wind. They fell apart as soon as they left her mouth. She knew they were hollow.

"Isn't it?" I nodded to my slashed robes. My voice changed shape to be an imitation of Nitham's. Not perfect, I admit, but close enough for my purpose. "*I want that Sullied trash dead.*"

Aram recoiled, then inclined her head as if conceding the point. "One person doesn't make up the Ashram, Ari. And Nitham doesn't make up the opinions of all nobles."

A truth I learned long ago in my life: Sometimes prejudice exists even in the most learned of places, because when not much else separates learned minds from others, and they all have access to the same knowledge, they still need something to desperately cling to to convince themselves they are better than others.

I noticed then what I'd been overlooking in Aram: She stood out of reach, eyes wide. Her lower lip shook.

I'd scared her. My friend. In the heat of my anger, and the depth of all the cold hatred a person could have for Nitham, I'd frightened my friend.

"Aram, I'm sorry. I . . ."

She didn't wait for me to find the rest of the words. "It's fine. I shouldn't have said what I said either. I know it bothers you." Aram didn't elaborate, and she didn't need to. We both knew enough to hear the things unspoken.

I suppose that's one of the signs of true friendship. You begin to learn the shape of one another's thoughts—their hearts. And in doing so, you learn to speak another thing. A new language. One unknown, and unheard by anyone other than the two speaking it. And sometimes, a great deal can be said within that stillness and silence.

Aram closed the distance between us and wrapped an arm around my good side, pulling me into a soft hug. "I'll see you tomorrow. Rest, and promise me you won't do anything stupid. That you'll stay away from Nitham."

I nodded.

She fixed me with a glare that brought back some of the iron resolution of earlier. "Say it."

"I promise, Aram."

She gave me a thin grin before finally leaving.

With her gone, I crawled into bed, slowly adjusting myself until I found a position that brought out the least of my aches.

Then I waited for sleep to take me. But my mind remained on thoughts of knives in the dark. Fire in my hand. And a single blow that could fell a full-grown man.

I dreamed of things. Of brilliant bright and shining white cloaks, and the ones who wore them. I dreamed of the Asir. And I dreamed of how to find them.

Because if they were really real, who else could help me find the Ashura? Who better to help me kill them? And, of course, I dreamed of fire. The night it took my family. And of the day I'd be able to call my own, true and proper, out of stories.

And finally, my thoughts turned to one last thing still.

I'd promised Aram to leave Nitham alone.

But as I'd learned a long time ago, some promises are made to be broken.

TWELVE

The Principalities

I'd spent the morning cultivating my reputation further—paying a monk five chips, their daily taking for begging, to let whispers about the attack on me spread. He'd made sure to add in details about how I'd called fire from my hands, and no knife could cut me.

While not true, I knew the tale would find its way back to Nitham, and might force him to reconsider another attempt on my life if he believed it would fail.

That done, I headed to pursue the bindings.

Students filtered out of the entrance to the courtyard where Master Binder taught, letting me know that he'd just finished a class.

Or, I hoped. He'd developed a reputation for leaving students to figure out his schedule.

My time with him had taught me it was just as likely that Rishi Ibrahm had spent the time rambling nonsensically at students, then told them he had no intention of teaching them anything useful in pursuing the ten bindings.

A few of the passersby shot me furtive glances that vanished as quickly as I laid eyes on them. Whatever they'd been saying died just as soon as it reached their lips, and I heard nothing.

I ignored them and went inside. Five students remained scattered through the tiers of ringed seating, making me wonder why they hadn't left with the rest of the departing class.

A sharp whistle pierced the air and drew my attention. I spotted the source and all thought left me, and any words that followed.

Radi sat there, one leg crossed over the other. His mandolin rested to one side and he laid an arm around it more possessively than I'd seen some men hold to gold with. He waved me over and I took the silent cue to join my friend.

He must have noticed my expression as I put down my sack and joined him. "What's with the look, *yaara*?"

The previous season Radi had made a small outburst in regards to the bindings, making it clear he didn't think well of them, and the same for Rishi Ibrahm's classes.

Radi opened his mouth to form a silent O, as if that was all he needed to say on the matter. Then he relented with a sigh. "It's complicated, but let's just say I figure I'd benefit from some extra tutelage."

I held my stare to make it clear I would have liked more of an answer than that.

He flashed me a roguish grin that said I would be left wanting, then proceeded to take hold of his mandolin, plucking a tune. It said: *Such is life, sorry—not sorry, grinning.*

I snorted and let him have his secrets then, turning to regard the rest of the small grouping of students.

Stillness—quiet hung in the courtyard for a full minute.

Rishi Ibrahm stood at the center of it all, almost seeming to hold that stillness as much in hand as within the center of himself. He was a pillar of stone before us. Unmoving. Solid. Silent.

No sign of blinking. No sign of speaking. Only staring at the six of us.

Moisture built within my mouth and I found myself swallowing the spittle in anticipation.

Finally, a break. Rishi Ibrahm's mouth moved. A whisper, one I couldn't hope to identify despite knowing how to read lips from a distance. Then, he spoke. "So!" The single word rang out like thunder in a cavern.

Every student straightened as if whipped.

"You're here to get a gleaning, the faintest better hint at the bindings. No more fiddling with the principles, no more trying your hand at glimpsing the folds of the mind. You want more. You think you're ready to bind. And maybe some of you are." Rishi Ibrahm pointed to a young woman sitting as far away from Radi and me as a person could.

She had hair cropped to a length no longer than my index finger. Black as starless night, and her skin held all the deep-dark warmth of the sun in its bronze. Her face had all the leanness and sharp, angular features of a feline. The young woman stiffened when Rishi Ibrahm focused on her.

"Rika has performed a composite binding of Wyr and Ehr—a short distance covered, yes, but nonetheless, a pair of major bindings." Rishi Ibrahm inclined his head toward her in what could have been a measure of respect.

I stared at her as well, stunned that another student had managed a pair of bindings. No word of her feat had traveled amid the Ashram's gossip. Or had I simply missed it in all my own rumor spreading?

Rishi Ibrahm then pointed to another. A young man who looked more like one of the shaven monks than a student. His face had some fat to it, like a child who hadn't quite let go of that early mass we are all born with. Soft, possibly portly under the layers of Ashram clothing, but there was a hardness—sharpness—to his brow. Deep-set eyes that told me he had just as much of that sharpness in his mind.

"Ishun performed the bindings of Ahn and Ahl." Then Rishi Ibrahm turned to Radi. "Our little singer has bound his voice to the wind itself—the air—and held the ears of all those in attendance one night in Stones."

I turned to Radi, staring at him with the obvious question on my lips, unable to give it voice. Was it true?

He shrank and looked away from me, possibly in shame for having kept this secret from his friend. The look he gave me next told me more plainly than if he had spoken the words: *Please don't ask me about it.*

So, I didn't, giving him a grudging nod of my head instead to let him know we'd bury the matter.

Rishi Ibrahm went on. Nila, a young woman holding all the fair features of someone from Sathvan, had performed one of the bindings—ahn. Raju, a man who looked to be twice Radi's age, with a full dark beard lining his face, had managed to call the counterpart to Nila's, ahl.

"Lastly, we have our young upstart." Master Binder waved a hand toward me. "Ari." No further words left his lips for a long moment. Then another. And longer still. The group sat there in the quiet as if it had been entrusted to us to hold it until Rishi Ibrahm found what next to say. He exhaled, then nodded more to himself than us. "Our young Ari, to the surprise of many, myself included, bound fire. He performed a composite binding of Whent and Ern, taking in hand not some simple thing—no. The little shit had to go and bind something living, something with a will and want of its own. Fire." The last word left him as a curse. "Damnable binding could have burned down half the Ashram."

I said nothing.

Rishi Ibrahm clapped his hands and took half a dozen paces closer to us, not quite reaching the first of the steps. "You are all here at my personal invitation . . . or to avoid having your head lopped off"—Rishi Ibrahm eyed me—"and to learn how to *safely* use the ten bindings all men must know. Mostly because you've all stumbled across them rather blindly, when I'd rather you not have found them at all. But, here we are. So, listen well, do twice better, and maybe you won't kill yourselves—and, more importantly, me—while we go about it, *ji-ah*?" Master Binder didn't wait for our assent before continuing.

"Right then, we begin with the beginning of the all itself."

Rika raised a hand, and when Master Binder paid her no mind, she voiced her question anyhow. "The all, Rishi Ibrahm?"

He blinked as if he'd forgotten he stood in the middle of a class, teaching. "Hm, oh. Yes. The all." He gestured around us, then to the sky. "It's everything. All things. The whole of it. All of it, Kaethar Rika, is the all itself. The world. The worlds beyond ours. The night sky and all its stars, and whatever is beyond them is the all itself."

The young woman nodded, and I couldn't be certain if she truly understood, or simply saw better to pretend she did.

But Ishun wasn't satisfied by the answer. Not in whole. "Worlds beyond ours, Rishi?"

"Mm." Master Binder nodded. "Was just coming to that, and it ties in nicely to what Kaethar Rika inquired about." Rishi Ibrahm went over to a trunk sitting by a stone table, kicking its lid open. He bent over and retrieved a number of tin plates and rods. A moment later and he'd arranged them neatly into an assembly that seemed better fit to a juggler or performer.

Three rods stood and held plates atop them, perfectly balanced, though they should have toppled. Another set of rods sat on top of those, keeping more plates overhead, then another, until they came to a single point. One rod. One plate above them all. Rishi Ibrahm muttered something under his breath, then lashed out with a kick that would have sent it all falling.

Only, that didn't happen.

His foot struck a rod and he let loose a string of profanities that had me torn between wanting to take notes, and finding religion in hope I'd be spared damnation simply for my proximity to Master Binder's cursing. I don't think any linguist ever imagined such combinations of actions and filth.

Once the tirade died, he recollected himself. "The reward for work well done is a bruised foot. Tits and ashes, I swear." He grumbled again before remembering we existed. "Right, the principalities. The pieces of the all. The worlds of ours and others. Magic."

Rishi Ibrahm motioned to the standing plates. "Pay attention now." He held up a pitcher of water and several of the students broke into low whispers.

Radi and I joined them. "Where'd he get that from?"

I shook my head, unsure. "I don't know. Didn't you see him pull the jug out?"

Radi mimicked my expression.

Was it one of the bindings? No. Nothing I'd seen indicated they could materialize something from nothing. But then, what did I know? Perhaps it was a stage trick. Sleight of hand.

Rishi Ibrahm gestured to the container. "The all." He motioned to the plates. "Also the all and . . . the principalities. No, no." He jabbed a finger at Rika, who'd raised another hand. "Not now. Not yet. I'm getting to it." Master Binder raised a balled fist to his mouth and coughed once to clear his throat. "The principalities are the larger worlds of worlds. Each and every all resides in a principality. All things across space and time among us sit within a principality." To punctuate his statement, he pointed at one of the plates.

"Imagine each of these as one. Each principality governs a modality—a way in which the magic of that space of worlds exists and shapes itself, and thus, comes to direct how the people and things live. How they grow. How they change over time, what they can do. The atham and Athir are part of it. The bindings are too." He jabbed a finger to the top plate then and began pouring water from the pitcher.

It splashed onto the tin surface, drops spattering off to pool in the plates below. A puddle formed on the top one as well until it overflowed. Then the inevitable. The excess ran off to flood the plates below, repeating the process until the water made its way through the entire assembly and hit the floor. He kept pouring. And the water never ceased to come.

"They are like so. The principality of the mind"—he gestured to the top plate—"the body." He took a breath and nodded to another plate. "And the soul." He finished by indicating a third plate. There were still more plates however.

I didn't bother with ceremony in asking my question, letting it blurt from my mouth instead. "That's all there are?"

He nodded, not perturbed by my interruption.

I looked at the plates again. "What if there are more?"

Rishi Ibrahm looked up at me and his gaze adopted a focus I'd only seen once before. It took in the whole of me with no room for anyone else—*anything* else. It was like it took in my form, my face, everything within me there and then, as well as all I'd been and done to that point in my life. With that one look, Rishi Ibrahm could have understood everything about me, if this was one of the old stories of magic and wonder. With that one look, Rishi Ibrahm would glean my future, and all I'd come to do.

But, no. Of course not. That's not what happened.

Even so, a stillness took me and buried my breath better deep below my chest, so far that I couldn't hope to call on it, much less hold it.

Then, he broke the stare and I could breathe again.

"What if there are." The words left him like a whisper in the wind. So low a thing that it couldn't hope to be heard, but somehow, I had.

He offered no further explanation, and the set of his face made it clear he wouldn't. So I chose something else instead.

"If that's how magic works across the worlds, which are we in? How do they work—their rules? What of where the magic comes from?"

At that he smiled. Bright and gleaming with all the mischief I'd first seen in him upon my admittance to the Ashram. "Ah, now that is a good question, Admitted Ari."

"Kaethar." I offered the clarification without any hint of irritation. "You . . . were the one who proposed my elevation in rank, Rishi Ibrahm."

He blinked. "Was I? Whatever possessed me to do that? Terrible decision, really."

I might have shrunk in my seat a bit, much like Radi had earlier. My momentary humbling didn't last, however.

Two monks strolled into the class, taking up positions at either side of the wide stone stairs. "Kaethar Ari!"

I stood, unsure of which monk to address.

The pair of men locked eyes with me. "You have been called to the Admittance Hall to discuss charges of performing an illegal binding while under suspension from the Ashram's studies. Under strict instruction *not* to attempt any major binding without the supervision of the Ashram's Master Binder. You will come with us now."

"What?" I couldn't manage any other words . . . or thoughts. *When had I violated my sentence?*

I turned to look at Rishi Ibrahm for some sort of help.

He flashed me a toothy grin, the light in his eyes burning brighter. And his lone offering of aid came in the way of raising a single thumb my way.

My stomach sank. I collected my things and followed the monks.

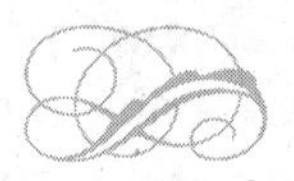

THIRTEEN

TERRIBLE TRUTHS

I arrived at Mines, its dark stone a deeper black than pitch in night. Yet, the surface held a sheen I hadn't noticed before, almost like glass in ink. The headmaster and other rishis save Master Binder sat in their usual places, all looking at me over low burning candles that cast odd shadows over their faces.

The monks stood to either side of me—two monoliths of tall muscle that I didn't think I would ever match no matter how much growth I had left in me.

"Kaethar Ari." The headmaster leaned forward, peering at me. "You are called here to answer claims that you performed a binding in the city of Ghal after explicit instructions that you were forbidden to attempt any major bindings until proving to Rishi Ibrahm and, by extension, us that you have mastered proper control over yourself and the forces of Brahm's teachings. Do you have anything to say for yourself?"

I didn't. I hadn't done any such thing, and I racked my memory trying to recall what I'd done in the city to have reached the masters' ears.

Realization thundered into me, causing my heart to lurch just as much as it sent chills through me. Master Spiritualist gave voice to my thoughts before I could.

"Kaethar Ari, by many accounts, was seen in Ghal at an establishment known as The Fireside. From there, he left in the night and came into an altercation where he channeled a binding injuring two men." The headmaster pulled his gaze from a piece of parchment he'd been reading off of and turned all his cold attention on me. "Is this true?"

I swallowed before speaking, searching for the courage to both speak the truth, and refute his account. "Yes . . . and no."

He quirked a brow and looked to the other rishis behind the long stone table. "Explain."

"I did visit the Agni-thaan, Headmaster. And I did leave in the night and encounter two men, but the details of the story that have reached your ears, respectfully speaking, aren't wholly true."

Silence. Another trade of looks, all of which settled back on me, telling me in no uncertain terms to continue speaking and clarify what I meant.

So I did. "Two men followed me out of the establishment and their motives weren't anything but decent, Rishis." The wave of a hand cut me off.

Rishi Bharia's voice cut through the second of quiet. "And how do you know what their intentions were, Kaethar Ari?"

I licked my lips. "Have you ever lived on the streets of Abhar, Rishi Bharia?"

Her mouth moved but she found no words to give voice to. She shot a quick look at the other rishis, but the stares they returned told her she was on her own. She had asked of me, and now she was to answer. Instead, she merely shook her head.

"I have. Three years as a sparrow"—I caught myself and realized they wouldn't know what I meant by that—"an urchin. I was taken in by a man who fed us, housed us, clothed us, with the sole requirement that we . . . come into goods through less than legal means."

"Stealing, you mean." The words came from Master Conditioner, his thick forearms resting crossed over the desk. Even sitting still, it looked as if the corded, knotted muscles he had visibly shifted and tensed.

I nodded. "Yes. I'm not ashamed of it, and I'd do it again if I had to. I'm not sure how many of you have lived under the thumb—no, knife—of a thug, one who sold children off if they underperformed, but I can tell you that most of your thoughts only go to surviving the day. Praying you don't get hit too many times by passersby, or that a kuthri doesn't lop off a hand and leave you crippled."

The quiet that fell deafened all within Mines. But I refused to let it rest and blanket all, even though I had an inkling that breaking it would be like shattering the thin layer of ice over unfrozen waters. The only thing keeping everyone from falling into a harmful winter's freeze.

"So, yes, I stole. And in the course of that life I learned how to spot the kinds of men who meant me harm. The kind who would skin a child for some coins, cut my throat and leave me bleeding to die in an alley, because who would mourn a street urchin? A Sullied one at that?" That last question hadn't been aimed at them—more matter of fact than anything else.

Still, it struck them, and their wide eyes and wordless mouths told me so.

I went on. "I left The Fireside, and grew uncomfortable, noticing someone following me. Soon enough, another man came down the alley after the first grabbed me." I took a breath and steeled myself for the lie to come. "I don't know what they wanted or why, only that they pulled a knife."

"None of this explains the bindings, Kaethar Ari." The comment came from the headmaster.

"In my attempts to free myself, I resorted to two pieces of cleverness I had on hand." I let the words sit, spread, and fill Mines, hoping to tempt the masters into further curiosity.

A dangerous game. And I knew that. But I needed the momentary leverage for my request to come.

"And what cleverness was that?"

I looked to the two monks at my sides. "Might we speak in private, Masters?"

A few arched their brows and exchanged silent looks before the headmaster spoke. "Why? The monks are here to ensure, should we levy punishment, that it is meted out."

"Headmaster, where would I go? They can wait right outside the doors. I came to the Ashram to learn, and I'm suspended from classes but for learning under Master Binder, which is where I was before summoned here. Many people can vouch for that. I can tell you why I wish to speak privately should you be kind enough to grant me that wish."

Another silence now. Another stillness. No traded glances. No murmurs. Just every pair of eyes within Mines staring at me. Weighing me. And deciding what to do next.

"Very well. You two may wait outside." The headmaster dismissed the monks and they bowed their heads, leaving as quickly as that.

"Thank you, Headmaster." I shuffled in place, my gaze falling to my feet for a moment as I thought over how best to present what I'd done. "I didn't perform any bindings, not exactly."

"Not exactly? How does one 'not exactly' perform a binding, Kaethar Ari?"

I dropped my sack and pulled free the kardan I'd stored in there, holding it up. "This is how. It's a kardan that I purchased from Holds. It's part of a project and theory I've been working on, Rishis."

"Might I see that?" Rishi Bharia held out her hand before she'd even finished speaking.

I ran over to her, passing it up over the lip of the high stone desk.

She inspected the warped metal with the care only a master artisan could manage. Slow, long, thoughtful stares. The Master Artisan wasn't looking just at it, but through it, almost into it. The same way Maathi had once looked at me. The same way I felt Rishi Ibrahm had at times. It was a look that spoke of an understanding you couldn't get from hearing a thing, or touching; it was something deeper—something older. Truly seeing. Much like a stare traded between a boy on a mountain and a dying old god.

"You've inscribed minor bindings on this, in the same language you used on your kite." It wasn't a question.

"Yes, Rishi Bharia."

She made a low noise of acceptance as she continued turning the mangled kardan over. "What happened to this piece of steel, and what was the nature of the minor binding you imparted on this? How does this relate to what happened to you?"

"The set of minor bindings I inscribed were fashioned to take in and store any momentum generated by my swinging arm, the one on which I wore that, Rishi. I duplicated the binding in hopes of storing twice as much energy within, giving me more to release should I need it." I caught myself too late, realizing I'd left myself open to a more difficult question.

The inevitable one of: Why would I need a weapon like that?

The obvious answer: Why, to use, of course.

Not how I wanted my inquiry to go.

"Sloppy." The word left her like a crack of stone on glass, jarring me from my own thoughts. "You cannot duplicate energy with a simple use of minor bindings. The minor bindings work in concert with the laws of the world and the all of all things. Not against them. Not to pervert them. *With. Them,* Kaethar Ari."

I nodded, deciding to pull on what little of the actor's arts I'd learned in my life in the theater. My stare fell on my feet and I tried to look properly chastised. "Yes, Rishi Bharia."

She went on. "You also left out a set of bindings to properly control the influx and discharge of energy, I take it?"

I had. I thought I'd accounted for that, but thinking back, what I'd inscribed ran counter to the double set of bindings. In effect, the second set completely negated my control. It was the equivalent of writing a sentence that makes the previous useless, or a lie that became the new truth. *Stupid.*

"With that, you told the kardan to accept *all* force it came in contact with. Not just that of your moving arm, but every footfall, every impact that rattled through your body and touched this steel."

My eyes widened as I realized just how my tool had stored so much force so quickly. "And it released it all at once as well."

She nodded. "Yes, though the idea was sound. There might be something to it, given greater complexity and time and more interlinked pieces of metal. Clever to consider steel for its nature. You seem to have a great interest in the storing and manipulating of physical forces, Kaethar Ari. As evidenced by your kite last festival, by any rate. Would you mind I held on to this for further study?"

What could I say? I inclined my head again. "Of course, Rishi Bharia. I can even walk you through the language I've been using."

She flashed me a rare smile that let me know I'd scored a minor victory.

I seized the opportunity to explain what I'd used the kardan for. "During the struggle, Masters, I discharged the kardan's built-up force to knock one of the men off me. The second piece of cleverness, one that I admit might have led to the stories running a touch out of hand, was my use of suthin."

And it certainly had nothing to do with me paying a damnable monk to spread word about this. I'd hoped my actions wouldn't have been seen as bindings, though. Brahm's ashes, curse my tongue. If I get out of this, I'll bite down twice as hard on it anytime I come up with even an inkling of cleverness.

When the masters didn't ask further, I clarified. "The strands of metal are highly flammable when they contact—"

"Water and salt, we know." Rishi Bharia waved a dismissive hand, her eyes still on the kardan.

"Right. And I used the salt from my sweat, and the snow. It created a flash of fire that terrified the men. They thought I'd bound fire in truth, but it was just a trick. After that, they ran off. But as people not of the Ashram and lacking the proper education, I can understand why they'd think what they did. And why rumors would spread then about me performing illegal bindings." I shrugged, hoping my story would appease them.

The headmaster frowned, lacing his fingers together before resting his chin atop them. "And that's it? A pair of cutthroats who wanted your . . . purse, your clothes, something in the night, and you fended them off with two pieces of artisanry?"

I nodded.

The headmaster exhaled before giving a long, searching look to the rest of the rishis. Then they broke out into low whispers that I couldn't hope to catch a hint of. And then they stopped. A decision.

I held my breath, waiting.

"In light of this evidence, and in lieu of any contrary information, we're given to accept your account of events, Kaethar Ari. You're cleared of any wrongdoing. And you will set about correcting the malicious stories about you—"

"No, please!" I forgot myself for a moment, quickly speaking up again to add the honorific. "Please, Headmaster. Let the stories sit, if you would? This is why I wished the monks gone."

More quiet.

I seized it, not giving the masters time to ask the obvious question. "I need people to listen to the version of the story that's been spreading—to believe that."

The headmaster spoke. "Why, Kaethar Ari?"

Not a refusal, at least. Good.

"Growing up how I did taught me something, Rishis. The power of reputation. It's a shield. On the streets of Keshum, I let certain stories spread and take lives of their own. They ended up keeping me and mine safe . . . as much as can be for children in our situation. Here, I've found it's much the same."

"Nonsense!" The single word ran through the room, and the headmaster rose halfway from his seat. "The students of the Ashram are among the brightest and best learned throughout the Mutri, and most certainly more so than many other countries. Mature! I won't—"

"Master Spiritualist"—Rishi Saira, the Master Lorist, placed a hand over the headmaster's—"are you telling me that every young student at the Ashram is more grown than child?" She gave him a smile that said plainly they both knew the answer to that question.

He stammered for a moment before collecting himself, setting a hand to stroke his beard. "Well . . . it's not unheard of for some students to take longer to mature." The Master Spiritualist gave me a sidelong look that made it clear I was included in his estimation.

Rishi Saira laughed. "I think you've forgotten what it's like to be a child. You know full well what any of us was like at that age. Sneaking kisses and plotting nights out in Ghal, away from our studies. Thinking of mischief and gossip as much as studies and prestige."

Some of the other rishis nodded, but looked as if they wished they didn't have to admit as much.

A sign to press my point. "And that's why, Rishis. Some students hate me. It's not said openly, but it's true. I've risen in rank within my first season at the

Ashram. I've called a major binding twice." The lie left my mouth easily enough, counting what happened in Sathvan—calling down the mountain, about which only Master Binder knew the truth. "Then I won the kite flying tournament, beating Nitham. You know how that turned out.

"Others think I'm a freak. I've heard some of what they say. But for all that, stories like these keep me safe. Would any of you try to make mischief with someone who's bound fire? Who called it in an alley at night against two cutters, and struck one hard enough to break bones?"

I knew I had them with that, though it pained me somewhat to have to speak the words. Sometimes, the truth is a set of shackles with which we lock ourselves into perilous positions in life, and the lies are the keys to freedom. Sometimes, sometimes the truth is better set to hurt us, and which of us wants any more of that? And the lies? They're the salve that soothes us. And sometimes the only protection from the terrible truths of the world are the lovely little lies we tell about ourselves.

For better.

And for worse.

Such is the way of things.

"That is why I asked for the monks to be sent away. The hope that I could share what I just have with you all and that you would let me keep that much between ourselves, especially after what happened to me. The longer that story holds the shape it does, the better the chance no one will try their hand at hurting me again."

Those last words had the intended effect. The masters gave each other long, silent looks, the sort that spoke loudly of uncomfortable thoughts. Finally, the headmaster inclined his head and spoke. "In light of everything you've said, Kaethar Ari, we agree to let the rumors surrounding your . . . cleverness stand. *But,* I advise you to take extra care to avoid future trouble, regardless of how well you can get yourself out of it. Our patience isn't inexhaustible, Kaethar Ari."

Fair enough.

I nodded my head and uttered my profuse thanks for their understanding. With that, I made my way out of Mines, my back straighter and chin held higher than when I'd entered.

If my story had reached the masters' ears so quickly, I wondered how much further it'd travel by the end of the day.

I supposed I'd find out soon enough.

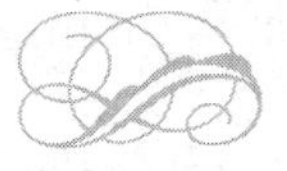

FOURTEEN

The Hurts We Hold

I let several hours pass after my run-in with the masters. Then I visited the Artinsanry, explaining my thought process behind the kardan to Master Artisan. We came to an agreement on how I could improve my bindings and what other materials I could use to get a better effect. In return, I taught her what I'd learned from Pathar the Tinker of his people's language. The intricate system of bars and dots that festooned the sides of their traveling homes.

That out of the way, I hunted down Rishi Ibrahm, hoping to catch him and learn what I'd missed with my abrupt removal from his class.

Only, he was nowhere to be found. And any attempt to hunt him down led to clueless students, all of whom had no idea where the Master Binder had gone.

Of course.

I walked through the main courtyard of the Ashram, trying to put the winter frost and its cold from my mind, but failing. What I would have given for a good fresh cloak to wear over my robes. The thought faded as I walked onward, falling under the looming shadow of a familiar building.

The place that could end up my permanent home should my probation go poorly. A prison for my future.

To call it a tower would have been an insult to any other structure that bore the name . . . and bothered to actually adhere to its strict shape. This pillar of stone stood like it had been constructed by a child. It shouldn't have managed to stay upright with all the uneven gray slabs that made it up. The place was held together by something other than mortar.

Something unseen.

Works of the ten bindings, I wagered.

It rose high into the sky, with rooms shooting out of it to hang over thin air, lacking any support to keep them in place. Anywhere else, they'd have toppled to the ground, shattering, and just as much the poor students housed within.

Students I could end up joining. Forever.

Only, something now struck me as odder than before, which said a great deal when considering the place. There were more rooms than there'd been before jutting out from the structure.

Will one of those be mine . . . one day?

And inside one of those rooms was a friend. One I hadn't visited since I'd bound fire.

I raced over to the doors of the Crow's Nest and made my way inside.

A young man dozed atop the wooden desk. He wore a sleeveless shirt, of a gray found in dark wet stone. His bare arms showed lean muscle and fresh scars that were not there the last time I saw him. The short brush of his black hair sported flecks of white paste that matted bits of his locks.

Mortar? Clay? I couldn't tell.

"Krisham?" I kept my voice low—calm, the tone best reserved for speaking to a skittish animal. A dangerous one at that.

The former student, and now internee of the Crow's Nest, roused with all the bleary-eyed energy of a cat long deprived of sleep. He blinked several times and put a hand to his temple. "Brahm's blood, what day is it?"

I thought on it then answered. "Pleaing, why?"

Krisham bolted to his feet, wobbling as he realized a second later where he stood. "How did I get back to the nest? Oh no. *When* did I get back?"

I opened my mouth, then paused. I had no answer for Krisham, only more questions. "Um, *where* did you go, Krisham?"

That seemed to bring him back to ground. "Huh—oh, you know . . . around." His gaze fell onto our surroundings, slowly taking in the circular room. "Hm. Someone's made the nest taller again. I should go check and see who's come. See who might have gone."

Gone? Gone where? The words left me before I'd realized and I voiced the question. "Who left—Immi?"

Krisham stared at me as if I'd decided to drop my pants and take a fresh shit right in the middle of the room. Eyes wide, mouth hanging loose. Then he threw his head back and nearly fell clear from the table. "Oh, gods, that's good. Immi, leave? No. No, Ari. She's nowhere near sorted enough to leave. Most of the old ones here aren't." Another sharp bark of laughter punctuated the statement.

I deflated at that. Not just in worry, but from asking something that might have cost me whatever shade of respect, or at least tolerance, Krisham had built up for me. Changing the topic seemed the best course of action. "May I see her? It's been a while since I've visited."

Krisham hopped down from the table and stood before the stairway. "I'm sorry, Ari, but you can't." His face twisted as if he'd been jabbed by something sharp and painful.

"Can't?" I echoed the word stupidly.

He nodded and informed that Immi had been in a bad way of late, and she required special care. Master Binder had expressly forbidden any visitors.

When I asked what had happened, all Krisham knew was that she had received a visit prior to throwing a terrible fit.

It had been Nitham. No one knew what occurred, only that it had gone poorly for the young girl.

I stormed out of the Crow's Nest in a fury, drumming up ten thousand curses for the spoiled sprat, and some aimed at myself. I hadn't come to see her at all over the season break. I hadn't been there for her.

It wasn't hard to once again lay the blame for this at Nitham's feet. No matter what I did, I found myself losing my life at the Ashram, and access to my friends. Aram's advice about Nitham came to mind, and she had a point.

Sort of . . . at any rate.

It's true, I had no idea how to act with nobles and their like. I didn't know how to bow and scrape to them. *I* knew another way to deal with them.

I knew how to rob them.

FIFTEEN

Intermission—Silent, Still, Alone

A heavy thud rattled the prison door, followed by another. "Lady Etiana?"

I stopped the story and eyed Eloine. "Your retinue's growing impatient. Evening plans?" I frowned, racking my brain to recall the time, but came up short. "Morning?"

Eloine reached through the bars of my cell and cupped my chin, giving it a gentle waggle. "My plans were to listen to you." She gave me a tired smile that faded just as fast as it'd come. "But it seems someone has other ideas in mind."

I quirked a brow. "Oh? Does this someone have a name? He wouldn't happen to be a dashing Etaynian prince, would he?"

Eloine pulled away from the bars. Just a shade, but noticeable all the same. Her gaze flicked toward the door, then back to me. "If he were, would that be a problem?"

I shrugged. "Not particularly."

A small spark kindled in her eyes and the edge of her mouth pulled into the beginnings of a teasing grin. "Jealous?"

"Nothing to be jealous of. I've killed a prince before, remember?" I'd meant it in jest, but knew I'd erred as soon as the words left my mouth.

Eloine stiffened, then rose to her feet. "You shouldn't joke about that. If the wrong ears hear you, you'll tie the noose around your own neck better."

I turned away from her. "Wouldn't be the first time I've been in one. And I've slipped them before." *But will you this time?* The question hung heavy in my mind.

"I'd like to hear that story." But Eloine's voice lacked the interest it had held before. "Another time. I trust I'll be able to find you when next I come looking."

I snorted. "I'm not the hard one to find. But, yes, I'll try not to break free and vanish into the wind."

She curtsied, half turned toward the door, then stopped. Eloine looked at me, long and deep. In that silent gaze we traded more than what we could have said.

Quiet sorrow over my situation, and what was to come. She promised she'd do whatever she could. The stare I returned told her I'd be fine, though it was quite obviously a lie. But all the same, I told her wordlessly to stay safe and not bother. I would handle this myself.

And the final glare she gave me told me I'd be better off sitting on my hands, and would do well not to tell her what to do.

Ever.

I decided to follow the advice.

Eloine then headed to the door and knocked. "I'm ready to leave." The guards ushered her through, not sparing me a look, then shut the door behind her.

And I was left alone.

The slow, steady sound of dripping water roused me from my sleep. For a moment, I found myself unable to do anything other than listen to the rhythmic drips against the stone. I lay there, watching the puddle where the beads of moisture struck and pooled.

My mind went to the folds. First two, then four. I held the image of the eroded stone in which the water sat. It wouldn't be a stretch to imagine the rest of the stone below me to fall into that sorry state as well.

To crumble away. Shatter. Fall apart. The iron bars could do just as well. Bend and break before my hands. After all, why not?

Otherwise I would remain here, and rot. And somewhere above in Del Soliel, one of the Tainted would be making dark plans. Twisting the minds of others, and quite possibly leading a country to ruin. And the lives of millions along with it.

I put my hands on two of the bars. Cold iron leached what warmth I had in me, pulling it from the deep of my marrow and bones. The metal was porous. Rusted. Hard. Resolute.

So was its nature.

It wouldn't bend easily. It would take a mind much harder and the will to follow.

A grin spread across my face. Stubbornness was a trait I'd been said to have mastered early in life.

The image inside my mind shifted, now showing the bars. First as they were, then as I wished them. Bowed out at the sides. Farther then, and farther still. Wide enough apart a grown man could step through them.

Two folds. Then four—quickly to eight. From eight to sixteen. Eighteen. I couldn't manage to double the previous set, settling for an additional two instead. "Start with whent, then go to ern." The words left me easily enough, but nothing happened.

I repeated them, grit and stone filtering into my voice. "Whent. Ern."

The prison echoed with the sound of cracking ice and a low moan of something else. Bands of rust snapped and flaked free of the iron bars. The metal shuddered and warped. . . .

But sadly not enough.

The rods barring my way had curved away from each other by the measure of a half hand.

"Brahm's blood and ashes!" I smacked a palm against one of the bars, grunting as pain radiated through my hand and settled in my wrist.

But I had been close. Close enough to affect something in this place of silence and stillness. No sooner than I had though, fatigue rushed in, and my mind grew fogged by all that had happened of late.

Had I ruined things between Eloine and myself? What *could* I do to better make my case at the trial? Would it even be an honest one? What happened to the three men who'd been sharing this place with me?

How long would I be stuck here without any sounds but those I could fight to make? A place of unmoving stone.

Quiet. Silent. Still.

And alone?

The perfect prison for me.

SIXTEEN

AN EXERCISE IN CLEVERNESS

Deep sleep kept me in its hold until the prison door opened with the grating sound of old metal that preferred to be left alone and shut in place.

I opened my eyes, shaking the bleariness from them. My head spun as something worse than tiredness set in.

Hunger.

I hadn't been given a sip of water, or food. Perhaps that was deliberate. Prisoners were costly to keep, and one charged with the murder of a prince? It might be easier should I never make it to my trial at all.

The boots of a visitor struck hard against the stone floor and I turned my attention to the source of the noise.

The man stood a head higher than me and wore tight, fitted clothing that showed heavy use. And he held to the youth of a man in his early twenties, despite having the severity of face and furrowed brow of someone decades older than himself. A fellow carved of sharp glass in features and dark tousled curls.

He stopped outside my cell with the abruptness of a wheel striking a rut. Or a soldier called to halt. "Storyteller."

I nodded. "In name and trade, though I didn't much get to ply the latter while in the company of your family. Apologies." I tried to give him a practiced smile, but fell short.

"I assume by now you know full well what's to come? What you've been charged with?"

The smile finally appeared across my face, though I knew it to be colder and sharper than I'd intended. A razor in ice. "Oh, a number of people have come through to make that very clear. I assume you're here to add to that?"

The well-dressed man betrayed as much as cold iron—nothing.

I looked him up and down, trying to take the measure of him—glean his story. Still. Nothing.

"I'm here to talk. To listen." The man made no move to sit or break from his stone-still rigid posture. "And from there, I will tell you what I think. What I know. And then you listen. *Sieta?*"

I took in all he'd said. Each word clipped. Purposeful. More and more like a soldier of experience.

And why would a soldier have any care for bothering with me? The cut of his clothes told me some, but not enough. Not a uniform. Simple, but quality material. That bespoke wealth. All of which left me with a guess. One I took.

"Forgive me, Prince, I don't think I caught your name." I tried to offer a more sincere smile than before, but fell short again.

He returned a minute twitch of the lips that could have been anything from bemusement reined in, to something close to surprise. "Efraine. Prince Efraine. Now you know my name, I would like yours."

"Storyteller."

His mouth twitched at my response. A hint of frustration?

"I think, if we're to be talking truths here, we should start with proper names, *sieta*?"

I blew out a breath and met his eyes. They were the same brown as found in most Etaynians, the deep dark of soil. But they contained a hardness not seen in many folks—a shortness of patience for games.

Shame. I was an avid player of them.

"I've had more names than most can count, Prince Efraine, and each has been plenty *proper*. Eagle of Edderith. Jade Sword of Laxina. The Ghost of Ghal. And I'm sure Prince Killer is now among them." *Again.*

He ground his teeth. "It is certainly being said among *some*."

Ah. Now that was something. "Some . . . not all. Are you among the some who are not saying that, Prince?"

"I am, as of yet, undecided. Though I am leaning to one direction the more you speak. And not a favorable one at that."

"Mm. Well, I'll have to see about changing your disposition toward me, then." I kept my gaze locked on his eyes, which never blinked as I spoke.

"The truth will help you a great deal in that, Storyteller."

A fair request. "The truth is . . . I didn't kill your brother. I had nothing to do with it besides being there, which I understand as a stranger—a foreigner—in your country, makes me someone people *want* to be responsible." Something of old fire and steel bled into my voice and eyes. I stared hard at Prince Efraine. "But I did *not* kill your brother."

He returned my look, holding it for longer than I would have thought. His eyes had the focus of someone poring over a tome they'd already committed to memory, nearly able to recite it without any effort. Whatever he saw in me prompted him to give me the barest hint of a nod. "I believe you."

I arched a brow. "Just like that? No trial for you. No deeper questions—prodding and poking at me, my belongings?"

"Just like that, Storyteller. You see, I'd like to think I have a gift when it comes to measuring a man and the words that pass through his lips. Lies and truths all."

"And how did you come by such a gift?"

Prince Efraine gave me his first full smile. Wide, curving, and all of white teeth. A wolf's smile. And utterly unfriendly. "I grew up among nobility. More than half of what's said is lies." He leaned foward, resting his hands on his thighs. "So, let us keep from the lies and trade more truths, yes?"

I motioned for him to continue.

"Why did you come here?"

I took a breath. "Answers. A story. The sort I believe best hidden and found in the most impressive of libraries."

"The kind only found in the wealthiest of houses." Efraine pursed his lips before going on. "My house."

"Where else?"

He rubbed his chin as he thought. "And what sort of story is so rare it's lost to you, Storyteller?"

Another truth, then. "The oldest sort. The kind that passed more by tongue to ear around old fires, and seldom made its way to scripts and paper. But, I know it's one that has taken many shapes and names across time. Fragments of it traveled across the world and its cultures. But it's all the same. One story. The first. It has to be somewhere."

"Mm. And where else to look but at the end of the world—the end of your road, I suppose. Etaynia is as far from your home of Mutri as a place can be."

Another truth, but I said nothing this time.

Prince Efraine now cradled his jaw more than stroked it as he fell into deeper musing. "And did you find it?"

I thought of what Eloine and I had come across, then shook my head. "Not what I wanted. Certainly not a story in full. Just a piece of promise, I suppose. Something to hold to, but not much still." I had learned something of the Ashura. That they had true identities—ones lost and overlooked. Their first ones. And those stories. But it wouldn't solve my worst problem.

It wouldn't help me with what I'd set free: the Tainted. And what shadows they could lay on men. What shadows they came from.

But the knowledge would help me kill an Ashura. Of that, I was certain. As much as one could be when dealing with storybook demons.

"And why is such a story so important to you? Merely a matter of trade—livelihood? A point of pride? Something more?"

All the years of playing at someone else, the theater skills I'd built, and the masks I'd worn, failed me then. I had no practiced face for him. No rehearsed expression to give. I stared as blankly as a person could, and no color filled my voice when I spoke. "A desperate need. A way to right a wrong. A chance to earn something I've been long in need of."

"And what's that, Storyteller?"

Forgiveness. The truth became a thing too heavy to share, and it felt better to keep held deep inside myself. Its own weight serving to hold it in place. So I lied instead. "Another chance."

Prince Efraine, for all his rearing among lying nobles, did not, it seem, have the talent to catch me then. He merely nodded in acceptance. "I suppose a chance to begin again in life is a thing many would ask for. Something worth seeking, even if it's taken you far from home. But it's also brought you here. My home. My family. My court. And my politics." Each word came hard as hammer on iron. Strong and ringing.

He took this personally. Not the murder of his brother, though I expected that to strike at his heart. But for all that, he didn't seem to be grieving. At least not outwardly. Though, the heart is a home of many doors, and our hurts can be hidden deep within many rooms of rooms, far from our faces, and the minds of others. But, no.

Prince Efraine took my arrival during the election as a problem. All of which raised a new question: Why?

"Your trial will be two nights from now. You don't have much time to gather your wits, much less make a case. You will, of course, be allowed to call your own witnesses, whatever you may have in that way."

I thought, and it wasn't a long list. "The Lady Etiana, for one."

"Mm. I remember her. She spent time in Ateine's company. . . ." A pause. Prince Efraine watched me then, waiting. "And in his arms. She seems an interesting woman."

I bristled, but for so fleeting a moment most men wouldn't have caught it. Especially under the folds of my cloak.

But Prince Efraine had quicker eyes than I'd first credited him with. "That bothers you? And what exactly is your connection to her . . . besides the obvious?" He didn't need me to take the bait and answer the question. "We all saw the performance you two shared. And the kiss."

I returned his words to him. "Does that bother you? She's an interesting woman."

"Why is that?"

I wholly wish I knew myself. Instead, I gave him a smile and shrugged.

He snorted. "I've known women like that. Fair enough. Back to the trial, then. Is there anyone else you can think to call on?"

I blinked as realization thundered home. There was one other person I could hope to name. There was no promise, of course, that they would aid me, but a chance. And that was worth taking. "Yes, he owns the Three Tales Tavern."

"Ah. How curious. Very well, I'll see him brought before us, then."

The prince's willingness to help didn't sit right with me. Since stepping into the palace, I'd been swept into their game of favors. Secrets and backstabbing.

Favors and scheming. All of which landed me into this mess. That, and Lord Umbrasio. Which brought me to ask two things.

"You never asked me who I think killed your brother. And why exactly are you helping me, Prince Efraine?"

"Good questions. Well, first, it's obvious, isn't it? You were found in a room with Arturo's freshly dead body. There was only one other person in that room with you barring the servant. Lord Umbrasio. If you didn't kill my brother, then he must have. Though, the question then becomes, why? What does he have to gain? And did he do it in a way to properly frame you? After all, the Game of Families was still being played."

A cold, leaden weight settled within me. Murder was permitted within their game so long as the responsible party did it so cleanly none could point a finger at them. At least, nothing that would stick.

"So it's on me to prove he's guilty?"

Prince Efraine shook his head. "It's on you to prove you're innocent, which . . . I should point out, does not indict Lord Umbrasio."

Of course. How convenient.

Prince Efraine smiled. "You'll need to make a strong case, my friend."

Is that what we are now, friends? I kept the question to myself. Instead I chose to ask something that'd give me a better idea of the quality of person Prince Efraine was. "You don't seem to be particularly upset about the passing of your brother." I ran my tongue along the backs of my teeth, debating how far to push him. "This is the second *efante* to die all too recently, no?"

He stiffened. Nothing so obvious as a straightening of his spine. Just a tightness that pulled his shoulders back. His neck lost some of the stoop he'd been holding to. And the line of his jaw hardened.

So, Prince Efraine did feel something about the loss of his brothers, though not enough to stop playing the game.

"Arturo will be missed, but I cannot say that a part of me isn't relieved he is no longer a candidate for prince-elect. He had a strong following—appeal. He would have given me much trouble in the election."

That was not the reply I'd expected, and it must have shown on my face.

Efraine's voice betrayed the most emotion since speaking to me. His lips pursed, and his brows rose together. "You're surprised by this. This is the way of things here, and among our line. It might seem . . . distasteful to outsiders, but it's for the best. Etaynia cannot be led by those without a measure of cleverness. The game allows us to exercise said cleverness, provided we are not caught."

I focused on a single word out of all that he'd said. Led. Not ruled. Not governed. "And where would you lead your country should you win, Prince Efraine?"

"Wherever needs be. The future. Across the world."

I heard what he said, and I heard the promise that went unsaid: *I'll lead them to war.*

But acknowledging that aloud would amount to an accusation, and I was in no position to be making those. "You seem confident you'll win."

The prince shrugged. "I'm a military man. I've soldiered for our people. I've been with the men in the dirt, and across the world's roads. And I've seen what's happening out there beyond our borders now."

I swallowed what moisture had built in my throat. I knew a bit of what happened out there as well, but perhaps the prince had heard more since I'd come to Etaynia. "Such as?"

"Amir is winning the war. As much as you can win so early on, that is. They're tricky things . . . wars. Gaining ground, taking territory, none of that means you'll win. It just means you look like you're winning. Up until you aren't. You never know until the end. And by that point, too many are dead." He finally rose, bent once as if to work out a stitch in his back, then straightened again.

"Baldaen might join the fight. For all their blind eyes to worldly woes, they have their bankers' brains. And they see what many of us do: opportunity. And what happens when a country of bankers decides to do more than fund armies? What happens when they come onto the field proper?"

I tried not to think about that. "What else have you heard?"

He shrugged in response. "Some are blaming the turmoil in your Mutri court for the instability out in Arakesh. A prince was murdered once upon a time, and an empire is in tumult. Trade flow has been hurt. Things have been bad there ever since the prince-to-be-emperor was murdered, and just before his wedding, at that.

"Laxina has locked its borders. To protect itself? Or do they too prepare for war? Sevinter and Tarvinter should be united against Amir, but they are not. Cousins are squabbling, and one wonders if a duke will make moves to become king? The world sits on a knife's edge, my Storyteller."

And it's no mystery who put it there.

"Do you mean to push it off that edge, Prince?"

"I mean to take the knife, whole in hand, and do what must be done with it. To do whatever is best for my country." He sounded almost as if he believed that.

Almost.

"I'll see that you are brought food and water . . . and a pot." He stared at a corner of my cell before giving me a knowing look. "And to answer your question earlier, why I'm helping you. Perhaps I have my own sense of justice. One I'd like to see played out, and until then, you just so happen to be the best way to see it done." Then, readopting the military stoniness of earlier, he left.

And I was once again surrounded by silence and stillness. Now with the knowledge that two nights hence, my fate would be decided. All by people who viewed me as a stranger, and as Eloine had learned, the Etaynians had little love for those.

So I'd have to better play their game, and muster all the cleverness I could to survive it.

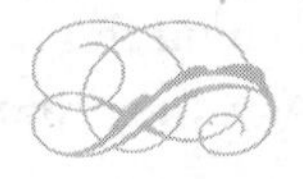

SEVENTEEN

PUPPETS ALL

She moves through the darkened library with all the careful quietness of a cat in night, doing all she can to keep from sharpest ears and even keener prying sight. There is a secret she is searching for, and now Eloine has seized the moment's freedom she has been in desperate need of.

Her eyes trail over countless books, but none hold the prize she seeks. "Where are you?" The question is as much a curse as a hope—that by simply asking she will find what she desires. Her fingers brush along the spines of stories, some untouched for a time so long forgotten that they give a touch of their own in return. It is a thing of soft worn leather and all the dust that they have come to hold in their loneliness—for she knows that even tales can feel the silent discomfort that sometimes come with being left alone.

No ears to hear these stories. No eyes to see them. And so there are no hearts in which to hold these pieces of history, once lives, and all the secrets they carry within.

If only she can catch sight of the one she seeks.

A song.

Something as old and bright as the moon itself.

One that she believes can save the world. Cast back the shadows that can take the heart of a man, and keep it in their blackened hold. Take their eyes and their ears, and feed them lies—trick them to do as they are told.

And then there is the subtle-sung call that reaches her soul and draws her from her own thoughts. One meant only to be heard by those that have the ears to catch it. Eloine looks down to the book that is pressing back against her touch. She pulls the tome free from where it rests. "Hello, little treasure." A smile graces her face as she opens the pages and takes them in.

It tells her a story she already knows and is too close to the heart. One that comes with a weight of hot iron and burns twice as fierce as coals. Worst of all, it carries memory. And that can hurt a person more than a knife. It is a pain that comes for the core of you.

It is a story of a young girl who had a shine as bright as the moon itself, but like all things set a shimmerant, their glow attracts more than admirers. It brings the monsters in the night, those all keen on stealing another's own emberling light.

And so this little girl learns a terrible thing early in life. To hide her own inner glow from all things, and in so doing, avoid a grasping hand or its knife. Worst of all, however, she hides her brightness from herself. A terrible crime, but sadly needed, because the minds of men can be more as wolves' from time to time.

There is a song for this girl who learned to hide herself in plain sight, but it is not the song Eloine seeks tonight.

But this book now knows a newer touch, and it is not one for wanting to be returned. To be put back in place to know another long and lonely rest. So she remembers things another performer told her once—the importance of these tales—and gives it then a longer look than she would have otherwise done.

Eloine pores over the song and recognizes a beat. Something old that has caught her ear before. Something lost in songs before and found again. She squints as she rereads the line and tries to rack her memory.

"Found something interesting there, Etiana?" The voice is smooth with a pleasant weight that many would find a treat to listen to.

She turns and finds a familiar face drawing closer.

He is dark of eye and of brow. His hair a shade deeper still, thick and tousled in a way that suits him. Prince Artenyo.

Eloine draws on her performer's art and turns to shrink away from him. It is a subtle thing and creates the smallest of distances between the two. In this, she adds another layer then—a smile, the sort to drive his curiosity away for simple acceptance of all she has to say.

"Something, but I wouldn't say it's interesting. It's certainly not what I am looking for." She meets his eye for a moment before turning from his look. Instead, she gives her care to what's in her hand, and returns the story to its shelf. "It's a sad story about a girl who, to keep from being chased, had to hide herself from all things. Most of all herself."

The prince moves closer now, pressing and prying as many men do—what she's said lost on him. His hand comes to rest on hers, and all without invitation. But she expects this, and does not brush away his touch. She knows a prince's prerogative, and how they view the world. Even so, one of her hands slides along her thigh, and her fingers touch the hilt of a weapon that can send one prince to join his brothers.

"It is one of the worst things a person can do to themselves—masking their truths. Sometimes I wonder if that's what life is: spending so long in the shadow of others, and their desires for who we should be, that instead we kill off our finest impulses. Our truest selves. And in doing so, only the mask remains. Few ever spend the rest of what life is left to them breaking off the mask. Trying to find all that they had buried." Prince Artenyo pulls away from her just a shade, perhaps realizing his touch had come without invitation.

For a moment, there is nothing between them but the stillness that can fall between two lovers who have not quite come to voice their heart's truths to one another. Though she knows this is a road only one of them has walked before. For hers was given elsewhere so long ago. But most men never have the eyes to see this thing, and even if they do, refuse to believe what they do not wish to hear.

And for all the smoothness of this prince's voice, he is like many young boys in other regards. He fumbles with his hands before finally finding something to say. "Are you finding everything well? I know you've come to the library often."

She smiles again, a shadow of her last. But it allows her to move a step away, and for once, he does not follow in kind. "Are you having me watched, then?"

He does not meet her eyes, turning instead to take in all the library has to offer. "Out of concern." He takes a step, and she takes two away in answer. Prince Artenyo finally begins to see the shape of the situation and remains in place. "I can have someone help you in your search. Tell me what you need? Anything at all, and I'll see it done."

Her mind has an answer but it is not one she can share: *A key to memory, a way to kill a wolf that cannot die, and a story that was never written down. Just the pieces of it. And the song from which they all come.* Aloud, she gives the prince an answer better suited to the happenings within the summer palace. "A distraction, Prince Artenyo. That is what I need." But she does not move to indulge in such, choosing to move farther down the stacks.

She trails her gaze over the spines of books, hoping to glean their secrets from just the look itself. Their names shift from Etaynian to a tongue she is better acquainted with, and all within the silent turnings of her mind.

"I think we are all in need of distractions, Etiana." He rubs his chin and his shoulders slacken as if under the weight of a burden. She supposes he is.

The loss of a brother is no easy thing, and she knows she can at least offer him a single comfort: kindness. So she gives him her hand. "Walk with me?"

"Of course." He takes her offer as well as the touch as they move through the library together. At first, there is nothing but another quietness between them, but it is soon broken by a sigh. "Arturo's death still weighs heavy on me."

"He was your brother. How can you feel any other way?"

He gives her a smile then, something meant to put her at ease. But for all the palace life he's lived, Prince Artenyo is not so good a liar as the Storyteller, or herself. His is the hollow lie—transparent as a pane of freshly polished glass. Something all too easy to see through. "I mean the game, of course. I do not know the truth of who did Arturo in . . . or why."

No tears shed for the loss of blood, but instead the weight of curiosity? This tells her more of the shape of these princes than if she had a way to look straight into their very hearts. So she says nothing, knowing now that this man needs a space to voice all that he's kept inside. She knows this secret truth: Sometimes all people want for is a place to share their hearts.

They do not need mouths of quick reply. They need ears that have no end of patience.

Prince Artenyo rubs a palm against his face, grinding into one eye as if the pressure can slough away all the fatigue weighing plainly on him. "Arturo was well-liked, even more so than me, though I am loath to admit it. He had a good chance of winning—a strong chance, truthfully. And he had no enemies but for our blood."

Eloine flashes him a look.

The prince catches this and waves a hand. "Not from me. I would never—*could* never—do that to a brother."

Which is the thing all brothers in this game would surely say. But she does not speak this to the prince. She is a stranger, and a foreigner, and those two things together always draw the suspicions of men, as well as their fears. And a man can be a dangerous thing when held hard in the grip of fear. Anger is never far away. And that itself is only ever one letter short of danger.

"No"—Artenyo places a hand to his breast before bringing it to his lips for a kiss—"none of my brothers have to fear me in that regard. But who else would have done it?"

An opening. One to pry at for an answer she sorely seeks. "The Storyteller?"

Artenyo laughs, and while this is neither the place nor time for it, it is a much needed thing. "Oh, yes. I know. He was found in the company of my brother's body, and with Emeris declaring him to be the murderer. All neatly packaged and sent down to the dungeons. Convenient. A touch too much for my taste."

"So you don't think he did it?" A chance for her to prod deeper then, and perhaps do what the Storyteller might be unable to: get out of trouble instead of getting himself into it.

The prince shakes his head, the lingering laugh still writ plain in the small smile he wears. "Oh, he could have, I suppose, but it would be a terribly stupid thing of him to do. Come so fresh into our company, and having just performed—all eyes on him, and next thing to murder an *efante*? And in the company of others? I do not think he is a man to have traveled as far as he has, and spent so much time among noble blood, to be so careless as that. No, I am thinking Emeris might have a better idea of who killed my brother. But was he himself responsible? A Talluv piece? Or someone else entirely?"

Prince Artenyo shrugs, and a better part of himself returns as he thinks on things. "I do not know for sure. But I think the Storyteller is just a piece himself. And likely just as clueless, and so, likely useless. Nothing more than a cat's paw."

She stiffens at this, and finds herself almost reaching once again for the knife she keeps in secret. But she remembers herself, and more, where she is. So the blade of moonlight bright stays where it is.

She turns to a different sharpness now. One in voice that can be far more cutting than any knife. "So, will you free him? If you know he is innocent of killing an *efante,* will you lend your voice to his case?"

Artenyo laughs. "Oh, Solus no. I am playing a long and careful game here, Etiana. And I am not one to throw away my throne for some foreigner, innocent though he may be."

She wonders if she should reconsider the knife. But no. She knows it best to play the game their way, at least within the castle walls. It will make it all the easier when comes the time to finally break their rules.

So she smiles, and says nothing, her gaze going far from the prince back to where it should have been all along. The books. The promise of a story. Of the song hopefully hidden within their pages.

One that will right a wrong done long before any of them ever drew a breath, but they all have come to bear the burden of.

She knows he senses something is wrong—has changed between them. Her feet carry her even farther from his reach, and he quickens to close the gap.

"Is . . . this what you would ask of me? Etiana?" He repeats her name again, but she has no ears for him. "Would you have me try to free the Storyteller? Come to his aid and declare innocence? And all without proof at that. What would I say?"

She does a better job of the false face he tried to show her earlier, wearing the practiced grin with masterful ease. "I would have you win the game. Or, at least I had hoped you were on the path to doing so." The hook she means to lay out for him will barb her as well, for she has no wish to sink it into him. But she has the want and need to continue the game beyond the one all played by princes. The one most needed, the one that could save the world.

And herself in the process.

"Am I wrong to wish for that?" she asks.

Prince Artenyo's mask cracks, and there is no feigned smile behind it. Only the hollow-made man who has lost a pair of brothers, and now is lost himself in doubt. The leaden-heavy doubt of whether he will win the game he's been long at playing. If he can win at all. The mask is shattered, and no amount of sweet words and plying will see it fixed.

But a prince is nothing if not an actor of another sort. All nobles are. And in this, Prince Artenyo remembers himself. His back straightens, shoulders squaring quick enough, and he assumes the role best known to him. The calm, collected confidence of a man born into ultimate power. "Of course. I've had it in hand since the beginning, Etiana. The deaths of my brothers will rally those looking for a steady hand to lead the future of the country." He reaches out toward her, almost as if to show her the promise of just how welcome his touch can be.

But she shies away from it, leaving the tips of his fingers to trail through empty air. "Then I suppose I worried for nothing. If you are so certain of winning, what will you do to your brothers' killer?"

He purses his lips and thinks on this. "There isn't a guarantee I'll even find who is responsible, even when I win the election." Prince Artenyo frowns now, and his eyes carry the light of someone who realizes what has really been asked of him. "But what you are really asking is what will the Storyteller's fate be, *sieta*?"

She nods.

"You care for him." Prince Artenyo says this with the quiet confidence of a man who already knows the answer.

Eloine does not deny it.

The prince takes a breath and inclines his head, more to himself than her—the look of a man deep in thought, and who will ask something else he already knows the truth of. "You love him."

Eloine's breath catches in her throat, but she is not given the chance to refute this claim.

"I might have known." A hand presses to the prince's face, as if wanting to push away a thing best left unheard—unknown. "I thought—never mind." Once again the practiced smile lights his face, and just as before, it is a plainly cracked mask.

One she sees right through, but so soon after hurting one piece of his heart, she has neither the will nor want to break another part of him. So she says nothing.

"You can't save him, you know? I cannot promise what will become of him by the end of all this, but you won't be able to help him. If he even lives long enough to make it to his trial. It is not uncommon for men to die of thirst and starvation in the dungeons."

This kindles a piece of the Storyteller within her. A piece he has always claimed to be his strength, and his flaw. His passion, and his pain. His fire.

For she has never been keen on being told what she can do. And what she cannot. Her back straightens, with all the bearing of Etaynia herself. Namesake of a country, lover of a prince of sunlight, and a hero all her own.

"Earlier, you asked me if there was a wish I would see done. I think I have decided."

The prince looks at her with expectation plain across his face.

Now she smiles full in earnest. "Who's your most traveled scholar? I'd like to ask them a question."

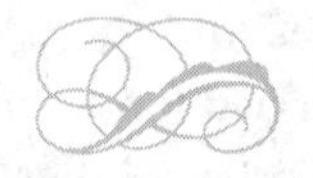

EIGHTEEN

Answers Earned

Eloine waits on polished wood with all the shine of rum in sun. Suits of armor and as many swords, all in the Etaynian style, line one of the walls—each of mirrored steel and silver gleam. Dark shelves run along the other side, betraying their age with the soft and subtle bow within each board. The kind of bend that comes from carrying too great a weight for a time too long.

The sound of boots comes her way. She's long since memorized the many noises a person can make, and the subtle things each one says about those they come from. These are the precise and clipped beats of someone hard in manner, and seeking perfection in all things.

Most of all—themselves.

The doors to the room open, revealing a woman much like herself in many regards, and in age. She is tall with all the poise found in Etaynian nobility. And twice as much all that in beauty. Hair pulled tight into a braid dark as shadow-swathed crow. Her features are as sharp and fine as a knife Eloine knows all too well. Her eyes are candle-brightened umber, a shade not so dark as some, but not quite as light as others.

She wears clothes befitting the explorer's life, not someone of her station. Hempen shirt and pants that look rough to the touch, the faded taupe of old-worn stone. "You are the one Prince Artenyo sent to me." It is not a question, but one hangs within the words all the same. And it asks beneath the breath and behind the breast for the heart of who Eloine truly is. The same prying demand lies within the woman's now narrowed gaze.

Eloine inclines her head in a gesture of slight respect, and never once forgets the role she is playing. A lady herself, and due just as much deference in return. "I am. He informed me that you were among the most learned of Etaynian nobles in matters of foreign arts. I wonder if that extends to songs, stories, and all the shapes they might take along the Golden Road—and among its people?"

The woman mirrors Eloine's earlier gesture. "I am, though it would be more polite to say Prince Arturo is as well acquainted. . . ." The words die in her throat, and her mouth makes the familiar tight line of someone who wished they'd stopped speaking moments earlier. She clears her throat and begins again. "I am Lady Solania. And, yes, I'm well-versed in many arts practiced along the Golden Road. Is there a particular one you are curious about, Lady . . ."

"Etiana." Eloine smiles. "Yes, I happen to be looking for a song."

Lady Solania arches a brow. "I'm not one for giving information freely, much less things I've found myself. In my life, they have to be earned." Her gaze drifts toward one of the walls. "And most especially to someone not a true noble, but veiled by one's mask." She fixes Eloine with a cool and knowing stare.

Eloine's mask does not slip. "Would you like to see how much a noble I can be? Would you like me to earn this information from you then?" Her grin is wide and cunning. And her eyes go to the lengths of sharpened steel hanging from one wall.

"Tell me, Lady Solania, how is your swordplay?"

Both women strip out of their more confining garments. As the Lady Solania's stiffer clothes pile on the ground, they reveal a blouse of plainest white, much like Eloine's own. Eloine's slippers join the noblewoman's boots seconds later.

Each takes in hand a *rispero,* the traditional Etaynian dueling sword. A length of mirrored steel shy of four feet, and just wider than a man's thumb. Not meant to hack one to pieces, but to deliver a clean and piercing thrust—to find one's heart. These are no blunted blades, but meant to cut—quick and to the blood.

The Lady Solania remarks on this. "These are not for practice, so, *not* of the *burgesa*. Etiana, how would you like to earn your questions?" She punctuates this with a light and practiced flourish of the sword.

So, she's well-acquainted with its use. I might have known. Eloine does not let this disturb her and answers the question instead. "I think a reply for every point scored seems fair?"

"It does, but it has me wondering how good your control is." The true noblewoman arches a brow.

"Better than a man's, and some women as well," Eloine says. "But you will see for yourself shortly enough."

The Lady Solania sighs and her posture softens as she stands sideways, positioned for the bout. "Shortly is what I'm all too acquainted with these days, and rather tired of." She gives Eloine a knowing look.

"I'll try to make a lasting impression." Eloine wastes little time and springs forward—the pure and perfect picture of an arrow shot forth. The tip of the blade catches what little glow it can hold of candle's light. But it strikes nothing but empty air.

Lady Solania's blade rests against Eloine's thigh, comfortably applying just enough pressure against her shift to be felt. "Point." She pulls the blade, cutting through the fabric with the measured deftness to spare Eloine's skin. "Why are you searching for information on these stories—these songs?"

Because there's a truth I've only heard of, but cannot find. Something I hope is real, because the danger very much is. Aloud, however, the songstress gives the practiced answer. "It is important to me and mine. Something as old as first voice, and the beginning of time."

The noblewoman's mouth purses at this, eyes gone deep to thought.

Eloine seizes the silent-moment stillness and twists. The subtle movement of her wrist snaps the blade diagonally, sending its tip along Solania's torso. It leaves a furrow along her waist that reveals tanned skin, but spares any harm or blood. "Point. There is a song, older than memory, and perhaps lost to it. Because it is the first there ever was. It is a story of a brother's love, and shadowed taint. Of jealousy, and a love lost. Of the binding ties, and later long-told lies. A song of sorrow, and of strife. A song of death, and of life. Do you know it?"

Solania shakes her head. "I do not. But I've heard tell of it, in stories, of course. Never the thing itself. It's been whispered about along the edges of the world, but never as anything more than a piece of a tale. A curiosity. A piece of wonder and magic in the old epics grandparents tell their children. Nothing more."

It's certainly a wonder, and most assuredly a magic. And if it is a whisper, then I will take it. Because even a whisper can bring down a world. Or save it. But Eloine does not speak these words. Instead she further presses the point. "What do you know of it, then?"

The noblewoman smiles and waggles a finger. "That is a second question, and must itself be earned." She lunges, but Eloine is the quicker of the two.

A side step, a ringing swat of metal against metal—a vibrating chime, and Eloine is closer now. The tip of her blade rests against the underarm of Lady Solania. No torn clothing, but the threat remains all the same. "Then I'll have my second question now." Eloine does not let the satisfaction show on her face. Only the curiosity—just the hunger.

The other woman steps back a pace. "Very well. I know its shape has been changed through time and along the Golden Road. I've chased it myself, once, hearing it first in an old Etaynian story. It's a tale of two lovers. One as dark and wild as the moon, but just as lovely. You know the sort of story. And the other as brash and burning bright as the sun. Courageous in heart, enough to make up for what they lack in wisdom. And it is a story of a kingdom having lost their king. A wolf who takes the throne. A shadow on the land. And with it comes the shadow's taint. Taking, twisting, and turning good men and women into little more than Tainted monsters.

"The song is mentioned. It helps the lovers save the day. Though there is a cost."

When is there not? But Eloine banishes the thought as quickly as it comes.

The Lady Solania seizes the moment and twists to bring the blade to Eloine's shoulder. A sharp pull and it severs more of her shift, once again displaying the comfortable control of someone long practiced with the sword. Her skin feels only the promise of the steel's heat, but not its teeth.

"Point," says the noblewoman. "Who are you, really? Some might entertain your farce, and you might pass as Etaynian under a certain light when you wear our clothes and carry our accent. But you are not." There is no judgment in the woman's words, only an explorer's curiosity.

But the question brings Eloine's deep-rooted fears back to heart—discovery, and the memory of those keen on collaring her not so long ago. The terror manifests itself as a tremor in her arm, settling into her wrist. But it is most noticed in the end of her blade, which now quivers.

"I have a suspicion," continues the Lady Solania. "You are a performer of notable skill. That much we all saw at the masquerade. You have a dancer's grace as much as a swordsman's, and you are interested in a thing spread across the world. You have traveled, and much. You are one of the traveling folk." She says this as a woman decided; there is no doubt in her mind, or her words.

Eloine answers with but a nod, for once at a loss for words. A moment of sympathy for the Storyteller passes through her as she realizes the pains she might have put him through in revealing his own painful secrets.

"And you've come here, in disguise, all for a song?" The lady frowns, not in disapproval, but in deep-full thought. Then a rare smile breaks across her face. "I suppose I can respect that curiosity—admire it, even." Then she catches what she has missed in conversation—the subtle tension still in Eloine's neck, and the set of her shoulders.

"Ah, you are worried I will tell someone?" The Lady Solania shakes her head. "I'm not so foolish as that. And you have my curiosity. Perhaps later we will talk more, and see what other secrets we may glean from one another. I do not hold the thoughts the *burgesa* might—nor their prejudices. You are safe from that with me, but perhaps not from this?" She raises her blade and gives it a little waggle.

It draws a fresh smile from Eloine, and she is back to their dance now. She hasn't quite finished all of her questions, and so she sets about rectifying that. She lunges and is met with a stunning swat—steel against steel—that sends her blade wide. The lady shifts her balance, narrowing her profile. A sharp thrust sails toward Eloine's ribs. She steps to the side and whips her sword back with measured control. The strike should graze the woman along her hip.

And it is a success. A sliver of fabric gives way, and Lady Solania hisses as she recoils. "*Tsst.* Almost broke my skin, but I certainly felt its heat. No, don't. I know—point. Ask your question."

Eloine straightens. "What do you know of where to find the song I'm looking for? Where *could* it be hidden—in what? How do I find it?"

The noblewoman exhales. "That is more than one question—"

"They are the same—or to the same end, at least," counters Eloine. Then she lets a plea fill her voice. "*Please.*"

The Lady Solania regards the songstress once again, then she nods. "If it is there to be found, then it is hidden in what survives—stories. And the songs of others. A thing older than record, and so it was passed by mouth—tongue and time, until it no longer held its first shape. It is in a story, overlooked, and thought little on. I myself, to my shame, cannot find it. If you wish to, then you'll have to find a special kind of story, I wager. And you'll have to sit. Be still. And be silent. To Listen. That is the price for finding what's lost to memory.

"I do not have the time to dedicate my life to searching for a single song or story. Not when there is so much more else on offer in the wider world."

Eloine's lips press tight and she bows her head in quiet acquiescence. Though she knows the disappointment is clear on her face. Closer than before, but still far from the truth she wishes to know. But if it is a story she must seek, she knows where best to look.

Or who to ask.

But the Lady Solania does not give her the time to think on this. Silvered steel flashes and this time there is no calm control behind its speed. It races toward Eloine, singing clearly it will end her pursuit here and now. And the frenzy begins.

She shifts her weight and the blade soars overhead, the threat of its passing just felt in the air. Eloine recovers and sends forth her own sword—a hornet's jab, but with none of the intent to harm. It slips and a wide-cast gleam arcs her way. She ducks and they fall back into the pattern of darting blades, giving and taking ground—foot by foot.

But it is Eloine that is driven back. A quick cut misses her waist, but forces her too many steps in retreat. She fumbles, and the sword is knocked from her grip before she falls. The Lady Solania stands over her now, and leans in. The point of the sword has not come to rest before her, but Eloine know it is what happens next. And she does not wait for it.

The game has changed, and she was always a better wrestler than a swordsman.

"I believe this is my point—the last point, *Lady Etiana*." The words come with no malice, however. "I'm going to ask a question now, and I would very much like an answer."

But Eloine moves, lashing out with her foot. Her ankle hooks around the noblewoman's calf, striking the knot of muscle there. She tumbles, and it is Eloine who surges to take control, rolling over and mounting the fallen lady. She takes the woman's wrists in her hands and pins them in place. Her mouth comes close to the noble's face, and Eloine's breath is pressed against the lady's skin. "If I didn't know any better, Lady Solania, I would think you were trying to kill me."

The noblewoman smiles. "More seeing what you were capable of. I didn't know the traveling people picked up skills as well as you do."

Eloine mirrors the woman's expression. "They don't. And I suppose the final point is mine, then." She releases her hold and helps the lady back to her feet.

"Very well. What is the last thing you wish to ask?"

Eloine needs no time to consider. "What do you know of the *Nuevellos*?"

The noblewoman opens her mouth then closes it in understanding. "As much as most, which is to say little. I know their stories, but who doesn't? Every child has heard their rhymes, and reasons to be afraid.

"*Worried, worried,*
in the night,
keep me safe,
quilt 'n' candle // light.

There's a shadow // 'cross my bed,
and the candle-smoke's // gone all red,
ma // ma, pa // pa,
hold me tight,
there are demons in the night.

Ma // ma, ma // ma, the thunder's loud,
and the moon's // behind a cloud.

There's a stranger red as blood,
and a thief with eyes of gold,
Pa // pa, pa // pa,
brave and bold,
help me, help me,
my heart is cold.

Stone and stave // start to crack,
and there's shadows,
tainted, turned,
in the black,

Dogs and crows // all gone mad
Nuevellos, Nuevellos,

Come for children,
who are bad!"

The Lady Solania finishes the children's rhyme. "Is that helpful?"

Eloine had hoped for something more to gift the Storyteller than little rhymes. So she offers a polite lie instead. "It is, thank you."

"And do you have any last requests beyond a tale told to children?" The noblewoman arches a brow.

Eloine smiles at that. "Yes, I do. For my next role I'd like to play a maid."

NINETEEN

THE TROUBLES WE BUY

I slumped against one side of my cell, letting the cold of the place seep deeper into me. My blood-red cloak did nothing to ward me from it. Or, better-truly said, I did nothing to tell my cloak how best to serve me then. So it did nothing.

A voice filtered in from the passage above and behind my cell, breaking the quiet that had shrouded me. I couldn't make out all of it, but the one that responded to the first speaker was certainly male, his cadence clipped and tired.

A guard. One who'd seen too many people come by to visit me of late, or was forced to work a shift he had no love for.

"*—efante ordenya quye me trajiya comdiya.*" A woman's voice. She spoke quickly, kept close to a whisper, with a slight shake in each word. Fear? Quite possible if the guard was an imposing fellow.

Silence.

Footsteps.

I waited, resting now against the bars, gaze on the door into the prison.

It opened, and the figure who passed through came without escort.

She wore a white dress, hanging low and wide, obscuring her feet. Were it not for the basket in one of her hands, the length of her sleeves would have fallen past her fingers. A hood and veil of the same color hid all of her face from me as well. Her other hand held a bucket in which something clearly sat. Its weight pulled on her, threatening to tilt her balance.

She moved closer.

I eyed the basket then the bucket. *Prince Efraine is a man of his word, at least.*

The figure stopped outside my cell, regarding me.

"I don't suppose Prince Efraine sent any of the food I was growing accustomed to when I was a welcome guest and not . . ." I trailed off, gesturing to my surroundings.

"I'm sorry, *sengero,* but I brought what I could." She spoke soft, still shaking in words. But there was something else in her voice. A hint of roughness, not in tone, but the accent itself. Etaynian, but not as smooth as I'd come to hear it.

I tried to peer at her eyes, but her hood hid them from me. "I suppose beggars can't be choosers."

She bowed her head, then knelt. First she placed the basket to one side. The bucket followed. Every motion precise. Almost ritualistic.

"If I didn't know any better, I'd say you were setting us a picnic, not leaving food for a prisoner."

"If the *sengero* objects, I can bring the food back to the kitchens. The maids and runners will appreciate the meal more than the good sir." Her response brought me up short, causing me to better consider what she'd said.

The staff above would appreciate it? No one enjoyed the scraps or worse given to prisoners. I leaned forward, peering at the basket, but a thin cloth rested overtop, hiding its contents.

"And if the good Storyteller does not wish for my company, I can remedy that as well. Shall I leave?"

I blinked. Her last three words came slower than before. They left her lips with an effort—practice. She was putting on the accent. But why?

The maid took my silence as evidence of disappointment. "It is a shame when a man isn't happy for a woman's presence. Especially when he's so deprived of company." There was that catch in her voice again. Just at the end. An edge—one that cut away at the attempt at an Etaynian accent.

Was that why she was afraid when speaking to the guard earlier?

My tongue however decided to take the lead without consulting my mind. "Well, I suppose I'll have to settle for what company I'm given then, no?"

The woman stiffened before one of her hands went to the hood, ripping it free and taking the veil with it. Her eyes were hard agates, brushed with old sage and flecks of brighter pear. They burned bright and promised to tan my hide with that heat. But I knew her by that stare.

"Eloine?" My voice echoed through the room, before her hand pressed to my mouth.

She let out a sharp hiss. "Do you want everyone to hear?" Eloine didn't remove her hand for me to answer. "Settle for company indeed. I should leave you here without a crumb to think on."

I smiled against the press of her palm, unable to help myself.

Her eyes held a dangerous light, and I knew from experience that I was better served by quelling any mischievous behavior. She watched me still. Then, content with whatever she saw, she pulled her hand from my mouth. "I suppose I should be flattered you didn't recognize me. My dear performer is slipping . . . or maybe he hasn't remembered enough of himself to catch another actor in the act, hm?"

I rolled my eyes. "Your accent was . . ." I bit off the response as the old flash of fire passed through her eyes again. "Fine. It was fine."

Eloine gave her head an imperious tilt, looking down at me. The expression faded faster than a blink. "I know, it's not my best work. For all the time I've spent here, I've never quite been able to wrap my tongue around it."

"I'm sure there aren't many things that can escape your tongue's wrap when you practice long enough."

Eloine's mouth twitched once, then pulled to one side in a wicked curve. But her eyes remained neutral, as much of the rest of her when she looked at me next. She gave me a knowing stare.

I returned it with all the blankness of her veil. Then what I'd said struck me a moment later. "Brahm's blood. I didn't . . . Eloine, that's not what I . . . I wouldn't . . ."

She arched one brow. "You wouldn't? A woman could take that as an offense. I kiss the man only to find after he's gotten his taste, he finds me sour, and what had been a romance promised long was just a flitting fancy, merely meant for but an hour."

"What? No, I . . ."

"You?" Her brow climbed higher.

My mouth ran dry and I ached to drown myself in the shallow puddle forming in the broken floor of my cell.

Eloine's mask cracked. Then it broke in full. She put a hand to her mouth, failing to fully stifle her laugh.

My tension fled, freshly bled and leaving me to cool. I sagged just a bit. "So much for my theater tongue. You had me properly out of sorts there."

"No more than you deserved." The hint of a smile returned to her face as she pulled the cloth from the basket. "Give me your hands."

I did as she asked, sticking them through the bars.

Eloine wasted no time with explanation, taking one hand in hers, while the other went to dip the cloth into the bucket. She squeezed it until most of the moisture had been wrung free. Then, still holding to my hand, she ran the damp cloth against my skin. The motions were slow, strong, and utterly consumed her attention.

We sat there in the shared silence, neither of us choosing to break the moment of quiet companionship. She sloughed the prison's touch from me, then attended to my other hand. "Lean closer, Ari."

I bent my neck, and brought my face closer to the bars—closer to her.

Eloine pulled free another cloth from the folds of her dress. Smaller, more fibrous than the one she'd cleaned my hands with. She wet it, then stopped short before touching it to my cheek.

I caught the meaning behind her pause and nodded, giving her the permission she was asking for.

The cloth pressed to my face just below one of my eyes and she rubbed downward. Her other hand came to rest opposite the cloth, thumb brushing away some of the water and grit from the floor. Her fingers came to a stop when they reached my jaw. She lingered there for a moment, tracing its line before bringing her thumb to the underside of my lip. "They're dry." She lingered on the spot as if to accentuate the point.

"A time uncounted in prison will do that to a man's mouth." I tried to flash her a quick smile, but her hand on my lips made it too awkward to attempt.

The expression I failed to make found its way across her face instead. A crescent sliver of a smile—half the moon in its curve, slowly spread to reveal her teeth. "Hardly uncounted. Just close to a day, my dramatic Storyteller." She punctuated each word with a slow circular motion. The cloth moved across my face, leaving clean wetness in its passing. Eloine then folded the cloth, resting it against the bucket's lip, content she'd done what she set out to do.

"You're looking a touch better now."

"I think anyone would be after your touch, Eloine."

A deeper smile then. A hint of color to her face. She turned attention to the basket, pulling free a block of white cheese. "I'm afraid the pickings from the kitchens weren't as grand as I'd have liked." She brought out a wooden plank, setting it between us. A silver fish soon lay atop it with the block of cheese. Slivers of what looked like cold sausage. Then followed a single lemon, a cluster of cherries, and some grapes.

I eyed the food, then her. "They're far better fare than what a prisoner might expect. I didn't think Prince Efraine would treat me with this much courtesy."

Eloine faltered for the space of a heartbeat before bringing out the knife to cut the fish.

The prince didn't send her.

She produced a bottle next, giving it a gentle shake. The dark of its glass turned away most of what light came into the prison. "And I believe you could do with more than water for a while, hm?"

"And what is it that's better than water, says the thirsty man."

She pursed her lips before bringing the bottle's head to her mouth. Flashing white teeth, Eloine bit onto the cork, freeing it from its resting place with a gentle tug of her head. She sniffed once before tilting the bottle back for a taste. "Acidic. Fruity. Good." She gave it another shake before passing its mouth through the bars toward me.

I obliged. And she was right. It sparked bright against my tongue. A lightning medley of sharpness, the sweetness of fruits, and a warmth of spice. "That *is* good."

"See how I'm right about many things." Her face remained neutral, but light danced in her eyes.

A dangerous precedent, letting someone like her know I agreed with what she'd said. So I offered her a grunting acquiescence instead.

She rolled her eyes. "It won't kill you to admit it, you know?"

"We don't know that with any certainty, do we?"

Eloine cut herself a piece of the cheese, taking her time passing it into her mouth. She chewed slowly—deliberately. After swallowing, she gave me a look that told me how much she'd savored the bite. "Save me from the stubbornness of men. That is what will kill you in truth. I swear it."

"No, it won't. I refuse to let it." I gave her my best smile.

She did not return it. Another motion of the knife. This time a piece of sausage became a smaller sliver, then skewered and brought back to her mouth. "This is good too." Again, chewing slowly. Again, savoring it. Again, that same look from earlier.

I waited for her to pass me a morsel.

She did not.

"All right, fine. You are right about a great many things, I concede it. And I would sorely like to find out just how right you are about the food. Will that—" I never got a chance to finish for a piece of the cheese had been pushed into my mouth as I spoke. I glared at her, but had the grace not to try to speak around chewing.

The cheese had no bite to it at all, complementing the wine. This was smooth, creamy, with a hint of nuttiness to its flavor. "Right again."

Still the neutral face, though the light in her eyes now became a smile. But she said nothing, and we fell into eating silently. Most of our time passed this way.

Passing glances. Savoring bites. Swallowing wine. Only once the latter had taken us did we break back into speaking.

She fiddled with her fingers, not quite meeting my eyes. "I've been hearing rumors, and some truths, up there." Eloine didn't elaborate.

I asked the question I'd been holding on to. "Up there with Prince Ateine?"

Silver-steel sharpness flashed through her eyes, then vanished. She exhaled. "Artenyo, and some of the truths came from there, as well as the rumors. The rest, from the staff. Maids, runners, kennel master."

All those people in so short a time? How far had she moved through Del Soliel? How quickly? But I didn't ask any of those things. "And what did you learn?"

"Some of what we knew already. Amir marches on Sevinter, only now they've properly begun a war. And Amir is looking likely to win."

Like Prince Efraine said.

"That's what the gentry speak of at least. But the common folk? They're telling the other sorts of stories. The sort that excite men like you, and worry others." She bit one corner of her lip, eyeing me as if wanting permission to continue.

The choice was hers, and I gave her a look that said as much.

She took a breath and went on. "There's a frost falling on small stretches of land from Zibrath to just before Etaynia's borders. Scattered patches. In summer? Outskirts of Amir have seen the same. Some villages frozen in the wake of a winter's wind that is unnatural. Homes abandoned. Children missing. All the while, those who've been spared these dangers whisper, *Shaen. It's the Shaen. Come for all manner of reason.*

"Vengeance. To take back the lands taken from them. Vengeance. Against the blood and kind shared by the one who killed one of their own. Vengeance. Stories of Black Riders seen at the edges of the horizon come evening twilight.

"Some say distant family act odd all of the sudden. Strange letters, stranger actions. Voices in their ears telling them things that cannot be, and never were. Lies. Seeing things they cannot see, but believe true as a thing can be. Odd sicknesses for which there are no cures. It's as if the whole world is going mad from prince to pauper."

Something twisting the hearts and minds of all things. *And imagine one of them taking a man of power. Like a general. An Ashura. Or a prince. The touch of the Tainted. And who knows how far that hold goes—and what harm it will do should it lead men to war across the world.*

I swallowed, and whatever fresh flavor and moisture the wine had brought to my mouth now fled, leaving it dry.

"I'm not sure how much I feel comfortable believing. It all sounds like a bad dream." She gave me a long knowing look. "But then . . . here *you* are."

I nodded. "Here I am."

Another pregnant pause between us.

This time, I broke it. "And have you heard anything about me?"

She opened her mouth to speak, but I waved, staying her for a second.

"About this, the trial. About what they think." *Anything I could use—leverage to perhaps escape. An argument I could make before the princes.*

Eloine pressed her lips tight before beginning again. "Some think it might be best if there is no trial. If you're visited in the night, sleeping and unaware, and your throat is slit. Some think that is too much and that you should be poisoned, or shot with a bolt before you can utter a word of magic."

I frowned. I couldn't blame the ones thinking that. Certainly not for what they might have been led to believe. I killed their prince. As far as they were concerned, their wrath was justified.

And that is often the cause of a great many problems in the world. How we justify the wrongs we do, and the ones done to us.

I blew out a breath and rested my chin on the back of one of my fists. "Our little performance has them wary, then?"

Eloine took another sip of the wine, then a piece of the fish. She passed the bottle back to me.

It tasted less sweet than before, and gave me more of its acid bite. When I tasted the fish she gave me, it carried more oil and coldness in its flesh.

"You conjured and shaped the light of the moon around them. Well, us. They take that kind of power in proper measure here. It awes them in performance, but they remember how unnatural it is once the act is done. They're afraid of you." She passed me a few cherries.

They tasted tarter than their promise.

"I suppose they would be once they were done being captivated."

She nodded in understanding. "Many are. They only tolerate the likes of us when we're putting on a show. Pushing away their pains, putting them to places past their thoughts. Then when it's over, the pain returns with their prejudices."

She plucked a grape before passing me one as well. Thankfully, a hint of its sugar burst through when I bit into it, washing some of the prior tastes away.

"So, they want me dead. Can't say that comes as a surprise. I don't suppose I have any supporters among the palace guests?" I gave her a hapless look, knowing it to be a foolish question.

"Some of the princes don't believe you did it." She paused and I took it to speak.

"That's wonderful, though. It means I have some support among—"

"But they'll keep those thoughts to themselves. It would be more convenient were you still found guilty. The game would resume, as would the election. The prince's murderer could be courted, allied with, and another brother could fall. And the election becomes easier to win."

I stared for a long moment, unsure what I could possibly say. The truth came easiest. "And they fear *us*? They have disdain for strangers when they're willing to kill their own for the promise of power. Even family. Or, at least turn an eye."

Eloine didn't meet my gaze, staring at the stone ground. "It's their way. We're strangers here. We play the game, their rules, and live accordingly. Or we're cast out easier. Worse, *cut* out easier. And that is not the kind of cut one heals from, Ari." Something had changed in her voice. A bitterness had crept in that could have soured the taste of even the sweetest fruits.

I reached out to her, not trusting myself to speak, and took one of her hands in mine. Just holding her there felt right. My thumb circled along her skin as we stared at one another. Finally, the moment passed and she slipped her hand out from mine.

"There's more. Some of the nobles consider you a tool to push and shape for their games. They might vote you out of trouble just to curry favor later. Some might believe you're guilty, but hope to steer you to another target."

That drew a ghost of a smile out of my mouth. "Is that right? Possibly free only to find myself back on strings—a puppet to another's desires."

"Isn't that freedom better than death?"

I frowned. "Is it really freedom? I've been offered my life before . . . and all for the price of answering to another. I suppose that's where my story really leads. Not quite yet. But eventually we will come to that part."

"Mm. Perhaps someone like you can only have that sort of freedom. After all, you seem to buy yourself the kind of trouble that can only be bought back out of. Usually out of another's purse." She gave me a knowing look, going so far as to tap a finger to her nose as if making a deeper point still. "I remember making the trouble with the clergos vanish like a dream on waking."

I narrowed my eyes. "With *my* purse, I believe. At least I guess. You never did tell me what you did with the coin besides the dress. Or how you got the clergos to stop."

"And what a wonderful dress it was, wasn't it?" She gave me no chance to reply. "Some things, my Storyteller, are better left a mystery." Eloine moved closer to the bars, nearly brushing her chest against them. Her hands clenched the rods separating us, knuckles going white with the strength and eagerness of her grip. "Now, tell me." Mischief and bright light kindled in her eyes. "You were about to buy another sort of trouble. Something about robbing a noble?"

I grinned. "Nitham had made a great many people's lives miserable since I came to the Ashram. Mine, of course, most of all. And he would do more soon enough. I was certain of it. So I needed little more motivation than what he'd already done to revisit a dozen kinds of hell on him.

"After all, I excelled at mischief."

TWENTY
Rumors and Hearsay

A few students filtered through the main courtyard, giving me long looks, passing whispers as they did. Were it a day earlier, I'd have been delighted. Put to wondering about what they were saying. Which rumors they traded. Especially after making the bargain I had with the rishis.

But at that moment? I'd grown tired of cultivating my reputation, and the consequences that came with it. I needed a night to myself to clear the fog threatening to take me.

I can't explain it better than this: My mind had found itself pulled in too many directions, and none of them had any clear paths ahead. I found myself thinking like a sparrow. Not in measure of all the cleverness I'd employed when I'd been one. But the comfort of identity it offered. The simplicity.

Only now, I had an identity in the Ashram. As a student. A rival to Nitham. Someone pursuing the major bindings. Who hoped to call them again. To bind fire and prove something close to mastery . . . and keep my neck intact.

Somewhere within that, there was still the nightmare of the Ashura. The night fire took my home, and my family. Then the night the fire nearly took me, and failed to take Koli.

The longer I stayed at the Ashram, that part of me drowned somewhere deeper within me. Lost. Without focus. And instead, I chose to exorcise this confusion with plans of mischief.

I say this to make it clear that my hatred toward Nitham could have easily been bolstered by the frustration I felt at other parts of my life. And at myself. After all, I was young, and nothing is as foolish and quick to wrongful anger as a young man.

❧

My arm had begun to heal, and I decided to break the tradition of eating in Clanks the next day. Radi and Aram had invited me to join them at a small tavern down in the city, and I jumped at the chance given the hole their absence had left in me. I wouldn't admit it aloud, of course. I'd built a great deal of pride to protect myself over the years, and it can be a difficult thing for a boy to voice his pains.

But I missed my friends.

Radi swallowed a bite of a rice medley, of chicken and vegetables infused with saffron. "And how bad was it this time?"

I told him all of it, which prompted Aram to remind us that I ended up in Mines more than any student in living memory. All on account of my mouth, and not having the good sense to shut it.

In my defense, I reminded them that I hadn't been at my best in recent sets. Mostly owing to having been attacked and nearly breaking my arm. This coupled with a healthy paranoia I'd kept to since being a sparrow. It had ensured my survival many times.

But all of this brought Radi to ask the obvious question. "Who would send cutters after you?"

Aram and I gave him a matching long look. Not that it mattered.

The doors to the tavern opened, and two of the kuthri entered. They informed us all of the growing concern among citizens of high standing that this particular tavern had been known to host folks of less than savory status.

The Sullied, who, of course, were well known for polluting the atmosphere. Never mind the fact they were believed to be thieves. And the city *had* recently experienced a string of thefts.

Nothing had come of those investigations, however.

What a coincidence . . .

But because of that, the tavern was now subject to search, and this of course meant the immediate rousting of all those inside.

It wasn't a hard guess to figure out which three were seized and forced out first into a gathered crowd.

And it wasn't a much harder leap to figure which concerned citizen of high standing had brought this about.

I scanned the crowd that had gathered outside the establishment, locking eyes on one individual who happened to linger at the edge of it.

Nitham.

He smiled before vanishing into the throng of people.

My friends and I tried to continue our conversation elsewhere. Only, this seemed to be the day any and every little tavern we visited happened to be harboring people of questionable character.

An oddity. One that saw us, and many innocent folks, rousted again. And again.

And. Again.

We eventually relented, sharing our defeat together at the hands of Nitham.

And the quieter pain it brought back to me, keeping me from enjoying time with my friends.

But I hadn't been his only victim. The Mutri Empire's quiet prejudice against those among the Sullied came back to light as another student suffered worse than us: Valhum. Another from my caste, who had been deep in debt the previous season. Someone Nitham had chosen to go after when he couldn't pursue me. A way to make his threat against me clear. The Sullied boy had lost some coin he couldn't afford to part with, and lost his places of peace within the city.

Radi's fingers blurred and the mandolin spoke in a jarring twang. It said: *bastard.* Then a sharp series of brightness. *I'd like to show him a knife.*

Aram, voice of wisdom that she was, reminded us that everything Nitham had done so far did not easily trace back to him. Oh, it was obvious, of course. But the Ashram couldn't act on it.

Which meant I couldn't get to him playing by the rules. I'd have to break them. To play dirty. And I most certainly had a better hand on that than him. When I smiled, I made sure my friends could see my teeth.

"I'm still not sure it's wise to try to do Nitham one over better than he's done you, Ari." Aram shook her head and took a drink.

Radi sniggered. "Might solve all our problems if they did just have the wherewithal to do one another and be done with themselves altogether." He plucked a few more notes. *Tension. Wry amusement. Release. Merriment.*

I stared hard enough to crack stone.

Radi remained unperturbed. "Hey, it's a fair method. If you can't beat them, seduce them. It works for me."

Aram choked, stifling her laughter quickly with a shovelful of food that she drowned in a deeper drink from her cup.

The mandolin let out an agonized twang as Radi's fingers stumbled, plucked, and chose a discordant set of notes. They could have said: *What? Bewilderment. Come again?* He turned only halfway to regard her. "What was that about?"

Aram said nothing.

"Oh, no. Come off it. What was that about? Are you saying I have trouble with women?"

Aram instead gave me fair warning. "Ari, you should stop thinking of Nitham. How about I go get us some rice pudding?"

A favorite of mine . . . and Radi's.

Aram left before my musical friend could find himself any more affronted. But Radi stared at her as she left.

I leaned in, keeping my voice to a conspiratorial whisper lest she hear. "How bad do you think Nitham will keep pushing?"

Radi still eyed Aram, aware of what she'd just done to us. He took a deep breath, then released it. "We don't have proof, but it is best to assume this is Nitham's work. Brahm's tits, man. He wants you dead. I don't think there's much further you can push him, or that he can push back. He's having you rousted now whenever he can. What if he worsens the rumors about you? The masters have a sword with your name on it, Ari. If you bumble . . ." Radi didn't need to finish that thought.

Aram returned soon enough with our desserts, asking what she'd missed.

Radi spun a lie faster than I could have. "Rice pudding, girls, and my wounded heart."

Aram passed him a bowl of the dessert and met his gaze. Then mine. It was a knowing look that quite obviously said she didn't believe a word of what my friend had said. "Ari . . ." She sat down, slowly, and stiff as a board. "If you continue to conspire with Radi, and follow his lead, you will have more than girl troubles in your life." Her tone was measured, but a hint of sharp-sweetness had bled through. The kind meant to barb in jest.

"I knew it!" Radi slapped a hand to the table in mock anger. "You think I can't—"

"It's not something to think when other girls—" Aram began.

Twang. A discordant note rang from the mandolin, cutting her off. "When other girls what?" Radi's eyes went wide. "You talk about me? What do you say? And you've the nerve to talk to me about conspiracy? Go on, tell me then. What do the girls say?"

Aram, it appeared, had gone so long without food that she couldn't help but finally indulge. And so she took a bite of her pudding, which of course kept her from speaking. Then another.

And another.

Radi glowered, then looked to me for help.

I might have taken a bite of my pudding then as well. But never let it be thought I wasn't there to support my friend.

In spirit . . . at least. Silent, still spirit.

Moments passed and the quiet finally gave way as the three of us broke into the laughter only close friends could manage. A sound I'd missed.

I finally conceded Aram's point, and we turned away from talk of Nitham. For now, it was nice to enjoy the company of friends. Aram spoke of her time in Master Conditioner's class, and how wrestling as a child with her father's soldiers had well prepared her for that.

Radi dragged his spoon through his dessert, not indulging in any. "I thought you said your father was a merchant?"

"He is," said Aram.

"He's well enough off to have a retinue of soldiers?" Radi frowned, eyeing his bowl, then finally took a bite.

Aram's eyes turned downward. "I don't like to talk about it, but my father's quite well off." Something in her voice had changed—gone hollow and distant, almost like an echo heard from the other end of a tunnel.

Enough of a sign to leave off that touchy matter.

Radi bemoaned the lack of proper musical attention and education within the Ashram. Then my friends spoke of philosophy.

That brought a bed of coals simmering to life in my gut, the heat quickly raising to the back of my throat. My pudding didn't sit well in my gut now and brought more stinging acid to me than sweetness. All I could think of was my former teacher in that subject.

Rishi Vruk. Vathin. Koli.

One of the Ashura. And I'd chased them like a fool to Ampur, coming up empty-handed but for the fact that they had been there. No idea of their purpose or what truly happened. All that time, Koli had been right in front of me, disguised as someone I trusted.

My ears turned from their conversation, and I wondered where the Ashura could have gone now. Farther north—into the pale mountains beyond the end of the Mutri Empire? South? They had been there once before according to Pathar the tinker.

How could I know without any new information coming my way? All I had was rumor and hearsay.

Then again, I excelled at trading in that. That would be my best course of action, I decided. To deal with the Ashura.

And to handle Nitham.

TWENTY-ONE

Sparrow and Crow

The first hour of third candle had just gone by, and I had till the end of the mark before class with Rishi Ibrahm started. Enough time for me to venture down into Ghal proper and tend to some things that had gone long enough unaddressed.

Namely, my cloak and cane. I'd grown more than fond of them the previous year. And being without them left me feeling naked.

I made my way down the thousands of Ashram stairs, giving thanks that much of the snow had been cleared by the minor bindings carved along them. They served to collect the sunlight's warmth as well as friction from the footfalls over the year. When they reached a certain coldness and came in contact with moisture, the stairs released a slow, safe current of heat to help melt the accumulated snow. Some of the Ashram's monks were also tasked with layering the steps with broken stone grit to help give students better traction when the surface turned to a slippery slush.

It didn't take long for me to find my way to a section of the city known for its garmentry. The layout of Ghal didn't adhere to the same quarter structure of Abhar. No. This place was like a pool of lotus blossoms. Bubble clusters that floated near each other with empty spaces for roads to go through them, creating further useless distances from other places.

I passed through one of these spots now, weaving my way through tightknit domed structures that stood close enough along the street to keep me from seeing other parts of the city. The blue stone of their roofs glimmered under the sun. I was trudging forward, kicking up snow, when a series of crunches sounded behind me. No sooner than I turned did someone crash into me.

I felt them before I saw them. Parts of my robes were brushed aside. Pressure built along one of my biceps from where they grabbed me—hard. Squeezing, more than necessary. All of which would have taken my attention from the defter touch being applied to the inside of my clothing, moving along my waist to where I'd cinched my purse.

Utterly ridiculous. Someone was trying to clutch from me? A sparrow? But it had been a long time since I'd plied my old trade.

I snapped back to clarity as their fingers worked the string of my pouch. My hand blurred and caught them by their wrist. I gave them the same measure of forceful pressure they'd applied to my arm.

"*Shad*. Ow!" The thief squirmed in my grip and batted their other hand against my flank. The blow did little against the layers of my clothing.

"Stop wriggling, you pissant!" I shook them once, brushing aside the bundle of rags they'd wrapped around their head to serve as poor-man's cowl and scarf in one.

He couldn't have been more than ten. Hollow-gaunt with the leanness I once knew all too well. The boy's hair had matted into ragged strands that looked like they'd break clean with one good tug. His skin held none of the color of those in the south. Pale. So much so he carried a ruddy red in his cheeks . . . where they weren't marred with sweat and grime.

"Oi, don't curse when you're caught lifting from someone, *ji-ah*? Your bloody hand wasn't up to the job and you're spitting about it? I should cuff you one." I did nothing of the sort, however.

"Isn't like I'm a one to know you're to catch me clean, is I?" He tried to shake free of my grip again, but failed.

"Hey, stop that." I hauled him off-balance. "What in Brahm's damn name are you doing?" I clamped my other hand to his shoulder, finally steadying the boy.

He shot me a glower and locked eyes with me. One had color like rum under light, now clouded with a touch of milk, leaving a shroud of grayness to the brown. The other eye was the color of swamp water and earth. A dark green of moss ringed with brown. "What's you want with me? Lemme go. I'll scream—promise on Brahm's tits I'll let loose. Make 'em hear through the pissin' city."

I let him go at that . . . after a fashion. My hand crashed into his chest, sending him off his feet and into the snow.

"*Gutiya*. Bastard!"

I kicked a mound of frost over the kid. "I am, as a matter of fact. Now where do you get off trying to rob me, eh? What's your name, sparrow?"

He shook his head looking at me like I'd switched to a foreign tongue. "Wussat, now?"

I sounded out what I'd said, slower, in case the ice had gotten between his ears.

"I isn't no sparrow. I'm a boy."

I sighed. "You're a presumptuous little shit is what you are."

He screwed his face tight, looking much like he'd enjoy taking a swing at me, but knew better than that.

"Do . . . you understand what any of that means?"

His expression darkened. "I know shit."

I'll bet. "It means you're too jumped up for your own good. Think you're better than you are."

That gave him pause, and his face lost much of the heat and stone that'd filled it seconds earlier. "How's a one like you catch me—what-how?"

I smiled and waggled the fingers of one of my hands. "Magic."

"Eat shit and piss mud." He clenched some snow, pressing it into a wet ball of slush that he threw at my feet. "Really."

I pressed my lips tight together in hopes of stifling a laugh. "I was once like you. A little bird down in Abhar. You know of it?"

He nodded. "Ways a way down'n south. Them's say it's always warm there. Some says you can lift fruit or veg off any stall and not one's a one to follow. People and places too packed—all next to one. No room for things. Just full of pluckings."

"Pickings . . . not pluckings. But, true, after a fashion."

The boy brushed some of the snow off himself and got to his feet. "They say . . ." His voice dropped to a hush. "That girls there show their arms and stomachs."

I rolled my eyes. "They say that, do they? And what's a one like you spending time worrying about girls for? Spend your time getting better at clutching first before you worry about women." It felt the right piece of advice to give the little urchin, in part because I'd been in his shoes, or lack thereof. And maybe just as much in part because I had little clue when it came to women, so anything I taught him should keep well away from that subject.

"I do fine 'nuff with me pickings. Been doin' right be me 'n' afore you came along."

Obviously. I didn't voice that thought, giving the boy a longer and better look-over. His feet were wrapped in strips of whatever clothing he'd come across, tied tight into misshapen lumps. Black sludge had hardened along lengths of the cloth and I figured it to be pitch.

"I suppose you have. You've certainly gotten by, hm?" The boy opened his mouth to respond, but I went on. "But you can always do better. I could teach you some things?" I'd spoken the words before I realized.

I don't know what prompted them, but looking back, I can only think it had been seeing a piece of myself in that child. I was still one myself in truth. But I knew that life. One without proper shoes, building callouses along my skin that took most men years of hard labor to develop. And that had been in a warmer climate, not one where too much time exposed could cost you a finger . . . or toes.

No man should ever suffer simply because of the place and position of their birth. Especially in their home.

I knelt, bringing myself closer to eye level with the would-be pickpocket.

"You says you was 'n grabber?" He looked me over much like I'd done to him. It left him pursing his lips like he didn't believe me.

"Never heard that term before, but I was, I think. We called ourselves the sparrows after the birds that roosted most commonly in Abhar."

His mouth formed a silent O. "S'at makes sense. We don't has 'em here 'n Ghal. Gots them big ones. Hawks." He spread his arms wide as if mimicking a large bird's wingspan.

"Falcons. Ghal doesn't have hawks."

The boy's face scrunched back into the tight mask from earlier. "S'what's the diffunce?"

It was a good question. "You know, I don't rightly know myself. They look different, though."

He seemed to mull that over, then decided that wasn't enough to constitute different names. "I looks diffun from Chapi, he's a boy. I'm's a one too. Don't mean we's diffun."

"I suppose that's true. But, having a name, an identity, matters when you're a band of little cutpurses. Gives you a sense of something more."

"What more?"

I blinked. "Family. A better identity . . . reputation. That matters."

"Why?"

Brahm save me from the stubbornness and stupidity of young boys.

I blew out a breath.

Eloine stifled a laugh and I glared. She fixed me with a stare of such practiced innocence it couldn't be seen as anything honest whatsoever. I continued as if she hadn't interrupted.

"If you have a reputation, sometimes other gangs leave you alone. Sometimes it means you're respected, and that can open doors to more opportunities. More work that doesn't mean clutching and chancing getting cuffed over your ear. Or worse. You risk the kuthri catching up with you every time you try to pick from someone, *ji*?"

He nodded. "S'true. But what's a one to do?"

"Be smarter. Work cleverer." I tapped two fingers to my temple. "Starts with getting a name."

"I's gots one of them, though? I'm 'n called Sham." He sniffled, rubbing the back of a hand against his nose.

I licked the back of my teeth, trying to remain patient. "It's a fine name. But I meant for your little flock. You've got one of those, don't you?"

He eyed me askance and turned his profile to the side as if trying to distance himself from me. "Says 'n who?"

"Brahm's tits, boy, you! You just told me you know another boy. That means there are at least two of you. Are you thick?"

"No. I'm 'n Sham. I's 'n just told you!"

Dear Brahm, spare me and my faculties today, grant me the better patience to deal with this thickwit, and I swear I'll leave off being a mischief and miscreant for as long as can be. Or so curse me with foul misfortune.

"Sham." I took another deep breath, using it to bring myself to calmness. "This is a hard life for a boy alone. Worse for two. It means there's just enough of you to worry about one another, but not enough to clutch coin easily if one of you is hurt or sick. Little birds prosper better with a flock. Even if you don't know why you're doing it. Most little thieves band together, yeah?"

He didn't meet my eyes, but a pained look fell across his face. "S'no. I don't have anyone."

What ache showed clear on his expression soon flowered in my heart. But I kept a steady voice then, for his sake rather than mine. "Having a name means you can build a reputation. The good clutches and impressive things you do can spread, and form a kind of protection." Like my own reputation had done for me. "Do you understand?"

He nodded again.

"Right. So, when I ran the sparrows in Abhar, eventually we built a good name for trading and telling secrets. Picking them up as much as we sold them. It made us a fortune."

"How much."

I had to appreciate the boy's directness when it came to the things that matter. "A lot, Sham. A lot. Have you ever seen silver? Gold?"

He shook his head.

"I have. A whole box of it. And I stole it from a merchant—"

"Liar."

I nearly cuffed him then, but as I'd sworn to Brahm, I resisted. "I'm not lying. I'm a fine liar when I need to be. But I robbed a merchant king from the west. Out past Zibrath. Does the name Ari mean anything to you?" Rumors traveled far, even to the low streets of Ghal.

He nodded. "Heard him a demon. He drank blood of folks down 'n south. Killed some too."

That's all the little rascal had heard. "And you didn't learn anything about him stealing a box of gold?"

He shrugged. "S'not really."

So I told him a bit about the sparrows. Of the family I'd made. Of Juggi. Of Nika.

"So's why 'n you leave her then? You's 'n here. She's 'n there."

The cold spreading through my core had nothing to do with the ice outside. Nor did it come from every frozen breath I sucked down.

"Sometimes you have to leave the ones you love to be who you need to be." I hadn't meant to say that aloud, much less for Sham to hear me.

"S'what?"

"Nothing. Look. Ask around, and you'll hear a boy named Ari ran off with a king's fortune of gold. Left them to the sparrows. It's true. And I'm that Ari." I then thought of what I'd told him about the power of reputation, and another story of mine I could further cultivate. "Have you heard about what happened on the streets near The Fireside?"

He squinted at me, then nodded. "'Bout some'un conjured fire. Did black magic."

I told him it had been me. It may have brought a small pleasure to me as I watched his eyes go wide. "I've learned a lot of things in my life, Sham. If you ever want to learn how to be a better hand at what you do, you come find me again on the streets, yes?"

He seemed to think that over, then nodded. "You's not gonna call 'n the kuthri?"

I shook my head. "No. And next time I see you, think of a name, *ji-ah*?"

Sham inclined his head. "S'only there's 'n no sparrows in Ghal?"

That wasn't wholly true. They just weren't as common and easily scared off by the larger birds here.

"We's a have crows, though? Them's taking every bit o' sparkle 'n' shine they's a find."

"That might do, Sham." I clapped him on the shoulder, taking the time to brush off what snow had accumulated on his clothes. "Now, go."

He didn't need another word from me, breaking into a run back the way he'd come from.

I watched him leave. Then, content I'd be spared from more sticky fingers and prying eyes, I went off to the shop I'd been looking for.

It stood a story taller than most of the buildings around it. A sign it did well enough to warrant the additional space, or that the owner had the money to make it stand out regardless. The walls inside were lined with endless raw material to stitch clothing of nearly any sort.

The thick woolen rug had been dyed the blue of sapphires and the white of fresh cream. A counter of dark wood ran perpendicular to the far wall.

"Haven't seen you before." The shopkeeper was a man late into his forties. His rolled-up sleeves revealed thick arms with the muscle of a hard worker layered under generous fat. Bald, with a thinning mustache that hung down past his chin, he had a brightness of eye that held my attention. "Need something sewn, then? Can make anything you have in mind, son. Go on, tell-tell, what would you have me make?"

"I was looking for a cloak, *sahm*. Nothing particularly fancy, just a piece to throw over my robes. Keep out the worst of the frost on the really bad days. Or if I take off to traveling, keep the road dust from my other clothes."

He nodded, bringing a thumb and forefinger under his lip, stroking the spot. "Simple traveler's cloak and that's all?" His mouth pulled into a frown. "It's not worth much to me to make those sorts of things, son. My time's worth a good bit of coin, and my labor more so, *ji-ah*?"

I nodded. "Then I won't waste any more of your time, *sahm*." Inside, I swallowed my disappointment, wondering if I should have ventured farther, to the clothier I'd first visited when new to Ghal with Laki in tow. The man had tried to gouge me with his prices, but had eventually come round to a fair enough deal.

"Oi-ah, wait a moment. I didn't say we couldn't do something for you, son. I'm not in the business of turning away customers." He placed a hand to his stomach as if to stay the sort of laughter that came from the belly. "I might have something that'll do, sitting around the place. Wait here, *ji*."

I gave him a thanks and he vanished into a doorway at the back of the room, reappearing quicker than I expected. A length of fabric lay folded over both his arms. It had the color of late-evening skies ahead of midnight black. He held it up for me to see.

The material wasn't thick enough to be of any use in Ghal's climate, especially in winter. A few threads had come undone along the hem, showing that it had seen some wear. But its shape and length were a near perfect fit for me.

He seemed to have the same idea, coming over and holding it just before me, sizing me up with a sidelong glance. "Looks like the piece was made for you, *arrey*, boy?"

I inclined my head. "That it does, good *sahm*. What happened, someone order the piece, then decided to raise a cry about it until you took it back?"

"Truth, son?"

"On occasion, but I've found it travels much slower than lies. And sometimes it's nowhere near as fun." I flashed him a smile that he returned.

"*Arrey*, that's true." He gave the cloak a little shake. "Made this for my boy. He didn't want something to weigh him down, see? He always wanted out of Ghal. Wanted adventures, like in the stories. Tried to teach him some sense, show him my trade, help make something out of him. But he didn't take to it. Always running out, getting into trouble. Boy would get caught in all sorts of trouble, and on all kinds of things. Tearing what I'd made for him. Figured he could do with a cloak to keep the worst of it off the finer things, *ji*?" The man pushed it toward me, turning to one side as if wanting to walk away from the conversation.

I took it from him, and only then understood what I'd missed at first glance. While its coloring and style weren't fashionable, its quality rested in its making. Light, so much so that it couldn't have weighed more than a breath on skin. A passing gust could have stirred it up if not for a shot of something heavier sewn into the hem, cuffs, and the collar. The cloth itself was soft enough to rival pricier materials without promising to be just as flimsy. "This is fine work, *sahm*. Really fine."

He waved a hand to dismiss the praise.

Something about the cloak left him uncaring for the compliment, but I didn't know what. I had only a guess. "What happened to your son, *sahm*? Why'd he leave the cloak behind? It *really* is good work."

The shopkeeper stared at the ground. "He . . . left. Long ago. Long ago." The man sniffed. "Ghal wasn't good enough for him, suppose. Said he was off to see the world—the Golden Road and all it had to give. Boy said he'd find a treasure, several of them. Wanted to ride out there past Zibrath. On golden sands he said. Golden sands. Not like here, white cold and old, old, old stone." He shook his head.

"But he left, and didn't come back. Don't know if he's still out there. Don't know if he's dead. Boy sends no post. None. Not heard a word. Not one." He cleared his throat, the sound wet and rattling, though the man had no illness that I could see.

"All I've got is the cloak he never took. Said he'd be back for it one day. Said it'd be something for me and his mother to remember him by. But, it's just a cloak. It's not my son. And he hasn't come back for it."

I didn't trust myself to speak after hearing that, pulling free my purse instead. Coins rattled as I fished for what I felt appropriate. A piece like this warranted a good bit of copper, at least. I produced them, then reconsidered, adding more until the sum totaled four and one bunt. More than enough.

It wouldn't soothe the pain of his long-gone son, but maybe it would bring just a bit of warmth, knowing the value of what he'd made for his boy. And that someone else appreciated it.

Maathi's old words echoed through me. So I passed the coins to the tailor.

He stared at them for a while longer than any shopkeeper should have, not moving to take them. After another moment, he reached out with both hands, taking mine in his and folding my fingers over my money. "It's fine, boy. Thank you for letting an old man talk."

I pulled my hand free from his hold, pushing the coins back toward him. "Someone once told me that anyone who tells you a good story deserves to be paid for it. Thank you for sharing yours, and this." I tilted my head toward the cloak.

The man still made no move to take my money, walking slowly back to the counter at the other end of the shop. "My son left to travel long ago, but his cloak never followed him. A cloak is made to be worn, traveled under, and keep someone safe." The look he gave me made the meaning clear.

I nodded, slipping into the cloak as I walked toward the exit. But I looked over my shoulder as I moved on.

He watched me all the while, the ghost of a smile trying to break across his face, but never coming.

I stopped near the door, eyeing a stand on which several bolts of cloth stood. There was just enough free room on the wooden surface for me to do what I wanted. I layered the five coins there in a neat stack. When I looked back, the man was still watching me. We locked eyes. "For your son . . . when he comes back. A gift." I moved to step out of the door.

While the man didn't say anything, his eyes spoke for him. In that moment, I promise you they said, *Thank you.*

I left the shop with my cloak, feeling it well worth the price I'd paid.

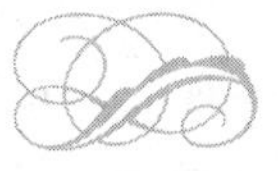

TWENTY-TWO

Of Stories and Other Things

My trip into the city took longer than I'd have liked. I raced back to the Ashram, biting off my fair share of curses as I climbed the countless stairs at a run.

The last third of the candlemark hadn't quite reached its end, leaving me just enough time to race across the main courtyard and toward Rishi Ibrahm's lesson. I slipped into the open lecture theater Master Binder taught in, not bothered by the changing sky above. It signaled new snowfall sometime today. But even if it broke out over the class, I'd stay in my seat.

Everyone else filtered in behind me, taking their seats. Radi looked like he'd just finished a wrestling bout. His hair was wild, tangled along his shoulders. The copper and brass bands had caught on each other, and he hadn't taken a moment to sort them out. He all but collapsed into place next to me.

"You want to talk about it?" I made a point not to stare at him as I asked the question.

He grunted. "Later." Radi then fell into the quiet motions of fixing his hair and accessories.

I finally realized what had bothered me about his appearance. It wasn't the disheveled hair and visible fatigue. It was what was missing.

His mandolin.

He'd been inseparable from it, making a point to bring it with him when we'd gone to Ampur, even though he had no idea what to expect on the venture.

I stared at the empty space beside him, then back at him.

He caught my look. "Left it in my room. It's fine. Appreciate the concern." Every word came harder than the last, and without a hint of his usual spark. Whenever Radi spoke, there was a hint of music in his voice. Even if he didn't try. It was as natural a thing for him as breathing. He simply had it in him.

"Damnable meddling-pompous-jackass-inflated . . ." The cursing devolved into dejected muttering, but we'd heard enough to turn toward the source. Rishi Ibrahm stomped into class, not bothering to slow or soften his stride as he slammed each foot down the stairs. He reached the center of the courtyard and whirled about, jabbing an accusatory finger at a student at random. "You, tell me how far you've come!"

Rika, who the gesture had singled out, shifted in her seat. She gave the rest of us a hapless look that said she wished she could have been anywhere else but here. "Um . . ."

"Um? Um! Um isn't far. It's not even . . . an anything. It's just . . . um. Nothing. If I wanted nothingery and empty words, I'd sit in on the other masters debating which of their thumbs they'd prefer to sit on today, so much so that they'd be shoving them up their own asses!"

Radi and I traded a short-lived wide-eyed glance. "What's burned his ass?" Radi whispered.

"*What* . . . has burned my ass, Kaethar Radi, is that I'm stuck having to watch a bunch of children meddle with things they have no business fiddling with. *That* . . . and the fact the Ashram seems to have more collective dung stuffed between the ears of those who occupy it than all of the manure fields in the empire. A considerable collection and feat, by the way."

Radi shrank in his seat and decided that his own twiddling thumbs were the most fascinating things in the whole world.

Glutton for punishment that I was, I raised my hand.

Rishi Ibrahm spotted me after a moment of gazing around the class. "You, of course." He breathed out a heavy sigh. "Go on, what is it?"

"What exactly do you mean when you ask us how far we've come? It's pretty vague, Rishi."

He crossed his arms under his chest, letting out a *harrumph* of indignation. "I thought it'd be obvious, especially for you, you little quick-wit." Something in how he'd spoken made me think it wasn't quite the compliment. "Your pursuits of the bindings. Anything. Everything. *What*—things! What have any of you done?"

Rika raised her hand again but didn't bother waiting for Rishi Ibrahm to call on her. "Um, I thought that's why we were here, Master Binder, for you to teach us?" The question should have brought us back to the realm of rationality.

It didn't.

He pressed his lips together and made a sound like someone breaking wind. "And are you all infants who need their hands held? Told when and how to piss and feed yourselves? You can manage that lot, *ji-ah*? To learn the ten bindings, a binder needs some gumption of their own. Some . . ." He trailed off, frowning like he was stuck looking for the right words. Rishi Ibrahm gave up seconds later and thrust a fist into an open palm, using the gesture to demonstrate more of what he meant. "That!"

I gave Radi another long look. "I think he's finally cracked."

Radi bit down on his lower lip to keep himself from speaking. A moment later, he finally mouthed back to me, *Finally?*

It was my turn to hold back a smile.

"Kaethar Ari!" The whip-crack sound of my name forced me to straighten up and bled the humor right out of me. Rishi Ibrahm's eyes held no amusement now, nor any hint of the mischievous light I'd long associated with him. They were the cold of mountain stone long held in ice. Heavy. Piercing. And for the first time I could recall . . . rational. He looked more through me than at me. "Have you learned anything of the composite binding you performed last season? A hint of the story of fire? If you can't understand the binding, at least *what* you bound?"

I licked my lips, looking at Radi for support. My friend returned his gaze back to his hands. I couldn't blame him. "Well, Rishi, the pair of bindings I used allowed me to manipulate a piece of fire that was within . . ." I broke off, thinking harder.

The fire had been out of arm's reach, hadn't it? I wasn't standing close enough to it to be able to touch it, and yet, I had felt the heat of it from where I'd been. Was that enough?

Rishi Ibrahm didn't push me for an answer. He waited, unmoving, stare locked to me as if no other thing existed in the world but for the pair of us.

I took a breath before continuing. "The fire was within my atham, the space I occupied larger than my bodily self."

The briefest hint of a nod.

Seizing that approval, I pushed on. "The binding I'd enacted served to bring the imagery inside my head into reality?" The words turned into a question halfway through me speaking.

"Close. Very close. Good. You're learning. But close is not correct. Do you remember what you saw in your head, Kaether Ari?"

I ran a tongue against my teeth, thinking. Nitham and his friends had taken my staff, breaking it. They'd taken Shola, throwing him into the fire. And I saw through Vathin's charade to find Koli standing so close to me. But most of all, I remembered the fire. Burning. The bright colors. Every movement of the flames that threatened to consume my cat.

And the heat of hatred that came with it. The desire to spread—grow. To take and consume whatever I could in order to burn brighter—harder!

I turned back to the candle and the flame, and I wish I could say it had been to gain a modicum of control over myself as I sat in class. But no. Truth? I missed a piece of the clarity I had found in the fire that night. The singular purpose to take everything I needed. What I hated. And reduce it all to ashes.

"Ari?" Rishi Ibrahm's voice sounded like a distant echo through water—warbling.

I looked in the direction he'd spoken from but my mind found better comfort in the illusion I held within. The blackness, and the lone candle and flame flickering at the center of it all.

"Ari. Look at me."

I did, this time properly. I saw him, eyes fixed on mine. My heart lurched once, threatening to break into a storm of a beat, but it remained steady. I felt most of my energy bleed from me, leaving me in a state of weariness. "Fire, Rishi Ibrahm. That's what I remember most. I don't know what folds I held to that night, just the flames."

I watched his mouth go tight and throat flex as if he'd swallowed. Rishi Ibrahm shut his eyes for the space of a breath, then nodded. "Don't think on it then. Just sit still for a while, Ari. Sit. Whatever comes to your mind, let it come, then let it pass, *ji-ah*?" His tone had changed to a father gently explaining something to a struggling child.

I nodded.

"Right. The bindings Ari performed are known as Whent and Ern. They allow you to manipulate the space within your atham with what you hold inside. As within, so without." He tapped two fingers to his temple. "This is why the Athir is so important. The faith the binder *must* be able to hold without fail. The irrefutable belief they can in fact force their thoughts onto the world and the world will obey. To a degree, at least. Even the bindings have laws."

As if on cue, Raju raised a hand. "What laws, Rishi?"

"Matter cannot be created from nothingness. Therefore, in the case of Ari binding fire, he had to have access to a living fire already. You cannot call it from a place that does not exist. And with the bindings he used, it must have been within the reach of his atham. Also, fire, like many things in this world, has a will of its own. Wants and behaviors. Dreams. And it has a history. A story.

"It is the same for sound, stone, wind, and water. To have a chance at binding them in any fashion, you must understand them as well as you do yourself—better, even." He pointed in my direction. "Ari gleaned just a piece of the story of fire. Some understanding that let him call it, but left him to lose control to the will of fire. It would have burned him from within as clean as if we'd dropped him into a kiln." He pursed his lips at that. "Mhm, maybe that would have been for the best. I'd have less of a headache to be sure."

For a moment, no one spoke. And Rishi Ibrahm continued his visible contemplation of a life where I'd ended up as ash.

"But Brahm seems to have a particularly cruel and confusing sense of humor, so he lives . . . to continue lighting a candle under my ass." Rishi Ibrahm sighed before moving to the lectern at his side. He rapped his knuckles against the cover of a leather-bound book. "Stories. To really become a great binder and understand the world, you need to understand the story of everything you wish to bind. Start small. Start with what you've done. Radi. Sound. Music. The air itself that carries noise to all ears. Start with music. *Ji-ah?*" Master Binder then went about giving everyone assignments.

Students were each tasked with pursuing anything we could to help us better understand the first things we bound. Not the bindings themselves, just what we bound. Myths, tales, rumors, our own musings on the matter.

For me? Nothing.

Rishi Ibrahm left me out of his instructions, then dismissed class before it had really gotten underway. A confused group of students slowly shuffled out, with Radi hanging back. He reached the exit, looking over his shoulder to me.

I waved him to go on. He gave me a reluctant frown, but left me alone with Master Binder. I went over to my teacher, waiting for a moment as he seemed fixated on the book he'd finally opened up. When he showed no sign of recognizing me, I cleared my throat.

Again, nothing.

I repeated the sound.

"Kaethar Ari, you grew up in a theater, yes?"

"Yes, Rishi."

"So you're familiar with the finer points of acting—performances." It was a statement, not a question.

"Yes . . ." I wasn't sure where he was going with this.

"Then you should be well aware of when someone is doing their best to intentionally ignore you."

My mouth opened but I found no words to voice.

He shut the book with more force than necessary, watching me stand there gawking like an idiot. "Well, how about that, there *is* a way to shut you up."

"Wish I knew how to do that to you." I narrowed my eyes at him, catching myself only after I'd spat my riposte. "Rishi! I mean, I'm sorry, Master Binder."

He laughed. Actually laughed. He leaned back, hand on stomach, and let loose a rolling howl. "Don't apologize when you're being honest, Ari. Good, seems like you haven't lost that little spark of fire in you."

The erratic change in his temperament sent my thoughts into a tangled tumble more than his odd mood had before. "Um, Rishi Ibrahm, are you all right?"

"What, yes. Of course I am. Why wouldn't I be?"

"You . . . haven't come off that way. You seemed to be in a bit of a temper earlier, and—"

Master Binder let loose a low growl that he swallowed just as quickly. "Yes, well, I suppose I was." He exhaled and rubbed a hand against his face. "The other masters have decided the next batch of students to confine to the Crow's Nest." A weight fell on the air between us as he finished speaking. It was a subtle thing, but felt nonetheless, like when clouds pass over the sun to cast the world into shadow.

"Oh." It was all I could say.

"Yes, 'Oh.'" He leaned against the lectern, using his arms to steady himself. "I had words with them. My opinions were discounted. It left me in a state, Kaether."

I nodded, knowing it better to simply hear him out and go along with things. He needed to vent his frustrations, and I suppose I could be that person for him.

"There are few things worse than watching someone become a prisoner of their own mind, Ari. Especially children." He took a long breath, pinching the bridge of his nose. "So you still want to chase the bindings, eh, Ari? Knowing what you do, knowing what happens to students who slip? Seeing the Crow's Nest and how more students slowly fill it?"

"Yes." The word left my mouth with the weight of iron and hardness of stone. It held all the fire I could have ever been said to have. And it came fast as lightning. "Yes." I said it again, making sure Master Binder knew it wasn't from impulse. That it wasn't a thoughtless response. And because things worth saying should be said in threes, I said it again. "Yes."

"That so?"

"I don't have a choice. If I don't show some form of control . . ." I didn't bother finishing the sentence, dragging a thumb along my throat instead.

"Mm, you could always renounce your desire to learn them right here and now before me. Swear to me you won't pursue the bindings any further, and I'll tell the other masters you've showed enough mastery not to be a danger." His look told me he was completely sincere.

"You want me to lie?"

The old dancing light of madness and mischief sparked back to life in his eyes, but his mouth remained neutral. "Oh, and that's something you're opposed to?"

I smiled at that. "I suppose not, but I can't. I won't." What heat and hardness had filled my words earlier now made up the stare I gave him. "I'll learn them. And I'll master them." *Like Brahm, I thought.*

"Good." He clapped me on the shoulder hard enough to stagger me. When he caught my wide-eyed expression, he laughed again. "What? Did you think I wanted someone half-sure of what they were getting into? If you're going to be doing this, Ari, I need to know you have zero reservations about what this will mean, about what you want . . . and what it might very well cost you."

I'd seen the last of those up close.

"So, here's your assignment."

I stood straighter, waiting with all the eagerness of a child being promised a treat. "Yes?"

"I want you to learn more than just the story of fire. I want you to learn your story."

"What?"

He looked at me as if I were rather dimwitted and he had only a half-frayed strand of patience left. "Ari . . . what does that mean? Who are you?"

I blinked and tried to find the answer, but he gave me no time.

"No, for once, don't speak. Just listen. Think. Every person's name means something, *ji*? Radi's name comes from Radhivahn, yes? To be *of* him. His qualities. At least, in part. Abrahm means to walk from Brahm. Not of him. From him. Almost like a son of himself, do you follow?"

I didn't, not altogether, but I gave no sign of that. Instead, I bowed my head.

"No . . . no, you don't." He sighed, putting his hands on his waist. "Names are just shadows of stories. The reasons we are given them, the hopes they carry in them from those who named us . . . and those who come to call us them. Love us. Believe in us. Hate us. Stories and deeds are bound to them. Shaped by them. And, sometimes we live up to the ones we're told to—named to. They are small stories. Do you understand now?"

I did. At least more than before.

"Good. You're shaping your own story now. I've seen pieces of it. The story of the Nagh-lokh, and the first binding. What you did with fire the night of the festival—"

"And with Koli." I spoke before realizing I'd said that name.

Master Binder arched a brow at that. "I'm not sure how you got that name on the tip of your tongue, Ari, but it's not one I'm familiar with."

I bit my lip, unsure of what to say. Did I tell my teacher all of what I saw that night? Trust him with the truth? After all, he'd known Koli as Rishi Vruk, a peer. Possibly a friend.

One now gone from the Ashram. Not a strange enough thing, however. Many rishis—masters, even—left eventually to find better pay or travel. Some rumors said just that: that Rishi Vruk left a note with the masters saying he was taking leave.

I thought then on what Rishi Ibrahm had said to me in the aftermath of me calling the binding. He'd promised we'd talk about what I'd seen. This seemed to be the moment for it.

"Koli is the name I knew that man by. The person who was there that night after Rishi Vruk's face looked like someone else's. You said you saw what I did?"

He nodded. "I saw Vathin's form change to another man's, yes." Rishi Ibrahm stared at me as if wanting to gauge my reaction when he agreed with me. "There are magics out there in the world that allow a man to do that. Old things. Forgotten things. These things are older than when Brahm gave man the bindings. I know of them."

It wasn't completely an answer, but enough to know I hadn't hallucinated that night. "I've seen that man before. He was in Keshum when I lived there. He was a drug peddler who sold White Joy, and children into . . . *soft* trades."

Master Binder said nothing, but his lips pressed into a thin line.

"He was there the night my family was murdered. The night my home was burned down and I was left an orphan."

Rishi Ibrahm's brows rose at that. "Was he now? And I'm assuming by the set of your jaw right now, that this man—Koli, was responsible for those things?"

I inclined my head. "*Ji.* Him and seven others." That was what I counted that night, despite all the lore telling me there were nine Ashura. I'd seen eight.

"And you think there's something more to this man, and Rishi Vruk, yes?"

I blinked. In part, yes. I knew Koli to be one of the Ashura, but I had never considered Rishi Vruk as anything more than a guise. What else could it be?

Master Binder seemed to have an idea of the thoughts on my mind. "I'm wondering if Rishi Vruk was never himself—always a mask for this man you're speaking of. Or, maybe he once really was a student of this place and later killed, his form and face taken by this Koli to use for his own means, whatever those might have been."

That thought chilled me. The idea of Koli gallivanting around, taking people's shapes as he saw fit, only after killing them. Treating them like an actor would a costume.

"There's more to this, Ari. Your eyes say so."

There was, but I didn't have the heart to face Rishi Ibrahm with what I knew. Not with half the Ashram thinking I was a threat, or already addled. With the probation hanging over my head, all it would take was some little nonsense of me believing in storybook demons for the masters to consign me to the Crow's Nest.

"Yes, Rishi, there is. But I think it's best if I keep that to myself for now. I have to. It's something I have to deal with alone."

I'm still not sure why, but he had no problem accepting that. No curiosity to push for an answer. What I had given him was enough. He clapped his hands together once as if officially ending the conversation. "Right, then. I can respect that. And if this is something you're going to pursue, Ari—"

"I will never stop pursuing it, Rishi. *Never.*" To say hate filled my voice is to misrepresent how much hate a person could feel. My voice held the sound of broken stone and splintered wood. Of fire-burned flesh and choking smoke. It was the kind of fury only a child could hold, with no care for the consequences—what costs to pay. It was bitter, bone-deep sorrow and a compulsion stronger than a starving man's hunger.

Rishi Ibrahm put a hand on my shoulder, giving me a light shake. "Then let me give you this advice: You're not going to find what you're looking for cooped up in one place. If you want to learn, *really learn,* Ari, you're going to have to see yourself far from safety's walls. To where no one knows your name, and no one knows your story. Those are the places you can start to shape yours truly, and learn what yours has been. A place with edges and sharp things to hurt yourself on. To slough off the things the world has put on you—rub you raw to the core of yourself."

He jabbed a finger against my chest. "You're going to have to go out there and look for stories. That is the only way to learn of them, do you follow?"

I thought I did and told him so.

"Good. So before you leave, let me give you another lesson then, and a story. Tell me, have you ever heard of Tarun Tharambadh?"

TWENTY-THREE

Tarun Tharambadh

Tarun Tharambadh stood at the edge of the world, far from the place that would be the Mutri Empire. High atop a tower of stone, black as night, and with nothing before him but wind and a treacherous fall. All he had to his name were his candle, cloak, and cane. The three things all binders must carry if they are to live up to the name.

The stone of old at his back and sides enclosed him in silence, for there was no breeze tonight. His world as quiet as a grave. So far up in a world where nothing moved, not even the fingers of the tower—all holding him with the stillness of stone.

Distant were the folds of his mind, eluding his grasp.

Smoke filtered into the sky from the wooded copse far below. None reached Tarun Tharambadh, though, so high was he. But where the sight of a campfire would fill most men with relief—a promise that rescue might be at hand, this fire brought no joy to him.

Because the smoke burned red. Red as blood.

Tarun knew what that meant, and that soon he'd be at battle, for which he was well prepared. So long as he could leave the tower of stone and stillness.

Not before long, a visitor came to his skyward cell.

A youth so fresh of face and frame he looked more the child than a man. His hair had all the color of long-rusted iron, and some of it had bled into the color of his skin to tint the bronze of it near to that of red clay. "Why are you here?" asked the child.

Before Tarun Tharambadh answered, he gave the boy a long look. Longer than any person ought ever give another. The sort of look only someone who'd learned to Listen and See the truth of things could perform. The kind that can glean the hidden story within.

And whatever he saw put him on his guard.

But while Tarun was many things, coward was not among them. No matter the trials and troubles come his way, he met them tall and proud. So he would not lie if it could be helped. And he told the boy in truth his reason for coming. "The king of Itragal was due to be wed. His wife-to-be, Shrutri, was taken by a monster of a man who has fled to the far end of the world. I have chased him here before falling to this fate. Trapped in his tower with but my three pieces of precious." He showed the boy his lone unlit candle, the staff of curdled midnight skies and wood as hard as stone. Lastly there was his cloak of brilliant bright, white morning clouds, and full-faced moonlight.

"Precious indeed. How could a binder with tools like those come to be bound in this place?" The boy wore a smile that no child should have known to make. A clever, tricky thing of wile-full deceit.

But no trick of this young man's could do worse than what had already befallen Tarun. So he told him true once again. "A misleading done with magic to make things seem what they are not. Three lies told among three truths. And a friendship not what it seemed to be, something hidden deep behind a mask of treachery. The last of which was worse a hurt than the rest. I saw so much of him over the years that I became blind to things that changed and saw then only what I wanted to, and not the lies once-buried deep, now come to surface, and all true."

The boy nodded in understanding. "King Thamar chose poorly then to have sent you in another's stead, to search for Shrutri, and the one who'd taken her from her restful bed. But this is not where you will find her. I can tell you where, but for a simple price and easy trade, one offered truly, and fairly made." The boy held up three fingers. "Give me your candle, cloak, and cane, and I will tell you where to find your missing princess. They are of no use to you. Surely you cannot call upon the folds of your mind in this place. Here there are no bindings you can do."

Tarun did not know what the boy wanted with his things, but no mere child should know what he could use them for. Or what held him proper prisoner within this place. And he would not answer until he got in turn what he had given. So he asked him then, "What of you, boy? You are here at the end of the world, all alone, in a tower no man ascends. What's brought you to the end of Carmeaum?"

"I am seeking something for myself, Binder. A flame that will not die once kindled. A flame with endless warmth to give. A flame no storm or wind could ever quench nor brightness dim. Would you give me one of yours? The one burning deep within?"

Tarun clutched at his breast. "No, I cannot give you that. Nor will I deal in trade with you. You seek something better left alone, and there is no warmth in your heart. A cold and callow place which no fire could ever bring a better light to."

The boy nodded as if he'd expected this. "Yours is not the first person's fire I've had to take for but a night's comfort. And yours will not be the last. I will ask you three more times. Three nights. Three chances. If you do not give me what I ask for by the third, I will kill you and take the warmth from your blood. This I swear."

Tarun did not doubt the boy. "I believe you."

"Good. Then know this: Shrutri has been taken far from your eyes onto the sea of Idhan-barahni. The Sea of Gold. And she waits now in the city of Iban-Badhur. You will not find her so long as you are kept here. But deal with me and I will set you free. Take a moment and you will find I speak truly."

Tarun did as the boy bade and found he spoke no lies. But still, Tarun would not give him what he wished for.

"Three nights, Binder." With that, the young boy left.

Now he knew where to find the missing princess, Tarun set about planning his escape. He watched the wind down below—waiting, Listening, Seeing the things only he could with his binder's eyes and ears. That night passed to morning with little sleep for our hero, and then day's light went by just as quick to darkness.

Again came the boy. Again he asked. And again Tarun readied his only answer.

"Will you give me your flame, Binder? You candle, cloak, and cane?"

"I will not. Will you release me for nothing in return, simply from the good of your heart?" Tarun knew the boy's reply before he asked.

"I will not. I will wait until this tower of stone, still and silent, saps you of your strength. Then I will take your precious pieces three from your quickly cooling corpse. And before you are as cold as ice, I will take what is left of your fire." And the boy left.

Tarun watched him go, still seeing more than most men's eyes could see. He saw the story of the young man. Who he was. Where he'd come from. And all he would go on to do.

The next day came and Tarun Tharambadh found no salvation in the folds of his mind. No bindings to call upon. No flame to light his candle . . . here. But the world below moved with the sound of all things, and it was a world he would return to.

Night fell and the young man returned with his offer of trade.

And again Tarun turned him away, but this time, he told him what he'd learned. "Your name is Bikhal, and in your seeking of a fire that burns forever, you've extinguished the flames of many. The innocent. The young. The mortal. But no matter how much you take, you will never find the warmth you lack within. You will be forever cold.

"Empty as a clay vessel—long forgotten, never filled. Until one day you take in more than your body can bear." Tarun's words were not a curse upon the youth, but a prediction he saw as clear as fresh water.

The boy named Bikhal did not react to this as a child should. He merely regarded Tarun and gave him an expectation of his own. "Maybe, maybe not. But you won't live to know if you do not give me what I ask for. And then come that time, I will walk away with another piece of flame, even if it flickers out soon enough."

Tarun accepted Bikhal's proclamation with steady calm, watching as the boy left once again. But he had no intention of being around for the final day and offer. For he had learned of more than just the boy. He learned of the birds below—how they rode the wind. And the pieces of fire's story that Bikhal had come to see through his own pursuits. With those, Tarun knew more than he had before, and could call upon the bindings to free himself from the tower.

He went to the open edge of all things and looked down, trusting the swaying wind to be there for him when he had need.

And then he jumped.

Whent. Wind below, wind around me, wind within, I bind you to my cloak and cowl. A current with which to see me safely below. Ern. And with those words he bound the wind to the folds of his cloak, and true to his desires, the air carried him down to the ground like a kite on a breeze. No sooner than he touched the ground did he call upon the hidden flame he'd found. The crown of flames bound within that only the most skilled know how to draw on. He breathed a breath billowing bright, and sparked a fire—like fresh candlelight.

In doing so, he understood a piece of Bikhal better still. The coldness within him that Tarun almost felt. But he had his own warmth now in hand on which to hold, and so he did. Tarun fled the edge of the world and raced east to the sea of Idhan-barahni. He sailed the treacherous waters, besting any beast that came his way, until eventually he came to the city he sought.

A thing of wonder, shining bright as a star low upon the world, sat perfectly on calm waters of an ocean that knew no swells or storms. A kingdom of brass and gold. Green life, and white-blue stone. But one thing was not there.

He scoured the empty halls and found no one. Echoing stone and barren rooms under brass roofs. No one but a lone boy.

"You're late, Binder," said Bikhal. The body of a woman lay prone in his arms.

Once, she would have been beautiful. Skin like the bronze above. Hair as dark as shadow's touch. The look of her limbs spoke of a dancer's. Only, now they were still. Unmoving. Lifeless. She hung limp in Bikhal's hold, and her eyes held no brightness now.

Shrutri.

Upon seeing her, Tarun realized what he had overlooked when he'd seen within Bikhal. Sometimes the stories we see in others are not the truth of all they are. Sometimes we see the stories they want us to see. The lies they tell themselves to better spread them to the world. And in that, Tarun had fallen victim to Bikhal's treachery.

"You've failed in your quest, Binder. You've nothing left but heartbreak and dismay. Will you not now give me your flame?" At this last request, the shadow over the city finally fell away, revealing the last of things Bikhal had hidden.

Every person who had once called this brilliant-bright place home now lay cold and pale. Their warmth bled from them to kindle fires that burned even along stone. The smoke above, red as the blood that had been spilled.

And in his wrath upon seeing this, Tarun came to understand a part of fire's story that he had not learned till that day. The wrathful hate and heat held in heart a man can feel. For all the life it can give, the flames can take them as well. So he called upon a terrible binding then, pulling a flame from his candle that burned bright, and breathing it to life onto the world around him. "I will give you the last flame you will ever see. A flame that will never stop burning. It will turn all things to ash and swallow you and this now barren city."

Tarun was true to his word. He summoned a hateful flame, using all he knew of the binding ways and what he'd now learned of fire. Tarun Tharambadh opened the doors to a place of ever-burning fire and called an inferno to burn the world away. The sea itself spat and cried—boiling into steam, until naught was left but sand and stone, as Tarun had opened the gates to hell itself.

But none of that would bring Shrutri back among the living. And Tarun would not forget the lessons he learned when it came to the stories of all things. A lesson for all binders going forward. For a lie told long enough and come to be believed can in fact come to be the truth, long-held, and used to deceive.

That day Bikhal got his wish. To see a flame that would never be extinguished. Some say those fires still burn today.

TWENTY-FOUR

GIFTS

Rishi Ibrahm smacked a hand against the cover of the book. "A great many secrets hide within these, Ari. Sometimes more secrets than you'd think to find. Same can be said to be behind a person's eyes. If you want to be a better binder, learn to Listen. Learn to See clearer."

I knew the end of a conversation when I heard it. "Thank you for sharing that story with me, Rishi."

"Don't thank me until you learn the many meanings of it. Now go." He waved his hand as if trying to brush away an irksome insect. "Think on what I said. And if you're feeling stifled like our intrepid Tarun once was, consider my other advice: leave."

I swallowed and nodded, leaving without another word. Though I did nurse the terrible ache to ask Rishi Ibrahm for help with one more story. One that I'd kept in my possession ever since I'd lived in the understage. The book Mahrab had gifted me that contained a story I desperately needed to hear, and that Master Binder had opened, only to bind it again.

I left the class, heading toward the Rookery.

"Ari!"

A young girl raced toward me. She could have easily been the same age as me, though her hair held the ash gray found in women decades her senior. A few streaks of black still shot through her locks, however. She'd dressed appropriately for the weather, clad in the thick woolen robes those farther north wore. What bits of her skin I could see showed pale splotches in places that stood out against the rest of her coloring.

Another woman trailed behind her. And it only took one look to know it was the girl's grandmother. Everything from the weathered old face to the stooped posture that comes with age.

"Laki?" I hadn't seen her and her grandmother since I'd gone to Ampur in search of the Ashura.

She threw her full weight against me in a hug that threatened to take me off my feet. "I'm sorry it took us so long to come and see you."

I embraced her in return. "I didn't know you planned to visit."

She let go of me and gestured to her grandmother. "We've been wanting to come ever since we were settled back home. Things aren't back to normal yet, we're still rebuilding, and we've had to shuffle between Volthi and Ampur. But the people there have taken in the refugees."

Her grandmother finally caught up, and I noticed she held on to a tightly rolled bundle. "Good to see you again, little *jadhu-wallah*. Are you stirring up trouble here like you did before?" She smiled. A wide-brimmed thing only an old lady teasing a child could make.

I flashed her one in kind. "No. I'm keeping well out of trouble." It took me considerable effort to keep my face straight as I said that.

The grandmother gave me a stare that had all the shrewdness of wise old age, and a light kindled in her eyes that said she might have known I was lying. But it didn't bother her. "Laki couldn't wait any longer, and snows be forgotten." She waved a hand as if she could banish the weather with just the gesture. "We've been working on this for most of the whole season, child. We felt it time to come give it to you as proper thanks for what you did."

That set the hairs on the back of my neck on end. I didn't know exactly what response to expect in the aftermath of all that had happened in Ampur. Yes, I had saved the village from the wrath of an old overgrown serpent, but the creature had been revered for a time. Laki's own grandmother had called the monstrous beast an old god. God Himself.

And in trying to survive the creature's wrath, I'd brought down the mountain on it. Killing a beast from another time and almost another world.

"There isn't really anything to thank me for. I—"

Laki's grandmother made a motion with her hand reserved for those who've lived long enough to quell any argument on account of their age and stubbornness. She had no time for an adolescent boy to bicker with her. "If you hadn't buried the Nagh-lokh, we might have stayed in Ampur and starved. Or it might have brought down our home on our heads. Either way, we would have died. And when it came for us as we ran, you stopped it."

Not entirely true. I'd tried to get the beast's attention, then struck it to draw its ire. But I'd learned enough to know I wouldn't win any battle of tongues with the old woman, so I simply accepted my fate and nodded.

The grandmother turned to Laki, giving her a knowing look. "You see, *golu*, they're really not so hard to rein in. You just need to know when to give them room, and when to take it away, *ji-ah*?" Laki inclined her head as if she understood.

I certainly didn't, at least then. But before I could respond, her grandmother pushed the bundle in her hands my way. I took hold of it on reflex. At first touch it felt like smooth stone. A longer look revealed the overlapping segments comprising the fabric.

"Go on, open it." Laki pulled at my hands, ushering me into unrolling the piece.

I did so, then let it hang free in my grip. The shape and cut were better than the cloak I'd just bought, almost as if it had been made for me. I opened my mouth to speak but the words caught as soon as I noticed what the thing had been made from.

Scales. Each as bright and polished as fresh snow and hardened moonlight, bespeckled with hints of dust that could have come from crushed pearls. Even the cowl was fashioned from the same material. I dug my thumbs into a section where the scales overlapped, testing their durability. They resisted the pressure and the touch of my nails.

"Laki . . . how did you afford this?"

She beamed and pulled a piece of the cloak from me, tracing her finger along its ridges. "Well, after we all went back to Ampur, people went to work on the Nagh-lokh's body. The meat, you know? Some started cutting around the scales, saying they'd fetch a big price with the artisans at the Ashram. We sold some off to passing tinkers too. Anything to fund rebuilding.

"But Grandmother convinced folk that we should do something for you who saved us. So we took the smaller scales we found near its tail, and sawed through some of the bigger ones—really hard to do—and, it took us a while. . . ." She gestured down at the cloak with her chin. "Do you like it?"

I nodded, too dumbfounded to say anything that would properly convey my gratitude. A cloak that had been specially made for me. And from the scales of an old god. My own piece of story—of legend. I may have clutched it tighter then, and brought it close to my chest. But only for a moment.

I won't cheapen the memory by overly fawning. Let us just say that for a young boy, holding his very own storybook item in hand has a particular power and weight. And whatever wetness that came across his face must have been from the flurries that started to fall then. Were anyone to say those were in fact tears, then let us forgive him for a young boy's joy.

He'd earned that much.

My voice ran dry but I finally spoke the least of the words I should have before. "Thank you. Both of you." I knew if I said anything else that the words would crack and fall apart.

Laki motioned at me with her hands. "Go on, try it on."

I didn't need any more prompting. I slipped out of the cloak I'd gotten from the tailor down in Ghal, passing it to Laki's grandmother. The white-scale cloak felt like a weight of air come to settle around my body. It fit like skin. Light, but sturdy, like wet sapling branches. You know they will bend and twist, but will not break.

Having fought the Nagh-lokh myself, I knew what it took to pierce its body. It had been the perfect angle between the scales, and no small amount of luck.

"You look wondrous, Ari! Like a hero out of the stories." Laki's eyes filled with gleeful light. Even her grandmother agreed how much that was true.

Those were the sorts of words to make a young boy's heart swell with pride. "Can I do anything in return? This cloak must be worth a fortune."

"No, Ari. It's. A. Gift." Laki said each word as if the slow enunciation would better drive them through my skull. "And we'll be fine. We made an appointment with the Master Artisan here to sell her some of the larger scales. They're sitting down in Ghal with Pathar."

That sent cold lightning running through me. "Pathar's here? Where down in Ghal?"

Laki and her grandmother told me.

I nearly broke straight into a run before realizing how rude that would have been. "Laki, I . . . thank you again. I mean, I could kiss you for this. I don't know how to ever—" Whatever I had been meaning to say died as Laki leaned forward, pressing her lips to the coldness of my cheek.

I know my cue.

I bowed low, the hood of the cloak falling perfectly to obscure the further flushing of my face. Laki's smile could be felt even if I didn't see it. I retrieved the black cloak from them, wished the pair of women farewell, and finally raced back down to Ghal.

Some of the other students watched me fly by, taking note of my new white cloak. I can't deny it brought me a wide grin as I made my way down the many stairs of the Ashram. *Let them whisper. Let them talk. Let them spread it wide.*

The black cloak I'd removed now hung in my hand, catching the wind and streaming behind me like a tail of shadow. I reached the ground below the mountain and took off into the city at a full sprint, having little care for the ache every breath of cold air brought to my throat.

I made my way past the first row of shops, looking for the section of crossroads where Laki informed me Pathar had parked his wagon home. A silhouette passed a wall at the corner of my vision, and it caught enough of my attention to bring me to a stop. I watched the space for a moment but saw nothing else.

My thoughts went to an all-too-recent night when I'd been followed along the streets. Men with knives in hand.

I walked on, now keeping my pace much slower than I'd have liked. Every bit of me wanted to hurry and not risk losing Pathar to the busyness of his trade. Tinkers were like summer storms, coming in a flash, loud and thunderous. Then they vanished just as fast, leaving a brightness in their wake, but gone nonetheless.

I crossed by a man selling *thori,* fresh and charred around the edges from too much butter cooked too long. A flavor I particularly enjoyed, though.

A child filtered through the crowd amassed near the vendor. They wore a poor man's shamble of rags and a matching hood. It was not, by any account, an inconspicuous outfit. And it happened to be one I'd seen before.

Brahm's tits. It can't be.

The child reached toward the flat stone griddle on which the bread sizzled, no regard for the heat the surface must have held.

The vendor saw what I had and caught the thief's wrist. His sleeve fell, revealing a thin arm of corded muscle.

"*Ai, gutiya!*" The curse left the child's lips with a speed that told me they were no stranger to spitting it. Their hood fell, revealing the youth's identity.

Sham. The little boy who'd all too recently tried his bad luck in picking my pockets.

I don't believe it.

The man who'd caught Sham raised his other hand, ready to bring it down in a stinging slap.

"Wait!"

He turned his head to look at me, but didn't slacken his hold on the child. "You want to beat this scoundrel?"

The question stopped me short, leaving me to fumble for words. "What? Brahm's . . . no!" I brought out my purse and opened it. "How much for the bread?"

"Two chips."

I doubted the bread was more than a tin a piece, but there was no point in bickering over a tin chip.

I passed him two. "For the boy." The stare I shot him made it clear that this was the end of the exchange. His meal was paid for, and he would remove his hand from his wrist immediately. Something else must have flashed through my eyes because he shied away from me, turning his gaze back to his goods.

He released Sham into my care, and I led him to the safety of a lesser-traveled street. My kindness prompted the obvious question out of him. Why had I helped him once again, especially out of trouble he'd bought himself?

What more could I say other than it seemed the right thing to do. I had the coin, and could afford to spare some in his favor.

He looked down as if considering what I'd said, then met my eyes. His were of bright curiosity and held a fire in them. "But you ain't'z givun me any coins."

I threw my head back and laughed. "Brahm's blood, you've got a pair, Sham."

He blinked. "A pair of what?"

I had the grace not to answer that. "You're not particularly bright, you know? Trying your hand at clutching when I caught you before."

He glowered at me. An impressive look for someone so small and who had been but a breath from a proper thrashing.

I decided not to chastise him further and ruffled his hair instead, blinking when my fingers came back with a smear of black along them. "What's this?"

Sham shrugged, then told me it'd be easier to show me.

I thought about Pathar waiting on the streets ahead, trading wares and peddling gossip. And I no idea how much longer he'd be there for. Then I looked at Sham, standing in the cold, and I saw him clearer than I'd seen him before.

Once, I too was a boy without anyone, on streets uncaring and not a clean stitch of clothing to my name. And no one to look out for me. When I did have that someone, he turned out to be a monster.

Sham would never know that pain. Or that loneliness.

The rags bound to his feet might have kept out some of the snow, but they soaked easily and held to the icy wetness left behind. It was no small miracle he hadn't frozen through to the bones and lost his toes.

I made my choice. "Yes, take me to your home."

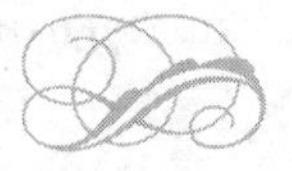

TWENTY-FIVE

A Cavern for a Crow

Sham led me through low domed buildings, passing through the empty spaces between I hadn't noticed were there. He led me to the rocky face of a frozen cliff, where a round door of old wood stood askew in a hole just a touch too large for it. More rags and tattered clothing had been pressed into the gaps to keep out the cold. Black pitch lined the fabric and must have served as fitting and insulation.

Sham ran up to the door and banged a fist. *Thump-thump, thump, thud-thud.* Pause. *Thump-thud.* A rhythm, fist to open-palm strikes, each bringing different noises.

A secret code. I thought of the language Pathar had begun to teach me on our ride to Ampur.

The little boy told me that the door in the mountain had existed long before he'd found it, and it took much experimentation before he found the trick of opening the door.

But the mystery behind who'd fashioned the mountain home still remained.

He wrenched on the door and led me inside, and I soon received my answer as to why all his hair was that shade black. Dust rained down from the cavern ceiling where he lived, coating him and his poorly fashioned wooden-pallet bed in powdered blackness. I might not have had a mender's training, but even I could tell that was not healthy.

Sham had all this to himself. Vast. Echoing. Still, silent, and empty.

No one to share it with.

No one but me now.

I realized what the little boy really needed then wasn't a mentor in the thief's arts. At least, not only that. He also needed an older brother. And I had a chance to be a good example of both those things.

. . . I hoped.

So I offered Sham my recently purchased black cloak, explaining the practicality of black clothing for thieves, especially at night. Not to mention the image he would cut with it.

Sham bristled a bit at the advice, informing me once again that he was quite capable of taking care of himself.

I informed him that he could barely speak intelligibly or enunciate his words.

This might have led to an argument that can only happen between a teenager, and a child on the cusp of puberty.

I was not proud of this moment.

But in the end, we bickered better than friends. We argued like family.

I offered to teach him. And it was as easy as that.

He informed me that sometimes he stole, not for himself, but the other urchins of Ghal. The ones with no one to help them, or no place of their own.

Dozens of them. And those were only the ones he knew about.

Sometimes, when the nights were too bad, they'd come to his little cavern hideaway to steal some shelter from the cold. The ones who didn't . . .

The kuthri found those the next morning, stiff as stone, and those children never had to worry about the cold again.

But the ones who survived were a skittish bunch, and scared of strangers.

Like me.

But that didn't mean I couldn't start with Sham, and set him up to do what I couldn't.

So I took count of what was needed, weighed my purse, and my conscience, and decided to do something terribly reckless with my money.

Old habits and all that.

I raced out of Sham's, praying Pathar hadn't left. Thankfully, the tinker had set up true to where Laki had said.

"Tinker, tinker, *Gadia Lohar.* Have knickknacks, trinkets-treasures-and-more! Pot-mender, salt-seller, message sender. Need some coin, come to a tinker, not a copper-lender. Fair trades, in and out. Come one, come all, and walk away with something to really shout about!" The tinker held up an oil lamp fashioned of brass, shaking it about in the air. Then he caught sight of me and some of his enthusiasm deflated.

Pathar stood in the driver's seat of his cart. A pair of dark bulls waited at rest before him, their horns painted in bright whorls of red. Beads in various colors had been looped festively over the bony protrusions. Heavy sacks hung from their sides, held in place by thick white rope.

The tinker himself dressed in robes with all the color and splendor of sapphires and fresh white cream. "Didn't expect to be seeing trouble so soon." Pathar grinned a smile short of all his teeth. "I knew those two women would rile you up and have you sniffing at my heels, eh? Looks like they gave you what they meant to, hm?" He inclined his head toward my cloak and I grinned back.

"Looks like," I said.

Pathar stuffed the lamp into a sack, away from the woman who'd been pawing for it in the air. "Never you mind it, ma'am. I've got more than that in my sacks. There's better to be found. Give me but a moment, and I'll be back with you." Pathar motioned for me to come closer.

The man had been carved from scrap wood, lean and knotted despite how snugly his heavy clothing fit him. You'd think it to be hidden bulk, but in truth, Pathar wore bundles under bundles when traversing the northern cold climates, and I couldn't fault him for it. "So, little legend, what's got you itching today, hm? No, wait, let me guess. A good tinker worth his salt can read the minds of customers with coin to spend."

Now that's a trick I'd like to see.

Pathar pulled his face into a pensive mask, looking me up and down as if appraising something to buy. "Gossip, isn't it. And . . . you'll be wanting to do brisk business in trade. No dickering for you, I wager. You've the look of a young man wanting to buy and be done with it."

He'd impressed me with that. "Well done, Tinker. Right on all accounts."

Pathar snorted. "Of course, it's what I do. So what first, trade or tales, hm?"

"Tales. Gossip. What news?" I reached for my pouch, but he motioned for me to stop. Then he gave me one thing I rarely expected from a tinker.

Free news.

Pathar explained just how valuable my story from Ampur had been, bolstered further by Radi's song. A tale Pathar peddled to great success, and coin. The boy who leveled Ampur . . . and brought down the mountain low.

No declaration of innocence on my part changed his mind. I hadn't leveled the village, the mountain avalanche had. Small distinction. Not that it mattered once the story had begun to spread.

Something he confessed to me. The further stories go, the more they twist. They changed shape and had it harder to hold their own. More mouths speaking, wagging tongues, and untrustworthy ears.

I had known this, of course, but only in terms of how a story could be twisted to benefit me. I hadn't considered that they could twist things to malign me. That could come to be used against me one day. And I might have wondered if the masters' concerns might have been well-founded, including those of my friends.

As you can imagine, the topic might have soured some of my cheer in found fame. Pathar spotted this and changed the subject, giving me the gossip he had. He'd heard tell of a caravan along the sands outside of Zibrath. They had a man with them who could read the future in the skies and stars. A man in search of a treasure in the heavens.

My face must have told him I didn't care for that.

He turned then to rumors of desert tribes at each other's throats of late. Tensions in the west.

But I redirected the conversation to the topic of what had led me to Ampur in the first place. Only, he had no news on that front.

Translation: no signs of the Ashura. No clues. No leads. Nowhere for me to follow them. I was stuck. But it wasn't Pathar's fault, so I kept from showing my disappointment.

All I could do was turn to the business of cloaks. While I couldn't tend to the many orphans of Ghal, I could do what little I could.

Foolish? Perhaps naïve? It might have been. But I had stolen a wealth of gold and left all of it but a single coin in the hands of birds before. What was a little more money gone now? Especially if it went to saving a life much like mine all those years ago.

Besides, as I had once learned: Sometimes kindness is a gift given meant to pass on once again. Sometimes that's all we can do, pay it forward. And so Sham would.

"How much for every black cloak you have, Tinker?" I grabbed my purse and opened it, rummaging through the coins inside.

Pathar pursed his lips in consideration. "Usually wouldn't let this go for short of twenty coppers. It's a lot of material, mind you. *Good* material."

I nodded. That it was.

"Then we'd dicker down to, say, sixteen. And it'd be skint on my end, there's that, too. But, truth is, you've already done me a good turn, Ari, and I'll never let it be said a tinker doesn't pay his debts—that I won't. So, I might be willing to let the lot go for, say, about fourteen coppers. It'll turn me a pretty piece, still, but not so much as to be unkind to you or me, *ji*?"

A fair enough trade. One I'd happily make, only I had a condition in mind. "Your price is generous, Tinker, and I'll pay it gladly, but I have another thing to ask."

"Oh?" Pathar's mouth curved into the makings of a grin. "What's that?"

I pulled out a single iron bunt. "I've got no copper left to my name, and no intention of walking from here short of fulfilling an obligation. So here's what I propose. I give you this bunt in full with the understanding that the change remains with you as credit for future trade. For the same goods. Should you come across any cloaks just like these, I'd like them paid for out of this bunt."

That ensured Sham would have a continuing supply to outfit other urchins in Ghal as needed. In time, he could become a fixture for them, just like I had once been for another group of birds.

"Oh-ho, and why's that, if I might ask?"

I let out my best mischievous smile. "You may. But it doesn't mean I'll tell you, Tinker. My secrets aren't for sale today, that's your business." Pathar broke into a full-bellied laugh at that, and I joined in. Once we'd finished, I told him about the door in the cliff face, and how to reach it. All he had to do was go there with the next bundle of cloaks he found and leave them wrapped outside.

Pathar agreed and I passed him the bunt.

I had four silver doles, nineteen pieces of iron, and twelve tin chips left to me. Still a great deal more than many a man ever sees in his purse in a lifetime. Plenty enough to be generous with, even if some would have seen it as reckless.

I took the cloaks from Pathar, and they filled me with a sense of lightness I hadn't felt in a good while. The lack of news about the Ashura bothered me, but the idea of being able to help Sham and the urchins of Ghal lessened the disappointment.

It would be a stretch to say I'd found another purpose for my life. I certainly didn't view it that way. Then again, maybe none of us do when we choose to do the things we do. We simply find ourselves swept along, and somewhere along the way, we realize we don't know if it was a purpose we chose, or was chosen for us. We were too busy paddling the current to notice.

But that was the true start of it.

The beginning of The Crow.

And the mischief he'd later help me make.

TWENTY-SIX

Passing

Time moved at a different speed after that. I'd fallen into an odd comfort with the newfound freedom of my life. I'd given Sham the cloaks I'd taken from Pathar, and spent that day teaching him what I could about how I'd once operated. That night, I returned to the Rookery and spent the hours before bed resuming my training with the folds. I pursued the candle and the flame. And when I could ill-manage that, I simply watched the flickering fire until my lids grew heavy, and I hoped to hear a piece of its story before passing into sleep.

The masters' threat still loomed over my head. As did their punishment.

My inability to attend regular classes save those with Rishi Ibrahm.

And those continued in the usual way. Little clarity, more oddities, and lessons that made every one of us question if he was insane, or we were for remaining dedicated to our studies. We made little progress in calling another binding. All of which led students to form their own little groups to pursue the bindings with added help.

Except one.

It wasn't a surprise to know that I had been excluded on account of my reputation. No one wanted a student who presented a danger, not to mention the number of times I had been called to Mines.

When I tried to at least partner with Radi, he informed me that he barely had time to dedicate to the class with everything else he was juggling. Another reminder of all that I was missing in the Ashram.

My friends.

And any effort to join them in public would just lead to the added frustrations of having them rousted because of my presence and the damage Nitham had done there. I know this because we had tried once again, under foolish optimism.

The results? Not only rousted, but this time . . . fined. Because it had been my idea, I'd cut the coins from my own thinning purse. I had the money, but investing where I had meant more risks would leave me dry sooner than later. But I had made a promise, and I keep my word.

The sets went on and Aram and Radi became distant faces, busied in their own pursuits and hardening classes. And I will admit that I felt that absence keenly.

So what was left to me, alone and with more time on my hands than I could account for?

Staring at a burning candle like a madman until I felt my folds would crack under the strain. And I along with them.

Is this what happened to Rishi Ibrahm? To Immi—Krisham? The flame soon burned its image into my mind until I saw it when I slept, yet I made no further progress.

So, frustrated, I ventured into Ghal and tended to the little boy who'd styled himself The Crow.

I taught him how to plea like a proper actor, and every other trick I'd learned.

In thanks, he taught me the many little alley paths I hadn't learned despite my time in Ghal. Sham had the same eyes for the city as I'd developed in Keshum and, soon enough, I saw the world through his lens. I knew pathways by night that many would never find by day, much less have the knowledge to walk safely through.

Sham grew to be more than he seemed at first look. Many would have dismissed him as an uneducated upstart, and to some extent, they would have been right. But he had a hardness to him you would struggle to find in tavern brawlers many decades his senior. A lousy thief, and he caught more than his fair share in beatings for it, but he bore them all for the sake of those he stole for.

I took it as a personal challenge to help him develop into a boy possessed of all the qualities polite society found distasteful.

After all, it is a big brother's solemn duty to be a terrible influence on his younger one. Ask any parent, they will tell you that is true.

And soon enough Sham could clutch a purse without alerting the target as often as he once did. But he still lacked in the finer points of education.

Namely being able to speak coherently. So we tended to that.

And I will say this on the matter: Fighting an old god on a frozen mountain is an easier task than teaching a little boy something he doesn't wish to learn.

But it wasn't long before Sham started asking for more than just letters practice and scribbled notes to study. He wanted stories.

So I gave him what he asked for. When I ran out of ones I knew, I scoured the Scriptory's records for more, committing them to memory.

It would be wrong to say these were the first performances I gave. They fell far short of that, but it would be fair to consider The Crow my first attentive audience in a long time.

For I'd told no stories among the sparrows. And before that?

Well, there'd been a lone girl, long lost in memory and my heart, who'd once listened to whatever I had to say. And in the moments I remembered her, I saw her face in Sham's. She had been a sister to me. In a way, I was trying to save Sham because I could never save Nisha.

Guilt is a powerful tool, and it never really leaves us, nor do the people we hold guilt for—to. We merely place their faces elsewhere, onto different people, and try to absolve the hurts we feel by trying to do right by others we come to see like them. I've never learned if that's the right thing to do; it certainly hasn't always been the smartest thing, but it has helped. I will not say it did not.

Even if it came to bring me later pains.

But for then, I had come to take The Crow underwing.

And he began to flourish.

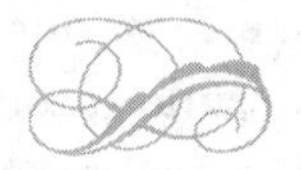

TWENTY-SEVEN

STONES

A full month had passed and I woke that morning to knocking against my door. Shola expressed his discontent at the noise as well as the audacity of someone daring to rouse him before his self-appointed time. He gave me a bleary-eyed glare that told me to tend to it so he could return to his slumber.

I grumbled half-coherent curses to whatever gods I could name. They all died a moment later when I opened the door to find no one there, only the delivered post.

A package. One the same shape and size as I'd received before and eventually discarded after the contents had started to rot. I leaned out into the hall, looking with a sharpness I shouldn't have been able to manage so early in the day, but a sparrow's fear had crept into me, and fear can hone your senses like few things can.

But no one stood anywhere I could see. Just the same smell from before. Lavender, orange peels, and freshly trimmed trees. I shut the door and sank to the floor to open the box, though I had an idea of what I'd find.

Like many a young man, I'd developed a fondness for being right, but I did not enjoy it then. The wrappings fell away, as did the twine. I opened the box to find what I had once before: a glittering mass of gold. All fake at that.

And the body of a dead sparrow.

Shola sauntered over to me, nudging the corpse with his nose in what could have been curiosity.

I turned the bird over in my hand and two seeds fell from its beak. Two more pips. My answer then. The three before had signified passing months. One month had passed and so two pips remained. Whoever had sent me this had just let me know their threat would be carried out within the season. Not a long time. I still had little proof it was Nitham, but I hardly needed much.

Not after the cutters in the alley, the fake investigation into Valhum for a string of thefts at the start of the season, the frequent rousting at taverns, and the targeting of the only other Sullied at the Ashram.

I couldn't wait any longer, and I couldn't deal with Nitham through the Ashram's laws.

But I have never been one to follow the rules.

I thrived on breaking them.

I rushed to Clanks for an early meal, managing to catch Radi and Aram shuffling through one of the long lines. They hadn't spotted me yet and I ran to get my own tray and sidle in alongside them.

A few students gave me bleary-eyed glares that could have passed for weak threats if they didn't look like they'd been thrashed the previous night and were functioning now off a handful of hours of sleep. But their looks were short-lived as they took in my cloak, and their grogginess slipped into recognition.

My reputation had been growing even over the quiet month's passing. And why wouldn't it? My stories had continued, even if they changed their shape along the way.

And now I wore a cloak that was a brilliant white like the heroes out of stories. It mattered little if people spotted the quality of craftsmanship or believed it was really made from the scales of a dead old god. The cloak *looked* the part. A storybook thing meant for binders of old.

And appearances are good as truths at times. Maybe more than truth sometimes.

The two students made no further protests, and I tapped Radi on the shoulder.

He had the same tired expression plastered onto his face. "*Nggh.*"

"Wow, a whole syllable. You must have had some night, eh?" I ribbed him with an elbow and he moaned in response.

"He's speaking truth enough for the both of us." Aram yawned, stifling most of it with a sleeve pressed to her mouth. "We've both been in the Scriptory for the last few nights into morning, studying. Midseason exams."

That was a reminder that perhaps my absence from classes could have been a blessing. "And that's going well . . . right?"

The both of them grunted again.

"Right, fair. Well, it'll be over soon enough. There's that." My sympathy needed some work as that did little to lift my friends' spirits. But gossip is a teenager's reliable gift when one is lacking excitement. So I leaned close as we moved through the line and told them what had happened.

"Nitham sent me another box today."

Aram's eyes widened. "What?"

"Like before. The one with fake gold coins and a dead sparrow."

Radi's eyebrows rose in understanding and Aram frowned. "If only you could actually prove it was him." Aram meant no harm by it. She spoke in pure logic and didn't mean to dismiss my beliefs. "Ari, with the weight of his family name, and the money he has, you have to go for him with perfect certainty. Evidence that no one can question."

A lump formed in my throat.

"My father talks about people who try to assassinate another man's character. It's common enough in court. Gossipers and people vying for another's position or fortunes. Or to curry favor with another. It's brutal. And Nitham's one of those, Ari. He's a prince. Don't forget that. He knows this game better than you. Before, you two fought in the open. On streets and on Clays. This is cat's paws—puppets that don't lead back to him."

The lump sank into a deeper pit then, drawing my attention to a hollow coldness in my body. I tried to ignore it and gave my friends my best practiced smile. "I guess I'll have to play a game of my own. One where the odds are stacked in my favor." And I was working on an idea for that.

"How well off is your father that he also knows how court politics work?" Radi looked to Aram as he motioned to one of the channels filled with food. A monk bowed his head and gave Radi a double heaping of chickpeas cooked in a red curry sauce.

Aram shrank a little and busied herself with her own meal. She chose half the helping Radi had of the chickpeas, and availed herself instead to twice that in brown lentils, a portion of buttered rice, and some lightly charred *thori.* "Father's worked with all sorts of people. He's a good merchant. He's been called on for rare goods before. You know how it is." The words came clipped—fast, yet close to a whisper, as if she almost didn't want us to hear them.

Then Aram turned her attention on me as we moved along the line toward the desserts. "You need to think about the long-term consequences of this, Ari. You make more trouble with Nitham now, it could buy you a lifetime of problems. It's no secret he's his father's favorite. Second son besides. If he's not chosen to take the king's place, he'll still have power enough to cause you problems if you ever set foot inside his family's domain. Then think of his friends, places he has influence outside his home." She had a point, though I didn't want to see it then. Besides, I'd suffered far worse than Nitham's ilk before.

"I've already had a lifetime of trouble." I let none of the mounting heat inside me flood my voice, keeping to the cool, taciturn calmness of stone. But still, my thoughts went to the Ashura. Fire. Crumbling stone and mortar. Bodies bent and broken in angles they should never have known. And the blood.

Aram reached out and placed a hand on my shoulder, giving me a look of both sympathy and silent plea. "Then stop asking for more. Take your lumps from him until he's done giving them. He'll find someone else."

And that's exactly what worried me. My thoughts went to Valhum, and what he'd already suffered. He wouldn't be able to weather more of the noble's ire.

But I could take Nitham's barbs, no matter what he tried. I'd survived his cutters, and scared them so well in the process, I doubted anyone else would come after me again. No. I had to go for the source this time, and find a way to send him a message that would keep him away from me for good. And do it in such a way that he couldn't trace it back to me.

"*Sathra,* please." Aram pointed to a recess in the stone channel that contained pounds of glistening brown gold: a pudding made from cream of wheat and dollops of clarified butter and brown sugar. White raisins and dried dates had been sliced thin and sifted into the mix. All finished with broken walnuts scattered throughout.

The monk gave her two large scoops for a serving, then gave us a look asking if we wanted the same. Both Radi and I nodded. The three of us then settled on our juices and found our way to a table that hadn't yet been claimed.

I'd opted for a warm meat stew, forgoing the vegetable-heavy choices available. I took a bite and savored the contrasting spices that brought a smokiness and a mild heat to the meal. "If you want to be fair about it, then consider that *I have* left him alone since he sent those knives. Haven't traded insults with him, crossed his path—nothing. And still I've gotten two packages with a dead sparrow inside and hundreds of fake gold coins, all making it very clear the amount of money he's willing to spend to have me done in for."

Radi frowned, poking at his dessert first with the tip of his spoon. "Ari does have a point there. He's left Nitham well-enough alone, and if he's still getting threats . . ."

"And you're, what, encouraging Ari to lash back at him? How do you think that'll go?" Aram scooped up some of her lentils, mixing them into her rice before taking a bite. "Ari, what can you possibly do to him that makes you think he'll leave you alone? If you have a plan that good, go ahead, share it. I want to hear it."

"Uh, I suppose if I murdered him he couldn't really do anything to me, could he?"

Radi sputtered, beads of mango juice showering the table. He pounded a fist to his chest and had to choose between laughing and breathing. "Brahm's tits, Ari. Yeah, that'd do it for sure, and you'd have the rope around your neck before you could dance to celebrate." Radi shook his head, the edges of a smile still on his face.

Aram sighed and took another bite of her meal. "That's my fault for asking you to be serious for a moment. I'm not sure what I expected."

I raised my hands in defense. "I was serious. . . . Dead men can't trouble you." I couldn't keep the grin from my face as I spoke, however.

Aram rolled her eyes. "Do you have a plan that won't lead to your arrest by the kuthri followed by being sent off to see Nitham in Brahm's bloody pits of fire for all eternity?"

"Oh . . . then, no. Not yet."

She bowed her head in a gesture of quiet victory.

I consumed half my stew with the same zeal as Sham when given warm food. My *sathra* lasted an even shorter time. I polished off what remained of my drink, a cold coconut and sweetened milk concoction infused with cinnamon and caramelized sugar. "What happens at the end of the three months, Aram? After the first package, men came to gut me in an alley. What's next? What's now? If I survive this, which I very much intend to, what will he do on the final month?"

Aram didn't meet my gaze then. "I don't know."

"But you can guess it'll be worse."

She nodded.

"Then I don't have much of a choice." I pushed my tray away from me and began to get up from my seat, but Aram spoke, stalling me.

"What do you need us to do?" Her words could have brought me to choke on air. The loyalty like that, to spend so much time and effort arguing with me to leave Nitham alone. And then seeing I wouldn't, to risk themselves to help me deal with them.

That is a kind of friendship not often seen in the world. It is rare. It is honest. And it is terrible. Because we are all willing to do monstrous things in the name of friendship.

But I couldn't do that to them. Aram and Radi had lives within the Ashram far different than mine. Neither were pariahs like me. They had futures laid out by either their parents or their own passions. Mine rested solely in learning the bindings, and not for the childish wonder I once held for them. I meant to master them in my pursuit of the Ashura.

For revenge. And I knew that was a path I could never take my friends down. Not if I truly loved them like I told myself I did.

"Thanks for the offer, but right now, I just need to think." I gave her a wan smile.

Radi took another swig of his drink, mirroring me in wiping his mouth clean with a sleeve. "Well, if you're going to spend time thinking, you should come by Stones later. I'll be playing. It'll be good for you, maybe lighten your dour murderous mood." He gave me a grin so boyish and full of mischief, I couldn't find the heart to say no. "Besides, there'll be others there. Music, a chance for you to spread some of the gossip you seem so keen on, and the most important thing." Radi's eyes glimmered then. "Girls, Ari."

Aram shook her head. "Ari, if you follow his lead"—she nodded toward Radi—"a woman's going to be the death of you one day."

"What about me?" Radi placed a hand over his heart in mock offense. "Why can't a lovely woman be my demise? Think of the story—the songs they'll sing about that!"

Aram waggled a spoon at Radi. "Oh, you're most certainly going to suffer at the hands of a woman. Maybe as much as you've made some of us lot suffer through. At least by the stories I hear."

"Ouch . . . that again?" Radi brought his fists up to his eyes like a bawling child wiping away tears. My friend opened his mouth to spit back a retort, and while I knew the two of them would bicker in good nature, I didn't want for things to devolve.

"Where *is* Stones? Master Binder and you have both mentioned it to me, but I've never been."

Radi finished his pudding then rose, beckoning me to follow. "I'll do better than tell you. I'll show you. Wait for me in the courtyard. I'll grab my mandolin and meet you. Aram?" He arched a brow at her.

She shook her head. "I'm heading to the Scriptory to study some more. Have a physical exam with Master Conditioner. Tomorrow, Master Mender will be putting us through questions on toxic compounds and improperly made medicines that can be as good as poison. What they'll do to a person, and how to counteract them."

I listened to what she said and realized the depth of her course load, now feeling that maybe my suspension from studies *was* a blessing in disguise. Aram and I traded farewells, with me wishing her luck on her test with Master Conditioner.

Then I followed Radi out of Clanks and waited for him on the frozen grounds of the main courtyard, ignoring the stares thrown at my cloak. An expected thing.

Word had continued to spread of it, and now, among the white ice and snow, it looked a thing crafted from winter itself.

Radi soon returned, mandolin in hand, and led me around the farthest side of the Admittance Hall and the building housing the Mendery. We went onward over open mountain ground, level—smoothed—but never paved or shaped to any purpose. A lone tower, its crown long broken, stood ahead of us. All that remained was thirty feet of rock, crumbled in on itself to form a new, shoddy roof. But the door hung straight as ever and looked like it'd been well cared for.

Radi went up to it and pushed it open. "Come on."

I gave the remnants of the tower another look. "You sure . . ."

"Oh, don't let the state of this place fool you. It's held through storms and ages of trouble. I heard it was only put into this sorry shape long ago. . . ." He stopped in a manner that let me know he had more to say, and had hesitated for fear of choosing the wrong words.

"Radi, what aren't you saying?"

"Binders. Well, binder students." He licked his lips and gave me a look. "This used to be . . . this was the place where people who got cracked ended up." Radi knocked his knuckles against his skull.

Realization thundered into me. "This is the old Crow's Nest."

He shrugged as he led me inside. "I suppose. The building is older than other parts of the Ashram, though. That's what I've heard at any rate. Though it wasn't made like the new one. For one, it was a singular tower of clean stone. Once, at least. Not that hodgepodge the new place is. Honestly, I can't fathom how it's stayed upright all these years."

I gave him a wry smile. "Magic."

He snorted, then sobered when he realized I wasn't joking. "Bah. The bindings. We're here for better reasons than that." He motioned to the stairs leading downward. "Down, down, we go. Underground, deep and dark, down below." The words left him almost a song, his voice rich and resonant.

I trailed just a step behind him, keeping silent the whole way.

Finally we came into a cavern much like what I'd found with Sham, only the place was large enough to easily swallow the biggest buildings in Ghal.

"Wow." I stared at the vast openness of stone, dark and smooth as ink made glass.

"Isn't it?" Radi grinned over his shoulder at me. "This place, this is my real home at the Ashram." He gestured around us. "Welcome to Stones."

Centuries of heavy footfalls had beaten the ground flat. Some mounds of rock sprouted to knee height only to be leveled off and hammered smooth, like a natural seat.

Radi sang a series of notes, clear and lemon-sharp bright. They hung in the air and echoed with a crystalline clarity. It was as if this place had been made for him. It caught and held the sound, bringing a better sweetness to it than anywhere else he could have brought his voice. And he must have guessed the thoughts on my mind for he explained. "It's like that nearly everywhere . . . except by the damn wall."

I frowned. "The wall?"

He picked up his pace. "I'll show you." Radi led me around a bend into another space just as large as the room we'd been in. A part of the stone face had been rubbed away into a smooth expanse of nothingness.

No, that wasn't true.

It was like a film of blackened oil made into a solid stony sheet—iron hard by the looks of it.

I stepped closer and the world grew tight around me. A pressure. A grip like the hands of God Himself threatening to squeeze the breath from me. The air itself felt thick.

"Ari?" Radi's voice sounded leagues away.

My mind was muddled and I reached for the folds, but found them impossible to call upon. The candle and the flame became my only hope for lucidity, but for the first time I could think of in a long while, I couldn't conjure a single image.

Nothingness.

My mind was held in stillness. My will silenced.

"Ari?" Radi grabbed hold of me, pulling me back a few feet with him. "Brahm's ashes, man, what's going on with you?" He looked at me as if I'd dropped my trousers and suddenly decided to piss all over the ground. "Are you all right?"

I shook my head. "I think so. How do you tolerate it here?"

He blinked. "Like . . . everyone else? What do you mean?"

I described the sensation I'd just felt.

"That's your mania catching up with you. All the pressure you're under, even if you're not thinking about it. Problems with Nitham. Problems to prove your control over a binding, or you're good as gone. And whatever you've been doing with all your time down in Ghal, so busy you can't see your friends."

That hurt.

Especially considering I'd been trying my best to stay in touch with the people I loved. But between my suspension from classes, and Nitham doing his damnedest to toss me out of any establishment, I could only catch Aram and Radi in Clanks. Even then, it was in passing unless I happened to meet them just at the right time. Add in the fact my free hours went to staring at a blasted candle, making little progress in the bindings—no thanks to Rishi Ibrahm, and raising a juvenile delinquent in Sham, I lost what time remained to give to my friends.

Including Immi. That thought brought me another pain. Was she okay? Had her condition improved at all?

I had tried to be everywhere for everyone, and in turn, I was left unable to be there for anyone at all. A cruel lesson for a young man to learn. I could conjure fire, if you believed the stories, but I couldn't spare a moment for my friends.

"Radi, I'm sorry."

He waved it off with a lazy, forgiving smile. "I know. Just giving you a hard time, and pointing out how much you've got going on. It's catching up with you. You look . . . not ragged, but like someone who's been working their mind and body as hard as they can, nonstop. Just drained, you know?"

I nodded. I didn't feel like it, but that didn't mean it wasn't the case. Often, we run ourselves dry well before we realize it.

"Yeah, you're probably right."

Radi gave me a look. "Probably? You know I am."

I laughed, and it felt good. But the little joy was short-lived as I traced my gaze along the odd wall I'd approached. Two lines of neat script, the height of the lettering matching me almost, ran along the top of the obstruction. "Can you read that? It looks like Brahmki, but wrong?"

Radi shook his head. "Older, I think. At least some of the students think so. Heard someone once say they think it means: 'A mind kept silent, and a heart held still, keeps the shadows of temptation at bay.' Something like that. It's old philosophical talk. You know how the old *yoghs* love that enlightenment stuff." He squinted, trying harder as he read over the text. "It goes: *Vala mouna. Daritha sathva.*"

"A riddle?"

He shrugged. "More like nonsense someone carved long ago. I mean, the wall's practically a prank made by some old rishi ages ago. No one can see through it, even though it's like black glass. No one's been able to find a way past it. It's just weird. Come on, I need to start practicing for tonight."

So I listened to my friend play for a few passing candlemarks.

Eventually, the crowds came.

TWENTY-EIGHT

Songs and Threats

Throngs of people packed tight, some availing themselves of the little flat mounds that passed as nature's seats. Radi hadn't exaggerated about the popularity of the place or the spectacle.

One student, a young woman possessing all the slender grace you could imagine, stood atop one of the low stone humps. Others had brought ceramic braziers, made in the Artisanry and crafted to hold great heat without failing.

Soon, Stones was aglow with the warmth and light to make it feel like a tavern. Bronze and orange danced along the rock faces and cast long shadows through the place. Students picked up in chattering.

The student who'd stood on one of the flat stone protrusions shrugged out of her robe, revealing clothing better suited for the south. Bare arms, and a skirt that left the length of one of her long legs exposed. Many a young man turned to pay her greater mind, and I too found it difficult to shy away.

Someone rushed through the crowd and passed her a rod of painted smooth bamboo.

Radi leaned close, cupping a hand to his mouth. "High flute. Alto. She plays classical. I've had a thing for Suri for quite a while."

That last line drew a smile out of me. "Is 'a while' a set? Radi, you've got a thing for every girl for too short a time to remember. For me . . . and for you. What's the name of the last one whose heels you were nipping at?"

He frowned. "That's not true. And her name was . . . Hennai." His brows furrowed. "No, wait, uh, Shari? Erhm."

I clapped him on the back. "Don't think too hard, you'll hurt yourself." I wanted to say something else, but a long bright note pierced the air.

Soon, others followed, trilling short and sweet and quick as can be.

Students settled down, and now Suri commanded our attention. She moved with the lithe grace of a dancer—swaying and playing. Her fingers moved with perfect pace, never too fast, never a slip. She knew her craft, and she'd given it the time to be masterful. Suri played, setting many feet dancing.

Clapping shortly followed.

Somewhere, the rhythmic beat of thunder drummed through Stones.

I searched for the source, but Radi spotted the boy first, pointing him out.

He looked close enough in age to me, but heavier and broader across the shoulders. Dark-skinned with short curly hair that looked like he'd slicked it back with coconut oil. His fingers and thumbs beat across white skin stretched tight over a wooden drum resting between his legs.

He played with the speed of rainfall in storm, beating a tempo unmatched. Face tight in concentration. His thunder a perfect harmony to the bright piping from Suri.

The dancing intensified.

Students giggled and laughed. I saw a few stolen kisses pass between the mingling bodies. More laughter. Spots of blushes and brushed hair in the awkward gestures the young make when feeling shy.

A hand clamped to my elbow and pulled me a half-turn from Radi.

I had called fire and bound it to thought and hand. I'd buried Ampur and killed an old god. So, few things could set my heart hammering into my throat.

She was in her early twenties at a guess. Her skin the color of sun-kissed teak, brushed through with touches of gold. She had all the warmth of honey and depth of molasses in the color of her eyes. Her hair hung loose to her shoulders, every tress a curled wave that she'd bound in bits of brass and a few blue flowers.

"Hi," she said.

I stared.

A sharp strike against my back drew a wince from me. Soft breath rolled against the base of my neck and a piece of whispered advice followed. "Say something, idiot." Radi's voice.

"Hi." I waved, then realized the stupidity of the gesture. "I'm, uh, Ari."

She smiled, wide and full-lipped. "I'm Shandi, uh, Ari."

That brought a measure of sense back to me and I let out a little laugh. "Ari, just Ari, I meant."

"I know. Almost everyone knows who you are." Her smile intensified, and maybe it was the brightness of fire spreading through the cavern, but her eyes carried a light of their own.

As extensive as my vocabulary had grown from my life in theater, some curse of the gods caused me to forget it then. There was no other explanation.

Shandi trailed her hand from my elbow down along the sleeve of my robe, stopping at my wrist to rub her thumb and fingers along it. "Would you like to dance?"

Idiot that I was when it came to women, I opened my mouth when it was best kept shut. "I dance." Nothing of the sort was true.

Her lips went tight like she held back a wry smile, amused at my struggle. "I certainly hope so, because I'm still wondering if you'd like to . . . with me."

This time, I'd learned my lesson and nodded without a word.

"Good." And with that, Shandi took my other wrist in hand, pulling me away from where we stood.

Just before I left Radi's reach, I felt a sharp smack against my rear. I turned to regard him. He flashed me a wink and a lecherous smile. It was a thing of as much mischief as confidence and cheer for a friend.

I couldn't return it, still not trusting myself with my own two feet, much less my thoughts. Thankfully, I needed neither of those.

Shandi knew the way and how to lead me. And so she did.

The piping picked up. Faster now and brighter still.

Drumming quickened in proper measure and thundered twice as deeply as before.

The whole of Stones became a concussive force, beating us with the full measure of music to be felt. And it *was* felt. To the core of us. You did not hear this performance of fluting storms. You moved to it. It settled in our hearts and made our feet light—fast, threatening to trip ourselves as much as running off with the joy.

Shandi skipped like a stone over water. Light enough to break again into airy movement as soon as she touched the ground. An unnatural fluidity in every motion. The wind itself trailed in her wake as much as it led her every step. She pulled me along with her, never forceful or throwing me off my balance. Just a gentle lead. The perfect amount. I was pulled into the flow of her like a leaf caught in breeze. She twisted, bringing me into it again. Then pulled me close—but no sooner than that, pushed away from me. Her chest rose with her breathing, and her eyes brightened.

And we grew closer in that moment, all while the music reached its peak, breaking soon to slow its pace and lull us out of our frenzied tempo. Shandi leaned in during the quieting moment, and the full shape of her lips promised to become better acquainted with mine.

"Shandi, there you are!" The voice had dragged her name out, in deliberate emphasis to draw more than just her attention. I knew a stage call when I heard one. Nitham, of course. Who else would piss on my fire? "Shandi, it's been more than a set since we last saw each other," he said.

Shandi froze short of bringing our mouths together. Her neck went visibly rigid. A weak and utterly hollow smile spread across her mouth. "Nitham."

He drew closer, arms spread wide in an offer to embrace her, which served to brush away the crowd at the same time. And of course, they moved for him. "That long without seeing you, hearing from you, it makes me think you didn't enjoy our time together." He pressed both hands to his heart, face falling into a wounded mask.

I'll give him something to hurt over. I hadn't realized how tight I'd taken to gripping Shandi's wrist. She winced in my hold, but gave me a look that said she did not mind. In fact, it said to me she would prefer I stay close.

So I did.

Nitham's gaze shifted from Shandi to me, and his face soured like he'd sucked a salted lemon. "Oh, *you*. Is that what's kept you busy all this time, Shandi? You've been slumming it with gutter trash? Every girl has her moments, I suppose, *exploring*."

Shandi's nails dug into my hand as she squeezed it in frustration. I couldn't blame her.

"I thought it was obvious when I didn't return your letters or come looking for you. I don't want to see you again." Shandi spoke with no venom—clear and without any inflection. The voice of someone speaking facts. That is all. "And right now, I just want to dance." She gave my arm a possessive tug.

Not that Nitham spotted the silent but obvious cue. He extended his own hand toward her in open offer. "So, let's dance."

I hadn't noticed it at first, but the music had died. All eyes were on us.

Shandi looked at his hand, then him. "I have a partner, thank you."

He gave her a piteous look, like someone sympathizing with a wounded animal.

"Really, him? Shandi, *tch-tch.*" Nitham shook his head. "You're of better blood than that. You know better. You shouldn't even be touching someone like him."

That brought me to bristling where I stood and my free hand balled into a fist. I took a step. Then another. Soon, I was between Shandi and Nitham. "Someone like me? You mean someone who made you look like the fool you are in front of a whole class? Or someone like me who taught you a pretty good lesson while everyone watched. You think you scare people. Think you can bully them around, like what you've been doing to Valhum. What do you think now that you've been given a burned hand as a lesson?"

I looked around the space, nodding at several of the fires. "Looks like I've got plenty to work with here. What do you say, Nitham, want a repeat performance? There's nothing I love more than putting on a *good show.*"

His eyes widened, and I saw him cast a wary look at each of the dancing flames. While his hand had healed from the injury, the memory remained. Not to mention the embarrassment he'd suffered. I doubted he wanted to suffer the same in front of another crowd.

Nitham licked his lips, eyes clearly calculating. "You know, *Sullied,* that sounded remarkably like a threat. In front of witnesses."

"You're the expert. After all, that's about all you can do. It's more your thing to have someone else do your work for you, isn't it?"

He took a step closer. "I'm more than capable of dealing with you myself, gutter trash."

I smiled, wide enough for everyone to see. "Then why don't you?" I leaned closer, letting my voice drop to a whisper sharp enough to cut through sinew. "Instead of sending cutters after me with your father's coin."

He leaned close and kept the smile from his face, though it burned in his eyes. "Prove it." The words had been kept to a true whisper meant only for us. "You just try to prove it, Sullied. Maybe you should learn to walk more carefully, and twice as much as so to whom you speak." His eyes narrowed and the firelight danced within their brown. "And how. Or I'll bleed you of your coin like the other Sullied. Poor boy's got nothing left to his name and is all set to go home without a bent chip in his pockets." His smile widened into the wolfish.

The threat was clear. But I have always been incapable of kowtowing to the privileged prats of the world.

"Of course, *sahm.* I'm so sorry. I *should* be speaking better to you." Nitham missed the dripping mockery in my voice and adopted a smile smug enough for a cat. "Brahm's teachings say to treat the infirm and malafflicted with the utmost of respect."

Nitham's face became a sheet of stone. "What do you mean, *Sullied*?"

I leaned close to Shandi, bringing my mouth to her ear. When I spoke, I made sure my voice carried in a perfect stage whisper. "I've heard it said, from many of his former lovers, Nitham's left them on their lonesome while engaging in shockingly amorous encounters with sheared and buttered goats."

Nitham's jaw ground tight enough I could almost hear his teeth creaking. "Stop talking, Sullied trash."

"Aw, I didn't even get to the part about why you need set-old coconuts." I turned to face the majority of the crowd and made several lewd gestures with my fingers.

A chorus of chuckles broke out.

"I'll . . ." Nitham stopped short, very well aware that we were surrounded by witnesses.

"Sputter off uselessly into dribble?" I made another gesture with my fist. "Nothing new there from what I hear."

Several of the women laughed, quickly stifling the sounds behind their hands.

Nitham huffed, his chest rising quicker and quicker. But he composed himself faster than I could have imagined. He reached into his pockets, scrounging around and pulling free a loose coin. He sent it my way with a casual flick. "Catch."

I didn't move, letting the piece fall against the ground. It shone gold in the light.

A rupai. He'd thrown a whole gold rupai like it was a piece of tin.

Like the coins from the box.

It said a great deal that he kept a coin like that as loose change in his robes and not tightly cinched away within a purse. He was making a show of his wealth. And I made the extra connection as well. *I have enough wealth to buy your death.*

"Your mood's probably foul from all the stress you Sullied go through trying to scamper about for coin, *ji*? You lot can't hold proper jobs, not that anyone would want to hire you other than for putting on an utterly shit play. As if you lot would know good literature from poor. Can you even read?"

I bobbed my head in the compliance he expected of my caste. Men used to the verbal abuse and quietly taking it all with practiced smiles and obeisance. I picked up the coin and stowed it like a good laborer would. "Yes, *sahm*. This one knows words like 'impotency.'" I motioned with my little finger while giving him a knowing look.

More laughter.

"And goat lover." I kissed the free air. "And this one knows—"

Shandi tried to pull me away from Nitham and my tirade.

"You think you're so clever." He seethed in place.

I grinned even while being hauled back, my smile answering him instead.

"What about your family of Sullied trash back home?"

The question sent hot steel through my core and set my heart hammering to the now dead drummer's beat. "What?" The word left me like a whip-crack against stone. Sharp and hard. "What did you say?"

His smile belonged on a snake and I almost expected his tongue to peek through his teeth, forked and all. "I started asking about you. There are rumors you had a family of orphans running around Abhar. Little sneak thieves plucking up coin and purses. Everyone knows Sullied steal."

That wasn't true. And not every one of the sparrows had been Sullied. They came from all walks of life. Orphans didn't choose their caste, and they didn't choose their fates.

I grew better aware of all the burning braziers. The flames within. Their heat. Their desire to consume more than they'd been given, keeping them low instead of how high they wished to grow. They spoke of anger and hurtful wrongs. And the ability to wipe all problems away.

A hateful hot thing.

"A word to my father and it wouldn't be so hard to send a letter to the king of Abhar. Our families go back." He pressed a hand to his chest and straightened as if reveling in the pronouncement. "It's bad business for a kingdom to let thievery like that go on. Maybe something should be done. I suppose they'd be rounded up and handled. They're not more than kids. So it wouldn't be bad. Maybe a branding. The older ones would be locked up if they're not already old enough to have their heads lopped off. The young might lose a hand."

Again the fires took me but for the briefest of moments. A heat. A spark. The first flashing of freshly lit flames. Something explosive.

I tore free of Shandi's grip and brought my face before Nitham's. "If you touch them. Think of them. Send *any* word about them . . . I will burn you. I will burn you and all you own to dust and bone and blackness. And when I am done, I will dance in your ashes. But before any of that, I'll show you the things I did back in that sparrow's life. I'll show you exactly why people thought me a demon. Why they called me 'bloodletter.'

"Saithaan himself will want no part of your soul after I'm through with you. The devil himself will know fear, and Brahm almighty will look away in horror."

All of Nitham's hot-faced bravado fled for the wide-eyed look of a child seeing their first frightful shadow on the wall. His lips shook, just enough to betray the fear. Then they parted, but he found no words to speak. He simply breathed. Slow. Steady. As if he'd forgotten how to do anything besides sit there. A mute, dumbfounded doll.

Everyone else had gone silent as well. All eyes stared, though not at us. Only me.

Nitham finally swallowed and looked around, realizing what had happened. He nodded more to himself than anyone in particular. Turned. And fled.

Radi came over to me and grabbed me by the shoulder, spinning me around. "What were you thinking?" His words were a rasping whisper, like weak wind through gravel and dead leaves. "You just threatened him openly . . . in front of a damnable crowd, Ari. He can bring you to the masters for that. You're already under suspension."

I hadn't even thought about that when I'd said what I had, and now wasn't the moment to lose face after having successfully driven Nitham off. "It wasn't a threat. It was a promise."

Radi shook me harder. "Brahm's blood, Ari. If word of this spreads—"

I pulled one of his hands off of me. "It won't. Just like most of the barbs and threats we've traded haven't. You think he wants it spreading further, what just happened? I whipped him bloody with words before he said what he did. I just won the fight is all."

Radi sighed and hung his head. "Brahm's ashes, man. I hope you're right."

So do I. I did not voice my doubt.

"Because if you're not . . ." Radi made the motion of a tightening noose, then snapped it tight. My friend nudged me an instant later, making a subtle look with his eyes that I followed.

Shandi stared at me with her mouth slightly open, flushed with color and wide-eyed. Several other students had similar looks on their faces.

Had I gone too far? Now that the fire had faded in me, I cooled and tried to think about the situation. Nitham had openly provoked me, not to mention made Shandi visibly uncomfortable. He'd developed a greasy reputation where women were concerned, and no one would have argued that fact with me. Threatening my family crossed the line, but would the masters see it that way if it reached their ears?

My family were thieves. But every city had theirs, and everyone turned a blind eye to them so long as they never reached too far into the wrong purses. I knew that for a fact, because I'd once done that very thing and bought myself a debt I couldn't easily escape.

But I didn't get to think through the answer as Shandi came over to take my arm in silence. And in that quiet, I couldn't read how she felt about the scene that had just happened, or me.

A tension had built through Stones, but now it quivered as weak strings, waiting to be cut. Others followed Shandi's lead to try to return to normal. The larger crowd broke back into little circles of friends. Partners hooked arms and pulled each other aside. The stage was set for another musician.

The right musician.

And Radi always knew his cue.

He flashed me a wide grin and leapt onto one of the flattened protruding stones. His mandolin came into his hands and he teased out a light and joyous melody. No true performance. Just something to whet the appetite and remind people why we were here tonight.

For some fun and good music.

Suri eyed Radi in appreciation, like someone who hasn't quite formed their full opinion yet, but was more than willing to take the time to figure it out.

He caught her eye and gave her a smolder that could have freed all of Ghal from winter's hold. "Oblige me?"

She nodded and brought her flute back to her mouth.

The student who'd been playing the drums picked up his as well, but he didn't set to playing yet. He watched Suri and Radi, waiting for a sign.

She began, low and slow. Each note long and pulling at us.

Then came Radi. He brought the mandolin to voice. It sang. Notes tripping like a horse in canter. Measured, smooth, and high. It worked well with the pace Suri set. Drumming filled the air to the beat of gentle rain on stone. Each person played distinct, yet together, and they made something greater than what each could do alone.

But even then, I had ears for only the best of them. For my friend. For Radi.

He took charge and led them faster. Bringing the gentle summer's rain into a full monsoon-season storm. They exploded to rock the foundations of Stones, filling us with a renewed vigor to dance and shout and live as only the young and careless can.

Shandi led me through steps I knew I butchered. But she didn't care, and neither did I. Under the firelight, and the excitement that had taken us all, her eyes held a brighter glow then, bringing out their lighter shades of gold. The trick of the fires' shine along her face brought out the rare metal color until it almost looked as if they took the whole of her eyes. "*That was wonderful.*" She let out a laugh, her breath catching and betraying how hard she labored.

The air between us grew heavy. It was as if she'd spoken those three words without edge, without inflection. Smooth and lilting like your first fresh breath or as if written with the wind itself. I felt as if the air had been pressed from me.

"I have my moments." Each word a strain to voice.

"I'd like to see more of those." She leaned close and I learned another thing then. That a young woman's kiss can make you forget a world of troubles. For a moment at least. And when she brought her mouth to mine, Nitham, fear of the masters, and even the threats on my family, all vanished for the space of that lovely touch. But as with most wondrous things in youth, they don't last long. She broke the kiss, smiling while the color rose in her face.

I'm sure the fire brought an embarrassing light to my own, and I had probably dressed too warmly for the night. What with the flames around us, one really didn't need the robes. It only served to bury more heat in a person's face and throat than any young boy really needed.

All the while, Radi played on. And then . . . he sang.

The dancing slowed and everyone's attention belonged to the man who truly deserved it that night. My moment with Nitham had brought folks some measure of entertainment. But afterward, Radi *was* the show.

He led the other musicians quicker now. Harder. Brighter—clearer until the music called all attention to them. To even think to look anywhere else, on anyone else, was an insult I don't think any of us was capable of inflicting on Radi and his fellow musicians that night. We stood, breaths held deep even though we ached for the reprieve of exhalation. No one dare let out a sound amidst the ones we were treated to.

He sang, crystalline clear, of Ampur. You know the song. Of my climb atop the snowy peaks and the old god that challenged me so. Of words screamed against howling wind and a serpent as old as time. Hardened scales of ice and white-snow bone and teeth as sharp as knives and tough as stone. Of bindings called and employed, and the village buried, and destroyed.

Radi held our hearts and breaths, promising not to return them until we could bear their loss no more. Quicker—he led the tempo. Harder. Sweat beaded his brow and he brought the music to a pace that teased to tell us it would not break. A speed with which no heartbeat could contend. Thrumming through the air like an unseen current against our skin. Strings that sang higher with no crescendo in sight.

He held the manic pace—all of us begging now to be let go from the spell. Radi's voice arced through it all and echoed bright through Stones, carried hard and full around us by the nature of the place.

And finally . . . it all broke.

The song ended and we felt our breath return. A lightning euphoria filled the crowd. Silence blanketed Stones.

Only for a moment.

And then we screamed.

Radi smiled, his face making it clear he'd rather have slumped on the spot. Performer first that he was, he found the strength to bow instead. That night, he was a king.

He deserved it.

One of my hands went into my pockets as I watched my friend mobbed by adoring students. My fingers brushed against a piece of gold, and I thought about what someone else deserved. Nitham and I had traded the last threats I felt we should.

I may have won the verbal jousting match with him, but Nitham had reminded me of what he'd shown over the season. His power. Privilege. And wealth. As well as all the troubles he could buy me with them. Left unchecked, he would find a way to win.

All I had were my wits, the stories about me—a flimsy shield—and my devilry.

If I wanted to survive, I'd have to be clever. I'd have to be a demon.

And remind him a sparrow keeps his promises.

TWENTY-NINE

Red Smoke and Flames

I waited for word to reach the masters about my verbal sparring match with Nitham, but it never came. Nor did any students mention it. What happened between us died that night. At least as far as gossip mongers of the school were concerned. Was it out of fear of reprisal from Nitham, or perhaps me?

He already had a terrible reputation for lashing out at those he deemed beneath him. And my own stories painted me as someone not to cross.

I knew the truth, of course.

Nothing would stop until one of us made sure of it for good. Being the enterprising young man that I was, I figured it best for me to make that first move. And I wasted no time going about it.

My mornings for the next several days were spent down in Ghal, hiding with Sham, and guiding the self-styled Crow through my plan. When he wasn't out on the streets plying his newly improved trade, he rehearsed with me. My little brother by bond, even if not blood, had grown in that time. He'd learned the art of eavesdropping and trading secrets. So I sent him on a little mission to see what he could glean about Nitham's residence.

And The Crow delivered.

Nitham had taken rooms at an inn called The Saffron House. A gaudy place by Ghal's standards of architectural beauty. Unlike the gemstone blue and trimmings of gold or silver found on most better-off buildings, this place had a domed roof of full golden foil. Something that made it easy to find even on days when the sun was but a shadow of itself. High-standing, with stone of past white that had slowly turned the color of pale yellow. Garish, ugly, and a monument more to the wealth it had cost to build than to any sense of taste.

So a perfect home for Nitham, really.

Afternoons had me back at the Ashram for lessons with Rishi Ibrahm, who for reasons of only his own knowing, spent the first of these meetings with his ear pressed to the stone ground, listening for something.

Half of the session passed this way. When we tried to ask questions, we were shown the sharper side of his tongue, then told to try it ourselves. A few students had the sense not to fall for the stupid act.

I wasn't one of them. After countless minutes, I learned that rocks sound a great deal like nothing. If you listen longer, you begin to hear your own mounting frustration. Beyond that, your breath, possibly the blood pumping in your own temples, until your irritation builds and you hear nothing once more.

Pure emptiness. A silence. And stillness.

But, knowing my temper had driven me to risky places already, I kept better control of myself. Partially to impress Rishi Ibrahm with my self-restraint. The masters' threat still weighed heavily on me, and then there was the fact that Rishi Ibrahm had bothered to give me the story of Tarun Tharambadh. It made me think that if I kept diligently to my studies, without complaint, he might aid me further in my pursuit of the bindings.

A private lesson. Maybe words of advice I could actually follow. The candlemark ended and the other students left in a hurry. I remained, however.

"Rishi Ibrahm?"

"Hm?" He blinked several times, staring more through me than at me. "Oh, yes, you. What is it?"

"It's about the bindings."

He nodded. "Well, I should hope so. I'm certainly not teaching you to sit on your thumbs here, am I?"

There was considerable debate on whether he was teaching us at all, never mind what. "Uh, right. I don't think any of us have been making as much progress as we'd like."

He pushed his lips tight together and blew out a sound like a horse. "I'm hardly surprised. None of you have even bothered properly applying yourself. You're doing things instead of *doing* them." I couldn't tell what he'd meant by that.

He must have noticed my lack of comprehension, because he went on. "Ari, what exactly is the Athir?"

I rattled off all I could recall. "The founding pillar of faith. The belief and mindset needed to hold the folds and imprint them with what we wish to see. That's part of how we affect things in the world. Employ the bindings."

"Right. Faith. Belief. The unshakable belief that you can in fact do the thing you wish to do, yes?"

It was my turn to nod.

"What do you believe, Ari?"

I didn't need to think long on that. The answers came to me quick as could be. The Ashura were real. The bindings too. Old gods and forgotten things rested in the world. Monsters. Fire. Koli. And I believed I would find the Ashura again, bindings in heart and held-in-hand, and that I would kill them. But I didn't tell him that. I chose the safer answer.

"That magic is real. That I've seen it. I've felt it. That there are things I don't understand out there in the world. And that I am terribly far behind mastering the bindings even though my life depends on it." I gave him a knowing look.

He met it. "That, Ari, is because you are remarkably thick. Listen."

"I am listening. I was listening." I jabbed a finger at the stone below us. "You know what I heard? Nothing, Rishi. Nothing. Quiet. I heard the empty sound of stillness. Nothing to help me. Nothing to teach me. Nothing to show me how to keep my head attached to the rest of me by the year's end!"

"That's because you were hearing, and not Listening." He sighed and put one hand on my shoulder. "Listen to me now. Do you believe in things you don't see?"

I shook my head. "Not really." I'd once operated on that logic and had been proven painfully wrong, but if I hadn't seen the Ashura that night, I wouldn't have believed they were responsible for the carnage in my home.

"Then you're pretty blind. After all, the moon vanishes from our skies some nights, and most mornings, *ji-ah*? And there are moments the sun is gone as well. Then . . ." His voice took on the weight of mountain stone and the dryness of ash. "Then there are truly terrifying moments when the sun and moon meet in embrace and cast the world into shadow. A false midnight tinged with light. Have you ever seen such a thing? A ring of flame around a pool of darkness." When he spoke, the world around me felt tight, as if the air held me hard. It was a thing of cold strength threatening to squeeze the breath from me, then break my ribs if I stayed too long in its grip.

"N-no." It was all I could do just to breathe that word.

"But it's true. They're out there, all of the things you can't believe. Even if you've never seen them. Never will see them. Seeing is not believing, Ari. The belief needed to be a binder must transcend the belief normal men and women hold to. And to believe those things, you must understand them. Because it is far easier to work with what we understand."

"And control them?"

"No, Ari. Never control. Binders do not truly control the things we work with. We shape them. That's what you are, a shaper, Kaethar Ari. For now, anyway. You can shape your mind and the folds, and you can call a binding under duress. That is not enough. And if you're thinking of control, it is most certainly not that.

"When you understand something, it is easier to bind the thing. Easier to believe you can. Something inside you understands a part of fire. Something inside of you knows how to Listen and See the truth of things. That is what you need to work on first. Then you can come to believe in the things it takes to be a binder."

I thought on that, and what it really meant. Immi, a young girl convinced utterly in the belief her fingers were in a constant state of repair. Thus, she could grind them to blood and bone and to her, they were never hurt. She wasn't wrong. Not when she could heal them to a state where they'd never been harmed at all. And with that logic and her binder's mind of conviction, she had told herself it was fine to continually tear them apart. After all, they were never in harm's way, were they?

Then there was Krisham. A boy only a handful of years older than me. Someone who never learned to master the bindings himself, so he taught himself to believe he was the old heroes from stories who could do the things he only wished. And his belief turned on him until his own mind made those thoughts reality. Now he went through fits of believing he was a storybook legend. Trying to harm others as much as himself. A prisoner of his own mind.

That is what belief can do to a man. Make you a danger to yourself. Make you convinced you're doing the right thing, even when it's wrong. Make you think you're a hero when you're the monster. Belief is a power.

If you spend long enough convincing a man he is a genius, you might well end up with an arrogant fool who truly believes the thing. Or you can break a child for life by telling them they are nothing. Convince them they are trash. And they will believe that.

Belief is the most powerful magic a person can wield.

And it. Is. Dangerous.

Which is why so many of us come to use it poorly.

"Ari, this is why I am urging you to listen to me now. For once. Slow. Down. Learn to understand things. Leave the Ashram and get a better appreciation for the secret truth of things. Shake loose the dung that's caking this up." He rapped his knuckles hard against my skull. "You don't know what you really believe yet, even if you think you can answer me."

I didn't know how to respond, so I merely nodded and left his class. But all the while, the words weighed on my heart. Leave the Ashram. The place that had become my home.

Maybe he was right. I'd only come here because I hadn't known where else to go after my home had burned down. I wanted to master the bindings to get revenge, but I wasn't making the progress needed here.

Why not take the chance? I could leave and pursue the Ashura myself.

But my mind went to the immediate threat at home. What Nitham had done to Valhum, an innocent Sullied student, and all to make a point against me. And his words against the sparrows. He'd sent knives in the dark, maligned my name, and wanted to see my old family hanged. . . .

I owed Nitham a visit.

That night saw me to the The Saffron House. A few other buildings stood nearby, closer than you'd expect from places wealthy enough to buy more space for themselves. A doorman waited before the inn and had a look about him that made it clear he would have no problem dealing with trouble.

By that I mean he stood as wide across the shoulders as some children did tall. His eyes seemed a bit too small for his face, and his forehead belonged to a lizard or some far-off brutish beast. Sloped, too large for the rest of his face, and shaped as if it had been dented flat. And he had a brawler's nose, set askew and never properly put back into its place.

Not the man I wanted to get into a fight with.

I skulked around the outskirts of the building, passing by with feigned indifference. My face remained forward while I watched the passersby out of the corners of my eyes. Sham had told me Nitham rented one of the side-facing rooms, three of his own windows along the street to take in the light.

A poor choice. Windowed rooms are the easiest for a thief to break into.

I moved around the perimeter until I came to the side wall where his rooms were located. The only problem rested in his chambers being on the third story. I'd have to climb. Thankfully, Brahm must have hated Nitham more than I did, because the walls were free from the frost and ice that had stuck to some of the other buildings.

I could scale them straight from the ground, using one of the ceramic pipes that ran along the side to remove old water and chamber-pot fluids. It was fixed to the wall by thick brackets. They would give my fingers purchase, along with the nature of the stone itself, and the lips of the windows. Still, it would be difficult, and a fall would leave me with a broken leg or arm depending on how I landed.

I rounded the building and took in the rest of it, my mind racing with how to tackle the problem. If I could manage the climb, then the matter of his room would be easy. A thin knife, or even a slender but strong wire would let me slip in between the window and trip its catch. After that, I could lift it open and slip in. Leaving would be the same.

Now all I needed to do was decide how best to send my message. And I had an idea for that. A good one. Fit for a performer. A storyteller.

I spent every night for a set trawling the grounds around The Saffron House, memorizing every road that led to it, and just as many that took me away. Any familiar face became burned into my mind. And all the while, Sham took note of Nitham's schedule, letting me know when next he'd be away.

The little urchin had taken quickly to skulking around in his black cloak, rushing out of sight whenever he feared discovery. Soon enough, rumors began to float about a figure in black spotted through the city, taking flight as soon as you saw him.

A crow.

For my part, I busied myself in my work, purchasing materials I needed from the city.

I couldn't risk buying what I needed from Holds. If things went poorly, and the particulars were discovered, it would be an easy finger to point my way. So, I shed my white cloak, given how much it stood out, and bought myself a large amount of rithra.

A powder close to the color of paprika, only discernible from it by its smell, something close to sulfur. The substance had little practical use besides a dye, becoming stable once mixed with water and drying to a fabric or stone mix. But when the powder joined fire, it had the peculiar effect of changing the color of the smoke. No longer were you given an ashen gray, but instead the color of blood. A red every child knew from stories.

The red smoke of the Ashura. And it possessed the remarkable quality of continuing to fill the air with the signs of demons long after its source fire burned out.

Performing troupes used it in plays when featuring the monsters. But Khalim never had the coin to spare for it, so we made do instead with the creativity he'd levied in building the understage.

The shopkeeper in Ghal had the wits to ask me why I needed the material, and why so much. I gave him the safest answer I could. That I'd been sent to procure it for a successful builder that was going to build a beauty of a building all in red stone. When I passed over a full silver dole for the amount, the man quickly lost all interest in my motive and sent me along with my powder in hand.

I'd gone down to under three doles of my own, not counting the coin Nitham had left me. But I had a special use for that.

And then there was the suthin, or flashsteel I had left over from the beginning of the season. A little wood and wool, easy to pluck for free. Thief's hands and all. Well, the necessary things all came together perfectly.

Content with my plan, I bided my time until the perfect night. And then it came.

Ghal had broken into light flurries by afternoon that day. The sun had retreated early behind a mask of gray clouds. Good signs. My white cloak remained bundled in my sack, but I intended to use it for the evening's work. I'd skipped class and made myself scarce, choosing to spend what remained of my free time with Sham.

My little brother had been shaped into something better than before. Still a far cry from what any of the sparrows had been, but his quality of life had improved at least. His hair now looked cleaner, no longer holding to as much filth. And Sham had learned to speak somewhat more properly.

Somewhat. He had a particular aversion to study and a stubborn streak that no other boy could match. Well, perhaps one other.

The little crow had learned to pilfer better purses. This had led him to having more regular meals, filling out, and procuring a feathered mattress for the cavern.

I'd also made sure to bring Shola along with me in case the night went awry. That way my kitten would be in the safety of the nearby cavern until I could get back.

I'd asked my little brother if he remembered the plan. If he didn't, I wouldn't be able to trust him with my safety. Not something I ever had to worry about with the sparrows.

But then, I'd had more time to get them to where I wanted, and Mithu had shaped them well enough before.

Brahm's blood, am I turning into him? Starting to think like he did? I shook my head clear of the thoughts, knowing I couldn't afford them in the moment. And that I didn't want to honestly entertain them. Too much time spent thinking like that could lead to opinions I didn't want to hear of myself . . . especially from myself.

Sham rattled off everything I'd told him. All of which put my doubts to rest.

After that, there was little else to do but wait.

❧

The snowstorm picked up, blanketing Ghal's sky and grounds in a shifting mosaic of white. Dark night, a wash of ice that blurred people's vision, and the overwhelming want to be inside and away from the unkind streets.

The perfect setting for a thief.

And, while I wasn't religious and supportive of Brahm in the same way as most other people, I had the awareness to at least give a quiet thanks for such helpful weather.

I donned my white-scale cloak and left the safety of The Crow's cavern. The streets of Ghal were lit in odd patches by the fire keepers—the men and women tending braziers—all offering to sell you a spot of warmth if you had the misfortune of being out during a storm. I made sure to stay away from their glow.

My robes and cloak did well enough to keep me safe from the worst of the cold, but errant snowflakes still blew their way into my face. The pathways I'd committed to memory from my training with Sham remained fresh as ever, and I navigated the empty spaces between Ghal's building bubbles, skulking with an ease I had long forgotten.

A trio of men huddling around a low brick pillar, taking in its fire, spotted me. One of them leaned forward, trying to get a better look at me through the storm.

I slipped away between the walls of two nearby buildings.

"Oi!" The voice came warbled, broken by the wind and weather.

I didn't answer the call and moved on.

"You see that?" another voice cried into the air, and I could have been wrong, but I heard a note of unease in the words.

I paid them no mind, taking the long way around to The Saffron House. The cold and piling frost along the ground meant it took me more than a third of a candlemark to trudge my way to where I wanted.

The crooked-faced doorman still stood before the building, but he wore a mask of complete disinterest for the goings-on beyond the front stairs.

Good.

I moved around to the buildings at The Saffron House's side. One roof jutted close enough to serve as a poor platform off which to launch myself. Not ideal, especially given the weather, but the buildings here were designed to shed most of the snow and ice. And as such, they weren't holding to much of that at all.

I scrambled my way up the side of the first building, biting off a curse as the cold made its way into my fingers. I couldn't stay exposed to the walls for too long, or I'd risk losing the strength and dexterity I needed.

My feet crunched against the snow as I made my way onto the roof. I leapt, arms outstretched to grab hold of the piping running down the side of The Saffron House.

My fingers closed around its bulk, and one of my feet struck a lower bracket. It squealed in protest, rattling against my weight. I'd damaged the bracket with my foot.

A dry pain built in my chest and my heart hammered from a mix of apprehension and the effort. I pushed it all away, focusing on the climb. I kept both feet pressed against the slick pipe, using the brackets as a rest. My fingers clamped to the next bracket above, and I pulled. The cold bit deeper into me, and I had to stop partway through my climb to risk letting go with one hand. I brought it close to my mouth and breathed warm against it, bringing it inside a pocket to give it some comfort.

I had to switch hands, working to relieve what chill I could. All of which slowed my ascent. Eventually, I made my way up high enough to reach the nearest windowsill. I reached out with a foot, tapping the ledge to see how slippery it was.

Just enough to promise me safety if I was careful. Which was also enough to throw me to the ground in a painful sprawl if I wasn't.

I took a breath and stepped out onto the ledge. My foot stuck . . . then slipped. I sucked in a breath but the limb steadied and I no longer risked falling. I pushed off the pipe and brought the rest of myself onto the ledge.

Still. I sat there like a cat, gripping tight to the sill below me. Shuffle. I moved my way to the edge, then crossed onto the next one. Then again. Each movement sent my heart lurching in fear that it would be my last leap. My fingers cried from the strength of which I held to the sill. A white-knuckled grip, made all the more painful by the freezing night.

Finally, I reached Nitham's window.

I knew he wouldn't be inside tonight. My ears had been kept to the ground for anything about him I could learn. I'd discovered a trio of things that would keep him far from his rooms this day. Exams, lasting from afternoon to evening. Then, Radi had mentioned there would be games and music down in Stones, and Nitham wasn't one to miss that. Especially with girls around. Lastly, he'd had a pisser of a week, on account of some family troubles back home. He spent the end of each night at a tavern he preferred in the company of his friends, drinking their way into a stupor just short of vomiting their insides out.

I reached into the folds of my robes with one hand, pulling free a slim piece of metal that I had shaved down even further. It slid easily between the window frame and sill and I pulled it along the edge until the curved end of the metal caught along the latch. Push, twist, pull.

A *snap-click* told me I'd succeeded.

I pried with the piece of metal, applying just enough force to press against the window without bending the thin steel. The window lifted, just a shade. I placed a palm against the upper frame and shoved. It resisted and my body shook. My feet scrambled and my other hand almost lost its purchase.

Kala mahl. The curse floated through my mind, but I dared not utter an errant breath as I hung there. I managed to steady myself and then reached out to apply a gentler, but consistent, pressure against the frame.

It shuddered, then lifted.

I clambered immediately into the room. Once inside, I turned to look out the window.

A small dark shape shambled through the storm, taking up places between buildings. They vanished as soon as I'd spotted them.

The Crow.

Brahm's tits. Sham was supposed to stay out of sight, not linger close by. The pair of us had scattered wooden bundles, strewn with wool, and what remained of my flashsteel. Once my job was done, the little crow would just need to sprinkle some salt on soaked bundles and the suthin would set them ablaze.

Smaller fires around The Saffron House to buy me time to escape. They would cause no harm, and burn themselves out soon enough in this weather.

My distractions.

More snow piled along the roads, and while it would make walking through the streets a greater pain, it would cushion my fall.

I hoped.

Nitham's rooms were everything I expected for someone of his background. Rich polished wood that caught the glow of the embers simmering in the fireplace. He had his own privy, not a pot. His bedspread was well-dyed wool, a shade found in carmine and beets. The royal color of Nitham's house.

There was no time to linger. So I tore apart his wardrobe, eyes sharp for what I wanted. Eventually, I found one of his purses in a set of drawers, kept nestled under a folded skirt that couldn't have belonged to him.

Either a keepsake or something stolen from one of his short-lived amorous affairs. It would probably be a great pain for him to lose that. I smiled at the thought and threw it onto the bed along with the rest of his clothes. The ransacking continued until I'd gone through most of the room, plucking up other pieces of his personal fortune: mostly coins, and a statue made of white stone, pearl, and gold.

Content with my findings, I looked at the mantel and spotted his oil lamp. Enough heat resided in the low burning embers to easily start the fire anew. It just needed some fuel. And there was plenty of that.

I poured some of the oil onto the coals, sending them sputtering spitefully before a renewed fire kindled to life. For a moment, I simply watched the flames, caught by their warmth, then their color. I snapped free from the trance and brought out the rithra powder. A pinch tinged the flames a color like roses washed pale. Too close to pink than the better red I needed.

So I fed the fire more. It hissed almost in protest, the color ebbing, as did the flames.

No, no, no. I lunged toward the bed, grabbing hold of one Nitham's personal robes. My foot bumped against something and I cursed. The oil lamp I'd rested on the floor tipped over, spilling some of its contents along the wood. I paid it no mind and tossed Nitham's clothes into the fire.

The flames accepted them, lapping up the new fuel in a steady burn. Soon, they resumed their previous strength. But the smoke they gave off doubled, its color closer to blood red.

Good.

I slowly fed the fire more of his clothes, making sure not to smother the flames. When it struggled, I gave it the last of the oil. Finally, it burned clear and strong.

I gave it the rest of the rithra powder, turning the fire's smoke and the flames themselves a bright hellish red. Content, I placed a gold coin on the floor before the fireplace. The same rupai Nitham had given me.

A little reminder that I pay my debts.

I grabbed Nitham's remaining clothes, but froze when I stared back into the flames.

I remembered the night it all changed. The broken wood and stone. The acrid smell of burned flesh, ash and smoke thick in the air. The color of it all. That horrible, hateful red. The blood from the ones I loved, and the streams of blood coming from the walls themselves. How the storm that night failed to quell the fires.

"Come on, just let me show you my rooms. I promise, just a look. I want to show you something." The voice was muffled, but it was clearly a young man's.

My heart somersaulted.

"Oh, I'm sure. I've heard that before. You're not the first boy to try that." A woman, not entirely excited.

"Just trust me." The male's voice loudened and the handle to Nitham's door jiggled.

I dropped the clothes and moved to run.

"Ah, Brahm's tits. Sorry, wrong room. I think I've had too much to drink tonight."

"I'll say," said the young woman.

Brahm's blood, I have half a mind to open that door myself and strangle the pair of you. But the thought died as soon as it'd come when I saw what had happened in my moment of carelessness.

A tail of one of Nitham's long coats had fallen into the fire . . . but the rest remained comfortably on the wooden floor. And they'd caught the flames and quickly went alight.

The oil, the fire! I had no time to stomp out the flames before the rest of his clothes went up with the first, and soon the fire spread along the floor.

I had only one thing to do. Scream.

"Fire!" I hopped over the flames, undoing the lock to Nitham's door and sticking my head through. *Dammit, Ari.* I realized my hood had fallen and quickly snapped it back up. "Fire!"

"S'what?" A voice carried through the walls, likely from a room a few down.

"Someone say fire?"

I shouted the cry again and again, red smoke thickening and filtering now out of Nitham's room into the hall. "Fire!"

"Fire!" The call came back this time as someone finally caught on. Others carried the cry. Doors flung open and people raced out to search for the source.

My cue to leave.

I turned, looking back into the room. The fire had begun to lap at his dresser, and the ends of his bed. *Shit.* I could clear the flames in one good leap, but it had reached a peak that meant no one would be able to put it out.

"Hey, who's that?"

I didn't look for who'd asked that, and I didn't need to know they'd meant me, still lingering in Nitham's doorway like an idiot. I bolted, voices screaming behind me.

"Hey, wait."

I leapt just as people reached his door. My body sailed through the flames and none of them touched me, only my white-scale cloak. I passed through them and struck the ground before the window.

"Did you see that? Someone jumped through the fire. Madman."

"All I saw was something white."

"What was that? Who? Nitham?"

I raced to the window and jumped, my arms flailing hard. My momentum carried me forward as the cries from The Saffron House loudened. The edge of the next building's roof closed in and I reached out.

A shame I'd forgotten the nature of Ghal's roofs when I jumped. I struck the edge hard, my hands slamming against cold, curved, and tragically smooth stone. My chest ached from the impact and I found no good hold as my breath was driven from me.

I fell.

Mercifully, I'd been right about the piling snow. Well, half right. It did soften the blow. But the remainder of the breath in my lungs left me.

I stared up for a long moment, watching the snow fall, and carmine smoke billow from The Saffron House. The flames spread, bright as blood. Red as children's stories. Red . . . as my nightmares.

As the night I'd learned the Ashura were real.

What have I done?

THIRTY

Intermission—for Coin and Country

Eloine reached through the bars, taking one of my hands in hers. "Oh, Storyteller." She squeezed me in her grip. "Vengeance of any sort never brings you what you want. Just more pain—more hurt. More fires." Her voice was free from any judgment, but I could feel the sadness behind her words.

I arched a brow and fought to keep my own voice as controlled as hers. But I failed. "And you've much experience with vengeance, then? Of having your family threatened by someone with the means and manner to carry it out?" Flint and steel bled out of me, bringing sparks and flame to what I'd said.

Eloine didn't pull her hand away from me, but I felt her stiffen in my hold. "I think we both know I'm familiar with the threats made to my people. The clergos." She didn't need to elaborate further.

"Eloine, I'm . . . sorry. I didn't mean—"

Her face remained free from hardness, but the fire I'd kindled between us now took root in her eyes. They narrowed just a shade. Enough to be noticed. "Yes, you did."

I nodded. "Yes, I did. I'm sorry."

She rubbed her thumb against the flesh of my palm. "You're quick to anger if you're poked the right way."

"Anger has its place and purpose. I can't say that I've always done right with my anger, but were it not for that, I wouldn't be alive. Though, I'm not sure if that's a point in anger's favor. I've caused enough trouble in my life."

Eloine's thumb dug hard into my flesh, and her eyes darkened to hold the fury of the wind in storm. "None of that."

"Ow." I tried to gently ease my hand from hers, but she held firm.

"You've done a great deal of sulking, Ari, and this place is bringing out the worst of your brooding." She picked up a grape and pushed it toward me.

I stared.

"I know you've held on to a great many things from your youth. The anger, the want for vengeance against the Ashura. But perhaps let a little of that stubbornness go. It will do you favors among the fairer folk." She smiled and pushed the fruit closer.

I glared but opened my mouth.

Eloine slipped the grape inside and shut my mouth for me.

I held my expression.

"You're supposed to chew it, Ari." She gave my cheeks a squeeze.

I breathed a sigh, wondering what god I'd offended to end up like this, then remembered the particularly impressive score of deities I'd irked over the course of my life. So maybe my current predicament wasn't as bad as it could be. I chewed, keeping my stare fixed on her.

She met it in kind, but just for a moment before the edge of a smile betrayed itself. "Better?"

"You're enjoying getting your way right now, aren't you?"

Eloine's smile broke free full and wide. "Oh, that obvious, is it?"

"Just a bit."

"Well, there's no sense being so dour, Ari."

A look at my surroundings was all I needed to make my point. "Isn't there? I'm in a cell, set for trial, and there's a good chance things will not go my way for once."

She pursed her lips. "I wouldn't give up all hope. You seem to have enough luck to survive even your own worst decisions."

That teased a small grin out of me. While that had been true, I'd also seen men too reliant on their own luck be hanged by the very thing itself when it decided to run out. Luck, as a rule, is a fickle beast.

And you cannot put your trust in fickle things or folk, because they will inevitably turn on you. It is not a matter of if. But when.

For Eloine, though, I agreed. It seemed the better choice to restore the mood. "I suppose you're right. Maybe I'll get lucky again, hm?"

"I'll make it so." No humor this time. Her words were firm as stone and held a promise in them.

I didn't have the heart to share my disbelief. So I merely nodded instead.

Eloine must have picked up on my doubt, and she changed the subject. "What were you hoping for . . . with Nitham, I mean?"

I took a breath and inclined my head toward the wine. She passed it my way and I took a sip to clear my throat. "To scare him shitless. To have him come back to smoldering embers and his possessions burned, with all the signs of demon smoke. I'd left the coin so he'd know who did it, and never mind if the masters found out. I wanted to take something away from him as he'd done to me over the season.

"And when he threatened the sparrows, I became one myself again, even if for a short time. I remembered the hatred I'd kindled and fanned into a greater flame for Gabbi and Thipu. And how I dealt with them. Once I had, they left me alone. I'd hoped the same with Nitham.

"Though he never seemed to learn. Then again, neither did I. I thought he wouldn't be able to prove anything with the coin. A gold rupai? Who would connect that to me? And the red smoke and fire were just a storybook fright that would chill anyone who saw it. Certainly no one would suspect me behind that. It's far easier a thing to blame the Ashura, even if you can't bring yourself to believe in them. Easier to garner sympathy when it's the unexplainable and frightful things from nightmares. After all, everyone is afraid of demons, even if they say they're not when they are awake. But get them alone in the dead of night? Kindle a flame, smoke blood rose bright? And you'll see if their words are really true."

Eloine took the bottle from me, tipping it back for a drink. Her other hand left mine to take up what was left of the cheese. It fell apart in her grip with the slightest pressure. She pressed one of the halves toward me while taking the remainder for herself. But she didn't eat it, breaking the cheese into smaller segments still. "I understand the drive, to do what you did. I do." She didn't elaborate, and seeing her face then, how her smiling mask slipped to a downcast gaze filled with tiredness, I did not wish to press it.

"I believe you. As much as we hate to admit it, there are moments in all of our lives where the call to anger seems the best choice. And there is never enough proof to tell us that it's not a choice to heed. Only afterward do we get a better sight of things. Sometimes, at least."

She nodded, taking a bite of the cheese.

I mirrored her.

"And sometimes anger is the thing that keeps you going." She didn't look at me when she said that.

"Yes." My voice was a hollow whisper that shouldn't have reached her ears, but it did.

"Did you come here for that—Etaynia, I mean. Your anger, Ari?"

A fair question, and she deserved what truth I could give her. "In part, but it might be more aimed at myself than anyone else. Though, I do have enough anger to give to those who've put me on this path."

"And do they have names?" The question came without the prying edge of those who want to wheedle more out of you without concern for your boundaries. She had none of that. Simply honest curiosity.

But I couldn't give her that answer. I had it, but not to share. "They do, but part of that rests in my story. And, if I tell you the later pieces now, I have no way of knowing if you'll come back to hear the rest. Then what will I do?" I managed a more honest smile than before.

Eloine returned it and lunged, reaching through the bars to swat me on the thigh. "That's a rude thing to insinuate. That a woman's only after you for the juicier parts of your tale."

"Oh, if it's not my story, then, what juicy bits of me are you after?"

She swatted me again, but the mock insult faded from her face. "Rascal."

"When I have occasion to be. Other times I'm a thief." My voice fell to a sound that should have gone unheard. "Sometimes a monster."

Eloine picked up on it nonetheless. "That's for me to decide, because you seem to be a rather poor judge of yourself."

"Well, there'll be no shortage of judging soon enough. And it would be all too easy a thing for the Etaynians to judge me so, and be done with me."

Eloine carefully collected what remained of our meal, stowing what she could back into the basket. The silent cue our dinner had concluded. "Well, if you're so sure your fate is sealed, then I don't see why I should bother doing a thing to change it." She rose and pulled down the hood to obscure her face.

"What can you do about it?" I hadn't meant a harshness or a heat to fill my voice, but they had regardless.

She stiffened. "Whatever I can. Whatever I want. You might be surprised, Storyteller." With that, she turned to leave.

"Eloine, wait! I didn't . . ." But she didn't wait for me.

The door shut with finality—the last drum of thunder just before a storm dies.

I found little solace stewing in silence, but in telling my tale to Eloine, a piece of my old fire had come back. So I gave way to old habits and fell back into the candle and the flame. I held it there, brilliant bright—full-flickering. The exercise in focus brought back the clarity of mind I needed for the bindings, but that was only the first step. The most important part rested in the belief. And that was something that had been taken from me long ago.

But I tried regardless. *Just let me be something more than a performer.* I picked up a loose piece of stone from the broken ground beneath me. A simple enough thing to bind. I brought up the folds and imagined the pebble hurtling toward the cell ahead of me and striking the wall. All through it, I would remain fixed in place—full-firmly rooted as if an extension of the stone below.

Two folds. Then four. No sooner than I'd begun did I bring the folds to sixteen. A multifaceted gemstone, each lens holding the mirror image of what I'd conjured. "Ahn." *I'm as solid as the steel before me. Unbending. Immovable.* "Ah—" I never managed to finish the last syllable as the door to the prison opened.

It took every bit of concentration to peacefully slip out of the folds instead of letting them collapse in surprise. One by one, I let each reflection of the image wink from existence before there was nothing but the candle and the flame again. And I'd only held on to that to keep me from reacting to the sudden visitor.

I opened my eyes and found one of the three men who'd been in the cells across from me earlier. The man called Satbien. His appearance left me wondering as to the fate of the other two men.

A pair of guards walked the man back to his cell, forcing him inside. They turned, regarded me, spoke something in a voice so low I couldn't make it out, and left.

I watched Satbien, taking in his details. The lines of his face seemed deeper than before. A hollowness framed his eyes and rested just as much inside. To say he was tired was to understate how much life could be taken out of a man in so short a time. "How are you?"

He didn't look up at me.

I'd seen that vacant mask on men before. The ones who've watched brothers chosen and those of blood die over unforgiving sands. Sands that would hold the better red of all they had to give . . . and forget it come the morning under wind and footsteps.

"Satbien, was it?" I spoke the name in the same manner you would to a strange dog you hoped to calm. "Satbien?" No response. A third time then, for there is a subtle magic in things thrice spoken.

Maybe I can manage this. Another little performance. I envisioned my breath blowing out—a thin unseen cord, not to fill the room, but to reach one man. Him. It touched the space just before him, well within what would be his atham. The folds came back to me and I made this image my sole belief. "Ahl." The breath blew along the path I'd set. Now to really do the trick.

The folds morphed to resemble my new belief. A current of air carried along the breath itself. Words. Mine. "Start with whent." I imagined me speaking what I wished to say, projecting it along the flow I'd conjured. "Then go to ern." I completed the binding and spoke the word for the third time now. "Satbien." It left me a whisper in glass. Low, caught along an edge, and holding to a hollow echo.

But it reached the man, and he roused. "S'what?" He looked up, blinking as if lost as to where he was. "Solus pound me." He brought a hand to his head.

"Sounds like a tiresome engagement with one's god." I kept my voice neutral as could be.

Satbien frowned, thinking over what I'd said. Then he tipped back his head and roared. It was the laugh of a man who'd long ago buried the sound and found himself holding on to an abundance of it. It became a cavernous echo within the prison, and the both of us were better off for hearing it. "Solus and shadow, boy, not sure a man should ever say things such as that." He wiped the back of a sleeve against his mouth.

I let out a little chuckle. "Technically, it was you, Satbien, not me." There was no need to speak his name again but for the simple, and overwhelmingly important, fact that some men need a reminder of who they are. And names are one of the best ways to do that. For all our names hold a piece of us. They are little stories with which we are shaped, and in turn, come to shape back. And they are the pieces of our story people can remember us by. Especially when they have lost us.

Satbien grinned and blew out a breath just short of a laugh. "True enough, Storyteller. Aye, true enough. I suppose it could be worse." He leaned back and stretched. "Ahh." The man rolled his neck then and winced. "You spend so long bent and huddled, standing straight, like a man, does your body no good. No good at all. Take me for my word, young man."

I nodded. "I will."

"Good."

An awkward pause fell between us, but I'd had enough of those of late, and wanted for no more. So I pressed him for what I wished to know. "When will your friends be joining us?"

The remnants of the smile on his face faded fast as that. "It's a bad thing, Storyteller. No, I don't think I'll be seeing Matio or Jencarlo ever again."

Ice and iron filled me, and I felt the bindings slipping. I knew I had a shaky hold on them right now, and perhaps the best thing would have been to let them fall apart altogether. So I did, slowly letting each of the folds fall from my mind.

When I spoke next, there was no magic in my voice. No promise of power. Just an honest fear.

"Are they . . ." I couldn't finish the question, but Satbien knew the heart of what I meant to ask.

"No, though were a moment a-few I thought that'd be the case. You hear me true, boy. I have no doubt that it was a near thing for him to kill us."

"Who?" The word left me before I'd realized it.

"The *efante Efraine*."

The cold metal inside me writhed, churning my stomach and pulling the warmth out of me. "Why?"

"To kill us? I don't know. He's a hard man, but he had such a look on him that I'd have thunk he'd do it just because he could. You don't doubt he could. I'll say it true, he'd have done it."

I nodded. "I believe you. But why did he want to see you?"

"Oh, that." Satbien coughed once into the ball of a fist. "He's fixed that he's going to win the election. Prince-elect then is as good as king before that's done, *sieta*? With that, he can do what he means to."

Which is what?

Satbien went on. "He fears the change in the world. And gave a speech about it in front of many of the *burgesa*. Heard tell that some of the missionaries sent by the church have been turned away. Some kicked from cities they gone to in good faith. Not that I mind that much. Now don't go thinking I'm not a good and godly man. That I am." He pressed a hand to his heart. "But I'm also not one for thinking o' telling others how to live. Solus never did as much to Antoine in the scriptures. Not once. He held him in good regard for living how he did, and never once told the man to be anything else."

I said nothing. An important part of listening, truly Listening, is knowing when to be as still and silent as stone. For stone has heard and seen the shaping of the world itself. And it remembers all things that have happened above it. In stone rests the stories of all things. And they are kept behind its silence.

"The prince Efraine is marshalling men. Anyone he can find that can stand straight and hold a *lanza*."

I could guess why, but I had to hear him say it.

"He says it's time to live true to Solus' word and Antoine's sacrifice. Jasir, son of God Himself's, sacrifice. To bring the sun and its glory to heathens out there on the sands. That god will surely turn his back from us, and withhold all the bounties we've been blessed to see as a people." Satbien turned and spat. "Bounties. *T'ch.* Haven't seen much of those in the whole long of my life. You tell me I'm lying, Storyteller. I've had a hard life, but not without its blessings. I've had those, aye. But bounties? Never. And the last man I saw chasing bounties . . . never . . ." The words died in his throat.

I said nothing, letting Satbien have his uninterrupted silence. Whether he needed it to cradle whatever he held in heart and mind, or simply needed freedom from the judgment of noise, I could give him that much.

He cleared his throat and ran a hand through his hair, making some of the locks stand up at odd angles. "But I did have me a treasure better than anything else. Little lad. Not my own, you see. My sister's son. Good boy. Raised him like my own, though. You ask someone if I didn't. Did as right as I could by the boy."

Satbien didn't say he needed affirmation from me. But any man watching him then could see the weight of guilt and hurt in his eyes. "I believe you, Satbien."

He nodded more to himself than me. "She named him after Solus' own grace, you know. Good boy, but he took too well to his name, I suppose. Went out east long ago. Long ago." He repeated the words, this time lower—almost a curse. "Never came back. The sands took him." Satbien sniffed and swallowed. "That's where Prince Efraine wants to send us now. Out there against the heathens. He offered Matio and Jencarlo freedom from this place. All they had to do was pick up a spear in name of god and country . . . and no small amount of coin. That's all."

That shook me from the reverie I'd fallen into listening to Satbien's story. "And they took him up on the offer?"

He bowed his head. "Course. What man wouldn't want to be free from here?" He gestured to the walls. "They got no family of their own. No kin to call on, or to miss them. Old men die just fine in war, and we won't lose a bit of sleep over it. And if we make it back somehow, well, a gold sobra is nothing to thumb your nose at, young man. You know what you can buy with gold?"

"I've held more gold in my hands than most men see all their lives, and all it's done is buy me a world of trouble." My words were a stone knife—rock hard and dry as ash.

"What was that?" Satbien tilted his head to one side as if trying to hear me better.

"Nothing. Go on."

He grunted and did so. "Can't say that I blame them, you know."

I wouldn't have either if I were in their boots, but for all his understanding of their situation, here Satbien sat. "I understand. There are many reasons why a man would be willing to go to war. I've had to choose some of those myself." *Once or twice.* "But why are you still here and not up there with your friends?"

Satbien gave me a thin, tired grin. It was the smile of a man who had a dark thought in mind, and the joke to go with it. The sort only he would know and could appreciate. "The last time the *efantes* meddled in the business of others, it cost me a nephew. Who's to say this time will be any different? Won't matter if it's my blood, a friend's, or some other fool of a boy's. It'll be someone's brother. Someone's father. Or their son. I want no part of it, Storyteller. I *won't*."

I respected that, and Satbien had the right idea of things. Would that I had thought and done the same once upon a time, the world would be a different place.

The man lost whatever fire had sparked him to speaking, and now slumped lifelessly. He needed something to hold to or else he'd soon become the man he'd been before we started trading stories. Broken. Hollow-hearted. And still of thought and tongue. Silent.

I moved to speak but the door to the prison opened again. One of the guards from earlier led in another man behind him. They stopped before my cell.

Both had the traditional short-cropped hair I'd seen among military men. Well-bronzed in skin, and sharp-featured in face. Handsome enough that neither man would have a hard time finding a lovely wife to go home to each night. The first of them motioned for me to stand. "Get up, move to the back of your cell."

I looked at Satbien, still bent like a man who'd lost what spine he'd had. For his sake, it would be better for me not to make trouble. So I obeyed the guards and walked until my back touched the stone behind me.

They opened my cell and tossed two empty buckets onto the ground. "Prince Efraine said you would need these." Then they shut the way and left.

Satbien let out a low whistle. "*Two* buckets. He must hold you in some regard." He motioned to the lone one occupying his prison. "The three of us only had the one."

"It might just be that they think I'm more full of shit than the three of you together." That was all it took to set him off into another bout of laughter. It was a good sound. You might take me to mean it was a beautiful laugh, a rich one. No.

His was a broken, choked laughter. Raspy in places like old parchment dragged along stone. It cracked high like a boy on the cusp of manhood. And it brayed in places closer to a donkey than a man. But, it was honest. And that is more than can be said for many a man's laugh.

But I knew he needed more than that. He needed a story. Something to rekindle what he'd lost, and give him just as much to hold to now that he was back in prison. I could do that for him.

I just needed a little something from him first. "I'm sorry to ask, I know it's a sensitive subject. . . ." I let that hang in the air, perking his interest first.

He looked up at me. "Hm?"

I licked my lips, making it look like I was hesitant to ask my question. "If it's all right with you, I'd like to hear more about your nephew?" All it took was a simple question, and he began to tell me.

THIRTY-ONE

Conjured Kindness

"Oh, well, mind you I don't have an ear and tongue for this sort of thing, Storyteller. I figure it more your . . ." He broke off and flourished a hand in my direction.

"I'll try not to judge." I gave him a wry smile.

"Well, so long as you won't." He cleared his throat and looked down almost as if reading a script only he could see. "Can't bring myself to say his name, you understand. But he was a good boy. Bah. That's not the place to start. He was . . . he was . . . I suppose he was everything an uncle could want in a boy, and for his sister's son to be. Looked like her, you see. Had brown eyes, like good farm soil after the rains—dark, rich. Hair was the same. Not so much the black you'd think. No, boy had a touch of the soft brown in it. The kind that'd make the girls give him long looks when he was older. You know the look." He grinned then, part in memory, part in a young man's mischief that seemed so far a foreign thing on an old man's face. And yet, it belonged to him. It fit.

And it was nice to see on Satbien.

"Boy was much like any young rascal. Ran around with a stick in hand, thinking himself a warrior. Not for god, but you'd think so, wouldn't you? No. Boy had one too many Shaen stories in his head. Wanting to travel the world. Wanting to fight monsters. Rescue girls, even though Solus knows it was the boy always needing rescuing. But he never gave his mother or me any back talk. My heart on that, Storyteller. Boy was an honest sort of good you don't see much these days. Reckless, but good." Satbien's face tried to return to a smile. His cheeks twitched, the edges of his mouth tried to form the shape, then failed. He fell short of it.

A piece of the hollowness returned.

It was my job to coax him out of it. But it was a subtle thing, an art, not to let the man know I pitied him. "I wish I could say I was the same sort of boy. He sounds like a great one. Truth was, I was always too reckless, starting trouble. Always trouble."

He snorted once. "Aye. Well, I suppose you would be." Satbien looked around to our surroundings, then tapped a finger to his nose. "Otherwise you wouldn't be here, ah, would you?"

I smirked.

"Ah, well, he grew into a well enough young man. Boy was quick on his feet, better though when a young girl flashed him a wink and twist of her skirt. Nothing set the boy set to dancing better than that. Solus and shadow, that's the truth. He helped his ma with the chores, came end of every set to help me with my business. Boy stacked the bottles, and whatever little pieces of precious I made. Was a glassmaker, you see. He never had a hand or eye for the trade, but once, just once, he really set himself to it. Spent a whole set trying to get it right. Made himself a little trinket, Storyteller, and it was something to look at."

A cue for me to ask the obvious question. "What was it?"

"Boy made a little bauble. All white. Looked like a star. Didn't have the details, you know. He didn't have the hand for it, like I said. But it had the shape, and it had his love in it. Bright as bright a thing could be, Storyteller. Don't rightly know myself how the boy did it. But when it caught Solus' morning light, I tell you this: The piece held starlight in it. Shone like diamonds. And it was just a thing, Storyteller. Just . . . a pointed star. But there was magic in it. I swear it."

"I believe you." The three words were enough for him to go on.

"Right, well I was proper proud of the boy. But then, it didn't last much, now did it. Call came down from the last Pontifex to start spreading the word of Solus far out past our borders. That it was a dastardly thing for us to be neglecting our duties to god above. That wasn't everywhere under his sunly light part of his domain? And if that's so, why aren't all the peoples out there under the sun praising his good name? So, they started asking boys to take up the call. Some took up the shield and the spear. Others turned to the cloth. My nephew . . . the boy, never had the sort of arm to swing a sword. He was a good boy. A good man."

"The best." I'd spoken without meaning to, but my words were what Satbien needed to hear.

He nodded again. "The best. Thank you. I know you didn't know him, but those words are true. Only would have taken you a moment, Storyteller, you tell me if I'm lying, but if you'd have seen the boy, you'd know it true. He was a good man."

I said nothing, giving him only an ear as he wanted.

"So, the boy goes to the church, and learns his scripture better than what he knew before. Then, 'I'm off to the east, Uncle,' he says to me. And true to that, boy goes off east. Out there in that desert. Those sands. No trees, no shade for a boy to hide from the worst of the sun. It's the worst of Solus' wrath out there. Truth of it, I tell you. No quiet dark spots to sneak a kiss with the prettiest girl in town, and that's what he ought to have been doing. Not running around sticking noses in other people's business. No good comes from meddling in others' affairs, Storyteller." Satbien's voice broke then, a ragged echo of what it had been before. "No good at all."

Most folk wouldn't have heard much in Satbien's story about his nephew. But those are the people who never learned to lend a proper ear to things. Never learned to truly see. I had. And I saw them then.

He'd told me enough about his nephew, and his silent-kept hopes. What he needed to hear in a story.

"It's a hard thing, losing family like that. I know that pain, Satbien. And I've never forgotten it, so long as we're telling truths."

The man looked up at me, staring long and like he hadn't quite seen me before then. Then he nodded in quiet understanding. "Suppose you do, Storyteller. Suppose you do."

"And I know the want to have those people back. But there's nothing you can do to change their fates. Few men venture past the Doors of Death and come back whole and sound. But, if you'd like, I can give you something else? At least a piece of my own talent."

He tilted his head like a dog hearing a new sound.

"A story. You gave me one, and an old friend once told me that any good story deserves to be paid for in full, and in proper kind." I made a show of patting myself down and coming up empty-handed. "But I seem to have been relieved of my purse. So, my trade is what I can give. Will you let me share it with you?"

Satbien rested his back against the wall, stretching his legs out straight before crossing one of the other. "Ah, well, now that's a thing, ain't it, Storyteller. Been a long time since I've heard a proper tale told by the sort of folk who do it best. *Sieta,* I'll take that payment, then."

I moved to the middle of my cell, shutting my eyes and stealing a breath for myself. This, I could do. A performance. One to help a man who'd given up on many things, and only just got a glimpse of what he'd lost, to be locked behind stone and steel again. For him, someone in need of a story, I would be who I needed to be.

So I believed. And so I was.

A storyteller.

I conjured the folds of my mind once again, envisioning nothing more than a lone ball of flame. It sat there, amidst the deeper dark of my thoughts, burning brilliant bright. A piece of my very own fire—my hand-held heart of sunlight. I folded my mind again, then once more. Again and again, until the folds numbered ten. More than enough for a little binding like this.

I breathed a breath, silver-shining and whisper-thin. "Ahn." I bound it still, a flowing band of air before me. Then I called on the crown of flame around my heart and pulled the piece I'd imagined free. "Start with whent, then go to ern." I blew the flame free.

Not like before—no. This was no gout of angry fire with which to burn a man or an inn to cinders. This was the hushed breath shared between two lovers not wanting to be caught in what they said. A spark of fresh orange graced the air, it wove around the flowing breath I'd bound in place. And thus there was a piece of the sun between us, hanging high in the cell to give me light and shadow.

That was enough to begin. "This is a story of a young man. An adventurer. Born of Solus' blood—fresh-given to this land and of Etaynia. A wayfarer. An explorer born. A man meant to travel and see the wide wonders this world has to offer, and bring them back home. A man of modest means with greatness in his blood, and twice as much as that of goodness in his heart. His name . . . is Sulvio. To those that know, it means 'of his grace.' For he held that from god above. And he lived up to it."

The ground trembled under thunder and drums, but this was no storm of wind and water to come—no! Horse hooves beat and sent loose stones dancing, so approached the horde.

I twisted and shaped my hands in an old trick I'd learned, making crude puppets out of them. The rest was a simple act of will—a performer's imaginings. New folds—fresh made, all while keeping the flame firmly held in heart and mind. Soon, one horse of shadow trampled along the wall behind me. Quicker then—now joined by more.

Howling cries pierced the air as riders, in shadowed black, surrounded the men of the west.

Sulvio, young in face and years, had never seen such a force before. But, like his namesake, he held to more wisdom than a man his age might have. So he bowed his head and submitted, urging his men to do the same. For Sulvio was no soldier, not like Antoine of old—Prince of Sunlight. Sulvio was an artist made man of cloth. And he was here by the will of god above.

Solus had spoken to him once a time not so long ago, back in the church sat square in his village center. Good god above told Sulvio to take but one gift in hand, and word in heart, to the wider world at large.

"And I tell you, child, that should you be lost, do not despair. Look up at night, and hold this high, and you shall find my light." And on those words Solus said, he pressed a piece of something silver bright into Sulvio's hand. Shining diamond white, and hard as glass, a charm of his love—cold-made starlight.

A work of glass, harder than any steel. A guide as said. And memory of Sulvio's little village. No small trinket indeed. For it held a binding to the stars across the sky all-black, and held the key to his return, the pathway home and back.

Thus did Sulvio not give in to fear, and openly welcomed the men around him. He spoke in the Trader's Tongue. "I come from the west, Etaynia, a simple man—" But the desert riders had no interest in what he had to say.

They rounded Sulvio and his men together, leading them to their encampment. Over shifting sands and sunbaked ground they went. The oppressive heat took one of Sulvio's men first, then another, and by the afternoon, a third. So Sulvio did what he could to slake his men's thirst, and ease their pains. But the one he had no salve for was the stone settling in each of their hearts. A heavy weight in place of the memory and love of home.

So he spent what time he could telling tales to his companions, reminding them of the place they'd left behind. He told them of the women and the wine waiting for their return. Of the fresh fields green and shady trees' respite. And he told them of Solus' promise, that all those within his blessed lands shall know no thirst or hunger. All they had to do was hold to that one hope.

The hope of home.

When the men fell to the blindness of the ceaseless sun, he told them tales of what lay beyond the merciless sands. Lies, but that did not make them any less true after a fashion. He conjured for his men dreams of golden-soft grains that did not hold a furnace's heat or threaten to pull them under with each step. He painted pictures of forgiving palm trees and their cooling shadows. And the maidens of the water—beautiful nymphs found within the Laps of the world and in the hidden oases of the deserts.

I worked another shaping of my hands then. The horses I'd cast along the walls melted away like shadow-darkened water, quickly taking shape as a lone maiden. Her form, lithe and languorous. She sighed once and beckoned Satbien.

This gave his men something to keep to, you see. For without hope, man is left despair, and in that, he loses all heart, and all care. He falls to darkness, and will want for reprieve, never mind the means. This leads some to madness, more to hatred, and a few to take matters into their own hands, and usher themselves off beyond the Doors of Death.

But no matter the hardship, Sulvio knew it his duty to keep to his faith, and so, keep hope for his men when they could not hold any for themselves. When that first night came, he pulled free his given gift from Solus, sharing it with his friends. It caught pale moonlight's glow, and shone silver-shimmerant in his palm. "You see this, men? This star here. This is a memory of home. The guide back to our sweet land." He held it up for them to better see, and the glassy star chimed like a bell as he lined it up along three more gems in the sky.

My fingers darted then, danced along the air, playing with what light the burning ball offered me. Three taps was all it took and I cast dots of darkness along the wall, a counterpoint to the stars in the story. Satbien followed them just before I reached out to the floating flame.

New folds then. Bands of flowing air around my fingertips. A binding just before my skin with which to hold the fire. And one to carry the flames along the breath. I held them all, then breathed them into life. I plucked three pieces from the minia-

ture sun and placed them along the darkened stars I'd shaped. "Ahn." Each of them floated still, new motes of light.

Three lights of purest white—glimmering diamonds in hand. Three guides to pave the way home. The Three Sisters, Solus named them, casting them from his own tears and water, breath billowed-blown through the night. Were they to be followed, they would lead all men back to Etaynia.

"So long as those three lights burn above, men, we have a hope for home. Remember that. So long as this white light shines within, we have a piece of God Above lighting our path." And Sulvio's words were enough to steady his men through the dark, and through the morning next. For they were brought before the leader of the sand-swept hordes.

The man towered several heads over any of the men in Sulvio's company. Broad of shoulder and hands large enough to crush skulls whole. A brutish savage if ever there was one. His skin, dark old clay baked long under the sun, marred with cracks and hard lines that bespoke no kindness. And there was none of the warmth of Solus' light in his coloring. None at all. Nor in his eyes.

I turned and let the bindings slowly wink out from my mind but for the one holding the burning ball. My hands joined and I worked my fingers into a set of shapes, playing with the shadows. Fast. Twisting and twining them almost like they were rope instead of shade. I formed a man who lived up to every word I'd spoken: large, tall, and broad.

"Who are you that comes to my lands in trespass?" asked the warlord.

Sulvio should have cowered before the giant's presence. Should have hung low and in fear. But with Solus' promise to him and his gift, Sulvio knew none of these things. He stood straight-strong and spoke with all the truth he could. "My name is Sulvio, born of Etaynia, far to the west. I came here with my men to explore. To see what wonders the world of our good God Above has for us men. And, we came to share what word of Solus we could." And Sulvio had erred in that, for the men of the desert had a lord of their own, and they knew no other word and story but his.

"I don't care for false and foreign gods from far off, nor the men who come to peddle their worship. These sands are sacred lands, meant for the hard and strong to brave. Not for soft-handed men like you. Not for liars like you. Not for heathens like you." And no sooner than that, the desert lord drew his long curved blade.

I shaped my hand into a crescent moon, casting a long-arced shadow along the wall.

But Sulvio still did not fear, for Solus had promised him a safe return. "You call me liar but you haven't heard me tell any untruths. You call me soft, but you do not know the hardships I can weather. And you call me a heathen, but you do not know me, or my god. Who are you then to pass judgment on me?"

And Sulvio spoke those words with such conviction that the desert warlord grew intrigued.

He spared Sulvio and his men under one condition. “You are to tell me of yourself and your god each day over dinner. And if I like what I hear, you will wake to feel another morning warm your face. If I do not . . .”

I slashed with the curved shadow, scything along the wall.

And Sulvio agreed to the terms.

That night he met the desert warrior. They feasted on lamb and warm mint tea.

“So, westerner, tell me of your god and why he is so great. And if he is so, why then do you find yourself at my mercy?”

But Sulvio was clever and knew he would not sway his captor’s mind, so he played a game of his own instead. “I can do that, but the story of my god is a story of many stories. Will you permit me to share them with you?”

The warlord agreed.

And so Sulvio began, and told him of Antoine, a Prince of Sunlight. But before he came to the conclusion of the battle between light and dark, Sulvio grew tired, as did his captor. The story remained unfinished, and the warlord asked him to end it the next night.

Sulvio retired to his bed that evening smiling, knowing he would wake again. And so he did. The next night again he met the warlord for a story. But as he finished the previous night’s tale, he soon then spoke of Jasir, son of himself. God Above’s envoy to walk among the world of men and remind them of Solus. Of kindness . . . and sacrifice. But before the new story reached its zenith, and the spears broke through Jasir’s flesh, Sulvio tired again and so did his captor.

For thirty days and thirty nights, Sulvio told every story he could conjure from Etaynia’s history, never finishing in one night. And when he could not think of any more, he made up new ones. Eventually, what he knew to be true came to pass. His words never swayed the desert lord to see the lord above, Solus. But, after hearing his gift for words and stories, Sulvio was welcomed to stay on with the lord and offered an adventure of a lifetime.

But his men were tired, and in want of home.

So Sulvio gave to them a gift that marked him a better man than most, for he bequeathed them his own silver shining star.

One of the men stared, nearly wordless. “But Sulvio, you said God Above gave you this, and you offer it to us?”

Sulvio smiled then. “He said it would lead me home, and it will, for you will bring it back to Etaynia. And it will still shine ever bright from there.” He pointed to the stars above. “And the Three Sisters will light the way from here until I return to join their brother with them.” Sulvio nodded to the glass star in the man’s hands. “Keep it safe for me.”

"We will." His men left with those words.

And Sulvio? He lived his dream of being an explorer. He traveled far and wide, seeing all the good world Solus had to offer. He crossed sands and over old forgotten stone. Dried seas and buried secrets. Collecting stories, and telling them along the Golden Road. But he never forgot his promise, the buried desire deep within. The call and star waiting for him. The call to home.

But every night he retires to sleep beneath the skies, still wandering far out there along the world, and he sees the Three Sisters. His reminder that he will always be able to find his way home. And he's on his way now. He's on his way. He's coming home.

I shut my eyes and let the last binding die. The ball of fire bled from existence as did the breath of air it'd been bound to. Darkness took the cell, and silence and stillness filled the space between Satbien and I.

It didn't blanket me so much as it did betray me. Spreading forth as if to dampen the area around me. There was little for me to do but wait for it to be broken.

Satbien sniffed then. A subtle sound. But sound enough. A tear trickled down one cheek and he did not bother to wipe it away. "God Above, man. That was a thing." He cleared his throat, hard and harsh. Then again, breaking the silence. He stood and clapped. Twin drums of thunder resounding through the prison.

And the stillness broke with it.

I inclined my head. "Thank you."

"No. Truth is, Storyteller, I should be thanking you. Was a near thing, me back there. Thinking of my nephew. Of the boy out there lost to sands and never coming back."

I smiled but said nothing.

He sniffed again. "But God's own truth, Teller, I never heard that one before. Can't think of where I would have. Shame it is, though. A good tale. An honest tale. Good man, Sulvio. Must have been a thing from when I was a child. Don't remember one bit of that, but it feels familiar."

And it was supposed to. For little of that tale had been true. But that wasn't what Satbien needed, and many a time, it's not what anyone needs. Sometimes people need the hope a lie can bring. A terrible truth, that, but a truth nonetheless.

Some people believe stories hold secrets. And some do. Some feel that they hold the keys to long lost things, or unlock greater meaning. That in them rests the truth unspoken. And some do. Some do. But some stories exist for no more reason than for us to share with others the breath we can give. What love we can pour into them. And what hopes we can kindle.

Stories are memory. They are love. And they are a kindness. Even when they are a lie. Sometimes, especially when they are a lie.

Because when I looked at Satbien then, I knew he'd gotten what he needed from my cobbled tale. Hope. The belief that his nephew might not be lost. That, like Sulvio, he might still be out there. Surely among the sands, but on the road home.

The story came from all the other stories I knew. The things that people need to hear in a tale. The bits they hold to, yearn for, and the silent hopes they keep tight inside, hoping to hear made true by the tale's end. I couldn't give Satbien back his nephew. No trick of magic could. But the magic of story could give him the hope and love of his nephew back.

No trivial thing. Sometimes all we have left is hope.

Satbien thanked me again, and we talked late into the night until we could talk no more.

When he slept, I stayed awake—awatch for longer still. Then, eventually, the night took me as well.

And when I dreamed, I dreamed of three things: a desert storm, black sands, and the doors to hell.

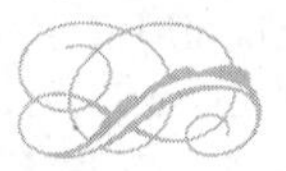

THIRTY-TWO

A Touch of Theatricality

Old metal groaned. Voices rose to a clamor, dying to whispers just as they reached the edges of my ears. Boots clomped against hard stone like distant drums.

I woke just as a cohort of guards stopped before my cell.

"Get up!"

Who could refuse such a polite request? I did as asked, going as far as clasping my hands behind my head. "May I ask as to why—"

"Quiet!" The word left the first guard's mouth like a whip crack. A long gash of puckered skin ran from his right brow down to one corner of his lips. It was a fissure in old stone when considering his leathery skin and hard lines of face. He had the look of a man who'd been in his job for decades, and relished indulging in its brutish moments of power.

I obliged, silencing myself in the process. Everything inside me dimmed. No fire. A pressure around me like weighted air, and the core of me strummed no longer. I stood there, waiting to be pushed along like a puppet.

The cell slid open, and three men built like the first rushed in. They grabbed me by the collar. They took me by the arms. And they took me by my hair. A hand pushed down hard, bowing me over at the waist until my eyes stared at the ground.

"Make any little cleverness. Say anything without being spoken to—you do that, *basha,* and I'll club you bloody to the ground. You hear me?"

I said nothing. A heavy fist slammed into the middle of my back, driving the air from me. My legs wobbled and I would have fallen if not held firmly in place.

"Oi! You hear me, *sieta*?"

"Yes." I spoke the word with the quiet venom to scald steel black and blister flesh.

"Good, good." The first guard's feet turned and he marched back toward the door. "Bring him."

"Where are you taking him?" The question came from Satbien, and I bit back a curse. There was no reason for him to buy any trouble now. Not after just being thrown back into this prison of still and silent stone. "Oi, where you taking him then?"

Metal clanged and rattled against metal. The sound of a sword along the cell bars. "Quiet! You don't shut your clep, I'll beat it so hard you won't have the teeth to talk, *sieta*?"

The threat did nothing to deter the elderly gentleman. I watched Satbien rise to his feet, spine straight—more strength in his back than before. "Beat me." He spat at the ground. "Aye, you're a proper man of Solus, eh? *Real man*. You'd beat an old man. Threaten your countryman. Go on then." Satbien walked to the front of his cell, placing his hands hard against the bars. He gripped them tight until I saw the knuckles whiten and the blood rise in his face. "Show your men what kind of man you are. Beat me bloody. But I'll say what I please. Solus will it, you won't take the good breath God Above gave me."

"Stop." The single plea sounded of sand and gravel, lacking the strength I wished it to have.

"Who said you could speak, *basha*?" Another fist crashed into my side.

I coughed, but did not still my tongue. "Let it go, Satbien. I'll be fine." Another blow. An ache along my side—deep tremoring through my ribs.

"He'll be fine?" I couldn't track whose voice it was, only that it came from another of the guards.

"Murderer takes an *efante*'s life, and he thinks he'll be fine?" Another pain blossomed, now in the small of my back.

I took the beating, not giving any man the satisfaction they sought. One thing held my attention. A candle and its lone flame. I poured every piece of myself into it. The tiredness. I fed it the pain. And the anger. A fresh-fanned forge-fire of hatred. The kind that could turn a man into a kiln within which to nurse a flame to burn him whole, and any who stood in his way. I bled it into the candle.

Another strike. A distant impact.

"God's blood, man." One of the guards broke his hold on me and he shook a hand. "Something's not right with that cloak of his. It's wet."

Another of the guards grabbed my shoulders, running his hands along my arms. "He's telling the truth. It's wet, slick like . . ." He never finished the sentence, but I knew what word rested on the tip of his tongue.

Blood.

My cloak was slick as blood. And it held all the color of it within its folds and shape.

"Shut your cleps and get him out of there." The guardsman who'd led the others stomped into the cell. His fingers clenched tight around my hood and he recoiled. "*Diavellos.*" He breathed the word like a curse.

I watched him even in my compromised position, his hand flexing as if he'd expected to have lost it on touching me. His eyes fixed on my cloak, then me. I managed to tilt my head just enough to regard him and meet his stare. He wore the look of a frightened child—wide and wary of what would happen next.

I smiled.

"Get him out of here." The leader made no move to help those under his command, keeping his distance as they finally led me from my cell.

But all through it, they left Satbien alone. I gave thanks for that, and since I was in Etaynia, it felt fair to offer that praise to Solus. *And I would take it as a personal favor if you could extend the small miracles toward what's to come.*

The guards led me, still in my bent position, by the crooks of my arms. Every few moments, they would change men, as if they couldn't bear the touch of my cloak.

I had the chance for another performance, and to steal a bit of something I needed as well. All it would take was a little theatricality.

I cleared my throat, making no attempt to hide that I wished to speak.

The leader stopped ahead of the group. He rounded, one of his hands going to a club at his waist. His fingers twitched in patient anticipation. The man wanted me to give him an excuse to draw it and drub me across the skull.

I'd be a poor entertainer if I didn't give him the chance. "Around him, the blood-red hame." All the words I needed to say, and all a hushed whisper.

"What was that?" One of the guards holding me paused, stopping his captain short of pulling his club. "What'd he say?"

"Said something about a blood-red . . ." The other voice trailed off, and the grip on my right arm slackened.

One of the men repeated what I'd said verbatim. Then again. "Like the one from the stories? Solus and shadow, I think . . ."

Their leader cut him off. "None of you are paid to think. Haul him where I say, or I'll see it that it's you filling his cell next, *sieta*?"

The men did as instructed, but I noted none of them held on to me with the same strength as before. And the pressure bowing me over was not nearly as firm as it had once been.

I allowed myself that little smile then.

"I don't like touching this thing. I swear it, Jacamo, thing's . . . *wrong.* Just wrong."

"*Tsst.* Captain'll do it too. I've seen him lock one of us down there for a day and a night. *Tsst.*" The man tried to quiet his uncomfortable friend.

"Don't *tsst* me, Jacamo. I'm telling you, this is . . . unnatural. I've heard 'bout this. And then there was that trouble in Karchetta, you remember?"

Ah. There it was. Another rumor worth listening to.

"Heard tell a man like him started a god-awful row down there," said the worried speaker.

"Of course. It's Karchetta. Bunch of village bumpkins." That was Jacamo, then.

"It's not a village. And it's not no lie either. Heard it from some of the . . ." A pregnant pause. I heard the man audibly swallow whatever had been in his throat. "The clergos were about today. Some of them mentioned the incident. Said the justice they were with got a mighty thrashing from a man in . . ." He trailed off.

The pause returned. Then deepened.

Jacamo had no appreciation for the stillness of the moment. The silence. Or its gravity.

Then again, I'd had my moments where I failed to recognize their worth as well. And it had cost me.

"What, Florenzo? What?" Jacamo's voice hadn't crept above a whisper, but a touch of tired acid had bled into it.

"A man in blood red. A storyteller." Florenzo's grip on me grew weaker still. So much so that I could have broken free had I wanted to. "They said he conjured a fire through the place. Like the devil himself."

Funny thing, that. One man conjures fire, weaves a crown of flames, and they name him god. A man of a different sort and shape binds it then and they brand him devil. The oddities of the world. The inconsistencies of man.

And, of stories.

"I've done more than that, gentlemen." My voice remained the breath below a whisper, just loud enough to reach the ears of the men at my side, but no farther. I did not want to draw the ire of the captain now.

"You hear what he said, Jacamo?" Florenzo's hands shook against my arm, promising to let go completely should any more frightful words fall on his ears.

"I heard him—*tsst.* Let it go. He's a storyteller. He's just playing you for a fool. All they do is that. Spin shit into golden . . ." Jacamo let his voice die off as if reconsidering. "Storyteller." A thoughtfulness hung in how he'd spoken it. "Like you were saying."

"I was too. That's what I meant. What if it's him?" Florenzo nearly broke his hold as he tried to convince his friend. "What if we're hauling some freak that can do something . . . unnatural?"

Unnatural, hm? My cloak was a thing well-worked and purely out of storybook fancy. A treasure as much a curse. But now it was nothing more than a performer's tool, and I could work small wonders with those. I closed my eyes and concentrated. No longer the candle and the flame or the folds. I called the first gift every storyteller learns to use. Their imagination.

I bled my will through the cloak and bid it to behave as it was wont to do without my control. Its shape rippled as if caught in an unseen wind, the ends of it lengthened—ragged streamers of fresh-spilled blood.

"You see that—Solus and shadow. Ugh!" Florenzo's hands came free of me and I staggered from the lack of support.

Only steady Jacamo remained in place, now gripping tighter to me as if he expected me to slip through his fingers. "What's wrong with it? What is it?"

"What in God's . . ." The captain never finished his thought as he whirled about to regard the situation. His eyes locked on my cloak, and the hand he'd grabbed me with earlier twitched again. But he never reached for his club. "Hurry it up. I don't care you how do it. You march him before the *efantes* or . . ." His gaze returned to my shifting cloak and he did not finish his threat. The muscles in his face tightened and he turned, as if by not looking at me, he could will me away from his thoughts.

One of the men bent, bringing his mouth close to my side. "If we let you go, will you walk of your own accord?" I realized the speaker was Florenzo.

I nodded.

"And will you stop . . . whatever is happening? God's blood."

"Yes. I promise, Florenzo." I turned to meet his eyes, smiling something crooked-crazed. A grin belonging to a madman who'd long ago left reason behind. A proper villain out of stories who burned villages . . . or buried them under a mountain of ice and snow.

That was all it took.

The men retreated from me and I righted myself, but did nothing to quell the errant motions of my cloak, or the appearance of rain-like beads rolling down its length. Only the sharpest of eyes would have noticed the rippling of liquid along it, but for those that caught it, it would look the run of fresh-spilled blood.

I had unnerved the guards, but not quite enough for my liking. Less for their treatment of me, in truth, and more for how comfortable they were to stand by and watch their captain threaten Satbien. A touch more theatricality would send the message properly.

The hall we walked through was narrow enough—just a pace to either side and I'd able to reach out and brush my fingers along a wall. All of which meant our shadows trailed by our sides in good form. And the space of my atham would hold them just fine.

To make light solid was a trick best left in stories, and required a sort of belief only a madman could muster, and the same could be said for shaping shadow from nothing. But manipulating them was no different than playing puppeteer. What better a thing for a storyteller?

I folded my mind, taking stock of the shadows of my thoughts. Each man's shape took form within my folds. I counted them there, then doubled the imagery. Then again. *Just another game. Another show for them to remember, and maybe a healthy dose of fear to keep them from trying to hurt the next old man.*

"Start with whent. Then go to ern."

"*Tsst.*" A dull pain plumed in my shoulder from where Jacamo cuffed me. "Florenzo told you to stop your . . . witchery."

I said nothing else, shaping the scene within my mind. Shadows lengthened across the expanse inside. They took twisted shapes better left to the nightmares of children. Limbs narrowed and elongated. Backs hunched. Mouths agape in the well-fanged mouths of beasts. And just like that, the darkened profiles along the walls became that which I wished them to be.

"Solus and sha . . ." Florenzo didn't have the heart to finish what he'd been saying. "Jacamo, look. Look, damn you." He pointed to the wall.

Jacamo turned, then whipped about the other way to see his own shadow now a monstrosity. It followed his every move, rippling as if made from ink, and tensing to leap from the wall. "God's blood. Captain. Captain!" His cry echoed down the hall, and surely reached through the doors of the rooms lining the passage.

"What?" Their leader spun on a heel, hand quick to his club as he raised it over head. The blunt weapon fell with a muffled thump against the carpeted floor. "The shadows . . . Solus." He reached for the pin on his lapel. The metal piece resembled a sun. "*Diavello. Diavello.*"

Devil. Devil. And so the cry went down the halls as the guards fled their duty.

As soon as they left my sight, I sighed and slowly eased out of the folds.

A clap sounded behind me. Then again before I could turn.

The noise continued as the man regarded me, a lopsided grin spread across his soft face. He was the antithesis to the hardened captain of the guard, lacking too the sharpened lines of face women want for. Rounded in cheek and chin, a man closer to beautiful than handsome when coupled with the darkness of his hair and brow. The traditional Etaynian features were strong in him.

He wore his clothes in a cut loose and flowing, betraying little of his build.

Soft pastels of seafoam green and polished turquoise. In all, the outfit made him look foppish. Why a prince of Etaynia had chosen to dress himself as such, I had no idea.

I bowed slightly, keeping my eyes on him. "Prince Ateine."

He inclined his head in the barest measure, though his eyes showed a more kindly warmth in them than when we'd met in my rooms. "Storyteller. That was a wonderful piece of magic there. I'd like very much to know how you did it."

I stole the grin from his face and wore it as my own. "We all have our secrets, Prince. And what would we be without them?"

"Terribly honest, I suspect. And how boring would that be?" His grin never faltered as he extended a hand.

I didn't take it.

He arched a brow. One did not refuse a gesture of courtesy from a prince.

But as I've said before, I never did learn how to behave with nobles.

He stared for a moment longer before nodding more to himself than me. "I suppose that's fair after what my family's put you through."

I hadn't expected that admission. I cocked a brow of my own, waiting for him to explain.

"I fear you've become an unwitting pawn for someone sharper than you and I. Someone with designs on my throne."

A wonder the Etaynian nobility ever got anything done. Every one of them seemed to believe the throne belonged to them, and after learning what I had, it seemed they weren't kings for long. Much less princes.

"And do you have a theory as to who that someone is, Prince Ateine?"

He shrugged, running a hand through his hair and sending his locks into rogue curls. "All the problem of the game, I'm afraid." Ateine let out a light and easy laugh.

"You don't seem afraid, Prince Ateine. With your brothers falling, and someone eyeing your throne, you should be." I hadn't meant it as a threat, but feared it left my mouth as one nonetheless.

Small fortune Prince Ateine had more the easygoing manner of a carefree child than a prince whose life could be at stake. "Why, should I be?" He held up a finger then as if making a point. "I know three things, Storyteller. One, you are not my brother's murderer. Two, I am no threat to Efraine's push for the throne, nor that of my other brothers'. Three, that is precisely why I will take it out from under them. Through the election, of course."

Of course. "Would you care to inform me why you're so certain I didn't kill Prince Arturo?"

Ateine finally looked at me with the calm and measured nature I expected of a prince. "What motive do you have? Were you hired by another of my brothers?

Hardly. You'd be a poor assassin, with theatrics like yours. You're not exactly . . . inconspicuous."

He had a point.

"No, I'm rather confident you were a convenient plod pushed to take the place of Arturo's murderer so the true killer could move freely to set the rest of the stage. One by one they'll do their deeds until their aims are achieved. That is what I wish to discover. Who, but more importantly, why? What is their aim? To see another of my brothers take the throne? I can understand that in part, but again, why?

"What could they gain from one specific brother that they couldn't from another? If it's not the power of the king . . ."

The truth struck me. "Then it's what the king stands for. His positions . . . and what he means to act on." A king could pass a great number of laws, execute favors owed, elevate rank, and properly start wars. *Or join them.*

What better a position for one of the Tainted to take? To be able to start wars, plunge a world into darkness.

And all my fault.

"My thoughts exactly. One of my brothers must be offering something more than just coin, or why not sell their services to each of us, vying for the biggest possible purse."

I'll give Prince Ateine this much: He certainly thought like a prince of Etaynia.

"So, your false charge might be my best chance to find the party truly behind this. And then, I can make *my* move." Now he looked nothing like the soft and unassuming prince. The rounded lines of his face betrayed a sharpness in him I'd overlooked. Nothing so obvious, but that his chin wasn't quite as weak as I'd first thought. His jaw had just the hint of a rougher angle hidden beneath the light fat. And his eyes no more held to a watery brown, but rather the brighter clearness of amber.

"And I don't suppose that means you'll be championing me at the trial? Since you're so convinced of my innocence, that is."

Ateine let out a better laugh than before. "Oh, no, Storyteller. I intend to leave you for the hangman from the start. You'll have to *publicly* convince me along with your other judges to spare you. I can't be seen sharing what I know or believe outside of what you present to the court. You understand, of course." The same clever smile returned, vanishing just as quickly, as if it had never been there.

I exhaled. Surrounded by shadows of a different sort in a country with no friends. If Rishi Ibrahm could see me now.

"As for your trial, Storyteller . . . well, that is why you were being escorted from your cells."

I frowned.

"You've run out of time, Storyteller. The pontifex and a few of my brothers have decided that we can't delay in returning to the Game of Families. Your trial is now. I hope you're ready."

I suppose we'll find out.

THIRTY-THREE

Truths and Trials

Prince Ateine led the way toward a set of double doors. The face of each had been carved from wood a color between burnt orange and dark cherry. Their inlay showed a scene of a powerful figure far in the distance, a corona of fire around his head, and within his breast. Below a man hung from a wheel whose edges were bent and pointed, stretched out in curving angles to resemble bands of flame. A sun. The hanged man's sides were pierced with a spear—run full through him and out the other side. Yet no blood showed but for on the faces of his killers.

Streams of tears down their mouths and their eyes. All the shade of my very own cloak.

The prince pushed past the doors and I peered inside to the room ahead.

One look told me beyond doubt it was the throne room, most obviously by the wooden seat far at its end. I paid it little mind, noticing the more essential features. Such as the rows of benches placed along the carpeted floor. And that, more importantly, they were occupied to the fullest by men and women dressed in the elaborate, and expensive, clothing befitting the gentry.

My trial looked to be a most popular affair. I would have been flattered under other circumstances.

A long wooden table had been set before the empty throne. And familiar faces sat behind the desk. The man I'd glimpsed at the dance; the Pontifex; Prince Efraine; his brother I'd met in the library, Prince Artenyo; another three men I guessed to be the last claimants to the throne besides the *efante* just paces ahead of me. There had been seven brothers in line for the crown. Well, before Arturo had been murdered.

Two women sat beside them as well, dressed in equal resplendence. Their sisters, then.

Prince Ateine eyed me out of the corner of his vision. He spoke no words, but the look itself said enough: *I will not acknowledge you. We are not friends. And be convincing. Both our lives depend on it.*

It wasn't an exaggeration. Were I to take the false fall for the true murderer, it would leave Prince Ateine with little to go on to find the actual perpetrator. All of which meant Ateine could very well be next.

All heads slowly turned to regard me. Their stares held the heavy silent judgment of those who had already made up their minds and shared a singular verdict: guilty.

How fortunate. I supposed it would save everyone a great deal of time if the outcome had already been decided before I opened my mouth.

I waited for Prince Ateine to reach the front of the room and sit with his kin before taking my own position. A simple platform had been set before the royal family with a large lectern, where I wagered I was to defend myself from. I came to think of it more as a stage, and with that, began to treat this farce of a trial very much the same.

It was just another performance.

And that I could do.

I took my place, resting my hands on the wooden lectern.

A few of the crowd murmured, speaking about the obvious lack of guards around me, and twice as much over my lack of restraints. They shared concerns for their safety, and who could blame them when they all thought me a murderer. What would keep them safe from me? The foreign demon in red who called down a spot of moonlight under which to dance, the man who sent shadow puppets racing across their walls!

As if attuned to my thoughts, a few guardsman filtered in from side entrances to the throne room. Each of them held a *lanza,* the traditional Etaynian polearm that could cut or skewer with uncomfortable efficiency if you happened to be on the wrong end of it. Which I was.

Two of these men came to either side of me, leveling their weapons at an angle that would run them through my throat, and my breast, should they decide to thrust.

At least it'll be quick if they decide I'm guilty. Or either man decides to sneeze . . .

The pontifex rose, clad in a robe the color of summer-cloud white. A wooden sun hung from his neck, the piece resting flat against his chest. His hat was nearly the length of my forearm, and the same shade as his robes. But unlike the sun at his front, the one fixed to his long cap had all the colors of flame.

"The accused before us, known as the Storyteller, stands charged with the murder of an *efante* of Etaynia." The pontifex took a breath and let the silence hang, surveying the audience as he waited. Content the scene had been set as he wanted, he faced me. His eyes were the color of water tinged with a strong dark rum. They held no brightness in them—no strength or shine. A weak, almost mutable brown that honestly failed to live up to the color in my opinion.

"You are accused of killing Prince Arturo of the God-chosen kingdom of Etaynia. How do you plead?"

When the highest member of your official holy body stands before the nobility in a god-fearing country, then accuses you like that, it sets the tone. I didn't see much point in playing the game his way.

"I was in the room when he fell to poison, your . . . I'm sorry, I'm not sure how to address you." Snickering spread through the room, quickly silenced as the pontifex glared. I hadn't spoken that in jest, but I welcomed the little moment of levity all the same.

"Holiness. You may refer to me as Your Holiness, as much as a heathen like you can come to understand the word."

I didn't let my reaction to that show, adopting a neutrality I'd learned long ago—my face hewn from smooth stone. "Your Holiness. I'd been invited to tea that morning at Prince Arturo's request. He'd given me his favor during the game, so my understanding was that I could not refuse."

Several of the crowd nodded, but I knew the pontifex hadn't been swayed. Mostly because I did not directly answer the accusation. But the question had been rigged against me from the beginning.

"That is not what I asked you, Storyteller. I understand people from the backwards Mutri might struggle with other languages, but I hadn't realized you might have issue with the Trader's Tongue. Because if you do understand me, then you'll understand I asked you a different question."

I exhaled and brought back the candle and the flame, focusing my agitation into the fire. "Then I plead innocent, Your Holiness."

He accepted my statement without showing much reaction at all. "Then let us begin. You were found to be in the company of the then dead Prince Arturo—"

"Along with Lord Umbrasio, Your Holiness."

The pontifex stiffened, and some of the *efantes* traded looks. The two women I wagered were princesses leaned in to whisper to one another.

Ah. Maybe some of them hadn't known that.

"Do not interrupt me, Mutri." The pontifex's mouth twitched. The only hint of expression he showed. Too subtle a thing to be caught by most, but when coupled with how he gripped the edge of the table, he may as well have barked at me. "You admit you were in the dead prince's presence?"

I repeated what I said, reiterating that Lord Umbrasio had been there as well.

The pontifex's face tightened, but before he spoke, Prince Efraine stood. "If I may, Your Holiness." The pontifex looked like he would snap at the prince for interrupting, but quickly reined in his worst impulses. He ceded his position to the prince, who adopted a similar neutrality when addressing me. "Storyteller."

I inclined my head in a measure of respect.

The prince clasped his hands in front of him and looked to his brothers before continuing. "You say you were called into the company of my brother, Prince Arturo, who also happened to be with Lord Emeris Umbrasio, correct?"

I nodded again.

"Why?"

I opened my mouth to speak but the prince waved me off.

"Besides the obvious request from my brother. *What* was the nature of the meeting?"

"Ah, your brother was fascinated by my background as a Storyteller, more importantly, what it meant for me."

That vague statement raised a few eyebrows, including Efraine's. "And what did it mean, exactly?"

"He believed I'd collected a great deal of stories over my years and travels, and he wished to explore a theory of his." I caught the change in Prince Efraine's expression. A thinning of the mouth, a narrowing of the eyes. More curiosity. So I fed it the truth.

Mostly.

"He believed many stories had unifying themes and inspirations that could, in some instances, be traced back to a singular source. He wanted to trade stories, as well as offer me the use of your library's collection in pursuit of this theory. He seemed very much the well-educated and curious man to me, Prince Efraine." I'd kept the better details of the late prince's thoughts to myself.

The idea that he believed more stories than most were comfortable with admitting all came from a single source. Something that could be seen as heresy in some circles of his country. After all, the church had their own stories, and just like the temples of the Mutri Empire, they were not fond of all of them.

The tales of Radhivahn came to mind.

And if something undercut the source of those stories, well, it could lead some men to begin questioning their religion itself. It was a short step from that to wondering if the church should hold as much power as it did.

Dangerous thing, free thought. Curiosity more so, because it is the well from which many a thought springs.

"So . . . you were there to only speak of your trade? And Lord Umbrasio . . . ?" The question hung in the air.

"Was a stoic prat, for the most part. Up until the moment he fetched the tea that killed your brother. Then he seemed a bit more lively." My words were echoed thunder in an empty room. They filled the hall and reverberated. Every soul heard them, and the next question was: What happened now?

Prince Efraine had better control over his face than the pontifex, showing me nothing I could guess of. "And you know my brother was poisoned, how?"

I swallowed a groan at the absurdity of this. "Because he died shortly after sipping the tea, bleeding from his face."

Some of the gentry in attendance gasped. A few invoked Solus' name.

Before anyone else could seize the pause and push for more pointless questions, I took hold of it and decided to better direct the trial. "Has your brother's body been inspected by a mender?"

The question drew a few confused looks.

"A mender?" Prince Efraine frowned. "I'm not familiar with the term."

I should have known that. "Someone who looks over the ill or dead. Discerns how they passed, tries to help the wounded."

"Ah, a *mederhia*. Yes. And he concurs with your assessment of poison. And you accuse Lord Umbrasio, a member of our nobility in good standing, of having done this?"

I ran a tongue against my teeth, taking in the whispers breaking through the crowd. If I accused Lord Umbrasio openly, I'd have to furnish the proof. Only, I didn't have much of that. No one but myself, the prince, and the lord had been in the room. It was Umbrasio's word against mine. And the word of a foreigner, no matter how well respected for his trade, meant little against familiar noble blood.

Nobility comes with far more than just wealth and title. It comes with a privilege of power that can spare them the consequences normal men would suffer. Or the justice. They're not always the same.

I cleared my throat and chose my words more carefully than I might have ever in my life. "All I am saying is this, Prince Efraine: Your brother asked Lord Umbrasio to fetch him another pot of tea. The lord obliged as your brother and I spoke. Your brother drank from the fresh pot. Lord Umbrasio and myself hadn't partaken yet. Shortly after, your brother began bleeding, then passed."

Prince Efraine pursed his lips, then nodded. The pontifex rose, but another brother cut him off, taking his place. This man had the square jaw and hardened lines many would picture of a storybook prince. Well-bronzed, and bright of eye. Hair cut fashionably to a length as long as his fingers. A touch roguish in places, but clean enough to be proper. He dressed in a sunflower-yellow shirt over well-fitting pants of black.

"I am Prince Emberdo."

I gave him a respectful bow of the head.

"I'd like to know, Storyteller, why you came here to our country, and most importantly, my family's summer palace, in the first place." A simple enough question.

"I believe your family library holds something very important to me."

He frowned. "And that would be?"

"A story." A few people laughed at my answer, but it broke the heaviness that had settled through the room. "I know, a silly thing to many of you, but remember, this is not just my trade." I created a pause. "It is my life. I'm known for my craft to the point the world only speaks of me as the Storyteller. I carry that name above all others, despite many sharing my profession. So when I say I believe your family, and culture, holds a particularly powerful tale for me, believe it, please." The little bit of flattery I snuck in did as I'd hoped.

A few nobles traded hushed remarks, now wondering what story I searched for. And the obvious reveling in that they had something foreigners would want. Theirs was a rich and wonderful culture, of course.

Prince Emberdo nodded at my answer. "And for all that you came into our home during the Game of Families, and decided to play?"

The whispering stopped.

I bit down on my tongue and kept myself from shifting in discomfort. "I didn't decide to play, Prince Emberdo, but was swept into the game, I'm afraid. If you'd like, I can tell you the whole story behind that, but I fear it will be a bit of a bore."

He gave me a thin smile. "Entertain me. After all, it is your trade."

I blew out a breath and decided I'd had enough of nobility. "I came to perform and was graciously given lodgings. I shortly received an invitation from Lord Umbrasio's wife—"

Some groans echoed through the crowd. A few snickers. And a low whistle or two.

Well, I had known his wife had cultivated something of a reputation. "Who wished to . . . assess my artistry in person."

That drew a great deal of laughter from some of the men in the audience. And earned them the scornful looks of the women beside them.

I might not have been the man in most danger at that moment, if the glares were any indication. It left me an opening to continue, however. "This earned me the displeasure of Lord Umbrasio."

"Who you feel left you to take the blame for his murder of my brother, yes?" Emberdo picked up quickly on the subtext I'd created.

But again, I couldn't exactly lay the full blame on the lord. "Well, it certainly would have been one way to exercise his wrath, wouldn't you say?"

Emberdo, to my surprise, nodded in agreement. "Though what motive would he have to kill my brother? Especially when Arturo and he got along famously—part of the reason he was invited to share a meal with him in privacy."

The crowd murmured. A few heads bowed in what could have been acceptance of that point.

I thought of what Prince Ateine had told me. "Unless he'd gained another *efante*'s favor."

The low chorus of whispers stopped.

Emberdo simply stared, but Prince Ateine broke into a smile and leaned closer.

I'd changed things, and I had more of their attention now. "After all, that's what the game is about, yes? Currying favor, trading opportunities, passing whispers, permitting . . . dalliances." I turned to regard the audience and managed to find and catch the eye of Lord Umbrasio's wife, Lady Selyena.

She apparently did not have the grace, or care, to shy away from the look. Proud as a cat, she met my stare, and gave me a grin wide and lascivious enough to make many a man in attendance uncomfortable. Some . . . a shade too eager for their wives.

Though it served to help my case, for everyone saw the exchange.

So I went on, choosing to play the card I kept in reserve. The one that could spare me a great deal of trouble here. The information I'd gleaned when I'd first come to the Three Tales Tavern. "There's also the fact that another of your brothers was murdered well before I came into your home. The last prince-elect."

The room erupted into chaos.

I hadn't intended for that to happen.

The pontifex seized the commotion to put himself back in position of speaker. He stood, smacking his hands against the table. "Settle yourselves!"

Nobody listened.

"Calm yourselves, by God."

I forced myself not to smile as the crowd continued its bickering and a few shouting matches took place.

Finally, Prince Efraine stood and barked a single command. "Enough!"

The audience seemed to recognize the *efante*'s authority, at least. The low grumbles dissipated soon after and the prince took over from the pontifex. "The Storyteller raises an excellent point. The last *efante* to pass did so *after* the previous game and election. And under circumstances in which the accused was not present. Though"—his gaze drifted over to settle on someone in the audience, Lord Umbrasio—"I do recall your attendance during the week-long game, Emeris."

The lord, to his credit, held his composure better than many would have, I'm sure. He merely met the prince's eyes, and inclined his head in acquiescence.

The crowd murmured again, but Prince Efraine had clearly heard enough for the moment. He clapped his hands twice to silence them all. "I believe it's time we take a short break for my family and His Holiness to discuss in private. We will resume once we've concluded our discussion." With that, the *efantes* rose, and everyone else at the table followed as they made their way out a side door. Prince Artenyo, the man I'd met late in the library one night, turned and flashed me a wolfish smile.

The pontifex, however, gave me a look that said he very much wished I'd kept my tongue between my teeth.

I figured I could live with the vast disappointment of another religious figure I'd managed to upset over the course of my life.

The crowd returned to their gossiping, occasionally shooting sidelong glances my way. Some of them rose and began to mingle. A shifting mass of people and their voices broke the stillness of the trial.

The guards moved a few paces away, but still kept their weapons leveled in my direction. I returned a look to let them know I had no intention of starting any trouble.

"You're not one for playing the game subtly, are you?" I knew the source of the voice and turned to find Eloine a pace from my side. She wore a dress of velvet, its color that of pine boughs and bright sage. It complemented her eyes. A scarf, more accessory than something to keep one warm, rested across her shoulders. Its crimson tails fell to her chest. A braid hung from either side of her head, tied off in a green matching her dress, but the rest of her hair fell in loose curls behind her and over her shoulders.

I turned my attention down to my blood-red cloak. "Is 'subtlety' an Etaynian word? Not sure I'm familiar with it."

She reached out and took a fold of my cloak between her fingers, rubbing her thumbs along it. "Mm, no, you wouldn't be, would you." The hint of a smile played at the edges of her mouth, but it never came in full. "The point about Lord Umbrasio, and the prince-elect's death . . ." She bit her lip and shot a quick look to the noble I'd implicated. "You rattled them with that."

"Good. They deserve to be. It's their damnable game. Not mine."

Eloine met my eye. "You came into it and their home knowing you'd be pulled into it." It wasn't a question.

I nodded, but kept the next thought from touching my tongue. *And I've meant to kill one of them all the while. If only I knew which.* Which among them was one of the Tainted.

Which one could topple a kingdom? Shroud a country in darkness?

"And you didn't expect this?" Her question held only simple curiosity.

"To be framed over tea? No. It doesn't happen often in a man's life, believe it or not. But I knew the game could be trouble, and had hoped to work it to my advantage."

The promise of a smile grew wider on her lips. "And how's that working out for you?"

I narrowed my eyes.

She returned the expression, but her lips finally parted into the grin she'd been holding back. A shame it didn't last. It vanished and she gave me an expectant look. "Do you think they'll find you innocent?"

I didn't have an answer she'd like, nor one that I did, for that matter. "I don't know. Prince Efraine . . . and Ateine made it clear I'm being pushed around in this game. They both have different goals in mind, but the end result is the same."

"The throne," said Eloine.

I nodded. "But it's how they get there, I imagine, that makes something of a difference. I just happened to be a convenient pawn for a moment."

"Which of the *efantes* do you think is responsible?" Eloine leaned in closer, keeping the question low enough so that the guards had no chance of overhearing. She hadn't asked if they'd done it, but which had. Eloine believed as I did then, that the brothers were behind this, and not some other party. Umbrasio was just another piece like me.

But what did he gain out of it? And which prince was protecting him?

A scream echoed into the room, and the guards nearest me moved closer, bringing their weapons into position.

I opened my mouth to chastise them, as I'd done nothing, but I never got the chance.

One of the *efantes* burst back into the room. Sweat beaded Prince Artenyo's face, and his collar had been undone. His hair matted his face and his chest heaved in effort. "Prince Emberdo has been murdered."

I raised my hands in defense and opened my mouth, though it was probably the most inappropriate time to speak.

"It wasn't me."

THIRTY-FOUR

A Deadly Game

The crowd gasped and more guards filtered into the room. The group that had left quickly filed back in—the remaining princes still among the living, and their sisters. The pontifex, notably, did not return.

Prince Efraine muscled past his brother, moving to the head of the table and taking charge with a soldier's efficiency. "Quiet!" He motioned to the guards. "Seal the room—wait, where is His Holiness?"

One of the guards opened his mouth to answer, but the prince waved him off.

"Find him. Bring him back here, *immediately, sieta*?" Prince Efraine gave the man a stare that brooked no argument, only obedience.

The guard ran.

"The rest of you, secure the room. No one leaves. No one enters but for His Holiness." Efraine hadn't finished speaking before some of the nobles protested.

His remaining brothers quelled that instantly, reiterating his orders.

The gentry took their seats, all adopting the still-silence of the wood beneath them. The quiet lingered, spreading through the room with the promise to choke out all thought and want for motion.

It grew to feel like a second collar around my neck, and before it became too tight a thing, I decided to break it. "I don't suppose this is a good time to mention that I was in here—under guard, mind you—while this happened."

A few heads in the crowd turned to regard me, but they said nothing.

Ateine actually smirked, but the expression disappeared as soon as he realized he'd shared it. Not the reaction I expected for someone who'd just lost another brother. Either he was complicit in the act, or Etaynian nobility had a tendency to cultivate insanity among its members.

Given my experience, both were possibilities.

Prince Efraine exhaled, but it was his brother Prince Artenyo who addressed me. "We're well aware, Storyteller. All of which makes you innocent, as far as we can see, of the murder of Prince Emberdo."

Not cleared of killing Arturo, however. But it did raise another question. "How did this brother die?"

Instead of an uproar at my indecorous question, given the timing, the crowd let out low noises of assent. They wanted the answer as much as I did.

Seeing this, Prince Artenyo bowed his head in concession. "We do not know as of yet. But . . . he began to bleed from his eyes, ears, nose, and mouth. He choked on his own fluids before . . ." The prince's jaw went tight.

"When their eyes begin to bleed. *Nuevellos. Nuevellos*." The voice came from the crowd, and someone else soon took up the chant.

"Run away. Time to leave."

I turned too late to catch who'd spoken, but it didn't matter. The voices shook, half hushed. These people were afraid. And they should have been.

I remembered a night, so long ago, when every face I saw had blood pooling from their orifices.

But the Ashura could not be here, or more than just a pair of princes would be dead.

"Ari." Eloine placed her hand on my arm, ignoring the guards nearby who gave her a look of reproach.

I flashed her a heated stare. "What?"

Her gaze tilted downward toward my hands.

I followed it to see my fingers clenched tight to the lectern, hard enough that my fingernails had created minute indentations in the wood. The small bones of my hand ached and I released my grip, taking a breath to still myself. "Thank you. I hadn't realized—" I stopped short when she gave me a reassuring squeeze.

"I know why. It's all right."

My mind reached for any witty remark. Something to brush off my discomfort and let Eloine know not to worry about me. I failed. "Thank you."

Another squeeze and she trailed her hand down along my arm until her fingers rested atop mine. "They'll have to let you go. If not now, then soon. I'll speak to Artenyo about this."

I eyed her askance and mouthed the word *Artenyo* without speaking it aloud.

Her glare wasn't a hurtful thing, only carrying the heat of freshly doused coals. But my comment had barbed her.

I inclined my head a half measure in silent apology.

She accepted it.

I think.

"Wait here." Eloine moved, but I reached out and caught her wrist, an action that did not go unnoticed by the guards.

Two of them stepped closer to me, pointing their spears my way. "Release the Lady Etiana immediately."

I did so.

Eloine adopted a look somewhere between smug satisfaction, and a moderate concern for my well-being. "It's fine." She placed a hand on one of the guards, easing his weapon away from me. Eloine looked my way. "He didn't mean any harm, did he?"

"No."

"See. He's quite harmless." She reached toward me, grabbing hold of my cheek and pulling it like a grandmother would a child's.

. . . before the entire gathered mass of nobility.

The two guards went through a series of expressions, trying to process what had just happened, but failed to settle on any one. They decided it then best to distance themselves from us and move closer to hear what the royal family whispered instead.

"*Tch.*" The sound was enough to get Eloine's attention and bring her closer to my side. "There's something I've been thinking about."

"Hm?" She tilted her head.

"This whole game. The princes have made it clear they can have one another killed so long as they're not caught. That's one of the easiest ways to take the throne while you're out currying favors."

She nodded, looking at me as if I were explaining something obvious.

"Killing one prince makes the rest wary. They waited to rekindle their game once the panic had settled, never finding out who killed the last prince-elect."

Eloine frowned. "What's your point?"

"I'm getting to that. Then, as soon as someone found a convenient pawn, they killed another prince and laid the blame at my feet. But things are changing. We've both seen the signs. Calls for Etaynia to go to war. A zealous pontifex who makes no effort to hide his disgust for those unlike him."

The comment made Eloine shudder and wrap her arms around herself. She knew the hatred men could bring on others different from them.

"Someone doesn't want to drag this out. To kill and restart the game each time, running the risk of being caught eventually. Whoever's doing this wants to win and be done with it, fast."

Her mouth twitched, and she looked down to the ground, deep in thought. "But they could win the election, and it would make for a cleaner . . ." She trailed off, realizing what I had. "They don't care about clean. They want to send a message, or leave nothing uncertain. They have something too important tied to winning."

I nodded. "It won't be enough to be a brother of influence to the next king. They have to be *the* king. In position to do something only he could."

Eloine's face asked the unspoken question: *But what?*

I answered it aloud anyhow. "War."

She took a deep breath and mouthed something I could not catch. Then she asked what I knew would follow. "But why?"

"There's a shadow that falls on some men's hearts. Others, their eyes. Some, their ears. It twists them. Turns them. Taints them." I'd spoken the words for myself alone, never having meant to speak them at all.

"What was that?" Eloine leaned closer.

"Nothing. I don't know why. And for the moment, it doesn't matter. There's something more worrying." I took a breath. "What would be the best way to get rid of the other princes during a game where everyone is moving about, hard to track, and in the company of others?"

"I don't know."

"You get them all in one place. One room. Like this. Then you continue your deadly game with your eyes on every piece, and remove them as necessary."

Her eyes widened, but she regained her composure instantly. "Do I want to know how you've come to have an assassin's mind?"

I gave her a smile with no warmth or humor in it. A gash in ice. But my mind went to a house buried in stone—behind shifting sands. A palace that promised paradise to some, and quick relief to others. Sending the latter well beyond the Doors of Death.

She took that as answer enough. "So what do we do now?"

"Survive."

Her eyes narrowed. "You are, at the worst of times, terribly unhelpful to a woman's spirits. Do you know that?"

"Would it help you to know that I have a plan?"

"Yes, very much so. What is it?"

I merely smiled again, this time with all the guile of a fox.

She did not appreciate that. "Careful, Storyteller. Men who get too clever for their own good find themselves in dangerous situations."

I'm very well aware of that. And have experienced it too often for my liking.

While everyone continued to speak in low-kept whispers, I took the opportunity to direct what remained of my trial. "Three princes murdered, and all during the game or its aftermath." I wasn't asking it of any of them, making it clear what I said was iron fact. "Who stands to gain from that?"

Some of the crowd began sharing their theories.

Prince Artenyo, to his credit, leapt to give the obvious answer. "We remaining princes, of course."

Silence. The open admission brought the crowd to stillness. Breaths caught in throats as mouths hung partially open, but with no words to share.

"You are, of course, implying that one of us had our brothers murdered." Prince Artenyo's voice remained level, though the lines of his mouth betrayed his latent anger. The corners of his eyes tightened. And the muscles of his cheeks twitched.

The accusation bothered him, but not in the practiced rage of someone trying to play the part of affronted. His was a quiet anger. The sort that burned over the idea anyone would harm his brothers, then blame another. A rarity within in his family.

The longer I stared at Prince Artenyo, the more I saw someone who couldn't act. A piece of me sighed deep inside that I couldn't glean his true story. But no matter the effort of will I extended, the depth of my gaze, I only saw him through a performer's eyes.

"Yes, I am saying that. The game is your family's best chance to trade favors and garner votes to win the election as much as it is the chance for the gentry to make moves of their own. But in the end, it is the princes with the most power, and thus the most to give. It's little effort to trade favors from a prince's seat for something as simple as a vote."

I had a point and knew it when much of the crowd nodded in agreement.

Prince Artenyo, to his credit, conceded as much with a quiet bow of his head. "Yes."

Another man rose to the prince's side, clapping a thick hand, wide enough to fully palm some men's faces, to Artenyo's shoulder. This *efante* had the build of a viper. Harshly lean of face with a long, pointed nose. A hollowness hung in his cheeks that brought out the curves of the bones, adding to the cruelly angular shape of him. His hair was the color of oiled midnight and tapered at the front to a peak. The narrow eyes did the severity of his expression little favor. "It is a bold thing to accuse one brother of killing another, Storyteller. Especially so when you stand here on trial for the very thing. Or have you forgotten?"

I gave myself a moment's consideration. I thought I'd done a fair job proving I had little motive in murdering the prince, as I had the least to gain from it. "I haven't forgotten, Prince. . . ."

"Emilio. Prince Emilio. And, good that you haven't. I—" The doors to the throne room opened, cutting the prince short as the pontifex entered, escorted by another cohort of guards. Only they weren't what gave me pause.

A woman led the group. She wore a coat dyed the color of dried plums, and pants a wash of olive. A thin hilt with a curving wire guard pulled my attention to the sword at her waist.

I remembered her.

The justice of the clergos, the knights of the Etaynian church. Eloine and I had encountered them back in Karchetta, and did not leave on the best of terms with the group. The men beside the justice wore chainmail with white cloaks hanging from their shoulders. A ring of gold with curved sharp edges decorated the backs. A sun.

The holy representative made his way to his previous seat, looking unbothered for someone who'd recently learned another member of the royal family had been murdered. I couldn't see any way he wasn't privy to the knowledge, having left with them to confer.

One clergos went to stand behind each of the *efantes* besides Prince Efraine, likely to ward them from any further threats. The one prince left without a guard seemed the most able to handle himself, being the only one who'd betrayed having lived a soldier's life to me.

Prince Emilio cleared his throat and eased Prince Artenyo back into his seat. "Your logic is sound, Storyteller, but it does little to answer who is responsible for killing Arturo."

The riposte left me before I could think. "It makes it clear enough that I'm not responsible for the death of the previous *efante*. And that I had no motive to kill Prince Arturo. It doesn't help you find the killer. . . ." I trailed off and gave Lord Emeris Umbrasio a long look that could have set his clothes aflame. "But I imagine it points you in the right direction."

Prince Emilio opened his mouth to speak, but the last of the brothers I hadn't come to know put a hand on the man's wrist. The remaining *efante* made it clear he wanted Emilio to sit, and then the final prince rose to address me.

He was an oddity when considered alongside the rest of his brothers. His hair lacked the rich blackness found in his brothers', betraying a dark brown under the room's light. His skin was lighter as well, more olive-reddened than a bronzed kiss of sun. But his eyes were the perfect mirror of the other princes'.

"I am Prince Estrevante." He offered me a bow that could have been considered polite if not for the stiffness of it. The *efante* dressed in close-fitting clothes of crimson threaded with gold. They flattered him, accentuating both his height and slim build. "I believe many of my brothers have made fair points. But I believe with everything shared so far, all we can conclude is this: We do not know who killed either of our brothers. And that is a problem, and it is not."

The last few words caused a great many of the nobles in the audience to trade quizzical looks.

Prince Ateine didn't rise from his seat, but leaned forward and spoke. "Estre has the right of it. We cannot let our brothers' murders go unpunished, but . . . we cannot punish incorrectly, for that too is a crime under Solus, is it not?" He turned his head to regard the pontifex.

The holy leader inclined his head, though the glint of his eyes told me he would have very much liked if that weren't the case.

"All we know is that the Storyteller did not kill Albero, and I am not convinced he killed Arturo. For that matter, beyond his story of the tea, we do not know that Lord Emeris was responsible either. All that can be deduced is that the tea led to his death. Who prepared it? Did someone else get to it before Lord Emeris served it? Too many factors. Let's call this trial what it is: a sham."

If that was a surprise to anyone, no one in the crowd showed it, which confirmed what I had thought.

The princes only wanted to find the murderer to discover who their enemies were as opposed to any true sense of justice. What brotherly love they held for one another ended when considering the throne.

But all they'd learned from this was that I wasn't guilty enough to condemn. If I survived this, I would still be looked on with disfavor until I was granted a more definitive declaration of my innocence.

Which I highly doubted would happen.

Prince Efraine clapped his brother Ateine on the shoulder. "Well said. I think we should use this opportunity with most of the notable nobles before us to make our cases and simply get on with the game. Perhaps by the end of this we can skip straight to the election." He gave the first enthused smile I'd seen out of the man.

A few in the crowd chuckled, as did some of the princes.

Ateine and Artenyo turned to face Efraine and the two of them spoke in near-perfect unison, one mere moments behind the other, becoming an odd echo. "You sound too confident for your own good, brother. It will be your undoing."

Efraine merely held his grin. "No, brothers, it's been yours."

The clergos standing guard behind the other princes grabbed hold of each of them by a shoulder, drew a short blade, and ran them across the mens' necks.

Only one prince remained uncut, unharmed, unfallen.

Then the screaming began.

THIRTY-FIVE

OUR UTTER CONVICTIONS

The princesses didn't join the cries of panic and despair. Each of them leapt with the bared-teeth spring-fury of wolves on a hind. They lunged for Efraine, the first signs of fresh grief finally showing on their faces as tears broke free. Each looked like they'd rend their brother to strips of red flesh and sinew, but they never got the chance.

The clergos interceded, grabbing each woman and restraining them.

"Take my sisters back to their rooms . . . kept under guard until the election is certified, *sieta*?" The clergos nodded and the pontifex bowed his head, making it clear he agreed with the order.

The palace guards stood like a blank monolith, every face a cold-hollow mask. Simply frozen in shock.

I suppose it made sense. Imagine spending your career dedicated to protecting the royal family, only to watch yourself fail before having the time to blink. And what then did you do when another prince was responsible and now the last living heir to claim the crown?

It certainly presented a problem.

The screams hadn't all quieted and the remaining clergos moved to ensure no one could leave. Or make any foolish moves.

Efraine knew how to steal a scene, and play a deadly game. He clapped his hands and ushered the pontifex to stand with him.

I turned a half measure to regard Eloine, but found no one by my side. *Brahm's tits. When did she leave—how did she leave?*

"My fellow lords and ladies, I think we can consider this Game of Families and election completed. I thank you all for your overwhelming support and votes." He smiled wider than before. "Some of you might be confused by this turn of events. After all, no *efante* has ever gotten rid of all his brothers before, and not like this. But as some of you know, I think it's time we take our country in a new direction. And it is one the pontifex and I have been long in discussion about. We've come to an agreement that too long we've sat by the side, taken too little interest in the world at large.

"We let its people, its influence, and its trade run our country. Every day more wonders from the Mutri take hold of our markets, our people, and even their foreign ways of thinking. There are monks and priests traveling along the Golden Road to our side of the world now, and they have convinced some of our folk to take up their religion."

Some of the crowd grew tight-mouthed at that, a few going so far as to openly scowl.

And like that, the last remaining prince turned fear into hatred.

Swept up in the fervor of emotions, it took little to morph their riled minds into the shape the prince wanted. They hadn't forgotten the horror they'd witnessed, only transmuted that intensity of emotion to anger. Disdain for and to the foreign.

Efraine nodded as if understanding their silent discontent. "I've seen it with my own eyes, wide and along the great road. I've traveled it, studied it, warred along it all in the name of our country, your prosperity, our people, and, of course, our lord and savior, Solus."

More of the crowd calmed from the excitement of murder—now bobbing their heads in quiet acceptance of what Efraine said.

He worked the politician's manipulation.

"And that is why I have made a decision, as your soon-to-be crowned king of our great country, to unify the church and the crown, to be in better service of our people, and our god, Solus. I, with the blessing and guidance of His Holiness, will lead Etaynia out across the road to all nations, foreign and unnatural, and bring them into the fold of our lord and savior."

Your. Prince. Elect. With those few words, he'd told them that they had in fact asked for this. Quietly nudged them into accepting the results of the game, and that it was by their unconscious blessing. He'd taken hold of their fear, repurposed it, given them a goal and direction for those feelings, and worked in the murderous results of the game.

Masterfully done.

Some of the crowd stood and began to clap. The agreeing voices loudened.

"I will free us from the grip of their tyrannical and godless hold over the Golden Road, opening trade without imposition for all our people. I will end all foreign wars threatening our borders, straining *our* traders, *our* merchants, and putting *our* people to fear, with this one move. I will take us to the one true war to end them all."

The rest of the crowd rose. A storm broke out of stomping feet—a chorus of screams. It was thunderous noise of one hundred clapping hands.

In the midst of it, I caught Prince Efraine's eyes. They showed no hatred toward me, nor a speck of measured coldness. Not even the sharp calculation found in a serpent's gaze. Almost an apology, a quiet request to be forgiven for the position I'd been in, and something else that drove an iciness to the core of me.

Utter conviction in every word he'd spoken. Unshakable belief. The heart of him held every word he'd spoken as purest truth, and nothing could convince him otherwise. Prince Efraine's heart had been taken and twisted by this cause. One with which he would lead his people to war.

Unless someone stopped him.

It is the things we come to convince ourselves of, so firmly so that nothing can dissuade us, that later come to define us. They shape us, extremity after extremity, left unchecked, and if not better honed for our proper growth, can leave us tainted versions of all we could have been. It is the problem all true binders face as well. When our beliefs come to shape us, rather than us them. And when we let them be corrupted by the wrong voices.

As I watched the remaining princes bleed over the table, I noticed a distinct lack of something I'd been hoping to find. The color black. For all the blood ran red as the color of my cloak and cowl. Red as the smoke from a night so long ago.

No sign of the Tainted. For any of the brothers could have had the capacity to ruin a kingdom in so many ways.

And so I realized that if there was a hint of blackness to be found, it resided in the last remaining prince of Etaynia.

I'd found who I had to kill.

If only it were that easy.

The room had been cleared by the guards and what remained of the clergos. Servants had been called in to clean the pooling blood and strip the now stained carpets from the room. Prince-elect Efraine had availed himself of what I supposed was now his proper seat—the king's own throne. He sat there, one leg over the other, with the pontifex by his side.

The rest of the nobles had left as soon as the speech had concluded, and by that, I mean were forcibly ushered out of the room.

"I'm sorry for the theatrics, Storyteller, but I'm sure you're one to appreciate a good show, even if a touch . . . overdramatic?" Efraine pursed his lips into an expression that could break into a frown, or a smile, depending on what I said next.

"It's not the first royal murder I've witnessed . . . Your Highness?" I hoped my confusion about Efraine's new title would keep him fixed on that topic, and less on me.

"Still prince-elect, I'm afraid, until the church and *congeriate* officially acknowledge the results."

I looked around the empty room. "I suppose it will be hard for your brothers to contest your election."

He inclined his head. "Just so. And, for what it is worth, I hope you can forgive me for the small inconveniences you were put through." Prince-elect Efraine did not voice that as a hopeful question. It came as a command.

So what could I do besides arch a brow and bow my head in quiet promise that they were pardoned.

"Leaving you to take the blame for Arturo's murder, for one, which led you to your accommodations in the rooms below."

I'd never heard of a prison cell referred to in that manner, but I knew enough that now was not the time to hold to my old habit of antagonizing nobles.

Even I can learn.

"I'll share a small secret with you now, Storyteller." He leaned closer, looking around as more a child afraid of being overheard than a monarch. "I have no idea who killed Albero, and as you said, it was before you had come into the country. I wager it was Arturo, maybe Ateine. They certainly did not get along." He clucked his tongue several times. "Shame. Arturo's passing however"—Efraine broke off to make a gesture to Solus—"did happen at my hand. Well, Lord Emeris', I suppose. You were a convenient mark following your arrival into the game. And for that, I am truly sorry."

I swallowed what moisture was in my mouth, wondering how best to play this new game I found myself in. "And Lord Emeris' enmity toward me? Was that also a construct from the beginning?"

"Oh, no. I do believe he despises you something terrible, Storyteller. I would not let that man get you alone in a room." He shook his head. "Emeris had my permission to dispose of Arturo as he best saw fit once I'd learned he'd been called to dine with him privately. I wager his use of you was also to satisfy his personal grievance."

I stared. "And . . . is that still going to be settled?"

Efraine laughed. "No. I have my own interest in you, Storyteller. As does my pontifex."

My pontifex, he'd said. Meaning he did not serve the church, nor did he truly work in tandem with them. The pontifex was his tool. I kept that firmly in mind.

The holy man took that as his cue to introduce himself. "Storyteller, your reputation has done you great favor, bringing your name to even my ears. An impressive feat given how little we care for news and folk from your home." His words held none of the malice or contempt he'd exuded during the trial.

An act? But which part, before, or now?

I said nothing.

"King Efraine's speech unnerved you?" The pontifex tilted his head, clearly watching me for visible reaction. And he already named Efraine a king.

Not if I can do something about it. Aloud, I spoke the best truth I could that would let me keep my head for just a while longer. "It's not an attitude I'd think for any in Etaynia to take. Your country has benefited a long time from the Golden Road. All have."

The pontifex gave a little shake of his head.

It was Efraine, though, who countered. "True enough, but there is unease building in the world. My heart tells me it will not be too long before that unease spreads. I can do a few things." He held up a clenched fist, raising a finger then. "Nothing." A second finger went to the air. "Protect our borders, but for how long?" A third digit. "Or I can bring my people to war first, and stem the tide before it reaches our lands. I will not make Antoine's mistake and wait for dark things at our borders."

I bristled at that. "And how do you take Antoine's story, Prince-elect?"

"A lesson. A metaphor. I know the invaders came to this land to plunder it, and it is a lesson in Solus' strength and grace to cast out the foreign darkness."

"Antoine died for his efforts." I kept my voice flat and empty of all emotion when I reminded him of that.

Prince Efraine nodded. "A possibility I too am willing to embrace for my country."

I'll bet you are. I took a breath and steeled myself before continuing. "He also lost Etaynia in the war." That struck him with the weight I'd hoped for.

His eyes lost the conviction they'd held seconds ago. His posture softened and he slumped just a shade. And the lines of his jaw lost their sharp angles.

The pontifex placed a hand on the prince-elect's shoulder, and Efraine's resolve visibly returned. But it was the pontifex who took the chance to question me now. "I think for the time being, we are, all of us, exhausted. Might it be best if we all take some rest, and if you wish to talk further with the Storyteller, to do so at a later time."

Prince-elect Efraine nodded, waving me off.

I turned to leave.

"Oh, Storyteller?" said the pontifex.

I didn't bother moving to face him when I answered. "Yes?"

"You were seen in the company of a curious and beautiful woman. Prior to that, she'd come to the attention of a few of the former *efantes*. And of course we all watched her at the masquerade."

My heartbeat was a bird's wings in storm. "Yes?"

"Where is she now?"

A basso boom sounded over the palace, indicating a storm to come. Only a breath passed between that and the susurrus of rain that followed. Another crack of thunder then.

"I don't know, Your Holiness." *But I terribly wish I knew.*

I left the throne room and hoped to find Eloine. Safe, and out of the company of any more murderous nobles.

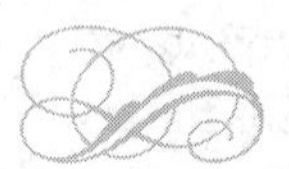

THIRTY-SIX

Forgotten Things

An escort led me back to the rooms I'd been given upon arriving at Del Soliel. My personal effects were soon returned to me as well.

A piece of me wanted to know the reason why, but it mattered little in the end. It meant I would be afforded at least one opportunity to be alone with the prince-elect, and then I could see for myself how far a reach the Tainted had come to get.

Another prince. Another death. Nothing changes. And so the cycle stays the same.

I exhaled and made my way to my bed, resisting the urge to collapse into it and wash away what was left of the dark evening in deepest sleep. It wouldn't do any good, however. So I reached for the sack into which my belongings had been stuffed, aside from my staff. The latter rested against the bedside stand, and looked to be unmarred. No one had bothered to give it too hard a look, not that it could be seen as such.

Staring too long at the wood left nothing for a man's eyes or memory. The wood and shaping seemed to pass by one's attention, blurring into the idea of a staff anyone could conjure for themselves. Unthought of. It was a thing made unordinary and worth no attention at all. One that could not be defined or recalled if you tried to, once having seen it. It was a staff without a story that could be told. Something that seemed made to be disregarded.

Just a staff, I suppose.

My hands went to the sack and I pulled free the tome I'd been questioned about down in the prison. A book almost like the one Mahrab had gifted me so long ago. It sat in my grip with the weight of a mountain, the stillness and silence of stone, refusing to share a story, and with the promise of memory long-hidden inside.

I pried at the covers, but they would not move. My mind went to the folds and I conjured imagery of the ends of the book falling away from one another, revealing the pages inside. Two folds. Then to eight. I committed the whole of my mind and Athir to the task. Sixteen folds. Soon to twenty, like I'd done so long ago.

"Start with whent, then go to ern." The pages were free. I willed it so. Then I pried. The book held firm, unmoving. The story remained shut, and so forgotten. Something inside me went hollow, growing wider by the moment until it threatened to swallow the whole of me into the emptiness within. The book slid from my grasp, striking the ground with a sound I was too far in mind to hear.

"You should be more careful with that. Someone once told me stories were important." Eloine stood in the doorway, watching me. The beginnings of a grin were plain in the lines of her mouth.

"You vanished after the trial." It didn't leave me as a question despite having been one.

"I did." And she made no attempt to answer me. Eloine moved closer, kneeling to pick up the dropped book. Her hands brushed along its spine, then cover. "This story has no name, no title."

I nodded, still wondering where she'd gone.

"There's nothing describing it at all."

I inclined my head again, not trusting myself to speak.

"What kind of story has no tell, no name, no sign?" Eloine brushed the cover again.

"The sort meant to be kept from people, and all the secrets within. If a story is forgotten, sometimes the pains within are buried too. When the memory of it is lost, so are the heroes, and the villains. And you can't chase after a story that's been lost to the world." I reached out without knowing I had until I'd taken the book from Eloine, placing it beside me.

She moved to the edge of the bed, pushing the book away from us. "Well, there is one I still need to hear." Her hands found mine. "I think after today, the both of us could use one."

I met her eyes then, and they had more the color of washed-out sage—so light a shade they were closer to gray-dusted green than the brightness of emeralds. Her face held all the marks of tiredness in it. And it looked very much like a story would offer her the most comfort.

So, what could I do but give her that?

I squeezed her hand and gave her the smile she seemed unable to share herself. "Of course. I'd just set out to pay Nitham back for every grief he'd given me, and the threats against my family. I'd robbed him, and I'd burned his home . . . more than I'd intended. What happens next wasn't planned in any measure, but it is an important part of understanding how the stories about me came to grow. And the wildness that came to fan them into greater mistruths.

"We start with The White Ghost of Ghal, the thief in the storm, and my departure from the Ashram to save a flock of birds that I'd brought trouble to. These are my last days for a long time in a place I'd come to think of as home. I suppose this is the part of the story where the complacency I'd fallen into is sloughed away, and I begin to rediscover who I wished to be. And then chase the being of that person.

"For better, or for worse."

THIRTY-SEVEN

The Ghost of Ghal

I lay there in the snow, the cold leaching what warmth remained in my blood. My body ached and the ice was no relief to the whole hurt of me.

The sky held nightmare's red and The Saffron House burned bright in the night. Screams echoed out beyond the building. The first escapees from the growing blaze raced onto the street. More smoke plumed at the edges of my vision. *The other fires,* I realized. Sham had lit the makeshift braziers we'd formed from flashsteel, discarded wood, and rithra. The immediate area around The Saffron House would soon bear the most telling sign of the Ashura.

And it wouldn't be long before the kuthri came to investigate.

I finally found the strength to get to my feet as the blizzard intensified.

All I could make of those fleeing were vague silhouettes against the blanketing white, and I wondered what they saw of me, clad in a cloak and cowl nearly shaped from the snow around us.

But my curiosity didn't last, and my feet remembered my sparrow's training better than my mind could.

I ran.

I blurred through the snowfall, passing through any side street I could, brushing by the unfortunate souls who still had business to conduct late into the evening and had not found shelter yet.

A voice shouted a curse at me as I went by.

Then another. "What was that?"

I paid them no mind, racing through the gaps between buildings Sham had shown me. But it did me little good as a pair of men in heavy fur-lined cloaks moved down the opposite end of the street.

Their armor consisted of hardened leather and layers of thick padding that could turn away most weapons. Each man trawled the way with spear in hand, and a small buckler shield in their other. For extra measure, curved long swords hung from their hips.

The kuthri. One of the men spotted me and shouted a cry. It was more surprise than accusation, but my life of thieving told me to run rather than try to talk my way out of this.

So I did. I bolted toward the closest building, planting both feet onto the lip of a window.

The kuthri screamed and raced after me, but the snow and wind were against them, and the weight of their cumbersome clothing did not aid them in navigating the piling frost.

I climbed to the roof, cursing every cold-needle sting against my bare fingers. My eyes burned with a newfound pain as tears formed and froze before falling from my lids. But still, I made my way up. The next building stood close enough for me to risk jumping.

The kuthri howled at me.

I broke into a sprint around the ledge of the domed roof. Enough frost had still built along the surface to threaten throwing me free, however. I reached the edge and leapt, striking the next roof . . . and sliding downward.

My hands smacked against the next roof's edge and found enough of a hold to let me haul myself up, but my fingers cried out from the effort.

One of the kuthri had made his way through the feet of snow and swatted at me with his spear. The blow wasn't meant to hurt me, but simply strike me with enough force to upset my balance and bring me down. However, the icy buildup below had left the man's footing unsteady, and he'd put too much force behind the strike.

My leg could not register the impact of the spear's wooden shaft striking it hard. The cold had numbed me to that, but the bladed edge of the weapon caught against my calf and dragged a furrow of fresh warm agony through me. I nearly buckled, my cry going far into the night.

The other kuthri reached his partner and had enough sense to reverse his hold on his weapon, thrusting the blunt end my way in an effort to dislodge me from my perch. It struck and slid harmlessly along the back of my cloak.

Ice-born fear galvanized me and I lurched away, ignoring the pain mounting in my leg with every step. Adrenaline had me in its hold, a familiar panic that had saved me many a time. So I let it have its way.

All the while, the sky filled with plumes of reddened smoke from the other pyres Sham and I had built.

Ashura. Ashura. Demons had come to Ghal. And they'd struck at The Saffron House—their ire aimed at Nitham. Or so people might come to whisper.

I skirted around the edge of the building, moving into the direction of the wind. My cowl kept the worst of it from my face, but the kuthri fared nowhere near as well. They had to raise a hand to block out the snow peppering their vision.

I leapt, this time not aiming for a roof, but the wall of a building that seemed close enough for me to hit. My body struck it—hard. My cloak and clothes buffered me from the worst of the impact, but I would feel the soreness later, especially in my side. I slid down along it and sank into the snow. Even with the frost-formed cushion, I wobbled before moving onward.

I slunk into the next bubble, taking twisting paths when and where I could. The kuthris had raised a cry, and it spread farther as the night went on.

Men and women had taken to the streets of Ghal. Candlelit glass lanterns hanging from poles swept along streets and touched to roofs to scour them through the storm.

Everyone soon searched for the shadow in white who'd leapt from The Saffron House as it broke into fire. Then they turned to the miniature fires The Crow and I had set as distractions, soon smothering them.

But I stayed on the move, avoiding the masses wherever they gathered. The night deepened and the hours passed. I'd been out for at least a full candlemark since the fire had started, and there seemed to be no rest in sight for me.

The storm held, and I remained a white-cast ghost running through it. Over rooftops when I could. Vanishing into what alleys and paths I remembered from the Crow's teachings. Sometimes a crowd would find me, but a chance gust of wind would kick up enough snow cover for me to use and pass from sight.

When my body finally begged for me to stop, I huddled close to the curve of one building's roof, digging a small hole in the snow for myself. I tucked into a ball and lay there, pulling my cloak and cowl tight around myself. This did little to keep the cold from me, and I shivered long until I thought I would never stop.

My rest could not last, though, and soon a crowd moved down the street where I hid. The glow of their lanterns and the calls of their voices reached me.

I moved to spring away, but my body would not heed my commands. Every muscle and bone had fallen into stone-stiffness and the shivering had stopped. My fingers were gnarled roots buried in the deep of my clothes, refusing to unclench.

"Sweep the alley-holes, any nook, and every roof." The shout came clear through the cold night wind. The bobbing lights inched closer, and I could see the distinct pale glow of a binder's lamp within the group. Someone with money enough to afford one had joined the patrol.

I must have really irked someone influential, then. Perhaps a partial investor of the inn, or the wrathful tenants I'd accidently displaced.

I breathed down my cowl, trying to bring a little heat to my throat. Eventually, my body found itself somewhat willing to respond to my thoughts, and I struggled to all fours. Each upward foot I climbed cost me in renewed agony, but I had no choice. I reached the crest of the domed roof, and rolled onto its other side. The ice and snow did as they were wont to and sent me sliding off to the ground.

I crashed onto more snow, this time almost content to lay there and let the crowd eventually find me.

Something moved ahead of my fading vision. A figure in black—shambling, all the makings of a monstrously oversized bird. The world darkened, but the shape drew closer—blacker in the white-washed storm of ice.

I saw a crow.

Then a hard jab made itself felt along my shoulders. The tip of whatever they used only barely reaching my awareness due to the solid protection of my white-scale cloak.

"Eh. *Tsst*. Ari?"

I groaned into the snow.

"You's wantin' ta stay'n here 'n' ta snow till it'n goes up yer ass?"

That voice. "Sham?" I sounded like I'd swallowed frozen glass.

"Been followin' since you's lit up the place like Brahm 'mself! Whoosh. Swear's 'n' thought ta'shura were comin' ta kill us."

My heart skipped a beat, but not in fear. And my stomach clenched in a manner that had nothing to do with the cold. Of all the people who could have found me, The Crow. If I could have laughed, I would have. I couldn't find the heart to chastise Sham for his abhorrent grammar in that moment. "Help."

Sham's hands clasped to mine, and another pair of hands joined him.

I managed to glance up and find a face hidden behind the dark layers and folds of the black cloaks.

The ones I'd purchased for Sham to give to the other homeless urchins of Ghal.

My vision clouded, and the shapes began to blur.

And another figure stood behind them, quickly moving to come to my aid as well. More blackened shapes filtered into view, all helping me to my feet.

Soon, I saw a murder of crows swarming my body. They took me in, shrouded me under the care of their wings, all as Sham led the way. A group of shadows surrounding the ghost in white. We might have painted an impressive scene . . . if I wasn't doubled over and being supported by a bunch of little birds. A procession in black, carrying a figure of white close to death.

White threaded my vision, and just as much as red from the inside of my eyelids as fatigue threatened to take me.

"Stay awake," said one of the crows. The rest cawed in unison, mimicking his cry.

It was a good suggestion. I would have terribly liked to follow it. But somewhere along the way, I failed.

The storm of snow beat against me and the whiteness took me.

Voices reached just the edges of me, and I couldn't tell one from another.

"Is he dead?"

"Don't think so."

"Pull him to the fire."

The fire. I opened my eyes, but the stark white I'd seen before had not left me prepared for the dark cavern. A wash of violent orange and red streaked across my vision so bright it brought knives of pain to me. I closed my eyes and held them tight. My skin prickled and I lay there, shuddering until I passed out again.

"*Tch. Tch.*" Each word came punctuated with a sharp jab.

I groaned and tried to roll away from the irritation, but my body refused to move. Every bit of me had locked stiff in place. My hands clutched to my chest and my arms had frozen into an awkward self-hug. I opened my eyes and stared at the fire that had been burning just outside my reach.

Its warmth passed to me and offered some relief from the cold. As I stared at it, I fell into a lull somewhere between sleep and lucid wakefulness. Each flickering tendril waved at me. Their very motions reminded me of the first time I'd paid a flame such mind: my exercise with Mahrab, when I'd been called to imagine a bulb of fire moving to its true nature—all without looking at one.

The fire promised me a gentle kindness. It spoke of reciprocity. For the breath that'd been used to fan it to life, it would give heat back. For the fuel it continued to receive, it would continue to burn and give light. For what food came to touch its edges and cook, it would take a piece for itself, and leave the greater meal behind. Fire was as destructive as much as it was a piece of creation—a tool to create.

I lay there, listening to the crackling as darkened shapes shuffled by, throwing pieces of old broken wood into the flames. Then a stranger's voice spoke to me.

They inquired as to my health given what I suffered from the snow, but I told her my cloak had kept me safe from the worst of it. That's when cold realization hammered into me and I understood why the fire's warmth touched me so.

My clothes had been taken.

I had been left, rather embarrassingly, naked. All of which gave me a better view at the sorry state of my body—a near uniform mass of purpling bruises.

But I didn't think long on my battered body, because a question remained: What had Sham done with my clothing?

A figure in black, standing on the opposite side of the flame, answered me. They told me that the kuthri hadn't stopped their search, so someone needed to lead them off our trail. And Sham had elected to do that himself.

The thick-witted, addlebrained, thought-curdled, half-toothed ghul had put himself in a world of trouble. Out there in my white cloak, he'd be targeted as the possible arsonist of The Saffron House, not to mention for evasion of the kuthri.

A crime in and of itself.

He'd had to don extra cumbersome layers to masquerade as me, which meant throwing away all his child agility and speed. Vulnerable. And the heavy snows would make him slower than the full-grown adults trudging after him.

The glare of the fire held most of my vision, blurring everything else at the edges. Weariness still begged me to rest, but I couldn't leave my brother out there. So I addressed the mass of barely visible children in the cavern.

But I was a stranger, and they took no orders from me—only Sham. And I could barely leave my bed.

In the end, the children forced me back onto the makeshift cot, bringing me a sweet soup that only managed to be edible due to the large amount of palm sugar fed into it. Moments passed before one of the urchins brought me Shola. Sham had tasked the little rascals to tend to my kitten while he and I started my business at The Saffron House.

The feline fixed me with a look somewhere between sympathy for my condition and disappointment that his preferred servant hadn't been here to attend his desires.

I gave him a look of apology.

He seemed mollified by that and came over to curl up against me, promptly falling asleep. His weight was a reassurance that salved the ache of losing my white cloak. A sonorous, resonant chorus of purring flooded me. Shola's way of telling me he cared. All was right in the world now as far as he was concerned.

Perhaps I could allow myself a short rest, and some hope that my little brother would be safe. Just as I was in a cavern of crows then. A fire's warmth, my cat, and the company of orphans.

While the Ashram had certainly come to be the place I lay my head down at nights, tonight, I truly felt home.

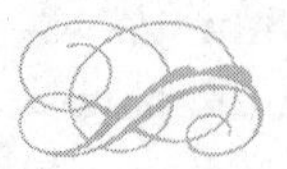

THIRTY-EIGHT
The Things We Believe

"Ari. Ari." My body jostled with each utterance as a pair of hands shoved me.

"Brahm's blood, what is it?" I roused and winced against the glow of the nearby fire.

Sham stood over me, looking more like a sentient mass of clothing than a small boy. My white cloak did not flatter his small frame, hanging over him like he'd been blanketed in a cloud of snow. You could barely see the child within. All in all, he did very much look the ghost.

Even if oversized for Sham, the snow-white cloak looked properly out of the old stories. The firelight brought a shine to the scales and made them look like moonlight and pearl-forged facets.

Sham threw back the hood of the cloak. His grin couldn't have spread any wider, or revealed more of the missing teeth he hadn't grown back yet. Sham sniffled, mucus dribbling out of his nose. "Yer alive."

I pursed my lips, not sure how to respond to his keen sense of observation. "I'm up." I gave him a long look. "You're wearing my cloak."

He nodded. "You t'wasn't needin' it I'a figured." Sham hooked a thumb to his chest, then puffed up like a cockerel, clearly proud of himself. "Gave 'em kuthris a'n' good run'a 'round." Sniff. "Ran 'em long 'round Ghal. Thems started calling me a ghost. Gots 'em lost 'nuff I could'n come home. Is'zat soup?" He tried to force his way past me but I caught him by the arm and held him still.

"Sham. Thank you for what you did." He brightened at that but I didn't let go. "But please give me back my cloak . . . and my clothes."

The one thing that could never be said of Sham is that he failed to obey an order. The boy instantly shrugged out of my cloak. Then my clothes. And then he proceeded to strip out of his own.

"Brahm's tits, Sham. Not yours!" I grabbed his shirt, pulling it back over his head as he struggled. His muffled complaints fell into incoherency as we wrestled. He slipped out of my grip and toppled to the ground. "Merciful Brahm." I sighed and fetched my clothes, summoning some of the children to help rig up a stand to dry them by the fire.

My white cloak, however, went back around my shoulders immediately. Patting myself down revealed that something had vanished. "I had purses on me when you found me, right? Right?"

"Sho' 'nuff," said Sham as he continued to flail on the ground. "Tooks 'em and put 'em in ma box o' precious."

I exhaled and sent of a prayer to Brahm that the coins hadn't been lost in the rooftop excitement.

"What's 'n 'em ?" Sham's question came from honest curiosity.

I smiled. "Bring them here and I'll show you." He finally got the better of his battle with his shirt, then donned his black cloak, now looking very much The Crow again. I ushered him off to fetch what I asked for while I watched my clothes dry. Sham returned soon and passed me the pouches I'd taken from Nitham's room. I held one of them up for him, then bounced it in my palm.

The unmistakable sound of clinking coins filled the air.

His eyes fixed on the bag.

I unfastened the pouch and pinched free a coin. In the light, the rupai caught most of the fire's glow, shining a color every child dreamed of.

"Is'zat gold?" Sham's eyes widened.

"That it is." I motioned with my hands, performing an old trick I'd learned as a sparrow. The gold vanished and he gasped. The coin reappeared seconds later as if springing out of my palm. A simple thing, but it kept Sham's eyes on me, and his mouth opened in glee.

The truth of the matter was this: The little boy would not be able to break a gold rupai, much less spend one, without drawing too much attention. It brought me no small amount of grief to think about withholding the coin from him. The money would benefit Sham, and thus, the other orphans he'd organized recently, a great deal even if they'd learned how to fend for themselves.

And I wouldn't be able to go into the Ashram's bank to break the coin. Word would spread, if it hadn't already, of Nitham's rooms, and what might have gone missing. If I turned up with gold I never had to my name, it would raise questions as much as brows.

I'd have to figure out another way to bring some extra coin to Sham's little flock and what to do with all I'd taken from Nitham. That's when I realized what had changed in the cavern.

Sham and I were alone. I'd asked him where the other orphans had gone, and he avoided my gaze at first. He eventually worked up the courage to tell me the painful truth.

While I had taken him under my wing, and even furnished them all with some clothes, I was a stranger. I hadn't earned their trust. Not like Sham had. This cave was his, as was its warmth. For the kindness he'd shown them, they answered him as a favor—to save me the night I needed it.

But they were gone now, and he was alone.

Because of me—my presence. In all my efforts to try to give him something, I might have just taken it away. That is when I realized another truth of why I'd taken Sham under my wing. The little boy—The Crow—lived a life I'd been coming to understand since Nitham had been turning the screws against me. Unable to see Radi and Aram. Unable to visit Immi. But nothing stopped me from seeing Sham. Perhaps I chose him for that reason. Perhaps, I needed a little brother as much as he needed one to look up to.

"You're not alone, Sham." I reached out and placed a hand on his shoulder.

He sniffed once. "I'm not?"

"No. You've got me, so long as you want—as long as you need. A brother." While I'd come to view him as mine, he'd yet to make that decision in return.

Sham frowned, thinking that over. "But yer s'not, though? My ma's differn' than yours, so's my da'."

I knelt, staring him in the eyes as I shared a truth I'd learned long ago. "Family, *real* family, isn't made in blood, Sham. It's not something given. It's found in the people who will stand by you when you've not a bent coin to your name. The ones who'll help you out of trouble . . . or start it." I flashed him a mischievous wink. "Family's chosen . . . with this"—I tapped his temple—"and this." I placed a hand on his heart. "No one ever tells us that truth is all. I've made my choice, little brother, what about you?" I watched and waited for his decision.

He smiled, and I knew his answer.

Then my little brother turned his Crow's mind to the problem of the remaining pouches. What would we do with them?

Count their contents, of course, and so we did.

Being a prince paid well. All in total, Nitham had five rupais' worth of coins in various metals, with only two in the prohibitive golden denomination. But the rest? I could work something better than mischief with those. And as I stared at the coins, I had a wonderful idea.

I waited till the next morning when the snows had settled and most of the streets that could be cleared in Ghal had been. I did not wear my white cloak as I returned to the Ashram, knowing it'd mark me and reignite the pursuit. Shola had put up something close to a fuss in leaving Sham, but eventually he'd resigned himself to the confines of my rucksack for the trip.

I did my best to keep my head down and met no eyes as I navigated the Ashram's main courtyard. Word had spread about what had happened down in Ghal, and even now, I caught the barest edges of whispers from students.

Something had struck The Saffron House. It wasn't mere accident. No candle flame gone wrong. One person had heard it had been a performer, too far gone into their drink, and not quite there enough in the head to know that fire should not be played with. In the midst of their juggling act, they lost control and cost everyone a reputable inn and tavern.

But those weren't the strongest of the rumors.

Everyone spoke in close-kept voices, not the sort to be heard past their little circles. Even so, I'd long grown adept at picking up on things not meant to be listened to. I made my way by one of these groups, pausing to fiddle with my robes and then boots.

"Red smoke. I swear it. Heard it from Qalbi himself. He left Nitham's party early—said he saw the fires too before they finally got put out. All. Red. Like blood."

"Like the . . . Ashura," said another voice. The last word left them like a curse, not meant to be uttered, and half-afraid some form of punishment would come down on them for uttering it at all.

The group grumbled in agreement.

So, Nitham's rooms had gone up, but the whole of The Saffron House hadn't burned down. That came as a relief. I had no intention of doing that much damage.

"They said the Ashura who did it wore white, like the snow itself."

That brought me pause.

"I heard they were like a ghost, moved from place to place, no wall could stop them, and no one could see their face."

"I thought the Ashura brought storm-rains and flood?"

"No, they turn fires and smoke red."

"Stone and stave begin to crack, and shadow figures on the wall, twisted—turned, and all black!"

"The walls bleed," said another. "Everyone bleeds!"

The group fell into bickering then about the many signs of the Ashura, and what reasoning the demons had for what they did.

I sighed, giving small thanks that no one had at least connected the figure in white to me and my white cloak.

It was one of my earlier lessons in a fundamental truth about humans. We simply do not believe in some things that might strain the edges of what we *wish* to believe. It is easier to tie a disaster to a group of infamous monsters, even if you do not think they are real, than to search for the truth.

Once we come to form our narrative of how the world works, and the truth of all things, we will bend any and all other truths to fit those we hold closest to. It is simply the way of the world.

I just didn't realize how powerful a tool that was in my youth. And I wouldn't for some time yet.

Another matter took my attention as the restless fidgeting in my sack intensified. Shola was growing agitated, not so much from his confinement, but from lack of food. Knowing full well the trouble I could get into if his royal highness wasn't catered to, I headed to Clanks.

Midday meal had just started, so I hadn't missed anything. Radi and Aram stood far to one side of the large hall, going through the motions of loading up their trays. They hadn't spotted me yet, and I didn't want to stop to chat. Settling Shola in my room, as well as hiding my white cloak, came as first priority.

I fetched a tray, ladling a medley of brown rice and chicken onto it. Then I spooned a helping of goat and rabbit stew. It would be enough for the kitten considering he'd already eaten something in the keeping of Sham's orphan friends. I made my way to my room, freeing Shola from my pack, then setting out the tray for him.

He gave it a perfunctory sniff before setting to the task of devouring it.

I pulled free my cloak then, sliding it between my mattress and the frame, knowing it would be safe there. Then I returned to Clanks.

Thankfully, the Ashram's monks never bothered if a student sought seconds. Our coin, including that which the Ashram brought in through many other avenues, more than covered it. I took a new tray and treated myself to much of what I'd gotten for Shola, only in larger portions, and making sure to treat myself to some *benkhbah*.

The dish consisted of several layers formed from flour, sugar, egg yolk, shredded coconut and its milk. It created a sort of cake after each section had finished cooking on the grill, soon to be topped by another bit of batter to cook. Some places went as far as to dip it into sweetened rose syrup and garnish it with nutmeg and slivered toasted almonds. The Ashram happened to be one such place.

I may have taken a few slices more than necessary. I'd been nearly burned alive, hounded by the kuthri, then a local mob, and been left to freeze. A little extra cake could soothe a great many sufferings. Or so I told myself.

Radi and Aram had taken seats at a table near the center of Clanks. Aram spotted me first, and I would have liked to say she wore the smile you'd expect when greeting your friend.

She did not. Her eyes widened, then turned to slits, before finally taking shape as a neutral stare that betrayed nothing.

Radi, for his part, puckered his mouth into a tight O.

I eyed the pair of them as I sat down. "So, the both of you clearly have something to say. . . ." I gave them a look, then reconsidered. "Many things to say. We can either start an awkward staring contest, or someone can say what's on their mind before the quiet kills us all."

Aram leveled her spoon at me. "Where were you the night The Saffron House nearly burned down?"

Straight to the heart of it then. I decided it better if I answered the question with some meal in my stomach, and it had nothing to do with stalling to find an appropriate response. The mild spice of the stew allowed you to appreciate the tenderness and full flavor of the meat. I spooned some of the rice medley into my next bite and found it much improved. "I was out." Aram stared at me, then Radi, then focused back on me. "Uh-huh. Out where?"

"About," I said through another spoonful of my meal.

Radi busied himself by idly poking at his food, but he mouthed the words *About where?*

I shrank a little in my seat. "I might have been in the general whereabouts of the inn that night. Why?"

Aram rose halfway and glared at me. "You know exactly *why*. What were you thinking? What did you do?"

I looked to Radi for support, but his full attention turned to his mandolin. He pulled it free and plucked a few notes: *Fair question. Answer her. I'd like to know too.*

"I thought I'd scare Nitham properly and keep him from making good on his threats." I glanced at Radi. "You told her, right?"

He nodded.

Aram cradled her head. "Ari, Nitham can't do anything to your family back in Abhar. He can't even touch you if you go back there."

I frowned, unsure whether she could be that naïve or just had a shocking amount of optimism about the turnings of the world. "One letter from his family to the royal family of Abhar, and he can have any of my family in rope and gallows like that." I snapped my fingers to accentuate my point.

Aram set her spoon down onto her tray and pushed it away from her with the smooth coordination that told me she'd done this before. She fixed me with an imperious look that belonged on a noble glaring at someone beneath them more than my bookish friend. "Ari, he can say whatever he wants to Abhar's family. It's up to them to decide what they will do about it. And Abhar and Thamar aren't on good terms. The families do not like one another."

Radi strummed a few more notes that could have said: *mild relief*, *I wonder why*, and *joy*.

"How would you know?" I tried to return Aram's stare, but couldn't manage it.

She fumbled when she took up her spoon, letting some of the stew slop onto the table. When she spoke, she didn't meet my eyes unlike before. "It's business. Father has to know everyone's situation among the nobles. Makes trade easier. You can predict if the roads between kingdoms will turn bad. Banditry coincidentally rises when neighbors are on bad terms." Her eyes narrowed in a way that said that was no coincidence at all.

I conceded that point. "Fair enough, but still, they're my family. What would you do if he'd threatened yours, Aram?"

Aram reached out to put a hand on mine and gave me a little shake. "I know,

Ari. I know. But he really couldn't have done anything. I promise." She'd spoken then with more confidence than in anything else I'd heard from her before. Almost as if she herself could have guaranteed it.

I thanked her, but couldn't bring myself to believe it. So far, Nitham had been able to make good on nearly every threat he'd made. I wouldn't have let him even make the attempt after the sparrows. Aloud, however, I confessed to something else. "I didn't mean for the fire to spread how it did."

Silence.

Then it broke with an irreverent *twang* as Radi pulled free a long sad note: *flaming pile of shit.*

I couldn't argue against that. "Is it true more than Nitham's rooms burned down?"

Both of them nodded.

"How bad?"

Radi set aside his mandolin and took a breath. "Almost lost half the place in the flames, and never mind the rumors that spread."

I arched a brow, hoping he'd elaborate.

"People saw red smoke in the air." He plucked some more notes that sounded like the beginning to an old song about the Ashura I'd heard. "It's been called an act of vengeance against the innkeeper. Someone said there was a new Ashura—one of white snow and half a ghost—half demon. The kuthri tried to find the ghost in white, only they couldn't."

I shoveled down some more food and shrugged.

Radi and Aram stared. The former pointed his spoon at me. "Hey, whatever happened to that white cloak you were wearing almost every day for the last month?"

Aram mimicked Radi's inquisitive look and turned it full on me. "Yeah, what happened to that? You wouldn't happen to have been wearing something so recognizable the night the inn caught fire, would you?"

I mumbled something through a mouthful of stew and rice.

Both my friends kept their gazes trained on me.

"I wore it that night."

Radi and Aram both blew out long suffering breaths and traded looks. "Brahm's blood, Ari, you don't do things halfway do you?" Radi shook his head and followed Aram's earlier move of pushing his tray away. "If you were caught—"

That brought a rare smile to my face. "Ah, but I wasn't. After all, I'm a ghost." I waggled my fingers in a manner that could have been considered magical. "Ow." My shin ached and I stared daggers at Aram.

She crossed her arms under her chest and fixed me with a look that said I'd deserved another kick.

It was a point well made, so I let it go.

"Nitham's put out word that some of his valuables were stolen before the inn caught fire." She raised a brow. "Do you know anything about that?"

I gave her my best nonchalant shrug. So well-performed a thing, a cat would develop jealousy at the level of uncaringness I showed. "Not a clue, though I'd be surprised to know how he came to that conclusion. Given that his rooms burned down, and there's not much left to sort from in belongings."

Aram pursed her lips. "If he proves it's you . . . Ari . . ."

I raised my hands in a calming gesture. "He won't, I promise." One of my hands then went to the hollow of my throat and I gestured pinching my windpipe shut. "Swear it, on my neck."

Three notes trilled into the air from Radi. *That might happen.*

I glowered at him.

"What did you take?" Aram hadn't been fooled whatsoever, and I figured it wouldn't be too much a risk to trust my two best friends with the truth.

I told them the amount of coin I'd pulled.

Radi let out a low appreciative whistle. Aram rolled her eyes.

Eventually we managed to direct the conversation to the important matter: What would I do now that I'd made off with so much money?

I had decided to breathe more life into The Ghost of Ghal.

And he had a job to do.

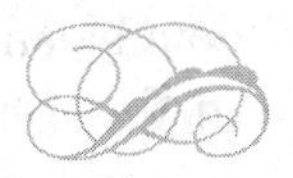

THIRTY-NINE

THE SIDES OF THINGS

What remained of the month passed in a blur too short to properly enjoy.

I attended my lessons with the other students in Rishi Ibrahm's binding class, doing my best to pursue the story of fire, in which Master Binder was little help.

My afternoons were spent slowly spending Nitham's gold on food for Sham and the orphans he'd taken in. Mostly I broke up the larger coins into pieces he could later spend more easily. And some of the money went to a few precious books I'd been able to procure from shops in Ghal.

Thus began Sham's true reading and writing lessons.

There are not enough gods and goddesses to ever pray to for the amount of pain that particular task brought me. Merciful heavens above.

But my nights? Those became the most special time for me.

I would make my way down to The Crow's cavern, slipping into my white-scale cloak. Once the deeper dark of true night fell, I would prowl the rooftops of the few buildings that had flattops for me to stand on. It didn't take long on well-lit and starry evenings for people to catch sight of me.

Then the games began.

I would run around the city, providing the streets were clear of snow, or at least enough to keep me from slipping. As the candlemarks passed, the kuthri failed to catch me. I grew better acquainted with every path in Ghal in a way I can't quite put to words. It became like breathing. An instinct. Soon, I was cutting corners and taking alleys in ways that had The Crow himself asking me for advice.

Between my nightly excursions, I made sure to make a one particular stop. Sham had learned that Valhum hadn't left the city, having taken to moping in a drunken stupor in a shoddy tavern near the outskirts. So I made sure that he'd find a special treat one night upon returning to his rented room: a whole silver dole.

Enough to pay his way forward for quite some time. After that, I returned to inciting the nightly crowds of Ghal.

Once I'd lost one mob, I'd turn to find another, this time roused not in fury, but curiosity. And into their midst I'd throw what tin chips and even copper rounds I'd been able to get out of Nitham's larger currency. I made sure never to give away too much, but soon, The Ghost of Ghal had as many supporters as he did detractors.

The city then tipped into a precarious balance of love and hatred for me. Two sides of a story of the same man. Well, the same ghost.

All of which meant my nighttime jaunts now came with a measure of protection from the crowds that would mask my passing, misdirect my pursuers, and soon take to spreading new lies in my favor that I would have struggled to come up with myself.

You would be surprised how clever people can be when coming up with stories, even if they have no particular knack for it. Some passion, a little bit of wonder, and soon you had an interesting cocktail that could catch flame with but a few sparks.

And if there's one thing I excelled at, it was starting fires.

A shame I never learned to excel at putting them out. Because some of the ones from my past were quickly catching up to me.

And fire always takes its due.

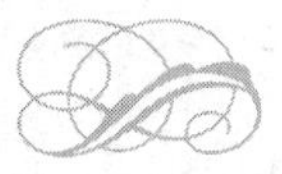

FORTY

A Debt to Call

The new month started with Nitham's threats coming to full fruition. And in the most convenient way.

I woke to a knife pressed to my throat.

My first hint to something being wrong was the smell that roused me from sleep: the scent of orange peels, something close to mint or the odor of a rich forest, and a smoky wash of lavender. I stirred, opening my eyes to find a shadow in the dark of my room.

Morning hadn't come, so no light filtered through the window, yet I could still make out the stranger's outfit. It was a swath of blues so black they could only be found in the deepest of night. Colors washed and whorled against one another so as to never betray where one dark shade ended, and another began. It made them a blackness to be lost in any shadow.

Save for their eyes.

They held a gleam like candlelight within their rum-brightened brown. And they held no love for me, if the sharpened edge against my throat hadn't been enough of a clue to that.

I dared not swallow, wondering if the simple movement would cut me. But the sheer knowing that the blade rested along my gullet raised an unpleasant heat through my flesh. Like the prickling I'd long suffered shirtless under Abhar's summer sun.

When I met their gaze, every sparrow's instinct rose in me like a wild dog, fresh cornered in an alley. They told me, never mind the knife, this person had a danger all their own. They told me to run soon as I could, and to keep running no matter what. They told me that this shadow in black would cut my throat as easily as some men relieve themselves on a tree.

My chest ached from the held breath kept deep in my core, building and burning in want to be set free. Even so, a part of me wanted to scream the feral child's cry I had inside me as well. I wanted to lash out, finger and nail, tooth and mouth against his flesh. Whatever it took to drive this stranger from my room.

Shola. The thought sprung a fresh flame of panic in me that quickly turned to anger. I could feel the heat flash through my eyes as I narrowed my gaze on the stranger.

They put one finger to the veil over their mouth, indicating for me to keep silent. "He said you were clever. Now we'll see if you are smart as well, little cub."

I nearly bristled at that.

"*Tch-tch.* Anger in your eyes, little one. Fire there. But no water in here to keep you cool, hm?" He tapped two fingers to the side of his head.

"My kitten." Each word took considerable effort to voice, and the morning's grit hadn't quite left my throat.

"Is dealt with." Three words, and not one of them gave me a clear answer as to what he'd meant by that.

Though I could guess what kind of thing a cutthroat would do. The fire kindling inside me flared to something terrible. A rage that could turn black iron the red of blood and a yellow inn to ashen gray.

I lashed out without any care for my own well-being, or a thought to how foolish that action had been. My palm struck the would-be killer's arm, batting it and the knife aside. I sprung up from my bed, a sparrow's fear and fury sparking full and sending me to attack.

I leapt at him, raking the air with a clawed hand. The blow would have taken him across the face, digging my nails into his flesh even with the garment protecting his skin.

Only if it had gone the way I'd intended. The strike never reached the man. He moved as shadow in night—gone from sight as if never there at all. Something crashed hard against my temple, driving a line of whiteness through my world.

I staggered, regaining my balance a moment later.

A crude shovel of flesh and bone struck my throat, driving the scream to come scattering from my mouth into a wet choking cough. The base of a fist slammed into the soft spot beneath my sternum, wringing all the air from my lungs.

I wheezed and collapsed against the edge of my bedframe.

And the blade returned to where it had rested not so long ago.

"*Tch. Tch.* Clever. Not smart." A disappointed sigh.

This time, I did not struggle.

"Do not move. Do not try to leave. No more cleverness . . . *ji* . . . *ah*?" He'd paused twice in giving the command.

He has to pause to think about saying ji ah? A sign that Brahmthi might not have been his native language, never mind how he spoke the Trader's Tongue. Then the rest fell into place. He had an accent I'd heard before, but I couldn't quite place it. Familiar, but different.

"*Ji ah?*"

The repeated question snapped me out of my thoughtful reverie. "*Ji.*"

He pulled the knife away from me, moving toward my desk and the lone candle set there. The shadow-cast stranger moved their hand just above the wick—

then whipped it fast the opposite way. The fingers brushed along the tip of the wick, or so it looked.

Something scraped. A crack like breaking twigs. Then came a hiss and soon a flash. A flame kindled in place and the candle's warm glow spread throughout the room.

I winced against the sudden light, my eyes sewing themselves shut. My mouth, however, did not commit itself to closing. A difficult thing for me even in the worst of times. "How did you do that?"

"Ah, ah. We are not to be talking of my secrets. We are here for yours."

I kept the scowl from my face.

He pulled away from me, having made the point at the end of his knife. He could best me any moment he pleased and my life rested utterly in his hands.

The only thing I did not understand was: Why not be done with it already? If Nitham had hired someone as skilled as this, why drag it out? He could have killed me in my sleep and left no one the wiser as to who or how it had happened. Nitham would have had his revenge with nothing implicating him at all. The perfect crime.

The stranger pointed the tip of his blade in the direction of my door.

I followed the action, squinting as my eyes hadn't quite adjusted yet.

A sack rested against the door. "Rested" may have been the wrong word. It sat there, but thrashed as if possessed . . . or something living had been stuffed inside.

"Shola!"

"*Tsst!*" The knifeman raised a finger to his mouth. "Your kitten is alive and well. His mouth has been bound to keep him from crying out, but he is fine."

Cool rationale washed out the fire that'd burned inside me. A sigh of relief left me and I found myself as tired as I'd been in the moments when waking.

"Good. Good. Now, back to your bed and all will be well."

I couldn't argue with the man, so I did as instructed, clambering onto my mattress.

He produced a small satchel that had been hanging over his back, undoing its flap and reaching inside to pull something from it.

A box.

One I had seen twice before.

He passed it to me.

I took it in both hands, undoing the twine wrapping to open it up. But I had already known what I would find inside.

The contents caught the candlelight and glowed the gold of treasure. Fake, as the coins before had been. A dead sparrow rested atop, and I prodded its beak to get the pip inside. Once I had, I held it up between my thumb and forefinger, letting the black-clad killer view it as well.

"Time is up, little one."

I arched a brow.

"Keep digging." He could have simply told me, but I suppose even murderers have an appreciation for theatricality and the art of building suspense. Though they had utterly shit timing in when to employ it.

But, given my situation, I felt it best not to enlighten him to that particular fact, and did as instructed. The coins parted as I dug around and eventually my fingers brushed against something sharp and flat. I pinched and pulled, drawing out a folded piece of parchment.

A letter.

I didn't need telling in what to do next. The message fell open as I ran my thumbs along the creased edges.

Ari.

I promised you a full year for your adventure and studies. You have had half of that already. I have need of you now, and you are in no position to deny my request. You have robbed me, and you will fulfill your promise to pay me back in kind. I am altering the deal, pray I do not alter it any further.

You will make your way to me. To Zibrath. I will find you there.

If you do not do as told, I will find your family. You will be sent the remains of every sparrow. Then I will find you myself.

Arfan, a robbed merchant king

Well, it looked as if the best bit of theatricality had been saved for last. The boxes, sparrows, and the false gold coins. But I couldn't wholly appreciate the long game and effort considering the cost . . . and at whose expense it'd been played, or would be depending on what happened next.

And in all my blindness and rage—however justified—I had suspected Nitham. Though, with the timing of the first box and the cutters on the street, something he'd all but admitted to, who else could I have thought of?

A young man's hatred is a terrible thing, driving reason from him. And I was a young and terrible man at times.

I finally found breath and sucked one down, trying to still my hammering heart. "Arfan." Everything that had happened since had nearly driven away all memory of the desert king and what I'd done to him. Including the deal I'd struck to spare my family—to change their lives for the better. I looked back up to the knifeman. "So . . . you're not here to kill me?"

He said nothing.

"I suppose if you were, you'd have done it by now."

Still shining the smile in his eyes.

"So why this—all the games. Why not just tell me true from the start what Arfan wanted?" I waggled the parchment in his direction, though I had no intention of turning away Arfan's demand. Not at the cost of my family. Nitham may not have been able to exercise royal power in Abhar according to Aram, but that said nothing about a man with the money to rival kings, and no concern for their laws.

The man in black bared his teeth. "I have been watching you on *Mejai* Arfan's request, and for his coin. I have seen you, learned you. You are brash, and stubborn. Arfan knows this too. You would try to find a clever way out from under his thumb. And you would not be the first to try."

Meaning Arfan's press-ganged others into his service?

"And so, little cub, this." He pointed to the box. "To make a point. To let you know you cannot hide from me. You cannot even see me should I wish it so. Yet I can reach you.

"If you run, we will send shadows like me to find your little birds. Then this knife will find other throats in the night. And in the morning, there will be no sparrows left to sing. When that is done, he will send you what pieces of them he wishes." Something in his eyes looked to glow brighter then, as if the smile he wore under the veil grew wider. "And then I will come back for you. I will find you. And we will see how brave and clever you are then."

His hand blurred again. Something *cracked* against my floor. A pungent odor filled the air just as smoke and ash plumed in the space between us.

I raised my blanket to shield me from the cloud of acrid fog, but it dissipated soon after, leaving only the smell.

The man in the shadows had gone like a dream on waking.

I searched my room for the space of ten long breaths, not quite sold on the fact I was now alone.

The bag against the door lurched to one side.

Shola.

I jumped from my bed and quickly reached the sack, opening it and freeing my kitten. His claws had caught against the lip of the bag and he refused to let go. One of the sharp nails raked my hand and I bit back a curse. The man had tied a thick wad of knotted twine into a crude gag, binding it to Shola's mouth. I saved him from that as well, clutching him close to my chest for a moment.

I rocked him gently for a time then, hoping the gentle motion would help soothe him. Once he'd properly settled, I returned to my bed and stared at the parchment until my gaze could have bored holes through it. Pale winter's light filtered through the window and cast a soft warmth through my room. All it served to truly do was make Arfan's writing stand out better. And the threat within.

Leave the Ashram or condemn my family to die.

Well, that wasn't a difficult choice for me.

Rishi Ibrahm had been right.

It was time for me to leave the Ashram, and face the knife from my past.

FORTY-ONE

PREPARATIONS

I wasted no time that morning thinking over all that had happened through the season. The many mistakes I'd made, and their consequences. But one thing had become clear: I had to leave the Ashram.

Maathi had advised me to do that. And Rishi Ibrahm had suggested a sojourn could help me in learning the bindings. Though, as with many things, he failed to be perfectly clear on just how a trip would help. So why didn't I heed them earlier?

For the same reason many a young man fails to listen to good advice. He simply cannot see it for what it is. And as I've grown older, I realize the same can be said of adults. We often don't know what is best for us until well after the fact.

But I did know this: By staying, I was endangering the sparrows, and that was *not* something I would ever do again. And there was something else.

The Ashura.

I had learned less about them than I'd have liked since coming to the Ashram—the only time even a hint of them had come my way had been my journey to Ampur. Another reason then to leave. At least, that is what I convinced myself of.

Resolved, I packed my coinpurse and coaxed Shola into my travel sack, leaving my white cloak behind. My first stop was a cross section of streets in Ghal well known for drawing traveling tinkers passing through.

Though, I had hoped to find one in particular.

I reached the spot, hands in my pockets. One of them clutched to my own purse, the other brushed along a lone gold rupai I'd kept. Today would be the day I chose to break it and get what I could out of Nitham's unintended generosity.

Low whispers, all carrying my favorite thing—rumors—reached my ears. An elderly man spoke of not seeing the ghost for a few days. A woman cursed the mysterious figure in white, condemning him to the fires of hell. I was trouble after all. And she thought me an Ashura. The man at her side dismissed that on account of the coins I'd given away.

Another passerby chimed in, asserting that I'd taken the coin from the kuthri. What else justified the amount I'd had?

And the gossiping continued. Some asserting that, like the Ashura, my motives had no real rhyme or reason. I was a ghost, of course. And the dead do what they do for knowings all their own.

Eventually, I turned my mind from the noise labeling me hero to demon, hoping only to find Pathar.

I waited for nearly a third of a candlemark before a few shouts from folks broke into the air.

"Tinker!"

"Tinker-tinker."

"Hoya, tinker coming."

I whirled fast enough to risk twisting an ankle as much as my torso, heart racing at the sudden fortune. But my excitement fell as I saw the bulls pulling the wagon home.

Their horns had been filed into rounded tips and were only half as long as the ones who led Pathar along. The whorls painted along them were not red, but a blue shy of sapphires. No beads decorated them. And the wagon home behind had been fashioned out of a wood burnt black by the looks of it. It held no shine in its color, more the dryness of ash.

"Tinker, tinker, bottle-cork and comb. Tinker, tinker, knives anew, pots for home. Tinker, tinker, paddle-jacks, copper-draws, gimgracks, and even geegaws! Come look, come look. Have wonders aplenty, something for all, spendthrift and wealthy! Tinker, tinker!" The moving salesman stood on the carriage seat, sending his cry as far as he could from between cupped hands.

The man could have been carved from the same wood as his home—a dark dry color to him and all of hard, knotted muscle close to the bone. His clothes hung from him so loosely, I didn't know if he could never find a belt tight enough to hold them close, or if he used the extra space to sneak more goods onto his person.

A shock of white hair, thin and blowing like dandelion fluff in spring, stood straight up from his head. It must have gone prematurely white given that I could not find a single line along the man's face, or speckling of gray thread anywhere else on him.

He caught me staring. "What's this? A little young man wanting to trade?" When I said nothing, he eyed me as if unsure whether I was deaf, daft, or dumb. "What's the matter? Never seen a *gadia lohar* before? You a shut-in? We're everywhere, boy-a."

I nodded and shook out of my surprise. "I've seen tinkers before. I rode with one a while back, in fact. I just . . . I was expecting someone else is all."

His mouth opened into a silent *ah* seeing my disappointment. "S'no worry, that. You've got another tinker you're wishing to see. It's a known thing 'mong our people. True-true. But, don't go thinking he's the only one who can do something for you. I've got trinkets aplenty in my packs and home. Surely-sure as can be, I've got what a young boy can hope to hope for and have in hand. Promise!" He put a hand to the space above his throat.

"Brahm burn my rump if I tell one spot o' lie." He then pinched his own bottom and yelped in mock surprise as if someone else had been responsible for the action. The silliness drew a smattering of laughs from those gathered around.

But not me.

He caught that. "What's the matter, boy-a? Someone steal your joy? I got something for that too—true-true!" He rummaged through one of the bags hanging from the side of the seat first. "Mm, no. That won't do. That neither."

I ignored him and moved to the side of the wagon home, glancing over the bars and knobs fixed to it. They read: *Bad business westward-ho. Bound easterly and northernly. Sadness. Sorrow. Mourning.*

Mourning. He'd lost someone. *One of the family?* That brought a cold spark into my gut and sent me running back to the front of the cart. "Tinker!"

"Oh-ho, back as quick as that? Told you, told you. Tinker's always have—"

"What happened out west?"

His bushy brows climbed at that. "What are you—"

I pointed to the side of his wagon and the secret script along it. "The message. I can read Traveler's Tongue. It says 'mourning.' Who died?"

His eyes now widened to owlish proportions and he stroked his clean-shaven chin. He was surprised by my understanding of the language, and prodded me about it. It was a short explanation as soon as I mentioned Pathar's name. He'd heard the story of Ampur, of course. Then he told me what happened in the sands beyond Zibrath. A gathering of tinkers had fallen under an awful storm that should never have happened in the desert. Come morning, every member of the traveling people had been slaughtered. Man and wife, mounts to children.

He told the story with white-knuckled fury, hands clenched hard.

Young faces found smiling in the grip of death, bleeding from every orifice. And he said the still smoldering fires sent up smoke. Smoke the color of blood.

All the warmth fled from my body.

The Ashura? It couldn't have been. So far from the Mutri Empire? But why? A dozen other questions ran through my mind, but one look at the tinker's face told me not one of them would be welcome. Not so close to having lost his extended family.

But the signs spoke of the Ashura as far I could tell.

And if they had left the borders of the Mutri Empire, then my best bet in finding them lay out there in the wider world. I could use my travels and work for Arfan to also position myself to hunt the Ashura. Find out whatever I could about them and their tales in other countries.

Like how to kill them.

I dredged up what pain and empathy for him I could muster, and it was a great deal. For I knew that horror well myself.

He accepted my condolences and muttered the wish to have that tragedy undone.

But wishes were Shaen stories. No amount of them could turn back anything you had once foolishly asked for.

I turned the conversation elsewhere to help distance the tinker from the pains of memory. "I'm going on a trip, Tinker. A wise man once told me every traveler needs a candle, cloak, and cane. I've got the cloak, and a fine one at that."

The man eyed me askance, clearly noting the lack of that very item, and close to remarking on it.

But I raised a hand and went on. "But I would very much like to see your wares, if you happen to have a proper staff for a traveler."

He disappeared into his wagon home, returning with three staves under one of his arms.

The first held the color of polished coal—a black so deep it pulled the color from the other pieces around it. But it was too short for me by the look of it. More a true cane than the one I wished for in heart and mind.

The sort best suited for a binder. As much weapon as traveling tool.

The tinker gestured to the staves bundled under an arm, explaining that a woodsman had gotten the wood from one of the Laps of the world.

I blinked, unsure what he meant of that. "Laps?"

"Oh, *ji*. Never seen one myself, but they're true things. You mark it so—true!" He jabbed a finger into the air to accentuate that. "Some say they're the places between places, coming through only in the oddest of times. The spaces between the neat little folds of the world in Brahm's shapings . . . makings. Though, some don't like talking about that. Think it means Brahm's bindings weren't as tidy and neat as they'd expect from Him Above. But, odd things, the Laps. Odd things. Places of magic." He lunged along the driver's seat, thrusting the tips of the staves toward me. "Places of wonder! And that's what these are—things o' wonder!"

I bit a reply as well as the smile wanting to break along my face. Good show, better performance. But I knew an act when I saw one. And it wouldn't work to skin me for more coin than any of the pieces were worth.

Another of the staves was of white oak, but hadn't weathered its own making, much less time. A binder's cane of all hard edges, unwieldy to hold, and just as uncomfortable to the cup of a hand. Its head, a knotted-gnarled thing that would prove to be of no comfort in any man's hands, but would make for an excellent club.

Not the thing for me.

The last staff could have been the heart of fire—cooling orange coals given shape and brushed with the red from cherries. A wood that would hold a light under the sun's glow of warmth and fresh amber. Brown and red, and something in between. A beautiful blend of rich wood. Smooth in all the right places, swelling to a proper bulb of a tip I could hold in my hand perfectly, and use as a blunt weapon should I need it. It looked sturdy enough to take the strain of a long journey.

Perfect for a traveler. Better so for a binder. I'd found my cane.

"How much for that one?" I pointed to the piece I'd picked.

No quicker than that, the tinker tossed the other two back into his home and pushed the staff I'd wanted toward me. "Four coppers for such a pretty piece."

I nodded. "Add it to the lot."

That sent both of his brows back to the air. "Oh-ho. The lot, he says. The lot. Looks like I'll be doing tidy business today."

I gave him a smile that let him know I intended to do just that. "How about some candles, Tinker?"

He returned my grin and vanished, returning just as quick with offerings. The tinker furnished three tapers. "Ruby red—bright as blood and will burn the same! Red light's easier on the eyes, you know. It's true. Might—"

"N-no." The word broke halfway through my utterance. My breath caught in my throat, and I thought back to The Saffron House—to the burning of the understage. Dryness took my mouth and I shook my head instead.

He pursed his lips, but didn't bother pressing the point. He returned with another three of cleanest white. Simple, well made, and promised to burn long by the look of them.

They looked ordinary. The wax held a clean and good shine to it, even in the cold and pale light today. That told me they'd been done with a steady hand. No odd bubbles or cracks along their length. The wicks stood straight and true—no show of bending or fraying, and the freezing temperatures had not made them brittle.

"These'll catch with just the faintest of sparks. Now, I know that's a tall tale to tell, but not much needed to get these a-goin'. And then? They'll burn cleaner and longer than any other. Don't rightly know the trick of it myself, shame as it is to admit, but I've kindled some myself to test. And blacken me if it ain't true. Swear it to Brahm Himself. These are *magic* candles."

I swallowed a halfhearted laugh. In all the stories I'd heard, I'd never seen a truth to magic candles. Oh, surely it had been said a binder should never be without one. But the reality of magic candles was a Shaen story—wishful fancy. Still, I was in need, and I had little desire to dicker with a tinker when it wouldn't be my coin to break.

I thumbed Nitham's gold rupai and grinned. "I'll take them, but do you have any more than the three?"

He nodded and had them out before I'd finished my next breath, dangling two more sets. "Three threes! Lucky number that, three. If ever you're a wondering how much of something small to bring, count yourself all the luckier if you can have threes of threes. Hear me?"

I barely made sense of that, but nodded all the same. I hadn't heard much in the way of luck and threes, but with my preparations for my trip weighing heavily on my mind, I didn't want to waste too much more time. "I'll take them." I thought on the coin and just how much more I'd have to break this down into.

How would I even get to Zibrath? A ship? It'd be possible to cut along the sea between the Mutri Empire and Zibrath, but it'd mean having to go south almost as far as Abhar again—near my family.

A familiar knife went through my gut at the thought. So close to them. And if I wanted, I could check up on the sparrows, watch them . . . but never bring myself to face them. I didn't think I could bear that.

A shameful thing to admit, true. But sometimes the best thing for a wound to heal is to ignore it altogether. It might not be the wisest advice, or the kind man's path, but sometimes all we can do is ignore the pains we've wrought until they became a forgotten scar. The mark remains, but the worst of the hurt will be gone.

Or so we tell ourselves.

"I'd like to buy one last thing from you, if it's not too much trouble, Tinker?"

He showed me a toothy grin. It said everything was for sale, and for the right price, he'd give me the clothes off his back.

Well, I couldn't argue with that logic. And had no desire to bargain. After all, it's always easier to be generous when you're playing with someone else's money.

"How about a name . . . and a ride?" I pushed the gold piece toward him.

He smiled. His name was Tarsh, and it meant "good fortune."

An auspicious start to my journey ahead.

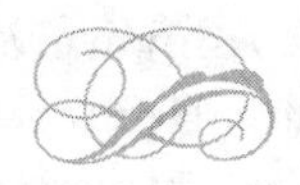

FORTY-TWO

A Brother's Farewell

I had never given the sparrows a proper goodbye. I'd elected to choose the coward's way out, I suppose. It had been a way to spare their hearts, I'd once told myself. But in truth, it had been a way to spare mine.

I owed another bird a better kind of farewell then. After all, he'd become my brother. And I, his.

And the bond between brothers is not easily discarded. Nor made. It requires hard sacrifices, and harder truths. Like telling them you have to go away, and leaving them alone once again.

Even after you promised you wouldn't do such a thing. . . .

"You's leavin'?" Sham sniffed, a thin trail of mucus slipping back up into his nostril.

I opened my mouth to reassure him somehow, but he didn't give me the chance.

"Is it cuz o' the cloak? Runnin' 'round like the ghost that night? Is my letterin' bad?" He blinked several times, and I could see the wet sheen forming in his eyes.

Brahm's blood. I put both hands on his shoulders, then cupped his face. "No, Sham. It's not that at all. I promise."

He sniffed again. "Then why do you want to leave me?"

I had suffered knives that hurt less than that question. "I don't, Sham. I *have* to." I explained the situation of the sparrows, and my debt to Arfan. Not an easy thing to tell a young boy. Especially when he realized I was choosing one family over another, in a sort of way.

But if I didn't do that, I wouldn't be the Ari he'd come to know, and the one who'd tried to be there for him.

"Will you come back?" he asked, and the mucus returned as he did.

What could I say? The truth of the matter was: I didn't know. But that is not what he needed to hear from his big brother. He feared for me, and sometimes all we can do is quell a little boy's fears.

Even if it's a lie.

So I reminded him that I was The Ghost of Ghal after all. And he of course knew the story of Ampur, and how I'd slain the mighty Nagh. Brought down the mountain low!

Battled an old god, and survived the Ashura twice. I called fire—bound it by breath and will to burn across the Ashram grounds.

But that wasn't enough for Sham. He needed a promise. His way of showing it was throwing the whole of his weight against me, and holding me with such ferocity I thought he'd never let go.

We didn't need words then. They couldn't say what either of us already knew had passed between us unspoken.

He prayed his big brother would come back, because he was just a boy—alone. And so many of us seldom ever get to be young. For life often finds a way to steal the child from us and force us to be the man well before we are ever ready for it.

Such is the way of things.

But I promised him I'd return, and that while The Ghost of Ghal was away, The Crow should learn to play.

He smiled at that. And the tears were gone.

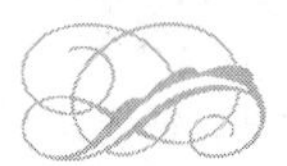

FORTY-THREE

Last Lessons

Master Binder paced in a small circle around his lectern, muttering to himself. His patchwork robe, holding all the colors of a forest in full-spring bloom, and just as much in autumn's hold, fluttered behind him in an unseen wind today. Probably from the speed at which he walked.

Seeing it move that way, with its torn sleeves, made me think of it less a robe, in truth, and more a poor man's cloak. He spotted me descending the stairs and shook his head, returning to whatever he'd been saying under his breath.

I stopped once I'd reached a space just outside of his reach. "Rishi Ibrahm?"

"Too soon. It hasn't settled yet." He spoke to himself, ignoring me completely.

I waited as he continued pacing, grumbling quieter under his breath. When more time passed and he showed no sign of recognizing me, I cleared my throat. "Rishi Ibrahm?"

"Hm—oh, you, right. What is it?"

"I'm leaving the Ashram, Rishi Ibrahm. I'm going to see some of the world like you suggested." I left out the part of Arfan's hold over me, and the sparrows.

He threw his arms wide and blew out a heavy sigh of relief. "*Finally.* Brahm be praised, the little upstart's seen the light." Master Binder leaned forward and rapped his knuckles hard against my forehead. "Dear me, is it ever hard enough to get a thought through this particularly hard coconut. Though, eventually . . ." He banged the joints against my head again. "Result!"

I took a step back and eyed him. "Right. Erhm. I wanted to talk to you before leaving."

He blinked as if unsure why I'd ever want that, then proceeded to make shooing motions. "Oh, no need. Go. Go. By my soul itself, our lives will all be easier if you leave now." He gave me a wide grin.

I frowned in return.

"What do you want to talk about?"

The rapid turnabout in the conversation left me wordless. "I . . . uh."

"You, uh? Well, with conversational skills like that, it'll be a long time before there's a lady witless enough to bother taking the time to teach you what's what. How are we ever going to get this boy's true fire going, ah?" He aimed that question up to the sky itself, looking in the direction of the sun.

I took a steadying breath. "I wanted to thank you too, I suppose, for the story about Tarun."

"Ah, stories." That seemed to bring him back from wherever the madman had gone in his mind. "Stories, Ari. I've told you about those, *ji*? The shape of names and such? The little pieces all stories themselves. Just fragments of it all. But, if you want some help as to the bindings, might I consider chasing those while you're out there—stories, *ji ah*?"

I nodded.

"Good, then let me give you some more advice, as you are remarkably thick of skull, so much so that I wager the Artisanry could use bits of your noggin to shape something stronger than steel. Wouldn't surprise me one bit."

I ground my teeth hard enough to chip them.

"You're not going to get any closer to learning how to perform any of the bindings by sitting in classrooms and looking at books, Ari. You need to wander, grow, think new things, and have your coconut rattled a bit." He rapped his knuckles on my head yet again. "See new places and learn new names for things you thought you already knew of.

"A name is a story, Ari. A piece of one, but has a story all its own, and is tied into the greater stories out there. Of a person, of a history, a world. But they're still pieces. If you want the truth to a story, start there, then dig deeper. Learn to Listen to stories, tear them apart, and find the meat of them. Most people are idiots, even the most avid of story readers. They never learn to read anything more than just the lines on the page, and so miss what's written between them, and lose out on the secret stories within. Sometimes in Listening to one story, you'll come to see the truths and secrets of another. Do you hear me?"

I did, but not wholly for the reasons you'd expect. Whatever crazed light filled Rishi Ibrahm's eyes moments before had faded. The set of his jaw and stare spoke of something intentional, hard, and sharp as bottle glass. He spoke with pure, controlled sanity.

And that more than anything brought me to attention. And maybe a little fear as well.

I nodded, not trusting myself to say anything else.

"It's all about stories, Ari." He broke off just before saying something else, then began again, though the touch of his voice told me the words were not meant for me. Such a hushed whisper, but I caught it nonetheless. "Sometimes it's just the same story. Over and over again. All the pieces scattered. Playing out the same way. Even when you push the pieces." He sighed.

"Yes, Rishi." I didn't know how else to reply, but offered a comforting agreement. The hint of oddity took his face again, making it clear the moment of lucidity had come and gone. A binder's curse. It took a slightly cracked mind, from my point of view, to truly understand the bindings.

Then, he did something so out of character I froze in body, mind, and heart. Rishi Ibrahm reached out and wrapped me in his arms, pulling me close. "When you go, remember this: Be ever wary of black sands. Beware the fhaalds on a moon-full sunny night. And a promise made in foolish love."

My mouth fell open and I settled for nodding as we broke the hug.

He patted me on the shoulders. "Good. Good. Now, before you leave, would you like to play a little game?"

The odd glimmer in his eyes made it clear I shouldn't refuse.

I walked up to the amphitheater, taking position near the middle rows.

Rishi Ibrahm stood below, bouncing three stones in the palm of a hand. Each looked to be close to the size of an eye. And each promised to deliver a good bit of pain if they struck soft flesh.

It didn't take much guessing to know what Master Binder had in mind.

"All right, Ari. Here's the trick. I'm going to throw these stones at you and bind them to pelt your coconut and see what shakes loose. Your job is to stop me." He bounced the stones again. "You're familiar with the game." His wrist snapped. The trio of rocks took to the air.

I fell into the folds. Two became four, but I knew it would not be enough.

Each held a muddled image, like dust swirled in water, of the stones falling to my sides without touching me. The rocks reached their apogee now, soon to hurtle down toward my skull.

Four folds to eight. I struggled. My mind felt leaden heavy and mixed with wet clay. No thoughts would form. No clarity could be found.

His binding caught and the stones sailed toward me. Their speed redoubled.

Twelve folds. I could do that much. The stones would fall away. I held the vision of their passing several dozen feet from me. They would have to sail through the point imagined.

And so I was right.

They struck the unseen space before me, and a mountain of weight came with them. It battered me and the folds I held, threatening to shatter the multifaceted lenses as if they were nothing but poor glass against stone's blow. I shook, more inside than in actuality.

The force rattled me. A burning breath billowed inside, wanting to cry and break loose in pained exertion. But I swallowed it back—held it like the hot air of a kettle, better serving to bring me to a faster boil. The pain—anger, offered a lucidity that pushed away the slowness of my mind.

I seized it, and held the folds against the weight. And it lessened.

The stones did not continue their original path, nor did they come to strike me. They rained down from where they'd hung as if dropped from that spot first and alone. I listened to them clatter—three beads of ice-hard hail against the ground below.

The effort brought me to my knees. Invisible hands worked and wrung my lungs like towels that had long been squeezed of any moisture, but still, they persisted. I sucked down ragged breaths.

"Throw them back, if you'd please." Rishi Ibrahm's command came calm and measured.

I found enough strength to scrabble to where the stones had fallen, and sent them hurtling in return.

His mouth moved. He muttered something. And the stones changed paths, careening toward his outstretched hand. A flick of the wrist and the rocks went back to the air. "Quick, Ari. Quickly now. Or so, as above, so below. These'll come down, and deal you a mighty blow!"

As above. So below. The words ran through my mind. Again. And again. I repeated them, a mantra. I spotted the point above that the rocks would inevitably reach, fixing that spot in mind as where I should expect my folds to hold and contend Rishi Ibrahm's binding. This time, I came ready.

I leapt to twelve folds faster than before, then pushed to sixteen. I knew he wouldn't go as easy as before. *Easy.* He'd nearly flattened me with just the weight of his will.

It had been some time since I practiced this exercise in earnest. And perhaps I'd grown slow in conjuring the folds over the season. But I remembered when Rishi Ibrahm tried this against me before I'd been raised to Kaethar, and how I'd stopped the stones most of the time. I remembered Mahrab's words. The lessons. And I remembered the names of the bindings.

Tak and roh.

I watched the stones, then brought new folds to life. Not just brushing aside their path in my mind—no. Now I chose where they'd fall, and how. "Tak." It left me in a whisper. The stones struck the point I'd envisioned. Our wills met, but this time his came a gentle ocean swell against the bedrock of a mountain. I'd barely felt it. *A trick?* "Roh." I bid the stones to fall where I'd hoped.

They did not, and my binding never took. Nor did my folds truly hold. Something was wrong.

The stones passed through as if I hadn't tried to alter their path at all, but they did not hurtle down against my skull. They merely went on their own way, landing over my shoulder, to the side of my head, and one skittered to a halt just before my feet.

For a moment, all I could do was stare in useless effort to glean what had happened.

"Confused?" Rishi Ibrahm didn't quite have a smile on his face, but the lines creasing his cheeks told me he wore one inside.

I retrieved the stones, taking my time to throw each back. Then I nodded to answer his question.

"You tried to match my will against my binding. Good. You could have just stopped the stones like last time, even if you can't manage the binding yourself. But then you tried to take control of them, thinking my binding would be weak after your contention, *ji*?"

I bowed my head again, doing my best to pay attention.

"Good idea. But the bindings are more than just the folds, Ari. Belief. *Belief.* Did you believe, utterly, without fail, that you could take command of the stones above and bid them down to where you wished? Not want for. Not demand or desire. Believed. Believed it as naturally as you draw breath?"

I shook my head. I hadn't even thought about that. I simply imagined the path I desired—and the outcome.

Rishi Ibrahm seemed to know what I'd been thinking without me telling him so. "Sometimes it takes great stress to make a man believe. It's when he has nothing left but death, and a world of fear, that he's given no chance but to have faith in the most maddening of things. But that kind of belief comes with a toll as much as power. You are not in control, then. Your feelings control you. Will you bind? Yes. But those beliefs and feelings will come to shape you more than you them. And what happens when your beliefs dictate who you are, and how you see the world, more than you them?"

I didn't have to think long and hard about that one. The answer lay in the Crow's Nest.

I suppressed a shiver at that. "I understand, Rishi."

He said nothing, tilting his head to regard me. "When you leave, take some time to look around the world, eh? The leaves. The birds. Look up as much as you do around. Then take some time looking down. It'll do you wonders to see all that you've missed with your head stuck in dreams and on fires. There is a gentle flow to all things that you've missed seeing." The stones leapt into the air again.

I had anticipated that. My mind tripped into a dozen folds. More partitions formed and I held sixteen now. Eighteen. Twenty, an old ease, now came slightly slower, but was there all the same. I held them, watching the stones meet the wall I'd set in my mind. They struck, only with a force I had no way to describe.

Or weather.

Rishi Ibrahm's will hit me like a hurricane in full force, and I stood the lone crippled oak before it. My bark was battered, beaten, and chipped away by axe, time, and storm. There was no resistance. No moment of contention where we bashed minds and tried to stave off the other's pressure. No. This was a wave to take a ship whole below and leave nothing behind. The hand of god himself come down to smack something as insignificant as an ant.

My folds didn't break so much as they reduced to fine crystalline dust, shimmerant flecks scattered to nothingness. For a moment, I stood still—silent—empty—free of all thought, until the first impact against my head.

The stone struck—sharp and heavy. Then the next. And finally, the third. I reeled, one hand going to my head to assuage the pain.

"How are you feeling, eh?"

My eyes hadn't returned to proper focus, still seeing the world through a muddy film. I didn't know if it was from the trio of impacts, or the absolute thrashing of mind I'd taken from Rishi Ibrahm's will. Possibly both.

I made an incoherent sound that could have passed for speech . . . among a populace just learning to string together guttural noises.

Rishi Ibrahm laughed. "Not so sure of ourselves now, are we? Twenty folds, though. Well done. It'll be a thing to see when you can push yourself further than that."

Some semblance of clear-headedness returned to me. Enough to really understand what he'd said. "How many did you just pit against me, Rishi?"

He grinned, wider than before. "That's the trick, isn't it? Let me know when you figure it out, eh?"

The man had stampeded over my will, with me nothing more than the grist on the road, kicked up and away in the beast's wake. How many folds would it have taken to utterly trounce me like that, or could it have been nothing more than the strength behind each one? Was that even possible?

I shook the thoughts from my head as I realized our little game had concluded. And it had been painfully obvious I had been a world away from ever winning. Still, I'd learned something else over my time with Rishi Ibrahm. Gratitude. Even if a little bit.

So I gave him some in return. "Thanks for the lesson, even after it's left me sore." I rubbed my head and made my way over to him, extending a hand.

The smile plastered on his face belonged more to a young boy, too full of honest excitement at good news, than a fully grown man. But it suited him. He met my hand with his and shook hard. "You haven't even begun to see the lessons yet, my boy. But you will. Now, get out of here."

I turned and followed his advice. Without complaint, for once.

I *can* learn.

"Oh, and Ari?"

I turned halfway to regard him. "Yes, Rishi?"

"Best of luck, Ari. Don't die. It's fatal. And if you happen to fall to a horribly gruesome death, don't bother coming back! We wouldn't want to put up with you after that. Some things should remain beyond the Doors of Death."

Unsure of how to respond, I left in silence instead.

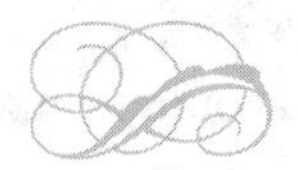

FORTY-FOUR

An Easy Bargain

Aram and Radi had asked around for my whereabouts, coming to wait outside the classroom. They were deep in conversation when I came out, and I told them my situation.

"Oh, Brahm's blood, Ari." Aram barely breathed the words. "You can't leave. If you don't show mastery, or some level of control with the bindings by year's end . . ." She didn't have to finish the statement.

She was right in a way, but if I didn't leave, the sparrows would be in danger from Arfan. It was my fault, after all. And I couldn't linger too much in thought on my old family, for all that would do is wring more pain from my heart, and in truth, I felt I'd hurt enough today.

I didn't want my friends seeing me a mess. A foolish thing, I know. For what else are friends for if not to take you as you are, without fear of recrimination, and to let you break as need be, because they will help you put yourself back together again. And all without a word as to what has happened. What you've done.

Still, I chose not to make them share in that grief. Not then.

And I learned to put on the first of my many masks that day. "I'll be fine. And I'll learn the bindings out on the wide roads of the world, just you wait and see." I let out a stage laugh—something practiced to go rolling down the halls and catch the ears of all. "It's me. What haven't I survived?"

Radi, performer that he was, caught on to my act. He flashed me a tight-lidded look, daggers behind slits, but he laughed aloud with me. "I mean, he's got a point, Aram. The lucky bastard's survived himself, and that's no small feat given the trouble he's prone to getting into."

That pulled a childish giggle out of Aram we rarely saw. She'd been so serious this season, so focused on studies. In that moment, she looked very much the happy youth.

For that, I loved Radi even more. He was able to do what I couldn't and set her better at ease. I may have come to be a famous performer in my own right, but much of what I've learned can be said to have come from him. And there will always be a space in my heart for Radi because of it.

In the end, both my friends embraced me in the way only the closest of hearts could.

And I walked to the one place I could think to help settle my heart before the journey. A place of stories.

The Scriptory.

I gazed through countless books, coming across the dangers out along the Golden Road: Raaga, singing shapeshifting demons that devoured men and wore their flesh as masks. Jahil, mischievous trickster spirits, tempting to lure men off course and into the sands never to be seen again. Qirin, fresh terrors of the night from beyond a place yet seen, slinking into the minds of men to haunt their dreams. And, of course, ghuls, ravenous half-men beasts that feed on the bones of the dead.

Shaen stories, the lot of it. Nonsense.

You thought the Ashura were stories once too. "And now I have to find them." The words left me without thought.

"Have to do what, Kaethar Ari?" The voice pulled me from my thoughts.

I turned in my seat, the promise of sweat breaking out along my neck as I realized who'd spoken.

Rishi Saira stood behind me, looking down her nose through a pair of wire-rimmed spectacles I'd never seen her wear before. The frames were drawn from thin gold. Their lenses, glass so thin they could have been pulled from a drop of clear water. Along with her hooked birdlike nose, they lent her an appearance more owlish than the hawk I'd thought of before.

Her skin had paled just a touch under the winter dreary, losing some of the bronze of her complexion. But what I noticed most of all was the lack of her traditional robe.

Every one of the masters save for Rishi Ibrahm, an oddity in so many ways he couldn't be used as a practical measure for anything, wore robes of black. But now she wore robes that resembled the headmaster's—garb bright as fresh powder snow, and closer to a cloak. Thin, with a hood along the back.

She caught me staring and gave a polite smile. "I suppose I can appreciate the curiosity. After all, this is a place for that."

Master Lorist leaned forward to peer at what I'd been looking over. "Mm. Interesting." Whatever opinion she held, though, remained between her teeth. She turned the conversation back to her clothing. "My master's robes are all in the wash. I've spent too much time of late in the underholds, storing and cataloging older works and those needing special care or treatments. I ended up covered in dust and smells no one would ever want on them. I must have changed through a set's worth of robes in days. All I had left were my headmaster's clothes."

I blinked several times. "You were headmaster?"

The smile now turned a tad coy, belonging more to a young girl of thirteen than the Master Lorist. "Once. Many years ago. It was after Rishi Ibrahm turned away from the post and Master Spiritualist still dithered around in his work. Davram, I think, still wishes he could be a student more than headmaster. Even a rishi's position left him little time for his pursuits. It's another reason why I eventually left the role as well. I had to return to my work here."

I eyed one of the books tucked under her arm. *Ashir ki Nayath.* Not Brahmthi, but Brahmki, and an old enough version that I had no hope of translating it. She caught my look, however.

"Another book destined for the underholds. It's sat so long and collected dust enough to keep the pages shut. I'm going to have to carefully clean this and get it back to usable order." She turned so that some of the folds of her robes obscured the book before looking at me in particular. "Now, what was this about what you had to do, Kaethar Ari?"

I almost frowned, then thought better against it. Rishi Saira would hear about my leaving one way or another.

"I'm taking a break from my studies to travel abroad. Rishi Ibrahm advised me that it'd be good for my work with the bindings. To see the world, grow a bit."

Rishi Saira pursed her lips. "Is that so? And do you plan to return?"

I hadn't expected that question and my response caught in my throat. "Y-yes."

"Good. Then wait here a moment, Kaethar Ari. I have something for you." She turned to leave down a row of shelves.

Rishi Saira returned with a new book in hand, holding it as if it were made of glass and not thick leather and sturdy parchment. She passed it toward me and I took it, eyeing her.

I followed her gaze and read: *Sashra ta-tathan kahniye*. The translation didn't come quite as easily as I would have liked, but I managed. "*A Thousand Tales?*"

She smiled. "Close. *Tales of a Thousand and One Things*. The title isn't literal."

I nodded, understanding. "I don't think I'll have time to appreciate it, Master Lorist, but thank you." I pushed the book toward her, but she stayed me with an open hand.

"I'm not asking you to read it now. Take it with you on your journey."

My hands shook, and I could not find a single word to say. My uncharacteristic silence should have made very clear just how out of sorts this was.

Rishi Saira must have known this because she crossed her arms and gave me a level look. "It's a temporary loan, Kaethar Ari. I fully expect you to treasure this as well as you do your own life." A pause. Her lips pursed, and I could see her reconsidering the statement. "Well, perhaps better than that, given your proclivity for recklessness." A hint of a smile touched her lips, but it faded fast. "You will bring this back to me unscathed, or you will be set to painstakingly transcribing, binding, and finishing an entirely new copy. *Ji-ah?*"

I had already struck one bargain before, and it had come back with teeth in my neck to drag me away. I could ill afford another. Then again, the promise of so many stories. A younger Ari would have ached and given much for this. With a long journey ahead, I would certainly make the time to give the stories inside the love they deserved.

So it was an easy decision.

I placed the book in my lap, resting both my hands over it in a protective manner. "Thank you, Rishi Saira. I'll take good care of this."

She watched me from behind her full-moon spectacles. Finally, she nodded as if accepting my promise. "Good. I wish you safe travels, Kaethar Ari." Master Lorist turned and began to leave, then stopped. She turned far short of halfway, looking over a shoulder to me. "And if you come across any new and marvelous stories on your journey, I would very much like to hear them. Keep memory of them." And with that, she left.

I still had one last person to see before I ventured from the Ashram. Someone I'd long ago promised to keep visiting.

And I always make good on a promise.

FORTY-FIVE

LEAVE-GOINGS

I walked into the Crow's Nest to find Krisham standing before the table he usually rested at . . . or atop when sleeping.

He stood sideways, a new wooden sword held in his grip. His face was a tight mask of concentration as he stared down a shadow on the wall opposite him. But that's not what held my attention the most. He wore a knitted blue cap that I'd never seen before, and a pair of curving tails hung from its sides that fell to his ears.

"Uh, hi, Krisham."

He ignored me, focusing on his own shadow on the wall. Only, unlike him, the shadow did not hold to the same stillness he did.

"Brahm's blood. What—"

Krisham lunged, and his shadow moved in kind along the wall. The two met, swords point-to-point as he struck the stone. Sweat shone along the bronze of his skin and shape of his brow. He pulled away from where he'd struck and turned a half step, freezing when he noticed me. "Oh, hello."

I blinked. "Hi . . . again."

Krisham adopted my confused expression. "Again? Did we already meet today?"

"I, uh, no." I hooked a thumb over my shoulder, pointing to the doors I'd just come through. "I just came in and greeted you—"

"Then why did you say 'again'? Are you all right, Ari? You should go to the Mendery if you're not feeling good in the head." Krisham tapped two fingers against his skull. "Lots of people start to lose their wits when they pursue the bindings. Sometimes memory loss is a sign of that." Krisham's eyes widened in sudden realization. The sword fell free from his hold, clattering against the ground.

"My hat!" He spun about, looking for the very thing atop his head. "Nobody move."

I swallowed half a dozen curses, then a dozen more, before finally speaking. "It's on your head."

Krisham stopped and clapped both hands hard to his head in a way I feared might actually rattle what was left of his brains. He held on to the hat as if he expected it to escape. "Oh, good. Can't lose this. It was a gift, you know?"

I pressed my mouth tight and ignored the sudden buildup of sharp pressure just behind my eyes. A headache of monstrous proportion soon to come, surely. "It's a very nice hat, Krisham. Who gave it to you?"

"A princess. At least, that's what she said when I rescued her from a monster. A princess of the Zahinbahari." He watched me after saying that, waiting for some recognition on my face.

I had none.

"Oh, I forget. You haven't really seen much of the world, have you yet?"

I shook my head, and knew it best not to argue with someone who'd lost a good piece of their mind.

"May I finally see Immi? I want to talk to her if that's all right?"

Krisham sobered somewhat, retrieving his sword and slipping it through a loop on his breeches. "Sure, Rishi Ibrahm's allowing her visitors." He motioned with a hand.

I followed in tow as Krisham led the way up the stairs and to Immi's cell.

❧

The walls were stained red, and Immi sat before them, fingers twitching.

She'd relapsed?

I took a few steps, then stopped. What should I say? How bad had she been this whole time, all while I'd been running off playing a ghost, unable to visit. I should have forced my way past Krisham, should have tried a dozen other things, but she didn't give me time to linger in guilt.

Immi turned, staring at me like she would a stranger. "Ari?"

I nodded, mute.

Then she looked at the wall and comprehension dawned on her face. "Do you hate me?"

There is only so much pain a heart can take in so short a time, and I had begun to become acquainted with learning that limit. I rushed to her side, falling to my knees. "Gods no, Immi. Never. I . . ."

"Then why haven't you visited me? It's been since last winter—Radhvahni. I waited."

And I left you here, alone. I shut my eyes and took a deep breath. "I am so, *so* sorry, Immi. Believe me, I didn't want to." I fell into telling her everything that happened at the festival and after. Nitham. The fire. My probation and the roustings. Soon, she knew all of it including Arfan's hold over me.

"Wow, Ari, you are terrible mischief." She giggled when she said it though.

I beamed. "I am." My travel sack shook and Immi noticed. I smiled wider and opened it, a blur of orange bounding out of it.

A delighted peal of laughter followed as Immi lunged after Shola. But through that, I caught a better look at her face and saw what I'd overlooked. Thin lines and a dark coloring under her eyes. A hollowness.

I asked her about it.

"Bad sleeps. It's been hard," she said. "Ever since . . ."

"Nitham?" I shouldn't have asked.

Immi froze mid-motion, hand hanging just above Shola's head in an effort to pet him. "Please don't ask me about him. He's bad. You know too, because of what he's been doing to you. You should leave bad people alone, Ari. They only hurt you."

I nodded, and lied that I would. But what I heard in her voice was: *They hurt me.*

Nitham had harmed her. My friend. In a way I didn't quite understand yet, but I made a silent vow some day I would learn that truth. And I would get even.

But pure soul that she was, Immi had little care for thoughts of vengeance, or dark conversation. So soon we turned to other things. She set her hands right again in a display of binding that never ceased to amaze me.

Then I told her that I would be leaving.

Unlike Sham, she seemed to take this in better stead. "For how long?"

"I'm afraid I don't really know."

She pursed her lips and thought on that. "Are you really afraid, Ari?"

"I suppose I am."

A tiny hand gripped mine and squeezed with the strength stronger than my own. "Don't be afraid," she whispered. "I'll give a secret." And with that, Immi furnished a crumpled piece of paper, placing it in my other hand.

I arched a brow.

"Open it."

I did.

"I spent a lot of time thinking it up, Ari. It was really hard to make the rhymes and clues to teach you without ruining how they work. Part of using them is figuring them out for yourself, you know?" She folded a hand over mine and the paper. Her little gift to me.

> *"There are ten bindings all men must know.*
> *From top to bottom, all things must go.*
> *Ten bindings for the wise man with which to go about.*
> *To shape within, and so without.*
> *Ten bindings to help the wise man stand tall.*
> *To push back trouble. And be safe from all.*
> *Ten bindings for man to share.*
> *And carry him from here // to there.*
> *There are only eight bindings for man to choose.*
> *The last two are ones he ought never to use."*

"Thank you, Immi. I'll treasure this. And I'll use the bindings to keep the people I love safe, promise."

Immi squeezed my hand again. "I know. Ari's going to be like one of the Asir, hm? Protecting people all over the world." Her smile showed no hint of mockery behind it. A gentle, faithful thing. The smile of a friend who wholeheartedly believed I would keep to my word, and keep the ones I loved safe.

How could I let her down after that?

"And you promise you'll be back, and that you'll see me?" Her eyes widened, and they shone bright with hopeful want.

"I will." I grinned and squeezed her hand back. "And I promise to bring you back something wonderful as a gift—I'll find you a better star than the one you asked for last Radhvahni."

She smiled, then looked deep in thought, and came to some decision. "Do you want to practice like we used to, one last time before you go?"

It was a wise suggestion. And I agreed.

❧

I left the Crow's Nest half a candlemark later and ventured back down into Ghal.

Tarsh waited with his wagon just outside the trader's circle, a place where traveling merchants and visitors all bustled about, catching the city's newcomers and those departing. All manner of goods were flung, passed, and bought. And ten times as many voices carried across the circle. It was a place of pinwheeling colors—every one you could possibly imagine.

A place of sweat, perfumed oils, and furs.

Tarsh saw me approaching and waved a hand.

I raised my staff and returned the gesture.

"*Sahm,* please." The voice brought me to a stop and took my attention.

I looked down to see a young girl, maybe a year or two younger than me, huddled on the ground. Her robes once could have been a brilliant white, if they'd ever held that shade in her care, but had now taken on so much dirt and grime they were closer to ash.

The girl's boots were leather that had long since cracked and lost their dark luster, but would still keep the snow out. Her hair was dyed the color of dried blood. A patch covered one of her eyes, and the one that remained free was in poor shape.

Someone had introduced something heavy and blunt, by the looks of it, to her face. The makings of a plum and yellow bruise.

The shape of her face and the way she looked at me brought to light an old memory of a young girl I knew back when I lived under a stage. "Have I seen you before?"

She shook her head. "No, *sahm.*" Her voice shattered the illusion that I had ever known her. All my years listening in on the plays Khalim put on left me with a powerful recollection for voices. And hers was one I'd never heard before. "Spare anything? Even one chip is a great grace. Naathiya's blessing on you for what you can give. I can even tell you a piece of fortune, *sahm.* I've been gifted with sight."

I took one look at her again and very much doubted that. That claim had probably earned her the beating that'd left her one good eye bruised, and quite possibly cost her the patched eye altogether. But I knew the hardships of a life on the streets, and she'd said something that pulled another mercy out of me.

I had once been told Naathiya looked out for those who never caught the eyes of normal folk. The ones forgotten. Thieves and ne'er-do-wells. People who worked soft trades and in the dark. The beggars. But the goddess also shepherded the Asir. And I supposed a piece of kindness done in her name wouldn't hurt anyone.

I knelt, meeting the young girl in the eye, its color like warm cedar with bits of muted orange in them.

Few people ever truly look the unfortunate in the eyes when they speak with them. Always choosing instead to shy away from them, as if by avoiding sharing a gaze they can wash away their existence completely. And with that, the discomfort they feel.

One of the truest and easiest pieces of kindness you can ever give a hurting person is to let them know you see them. See them whole. See their hurt.

I reached into my purse and drew out one chip, then a copper. A piece of iron followed suit. Then I went to pull a silver dole, but her hand quickly clasped mine, folding my fingers over the coins.

"Please, *sahm,* nothing more. Too much and someone might notice." She whipped her head around, taking in the moving masses of the trader's circle.

I knew that fear, and the wariness of too much coin in your pocket. You never knew who was watching, and how keen their eyes were.

I sighed and pushed my hand toward her still, offering what passed as a small fortune to someone in her position. "At least take this. I can afford to give you that."

She shook her head. "Not for free, then. A trade."

I frowned. What could she possibly have to trade? But, if it would get her to take the coin, I wouldn't argue. "Fair enough. A trade."

The coins left my hand faster than I could have ever managed in the best of my sparrow's days. No sooner than they'd vanished, she produced something from within her robe. "This, first."

A candle. It had no base, just the lone length of wax. Its color was that of spring morning's sky. I turned it over in my grip, noticing a small imprint in its shape. It looked to be some sort of bird. Longer inspection showed it could have been an owl, or a squat and portly hawk. But I placed it into my sack and thanked her for it.

"And two more things." She pulled out something else, pressing it into my hands before I had a chance to look. "Not here. It will draw the wrong attention."

I nodded, and moved it to my bag as well, but I snuck a peek at it as I did so. A handle of black horn, shining as if freshly waxed and polished. The sheath a leather black as midnight drawn from ink. A blade of some kind rested within. She'd been right to warn me.

That would have drawn attention.

But still, I smiled to myself. This exchange reminded me of the old stories. The hero always meets someone just before departing who gives them special items for their quest. While these were nothing magical by any means, I allowed myself the illusion. I was young, and of course fancied myself the hero.

"And now for your piece of future. Stand amongst fhaalds when comes the time. They will lead you where you need to be. Don't fear the noose. And remember the power a story can hold."

"Right. Of course." I had no desire to offend the young girl, but as far as futures went, that was particularly unhelpful. So, gifts in hand, and goodly deed done, I backed away and walked to Tarsh.

I climbed up into the seat behind him and gave one last look to where the young woman had sat.

The place looked as empty as if no one had been there at all.

Tarsh caught me staring. "You fine, boy?"

I nodded my head. "Yeah. Let's get going, shall we?"

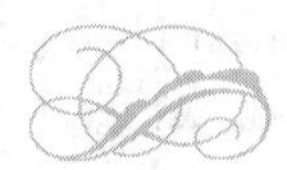

FORTY-SIX

The Journey West

Tarsh did not have as loose a tongue as Pathar. We talked less, though we did pass what gossip we gleaned along our stops. He did, on occasion, help me refine my understanding of the Traveler's Tongue. Eventually, I graduated to being able to speak it at a level Tarsh judged to be only mildly incoherent, rather than wholly incomprehensible.

Tiny victories.

The path Tarsh suggested carried us down toward Thamar, then to the port city of Summinth. From there I could book passage across the sea straight into Zibrath and save myself a great deal of time, and trouble.

I didn't explain my whole history with Nitham to the tinker, but made it clear that bringing me into that kingdom could stir up trouble Tarsh wanted no part of. I thought this would bother him, but the tinker merely shrugged it off.

If he couldn't travel to one place, he'd find us another route, and business was always good for a tinker quick of tongue and mind. So we rode the long way, skirting along Ghal's border westward, picking up tidbits of news along the way.

The royal family of Thamar sought to broker a marriage between one of its children and another from Abhar, thereby solidifying an alliance between them.

Merchants had been losing ships south of Emperor's Cradle to a group of pirates. Myrath, a country I knew so little of that I hadn't even known of its existence, had undergone a coup, and was under the leadership of a military general. And a group of bandits had begun raiding traveling parties through a desert whose name I had no hope of pronouncing.

All problems of the usual fare, and the people speaking of them seemed to have little care for news from far off.

True to Tarsh's words, we eventually crossed paths with a caravan heading west and south. They would travel to Tikhar, making their way into Koshtesh, and finally Zibrath. A long journey by road, but safe by all accounts.

And it would mean avoiding Thamar altogether.

I bid the tinker farewell and joined with the caravan.

It would be the first of many mistakes I'd make on the way to Zibrath.

The journey westward had as much drudgery as it did disaster and danger. And to fully share those with you would lose the heart of the true story, and what really matters.

The caravan drivers fell into heated debates on routes and schedules. Someone's wife insulted someone's son. This led to one man threatening her, which drew the full ire of that woman's husband. The caravans split, halving our collective resources, as well as our protection.

In short order: We were robbed by bandits, during which I miraculously managed to save Shola and my possessions, though not all of my coin. We were driven off the road by a traveling mercenary band, leaving us lost for some time.

And through it all, I added rather wonderfully to my already growing reputation. My white cloak, combined with all of my usual cleverness and skill in spinning stories, aided a great deal in this.

So I arrived eventually in Zibrath. Close to penniless, but at least holding to everything of import. Namely: Shola, all my belongings in my sack, my scaled cloak, my staff, the candles I'd bought and been gifted, and of course the knife. The latter of which sadly saw some use of the hard sort over the journey west.

It had taken me several months to arrive, and I hoped very much that Arfan had developed a great measure of patience in that time.

FORTY-SEVEN

Just Rewards

The trading city of Mubarath lay at the end of Zibrath. The first place of entry for those coming from the east by land, and as such, a haven of all delights. And the best vices you could hope to find. The influx of wealth and taxes on such made me feel reminiscent of my old home of Abhar. A comfort hung within its sandstone walls.

I passed through a large archway, admiring the nearly seamless shaping of the stonework, almost as if someone had formed it from a single block of clay than rock and mortar. The city looked to have been designed by a child who had a master's eye, but still kept to some youthful ignorance. By that I mean many buildings loomed next to one another, leaving narrow passages between, fit for only the slenderest of youths to slip through. Large portions of streets were cast into long shadows at certain times of day, and then other places had enough space between buildings that you could set up an entire trader's circle on the spot, only to whisk it away come evening.

And I loved Mubarath for it.

It had a liveliness—a dynamism. The kind of life only found in certain cities where anything was possible. Strings ran across homes to the windows of others and all manner of colorful clothing hung along them. Neighbors over the way would pull and pass bits along, mending things and shouting from windows any gossip or news. A few youths would linger atop flat roofs, flashing winks, and maybe, if they could sneak over to one's place, share a few kisses in the shade.

Colored kites took to the air, much like at home. Children at play, or old men passing candlemarks. They all enjoyed the simple pastime. And the familiarity of it brought me another layer of comfort despite being in a foreign country.

The road wasn't paved, and it had no need of it. The constant travel had beaten it smooth and flat to a point it barely kicked up any dust.

I walked on, keeping my sack tight in hand, and muttering sweet whispers to soothe Shola inside. The pack juddered twice, letting me know the cat had taken to batting against it out of bored discontent. "Relax, I'm hungry too. We'll find something soon enough. I've still got some coin on me. Worse comes, I can always clutch more."

A man teetered into the circle ahead, ignoring all the passersby. His skin held all the dark one's could, and a smoothness some would have killed for. A short brush of curling hair, as black as him, sprouted out from beneath his flower-shaped cap. He moved like he'd drunk a cup too much and had never quite learned how to work his legs. Dressed in robes of mustard yellow, he swirled like a top about to topple. Only, he didn't.

The man collapsed to one leg, quickly pirouetting and coming back to two feet. A small cone of brass appeared from out of his sleeve in a trick even I had to applaud him for. He tipped it to his lips and spoke. "Hanging! Hanging! Tricksters and deceivers. Malcontents and mischief makers. Troubles bought—now they're caught. Come see them get their penance. See the rewards of clever hands—not quite quick enough to escape the law! And the big heads of the little minds whom they belong to."

The man then took to walking in long exaggerated steps as if led by an invisible string.

Some of the crowd followed him. A few cries took the air.

"Hanging!"

"Already done with market, might as well."

"Haven't seen a good one in a while."

Through the crowd moved a small shape. The girl couldn't have been more than twelve, wearing a baggy shirt that hung to her thighs. The white of it had slowly shaded to road-dust brown. Probably years of dirt that had never properly washed out of the piece. She moved barefoot, slipping by with the ease of someone who'd long navigated this flow of traffic. One of her hands blurred and slapped a man's flank.

The passerby turned to look to his side but the girl had gone.

And a young boy moved in her wake, coming to the man's other side. Hands moved, steel flashed, and the purse tied to the man's waist came undone. The pair of children sank into the crowd, moving with the flow until they came out of it again, quickly breaking into a run the opposite way.

That brought a grin to my face. Even with a hanging set to happen, the children of the streets would not be deterred. The fact little thieves could be found here, too, came as another relief, horrible as that may sound.

After all, I will always be at home around thieves.

I walked on, deciding to follow the crowd and catch my first public execution. I'd done what I could to stay away from that sort of thing back in Abhar for all the obvious reasons. Then in Ghal, it simply had no appeal to me with my studies ongoing and being constantly on guard from Nitham's provocations.

The sound of strings carried into the air just as I reached another high archway. The music hung under the curved stone walls, almost as if favoring the place. And the notes carried a warm brightness and silver-high sharpness in them.

I turned to regard the source.

The girl looked like she was somewhere well into her teens, but not quite close to leaving them yet. Her hair had a color found in dark cherry wood. A brown that carried more the promise of red in it. She wore it down to her shoulders, the greater lengths of it kept from her face by the green sash tied around her head. The girl's features had been chiseled to a sharpness that gave her an angular beauty. And bright eyes of light amber only served to enhance that.

Her clothing, however, told another story.

A single long shift the color of night sky. Its hem showed a few loose threads and she wore no sandals or boots. A thin bracelet, strung from many thinner strings, hung around her wrist. Its color was much like that of the road below, a dirty brown of all the sand and grime one could track along. She met my eye, her fingers returning to the mandolin resting on her thighs.

Its wood was muted honey. And just as much as rich burnished cherry.

"See something you like?" The musician didn't smile, but the hint of one could be found in her eyes. One of her hands pulled away from the mandolin and reached behind her back. She pulled free a clay mug, giving it a little rattle. The unmistakable sound of coins.

My purse had thinned considerably on my trip here, mostly due to the banditry, and then the usual cost of survival on the road. Nitham's coins had run out entirely. All I had to my name now came in tin, copper, and a lone piece of iron.

Enough to get by, but I would have to be prudent in a new country with no friends to help. Not to mention the difference in currency. I hadn't had an opportunity to visit a financiary to exchange my coins.

The cup shook again. Another jingle.

I drew my purse and pinched a few pieces of tin. Enough for some food. The state of her dress said that much would at least be appreciated. I dropped the coins into her mug.

She smiled now in earnest. "Thank you. Do you have a song you'd like to request?"

I thought about it, but couldn't think of any at first. Then came an idea. "There's a song back in the Mutri Empire I've heard a few times. Something about a young binder high up in the mountains of Ampur, and the monstrous serpent he bested up there."

She ran one hand through her hair before setting it to the mandolin. "I've heard that one. Can't say I believe a word of it, though."

I stood there, wearing my white cloak made from the very scales of the Naghlokh, an old god. She took in the whole of me, and she couldn't believe a word of the story.

"But, I hate to say I don't think I'd do the song any justice. Hearing it a few times isn't the same as playing it well. Anything else?"

I thought, but drew up short. "Nothing at all. Just the kindness then, and maybe your name?"

"Radika."

That raised my brows. "That's Brahmthi, not Zibrathi."

"My father's from by that way. Mother . . ." The sentence trailed off into an expression and tone I knew all too well.

"I'm sorry."

Radika tilted her head in the direction of the crowd filtering by. "There's a hanging today. If you stay here too long, you'll miss it."

I turned to watch the goers-by, then back to her. "Come with me?"

She extended a hand and I took it, easing her to her feet. "Sure."

We followed the crowd, eventually making our way to a large clearing. A wooden platform had been erected long ago and showed the signs of weathering from sand and rain and all the steps taken over it. Another color had tinged the wood, one that needed little imagination to guess the source of. An old burgundy that had stained some of the planks.

The group of gathered people easily outnumbered those in the trader's circle I'd left behind. Nearly a hundred had packed close together to watch the proceedings.

Three men and two women, their hands bound behind their backs, stood along the platform. The last figure caused me to grind my teeth. A boy, showing all the hard leanness that came from living on the streets and resorting to the thieving arts.

I leaned close to Radika. "They can't be serious."

She shrugged and didn't stare at the boy. "The laws are the laws in Zibrath. You break a big enough one, and you hang for that here." Radika shifted from foot to foot, and one of her hands went to her other arm, rubbing a spot.

I eyed one of the bloodstained patches along the stage. "And where's that come from then?" An unintended edge had slipped into my voice.

"Sometimes people lose a hand—the offending hand. But you only get off so light if you've some penance coin to ease your punishment, know someone, or the Bloodcoats are feeling nice." The look she gave me told me that the Bloodcoats did not feel that way often.

I turned back toward the boy. "He's barely thirteen by the looks of him. What'd he do, tup some noble's mother?"

"Got caught stealing something, probably. And he's from one of the bands, so they'll count that against him as hard as they would any grown man."

"The bands?"

Radika chose that moment to become both a mute and deaf, and the newly fallen silence seemed the cue for the executioner to arrive.

He looked like any other Zibrathi, which is to say not all that different from someone from the Mutri. Tall, holding a deep and rich brown in his skin that shone under the afternoon sun, but he wore clothing more to the local fashion than of home. Broad shouldered, and sporting a long mustache that had gone gray early in life. He moved without ceremony toward a lever, and while it was my first hanging, I could hazard a guess as to what the rod would do when pulled.

The hangman addressed those lined before him, asking if they had any final requests. He was answered in kind, then set to meeting the most reasonable of things asked of him. One of the doomed wished for one good long puff from a pipe, and he was treated to it. Another wished to just see and hold a real piece of gold once in their life. A coin touched his hand, and he clasped to it before it was wrenched free and back into the pocket from whence it came.

The other dead-to-be were denied their wants.

One of the women with a noose around her neck tilted her head back and broke into song.

"Hangman, hangman,
comin' for the damned.
Nicked a little silver,
or a golden band.
Out to take your head,
or just as much your hand.

Hangman, hangman,
take you to the pole,
hangman, hangman,
come to claim your soul.

Oh, headsman,
deathsman,
will you wait awhile?
Can you stay the noose?
Hangman, hangman,
will you let me loose?"

Some of the others joined in now, including, I noticed, the young boy.

"Gallowman, hangman,
Listen to my plea
let me out of irons,
will you let me free?

I've got a little somethin',
nestled in me pocket,
piece of mother's silver.
A treasured ole locket.

Hangman, gallowsman,
will you let me go?
Spare me death's own gaze—"

They never got to finish the song. The hangman pulled the lever. Again, and again. Six bodies fell.

One. By. One.

A snap. Crack. Someone screamed. A thunder. The crowd cheered and clapped. But I found the same deaf muteness Radika had as the young boy's eyes touched mine. They didn't move. They didn't shine anymore. And whatever mischievous light they'd had now faded to nothingness.

My first lesson in Zibrath was that thieves did not prosper.

As far as the law was concerned, they were given their just rewards.

FORTY-EIGHT

BANDS

The edges of the crowd broke to leave. A portion remained to speak amongst themselves in all manner of gossip and condemnation of the freshly dead. But another group moved within the larger mass of people.

A secret one. All young, much like the boy still hanging from a noose.

One of the children sported a band of blue along his wrist. Some of the others wore the same accessory—the only similarity between any of them beyond their close age. They slipped through the crowd with the practiced deftness of thieves.

A tap. A squeeze. Pulling here. Patting there. All misdirection. And in the confusion, clutching goods from the tightly packed gathering.

Oh, Brahm's blood. They're running a damn game . . . right where six people were just hanged for it. The level of idiocy in that turned my mind to a storm of windblown sand—scattered thoughts and particulate grain whirling about to drive all clarity from me. For a moment, I stood a mute and immobile puppet.

Finally, I managed to regain some of my wits. "Radika, do you see this?" She had gone, and the man who'd been standing closest to us went through the motions of patting himself over. *Brahm's tits. She didn't.*

"My purse? Alum Above, where is my purse?" The man reached out to someone nearby, tugging on their shirt. The two whispered low to one another.

I caught more of the child thieves slinking through the crowd, working their mischief and trade with an all too comfortable ease. That sort of overconfidence would lead them back to this place, only with a better view of the group from atop the platform. A short-lived view at that.

The man whose purse had been plucked rounded and trained his gaze on me. The nearest of likely people who could have robbed him.

I raised my staff and my free hand. "N-no. Good sir, I didn't—" Shola had picked up on my distress and decided that now, of all times, would be the best moment to voice his displeasure about being kept in the travel sack. He let out a sharp *mrow* and batted at his cloth prison.

The man leveled a finger at me in accusation. "He took my purse. Thief. Peacekeepers!"

At that cry, a group of men who'd been lurking at the far outskirts of the proceedings closed in. And I was treated to a quick understanding of why they'd earned the name Bloodcoats. They wore long coats of woven fabric the color of heart's red. The material looked durable enough to turn away the curve of a sharp blade with relative ease. A veil the same color as their uniform obscured all but their eyes, which were ringed in dark paint.

The men moved in with uniformed synchrony, their long spears parting the crowd with gentle motions.

I knew enough not to bother trying to explain myself. A stranger, freshly come into a new land, and I barely spoke a smattering of the language. Trader's Tongue might have been of some use, but only if they let me live long enough. Given the narrowed-eyed look each Bloodcoat wore, I had a feeling I would not be so fortunate as to be able to argue my case.

I turned and ran.

This, of course, set off Shola. The cat tilted into a proper frenzy. My travel sack jolted and moved with the spasmodic motions of a cotton-eyes in the mania of white-joy withdrawal.

"Get him!" The sole shout soon became carried by others, turning into a wrathful chorus.

I ran through the archway I'd found Radika sitting under, cursing her silently all the while. A passage lay ahead between two buildings that looked just wide enough to grant me freedom. I pivoted, letting my momentum carry me hard into the wall.

My shoulder ached, even though part of my white cloak absorbed some of the impact, and I staggered forward, redoubling my speed and making my way down the alley.

"Down that way!" The cry echoed after me, almost threatening to brush my collar as if the speaker raced on my heels.

If I find Radika, I'll tie her to a chair and do something utterly torturous to her. Like play her mandolin and make her listen to me sing.

I looked over my shoulder, seeing the shadows of my pursuers, long and looming across the walls.

"There, in white. That's him!"

Not one day into Zibrath, and I'm in trouble. Brahm's blood. I ran onward, feet beating hard.

A child leaned out from the side of a wall I couldn't see beyond up ahead. He spotted me, then the crowd behind. The boy waved and drew up a poor cowl, more a knotted mass of fraying scarves, and a hood much the same. He sank back from where he'd popped out from.

I sped up, reaching the turn, and took it. My feet fumbled as I found myself on old stone stairs. Only my staff saved me from toppling properly and striking the ground hard enough to drive the light from my eyes. I regained my balance, hobbling up the first steps before picking up speed again.

"This way." The child had reached another flight of stairs breaking off to the right. He vanished again.

Little choice left to me, I raced right and followed where the child had gone . . . right into a solid wall.

It stood there, too high to properly scale, and with no gaps to squeeze my way through to anywhere else.

"*Ah-ch!*" The sound had come from below.

I looked down to see a small opening carved into the stone. Its edges jagged in some places, smooth in others. It looked as if it had been broken and beaten into that shape rather than truly cut.

A face appeared in the opening, betraying only eyes a color somewhere between shale and worn jade. "Come on." The boy beckoned me with a hand.

I gave the crude entrance another look. It had been shaped for someone small, or an adult of slender build. My sparrow years would have seen me through it with relative ease, but a full diet at the Ashram, and my growing age, had seen me slowly filling out.

"Up ahead. He went off to the right!" The echoing shouts grew closer.

I unslung my pack, pushing it through the opening. "Careful with that." A quick toss sent my staff through afterward.

"Ow!" The cry came from the young child, likely after my binder's cane had struck him.

I fell to all fours and wriggled myself through the hole. My shoulders brushed against the sides of the entrance, and I had to suck in a great breath to get most of my upper body through. Eventually, I tumbled, all without a shred of grace, to the hard ground below. Feet scrabbled by me.

"Hurry," said a voice clearly belonging to another youth.

"The boards." Another child chimed in.

I turned to see two youths, dressed in shabby layers that obscured most of their features, climbing on a pair of rickety stools. One held a heavy board before the opening while the other looped twine through pegs that had been fixed to the wood. That done, they both looped the rope around a series of nails that had been forced into the walls. It served as a poor lock of sorts, and it wouldn't hold up to a strong boot giving the board a few good kicks.

The footsteps outside told me the men had just reached the wall above me.

"Wrong end. Probably went to the roof, or back down below."

I waited.

They didn't move away, however.

Every child stood still as the breath in my chest.

An aching. A burning then. My body shuddered in anticipation, and a sweat not drawn from the heat broke around my collar.

My travel sack shook.

Merciful gods, Shola, please be quiet. And as proof of miracles, he listened.

Boots plodded outside in the familiar noise of moving away.

I let out the deep-held breath, and the children followed.

One of them leapt free from the stool, running his hand against his other wrist and scratching himself. The action revealed a grimy corded band of scuffed brown. The other child wore one identical.

"Where am I?" I got to my feet and snatched up my staff, leveling it toward one of the children who'd come too close to my pack for my liking. He backed away, allowing me to retrieve it and finally give Shola the break he deserved.

My cat leapt out of the bag, letting his disdain be well-heard as he loosed a long, droning *mau.* He looked at our surroundings, sniffing the place in consideration, and sneezed to let us know his opinion.

"Cat." One of the children walked toward Shola, meeting resistance in the head of my staff as it thumped against his chest. "Ow."

I glared hard at him. "No. Answers. Who are you? Where am I?"

"Well, I'm a little upset you've already forgotten me." The voice came from far to our side, but I knew to whom it belonged.

I turned to find Radika standing there, two purses hanging in a pinched grip from her left hand. Her mandolin rested atop a bench mostly made from woven cloth and scrap wood.

"You're in our home."

I stared at the purses she'd clutched, then the surroundings, much like Shola had done. "You ran a game during a public execution and you left me to take the blame for it."

She shrugged, tossing the pouches to another shrouded child, who caught them with the awkwardness of youthful incoordination. "Shawbi also helped you ditch the crowd chasing you." Radika offered that as if it were an apology.

It wasn't.

"I wouldn't have had to slip them if you hadn't robbed that man and left me to take the blame." My words could have cut a deep furrow through the stone around us. "You don't do that to one of your own, *ever.*" I didn't raise my voice, but dropped it to so low a whisper it was the sharp bite of quiet winter wind along already frozen skin.

Radika, for her part, took a step away from me. Her gaze drifted to her feet and she shuffled in place much like she had before. "I'm sorry." More of an apology than before, but the look of contrition died the next instant when she looked back at me. "What do you mean, 'one of our own'? You're not one of the banded." Her eyes turned into thin slits. She took in the whole of me, top to bottom.

"You're thieves. So am I." I should have probably said, so *was* I, at least once upon a time. It had been a long time since I truly lived the life the way these people did. My time with The Crow was more as mentor, brother, than burglar and purse-clutcher. Though, my activities the night I'd burned The Saffron House surely counted.

One of the children, still hooded and masked, came over to my side. They reached out with a tentative hand, first brushing the backs of their knuckles along my cloak. "It's soft, but hard. Smooth . . . and rough." Then they took a piece of its length in their grip, tugging on it. "What is it?"

"The skin of an old god. A Nagh-lokh. I killed one high atop the mountains of Ampur, on the ice and snow."

Radika snorted, and some of the other children quickly fell into laughter too.

I didn't join in, adding a small silence within the bubble of amusement. In the end, the quiet won, drowning out the other noise until only it remained.

Radika met my eyes again. "You're serious." She blinked, looked away—reconsideration plain on her face. "You're the one from the song?"

I inclined my head. "I am."

Mouths parted, and the familiar look of recognition dawned along the faces of some of the children who'd lowered some of their obscuring garments. They all took measured steps away from me.

But it was Radika who voiced the question likely on all their minds. "What are you doing *here*?" One of the children came to her side, then shuffled behind the folds of her shift. Their head peered out from the side, still watching me, but keeping to the better safety behind the matron of their little group.

The tone of her question said much. It came on the current of thinly veiled fear. Tremulous strings, caught-a-quivering, waiting to break at the wrong answer. It was a thing of hearts on edge, quick-set to beating hard at a moment's notice in cold concern. And the setting of feet, all turned to break loose in full run—fast as a child driven by fright could be.

I knew that feeling and the drive. It had carried me one night so hard all I could think to do was run. And run. And run.

"I came to fulfill a promise." My words did not set the children or Radika at ease.

She shifted a bit, putting the cowering child behind her. A simple change in posture to put more distance between us. She worried I could be a threat to them.

I suppose with the stories that had been brewing about me, it wasn't an unfair concern. Though it did bring a sting to my heart. So, I did what I could to clarify things. "Long ago, I played what I thought was a clever game on a man I shouldn't have. For he was playing a different one altogether. More dangerous. With more traps than I could see. He caught me in it, and I only left with my life at his mercy, and under his conditions. I'm here to meet those. It's a personal matter. None of your concern. And you have nothing to fear from me."

"*P'tch*." The sound came from the child behind Radika. "But he knows where we live now?"

Radika arched a brow, asking a thing of me in silence.

"I told you before, I'm a thief as well. And we don't put each other in harm's way. At least we didn't back home."

A thin and brittle smile. Bottle-glass sharp, and just as fragile. It cut along her at a crooked angle. "We're not in your home. This is Mubarath. And here the bands hold only loyalty to themselves." She raised a hand, the corded bracelet of road-dust brown shaking on her wrist. "Another band will cut your throat if they can, or turn you in to the Bloodcoats just to thin the number of mouths on the street to feed. Makes it easier for them. Some bands that were here months ago are here no more."

I frowned and asked the question before realizing the obvious answer. "What happened to them?"

"The same thing that happened to that boy from the Blue Hares."

Brahm's blood and ashes. In all my time running the sparrows, not one had been lost to an executioner, or even the kuthri.

"And how many bands are there? Are you all on bad terms with one another?" I swatted without thinking toward the child who'd been fondling my cloak. Their hands, driven by cultivated impulse, had worked through the folds of my clothing, searching for my purse.

"Ow." The child reeled, pawing at where I'd cuffed him. "I don't like him."

"The feeling is mutual, you little sprat. Try to clutch from me again, and it'll be the staff walloping you, not my hand." I gave him a look down my nose, doing my best to adopt the imperious stare Aram had given me back at the Ashram.

It seemed to work, and the young boy shied away from my look. He muttered something under his breath that could have been an apology or a curse.

I decided to believe it the former and save myself a touch of further aggravation. A pressure built along the bridge of my nose and between my eyes. Pinching the spot and rubbing it did little to alleviate the feeling. "I don't have time for this. I'm in enough trouble as it is."

Radika watched me, not saying anything for a space of long breaths. "You said you were, but you never said with who."

I eyed her, the look a clear message that it wasn't any of her business.

She matched the stare in kind, saying that she wouldn't drop the subject.

So I would take the matter out of her hands completely then. I turned, motioning at Shola. "Come on, boy, we're leaving."

"*T'ch-t'ch.*" Radika clicked her tongue twice in tandem with each warning sound. "I wouldn't go so quickly. They'll still be looking for you on the streets. Robbery during penance is really looked down on. And you're not going to be hiding anywhere with that white cloak."

I frowned. She had a point, but it wouldn't be an issue for me to hide it in my sack. However, if the man had even the barest recollection of my face, then my clothing wouldn't be enough to obscure me. Especially if the Bloodcoats decided to search my belongings on catching me. A hard knock came at the board behind us, stopping my thoughts before deciding what to do.

We all turned.

The knock came again followed by a poor trilling whistle that fell into wet sputtering. Then it came again, falling into the same broken noise.

Radika rushed past me, motioning to some of the veiled urchins.

They returned to the chairs and stood to undo the shabby bindings holding the wood in place.

A small figure inched through the opening with all the lifelessness of an old leaf caught in too weak a wind brushing it along the street. Their slow and feeble movements made it clear what would happen next.

I ran over, letting my staff clatter hard against the ground. The child crashed into my arms, forcing me to grunt and sink against their weight, but I held them firm.

Radika slipped her arms under mine, helping me ease the child to their feet.

Which was a mistake.

They collapsed to the ground, breathing hard and dry like they'd lost all moisture in their throat and their lungs. Radika pulled them up and cradled them, but my curiosity in the moment kept me from the compassion I should have showed.

I reached out and pulled free the child's hood, wrenching down their cowl. A sharp breath passed in through my teeth as I sucked in the air.

Their face carried more black and blue and red than any child's should have. A swollen mass of battery and blood that made it hard to tell if they were a boy or girl. Small mercy their nose or ears hadn't been broken or savagely torn. That sort of mess so young in life rarely healed well and straight.

"Oh, Alum." The words left Radika in a low breath. "Alwi, what happened to you?" She brushed her thumbs along their cheek, trying to clear some of the blood. All it served to do was smear it across their face. "Mahli, Salim, go fetch water, *nahbya*, and a clean towel."

Two of the children ran off to do as bid.

Alwi coughed, a sound better come from a drowning man than a child. Wet and buried low in the throat. Blood spilled past their lips.

Radika hushed the child, urging them to stay quiet.

They didn't listen. "Black . . . Towers . . . Band."

Radika pressed her hand to Alwi's mouth, hushing them. "*Ssh,* please stop."

Brahm's blood, seeing a child put in that state did not do good things for my already high temper. A deeper fire blazed to life inside me, and I did not foresee it calming anytime soon. "What are the Black Towers?"

Radika whipped her head to give me a glare that could have matched the flames inside me. Hot and scalding, and speaking silently: that this was not the time for questions.

Nevertheless, I asked again.

She relented. "Another band. *The* band that runs roughshod over Mubarath. We all live at their pleasure, according to them."

I never did like bullies. My mind went back to two boys back on the streets of Keshum. They'd left me alone after I taught them a painful lesson.

Looking at Alwi made one thing clear: My meeting with Arfan would be delayed a bit longer.

I sighed. "Looks like you're going to need some help."

Radika tilted her head.

"But first, I need to send a letter."

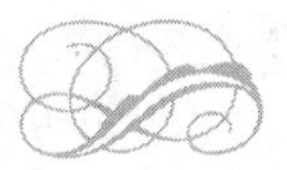

FORTY-NINE

Bullied, Beaten, Broken

Two of the children Radika had sent off now shambled back into view with a bucket, a dusty glass bottle, and rag. I took the bucket and rag, Radika accepting the *nahbya*. She unstoppered it and motioned for me to help.

I wet the rag and fell into the soft smooth motions of cleaning most of the blood off Alwi's face. Soon, he looked more young boy than beaten mass. Some red still marred the brown of his hair, crusting it to his skull. Radika applied the *nahbya*, a weak wine, to the boy's head. He winced through it all, and soon, tears welled at his eyes. I drenched the rag again, wringing it until lightly damp, before pressing it to his face.

A silent understanding hung between us as I blotted the tears away, and I acted as if I hadn't seen them.

He had full cheeks, and his eyes were the brown of dark tea without a touch of milk to soften the color. The brown of his hair was shades darker than the lighter grains of sand on the streets outside.

Alwi spit up more blood and I wiped it away just as Radika cupped a handful of water, bidding him to sip. Soon as he did, she offered him some of the weak wine. He coughed again. "It burns."

She nodded. "A little. For now. Soon, it won't hurt." Something in her voice wavered, too close a note to breaking. A tone I knew.

I reached out to place a comforting hand on her shoulder, but Radika shifted away from me.

A sniff. A cleared throat. And beads forming at the edges of her eyes too.

Just then, another child shuffled into the room. Their face remained hidden behind their cowl. They held up a piece of broken charcoal and a sliver of parchment that had more creases to it than smooth, flat edges.

I supposed it would do.

The child traded places with me, tending to their adoptive brother as I moved to a desk with only three legs. After applying a little pressure to check if it would topple, I laid the paper down and wrote.

Arfan, I have arrived in Zibrath with all possible speed. I am in Mubarath in the company of children much like the sparrows.

I am here.
I am willing to do whatever you ask.
I might be delayed in the city, but I will find you if you do not find me first.
Do not harm my family.

Ari

I had thought about adding an extra line of threat, then decided against it. I'd antagonized many powerful people over my life, and Arfan was not one to push further. But I had no idea how he'd take my delay. Then again, he hadn't made it easy to find him. All I had known was to search for him beyond the country's border, venturing well into the desert.

And that is not a journey easily taken. Or without proper supplies. My trip here had robbed me of those, and I had little left to provision myself with.

The choices before me: venture out regardless of my coin and subject myself to the desert, all at the cost of leaving the little rag-band of thieves on their own. Or, I could stay to help them, and they sorely needed that, as well as refill my purse enough to withstand the next part of my journey.

Alwi coughed, and thankfully, most of what came out looked to be wine and water. Though they bore the unmistakable tinge of blood.

I have always had a soft spot in my heart for the beaten, broken, and bullied. And I had a particular way of dealing with the men who did that sort of thing.

Radika came to stand by my side, looking down at the letter. "Arfan. I know him."

"I didn't know you could read." I hadn't meant it as an insult, more an honest curiosity, as not many thieves ever learned their letters.

Radika bristled. "I can do a lot of things that might surprise you."

I raised a hand in a gesture somewhere between placation and apology. "I believe you." My mouth tightened as I thought on something. "How do you know Arfan? *What* do you know about him?"

Radika licked her lips. "You don't know? But you're indebted to him?" It was half question, half statement.

I nodded.

"*Mejai* Arfan is one of the *Shirs* who rule Zibrath. Even if they live out there." She motioned to the farthest corner of the room, which I took more to mean beyond the sands. "They have the money to buy whoever—whatever—they want. Even the sultan heeds the *Shirs'* words and advice. And every one of the *Shirs* has hands and eyes on every street in the whole of Zibrath, not just Mubarath. Even here. Some of the bands even work for them. Others pass things on to them." She rubbed a hand to her brown band.

I looked back down to my letter. "So could you get this to him?" I pushed it her way.

She backpedaled and waved her hands, wanting no part of it. "Not for all the coin in the world. No good comes from those men. Anything they give you comes with hooks."

Don't I know it. "All the same, I need to get this to him or some people I care very much about will be hurt."

And this also settled the matter for me. Radika and her thieves knew of Arfan. She could read. With some time, I could quite possibly find a way out from under Arfan's thumb with her band. Teach them what I knew, help glean Mubarath's secrets, as well as those of the merchant king. With a little training, and some help, I could do here what I hadn't been able to with The Crow, as well as save the sparrows.

And myself.

Radika looked down to Alwi, whose breathing had steadied as he rested comfortably in the arms of his family. The look on her face told me she knew my fear, as well as my pain. She nodded.

"Sadi, run the letter to the post for him. Take off your band, you don't want any Bloodcoats recognizing it. If you cross any of the banded, just run. Don't sign any of the others, pretend like you're alone. Do you hear me?"

One of the veiled and hooded children bobbed their heads. "I hear you." They reached for the letter, which I passed to them. The child remained, staring at me.

It took me a moment to realize why. "Right." I fetched my purse, drawing out one of the few remaining coppers. "That should be more than enough to cover a courier."

"They won't have to look far. Just his name will get it to his hands . . . eventually." Radika took the letter from Sadi, sealing it in on itself with a creative set of folds that meant its edges would tear once opened. With that done, she scribbled Arfan's name atop the length of the one side in a script neater than I'd have guessed her capable of. "All of the *Shirs* have posts within the city dedicated to their affairs. Messages are delivered there, some get them when they come back from the desert to do business or collect."

I raised a brow. "Collect?"

She looked at me the same way you would a dimwitted child. "Taxes."

I sputtered. "They have the power for that? I thought the sultan . . ." I trailed off.

She rolled her shoulders. "The royal family is only in place so long as they have the support of the *Shirs*. The money is really managed by them, and the foreign business. Trade. Travel. *Shirs* rule Zibrath, not the sultan. But *Shirs* are busy dealing with their own business outside the country. Here, they can't take out old family problems on other tribes. In the desert, they can. And their anger makes it worth living out there to settle old issues than staying here to run things. So, the sultan handles Zibrath . . . with their blessings, and they stay in the desert mostly to handle what they want."

That explained a good deal more about Arfan's wealth, and why the man would style himself a merchant king.

Sadi plucked the letter from Radika and scampered up to the crawl hole, leaving the burrow home.

The action spurred me into finally taking better account of my surroundings.

The place could have once been a home that had fallen into disuse and been abandoned. Its walls were of the same stone that made up most of the structures I'd seen in Mubarath, a pale rock shaped from the sands and some kind of adhesive to form the sturdy slabs. It served to keep out the heat and hold in whatever natural coolness could be found. A doorway, lacking the thing for which it was named, revealed a passage that likely led to other rooms.

"Neat place. How'd you come by it?" I tapped my foot idly against the ground.

Radika pursed her lips before speaking. "It used to belong to a tile maker. He made colored pieces for fitting in better homes. They sold well enough, traded as far as Laxina, I heard. He used to show all the children nearby the pretty colors and pieces. Sometimes he let them play with tiles. And if any child came to him with a problem, he'd flick drops of sesame oil on their face, then mutter a prayer. He said it was old magic, and it would open the way to blessings for them. Then he stopped."

I blinked. "He just stopped?"

She gave me a look sharp enough to break skin. "It's hard to work when you're dead."

"I'm sorry."

"The Black Tower Band had decided he needed their protection services. He turned them away. They returned one day to show him, and other tradesmen, why he'd been wrong." A silence fell. The quiet of words that do not want to be said, but if kept held within, will soon burden the heart with an ache no one wants to bear. "And they showed him."

I shouldn't have asked the next question, but my curiosity had gotten the better of me. "How?"

Radika nodded down the way.

I extended a hand, which she took. "Show me."

She did.

First came the smell. A thing of oil gone too long and set to smoking until well past the point of being considered fragrant. Thick, clinging as much to the walls as it did the air itself.

The shop floor couldn't have been from the same building. No speck remained that held the color of sand above. Every visible space was the color of deepest dark-kept black. A color found in a crushed coal smeared so densely along the place that no hope of once-brown walls would ever be found. This was the shade of a world that knew the touch of one thing in excess, and would never be able to shed its shadowed hollow memory.

Fire.

The tile maker's shop had been burned to a heat so hot even bones would char to black crumble, leaving nothing behind to find. No comforts for friends. Or family.

The street-level entry to the shop stood ahead. A door that had been so heavily boarded it would take half a day of solid hatchet work to break through the barricade.

A message meant to warn all. And likely why none of Radika's little band ever came down here.

Because the message remained.

The Black Tower Band had writ it plainly: *Stay out.*

I decided to send them a reply.

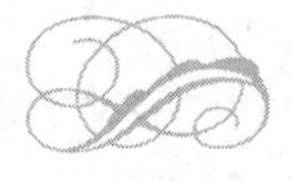

FIFTY

THE HONING EDGE

We waited till Mubarath fell under the cloak of darkness. A coolness washed through the world that was a welcome relief from the morning heat.

Shola had taken to his temporary lodgings, making himself well at home. It didn't hurt that he had company in a few of the children he deemed worthy enough to share his presence. The rest would have to make do with all the accompanying glory and gratitude in serving Shola his meals.

I kept little on me tonight: my purse, mostly to keep it out of the hands of a bunch of thieves I knew little about. A candle, out of old superstition. My white-scale cloak, for the protection it offered. And obviously, my binder's cane.

Lastly came the knife I'd been gifted back in Ghal.

The sheath had all the dark of the sky above with a shine like fresh black ink. I drew the blade, marveling at the metalwork. Its shape was the truest thing a knife could hope to be. The purest imagining of sharpened form. A ripple of darker gray ran through the bright moonlit silver of the blade, forming a pattern like waves.

Arasmus steel.

Sharper than a lover's scorn or a theater-man's tongue. I slid the knife back into place, fastening it to my hip. It had quickly grown a comfort in my hand on my journey to Zibrath, and I didn't know if that was a good thing.

How the young beggar girl had come by it still remained a question. Likely stolen, and something she'd never be able to sell for the questions it would raise. So why not trade it away? And of course, the little convincing I had done to myself that she was in fact a guide in disguise, helping my quest.

Just like in the stories.

I looked back at Radika, flashed a wink and a smile, and headed toward the crawl hole. "Wish me luck."

Her words came a whisper too soft to be properly heard, but they came all the same.

I figured that counted well enough. And her band of thieves had drilled me on the streets so well that I could recite them from memory. So I wormed through the small space and greeted a moon-full starry night. Just enough light to work with, and dark enough in sky to lend me the cover I needed.

There was thief's work to be done.

And The Ghost of Ghal had come to Zibrath.

Mubarath did me the merciful kindness of consisting of nothing but buildings with flat roofs and terraces. That, along with the close proximity of structures, and the long washing lines running from them . . .

Well, I had a playground any quick-footed and nimble-fingered thief would give thanks for. And I certainly did.

But Mubarath's thieves were a different breed than those in Abhar. Here, crime kept to the streets, and never above them. So no one would think to look up.

I raced over stone tops, feet striking light as a cat's—tripping back into the air no sooner than I touched ground. My eyes stayed wide in alert, taking in every moving shape in the world below. An old game came to me then and brought with it the cost of memory.

Pains. An old face.

And a name: Nisha.

I tried to bury it, but the weight persisted as I played the game, realizing the aid it now was. I'd long grown into a keen observer of people, and now I could make out the likely stories of those moving along the ground of Mubarath.

A late-night drunk—a husband, teetering about in hopes of finding the things his wife had asked for, and that he'd forgotten. He hobbled along in absent thought, driven more by fear of returning emptyhanded than any hint of clarity in what to find.

Two children chased each other just below a second-story window. A woman leaned out to watch them, her hair bound tight under a wrap of mustard yellow. She had the ghost of a smile along her mouth that said she would have taken a greater pleasure in their activities if not for a greater hardship she kept all to herself. Nothing betrayed what that weight could be, only that she carried it in the tired lines of her face and low stoop of her shoulders.

Her eyes drifted upward, taking in the buildings across the way, then the roofs. She spotted me perched like an ornament of moonlight marble—snow-white and stone-still.

I returned the calm and measured gaze, giving her no reason to fear me or report me to the Bloodcoats.

A heavy sigh left her lips and she hung her head with the resignation of one who couldn't be bothered with anything other than the mountain-heavy burden within.

I moved then, darting along the roof to the lip of the building. The next structure stood just a short jump from me. I leapt, bracing myself for the impact. My feet struck ground and I toppled forward, letting my momentum carry me on. I rolled, came clean to my feet, and raced onward.

I reached another edge and looked below to find what I'd been looking for.

Two men, older than me by a handful of years, moved along the corner of a building. Each had a lean and scrappy build that came with much work done and little food consumed. They each held a hand to the shoulder of another man.

Clean shaven of head and beard, he had as much of the sun as one could hold in their skin, bringing him a golden-bronze darkness that almost shone even in the late of night. Glints of light drew my eyes to his hands.

Rings. Gold. Someone wealthy enough to afford flaunting it.

The men leading the bald gentleman into an alley had accessories of their own. A single band on each of their wrists. The dark gave me little hope of making out the color from here, but they weren't part of Radika's group.

My problem rested in getting to the other side of the street unseen. I could risk climbing along some of the thicker lines hung from roof to roof. Some existed to support no end of drying laundry, but a few had been placed for vines to creep along. And those had been fashioned from a thicker twine that, in theory, could bear my weight.

The two banded thieves shoved the man hard, bouncing his head off a stone wall before ushering him into the darkened alley.

"Brahm's blood." I spat over the end of the building and stepped out onto a thick line. My body teetered, and while I may never have nursed a fear of heights, I learned it's never too late to develop a healthy appreciation for steady footing when so high up.

And I certainly did not have that in the moment.

My staff served as a poor acrobat's ballast. I teetered again. Then tottered. I'm not sure what the technical difference is, but given that I shook and tilted in new ways each time, it is a safe assumption that I went through every form of nearly toppling known to man.

Halfway along the line, I am young again. No more the cool night of Mubarath, but the hot peppering sun of Keshum. Not a bending bit of twine underfoot. It is a plank of hard wood, though not wide enough to be a comfort to walk across. A man, brown as one could be living a life under the heat, and lean of limb and muscle, schools me on balance. He wields a wooden sword and has more the grace of a dancer than a soldier. But his discipline is one found in hardened veterans.

A man of singular mind and movement in every step and swing of sword.

I mind my footwork and move better assured than before. A step, retreat. My staff—a sword, and my balance steadies. A low fire builds in my feet, running up the thin tendons that join my heels and muscles. Soon it rises to settle in my calves. Breaths come shallow and my heart thunders three times as fast a beat could be. My core tightens and I am reintroduced to pains in places I'd long forgotten could bear a hurt.

Vithum moves a memory of shaded fog—condensed breath on winter winds. A gentle glide away from me, pulling me along as if on strings. I follow, smooth as once-child's grace and training can take me. My sword moves forward, straight and true. Its head coming to strike a blow that could never have landed in reality.

The shock of it sets me free.

I took a harder breath than before, cold lightning racing through me and bringing me back to clarity. My feet had just touched the firm lip of the building I'd been eyeing from back across the way. I'd progressed along the rope without falling, though my stomach and heart had not come to understand that fact yet themselves. They sank somewhere far below me and kept chains tethered to my hollow, threatening to drag me down as well.

I swallowed and stepped off the ledge, landing on the roof. My legs shook and wanted to buckle. *Brahm's tits and ashes and all the other clever pithy things I'm too shaken to think of.* I took a few steps as the ground ceased spinning and made my way to the other side of the roof. It offered me a view of the happenings below.

The banded thieves pressed the man against the wall, one pinning him in place with a forearm to his throat. The victim raised both hands and offered no resistance. Only a quiet plea of mercy.

The thieves had none. One of them launched a fist into the bald man's belly, doubling him over. Spittle left his lips. More solid blows struck, and the man finally cried out. They muffled the sounds by shoving a wadded rag into his mouth.

That had been enough for me. I turned and climbed down from the ledge. I tied my staff to hang from my back with a piece of line, and did my best to keep its head from clattering against the wall I descended. My fingers held to one window ledge, then another. Feet fighting for whatever hold I could find: sill and lip—holes in old stone.

I looked over my shoulder and saw the familiar glint of flashing silver in the night. A knife. One of the men raised it by the victim's face, waggling it to make a point that did not need further elaboration.

"*Nabey, nabey,* Rakhim. You're late with this week's money. It's hard to be in business with broken hands, *naeh*? Or . . . missing fingers." The thief with the knife tapped the flat side of the blade against Rakhim's thumb, then touched each of the digits on the hand until he stopped at the pinky. He pressed the tip of the weapon against the soft flesh, drawing a pinpoint of blood.

Rakhim winced and whimpered.

I'd seen enough and let go of the lip I held to.

If you listen to the stories of The White Ghost—The Ghost of Ghal—you'll hear that I moved ever-soundlessly. The wind itself at my beck and call, and set to never betray my movings. No whisper of my passing, nor my each and every step. Silence.

A lie.

I landed harder than I would have liked and sucked in a breath. The head of my staff clattered against the wall behind me, alerting the two banded men.

They whirled. The edge of the knife held my attention, and I remembered not so long ago when I'd been in another alley and a pair of cutters had nearly succeeded in doing me in.

"Who are you?" The speaker looked in his early twenties. Lean and hard of jaw. The shape of his head had been taken from a brick, and the short cropping of his hair did him no favors. He wore a simple black shirt and matching breeches, and his sandals looked nearly worn through.

His partner wore the same, only having extra in way of the weapon.

The bands on their wrists were black as the anger swelling inside me.

"Who are you?" The first speaker thrust his chin toward me.

I refused to answer, pulling free my staff instead. "Let him go. He doesn't owe you money anymore." I hoped my voice didn't shake as much as the muscles in my arms. Small mercy the binder's cane showed no signs of quivering despite my weak grip.

Rakhim tried to shuffle by the distracted men. It didn't work.

The one without a weapon turned and shoved a palm hard against the man's head, driving it into the unforgiving stone.

A yowl of pain. Red smeared along the wall.

Something hot seized me tight. It fanned and screamed a wordless cry in the hollow of me. I gave voice to it then. "No!" I lunged, thrusting with the head of the staff. No proper attack, but more than enough for a man unsuspecting.

It smacked true into the soft flesh of the first man's ear and cheek.

He staggered and fell to one knee, a hand pressed to where I'd struck. The man motioned with a snap of his hand in my direction and a pained scream. "Get him."

The other thief with the knife moved. Steel scythed through a series of patterns that should have dazzled me in the midst of my anger.

But it did not.

For anger is a honing razor of its own when held proper. And then, seeing the blood along the stone, I took it in whole and made it mine. I swatted with the staff, more a club in my grip now than a rod. It struck the man on his shoulder and threw him off-balance.

But still he came. A lunge.

I leapt back, trying to poke him with the head of my weapon again. I failed.

Another dizzying array of flashing silver. This time, I did not see the trick of it.

Vithum's training seemed another mind away—far from recall.

The man closed in and I tried to bat him aside. His larger size and strength made it a simple task for him to break my hold and send my staff to the ground. One of his forearms crashed into my nose.

Crimson streaked my vision, banded with stars of white. I reeled. One palm struck my chest hard enough to send me into the wall.

The knife moved.

I turned.

A hard point dug into my ribs and forced the breath out of me. I gasped.

"Stupid shit. I'll carve you—"

I turned and dashed my head against his. My forehead met soft mass and a muffled cry went into the night. Breathing heavy, I managed to get a hand to my side. No flesh broken. No warmth of blood. Nothing.

A look at my cloak showed me what had happened.

The scales had cinched tight around where I'd been struck, but they had not broken. I'd felt the force of the blow more than the knife itself.

A dark-edged laugh left me. It was sharp glass and broken stone echoing deep. I laughed it again and spoke. "You can't hurt me with knives and swords." The words left me in my best demon's voice, something I'd heard over and over in the understage, and repeated to myself in a child's game.

The man cupped a hand to his nose. A color like dried cherries spread through his fingers. The knife shook in his hand, and one look at it told him the truth of things. It remained clean. No blood of mine.

I lowered my cowl but for a moment so that he could see my smile. It was silver-bright shining, like the moon itself. Like a wolf.

"Who are you?" The first man had risen to his feet, leaning hard against Rakhim.

I thought then of the myths already spreading about The Ghost of Ghal. "I am vengeance."

The thief screwed his face tight, lost in thinking. "Is this because of Jalil? Little blue-banded shit borrowed our coin. He brought it on himself." The man spat. "Got off easy being hung. I'd have taken his stones for what he owed."

Jalil. He must have been the boy I'd seen at the hanging. Of all the things the thief could say, telling me that he would have done worse to a child who'd already had it hard?

I have never claimed to be a good man, though Brahm Himself knows I've tried. And I have certainly fallen short.

This was one of those moments.

"He was a child." Each word came a hushed curse. I lunged, striking out with an open hand—more driven from bone-deep fury than any skill or plan. It struck—full-flesh against the soft of his face, rocking his head.

The man with the knife had found his courage and charged me. His shoulder connected hard and forced me against the wall. Knife overhead, he swung it down like a hammer, the tip promising to bury itself in the hollow of my throat.

I turned, just enough to bring my covered shoulder in place of the strike. Another dull ache flared, settling in my collar. The force of that could have fractured the thin bone. At the least, I would have an impressive bruise.

I shoved hard, but the man resisted, bringing the knife back. This time it struck beneath my ribs. I winced and wondered if I would piss blood the next morning. Blinding light came again as the man struck true with a fist to my cheek.

My hands moved, as much in panic as a newly honed reflex. Something smooth and firm came into my grip and I pivoted. I felt a sensation like meat parting under knife.

A warmth. The sticky liquid feeling I'd feared I'd find earlier along my body. Only it spread over my fingers and wrist.

The man with the blade blinked before breaking into an open-mouthed whimper. He collapsed, clutching to the space I'd buried the Arasmus knife.

I looked down at it.

My hands did not shake now.

"Alum. Alum. Please." The bleeding thug spoke a plea, but he would find no mercy this night. Not from me.

The other man raised a hand as if hoping to stay me with the gesture. "Please, stop. Who are you? What are you?"

I needed no instruction how to play the role given me. I kept to the voice I'd used earlier. Theater demons. The sort out of the best stories, and utterly fictional to those who didn't know any better. "I'm The Ghost of Ghal. The ghost of every life you've hurt and taken. I am their retribution. I am their vengeance. Tell all of the Black Tower Band that I am coming. Tell them!" I lunged, brandishing the reddened knife.

The man turned and ran. And ran. And ran.

Much like a boy who'd seen demons so long ago.

The thief on the ground moaned and crawled, still clutching to his wound.

I looked to the knife in my hand. It did not feel as heavy as it once did. A simple application of my weight. Just press down, and I could bury it hilt deep in the man's chest. Or his throat. The power and choice rested in my hand.

So easy a thing.

I took measured steps toward him.

He crawled away, taking a movement for each of mine. One hand rose to the air. He begged. He cried. He did all the things men like him do when faced with their own actions at the hands of another. All the noises the people he'd hurt had probably made.

I caught up to him and I brought a foot down hard on the small bones of his ankle.

The stories have grown to say I had a strength like several men. Perhaps one day that would be true. But then? I did not. So it was not a clean break. I stomped again. Then again.

He screamed.

But his ankle did not. It broke with the soft wetness of drenched twigs underfoot.

I knelt, holding the knife's bloody point toward him.

"Please, *asahb*. Please. I'll go. Let me live. I'll never—I'll . . ." He fell into sputtering and raised an arm. The one from which the black band hung. His other hand moved, fingers hooking around the string. He tugged on it. "I'll leave the Black Towers. I swear on Alum Above."

I brought the knife under his chin. The soft meat, that with but a push, I could pierce up into his skull. "Swear to me." It left me a whisper, but not without its edge—just as sharp as the Arasmus blade in hand.

"I swear it." Tears now streamed from his face.

"Your purse."

He blinked. "What?"

"Your. Purse." I didn't wait for him then, kicking him to his side and rifling through the folds where his shirt and breeches met at the waist. A quick pull of my knife and it separated the weak string holding his coin pouch to cloth. "Start crawling. Scream. Get your friends to help. Let them know who did this." I thought of something, then bent again.

The man flinched as the knife neared.

I slid it against the black band and freed it from his wrist. A keepsake.

This is the point of my story where I suppose it can be said I began to hone my anger into a razor's edge to serve me.

"You should return home, Rakhim." I collected my staff, fastening it over my back.

"How do you know my name, *asahb*?"

"I'm no sir. *I* am a ghost." And I ran down the alley away from him and the man I'd nearly killed.

FIFTY-ONE

GHOST STORIES

A cry rose through the city in the wake of what I'd done. The Black Tower thief must have found his friends, or a Bloodcoat willing to hear what had happened.

Bells chimed.

A loud horn blared from a stone tower in the center of the city.

And I ran as hard as I could.

I made my way up to a roof, this time choosing one better connected to a landscape of other buildings I could navigate. Not one piece of me wished to tight-walk another line tonight. Especially with the guards looking for me, and likely the rest of the Black Tower band.

The Ghost of Ghal had gotten lucky, but those were odds well beyond what I knew I could handle. So I ran on, leaping small gaps between rooftops.

I confess, it must have looked far more impressive to those on the ground pointing at the figure of trailing white rushing overhead. In truth, any child could have made those jumps. The blessing of Mubarath's crowded layout—a place well made for thieves and cats.

My lungs ached, and my heart hadn't settled from the thunderous drumming it'd been set to during the fight. And now the reality of what I had almost done to one of the men sank in.

So close to taking his life. I had done that before, and in a similar enough situation.

Mithu. Askar. And Biloo.

The action had left me unwell for a short time. Eventually it had become distant memory, better-buried and to be forgotten. Now it resurged.

The flash of falling men and the blood below. The broken canted angles in which their bodies lay on the street.

My stomach tightened, throwing off the soft fluidity in body I needed to keep my pace and flexibility. I faltered. A footstep failed me. I tumbled—hard.

My cloak did not absorb all of the impact, but it kept me safe enough as I rolled to hit the lip of the roof. For a moment far longer in thought than reality, I rested there.

Still chiming bells. And the long drone of a horn. Most of the city would be roused by now, resentful of what had stirred them.

I wouldn't win any love for waking every sleeping citizen. Something I'd need to rectify after I'd gotten to safety. A look over the edge showed me prowling Bloodcoats, but no signs of any wandering Black Tower thieves.

Maybe he hadn't told them all of what happened.

The guards stared along the streets, not turning their gazes upward.

. . . yet.

I seized the good fortune and got back to my feet, mantling over the edge and then onto the next roof. It became a familiar and repetitive thing: run, leap, roll. Soon to be no different than breathing.

I made my way back to the alley where I'd first found the crawlspace and stood before the dead-end wall. A series of short knocks was all I could manage, never having learned their proper call.

No answer.

I kicked the wooden board with the flat of my foot, then knelt before it. "It's me. *Kala mahl,* let me in." They wouldn't understand the foreign curse, but it left me regardless.

The board juddered, then slid partway open to reveal a pair of eyes. Then the wood moved.

I slid my staff through first, following on hands and knees. A low groan left me when I landed. "There has to be a better way in here, especially when I've Bloodcoats on my heels."

The mass of masked children said nothing, watching me instead. One of their gazes fell on my left hand and the crimson spread along it.

I looked down and raised my other hand in a gesture of calm. "It's not mine." That did not placate them.

Radika came into the room then, spotting what her children had. "What did you do?"

I said nothing.

"What did you do?" She crossed the distance between us, reaching out to take my throat in her hands, but stopping short of applying pressure.

"I went out looking for the Black Tower Band. Any of their members I could find. I wanted to watch them, see if I could find out where they call home. Learn what I could about them. But then I saw what they were up to. . . ."

Some of the heat fled her eyes and the lines of her mouth pulled into a crooked curve. Half curiosity, half concern. "And?"

I told her about what I'd seen with Rakhim. "I intervened."

Her stare went to my hand, then back to my face. She didn't ask the question aloud. But then, she didn't have to.

"Things got out of hand. We scuffled. They tried to knife me. It didn't work. I tried to pay him back in kind. My try went better than his."

"Are they . . ." Radika put a hand to her mouth.

"One got a little beating that a night will cure him of. I stabbed the other pretty deep, but I don't know if it was a killing blow. If he can see a mender, he'll live." I chewed over whether to tell her what else I'd done, then decided there'd be no point hiding that after what I'd already shared.

"I broke his ankle. He may never walk again. And there's this." I reached into a pocket and pulled free the cut black band, holding it up for her to see. "Took his band. I'm not sure why I did it, but I did."

Radika reached out to take it, then stopped just before her fingers touched it. "Do . . . you think they knew you were with us?"

I shook my head. "No. I made sure they'd think of me as something else." And so I told her more about The Ghost of Ghal, and what I had said to the men.

Once I finished, I pulled out the purse I'd taken from the Black Tower thief. A single bounce in my palm drew the ears and eyes of all the little brown-banded children. "Let's see what we came away with, eh?"

Radika mouthed the word "we," but only for me to see.

A fair point, I supposed. Technically speaking, I was not a member of her little group of thieves. And I had in some sense forced my way into their life. Though, one could argue it came by way of them leaving me in dire straits, and then inviting me into their home. But much of life's stories happen in such fashion.

It's rarely a clever and well-planned thing. Only in the aftermath do we begin to draw strings from point to point in some vague hope of better rationale and understanding. There often isn't any. And that uncertainty terrifies us. So we fight and bridge chasms with whatever piece of convenience we can. Anything to make a story make sense.

I upended the pouch and spilled out the contents. Pieces of copper, white discs closer to crystal than metal, and a single silver coin. I thumbed through them, still not savvy on Zibrath's currency, or the conversion.

Radika's eyes widened as if she'd never seen money before.

The rest of the children moved just a shade closer, craning necks to get a better look.

"Copper, these white bits"—I nudged them with a thumb—"and a single piece of silver. I know silver's traded by weight country to country. But I don't know much about these other two?" The look I gave her asked the question for me.

She took the coins in hand. "This is a copper barinth. It's worth almost what a copper Mutri round is. Almost. The white is radham. I don't know how they make it. It's this crystal with"—she tugged on her hair—"little metal hairs in it? But it's close to an iron bunt if I remember. The silver is called a dhiran."

I made note of that.

She continued. "This is more than we ever see. It's not much for the Black Towers. A lazy few days of pushing for what they can. Bullying people. We usually take food, beg for alms and charity coins. Sometimes we pinch from crowds like what you saw. But most crowds midday don't have lots of coin on them. They've spent them at the market, or only have carrying-around money."

Carrying-around money usually consisted of the lowest possible currency one could have. It was just enough to buy a fruitless piece of idle fancy.

I eyed the coins again. "So the silver dhiran will keep you lot fed and clothed for a while?" I had a good idea of the answer, but had to ask it anyhow.

She nodded. "A long while. But we'll have to break it at a financiary. It's not good for us to be seen with this much money. I'll do it tomorrow." A frown. Radika looked at the coins again, motioning toward me with her palm.

I accepted the silent request. An even split. "That's fair, but I'd appreciate if you could do me a favor in turn."

She tilted her head.

"I'm going to need you to come up with some songs, and spread some stories in places they'll catch best." The wolfish smile from earlier in the night returned. "Ghost stories."

Radika grinned back.

FIFTY-TWO

MOUTHS TO SHAPE

I woke to find I'd been right about the bruise. A hideous spread the purple-blue of plums. Tender to the touch or any roll of my shoulder.

Perfect. That'll make climbing and fighting a treat.

Radika came into the living room of the abandoned home. Today she wore a simple shift of secondhand homespun. It was a color somewhere between sunflowers, full in bloom, and burnished gold. It drew out the best brightness of all her amber eyes had to offer. Her hair had lost its tangles, now brushed smooth and straight. She caught me staring, turned her head to not meet my eyes, and smiled for half a heartbeat.

"You look . . . good." A bit too late to the compliment . . . and awkward.

The smile returned, lingering just as shortly as before. "Thank you. I hope it was fine to take some of the money and . . ." She broke off and pulled at the sides of her shift. "I needed a new one, and a good bath at a bathhouse."

I nodded, not trusting my tongue in the moment.

"I made food?" It came more as an offer than a statement. The invitation to join her and her little band for morning meal.

I accepted with another gesture of my head.

We shared the quiet morning meal together while Radika told me of the various children she'd scooped up into her care. Though she avoided any mention of the tile worker whose home this had once been.

"This is Baba." She waved to one of the children who'd forgone the usual obscuring attire.

Baba could have been ten at a guess, possibly a few years older. But he didn't have the look of a boy going through the flowering of adolescence yet. Round faced, with thin brows and hair dark as could be. He wore it in a shaggy cut that had likely been done himself or by Radika. As trite as it may sound, a kindness hung in the warm brown of his eyes. An honesty. The sort only the best of children had, and some rare few managed to keep over the course of their lives.

"Hello, Baba." I smiled and offered a hand.

He didn't take it, looking to Radika for direction. She nodded and he followed through. His hand clasped mine and he squeezed with a grip made for a wrestler twice his age.

I did not wince in the hold of a child. I simply gritted my teeth and forced a smile. "You've a strong hold, little man."

"*Bah. Bah.*" Each word sounded more a sheep's cry than an attempt at his own name.

I looked to Radika for explanation.

She exhaled and some of the brightness fled her face. "He's . . ." She stopped. "Baba . . ." Another false start. Radika took a breath. "We don't know what it is. Ever since I've known him, that's the only word he can say. He's not dumb. Not really. He understands things. He just can't get other words out."

"And his name?" Perhaps I shouldn't have pried, but the question came to me.

She shrugged. "It just made sense. That's what he said when I asked him, 'Bah-bah.'"

At the exaggerated sound of his name, Baba laughed. I joined in, feeling relieved the boy didn't find it a mocking thing. I had no desire to add a hardship to one who'd already had his fair share. One of my hands went to his head and I ruffled his hair. "Boy with a grip like that doesn't really need words, ah? You'll make a scary strongman one day if you've got the want for it, Baba." I brought my hand to his cheek and gave it an affectionate pinch much like a grandparent would do.

He laughed again. "*Bah. Bah.*"

We finished our meal and Radika offered to take me out to see Mubarath proper.

I couldn't refuse that, so I trusted Shola to the care of the rest of the little urchins, and headed off with Radika.

We'd left my cloak and staff behind, and I confess that doing so brought me a deep unease. Both things had slowly grown to become part of my own personal legend.

A silly thing when thought of, I suppose, but all the same. The Ari who'd been building a reputation had always carried a candle, cloak, and cane, much like the heroes of legend I'd grown enamored with.

But I did keep the Arasmus steel knife bound at my hip. Mubarath had no law against wearing weapons. Not with the influx of traders coming off paths rife with banditry, and the fact the city harbored more than its fair share of thieves and bullies. A man could take some level of justice in Mubarath on his own, so long as it was properly warranted.

I hazarded a guess that my late-night activity did not count as such.

Radika led me out onto the streets and we took in the market's morning affair.

People had let early morning laundry fly along lines, soaking in the sun to dry. It created a sky-thrown canvas of all colors. A patchwork cloak thrown to air, after a fashion. Merchants stood outside their own homes, some before stalls and carts, crying for all to hear.

Hands waved, people shook wares, pinches of spice thrown to the air for a sniff or a color to catch your eye. Every hot and flavorful smell you could conjure. Any attempt to turn an ear, then to take that instant to sell you something. A dynamism that reminded me of Keshum in the best of ways.

Radika had brought her mandolin. It hung against her back, exposed to the elements.

I frowned and raised the subject.

Radika merely shrugged it off. The heat would stretch the strings, but it wasn't anything she couldn't fix with some tuning. She did the best she could to care for it.

Radika led me to a single-story building made of the same pale yellow stone as much of Mubarath's structures. A rope ran along the front's perimeter, creating a simple fencing before the walls. Tables had been set outside with poles and tenting stretched across them to create spots of shade. The low-squat place had a filtering of people passing through in both directions.

"This is where we can start what you have in mind." Radika's smile almost touched on mischievous, but it lacked the gleaming edge that true mischief carried. It was closer to a child's enthusiasm to try their hand at something new, the results unknown.

I almost asked her what she meant, but she led me by the arm into the building.

The smell struck me. It was of warm nuts and something sweet cooked low to caramelizing. A long trough ran from one side of the place to the other. Men stood behind it, gripping metal cups with unnecessarily long handles. They moved the cups in circular motions through a bed of sand.

I arched a brow at Radika as she led me to the counter.

"You've never been to an *awfhar*?"

"I don't rightly know what one is, though I have a feeling I'm standing in one?"

She nodded. "They're named for the drink." One of her hands gestured to a cup.

I watched a substance like dark tea quickly come to boil in the metal, then froth to a softer-colored cloud atop.

The man pulled it free from the sand and tipped it into a clay cup. He turned then to a pitcher and scooped a ladle of milk, spooning in a bit. A customer reached over, hands cupped to the drink in a gesture that almost could have passed for prayer. Coins changed hands and the client returned to a table with their drink.

While the beverage held some of my interest, more of it rested in the trough itself. I took a hard look at it, wondering where the heat came from. I saw no flames, nor a bed of coals. Kneeling, despite the whispers of protest from Radika, I saw the trick.

A script ran along the underside of the stone tray. It had been carved deep enough to withstand erosion of time and weathering. But the writing itself was in the language most commonly used for minor bindings at the Ashram.

I smiled, taking more than a little pride at the wonders that came out of the Mutri Empire.

Radika pulled me back to a stand. "What are you doing?"

I explained myself and she looked at me in part disbelief, and a healthy amount of embarrassment on my behalf. I didn't see anything odd with what I'd done.

"Ah, *nabey, nabey,* Radika!" One of the men beamed at her. Closer to his forties than thirties, bald, and only keeping a dark brush of stubble along his face. His brows were thick and heavy. He had the build of someone who had once worked heavy labor, but had since indulged in many years of a softer sort of life. "How's my favorite little singing bird, *nabey*?"

She returned the expression. "Good, Abil. Good. I bought new clothes." Radika accentuated this by pinching a piece of her shift.

Abil grinned wider. "That you did, and it's almost as bright as you. *Awfhar*?"

She held up two fingers. "One for me, and one for my friend." Radika pulled my hand up, showing both our fingers were interlaced.

Abil's smile dimmed at that and he may have let his gaze linger on me longer than polite. He gave Radika a quiet stare that spoke of a question being asked.

Radika shied away from the look and shifted in place, but said nothing.

After a moment, Abil blew out a breath and nudged a man at his side. "Two *awfhar.* Milk, honey? Palm sugar?"

"Palm sugar and milk, yes." Radika looked at me for confirmation, which I gave via a weak nod. She turned back to regard Abil. "I have a new song?"

That brought back the brightness from before and he broke into a true grin. "*Nabey?* Alum Above, this'll be good for today. Been doing brisk business before midday, but a song will bring in a good lunch crowd. You need time to practice on the dozy-headed drowsers?" He jabbed a thumb in the direction of the customers along the opposite wall.

Many sat slumped against tables, blowing shallow breaths to cool their drinks. A few took pleasured sips that led to fluttering lids and sighs of relief.

It must have been quite the drink.

We waited for a few breaths shared in silence as our beverages were made to order, then, taking the cups in hand, walked to an unoccupied corner. Radika didn't wait to indulge, blowing deep, long breaths over hers before taking a sip.

"Mm. Finally, I can wake up." She then urged me to try the drink myself.

So I did. The heat radiated through my hands as I held the beverage, promising a scalding touch if I didn't do my best to cool it. Content that I'd breathed enough air over it, I took my taste. It brought notes to my tongue close to the smell of the thing itself. A warm nuttiness with a slight bite to it. The honey and milk softened what could have been an undercurrent of bitterness, and brought a creamy smoothness to the delivery of other flavors. I likened it to something like fire-borne lightning. A jolt with a deeper warmth.

We sipped the drinks without word, treating ourselves to the quiet pleasure of each other's company, as well as a stillness that had been filling my life of late. Though, I confess, as a burgeoning binder quickly growing his own myth, the inactivity I'd grown accustomed to rankled me.

If you don't know how much you crave to be in motion, it is like this: Imagine a badly sprained ankle that has developed a murderous itch. No amount of scratching the thing will soothe your irritation. The only way is to walk, only then does it cease. But your foot is in no position to do such a thing. So the itch persists, as does the deep-in-mind knowing of it. Twice the annoyance.

A part of me knew I needed to be doing more. The rumor of the Ashura still hung in my heart after the months of travel. And the threat of Arfan, even if I had sent post to alert him to my position.

The merchant king hadn't come to look for me still.

Then the threat of the Black Tower Band's oppression over Radika's family still weighed on me.

Too many strings pulling on me, and yet I sat immobile. Sometimes stillness, as needed as it is, can be a quiet death to someone so keen on action. A prison of quietness as much to the body as it is the mind.

We finished our drinks, and I found the morning's grist cleared from my mind—a better, brighter clarity than I'd had before, as well as the uncanny energy that manifested in one of my hands. It twitched with nervous energy. I eyed Radika.

She grinned. "*Awfhar* wakes you up and makes the tired go away. Someone on *awfhar* can stay up for a day and a half if they wanted. I've heard of some going days without sleep."

I felt my pulse throb inside my throat, and pressed two fingers to the spot to see if it were true or a hallucination. "Three heartbeats for every one. I didn't know there was a drink that mimicked the feeling of fright."

She laughed. "It lets you do more work in a shorter amount of time, and makes mornings less miserable."

I joined her in the short-lived cheer. "Well, that alone might be worth it. Most mornings are insufferable."

Radika murmured in low agreement, then pulled her mandolin to her chest. Its curve rested along her thigh and she slowly drew her fingers along it, pulling free smooth, lilting notes. At first, they sounded a foreign tongue, too fluid a thing, unlike Radi's voice when he played. This was subtle smoke on gentle wind.

It would be wrong to think it aimless or without body—swept into the current of air without direction. It was too ephemeral a noise to be bound in description is all. I couldn't give it name.

She hummed with it, a tuneless thing that still said much, only beyond my ears to hear properly.

Some of the patrons stirred, turning appreciative heads in her direction. Fingers drummed along the tabletops. Feet tapped against floor-bound stone. A low chorus of breaths pressed through tight lips—hums of their own, a touch discordant, carried over from behind the heating trough.

"He came from the east,
so far now from home,
to Mubarath,
of spice, and warmth,
and of stone.

Over roofs,
and under eaves,
he moves like fog
a shapeless ghost,
borne by the breeze

His skin a cloak,
of moonbeams and pearls,
all brilliant bright,
a spirit of vengeance,
let loose upon the world,
carried on wind,
and under moonlight

His skin a cloak,
all silver hard,
his form white shadow,
no doors or walls,
be his bar

The Ghost of Ghal,
come far from east,
come from afar.

Be he friend,
or be he foe,
this spirit of justice,
of white skin-iron,
and of snow

The Ghost of Ghal,
be he friend,
or be he foe
a spirit of vengeance,

where will he come next,
where will he go?

Silent come,
silent go,
whisper quiet,
white as snow

Not a man,
nor just a ghost,
mayhaps something more,
de // mon, de // mon?"

The crowd had fallen silent as Radika limbered through the song. It had come softer, slower, than anything Radi had ever sung or played. No quickening tempo or beats of broken thunder drumming at the heart of you. It was teased, almost pulling at the breath held within your throat. The pulling kiss of a lover pressing the wind from your lungs with but their lips and a simple inhale of their own.

It drew you—lulled you.

It whispered and asked questions you thought best not to think of, but now you had no hope but to do the very thing and wonder.

A few men put fingers to their mouths and let loose shrill-sharp whistles. Some of the workers behind the troughs clapped, low and respectful, far short of the raucous applause Radi drew.

Two women smiled and bobbed their heads to Radika in silent respect.

But the girl herself squeezed her arms tight around the mandolin as if trying to shrink away from the moment of adoration. Her face caught between a smile and fresh embarrassment. Eyes flitted toward me then back away. A concern, or a question hung in her face.

I didn't know if she was asking it of me, but I felt pressed to speak and answer. "That was great. Really."

Radika shrugged. "Thanks, it's all right, I guess. I didn't have long to think on it. It's a bit . . . canty in places. Sharp, but like a broken stone, all jagged. It's not smooth like I wanted."

"That's not true at all. It was wonderful." Then I thought on the word she'd said. "Canty?"

She frowned and thought for a moment. "You know how when a cat gets scared and makes its back like this?" Radika formed an arch with her hands.

I nodded.

"It's like that, but then the cat walks all . . . canty. It's just the word that makes sense." Radika's hands moved from the mandolin, fiddling with herself for a moment with the nervous energy I'd felt myself from the drink. Then they retreated to rest along the strings—they moved, slowly tripping back into song. This one lacked her voice, just the words the mandolin brought to life instead.

I heard them now, clearly as a story spoken aloud.

Worried. Nervous. Things too good to be true.

I reached out, just managing to brush my fingers against one of her forearms. My touch stilled her and she regarded me. "Don't be afraid. There's nothing to worry about."

Her eyes widened at that. "How did you know I was . . ." Radika pulled free from my gentle touch, holding to her mandolin tighter than before. Hands moved. A broken note. *Frightened.*

Not of anything else at the moment, but of me.

She was frightened of . . . me.

I pulled back, and for a moment, my hands fidgeted much like hers before I stowed them in my pockets. "Are you . . . afraid of me?"

Radika shuffled in the seat. Her hands ran along the shape of her mandolin, never coming to rest in any one place for long. The lines of her mouth tightened, broke, then tried to find some expression to fix in, but failed. In the end, she nodded.

The question left me in a broken breath. "Why?"

"It was just when I was singing the song. It came too easy in places. Like I knew you, and the parts about the ghost . . ." She dropped her voice to a whisper meant only for us. "They all came to me, but when I said the word 'demon,' I almost believed it. I'm sorry. I know it's silly, and doesn't make sense, but it scared me for a moment."

De // mon. De // mon. She'd sang it so, with the breath of pause between, stressing the syllables. I'd heard another song that held a note like that not so long ago. One that had carried far along the Mutri Empire, and maybe farther still.

"Radika, do you know anything about the Ashura?"

She pursed her lips, looking at me in obvious confusion. "Yes? My mother and father told me stories growing up. But we came to Mubarath when I was little, and here they don't believe them. They have their own Shaen stories and monsters. They call the demons here *bhaalghul,* or Ajuura. Like *ajuur,* those who rejected Alum Above's offer to walk with him in heaven's light. The first nine to embrace darkness, shadow, and to use black magic."

Like what Maathi had once said, though I'd only ever seen signs of eight. The ninth Ashura had not come the night my family had been murdered. "Do you know anything else?"

"A song about them? That's about it. Everyone's heard one or two, but I won't sing it here. Not with people listening. It's bad luck, Ari. And it makes people uncomfortable. If I'm going to sing, it should be more about The Ghost of Ghal." She flashed me a smile equal in good nature and childish mischief.

I couldn't argue with that, though my heart ached for want of more about the Ashura. I'd come this far chasing but a rumor, and if their stories lived in Mubarath, then I would find them.

Somehow.

Out there, beyond the country, they had struck a group of tinkers in the very sands Arfan bid me to. They were there.

I knew it.

And his service could bring me closer to them. I just had to get to him, or have him find me.

Where are you, damn merchant king? I had no time left to my thoughts as Radika pulled me to my feet, leading me out the way we'd come.

She bid farewell to the owner of the *awfhar* house and the patrons, then stopped outside. Radika motioned for me to take a seat at one of the outdoor empty tables. Once I had, she fell back into singing and playing.

She played as soft as before—sweet melody and quiet harmony to draw the heads of those not caught in the frenzied morning rush of busy trading and pressing matters.

And sure enough, they came.

So she sang to them, all of The Ghost of Ghal. The stranger come in from the east. White-cloaked and iron-skinned. No blade could pierce him true. No walls or doors could bar his way. He moved a wraith of moonlight shadow, white mist on the wind. But wasn't he a demon? A monster?

Oh, certainly it could be argued. But if he was a spirit of vengeance, then he came for the wicked, and none of the audience would ever be among those. Oh, no. So they cheered and nodded in approval. For who else could he, The Ghost of Ghal, come upon them for?

The thieves. The ne'er-do-wells. The cutthroats and bandits who often ended up too late on the gallows, all after hurting the innocent folk. This spirit had put a stop to a thing much like that just a night before.

Of course they'd heard, hadn't they? They'd been roused from their sleep to see it. And true enough, some watched him race along the sky above—white wind on his shoulder and at his back—the gust of air bringing him along as much as he brought it in his wake.

No one caught him.

And he *did* stop two of the Black Tower Band from hurting a poor shopkeeper. His skin *had* turned a knife's edge away. And he'd left with the only blood spilled being that of the thieves.

Soon, there were as many stories of The White Ghost of Ghal as there were mouths to carry them.

To shape them.

And to lie.

FIFTY-THREE

GLEANINGS

The Ghost of Ghal returned to the rooftops of Mubarath that night. The day had passed in a sweetness out of old stories. A young boy, a girl the same age, sharing drinks, songs, and soft touches when they could. The awkward shy stares as well.

But the darkness belonged to other side of that boy. Old memories, and their angers.

I peered over the edge of another roof, watching a trio of men walk with the wary alertness of those who knew trouble would come to find them.

And I would.

The Black Tower Band had heard of what happened to their two men, and now moved in larger groups. The three men left a shop, tossing a freshly plucked purse between themselves. They laughed. One hooted a whooping cry, more a bird's than a man's call, long into the night.

One of them pulled a children's wagon behind him, atop it resting two barrels that came up to my knee. The contents could have been drink, or some sort of spice. It must have been a small fortune in value if that tightly packed into a tiny container.

I watched them pass an old man's cart, its shape much like that of one I'd seen years ago in Keshum. Script ran along its edges that I could barely make out from where I sat perched. Smoke rose from its ends as one of the Black Tower Band asked the man to open it.

Not smoke. Mist. I recognized the contraption for what it was: a costly device, more for the writing along its side and bindings imparted on it, than the frame itself. The Ashram's artisans crafted ice boxes for many merchants, allowing them to lower the temperature within the device to a chilling climate like Ghal's in winter.

This may have been a city of crime, but it was also one of coin and commerce. And places such as that never truly sleep. There are always customers to be had, and business needing doing. That necessity meant there will always be those forced to work the late hours of the night and put themselves in harm's way for a piece of precious more.

One of the thieves grabbed the man by the hair and exchanged words low under breath.

The merchant quickly went about the business of serving them his goods: mounds of grated ice in tin cups, followed by ladles of sweetened syrup to give the cold dish flavor. Then the black band fell into the tidy work of relieving the elderly man of his coins. They moved with practiced efficiency, pinning him in place before pulling his purse from him. Fingers moved, metal flashed in the night, and the man soon found himself poorer for it.

The Bloodcoats, if ever they could be found diligent in their duties, should have stopped them. But much of the Black Tower Band's pickings went to buy a different sort of protection from what they offered. Payments to the "right people." The ones who held sword and spear in name of the law.

The Bloodcoats were as good as thieves in a way, even if they didn't take the coins directly out of a person's pockets. They profited all the same.

So these little mishaps happened much too often on the streets of Mubarath.

I watched them go, then crossed the way along the roofs over to where the old man rested.

We traded talk. Small comforts, and what I could offer by way of coin to salve his hurt. In exchange, he told me what he knew of the Black Tower Band. Just enough to further my prowling for the night.

The treatment of the old vendor would be the first of many injustices I'd witness that night. I would learn more about the shape of the world then, and that of myself. And who I wished to be, versus who I chose to become.

Those two are not always the same thing.

We forget it at the cost of ourselves.

❦

I caught up with the Black Tower Band as they paid a visit to another shopkeeper, banging fists against the door until a young woman greeted them.

Dark of hair and brow, with the complexion of those who spent much time in the sun. She had an angular face and a sharp-featured beauty, softened by the roundness of her cheeks. The woman wore a long dress the color of saffron trimmed in cream. It suited her.

One of the thieves, a man with his hair pulled into a long raggedy tail, placed a hand against the stone frame of the woman's shop. He leaned. And while I couldn't see his face, I knew it had the makings of that curved and greasy smile some men made when eyeing a woman with particular thoughts in mind.

She pulled her arms around herself and recoiled just enough to be noticeable.

I watched her harder, my mind tipping back to the game Nisha had taught me.

It didn't come with the ease it had before. I took in the lines of the woman's face—her shape, and the way she held herself.

Strong. Confident. But not without her fears. Something the Black Tower men knew in heart, and meant to use against her.

She shifted away from their looks. First to one side, then to her feet—anywhere but at their faces.

This woman lived a simple life. One without riches, and she had people that depended on her. The weight of the look in her face spoke of the heavy responsibilities of someone torn in two ways. The burden of elderly parents. And perhaps younger siblings. It was her steadfastness, and her strength, that saw them all to comfort and stability.

And these men threatened that.

One of my hands gripped hard to a handle made near-perfect for the shape of my palm. An ache built in the spot before I realized what I had been holding. The knife felt much like a limb I'd used all my life. An extension of me, and my will. I released it and took a breath to calm myself.

Every muscle in my legs flexed, screaming for me to spring from the roof and find a way to the ground. To rush and close the distance and bury my knife in the back of one of them. A quick twist and I could send the head of my staff crashing well into the skull of another. After that, it would be a lone fight against the remaining man.

If only the scenario would go as smoothly as I imagined. I was no soldier, and most of the fights I'd won came with their fair measure of great luck. I had no illusions about that.

One of the men stepped closer, almost coming into the doorway.

The woman retreated into the shop, but she did not shut the door behind her. She returned a moment later, flashing coins in hand. They left her palm in a quick swipe by one of the men. A pair of them left the moment they'd taken the money, but the one with his hair bound in a tail did not.

He lingered, leaning close. One of his hands went up to her face. A finger trailed along her cheek and she turned from the touch. He did not like that. His grip came strong against her chin, holding her tight.

Her eyes widened, and she flinched. A balled fist went into the air, and for a moment, her glare held a heat hot enough to turn sand to glass. But she remembered herself and who the men were. The clenched hand fell to her side and she resigned.

I waited for the man to act further, but the long-haired man shoved her back and left. The heavy drumming in my heart slowed, and I waited till the thieves vanished from sight.

The way cleared and I skulked across buildings until I reached the roof above where the young woman sat.

She'd taken to hunching on the lone step up to her shop door. Arms tight around her knees. No sounds of sobbing, just a quiet fatigue and the deep-buried weariness of having to deal with men like that.

"*Psst. Psst.*" I cupped a hand to my mouth, hoping to direct the sounds solely toward her, and not catch any other ears that might be listening elsewhere along the streets.

The woman shuffled, then looked around.

I made the call again.

She finally turned to look up, then gasped.

I splayed my fingers, making a universal gesture for calm.

Merciful gods above, she understood it, and did not scream well-wide into the night. "You're him. The ghost."

I nodded.

She licked her lips, then looked around as if she expected the men to return. "They were asking about you." Her glance now carried a weight of expectation—a silent question that I could not glean.

I waited in silence, hoping she would explain.

"The Black Band ones. They spread word about you, the ghost who attacked two of them. One of them died."

That revelation fell with the weight of stone and the coldness of ice. I hadn't meant to do that, and while my anger had asked it of me, I had done all I could to resist that particular impulse.

"But I don't believe it." She spoke the words with utter conviction. "I heard from a friend who heard it straight from Rakhim. You saved him. You helped him. And you hurt the men who did that to him, but you didn't kill him. You let him go."

True, but it left the question of how the man had died. Had the knife wound soured? Did I cut too close to something important and, with his broken foot, he couldn't get to a mender in time?

"I'm telling you that it was one of them that did their friend in. Probably didn't want the word spreading that a Black Tower's man had been given the rough of it. Or someone just did it to have one less mouth to feed and purse to pay for." She spat to her side. "Good riddance."

"And what did you tell them about me?" My voice remained practiced, deep, and perfectly neutral. The very tone expected of the mysterious strangers in the old stories and plays. The wanderer, the demon in disguise, or the hero playing the rogue.

She crossed her arms under her chest in the same defiance she'd shown the thieves. "Nothing. I'm not one to turn on the only one doing something against them."

"How much did they take from you?"

That drew her short and she fumbled for the words. "I-I, not even a barinth. Just a few soft qitha."

The qitha was a coin fashioned from a metal close to tin in construction, and near enough in value along the Golden Road.

I didn't have any of those smaller coins on hand, and had to make do with a single barinth. More than the shopkeeper had lost, but I figured a little generosity in the midst of being a criminal would serve me better than stinginess.

The common folk remember a kindness done. And when given freely, it has interesting ways of coming back to a man. Not that that's why it should ever be done.

I tossed the coin toward her. "For your troubles, and another piece of information?"

She caught the copper piece, stammering through all the nonsensible things someone freshly given money in surprise could think to say. I waited till she finished and asked the question I expected. "What do you wish to know?"

"Where do the Black Tower Band call home?"

She pointed.

I followed the gesture to an old structure standing taller than any building in sight. Far at the end of the city itself loomed a building of solid black, casting a deeper shadow along all things before it, even in the dead of night.

A tower that took its color from the deepest of shadow-darkened dreams.

I thanked the woman and headed toward my new destination.

The tower of nightmare black.

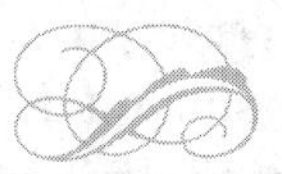

FIFTY-FOUR
Plans of Flight

The journey took nearly a candlemark, moving across the roofs with all the care I could take.

At first glance the structure's form mirrored many of the other tall and similarly shaped buildings dotting Mubarath. Towers raised high, rectangular instead of the cylinders of Ghal, but the reasoning for that lay clear on second look. They boasted long slats cut deep into their heads, and I knew those to be by design. They caught all passing air, funneling it down deep channels in the tower until blown through lower passages and into other buildings, sometimes straight onto the streets themselves.

Much like Ghal had its resident fire sellers and keepers, offering bits of passing warmth to travelers, Mubarath shaped and sold the wind. Wealthy merchants oft paid to have buildings adjoined to a wind catcher, always bringing cool air to customers. The rest merely made do with walking by the small vents along the tower to catch errant breezes to drive away the worst of the heat.

But the black tower, highest of all, was no wind catcher. Solid in shape with nothing to betray a look inside, it rose to a broad head with a ridged crown of stone atop. Almost a prison from where a man could look down, but had no hope of mantling and descending. The tower's surface had the smoothness of glass, offering little by which to climb.

Except for the lengths along it that looked as if they'd been struck by the fist of god himself. Portions of the tower sides revealed missing sections and crumbling stone, but only a madman would try to use them to gain entry. One misplaced foot, and the climber would need to sprout wings to survive.

And in my experience, men could not fly. Even those who once styled themselves sparrows. They fell all the same. And they died.

I moved farther along rooftops, eyeing men who I guessed to be members of the Black Tower Band. They met with others, traded coin, gripped hands, and a few laughs. But eventually, all men headed toward the old stone tower.

I counted at least seventeen men walking into the place, and ghost or not, those were not odds in my favor. A poor demon I'd make going up against that many.

I didn't think my growing reputation needed stories of thorough trouncing. Besides, I'd had enough of those over my life to know I wasn't eager for another.

As I tracked the comings and goings of the thieves, I spotted several more of the barrels I'd seen the first trio bring along with them. All the same height, and wrapped around top and bottom with a braided dark cord.

One of the men had a lit pipe between his teeth, and moved to inspect a barrel. He was met with a quick cuff along the head and shoved back from the container. Shouting followed, and the pipe was pulled clean from his mouth and thrown to the ground by the thief who'd struck him.

The Black Tower Band continued to haul more of the small barrels inside.

My gaze filtered back to the broken section of stone along the tower. I spotted children's kites that had likely been caught in too strong a wind and gotten lost in the openings. And a few left trailing strings down below, but the angle of their landing left them hard-wedged against the broken stones, making it impossible to pull them free.

Realization hammered into me and I almost laughed at the solution that came to me. An old game, a sparrow's cunning, a bit of clever student's knowledge, and The Ghost of Ghal could very well scale the tower and right some wrongs.

I just needed more of a plan. Some supplies.

And a kite.

Morning saw me back at Radika's home to share a breakfast. I told her what I'd learned, and my plan. The look she gave me told me she thought it monumentally stupid.

"You're just going to sneak-thief your way up an almost impossible-to-climb tower, look around without being seen, and then make off with their coin?"

I shrugged. "More or less."

"How have you stayed alive for so long?" She eyed me in genuine awe.

I sipped the broth. "There's considerable debate on that account, and depending on which stories you listen to: I'm magic, a demon, a scion of Brahm himself, or . . . incredibly lucky."

Radika snorted and pushed her own bowl aside. "Luck runs out, you know?"

I did, but thinking on it did little to help.

"But, if you're going to do this, you can't just rob the Black Tower Band. They'll hit people twice as hard to get the money back."

I frowned, not having considered that. The thieves here worked differently than back in Abhar. When sparrows pulled low tithings, we suffered a rough night and an empty belly. We could always make it up over the long term. But the sparrows never took out low earnings against shopkeepers with force.

"So what do you propose I do?"

Radika took a deep breath. "Some of the Bloodcoats are on the take, so if you really want to hurt the band, you'll have to make sure the Bloodcoats have reason to go into their home. That's the hard part. They don't have one. You'll need to search the place, and then do something that the Bloodcoats *must* come looking into."

"I think I can manage something." I pulled free my purse, upending all its contents onto my palm. "I can't go far with this, but maybe just enough to start some trouble. Do you know where I can get a kite?"

Radika smiled, and it turned out, she knew exactly where to find what I needed.

We wasted little time, and set fast to work at smoking the Black Tower Band out of their home.

And their riches.

I ventured out with Radika and Shola, who decided that today he would be on his best behavior.

Miracles do happen.

The cat stayed several steps behind me as we visited the various shops I needed for what I had in mind, including a few projects I'd been thinking of since leaving the Ashram. And, Shola's presence earned me extra consideration from many vendors. It certainly was no imposition on Shola that everyone seemed delighted to see him, and some went as far as to offer him little treats.

And I might have detected an extra spring in his step at the pampering.

This place would prove to be terrible for his ego, I feared.

We spotted pieces of parchment pinned to walls along the way and anywhere that might catch folks' attention. All of them bore the same message. An offering—a bounty for the capture of The White Ghost. The Ghost of Ghal.

I pointed them out to Radika, who gave me a wry smile, musing at how much that fortune could turn the course of her life, and that of those under her care. My frown wiped the smile from her face and she reassured me she'd only been joking. The tension short-lived, we went on to gather all that I needed.

Radika and I collected thin bands of steel that a smith kindly agreed to shape into rings that would easily fit to the head of my staff.

Baba had been sent out to fetch me a kite from some of the other children he knew, and we'd given him one of my last remaining copper rounds to purchase it with. A tidy sum for any child to part with for a toy.

But I would have to replace the weak and thin line with something sturdier that wouldn't hamper the kite's ability to catch the wind. And I would need the materials to etch and inscribe the minor bindings to fulfill my plan.

That required ink and a fine brush, which thankfully did not cost me much at all. For carving, I resigned myself to the use of a sharp chisel I'd bargained for when dealing with the smith. Its tip proved hard enough to engrave metal the way I'd need.

Lastly, I purchased several powder matches, and several pounds of *achuur* resin, a crystalline amber that smoldered and kicked up an awful stench, but more than that, created an inferno's worth of smoke all without a hint of fire.

Materials all accounted for, I decided to head back and leave Radika to her own dealings. She had a plan to further spread The Ghost of Ghal's mythos, and in doing so, better set the stage for my game.

FIFTY-FIVE

Motions

"*Bah. Bah.*" The young boy passed me the kite.

I took it from him with quiet thanks, patting his shoulder.

He spoke half his name and smiled in obvious pleasure.

"Would you like to sit with me and watch while I fiddle about, Baba?" I didn't look at him when I asked the question, focusing on restringing the kite with what I'd purchased. A braid of cotton, hemp, and linen. Quite strong enough to support a good deal of weight. And it remained light enough to let a kite do its job and soar as high as needed. There was, of course, some disagreement as to the maximum weight the line could bear, such as that of a person's. But I had some ideas on how to deal with that.

Lessons from my past seemed as well earned as they did learned. And now I could put them to use in a manner the masters of the Ashram would certainly frown on.

I examined the kite. A simple thing styled to the shape of a bird when viewed high in the sky. Two canted angles that met at a point in the middle. Its colors were that of a bouquet of bright flowers: rose red fringed with sunburst orange, and a wash of strong yellow. It would do.

Content that I'd done the best I could with it, I fastened it to the reel and began the painful process of setting ink to line. No dot or dash could be mislaid as I used the Traveler's Tongue to bring meaning to my minor bindings.

The same sort I'd once used to transfer incoming force against a kite to store in its spool. Only now those bindings and materials would have to endure a great deal more weight, and for nearly as long as the entire festival fight had lasted. A lot to ask of string and wood. So I would need to enlist the aid of something else.

Something with the weight and strength of stone.

A full candlemark passed with me going through the artisaning process of holding my folds and imbuing the string with what I required of it.

I then set to the task of engraving the frame of the kite with a series of bindings to affix a small flat stone to the center of it. I'd plucked the rock on a quick return trip to the black tower, ensuring it was the same material as the structure itself. There had been an ample amount of tiny debris at the base below where the broken section sat. That would add some weight I would have to account for, but it was a necessary component for the plan ahead.

All the while, Baba sat company with me, pointing and delighting in the simple things of the world around us. Petals falling in the wind from rooftop gardens or from strung vine blossoms between windows. Once, he pulled on my sleeve, drawing my attention to a particular few pieces of once-flower coming our way.

I smiled, watching them with him as they flitted, caught in unseen breath. Their motions almost reminded me of the candle and the flame—the ebb-and-flow dance of flickering fire, caught in breathing to stay alive. The subtle motions of snapping and pulsing almost like a heart in excitement. Soon, I found myself as entranced as Baba.

The longer I watched, the more I began to see not petals, but light stones thrown carefree into the air. Much like what Rishi Ibrahm had done, and Mahrab before. With time, and nearly another third of a candlemark gone as well, I felt comfortable enough to predict where some of the pieces would fall.

Baba and I soon made a game of it. He hooted and pointed to any petal that landed where I'd said it would. And he chuckled twice as hard when I failed to accurately call them. In my mind, I fell into the folds, envisioning the flowers as stones coming to a point I wished. I did not try to extend my will further than that. No attempt to actually bind them.

I simply watched. Mused. And guessed how they would fall. Just the motions of it all.

Eventually, Baba grew discontent with being a spectator, and decided to throw his own things into the mix. He'd toss a stone and declare with a bellowing "Bah. Bah!" as to where it would land.

To my surprised, Baba had a better grasp of the weight of the world and falling matter than I'd credited him with. By the end of it, I may have guessed the proper placement of the petals perhaps three out of every five fallen pieces. Not bad at all.

Baba called every single one perfect to pinpoint spot.

He may have been tied of tongue, but the boy had a sharper eye than I think anyone else realized, and maybe another gift altogether. One I couldn't make the shape of yet.

The hours passed and my brow broke full into sweat from the heat and extent of effort when I returned to applying my minor bindings. All of which left me able to then begin etching the bands of steel I'd fastened around the head of my staff.

My early experiment with the kardan had taught me that my thinking had been sound, just not my execution. I sought to remedy that now. The thicker steel would hold a great deal more force, and with several pieces of the metal fixed in place, I didn't run the risk of overtaxing any particular band. Much like my first working with my kite, I turned to the flexibility and strength of wood to add to the bindings. A conduit to channel the backlash and help bleed out the excess energy to keep from disaster.

Eventually, the work was done. Well, a part, at any rate. I had more to do.

Legends and misdeeds don't build themselves.

That night I made my way back across the city, forgoing my white cloak and ghostly guise. Every motion of my arm, touch of the staff against ground, or turn of it through air sent force into the tool.

It built, held, and waited for the proper moment.

Brahm Above, please don't let this blow up in my hand.

The black tower had been built near a wind catcher, and so I had all the makings of my own storm.

I surveyed the area to make sure I wouldn't be disturbed by late-night passersby, and once content I was alone, I set to work. A nail and chisel allowed me to carve the script I thought would bring me the current I required.

A wind catcher's nature is to channel fresh air from its head, funnel it downward, and gust through buildings for cooling, or fan wide into softer breezes through some streets. I needed a consistent upward draft that would allow me to sail my kite up into a broken part of the tower. But I couldn't run the risk of diverting so much of the wind that people would notice and look into the channels.

So I created a long but crudely written script that would siphon the air from other channels and carry it along the particular one venting to the street I would be overlooking. More than the usual current of wind would strike the building wall, and that air would rush upward. The powerful draft would be all I needed to sail my kite up and into the broken sections of the tower.

The only thing remaining was the use of a good brick. And I could see to that later.

A cavernous groan, better belonging to a beast from story, echoed through the bottom of the wind catcher. Wind sailed through the tunnel, buffeting me.

Nothing that would throw me from my feet, but it had a weight like a grown man pushing against my chest.

Happy with my work, I made my way to the roof from where I'd strike come the right night. True to my design, some of the excess air rose along the building's side and up to where my kite would make the proper use of it.

The stage was set.

A cast of villains was already assembled. All the play needed was one actionable hero. And one brilliant smoke show. Because nothing brings a crowd like a fire.

I would know.

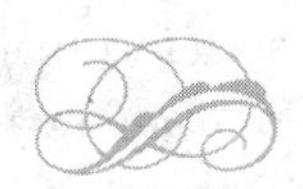

FIFTY-SIX

Smoke, Wind, and Kites

I sat on the roof of Radika's thiefling den, watching the falling flower petals drift downward in the wind. The exercise had grown to become something of a comfort of late, much like the candle and the flame.

Eventually, Radika visited the roof, passing me the brick I had asked her for. "Are you going to tell me what this is for?"

"I'm going to inscribe it with a small magic, and it's going to take on a property of physical adherence to another material like it. It's how some people at the Ashram can join stone to stone without mortar."

She looked at me as if I had spoken a fictional language, and wore the patient smile of someone who decided that it was impolite to point it out to me.

I opened my mouth to apologize, shut it, then reconsidered. "You know how a large stone breaks into a dozen other stones if you smash it apart?"

Radika nodded.

"Right, it's all just one big piece. What I'm going to do is write something on this brick that helps it remember it's another piece of something else. So, say, the roof of a building. Once the side with the . . . magic words on it touches another bit of stone, they'll join together like they were always meant to be. The only way to separate them will be by breaking the brick." I hated simplifying the minor bindings to something akin to storybook magic words.

Though, I suppose to the uninitiated, they may as well have been.

"Will you be safe?" Her voice remained level—the calm, practiced measure of a musician who always had the hold of how they sounded. But behind the question, and her eyes, I caught sight of her concern.

I placed a hand on her shoulder and gave it a firm squeeze. "Obviously. I mean, haven't I been?" I smiled.

She did not return the expression. "Ari, you say that like it's supposed to make me feel better."

I kept the grin plastered on my face. "Doesn't it?"

Radika shook her head. "No. It makes me think you're reckless. And you think being clever and smiling can get you out of trouble."

That stung. Particularly because it was true, and doubly so . . . because it *had* been true. Most of my better moments were born out of no small amount of cleverness, and the occasional well-timed smile. Saying nothing, of course, about the extraordinary amount of luck I'd been fortunate to have at my back.

But none of that meant I wanted to add extra weight to the heart of a friend.

I reached out and wrapped an arm around her, holding her there for a moment of long-drawn silence. Finally, I found the best thing to say. "I don't know, Radika. But I promise you I'll do my best to come back safely. Is that better?"

She nodded. "Much." Her lip folded under her teeth and she lightly chewed a corner before catching herself in the nervous act. "You think you can get the Bloodcoats to storm the place?"

On that, I had more certainty than of my own safety. "Absolutely. I'm a particularly industrious fellow when it comes to, uh, inciting disaster. Just ask the people of Ampur." I grinned. It didn't last long as a sharp pain sparked along my thigh. "Ow." I rubbed the spot where Radika's nails had dug in.

"It's a pinch for luck." Her face remained as perfectly emotionless as the brick in my hand.

I glowered. "Uh-huh. First I've heard of such a thing."

She held the stoic expression. "That's because all your luck's come from Alum Above until now. I'm just giving you extra." Then she leaned in and gave me another piece of luck in a manner many a young man would want to experience again. For the extra luck, of course. Her lips brushed mine, and she pulled away, watching me.

By now, I'd grown a bit better at hiding my surprise when a girl decided to show me a hint of her affection. Consider it just another piece of youthful serendipity. Sometimes, many times in fact, life treats you to enough little surprises that you come to learn how to just enjoy them. The questions of how and why fall away, and you are left with just the pleasantness of the moment.

And how I wished it could have stretched on. But, like most stories, it was not meant to be.

Afternoon passed into darkness and The Ghost of Ghal went to work.

I'd left Shola in the care of Radika and her band, bringing with me only my tools of mischief. My candle, cloak, and cane. Kite, brick, and knife. And of course the trinkets I'd purchased with which to bring about a world of smoke and promise of fire. My only regret was that I had no access to more rithra powder. I would have loved to set the top of their tower burning with red flame and smoke, just for the dramatic effect. That would surely have brought the Bloodcoats quicker than anything else.

But a performer makes do with what he's given.

And I had every intention of giving the Black Tower Band, and the people of Mubarath, a great show.

The trek and rooftop climb took till near the end of eighth candle. Once in place, I unslung my kite and let it loose. The wind did its job and took the toy to the air. Old motions returned to me as I guided the kite with the wind, shaping its path toward the broken section high above. This time I worked with a more forgiving line than before, letting me use my wrists and turn of a hand to better control my tool.

Eventually, I edged the kite up the way I wanted, letting its underside brush against the broken-stone opening in the tower.

Snap.

A forceful pull as the stone I'd bound to the bottom of the kite locked in place. The exact same binding I'd carved into the brick. Now the device would remain firmly anchored. All I had to do was weigh down the other end, and I'd thought of a solution to that as well.

I laid down the spool, pinning it in place with a foot before removing the inscribed brick I'd shown to Radika. Bending low, I brought it close to one of the flat end of the spools. The block clacked hard against the stone of the roof, pinching the wooden handle of my kite down between the roof and itself. I gave the line a forceful tug, seeing if the spool would slip free from the makeshift clamp I'd fashioned.

It did not move.

Now all I had to do was scale the string. The *long* string hovering over thin air and a drop that would break most of the bones in a man's body, if it didn't kill him outright.

I stepped onto the ledge, dropping to all fours and grabbing on to the hempen-blend line. It shook under my weight, wobbling just a bit, but did not snap. You would think this brought me some measure of calm.

It did not.

I could have easily fumbled my script somewhere along the long length of the cord. Part of the line could fray somewhere along its shape, and if that piece happened to take some of my inscription along with it, well, the whole script would be buggered. And I would go hurtling to the ground, The Ghost of Ghal ending up flatter than a piece of *thori.*

It wouldn't make for a good legend, that.

I clung to the line, hands fastened hard to it, and my legs crossed below. So far, it held as I inched my way forward.

The sky above rumbled in discontent, and I'd grown to know the sound and what it foretold.

A storm.

The low drumming signaled that it would come hard and fast, as they are wont to do along the desert places of the world. It lived up to that and there was no gentle wash before it peaked. The storm struck in full, beads of rain stinging like glass instead. My only comfort came by way of the relative warmth of Zibrath's climate. Had it been any colder, the water and air would have brought an ache to my hands that would have caused me to slip.

My mind went to the candle and the flame to distance me from my discomfort.

I climbed. My arms ached, as did my legs. A low fire built throughout my muscles, reaching the deeper bones of me as I went on.

The wind intensified, promising to throw me free of the line if I didn't quit and let go myself. My eyes cried out as harder rain struck them, minute whiplashes against the tender parts of me. All I could do was hang there and absorb the length of pain from all places around me, and just as much inside me.

The candle and the flame became my reprieve. I poured into it all of my hurt. My desires to make this climb, and to see Radika and her little nameless group of thieves freed from the Black Tower Band. And, I will confess, that a small part of me wished to pluck all their coin and recoup my dwindled fortune.

Arfan hadn't responded to my post, if he had even gotten it. Radika's thieves had made little progress in learning any secrets about him. And I had no idea where across the desert I would have to search for him. How to navigate the shapeless landscape and its rigors, or the cost. I may have been reckless, but I wasn't so much the fool that I'd have ventured out there so woefully unprepared.

The thoughts steeled me as I climbed on, giving little care to the time it took. My cloak whipped about as the storm hardened, now beating down with near sheets of solid rain. Every bolt that struck me turned to mist as it met the white-scale cloak.

I had made one grave miscalculation. Yes, the wind catcher would funnel more air along a particular channel to aid my kite flying. But I hadn't counted on a storm to fuel its currents. The result came as monstrous breaths along the underside of the line, sending it swaying in all directions.

I bobbed, rattled, and occasionally spun as the cord tried to return to some semblance of steadiness. I say some, because there had not been one moment where it stayed true-still. My fingers slipped, and one of my hands fell from the line. I gasped, taking in more water than air, and turned the breath into a hard coughing choke. That did not help me maintain my hold.

I hung from crossed legs, the stretch pulling the muscles along my torso and my spine. For several uncountable breaths, my heart beat to a tempo too fast to track, and was the only salvation I had from a deeper fear taking root in me. The whole of me shook. My staff vibrated against me, and I worried that it could slip free from the fastenings keeping it in place. Go tumbling down to the ground and shatter from the fall.

The sack hanging from my shoulder now grew to be an added weight, and the temptation to cut it free to spare myself the burden built. But that would render the whole plan useless as quick as that. And then what?

I could return to Radika, safe and sound. She would be happy with that even if it meant the Black Tower Band went on to give grief to her as well as all the other thieves of Mubarath. But they would live, and so would I. Not so bad a fate, was it?

Fear has a way of making the little deaths of ourselves, and our desires, seem palatable. We will sacrifice our greater wants for the ease of smaller options that bring us peace of mind, but kill our better impulses and wants.

And what I wanted, more than any measure of safety for myself, was Radika and her family safe. I wanted an end to the Black Tower Band—people of cruel position and power, to lose their hold over the less enfranchised. I knew that sort of power imbalance from my time under Mithu, under the heel and fear of Gabi and Thipu.

No one else would suffer that while I could do something about it.

And I wanted to live up to the dreams of Brahm the Wanderer. Of the Asir, the free-roaming heroes who righted wrongs. I'd bound fire, so I knew those things to be true and within my power. All they required of me was to hold to those desires more strongly than any doubts that tried to wrest them from me. And to hang to the line just as hard.

I bent, flailing and sending my hands scrabbling for some purchase. They found hold and I resumed my climb.

Brahm's blood. I went on and reached the ledge where my kite had fixed itself through the minor binding. The only way to free it would be to elide the script along the bottom of the stone, but seeing as how that had now joined the rocks below it with the weight of a mountain holding it in place, it'd be simpler to leave it all alone.

I took in the place around me. Nothing but charred walls. I went to one corner safe from the wind and cold, opened my sack, and pulled out some hay and other cheap tinder that I'd scrounged for free. My powder matches had been stored in a waxed wrap of cloth, and it looked to have done the trick in keeping them dry. Lastly came one of the three white candles I'd purchased.

I laid the head of a match against the hard stone below me, and a quick snap of my wrist brought about a bulb of flickering flame. It touched to the wick of the candle and brought it to light. I brought the fire to the kindling and set it ablaze. With that, I sprinkled some of the resin atop it. It sizzled like water on hot oil, and quickly turned the amber material black.

Acrid curls of smoke wisped up from the little crystals and soon billowed into a mass of smoke to rival a full campfire.

An opening ahead revealed a hall beyond, which would let me navigate my way along the upper levels to set more fires. Though it would all amount to little should the storm drag on.

I picked up my candle, holding it by the clay base it rested in. The curved edges would keep most of the wax from dripping down onto my hand, but some would inevitably touch my skin. I could only hope that by that time it would have cooled enough not to be a serious problem.

I inched my way along the curve of the tower's hall, watching for any sign of movement. But what gossip I'd overheard about the Black Tower Band indicated they mostly kept to the better preserved lower levels. And it made sense.

My count of them numbered from twenty to possibly somewhere in the thirties. The height of the tower would make it impractical for them to spread themselves out too far through the place. It would make communication nearly impossible if any speed was required, not to mention rallying in case of an emergency. But it also meant that any bits of precious would be far below me, and closer to their hands.

I would have to get close and personal at some point. Most of the rooms I peeked into were empty but for windows that led back out to the world in storm. Some of the rain occasionally filtered in, and the sound of rushing water prompted me to look into the noise. Small channels had been built along the walls nearest the window. This tower had been built to account for storms and likely led the rain somewhere, but I hadn't a clue where.

I continued walking, wondering if the small patch of resin I'd lit had kicked up enough smoke to filter far out of the side of the tower, or if the storm had smothered the worst of it. Thankfully, the weather seemed short-lived, as I could hear the sound of rain thinning while I navigated the tower. The breaks of thunder softened and grew father apart, and it told me that I would be able to complete my plan with a little more patience on my part.

I moved down a set of stairs, but found nothing on that floor. Each room burned as black as the rest, and all without a thing in them. Floor after floor brought the same result until I neared the bottom third of the tower. The first room might have been empty of people, but not possessions. Nor lit torches in sconces outside. Signs these floors must be occupied. A few cot beds that offered little comfort to those who used them, clothes strewn about, and bits of broken bottles and pitchers still intact.

I rifled through everything, looking for whatever I could find. As I did, the storm continued to dwindle. My searched turned up little in the way of fortune. Some spare coins, all copper. So I brought all of the clothing to the nearest window, wadding it along with another clump of tinder. It caught fire and I fed the resin to smoke, thicker than the last batch I'd set off.

Encouraged, I set off to check the rest of the floor, finding much the same. Some rooms were better with their offerings, leaving me with at least two full pouches of coin. As thanks for their generosity, I did the Black Tower men the favor of not having to launder their clothes, burning them and setting off more smoke.

Voices filtered up to me as I neared the stairs to the floor below. Laughter. The familiar sounds of men too deep into their drink. I crept down and peeked around a corner to see one approaching me.

I fumbled, nearly dropping my candle as I reached for my staff.

The man rounded the end, spotting me. He moved in the uncoordinated stupor that said he'd been long gone in the grip of alcohol. And it took him a longer moment still to register the oddity of me standing there. His eyes widened, mouth slowly opening into a stupefied O.

I brought the staff crashing down on his head, not bothering to trigger any of my minor bindings I'd set to it.

The blow did the trick, and the man fell. Though, in all fairness, it was just as likely that he'd already been close to falling over of his own inebriation. I grabbed him by his ankles, hauling him into the closest room, and praying it did not have anyone else inside.

Brahm's tits, my luck is something else. The room was exactly as I'd asked for, empty—mostly. . . . The room contained several dozen of the barrels I had seen the Black Tower Band bring into the structure over the course of my spying excursions.

I let go of the man and went over to inspect the barrels. The room once had a few arched windows along its curve, only they'd been boarded up so well that not a drop of moisture found its way through despite the storm. I reached the nearest of the barrels, spotting it to be tightly corked. My Arasmus steel knife came to hand as quick as that and I pried the cork free.

"Oh, god . . ." The shock of what I had found made dropping the candle seem like a good idea, though that would have sent me off to meet Brahm far sooner than I had any desire to.

A familiar fluid rested inside the barrel. The same material that once killed a brother of mine, and addicted the minds of many in Keshum.

Unrefined white-joy.

Every. Barrel. Contained. White-joy.

Enough that, if set off, would reduce a good chunk of this side of the tower to dust and crumbled stone. A sound so loud that no amount of thunder could compete with it. And so much smoke the whole of Mubarath would see it, despite the dark.

I couldn't fathom what they needed so much of this for, and the terrible use it could all be put to. But the value of it far outstripped the small coins the band had been lifting from shopkeepers, and if the Bloodcoats learned the thieves had been storing this . . .

One solution to many problems.

I dragged the man back from the room, making the aching effort of hauling him up the stairs to the floor I'd come from. While this may have seemed like a small mercy because of what I had in mind, I will admit that I gave little consideration to keeping his way up bump-free. Though, you could blame the unforgiving stairs for that.

Content that he would be a decent distance from the disastrous outcome of what I planned to do, I returned downstairs. I upended one of the barrels, taking the time to wind a trail of the white-joy from one corner of the room back toward the mass of other containers. Then, I set a new candle in place on the ground, removing its clay base. Once lit, it would last a full candlemark, near three hours.

Too long.

So I pared it down with my knife to my best guess at a quarter of an hour. More than enough time to skulk about, set off more smoke, and get out.

The storm had finally stopped and I lit the candle from the head of the one already burning. That done, I made my way back into the hall, circling around to the other empty rooms. The process came naturally to me now.

Cleaned out what I could, searched for loose coin, and set a small fire that would use the resin and bleed more smoke out into the world. That done, I made my way to where the Black Tower Band had gathered.

A pair of double doors led to a room ahead, and the loudest of the noises came from there.

I knelt, deciding it best to shroud the passageway in case I needed to fall back. So I set off the last of the resin in the hall, waiting for the thick black smoke to obscure the length of the hall. Some of it filtered under the shut doors, and I followed it until I came to rest against the entry.

"Fire!" My call echoed into the room, but no one stirred inside. I cupped a hand to my mouth, and almost shouted again, but some of the smoke had made its way through the covering over my mouth. I choked. "Fire." The word came more a sputtering cry.

Again, nothing.

So I leveled the head of my staff against the doors, focusing my will on the bindings I'd imparted into the steel bands and the body of wood. *Just one band's worth will do,* I thought, and struck the staff against the doors. The force of a hundred men, all kicking at once, reduced the barrier to splinters and all to the sound of a thunderclap.

The men inside roused, and the smoke began to rise up from the ground, filling the space between us. Not so thick a thing we could not all see each other.

Nearly twenty men, all in various states of bleariness, just rousing from drunken sleep or well close to voiding their guts. They staggered to their feet, and a few pointed at me while dribbling incoherent mutterings.

"The Ghost? S'it's s'him." One of the men staggered toward me, fist raised. He swung. The blow never would have reached me, but I stepped into it, taking it on my shoulder as I brought my staff up between his legs.

He toppled.

"Smoke?" One of the men turned his attention from me, just realizing the happenings around us. "Fire? Alum, what's happening?"

And the opportunity came clearer than if it had been written by the hand of god. I must have looked quite the sight to them: brilliant bright white cloak. Staff in hand. A burning candle in the other. A world of smoke growing around us. And the door had just shattered at my touch, as far as they were concerned.

Sure, it may have been the work of happenstance, a little planning, and some creative use of the minor bindings, but drunk men are not sober judges when it comes to the truth of things. So, I seized my moment.

"I am The Ghost of Ghal, and I conjured the smoke and the fire. And if you do not leave your home, I will bring down a thunder that will shake the very foundations of your tower. I will call fire and a force of wind so strong a thing to break the stone around us." I gestured to the door as more smoke filled the space.

I'd made a good performance. Khalim would have been proud.

Small shame the men had drunk too much to care, or be properly frightened.

They screamed and charged me.

Oh, Brahm's tits.

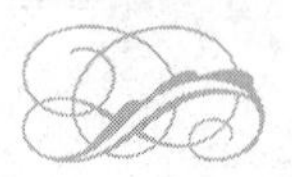

FIFTY-SEVEN

FIRE AND THUNDER

The first of the men kept his balance better than I'd have imagined for being drunk. He swung, wide and hard. The blow struck my shoulder, sending the candle from my grip. It tumbled, the flame snuffed out as soon as it struck the ground.

For the space of a heartbeat, the thought did cross my mind that my own fire could very well be put out if this went poorly.

I twisted, taking the staff in both hands and brought it against the man's ribs with all the force I could manage. And, a little bit of binding help. I triggered another of the rings, giving thanks that this time I'd taken account of how to control the flow of energy, both stored and released.

The impact sent him flying to one side. His ribs wouldn't be broken, but certainly cracked.

The quick exchange brought all the other thieves to a stop. They watched what had happened, and now traded silent looks.

Brahm, if you can hear me, please let this next bit go my way. I cleared my throat, putting on my best ominous voice. "You can't hurt me. Your own men have seen that I cannot bleed. No knife can cut me. And I strike with the strength of a dozen men."

Some of the men placed hands on each other, fighting to shove another person my way. One unfortunate man stumbled forward, freshly pushed by his generous friends.

I thumped him the same, taking him at the arm with a proper crack that broke the limb by my guess.

He collapsed and howled. The man writhed, cradling his injury, screams loudening.

Just stall. If I can keep this going long enough, I can swing at them one at a time. Or talk my way out. I tried the latter once more. "I'm giving you this one chance to leave." My theatrical voice cracked as more smoke filtered into the room. Not exactly great acting. I coughed, and some of the men joined me. "If you stay, the fire will take you, flesh, bone, and marrow. The smoke will choke you, and the thunder I bring—"

"Fire!" One of the men's eyes widened larger than they had before, and he pointed behind me. "The white-joy. The white-joy!"

And realization struck all of them.

Panic.

Men broke into pandemonium. Some grabbed whatever pieces of precious were nearest, running not toward me, but past me. The passage had grown thick with black smoke, and I doubted they would make their way to anywhere but safety.

A pair decided to try their luck to avenge their injured comrades.

I was no real fighter, and took a couple of heavy blows that reminded me of my youth. But for each hit, I struck back. The staff worked as I'd hoped and I sent two more men to the ground in agony.

"This is your last chance to flee, or I swear to Brahm, I will call down a thunder to destroy you all!" I raised my hand above, and then spoke the words I'd heard so long ago. "Tak."

Some of the men looked around as if expecting the storm to break out in the room itself.

But I never got to speak the second binding.

Thunder. The weight of the world rolled through. And stone gave way.

I had gotten my timing wrong, and shaved off too much of the candle. The fire had caught the white-joy, and the barrels had gone off.

Everything rocked hard and I flew to the ground. The men remaining in the room followed me down. Bells chimed in my skull, and my eyes spun without relief.

Smoke continued to fill the air.

I coughed, struggling to my feet.

Some of the men mirrored me. Two only managed to get to all fours, then voided their bellies' contents.

"He . . . what happened?" One of the men looked to another for answers.

I wish I had regained enough clarity to make good on the obvious opening, but a new fear had found me, and I turned and ran. The way I'd come from had now been reduced to collapsed stone and piled rubble. My only path was the other set of stairs, leading down through the remaining floors of the tower. The explosion of the barrels had left a gaping hole in the tower that could fit a single-story home.

I coughed, the smoke now threatening to choke me fully. So I ran on. Some of the other banded thieves were ahead of me, and the one thing that unites men is the panic of the world falling apart.

We ran together, soon breaking out through the front of the tower and onto the streets, but I didn't stop. I made my way off to a street I had committed to memory. The world now a blur.

All that remained was the frenzied race along the paths I'd traveled so many times in scouting the tower.

The night passed in a darkened haze.

But all through it, I heard the cries of thieves, loud in the air. The shouts of the confused populace, roused by the explosion, and the smoke trailing high above. Horns followed. And the Bloodcoats took to the streets again.

And I'll give you one guess where they marched toward.

Tower posts rang a cry of beaten brass and panicked voices. Some spread word of a fire. Others shouted warning of the clouds of smoke, and that they were a portent of worse things to come.

They weren't, but how was anyone to know?

And lastly came the screams about the man in white. The ghost who'd been spotted fleeing the aftermath of the thunder that broke apart a side of the black tower. White cloaked and all. A miscreant who'd been said to have attacked men in Mubarath. A thief, according to some. And a hero to others.

The Ghost of Ghal.

I ran, doing my best not to pay mind to the shadows cast along walls under torchlight. Trailing figures—the mob on my heels. The paths were not as easy to remember as I would have liked. I owed some of that to my learning them from rooftop vantages, not having navigated them on foot below.

So I found myself chancing looks above, to familiar ledges I'd mantled before, giving me a better idea of what streets I raced between. Bearings in mind, I took a set of turns that would lead me to stairs I could take to a roof with. From there, I'd have a better chance to make my way to Radika's home, and without the Bloodcoats on my tail.

I veered off down the way I needed, coming face to face with a vendor.

In a city of trade and prosperity, even the aftermath of rousing disaster presents economic opportunity. And this man knew it. Out and ready to capitalize on the moment.

A shallow wooden crate rested atop his cart, set to an angle to display his wares. Dates. Endless dried dates.

Lines littered the man's skin that could have come from a combination of his age, years under the unforgiving sun, and no small amount of stress. He dressed in long clothes to shield himself from the worst of Mubarath's dust, but the excess shape of them told me the man had missed a meal on too frequent an occasion. A single word left his lips as he stared at me. "You."

I didn't turn from him, but did cast a sideways glance to the street I'd come from. Shadows loomed closer along it.

The Bloodcoats drew nearer, and whatever mob they'd rallied with them.

I fumbled for one of the purses I'd plucked in scavenging the Black Tower Band's rooms. A thumb and forefinger went into a pouch, pinching two coins in my grip. I didn't bother looking to see what they were before tossing them toward the late-night worker.

He caught them between clapped hands, giving them no mind as I had. "Thank you, *asahb*. But you don't need to do this." He pocketed the money just as he told me that. "You saved Rakhim." It wasn't a question.

I nodded, then broke his gaze to look over my shoulder again. "Yes."

"He is my sister's husband." The vendor joined his hands in a gesture of thanks, or just as much a silent prayer. "Go. Go." He ushered me by him.

I needed no further urging. I moved, quick as I could, whispering a low thanks that I hoped reached his ears. My path led to the left, and I rounded the corner, stopping to peek behind me.

A loud crash sounded and I watched as the vendor tipped over his cart. His cry of dismay carried wide into the night, and one hand went to his brow as the other went to his mouth. The man could have had a future in theater if he so chose it. Dates scattered across the ground and he broke into weeping. "Alum. Oh, Alum Above. My dates!" He cast a piteous look to the sky above.

The Bloodcoats came down the street then, rushing toward the man, with every intent of moving by him.

The vendor lurched toward the group of city guards. His hands closed around the crimson coat of one of the men and he begged. "*Asahb. Asahb,* please. I'm ruined! Look at what he did."

The guard moved to shove the elderly man, but the vendor would not be dissuaded.

"Thief. Rascal. Damnable ghost!" He shook a fist down the street my way, only the turn of his body better faced him down the path to the right. The one I hadn't taken.

Clever old man.

"Help me, sirs. Who will buy my dates all covered in road dust and boot muck? I can't pick them all up. Help me sort the clean from dirty, sirs."

One of the guards finally managed to break the man's hold. But another stayed the first man from striking the vendor. Conversation. They spoke in tones too low for me to hear, and the old man began his pantomime of what had happened between me and him. He finally gestured down the wrong path for them to take.

Heroes are not made through stunning brilliance and inherent betterness. All too often our stories are made by the charity of others. The ones gone overlooked.

Do not forget this.

I'd seen enough, breaking back into a full sprint up to a second level of buildings—single-story homes sitting squat above others. I passed them by and headed to the roofs. Once there, I returned to the route I'd memorized.

Low leaps over close-knit ledges, to mantle this higher wall, and when to tuck and roll. The pattern of familiar motion took me, and I fell back into the candle and the flame. The black void and flickering fire took the fear from me. It took the question of why the Black Tower Band had such a quantity of dangerous powder. And it washed me clear of my concerns for what came next.

Only the clarity of the night remained, and what I was to do in it. I crossed more roofs, developing a tightness in my chest I knew to be from exertion and hard breathing. But Radika's home would come into view soon enough. I just needed to endure.

"There!" The voice came from below. Torchlight revealed a trio of Bloodcoats on the street below. One of them had spotted me leap across the previous roof, and now he pulled free a short bow.

Brahm's blood. I hope it's not too much to ask he's a poor shot.

It had been, in fact, quite a bit to ask from good god above.

The man drew, nocked, and loosed in the smooth motion born of long practice. Silver glinted in the night.

There came a time between my last breath and the next, in which I could almost see the full path of the arrow, even though it still sailed high above. It was like the game Rishi Ibrahm had played with me so many times before. A stone set hurtling through the air, only now I didn't trip through the folds. I simply watched and knew where the arrow would land before it did.

I shifted, still at full speed, and my actions threw me off proper balance. My body went sideways. Something hard struck the space along the back of my shoulders. I staggered again.

"Again. Hit him again!"

The words registered and I realized I'd been shot. Cold panic seeped in and washed away the candle and the flame. The fear—a quickening heartbeat. The questions, drums against my previous clarity. And now all the concerns for what came next thundered into me. In the dizzying moment, I looked around in hopes to find something to fixate on. Anything to better ground me and let me return to that stone-steadiness in heart and mind.

I saw the arrow that had lanced me, only no blood tinged its shaft or head. It lay on the ground, as perfect and unmarred as it had been when it left the bowstring. The sight of it pulled free a deep and echoing laugh. I marveled at the luck, and gave twice the thanks once again to Laki and her grandmother. The arrow rolled under my boot as I nudged it back and forth. It was the wrong thing to do, but I knelt, took it in hand, and tossed it back the way it'd come.

The Bloodcoats could think what they wanted of it, but I knew it would send a silent message: The Ghost of Ghal could not be harmed by conventional means.

Another arrow took to flight, but this time I would not risk it striking me.

The Nagh-lokh's skin might very well have rivaled the hardness of diamonds, at least in my mind. But I knew it could be broken as well. I had done so, more by chance, when I struck the beast just between its scales. It would only take a single lucky shot, and I felt I'd used up most of mine already. No need to test that to see how much I really had.

I crossed onto the next roof. Then the next. A mad dash of white in the dark sky. Eventually, I lost the Bloodcoats and found myself at the little crawl space into Radika's home. The butt of my staff banged against the wooden planks barring the way.

"Password." I recognized the voice as belonging to Alwi, the child I'd first met when he'd been beaten to a mass of blue and black.

"What?" I banged my staff against the boards again. "It's me."

"Password. We got one now."

"Oh, Brahm's blood and ashes. Open the damn way, Alwi. It's me." I hoped my voice did not carry despite my rising temper.

The boards slid open to reveal a veiled and hooded child staring up at me. "Alum." He breathed the word more like a curse. "You do look like a ghost dressed up like that."

"Let me in." I motioned with the end of the staff, making it clear that if he did not move, I'd thump him on the forehead to get him aside.

Alwi moved and I got to all fours and dropped down inside.

Radika rushed into the room, the fingertips of one hand close to her lips. She'd been chewing on the nails by my guess. A nervous habit. "Are you fine? What happened?" She came closer. "I thought the storm was over, but then we all heard this huge boom like another thunderclap? I heard the horns, then even prayer bells sounded."

Alwi and another of Radika's band rushed to seal up the board behind me, but I could tell their attention and ears were on me.

I reached out with my hands, taking Radika's shoulders in my grip. Then I slid my palms along her bare arms, hoping the slow and gentle motions would bring her a measure of calm. "I'm all right. Mostly, anyway. I had to . . . improvise."

She didn't pull herself out of my grip, but I felt her tense and knew my answer hadn't been enough. "What. Happened?"

I exhaled and told her the whole of it. First the cursed storm that made it so my smoke plan almost didn't work until the weather had calmed. The realization that all the barrels I'd watched the Black Tower Band smuggle for nearly a set were filled with white-joy. Something that made me think of the Ashura—of Koli, and how the same drug had once been a staple of his. But I did not tell Radika that.

I shared the details of how I'd set off the explosive contents while getting many of the gang to leave. A few stayed around, but thankfully the eruption had been contained to just that side of the tower.

Though, it had kicked up an almighty thunderous force that shook the world for a moment. And, I told her that the Black Tower Band just might have come to believe even more of the lies about The Ghost of Ghal's abilities.

After all, I had just conjured fire, smoke, and a storm to sunder stone.

Neither of us knew what it meant then, but we shared the quiet hope that so long as the figure in white raced along rooftops, the Black Tower Band wouldn't be so bold in their behavior.

After all, they'd been given good cause to fear the ghost, and the city of Mubarath had seen that he could not be killed.

If only that myth had persisted . . .

FIFTY-EIGHT

Measure of Trust

The next few days passed in a quiet hell of stillness and silence. Radika, with the support of her band of little upstarts, had insisted that I not leave. There was no telling who would recognize me, white cloak or not. A larger bounty had been placed on my head immediately following the explosion at the black tower, and some of the thieves I'd fought claimed to have seen my face.

The details were all given to the Bloodcoats, she'd heard. And various crude charcoal sketches had been placed around the city. I'd asked her to lift one so I could see for myself.

She refused.

There was good news, however. Most of the Black Tower Band had been forcibly rounded up. No word on if they faced execution for their crimes, and it had been implied that their years of bribery had left them in an odd place within the law. Their home had been raided on account of the disastrous explosion. And it wasn't their ill-gotten coin that landed them in trouble, but the fact they had been stockpiling a dangerous thing like white-joy. The Bloodcoats couldn't ignore that.

This, in addition to the fact they had in their possession no end of stolen personal goods belonging to all manner of citizens in Mubarath. The wealthy and connected. The low and impoverished. Those in good regard. And some not so much.

Worse, some precious family heirlooms, old woven rugs that apparently carried far greater value in Zibrath than I'd have ever guessed, and shawls were said to have been irreparably damaged by the thick concentration of smoke through the tower that night. Fabrics caked in darkness that would not wash out, having stained the lighter colors. No treatment would save them apart from being taken to the Mutri Empire and into the hands of a master artisan.

Not a cheap or easy measure, even for the wealthy.

To not act then would have been a public embarrassment to the Bloodcoats on a level they simply could not ignore.

And so the Black Tower Band found many of its members relocated to rooms of similar stone, but the prison lacked the comforts their tower home had.

What did this mean for the streets of Mubarath, however? Well, for one, the single most threatening presence looming over the populace and other bands of thieves, apart from the Bloodcoats, had vanished. A hole of absence that, in time, would want to be filled. But for the moment, the quiet echoing space remained.

And the question: Who would come to fill that hole?

I had an answer.

But first, it required waiting.

And perhaps another hand of mischief.

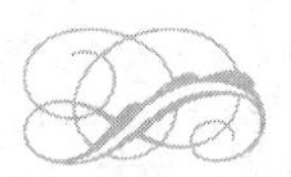

FIFTY-NINE

GAPS AND LINES

I'd earned the trust of everyone under Radika's care, and so had little difficulty in asking a small favor from her band. We had enough coin from my recent debacle to afford a few dozen charcoal sticks. I ran them all through the plan and they agreed it would be easy enough.

They would go out in pairs: a spotter and a scribbler. One would find a sketching of me and take some artistic license to amend it, and the other would keep watch for any Bloodcoats or those who might take issue.

Radika didn't wholly approve of the idea, but she agreed it had some merit, especially since I couldn't spend the rest of my life cooped up.

Shola might have taken well to a life of rest and being fed affection, but I grew more agitated by the day.

Every time a pair of children returned from their task, they would feed me little rumors of what they'd overheard on the streets. Sometimes they'd run into members of the other bands, now freed from the worst of the Black Tower gang's abuse. The gap in power worsened after a fashion. No one rushed to fill it, which left most of the other thieving groups too terrified to work at all.

It sounded like a good thing as far as many of Mubarath's citizens were concerned, especially the traveling traders. But I knew what trouble this would later bring.

Eventually, everyone has to eat. And what would happen when the tentative stillness and silence of nearly a dozen thieving bands broke at once? A free-for-all with nothing to hold anyone in line.

The wrong purses lifted, or worse? How badly would some jobs go? And just how would the Bloodcoats react? It wasn't a stretch to think that lines would be crossed, and in retaliation, the full strength of the law would come down on any banded thief.

They needed a structure—a unity that would keep them from tearing each other apart as much as turning on one another. It would also keep them working in concert well enough that none of their actions would get them sent to the gallows.

That meant someone would have to talk to the various bands, give them a reason to gather, and draw some lines in the sand.

I drafted letters to the various band leaders I'd learned of and discussed my plan with Radika's family.

She heard me out, as did the rest of her crew. Radika then read over my letters and looked at me. "Do you think it's a good idea? Do you think you'll be safe?"

I'd already worried her enough with my antics, but I knew she deserved the truth if I would be lumping in her group with others. "Are the other bands anything like the Black Tower Band?"

She shook her head. "The Red Falcons are on the rough side, though. They have toughs and can get aggressive with people, but they're not like the Black Tower Band. Blue Hares are all fast runners. They sneak-thief, but they're better at just grabbing and going—*fast*. The Yellows don't have a name, kind of like us. Just Yellow Band, really. But they're a little bit of everything, same as us too."

Brahm's blood, if I had more time, I could do more to really shape them into something. It wasn't as if I didn't have the practice for it, especially after my time with the sparrows.

I could make that difference again, and see to it that Radika's group never found itself under the heel of others, or without food to last a set. And, try to further my goals of learning something about Arfan in turn. Perhaps my own leverage. With that many trained eyes and ears, there was no telling what they could dig up. Every man had his secrets, after all. Though my time here had revealed nothing on Arfan's.

"Then I don't think I have much to fear at all. And, if they have enough brains between them, they'll see what I'm proposing will keep everyone safe." I passed the letters toward Aya, another urchin, who in turn handed half to Alwi.

Radika pursed her lips, then nodded. "I guess it can't hurt to talk."

Sometimes it can. I kept the thought to myself, however. "Speaking of talking, I've got a job for you too, if you're up to the challenge?"

The glint in her eyes told me she did indeed feel up to it, even without knowing what it was.

"Good. Because I'm going to need you to work up some more songs about me. If we're going into this meeting, The Ghost of Ghal's going to require a better reputation than he's already built."

She smiled and fetched her mandolin, teasing forth a long string of notes that spoke for her. *I can do that. Let's make a legend,* they said.

I grinned back.

❧

Alwi and Aya delivered the letters while the rest of the band finished altering my various bounty posters. Radika had gone out in front of the home, strumming to a public crowd while I sat on the rooftop. I didn't dare peek over the ledge, even though I'd taken off my white cloak. Call it an extra touch of paranoia, but with everything that had happened, I figured keeping my head down a little longer couldn't hurt.

I fingered the scales of my cloak, tracing a lazy circle around the spot the Bloodcoat's arrow had struck. My guess had been right. It hadn't pierced the material, but it had left a mark. A speck of the scale had been discolored, a portion of its surface chipped away much like if someone had scraped their fingernail against dried paint. So, the cloak wasn't as impervious as it seemed. As long as I avoided standing before a hailstorm of arrows, I would be fine.

Enough strikes to the same spot would likely damage the scales' integrity, and in the event of a lucky blow, tear through the space between the hardened skin and find my softer flesh beneath. The Ghost of Ghal's reputation would have to become his shield more than the cloak.

And Radika saw to that.

First she played idly, smooth and lilting tunes that turned ears and drew attention. Nothing so hard it required people to stop their goings-on. All the while, she sang slowly about a figure in white. A mad blur across rooftops, threaded in moonlight and pearls. She didn't use the moniker. Not at first.

She sang of my doings, and some of my myths. Quicker now. The tempo sped up. She sang of my speed, with which I came to the rescue of common man and woman alike. The story of Rakhim, all without names. How I leapt from the rooftops, how I sprung out from shadows, long across alleys, and struck down thieves.

How coins sprang from my hands, and I salved the poor folk's troubles. Louder. Louder she sang of how no knife could cut me.

The crowd gathered now, forming a crescent moon around her.

Higher. Notes rang brighter now, and her voice matched them in kind.

She sang of my climb atop the tower, doing only what a ghost could do. Silent going through the place, and when confronted, living true to my claim and calling down a thunder with which to shake the world. I broke stone with just a word, and brought fire to a tower already once blackened by it.

On Radika went, silver-string sweet, her voice pulling in more ears. I could hear people trading low gossip throughout her performance.

And soon enough, Radika finished her song. People clapped. A few coins came her way, while some others offered small treats of food. Radika took them all with gracious thanks.

A woman stepped out of the crowd. "Every word of it's true. I saw him myself. He came to me when those godless thugs took my coin, and they wanted to take more." She touched herself along her throat, and I recognized her. The same woman pointed me in the direction of the black tower. "The Ghost of Ghal gave me coin, and had a look about him I knew meant he'd stop those men. Then look what happened." She gestured to the large monolith across the city.

The one I'd climbed and ruined not so long ago.

"He brings down fire and smoke in their home, and thunder that only Alum Above could have granted him. You all heard it after the storm had gone. Some of you saw it."

Some of the crowd nodded in agreement.

"I'll say this too, though not one of the Bloodcoats'll let you believe it if they have their way, telling tall tales and lies 'bout him. The ghost's a hero. Everyone's heard, anyone that has ears, that is." She rounded to stare at people in the crowd, all of whom recoiled from the look. "Those of us with some sense know what he's done. Anyone hear of one of us he's hurt?" The woman slowly turned in place, turning the defiant glare on any—an open invitation to challenge her claim.

But the crowd shook their heads.

"That's right. Not a one. But we've heard what he did for Rakhim. I'm telling you what he did for me. There are stories coming in now, slow, but surely from the Mutri. Sure you lot have heard some of them too."

More nodding.

"Said that he'd been robbing nobles and the crooked like up there. The coin he took? He gave it away. All to the poor."

I thought on that. Nobles, she'd said. Plural. I'd only robbed Nitham, and while he'd certainly had a hefty weight of coin on him, it certainly wasn't enough to make up several of his ilk's worth of money. Then I remembered what it had been like being a sparrow, and just how much a single rupai had changed my life.

Enough wealth to fund my trip to the Ashram, pay for it all, new clothes, and plenty left over to be reckless with. What would a few handfuls of silver, iron, and copper be to people who mostly lived in tin?

Brahm's blood, the story had grown more than I thought. I knew the shapes stories could take, of course, but I had thought the coin would only win over the locals' approval and keep me from a noose. The myth of the ghost worked to keep my identity safe, and surely some small pleasures for myself in it as well. But they'd turned me into something of a folk hero.

Robbing the rich. Giving to the poor.

The crowd broke into low murmuring—various sounds of agreement.

"It's true," said one voice. A man in robes that looked like they'd seen fresh travels and not a wash they sorely needed. "I saw him over a set ago, I did. Saw him giving a man coin from up on a roof, like some kind of animal. Though you wouldn't think it looking at him, all hunched up there like a cat ready to kek up its supper."

Not the most flattering portrayal, but I couldn't be choosy, could I? I supposed it was a miracle enough they saw me in a good light.

"I was peeping that night, when the tower got struck by that lightning and flame," said another voice.

There hadn't been a single bolt of lightning that I'd seen the entire night. The fire must have come from the white-joy bursting, but that had happened after the storm had died.

"Was watching the streets for a long while. Not ashamed to admit I was proper scared to see what done it all, but I kept watch. Saw the ghost coming down on the street, much like I see you all. Ran across a vendor selling dates. He stopped and gave the man coin. No reason to. Just like that. Like you've all been sayin' and we've all heard. It's true."

Oh, blood and ashes. I had half a mind to cup a hand to my mouth and cry out the truth. It had been a bribe. I meant to convince the old fool to keep his mouth shut about me, not carry out an act of charity.

In a way, this is what I had hoped for. More stories about The Ghost of Ghal. But I admit it was an unexpected lesson seeing how the people of Mubarath, and those of Ghal, filled in the gaps of my story as the ghost. New lines found themselves added by each person's account, faster than I could believe.

As much I could be credited for slipping my own creativity into the mythos about myself, people now carried it better than I had ever hoped to. The seeds of truth ran through it all, giving better claim to the lies.

"I heard he has a thousand faces," chimed a man far back in the crowd. "That's why no one ever gets a good look at him. What you see under that hood are the faces of all the lives taken wrongly. Innocent men and women done wrong turns. Children punished too harshly for small crimes. He's got all their faces to show. That's why no one can tell what he looks like."

That particular claim drew an angry chorus of shouts, shutting it down almost instantly.

But like I said, a little bit of truth can give way to better lies. And so the lies sprouted.

"Well, how else do you explain the changing faces on the signs, huh?" This question came from someone else hidden among the crowd.

Someone echoed the sentiment.

Then another.

And it wasn't long before another gap in my story had been filled with lines of lies.

I *did* possess a shifting face, plain for all to see, made from all the ghosts given second life after their first ended at the gallows. I was the daughter who killed herself in secret shame brought to light. The son beaten to death by the wrong crowd coming across him at the wrong time. The forlorn father, without wife, caught stealing just to feed his children, and instead given a rope to choke on.

I was all of them. And I was none of them.

More than enough half-truths and whispers to give anyone a second's pause when dealing with me. Just what I needed for the next part of my plan.

SIXTY

Mutually Beneficial

Alwi handed me a fan of letters the next morning.

Each note had been written in charcoal, betraying nothing of ink or graphter. So the letters had come from the various heads of the thieving bands left in Mubarath. Well-to-do folks, and in possession of sufficient coins, preferred to do their writing with proper tools. The leaders of the respected bands had received my offer to meet, and each of them had agreed. They promised safe conduct, a location and time to gather, and that they would hear me out.

That was all.

As far as promises went, I supposed I couldn't complain. The fact we wouldn't have to expect threats was no small comfort. My biggest concern about leading Radika and her band into a gathering of thieves had been exposing the children to potential harm. So long as that was off the table, I had a good feeling that The Ghost of Ghal's reputation would keep others from trying anything stupid.

Unless they decide to test you and see how much stock they should put into those rumors. I banished the thoughts, not wanting to carry doubts into this meeting.

"The gathering's tonight." I waved the various letters before Alwi. "Every one of the bands is going to be there, which means the rest of you lot will be expected to show up too." I gave him a long look, devoid of any emotion, but still held a note of question within.

It spoke silently that I would understand if he or any other of Radika's crew wanted to remain behind. Her group had the fewest in number, as well as were lowest in age and strength. While they had little concern going about their clutching, most members had a healthy fear of the other groups, and preferred to run away than engage. Their skittishness, while justified, could also make us all look weak when confronting the other bands.

But, in the end, they were still children. And I could never hold a child's fear against them.

Alwi looked at the letters as if they held the answer for what he should do. Then he turned his gaze back on me, meeting my eyes and nodding. "I'll come. Baba will too. I know it."

I smiled and placed a hand on his head, ruffling his hair. "Good man."

He clamped his hand to mine, holding it in place for a second, and flashed me a beaming smile. Then he tore off to spread the word to the rest of the crew.

Shola let out a low rolling *mrowl* of curiosity, matching my bleary-eyed stare. He looked to me as if asking whether there was anything he should be concerned about. Then, without waiting for me to say so, he decided that, no, there wasn't anything he need bother with at all. So he returned to sleeping.

I left him there, making my way to a small bowl filled with petals and water. Radika had purchased it as a treat for the band from the spoils of the Black Tower job. I used the scented water to slough off what dust might have been on my hands and face. After that, I dressed, keeping my white cloak in my travel sack as I had no need for The Ghost of Ghal to make an appearance.

Instead, I brought out the book Rishi Saira had lent me, as well as the notes Immi had scrawled down in regards to the bindings.

I exited the tile maker's home and went to the roof, taking in the early morning all to myself. The sun hadn't risen yet and left me with the endless view of sandstone buildings caked in an eerie blue of early twilight. I thumbed through the pages of the book, content with the silence given to me. For a moment, nothing existed but myself and the world of stories within.

No Ghost of Ghal. No burden to Arfan and my duty to save the sparrows. No counting coins and wondering what hardships the desert ahead had to offer. Or the threat of death or being confined to the Crow's Nest if I didn't show some semblance of control in the bindings.

Just stories.

Just me.

In a way, that moment, and that Ari, was the closest to being the boy I wanted to be. A piece of place and time where I absorbed the greatest legends. Athwun, a soldier pressed into the service of Brahm against a war of ten shadows. The enemy had no name or description in these legends, left to the reader's imagination as wraiths of black in whatever form you best deemed them to be. He'd been gifted a crown of flames from which to draw ceaseless fire. Imbue his very blade from that light itself to cut through swathes of darkened monsters, and their tainted servants.

And for a short, but important time, Athwun burned brilliant bright. A piece of Brahm's own flame—his morning star and light. He cast back shadows, until he himself fell valiantly.

I read of Sakhan, the boy prince who'd run away to find fair fortunes across the world. He sailed the many seas, learning swordsmanship, archery, and whatever else his travels had to teach him. He ventured south as far as southern waters could take him, finding lost lands, courting pirate princesses, beings of myths, and once, while wandering wastes lost to man, he stumbled through a doorway hung in the sky and ended up in the Shaen lands. And he met with a temptress out of story.

Some exaggeration always made their way into the old legends, and I did know something of that, of course, but after learning that the Ashura were real, I could not turn away from the magic these tales held.

The book held a thousand and one stories in it. More than I could hope to devour that morning, but I would be away from the Ashram for time uncounted, so I held to the hope that I would eventually learn them all over my travels.

But as I read through the pages, not one held a story about the Ashura. This pulled my heart down low into my stomach.

But I found another tale—a surprise.

A single story about the Asir. One of the authors of the collection had even gone as far as noting at the beginning of the tale that any stories considering the Asir should be regarded as purely for entertainment reasons, and had no respectable basis in recorded history to be deemed otherwise.

I ignored their words and dove into the story with an open mind.

A tale of a young rascal boy, more criminal than hero. He'd been caught one too many times pulling at the purses and precious pieces people kept to themselves. But, he had the uncanny luck of the devil. Not one person had been able to keep him in chains, or from stealing again, until he crossed paths one night with one being even he would have to show a measure of respect to.

Unless he wanted to find out just how quickly he could in fact be put to rest.

Naathiya, goddess of wisdom, rogues, scoundrels, and the caretaker of the Asir after Radhivahn had formed them. She'd extended her hand to him in fair offer: Put aside his thieving ways for a chance to serve her, and his reward would be something greater than pocket gold.

Legacy. Immortality. The sort of renown most thieves never come to know, as their lives are usually short-lived and terminated at the end of a rope or sword's edge. By accepting, she would tutor him in the ten bindings all men must know, and set to shaping him into the cleverest Asir.

And he rose to the occasion.

Eventually.

The boy was stubborn, and couldn't quite get the larceny out of his heart, using what guile he had to continue running games on unsuspecting merchants, leading other children soon in miniature bands of his own. But, with time, he came around to Naathiya's guidance. Armed with candle, cloak, and cane, he set out across the world to right what wrongs he could.

Crossing paths with sorcerers who had taken Brahm's gifts of magic and turned them to evil purpose. Battling them with a source of flame in hand, and light to call on. Nasir the unjust, a tyrant from the east who'd fled west, matched the nameless Asir, binding for binding. The two battled hard enough, drawing enough wounds that it was said the walls themselves began to hold the blood spilled. It bled in kind, and wept for the two men set on killing one another.

In the end, the sorcerer fled again, setting fire to the village in his way, hoping that it would deter the Asir from hounding him down.

It only slowed Naathiya's champion in that he had to pause in order to put out the flames that risked harm to people. For the rest, he raced through them, stepping over smoldering ruins without care for his own feet. And he emerged unscathed, unharmed, unburned. For no Asir would come to fear Brahm's own gift—fire.

But the delay had been enough, and Nasir had fled. The thief-knight took to wind with wings of lightning and set after in pursuit.

A high fantasy of a story, giving me little beyond a sense of wonder. Still, I cannot deny that it filled me with hope that there could be something like an Asir out there in the world.

If the Ashura were real . . .

"Thought I'd find you up here." Radika came to my side. Her gaze went to the book, then to me. She sank down to the ground and placed an arm on my shoulder. "Alwi told me the heads of the other bands agreed." She'd spoken it as a statement, but an undercurrent of question hung within it.

I nodded. "You not sure about it?"

Radika pursed her lips and turned her gaze toward the horizon, the promise of the sun casting a muted orange glow as far as we could see. She didn't speak and instead waited as more light crested over the distance.

So I didn't push her, and for the moment, waited in shared silence.

The sky grew awash with lavender and a color closer to white-brushed rose, all stroked with warm tangerine. It belonged more to a painting than above a city like Mubarath, at least when you think of the place by reputation. A city of dust-swept streets on the threshold of where the world turns to an ocean of sandy grains. You wouldn't think it could produce colors like that, or you wouldn't think of it at all.

Over the course of my life, I have seen many kinds of wonders. And I can say full-assuredly that that was one of the moments I felt a different, subtle kind of magic. The kind found in just being. In something being beautiful just because it was. It needed no other reason than that.

Finally, Radika pulled away from me and wrapped both her arms around her knees. "I don't know, Ari. It'll be good, and we need it. A peace between the groups will be good. Right now, everyone's too scared to pluck. Groups are running off what they have saved, and when that stops . . ."

I nodded again. "Someone does something risky—something stupid, and then they get caught. If they do something dumb enough, it brings down the Bloodcoats on all of us."

Radika said nothing, but the look on her face told me I was right.

"I'm scared of that too. I don't know the rest of the bands, but I've done this kind of thing before."

She snorted. "Obviously. You show up in Mubarath and start thieving better than some who've been at it for months. You're a thief, Ari, through and through."

I took that as the compliment it was and smiled. "Thank you. But I meant that I've seen how this sort of thing can end." That brought her back to sobriety. "That's how I ended up on Arfan's string, you know? I ran too big of a game, and I got caught in his snare."

What remained of Radika's grin faded at mention of the merchant king's name. "Yeah. The *Shirs* can get their hands on anyone or anything." She didn't elaborate. Radika simply sat there and rocked in place, holding her knees—gaze on the horizon.

"When I first mentioned Arfan's name when we met, you went all stiff. Now again." I watched her as I spoke. "He has something on you, doesn't he?"

Radika adopted the stillness of the hard sandstone beneath us. It didn't even look as if she'd taken breath—such was her unmoving quiet. Finally, she broke it. "Yes." The word left her with a weight that brooked no further investigation, so I didn't push, choosing to at least share what I had done.

"He lured me out back in my home of Abhar. One of my sparrows, the thieves I'd come to take care of, found out about a treasure of gold." At the word, Radika perked up, looking at me out of the corners of her eyes. "I thought it would save my family in the long run. Keep them fed without ever having to clutch again. Buy some of the smarter sparrows appointments they could use to earn real, clean money."

"But it was a trap," said Radika.

"Yes. I got the coins, but only after Arfan had me cornered. He'd heard about how I'd been trading secrets in the city, making coin off it, and thought someone as clever as that should be in his service. He let me keep the money, but—"

"You'd have to pay it all back one day . . . somehow." Radika's face told me she knew that bargain as well.

I inclined my head. "A whole box of gold rupais, conveniently converted from Zibrathi currency to Mutri." I laughed as realization struck me. "And I never wondered why until now."

That set Radika off as well. "Arfan knows how to get at people in the way that hurts them most." She realized she'd spoken, betraying something that she had meant to keep quiet.

I acted as if I didn't hear it. Some secrets are meant to be shared. It's the unspoken truth of them, but you do not keep those. Instead, you must go and speak them to those you trust, all with the agreement they will carry to another set of ears. But this was one of those secrets you pretended did not exist, mostly to spare someone you cared about a measure of discomfort.

"I'll make sure this doesn't go as poorly as my last gamble." I reached over and took Radika's hand in mine. She returned the squeeze.

And we shared the morning together.

Evening came and we found ourselves walking through a series of alleys just as sixth candle ended. Radika moved at the end of the band, keeping all the children in a tight pack around her, with me at the head. Clad full in my cloak and cowl, I'd become The Ghost of Ghal again.

That alone would offer us some protection on the streets tonight.

So long as we don't come across any damn Bloodcoats.

We moved down another pair of streets until we came to an old stone building that had lost much of the red clay coloring it once held. Now closer to something like a pale sand with flecks of wine throughout it.

A storage warehouse. The door groaned as we approached, slowly sliding to one side to permit us access.

I led the way in, shooting a glance to my side to see who had opened the door.

A quartet of young men, all under twenty by my best guess, hauled on a block and tackle that pulled the door.

The inside of the building had been given light from sconces along its wooden rafters and support beams, as well as a smattering of candles placed in the spaces left unlit by other means.

I counted nearly ten bands of people, all staying well outside of arm's reach of another group. The various thieving families of Mubarath.

One of the men, someone closer to his thirties than twenties, broke from his crowd as he noticed me. He wore only a vest that showed arms made of thick corded muscle, and a chest built from hard work. The outfit had been purposely chosen to reveal the faint scars that raced along the exposed skin.

Not exactly subtle.

He stood a full head taller than me, and by the straight posture he adopted as he neared, it was clear he wanted to make that fact obvious. His face reminded me of poorly shaped and lumpen clay. An overly round head with a chin and jaw left to the curve of a vase.

It did not do him a favor.

He stopped a few feet from me, looking down his nose in another quiet play to accentuate the difference in our height. "You're The Ghost of Ghal?"

My hood and veil obscured all but my eyes, and I did the best I could to flood my stare with all the anger I'd built over the years. "I am."

The man grabbed the crotch of his dark pants and gestured to the crowds. "Pisser looks like his stones ain't drop yet." The comment drew a few chuckles.

I showed no reaction, but I clenched my staff tighter. A hint of my will bled into the weapon, and I had to resist the urge to trigger the minor bindings I'd laid into it. But I remained prepared for the inevitable test I knew would come.

The man then ran his fingers through the lank strands of his dark hair. "How old are you—" His hand blurred as it left the side of his head, forming a tight fist as it shot my way.

I couldn't move fast enough to slip it unharmed, so I took the blow across my shoulder as I snapped the butt of my staff up between his legs.

The man learned that he should have been more concerned about his own stones than mine. He crumpled, letting out a sharp long wheeze. Some of the crowd he'd been with moved in closer.

I held up a hand, staying them. "It's all right. No real harm done, *ayam*?"

The man writhing on the ground let out another choked noise before managing to wave his crew off.

I appreciated the gesture as I didn't want this to erupt into a full brawl. "I'm going to guess that was just a little test. Just to make sure I wasn't someone pretending to be who he's not?"

No answer.

I could prevent the situation from worsening by making a statement now, but it would have to be done with care. "Would anyone else like to test me?"

The man who'd fallen returned to his feet. One hand kept to his groin, but the other balled into a fist again. A red band hung from the wrist of the clenched hand.

"Again?"

The man answered with guttural growl and a charge.

This time I fed my will into the staff, keeping every intent to only let one ring's worth of momentum free.

He came within reach.

I twisted, lunged, and sent the head of my staff into his core. The force of a thrown body struck him.

He toppled back the way he came.

That made the impression I'd been hoping for. But I knew the numbers here meant it wouldn't be long before they reached the same conclusion I had. If enough of them charged me, I wouldn't be able to do a thing. So I'd dissuade them from that before it reached that point.

"Alwi?"

The boy raced to do what we'd discussed earlier. He drew a small knife, rushing me with the blade held in an overhand grip. Its point came down at my back with more force than expected out of the little urchin. It sent me staggering several feet forward, and I gave thanks that the child hadn't gotten lucky and struck between the scales.

Every breath stopped for a moment as people watched to see what happened.

Alwi held up the knife, clean as it had been before. Then he held it up for all to see just as he brought it to a length of his hair, cutting it free with ease.

Low murmuring spread through the crowd.

I pointed my staff at the man I'd knocked to the ground. "I think that's enough, isn't it?"

Several of whom I took to be the bands' heads traded looks. Silent exchanges. A few of them nodded, and I took the matter to be settled.

"You all know why I asked you here." I took a single step forward, banging the butt of my staff against the ground. Its clap served as a theatrical emphasis—a trick from my time in the understage so long ago.

Another group leader took a step toward me in kind. Lean, like a starved hound, and pinched of face. His chin and nose protruded too far to lend him a look anything but comical. The man's eyes were a bit too wide apart, and it gave him the appearance of not being able to properly glare, at least in a manner that seemed intimidating. "You want us to work for you."

"No, I want us to work together. All of us." That caused everyone to straighten further. "Right now, you're all scattered, and you're afraid."

The man I'd sent to the ground spat to the side, narrowing his gaze on me. A look that said he had little to fear.

So I addressed that point. "If I'm wrong, then why haven't any of you been running any games? Every band's been holed up—waiting, watching. Suddenly Mubarath is thief-free? You're scared. And you're wondering who's going to step up and take the Black Tower Band's place? Are they going to be just as bad, or worse?"

Now the stares held a hint of trepidation. Wide eyes, and everyone asking the same questions I had. Suspicion built among them, but I needed them to trust one another, and turn any doubts onto a singular target.

And I had just the one.

"Who did the Black Tower Band pay to smooth things over? Who finds it mutually beneficial if a few of you lot get to clutch and take pickings, so long as they get their cut?"

The answer came at once. "The Bloodcoats."

I nodded. "And right now, they're sitting on nearly everything they could keep after raiding the black tower. That's a lot they're content with. So, if that's true, what use have they for us?"

The same pinched-face thief from earlier spoke up. "Who's *us, ayam*? You said work together, but now it's us?"

"It is. That's the only way this works. Otherwise, the Bloodcoats will come for you. Each band. One. By. One. How will you fare against that?" I let that hang in the air as the doubt settled into them. Then I went for the piece I knew would put them in my hands. "How did the Black Tower Band handle it?"

The starved hound of a man crossed the distance between us with long strides, bringing him within arm's reach. "You mean how did they handle *you*." A heavy accusation.

I inclined my head. "All the same. And here I am now. So . . . are you going to handle me, then?" I tilted the tip of my staff toward the man I'd toppled earlier. Not quite a threat. I didn't want them to fear me, or feel bullied, but rather that I could help them. Shield them.

"You know what I've done. You know *who* I am. And you've all heard the stories. So here it is, now we work together. No more colors. Just all of us. We share resources, information, and coin. Everyone gets fed. Anyone gets caught, everyone works to help them slip the hand that's got them. One band. One family."

I gestured to the warehouse in which we stood. "And we have the perfect place to start storing what we take."

Every one of the leaders left their groups, forming a circle with each other that notably excluded Radika—and me. They conferred in whispers just loud enough that I could catch the edges of things, but nothing near enough to get the shape of what was said. Finally, one of them turned to face me.

A young man, closer to my age than twenty at first look. His head had been shaved clean, leaving the most prominent feature to be the bushy brows I could have taken for caterpillars. He'd just begun to grow a scruff of hair too thin to be considered a beard, but you could tell he took pride in it. One of his hands constantly brushed it in an effort to draw attention to the patchy mess. "And . . . you'll protect us?"

I nodded.

"And you'll be in charge?" That question brought all heads to slowly turn on me. A weight settled into the air—unseen strings touching the ears and hearts of everyone in attendance. My next words would decide everything.

"No. *We'll* be in charge. The heads of every old band. You all have experience and know your families better than anyone else. It would be stupid to ignore that. You know the streets, what you're good at, and have the respect of everyone you care for. So, we decide things together."

They turned back to the circle. More murmuring. Finally, the pinched-face thief broke to address me. "So, there are ten of us?" He pointed at the leaders and did a quick tally, making it clear he'd entirely missed my point.

While the old heads would decide things, we were no more important than anyone else running a game and putting their lives at risk. And I would make that clear now.

"No. There are a hundred of us. From this moment on, we're one big group." I tossed the old black braided cord I'd cut from the man I'd knifed. Radika mirrored this by throwing her brown band to braid it.

I stared at all the other thieves. Soon, a mountain of colored bands sat in the warehouse. No more colors. No more separate groups. Just the one.

"Now, we are The Hundred Thieves."

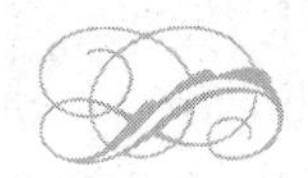

SIXTY-ONE

The Hundred Thieves

You've heard the story of the sparrows, and how I came into their care and, in time, how they came into mine. I suppose my time with The Hundred Thieves was much the same. Only I was cleverer by far by now, though, sadly, still far from wise.

The sparrows had taught me the power of a large family, and how to use them. And thus I put The Hundred Thieves quickly to that task.

They flourished at it. We returned to the streets, running games and pulling purses. Every thief and their once-band played to their strengths, and without the Black Tower Gang to stop us, we turned a tidy profit.

The Hundred Thieves had established something of a headquarters in the warehouse we'd first met in, and it worked for a time being. Though I preferred to keep to the old tile maker's shop Radika's band had once called home. A place of familiar comforts . . . and damnable passwords, all under the unearned and overly enthusiastic tyranny of the self-appointed Lord Alwi.

Small boys are always prone to delusions of grandeur.

I would know.

"Password!"

I narrowed my eyes.

"I have sweetbreads, Alwi. Let me in." My argument would surely persuade any starving boy. And I was right. The board moved, and I soon slipped inside.

"The password's 'Open Sesame'!" Alwi made a flourish with his hands, then noticed the distinct lack of treats in my possession and commented on it. "You said you had sweetbreads." Baba watched me from the sides.

"I lied." My attention remained on Baba, who now fixed his gaze on me and flicked his fingers. Droplets the color of amber arced toward me, striking my nose, lips, and the underside of my chin. I eyed the child.

He, as you would have expected, merely held the same grin he'd had moments earlier. "*Bah. Bah.*"

I looked at Alwi.

"It's sesame oil. You know, for good luck, like when . . ." He trailed off, gaze going to the ground. His mind had clearly gone to the old tile maker and his ritual of blessing children with the oil.

Brahm's blood. I took another breath and lowered the box to the ground. "It's all right." One of my hands fell on the boy's shoulders. "I understand. It's a clever thing, and we could all use the luck. The password was a good idea—keeps people we don't want from coming in, and it's a good way to honor that man."

Alwi looked up to me—the expression more expectant, seeking validation. "Really?"

I nodded. "Sometimes the best way to keep someone alive is in stories. Stories never die, and so long as you keep the stories about someone you loved alive, then they stay with us too."

That drew the cheer back onto the young boy's face. "We'll keep telling stories about him then, right, Baba?"

The other boy gave an affirming cry.

That's how I would like to remember my time leading The Hundred Thieves. The quiet moments between the jobs, making a difference to the lives of little children who so desperately needed it. I wanted to preserve that.

And not think of what would come to break us.

Nor the truth settling deep in my heart. The repetition of it all. The trapped feeling like my life had become a circle, searching in desperate vain to find a family like I had once had, but never been able to fully grow with. Something taken from me.

Radika could have been something close to a Nika, when I look back on it. Alwi and Baba, both taking two heads, albeit, to be a replacement for Juggi. I had begun to fill the holes in my life, and myself, with whomever I could. Not the healthy thing—the right thing, but for a boy who'd lost much, perhaps the only thing I knew to do.

And cling to.

So I set The Hundred Thieves to remedying this hurt. While they pinched and plucked precious coin, they kept ears honed, and eyes even sharper, for any signs of rumors.

About the Ashura—the Ajuura, or *bhaalghul* as known here. And, of course, Arfan. Anything I could use.

But, as I said, I was clever, not wise. And so didn't think that my own cleverness would come to be used against me.

Things were smooth for a few sets. I sent sneak-thieves out to peddle rumors and glean secrets. Listen in on whatever gossip there was to trade and all in hopes of learning something of Arfan. He, however, seemed to be among the few topics too taboo to speak of in Mubarath. At least openly. So I was left with nothing but empty air, and thinning pockets.

We plundered, pilfered, and plucked—all the various words you can choose from to mean "steal." It all depended on the complaints from those we relieved of burdensome coin. But it wasn't enough. Not for all of us. While The Hundred Thieves tried to recover from the period of inactivity before uniting as one family, the lull had damaged finances. And the strain began to show.

Most of all . . . in Radika. I caught her fretting in quiet moments, muttering to herself. She wouldn't admit it to me, of course, a thief's pride and all, but the worry was there. And I'd seen it plainly.

Had I had the time, I would have done more to help her, but we were soon given our first real challenge as The Hundred Thieves.

The Bloodcoats had captured nearly a dozen of our members and taken them to their most impregnable prison: the Bloodfort. A place, I later learned, that sadly lived up to its name more in the metaphorical sense—mercifully, than the literal, owing to the blood-red stone used in its form.

And as befit me, The White Ghost of Ghal, I made a plan to rescue them.

One that was nothing short of monstrously stupid. But, all the same, succeeded.

And led to a lesson I have never forgotten.

Much like the night I stormed the Black Tower, I broke into the Bloodfort in a fashion far gone from how you hear of it today. But I'd freed them, and lost Mubarath's constabulary in the aftermath as I returned to the old tile maker's home in want of respite, only to find something amiss.

A single source of light. A candle, long burning in anticipation.

Of me.

It glowed in the corner, bringing out the silhouette of a man seated there. "She said you'd come here." The man rose, keeping himself to the low light and shadows so I could not make out his face.

She? I didn't get a chance to voice the word as the tip of a spear came to my throat. Then another.

. . . Then another.

My eyes adjusted to the poorly lit room, and I made out the distinct color of a uniform I least wanted to be confined with this night.

Bloodcoats.

"I'm sorry, Ari." The voice came clear and belonged to the one person I could not bring myself to believe would be here. Be behind this.

"Radika?" Her name left me in nearly a breathless whisper. Jagged, cracked, and with all the dryness you'd imagine of a man who spent the night running. "Why?"

"It was the only way . . . the bounty."

Something broke in me, but I didn't get the chance to feel the pain in full.

"Take him." At the shadowed man's command, a hood slipped over my head, shrouding the world and all light from me.

Something struck the side of my head. Another blow followed suit. Then came the deeper darkness still, washing away the blackness to a color so vast it could swallow all other shades within.

I fell through the doors of darkness then, well beyond my pains.

And all the hurts a loved one can do to a heart.

SIXTY-TWO

Hangman's Judgment

The great epics have their moments that rouse the spirit and stir the soul. The twist that comes when the hero is betrayed, for it is always from a likely source.

But that is not the truth of betrayal. We expect it from the ones who mean to harm us—the monsters—demons in the dark. Open schemers, and forked-tongued characters. But to hurt us is the truth of our enemies, and so, they cannot betray us. They will only ever be true to the harm we know they mean us.

Betrayal, then, can only come from the ones we've welcomed close in arms. Shared the secret trusts of our hearts with. True betrayal can only come from the hands of loved ones—our family, and our friends.

That is why nothing hurts quite as much as that. And that is why, long-left in heart, it begins to fester and poison our soul. Few wounds scar the way betrayal can.

It would be very much like the old stories to say that I woke with this realization in mind, but no. Then? I came to with only the muddled mind of someone who'd been put to sleep at the end of a cudgel.

The hood had remained over my head, left loose around my collar so as not to choke me in my sleep. I supposed the Bloodcoats didn't want their prized catch to die in captivity. I had spent a decent bit of time making idiots of them.

Though, I would argue my antics only revealed what most people knew to be true: The Bloodcoats *were* idiots. I only removed the thin mask of competency they chose to wear.

Keeping that in mind, I thought my treatment seemed rather unwarranted. If we were to consider matters of fairness, which, I noted, the Bloodcoats were not keen on. Maybe the word simply didn't have a translation into Zibrathi.

"He's moving." The voice struck me with the jagged weight of broken mountain stone, making it hard to discern who it belonged to. Though, it had to be a Bloodcoat.

My head spun and begged me to return to sleep, though I couldn't find the comfort to do so. And I found less the moment after as my ribs brightened into fresh agony. The tip of a boot bounced off the bones, jarring me to a wakefulness I wished I could ignore.

"Now he's moving more." A broken laugh—cracked-stone rough and holding all the malice you could imagine. "Let's see how much of a morning person our little ghost is. They like the nights better." Another blow punctuated the final word. And, just for good measure, likely to test his theory of which I preferred, another kick.

My pained groans spoke clear enough. No, I was not a morning person.

"Careful." Another voice now, holding the dryness of someone who indulged in frequent smoking. "Need him alive until we can make a show of it. Then, if you want, you can be the one to pull the lever."

"I'd give ten rayhals to be the one to send him off to Alum for judgment. Ten, mind you." A third speaker, holding all the excitement in him of a child given a new toy, but not yet permitted to touch it. The edge of anticipation clear like quivering strings.

"You've never had a whole rayhal to your name. Alum Above, where would you get ten from?" The speaker I'd now dubbed as Boots, for obvious reasons, let out a little laugh at the expense of his fellow Bloodcoat.

"I'd borrow it from your mother. She's got a load of gold on account of the sopping wet spot on her bed." The third speaker quickly came to be known as Penniless in my mind. Though, after hearing what he'd just said, I suppose Tactless could have just as easily suited him.

Silence fell around me with the weight of lead.

Then it broke under the sound of scuffling boots, the grunts of exertion I knew well to be men locked in arms, and low muttered curses that would soon break to louder shouts.

"Bastard!" Boots spat as a fleshy smack filled the air.

Penniless said something in Zibrathi that needed little translation, mostly on account of the acid in the words. Whatever it had been, it sent Boots into further rage.

He screamed and I heard more feet stamping across the floor.

"Enough." The word left the smoke-voiced man in a whisper sharp enough to score steel.

The noise of struggling men ceased and the silence returned.

"We have people putting out the word he's to be done in today?" The question came from the smoky-voiced man.

Penniless and Boots grunted in unison.

"Good, good." Something tapped, metal on wood. Given the man's tone, and what I'd already guessed about him, I wagered him to be stuffing the bowl of a pipe. "We'll make a good show of it. We picked up those two traders, *ayam*? Men were trading in shaved silver coins. How much weight were they off by end of trading?"

"Enough to make up a whole silver piece," said Boots.

"Mm." Smoky took a long lungful of air, breaking into two dry coughs. "That'll earn them the rope too. Could take a hand from each man, but it wouldn't send the message when we've got this one to deal with."

I knew who he'd meant by that. Even so, Boots decided to live up to his given name and drove a foot into my gut.

"He's talking about you, ghost." Another kick.

I grunted, warm saliva trickling out of my mouth to pool inside the hood. "I gathered." I'd barely managed to voice the words around the ragged edges of the pain filling me.

"What's that? The ghost speaks?" Two more solid introductions of his boot to my side.

I knew enough when to be quiet.

"I'd like to hear what you have to say, ghost-*asahb*." Smoky had added the Zibrathi honorific to my name, and all without a hint of mockery to it.

I thought then on what my first words to the man in charge should be. "How many others did you pick up?"

He laughed, breaking back into coughing. "Alum Above, you're a bold one, *ayam*?" Smoky didn't wait for me to answer. "Just you. No one else. Don't know where the rest got off to—don't care, truth. Catching you does me well enough as far as the Sultan's concerned. Your name's spread a good deal, ghost. Even after paying out the bounty to that little rat, the Sultan and *Shirs* will set me up for life for putting you at the end of a rope."

So, The Hundred Thieves had evaded the Bloodcoats. A minor relief, though I could not bring myself to enjoy it.

The bounty.

Radika.

She'd traded me off for a bag of coins. No amount of questioning would answer me why, but I asked all the same. For moments uncounted, I lay there, running through every possibility. And they all left me with as much as I'd had before.

Nothing.

I had no ache left to give voice to. And whatever had been there before had already been taken out of me by Boots' enthusiastic kicks. No tears to shed. Only tiredness. And another question for Smoky. "I'm entitled to one request, yes?"

Quiet. A long breath which I took to be another inhalation of smoke. Finally, he answered. "Yes."

"And I don't suppose I can ask to be let go?"

Laughter filled the room and it took a long time to die. "Alum Above, I was right. You *are* bold. No. You cannot ask that."

"Then I'd like to go with my cloak and cowl still on. Don't let them see my face." A fair thing to ask, or so I thought.

Fingers clenched the hood around me, pulling it free.

Smoky sat in a simple wooden chair, one leg crossed over the other. He wore the typical fare for a Bloodcoat. A wrap of red cloth had been wound tight around his head, more to distinguish himself than to bind his hair. He had the hard lines of face you'd expect for a man long in service in his line of work. More gray than youthful black in beard and brow. Eyes closer to watered old iron than the typical brown found in Zibrathi. He held more smoke to the look of him than just his habits, it seemed.

Everything about him spoke of a man long accustomed to authority—its weight . . . and its privileges. He leaned forward. "And why is that? I'm curious."

"Please." The word left me before I realized I'd spoken it. "If you're going to kill me as a ghost, then let people remember me as such. I know I've caused trouble, and I know it won't matter to you whatever my reasons. Even if I told you I did it all to help people."

"You caused the trouble of all troubles last night, little ghost. And the same the night of the Black Tower fire. That was you, wasn't it?"

I nodded, taking care not to let the hood of my cloak fall free and reveal more of my face. "It was me."

Smoky stroked his neatly trimmed beard. "Some of my men were on their take, you know?"

I bobbed my head again, not seeing any point in playing stupid.

"What you did gave us cause to investigate, but you knew that going into it, didn't you?"

"I did. I had hoped you'd round them up and no one would have to deal with them again."

Smoky continued rubbing his beard. "Mm. And the people of Mubarath loved you for it, so there may be some problem in executing you."

That gave me a thread of hope, and sometimes, a thread can be more than enough. It may not bear your weight. It may come undone, but all the same, the thread remains. And you cannot but grab for it. So I did.

"You don't want to sour their opinion against you. Especially after the Black Tower Band hurt so many people, and your men looked the other way—took a cut, even."

Smoky nodded. "Yes. But in Mubarath, the people's opinions are a luxury. The Sultan's is law. And he says you hang."

The bottom of my stomach gave way, and my lungs and heart sank to fill that void. I made no sounds, no pleas. We locked eyes and stared.

"You want to keep your face masked, why? Spare your family the sight of you crying before you go? . . . No." Smoky frowned, the expression drawing out more of the hardness in his face. "You don't have a family. But you're no street rat from Mubarath either. You'd have been picked up by one of the bands long ago. It's true, then."

I didn't have the strength to raise a brow in question. My silence spoke for me.

"What the songs say. You came from Ghal—out there in the Mutri." He motioned off to one side.

"Yes."

"And you came here to . . . ?"

I smiled, knowing he couldn't see the expression behind the cowl hiding most of my face but for my eyes. "Pay a debt."

That sent Smoky's eyes wide and he leaned forward, finally lowering his crossed leg. "Oh-ah? Well, you'll be paying for many debts, ghost. Many. But I can grant you your request. A dead man is a dead man to me. I don't care for your name. And I don't care how you die. So long as you do. Make a man a ghost, and he comes back to haunt you. Kill the ghost then, and does something else take its place?"

The oddly philosophical question brought me to blinking, unsure if he wanted an answer to that, or had been merely musing aloud.

Smoky sighed, placing his hands to the chair's armrests. "Ah. Doesn't matter. You'll be dead by afternoon, and fourth candle's nearly ending. It'll be time enough. You should make your peace with Alum . . . or whatever Mutri god you pray to. You lot have too many for me to count." Smoky rose, pretending as if the other two Bloodcoats weren't in the room at all, and he moved toward the exit.

"See him granted his request. Keep him masked. Let him die with some dignity. My gift to you, ghost, for ridding me of the Black Tower Band. When you get to hell, may you be in the company of all your kind—thieves and scoundrels alike."

I don't know what possessed me to speak, but perhaps it had been what he'd said last. Damning all thieves to a place like hell without ever knowing the lives those people walked. Most don't turn to the cunning art out of greed. They do it out of desperation. The pains most people never come to know.

"I'll be waiting for you there, Bloodcoat."

He looked back at me one last time, letting out a short laugh. "Bold." With that, he left.

And Boots realized that he hadn't been told he couldn't continue beating me. So he indulged.

I lost much of what happened then.

The vague awareness of being dragged filled me. A pressure on the sockets of my arms as people pulled me along by my wrists. My knees and legs took the roughness of the ground in full, making me glad I'd worn a sturdy pair of pants as opposed to the breeches many of The Hundred Thieves preferred. The old hood

I'd been shrouded under by the Bloodcoats had returned, but bands of brightness made their way through regardless.

Midday sun in Mubarath.

My breath left me shallow-worn, each gasp bringing new pains to my chest. Much of that came by way of Boots' beating. The rest, well, that was the simple weariness found in the lungs of any man who knew he was close to dying.

Even waiting to die can be tiresome work. And your body realizes this before the rest of you.

My knees struck something flat and hard. Then again. *Stairs.* They dragged me up a short length of steps, and I had a good idea to where.

Hands yanked my hood free, leaving me to squint as bright pinpricks jabbed my eyes. Mubarath's sun stood out—far overhead in the fullness of itself. I wouldn't be able to open my eyes for a while, finding some solace in the soft pink of the insides of my eyelids.

A lesser pain, but with all I'd taken in recently, small pains were a touch of mercy.

Something fell onto my shoulders, then cinched tight around my throat. Not so much to hamper my breathing, but certainly enough to make it felt.

Hangman's rope.

"Good people of Mubarath." I recognized the voice as belonging to someone who'd lived a life of theater. Dramatic, boisterous-booming in all the best ways. Someone who knew how to work a crowd. Likely an out-of-work performer deciding that to cry for the Bloodcoats and city affairs was not so bad a way to make extra coin.

I couldn't fault him for it.

"Today we have a special treat. Two tricksome traders, come into our country—*your homes*—to rob you of your hard-earned money! They were caught shaving coins and passing them to you good folk."

I couldn't see the crowd, but the collective weight of their jeers and displeasure drubbed me like ocean waves.

"And"—he dragged the word out, clapping his hands in the aftermath to bring about a measure of silence—"we have a cutthroat. That's right. Some gutter-swill who took the throat of a lovely young lady not more than a few streets from here. He's spilled our blood, people. Your blood. What a long life that woman was to have, all taken by him."

The angry cries doubled in intensity, making themselves hammer at the heart of me.

"Lastly—quiet down now. Quiet!" The announcer's demands were ignored, and I'd finally acclimated to the brightness enough to risk a moment's look.

Stones had taken to the air, all heading toward a man at the far end of the wooden stage.

I watched them all, even in the grip of my fatigue, and senseless, and fell slowly into the folds.

How many had it been again? Twelve? Rishi Ibrahm had failed in that before. But then, he'd tricked me once too, hadn't he? Was I ever able to reach twenty during our little games? I believed so.

All the while, my mind caught each of the stones in the air. Tracing exactly where they would land. I fell into the folds more deeply then, holding the spaces I knew they would pass through, and imagining where they would fall.

They wouldn't, of course. I wasn't attempting an actual binding to alter their paths. Merely a game, because I was left too tired for anything else. And so the stones fell, striking the man at the end, of whom I could not get a clear view with the two traders in my way.

But I could hear the noises of his fresh hurt as everything hit him.

I may have been a thief, and a murderer too, depending on the accounts of things. Mithu and his friends would have argued so if they could. But everyone and everything I'd killed to date had deserved it.

Then, many a man who does and says such things comes to believe it. Does it mean he's right—justified?

I certainly thought I was.

"Lastly—settle down, you uneducated, witless—ow!" The actor broke into a string of colorful profanity that lost much of its venom given his choice of flowery language.

It's a simple art, but sometimes cursing a man should be no more complicated than spitting.

"Might be witless, you whore's son, but if you don't get on with it, you'll be toothless." The voice came from the crowd, and the rest of the mob laughed and cheered with the speaker.

"Fine-fine." The actor composed himself. "Lastly, we have the wraith in white." He made a sound like a parent trying to frighten a child—the long drawn-out *ooohs* of anticipation. "The ghost skulking over roofs and setting our fair city ablaze."

Quiet. No jeers. No excitement. Nor a plea in my favor. The leaden heavy weight of expectation—and waiting could kill a man.

"The Ghost of Ghal!" The actor's pronouncement did nothing but punctuate how strong a silence had fallen over the place. A stillness so deep no one dared take breath.

This was the quiet unmovingness of people watching the end of something they did not want. The noiselessness of those who knew the coming of a horrible thing to be, and nothing they said could turn it away.

The grim gallows quiet of the hangman's judgment waiting to come.

This was the quiet of a place built for one purpose: to take the voices of all men, just as much as it would take their bodies, and soon, too, their souls.

This was the stillness of men who knew their stories were coming to an end.

The hangman's boots plodded along the wooden stage, but I had no ears for them. Or the eyes once they passed the corners of my vision.

I looked above, taking in what I could of the sun.

One man broke into song.

"Hangman, hangman,
comin' for the damned.
Nicked a little silver,
or a golden band.
Out to take your head,
or just as much your hand.

Hangman, hangman,
take you to the pole,
hangman, hangman,
here to claim your soul.

Headsman,
deathsman,
can you wait a little while?
Will you stay the noose?
Hangman, hangman,
death's own ferry man,
will you, will you, let me slip loose?

Gallowman, hangman,
please hear my little plea,
slip me out of irons,
won't you let me free?

I've got a little somethin',
a gift of treasure proper,
a piece of precious silver,
and a little copper.

Hangman, deathsman,
oh what do you say?
Will you set me free,
let me get away?

Hangman, godsman,
will you let me go?
Hangman, hangman,
is it yes,
or is it no?"

The whole-hollow sound of a lever *thunking* against a stop. The stage creaked. I watched a line go taut, and heard the unmistakable wet-bone sound of a man who'd gotten his answer.

I guess he says no.

And the hangman moved in kind to give us all the same answer. He seemed to be in no mood for last requests. A small bit of luck mine had been asked in advance.

Two more pulls.

Two traders died.

Then he pulled once again for me.

And I learned that a ghost, can indeed, feel fear.

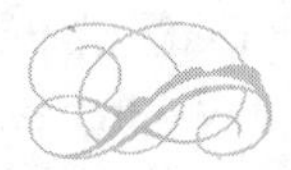

SIXTY-THREE

Intermission—the Appreciation of Things

"Did you die?" Eloine's voice quavered. Her eyes were wide with the eager anticipation of a listener wanting to know what happened next.

I blinked, opened my mouth, then stared at her.

She finally threw back her head and laughed. "Oh, my Storyteller." Eloine reached up and pinched my cheek. "You were being dour again. It's not healthy."

I frowned, as much as I could with part of my face still in her grip. "You enjoy teasing me. Here I am, laying out my heart, all my deeds laid bare—good, and all the ones far from that. And you make jokes." I pressed a hand to my breast.

Eloine's touch fell from my face and she pursed her lips. The corners of her mouth betrayed a smile she fought to keep back, and her eyes held the light of mischief. "Oh, now you're being overly dramatic. Save that for the stories."

I let out a long, low sigh. "First she worries I'm too serious, then I'm too silly.

How's a man to know what a woman wants of him?" I raised my hands, shrugging for an unseen audience.

Eloine placed a palm to my shoulder and pressed me away in a stage shove, meant to topple me without any serious force behind it.

I rolled with it, tumbling to the flat of the bed. "That was rude."

It was her hair that first fell atop me, trailing along my brow and the sides of my face. She leaned over me, her nose a mere inch from mine, bringing me closer to the depths of green her eyes held. Her smell hadn't changed since the last time we shared closeness, keeping to all the notes I'd remembered, and striking me in full. Eloine smiled, her lips close enough to mine that we shared breaths.

"A man could come to know what a woman wants of him if he uses these"—she touched my ears with her hands—"or what's between them." Eloine tapped a finger to my forehead, a light smile playing about her face.

"Or . . . you could just tell me plain."

She pursed her lips, gaze turning to one side as if deep in contemplative thought. "Mhm. It certainly would make things easier, but knowing *you*, you'd still find a way to glean the wrong intent behind our words and thoughts. Then all our communication would be confusing, and anger fraught. You've certainly ignored clear advice before."

That pulled a deeper frown out of me. "Oh, it's always my fault, hm?"

Eloine leaned away, just enough that I no longer felt the warmth of her breath against my skin. "Well, otherwise it would be *my* fault." She placed a hand to her chest in exactly the same manner as I had. "And that certainly *can't* be right." Her eyes shone now bright, close to emeralds, showing less the shadow of gray I'd seen before.

I couldn't match her stare, at least the kindled humor within—not now. But I could give her as much in theatrics. "Oh, of course. We can't have it be your fault." I grinned and leaned up—leaned closer.

She pulled farther away. "At last, he understands." Eloine stood, twirling once before falling back to the end of the bed. "Enlightenment. So hard to teach a man things he ought to have been taught so long ago."

I arched a brow. "Oh, are we teaching me, now? Here I thought I was telling you." I moved closer.

Eloine managed to give me a long sideways look despite our closeness. "Now he's presuming."

The old frown returned. "He's . . . not trying to?" I didn't know what had prompted the sudden change in her, and while my hand wanted to take her shoulder in a comforting touch, I felt much like a child reaching out to a candle flame.

The heat radiated into my flesh, past sinew and to the bone. I knew I could be burned, though, much like the child, I didn't understand the why of it, or the how.

Eloine's posture softened and her shoulders slumped. "I'm sorry."

I didn't know what went on inside her then, but I knew enough to not make an issue of it. "There's nothing to apologize for, I think."

A ghost of a smile, pulling along one side of her mouth, before vanishing as quick as it'd come. "You're sweet."

That teased out a grin of my own. "It's all the rice puddings I snuck extra servings of as a child."

She rolled her eyes. "Oh, is that all it takes?"

I made my face one of stone—somber-still, and unmoving. A nod.

"Mm. I liked you better when you were somewhere between dour and sweet, but not as dramatic. Find that again for me, will you?" She motioned a lazy circle with her finger.

I inclined my head, hand to heart, and bowed. "As you wish."

Eloine rolled back onto her stomach, body propped up on her elbows. "Oh, my. As I wish? Mhm. I could get used to that. That's a dangerous promise to make to me, Ari." Her mouth went wide into a wicked curve—sharp and lovely as a crescent moon, with all the brightness behind it.

"If you'd been listening at all to my tale, you'd know I'm quite fond of my danger."

Her eyes lost the smile within, holding hard-steady as ice. "Mm. Very fond of it. So much so you were willing to put your neck into the noose."

"I had my reasons."

Eloine crept closer. "To save your new family, however short-lived that relationship might have been." Her tone turned to brittle bone, broken beneath something heavy, leaving only the jagged edges behind. "You put yourself before blades and arrows and the noose, all to save her."

There was little question as to which *her* Eloine referred to.

"You're angry at her."

Both of Eloine's brows rose at that, and she fixed me with a stare better left to an affronted cat. "Of course I am. Weren't you? . . . Aren't you?"

Ah. So that's why. "No. Not then, and certainly not now. We all get our wounds when and how we do. Not all of them heal, but the rest? You can only give them the one thing that heals most things at all: time. Some wounds cannot, of course. They fester, you pick at them, unable to leave the mass alone. They remain ever-open because of it, and you bleed all the while—forever long.

"But Radika? What she did to me became what most wounds do. Scars. It healed, but the memory of the trespass remains. Besides, knowing why she did it helped keep the anger at bay. It did nothing to soften the hurt, but I could at least understand her reasons. Not knowing that would have eaten at me worse than the pain of what she'd done."

Eloine's mouth went tight, her gaze dropped low. "Why did she do it?"

I waggled a finger in admonishment. "That would be telling."

Her mouth thinned further, and her eyes narrowed, but none of their sharpness filled her words. "And here I thought you were supposed to be telling me, while I thought I'd been teaching you. Am I to do the telling now, and you the teaching?"

I blinked, caught in the twisted tangle of what she'd said.

"Oh, he's stuck. He doesn't like this. Watch now how our clever Storyteller ties his tongue in knots, not knowing what to make of what he'd heard but couldn't hear the truth of. Even though anyone could see it's plain to see." She pressed both hands to her chest. "Even me."

"I . . ." The only person who'd ever been able to trip me like that had been Radi. His name then at the tip of my tongue, and so close to mind, brought another memory to me. Cut strings. Discordant notes. And broken wood. But I didn't have the heart to sit in it then.

Not with Eloine so close by.

I became acutely aware of how intently she watched me.

A silence fell between us, born of strings. Too delicate a thing to pull on for fear of breaking them, and something worse then would come to fill that space. A poet would have said they were tied to our hearts, linking us someplace deep, so that we dare not breathe lest the motion of our chests send the strings apart.

And that is why many poets are simply fools.

There were too many strings to count. That is all. The quiet ones held in our stare and kept us held in turn, not daring to blink as if we would never see each other again should we do so.

The strings binding our hands to the blanket, though they wished to move along its surface and touch one another.

And the strings sewn through our lips, keeping us from saying anything to break the quiet between us, keeping me from asking for something I'd been given before, but knew not whether I'd have again.

The sound of a heavy fist on wood roused us and the quiet died with it.

I finally drew breath, and Eloine turned away from me, taking with the motion of her head all the strings that we had held between us. As well as what hopes they'd carried for that moment.

I followed her gaze to the man at the door.

The old tavern keeper had changed since I last saw him upon coming to Karchetta. He wore a shirt the color of pressed olives, though it stretched tight against the broad of his chest. His hair held more chalk and iron than last I recalled, and it was already lined with more than enough of that for his age. Even the creases under his eyes seemed deeper.

"Dannil?" I rose from the bed, stopping halfway. "What are you doing here?" Realization came to me. "The *efante*. The letter. My witness of character."

Dannil didn't respond, looking to me, then to Eloine with the eyes of a man clearly coming to a conclusion. His mouth twitched, telling the story of someone who had many things to say, all of them clever, and knowing better than to voice a single one of them. "Should have known if you were going somewhere that it'd be into trouble, and that you'd be led around your nose by that one." Dannil inclined his head toward Eloine.

I could see all the makings of a smile behind Eloine's eyes. "Oh, I wouldn't say I've got him around the nose quite yet," she said. "It takes time, you know?"

Dannil nodded as if he understood.

"This might come as a terrible shock to the both of you, but I am, if you care to see, right here." I pulled at the sides of my cloak, using the motion to draw some emphasis to myself.

"Besides, he gets into trouble just fine without me. Or haven't you heard." Eloine went on as if I hadn't spoken at all.

Dannil took a deep contemplative breath. "Oh, I heard. No way I couldn't have. Not with men in armor showing up at my inn, what, at an hour even Solus Himself would be in bed at.

"Had *lanzas* pointed at me, mind you. At me. In my home. What kind of world is it when a man has steel drawn at him when he's wearing his small clothes? It's . . . indecent. It's . . . Solus, they really . . . you killed an *efante*?" Whatever he had been thinking to say fell apart at the end of his rant.

Now, Dannil had all the look of a father who'd come upon his child fresh in the act of some terrible mischief. Wide-eyed weary, and mouth hung slack.

I shook my head. "No. That was part of why I first thought to ask you to come as my witness. Only, I thought you'd come sooner."

Dannil took a breath, then lost it. His chest heaved as he turned, gesticulating toward the entrance to my room. "You'll have to ask them that brought me then. Took their time, that they did. Were quick to point at me with *lanzas*, don't you doubt. But make any kind of quick to get here? No." He shook his head as I'd done. "Not at all. Though, I told them on the way, and you can ask 'em if you don't believe me—"

"Dannil—" I didn't get a chance to finish voicing what I wanted.

"I said it to them. I did. I told them couldn't have been you. What, you just came into my tavern not knowing the last *efante* had been done in. How's one to finger you for it again? Solus, his grace and good sense has left many folk. I'm telling you." His voice dropped to a conspiratorial whisper. "Though, don't tell anyone I said that. Not a godly thing for a man to say, that his fellow people don't know what from what, *sieta*?"

Eloine tried to keep the smile from her face but failed.

I did as well, letting out a light laugh. "Dannil, it's all right. I know. That's what I'd hoped you'd tell them, but it doesn't matter now."

He opened his mouth as if he had more to say, completely unaware that I'd spoken. Then it struck him. "What?"

Eloine and I told him what had happened. Being manipulated by Lord Umbrasio to take the fall for one *efante*'s murder by poisoning, then led to trial. That being just a plot to get the rest of the princes in one place—all the easier for Efraine to do what he desired, and secure the election.

Just a game, of course. Even at the expense of family. Of blood.

Dannil buried his face within the cup of his hands. "Solus and shadow. I can't believe it."

I reached out to comfort him. "Men kill for all manner of things, and power is one of the most tempting reasons of them all. And few things offer the sort of power that comes with a crown. Some think it's a gilded cage, but a man within that can still cast a long shadow . . . and in that darkness, take up a good deal of the world."

And the people within it.

Dannil shook his head and blew out a heavy breath. "Solus. And. Shadow. I heard stories they played the game, but not like this. It was supposed to be just a thing that made people think them up high were the same as us. That's all. Just rumors. You don't . . . The game isn't supposed to be for this."

Eloine and I traded looks, then I rocked Dannil's shoulders with all the gentle care I could manage. "What do you mean? I thought the game was only for the nobles?"

He looked at me like a man who'd come to realize a lifelong truth had long been a lie. "That's not how it started. There's a story—old one, mind you. The game didn't start with the families. It's out there." Dannil pointed to one of the tall glass windows. "It belongs to . . . us. Them. Just the folk.

"It's when a boy sees a girl he's too sweet on, but he knows he's still got more wool in his head than proper sense. So, what's he to do or say without making a fool of himself? He gives her a flower. Now, if she's all sunkissed bright and like a gift from Solus himself, he gives her a yellow flower. Something bright, like the sun, see?"

I nodded.

"You give her a sunflower, a pansy, maybe a daffodil if it's turned the color. A boy might find himself a man one day, blood-red and hot, and realize it's time to give a girl something more. A rose. You give your mother something green, a kindness for all that she's done for you, and you remember. The work, and the love, and the patience only a mother has. You give your father something blue, like the sky. Something like . . . that blue one that grows about all the fields here. Thing like that, of the earth, solid and sturdy. Like Antoine, born beneath our blue skies."

"Cornflower," said Eloine.

Dannil snapped his fingers. "That's the one. And it's been like that always. Just little ways the common folk all give thanks and blessings without playing fancy behind pretty words. Just a game. And it takes away all the things you leave in here." He tapped the space above his heart. "Not too hard to give a flower. But then nobles took to making pretty pieces of precious of it. Gems and jewels. Secret meanings and the like. And for what?

"Solus and shadow. To . . . play games like this. To kill each other. To kill blood? That's not what he taught us. That's not how the game began. There's a story 'bout that too, though I don't remember the right of it.

"But the nobles heard of our giving of gifts, and decided that they deserved it better, no? So they made a game out of the giving of flowers. Prettied it up, made 'em pins. Fancy, all to hide . . . this kind of thing, I suppose.

"And you said the pontifex himself was fine with all this?"

Hard thing to tell a man the embodiment of his faith, all he held whole in heart dear and holy, hadn't even batted an eye at the murder of several people.

"He was."

Dannil heard me, but had become lost in himself. "Some girls, fair and pretty as the moon. You give 'em something white. Like the stars, see. Something like that weed that grows in on dark. Moonflower?"

Eloine laid a hand over his, squeezing it tight with all the visible reassurance she could offer the man. "The Goodnight flower grows on vines, and it's not a weed. That's jimsonweed. They're all poisonous, though."

Dannil came out of the reverie for a moment, eyes wide as if Eloine had slapped him. "Solus and shadow, girl. Poison? Where's about you get on thinking like that? They're just gifts, we're not doing what—"

It was my turn to put a hand in comfort to Dannil's arm. "She didn't mean it like that. She was just saying, is all. That's all, Dannil. She didn't mean the common folk would do something like that with that flower. You know that."

He took a few steadying breaths, nodding to himself. "Yeah. S'pose I do, that." Dannil rubbed the meat of one palm against an eye. "Solus and shadow, boy, what kind of trouble have you gotten yourself into? Thought it was plenty bad enough when you kicked in the clergos' teeth."

"I'm not entirely sure myself, Dannil. But, if there's one thing I'm good at, it's getting out of trouble I've gotten myself into."

"Don't suppose I could convince you to come back and take on a less dangerous game? The pair of you? The sort that involves two insufferable performers living up to their trade and making us all some tidy copper, eh?" Dannil leaned to one side, nudging me with an elbow, making a silent plea with his face toward Eloine.

She and I spoke in unison. "I can't." We traded looks, broke the stare, and found everywhere else in the world to look at but each other.

"I'm looking for something." Eloine's voice held a touch of smoke, born more from want than any dryness. And I knew that because I would have said just the same as she did, and sounded no different.

For I was looking for something as well. Of the Ashura, and the Tainted. And the hand that shaped them all for a purpose I still did not know. Only the harm that came from them.

Kingdoms fallen. Hearts taken, minds twisted, and promises of war across the world.

Dannil regarded Eloine. "And what are you looking for, dear?"

"Something important to no one but me. Just a song. Something I heard once before, but cannot remember, and it's the memory of the thing that's been weighing heavily on me."

Dannil and I nodded in understanding. Remembrance carried a heaviness like the whole of a mountain pressing down on you. Remembrance could eat at you like moths to clothes. And certain kinds of remembrances can kill you when they're given the proper thought, which is why some memories are best locked away behind the doors no one will look behind.

Especially when those memories hold the key to opening the very doors they were locked behind, and to the thing themselves that's been forgotten.

"And you, Storyteller. You're set on staying here until the *efante* . . . prince-elect, I mean, finds a new noose to tie 'round your neck?" Dannil gave me a long knowing stare.

"Of course. It wouldn't be much of a story to walk away from without a little more danger now, would it? Besides, I'm a fair hand at slipping nooses."

"There's a fair hand, Storyteller, and there's dumb luck. My Rita once said something like that to me. Just don't get the two confused, *sieta*? A man goes long enough running on the second, he starts to think of it as the first." Dannil tapped the side of his nose. "You follow?"

I inclined my head. "More than you know."

Dannil grunted as if he didn't believe me. But he turned the conversation elsewhere. "Suppose I don't have call to ask you for a favor after comin' late to your need, Storyteller. Maybe it *is* more than fair if you stay here, I suppose."

I smiled as I thought of something the innkeeper had once mentioned. "I've got a way you can make it up to me, if you're up to it?"

He arched a brow in silent expectation.

"There's not much a good story can't pay for. You once told me the Three Tales had one." I didn't need to say anything else.

"Well, seeing as I don't rightly know when I'll be seeing either of you again, might be sharing this gets your noses itchin' and you'll be comin' back to hear more. Maybe listen to an old man's offer to perform again . . ." A spark flashed behind each eye as he made the request again.

Eloine and I could have been tethered in heart as much as mind then. We both flashed him the same sincere smiles that said we would love to, but we cannot.

He blew out a heavy breath and nodded as if he'd known the answer was coming. "All right. All right. Everyone knows . . . nothing more stubborn than a performer, 'specially a pair of them. Doubly so then some if they're in love."

Eloine spoke, but I lost the sound of her.

My own words caught somewhere between my throat and tongue, deciding to leave me a stumbling mess no man could make sense of.

Dannil, as it turned out, had no ear for what either of us had to say. "I heard this tale by way of the man who held my home before me. Some off-on foreign fellow. From the Mutri, like you. Abraham. Ibriham? Ahhh." He shook his head and motioned with his hand again, dismissing the name.

"Doesn't matter. Goes something like this." He pulled something from his pockets.

> *"It all began with tales a-three.*
> *That which was.*
> *Those which are.*
> *And what tales would come to be.*
>
> *A binding of three stories. Three names.*
> *Twined full in des // ti // ny.*
>
> *A man of past lives many,*
> *set lost to wandering through more than he can see,*
> *and hoping full,*
> *and foolishly,*
> *for a future that would not be.*
>
> *A woman whose past,*
> *was set-defined,*
> *now put to hiding,*
> *pres // ent // ly,*
> *yet full in plain,*
> *and before you all o // pen // ly*

Two souls set on paths,
and bound in hand,
for paths that they could not see.

And marked in whole,
by things unseen,
shadows scheming,
malevolently,

who seek to twist,
taint and shape,
to malign all things,
and his // to // ry."

The sound of folding parchment touched my ears before the jarring noise of it being crumpled in hand and unceremoniously stuffed away into the pocket it had come from. Dannil blew out a breath before turning back to face us. "Ah, I don't have the ear or tongue for this. You lot make it sound easy. Had to write down what I remembered, and not sure I got that much right anyhow. Last man who owned the place before Rita and I took it over told me to pass that on to someone who'd appreciate it. Figured it'd be you."

I inclined my head, putting as much quiet respect into the simple gesture as I could manage. A thanks for sharing another story with me, and one personal to the history of his home.

Dannil said nothing further, choosing to give the pair of us one last look and a bow of his head as he turned to leave.

I had just turned back to face Eloine when another knock came at the door. It would be an exaggeration to say the all-too-soon disturbance lit a candle under my ass, but it wouldn't be far from the truth either.

I turned. "What?"

The man at the door was the same who'd first been sent to wait on me by instruction of the former princes of Etaynia. "I'm sorry for disturbing the pair of you, but the Lady Etiana's presence is required by *Vizconte* Tario. I was told she has been expecting the summons."

"You are? You have?" I looked at Eloine, but she'd already risen to leave.

She moved to halfway between me and the doorman, turning slightly to regard me over her shoulder. "I trust I'll be able to find you again soon enough?"

"Of course." The words left me before I had the wit to think of something else—something better.

She smiled earnestly. "Good. And if I don't find you, I presume you'll keep to your promise to find me." It wasn't a question.

I nodded.

Eloine left me with nothing else, passing through the door and out of sight.

I would have cast my gaze to the ceiling and let out a long-suffering sigh at the turn of luck, but the doorman remained. So I turned a different look on him. One that spoke my question for me.

"Ah, Prince-elect Efraine says he wishes to speak with you, Storyteller." The words came without a hint of edge to them, but a weight hung in them all the same. And the true translation as well: He wishes to speak with you . . . *now.*

This was a demand, politely put.

And I had seen how he'd treated his own blood. So perhaps I shouldn't keep the murderous king waiting.

I rose, moving to fetch my staff and taking it up in hand. "Very well. Shall we?"

The doorman nodded and led the way.

I followed behind to meet the man who'd killed his family, and wanted to begin a war.

SIXTY-FOUR

THE THINGS WE CLAIM

The porter led me to a pair of double doors and motioned for me to enter.

I did.

Every inch of the floor was covered in a rug made to the shape of the room. The tassels at the ends just brushed the walls, and the colors matched those of the royal house of Etaynia—the red of lion's mane and burnished gold. But the shape and style were not native to the country—no. The people here may have had an appreciation for fine rugs, but the means to afford one such as this was beyond many.

And Etaynians had little love of foreigners, which is what brought me to wonder why Prince-elect Efraine owned a woven rug, tailored to this room, that came from Zibrath. Especially considering the speech he'd given before the rest of the gentry.

The full glow of a proper sun eater radiated from a shelf above, casting rays of gilded brightness over much of the room, as well as Prince-elect Efraine himself. At odd angles, it brought out some of the gold hidden in his skin.

The rest of what I took to be the prince-elect's study had been appointed in similar fashion. Woodworks in differing styles that spoke of other parts of the world. A statue, carved in the image of Hahnbadh, down to the painted cloak of white. A tall figure, half man, half ape, with a tail wound around his waist. Muscles that belonged to a wrestler had been etched in every detail.

Another piece rested beside it. A woman in a flowing dress, formed out of a wood the shade of summer clouds, and its bark promised to be as smooth as ivory. She held a painted fan in one hand, its colors drawn from every shade of red imaginable. In her other grip rested a weapon.

The sword, even in this carving, spoke to the idea of all a sword could be. Clean, and shaped to purpose—that purpose set to killing with but a stroke. Its form as if someone had pulled free shimmering water and let it crystallize straight and true. When it was done, only the sword remained.

Too much detail for a statue of just any woman. But then, it told a story that didn't belong to just any person. For a moment longer than anyone should have thought to give to such a piece, I stared, whole-caught in taking in the shape of the woman.

And the sword.

"I see something has grabbed your attention, Storyteller." Prince-elect Efraine steepled his hands, resting his chin atop them from behind the desk. He hadn't changed his outfit since after his coup.

I gestured to the statues, then tapped my staff against the rug. "I didn't take you for a man who—"

Prince-elect Efraine waved me to silence. "You didn't take me for someone who takes interest in the finer points of other cultures, *sieta*?"

I didn't speak the words, but the look I gave him said it for me.

Efraine clicked his tongue. "True. I am not. While I appreciate them, it's as a point of curiosity, not honest love. My brother was more the artist, I'm afraid." He motioned to most of the room with a hand. "Arturo loved collecting things from far off. Same with Artenyo. Many would argue they were better learned. And they were certainly loved for it." The way he said that invited question, so I asked what I felt he wanted from me.

"And you're not?"

He pursed his lips, not going quite as far as a frown. One of his hands brushed against the surface of the desk, more an absent gesture than to wipe anything away. "If I ever was, it wasn't for that. And if I ever was, I am certainly not now, am I, Storyteller? But one doesn't need love to move a people." A thin smile, curved and sharp as a fresh-stoned sickle, keeping to all the metal-coldness you could hope to find in such a thing.

But I heard what had gone unsaid in his words: One doesn't need love to move a people, not when you have hate. Hate for the different. The foreign.

"You didn't ask me here to lie to you, or respond to questions you have answers to." My voice remained level, making sure not to invite the prince's anger.

"I did not." Prince-elect Efraine leaned to one side, pulling on one of the desk's drawers. "Do you like my brother's study? One of them, at any rate. He had many."

A simple question, but I didn't see the point of it. Why bother to invite me before him only to ask my opinions on décor?

Is he testing me? Prodding me? Or leading me? Worse, I realized, it could be all three. And none of that told me his purpose. But I'd already seen the measure of the person he was—the manner in which he took the crown had revealed that. And, if my other theory held true, I knew what he was deep behind the mask he wore.

One of the Tainted. Now able to lead a country to ruin.

But the only way to know for sure would be to play the little games, and the larger ones he had yet to share.

"And what did your brother have to pay to acquire something like this?" I moved to another side of the room, examining the shelf that ran the length of the wall. Dark as pitch, the wooden board had been fixed in place with two bands of gold. Atop it rested another piece of wood, nowhere near as polished or worth remark compared to what it sat above.

A piece of cloth was spread beside it. Most of it looked to have survived the hungry attention of an overzealous hound. But what remained told another story. A field of red the same shade as my cloak—the color of blood. Emblazoned on it was a serpent drawn from brightest gold. Only, it had a body longer and thicker than most beasts by that name, and scales given special attention to stand out in greater detail. Most of all, two legs that sported the claws belonging to lions.

"Arturo paid good sums for every piece in here, including that which has caught your eye. The Dragon's Banner, held by the last dragon himself. Are you familiar with his legend? I admit I've only studied his campaign, less so the history of the country's turn and his rise to power. Though, I sometimes wonder if I should have. Then again"—Efraine leaned back in the chair, gesturing wide once again, the message clear—"my way seems to have worked fine."

Temptation is a terrible thing. It is how the little evils begin to take root inside you. The little steps they ask you to take. Just a grasp of the wooden shaft; its broken jagged crown would pierce skin easily enough. Never mind the spear tip fixed to head of the banner. No more than a few steps would put you close enough to the prince-elect's form. Just one perfect thrust would send the tip through his throat.

Each motion, simple enough. Each reason to do them, simple enough. The end result, simple enough. And the last prince of Etaynia would die, possibly ridding me of one of the Tainted.

If he is one at all. And how easy it would be to be wrong, and kill an innocent man in the process?

My fingers flexed, coming to rest on the broken banner. "Your way has certainly gotten you what you wanted, Prince-elect Efraine. But it leaves me with this question: What do you want from me?"

Prince-elect Efraine pulled something from the drawer. A box. The flat top of the container had been fashioned from smooth glass, carrying every shade of green imaginable along its length. The surface had been painted with lines in white to divide it into a board featuring close to fifty squares. "I'd like to play a game, Storyteller, and there aren't many who I feel are up to giving me a challenge."

I eyed him, then the Talluv box—the game that had spread wide across the Golden Road. A chair waited for me opposite him. An obvious invitation. So I sank into place, resting the head of my staff against the table.

"Excellent." Efraine placed the box between us, pulling on a brass knob fixed to one side. The tray slid open and revealed a mixture of pieces within. Towers carved from polished black stone. White bone pieces followed—their shapes made to look like small arches formed of smaller rocks. Some sets of Talluv used simple humped discs in place of these.

The prince-elect went about setting the board, casting fleeting looks my way when he thought I'd turned my attention elsewhere.

And a game was a great way to learn about a man. An excuse to watch him, see how he reacted to things such as loss, frustration, and how he thought.

He gestured with a hand for me to take the first move. "What rules do you prefer?"

"Zibrathi." The word left my mouth without thought.

Efraine's brows raised. "I wouldn't have thought that. I'd have figured you for the Mutri variant." He watched me—a hawk's eyes, slow to blink, and taking in any hint of motion I might betray.

I gave him none. Slowly falling into the candle and the flame, though it did not come as easily as it always had. The lone flickering fire took my thoughts. I became a stone before the flame, in face as much as heart. Impassive.

"Very well." The prince-elect retrieved a die carved from the same material as the arches, placing it at the center of the board.

I reached for the piece and cast it into a roll no sooner than it touched my hand. It landed on a three, and I made the appropriate staggered moves along the board befitting the curved piece I chose.

Efraine acted in kind. His roll a four, and he chose the straightest path ahead with one of the towers.

The game progressed in the silence kept between two men who studied one another, wishing to glean the other's secrets, all while keeping their own. It was the sort of quiet between two wolves, unfamiliar with one another, who had crossed paths. And they did not intend to form a friendship.

"I've ventured eastward far as a man can dream to go, and in that time, I've seen a man born of dragon's blood, a woman who could step as lightly as a feather and fly as freely as a bird on the wind. And last of all, I have seen a serpent large enough to swallow ships whole." Efraine rolled the die, covering it with his hand. "Four."

I frowned. "Liar."

Efraine broke his hold on the die, revealing it to be a two. "If I hadn't lied about the roll, you'd be in the wrong, unless you're saying such creatures and feats are not real? That would be an odd admission from a storyteller of your reputation. After all, you certainly speak and perform about such things as if they're true." He smiled a cunning thing.

I shook my head as I pulled the die into my grip, rolling it across my palm. "Not the things themselves, and we won't touch on that. You said you'd seen them. I don't believe you have, Prince-elect." I rolled the die as he moved one of his pieces back the way it'd come. My toss brought me a three, but I shielded it before he could see.

"I've seen the last dragon, and took their flame, full in hand, after I took their life. I've ridden on an eagle's wings of lightning, far across a sky with no stars. And I've steered the wealth of a kingdom whole into the very mouth of the serpent you've claimed to have seen. Three."

"Liar . . . but on your claims." Efraine narrowed his eyes, staring at my hand cupped around the die, then to me. "Not your roll."

If only . . .

I grinned, revealing the number to be as I'd spoken it. "You're good."

The prince-elect's mouth pulled into a thin frown as he regarded me in a stare I hadn't seen before. It was the careful look of a man who'd been wrong about something, and now had been forced to reconsider his plans. "Why did you say that?"

I blinked, pausing before advancing my piece the number of spaces I'd earned. My lies wouldn't penalize me as my roll had been true, nor would they earn a mark against him for accurately calling the situation as it was. In Talluv, the truth of the roll is what mattered. Or that is what most players have come to believe. "What do you mean?"

He motioned to the die, then me. "You could have told me any number of lies, or even truths that sounded like lies. You're a storyteller—the Storyteller. Surely you can do better than that? It was too easy, and you know that."

I thought then on all I'd shared with him, and how easily he'd called them false. He was right after a fashion, I could do better, but sometimes the truth itself comes in the shapes of lies, and it's scarcely believed. Far easier than to believe life's convenient little lies. Many times they're easier to swallow.

"Well, Prince-elect, what kind of lies would you have me tell, then? If I told you I'd marched besides the last dragon, would you believe me? If my hands had once held that very banner your brother had there"—I pointed to the broken standard—"would you believe me? What if I told you *I* killed the last dragon, and it had been a mercy? But the world remembers it a crime? That in the end, I stole their very fire, that fanned and fueled the flames of their world, as much as their dreams? Which lies can you believe?"

Prince-elect Efraine reached out to take the die, throwing it in a callous roll that made clear I'd trod on his patience. "Now you're being pedantic, Storyteller. I am not the sort of man to play *those* kinds of games with, *sieta*?"

I inclined my head.

"Good." Efraine interlocked his fingers and stared hard. "Now, you tell me you knew the last dragon, but that would have made you a very young man at that time. Too young to be marching into war, or at least serving the dragon properly. At least, too young for *my* army." He pressed one of his hands to his chest.

"And how old are you now, Prince-elect?"

He moved his piece three squares, positioning a black tower along one of my arches. "I will touch my fortieth year in a few months. And yourself?" He never finished his move, turning his attention on me. When he did, it was with a stare of frozen needles—cold and piercing.

I didn't smile, and kept my voice pitched to match his expression. "Old enough to know better, young enough to not do as I know I should."

Efraine watched me longer then—finally, a break in the mask. The shade of his eyes remained the same brown as they had throughout our conversations, but now carried a touch of gold on account of the sun eater's light. But not black.

Not taken in sight.

He relented with a sigh, gesturing with his hands as if the matter couldn't be helped. "Sometimes I think too much cleverness is wasted on a man. We have no need for it. Sometimes the straight way is best." He used the positioning of his tower near my arch to gain an extra move, inching farther up the board.

"Sometimes, Prince-elect. Other times it's a blessing. It can get you out of trouble as much as in. Do you want to know what happened to someone who wasn't so clever?" I took the die and rolled it, scoring an even six.

The prince-elect waved his hands, a silent gesture for me to continue.

I made my move and elaborated. "The person who held that banner by right and claim. The last thing that happened to them, and the banner, was to be found in a pool of their own blood. You can't see it now. But once that red was not from dye. They were not a clever dragon. Not before, and not in the end. Though, I bet they wished they had been." A pause. We watched other, and I realized what I should have added. "That's what I heard, at any rate."

"And here I thought I'd be getting the better measure of you, Storyteller, but I have the feeling you've been taking the length of me." A practiced smile—quick and too stiff to be genuine.

He could act to fool many men, but not me. It didn't answer the question I'd been holding back, however.

"I think we've been watching each other as carefully as anyone could, no?"

He didn't answer, choosing to lick his lips instead. The color of his tongue was that of every man's, and so the game went on.

Not taken by mouth then.

Eventually, I lined up my pieces where I wanted, and all that remained was one last toss, and the right lies to win. I rolled, landing me a solid four. All I needed. My hand came to rest on the last tower in my possession. "I have held the moon, twice in hand, and lost her both times. I have walked through and back from beyond the Doors of Death, and took my prize in the shape of a feather. And I have held a world of worlds bound in stone, one for every finger on this hand."

I held up my left index finger. "One heaven sent, the next born of blood, one pulled from the heart of fire, and lastly the one shaped from sand. And I've walked the world where every man finds himself at night, but wakes from come the morning to find it naught but the realms of vanity."

Efraine blinked several times and looked everywhere but at me for a count of several breaths. When his gaze returned to me, his mouth worked wordlessly, searching for something—anything, but I knew he wouldn't find it.

Finally, his hands moved to the Talluv board. The back of one of them brushed against my pieces and, in one gentle motion, he toppled them all. "You had already won, but if not for your lies. Those were too many for me to think on, and too artfully told to be true. What I don't understand is why throw the game when you could have told me you wear a red cloak and carry a staff. All true. And the game was yours."

I looked at the scattered pieces. The towers and the arches—folded stone. "It's just a game, Prince-elect. What good is winning?"

"Spoken like a man who has little interest in gain." The voice had come from behind me, and I shifted to see who'd been able to approach so closely without me noticing them.

The pontifex, dressed in his traditional robes. He moved to Prince-elect Efraine's side. "I can appreciate a man who has little room in his heart for desire."

I gave the man a thin smile. "Oh, I have wants, Your Holiness." My gaze flickered to Efraine. "Such as wanting to return to my studies of a book your late brother allowed me to translate, and access to peruse your library at will."

Prince-elect Efraine granted the request with a wave of his hand. "Of course."

The pontifex leaned in and whispered something in the man's ear, all behind a cupped hand.

I kept the frown from my face, having hoped to read the man's lips as he spoke. But I caught no sound of what was said.

Efraine placed his hands on the table and pushed himself to his feet. "It seems I'll be entertaining other company later tonight, and we will have to conclude our talk soon." The skin around his eyes tightened as he gave the pontifex a look that carried all the irritation only a prince could muster.

He wasn't happy about being pulled along by the holy man's string.

I rose as well, knowing I'd be better served leaving while still in their collective good—or tolerable—graces.

"You should tell the pontifex some of what you told me, Storyteller." Efraine hooked a thumb in my direction. "He's a marvelous cobbler of tales, even on the quick. Little lies that had me wondering if there could be any breath of truth to them."

The pontifex arched a brow. "Oh?"

I made a motion that could have been taken as dismissal by those not paying careful attention, but in truth was the sign of someone playing humble at the praise being given.

"He claimed . . ." Prince-elect Efraine trailed off, a hand on his chin as he thought.

All the while, I moved to the broken banner of the dragon. My hand gripped the spear-tipped shaft, tight-held so as not to shake.

Memory came to me like waves in storm, hammering hard against a stone that remained firm to all who looked on it. But they never saw how the sea took its toll. Every wash against the wall scraped flecks of it away. And over time, the stone was no more.

I remembered the shaping of the banner, and the breaking of it. I remembered the one who carried it, and the one who used it last. They were not the same. And they did not leave those fields together. Or at all.

"He claimed to have sailed into a monstrous serpent with . . . ah, what was it?" Efraine snapped his fingers. "God Above. It was something. He claimed to have held the moons—two of them, if you can believe that, in his hands."

I turned to face the two men, shying away from the pontifex as he stood within the strongest of the sun eater's light.

He watched me as I moved closer with the spear. His eyes not hard with suspicion, but simple curiosity. Their brown as bright as all the gold I once owed Arfan, and many others over the years.

"Is that so, Storyteller?" The pontifex pursed his lips in polite surprise, but the expression came too stiff to warrant true belief. Merely humoring me.

"It's what I said during the game, Your Holiness. That much is true." I moved closer, spear's head pointed toward the prince-elect. The muscles through my arms quivered.

"And what else did our performer tell you, my king-to-be?" The pontifex held no amusement in his voice. His tone had all the cold measured flatness of a lake frozen over so deep that you could not hope to find a hint of moving water within. The exacting edge of a razor, honed to so fine a thing it could cut the air as much as your skin.

"He made claims of knowing the last dragon, and taking his fire. I don't understand it myself, but it is a wondrous lie if he can spin a larger story around it."

"Is that so, Storyteller?" The same words, all spoken in the exact same way as he'd said them before. The pontifex even managed to bring back the earlier expression of surprise—still feigned, but a perfect mirror of what it had been before.

I nodded. "Just plying my art, Your Holiness." I shifted to face Prince-elect Efraine, pushing the banner in his direction. "If you care to look at this, you might be able to make out where it's been stained." I inched it forward.

The prince-elect reached out to take it in his grip.

I shuffled, trying to hand it to him, feigning more excitement than necessary. My body met the desk and the spear rolled in my grip.

"*Hssch.*" The prince-elect pulled his hand back, bringing his thumb and forefinger to his lips with the speed of a striking snake. He sucked on his cuts before lowering to take the spear from me properly. "Careful there, Storyteller. You're a performer, but I don't think you should be handling something close to a *lanza*, *sieta*?"

I did not give his words any more attention, keeping the whole of myself focused on his lips.

What blood he'd missed smeared along the corner of his mouth, and its color was that which I'd seen spill from two men back in Karchetta. Two men who'd come looking for a man named Ari. Two men with blood black as night.

And they were demons.

The sudden coming of thunder signaled the storm and roused me from my troubled thoughts.

"Ah, I suppose we will be dining indoors then. Shame, these warm weather storms are frequent enough, but bothersome when you want to enjoy the stars, no?" The prince-elect reached out to take the sun eater in hand, operating it with practiced care unlike his brother. The light dimmed, and all of the golden glow fled the room, and the faces of the two men with me.

I wasted no more time, and made no farewells as I turned and left.

Prince-elect Efraine was one of the Tainted. Taken somewhere in the deep of him so much so he bore none of the most visible signs. But his blood ran black as sin. So I would have to kill him.

When and where I could get away with it.

Because how many would perish if I failed?

SIXTY-FIVE

Invitation

The remainder of my night passed in the library as I didn't have it in me to sleep. Not with having confirmed my suspicions about Prince-elect Efraine.

One of the Tainted, in so high a place of power that he could shape the future of his country. And he meant to. With war.

A man with supreme power, shadow-taken in mind and heart—so far gone he could not hope to do anything but wrong. And the world would pay for it.

Blood and ashes. I pressed a hand to my head, unable to focus on the row of titles along the shelves. They became a washed froth like the head of ocean waves, and I could not make out any of them.

The flickering candles along the walls became my point of fixation, and I walked over to them, finding a spot to rest at one of the tables before one of the many glass windows. I laid my staff across the table and took a breath.

"You look like a man who's had more hard times than he's had time to rest, my friend." Dannil ambled over to me, stopping short of taking a seat at the table. He placed his hands on the corners of its wooden top and leaned forward. "Don't seem to be holding much of that fire you had back when you first walked into my home." A curved smile, holding all the warmth and worry of someone I suppose you could call a friend.

I wanted to return one in kind, but in truth, I couldn't manage it. So I settled for giving my words. "I suppose most of it has been squeezed out of me."

"Ah." He waved a hand. "Thing like that doesn't go away so easily. My Rita had her moments, much like you now, that's the truth. But you'd be a proper fool if you think her fire had gone out. Sometimes I wish I'd remembered that." The smile returned, then faded. His eyes went to a place somewhere between my face, the table, and the wall. Somewhere only he could find. "But there were moments where it'd come back proper powerful, and frightening. You believe me on that."

"I do, Dannil."

He nodded. "It never went away. I think it just needed to rest, went to sleep. Then it came all up roaring and angry when it needed. Other times, the good times, the ones I like to remember, it was just warm. The kind of fire you fall asleep watching late at night. You know the kind?"

I did, but didn't say it.

Dannil's face lost some of the sobriety that'd come across it, slowly turning into the guilish look best found on a young boy about to talk as much mischief as he is keen to do. "So, where's our lovely little songstress? I'm sure she could find that smile you've lost, and that quickness of tongue you showed me not so long ago, eh?" He leaned forward and ribbed the air with an elbow.

"She left not long after you did. A summons."

Dannil clicked his tongue in an unspoken *ah*. "And she hasn't come back . . . or you haven't gone looking for her?"

I opened my mouth but never had the chance to speak.

"She's come back, but he didn't go to look for her—as he promised." Eloine walked toward us, a basket hanging from the crook of one arm. "A woman might take that personally. Broken promises, hearts"—she touched a hand to her breast—"and all."

I had the grace not to gawk in surprise.

She seized the opportunity to give me more grief than I needed. "Oh, I've broken him again. Not sure what to say? Is it because you forgot to look for me? Found books more interesting? Or decided to go back to being dour?" Eloine stopped beside the table, placing the basket atop it.

"I'm sorry." I rubbed a hand against my forehead almost as if the action could grind away the thoughts plaguing me. "I lost track of . . ." I resorted to gesturing at my surroundings.

Eloine nodded, moving past Dannil and giving him a quick look that turned to the chair.

He inclined his head and went as far as pulling out the seat for her.

She thanked him and sat opposite me, opening the basket and setting the table for us.

"Where did you get the food?" I leaned forward to peek at what else she'd brought.

"The same place as before, and I knew you would forget to take a meal." Half a loaf of bread had been placed onto the table, with a crust that looked firm and how I liked it. She added cheese, a baked squash, and more than enough grapes to be a meal themselves. Lastly, a bottle that held more dust to its surface than visible glass. So it was either something well-aged and tasty, or something that soured so far it would remove all of the thoughts bothering me . . . for good.

Eloine pulled the stopper from the bottle and brought it close to her nose, taking a deep breath of it.

"What is it?"

"I don't know, but it smells like fruit." She took a sip. The corners of her mouth showed the first signs she'd enjoyed it, pulling up and taking the rest of her lips into a wide smile. "And it tastes like it as well." She passed it my way and I took it with quiet thanks.

True to her words, it touched my tongue with notes of strawberries and apples as well an acid bite that complemented the flavors well. "Sweet and sharp, like many of the best things." I tipped the bottle in her direction but didn't pass it to her.

"We haven't started our dinner and you've already started the flattery." Her eyes shone.

Dannil's gaze went from me, to her, then to a space between us both. "I know well enough when to leave a man and woman alone." He fixed me with a look that could have said something under it, but I couldn't find the meaning of it. Then he gave Eloine one as well.

"You could always stay, Dannil." Eloine's words, sweet as they were to hear, however, did not ring of honest invitation. "The storyteller here has been entertaining me with tales of a particularly enrapturing man out of legend. Not the same sort of performance as he put on back in your home, but I'd say even more . . . interesting." The light in her eyes burned brighter than any of the candles around us.

The bottle rolled in my grip, promising to slip free if I didn't redouble my effort in holding it firm. So I did, catching it just before it left the tips of my fingers. I eyed Eloine, then Dannil, but fortunately the tavern owner meant what he'd said moments earlier.

He raised his hands and stepped away from the table. "My Rita would twist my ear clean off if she knew I was ruining a dinner like this." Dannil took one of his earlobes between his forefinger and thumb, giving it a little tug to make his point. Then he backed away from us before vanishing deep within the rows of shelves.

Assured that Dannil had moved far enough away not to overhear us, I placed the bottle down and regarded Eloine. "What was that?"

She reached for the bread, breaking free a piece and then doing the same to the cheese. "What?" The way she'd said it told me she knew exactly what I'd meant.

I stared.

She returned the expression, indulging in a bite of the bread and cheese together, washing it down with the fruity wine. "How would you have reacted if he'd agreed to listen?"

I blinked, thought on it, then decided it better not to answer.

She watched me all the while. "So, your story isn't for everyone then?" A teasing smile, but it faded soon after. One of her hands reached out to brush against the top of mine. "He wouldn't have sat in, Ari. Dannil isn't one to intrude on this." She motioned in a small circle with her hand at the spread set before us.

"And what exactly is *this*?" I mimicked her gesture.

Eloine plucked free a single grape, taking her time in bringing it to her mouth. She chewed it, still holding her gaze locked on mine as she did. "That depends." She leaned forward, close enough that were I to meet her in kind, our lips could almost touch. "It's a dinner. A story I hope, and . . ." She broke off to lean even closer. "An invitation."

I didn't need any more prompting than that. My face came to hers and I found something sure-sweeter than the wine she'd brought. The taste of it lasted longer than that of the drink, and I did not wish to spoil it so soon with any of the food.

Eloine said nothing, bringing back *that* smile, silver-moon sharp and bright. I wished for all the life of me I could have gleaned her thoughts then. "And what's going on inside that mind of yours?" Eloine plopped another grape into her mouth, watching me as she chewed.

"I'm thinking that I once kissed a girl and gave her my trust, only to find that she'd broken that and left me to face the noose. And now I'm thinking there's a woman I've kissed twice, and wondering when she'll th—" A sharp lance of pain shot through my shin and I winced. "Ow."

Eloine's face remained as it had, a smiling mask that said nothing of the kick she'd just dealt me. "And I've given you reasons not to trust me? Or are you afraid you'll end up in a noose for having given me that much?" A dangerous tilt to her head and a sharper look in eye than before.

I said nothing, but mimed wrapping a rope around my neck. I did not finish the gesture as another bright pain raced along the same spot as before. "I suppose I earned that one."

Eloine took another grape. "I suppose."

Silence, but I did not let it linger, knowing once it set in full it could be too hard a thing to break. "You said you were looking for something, earlier in my room."

She inclined her head but did not elaborate.

"What song are you looking for, Eloine?"

"It's a little thing, really." The tips of her thumbs brushed against each other as she fiddled. Her eyes fell from mine and she looked everywhere but at me. "The song."

I waited.

"You have your art—your trade, I have mine. It's a curiosity. But I think there's something special in it, as much as the thing itself is special. I think you understand."

I did, and I told her so. But I knew she had another reason than what she'd given me. I couldn't tell what it was, only that it existed. Because something in her voice spoke of it, just as mine did whenever I told someone what I sought.

A story.

The most special of them, and while all stories held that specialness, this one just happened to be worth more to me than the rest. I didn't speak of the worth of all stories in the grand place of all things, just for the space in my heart. The one left to me. Because of what I needed it for. And what I wanted it for.

And the wants of some men can be terrible things.

"I hope you find it." I paused, taking a sip of the wine. Its taste did not wipe the one Eloine had left, and for that, I gave silent thanks. "Is there anything I can do to help?"

A smile, telling me my words were welcome, and then it faded, giving me the answer before she'd said it. "No, but thank you. Though, there is something you can give me."

I straightened, waiting for the answer.

"I seem to recall a young boy, with a heart too big for his wits, and not wits enough for his eyes to see the trouble plain before him. *Trouble* that he seemed quite keen on making. And for it, he bought himself a collar too tight for his liking. But I've been kept wondering about his fate. Did he live, or did he die? Mayhaps that boy never slipped the noose at all, and I've only been led to listen to a lie. What if you're not him—Ari, and just someone putting together his stories?" She reached out and tapped a finger to my nose.

I rolled my eyes. "I've been sentenced to death by many men over the course of my life, and some things more than men. None of them have ever got the better of me in the long of things. I am still here, and many of them are not. But that day I learned just how much some men can tie the strings to your life, and how long they come to pull on them, letting you think you were in control the whole time.

"But that's the lie itself: control. Some realized this earlier than others, and take your threads in hand before you ever know, and with it, your freedom."

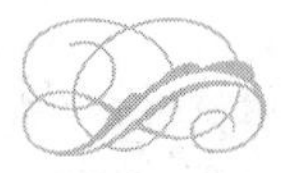

SIXTY-SIX

Strings Unseen

Something arced through the crowd—a silver-tipped shaft holding the full glint of the sun along its edge. For a moment, in the space between falling and dying, I had eyes only for that moving thing.

A stone thrown at me.

The shaft of an arrow set to take me.

A form of a crow—an eagle, some bird of prey rushing to take me in its hold.

Realization: It *was* an arrow.

The shape of it took me as it drew closer, moving too slowly to be real. There is a world we go to just before we die, and then, I hung there as the rope continued to lengthen. Time did not flow as it should have, and I kept to the awareness of a man listening to a story, wondering—waiting, when the next sharp turn would come.

And if the arrow would spare me the pain of a broken neck.

As it just so happened, it did. And traded me that for a different pain.

It cut through the rope, and I fell full now in the fear of realizing what was happening. No longer did I hold to the slow space I'd been in. The world rushed upward and my knees ached as I struck the ground. The pain then settled in my skull.

My vision streaked red, then black, all before returning to a blurred wash of golden brown—the hard-packed sand roads of Mubarath. The crowd stood on their sides, until I realized it was me on mine.

Figures broke through the crowd, drawing close to me.

Voices sounded and I did not have the wits to make out whose.

One of the faces came to clarity as it drew nearer. The man was in the fiftieth year of his life. His face shaped from hard wood, and the lines of it spoke as much of that in their severity. Bright-eyed—warm and honey-shine-touched. I did not see a strand of hair beneath the red wrap tied to conceal it all. And his clothing was the same shade as the Bloodfort's walls.

A coat that flattered him and fell to just above his knees, tied tight to show the breadth of his shoulders by a sash the white of fresh cream.

And he moved with the quiet surety of a fox, keeping the look of one in face, and the guile in eyes.

Every bit the king without the crown.

A merchant king.

Arfan. Brahm's blood. The world still teetered as if set on edge and promptly swatted off by the hands of an all-too-curious—and petulant—cat. And I knew the habits of that sort of creature well enough.

A cat. *My cat. Shola!* I rolled onto my stomach, trying to find the strength and wits to get to my feet, but most of my better senses hadn't returned.

Arfan came to a stop a few feet from where I lay. "*Tch. Tch.* When I thought you'd bring yourself to me, I didn't think it would be like this, little bird. You've made quite the problem . . . and the opportunity." He beckoned me with a hand. "Up." It was no simple request.

It was a command. And Arfan did not care if I hadn't found my legs, much less the direction of above from below.

My hands scrabbled against the ground, pulling me more forward than upward, but all the same, I got to my knees. Then to my feet. The world did not stop tilting, however.

Out of the crowd came another—a girl close to me in age. Her figure did not sway in my vision then. She had hair as dark as starless night, with a shine like the moon's own glow to its strands. The lines of her face a hawk's, sharp and angular—fiercely striking and holding my attention more than I would have thought them to have. Her nose straight, and her eyes as bright as Arfan's. She wore clothes fit more for a rider than someone in the city.

A split skirt over pants, both the color of tanned hide. Her shirt held more the brown of road dust and grime than the white it should have, but the look suited her.

One of her hands held a bow, and her other rested on her hip. "Him?" The question had been addressed to Arfan.

It took me a moment longer to realize that she'd been the one to shoot the arrow clean through the rope that had been meant to end me.

Arfan spoke to the young woman without breaking his gaze with me. "Him. The little sparrow took a great deal of Mutri gold from me, and bought himself time to play at being a magician. And now his time is up."

His words brought to mind what I'd forgotten. "You said I had one year." I stared at him, and it would have been generous to say that my look had a razor's edge of sharpness to it, but it was a look only playing at being harder than it could have been. "But you sent a knife to threaten me—in my home, and call me before my time was up."

"You had the time I allowed you. That is all you were ever to have, and careful, little bird." Arfan nodded to the gallows just behind me. "My daughter cut you down from that, and it is my name that keeps you from returning to it. Or, can be the very thing that sees you back in rope . . . ghost."

It is rather hard to argue with a point like that. My gaze turned to Arfan's daughter, and she held my look with all the attention of someone carefully weighing something to be bought or traded. Taking the value of me faster than many did a horse they already knew they wanted.

I inclined my head, making it clear that I took stock of my position, and Arfan's over me. I chanced a glance over my shoulder to the executioner, but the man found a space to look at that fell nowhere on me, the crowd, or the merchant king.

It was as if by keeping his eyes elsewhere, he could ignore the utter existence of the scene playing out before him, and the consequences. Several Bloodcoats followed suit, staring off as well. No one met the merchant king's eyes.

Radika hadn't exaggerated the man's influence, or power.

"Quick eyes, little bird. Are you beginning to see the shape of things?" Arfan's stare followed mine, and told me he'd taken in the scene same as I had. "And what do you think now?"

It was as if the world waited on the one man's opinion before deciding one of its own, and I very much had the feeling that it would be the image of whatever Arfan's was.

Funny, how power can do that.

"I think that maybe my best chance of freedom died with the breaking of the rope." I watched the remains of the swaying noose, then the ones that still held the men's bodies who hadn't been as lucky as me.

And I remembered then that luck had two faces. The one that greeted the hanged, and the one I'd been shown.

. . . The face of bad luck.

"He's bold," said Arfan's daughter. Her voice cut as sharp as her arrow.

"And that is what I hope he'll be in my service. Come." Arfan's tone brooked no argument.

I turned and joined him, moving just a step behind him as he led the way.

The crowd parted and gave us a path—all eyes avoided the pack of us now.

"What happened to my things?" Not the question I should have asked then, but my thoughts went to the most important one. "Where is my cat? Where is Shola?" My voice could have cracked the ground beneath us as well as the stone walls along the streets.

Arfan said nothing, as did his daughter. Good to know they shared similar tastes of tongue, and when to keep them still.

That did not, however, bury my question the way they would have liked. "Where. Is. Shola?"

We reached the edge of the crowd where I found a half dozen familiar faces. Among them, two boys I'd come to care greatly for.

Alwi and Baba avoided meeting Arfan's and his daughter's eyes, but they held mine.

And their looks said much.

They told me that both boys had been worried about me, but also that they had known. They had known what would happen to me *before* I returned to the tile maker's home. That I'd been set to fall for the rope. And they hadn't told me. So now they held to the shame only secrets could bring. But my gaze turned from their sorrow and the truth they too had turned on me, and to the bundle of flame held in Baba's hands.

Shola rested there, comfortable as a cat could be, full asleep. Alwi had my travel sack over a shoulder, strung 'round the head of my staff. And by his side stood a girl I had come to trust almost as much as I had Radi, Aram, and The Crow I'd left behind.

I had given her as much as I had Sham, and he would never have done this to me.

Radika, to her credit, found the courage to look me in the eyes. And hers told me that she knew all the anger I'd hold in heart, and just what I was capable of. She'd seen as much in my time as The Ghost of Ghal, and against the Black Tower Band.

And while I burned with the full fire of my anger then, I found a space to place it aside in favor of something else.

My curiosity.

She stood here now in Arfan's company, and with all she'd said before, that left me with a piece of the answer to my question. But I needed to hear the whole of it from her now.

"Ari." My name left her in a breath caught between curse and relief. "You're—"

"No. Don't. You don't get to say my name. Not now, not again. As far as we're concerned, I *am* a ghost to you, and you to me." To make my point, I resettled the cowl that had fallen free during my short plunge. "When you spoke about *Shir* Arfan, it was obvious you knew him better than you let on."

The assassin in black who'd come to my rooms had warned me as much, and I'd paid little mind to it. Arfan had others on his strings. I gave the merchant king a sidelong look, but he paid me no mind. "I just never thought you'd use me to pay your debt . . . especially after all I've done to try to help you." I eyed Radika.

She nodded. "Yes. But . . ."

I didn't need her to finish to know what came next. "It's not enough." I turned to face Arfan. "Is it?"

The old king didn't look at me, and he didn't need to, because I could almost see the foxlike smile across his face regardless. "No. But she played her game well enough to let me know she has a keener mind than I'd first given her credit for, and you . . . perhaps not so much."

Her game? Of course, it came to me then. Everything she'd said, she'd nudged me toward. "The Black Tower Band wasn't just a problem for her or the other thieves of Mubarath, were they? They were a problem for *you*. And—"

"Radika found a tool sharp enough to handle them, yes. The Black Tower Band was a problem for many a *Shir*, and we could not make the time to deal with them without . . ." Arfan never finished the sentence. "But you've done what many couldn't. You removed them, and in doing so, brought the remaining bands together, and in one place."

Oh, no. Blood and ashes. I'd formed them into a single family, and delivered them right to Arfan's hands. "And now all the thieves can be picked up by the Bloodcoats." I kept my teeth from grinding.

"You're thinking this wrong through, ghost—sparrow. You didn't collect them for me to throw away." Arfan finally turned a sliver of his attention my way.

The rest of his game came clearer to me than before. "You're going to use them—expand your group of spies, thieves, secret sellers." It had always been a part of his power, and he'd confessed as much back to me in Keshum. I had just forgotten, and in that mistake, not seen what should have been plain before me all this time in Mubarath.

Arfan smiled. It was not a kind thing. "I'm going to pull this one's strings." He made a callous motion in Radika's direction. "And she will run your Hundred Thieves as I need."

I eyed her, then Shola in Baba's care. Making more of a scene now wouldn't help. "It won't be The Hundred Thieves without me, you know? Ninety-nine doesn't have the same ring to it."

That drew a wider grin out of Arfan. "I still don't think you understand what you've given me, Ari. You've given me a secret—a myth, the best sort. The kind that creates itself. The Hundred Thieves are much like you've played at being—ghosts. There never needs to be that number now. Only the name. Only the deeds they've done, such as breaking into the Bloodfort. And the deeds I tell people they will do.

"A hundred. Ninety. A thousand. It doesn't matter anymore. They're stories. And they're mine. As are you." Arfan reached into his robes and pulled free a knife I recognized.

After all, it had been mine up until a short time ago.

He reversed it in his hold and passed it to me. "Don't lose such a blade again. It is a precious thing. You will need it. And getting this back from the Bloodcoats cost me more than gold, and my time is not something to be wasted, understand?"

I took the Arasmus steel knife from him, inclining my head in thanks.

"Good. Now gather the rest of your things." He motioned to the sack Alwi held, then to Shola.

"Why?"

Arfan cast a look over the tall sandstone buildings and into the horizon. "We're going to the place I truly rule. My kingdom. My home. I hope you are ready because, ghost or sparrow, the desert can kill you all the same."

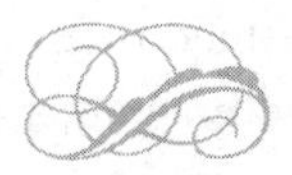

SIXTY-SEVEN

BLACK SANDS

I was given no chance to make farewells to the men and women I'd brought together into The Hundred Thieves.

Arfan had no time to spare, and so Alwi, Baba, and myself—with Shola in tow—followed him to the city limits. A caravan comprised of camels waited for us, along with his retinue of men and women that ranged from those carrying an assortment of weapons, and those bringing packs of everything we would need to survive the desert.

The merchant king's daughter broke from our group and went ahead, securing a mount for herself while I remained by Arfan's side.

"Where's Radika?" My question hadn't come from concern, not so close to her betrayal and the wound still raw. Shola picked up on the agitation I'd kept swallowed deep in my chest. He nudged his head against my shin. A curious look took his eyes. I reached down to scratch the top of his head, which he seemed to appreciate. I bent to scoop him up and carried him in the crook of one arm.

Arfan leaned to one side to run a finger along Shola's fur.

I eyed him, but said nothing as the cat didn't protest.

"Radika is staying behind. She will be in charge of your Hundred Thieves while we handle more important business. Your concern from now is repaying every last piece of gold you have taken from me. And you will do that in any manner I wish. Do you understand?"

I clenched my jaw, but nodded.

"Good." Arfan watched me in silence as we walked toward the convoy. "You are not happy about this."

I didn't answer, but then, I didn't have to. My displeasure radiated from me, and anyone with even one good eye could have seen it.

"That is earned, I suppose, just as much as your situation was. You will be happy to know that by coming here you have spared your family. I gave you my word, and I keep it."

"Even though I'm late?" I didn't look at him, keeping my gaze on the animals ahead.

Arfan didn't answer. He caught my stare and nudged me with an elbow. "Can you ride?"

I shook my head. "Not well. I had some practice on my way here, but it didn't last. I trust my own two legs more than . . ." I nodded at one of the camels, which had decided to leave droppings where it stood, and if that wasn't enough, let loose a wind that sent the nearest man leaping from its side.

The merchant king snorted. "Then you're not as smart as I thought, sparrow. They're clever beasts, and I think you too can be one. I need clever beasts. Do you understand?"

I didn't, but I nodded. "You didn't answer my question."

Arfan smiled. "Clever beast." He reached out and a put a hand on my shoulder, giving me a shake. "I wanted you here, in Zibrath, where I could watch you."

I took a long breath. "You didn't want me heading out to you immediately. You knew I'd have to find my way—gather coin, and in doing that, I'd be stuck. For a while at least." Arfan remained quiet, but the set of his mouth told me I was right, so I continued. "You were watching me?"

He nodded. "The moment Radika learned you were bound to me, she left a letter of her own with yours. You thought to turn the thieves of Mubarath against me—learn my secrets. But I have been playing this game longer than you. I told you once, I wanted to see the sort of cleverness you have in you, boy. And now I've seen the shape of it, and I have use for you. In Mubarath, you are a thief, a clever ghost and story. Out there, I will need you to be more."

I frowned as we reached the caravan. "Of what?"

Arfan took a breath, and the wind picked up loose grains of sand and dirt, twining them together as they sailed before us. "Of everything, Ari. Everything. Out there, I will see the truth of who you are. Or you will die. Either way, I will have my gold out of you." He clapped me once on the back. "May you walk on firm sands, Ari."

❧

Alwi and Baba had been fostered off to a tinker who'd been lingering with Arfan's caravan, their way paid for by the merchant king.

As for why? Arfan saw them as a check on Radika . . . and me. Hostages, in a way, as much as they were extra arms to put to task as needed.

The merchant king saw the use in everything, and everyone.

The tinker had something that resembled the typical wagon home I'd seen in the Mutri Empire; only four curved boards rested before the wheels. When I'd asked him their purpose, the tinker had told me that come the soft and shifting sands, the boards could be put into place of the wheels. Then, a group of camels would be able to pull it atop the grains with ease.

Watching Alwi and Baba talk the man's ear off, riding in comfort, made me wish for a moment that Arfan had bought me a place with the tinker. But it was enough that the traveling trader had allowed Shola to stay in the safety and cool confines of his wagon home.

I'd taken to a camel whose name was Anedi. It meant "stubborn," at least as far as I could guess. It certainly fit the animal, and while I'd made an earnest attempt to build some semblance of friendship with the beast, he seemed rather resolute on spitting on my efforts. Quite literally on first meeting.

Arfan assured me the animal would warm to me eventually. If not, well, camel meat could keep me fed a long time. I thought he'd been joking.

I would learn that Arfan didn't have a particularly good sense of humor.

We'd been riding for four days, and still weren't into the desert proper. At least according to Arfan's idea of what the desert was. All that lay before us looked of salt turned gold, flecks kicked into the air with every errant breath of wind, or beat of hoofs.

My ass had formed a list of complaints after many days spent in a saddle. While camels moved with a gentler ease than horses, my legs were not so fond of being stiffly kept in place.

I led my mount forward, trying to catch Arfan's daughter. She'd stayed near the head of the caravan for as long as we'd ridden. I came by her side and leaned close. "How much longer will it be?"

She didn't look at me when she answered. "As long as it takes to get there." Arfan's daughter had shrouded much of her head and face underneath a hood and cowl of black. She now wore a robe of the same color as well, mostly to take the worst of the sun's heat away.

I'd been advised to do the same and forgo my white-scale cloak, and in truth, the temptation grew each day. But I couldn't. You'd think it a child's fancy, or something equally as silly.

Maybe.

But it had been a gift, and a memory. The piece had saved my life, and added to the growing story of myself. And in that, it had a bit of magic to it. The kind found in stories, and the sort found in a serpent large enough to swallow the head of a mountain.

The Nagh-lokh. A creature of stories. An old god.

My hands brushed along the scales for a moment.

"I've never seen something like that before." Arfan's daughter motioned to my garment with the slightest shift of her head. But she still did not look at me.

"You wouldn't believe me if I told you."

She finally turned and regarded me. "I can believe a lot of things. I've *seen* a lot things, thief."

That brought me to sit straighter, the muscles of my back going stiff as rods. "I have a name, and it's not 'thief.'"

She tilted her head one way, then another, as if my words meant nothing to her. I suppose they didn't. "Would you prefer King Sparrow? Sparrow Thief? Maybe, Ghost of Ghal?"

I glared. "I'd prefer to be called Ari. At least here. We're far from the stories about me, and I have a feeling we'll be going farther still."

"We are." She nodded. "And you're right, I should call you by that, Ari." She maneuvered her camel closer to mine, leaning out to extend a hand. "My name is Qimari."

I took her hand and shook it. "Thank you, and it's a pleasure to know your name, Qi—" My body lurched and if my other hand hadn't kept tight to the reins, I'd have toppled fully to the ground. Instead, a tight pain lanced through one side of my torso before I managed to steady myself. I glowered at her.

Qimari laughed. "Good, he can at least keep himself in his seat. If you're going to be living with us, and serving my father, you're going to need to learn how to stay in your saddle."

"And how exactly will I be serving your father, then?"

Qimari gave away nothing, her expression turning to the stone-faced flatness of Mubarath's walls. "Whatever he needs, whatever he wants."

I looked over my shoulder to Arfan. The man's face held the severity of a knife, and the sharp focus of one as well. I thought then that it was the look of a man for whom needs and wants were never small. "I have a feeling your father wants a lot."

Her mouth pulled to one side. A dagger's curve of a smile, and just as sharp. "He does."

My camel, Anedi, stopped of a sudden, jarring me. "What's wrong?" I urged him onward, but he protested with a guttural snuffle. "Oi, *ksthi-bhaag, ksthi-bhaag*. Tut, tut."

Qimari stopped at my side and looked at me as if she hadn't seen me before. "What was that you just said?"

I repeated myself.

Her lips pulled into a frown, pensive as if rethinking something she'd already decided. "Who taught you that, *ksthi, ksthi*?"

I shook my head as I reuttered the words to Anedi, coaxing him on. But the camel resisted. "No one. It just . . . sounded right. At least when dealing with this stubborn ass." I nudged the beast again, and one of his front hooves beat against the sand.

"Wait!" Qimari reached over to squeeze one of my arms. "Look down."

I did and found something pooling beneath the sand's surface. Dark like pitch and with a consistency thinner than tar, but holding its color. "What is that?"

Qimari let out a sharp breath between her teeth. "Black sands." She said the words more like a curse than to explain the substance. The young woman waved a hand, ushering me to move away from the path ahead. Then she turned and shouted over her shoulder. "Black sands! Black sands!"

The party stopped, and several men dismounted, running ahead to begin prodding the ground with sticks. "Clear way here," one of them said. That man remained on foot, sweeping the stick as he led the way. We moved behind him in slow silence, a tension in the air, like strings pressed tight against a board—held so as not to betray a hint of sound.

Qimari finally leaned close to me, pulling on the edge of my cloak. "We don't know what it is, but it rises to the surface at times. All through the desert. You can sink down to your knees, but it doesn't swallow you whole. You can get out of it if you're careful, but that's not what makes it dangerous."

I eyed her, waiting for the rest.

"The air around it at times is hazy, like a mirage. It waves, and then if you strike a powder match, or light any kind of fire—" She clapped her hands together, spreading them wide to mimic an explosion. "Sometimes it's the air that catches and brings the fire into the black sands. Other times, a man is smoking a pipe, or someone throws some coals after cooking. They sink low, still hot—spark, flash, and then fire. It can burn for hours, sometimes days. I heard once a place burned for a week before all the black sands were gone. All that they found in the end was glass . . . and the bones and burned flesh stuck inside."

I looked away to the man still prodding the sands, kicking away at the surface to free up whatever he could from below. "Brahm's blood. One spark . . ."

"And we're all kindling. Have you ever been on fire before, ghost—Ari?"

I shouldn't have grinned when she asked me that, but it was too easy a thing. I looked at her, smile wide and full of mischief. "They tried, but I didn't burn."

Qimari's eyes sparkled but the rest of her betrayed nothing but quiet, careful consideration. She was forming a new opinion of me.

I hoped it was a good one.

We didn't speak much after that on the way to Arfan's home. Eventually, I ended up falling back to the caravan alongside the tinker. Alwi and Baba had called it an early afternoon, retreating into the trader's wagon home for a nap.

Gushvin was younger than most tinkers I'd met, having only reached his thirty-second year. His hair fell in waves and curls to his shoulders, dark as the black sands we'd seen. The line of his jaw seemed shaped from stone, and his nose had the straight symmetry all too rare in the world.

"Been eyeing your cloak for some time now, boy, and it's a fanciful thing. Looks straight of the stories." Gushvin kept his attention on my clothing. "You going to tell me there's a story just as magical behind it—as much as it looks, eh?"

"There is." And I could see the light blossom behind Gushvin's eyes when I said that. So I told him the whole of it. What brought me up to Ampur, apart from the bit of chasing the Ashura. I told him of red smoke and bleeding stone, and the serpent that came for us in the wreckage. Of how we survived it up the way until we reached the top, and the binding I'd called to bring the mountain down.

He'd heard a piece of it already, of course. The song Radi fashioned had traveled farther than either of us had ever imagined, and where it wasn't sung, it passed from lips to ears in idle gossip. But no sane man would believe it, of course.

That is until you saw the cloak. At first, nothing special about it to mark it as it was. Perhaps the scales had come from a family of white snakes. They were rare, but not so much you couldn't make a cloak from them. But then you looked again and you saw the truth. The shape of them and their color. Too bright to be ordinary scales.

Gushvin had pulled a knife and tried to jab at a piece of the cloak dangling behind me. The garment brushed the knife aside. "Heard from Arfan's men that you're a ghost too, huh? You've been running along roofs and plucking purses?"

I nodded.

That didn't draw a smile from the tinker. "Well, just don't go about doing that here. These lot catch you in that, they'll not stop at taking a hand." He drew an index finger along his throat. "And if I ever catch you rummaging through my packs . . ." He never finished the threat, but the tinker's eyes burned with a fire to turn sand to glass.

"I won't, tinker. Wouldn't dream of it. Your folk have been mighty kind to me." I reminded him of my trip with Pathar, then elaborated on the details of that journey. How he'd taught me some of their tongue and how to read the symbols along their homes. Then how I'd formed a lighter bond with the tinker who I'd bought my staff from.

That warmed Gushvin back up, and soon we spoke more as long lost brothers than newly met acquaintances. Now comfortable enough with one another, I could start steering the conversation toward the question I'd been keeping quiet in my heart since coming to Zibrath.

"Gushvin, how much of the desert have you seen?"

The tinker stroked the side of his chin with a finger, lost in thought. "Hm, not as much as I'd have liked to, but more than many—that's the truth."

I suppose it was a fair reply, though I'd hoped for something more solid than that. "Did you hear about the rumor many months back about a band of tinkers who'd—"

"Lost everything they had. Found them and their wagons all burning still, red smoke and blood all through." He lowered his head, lips parting to murmur something far below his breath I could not catch. Perhaps a prayer? "I heard. And I'll be telling you this to keep between the two of ourselves, yes?"

I nodded.

"I went looking for them that did it." Something cracked in his voice, but it was not the sharp, high-breaking found in a child's throat who'd just begun to change. This was long-old ice that had hardened to something like steel, breaking deep in fissure. An ugly crackling sound that was a warning as much as a hateful hissing thing. This was the sound of a man bone-deep angry for the loss of family, and who wanted revenge.

I knew that feeling all too well.

"But I never did find the lot of 'em. Not one. You think the sands here are something, Ari?" Gushvin shook his head. "No. You wait till we're out in the desert proper. This is just the road to get to where there are no roads. No maps that'll help you. There? Those sands swallow people, horses, wagons . . . and over time, even cities. If you're not careful, they'll take all of you till there ain't even a memory of you. In time, they'll swallow those too. And no one will ever find the bones of you."

That should have been warning enough, especially to a young man like myself. But I didn't take it to heart as I should have. Instead, I kept my mind focused on what he'd told me.

Another confirmation of the Ashura's passing through the sands. They'd been there. And now I was heading toward their last known location. With any luck, I'd find them out there.

Far beyond the lands and laws of men.

And this time, I would do whatever it would take to kill them.

I should have listened to Gushvin.

The desert showed me its true nature not long after.

And it was a perilous place.

SIXTY-EIGHT

Clever Strong Hands

We arrived at Arfan's encampment after nearly a set of travel. Though, "encampment" might have been the wrong word. A tent city seemed more fitting. Long sheets stretched out far enough to encompass fifty people under some of the structures—canopies interlinked with others, forming covered passages of cloth. Others were just big enough to house a person or two. And you could find every size between those in which to settle for the day.

I counted at least two hundred shelters, but Qimari told me there were more over the next dune.

Makeshift pens had been set up in which to keep livestock of goats and sheep.

A canvas city of mostly storm-cloud black. It looked a relief as much as it did a hallucination after all our long traveling, especially when the wind blew through to send flaps swaying in its wake. It seemed as if though with but a billow of better breath the whole camp would blow away—a thing of smoke and dreams.

Arfan waited ahead, motioning for me to come over to him.

I did.

He gestured to the wide expanse of fluttering black and bustling people. "Welcome to my family, Ari. Here, you're no more a sparrow, and not a ghost. Do you understand?"

I nodded.

Arfan then explained my role here—to serve as a hand. If something needed fetching, I did it. Letters written, I wrote. And a mess made . . . I cleaned. A glorified servant kept under watchful eye. Mostly owing to the fact that left in Mubarath, only Alum Above could know what other mischief I'd get up to. And the merchant king had no need of that. He wanted me to repay him, and for now, that meant through work.

And then there remained the matter of training.

I straightened at that. "Training?"

"Can you use bow and arrow? Can you ride a horse hard as can be without falling from your saddle? How long can you walk through a place like this if you need to? Will you be able to find water on your own?" Arfan gave me no chance to answer.

"After that, you will work."

I looked far out to the hundreds of tents upon the sands. "What kind of work?"

"Anything I can think of. Anything that needs extra hands, or can free a more important pair for better tasks. And most of all, I want you to keep your eyes and ears open. You are a clever little thing, so do not disappoint me in this. Go, be clever, and survive." Arfan dismissed me with a hand.

I inclined my head and turned to Qimari. "Where should I meet you?" I hooked a thumb over my shoulder. "I just need to see the tinker before I catch up."

She nodded, understanding full well, having seen me put Shola into the traveling trader's care. "The largest tent." Qimari gestured to it—one large enough to house at least fifty people. Plumes of smoke rose though a cutout high above in the desert shelter.

She tipped two fingers to her forehead in a salute as she led her camel forward.

I steered Anedi around, heading toward the oncoming tinker's sledge.

The wagon home had been converted as he'd said it could be. The wheels had been fastened still and rested above long curved boards that reminded me of something like a fisherman's boat. Now, the home slid atop the sands as the team of four camels pulled it along.

I'd missed the script running over each of the wooden boards before, but now each line caught my eye. I recognized the style, and the language. The latter came in the form of what Pathar had taught me, the secret way tinkers communicated. But the markings had been burned, not carved, into the wood.

Gushvin caught me staring. "Ah, caught the little trick of it, have you?"

I nodded, more in acknowledgment of having heard him than in answer to his question. "They look like Artisaning script, but the language is yours." I arched a brow, hoping he'd catch what I'd left unsaid.

Gushvin tapped a finger to his nose as he gave me a knowing look. "That they are. Long while back, maybe fifteen years or so, my *ba* came across one of those traveling *mejais*. You know, the ones from off foreign." He pursed his lips for a moment. "Wait, you're out there from the Mutri, aren't you?"

I inclined my head.

"Right, there's that school up there somewhere, where people meddle in those kinds of things. Unnatural and whatnot."

"A binder? You met a traveling binder?"

He snapped his fingers. "That's it. One of them. My *ba* traded him a good deal of precious to get his help. We worked for nearly two sets coming up with these." Gushvin waved a hand to the boards. "He worked his magic on them, and they've helped us move along the desert ever since when we can't trust our wheels. No sand ever gets kicked up and over the wood, and they never bog down."

He spoke the truth. Not a grain found its way above the head of the boards or onto them. They should have been shoveled onto the wood, occasionally leading the ends to jam into a hump of sand. But it never happened.

The minor bindings burned into the wood must have had something to do with using momentum to redirect the path of oncoming sand.

"So, what's brought you back, Ari?" His question pulled me from my thoughts.

"I need to grab Shola before I head off."

"Ah, easy enough a thing. Oi!" Gushvin took the stick he'd left resting against his seat and thumped it against the small crawl-doors fitted at the head of his wagon. "Oi, you shitless layabouts." He thumped again. "Oi!"

I had to bite my tongue to keep from laughing. "Shiftless, Gushvin."

He tilted his head in my direction. "Ah? You sure on that?"

"Pretty sure."

He frowned as if considering, then shook his head. "No, I think I've got the right of it. It's shitless. These two couldn't be forced to give a shit if their lives depended on it. Put a sword to their bellies, and their pants'd be dry, not on account of bravery, mind you. But because they couldn't be assed to have the wits to be afraid. It takes work to use this, you know?" He tapped a finger to his temple.

I shook my head and swallowed every ounce of the humor that wanted to break free.

The doors opened and Alwi stuck his head through him. The morning had taken its toll on the boy, leaving him with the narrow-eyed gaze of someone who still clung to sleep, and hadn't been prepared for the sun's bright intensity. "Alum Above, Gush, what is it?"

"Oh, a thousand apologies, my *Shir,* I hadn't known you were resting." Gushvin prodded the boy with his stick. "Get up and get the cat."

"Huh?" Words seemed to be far from Alwi's morning faculties. "What?"

Gushvin prodded him again, each time for every word he said. "Get Ari's cat. Now."

Alwi seemed to finally register that and vanished into the home, appearing a moment later. He held Shola, bundled tight in a scarf the color of the sands below. "He's sleeping."

There is a wisdom in leaving a cat to sleep, and just as much kindness, though the people who came up with those thoughts had clearly never met Shola. If they had, they'd know my cat could sleep through a white-joy barrel bursting into flames if he had the mind to.

And he often did.

Gushvin passed my flame-furred kitten to me.

I brought Shola into the folds of my cloak to shield him from the sun, then rode toward the tent Qimari mentioned.

Qimari led Shola and me into the large tent where a gathering was underway. At least twenty people at rough count, all various ages, and dressed similarly to Arfan and his daughter.

One of these, a woman I put to be at about her mid-twenties, spotted Qimari out of the corner of her eye and turned. She had a slender mouth that broke into a lopsided smile, all warm, at the sight of Arfan's daughter. "Qima!" The woman spread her arms and raced toward us. Her hair, bound into a tight braid, bounced a bit behind her as she did.

Qimari picked up her pace as well to meet the woman in an embrace. "Aisha!" She held her tight for a space of five breaths before letting her go. "I'm well. Just picking up Father's newest stray."

Aisha followed Qimari's stare to me, then down to Shola, who'd now taken to walking at my side. She then gave Arfan's daughter a sly, canted stare. "Just to be clear, are we talking about the boy, or the cat?"

The two women stared at Shola and me, then each other. They broke into a torrent of giggling immediately after.

Shola tilted his head side to side, eyeing me all the while as if I'd supply the answer.

I had none, and told him this. "No idea, friend."

He released a low *mrrip* that said he didn't much care for what the two women had to say if it wasn't his well-due praise.

Qimari waved a hand in my direction. "This is the one Father was talking about."

Aisha opened her mouth and let out a low sound. Her gaze changed and I felt like a hare fallen under a hawk's keen watch. She took in all of me then, and I tried to do the same, mostly in hopes that it would keep my mind off how heavy her look seemed to be. Soft candle flame came to light behind her eyes, and I noticed the brightness of them then, close to rum in sun.

She had the full glow of gold in the brown of her skin, and the whole of her face held a stunning angular beauty.

Radi could have composed a song on the spot to compliment the older woman's fierceness in look.

Myself, well, I simply stared much like a young man of my age would have.

"Him?" Aisha's words broke me out of the trance. "This is the one who robbed *Mejai* Arfan? Who ran a city full of thieves? This one?" Aisha fixed Qimari with a look that asked if the younger woman was playing a joke on her.

Qimari presented a hapless apology. "It's him."

"And . . . everything with the ghost as well?"

Qimari nodded. "Not anymore. Now he's here to work off his debt."

Aisha pursed her lips and shot me a sideways look. It spoke of silent understanding, and a decision being made. A shame she didn't feel fit to share it with me.

I watched the two women in silence and Shola followed my lead, holding them in quiet regard.

Finally, Aisha gave voice to what she'd been thinking. "You want me to teach him . . . while managing my duties as *Al-sayidha*." Not a question.

Qimari had the grace to shy away from the older woman's stare but for a moment. Then she remembered whose blood she carried, and the young girl straightened then, looking all the taller for having done so. She managed to look both straight ahead and down the length of her nose as she addressed Aisha. "My father, the *Shir,* wants you to teach him. He will also be your hand."

That brought a light to Aisha's eyes, and the curve of her mouth twitched ever so slightly. Enough to betray the hint of amusement. "Will he now? I suppose that will be worth some of my time. I won't promise that he'll be good, or that he'll live . . . long."

My teeth grated and I decided to remind the two women that they weren't discussing my fate alone. "I think I might surprise you, so much so because you seem to have forgotten that I'm standing right here."

Aisha frowned, cupping a hand to one hear. "Did you hear that?"

Qimari smiled, joining in quick on their little joke. "Whispers on the wind? Just a noise. The desert often brings echoes of things that could pass as voices."

Aisha nodded. "Mm, must have been."

I glowered at the two of them, and they both matched my stare, but theirs soon gave way to laughter. Surprise that it may be, I didn't find them terribly funny.

Qimari embraced the older woman in another short hug. "I'll be back for him around end of seventh candle. Father will have errands for him." Arfan's daughter left, but not before stooping to give Shola a scratch on the underside of his chin.

"Well behaved," said Aisha.

"Thank you." I gave a curt bow.

"I meant the cat." Her lips twitched again, but whatever smile she'd been keeping back didn't show this time. "You can leave him here if you wish. No one will harm him. Cats are the blessed makings of Alum. He will be well cared for."

If Arfan or his people meant either me or my cat harm, they'd be able to carry it out regardless of us being together or not. "All right." I knelt and rubbed Shola's ears, my voice dropping to a whisper as I spoke to him. "Give them twice as much as hell as you've ever given me, *ji-ah*?"

Truly my cat, he had the wiles to pretend to be stumped by my request, staring at me as if I'd said something horribly incoherent. But he released a low, drawn-out *mrrrr* that I took to mean he'd do as I'd asked.

I may have been laboring under a grand delusion of how willing a cat is to do anything other than it wants. I *was* young.

Aisha beckoned me with a hand to follow. "Leave your things."

I did as she asked, putting down my sack and staff, keeping only the Arasmus knife fastened to my pants and hidden under my cloak. Then I fell in step behind her. "Where are we going?"

"To your first lesson." She didn't look back at me as she spoke, parting a flap in the large tent as she stepped out into a canopied walkway of sorts. Stretches of canvas and other material ran along from other nearby tents to form a shaded covering we could move under.

Several folk sat outside their makeshift homes, going through the many small errands or ways to pass the time you would expect. One man, all made from gnarled wood and lined leather, smoked a pipe. Two young women spoke to one another in low voices as they worked needle and thread, mending fabric. Another woman sifted through a basket of what looked like dried dates.

"And what's my first lesson, Aisha?"

She didn't answer, smiling and inclining her head to anyone who addressed her as we passed her by. And everyone took note of her, which told me something.

"You're popular."

"And you're trying to make conversation." She still didn't turn to look at me.

"Shouldn't I be? This is going to be a boring lesson if we're to keep silent through most of it."

Aisha's back and shoulders straightened more than before as she inhaled and let loose a long suffering sigh. "Do you know how much easier my life would be if more men would choose to keep silent through most of anything?"

I opened my mouth to bite back but realized the trap of words and decided to keep quiet.

Aisha turned halfway to finally look at me as she touched a finger to her nose twice. "Quick. I like that." She moved on, leaving me to fall back into tow.

We eventually left the stretched cloth roof of sorts and made our way onto flat open sands. The ground held a firmness here that I hadn't felt on the journey to Arfan's camp. Solid, not threatening to swallow as much of your weight.

"Over that crest there." She pointed to a sand dune that stood at least three times my height. "Come on." Aisha picked up her pace, keeping to something just short of a full jog as she went over the rise.

I followed, reaching the top to stop by her side.

Aisha held out both of her hands, palms up. "Give me yours."

It took me a moment to realize what she'd meant, but I soon placed my hands atop hers.

She trailed her fingers along my palms, the soft skin tingling almost as if brushed by grains of sand. Aisha's eyes remained closed as she did this. "You have callouses. No stranger to hard work. But you have slender fingers." She took mine between hers, moving each digit around as if unsure whether to bend them far enough to break them, or just see the measure of flexibility they possessed.

"Strong, clever, calloused. How did your hands come to be like this? Do you fight? Have you used a bow before? What of a sword?"

I blinked at the succession of questions. "I'm not sure. They're just like that from how I've lived, I suppose." I told her of my life in the understage, working all the contraptions to make the theater above come to life. Then my time with the sparrows, and how clever hands became more of a necessity than strong ones. But they'd certainly earned their callouses as well. Climbing over rooftops and scrabbling across hard ground did not earn you soft skin.

Lastly I told her of my work in the Ashram in the Artisanry as well as the time kite-fighting. But I left out my time and training with Vithum. Stage swordsman choreography had little importance here, but with as many secrets as Arfan and his tribe seemed to be keeping from me, I felt I could do with at least one of my own.

Even if it was a small secret.

"And you've spent your life thieving and using these hands to hurt people." Not a question, but a statement. One holding judgment as rough-coarse as the grains beneath our feet.

"I used them to do whatever I had to do to survive."

"Like robbing *Mejai* Arfan."

I bristled at that. "His gold saved my family. More children than you can count. It kept them from ever having to do that sort of work again. Never catching a beating or an errant hand from someone on the streets of Abhar. Never again. I'll take chastisement from him because I have to. We have a deal. Not from you. Never from you." I took a step closer to her.

Aisha, for her part, merely looked me over again. "So, you have a fire in you. Good. You'll need that as much as you will the clever strong hands."

And that is when she tried to kill me.

SIXTY-NINE

Candle, Flame, and Void

Aisha made no sound as she leapt, moving with the silent speed of a hawk diving for a sparrow. She raised her hands, fingers wide like claws ready to rake into me. Only that never happened. She grabbed hold of me, one hand clenching the collar of my cloak, the other grasping it at my waist. She shifted. One of her feet moved behind mine and the full force of her heel crashed into just below my calf.

The world slid from me and I struck the sand. Golden grains danced past my eyes in front of the slow-moving clouds above. She gave me no time to register what had happened.

Aisha sank to the ground with me, arcing one leg over my torso to straddle me. A hand went inside her robe, pulling free a handle of polished horn. Only, it was what protruded from the handle that caught my attention. A length of curved silver, holding an edge so sharp that it promised to cut before even touching its mark. She brought its point to rest along my cloak just over my ribs. Aisha ground the blade in place.

"What's this?" She leaned in. Not hard enough to risk the knife breaking flesh had it been against my naked skin, but certainly enough for the pressure to be felt through the white-scale armor protecting me. Aisha dragged the blade's edge against the cloak, drawing a sound like a nail on glass. She then pinched a piece of my garment between the fingers of her free hand. "A special thing. What is it?"

One of my hands moved under the cover of the cloak as I explained. "All that's left of an old god. I killed it back in Ampur." My fingers clasped around something smooth and hard.

"And how did you manage that?" She moved her knife from where it rested to trail along my torso and up toward my throat.

"I dropped a mountain on it." My words broke her composure, and she lost some of her coiled-serpent grace. Meanwhile, my hand freed the one thing that could change the situation. I moved it into position and brought the edge of my Arasmus knife to rest against the side of one of her thighs.

Both of her brows rose. "I hope that is a knife you cleverly pulled while telling your story." She brought her blade to rest against the hollow of my throat while giving me a long and knowing look.

"I am going to get up now, unless you would like us to stay stuck like this for a candlemark. But then neither of us would get anything done, and *Mejai* Arfan would punish us. I'm not one for wanting that." Aisha pulled her knife away, sheathing it.

I slipped my own knife back into its resting place.

"Good." Aisha rose, offering her arm to help me to my feet. "Like I thought, clever hands."

I took her in my grip and hauled myself to my feet. "Is there a reason you just tried to kill me?"

She rolled her eyes. "I wanted to see what you were like when threatened."

I arched one brow. "And?"

Aisha shrugged. "You've been threatened before. Your eyes were wide, but they were like a cat's. Shocked, but angry. You were thinking the whole while, working for a way out. You didn't panic. That's good." She moved down the dune, motioning for me to follow.

I came to her side and watched her for a moment before deciding to speak. "Is that something you do to everyone Arfan asks you to teach, or?"

"*Mejai* Arfan. You're in his service now. Call him properly, even if you are not a member of the tribe. And, sometimes. Depends on the person. I am *Al-sayidha*. His eyes, his first among hunters, and if we go to war . . ." She trailed off, a hand going back to where her knife rested.

I caught the unspoken meaning.

"And that means when Alum favors us with moments of peace, I teach those *Mejai* Arfan asks me to."

I thought on what she'd said. "You're a soldier? And . . . something else?"

She shook her head. "I will ride with anyone to protect the tribe in war, but no. I am not a soldier as you are thinking. There isn't a word for it in Trader's Tongue. It's like being a knife, but also the arm that uses it. You can do many things with them both, and you cannot put a label to all of them?" A question, and she looked at me in waiting for the answer.

I nodded. "I think I'm following."

"The knife can cut an enemy as easily as a branch, or a fruit, or meat for a family. The arrow can pierce the heart of a man who wishes you harm, or a desert hare for a meal. I am what *Mejai* Arfan needs me to be." She gestured with a hand to the way ahead. "There."

My gaze followed to where she pointed.

A row of people stood several feet apart from one another. I counted an even six of them. They varied in age from some close to me, and others closer to Alwi and Baba—just children. All of them carried two things. A bow, and a quiver of arrows.

Twenty paces beyond them stood wooden poles that had been planted into the firm sand, with a beam running horizontally atop them. Small sacks, each just larger than a man's head, hung from the structure. One sack per archer.

They all drew at their own measure and loosed. Some connected, some did not. None found their true mark at the painted center. Sand poured out from wherever an arrow struck home.

I watched the scene, then turned my attention on Aisha.

She didn't have eyes for me at the moment. Instead, she brought a thumb and forefinger to her lips, letting loose a sharp whistle.

All those practicing their archery stopped, turned as if on the same puppeteer's strings, and raised one hand to press flat against the hollows of their throats. "*Sholkuh, Al-sayidha.*" They spoke the greeting in perfect unison, all carrying notes closer to reverence than mere respect.

"You're doing well, but I need the space for myself. Return after dark for those of you still set on learning."

No words of protest. Not an utterance of confusion. Or any questions as to why. Every person lay down their bow, *gently*, on a sheet that had been set behind them. Their quivers and arrows followed. Each archer walked by Aisha with the slow, measured air of caution and deference you would expect more if navigating around a queen than how she'd described her role in the tribe. Hands touched throats and low words were spoken to her as every person passed.

Aisha kept the somber mask of stone on her face, taking their words with quiet thanks and minute bows of her head. Once they'd all left, she moved over to the long sheet atop which the weapons rested. She gestured to the wide sweep of bows. "Pick one."

I made my way over and looked at them. At first glance you wouldn't notice any difference between them apart from some variances in size and thickness. All of wood and horn and sinew. But a longer look showed me the subtle ways their shapes changed.

One bow had a slightly sharper curve than the ones beside it. The sinew string of another was clearly thicker than the rest by a good measure. And the limbs of another bow still looked to be more solidly built than any of the remaining weapons. Something that would surely tax the muscles of the one who used it.

I stared longer, unsure which to take, much less why. My gaze passed over them all. Then again.

"You've a careful eye." She watched me while I deliberated.

"I try to." My attention remained on the bows, though, and I settled on one. The wood of it held a color found in coals. Dark, brushed with strokes of night itself. A black that held no shine or promise of light within its grain. This bow held to the shade of charcoal and shadow. It was wood that had known fire.

I bent over and closed my fingers around it. There are many things I could say now about what it felt like. They would be wasteful poetry. The bow was right. And that's the only truth that matters. It fit in my hand like it had been made for the shape of it. Its weight, a comfort.

Aisha watched, taking in both the bow and me together. The pair of us said something to her, but whatever that message was, it went unheard by me, and she did not feel to share it.

I raised the bow and looked down where I felt the sight rested. Not that I knew how to use one. To me, they were things best known in story, held in hand by those who could fell a man at the edge of what your eyes could see. They could take a feather in the wind with but one shot, or the heart of someone set against you. Wars were waged with them, and won by them. More than any sword.

According to some of the stories at any rate.

All I know is this: I held the bow, and as it sat in my hand, I felt as if it wanted to be there. A story sat within its burnt-black length, and it asked me silently to listen for it. To find it. And once I did, to keep it in mind as much as heart.

A silly thing to admit, perhaps, but that doesn't make it any less true. Sometimes, life is made of the foolish things and moments that we dare not share with others. And in doing so, we bury the magic of them as well as a piece of ourselves. That was one of those moments.

The bow had something special to it, and I would uncover it. With time.

"What made you choose that one?" Aisha's voice gave no hint as to if another question hid beneath the one she asked.

I shrugged, turning the bow in my grip. "It just felt right. Why, is there something wrong with it?"

Aisha shook her head. "No, it's much like the rest we use to train." The words were measured, practiced—not quite recited, but she'd said them before to someone else.

I ran my fingers along the limbs of the bow and realized the wood hadn't been burned. It held a smoothness that should not have been there—only the rough porous surface of something touched by fire. It had been blackened another way, but how?

"What's the story behind this bow?"

Aisha came to my side, pulling up one of the quivers and taking an arrow from it. "In some ways, the same as any other bow. In others, it's a story about the person to whom it belonged."

I waited for her to tell me, but she didn't. Instead, the woman pressed the arrow toward me, inviting me to take it from her. I did, understanding what I was to do. The shaft rested in my hand but for a moment before I brought it to the bow and nocked. A pull and I drew it full, the muscles in my back straining with the effort. My eyes fixed on the target ahead and I envisioned the arrow driving home.

The folds came to me. Two, then four. Six soon enough. Then to eight. More than enough for something that required just my concentration. All of them showed me the image of the shaft burying itself well in the center of the sack. One perfect shot.

I released.

The arrow wobbled, arcing up before careening toward the ground as if it had been thrown from the hand of a child. The string struck full force and brought an ache to the soft meat of my forearm I knew would leave a bruise. The shock of it bothered me more than the pain.

Aisha pursed her lips, her gaze going from me to the fallen arrow, then back to me. "I suppose it could be worse. You could have stuck your face in the path of the bowstring and lost a piece of your nose when you released."

I stared at her.

"Oh, it's happened." She shook her head and moved to retrieve the fallen arrow. "Again." Aisha passed it back to me.

I nocked, but one of her hands touched my elbow as I drew.

"Keep your elbow higher. You're standing wrong." She tapped the tip of a foot against the side of mine. "Shift." Her hands came to my waist and she gently pulled me to stand in what she deemed proper. "Relax."

"How can I relax, shift, hold my arm higher, and keep the arrow drawn?"

Aisha jabbed my ribs with a finger.

The surprise of it forced me to loose the arrow. Once again the string struck my forearm. The bruise-to-be would be deeper still from the repeated blow. "What was that for?"

"You're overthinking. I can see it. You have a quick and darting mind—clever, but you haven't learned how to be still. How to be silent so you can hear it."

I frowned. "Hear what?"

Aisha pointed far out along the way.

I watched the space and saw the full spread of the sun, pooling along the horizon like a wreath of copper-brushed amber. The golden brightness could have touched the ends of the world from where I stood. There seemed no end to its light.

And then I saw the sands.

The journey to Arfan's camp hadn't given me a proper appreciation for all that they were. Before, the sand had been nothing but irritating grains offering little but uneven footing, and no signs of green.

Now, I saw a new shape of the world. Hills of once-stone turned to dust, but small mountains all the same. Somewhat like Ampur. Flat plains of firm sand on which a horse could gallop, or children play. Here, you could almost see the breath of the wind roll along the open, empty space of it all. The longer I stared, the more I came to see something gone unseen by many.

The desert had a movement to it even within the great stillness in which it sat. The way the wind passed through, taking along subtle grains of sand most would pay no mind to. But in that, the home of the sand shrew was disturbed. And so, it moved as well, and skipped to somewhere else. Its feet upon the ground stirred the scorpion that sat nestled beneath the golden blanket of the place.

Agitated—excited, it comes to life and looks for what bothered its rest. What meal could be there?

And it is not the only one. A hawk soars above, watching the field of glimmering grains with eyes to take in more of it than anything else could match. And so it knows it is the king of all below. The greatest of hunters. All this and more occurs in the moment it takes to breathe but a few breaths.

What else happened that I didn't have the eyes yet to see?

"*Irrum Al-durahn.*" Aisha's tone mirrored those who'd been paying her hushed respect earlier. Low and reverent.

I turned to her, a piece of me regretting doing so and breaking the view of all I'd taken in. "What?"

She repeated the words and gestured to the expanse. "The breath of the world. The gentle flow of all things—most seen here, in the desert. There is a law to living here, *in here.* There is a secret shape to things here, and in watching long and hard, you come to see how all things flow. You live with it, move with it. The desert has a breath of its own, and you must learn to breathe with it if you want to survive." Aisha punctuated the end of the statement by taking another arrow from the quiver and snapping its shaft against the exposed back of my hand.

It struck with a fleshy crack that sounded far worse than any pain it brought me. I winced, but made no sound.

"Again."

I took the arrow from her, but she stopped me before I could nock.

"Look where you want to shoot."

"I am."

She shook her head. "Your eyes already know where you want the arrow to go, the rest is telling your body how to send it there. Point." Aisha gestured even though I didn't need a demonstration.

But I did as instructed, sticking out my index finger from the hand holding the bow. The tip of it lined up with where I wanted the arrow to strike.

"Draw and loose."

I followed her commands and the arrow launched forward, still falling short of the mark. But it went farther than before and all without the bowstring striking my arm.

"Good. If we keep at this pace, you'll be sure not to shoot your own foot by the end of the month."

I glowered at her. "It's not as easy as point and shoot."

Her mouth parted in mock surprise. "Oh, it isn't?" Aisha stripped out of her robes. She wore shirt and pants the color of slate and kept tight against her body. Even with the clothing I could see she had a firmness of muscle that came from long, hard work. Her back had the width of someone who put it to work, and her shoulders and arms had a solidness to them. A leather guard rested against her left forearm.

Aisha picked up one of the bows and slung a quiver over the back of her hips.

"Let's see, then." She raised the bow in one fluid motion and pointed her index finger to the target. An arrow came to rest in place and was soon pulled back as she drew and released.

I watched it spring foward and strike the target dead center.

She lowered the bow, pulled an arrow, and repeated the movements as if she hadn't just done so before. The arrow flew. It struck. And before I registered it, she'd drawn and launched another. Then another.

No sand remained in the hanging sack before long and it only stayed in place from the weight of the many arrows that had found home there. The last shot sank in and Aisha wasted no time bringing the bow to the ground, resting it between a hand and the sands beneath.

She slipped a leg through the open space between the bowstring and the bow's limbs, sinking her weight to bend its arms. With a quick hook of a finger she freed the string and the bow snapped straight. "Looks as easy as pointing and shooting to me." Aisha didn't smile, but she kept one burning bright in the light of her eyes as she stared at me.

"Show-off."

"And you could be too if you practice." She went to the next bow and unstrung it as well, going through the lot of them until they rested in a neat row. "Again." Aisha nodded to the target.

I sighed and tried again.

I did not fare any better.

"Do you have any way of clearing your mind?"

That brought me pause, and I thought on it. "I do." And I told her of the candle and the flame.

"I was taught something similar." She held up her thumb, positioning it in front of one of the targets. "I imagined this as the head of a flame and the world around it as a void. There is only the head of the flame and emptiness. Focus on the flame. Feed it everything, then do as I say."

I nodded, raising the bow and bringing up the candle and the flame. Once I'd done so, I cast the world around me into darkness. A stillness. The same drubbing silence I'd felt around Stones.

All that remained was the candle, flame, and void.

I fired arrows until the sun fell behind the dunes.

SEVENTY

Set to Seeking

By the time Aisha and I trekked back from practicing, the muscles of my back and arms burned in newfound pain.

"It's not as bad as you think. You could have done far worse." She smacked a hand to my sore back and I staggered forward.

I shot her a look, but she'd already turned to gaze everywhere but at me.

"See me tomorrow after fourth candle's end. Same place." She dismissed me and took her own path through the canopied way.

I thanked her out of respect for her time as she left. While teaching me might have come on behalf of Arfan's orders, having seen the way other members of the tribe treated her, it was clear her time had a value no small words could pin down.

After she departed, I headed back to the tent where Qimari had first introduced me to Aisha. I parted one of the flaps and entered to find it better appointed than it had been before.

Woven rugs covered the floor, each a color found in earth. Deep browns, bright brass, and the best black of rich soil. This created a backdrop for the working of white yarn through it to create scenes of people I did not recognize.

Several trunks rested far to one side of the tent. Their wood held the polished dark shine that spoke of expensive material and well-kept care.

Half a dozen men sat at the other end of the tent in a tight circle. Trays of food rested between them as well as a set of white porcelain cups. A black iron kettle stood atop a stone block, wisps of steam still billowing from its mouth.

I did recognize the man at the center of the group.

Arfan.

A streak of orange bounded by, batting a wooden ball through the tent. Qimari trailed behind my cat, keeping her lips pressed between her teeth so she wouldn't laugh. She noticed me and stopped.

"Come, Father's waiting." Qimari tapped the ball one last time, sending it farther for Shola to chase.

I followed her closer to Arfan and his group.

The merchant king finally looked up from the conversation. "Ah, Qimari told me you were with Aisha."

I nodded.

"And how did you find your first lesson?"

I rubbed my forearm and rolled my shoulders. "Much like having aching arms and a sore back."

Arfan let out a low chortle that some of the men around him shared. The rest made content with half grins that fell from their faces as soon as the expressions came. "Life here can leave you sore, Ari. And that is preferable to the alternative. If you feel little to nothing out here, it means there's nothing left for you to feel. Remember, only a dead man feels nothing. If you hurt, rejoice, for you are alive."

I didn't know I agreed much with that, but I decided to keep that thought to myself.

"And what did you make of her?" Arfan poured from the kettle into one of the cups. A liquid the color of white clouds washed with a hint of pale gold. Just enough to bring some yellow to it. The merchant king raised the cup, turning it a quarter in his hand and blowing on it. Then again, repeating the soft breath. Again. And once more, almost as if it were ritual.

"Of . . . Aisha?" I wasn't sure what he was asking, and kept my words cautiously guarded.

He nodded, passing the cup toward me.

I accepted with thanks, but did not take a sip. "She's well respected—revered, I'd say. The men and women address her the way someone would nobility. Maybe more."

Another half smile. "I told you he had a quick mind. Not a wise one. But a quick one. He sees, and he listens . . . *sometimes.*" Arfan watched me with eyes better suited for a fox, with all the weighted cunning behind them. "And he doesn't know well enough not to refuse a man's offer when in his home." Arfan's attention settled on the cup. "Drink."

The other men went silent, all staring at me as well.

And the quiet that had grown between us spoke volumes.

One did not refuse the *Mejai* Arfan's hospitality. I had a feeling no one refused him anything, but at the very least, a kindness on his part should be taken, and gratitude given for it.

So I did just that, taking a sip. It brought the taste of fresh lemon to my tongue, a spark of ginger, the touch of cloves, and just the right amount of bright sugar sweetness. "Thank you."

He made no note of having even registered that. Instead, Arfan brought the subject back to Aisha. "What else did you glean about her?"

The way he'd asked it told me Arfan didn't want simple answers. He was looking for something beneath my responses. But what? I wouldn't know unless I played the little game, and the best way for me to do that was to give him the truth.

"She's bold. Well skilled with the bow, but you already know that. She's smarter and cleverer than many her age, and she must be even better than I think at working in your service or she wouldn't have been treated the way I saw earlier. And you wouldn't have placed her in the position she's in."

He waved a hand. "I know all this. What did you make of her? Not what she does, but *her,* boy."

I frowned and thought back to our day. "Loyal. She holds you in high regard, and I don't think it's only because of who you happen to be, but something else. The way she spoke says she'd do anything for you, and it's not for the reasons I will. You don't have a hold on her, she chooses to follow you."

He nodded. "What else?"

"She's a keen observer of people." I told him almost all of what happened atop the dune when she'd pounced and tackled me to the ground. "Which is why she's your . . . *Al-sayidha.*" I remembered the word's pronunciation well enough.

"Yes." Arfan took a sip of the lemon-accented beverage. "And do you know what that means?"

I saw no point in denying the truth. "No."

He pursed his lips as if he expected my answer. "You will learn." He took another sip before placing the cup on the ground. "Ah. Have you eaten?"

I shook my head. "No, but I'll find—"

"Sit." Arfan gestured to an open space between his group.

I sank to my knees and joined them. The spread before us consisted of dried dates, a crumbly cheese that looked like broken pieces of morning clouds, a mash of spiced and oil-topped chickpeas, and thin strips of meat—cured and smoked. A stack of flatbread rested by the side as well.

At first look it could have passed for *thori* or *fahaan,* but each piece was bigger than the other breads I thought of. Just as flat in most regards but for small bubbles along the surface carrying a slight char. Likely pockets of air that filled and didn't burst as they cooked.

I reached out, breaking off a piece, shoveling it through the chickpeas and bits of cheese. It tasted of once-warm smoke's bite, in a good way. There is a flavor to charred things all its own, and it is one I long ago came to favor. The chickpeas had a comforting weight, almost a meatiness to them, along with the spices and smoothness of oil that had been added. And the cheese brought a soft saltiness to it all that completed the fullness of flavor, especially with the still lingering hint of lemon from the drink.

"Tell me how you find it, Ari?" Arfan hadn't taken any food. No. He kept his attention solely on me.

I was still being weighed, but for reasons I couldn't guess. So I told him how I found the food.

Arfan nudged one of the men by his side with an elbow. "See how he speaks, what he notices. This is what brought him to my attention last year. Tell me, Ari, do you know what it was that brought you into this?" He motioned to the tent around us.

"I robbed you?" The look on his face told me that he wanted to hear something else, leaving me to think back to what had led to us crossing paths. Then I had it. "Secrets. My sparrows and I were trading secrets in Keshum."

"Mm." Arfan then looked at the men surrounding him. "Leave us."

All did . . . save for one by his side.

The merchant king continued as if nothing had happened. "You have the ears and eyes for secrets. And this is what I want from you. You will live here with my family, my tribe, and you will see and hear and report back to me at the end of every day. You will tell me everything you glean, and your thoughts. You will do all this while you work to whatever task I, my daughter, *Al-sayidha,* or my *Maathi* has for you." The last name he said took my attention.

"Who?"

Arfan clapped a hand to the shoulder of the man next to him.

Lines of ash threaded his brows as well as his beard, but not one crease banded his face to mark him as old. Even in the candlelight, the pate of his head carried a shine almost as if it had been oiled, and the rest of his scalp only betrayed the barest hint of stubble. He must have shaved it within a day or so.

He looked like someone who'd lived a comfortable life by the set of his body and the softness of his face. Not quite plump, but close enough. But his eyes had a brightness in the dark of them. They spoke of cleverness, quick wit, and the mind to put those things to good use.

"This is my *Maathi.* At least, until he grows tired of curiosity and the wonders of the world."

The *Maathi* snorted. "There is too much in this world of ours to ever be tired of it. I will live a thousand lives and not see a piece of all its mystery."

Arfan reached to take a sip of the lemon-infused drink. "*T'ah,* all I need of you, *Maathi,* is to find one piece of mystery first."

The *Maathi* waved a hand. "*Zho. Zho.* I will do it, my *Shir.* And this you know. Besides, I'll not be able to keep my own head down at night until I find the Lap. And then—and then there is the study of the shadow of the moon, *Shir.* You remember my—" The man's voice had quickened but Arfan raised a hand, silencing him.

"I remember. We will concern ourselves with the Lap first." He gave the man a stare that said it was not up for discussion.

The *Maathi* inclined his head. "Of course, of course."

"Mm. And for your troubles and work, *Maathi,* you may avail yourself of the boy." Arfan looked to me. "You will do whatever he needs to further his research."

I nodded.

"Good. Now go." Arfan dismissed me with a curt motion of his hand. "Take him with you, *Maathi.*"

The *Maathi* rose and bowed, one arm across his belly, the other wide out to his side. "Of course, of course. Come now, my spare hands. We have things to do, ah?" The *Maathi* gripped one of my shoulders and pulled at my cloak. "Oh, but what's this? Ah, no small wonder, ah? Come, tell me of it. Come." He wasted little time and walked off at a pace faster than I'd have credited him capable of.

I got to my feet, bid Arfan farewell and thanks, and moved toward Qimari. "Would you mind if I asked for my belongings?"

She gestured to a side of the tent where my staff and travel sack lay. "I'll walk with you to *Maathi*'s tent."

I fetched my things, stopping to scoop Shola into the crook of an arm. He snuggled into place as if expecting my hold to be his bed for the night. Not being one to want to disappoint him, I moved with a more careful pace.

"Father wants you to spy for him."

"Yes." My history with secrets, and general wariness built from my time as a sparrow, would all come in handy for a man wanting to know the happenings in his own home without having to look himself.

And it removed the obvious fact that people would step twice as carefully—silently—in the *Shir*'s presence. Maybe less so a young man. Though, I was still a stranger. Few people shared secrets in the company of those they didn't know. Meaning I would have to earn their trust.

Games within games, and all to please Arfan. But he had another motive. He was searching for something, and in that, he wanted to be sure of what the people in his tribe were up to.

But why?

Did he fear betrayal? Just a general unease? And through it all, I still had to find a way to use Arfan in return. I hadn't forgotten that the Ashura had struck in the desert. They were out here—somewhere. And I had to use the desert king in kind to find what I wanted.

Qimari watched me like someone poring through a book.

"You're wondering why Father wants you to spy for him?" She reached out idly to stroke the sleeping Shola.

I nodded.

"I wish I knew too." She sighed, her shoulders drooping a touch.

"He hasn't told you?" Odd, considering Qimari was his daughter. I felt there would have been at least a measure of trust between them.

She shook her head. "No. Father's bothered by something. It's taken him at the root, and ever since the betrothal . . ." She trailed off. Color touched her cheeks, and I would have wagered it to be a young girl's blush, but the set of her mouth said something else entirely. A crooked gash in stone.

Tenseness. Frustration. And the heavy disappointment that comes with duty that one does not want to fulfill.

"But, no, Father's kept this to himself. His mind is split between the welfare of the tribe, and then his blood feud with Sharaam and his ilk. Then there's what he has *Maathi* searching for. I've never seen him like this." A brittle sharp note filled her voice then. It was the edge of glass, quick to cut, but could be broken with just the right touch. She was worried, and that gave rise to anger in measure.

"I'll do what I can to ease his mind then, Qimari. I promise." I'm not sure why I said that to her, only that it felt right. And maybe that is always reason enough to say the things people need to hear. At least in the moment.

The weight of unease lifted from her face, and she looked very much the young girl then and less the proud daughter of a merchant king. No burden of duty. Just someone relieved to have heard what they needed to. "Thank you."

I gave a half bow.

Her eyes slowly trailed over me, settling once again on my cloak. "It looks different now. Under the starlight, I mean." She pointed to the gaps in the tent canopies above where errant bands of pale moon's glow filtered through. "It's like it was woven from white thread and light. Like diamonds. Or moonlight made hard." She ran a finger over some of the scales, then flicked a fingernail against one of the hardened bits of skin. "What is it?"

I told her the truth.

She had an easier time believing it than Radika, and when I asked why, she merely turned the question back on me. Qimari had no problem accepting the wonders of the world.

In time, I would come to learn why. But then, I didn't press the point any further.

She left me outside the *Maathi*'s tent. "I'll see you in the morning for your duties."

"Wait." I reached out, stopping myself short of taking her arm in one of my hands. "The man's name—title, *Maathi,* what does it mean?"

"The way-finder, or lighter, depending on how literally you want to take the translation to Trader's Tongue. The guide. One who paves the way. A seeker. A *Maathi* shows the way to something. Ask him about it, he knows more and has a scholar's mind. In our tongue, that is what it means, though."

"Your tongue?"

She shrugged. "We speak a version of Zibrathi older than what is left behind to the people who live behind walls and stone. Ours is truer. From when our blood only knew the skies and sands. *Maathi* isn't Zibrathi at all. He came from the Mutri. He's looking for something and has been for a long time. It's through that he came into Father's service. Why the questions on his role?"

I shook my head, not wanting to share what I had in mind. "Nothing. Just struck me as odd is all."

She watched me as if weighing whether or not I'd spoken truly. Whatever she decided, she kept to herself. "Until morning then, Ari." Qimari gave me the barest inclination of her head, something that I took to be the first measure of real respect from her. Then she left.

I slipped into *Maathi*'s tent and stopped as I caught sight of everything inside.

It was a mad magician's study out of the old stories. Brass frames and glass lenses littered the floor. Parchment, tools of all manner, and unceremoniously stuffed clothing spilled over the edges of open trunks.

A large cloth hung across a good span of the tent's width. Lines of charcoal raced across it to form a crude map of sorts. Small symbols dotted far-flung regions of the map's surface, and serpentine lines traced a border to frame it all. Perhaps the outskirts of the desert?

"*Zho. Zho.* You see something on the map?" *Maathi* rested his hands on the slight swell of his stomach. Glints of gold and silver drew my eyes to his fingers, and I counted at least five rings over both his hands, each band set with a jewel.

Wealthy. And feeling safe enough to show it. No one with any sense would have worn such on the streets of Mubarath or Keshum when I'd been leading bands of thieves. With just a touch you would find yourself with fewer pieces of precious when next you saw your hands.

Maathi gestured to a makeshift table he'd formed out of several trunks set side by side. Various scrolls and parchments lay atop, along with a graphter and drawing compass.

"Come, come." He motioned me closer. "Look and tell me what your young eyes see."

I set my staff and sack down.

"Ah, what's this?" *Maathi* wriggled a finger toward Shola. "You brought a piece of luck and fire, ah? Good-good. Be it Brahm's blessing, or Alum Above, I will take it."

"What do you mean?"

"Oh, ah. Cats." He still shook the finger in Shola's direction. "It's said that Alum created them as his little treasures. Wild, free things with a will. Curious. Explorers. And wise."

I thought on Shola's many actions since coming into my care. Wild and free? Certainly. Curious? Absolutely. Wise . . . was a matter up for considerable debate, and given what I'd seen, it would be a short one at that. And nothing much to consider at all.

It didn't make me love him any less.

"Ah, I forget myself. Look-look." *Maathi* waved at the papers. "What do you see?"

I pored over the papers. "What's this about Laps? The Water Tree?" I'd heard of the latter before, but I couldn't recall all of when and where. Some parchments detailed the faces of the moon and turnings of the sun. And the words along the pages were in languages I couldn't recognize.

"Ah, the Laps. No, not the Laps. *The Lap.* The one *Mejai* Arfan is looking for, ah?" *Maathi* brushed aside some of the papers, pulling out a map that resembled the one hanging high along the tent. "Look-look." He tapped a finger to a spot. "Twenty years ago, a group of men claimed to have stumbled across the Lap in where the Water Tree rests. Then again, years later. But it is somewhere else, you see?" He tapped another spot.

Maathi grabbed the graphter and slipped it through the hooked protrusion on the drawing compass. He pressed the tools to the map and traced an arc. The points where the two sightings of the Lap occurred now connected, but *Maathi* continued dragging the line to other points. "See?"

I did. "It moves, but it's not random."

"Ah! Yes. Much my thinking. And see here?" He prodded some points left out by the line. "It changes after forty years and a new path comes. These are older, much older. I paid good money and traded treasures for just the whispers and words of this knowledge. And soon, I will be the one to find the Water Tree. I will find the lost Lap, and seek my fortune in its waters."

Fortune. A thing many men would risk a great deal for. Its promise took families, hearts and mind, and in the end, some fortunes took their tolls in lives. And while many men find what they are looking for, they come to lose much in the search. Sometimes, what they lose can never be recovered.

Sometimes you lose yourself.

"And what is it you're looking for, *Maathi*?"

"Ah." He drew the word out, raising an index finger. "Much the same thing as our *Shir*. It is this why he keeps me around, you see. I am a seeker. A looker. A finder. I think." He tapped his head with two fingers. "And only he who looks and seeks to find can find a thing left lost but to be found, ah?"

I blinked, trying my best to parse what he'd said, though it sounded much like nonsense Rishi Ibrahm would have spouted.

"But what I am looking for, young one, is a piece. A piece of prophecy."

I didn't want to laugh, much less at a man who'd welcomed me so warmly after only just meeting him, but prophecy belonged in children's dreams and Shaen stories.

But a night of red smoke and flame had been no Shaen story. And a man with burning yellow eyes, who claimed he could not be killed, said that the stories were real.

I reconsidered what I'd been about to say and settled for a respectful nod.

"The Water Tree is the center of the moving oasis. A place where all can find succor in the hardest of places. And at the heart of that itself? Well, my friend, there is a special woman. She will give the worthy a piece of their future. And it is said the greatest of men and women, heroes . . . and some who have fallen, my friend, far-fallen down from heroes, all have spoken to the Water Tree's maiden. For you are given the chance to ask of her—whatever your heart desires. And she can put you on the path to greatness if you listen." *Maathi* may have been a man whose years had brought him touches of grayness, but in that moment, he held to the youth of a man my mirror in years.

Young, bright in eye, and kindled of the fire with which a man could do many a thing. His hands shook ever so slightly, and his look spoke a touch of manic energy.

I finally noticed the small cup resting at the edge of the makeshift table.

It held a liquid that looked to have gone cold, but I did not mistake its color, nor what it was. *Awfhar.* The substance Radika had introduced me to, and could give a man the mind to go without sleep for a time I had no desire to test.

All of which explained *Maathi*'s fervor more than impassioned excitement.

"And Arfan wants a prophecy? He wants greatness?" I measured my words to be free of prying curiosity or any hint of judgment.

"Ah, yes. What he wants is to lead his tribe to be the tribe above all tribes. He wishes to break the cycles of bad blood between them all, and to unite them. It is said, or so he tells me, that there will be one who brings them all of one blood of the desert back to being one blood. To bury old shames and wrongs beneath the sands, and be one family once again.

"But that takes more than prophecy, it takes tools. It takes a name that I am afraid good *Mejai* Arfan doesn't have. At least, not in the measure he requires. He will need more." The last word hung in the air like the aftermath of the final struck chord, left to vibrate and invite inquiry. It was the setup for an obvious question.

What could I do but voice it then? "What more?"

Maathi smiled, showing all white teeth. "Ah. Tell me, what do you know of the Horn of *Dhilare*?"

I frowned, thinking it over. The name had come up a few times in old stories, but I had always passed over it. I shrugged. "Not much. Something old? It's a tool out of legend. Sometimes a hero blows it and their enemies are vanquished. Sometimes the one who blows it is promised glory. One story I heard said it's been blown many times, and each time it binds both the dead to serve again, and the heroes of today to serve when called in the future. It can still the tides—wash away sin. Doesn't make much sense."

Papers flew from the trunks as the *Maathi* brushed them aside without care. "Ah, ah! Yes. But, look at this." He punctuated the word by smacking a new sheet down on the surface.

A dark sketch of charcoal. The image resembled a horn that must have been shaped from an elephant's tusk, banded top and bottom with black and pale whorls.

"There are many pieces of truth and stories about this, my young friend. Enough so that I'm thinking it is not tall tale. And I would very much like to see it." The look in his eyes told me that much was true, but upon a longer stare, I noticed that he did not hold to greed. Nor did the tribe's *Maathi* keep the same ambition as most men who'd seek a thing for power and fame. This was the light of curiosity: of a man who simply wanted to see a piece of story come to life.

A dreamer. Someone who had been caught up in the promise of magic old legends held. I knew that desire all too well.

And I knew what it felt like to have them play out before you, and not in the way you ever hoped for.

But seeing him then, and the brightness take his face as he looked down at the horn, I couldn't bring myself to give him the word of caution I once wished someone had given me. Instead, I placed a hand on one of his arms. "I'm sure you'll find it, *Maathi,* and if I can help, I will."

But in my mind, I thought of what he'd told me. I could ask a question at the Water Tree. And I had just the one.

One about the Ashura. And how to kill them.

So I resolved to help him find this tree.

"Ah, *we* will, friend. Of this, I am sure. *Ikthab.* It is written—ah? It will be." He grinned wider now. "So, let me have your eyes for the night, and we will search for all the mysteries of the world, yes? All the things great and wonderful and meant to be hidden from us." With that, the *Maathi* fetched several bound books, slamming them onto the table.

He tapped the cover of one of the books. "Tell me, have you heard of Tarun Twice Born?"

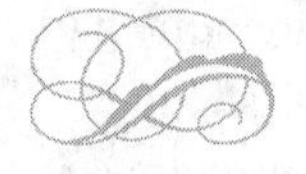

SEVENTY-ONE

Twice Born Again

Tarun Tharambadh, Tarun Twice Born, was a binder born. They said he showed the gift from the moment he could speak—no, not speak. He sang. The first words from his mouth were fluting, lilting things. Words without edge. They seemed to shape the world around them as time came to pass. He began to bind the world around him before he could run, it was said.

As he grew, he took to wandering, seeking all he could about Brahm's makings left to the world of men. And this is the story of how he came to wander through the unseen doors—those from when our world was more than it is today. The paths between the sun and the moon. Far beyond the folds of all we know and can see. Of how he brought with him only binder's cane and cloak and candle-light.

Of how he lived and died and lived again, and became one of the few to journey through the Doors of Midnight.

Tarun Tharambadh was a curious youth, and more than that, and worse by far, was a young man cleverer than most. And he knew it.

And in his cleverness he came to strike a bargain with a man many would not deal with under the worst of needs. But he did. In doing so, Tarun Tharambadh found himself far from his home in the northern cold of Uppar Radesh—the kingdom of Usaf Ghal.

Now he rode across lands of golden grains and heat unfelt by him before. The man he'd sworn a debt to ruled these plains and had need of his mind and body, but more than that, his bindings. For Tarun had already learned the ten bindings all men must know, far younger than any before him. And he would put them to use in war. All because he had need of something himself.

Answers.

For Tarun wished to venture far beyond the lands of men and into the place where it was said more than bindings still shaped the world around it. He wanted to find the *Behel-shehen*. The people before. Those born of smoke-washed flame and shaped of ash. Hair brilliant bright and strung straight from pale-star glow and fair moonlight.

"When will you show me the way to what I seek?" asked Tarun.

The warlord, a wiser man than most, knew telling Tarun what he wanted would send the young man quickly out of his service. And without him he could not win the battle that would come to be. So he kept a secret he had no knowledge of, knowing better not to let slip that he had lied to young Tarun.

"The way you wish to pass through is not open for men like you and I. It only shows itself as the world is given a scar upon its face. It is only when the moon and sun come to embrace and look on us together that you will find the way. It is like an eye that has come to see, and only then may you pass through the doorway hidden in the eye of heaven."

And so Tarun resigned himself to the warlord's yoke until such a time could come.

He learned of the bow, and the arrow, two things twined in service, but of different natures though they seem to share the one. He learned to catch the southern wind itself, swept long and hard against these bright open plains, and found the way to shape it still to his desires. And he learned the sword, and the falcon's call. Soon, he became more than just a binder, and that is no small thing, but a man grown and ready for war.

And that is what would come to him soon enough.

But before that, he would find the thing that all men seek, and fewer find still. The one that breaks many doors, and is worth returning from beyond the last of them for.

Love.

On a night more silver-shining than most, Tarun came across the caravan of the folk first formed by Brahm long after he shaped those that would leave him behind. The ones who felt best bold and bright under guide of dark and moonlight. The ones who brought first voice to songs and sang them for all to hear. Long lived since before there was ever a hint of fire in our world.

The warlord greeted them. "I offer you warmth and hospitality in all my lands, and all you can see of these golden fields are mine to share. Now, and for as long as I have sons of my sons."

The *Mamman* of the caravan smiled. "Men are always thinking things are theirs to give and share, and never seeing them for what they are. Just there. Always for anyone to pass through and over and take what they need, so long as they have the heart to give back that and more. And so few ever do. But I thank you for your hospitality and offer you that of ours as well." And she invited them into her home.

It is there where Tarun's path would begin to change from clever troublesome binder, to something more.

The *Mamman* celebrated the arrival of new friends with a night of dance. Music set to bright brass and silver bells. Young women and older alike donned dresses and gave to moving in ways that set many cheeks afire, and all in the warlord's tribe found themselves under a different sort of spell then.

But most of all Tarun.

Her name was Esme. And it meant "loved." Esteemed. And so she was.

Hair brushed black by strokes of midnight and eyes of pale gray stone. She had the full kiss of the sun's bronze in the deep of her skin, and a smile silver-moon sharp. Like all the others, she danced for them in welcome, but it was when she sang that Tarun's heart went from quivering strings to still standing transfixed by her voice.

And soon, the two of them shared more than time in dance and song. They shared dreams and desires and all the things young lovers do when full-fresh in the beginnings of passion.

But, like all good things, there comes a point past which they are not meant to last.

And so it came to be.

Warlord met warlord, and for a time, Tarun turned the tide away. He kept safe the men of the tribe, and the wandering folk who'd come across his path. Most of all, Esme. For she joined him at his side as he waded into the thick of every fray, and all the while, the two searched for their dreams. And the both of those waited beyond doors no man can open.

But then came the battle that would change things.

Deep over the land where once Iban-Badhur stood long ago, now waited an army as dark and terrible as a night with no stars or moon. Tarun waded to battle as enough arrows-sharp showered the skies to shadow the sun.

But none struck him.

Men fell around him until the fields gave up their gold to bleed a shade of red bright as blood. Arrow after arrow dotted the sky and pinned men to the ground.

But none struck him.

He went forward, striking down foe after foe with sword, horse, and his bow. All the while, archers fired down on him. Arrow. After. Arrow.

But still, none struck him.

Not with Esme by his side, she who sang sweet, and tremulous, and something otherly—something dark and terrible as much as bright and beautiful. She sang. Hard as hailstorm and silver strings shaking.

But in the midst of the battle, Tarun faced a foe who would match him in kind.

A man before whom shadows would turn away and face wrongly. Even his own, so to betray his coming. A man in blood red who was every bit the binder Tarun was.

And they fought. They shook sky and stream and stone with their words. The world bent and bowed and quaked beneath them. And when the fire 'pon which Tarun had always drawn ran dry, he took the candle Esme had crafted for him.

Bright as sky blue and burning clean and long. He called on that flame, and the battle continued. Long through morning and into the deep of dark, Tarun bled and breathed fire to fight his foe. Long through it the flames burned. Long through it the candle dripped its wax, hot and fresh, down onto his open palm. But he did not flinch. And he bore the pain.

Through it all, the war raged on around them.

Arrows fell.

But none harmed the two binders.

And through it all, Tarun remained: unstruck, unharmed, unfallen.

Seeing that his foe would not fall, the man in red finally fled, and the battle was won. But it did not stop quick enough.

For one last arrow took to the air.

And one struck home.

Tarun Tharambadh fell. And he would not get up.

But sweet Esme was the first by his side, and she heard his echoing call from beyond the last doors through which all men must pass, never to return again. But she would stop Tarun's passing then.

And so she sang. She called to Tarun and urged him back to life. "Please come back. Come back to me, my love. Take breath again."

But Tarun lay dead. And he would not move.

So Esme sang brighter still—harder than stone, and steel, and sharper than sword's edge. She poured every piece of her heart's song out into Tarun. "Hear me. Hear my words. Hear my heart and its song for you. Please come back again."

But still, Tarun lay dead. And he would not move.

Esme shed her blood and burned it with her voice into a song that was like no song before. Too terrible a thing to tell and share, the nature of that song. But she sang it loud and hard for all to hear. To and across all skies and across the folds of the world Brahm left behind in his making of things. "Hear me, Tarun! Hear me true. Hear my grief. Hear the ache and the pain. Hear the hollow space and what in it cries for your name. Hear me, Tarun. And please come back!"

And yet . . .

. . . Tarun lay dead. And he would not move.

With the blood and life shed 'cross the ground, the sun and moon had seen enough, and came to embrace each other that bright day to bring the world into an early night of mourning. And the eye above the world took in Tarun's sacrifice and Esme's love, and the door unseen opened during that night in mid of day.

Through it she heard a voice. A telling. A song.

Esme sang one last time. Twice as hard and bright as before. She sang true and terrible and to Tarun. She bid him back for love. She bid him back so they could follow what desires they'd shared. And she bid him back for one last song—one last dance.

"Hear me, love. Hear this song. What strings of mine bound to you from my own heart. Strings red as blood and bright for you as my love. Hear me, Tarun, and you will come back!"

But still . . . Tarun lay dead.

Yet he did move.

And then, he walked back from before the Doors of Death, and was born anew again.

Eloine's hand reached out to take mine in her grip, digging her nails into my flesh.

"Ow."

"What song, Ari? Tell me the song." Her voice then was acheful desire, longing pain, and hopeful plea.

I wish I could have given her what she wanted.

I couldn't. "I don't know, Eloine. It was a story, and the Maathi *never shared the song. It's just a tale."*

She frowned. "Someone once told me stories have secrets within."

"They do. But some are lost between the lines and to translation. Many then fall to time. And what remain are lost still in memory. And not everyone has the heart to open those in search for the secrets lost." I continued the story as Eloine fell to silence.

In watching this the moon and sun rejoiced and opened up the dream that both she and he had held together. As the warlord's army watched, Esme and Tarun now Twice Born Again, walked through the doors hung in the sky while the world stood under a moon-full sunny night.

Through the door that is not a door they found what walked before mankind. The earliest of Brahm's shapings. One of the *Behel-shehen*. The beings of shadowed flame and ash.

The temptress. En-Shanaiel. The one whose voice and songs could twist the minds of men and things that were not men. The one who could shape and bind among the best of all *Shehen* folk.

"Strangers in my midnight grove. How come you here?" En-Shanaiel looked to the sky and saw her answer. "Ah, the doors have opened and passed you through the first of folds. You still have time to leave."

But Tarun and Esme, now free from the warlord's hold, and his promise to show them through the very way they now crossed, decided to stay.

"No," said Esme. "We have been looking for this. For you."

"And why is that, sweet child?" En-Shanaiel cupped the young woman's chin in hand and examined her. "My, you are as lovely as the moon. And you, young binder, are as burning bright as the sun. What do you seek here in my home? Ah, I know. Secrets."

For En-Shanaiel, among many things lost to and through time, knew the desires deep down in every man and woman. For she had come to Listen to all men's hearts, and through it, tempt them with the things that held their hearts best.

"You, sweetness, seek a song older than all recorded memory. And you, bright sun, want to find bindings lost to time and chase a greatness that would bind you two in love and history. So as to never be apart, even in stories to come, from your lovely moon."

The both of them nodded.

But En-Shanaiel did not smile, though she had the answers they sorely sought. "I can give you this, but there is another secret you should know. There is something else the two of you seek to find and undo. Something to unmake. For you are but shadows of something more. Bound to time and time again the two. A wheel old made, long in turning, and in desperate need to break.

"Stay with me then long after the doors above have closed, and I will teach you all I know, and I will help you find what you seek."

And Esme and Tarun Twice Born Again agreed.

They spent one thousand and one nights with the *Behel-shehen* maiden of midnight. And in doing so, they came to learn the many knowings of the world, and what had been lost to memory. In that time, En-Shanaiel, so deprived of company in her lonely darkened grove, came to care for these two mortals. So when the time came for them to leave, she offered them three gifts.

One for Tarun. A cloak she wove, all of shining white. Of diamond glimmer, pale star glow, and silver bright moonlight.

One a thing for Esme then. A mandolin, of silver strings and beaten brass, to sing and speak as bright as sun—and shine golden.

And last a thing for them both, so that they might never be too long from the *Shehen*'s sight. Whenever the sun's own blood is spilled before the eye above, she would open a path to lead to her own shadowed garden kept in ever-midnight.

So Tarun and Esme passed back from behind the doors which no man has crossed before, and . . .

"And what, *Maathi*?" I leaned over in an attempt to peer at the book.

But the man simply shut it. "Nothing. Nothing. Just a piece of the story I . . . it's childish, is all. It cuts short. 'And they lived happily ever after.'" He gave me a wan smile and pushed the book aside.

Something in how he'd said it didn't sit right with me, but before I could push the point further, he rounded back on me. The old crazed light rekindled in his eyes.

"*Zho. Zho.* Tell me what you think, ah? There are secrets in there, yes?"

I frowned, not having come to the same conclusion. "What, that a beautiful lady can sing someone back to life? I don't think that's true, much less—"

He waved me off. "No, of course not that. Don't be slick."

I blinked. "I'm sorry?"

The *Maathi*'s lips pressed tight. "Hm, that is not right, is it? What is it like when a young man is being as . . ." He mimed stirring something with difficulty. "Too . . . fat to stir. Your arm aches. Like pudding, but of the mind. Fattened, but not that word. *Ackh.* The Trader's Tongue is a terrible thing and a curse on the man or woman who shat it out."

I tried not to laugh.

I failed.

When I composed myself, I finally had enough air to give voice to the answers I think he wanted. "Thick? He's being thick? And I think you meant spat out, not shat out."

"Don't tell me what I meant. Do you know how many tongues I speak? And I am smart in every one of them—ah!" He held up a finger. "And clever in them as well. Oh, yes, I meant thick. But also shat. No man or woman with brains would have thought to cobble up a language that is so many others pretending to be one in goat's clothing."

I left that particular phrasing alone, having lost any hope of trying to glean what he meant. So, a polite nod had to do instead. "Right."

The *Maathi* watched me, weighing me, then decided whatever he'd seen, it was enough for him to confide in me the secrets of the story. "There is a door, truly, my good boy. A door that leads beyond this world. And it can be opened. Look."

His hands blurred. The sounds of rough paper being drawn out, sliding against each other, and brushing wind as they came to press hard against the solid trunks.

Sketches of the moon littered some. Others the sun. And one image looked like a darkened eye surrounded by a ring of a fire. A burning crown of flames.

"What is that?" I leaned forward, trying to make sense of it.

"I've studied the stars a long time, good boy. And the sun. And the moon. Sometimes, they all come to share the same sky. And when that time comes"—He clapped his hands hard, then spread them wide, eyes going large as an owl's in wonder—"magic!

"And I am very much waiting for that day. If my studies are correct, it is coming. And that day I will do something very few have done before. I will do that, and many other things, my boy. And you will help me."

He was right.

This *Maathi* would come to walk through places and legends as few had ever done before. And he would take me with him.

In time, I would come to regret them all.

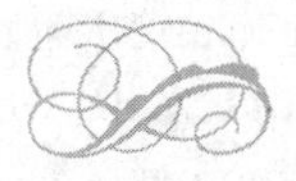

SEVENTY-TWO

TRULY LOOKING

The tribe's *Maathi* took up most of my night with theories and stories. In the end, I left with Shola in arm and a headache twice as large as any I'd ever had before. But it had been worth what I'd learned from him. Arfan sought something so valuable a thing that it would indebt him to the man who found it.

I could think of no more perfect a way to free myself of his hold. Much like in the story, a binder—in training in my case—serving a warlord until his needs were met. No point in trying to earn back every piece of coin for him if I could help deliver him to the Water Tree he searched for. That prophecy. A question.

My situation in Arfan's service could be twisted to have the *Shir* help me as much as I was him. Have his tribe deliver me across the desert to the Water Tree, and then ask what I sorely needed.

Of the Ashura.

After all, why not? I had bound fire and killed the mighty Nagh-lokh. Wasn't I already making a story of my own? What hero's journey would be complete without prophecy?

The thought kept me company until I passed into blissful sleep.

I only wished it could have lasted longer.

A sharp jab woke me from dreams of falling arrows, much like what Tarun had avoided. A crown of flames around darkened moon, threatening to take the heavenly body within itself. And I dreamt of red smoke and blood along the sands.

The Ashura that had been out here in what now seemed so long ago. I'd been on their heels before and come close enough to see the still smoldering wreckage of Ampur. This time I came too late, but I could find their trail again.

Somehow . . .

Provided I could use Arfan in turn.

The jab came again, this time digging into a space between my ribs.

"Brahm's blood and ashes—what?" I whirled to find Qimari standing over me.

She'd forgone the black robe and covering many wore to keep the worst of the sun from themselves. Now she'd chosen the comfort of riding breeches and a loose tunic of cream white. Her hair had been pinned up in place with a straight rod the color of copper-caught sun.

"Father sent me to get you." She prodded me with her foot this time. "Get. Up."

I groaned and rolled to one side in an effort to rise. My movements were hampered by my care in moving around Shola, who had tucked himself into a ball against where my chest had been moments ago.

The cat woke as I did, holding as much hatred for the early morning as any sane person should. But his was a short-lived irritation that vanished upon seeing Qimari. He quickly crossed the distance to her, nudging her shin with his head.

She returned the minor affection by running a few fingers across his skull, giving him light scratches. "What a sweet little prince you are." Qimari clicked her tongue together several times, continuing to praise Shola.

I got to my feet and fetched my cloak, throwing it over my clothes. "Don't feed his ego. The little beast already acts as if he owns every piece of ground he walks on." My staff came in hand next, then I checked to make sure my Arasmus knife stayed bound in place against my side. It did.

"Where am I off to exactly?"

Qimari informed me that it was time to begin serving Arfan in the capacity he'd desired. Guising myself as a pair of helpful hands among the tribe, and through it, learning all the secrets they carried.

I wasted no time getting to work.

Dubar was a man just shy of his fortieth year. Hair and beard dark as could be, with both bound into braids with red string. The man was dressed in a loose sarong as black as his beard, and a flowing shirt the color of pale olives.

The sun didn't bother him, nor did hard labor. I soon learned this tending to his goats. His daughters kept to the finer work of weaving. Why? Because they were crafty things, while us two, well, he wagered I had more brawn than brains.

I tried not to take it personally.

"*Zho. Zho.*" Each word came punctuated with a flick of Dubar's wrist. He tossed clumpfulls of dried shrubbery, oats, and soybeans. "*Zho. Zho!*" He motioned at the penned-up goats, but they seemed interested in doing anything but accepting the food he offered. Two, in particular, had decided that this early morning happened to be the most perfect day to butt heads.

And so they did.

I gleaned little the first day with him. But eventually, he warmed to me, and that is when secrets began to spill. Talk of the *Mejai* Arfan's plans to wed Qimari to the son of another *Shir*. Something that clearly unsettled Dubar.

Why, you ask? Especially when the action would unite two tribes, all hopefully under Arfan's thumb more than the other *Shir*?

Because the other tribe, and their *Shir*, were not good people, obviously.

One of my earliest lessons in how quickly we come to demonize the other.

No matter who they are. So long as they aren't us, they are all the more likely to be wrong in some way. If we cannot find it, we will create it.

Arfan's designs were not small, according to Dubar. And he would begin broadening his power the way many men did.

Through their daughters.

The thought shouldn't have bothered me. I'd known of people doing as much long throughout time. It was common enough all across the Golden Road. Then there was the matter of Qimari herself. I barely knew her, and we hadn't exactly taken a liking to one another, but all the same, hearing her being spoken of as a package to be bundled off like that . . .

It kindled a fire in me.

But Dabur, as he said often, had a solution for everything. After a fashion, the man was right.

He had me collect and shovel every bit of goat dung I could find. All the while, he spoke about his wife, and the argument they'd had the previous night. He'd gotten over it, of course, and nothing made that clearer than the fact he refused to stop speaking about it. The man had so wholly forgotten the ordeal that he certainly didn't need me to weigh in on the fact that his wife had been utterly wrong.

I gave him the opinion he wanted to hear.

And that put the matter to rest.

So we soon returned to something else.

Gossip.

About his own personal discontent of late. You see, he had grown used to the nomad's life. Living by the grace of Alum Above. Following the gentle flow of things in the desert. But to chase the Water Tree—chasing stories? Well, it was certainly a foolish thing to do. There were more practical needs than the promise of prophecy.

Like rearing goats, of course.

Dabur continued talking through our work, telling me of the decades of traveling life across the sands. Never in this manner, however. Seeking a story. They'd lived with purpose, and now he questioned it. "Sometimes good men do bad things for the greater good. And it is only the good they tell themselves that they're doing. So all the bad that might come to pass will be good as well. But no. Sometimes a bad thing done with good reasons is still just a bad thing." He sighed.

"No good comes from chasing glory. Do you hear me? None at all. It is a fool's desire." The way his shoulders stooped and his head bowed spoke more than his words. They told the story of a man who knew this to be true in a manner that could have only come from having made that chase himself. This was the silent bent spine of a man who had been cowed by a moment in life, and it had broken him.

He had never been the same since.

During that exchange with Dabur, I came to understand him in a fashion I can't explain. I simply did. And sometimes, that is enough.

Our work ended shortly after that and he bid me a good day.

I thanked him and left to find my way to the bowyer.

Qiran was a man in his late twenties. Lean and hard-knotted muscle made up most of him. He wore an open vest that didn't reach halfway down his torso, exposing a tanned midsection that could have been carved from hammered bronze. The muscles in his arms swelled as he worked wooden limbs. He held them before fire—not so close as to let the smoke permeate the bow to be, but enough for the heat to soften the wood. All the while, he held them with the care of a father carrying his child.

Every so often he would bend wood.

We did not speak at first.

Eventually, he asked me to hand him a blunted tool much like a hammer. Every strike of its head served to tear as much as flatten the length of old sinew Qiran had laid out against a block. "It's for the bowstring."

I nodded. The man didn't have a tongue that offered loose and easy conversation.

The steady tapping of the wooden mallet continued, serving as an odd rhythmic drum as I watched. "Every bow is a little different. Every one. Even when they look the same. You can see the mood of the maker in them. And their intent. Some have a bit more sinew in the string. Maybe he was tired that day, and thought, *Just a little more won't hurt*. But really, he was angry. And sometimes shredding sinew is the only way he can free himself from that anger."

I listened, not sure what Qiran meant, but I saw no reason to tell him so.

"Some bows you know are going to a monster of a man. Someone broad of back and with the strength to bend the wood and string more than they ever should be. So you make something stronger, something to hold that man's anger. Because some men don't know how to hold it themselves, and they take it out on the wood. Every pull, too hard. Too quick. Some men never learn to take care in the drawing of their bows. Some never learn at all."

I nodded again. And soon, Qiran's droning grew to be soothing. I didn't work, nor did I really help him at all. I sat. I watched. And I listened.

I suppose as far as working off my debt to Arfan went, this wasn't a particularly painful way to go about it.

"Hand me the plane." Qiran gestured to a canted metal blade held within a wooden frame.

I did, passing it over to him.

"Mm." He ran the plane along the body of another bow with the measured care of a man who'd made that motion tens of thousands of times. Only the barest sliver of wood shaved off. "You have to be careful when shaping something. If you take too much the first time, you can never fix it. It is ruined. All it takes is one wrong pull to ruin something. Do you understand?"

I nodded for what might have been the hundredth time.

He watched me for a moment, then mirrored the gesture, pleased, I suppose. And silence fell between us. He finished his work before turning to regard me over one of his broad shoulders. "You . . . cannot use a bow." Not a question. A statement.

"No." I dragged the word out, not meeting his eyes. "But Aisha is teaching me."

The muscles along his neck and back visibly stiffened. One of Qiran's hands clenched tight to the length of wood he held. "She is a good teacher." If Radi had played those words out on his mandolin, they would have come stiff, strummed to thrum for only an all-too-short second before being choked out.

"I wouldn't know. She tried to kill me pretty early on, then she told me to point and shoot." I smiled, hoping what I said would tease one out of the stoic man as well.

He looked me over. His mouth twitched. Then cracked wide open to reveal white teeth. And mercifully, a young and braying laugh rolled out from him. You wouldn't have expected it to sound like that coming from so somber a man, but he had the laugh of a child whose voice hadn't quite settled into its proper pitch.

"Ah, yes." He wiped his eyes with the back of a hand. "She would do that." He took a breath that brought his thick chest to swell. "She is a good teacher, Aisha. She is . . . she is . . ." Qiran finally released the breath he'd taken, looking more deflated than he should have for doing that. "She is good."

But something remained unsaid in the words. *Regret. The weight of missing someone you once held close. And the quiet distance that can come to fall between even the fiercest of lovers when that love runs cold and there are no embers left in its fire. Not even warm ashes. Just nothing.*

Qiran laid one of the bows down and the smile faded from his face. "How did you like the bow you practiced with?"

I told him I didn't have the depth of understanding to really appreciate it, or any of the ones Aisha had put out for me. And I hadn't chosen the one I had for any good reason. It had simply seemed like the right one. I described it for him.

"The black bow." He inclined his head. "It is good wood. Not one of mine, I am ashamed to say. I know the making of it, but not how it came to be made, if you understand."

"I think so."

Qiran motioned for me to sit beside him. Once I had, he reached into a small pouch and handed me a piece of dried meat.

"What is it?"

He took a bite and chewed. "Here, we have an abundance of things. We have sand, and that is wonderful for those who wish to make glass. But you cannot eat sand. And we have camels, more than any other beast, except maybe horses. But those are a gift from Alum like no other. And we do not eat those."

I looked at the piece of meat, then decided that I had probably eaten more questionable things back when I was a sparrow. What was one more in the course of my life?

I chewed it. Hard, but filled with the hot spices you would expect to find in preserved meat like this. I liked it.

Qiran smacked my leg to get my attention. "The black bow isn't the strong man's bow. It can't put a shot out farther than any other. In many ways, it's not so special a thing at all. It looks different—very different. But it is in the care given to the wood itself. There is something done to it that I don't have the mind for. But I have shot it a thousand times. And a thousand times again. So has Aisha." Something hung unsaid again in his words, and I waited for him to speak it.

"This is a bow of magic. I know you might not believe in the thing. I have never seen a piece of it myself. But this bow will not break. The string has never frayed. No water will bring its shot to falter. And in the right hands, I believe no shot will miss the mark.

"I know its paint was made from smoke and ash and ground charcoal. That it sat beside flame until it began to hold the shadow of the thing itself deep in the grain of its wood. And then all the black you can find from fire's passing came to make the color of it. Or, maybe it's just a silly story." He laughed again.

A rare sound.

And it was just as short-lived as before. Then he sobered.

"I think when we don't know the truth of things we come to make little stories to explain the things we can't explain. We've all told tales about the black bow. I'm sorry if you believed me in what I said."

I almost had until he'd told me the truth. And I confess, a piece of me sank at that. At knowing that something I had felt compelled to pick up had been nothing other than a black-colored bow. All that after I had seen *real* magic. After I had called a piece of it myself.

But no, sometimes a bow is just a bow. Sometimes there is no magic but the bits we give to things ourselves. Sometimes, that might be the only magic we need.

But there, I saw the need for a bowyer to have some for himself. He held to secret pains that he did not want to share, and so he buried himself in his work. And when he faced a problem in his work, like being unable to work out the crafting behind an interesting bow, he turned to stories.

So I told stories back, mostly the same sort Dubar had. The little kind. The gossiping kind. And in turn, Qiran paid me back with just as much.

"We're all nervous. I've been making more bows than I know what to do with. Sometimes I fix what's broken. The broken strings. Some strings cannot be fixed, though. Not the ones in the heart. And when we can't fix those, we turn to fixing whatever else we can so as not to hear their broken quivering sounds." But Qiran didn't elaborate, instead speaking of other strings then. "Something bad is in the air, Ari. It's like a string that is too tense. You feel it wanting to pull away from you, or . . . break loose.

"There is a storm coming, Ari. And I think *Mejai* Arfan will lead us into it. But I do not think he will lead us out." He sighed, pressing his hands to his face. "He has always been a good *Shir*. He is not my *Shir*, but he is in a way. But he's seeking to be the *Shir* of *Shirs* so hard, and I don't know if that is a path a man can walk without great cost."

Qiran didn't speak after that. He didn't do much at all. The man only returned to his bows, but he didn't shape any. He didn't touch them. He merely watched them.

Eventually, I took that as my cue to leave earlier than I'd expected.

So I went to go look for Qimari.

SEVENTY-THREE

To Take the Heart

I found her sitting on a low-rising dune, staring out far into the horizon. Her bow lay beside her and a line of arrows had been planted head down into the sand. A slender pillar of wood rested in the ground ahead. It stood littered with shots that could have only come from one source. But whatever had driven her to pepper the pole had now left her. She looked much like a doll without the hand to hold her upright. Lank and hanging free.

I walked over to her side, not taking the care to move silently. She had the look of someone who didn't need any sudden surprises.

She turned her head toward me. Beads of moisture glinted for the briefest of passing seconds before vanishing in the dryness of the desert.

Tears, I realized. But I made no visible notice of them, and she, for her part, did not go through the motions of wiping their remnants away. "I finished early."

She sniffed to clear her nose. "I see that."

I gestured to the side of her that didn't have a half dozen arrows sprouting from the ground. "Mind if I sit?"

She shifted slightly away, not that it was necessary, to give me space.

I joined her. "Are you all right?"

Qimari ran her tongue against the inside of her mouth before sighing. "I have a lot on my mind."

"Because of the marriage?" I shouldn't have said the words, but they were out of my mouth before I knew I'd spoken. But in the saying of them I saw what I'd already known to be true.

She stiffened as if one of the arrows had pressed into her side. Her jaw tightened, then worked loosely to say something she couldn't quite find the voice for. Finally, she nodded in resignation. "Yes."

"You don't like him?"

Her mouth twitched and she gave me a sidelong look. "I don't even know him. Not beyond reputation. He's the son of another *Shir.* As close as you can get to a prince, I suppose."

"A fitting match for someone who's supposed to be close to a princess, no?" I'd hoped the compliment would at least soften some of her aching.

It didn't.

She let out another heavy, weary breath. "In Father's eyes, perhaps. But when I look in his eyes, I see them changing. Something's taken him. He's possessed by the glory of the tribe. His years are waning, he says. He wants the Horn of *Dhilare,* he wants to find the Lap, all these things out of stories and legends that we've never even seen a hint of all the time we've lived here. Not one. All to be the *Shir* of *Shirs*. And if he has to—"

"Marry off his daughter to start that, why not?" I'd kept my tone respectful, not wanting to sound like I was reducing Qimari to a bargaining chip. No. Because her father had done that quite well enough already. So I reached out and placed my hand just near enough hers to offer the silent invitation of comfort.

She moved hers closer and soon we twined fingers. "I don't want to. I mean, I'd do it, for the good of the tribe. I would—" Her voice broke, sounding like already shattered glass under the heel of a boot.

I squeezed her hand, hoping it brought her a touch of relief. "I know you would. And I'm sure your father does too. But . . . what do you want?"

Her mouth parted, but she said nothing. Finally, another breath—short and measured as if in doing so, she could give herself the time to think of something to say. "No one's ever asked me that before. It's always been duty. Dedication to the tribe. My responsibility." She looked away, but not before I caught sight of her face.

It was the mask of someone who'd long ago buried passion and desires beneath the needs of others. The heavy mask that falls over your own excitement for knowing that others will dismiss it.

Qimari, if close to a princess, wasn't so because others saw the value in and of herself. But more what she could do. For the tribe, for Arfan—even with a father's love, she was a tool, and for outsiders.

In some ways, I saw her as something similar to one of the Sullied then. Cast in a role through no choice of her own, and because of it, she received a different treatment from others. And it brought her no joy.

"Well, Qimari, I'm asking you now. What is it that you want?"

She pointed above and I followed the motion to find a bird circling in the air.

Larger by far than many I'd seen, though at the height it flew, I couldn't make out much of its form.

"Freedom. Like that. The falcon is the king of hunters. It can do as it pleases, and it never does any wrong. It lives with the gentle flow of all things. When it needs to hunt, it hunts. When it needs to rest, it can. No one expects anything from it other than to do what it is meant to do." The way she spoke invited another question, one I knew she wanted me to ask.

So I did. "And what is it that you're meant to do, Qimari?"

She rose in a fluid motion, hefting the bow and pulling free three arrows. The first blurred up to her cheek before shooting forward. The second followed the one before, and all sooner than I could register. By the time I watched her raise the third, the other two had struck home in the pole. And the last sank into place beside them.

"That. Hunt, practice what I love, watch the desert . . ." She went quiet. Her voice returned, but now so low it was a match for the breeze sifting through the sand. Almost a thing gone unheard, but if you had the patience to listen for it, you could just make out the barest hint of its breath. "To paint it. To paint this." She motioned to the scene all around us.

You would have never known it looking at her. The stoic woman raised by a merchant king. But she had the heart of an artist, and the desires of one as well. But life had seen fit to steer her down a path away from that, and that was something I understood well.

"Is there a way for you to get out of the—"

"No." The word fell with all the finality of a hammer driving in the last nail, and silence followed in its wake.

For a while, we sat together and watched the sun reach a brightness you would only find in the deep of the desert. Then, when sitting became too much, Qimari broke that quiet and got to her feet. "I wish I'd been named after the falcon. Maybe then things would be different."

I arched a brow but didn't press her, feeling that if she wanted to share what she meant, then she would. After all, Qimari wasn't shy of speaking her mind.

"They say whenever one of us is born here, that we're given a name that holds some of the desert in it. A piece of its story." Once again, there were words unsaid, and this time, the look in her eyes told me she wanted me to be the one to ask.

"And what does yours mean?"

"There's not a clean translation to Trader's Tongue, but it's about the way a sliver of moonlight glints along the sands at night. A piece of the moon, if you wanted to get close to literal."

"I think it sounds beautiful."

She sniffed, not quite dismissing what I'd said, but making it clear she didn't think so fondly of her own name. "I should be named for something better—fiercer." Her eyes went back up to the falcon as it flew away, soon becoming nothing more than a blot of black against the orange burnished sky.

I wanted to offer her something more to lighten her mood, but she never gave me the chance.

"Come on, we'll be late for your lessons with Aisha. And I'm very much wanting to see her work you over."

She was not exaggerating.

"Ow!" The bowstring smacked into my arm again, and with so short a time for relief between blows, the pain worsened. "How come I don't have one of those?" I pointed to the leather guard along Aisha's arm.

"Because you failed to ask." Her lips twitched, but she didn't smile.

Qimari, however, who'd decided to sit and watch, gave way to the grin for both women.

I, of course, was all too glad to be the source of amusement for the pair. . . .

Aisha came over and tied a guard to my forearm, still not quite smiling. "Now, again."

I sighed, going through the motions as she'd taught me.

"You're tensing."

I released my hold on the string and arrow, lowering the bow. "Of course I am, what am I supposed to do?"

She motioned for me to hand her the bow, and I did. "Hold out your arms."

"What?"

While Qimari may have wished to be the king of hunters, Aisha's face held more of the bird's fierceness than I'd ever seen from Arfan's daughter. Sharp-eyed, and the light of their brown carried more the hint of bright gold in the light. And in irritation.

I had the feeling that Aisha could have been born of Arfan as well. He too was not accustomed to repeating himself, and the thought of doing so brought rise to his anger. So I blew out a breath in frustration and did as I'd been asked.

"Palms up."

I obliged.

"Good." She placed the bow in my hands, and then the arrow I'd been readying to shoot. "Now, hold them."

"For how long?"

"Until I tell you to stop."

That tells you all you need to know about Aisha's methods of teaching, which is not to say that they weren't effective. I didn't have the breadth of understanding to see it yet is all. But I would come to, in time.

Aisha laid another arrow from my quiver atop my palms. Then another. All the while, she watched me for the slightest hint of irritation along my face.

I refused to show that, adopting all the expression of worn stone.

But another arrow joined the rest. And another still. Time passed, and soon, the muscles of my back turned to fire. My arms soon joined, and it was all I could do to keep myself breathing deep and heavy, all in hope of assuaging the agony flowing through me.

It did not help.

I reached then for the last refuge I could think of: the candle and flame. All my pain, the shaking of my muscles, and the long-suffering question of why

Aisha put me through this bled into the flickering bulb of fire. I fed it everything. And in return, it brought me some measure of relief.

But eventually, even the candle and the flame failed me. My muscles followed. And the bow and bundle of arrows fell to the ground. My arms burned like never before, searing past the muscle and down to the marrow of me. "What was the point of that?" Each breath came with the effort of taking twelve, and still only served to bring me the air of half of one.

"The point"—Aisha knelt to retrieve all I'd dropped—"is to show you what tensing does. Now"—she placed the weapon back in my hand—"shoot." The look she gave me invited no argument. Only strict adherence.

I stole what few extra breaths I could and raised the bow. My arms quaked. The small muscles in my hand tremored, and I didn't have the strength to hold. I knew that before I'd even nocked the arrow. So I raised the bow, pulled, and released. The motion drained me.

But the arrow sailed forward and struck the sack target.

I stared at it, then her.

She finally shared the smile she'd been keeping hidden. One of her brows arched enough to turn the expression to smug rather than merely amused.

I relented and told her what she wanted to hear. "You were right."

Aisha flexed the fingers of one hand, asking me to pass her the black bow.

I did.

She went through the same motions I had and, in them, they held all the smooth fluidity of water. Fletchings came to cheek, but not for longer than the space it takes to let loose a heavy-held breath. Fingers spread. The arrow went forward.

And it was a single perfect shot.

It struck to where the left breast of the sack would have been, if it had any to speak of. And, it may come as a surprise, but sacks were known to be lacking in those, as well as many other anatomical parts to properly constitute being a person. But if it had had a heart, Aisha would have pierced it from a several dozen paces away.

"That's what you should be aiming for, Ari. The heart of things." She tapped her own chest, just above where her blood beat best and reddest. "Make it quick, both in the firing, and the death of a thing. And give them no chance to shoot back." The sudden iron-straight coldness of her voice rattled me.

"What? I thought we were just . . . I mean, this isn't for—" I never got to voice all of my confusion.

"You thought what? That this was just passing time? That I was training you to shoot a hare? To impress *Mejai* Arfan with some sunk shots into wood or canvas? Ari, when next we move camp, we will be across sands that change. The people above them change. And not everyone is a passing tinker or one of the tribe. We are not alone out there. There are bandits and worse than those."

Worse than bandits? I thought.

"The other tribes. None have forgotten old debts made in blood. *Mejai* Arfan has not. And they will all seek to see those debts paid . . . in the same manner as they were forged. Do you understand?"

I inclined my head. "Yes." I could almost see Aisha out there along the sands, among others—bows all ready to loose a volley of arrows so great that they would shadow the sun itself when they took to air.

"Good. Remember, Ari, if you don't take the heart of a thing, it could very well take yours."

"I'm not afraid of that." My voice had risen, and I don't know what brought me to speak with such hardness and heat. But it was the truth. I'd been put in that place close to death, and once near enough that I'd thought I'd died proper.

"No?" She looked me over. "I suppose not. You've killed before?"

I opened my mouth to answer.

"People, I mean."

My mind went back to Abhar—to Keshum. To the house of sparrows and the roof from which three fell, and not a one could fly. I thought of the Black Tower Band thief I'd stabbed. The bones I'd broken. And how close I'd come to ending his life myself. It had been such an easy thing, and my anger had made me want for it so badly.

In the end, he died anyways, even though it wasn't by my hands. But, I suppose I could have shouldered the blame depending on how you looked at it.

But for Aisha, I had only the simple answer. "Yes."

"Then you understand something more than most people ever will. So I will tell you this so you can understand it better. It never gets easier. Only more familiar. They are not the same thing. Understand that. And now understand this." She pointed to where she'd sank the heart shot. "If you do not make that shot, then the hearts of everyone you love could face that fate. If you do not strike the heart, it will take the one of a child in the tribe. And then a husband. A father. A daughter. Maybe your lover. But someone.

"What will you do then? Will you miss? Will your hands be unsteady, will they shake? So, we will train, and you will learn to make one perfect shot."

She was true to her word. We trained and trained until I could not feel my arms, and all I could come to see was the beating heart I was told to take. All in one perfect shot.

And in time, I would be called to that task.

To take the heart of a thing.

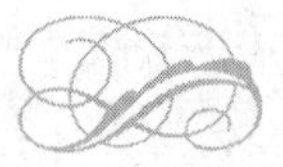

SEVENTY-FOUR

The Weight of a Crown

I was let go early that evening before the sun had sunken past the horizon. It left a smear of softer light in its passing—the colors of crushed strawberries over a bed of lavender.

Aisha had left, wanting some solace for herself, and she might have given hint that she could only endure so much terrible marksmanship in one day.

In whatever I do, I strive to make a powerful impression. And it seemed I'd done just that.

Qimari, however, elected to stay with me, so we sat and looked across the desert. But the silence eventually brought my mind toward something else. Stories.

I had two books with me. One, the tome Mahrab had given me so long ago, which still remained bound. The one holding the truth of all I was inside it, at least as far as he'd said. And then the collection of stories Rishi Saira had loaned me.

I caught Qimari staring at me out of the sides of her eyes, then explained the differences and history of each book.

The idea that Mahrab's couldn't be opened intrigued her, and she tried her hand at it, only to be met with the same result as everyone else.

I told her of the bindings, and that it had been sealed by one.

Surprisingly, she'd more than heard stories of binders through rumor. Her own father had encountered one. And she fell into the tale with little prompting.

Qimari told me of Arfan's first attempt to find the Lap, and the Water Tree—to grab hold of prophecy. And of the man who stopped him. A binder in red, casting a shadow larger than any across the desert. A shadow that looked eager to swallow those made by other men, as much as the men themselves. The man in blood-red slew Arfan's soldiers, leaving only the merchant king to survive the tale. In the end, the binder warned Arfan to never again search for the tree.

I wasn't sure what made the desert king change his mind after all this time, but I had a feeling I would find out soon enough.

In return, I told her some of the highlights of my own growing story. You know the ones.

Qimari's hand came to touch my cloak. Her fingers trailed the line of it until her skin brushed mine. For the space of a heartbeat, she lingered there, before pulling away. "Sometimes I find it hard to believe."

I smiled. "If it makes you feel better, it's hard for me to believe too, and I lived it."

That sent us both into fits of laughter that carried wide across the sands. Qimari's hand found mine again, and this time she held it.

It is worth saying that I think back to that moment many times. A moment when the world seemed truly still, and we were the only two in it. Golden copper-cast skies and sands. Quiet company, and a stillness that could almost be seen as much as felt. It didn't last, but while it did, it brought me a peace I seldom ever enjoyed in my life.

Or maybe it was something else. Perhaps the all-too-still-fresh wound from Radika, and what she'd done. Maybe in sharing that moment with Qimari, I could find quiet comfort in another, and a distraction. Perhaps not the right thing, but maybe it wasn't quite so wrong either?

"I think I'd like to see some of that storybook magic from you one day. Maybe if Father leads us into a spot of trouble, you can stop some arrows from piercing my heart, huh?" She snorted and shoved me a little.

I returned the gesture. "No promises." I gave her a roguish grin that I knew she would recognize as nothing more than a teasing joke.

"You might have to start with saving your own ass from me if you say things like that. I'll put a dozen arrows into it and leave you sleeping on your stomach for many sets."

I stood, turning around and patting my backside. My hands touched the cloak that fell over it and I flicked some of the scales with my fingernails. "I'll have you know my ass is particularly arrow-proof."

The sound of dry bone breaking. A pressure against my rear.

I whirled to find an arrow shaft splintered in half, one piece still resting in Qimari's grip. The other hung limp by a few strips of wood that hadn't fully given way. And the dull pressure in a part of my ass told me she'd jabbed me with the arrow—my white-scale cloak having spared me from a rather pointed demonstration.

"You didn't just say that." Eloine stared at me, flat-eyed and with her lower lips pressed under her teeth, almost as if biting back more of a reply.

"What?"

She held the stare, and all the judgment that came with it.

I apologized for the pun and returned to the story.

Qimari stared at where she'd struck. "The arrow broke."

"What if it had been my ass that had—"

"But it didn't!" She tossed the arrow to the ground. "Let me see."

I blinked and found whatever I'd been about to say next had gotten lodged in my throat, deciding that, no, now was not the appropriate moment to respond.

Qimari reached for my backside.

"You want to see what?"

She caught the reason for my surprise and fell away from me, clutching one hand to her side. "Oh, Alum Above, no. No, not that!" Her laughter rippled through the air, and she balled a fist to rub at one eye. "If Father had heard me say that and thought what you did . . ." Her words died under another torrent of chuckles. She composed herself seconds later. "I wanted to see where the arrow had struck the cloak."

"Oh." I had known that, of course. My hands pinched the section she'd stabbed at and I held it up for her inspection.

She squinted at the material as she leaned closer to inspect it. "It's like when you scratch a piece of glass. Just a shallow graze. Some of the scale around it has peeled away, but you can barely see it." Her eyes widened and I caught the shadow of a different thought behind them.

The understanding that maybe there had been some truth to my tale after all. I had seen magic. I was one of *those* men. A man in red, only I happened to be cloaked in white. A man casting a long and terrible shadow across the sands of the desert, far over the bodies of the men he'd killed with magic. I bound fire and set a student aflame, but that was not all. In my wrath I buried the village of Ampur and killed their god.

I saw all those things and more flash behind her eyes. Stories. And the promise of all the ones I could still give birth to. Some grand. Others terrible. For the future is always shapeless, waiting for our hands to give it form. And the hands of man can always come to craft something horrible should they have the will.

Qimari returned to where she'd sat before, and I noticed something in her then. The same discomfort showed plain across her as when she'd spoken of the man in red who'd slain her father's forces years ago. I had no way of knowing how to set her at ease.

Except one. More a hope, but sometimes hope is all you need to mend a thing.

I reached for the other book. The one containing all the stories Rishi Saira told me to study along my journey. I thumbed it open and began to read aloud.

I wasn't reading it for her, you see. I loved stories, and she just so happened to be within earshot. Never mind the fact I happened to be orating in my best stage voice, ensuring my words carried deep and far across the dimming sky.

After the tribe's *Maathi* had told me a story about Tarun Tharambadh, I felt it fitting to find another of the wandering binder. I had, and now it was Qimari's turn to hear it, and hopefully see that maybe we weren't all as bad as the binder she'd been told of.

I read to her about his voyage of the then nameless sea toward the south of what

I guessed was now Emperor's Cradle. Of how he sailed into the belly of a serpent king so large it was said the ridges on its back passed for floating mountains on the sea. Its mouth so grand-gaping a thing it could swallow ships whole. Its coming signaled lightning, storms, and ocean waves that would sink a fleet, leaving men and treasure alike to be taken deep below. And never again to be found.

She watched me with the wide-eyed enthusiasm of a child caught fresh in the hold of the most gripping story they'd heard.

Seeing her like that brought a different joy to my heart. I didn't know why, only that being able to share a story with someone so receptive brought something to life in me.

So I continued. After Tarun's journeys over the seas, I turned to Anjya, the runaway princess who wished to make fortunes of her own. She crossed a land once an ocean now burned away. Walking over hard barren grounds, all lifeless still, until she found a house held in blackness. Home to wraiths and shadows. Those who worked the silent trade. Quiet come and quiet go, but in their passing, death's own hand would show.

We spent nearly another candlemark like that. Together, me doing my best to live up to a past life in the theater. To what a wandering storyteller had done for me. I would like to think I did a fair job of it. I will never know.

All that mattered was how Qimari looked at me. I still remember the stare. And when we finally parted that night, I wish I could have taken that memory to bed with me.

But I had other duties first.

Arfan summoned me on my way to meet the *Maathi* for the night.

I found him in the tent I'd met him in before, Shola resting in his lap.

He sat before a brass bowl from which a long flexible stem protruded. Smoke filtered out from the lip of one end. A series of etchings ran along the widest part of the bowl, and I recognized the markings as well as the language.

"Artisanry." I hadn't meant to say the word aloud, but Arfan heard me and nodded.

"A treasure well worth its price, at least my men and I certainly think so. It always keeps the perfect heat for the smoke, you see." He took a long puff and blew out a breath tinged violet. The air smelled of tobacco, lavender, and a sharp bite of spice, which brought my nose to twitch. "Sit." The merchant king patted a cushion by his side.

I joined him and didn't wait for invitation to speak.

Another puff. A long stare.

Did I tell him what I'd learned—the concern and discontent growing in his camp? Arfan was not a man to be trifled with, and he held more than the lives of his own tribe in hand. He had those of the sparrows as well. How would the truth be taken? Would I be consigning simple men, and sparrow children to death?

In the end, I knew lying to him would only bring about what I feared. He'd bested me before when it came to secrets, so there was no point in keeping them from him. Thus I told him of my time with the goat herder, Dabur.

Arfan watched me, eyes half-lidded. Whether it was from fatigue, or whatever the smoke happened to be, I didn't know.

"While we talked . . . he spoke about your desires."

Still nothing from the merchant king. Only quiet awareness—the weight of knowing the man heard everything I said despite how he looked. And whatever thoughts he had remained firmly kept between his lips.

"Dabur spoke of Qimari's marriage." I shared that to test Arfan's temperament, but still, he betrayed nothing. No stiffness of body, no sharpness in eye. He watched me, and I returned the look. Relenting to the quiet stalemate, I went on. "He hopes the arrangement goes well for the tribe, but he worries. He's used to the nomad life, but he's not so sure about—"

"My want for the Water Tree, the Lap—prophecy." Each word came with the dryness of old leaves and coarse sand. The hard rasping you expect from a man with more smoke than clean air in his lungs. But there was no note of judgment in the words. Only understanding.

Arfan had already known.

I kept that in mind as I spoke of Qiran, the bowyer. At first, I eased into our discussion by sharing the story he'd told me of the black bow.

Arfan didn't laugh. Nor did he think me crazy for first believing what I'd heard. "Qiran is no fool, but that does not mean he is as wise to the ways of the world as he, or anyone else, might think. Bows are special to him, and they should be. And they will always be the more so to him for what they mean to Aisha." Arfan didn't explain the point, only moving on to the next. "But Qiran is wrong, Ari. That bow *is* special."

I looked down to the weapon I'd brought with me and had set down with my staff. The black of it called to me. It said nothing, however. No gleaning or understanding. Not then. Only blackness. Just quiet. But all the same, I looked and waited—hoping it would speak to me.

"I know this to be true, Ari, because it is the only bow that made it back from a foolish journey of mine long ago." Arfan undid part of his robe, then pulled away the collar of his loose shirt to reveal the bare chest beneath.

He had the build I'd expected of a hard-made desert king. Lean, holding only to a little fat that came more by way of old age than poor diet. But you could see the old lines where a more solid man had been. And the muscles left behind. That is not what I noticed most of all, however.

The man tapped two fingers just below his left breast. A line of skin had puckered long ago, carrying a stretched shine. A scar. He'd been shot through the heart.

No, not completely through or he'd have died.

"You are thinking about the shot, yes?" He tapped the spot again. "You are right in what you first thought. I can see the turning of your mind behind your eyes. It took me true, and I should not have walked away."

"What happened?" My voice, a whisper, something so quiet a passing breeze would have stolen it from people's ears.

Arfan grinned. A fox's smile. All bright-eyed cunning and sharp teeth. "A binder. One of yours who'd gone wrong. I understand why so few come from that place. Many go mad. And if their minds do not break so far that they are left crippled, they are likely killed rather than be let loose on the world. Some might still slip free, or have masked their madness until they can be let go. I wonder if that is what will happen to you one day?" He'd meant it as a joke.

He must have.

But it didn't matter then. For the thought settled deep into me, and I knew eventually it would take root as a long-held fear. I washed it away in the moment, keeping it for another time.

"The man killed every one of my men. Then he killed me too." Another tap to the scar. "Not with his magic, you see. He decided to do to me in turn what we tried to do to him. We shot him with arrows. But not one found him. No matter the harm we sent above, none came to him below.

"The air before him bent and bowed. Arrows fell to everywhere but his body. Next, the storm of arrows turned on every man but me. When that was done, he ripped the bow from my hands with but a word. He turned it on me, and in the end, he fired one perfect shot through here." Another tap.

"Then he told me what would be my fate. He breathed a fire to life and set my own bow in it. He worked his magic and told me he would blacken the bow eternal, as dark as his shadow—dark as dark can be. And that he would lay a powerful spell on it still. The bow would be forever unburned but treacherous to shoot for long. No blood of my tribe would ever find it to shoot true in war. But glory to the one who it would choose. And if I were ever to set out on my quest again for the Lap and Water Tree, its touch would take the heart of someone and set about a tragedy."

I looked at the bow, my mouth hanging open. "And do you believe it?"

Arfan looked me in the eyes then, and all trace of cunning and old man's wiles had left him. "I believe if I ever see that man again, he will kill me. I believed in the things I saw him do. A bow blackened but unburnt from flame. The workings with which he turned aside my arrows. But no, Ari. I do not believe in an old man's curses. I have spat my own many a time at men, and the whoresons still live. May sand fleas and scorpions take root in every one of their asses."

I saw his point about curses, but then, I knew better, didn't I? I certainly thought so. I almost told him then, of the Ashura. Of all that had happened. But the words never quite formed, and instead, I found myself telling him the rest of what Qiran had shared.

I confided in Arfan the man's fears of the merchant king's pursuits. That while he knew it was for the best of the tribe, he feared Arfan's obsession, and what else it could mean. And lastly, I told him the fear that I might not have shared, but I felt I had no choice to. For I held a fear of my own within it.

And so I told him Qimari's concern, the situation of her marriage.

Arfan didn't reply to that. Instead I saw a new face to him beyond the mask he'd been wearing. He was the *Mejai,* and though I didn't know what it meant, it carried great importance to his people. Their leader—the *Shir.* A father. And I realized then that I wasn't meant to pry for secrets and uncover treachery.

The man looked down with profound sadness. His shoulders lost what strength they had, and I saw this proud merchant king sit with a stoop in his back. All of the iron had left his spine.

This was a man who knew his people had come to doubt him where they once had not. But because of his many faces and positions behind them all, he would never be able to hear the truth from them. Their doubts, even those of his own daughter.

I watched a man who held the power of a king, but could not be given a simple answer from those he shepherded—those he loved.

"Sometimes, Ari, a crown, even an unseen one, is more a weight than any amount of steel and iron. Do you understand?"

I didn't, but the long look in his eyes told me this was not a moment for honesty, no matter how much Arfan might have wanted it. "Yes."

He nodded, more to himself than me. "Thank you for your truth, Ari. You may go."

I fetched my things and turned to leave, then cast a look at the still sleeping Shola.

"One more thing."

"Yes, *Mejai* Arfan?"

"Does Qimari hate me? Does she . . . for . . . ?" The words left half-formed, and I couldn't tell if it was the smoke leaving him in a stupor, nightly fatigue, or a man with the weight of a tribe on his mind, with a heart grown too heavy to bear it all.

I shook my head as answer. "No, *Mejai* Arfan."

When he slumped, I could tell it came more as relief than tiredness. But the old man had noticed my look to my cat. "He will be safe here with me tonight if you wish not to disturb him. I give you my word."

I looked at Arfan, and some of the old iron strength returned to him when he made me that promise.

I believed him.

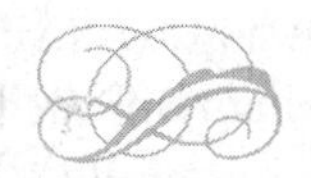

SEVENTY-FIVE

Quiet Spaces

That night I dreamed of Tarun Twice Born Again. And a world beyond ours—the mystery the tribe's *Maathi* wanted to solve, among others. I supposed it was a fitting thing to see in the sleeping hours, but a pair of hands took me by the shoulders and shook me free of the reverie in the morning.

The sand and grist that had settled between my ears had no way of clearing so soon, so I could not make out whose voice had spoken. Another shake, then a pinch.

I rolled to one side, pushing off one arm to rise. Sleep had sewn my lids shut, and no amount of grinding palms would free them.

Qimari had little regard for the sleeping. She informed me that we were to leave camp, heading toward another. The urgency to depart came from the *Maathi.* His reading of signs in the stars brought news in the pursuit of the Water Tree. And so we had to leave.

I rose, throwing free my covers.

Qimari advised me on bringing everything that I'd come into Arfan's service with, and the rest would be provided. Our destination? Iban-Bansuur, one of the fabled cities in the sands. Farther into the desert than most ever venture. A city of old stone that had once suffered the wrath of fire, and yet resisted its blackening touch.

And, a place many tinkers and wandering storytellers visited to peddle their wares and trades. I could think of no better place for me to visit.

A place perhaps to tease out a story about the Ashura.

So I gathered my things and set out to find Arfan.

The merchant king pored over several pieces of parchment. The tribe's *Maathi* pointed and gesticulated like a man who'd drunk far too much *awfhar* for his own good.

Shola contented himself lying in a corner of the tent, clinging to half-lidded sleep.

"*Zho. Zho.* See. It is like I've been telling you. The path adds up, and if we follow it before the new moon, we should find where the Lap will come to."

"And the Water Tree." Arfan ran a thumb and forefinger against his chin. His other hand came up and I caught a glint of silver. He held a piece of horn and silver inlay with a tip that somewhat reminded me of a graphter. The merchant king pressed the tool to the map and drew. A smooth line of ink flowed freely from it.

I'd never seen something like it, but it spoke of having come from the Ashram. It must have. But I didn't understand how it worked from a look at it.

"Ah." Arfan glanced up at us. He made a dismissive motion with one hand to the men, but the *Maathi* remained. "Come, Ari." He beckoned me closer. "Look at this and tell me what you see."

I gazed at the maps and drawings. A cycle of the moon's many faces. The sun and small scratches that looked more like half-recorded pieces of story. They spoke of the sun and moon bound in place, tethered to an unseen string red as blood—made from Alum himself. Though one conflicting piece said that it had been Brahm who'd done the act. On occasion, the two bodies shared not only the same sky, but the same place—meeting in heavy-held embrace.

Dots raced along the maps in the patterns I'd seen before in the *Maathi*'s tent. Arfan had drawn a series of lines connecting them, and beside it all, the various days and times of the sets used in Zibrath.

The last sheet was nothing more than a scattering of ink pinpricks. But a longer look revealed the truth to me. A map of the stars.

I told him all of what I understood, which wasn't much. The connection of the past places the Lap had been stood out rather obviously.

The *Maathi* smiled and quickly fell into telling Arfan the best-laid path to find the Water Tree. Only, he was wrong.

The longer I stared at the parchment, the more something began to shape itself. A path. A story, one hidden between the obvious inkings and marks made by the *Maathi.* A story within the story. And one that led in a direction away from the *Maathi*'s recommended route.

A dangerous thing, contradicting Arfan's wisened *Maathi,* but I'd been forced into service and lost much of the freedom I'd long fought for—and cherished. It was time to take some back, and set Arfan to meeting some of my needs in turn.

It was one of the few opportunities I could think of that might lead me to the

Ashura. As much as Arfan wanted to find the Water Tree, I *had* to. A chance to ask my question of it.

I voiced what I found, tensing in anticipation of the desert king's wrath.

Only, it never came.

The *Maathi* frowned, reexamining the maps before breaking into delighted glee and agreeing with my assessment.

Arfan eyed me, long and heavy, opinion forming behind those eyes. "I'm very glad I took you into my service, Ari. You will be riding with him—" he gestured to the *Maathi* "—and helping with research each night. The rest of your time will be spent doing whatever needs done on our journey."

I nodded and studied the look he gave me. He had not freed me of my obligation of learning what I could about his tribe's opinions of him. "And my training with Aisha?"

"Will continue." He gave a nod that concluded our conversation.

The merchant king's nature had changed since I'd spoken to him last night. Odd, perhaps, but it could have simply been his current preoccupation with finding the Water Tree. But, still, I kept track of the difference in behavior.

I made a half bow and went to retrieve my cat. Shola roused from his drowsy state and bumped his head against my shin in greeting. I scooped him into my arms, drawing only a small *mrow* of protest, but he soon settled into place and decided that more sleep would benefit him.

I couldn't begrudge him that.

Qimari and I left to prepare to head out with the caravan.

Gushvin was kind enough to take Shola back into the shaded safety of his wagon home. Alwi and Baba, lovable layabouts that they were, rested within as well, caretaking his majesty, my cat. The tinker and I traded the gossip we'd learned during our stay in Arfan's camp.

Qimari's upcoming marriage wasn't quite the secret I'd thought, nor was Arfan's changing reputation. Though, many kept silent for fear the wrong ears would hear their opinions.

Gushvin shared further bad news. Odd storms had wracked parts of the desert, bringing rains that few people had prepared for. Usually a blessing, but everything had a point at which it became too much. And the storms had provided shelter for bandits to carry out aggressive night raids on some of the other tribes. One such raid had left behind a truly horrible mess.

Mangled bodies and sands run red with more blood than anyone should ever have to see. Shattered wooden wagons and tenting. Broken stone. Odd smoke, the color of nightmares, from still smoldering campfires and burning wreckage. And a mess of bleeding faces.

Signs of the Ashura.

The path they'd been on only seemed sets ahead of mine. Were they also chasing the Lap—the Water Tree? Was it something else they were after?

But any attempt to get more from Gushvin resulted in an immediate change of topic. He simply would not discuss something so terrible, a crime done to innocent peoples. And he had no room to entertain my theory that it might not have been bandits.

"Even other tribes would not do such a thing. Not even in war or over blood debts. There is no honor in behaving like that. There were women and children slaughtered. Even lambs and goats are shown more respect when killed. There was none of that. No decency. No human thing." Gushvin spat to one side. "Monsters, only."

I think you might be more right than you realize.

That ended our conversation and left me to find Aisha. Qimari had already been keeping her company, and the two women were deep in conversation and loosing arrows when I arrived.

Rather than let me join their whispers, the pair decided I could use more training.

A last effort before we departed even deeper into the desert, and I would need my skills to be sharp.

I sighed and fell into the task.

The black bow had grown to be a comfort now in the cup of my hand. It would be a lie to say that I had improved greatly. But, I made more shots than I missed, and that in itself was progress.

Slowly, my mind would tip into a space much like the candle and the flame, only now it rested far from the center of my mind's eye. It floated above where the heart of a man would be. It drew my attention, my anger, my fatigue, and all the many questions flooding me.

There was only the candle. Only the flame. And the promise of an unseen heart to strike.

My mind numbed to the pains of my muscles and the callouses that formed on my right hand from every arrow I nocked and released.

A slow chorus of *thunk, thunk, thunk* came to dominate my hearing. It turned aside the women's whispers, and I became obsessed with the sound.

Nock. Release. *Thunk.* Soon, I had no room left but for the simplicity of the motions.

Another shot.

"Well done, Ari." Aisha's voice tore me from the lucid dream I'd been floating through.

I blinked and looked at the sack that had been pinned to three poles. Most of the arrows had found their way into its body. But my last shot had rested perfectly where the would-be-man's heart lay.

One. Perfect. Shot.

I hadn't even known I'd made it—so caught in the motions of just doing the thing was I.

The desert journey would call on me to make that shot again. And it would come with fame, and misfortune.

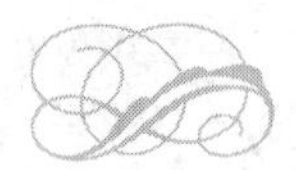

SEVENTY-SIX

FULL AND FOOLISH

We journeyed a set before the first storm came upon us, and it was a thing to remember. And certainly not one to endure. You sheltered from it. Only a fool tried to pass through.

The caravan moved into a canyon of old worn stone where we found a network of caverns—all varied in size.

I led my camel to one of them and hitched him in place. Shola had shown little care even as the world above sounded as if it had split open. To him, it came as nothing more than an irritation from a proper night's sleep.

I left him in a bundle of blankets that would make do until we settled in proper.

Fires had been started outside the cave entrance and no man bothered with a tent. Cavern camping, as I'd been told, came with few niceties of its own, and one happened to be that you didn't need to bother with extra shelter when surrounded by good stone.

I helped some of the tribe we'd traveled with unpack their belongings for the duration of our stay. Most of it yielded little conversation, and what bits came up only reiterated the same fears many seemed to share.

Arfan's obsession with the Lap and Water Tree. Chasing glory, and a mythical horn that few believed had ever existed. But a few things of a different sort slipped through.

The *Shir* of the tribe to whom Qimari would be wed carried a cruel man's reputation. He had a monster's cunning in his eyes and took part in some unsavory practices no one wanted to even speak of. Likely rumor, and I knew well enough how those things spread. But the single truth remained: Not one person spoke of him in a kind light. That in itself told a story.

Who was Arfan really giving his daughter away to? Especially with the history between the tribes—a blood feud that did not seem like an easy thing to forgive the more I asked around. Yet none disclosed its full nature. And I couldn't fault them either.

At the end of the day, I was in many ways as foreign as another tribesman. Just an outsider who hadn't earned any of their trust.

A hand fell on one of my arms and squeezed tight. I turned to find the *Maathi* standing by me.

"*Zho. Zho.* Come with me, Ari." The *Maathi* threw an arm around me as he led me away. "We are to be talking of treasures tonight, and more importantly, finding them!"

One did not argue with the *Maathi* of the tribe. Mostly because the man got in a dozen words for every one of yours you tried to speak. Hard to argue with a man who never let you say a thing.

"Oh, I am well aware of that." Eloine's eyes sparkled and the curve of her mouth pulled more to one side than the other.

I stared hard for the interruption, but the longer I did, the more I relented. A low sigh left me and I resumed the story.

The *Maathi* brought me to where he'd set his personal camp for the night. Parchment had been laid out along the surfaces of trunks and across the floor.

Soft candlelight pooled over the papers to give us a better view of them, as little starry glow filtered into this part of the cave.

"Careful, careful. This research is years in making." He pressed a hand to my chest, stopping me from stepping on anything. "*Zho. Zho.*" He gestured to the spread along the trunks. Each piece detailed a phase of the moon. Below it, a series of dots trailing a different path through the sky, but I recognized the word "sun" written in Zibrathi. "Do you see?"

I did. The paths of the sun and moon would eventually conjoin—meet in the sky a few sets from this one. At least at rough guess. "What's it mean beyond them meeting? What else happens?"

The *Maathi* opened his mouth, then shut it. He held up one finger, then lowered it. And finally, he gestured both hands to all his work . . . then dropped them back to his sides. "I have no idea."

All of the air left me as well as the excitement that had been building.

"But"—his index finger went back to the air—"I know this much, young one, it will be important! The sun and the moon embracing is in too many stories to ignore. The signs are coming. Omens, young one. The shape of the world is changing around us, and even if it is but for a moment, that moment will be *magic*!"

I had no idea what that magic would be, and in truth, I was better off for not having known. Because when it came, it would change everything. But for that moment, I simply enjoyed sharing space with someone else captivated by the promise of what else lay in the world. The stories, the truths behind them, and possibilities for wonder.

And in that, the *Maathi* did not disappoint.

"This is what I wish to show you, though." He tapped a foot to the papers I'd nearly stepped on. "See?"

Each sheet depicted a cloaked man. The first showed him kneeling before a box that had just been opened. Light shone through it and cast bright rays over his face. The second had him risen to one knee, holding a horn in his grip for a crowd to see. By the third, the man had risen fully and brought the horn to his lips. He blew on the fourth, and by the fifth, bright shadowed figures surrounded him. They bore swords and shields, spears and lances, and a few carried bows.

A piece of script ran above each sheet, and together, they might have formed a sentence. I couldn't decipher it, though.

"What's that say?"

"It's older than Zibrathi, even Brahmki. Something that sounds like both, but also neither. Old—old, my friend. But what I have gathered is this: *He who will answer the brave man's call will know glory. He shall live eternal and be bound to greatness and in memory, to live again, for the last calling of names. Nahma Gaithan* in old Brahmki. *Shal-kayib* in Zibrathi. *Dernem Gadstohn* to those in Baldaen. *The end of days, the day the last names of men will be spoken for any to hear, and all shall end in shadow. The end of an age. No more stories to be told, none to be remembered. And even stone will forget the tales told to it, for there will be no stone left.*" The *Maathi*'s voice fell to a whisper between reverence and fear. "The Horn of Dhilare, my friend. The Horn of the Brave. The more I read, the more I am sure it exists. And it is lost to us somewhere along these sands. Unlike the Lap, the Water Tree, there is no knowing where it has been, and where it will be. But it is here for me to find."

I looked back at all the parchments. "Shouldn't you be focusing just on the one thing?"

He looked at me as if I'd told him that he'd find drinking his own urine as helpful. "What a terribly stupid thing to say. Do you know how many things I can think? How some mysteries hold the keys to others, or in the thinking on one, you may think the thing you need to think to figure out another?"

I regretted the decision to question his obviously clear line of thought. . . . "Uh, no, but I gather it's a great many things."

The *Maathi* squinted at me, knowing that I was patronizing him. "Yes, a great many things. And in that, I will not compromise in the finding of any one of these mysteries. *Ikthab.* It is written. It will be. And I"—he hooked a thumb to his chest—"will be the one to find these things. *Mejai* Arfan can have the treasures and glory themselves, but the world will remember it was I who brought to light old treasures."

And suddenly I saw him. The truth of the *Maathi* and all he was came to be clearer than it ever had been before. I understood the man better now. His wants and desires—what he truly lived for.

Knowledge.

And he would do anything for the sake of uncovering a treasure lost. The greater the prize, the hungrier he grew for it. And in hunger, a man will do terrible things to sate that hollowness.

This I know.

And both the *Maathi* and I would learn where that thinking would lead us.

But for that night, we contented ourselves with trading theories. Discussing the history of the horn, which was really a collection of lies and rumors, leaving behind little truth to sort through. But we took to that task with childlike enthusiasm. A delight in dissecting what we could and why the stories had been birthed at all.

I came to learn of the men and women who'd blown the horn through stories I'd never heard before. The horn never kept the same name, but it did its shape. And what it professed to do. Confer greatness and glory on whoever blew it. It offered salvation. It changed the tides in war. It raised the dead.

Still storybook magic, but it was a wondrous thing for a young man stuck in a cave while on the hunt for another piece of Shaen story he couldn't quite believe.

But that is the thing about magic. It doesn't need you to believe in it for it to exist. It simply does. It will be there whether you have the eye to see it or not. And it will shape the world under your feet all without your knowing. So grow wise to it, and learn to find it. Or don't, and forget it at your peril.

Somewhere through it all, I began to see another story hidden in the shapes of all we searched for. And when I told the *Maathi* my suspicions, as well as my recommendations, he heeded them.

Because I would not allow us to lose the Water Tree. It was my chance at a question about the Ashura. I hadn't forgotten them while in Arfan's service.

And I hadn't forgiven them. . . .

By the end of our conversation, and a few cups of a raisin-date mulled wine, we wagered over who would find the answer to the *Maathi*'s questions about the sun and moon meeting in embrace.

We were both foolish and full of the bravado only drunk men could muster.

Only one of us would be proven right.

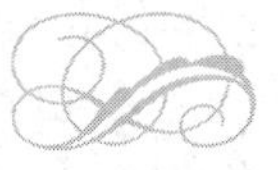

SEVENTY-SEVEN

Rogues and Princesses

I found my way back to where I'd set my bedding for the night—far back against a wall away from most of the other low burning fires. It should have been empty save for Shola. Only, my cat hadn't returned from wherever he'd taken to exploring. That should have left me worrying, but Shola had a knack for surviving anything.

We were kindred spirits in that regard, and I suppose that may very well be part of why we came into each other's lives.

But someone else waited for me by my bed.

Qimari stood there, dressed differently from her usual attire. Most of her face remained shrouded behind a veil of shadowed black, hemmed with moonlight silver along the top. The glint of brightness did wonders in drawing all attention to her eyes. She had donned a pair of chiffon pants, loose and billowing, the color of pressed lavender softened by brushes of winter's white. Her top had been made of the same gauzelike material and shaded the soft red of watered strawberries. It accented her skin wonderfully, and the clothing was thin enough to offer a better idea to the shape of her beneath it all.

"What are you doing here?" I gave thanks that, while my drinking had blunted some of my usual sharpness, it hadn't turned me into a total dullard.

"I wanted to see you once when you didn't have to train. I was hoping we could just talk, maybe you could read from the book." She nodded toward my belongings, and I knew which tome she'd meant. Qimari slowly walked away from me, keeping her eyes fixed on mine as she did. "Come with me?"

How could I refuse a friend? Especially one I'd come to care for so strongly.

I set down my staff and retrieved the tome Rishi Saira had lent me.

Qimari lingered near the bend ahead that led down another path.

I made my way over to her and she extended a hand. What else would any young man do but take it? I let her lead me along, far from any of the other flickering fires or their long cast shadows across the walls.

She had set her bedding for the night in a dead-end tunnel, hers being the only one in sight. A half dozen candles formed a crescent moon of copper-flame light that washed over us.

Qimari's blankets were made from linen the color of bronze-cast gold. They looked soft to the touch and inviting.

She sank onto a bundle of thick cushions. One of her hands came to rest by her side and she patted the ground. "Join me?"

I took care to measure my steps, more out of uncertainty than loss of balance due to the drink. Once close enough, I sank to my knees and joined her.

"Read to me. Tell me of anything, everything away from here. About the stories with Tarun and Esme. Of anyone else who found . . ." She trailed off and never did say the word left unspoken. "Tell me about people who live how they want. Take what they want. Free from anyone's whims and desires but their own." Her hand found mine and slid along the length of my arm until it rested against my elbow.

She took the joint then, squeezing hard enough for me to think her in the grip of fear. Then I realized it was something else. It was the desperate want for escape. The silent plea of someone asking for help but unable to give voice to their cry.

Hers wasn't a simple request. It came from a place of deep desire and need. Qimari *had* to be far away from this place and the one taking her mind and heart whole in hand. To be free of whatever had sunk into her, held her firm, with no sign of letting go. And that brought her to this state.

I nodded, thumbing open the book. It takes special skill to truly hear someone, much more their heart's silent wants. And doubly so to then find the proper story that they might need. It would be a great lie to say I had that ability then, but I'd found an inkling. Sometimes simply wanting to do right by a person opens the way enough. The rest falls to you to step through it.

So I did. And I found a story I believed as much as hoped would set Qimari's heart at ease.

"This is a story about a rogue of lowly birth and little means. A young man with a world of wits and wiles, and just as much a heart wide and wonderful. But one he'd shut long ago to spare him the pain few can ever take again. And again. The broken pain that leaves you hollow.

"And this is the story of a princess kept, long high-held in her father's tower of ivory stone and gilded roofs. The world she saw only by starlight from on her pale moon terrace, and the kingdom she wished to walk.

"And this is the story of how these two unlikely souls meet: princess and pauper-rogue. The love that would be denied them. And the love that they would take. The love that they would make. And all for themselves.

"This is the story of Arun and Leilah, and a love that defied kings and copper-lord cutthroats."

❧

Once long ago stood a kingdom nowhere now in being but for in name and memory.

Aramdhuur.

The highest and most exalted of places, so aptly named for it sat at what would become the heart of the Golden Road to come. But this is a time before all roads met in this kingdom. So let us focus on what else it had to live up to its name.

High walls of stone and brick—all perfect made, and kept.

A place sun-touched by day and moon-kissed in night. This was a place of much means for the many, and little to naught for the rest.

And Arun, unfortunate as it was, happened to be among the folk not so blessed to be born to a family of silver, or of gold. Much less copper. The only bit of that to his name rested in the color of his skin. For if any man could have been said to hold the sun in him, it was Arun.

Bright as a boy could be, both in spirit and in mind, he held the morning's own shine in the light of his eyes. With all the mischief you could imagine a child like that to have.

And it is this that brought him all the trouble only a thief could steal for himself. But it would be the greatest of things he'd come to take. It would come in time, and it would be a piece few could ever truly grab hold of and not let go.

A heart.

Arun had been left to himself for as long as he could remember. Some said he'd been born of himself, for no one else had wanted him in heart, hope, or in wish. No parents had desire of a child whose hands were quick to pick your pocket or your purse. Guile in eye as much as on tip of tongue. And when he was nothing more than a thought in the minds of gods above, it was said that even then, the very idea of him was a problem grand.

For any thought of him robbed the gods of other things on which to think. So, they placed him into the hole left in the world itself, all waiting for him to come and fill it. Though, it is fairer said that he stole his way into creation by knowingly being a thought so vexing the gods gave him a birth of himself.

So Arun came into the world, a boy meant to vex your heart and mind, and pick and pluck you clean as could be. The first things he stole were the words off women's lips and from behind men's ears, and all before he could walk.

By the time he could run, Arun had grown into a boy so larcenous that he would steal the very moon and all the stars just because he could.

Even if it meant he'd be lost in darkness for the rest of his days.

Not a boy born to like stealing—no. But one who needed to. And the needs of some boys can be terrible things. But, with time, things and people change. And this isn't a story about who Arun once was, but of who he came to be.

Arun, like many at the time, did not live set to set, or even day by day. He lived by tin chip to chip, for his life hung in the hands of another.

Karulthi, the copper-shark king of the streets. Or so he styled himself. A little lord of littler people still. If you needed coin to buy a loaf or cup of stew, he would be your bank. Pair of shoes, or new shirt whole, he would be your man. And if you were in need of a man to go missing or a dark deed to be done . . . he would be your hand.

For Karulthi had eyes as bright as Arun's, but they were the bright of burnished gold. Holding to the whole-shine gleam of coin. And it is through the crooked man's cunning that everyone who came to take a coin in need from Karulthi found themselves bound to pay it back with the hangman's interest. For any load of his quickly grew to be a burden few could shoulder.

And Arun, in the child's need of the first few things—loaf of bread and of stew; brand new shirt, and less-holed shoe, took the coin that made him Karulthi's toy.

One night Arun returned with a day's work in hand. "Here are today's pluckings, Karulthi-*sahm*." And Arun passed him one man's candle, its base black pewter set with gold. Then he gave the copper-shark a length of wood, burnt stone dark, and clearly a lame man's cane. Lastly came the gift of cloak, thinly hanging and very old. Threadbare-ragged but deep in color, and once-richly made. The pitch of night and shadow-dappled shade.

Karulthi gave each item a long look then. First the candle held in hand and touched bright to life with a spot of flame. "Good candle, but nothing special, and not worth even a chip itself."

Arun knew this, but he had hoped it would be enough for something.

"But the base is good, metal set with better gold. Hm . . . four chips."

Arun's heart sank, for he knew the gold had more value by weight. But what could a fledgling bird do against a shark?

"And after the changing fee, because you cannot go sell what you stole yourself, can you?"

Arun shook his head.

"That leaves you with two chips for this." Karulthi put down the candle and its base, snuffing the flame from its head. "The old man's cane, no special thing, but the wood is solid. I can sell this and have it turned to something else. Or, maybe I'll sell it back to the cripple you took it from." He laughed the cruel man's laugh, dark and jagged the thing. Bitter sharp and sharply broken of a noise.

"One chip." He waved the old staff before tossing it into a pile of precious pieces and worse odds and ends. "Ah, and this cloak." He held up the breath of darkness loosely between his fingers. So thin and lank a thing it was, as if someone had pinched free the thinnest band of shadow. "It's a flimsy thing and no good to me or you or anyone as a blanket or shirt. Just a sneeze will have me blowing through it." So Karulthi tossed the cloak back to Arun.

"Take it and go."

So Arun did, choosing to hold this piece close at heart, as it was the first thing Karulthi had ever given him after taking him in his debt. Frustrated at the state of things, he decided to go back out onto the streets and risk a bit of daring in the deep of dark.

Now shrouded in a cloak as black as shadow, he moved about the roofs until he came upon a piece of brass shining bright. It caught morning's glow that wasn't there and just as much of pale starlight.

And so into the window he stole, light as feather and soft kiss of wind, all to make away with the burnished lamp. Up, up into the night he climbed, to a place no one could find him high above the roofs. To a place in the sky where he could hide behind his cloak, and not any an eye could see past that darkened veil.

Atop the heights on high, he held up the lamp to see, and bring its secrets to clarity. But he spotted a dullness along its shine and brought a breath to his cloak with which to rub and brush this spot clean. "Whent and Ern," said Arun. But the spot remained as fog-born as before. He fixed firm his mind and uttered once again the pair of lucky words he'd conjured up. His own little secret language. "Whent and Ern." But the spot would not clear. In his frustration, he rubbed harder than before and held a fire in his heart when next he spoke the command. "Whent and Ern."

And the spot bore the brilliance of the rest of the lamp. But that was not all that happened. A cloud of blue smoke filtered out into the air, slowly coalescing to take the shape of something close to a man.

"Brahm's blood, who are you? What are you?" Arun had half a mind to throw the lamp, but then he remembered an old lesson about clutching tightly to something once plucked. And so he kept the lamp hard in hand.

"I am Bhaarbhaar, the one outside the folds of your world. One of the earliest-shaped things in all creation. Bound in brass, enclosed in silence, held in stillness. Born of smokeless warmth and flame. What is it that you desire?" The being spoke with a voice of thunder kept in throat and chest.

"Desire," asked Arun, unsure of what Bhaarbhaar meant.

The being of smoke and fire held up a finger. "I've been bound, thought and form full within that vessel. Your words and actions freed me. For that, I will bend and bind a piece of fate to give you but one desire. Name it."

Arun found his voice caught tight in throat as he thought. With just one wish he could free himself of Karulthi's grip. To be a thief again for his own whims and wants, never again held under the thumb of a copper-shark. But there was surely more to steal in the world than just plump purses and the occasional piece of brightness.

And then he heard it—a voice break out across the sky. It was strung of silver cords and soft as moonbeams.

Arun followed the sound to a tower of white stone and gold. There he saw her.

Leilah, holding all his sight under the late hour and starlight. Shadowed hair and brow, burning bright in light brown eyes. She had all the majesty of the moon in her. That is all that needs be said to understand her.

And Arun had finally found the greatest thing worth stealing, though it would be wise to consider that it was he who had been robbed first. Of his heart.

But he sought to return the favor.

"Who is that?" The boy's question touched Bhaarbhaar's ears, but the being of smoke and fire knew it was a waste of a wish to answer this.

"Is that what you want of me? A simple answer, or is it something else?"

"I want to be with her. Just her. Even if for a moment. I want the chance to win her. I've stolen almost everything these two hands can." To make his point, he held them up for Bhaarbhaar to see. "I've stolen a key that lets me walk through dreams, and I've pinched a piece of ever burning fire. I've taken one man's kite that let him fly through rain and storm, over mountains—through hard lightning. And I've even clutched a stone that one man said will let you speak to the dead.

"But I've never seen nor heard a thing like that. And I'd like to very much do something that these hands have never done before, and hold her only because she wants to be between them. Tell me how? Help me."

Bhaarbhaar clapped his hands once for having heard. Twice for having agreed. And thrice still for the deed being done. "As you wish. And wise for you not to try to take and twist her heart, for tainting someone's will like that leads to disaster. Never try to force the mind and love of another person, or you will cast a wrong shadow on their soul that no amount of magic can cleanse.

"Now, for this girl of yours . . . I will tell you how to have her choose to come between your hands, all her own, and whole in heart. Go to her when next she sings and listen. For that is the secret to understanding anyone's heart—Listening. Hear what it is she yearns for, and then give it to her. Bring her the thing she seeks, and in time, she will be yours. And to do this thing, one last piece of advice. You have stolen candle, cloak, and cane. Make those your tools and you will succeed. And, perhaps, remember the other things you have taken too."

Bhaarbhaar then vanished into the sky as if he had never been there at all.

But Arun had work to do. He spent the following day picking as many purses as he could. No cleverness today. Not one special item or promising piece of treasure. Just coin. And in doing so, he brought a larger smile to Karulthi than any of late. Enough so the copper-shark lord offered him a whole eight chips for today's cut of coins. The rest of course going off to pay the interest that had been added to what coin Arun had borrowed.

And interest . . . had quite an interesting way of multiplying into the unbelievably burdensome when in the hands of a man like Karulthi. But the money lender and streetly lord was pleased, and retired early for the day.

All of which left his many other wares unattended. And there is never quite so much a gift as precious pieces left unguarded. So Arun took the other two things he'd been forced to give to Karulthi. He took his candle, now without its base, and he stole away the old man's cane. Complete with his darkened cloak, he now had the three things Bhaarbhaar promised him would help in his aim.

Candle, cloak, and cane.

But Arun had a thief's eyes and heart, so he didn't stop with these things. No.

He stole a kite in the shape of a bird. A special thing told to hold the wind within its wings, and which could carry a man across a city or a country but with the right air.

Things in hand, he waited for full night, and then made his climb to that rooftop of before to watch that sweet songstress sing silver sharp and just as bright.

And Leilah came. She brought her voice loud and sent it wide through the sky, almost as if inviting Arun to come closer, the better to hear.

He obliged. Arun took the pinch of fire he had stolen and breathed it out to light the naked candle and enbrighten his way ahead. With two magic words he'd been gifted long ago, he pulled out his thief's trick of old and sang words of his own. They brought the wind to bear—billow-best and breathe, against his kite. To carry him high into the air, from where he sailed to Leilah's tower of white stone and gold.

His cloak kept him from being seen, a shadow against a dark as deep as the covering itself. Once atop her roof, he followed Bhaarbhaar's advice and listened to her secret desires.

She sang them for him. For any who would hear. And for the one that could find it in his heart to care.

Leilah cried with the want to see a city that was hers in name but never could she look upon from anywhere but her tower high. A wish to walk low among the people that were hers, never knowing them but for in number, and not by face. And she wished to be as free as any caged bird should be, to fly and soar so very far.

All things Arun realized he could give her. But it would take a measure of her trust. And trust is not a thing that can be stolen.

Only given.

Only earned.

So he set to earn hers and hoped she would give him that chance. Arun pulled low the black cowl and kept his face hidden. He called to her. "I heard your singing and couldn't help but come. I heard your wants and I'd like to help you have them. What can I do for you?"

Leilah did not shake or scream up a fright at finding a stranger high on her golden roof. She was a princess, and that meant being as brave as it meant being wise, and she was both those things. And many other things besides. "Who are you?" she asked.

Arun, afraid to name himself, knowing it would betray him as nothing more than a scoundrel from the streets, turned away her question. "Just a shadow. Just . . . a thief." In that moment, he let one piece of honesty through, and he cursed himself for it.

But Leilah was not one to judge a man for things such as that. As it was said, she was wise. And she knew the stories of some thieves who dabbled in the low trade, but were as good as gold in heart. So she would take the measure of this man and come to see the shape of his soul. "I want to be free of this place, but I cannot leave. I want to be gone even if just for a night."

He held out his hand. "Then let me take you. Do you trust me?"

Leilah smiled, curved sharp and sly as the moon that night. "No." Her smile deepened and she laughed. "Not yet, at least. Do you want me to?"

Arun nodded. "Yes."

She held up three fingers. "Then bring me three things. I've long heard stories of my own people and their lives, all from servants—Father's minions. I know them to be but fables—lies. I want the truth from you. Find me every night for the next eleven days, and tell me at least the story of one person you can come to learn by each night. Eleven nights. Eleven tales. And I'll count every extra a blessing in your favor. Let me know my people better.

"I wish you to bring me something you think a treasure from your own life lived down below my tower. Whatever it may be, just something meaningful to you. And lastly, when you've brought me the last two, I would ask you for your name. Your story."

Arun almost opened his mouth to argue that last piece. If he told her his name, she could surely see him put in irons. But what else could he do before his heart's greatest want? "As you wish."

He set to the task with every waking moment he could spare. By morning, he clutched what he could to appease Karulthi, but the rest of his attention went to taking in the stories of every person who fell under his eyes in the kingdom of Aramdhuur. He counted them all, names, tales, and all things. Trying to find the best in each day. The eleven most worthy. And when he couldn't find these things, he came up with his own, hoping they would please the princess.

The second thing he thought long and hard about, but he had nothing to offer that a princess could come to value. Then he remembered her words and turned his mind to the three things the spirit of smoke and flame had told him to carry. And he knew which of them he held most precious, but there was something still precious more.

So he returned high to her tower at the end of every night, keeping high atop to the gilded roof. A shadow against gold foil.

"I've done as you asked and come with stories," Arun said. "But in my searching came to know that there are none worthy of the eleven you have asked, because every one I have learned is worthy of being told, and being heard." And so he told her them. As many as he could, as many as he'd learned.

First of the elderly man who Arun never robbed. The man had nothing left but his name, and no one to carry it on. All that remained was the craft in his hands. An iron worker, pot mender, knife grinder. A man who could do naught but tinker. For this he earned a meager living, but many did not have need of his services, and he did not have the coin to leave the kingdom. And if he did, how could he bring his tools and home with him?

But this man held to the tired resilience most found in the bent of back and aged, but with spirits strong as oaks. He walked the same streets every day in hope that one person would need his services. He rarely found them. However, once a set, he would come across a poorly bundled purse stuffed with the sort of coins only a beggar could consider a treasure.

The size of said pouch happened to coincide rather perfectly with the missing number of coins Arun would have in hand before turning in his daily due to Karulthi.

The oddities of life and coincidence.

The next night Arun told her of the young woman bound to marry the spice seller's son across the way. He was a loveless man who held more interest in counting coppers than honoring a wife. And this fate broke her in places you could not see unless you had the eyes to look into the heart of a person. Because she wore the proud smile of a woman who'd been through much, and knew she wasn't done by far with what was left to endure. So she only had the mask to hold to. And she kept it strong.

Arun told Leilah all eleven, and then more still until the princess leaned against her balcony.

"I never knew." She breathed a strained sigh. "All my life I grew up hearing stories of how wondrous this place is. That the wealth was something everyone enjoyed. I never knew the suffering. The secret pains."

Arun so wished then to find a way to heal her ache, but he didn't know what else to tell her. So he chose then to grant the princess' second wish. "I have something to give you. You asked for the most important treasure that I have."

She perked up at this.

"I've stolen many things, and I can't think of any one I value so much as to be worthy of you. So I will give you these." First he held up his candle and sparked it aflame with the pinch of fire he'd once taken and kept within the seat of him. "A candle and the flame to go with it. If you ever find yourself in a darkness you cannot see your way out of, speak these words, and the candle will spark to life, and my fire will be with you. Always." And he told her the magic words.

Next he undid his cloak—shadow-shaped, and darkest black. "I stole this shadow when bored and bound it fast-tight into a cloak of my own, never having had one. If I wear it, I can pass for the night itself. No man or woman may look on me, even with eyes to see. But I want you to see me now." And he shed the cowl to reveal his face.

"I give you my name." And so he did. "Arun, without father, without mother. I am a son of myself, or so I've been called. I give you my cloak, so that you may fulfill your fantasy to fly free of this place without being seen." And so he did, passing her the shroud of midnight deep. "I give you my heart, because that is all I own that I have never taken, but wish to give to you. The greatest of things I think I own." And so he did, falling to one knee and pressing both hands to his breast before passing them to her.

Leilah smiled and took both hands, helping him to his feet. "I accept these things and your love, and in return I give you something back." Her smile widened, and Arun thought then that it was as bright and shining and lovely as the moon. "My trust. Take me away from here for just one night."

Arun wrapped his cloak around her, pressing the candle into her palms, and fetched his kite of wind. "As you wish."

He was as good as his word.

They sailed high as clouds and took in the city she had only ever seen from behind stone walls. He took her across rooftops and down low through streets, so safely hidden was she under his cloak of shadows. But in the end, while the lovers-to-be grew closer, a shadow of something fouler drew near as well.

For Karulthi was a jealous, hateful man. And he kept a tight string on every thief, Arun most of all, because he knew the boy's heart held larceny whole within it. A boy who would make him rich for all time as long as he remained in his hold.

And tonight, Arun raced plain-openly for all to see, no longer shrouded in darkness and mystery. Karulthi watched him, and watched still when the princess undid her cowl to kiss our rogue.

The copper-shark had found something he wished for himself that was no easy thing to steal. So he set about in the foulness only someone as dark and tainted as he could manage. He sent word to the princess' father and decided that a trap would do very nicely. Everything and everyone put perfectly in place, and when all was said and done, Arun would be back in his hands, as well as a princess lovely as the moon.

And so when Arun met Leilah next again, he came to whisk her away for another night among the skies and her city.

But it was not to be.

The king was waiting with his guardsmen. "You will not take my daughter anywhere. I know who and what you are: thief, rogue, scoundrel. You will leave or I will take your head from your shoulders."

Leilah tried to plead on Arun's behalf, but her father would hear none of it. "You are not to be wed to some street thief. I gave you too much freedom it seems, even letting you come up to your high tower where rogues would try to steal you away. Take my daughter below, gently. Get rid of the thief, however it pleases you." The king turned and left, but his daughter would not be so easily commanded now that she had breathed the free air.

She slipped into shadowed cloak and cowl and made one last wish of Arun. "Fly me away. Forever away—with you. Take me, now!"

Arun, loyal servant to the crown that he had just decided he ought to be, could not refuse a princess. He pressed a hand to his heart and bowed. "As you wish." He grabbed his kite blown full of wind and raced to the edge of the balcony. "Take my hand."

And the princess did.

Together, they leapt from the roof and soared as far from that place as they could. Arrows rained from above all in hopes of shooting Arun and Leilah down.

But none struck them.

They flew and flew until they felt safe to land, back at Arun's secret spot high atop the city. The place he'd first called Bhaarbhaar and been instructed how to find his bliss. The place he spent every night wondering how to free himself of the copper-shark who held him in bondage.

And the place Karulthi had long since watched Arun retreat to, and where he now lay in waiting.

Leilah undid her shroud and kissed Arun firm and deep. The kind of kiss that presses warmth and lightning down any young boy's throat and holds it there until it fills the whole of him.

But in doing this, she'd erred.

Karulthi's claps rang loud through the night. "Well done, Arun-*cha*. My boy. Look at last what you have brought me in treasure." He pressed the fingertips of both hands to his mouth and blew a kiss. "*Wah,* and look at her. A princess, my boy. As bright as gold and pretty as the moon. I think I shall have her from you now, and if you wish no harm to her, you will give her to me. And she will be mine from this day, until the end of days. You do this, Arun-*cha,* and I will let you live. If you do not . . . I will see the king finds you, but he will not find the princess. I give you my word."

But Arun would not bend. "You have more than enough in your life to have gold so deep in pocket and in hand that it even takes your damnable eyes. But no. You won't have her. Now. Or. Ever. She's meant to fly free, even if that means far from me." With that, he pushed his kite into Leilah's hands and told her to go, to fly, and that they would see each other again. He promised her this.

For the sun and moon rarely ever share a sky, but they always find a way back to each other. And when they do, true magic happens. Eventually, the sun always finds a way to embrace the moon high above.

But Leilah would not go. She pulled free her candle, and Arun raised his old staff, and together . . .

"What is it?" Qimari rose from where she'd lain, looking at me now through eyes holding candlelight and curiosity.

"Nothing. Sorry, just lost my place." I reread the lines to come and took a breath, deciding that sometimes a story could do with a lie.

They fought hard and valiantly, making room to escape together. And Arun made good on his word to Bhaarbhaar and the princess. He delivered Leilah her greatest desire, a freedom no man could take. He'd come to hold within his hands something given freely, not stolen. And in return, she welcomed him into her life, her love, and her heart.

They sailed forever high and farly free.

Some say they still ride through the skies above on a windblown kite, candle spark of light their sign, and a trail of shadows in the night.

. . . And they lived happily ever after.

SEVENTY-EIGHT

Candles, Caves, and Kisses

Qimari came closer to me as I shut the tome and set it aside. "Do you think they really did live like that? Happily ever after, I mean?"

I couldn't give voice to another lie so soon, and not to her. So I nodded, not saying anything at all.

She blew out a breath I hadn't known she'd held. A thing born of relief. "I think I understand Leilah." Qimari pulled her legs close to her chest, her fingers twining with one another.

I reached out and offered a hand, hoping it would at least give her a touch of comfort. She smiled and took it.

"Thank you for that." She moved closer and I became aware of the intensity of warmth in her eyes. The candlelight did wondrous things to them, bringing out a glow of soft brown fire I hadn't seen in them before. You could lose yourself in their depths the longer you stared.

I know that I began to.

"Do you think what they did can be done by us?"

I cocked my head to one side, unsure of what she was getting at.

"Getting away—freedom. Not being bound to the whims and wants of others . . ." *Like my father,* she'd meant to say, but the words never came. Hidden, unspoken—buried deep within.

But I heard them all the same, though I sorely wished I had a Bhaarbhaar of my own to tell me what to do next. Instead, I reached for something sometimes better than truth.

Hope.

And I gave her that—I gave her mine.

"I believe so. I don't know why I think that, I just know I do. I don't want to be bound to another man's plans." I gave her a knowing look and she took the meaning of it.

"My father has a way of getting many people caught on his lines." She mimed tangling a cord around one of her fingers. "And it's not an easy thing to slip."

I grinned. "Oh, well, I have some experience slipping nooses."

The light in her eyes spoke of her matching my grin. She leaned closer. The fullness of her breath passed through her veil and touched me along the throat.

And its warmth brought a quickness to me both in blood and heart. I didn't know why, then, but I'd learn soon enough.

"I think you had some help in that, no?" Qimari placed one of her fingers against my neck, taking her time in drawing along the shape of it. Her touch brought grains of lightning skittering across my skin and left me breathing harder.

"You're not the first woman to save me from a spot of trouble, you know." Another smile.

"Am I the first you've spent the night alone in a cavern with?"

The question drove all the wit from me, and I had no room to answer. "What?"

She pulled away, but kept one hand tangled in mine. "I want you to do something for me, Ari."

Some of my quickness returned and I found myself speaking the lines from the story. A hand went to my chest. "As you wish."

"Mm. Take me away from here, like Arun did Leilah, just for a night. I don't want to think about my father, about the . . . marriage. I don't want to think about hunting Laps and Water Trees, Ari. I just want to be away from everything, and here."

I blinked, clueless how to give her what she wanted. "Qimari . . . we can't just leave. Your father . . . the people watching outside. There's a storm and—"

She guided my hand, still held in hers, and pressed it to the flat of her stomach, slowly pulling it up and along the shape of her.

As you can imagine, I lost all reasoning for any argument I could have had.

"I'm not talking about that. Just help me forget. Everyone has always seen me all my life as something else to be. A princess to be wed off. A tool. A daughter. An influence in the tribe. But I am more than that, Ari. I'm me. I'm many things. And . . . I want you to see me." She reached up and undid the veil.

And she leaned forward to bring her lips to mine and gave me the first piece of seeing her properly. It was soft-touched heat against my mouth. She held the lingering taste of sweetness and mulling spices, likely from some wine she'd drunk earlier. Qimari pulled my hands to her and slowly shaped me in what to do next.

Shadows danced and played along the cavern wall as I slipped from my cloak and clothes. She joined me and soon the gauzelike chiffon she'd worn was piled beside us.

There was laughter as much as there was passing-shared breaths.

We were pressed copper and warm brass held tight against each other until we made something else—something new. An alloy of sorts born only of the passion two young people, very much swept up in carnal desires, as much as the moment, could make. It was not something found in the great romances.

No.

This was what you truly expected of two inexperienced lovers caught in a tangle of limbs. Breathless rise in breast and pleasure. Just as much giggling and fresh exploration. But our passion then could have matched the stories of old. Of that, I am certain. That is what I choose to believe mattered. That is what I would like to remember.

If you think this was love, however, you are mistaken. No, not love. Maybe not even close to that thing. But in the moment, it was enough. It was fire-warm bliss against skin that had been long too cold. And all the excitement of a new beginning. A dream—deeply kept, distant held, and now realized.

Maybe you think I'm doing our night a disservice remembering it this way. That it is too idealistic for a boy of sixteen, and a girl much the same. But no.

Because Qimari, that moment in time, our space, and the night of it all deserves to be remembered in the best of lights.

Ours was a candle-cast and golden glowing night at that.

And in the end, I made good on my promise, and I took Qimari very far away from all her troubles. She did the same for me.

It would be one of the first . . . and the last, we would be able to share as such.

So I will remember this memory, and treasure it always this way.

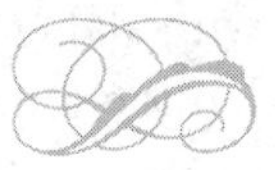

SEVENTY-NINE

Candle Cast. Candles Cost.

There are few better ways to wake up than in the warmth and comfort of another person. The candles had all burned low to pools of wax against the surrounding stone, so we had no light to ourselves so far back in the cave. But it didn't matter, because in the moment, we had each other.

Qimari moved under her blankets with the slow languid grace of a cat just beginning to stretch. Every motion of her seemed perfect-drawn as if by a painter full-fluid in the grace of their strokes.

I wanted very much to lean over and kiss her.

"Mm." She smiled at me, her eyes half-open in the look of someone who could just as easily return to bed for another whole candlemark. "I don't want to leave this cave. Not now. Not ever." Qimari rolled over to me, one of her hands trailing along the length of my torso. The touch sent bright sparks of gentle heat through me.

This is the part where you say something clever and romantic. That's what the heroes in the story do. It would have been a wonderful thing if I had done just that, and just then, but my moment of stillness cost me.

Qimari caught my tied lips and decided she should pry them open. So she did. Hers pressed against mine—soft-supple pliant, and bringing one last taste of the previous night to me.

"You'll have to leave the cave. Both of you." The words came hard, with full winter's bite, and the hateful glare of firelight.

Qimari pulled away from me, taking some of the blankets with her.

I whirled and took just enough covering to make sure I wouldn't give someone a view of me they'd remember more than my face.

An oil lamp, held in hand, illuminated the figure who'd spoken.

Aisha looked down at us—eyes holding all the brightness of candle flame touched with oil. A spark-sizzling hate that could have scalded the stone behind us. She looked every much the hawk as she glared down her nose at the pair of us. "Qima . . . what are you doing? What did you do?"

And the fullest of her fury turned on me. One of her hands went to the small of her back and the cavern space echoed with the unmistakable sound of sharp-drawn steel. She came at me then, falling atop me as I tried to scramble free.

"No, Aisha. No!" Qimari wrapped her arms around the woman's chest and throat, trying to push Aisha away with all her weight. The two of them wrestled in place for a moment that stretched too long for my comfort. "I asked him. I wanted—"

That brought Aisha to pause. She turned toward Qimari. "You *wanted*? You wanted. Qima . . . that's not your—"

A flash of Aisha's fire from earlier now filled the younger woman's eyes. "That's not my what, Aisha? My choice? My right? Is that what you were going—"

The knife slipped from Aisha's hand as she brought both palms up in a gesture of placation. "I didn't mean it like that."

"Yes, you did. Father's words. His good little *Al-sayidha,* dancing to whatever strings he has you on. But what about my strings? Have you ever once cared about—"

Aisha cupped Qimari's face, stopping her words and staring deep into the girl's eyes. "Of course I have. Always."

"Then why does this bother you? Why am I supposed to wait until I'm sold off like—" Moisture lined Qimari's lids, and though in another moment I would have looked away—as it would have been the polite thing—I watched.

My hand found one of hers and held it tight.

"It's not—your father doesn't mean—" Aisha never had the chance to finish.

"Mean what? To trade me off? He does, and you know this. He loves me, I know this, and he has his duty. And would he break his duty for love?"

Aisha's gaze broke first and fell away from the heat of the younger woman's. "No."

"No, he wouldn't."

Qimari's reply brought rise to Aisha's ire, however. My teacher stiffened and rekindled her own heated stare. "But him? Why? Why risk . . . if anyone else had come?"

"But they didn't. Why not? Why not him? I thought you said you cared about what I wanted? Last night, I wanted him. Wanted anyone but who Father has in mind for me. Is that so bad a thing?"

The words should have dealt some measure of blow to my ego at the time. You would think so, after being talked of in that light, all while being naked under the same sheets as her. But no.

How could I, when upon reflection, you see that I had lived with more freedom in some ways than Qimari ever had? And I knew some of the same restrictions as well. My life in the understage had taught me that. Being Sullied showed me how far the kindness of others went . . . when it was shown at all.

So, no. I couldn't blame her for wanting something for herself. Selfish? Perhaps. But was it an unearned selfishness? I can't say. Nor will I.

She wanted something. So did I. In that shared moment, we agreed to give it to each other. And from what I saw, neither of us came to regret it.

Aisha gazed at me out of the corner of her eye, almost as if she couldn't bear to look at me directly. Perhaps out of some misguided blame she could conveniently place on my shoulders. Maybe something else. She didn't say. And her attention remained on Qimari.

"When your father learns of this . . . Qima, I won't be able to—"

Qimari cupped Aisha's face in return. "He won't learn. He doesn't need to know."

Aisha pulled away from the girl, not quite breaking the hold on her face, but just enough to make it clear she could slip free with just a bit more effort. "I can't lie to him, Qima. You know that?"

"It's not a lie if you don't tell him. Never say a word. *Please.*" Qimari's was the heartfelt plea of a deeply cherished friend.

Aisha's gaze fell to the ground, and I saw then in her the long-hollow look and weight of someone forced into the terrible position of choosing between the love of a friend, someone they might have seen much like a sister, and the person they served. Loyally. Aisha believed in Arfan, even if she doubted some of his decisions. And she loved Qimari with all the fierceness a person could.

"You're asking me to keep a secret from your father. My *Shir.*" The word fell with the weight of old tower stone—colorless and dry. The strength left her back and shoulders.

"I'm asking you to keep a secret for a friend—a sister." Qimari's hand left mine, and she took both of Aisha's in hers. She gripped them tight and pulled them close to her breast. "For me. Please?"

Aisha nodded, saying nothing.

Qimari wrapped her arms tight around the older woman and breathed something too low to be heard. But I could guess the shape of the words all the same. The hushed *thank you* of a great kindness done.

Aisha repeated her earlier gesture and leaned forward to press a kiss to Qimari's forehead, then both her cheeks. Lastly, she cupped the young woman's chin between a thumb and forefinger, giving her a little shake. "I can't protect you forever, you know?"

Qimari gently brushed aside the older woman's touch, moving to return the carefully placed kisses. "Who says you have to?" She smiled.

Aisha let out a harsh breath through her nose that wasn't quite a snort, but was close enough. "I'm protecting you now." She retrieved her knife, sliding it back into the sheath with a noise that passed as an unspoken threat toward me. And as if having read that very thought, Aisha rose and flashed me a look sharp as any hawk could manage. She left our company without another word.

I let loose the breath I hadn't known I'd been holding tight. "I really thought she was going to kill me."

Qimari didn't look at me as she spoke. "I thought that too. I've never seen her like that before. She never gets angry. She's always calm, in control. Sometimes her temper flashes hot, but never cold like that. Never cold." She said the last two words as if trying to convince herself she hadn't witnessed Aisha behave like that.

"Do you . . . about last night. What I mean to say is . . ." I couldn't find the right words.

Qimari gave me a lopsided smile. "No. It was a good night, Ari. Thank you for it. I needed that." She bent toward me and reminded me once again of last night's first shared touch as our lips met.

"*Mrrrp.*" The inquisitive noise came from the end of our sprawl of bedding. Shola's eyes caught mine and my cat gave the pair of us a look that carried no judgment, but certainly held a weight of curiosity and an opinion.

"*Psp-psp,* Shola." Qimari beckoned the cat, motioning her fingers.

Shola gave her a long look, then decided, for reasons he deigned not to share, to ignore her and head over to me. He rubbed his face against me, and I, knowing full well my role in the relationship, ran a hand affectionately between his ears.

Before I could say a thing to Qimari, she'd already fetched her clothing and begun slipping into it. "We should go before anyone else finds us, Ari."

I wanted to protest. I wanted to say a hundred different things that could have had us stay under the covers and give truth to her desire of never having to leave. But I knew after what had happened with Aisha, I couldn't argue. So I hung my head and got to the cold task of dressing myself.

We cleared and packed most of her bedding and lit a new candle from her belongings to help light our way. The short walk back to where I'd left my things seemed longer for the silence carried between Qimari and I.

When I reached my space and started the slow process of packing, she brought a hand to the back of my neck. Her touch came as soft as I remembered from last night. The warmth of her breath washed along my collar as she leaned close.

"I don't know how much time we should be spending together after what happened. For a while, at least. My father . . . Aisha, you know?"

Something sank inside my chest, but I knew she had a point. Arfan had a terrible rage when pushed to it, and I could not begin to imagine the shape of his anger if he learned what Qimari and I had done.

There was no parting kiss. She touched my shoulder, more like a friend, and left.

Shola continued watching me with all the waning patience of a cat that is in need of attention, and more so food.

I saw him tended to, wondering what the cost of last night would come to be.

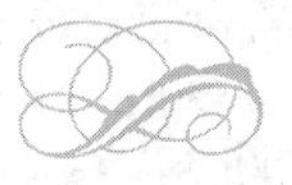

EIGHTY

A Dream of Glory

We left the safety of the cave well into desert noon, the sky above a burnished foil—copper beaten bright. No one spoke to me when we left.

And that set much of the tone of the way ahead.

The first day passed in the quietness only found in places like that, swept clean of man's mark and standing stone. Nothing but wind and footfalls against soft sand.

When we made camp that night, I kept to my own fire and drank little, eating even less. I'd been given apricot leather, dried and pressed until it could be rolled almost like parchment. It tasted sweeter than a bite of the fresh fruit itself.

I contented myself then with Shola's sleeping presence, the tome of stories Rishi Saira had let me borrow, and the flame itself. Every tendril bowed and bent in a familiar shape to me. It was as if someone had given the wind itself three colors, and I knew them all. And in that knowing, could come to see its every streaking movement along the horizon. Only, it rested just before me. Within hand's reach.

The space of my atham.

All the madness of leaving the Ashram, The Ghost of Ghal, and being under Arfan's thumb had kept me from what I'd set out to do in truth. Learn the ten bindings all men must know.

So I spent the night looking lost into the flames, hoping they'd bring some missing piece of the bindings to clarity. I conjured the candle and the flame, holding the image of fire deep inside me. It helped, at least to numb the disappointment of what had happened with Qimari, but achieved nothing else.

I brought up the folds, and visualized the fire before my hands creeping closer. A gentle thing. I pulled it. I breathed life into that reality and fixed my Athir so strong a thing I could break stone.

"Whent. Ern." The flames would move. They would bow and bend, spread and burn.

I fell back to the old pains of mind as when I'd first begun the training with Mahrab. For the folds, and imposing your will so rigidly on a thing like fire is not for the weak of thought. Salt and water touched my upper lip.

The taste of sweat.

I banished it and continued.

This is the part of the stories, of course, where the hero, alone and in the dark of the desert, uncovers some secret truth. I learn the story of fire in fullest and bind it where no one can see. I pull it free from its bed and send it dancing along the sands.

But no.

Instead, I slowly fell from the folds, unable to manage any longer. But I didn't give up. I remained seated in place, resting my head on balled fists, and watched the fire for as long as I could. For as long as it took me to fall asleep with flames dancing before my fading vision.

And in my dreams.

The next few days saw me free of training with Aisha, and I felt that had a great deal more to do with her mood over what had happened than any order from Arfan. So my time went to handling my other duties.

I tended to anyone that needed a hand with anything mundane. Rubbing down camels after a day's ride, and feeding them. Setting fires and raising tents, talking all the while, and coming away with more of what I'd already heard.

Qimari's marriage. The hunt for the Lap and the Water Tree.

The only useful information came from talking with Gushvin, and doubly so when we crossed another tinker on the path.

Their wagon could have been a mimic for the one Shola currently rode inside. The same curved wooden boards to glide along the sands. A team of camels to pull it along. And the familiar wagon home behind it all.

The knobs and bars that ran across its sides told a story. They spoke of thick rumors, juicy as could be, and bad omens down-aways-away.

"What's that, Tinker?" I pointed to the script on his home.

"Oh, nothing for you." The old man, leather-faced and lean-limbed, waved me off. "Just for us—"

"Boy's as one of us as a boy can be, short of being born in or under wagon, Shavam." Gushvin laid a hand on the other man's shoulder, calming him. "He can read our language just fine. Tell him."

Shavam ran a finger along his great mustachio of feathered white. "Fair enough. Well, heard rumors back by way of the Mutri. Princess of Abhar came home after a long trip away, traveling and studying to do whatever it is princesses do. Not that I'd know. I'm no princess, you see."

And I never would have confused him for one, but I felt he didn't need me to point that out.

Shavam pulled the sides of his baggy pants, and gestured to the rest of the motley ensemble to accentuate his prior claim. He wore a patchwork of nearly every color imaginable under his traveler's robe of black. "Now, as I was saying, rumors of mending ties between Abhar and Thamar. Heard said a betrothal might not be so far off in the future. One's got a daughter. The other, several sons. Might do them some good to tie blood."

I tuned out the rest of the words, my heart and thoughts going to Qimari.

Eventually, my attention turned back to the tinker as he continued.

"Like I was saying, odd storms from ways I've been coming. Ahead of you all. More than I've ever heard of in this place, not that it couldn't do without more water. Did a brisk business with *Shir* Sharaam's tribe before another rainfall came in. Saw some odd things in their camp, though. Barrels of something that I didn't like the look of too much. And I don't know if they've been following the storms, or the storms, them, but bad omens that. Storms and storms mean war, and don't you forget it."

"Anything else, Tinker?" I kept the urgency from my voice, knowing the man had already taken a prickly disposition toward me.

Shavam brushed his mustache with an index finger. "Passed by some odd fhaalds on the way here, though nothing so strange about them. Them's all over the world, they are. But never seen a row so large as these. Could build a house under their archways, not that any sane tinker'd do that. No sense in letting the grass grow green beneath your feet when you can move to fairer weather as the mood strikes, ah? Not that any grass'd ever grow here. Still, never seen any so large before. Figure I won't see any more like that again."

As far as news went, it failed to be what I considered to be juicy: news of the Ashura. But as it's been said before: The best things are saved for last.

"Now"—Shavam pulled one of the ends of his mustache, twining it a bit—"this bit's a touch interesting. At least to me it is, and I've been dabbling around in the secret trade to know a piece of good gossip when I hear it, don't you doubt it."

Given what he'd shared so far, I did exactly that, and didn't put much stock in what would come next.

But Shavam proved me wrong. He relayed how Sharaam's tribe had ended an old blood feud with another. How, you ask? The easiest way: murder.

A raid, masked under the cover of night and storm, on the other tribe. Something considered a crime by both tinkers' standards. But for the *Shirs,* it was a crime of honor and heart, and nothing could be done about it. At least without witnesses. After all, it was gossip.

But it spoke loudly to the sort of man *Shir* Sharaam was, and what he would do to settle grievances . . . or achieve his goals.

The man Arfan wished to tie his family with . . .

Shavam, however, had been wrong as to what the best bit of his gossip would be. He had been keeping another piece back. A tale of red smoke from smoldering, ruined campsites along the desert. Smiling victims of broken bodies and blood-soaked faces. And crumbling stone and splintered wood.

The Ashura had struck again on the way ahead. But not on the path we traveled, to Iban-Bansuur. Days off from it in fact.

Would they cross my path anyway? Could I try to coax *Maathi* into taking another way in pursuit of them, especially with us so close to the city? I wasn't sure, and another question sat heavy on my mind.

Was I ready to face the Ashura?

In truth, no. But I was young. And nothing is as confident—and as foolish—as a young man holding to years of wrath.

And there is little a foolish man will not do to see their vengeance sated.

If we couldn't set chase to the Ashura, I could perhaps redirect our efforts to learning how to defeat them. The Water Tree. A magical maiden, and the chance at a question.

So that night I sought the *Maathi*'s company.

"Ah? You wish to discuss this now, when we are so close to Iban-Bansuur? Why, my friend?"

"I'd just like to look at the maps again, maybe see something we missed before—that *you* might have missed." I hated saying that, but implying the wisened *Maathi* might have overlooked something led him to do as I hoped.

He whipped out every note he could, throwing papers, and caution, to the wind. And so we pored over every detail we could until our eyes ached, and minds followed.

But eventually.

"*Zho. Zho.* Look at this now." He gestured at the sky, waving an index finger as if trying to cover every inch of the endless expanse.

I had no hope of following the frenzied movement. "What exactly am I looking at?"

"The stars, boy. The stars. Our true guide to the Lap. Any man's guide out here. You cannot hope to walk only by day with luck. You must make the knowing of where you are beneath the stars. Watch." At that, he reached into his satchel and pulled free a disc the color of worn brass, more the shade of pale gold found nearly in the sand we walked over.

The shape of it held more within itself. Small ringed grooves featuring symbols I didn't understand. A flat bar had been set into the channels that the *Maathi* could maneuver with the press of his thumbs. The configuration of the device changed as did the alignment of the rod.

"What is that?" I leaned closer trying to make better sense of it, as if that ever helped a man come to understand anything.

"Ah? Ah! This is an *Al-Nazhuum,* my friend. Come, look." He beckoned me closer and worked it again for my inspection. "With this, you can line the stars to your need. They are always moving, the stars, but not so much that you cannot figure out how to move with them. And in doing that, you will never lose your way. We can make the measurements of them with these." His eyes widened and he stored the device back in his satchel, drawing free instead several rolled pieces of parchment.

"Like this. Like this." He stretched one open for me to see. "*Zho. Zho.*" His fingers traced the shape of a few stars dotting his sheet. "This is the movement of them over time. But some paths stay the same, and some stars do too. Knowing this lets you know where all . . ." He trailed off, smacking a hand to his forehead. "*Vala mouna. Daritha sathva.*"

The words struck. "What did you say?" Mahrab had once said those words.

"Ah. Nothing, nothing. Just an old wise man's thoughts. Keeping silent and being still. It is good for the mind to think. Foolish me, I missed something so clear. Look." He pulled another sheet from his satchel, letting the parchment hang from his grip.

It was a charting of the historical sightings of the Lap and Water Tree. All the places it had appeared along the desert. Though whatever revelation the *Maathi* had come to still eluded me.

My silence made that clear.

"Don't you see? *Zho,* boy. *Zho.* Look. The path of the Lap over time? The shape of the stars." He nodded to one sheet. Then the other. "They are connected. When the Lap appears is dependent on the stars and the year. I can see it. If I take the old paths and . . ." He trailed off, soon devolving into a low mutter that only he could hear.

I studied the maps until my vision blurred at the edges and the two pictures merged to one. It yielded nothing but a greater headache, yet I remained fixed on the images. I saw nothing indicating clear paths like the *Maathi* claimed. All that stood out to me looked like an unseen road passing through the points. Almost as if a child had planned out the map of places to be, but only ever bothered putting down the notable stops. They had decided halfway through the process to do away with any way to connect them all. However, the path remained.

A story of sorts. The promises of what and where to be, and how to get there. Only, the last part had never happened. That didn't mean you couldn't see the intent if you had the way to look at it.

The Lap and stars looked to be going through journeys of their own, but all bound to one day return to where they'd begun. And then they'd start the trip again. Like a circle. *Or a wheel.*

The *Maathi* was looking for old roads to retread, but in truth, we were searching for a pattern.

One of my hands touched a point on the map and I slowly traced along the forgotten paths, and when I reached the end, I went on.

The *Maathi* stopped his half-whispered mutterings. "Boy, boy?"

I didn't have ears for him them.

"What you . . . Alum Above." The words left him now a breathless curse, nearly too low to be caught. "Do that again. The same path."

I did, less so because he'd told me to and more because I remained in the grip of whatever pulled at me. It felt like being an artist, stick of charcoal in hand, and following faded lines in the ground, bringing them back anew. Like repeating a story so old I'd heard it enough to tell it without thinking.

The papers fled from my touch, snapping me free of the lulled state. The *Maathi* rolled them and pressed them back into his satchel. "Boy, we are destined for something great. Alum Above is my witness, I say it to you here and now. Glory, boy. We will find the things left lost to time and many, ah?" He leaned forward to pull one of my earlobes, breaking into a wide grin as he did.

"Now, *zho, zho*!" He shooed me with both hands. "Go, rest. The both of us have earned it."

I finally regained a better clarity of thought and had the wits to ask him something. "What about you?"

"Me? Ah. I am going to get so drunk that I will not be able to find my own . . ." He frowned if reconsidering. "Ah, my feet. I'm going to drink until I cannot find the feet to walk with tomorrow. But first, I will tell good *Shir* Arfan of what we have found, and where to go. *After* we rest at the city."

I frowned at that.

The Ashura were out there. And I knew I couldn't force Arfan to break course and pursue them so close to the city. But perhaps I could get him to set after the Water Tree now. Especially given its moving nature, and the fear of missing it . . . forever.

A concern I gave voice to. "What if by going to the city, *Maathi*, we lose the chance to find the Lap. It moves, doesn't it? The city, however, will be there after we are done." I kept my voice as steady as possible, not wanting to betray my hunger—my own need to find the tree. But I knew the man needed more of a push to send him over the edge. "Didn't *Mejai* Arfan task you with finding the Water Tree? Can you risk the Lap moving again?"

My question worked. *Maathi* stiffened and his eyes widened. "Alum's blessed breath. *Zho,* what if we lose it? No, no, I cannot have it—*will* not."

I cut him off then, sensing opportunity. "And if we're so close, others might be too. What if they find it first . . . before you?"

That did it.

Maathi gave me a look that said I might as well have offended his entire ancestry and done him terrible insult. A pained expression then followed, and I knew I'd struck the man in a place that would cause him ache within for a time. His identity, desires, and efforts had come under question, and a threat of a sort. Not to mention one of the best motivators a man can feel—fear. The threat of losing all he'd dreamed of. And I'd used that against him.

My stomach knotted, and I tried to keep the discomfort from showing on my face.

"Blood and stones, boy. No! This is a chance for glory. Glory, boy. Say it as you go to bed tonight. Remember it, and keep it close to heart. Ah? For Alum always answers a prayer kept at heart. And I will not have it taken from us. Go. Go."

I did, and that night when I slept, I kept the thought close at heart.

One word echoing through my mind.

Glory.

And why not? I was a child, still held by the promise and magic of stories. And the hope they offered.

What harm could the dream of glory do me?

I wish I had never wondered.

EIGHTY-ONE

OMENS

Arfan left us little time to rest after hearing the *Maathi*'s findings. Ones that I helped with, and thankfully, the tribe's way-finder gave me this credit before the merchant king. After all, I had found the path between paths in the map.

But a stone had settled in my gut over how I'd manipulated *Maathi*'s emotions, someone I'd come to care for as a friend. We'd been close to refuge from the desert, and my comments had led to *Maathi* urging Arfan to steer us off our previous course.

I could not risk losing a chance at the Water Tree however. It might have been a dream, a Shaen story, but it was the only hope I saw at learning of the Ashura while in Arfan's service.

We traveled a hard set and took a route away from our destination of Iban-Bansuur.

And hopefully toward answers about the Ashura.

My days went somewhat back to normal, if you took that to mean training in a sullen silence that came from a young woman's rather loud ignoring of you.

My relationship with Aisha had not improved in the time since she'd found Qimari and I abed. But at least she'd taken back to watching me perform my archery exercises.

I raised the bow, nocked, and released. The motions had grown smoother than before, and all the time of working with the bow had brought small changes to my body. My arms had grown a touch thicker. Not so noticeable to any girls my age, of course, but any sign of growth is noticeable to a young man. My back had broadened a shade, and I felt it in the fit of some of my clothes.

But more than that, the changes that happened most were inside me. I found myself more and more falling into a space that held all the folds as well as the candle and the flame. A soft surface of floating much like resting atop a deep pool of water. I could envision my shot, and pour all other distractions into the head of the candle and the flame. When I released, a shaft would be buried in a length of wood. Other times, pierce pure canvas.

I did not miss so much as I had when I'd begun.

Now, I barely missed at all.

Which was still a far cry from one perfect shot. The sort that took the heart of things.

"Better." The word was a crack in stone.

I looked to Aisha, my bow arm coming to hang by my side. "That's the first thing you've said to me in days." The weight of the weapon, now a comfort, did not sit easy still. The bow was meant to be put through these motions and had become familiar with them. It was a rhythm best left unbroken. So I glanced at my target, drew, and fired. My eyes returned to Aisha before I heard the shot strike home.

"I've needed days to really think about what I wanted to say, if anything. And I felt it best to watch you in silence and see where you were with your training."

The black bow called again to me, and voiced a subtle discomfort of now sitting so still. I turned a half step, and a breath later, another shot sailed forth. "And what have you seen?"

Aisha didn't look at me as my eyes touched hers. "You've improved. Quicker than I'd thought. Not quite so good as you might think you are. But better. About as good as I'd hoped for someone with as little time as you have to practice. You haven't sank the perfect shot again, though."

I took a breath and took her cold, measured words, deciding to place them into the candle and the flame. My mind remained clear for only the image of a perfect shot. I loosed another.

It struck, but was no story-fit strike.

"That's all? What about what you saw with Qimari and me?"

Aisha's chest rose and the beginnings of an angry word formed on her lips. But it died just as quick. "It's hard to look at you at times."

The muscles in my arms shuddered and my next draw faltered. The shaft slapped against the limbs of the bow, and I couldn't quite settle the arrow into place. "What?"

I knew she had slipped into a terrible rage that night, but for it to manifest in a way that she had to avert her gaze from me? That was a different kind of wound entirely. "Why?"

"Ari, Qima is like a sister to me. What you did—"

"What I did?" A new shot snapped free of the bow. It struck home with a solid thunk, but fell far quieter than the leaden-heavy hardness of my words. They held the edge of Arasmus steel, and cut just as sharp. "You were there. You heard what she said. We both wanted it, Aisha. And I think maybe that's what bothers you." One. Perfect. Shot.

I hadn't meant to say it, but the thought left me before I found a drop of caution. And now a fire had kindled inside me, and the only thing to do was to let it out.

"She's right, you know? Who are any of you to ask her to give up her wants in life to appease you? Did you ever think that maybe if you didn't ask all that of her, for her to be all those things, then maybe she wouldn't have wanted what she did that night? That maybe I was the only way she felt she had any control of things? To take that, and take something away from her father?"

Aisha's hands balled into fists, flexing a few times before she released them. The curve of her chest rose several times as her breathing quickened. "And who are you to decide what can be taken from her or not?"

I took a few steps closer to Aisha, bow tight in my grip. "I'm not. And I didn't. She did. I just gave her what she asked for." My arms blurred and another arrow went into the air. It struck with the sound of a hammer on board.

And it struck the perfect heart of the thing.

One. Perfect. Shot.

Just like before.

Aisha had no eyes for me then, attention on the arrow buried in the wooden pole. After a long moment she turned her gaze back to me. "I want you to be able to do that every time you fire. Keep practicing. I can't be with you right now." She wasted no more time with words, turning on a heel and leaving.

I watched her go as the sun of fourth candle's end reached its zenith. Its face hung wider and larger than it ever had—so great a thing that it dominated the sky. And the color of it held a violent shade of red, as if someone had pressed a freshly blooded thumb to it.

Red as some smoke.

I felt if anything was a bad omen, it was what I saw then.

I tried to put it from my mind and returned to practicing with the black bow. A steady breath, and then I pulled and released.

I missed.

The next days passed much the same as the ones before. Chores in the morning and gleaning gossip anew, and then training until night. My evenings with the *Maathi* had fallen into mostly the same quiet that filled my time with Aisha. He needed something, I fetched it, and the *Maathi* continued his scribbling and tracing the stars. And I did nothing to disturb him, for I desperately needed the Water Tree to be real.

Otherwise I'd have let the Ashura get farther away for nothing.

All the while, Qimari had put the greatest amount of distance between us. I barely saw her on rides, and if I did, her head would turn to face everywhere but my direction.

The cost of our night together, I suppose.

I'd been asked to get a girl, a princess of sorts, away for just the night, and it ended badly for me. Just like in the story.

So my training became my solace. The black bow came to fit me as much as my cloak and staff. I no longer tired as quickly in practice, and I found a new comfort in simply looking at the weapon when I finally had to take a break.

It was the black of fire's passing, yes. But something else as well. It was the black stone clarity of a rock turned smooth under a river's water. With it in hand, I had no errant thoughts.

I could fall into the candle and the flame more easily than ever before.

With the bow, I knew exactly what to do.

And so I brought it to my campfire each night, holding it across my lap as I watched the flames. Eventually, I would sleep.

But I would never forget what I came to see each morning and night.

And eventually they would save my life.

More days passed, and we came no closer to finding the Lap and Water Tree.

The fear of being wrong, the worst kind a young man can feel, soon filled me. This was my fault, and I had cost us the safety of the city, and we would die searching in vain for a story.

I'd let the Ashura slip through my fingers—again.

But then came a call that brought us all to action.

"Riders!" I didn't recognize the voice, but it came from the front of the caravan. A horn sounded. Screaming followed.

My camel lurched and I fought to steady myself. I hadn't practiced firing from the beast's back, but now I sorely wished I had.

Other men had drawn bows and shouted directions to one another.

A flash of shadow crowded the western edge of the horizon and grew larger by the second. Soon I realized what the mass of black truly was.

Horses.

More than I could make out.

Riders as dark as their mounts sat atop, and a horn much like ours blew back in reply . . . or challenge.

And from where I sat, it felt very much like the second.

They raced toward us, the head of a black wave that promised to crash against us until we were grist in the sand. No banners to mark them. Only their swords, each a curved length of steel that looked like water-drawn glass—silver-shimmerant and sharp enough to cut at a glance. I fumbled to draw the black bow, and my camel, Anedi, decided to make things more difficult than before. He huffed and shifted, causing me to nearly lose hold of the weapon. The head of my staff slapped against my thigh where the tool hung loose, strapped through a loop in my saddle.

The riders closed in and a few shots took to the air. Only one shaft found a home in the flank of the oncoming horses. The beast jerked before sinking hard to the ground, a plume of sand showering forth. The rider fared worse. They sailed free of their mount and landed flat against the dunes.

A shower of arrows pinned the stationary and easy-to-hit target in place. Even from where I sat, the vision of red bleeding through the golden grains was as clear as could be.

More volleys took to air and some of the riders fell, but not enough.

Then came the part from the stories. The men around me drew steel of their own and several cries rang louder than any clash of swords could be. "Alum! Alum Above!" And through it all, three distinct screams of a word I myself had held to of late.

"Glory! Glory! Glory!"

There is a mania that seizes all caught in the passing of it. It is the frenzied rhythm of war. Strings set to a speed that can raise your heart to thunder and hoof beats. You are moving before you can think and your hands know what to do, even when the rest of you does not.

And then, my body did what needed doing. The black bow returned to its rest and I pulled free my staff. Anedi carried me forward and the tawny sea of camels rushed to meet the wave of black.

The horses broke and took to our sides, fewer in number, but they had a speed we could hardly match. And on the firmer sands we traveled, their beasts would have little issue keeping a pace well above ours.

Then I saw Aisha. She turned a half quarter and loosed a shot. No sooner than it had left her bow did she shift to another half position, sending free another. Then the third. Each so fluid a motion it was as if they were all part of the same song, only separated by the breath needed to break into the piece. And three arrows found their marks.

Another of the riders broke free from their ranks and charged toward a familiar sight. A tinker's wagon skiff, sliding along the sands far back behind the safety of the greater group.

Alwi. Baba. Shola!

Anedi, having a willful mind of his own, raced to meet the challenge. Stubborn beast that he was.

But for once, we were in firm agreement of what to do. "Brahm's tits, faster! Faster!" Of course my words fell on deaf and dumber ears.

The oncoming rider drew a sword that looked like it wouldn't care much for the protection of my white-scale cloak, especially if it took me along the neck. Fortunately, his attention remained on taking the tinker's wagon home as an easy target.

He would not find it so.

I held out the staff more like a spear, unsure what else to do. Anedi did not have the speed to match the horse, but between the hail of arrows and other riders, the one charging the wagon didn't gallop as hard as he could.

Small blessings during bad omens.

The tinker caught sight of what was coming his way and urged his team of camels into another direction, bringing him closer to the rear of our caravan. But it wouldn't save him fast enough.

"Come on, Anedi." I remembered the word the *Maathi* would always use, urging, chastising, and for anything he could, really. "*Zho! Zho!*" It seemed fitting then. I urged Anedi on. "*Zho! Zho!*" And the camel responded.

The rider moved alongside the wagon just as Anedi put me on a course that would have us crash.

I did not think my camel understood what would happen if all our bodies met. It may come as a surprise that the realities of physics elude some animals, and thus, we all come to be victims of it.

Anedi's neck and chest slammed into the horse's side just as the tinker's wagon passed by. Both I and the other rider fought hard to hold to our reins and keep our balance. Neither of our mounts fell from the impact, but they staggered as they tried to recover their solid footing.

The black-clad man had years more experience and quickly brought his horse around to circle me. A trail of whisper-thin silver almost seemed to follow in the passing wake of his sword's movement as he sent it scything through the air. A dizzying display, more meant to distract me than anything else.

He swung.

Panic, rather than clear thought, drove me to retaliate. The thick wood of the staff met the blade's edge like a club. I triggered the latent minor bindings.

There had been no way to know just how much force had been stored within it after all the time since its last use.

The answer came.

A clap of thunder sounded from the impact and flashing steel shattered like cold glass under stone. Flecks of former sword showered us both and the grip had been torn free of the man's grasp. He rocked back in his saddle, but he did not fall.

The blowback took me as well, threatening to send me toppling. Only my firm grip on the reins and saddle's horn kept me in place. Anedi finally found better footing and brought me around to take another heavy swing at the rider.

The strike sailed wide above him, and the rider sank to one side, drawing a knife near as broad as my hand. It tapered to a point that would have had no problem sinking deep into me. He whipped his hand, trying to bring the blade's edge along my exposed thigh.

There was nothing for it but to jab the head of the staff against him. Another half-thought focus of will. The minor bindings triggered, and another pillar of force rocked the man.

He flew free of his saddle and to the ground. His horse, which had already had more excitement than it must have wanted, ran clear from the exchange.

The man didn't get back to his feet, but writhed in place.

I leveled the staff, torn between taking another swing at him and the right thing to do. He'd been bested and now lay on the ground, little threat.

The choice had never been left to me, and would be made moments later.

Another horn sounded and all eyes turned toward the source.

A mix of camels and similar horses crested the dunes. Their riders were upon us in the space of ten breaths.

Reinforcements? The motley assembly had come to the bandits' aid, and would cut through us like harvest wheat. My heart could not sink—already tuned to the drummer's thundering beat. But all the same, a part of me braced for the dark reality of the losing battle we had ahead of us.

Only, the new riders wove through our caravan, quickly setting upon the men who'd attacked us. And in doing so, a rider passed by me.

Silver flashed. A sword leapt. And took the head of the man who'd risen from where I'd knocked him moments earlier.

Once again, red touched the gold of the desert and turned it to a shade it ought never have held.

The swordsman brought his horse around, circling me in a slow canter. Shrouded in robes and veiled in the once-white of fresh cream, now carrying a touch of gray, he stopped ahead of me. The man lowered his hood and the cloth obscuring his face.

He couldn't have been more than a year or two older than me. Dark hair cut into neat tousles that framed a face too pretty for any man to have. His eyes were ground jade touched with old stone. The sun hadn't quite brought his skin to the same shade as many of the other men in the desert, giving him a look close to as fair as could be found in these sands.

"You are a *Shir*?"

The question pulled me back from where I'd gone lost in mind. "What? No . . . who are you?"

The boy looked me over again, weighing me with the quick efficiency of someone who took stock of every person they came across. And all in the time it took to exhale. "I am Shareem, son of *Shir* Sharaam." The words left him with the measured confidence of someone who had known power and privilege all his life. So much so that it defined him more than he carried the trait. "Who are you?"

Shareem. The one Qimari's supposed to marry. The thought shouldn't have been what first crossed my mind, not in the midst of everything going on. But it did.

"Ari, son of myself."

Shareem looked me over again, all cool eyes and cold calculation. It reminded me of how Aisha took someone in. "*Hrmph.* May you walk on firm sands, Ari, son of yourself." He turned his horse and rode off to meet some men at the head of our rescue party.

I nudged Anedi into step behind him. The camel made a sound like something had lodged in its throat and couldn't be spat free. I took it as a minor protest. "Brahm's tits, just follow that sprat, will you?" Anedi trudged after him, making it clear every step was a begrudging one.

We eventually caught up to where several people had formed a close-knit circle. Qimari and Aisha were on either side of Arfan, the three of them looking across at a group of six. I joined them, taking in the other members of Shareem's party.

One looked close to Arfan's age, and I noticed every man gave him the breadth of space that comes with fear, or respect. And sadly, there are times the two are indistinguishable from each other. The *Shir,* I suspected.

A man by his right, however, took more of my attention. Lean, with the hard angles of an even harder-lived life to his face. Grizzled with a patchy growth of hair that should have long filled in along his cheeks. But it never did. And the set of his mouth, in a curved smile, reminded me more of a wolf's than anything else.

I had no proof that he was the *Maathi* of *Shir* Sharaam's tribe, but I remembered all I had heard about the man and his nature. I guessed it might have been him then.

He caught me staring, and the blood-red sun cast a bright light against the faces of everyone caught in it. His eyes lost most of their brown and held the deep burnished light of flame and gold. But the look didn't last, and he too turned his attention to Arfan.

"*Shir* Arfan," said the man I took to be Shareem's father. "You're the wrong way from Iban-Bansuur. And you've no horses with you?"

Arfan bristled, and I noticed that his eyes were not on the man speaking to him, but on the man I assumed to be the other tribe's *Maathi*. "No. I had not thought to bring any. Ours are at our home camp. I did not think we would need them. The problem with bandits has gotten worse. Thank you for your aid, *Shir* Sharaam."

The other man inclined his head, but it would have been a mistake to take it as a gesture of respect. A cold wind hung between the two men, and anyone with skin to feel caught its winter edge against their flesh.

"Ah, but you didn't answer the question, *Shir* Arfan. You're heading the wrong way. We are all to be at Iban-Bansuur, are we not? There are dealings to be done." Sharaam cast a look to his son, then Qimari.

It might have been my imagination, but she shrank in her saddle a bit. The motions of someone trying to go unnoticed, but knowing they could not, no matter the desire.

"It would have been a small thing, with you here unprepared for something like this, for my people to . . ." *Shir* Sharaam gave him a smile better fit for a shark, and with all the teeth to match.

Arfan's sword hand flexed, and it came to rest on the pommel of his weapon. But the wisened *Shir* never drew, nor made the motion any more obvious than need be.

The man I took to be the other *Maathi* nudged his horse forward just enough to make it clear he meant to address Arfan. "My *Shir* is still wanting to know why you are headed the wrong way from the city, *Shir* Arfan?" The words were sharp-tooth-edged and just short of biting.

If the man's tone bothered Arfan, he didn't show it. "I have other business I must attend to first. Something personal. I will join you at the city to discuss the future of our tribes. And"—he faced the *Shir* Sharaam—"I thank you for your aid. *Sholkuh*." He inclined his head and nudged his camel to move to the side.

"*Tha-tha*." Each click of tongue came with a waggling finger of admonishment as Sharaam moved his camel to head off Arfan's. "We will travel with you. As one family . . . to be, at least. It will be safer this way."

Arfan betrayed a better sense of the quiet anger rising in him then. The line of his jaw showed its sharpness, and the jaw hardened. His eyes held a brightness in them that was not kind warmth. But something to scald. None that touched his voice, however. "Of course." He motioned with a hand. "Join us."

Shir Sharaam inclined his head in stiff acceptance and gratitude. His men moved along to join the caravan, and I noticed that there weren't so many of them as there were us.

Which raised the question: Where was the rest of his tribe?

The *Maathi* of the other tribe stopped just as he neared Arfan's mount. "For you, *Shir* Arfan." The hardness held in his voice had now left, and something softer took its place. He passed over a glass vial that Arfan accepted, quickly slipping into the cuff of his robes.

But I had seen a vial like that before. No special thing on its own. The color within, however, could not be mistaken for anything else. A cloudy white like milk-strewn cotton.

White-joy. But why?

Arfan had none of the telltale signs of abusing the drugs. His eyes hadn't taken on the coloring that befell any cotton eyes after long use. Nor had he shown the diminished mental faculties of one. But I began to wonder.

The *Maathi* watched me take note of the quiet exchange.

I averted my gaze first, turning instead to look to the horizon.

Black clouds gathered early in the day. A clear sign of what was to come.

We all headed toward the gathering darkness until we were forced to make camp.

What had Shavam said about bad omens? He spoke of desert storms being among the worst.

I set up my tent that night and waited to see what would come of the change in weather.

And the storm came.

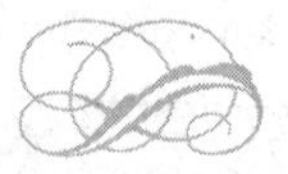

EIGHTY-TWO

The Shadow of Things

The journey to find the Lap did not go smoother with the addition of more men to our caravan. Arfan's tribe gave long eyes to every one of Sharaam's men. And the same was true in return. Through it all, Qimari spent every day in the company of Shareem.

He rode close to her whenever he could, taking small liberties to hold her hand in his. Any time we stopped, he made a point to bring out his bow and practice where she could see. And a few times, he stripped to his bare chest and went through a series of fluid motions with his sword, showing lean muscle and a body I supposed many girls would find alluring with his pretty face.

I found myself developing the sort of irrational hatred that had me wondering what it would be like to bury him in a shallow grave of sand. No one would miss him. At least, I was beginning to convince myself of that.

Aisha caught my stares and came over to me one day as I sat on a low mound of sand, reading to myself. "You hate him."

I didn't look up from the book Rishi Saira had given me. "I barely know him. You can't hate someone you don't know."

Aisha joined me, sitting by my side. "I wouldn't say that. And you hate him for other reasons." Her gaze fell on Qimari, and Aisha knew I followed her stare. "But you don't love her."

I opened my mouth, then closed it. I had to think a moment before I found the answer, and the truth. "I barely know her too. I thought for a while I was getting close to her, but . . ."

Aisha nodded. "What happened that night. The cost of your pleasure, and now you're without her presence. You feel for her, but it is not true love."

The comment barbed me, and I can't tell you why it did. She was right, what did I know of love? But I was young, and I'd just experienced a new kind of passion with Qimari I hadn't felt before.

"How do you know what true love is?" I let none of the heat in my heart make its way into my voice.

Aisha didn't miss a beat. "How do you?" A thin smile. "I know because I have had it once before, Ari. And I have lost it."

Just once? The weight of that brought low all my anger and I sat there—quiet.

She caught my silence and its meaning. One of her hands came to rest on my bicep, giving it a squeeze. "You can't have known. It was long enough ago that it doesn't hurt like it used to. Don't be upset with yourself. There's more than enough of that in any love lost. And no one needs extra." Aisha took a breath and looked back at Qimari and Shareem.

"You do not love her, and she doesn't love you. Not in the way it should be. And that is simply that. And that is fine. You two care a great deal. That sometimes matters more. But I see the way you look at her, and it is fear and caring together. You can't have them both if you truly love someone."

I opened my mouth to speak, but she held up a hand to stay me.

"And I know what your fears are. They are fine, and they are just. But I will tell you this now, take one more look at Shareem and tell me what you see."

I looked and took in the young man. My gaze fell as much on him as through him—the sort of halfhearted stare found in people looking off into the distance.

What I saw was the same as before: a young man, born into the power and privilege that comes of being a *Shir*'s son. Set to inherit something, at least. Though Arfan had once told me that power and rule weren't as straight-set as that. But Shareem knew the confidence of nobility, and taking what he wanted.

And this meant Qimari. He bore no love for her, as Aisha had said. He saw potential, and the fulfillment of his father's desires. Uniting two tribes under a rule that very well could be his one day. It was hot ambition and the want of a thing simply because he might come to have it. Nothing else.

"So?" Aisha watched me with all the careful patience of a hawk.

I exhaled and told her all of what I thought.

She pursed her lips, then nodded. "You've taken quicker measure of him than most, then. Impressive. Maybe your eyes aren't so bad after all, though with how you shoot a bow at times . . . I still wonder." A ghost of a smile played across her mouth.

"So do not worry, Ari, because he does not love her either. In fact, he knows even less of her than you've come to."

I blew out a breath. "I think that's obvious, given what—"

The shaft of an arrow smacked against the back of one of my hands. I never saw it come to her hand, much less lash out at me.

"Ow." I rubbed the spot, watching a portion of the flesh redden.

"You know that is not what I meant. Qimari has grown close to you in a way she doesn't with many. She is a *Shir*'s daughter. She is of the tribe, and yet, she is never *one* of the tribe at the same time. They do not, nor will they ever, speak to her the same as they do one another. How can she be close to them?"

"For as close as we've gotten, it seems all that is ruined now." I gestured back to Shareem and Qimari.

Aisha frowned. "Not of any of your doing. As young boys will be boys, so will young girls be themselves. And the three of you are all still young. You have only ever stood in the shadow of love."

I bristled at that.

Aisha caught the frustration building in me and rose to her feet. "Come, show me how your shot has improved."

I sighed. "Do we have to? I don't suppose I can have a break from it?"

The old whisper of a smile returned, now full-wide. "Of course . . . after you loose, say, a thousand shots?"

I gaped.

Aisha had little time for my hesitance, and quickly marshalled me into practice.

And we went deep until evening that day. It would be wrong to say our relationship had been repaired. We were not what we had been before. And every now and again, I saw her watching me with the same look I had turned on Shareem.

The careful, penetrating stare meant to see as much through me as at me. I don't know what she saw, but the shadow of distance between us remained.

And it would only grow with time.

EIGHTY-THREE
LOST-LOOKING. FOUND.

Days passed and the *Maathi* continued to lead the way ahead by morning, and many times now by night. He constantly reassured Arfan that we were on track. All the while, *Shir* Sharaam and his *Maathi* remained close at hand—listening.

Though the two *Shirs* began to wonder, would their other goals be better served by heading back toward the city? Finding respite, and perhaps hurrying along the joining of their families.

And there I stood, between them all, urging the pursuit of the Water Tree. Of Arfan's greatest desires, and of course of the glory. Behind it all, my desire to ask my question about the Ashura, and perhaps . . . delay Qimari's marriage as long as possible.

Occasionally, the other tribe's *Maathi* could be found riding aimlessly, eyes cast to the sky, trailing stars and moonlight. I attributed it to his role, as our *Maathi* did much the same. It could have just as much come from the fact he traded in white-joy. The man could have occasionally enjoyed the drug himself, and I had seen what its usage did to the mind.

Something in the way he looked at me, when passing glances over the caravan, stirred a buried memory. But which? Was it the lines of his face I found so familiar, or was I simply making a connection where there wasn't any? Much like when I'd first heard the *Maathi*'s title spoken aloud.

"You're too far gone in your head, my friend." The *Maathi*'s words jarred me from my thoughts.

I looked around and realized that I had wandered toward the front of the caravan.

Arfan's *Maathi* recognized that I still hadn't quite returned to my senses and carried the conversation. "The stars are giving us good omens."

I nodded, still not quite giving him my best attention. That remained on the couple sharing a ride on a single dark horse.

Shareem had somehow coaxed Qimari to join him for a little trot away from the caravan. A red thread had been fastened to the young man's right hand, the ribbon's tail trailing free and long behind him. Qimari's gaze flitted to the length of cord every now and again, but she adjusted her posture to avoid it touching her whenever it drifted close.

"—And that is why you should never linger in the Lap, friend. There is a cost for knowledge. Prophecy more so—ah, are you listening?"

"Yes, *Maathi*." Though I wasn't doing anything of the sort. Instead, I found myself occupied by the fascinating thought of what would happen if Shareem were thrown free from his horse while it galloped at full speed.

Aisha led a splinter group that moved along the side of the main caravan. Several members of the currently conjoined tribe rode ahead, throwing wooden hoops through the air. With every toss, another rider fired a shot through the passing ring.

Someone hurled a hoop hard and high into the air. Several arrows raced ahead to try to pass through it. Many failed. One managed to nick the hoop, but not break it. The impact sent the ring tumbling over itself as it fell, now becoming too hard a target.

For anyone but Aisha.

"—Because some say the longer you stay, that more of the shape of the world begins to change. But no man can pull another out of the pool, or may enter at the same time. It is the way of things. *Ikthab.* Or maybe that is just what the stories say, ah?" The question came punctuated with an elbow ribbing me hard.

"Huh? Ah. Yes, *Maathi*." My eyes hadn't left the scene of falling arrows. Rings dancing through the sky. They'd made a game of it, taking sport and trading coins over whoever failed to call a shot properly, or made it. All of it only reminded me of one thing. Stones in the air—moving, falling, and watching them pass through points I could perfectly pick out.

"That is what they say, though. And you've never seen such a thing as it. The Water Tree is so grand and large a thing that it is bigger than many towers you have ever laid eyes on. They say the water of its pool shall never run out, even if an army of men were to set camp and drink every day for a thousand days. But the touch of man too long there sours the place."

"Does *Shir* Sharaam already know what you're looking for?" Some of my attention had now returned to the *Maathi,* but I still gave the occasional glance toward Aisha, then Qimari.

Shareem brought his horse around to head back toward us. One of his hands reached back to rest along Qimari's thigh, but she swatted the blow away as if on reflex. The *Shir*'s son reined his horse in and they stopped. He shifted halfway in the saddle, giving Qimari a look of sharpened iron.

One of my hands fell to the black bow, and I wondered just how much truth rested in what Arfan had told me. It had been cursed, but the one it chose would never miss a shot.

"Ah, well, yes. But we are all lost looking for things to be found, and in that, truths eventually spill. You see, it is a hard thing keeping secrets from another *Shir,* especially when you are to wind your families together."

I blinked and my hand fell from the weapon. "Huh?"

The *Maathi* repeated what he'd said.

"I think you mean bind the families together, *Maathi,* not wind."

He pursed his lips as he thought on that.

"Bind means to tie together." I motioned in the air as if wrapping an unseen cord around my wrist. "Wind means . . ." I trailed realizing that if I demonstrated the action, it could come off as no different than bind. So I took a thumb and forefinger and pinched a piece of my cloak. I wound it sharp in my grip. "Like that, and you can do it to people too."

He laughed when he understood what I meant. "Then maybe, friend, I meant just that. Have you ever been married?"

I gave him a look that made the answer obvious.

"Well, let me tell you then. There is much of that"—he mimicked my gesture—"in marriage. The winding of one another, and the binding too. Sometimes I think your tongue is a terrible mess of words—all stolen and used wrongly. Then I think in moments like this that it is not so bad."

I frowned. "The Trader's Tongue isn't my . . ." I stopped, realizing that wasn't wholly true. "Well, I suppose it is, but I'm from the Mutri Empire. I can speak Brahmthi too."

The *Maathi* waved a hand to dismiss that. "Ah, I speak as many languages as you are years old, boy. *Tuam appan mainye nae jahn. Ickumainye—*"

I didn't let him finish. "Yes, yes, very impressive. I got it." I repeated the words back in my head, trying to take them apart. "Was that Brahmki?"

He smiled. "*Zho.* First guess, ah?"

"What was that last bit you said?"

"What I was trying to say, friend, before you showed me the rude side of your tongue and interrupted, ah? I was saying you couldn't even tell me your own name if I asked you. Much less one name. *Dohmaine.*"

I understood the last thing he said. A truncation for the words "two names," though it had been said in the more commonly spoken Brahmthi. "I don't have two names."

Both of the *Maathi*'s brows rose at that. "Hm? What happened to your last one, ah? Did someone take it for their own?" He laughed, one hand pressed to his belly. "Someone didn't feel two enough? Maybe they wanted to hide their own name so took yours to run some mischief with, hm?" Another chuckle.

I told him of my upbringing, not bothering to detail what happened to my family or my years spent in Mithu's care. Just the fact I was orphaned by my birth parents.

A heavy hand clapped itself to my shoulders. "Alum Above, I pray for you, friend. That is a hard thing." The *Maathi* gave me a little shake. "I have seen many wonders with my own eyes, and many mysteries are still left to me. One of them is the wonder of why good Alum, Brahm, whoever you choose, friend, leaves children to suffer as they do. There are terrible things out there. Monsters. And there are great treasures. But none so rare and special as children. And still, they come to harm in this world of ours."

He had seen many things, he'd said. Among them, monsters. How true was that, though?

"*Maathi* . . ." I chose my words carefully. "What do you know of the Ashura?"

His eyes widened. "*Zho! Zho.* Now you're thinking like a *Maathi*! Questions, and interesting ones. Yes, yes. I have heard of them. And I know a secret of theirs. Would you like to know?"

I nodded, not wanting to betray by tongue just how badly I wished to hear what he had to say.

"The Ashura are everywhere. They have touched every land, but they always change their names wherever they go. And they change their stories. How can you hurt the thing you do not understand? Understand? Here they are the Ajuura—the *bhaalghul,* but do not mistake, they are the same, ah? They are clever, always—always. They know how to hide their signs. But not well enough. I have made study of these things. And . . ." He broke off to look around in case anyone decided to listen too closely to our conversation.

The *Maathi* leaned toward me, cupping a hand to his mouth. "I have seen them, friend."

I pulled hard on Anedi's reins, bringing the camel to a frustrated stop. "Sorry." I patted him in apology. "You've seen them?"

The *Maathi* gave me a smile halfway between apology and a sheepish "no." "I have seen what they have left behind, I mean. I've seen the signs of their passing. And I tell you that true, friend. No lie, or Alum Above take my voice."

"What did you see?" I knew the answer, but I needed to hear it aloud from him.

I had to.

"Oh, a terrible thing. Not for someone like you to think on. Best to be keeping eyes on pretty girls, ah, and—"

"Please." The word carried all the heaviness of a sunken stone and the hard dryness of gravel.

The *Maathi* looked at me as if finally seeing me for the first time. The long, searching stare. Finally, he sighed, relenting. "I saw the bodies of men and women, some like you, friend. Young. Too young to be found broken and twisted like old dolls. Their eyes . . . Alum, all bleeding. And from the mouth and nose and ears too. Died smiling, like they had been watching a story, or a puppet master." He shook his head.

"Their home, shattered like a summer storm came over. But what storm breaks stones as easy as wood, ah? And the smoke. Alum. The fires burned low, but the smoke—"

"Was red as blood."

The *Maathi*'s lips pressed tight and he nodded. "You know this?"

I bowed my head as well. "I know this. I've seen this."

His hand returned to my shoulder for a hard and reassuring squeeze. "I am very glad they did not take you then, hm? Otherwise I would be needing a new assistant. Then who would be grabbing things for poor old *Maathi* when I am needing them, hm? Boy, fetch me the *Al-Nazhuum*. Fetch my boots."

I laughed. "Fetch your wits?"

"Ah!" The quip struck him later and he narrowed his eyes, raising the riding crop in his hand. "Oi, *zho*! *Zho!*" Each word came punctuated with a sharp swat of the crop. Though the blows had intentionally been struck against my cloak.

"But I am thinking maybe you do not need to worry so much if we see these *bhaalghul* again, ah?"

I wasn't sure about that, and I focused on the Ashura's signs he'd spoken of. Would I see them again, and when? What would I do? But his next words tore me from my thoughts.

"Maybe you too are going to give them trouble one day." He swatted the cloak again. "You are taking yourself to be a *Shir*, and so young, hm?"

I tilted my head, making it a silent but obvious question.

"You don't know? Look at—"

The world lost all trace of golden light, and the coolness only found in shade washed over us. The shadow of a mountain fell across the caravan.

I looked down first, unable to believe the breadth of spreading darkness.

"Alum . . . Above." The two words were so lowly spoken that my own exhalation could have drowned them out. The *Maathi* pressed a hand to his breast. "We've found it. *I* . . . found it."

I turned to see what he had.

The man had done the rumors a grave injustice.

It towered well over any building I had ever seen, and then some. Taking on a height to brush heaven above.

We had done it.

We'd found the Lap. And the Water Tree.

I would come to wish we hadn't.

EIGHTY-FOUR
A Piece of Prophecy

The canopy of the Water Tree took the attention of every person who'd fallen under its shadow, and given the size of the thing, everyone had. Its leaves held every color imaginable, and then some shades that had no names or were pulled from Shaen stories. Some had more than one hue to them. Others, dizzying patterns like the sort found in quilts and tiles. So bright, and yet, it did not bring a soreness to your eyes to look upon.

It held an odd beauty. Almost like a brand new cloak, patchwork-made of the finest materials and all the colors you could source.

The trunk of it so thick a thing it could have held several of the black tower of Mubarath in itself.

There were no words in any language to properly describe the enormity of the tree. Everything else failed—paled to color it full to life. It had been pulled from the brightest and wildest of dreams. A tree that dominated all the eye could see—cast a shadow over the very world.

The canvas of its leaves looked to bleed and blur together—to almost breathe before your eyes, the very air bowing to its presence, and all visible to your gaze.

"How does it stay hidden from anyone. . . ." My words died on my tongue.

The *Maathi* had no answer for me. Instead, a hand crashed to my back, nearly toppling me from my mount. Other hands joined in, and I realized a group of the tribe had ridden up on me.

"*Zho. Zho!*" Each of the words rang like thunder across the sitting silence of the place. Cries of triumph. "Look at what my little hands have found, ah?" The *Maathi* motioned my way. "Clever, and with my knowings and his sharp little eyes, we've done it. Ari has led us to the Water Tree—but, ah, you are not all to be forgetting who started this chase, huh?" The *Maathi* beamed in both self-congratulation, as well as with a father's pride as he stared at me.

Cheers took the caravan with all the force of rolling thunder—one that quickly died as the enormity of the tree further sank in.

Our procession continued with all the somber slowness of those marching toward certain death. No one spoke. And the wind never stirred. It was almost as if the desert itself had respect for the stillness of this place, and for that, refused to move in accordance of its nature.

We crested a dune that gave us a sight of the rest of the Lap. True to the *Maathi*'s description, a crystalline pool spread from the tree's base. Its water held a clearness unfound in anything but glass and brightest diamonds. You'd think me waxing poetic for saying that, but then, even shrouded beneath the expansive canopy, the water's surface glinted like gemstones, all while giving us the truest of views down past its surface.

The *Maathi* had told me that no man could drain its waters. And the longer I looked, the more I believed it.

"Good *Mejai* Arfan is calling. Come now, or you'll lose your chance to see history being made. *Zho. Zho.*" The *Maathi* pulled my sleeve once before riding ahead.

I nudged Anedi to follow, not wanting to fall behind. Not now. A piece of true storybook wonder stood before us, and I would steal my chance if need be to see it for myself. And walk away with a piece of my own prophecy.

"You did it. Praise Alum . . . you did it." Arfan's tone hung between disbelief and the joy of someone fulfilling a long-held dream. His words had been meant as much for the *Maathi* as me. "No weapons, yes?"

The *Maathi* nodded. "And remember, my *Shir,* the questions you—"

Arfan waved him off. "I remember. I have been waiting for this moment longer than some men have been alive. I remember." The merchant king turned to Sharaam and the other tribe's *Maathi.* "I will go first. It was my *Maathi* who led the way and brought us here. It was my chase. My question. My answer." The words were steel-edge sharp and old-stone hard.

A challenge if ever I'd heard one.

Sharaam's hand fell to the curved sword at his hip, and his own *Maathi* reached for a wide knife resting along his thigh.

"No! *Zho. Zho.* Fools!" Arfan's *Maathi* bulled his mount between the trio, one hand in the air as if hoping to stay them with that simple gesture. "You cannot fight within the Laps. Any of them. Should you even bring a weapon into the waters . . ." His eyes went wide and I very nearly saw the man's pulse come to life in his throat. The sweat along his brow did not come from the desert heat—certainly not under the thick of shade over us.

"You will have us out of the Lap with that . . . and worse. There are stories of men who draw blood within a Lap." The *Maathi* swallowed.

Arfan came to his senses first and asked the obvious question on all our minds. "And what happens to them?"

The *Maathi* gave a smile only found in the sickly and dying. "Bad things. Alum preserve me, but I would not speak such horrible things. And not even in the face of Saithaan—*Bhaal,* may god above save me from the devil's stare. But even he, most foul, would turn away at the things I have heard happen to men who fight inside the sanctity of a Lap. This is a place touched by god's hand in the shaping of all things.

"This is a piece of the world before it was split, one of the many spaces left between the folds, forever moving to keep its place. And we are now in that world between worlds. To act wrongly here . . ." The *Maathi*'s gaze fell away from all of us, and that set the tone.

Some must not have believed in stories and their curses. A shrill cry pierced the silence, and we all turned to find a rider from *Shir* Sharaam's tribe—bow in hand—fall from his horse. He writhed like a man in a fit, screaming like one freshly cut to the bone. But soon, his protests died and we returned to the silence of a grave.

Fitting, as the man no longer moved and adopted the stillness of the dead.

Yet no one else had laid a finger on him.

Hands fell from weapons and everyone readopted the quiet that had hung around us.

Arfan looked at the various men of both tribes, then the one who had been struck down by the unseen hand of God . . . or perhaps another power. "There might be a better way to settle this."

Shir Sharaam, to his credit, bowed his head in agreement. And so lots were drawn. I found myself included, thankfully owing to my aid in finding the tree. Which meant I would get my answer.

I would ask of the Ashura.

Arfan took the lead, stopped just before reaching the pool to dismount. One of his hands went to the air as a signal for the rest of us to stop.

"No one will take a drink until I have left with my answer." The merchant king stripped out of his boots and his robe, leaving them on the bank before wading into the waters.

Arfan walked through the shallows until the water came to his chest, but he didn't slow. Eventually he reached the trunk of the Water Tree. One of his hands pressed against the bark and he leaned close, much like someone whispering into the ear of a lover.

The *Maathi* quivered beside me—a leaf in gale, visibly vibrating with excitement.

I watched Arfan, but no storybook magic came to life before me. So my gaze slowly filtered up to the canopy of countless colors. Some from a painter's palette, the rest born of a child's imagination—combinations and shades that should never have been possible. Then, something happened.

One of the leaves fell.

I watched it drop, a feather-weighted stone. So slow a fall. Giving me all the time in the world to track it and take in its shape.

It had the color I'd once found in a box of coins. The shade of brightness that gives birth to greed and envy. The better burnished gold of treasure. Dreams.

And desire. It was as if the leaf had been shaped from the metal itself. It tumbled until it touched the surface of the pool upon which it furled in on itself as if set ablaze by an unseen fire. Curls of black smoke took to the air and, eventually, the leaf turned to nothingness.

"Too long. He has been in there too long." I realized that the *Maathi*'s shaking had not been eager anticipation but the frenzied hold of fear. "He must leave. Too long!" His hands cupped to his mouth and the cry went far and loud. "*Mejai* Arfan! My *Shir*! You must leave!"

But Arfan didn't hear the man. And he did not leave.

Soon, another leaf broke free from above and made its slow fall down. It had all the colors you'd find on a desert hawk. A brush of brown, found in tanned hide, over pale moon white. Touches of black as dark as starless night. It twisted until it touched the ground. This leaf did not cinder-smoke and burn away. Its color bled from it as if it had only held to a painter's touch, and soon nothing but red remained. Then, that too faded and the leaf was but dust.

The *Maathi* leapt from his camel and ran to the shore. "*Shir* Arfan! You must get out of the pool. You have been in too long. Please!"

I followed him, coming within a dozen feet of the water's surface before a pressure fell on me like being cast to the depths of the ocean. A blanket, bound tight around me, stole the sound from my ears. It was all I could do to remain upright. The quietness of the Lap loudened around me.

You might think that a foolish thing to say, but it is true. Such an intensity of silence it drubbed at me, threatening to push its way through flesh and sinew until it touched the marrow of me. And once there, would sit to still me whole until nothing remained in thought and heart. Mute of mind and soul. It promised to silence me in full.

I had only felt close to that way once before. My stomach knotted with the urge to retch up everything I had ever eaten.

"Ari?" The call of my name, and I remembered it then.

It seemed so long ago that someone had used it.

"Ari!" A hand fell on my shoulders, and I remembered the feeling of being touched. Once a warmth that I had known even against my bare skin. "Ari!" The world shook at the sound of it, and I followed. "Ari!"

The first breath came ragged, as much as an edgeless thing could be, and brought about a coldness in my lungs that shouldn't have been possible in the desert. "Qimari?" I heaved, trying to steady myself. "What happened?"

She took my chin in her hands, tilting my head one way, then the other. Concern touched her eyes, but whatever fondness she'd once held for me remained clean from her gaze.

I understood why a moment later.

Shareem lingered paces behind her, watching with the measured stare of a hyena eyeing a prize.

And the treasure he had in mind was certainly not me.

"You went still like you'd taken a blow to the head. I couldn't even tell if you were breathing. What happened?" Qimari pulled her hands from my face as if they'd been touched by fire. Her eyes flickered to one side, suddenly remembering Shareem, and she took one careful step away from me.

"Nothing, nothing. I'm fine." I brushed myself off and returned my attention to the pool.

Arfan had reached the shore, where the *Maathi* continued urging him to leave. Moments later, the merchant king exited the water. "Thank you, friend." He clasped the *Maathi*'s hand. "You have made an old dream of mine come true. Whatever it is you need for any of your hunts, tell me, and I will see it done."

The *Maathi* bowed his head. "Of course, *Mejai* Arfan. Of course. Thank you. I have a thousand questions to ask you. Come, come. *Zho*." He beckoned the merchant king to follow as they headed away.

Everyone kept their eyes on Arfan.

I did not.

My gaze remained on the tree. What had he seen? Why did the *Maathi* call him back so soon?

There was only one way to find out.

My lot allowed me to go second, something that had earned me Shareem's baleful glare during the choosing, and his father's still-silent condemnation.

I headed to the pool and undid my boots. My staff and bow remained hanging from my saddle, leaving me free from concern about weapons in the presence of the tree. The first touch of water washed a gentle coolness against the skin of my feet. I waded in, letting all the tension and warmth bleed from my body. My lips hadn't dried in the heat, but they'd come close enough that I knew taking a sip would alleviate much of the problem.

So I did. And it carried a sweetness. The floral smoothness of rose petals steeped in drink. And the sharp biting savoriness that comes from the first taste of a cold citrus fruit.

"Ari?" The name fell—a distant call, almost as if said in dream, and just as much through water. A trick of the mind. I paid it no heed as I neared the trunk of the Water Tree.

Something shifted along its bark. The air shimmered as if strung with beads of golden sand in light, only to shine back to me. I blinked, trying to dispel the illusion. But it did not fade. The skin of the tree rippled and slowly shaped itself as a young woman.

Her face had the pale smoothness of ivory. Her hair, ashen strands of ivy. Her body pressed itself free from the form of the tree to reveal the curves of someone who had reached full womanhood, but still held to a youth found in those just a few years older than me. The lines of her face had been carved to hold angular beauty as much as the softness of childhood innocence. Nowhere was this clearer than in her eyes.

They were pools their own of shadow-cast jade. No. They were hard-born ice, shaped grayness that had then been touched with a promise of blue found in sapphires. A lie. They were then the yellow-washed browns of tiger's eye. Amber bright, fading fast, then sparked to life as golden-bled citrine.

I fell entranced and lost all thought as I watched her eyes shift, no set look to them.

"Ari!" The name again. An echo of something far behind and forgotten. There was only the tree, and my standing in the waters.

"What is it you seek, castaway flame?" She spoke with the softness of spring's first breath passing over freshly brightened green. Grass that has just given up winter's hold.

"Answers." My throat had a hoarseness it should not have given how recently I'd drank.

"You are but a castaway piece of fire, thrown free from a forgotten whole only to be much the same—forgotten. Born and born again. Forever-lost to the cycle of time, and of birth." Her words held no mockery. Only the weary sorrow of someone watching a tragic play they had seen once before, and knew how it would end.

"No riddles, please. I want to know how to find the Ashura. I'm already far behind their trail. What happens next?"

The woman inside the tree gave me a smile. It held sympathy and tiredness. A grandmother's patient smile. One given to comfort someone in the midst of their hurt. "You already know the answer to some of what you seek. But you are here for pieces of the future, and that I can grant you."

Hope blossomed within me like fresh fanned fire. I fed it with the knowing that I stood right here, in the middle of a story—of magic made before me and hung just moments from getting the answers I sought.

"I see you caught at crossroads betwixt days past and days to come. Lost among a world hidden-hung between the moon and the sun. Whisper thin, the blood-red cord, to bind you hand-in-hand, reborn flame and pale-moonflower."

I didn't understand a thing she said, but I could not pull away. Something flitted at the corners of my vision and I tracked a falling leaf. It was the once-white of fresh cream, now touching gray—darkening the farther it fell. Leaf touched sand, ran red as blood, and then was no more.

"A circle of crows all around you, scattered far from the ruins of the broken tower."

"Ari!" The name came again. I remembered it. It had belonged to someone once long ago. A sparrow. He had run long into the night, not so far a distance, and shortly still through the streets of Keshum. He had been swept up into the care of another sparrow, a man named Mithu.

"You chase a wolf in waiting, seeking the same prize you do, and you ever fail to catch him. The man in red is your shadow, your past, and your future. Shaped you to falter, folly, and to fail. I see more things still. Do you wish to know?"

Nothing she said made sense, so I hoped the next words would. I had to know. "Yes. The Ashura, damn you!"

"Ari!" The voices now mingled, but I had not the ears for them.

Another leaf fell, and it was the dark of crow. Then another, this the color of twilight darkness, and all the blues you could hope to find in the deep late of night.

"Bound for glory, and in glory bound, to take up the call all brave men seek, and to answer it still. Once in desperate need. Twice to quell the shadow's greed. To catch and tame a southern wind and rush to treasure's sight. And fall full-fast in righting the wrong you thought first right. To hold and let loose the kind man's wrath, and pay its price."

If this had in any way been a normal place, I would have fallen into the fullest of my anger by now at the riddles—the lack of clarity. But no. A piece of me had been silenced—stilled. And I stood nearly mute, waiting—listening.

Next came the leaf black as raven's wing. It broke free from the canopy and sank. And upon touching the ground, it too turned a shade of red from night-mare and demon's fire smoke. Another followed. This leaf, shadowed honey, soon drenched another color, the drowning red of rose.

"I see you walk in the liar's shadow and set free that which must be bound still, and kept silent. To ride aback the man's eagle through storm and lightning, and lay low that which must stay standing. And divide—break, shatter, and cut the bond of brothers that must remain steadfast—true."

This time the leaf that fell held the colors of sunburst orange, so bright-enrosened you'd think it a piece of flame pressed flat. And it carried just as much the black of rich tar. The leaf struck the ground, splitting in half along its top as if torn by unseen hands. Then it faded as fast as the other leaves had.

"Ari, too long have you—" The voice fell to that distant thought-held place where it would soon fade to nothingness.

And I was resolved to keep it there. No distractions. Not now.

The irritation gave me something to draw on—speak with, and I brought it free to mouth. "What about the Ashura? How do I find them? How do I stop them? *Please.*" The last was the broken plea of a child still kept whole in the hold of broken glass-sharp memory, and all the pain it continued to bring.

"You find your answers beyond a pillar of flame—born from moon-full sunny skies. One accursed falls, and another takes its place. Bound in collar bright blood-red. Betrayed by silence, plagued by stillness heavy, know the last of them, first new to be, by his signs to come."

The newest leaf broke free faster than the ones before. This carried the red born of blood and beets, a carmine that shone through the whole of it. It, too, died.

"You will walk old paths, best left forgotten, and left to be walked anew, to once again break the wheel that has gone unbroken. You will dance, flame in breast, and light in hand, against the shadows that Taint all men. To hold in a heart a story, best left unspoken, but then remembered, and give voice to the last of ten things all men must know. To hear a song silver bright and sweet. Terrible and tremulous. To fix once and for all the sins of the son, the father—and him forgotten—the long-lost brother."

"Answer me, burn you! Tell me something I can use!" My hands clenched, nails dug into the soft flesh of my palms with a force that could soon break skin.

The lady of the Water Tree did not care for my demands. Or my temper. She continued with all the cool calmness of the pool in which she resided. "I see you taking the heart of a prince, not a prince, only to take the one of a prince seeking to be more than one. Steady-handed, cold as ice. And you will do so once again, to take the blackest of all hearts there can be. To take a prince electing to be a king.

"The Ashura. Koli!" I brought my face to within an inch of hers, my breath hot as coal smoke and old fires not forgotten. "I have to find him."

"I see a flame born in heart and passed to hand, only to be lost again to the hands of another. And then a flame born in breath to be taken by you, kept where yours has gone from."

"No. More. Riddles!"

Now the leaves fell in full—no longer one at a time. One, the color of wolf's gray and touched with golden rings bright. Then the one white as moonbeams pale, and pearl-set shimmering. Another the royal red and golden bright of noblest blood.

"—And take a piece of shadow to call your own, to then sacrifice it to a flame that knows no end in hunger. You will long-lost wander in search of that you seek, and—"

"Ari!" The name came with the weight and echo of every voice I'd ever heard. A flash of Mithu's, then a man who'd become a teacher and a friend—Vathin. I heard as much of Radi, as I then did Aram. Rishi Ibrahm, and Aisha. Qimari and Alwi.

It weighed on me and my anger touched the surface now. I tore myself from the grip of the maiden's words. "What?"

The whole of our joint caravan had gathered at the shore, calling to me.

More leaves rained down around me and I realized what had happened. How long had I been lost in the stupor of hearing her speak?

"Come back. Too long have you been in the waters. Too long. Come! Back!" My friend, the *Maathi,* beckoned me.

I looked back to the woman in the tree and water.

She gave me a smile better fit for someone relieved in dying. The weak and tired grin, finally finding peace in silence and stillness.

Enough of a sign for me to leave.

I waded away from her, slowly coming to shore.

The *Maathi*'s hands took me at the shoulders and he hauled me out of the water. "What were you thinking, boy, ah? *Zho.*" He shook his head. "Too long were you inside. Too. Long! Do you know what you risked? No. Of course not. I am speaking to a boy, not a man." His words fell apart into broken strings of some languages I knew, then several I did not. Then . . . several more.

I couldn't parse much of what I heard, but I didn't need to know much to understand it amounted to a great deal of artful profanity.

Arfan brushed the man aside with a measure of gentleness and the weary impatience of a man who had been waiting to speak. "We will talk later of what you learned." It was not a question.

I nodded.

"Good." Arfan turned *Shir* Sharaam. "You and your son are next to enter the waters."

The other leader nodded. "Then my *Maathi.* And yours."

The merchant king grunted. "Then let it be. *Ikthab.* I have learned what I needed. Ari, my tent." Arfan turned and headed toward the new and larger shelter that had been set up for him while I'd been in the pool.

I followed him inside and took a seat on a pile of cushions.

Arfan sat opposite me, watching me with all the careful calculations and intensity as he'd done when first meeting me back in Keshum. "Do you take tea?"

The question caught me off guard. "Yes."

He lifted a kettle that looked fashioned from clay or stone, a thick rag wrapped around the top of it. Dark tea filtered out into a clay cup. Arfan then pulled out a disc the shade of honey-washed amber. "Palm sugar?" He waggled the wheel.

I inclined my head.

He drew a curved knife, blade longer than my hand, from a place along his hip. Its edge parted some of the sugar, letting it fall into the hot contents of a cup. Arfan then pushed the drink toward me before busying himself in doing the same for his own beverage. He stirred the contents with his blade before wiping it clean and sheathing it. "Ari . . ." He took a tip, eyeing me over the rim of the cup.

I did not drink, and waited to hear what would come next.

"You asked of her, and she answered."

Another bow of my head.

"You stayed a long time, Ari. Longer than most men ever have. The ones who would not risk a madness, at least. Prophecy can weigh on a mind. Some, it breaks. The thinking on it, trying to understand it, it is like pulling on all the woven strings in the world. Every time you tug, you pull on others, unknown—unseen. The threads are all connected, according to my *Maathi*. And when you begin to tear one, the rest fray too. I'm sure it is already falling heavy on you, hm?"

In truth, I hadn't reflected much on what she had said. Some of it had already turned to cotton fluff in mind. Cold realization bled through me and I seized the candle and the flame, bringing it back to help hold what clarity I could. The words the maiden in the pool had spoken to me returned.

Some of them, at least.

"Ah, there it is. Too much of a thing, Ari. Like the hunger for gold. Still your problem, hm? Too eager. Too quick. Too hungry for knowing today." Arfan took another sip, and the look he gave me said I should follow suit.

So I did. The tea had cooled just enough not to sear my lips. Black, with a hint of something close to lemon in its taste, made all the brighter by the sugar.

"What did she tell you?" Still the careful look in eye as he watched me over his next sip.

I told him what I could remember, leaving out my questions of the Ashura. Not that she had answered any of them.

"You realize she is not an oracle or a seer, at least in the storied sense? She does not give you answers to what you wish for. She reads you like some read the omens in the sky. Only, she does the true reading of things. As true as true a thing can be. And comes to see what path you put yourself on, and the rewards . . . or consequences. And there is a cost for prophecy, Ari. Always."

I did not drink further upon hearing that. "Like what?"

Arfan laced his fingers together and looked down, a sigh escaping his lips. "Heavy ones, according to the stories. I have heard them, and I am not so sure I believe them all. I hope the ones we pay will be small. But we will pay them all the same."

I finally found it in me to finish draining my cup, and once I had, my mind turned to the question I'd been holding off from voicing. "What did she tell you?"

Arfan arched a brow, the curve of his mouth breaking to one side in a lopsided grin. "You do not know when to stop poking at secrets, hm?"

I returned the expression. "Never."

He laughed, setting down his cup. "She told me that a little bird would show me the way to treasure and trouble. That they will break many things that have gone unbroken for so long a time most men do not remember. And they will bring me in hand the things I desire most. More than any gold I've come to lose in my ventures and gambles. A horse to bet on, if they weren't a bird. And will tame a southern wind in my service, bringing me a new power I can only dream of. That is something to be sure. For my dreams are large, Ari. Very large." The smile now grew to carry all the cunning of the fox I often thought him to be.

His prophecy had been so short, but knowing Arfan and how powerful his wants were, why not stay longer? Something I asked.

He smiled, a fox's cunning once again. "You heard *Maathi*'s warning, and saw a man die from no cause—here in this world between worlds. Am I so much a fool to ignore that advice?"

Then it struck me. "You . . . counted on me—my curiosity to keep me in there longer, and then—" *Brahm's blood, this!* Our conversation together, where he had just gleaned more about me and my fate, perhaps, all while in his service. A way to get more answers without putting himself at risk.

Clever. And still beating me at my own game.

Arfan smiled. "It is time to return to your duties. My *Maathi* will want to talk to you, and I still wish you to glean what you can from my people. More than ever, I will need it."

I thought on that, and then the white-joy he had been slipped. Bringing up the vices of a man as powerful as Arfan did not seem wise. But another thing came to mind. "Because of Qimari's marriage to Shareem?"

The smile slipped from Arfan's face finally, leaving behind only something old-stone made and just as flat—emotionless. "And what do you know of that past what we've already spoken of?"

I shrugged. "I know there's a blood feud between you and *Shir* Sharaam's tribe. This might quell that . . . at the cost of putting your daughter in their hands."

The knife came back to Arfan's hands. So fast the movement that I hadn't tracked it. Its edge now rested against the lip of the clay cup that sat firmly in the merchant king's other hand. He raked the knife slowly along the drink, slicing free a piece of hardened earth with the ease of parting butter. Then again. Soon, the cup bore countless notches.

"There are things to be concerned with, Ari, that are not my daughter. Do you understand?" The knife took another piece of clay. And another. "You do not understand a great many things, and you do not understand this one. Do not presume to."

I'm not sure what caused the rapid change in behavior, but I had my suspicions—

and my fear. The white-joy. Had he fallen further than I imagined to its hold? Was I in service now to a madman—as temperamental and quick to betray me as Mithu had been? I swallowed and tried to keep a more level tongue in mouth.

. . . I failed.

"I'm not presuming anything. These are facts. You're trading her away to settle an old score. But have you ever once thought of what she wants? Or, do only your needs matter? I'm sure *Shir* Sharaam's son is a very good man."

The cup struck the carpeted floor, spilling what remained of its contents. Arfan had bolted upright, the knuckles of one hand going near white against the hilt of the knife. "Out." It was not the cry of a man held in the whole of his rage. But the quiet whisper of someone holding back a sword-sharp fury. Full-toothed and edged—meant to cut.

I bowed, my back keeping to a stiffness born of my own anger. My eyes never left his as I retreated.

And Arfan never broke our stare until I reached the rear of the tent.

Just before I left, I watched the old *Shir* pull something from his robes. A small vial of clouded fluid. A few drops splashed across each eye, and a heavy sigh left him.

I knew what white-joy did to men. And what it had once done to my own adoptive father. Would Arfan soon go much the same way?

And would I have to kill him before he decided to kill me?

I stripped out of my cloak in the tent that had been set for me. Shola had already made himself a bed in the folds of my blanket. I moved around him without disturbing his sleep. My staff and bow were left to one side, as well as my travel sack. I unbound the Arasmus blade from where it rested on my hip, stopping as I realized that I hadn't gone unarmed into the waters.

But nothing had happened. No curse upon me. No ill fortune.

Just a piece of superstition then? There had certainly been those just as much as there had been moments of real magic.

My thoughts turned from that worry to trying to make sense of what I had learned from the Water Tree.

I lit a candle and found little sleep.

Instead, I spent the night with fire.

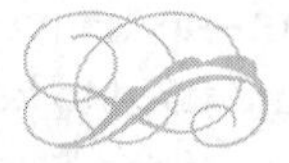

EIGHTY-FIVE
WEIGHING HEAVY

We did not linger at the Water Tree long. Only a handful of days.

Days I could have used to pursue the Ashura, had I better clue how to go about it. But the maiden had given me little there. My best hope remained in setting off in the direction of the rumors the tinker had told me. But Arfan could not be convinced to do that. Others wished to approach the legendary tree.

So Arfan allowed enough time for everyone who wished to risk a visit to do so. We replenished our water and gave everyone some much needed rest, and took the time to allow for more conversation to break out between the two tribes.

This did not help things.

Spilling blood may have been forbidden in the Lap, but apparently blackening a few eyes and knocking some teeth loose fell within what was permitted. The laws of violence often aren't clear. And many men will use this liberally to their advantage.

And their pleasure.

Eventually, we left, riding toward Iban-Bansuur.

I hoped I hadn't set us too far back behind the Ashura's trail.

I stayed by Gushvin for the first few days of the journey. Trading my own stories that had been growing about me for ones the tinker knew. Some of the world at large, some of his own people. Their history, teaching me more of their silent language, and eventually, what stories he had of the Ashura.

He told me that he had heard the Ashura chased bad omens as much as they brought some of their own. They were responsible for bad weather and worse harvests in some parts of the world. Things I'd already heard attributed to them, but I put little stock in. Gushvin mentioned that some of the Ashura were cursed to wander the world eternally, each in search of something they could never have.

I liked that theory more, only, it didn't sit right with me. If they were forced to move in that manner, it would make organizing all but impossible. But they did. And they had.

At least, eight of them had. All of my travels so far still hadn't brought to light the slightest clue as to the ninth Ashura. But all the stories confirmed that much at least: There was a total of nine. And the only one I could truly recall was the man with golden eyes and the smile of a wolf.

Koli.

Every time I tried to rack my mind for the other faces from that night, they blurred into horrible distortions. Like paintings that hadn't dried, come quick under rain. Soon enough, faces became smears only holding to a piece of their former selves.

I remembered only the faces of the broken. The beaten. And the bloody.

And the fires, of course.

I'd asked Gushvin why he thought they did the things they did.

To that, the tinker had no answer, saying that the question was the same as asking why it rained sometimes, and others, it did not.

Eventually I left to find Arfan's *Maathi*, and he and I spoke of the Water Tree. I had been expecting this talk.

I told him all I could recall.

He made as much sense of it as I had, which was to say, very little. Instead, he told me more of the history of the Water Tree. Much of it aligning with what Arfan had to say. That terrible costs came from lingering too long in the waters. And that no man had yet avoided paying them.

Not what a young man, who had survived all his own foolishness to date, wanted to hear. I pressed him for his piece of prophecy then, and he told me all of it.

"I am to find greatness still. And this pleases me. Not in the way you are thinking, of course. I do not covet fame—no. What I am seeking is the things themselves, but you see, she did not tell me I would become great. No. She said I would find the greatness. Many of them. This leads me to thinking that I will find the treasures I still seek—all the wonders of the world are waiting for me. And that a small bird will bring my glory, and steal a greater one for itself. History will remember my doings, but remember the bird all the greater."

"Do you know what any of it means?"

The *Maathi* inclined his head. "Oh, of course. I would not be *Maathi* if I didn't have the quickest of thinking." He rapped his knuckles on his head. "But more importantly, I know the secret of some prophecy." The man curled an index finger, beckoning me to lean closer.

I did.

"Much of it is up to you to shape, ah? And most of destiny is how you choose to make it—shape it. Prophecy lies in this." He flexed his hand.

I stared, unsure of what he meant by that.

Only when he did the motion again did I realize he meant for me to emulate him.

I opened my palm, but he placed a finger atop it before I could close it.

"Ah. Ah." The *Maathi* traced a small circle along my skin before slowly following the many creases that rested there. "There are many roads for a man to take. But, in the many of them, he is free to choose one. *Zho. Zho.* So choose. Never let someone make you think that you do not have all the roads you do. Even prophecy."

I looked down at the many lines he'd run his finger over, taking them in after a fashion I hadn't before. Mahrab had taught me how to give things a better focus and clarity. I gave them then to my hand. Though it brought nothing special back to me. So I turned to questions instead. "Then why did you seek out the prophecy at all?"

He smiled at that. "*Zho.* Ah, the right question now. Good. Good." The *Maathi* rubbed a hand along his chin as he thought. "Well, my friend. Magic is real. And even if a man wishes to make his own path in life, there is never too much harm in getting some help. Sometimes prophecy gives you something more than directions."

I wondered where he had gotten the idea of directions from, because I had received nothing of the sort.

"Sometimes, they offer a man hope. And that is something always worth keeping to. So I know I am to find treasures still."

"*How* do you know that?" I'd finally taken my hand back from the *Maathi*'s grip.

"Ah, friend"—he held up a finger—"after talking to you, little bird, I have come to find the Lap, have I not? I have a feeling we will find many things still. Like this wonderful sight."

Then the *Maathi* pulled a roll of parchment from a satchel along his camel. The same image I'd seen before. The moon and sun close in embrace, leaving only a ring of flame around the darkened smaller astral body. "It will come. And I have the piece for that as well, from the Water Tree, of course. That much she was clear on. Soon, just a set of days. Mayhaps shortly after we reach Iban-Bansuur. And then you and I will dance in the shadow of the sun and see what more magics await us."

A part of me liked that. The sense of wonder, and the adventure. It reminded me of the stories I'd come to hold close in heart. Of Brahm, Tarun Tharambadh, and the other legends I'd grown to hear of.

"But your prophecy, friend, is a special one. You lingered in waiting too much. Too long. So you have come away with much to think on, and I am wondering how much will come true. What we can shape, hm?" A frown broke across his face. "And what costs there might be to pay, you lingered too long." The last words seemed meant for him, but they left me thinking on them.

I wonder that too, Maathi. I wonder that too.

A darkened shaft soared along the edge of my vision, taking me from the conversation with the *Maathi*. The arrow sailed high overhead, no clear target in sight. Even still, I made out the shape of its trajectory. It struck where I had imagined it would, sinking into the sand until only the fletchings remained visible. Another followed it, striking just beside the first. Then a third.

Much of Qimari's face remained obscured by the hood of her robes, but I recognized her regardless. She drew and fired exactly in the manner Aisha had been teaching me: a finger straight to point where she meant to target—then the smooth and fluid motions that sent arrow through air.

Shareem rode beside her, speaking something too far away and low for me to have hope of hearing. She had no mind for him, though. And the stiff set of her body told me that the two had had a row. As much as she had no thought for him, he seemed to have less for her unspoken boundaries. The young man reached out, taking hold of her sleeve, giving it a light tug. She brushed it off in a quick and callous motion that said more than words could.

The *Shir*'s son did not take kindly to that. His light grip now turned to one of steel.

The hood fell from Qimari's face, and I saw the tight set of her jaw. Her eyes narrowed in a short-lived wince.

Shareem had hurt her. Perhaps still was.

My knuckles throbbed against the wood of the black bow, and one finger pointed toward the middle of Shareem's back.

"*Zho!*" Fingers clamped tight to my collar and pulled me from the waking dream. "What are you doing? Do you see danger? Or a hare?" The *Maathi* looked at me, not to where I'd aimed.

I blinked, realizing that in the stupor of my anger, I'd taken the black bow in hand and nocked an arrow. So quick a thing, and all ready to loose it into Shareem. The action hadn't been born of conscious thought. Something subtler than that. A quiet pull. Almost natural.

It had little to do with my dislike of Shareem. I confess it does not sound that way, but it's the truth. Then, it was more a hidden urging. But from where?

When I looked around, I saw nothing but the passing breath across the desert. Low whispered air brushing along the surface of loose and golden grains. A gentle flow of things.

I released my hold and stowed the arrow back in the quiver. The bow followed. "Sorry, *Maathi*, I think . . . yes, I saw something. But it was gone just as quick."

His lips pursed and he nodded as if understanding. "Mm. The desert plays tricks on the eyes of many, friend. Don't let it take you too much here, ah?" He jabbed a finger at my heart. "You stare too long at the sun, and you see many odd things." A toothy grin punctuated that.

I returned it. "Like a tree larger than anything in the world—a canopy of all the colors you can imagine?"

He snorted. "And sometimes you have to believe in things before they can be seen. This, I know. *Ikthab*. It is written. It will be."

As the journey to Iban-Bansuur continued, the prophecy weighed on me heavier than before. It was written.

It would be.

How much of that would come to be true?

And what of the Ashura? Had I squandered my chance to find them?

I would come to find out.

EIGHTY-SIX

Shade, Storm, and Knives

Both *Maathis* had foretold of a dangerous sandstorm, a thing I'd only heard stories about.

I didn't know how they could predict something like that, and I received no answer. But my question had drawn the attention of the other *Maathi*. The one who had given Arfan a vial of white-joy.

He turned his gaze on me, the sun bringing out the tones of yellow in his light brown eyes. "You have been riding with *Shir* Arfan for how long now?"

I answered him.

"Not long enough to be in the tribe, then." Another of his odd looks passed over me—taking me in whole as much as going through me. It was the stare of someone deep in thought as they pored over a book and had no room for anything else in their periphery.

"And since coming into it, you have, by the words of *Shir* Arfan's *Maathi*, come to help him find the Water Tree, a thing many men spend their whole lives dreaming of. What did you learn from the maiden in the pool?" The question came on the edge of a knife—so sharply said that it would certainly cut me if I answered.

So I deigned not to.

If my reticence bothered the *Maathi*, he did not show it. Instead, the curve of his mouth revealed amusement. "Very well, little sparrow, keep your secrets. But I will tell you mine." He took a breath, holding it deep in chest before letting it go. "I will have the greatest chase for my heart's desire I could hope for.

In the end, I will hold my prize in hand, after many years of chasing. As bright and shining as diamond. A treasure worth my attention and passion. One I've long sought. And then it will be taken from me. By a castaway flame and lightning. By memory. And by a tale." The man's smile turned thin, into the frown of someone who had already lost something dear.

A shadow of something else showed across the *Maathi*'s face. The mask slipping and revealing a truth beneath. A shine of eye, wolf in smile. But it faded just as fast.

The sun pricked my eyes and I winced through the brightness, remembering what the other *Maathi* had warned me of: that the desert brought out odd things to see. And I saw them now.

So I focused on the question on my mind. "What do you think it means, *Maathi*?"

"That I will have to guard my prize . . . very carefully—ruthlessly. And, fortunate for me, I am well skilled in that." The smile he gave me was no kind thing. "Come, we should find shade, and water. There are old cliffs we will reach shortly. And the storm will come on us soon."

He had been right.

It came with the drub of distant drums, rolling forward with a blanket of dark sand risen to a curtain that shrouded much of the horizon. It threatened to wash over everything, and leave nothing behind.

But Sharaam's *Maathi* had spoken truly about what shelter we'd find, and so we led our caravan down into a recess in the sandy valley. Most of the storm would blow overhead, we'd been told, but a network of caverns ran through the base of the cliffs we could take better refuge in. Tenting and canvas would be rigged as best as possible to keep what sand we could from filtering into the tunnels.

So we staged the campsite for the duration of the sandstorm.

I had managed to get a peek at the oncoming weather before we sealed ourselves in, and my look revealed something I hadn't expected to see. Violent bands of brightest blue and starlight-touched lavender raked the sky. Lightning, without the rain, and none of the thunder but for the rising howl of wind.

Candles had been lit, and men and women went about seeing to the camels and horses. Others set about preparations for meals to come.

Shir Sharaam gathered his own cohort of men, including his *Maathi,* and headed off with them all in tow. Likely for a private meeting.

Arfan had done the same.

That left Qimari, Aisha, Shareem . . . and myself.

Not exactly the group I wanted to be left alone with, for obvious reasons.

I decided to fetch Shola, giving me a perfect excuse to distance myself from the trio.

Shola, at least, would make remarkable company for the duration of our stay. And I could be mostly assured of his disposition toward me. I could always coax him with an extra portion of something tasty if need be. He currently kept himself curled in a tight bundle, his front paws cupping the sides of his face. So I moved with the utmost care to ensure he remained restfully asleep until I brought him to where I'd make bed for the night.

I set my blankets and roll before placing Shola atop them. Then I settled my staff, bow, quiver, and most of my belongings. Girad, one of Arfan's riders, and nearly as skilled a shot as Aisha, had offered me use of a lit candle so I could kindle one of my own, using its light to read by.

Shareem and Qimari walked close enough to be hand in hand, but their fingers were not laced together. Despite their proximity to one another, a world of distance visibly hung between them. Enough to be felt.

Alwi and Baba remained close by, and I realized Qimari had kept them at hand to be something of a buffer between her and Shareem's boldness.

But it wasn't my problem. Or, I tried to convince myself of that. I brought my attention back to the sheet I'd pulled to study. The rhyme Immi had written for me in order to learn the bindings. The more I stared at it, the less I came away with. But the light before me brought me to bring one to life inside me, and soon there were two candles and flames.

I kept the one in mind as my primary focus while thinking on the bindings.

"There are ten bindings all men must know.
One for tak.
Another roh.
As above.
So below.
Ten bindings for the enlightened to learn.
Start with whent.
Then go to ern.
A way for the wisened to shape this world,
to how they yearn.
Ten bindings answer the wise man's call.
Stand firm with ahn.
Push danger with ahl.
Ten bindings given to mankind's care.
Stay for wyr.
And travel ehr.
There are only eight bindings for man to choose.
The last two are ones he ought never use."

I knew their meanings, even if I couldn't make sense of them. I'd seen them work. Some of them, at least. I went over the first few lines in my head. *There are ten bindings all men must know. One for tak. Another roh. As above. So below.* The rhyme stuck, and I repeated it, choosing to stick only to those until I'd committed them to memory.

"Ari?"

I slipped from that thoughtful place and shifted to face Aisha.

She had stripped out of her robe and riding clothes, wearing something softer than I'd seen her in before. Nearly the same outfit as Qimari's the night she had decided to get . . . cordial with me. Which, you can imagine, raised an alarm within my chest.

I was young, a boy, foolish—and two of those things more often than not are the same; I will leave you to figure out which I mean—and rather inexperienced in a great many areas of life.

She wore a top that hung loose around her arms, leaving parts of them bare, and letting me see through the fine mesh of shadowed gold. The color of it complimented her skin. Her pants were of the same fabric and shade. All of this was accentuated by the shining bright metal along her throat, wrists, and ankles.

Aisha had never dressed in anything other than the toughest of riding clothes. Made to travel, endure any of the harshness of the desert.

Her hair fell loose in ringlets and the glint of burnt orange pulled my attention to the folded copper bands she'd layered through it.

Much like Radi.

"You . . ." I didn't have the words.

She arched a brow, waiting for me.

"You look different."

Her mouth pulled into a slow and lazy smile, more to one side than the other. "I suppose that's true." She nudged a corner of my bedroll with a foot, asking for silent invitation.

I patted the spot and gave it to her.

Aisha sat cross-legged, one of her hands going to her left hip to slip something free. She held it in both palms almost as if meaning to present it to me as a gift. The sheath, curved and polished ivory. The blade's hilt looked to be ebony set with gold. When she pulled the knife free, the whole of its form caught and held the nearby candlelight, sending a soft orange through its silver.

"Is . . . this the part of the story where you stab me in the dark cave, and no one finds out about it?" I managed a smile.

Aisha breathed out a light laugh. "No, Ari. Take it. Hold it." She passed it my way, handing over the sheath as well.

I took them both in hand. The hilt had warmth to it, some from Aisha's grip, but some that belonged to the weapon itself. Mayhaps from all its time in the desert and heat, it'd come to simply keep some of that. Or, it could have been something in the wood. I couldn't say, but I knew I felt it.

A smoothness had taken the wood that I didn't expect to find there. Something as much done in the initial shaping of the grip, as well as all the hands that had held it for so long a time. In the end, all that remained was the passing lines of their touch. It felt like it had been made to sit in the shape of a specific person's hand.

Just not mine.

One of my thumbs skirted atop the knife's edge. It had been honed to a razor's kiss of sharpness, so cutting a thing that I knew should I lose my caution, my thumb would be sliced well down to the bone. This blade may have been made that way, but Aisha's diligent hands kept it that way.

The sheath had been fashioned to complement the knife's dark hilt. The ivory showed no sign of the desert against its grain. No discoloration. All holding to the shade it likely had the day it was shaped. A day long ago.

"How many hands has this been passed down?" Another mind, buried beneath my own, had prompted the question. And I had no time to ponder what had driven it. It had been asked, and Aisha had been waiting to answer.

She held out a hand, a quiet request for me to pass the blade and sheath back to her. "What makes you think it's known more than one owner?" She slipped the knife back into its cover but didn't tie it back along her hip.

I opened my mouth, then paused. I hadn't known that at all. The idea of it had simply come to me. So I confessed that instead.

"You're right, even if you don't know why." Aisha held the sheathed weapon up to catch more of the candlelight. "This was made long ago for my great-grandfather's father. It's been handed down to the eldest of each generation. There are as many stories behind it as there are hands that have held it, shaped its edge, and kept it clean. Things it's cut. People, or bowstring, or food. It is special. It is treasured." She sounded more as if speaking to the knife about itself than teaching me its meaning.

"They are sacred things—knives. Everyone in the tribe has at least one, and it is always carried. It is memory. And it is a closeness to all the ones before us. Some have been here among the tribe so long that the metal's edge remembers more than some things told aloud and remembered in ear. Some knives have forgotten more than we shall ever know."

I thought hard about my next words, unsure if they would cause offense, because that was not my intent. But I wondered what gave knives this prominence in their culture over something else more useful. "What of the bow?"

Aisha shook her head. "Important, but not like a knife. Everyone knows how to use a knife, but the bow must be learned. You can use it to hunt a man, or a hare. It has little use beyond that. But the knife? It can make a meal, it can shape kindling, cut many things to hurt or create. It is a tool with which you can survive in this place. Build. Thrive. And it is a gift. To be without a knife here is to be a sort of poor that I would not wish on anyone."

My gaze drifted past her to where Qimari and Shareem stood. Alwi and Baba were there as well, the former's mouth moving so quickly I wagered even Qimari struggled to take in all he said. But she wore a patient smile across her face. Unlike Shareem. The *Shir*'s son instead had all the makings of a scowl that he barely kept from showing. His hands flexed in the clear signs of wanting to throw a punch, but laboring under restraint.

"No, not even Shareem." Aisha's words brought me back to the moment. "It still bothers you that he and Qimari are meant to be married." Not a question. "Or is it the truth you learned, that he does not love her?"

"She doesn't love him either. You said so yourself."

Aisha smiled, and I noticed it was much like Qimari's then. The careful, nearly motherly level of patience in it. "No, she doesn't. Love is a tricky thing, and it is a fragile thing, for as fierce as it can be. Love is like a candle flame." She reached out with a hand to cup the flickering fire. "There is warmth, but you must keep the right closeness." She moved her hand again and most of the light vanished.

"Too close, and you smother a thing's fire, and you feel the worst of its heat. How can a flame not bite back when you threaten it so?" Her hand then moved back to her lap, but remained in the shape to try to hold the candle's glow. "But so far back? This timid. You can never hope to feel her warmth, her love. All you do is cast a shadow against her light. And there is no love in that."

She looked back down to her knife and her gaze wandered from there to the black bow I'd set beside my bedroll. "The best way to love is to know where to keep your hands—the perfect touch, warmth, and space." Aisha cupped the flame again, giving it a gentle, steady breath. It grew greater and did not risk blinking out of existence. "But sometimes you do not get a flame that understands you, or you don't have the eyes to see what it needs. So you turn away from the candle and put your love elsewhere.

"The knife. The bow. The needed things. And they love you back in return in a different way. If you are going to travel longer with us, Ari, you too should find a good knife. Keep it close. Treasure it. And love it."

I know a sign when I see one. So I drew my blade of Arasmus steel, holding it in invitation. "Already have one."

She did not quirk a brow this time. The slow pulling of her mouth to one side said much the same, however. "May I?"

I passed her the knife before she finished asking.

She took it, drawing the blade out to inspect. Its metal chimed—no, that is the wrong word for it—as it left the black horn hilt. It vibrated, much like strings freshly plucked and left to reverberate in the perfect space to catch and echo the sound. They rang. Its edge sang.

But the length of the blade carried none of the candle's copper foil light along its shape. Instead it held all the pale gleam of white glass and starlight. Even in the ripples of the pattern along its side. This was a blade just long enough to find the heart of a thing should it ever be put to that use.

Aisha let out a low breath. "Arasmus steel."

I nodded.

"Where did you get a blade like this? Did you steal it?" She realized what she had asked. "I'm sorry. I shouldn't have said that. It's just that I remember you . . ." Aisha trailed off, and she didn't need to elaborate.

"I know. And for what it's worth, I *am* a marvelous thief, but no. That was a gift, believe it or not."

She turned the knife over in her hand. "It's well made. Old. And it's touched a great many hands, though it hasn't stayed in them long. This knife is a traveler."

It was my turn to raise a brow then. "And how do you know that?"

Aisha gave a smile, more aimed to the weapon than me. It was the expression of seeing someone old and familiar for the first time in many years. Warm. Welcoming. And tired. One of her thumbs ran along the flat length of the knife. "Like things, I suppose. I am much like this, or it is like me. I don't know which."

"So . . . you're not one for one set of hands then? A traveler too?" I made sure to keep my voice neutral, not wanting the question to carry a note of judgment.

"Mm." A light laugh. "I was. Once."

I didn't know which piece of my question she'd answered. "What happened?"

The smile did not leave her face, but the lines of it changed. Just slightly. In the manner you could only notice if you had spent your life watching the many shapes a person could make with their mouth on stage. More tiredness crept through, and some of the warm welcome bled from it. "The flames and hands grew too far apart—cold. But sometimes you remember the warmth. And you wonder about going back." Her eyes flitted back to the black bow, then away to the candle.

"Why don't you?"

Aisha reached out to almost take the bulb of fire in one hand, stopping just short of it touching her skin. "Because no matter how much you wish to feel an old warmth again, you should be wary. Never let the want of warmth lead you to be burned again by an old flame." She sheathed my blade in one smooth motion, passing it to me before reaching out to take the side of my face in her hold. Aisha trailed one of her thumbs along the side of my jaw, but the touch was not like Shandi's had been, or Qimari's. This had all the affection and care of an older worried sister behind it.

I reached up to take her hand in mine, but she pulled away before I could.

"Spend time with your bow, and your knife, Ari. They will not let you down. Learn them. You will be with them a long time, and they you. So give them your time, hm?" She turned to leave.

"Wait . . ." I didn't have a question in truth, just a knowing that I should stay her.

She didn't face me, though. "Yes?"

"Thank you for telling me what you did. And I meant what I said earlier, you *are* dressed nicely."

Aisha looked over her shoulder at me, the makings of a more honest smile there. "You're sweet. Thank you. And, for this." She pulled at the sides of her pants. "This is for tonight. *Mejai* Arfan wants a *Saraansar* tonight in honor of . . . our *guests*." The last words left her like pulp wrung through too fine a sieve. "Since the tribes may one day be joined." Her gaze flickered to Qimari, and mine followed. But she said nothing further before she left.

I stayed there, watching as Alwi did something with his hands.

Qimari stifled a laugh, and Baba joined in. The boy teetered in place, and rested a hand on Shareem's side. The *Shir*'s son, and Qimari's husband-to-be, lashed out, cuffing the simple boy across the side of the head.

I rose to my feet, Arasmus steel singing once more as it left the sheath.

Alwi moved toward the *Shir*'s son, then reconsidered. Instead, the young boy wrapped his friend in his embrace and tried to console him.

Qimari, however, tended to the situation in her own way. Her arm blurred, the full length of it in hard motion. The flat of her palm struck Shareem along his cheek and jaw. He would be seeing stars despite the cavern walls above us, and they would follow him long into sleep after a slap like that. The desert prince did not take kindly to her treatment, though.

He snaked out with a hand of his own, taking her wrist in his grip and holding tight. But something drove realization into him the next moment. Shareem saw how quickly the scene could get out of hand, or how many passing eyes could fall on them the longer it continued. So he let her go and stormed off. All the while, I caught the subtle motions of his other hand. It flexed and tensed, itching in silent want for his sword that hung just within its reach.

Qimari reached out with all the tenderness of a mother toward Baba, cradling his forehand in her hands before bringing her lips to the spot where the small boy had been struck. It did little to solve the problem, but it stilled the worst of Baba's sobbing. He stopped as she wiped away the tears. A moment later, and she'd drawn out a few rolls of apricot leather, passing them to both of the children.

They accepted them with delight and ran off at her urgings. When they left, her gaze drifted with the aimlessness I knew too well. All searching for a place no one but she could see and settle on. But that is not what happened.

Her stare fell on me, and mine her. She watched me for a time we could not count, and I realized she noticed the knife in my hands, and that I had been watching.

I opened my mouth to speak, but Qimari was in no mood to listen. She turned on her heel and left. I stood there, blade in hand, mute and still as stone.

Eventually, I managed to free myself from my hate-filled stupor and confusion. I returned not to the binding notes Immi had left me, but to contemplating the candle and the flame. Of turning my knife over and over in my hand.

And starting to wonder just how many princes of one sort or another that I could come to hate.

I slept, and I dreamed dark dreams of Shareem.

EIGHTY-SEVEN

DANCE, RUMORS, AND WATER

"*Tsst. Tsst.*" A small hand pressed itself to my shoulder, shaking me.

I groaned.

"Ari? Are you awake?" I recognized Alwi's voice.

"No, Alwi. I'm dead, and I prefer it that way. So let the dead lie, and have some respect."

As it so happens, children are utterly without any measure of deference to their elders, and the same toward the dead. And so he shook me anyways. "Everybody's going over to the opening of the cave. The storm's over."

I grunted, deciding that I was in no mood to be near anyone. Especially after what I had seen earlier. "Are we riding out?"

"No. *Shir* Arfan's having a feast. It's starting soon. Everyone is supposed to be there."

"I thought you just said everyone was." I tugged my blanket tighter.

This did not deter Alwi. Rude boy that he was, he chose to nudge me with a foot. "He'll notice if you're not there."

I took a deep breath and realized he was right. "Fine. Give me a moment to drink something and—"

The boy offered a drinkskin. "It's water with brown sugar rum." His tone suggested two things. One, that he should not have had this in his possession, which raised the question, why did he? And two, that he had already discerned what it was by testing it . . . thoroughly.

I bit down on the stopper, pulling it free with a tug. My lips felt the wash of the rum a moment later. It tasted as I expected: a sharpness that came as much from the alcohol as it did sugar, and the subtle spices that added a better body to it. I pushed the skin aside after taking my fill, and I rolled to one side in an effort to rise. There was little point redressing when I had a cloak better than the finery of many men.

I donned it, fetching my staff as well. The binder's cane was less to mark me as someone who studied the arcane, and more to prop my bedraggled self up with. Standing so soon after waking from sleep was not meant for us.

Shola roused from his rest as well, and mirrored my unbalanced motions as he joined me in the regrettable world of the conscious. He blinked and looked at the bed as if wondering whether to return to it. Seeing me readying myself made the decision for him. Clearly anything that required my attention just as much *needed* his. He bumped his small head against my leg, informing me that he expected me to carry him.

"Come on, Ari. We'll miss it." Alwi's voice carried the impatient demand of a child. Or someone who'd long lived in power.

I bowed my head. "Of course, *Shir* Alwi. I forget myself."

Shola *mrrowld,* reminding me of my duty to him as well.

I looked at the both of them, stifling a sigh as I gave way to the demands of the two tiny tyrants. Cat in arm, I prodded Alwi with the head of my staff.

The boy took the cue and led the way.

I trundled behind him, my eyes weighted with stone and refusing to stay open.

Bulbs of orange strobed ahead, each flicker seeming no larger than the tip of my thumb. Candles, running in rows along the sides of the cavern as it opened to its mouth. Several dozen people sat between the lights.

I counted men and women, children in laps, and some by themselves. Some had the comfort of small rugs on which to rest. Others made do on hard stone, such as it was. Larger light flashed beyond the cavern mouth.

We exited to find proper fires burning and at least two goats that had been spread and fastened to crude crosses. Each hung an arm and a half in distance from the flames. The perfect place from which to cook in a slow and measured manner.

A few women and men alternated in a process of dipping their hands in a tin pail, soaking them with water, and flicking it across the meat. Someone else occasionally added salt, powders, and more water back to the container.

A brine, I realized.

Both the *Maathis,* the *Shirs,* and their children sat in a semicircle by a fire farther back still. A spot from where they could watch everything. Arfan noticed me as I approached, and the merchant king raised two fingers into the air, beckoning me with a gesture.

Alwi noticed the invitation and quickly ducked away. "Take care of yourself, Ari. I don't want to be anywhere near him." He gave the merchant king one last look, then sped off.

I made my way over to Arfan, but the desert lord stayed me with a hand, then motioned to a hempen mat that had been placed near the end of the group. A silent message as to where my place among them was.

Fair enough. I knew I wasn't one of the tribe. Most of what I'd offered the *Maathi* in conversation had been guesswork, or recognizing a pattern I couldn't have seen without his notes. Regardless, I *had* led them to the Water Tree, even if it had been out of my own desperate want to ask about the Ashura.

But as far as most were concerned, I was still a thief that owed Arfan a king's fortune, and I still had no way of seeing how to pay for it. But as long as the merchant and desert lord stayed fixed on other pursuits, perhaps it wouldn't matter?

Keep believing that, and it just might happen. I dismissed the thought, raised my hood and cowl, and took my place.

No one had changed their clothing despite this being a feast, though I finally realized what I'd overlooked.

Most of the young women all wore their robes tonight, but I saw nothing betraying their usual outfits below.

A man in the circle, who I didn't know, leaned close to me. He could have been somewhere in his fortieth year, but had lost all of the hair from the top of his head. All that remained came in the form of a thick beard of ragged weeds, coarse, but holding to a rich dark. A thick neck and just as solid a head, all set atop the build of someone accustomed to working hard, and eating just as well. "Your cloak . . . you are a *Shir* of another tribe? You are come here to . . ." He frowned for a moment. "To *dulhaan* under the good *Shir* Arfan?"

I shook my head, not exactly sure what the man had asked me. "I'm not a *Shir.* What about my cloak makes you think that?"

"You are young, but not so young as not to be a *Shir.* It has happened when a father dies, and the son has good reputation to succeed him. If chosen by the others, of course. The young ones, though, they don't always have the way of leading and doing what needs to be done. So, some of them are sent to other tribes with good relations. You learn from an older *Shir* if your father is gone."

I didn't know how that led him to assume I was who he'd thought I was, though.

The man must have gleaned that from the look on my face, and he went on.

"The cloak. The *Shirs,* the first—old ones wore them before we really shaped ourselves to the desert. All our people. Before this place was all sand. Now, if you are become a *Shir,* you wear the cloak the day you are chosen. And the young ones"—he gave me a knowing look and smile—"like to wear theirs more. A reminder, and to show the young girls who they are." The grin widened.

That comment did draw a bit of my own humor to show on my face.

"But if you are not so, then why do you wear something like this?" He reached out, a thumb and forefinger stopping short of taking hold of my cloak.

I bowed my head, giving him the silent invitation to touch it.

He did so. "It is like pearls and leather. Scale." He breathed the last word half in disbelief, just as much in awe.

I nodded. "Of a . . ." I let the words die, realizing that maybe tonight my reputation didn't need any more help. Let the man think what he would, perhaps things would be better off for it.

He waited for an answer, and I reconsidered my silence. "What do you know of—"

Arfan rose, his voice booming over all conversations. "Tonight we are to celebrate the finding of the Water Tree, and my dream come true. The guidance I have received in it. And the visiting of another tribe, to hopefully put aside old wounds, and let the sands bury bad blood. To set the path ahead for our families to be joined."

Several in the audience clapped, but just as many watched in silence.

Which said all that needed to be said about the marriage.

Both tribes had their fair share who did not want such a thing. A look at Qimari made that obvious as could be. Though Shareem's mouth had adopted the lazy smile found on a rather contented cat.

"We will share water, and there will be *Saraansar.*" Far more enthusiasm showed at that pronouncement. Especially from the men. Though, I noticed a trading of knowing smiles from the older women in the crowd. Many of the girls my age went through familiar flushes in face. Some with expressions wicked enough to set any boy's face aflame. And some still held the quiet confidence you'd expect from someone years their senior.

A few men, varying in age from near my own, to ten years older, spread through the crowd. Each carried an instrument. Some were bowed in shape with strings running along them. Close to a mandolin, but different enough in form to be noticeable even by me—a person with no musical talent or knowledge.

Two were drums the shape of goblets, their colors the blue of first spring.

And then there were the pipes fashioned from something that could have been horn, or a wood I couldn't recognize.

They fell into playing, and the desert came alive to rhythmic basso beats—the quiet *tappering* of hail on glass. Measured. Comforting. And, at the same time, rousing. The strings sang then, sharp and silver-bright. They fell into something like a horse's canter. Quick, but kept held in pace, all until it skipped and quickened once more. Then soon back in control.

And the pipes added their wind-hollow-whispering and echoed-golden voice to the music. Soon, everyone rocked in place, enjoying the performance. Some of the older couples joined hands and took to their feet, dancing only for themselves.

But it was what happened next that took best root among my memories of that night. Every robed young woman suddenly shifted free of her coverings, revealing outfits like what Qimari had worn the evening we'd spent so closely together. Every girl rushed into a line, each person hidden behind the one that stood before them.

At least from where I sat.

The music changed—slowed. It pulled at you like unseen strings, tugging with just enough weight to make you aware they were there. Then the drumming brightened—quickened.

The women moved in tandem. Smooth, rhythmic, but their bodies flashing color—bold and sharp. All moving hips and waists in a way that captivated everyone.

And I was no exception.

The line closed in toward the *Shirs*' half circle, and the head of the line leapt to one side, only for the woman who took her place to move the other way. The procession fed itself as the women fell back into place at the rear—then fast breaking apart into position side by side.

I spotted Qimari, even with the sheer veil over her face. The blood-red of it, hemmed in gold, only brought out the brightness of her eyes in the dark. And I now understood why Aisha had dressed the way she had earlier. Every woman's lashes held a rich shadow to them. *Kahal,* a charcoal-like spread that lengthened their appearance to draw your attention to the eyes.

And give shape to a look that could take the heart of any young man watching. Or older.

Many of the women who had not taken part in the dance traded whispers and smiles at the sight of the dumbfounded or shy expressions over many of our faces.

I may have been very glad for my hood and the white face covering I'd adopted.

The music sped and the women matched its tempo. Golden bands and bangles chimed and flickered under firelight.

Some of the dancers moved from the assembly, never breaking their performance, and took up small bowls of water from older ladies. They made their way to certain men, offering them a drink.

Many knew what to do, and smiled and accepted. Some of the boys, flustered for obvious reasons, failed to make good use of their situation. And those men who'd given up youth's excitement long ago merely watched and chuckled at the confusion of us all.

But I lost interest in the rest of the scene as Qimari headed toward our group, bowl in hand.

Shareem rose from his lounging position, sitting straighter in anticipation.

Only, she continued not toward him.

But toward me.

Arfan and *Shir* Sharaam did not notice right away. And Qimari moved on regardless, soon making it obvious to whom she wished to share her water with.

Shareem's eyes caught mine, and my heart leapt as I wondered how long before Arfan and Sharaam realized the truth of what was about to happen.

Aisha's form came into view, dancing harder, with bolder movements that drew the eyes of many.

Including Qimari. The girl faltered as the older woman moved past her, taking up the whole of my view, and offering me a dance that brought my heart to several places at once.

It beat four times as hard as a storm in my chest. But so large a thing that it took space in my throat as well. And soon my temples.

She bent at the waist, pushing the bowl my way.

Qimari remained the only dancer out of motion, still-standing like carved of stone.

Arfan and Sharaam leaned forward, finally realizing something had gone wrong.

I lowered the white cloth and hood, taking the bowl from Aisha in both hands. She tipped it to my lips, and I drank.

And I saw the hurt in Qimari's eyes. And I watched the confusion. And I looked on as it turned to the anger of a friend who had had another choice taken from her. She composed herself with all the practice of a woman used to wearing the mask others wished her to, and made like a hard wind toward Shareem. She found her rhythm, and offered him the bowl.

The young man accepted, and everything soon returned to as it should be—as the two *Shir*s would have hoped, with neither the wiser as to what had almost happened.

My attention turned back to Aisha, but she had spun away, returning to the larger group of dancers.

I found myself quickly friendless for the remainder of the feast.

⁂

The goat should have tasted wonderful, but I didn't have the heart to appreciate it. Warmth, the familiar flavor of red meat, and some spices. The flatbread provided a textural contrast and touch of clarified butter that should have been savored. But I couldn't manage.

I left most of the meal for Shola instead who, unbothered by my trivial problems, found it both a welcome boon, and a surprise, that my food went to him. I kept to a skin filled with more water and brown sugar rum. It helped settle the many thoughts that were taking me then.

"You don't seem too happy for a man who just saw what you did." Aisha bent to look at me, her face a finger's breadth from mine. "What's wrong?"

I stoppered the skin and shrugged. "I think you have a good idea."

She sat by me, putting one arm around my shoulders. Her touch was warm and comforting. Though I wished in part it wasn't. "The business with the water giving in the *Saraansar.* Do you know the point of it?"

I shook my head.

Aisha blew out a breath, resting her arms on her knees. "It's close to a commitment, you can say. Far short of a proper betrothal, you understand. But it is the closest a woman can come to saying she's chosen a man to . . . pursue." The last word came with smoke and a dryness that was not husky or inviting. It was forced, and hard.

I opened my mouth in a silent *ah.*

She caught the gesture. "And now you're wondering what it means for us?"

I shrugged again.

"A smaller problem than what would have happened had I not done what I did." She reached out and took the skin from my hand. With a tip of her hand, the brown sugar rum passed through her lips. "This is watered down." She gave the skin a jiggle.

"Would you rather it not be?"

The smoldering heat of the fire before us found its way into her smile. Lascivious, and full of mischief.

It caught me off guard.

"I suppose if it were something stronger, it would make many things easier. Or more exciting." The smile held, but something burned brighter behind it.

I blinked. "Like what?"

She sighed, and the expression faded, turning to one of patient understanding. "Nothing." Another sip. "Qimari would have given you her water, you know. And if everyone had seen that, you would not be here to sulk. You would be out there"—she gestured far beyond the cliffs—"buried in shallow sands left red with your blood."

"So you did what you did to save me?" I couldn't wholly believe that. Aisha hadn't come to hate me for what had happened between Qimari and me. But I knew I'd lost some of the kindness she'd held for me before.

Aisha nodded. "In part. More to save Qimari. The scene would have caused as much trouble for her as you."

I gave her a look that told her I didn't believe that.

"*Almost* as much trouble. The two of them are near enough betrothed. Breaking that now would lead to war between the tribes. The blood feud's too old. And this is the only peace they can have. And when Sharaam dies, Shareem will not inherit his father's tribe. In fact, they will all join ours."

"Under *Shir* Arfan. Except this is all under the assumption he doesn't die first, or at all."

She stared at me, then broke eye contact, gaze falling to the floor.

Unless she and Arfan are planning to murder Sharaam? I thought back to the man who'd first told me of the merchant king's desire for me to come to Zibrath. The man of shadows and spice who'd broken into my room. I had heard of such men before, and for the longest time, I thought them nothing more than stories.

I told her of this.

She inclined her head. "I know of them." That answered a part of my question, but not if she or Arfan had employed these living shadows to make sure things played out as they hoped. "Qimari's marriage to Shareem is a must as far as the *Shirs* are concerned. And she is too young to know what is good for others when it flies in the face of what she wants."

"And that's all that matters?"

She shrugged. "Sometimes when we do things for ourselves, all we do is bring about more hurt for many, but sometimes when we do things for others, the only one hurt is us."

I thought on what she'd said. "And how much is tonight's performance going to hurt you?"

Another thin smile. Practiced. Fake. "Not much. Just rumors. And people always have those to spread."

She was right about that. "I'm no stranger to those."

Aisha looked me over again. "No, you aren't, are you?" Then she leaned forward and I finally found my taste again. Her lips touched mine and they were warmth, brown sugar rum, and spice.

She left then, leaving only the lingering taste of herself.

And the thoughts of what rumors would spread about the two of us.

EIGHTY-EIGHT

Blood, Smoke, and Flame

We set out hard the next morning. Back on the road to Iban-Bansuur, the fabled city among the sands. The aftermath of Arfan's feast could be felt through our joint caravan. Quiet allegiances had been drawn that night.

You wouldn't think it possible from dance and food, but more alliances are made over shared cup and meal than any special meeting.

Bolstered by the union-to-be, members of both tribes now mingled more than before. None more obvious than Qimari and Shareem. Though it would be a tall lie to consider them close in anything other than proximity. The *Shir*'s son rode his horse by her camel close enough to reach out and touch her anytime he wished. Something that he made great show of, though his hold never crossed into indecorous anytime he displayed a hint of affection.

Qimari, for her part, put on the fine act of reciprocating. Half smiles, that to anyone untrained in the theater arts would believe as sincere. A performance, and nothing more.

Anywhere his hand fell, hers would come to rest atop. But again, for the briefest of moments.

Occasionally, her eyes met mine, and those looks could have lived as long as eternity, and faded as fast as short-drawn breath. How can that be?

Consider the odd space occupied only by those caught in the confusion of attraction, childhood, and not quite understanding what love could be, much less *should* be. All the two of us knew was that for a moment, quite a few of them, we had at least wanted to share that misunderstanding with each other.

And everyone else saw fit to deny us that.

Though I had certainly played my part to do so at the feast. Had I not accepted Aisha's water, perhaps things would be different.

Qimari had not forgotten. And I could see the quiet hurt, as much as maybe the early shapings of something close to hate, in her stare. But there remained a spark of affection as well.

I think that is what made it hurt the most.

Aisha only saw me during training, which of course continued at every stop along the way. By now the black bow had almost taken on subtle grooves to fit my hand over the ones that had held it before.

Was this wholly true? No. I suspect I had simply grown more accustomed to it, developing a subtle knowing of just how to hold it so it felt more an old weight, well-known, in my grip. My fingers and palm had just found the perfect place to rest is all.

Aisha noted this, and remarked on it. A compliment of sorts. Though she warned me that the familiarity of the weapon did not mean I would have the same comfort of using it against another person. Especially if they were trying to take their own perfect shot at me.

And the old curse of the weapon hung in my mind as well. Arfan's words. The bow had failed a great many people, but the one who earned its trust could not miss their mark.

If my target practice were any indication, the last statement had little truth to it. For the first salvo of many days seemed to miss wherever I aimed. Something that had not gone unnoticed by Aisha.

"You have too much going on in your mind." She swatted my rear with a bundle of arrows.

"How can I not?" I loosed another shot.

A miss.

Though the motions came to me now as easily as breathing. I pointed as I nocked. Drew. And released. A hit. But far from the heart of a man.

"Better. You still remember the candle—"

"Yes." But I hadn't been calling on that empty space or the clarity it offered. I should have been, but given all that was happening, I couldn't put my heart into my efforts.

My gaze faltered and I watched as Qimari shared a meal with Shareem atop a low rising dune. Dried fruits and nuts. Flatbread, and yogurt made from the milk of goats. Alwi and Baba hovered around the desert princess, not partaking in the afternoon snack themselves. But they seemed to delight in her company, and she theirs.

Shareem, like before, did not find the two boys anywhere near as tolerable. He waved a hand in the same manner of one rudely dismissing an irksome street vendor. When that failed, he raised to his feet, giving them an imperious glower.

The boys cast a look to Qimari, and whatever she said had comforted them into staying. She clearly kept the pair around to stop the best of Shareem's boldness, I wagered.

Shareem quenched his disappointment, and likely a touch of anger, with a long drink from a skin. I didn't need more than a guess to figure it alcohol of some kind.

"Ari, your shot." Aisha's words pulled me from the scene.

I sighed and continued firing.

I did not improve much over the day.

Part of the journey entailed going over notes and drawings with Arfan's *Maathi*. While I had little sense for the work, I confess I enjoyed it. Especially every time the wizened man showed me a new piece of technological wonder.

"*Zho! Zho.* Look." He pointed up to the diamond-cast stars. His hands worked a segmented tube of engraved brass. Each cylinder had a slightly larger circumference than the one it protruded from. A collapsible device engraved with writing I recognized.

Minor bindings. The *Maathi* explained that they had been fashioned to help the device preserve a view's integrity in low light situations. Not much of a feat in and of itself, but invaluable to those that relied on such lenses. This ensured someone like the *Maathi* could always have the best look across the desert or up into the sky.

The wealthiest of merchant captains and sailors relied on these for navigating across seas. The rest made do with their eyes and some, it had been said, pricked their skin with ink until a secret map of the world rested along their body.

I didn't believe that one.

The *Maathi* felt as I did, and instead took the time to teach me how to look at the world with a thinker's mind. Something I enjoyed, and a thing that had assuredly been bolstered by my time with Rishi Vruk.

Koli.

But the lessons I'd learned favored me then as the *Maathi* showed me more of the moon's passing, and the turnings of the sun. I did not understand them near as well as him, but I didn't need to. My interest rested in what else the *Maathi* knew of them.

Stories.

He shared some with me. Small things. Almost akin to Shaen stories. Fables. But the one I cherished most . . . was the one about the boy who fell.

"*Zho.* Do you see them?" The *Maathi* pointed to a cluster of stars, their shape almost like an arrow in flight, pointing the way to something unseen. He handed me the lens and I took it in hand.

I pressed it to one eye and looked. "I see them." He motioned for me to pass the lens back, and I did.

"There are many stars like that, ones that show the way to something. But this star—story—is not of that. No. This is of a boy who fell in a quest. A noble one."

That caught my attention. "What was he trying to do?"

"Rescue a lady. But not one of our world. Oh, no, my friend. This is of a boy who fell through the doors hung between the sky. And the Shaen maiden he found trapped there. One needing rescue. And how he failed to free her."

Beyond nine dunes, and then past as many hidden rivers. Through nine sunken stone valleys, and nine still-hidden oases, there was a boy.

The boy was Feroz, and he was considered lucky in all things. Young, but maybe not so young as to be a child. But certainly not much older than you by guess. Maybe it is best to just say he was a boy, not yet a man.

Yes.

He grew up on sands like these, a long time ago. Not so long that the world hadn't come to take the shape it has now, but long enough that there were not the proper names of things today.

That's right.

Feroz had the good fortune that many men wished for. It was the kind that let him wander the desert without ever getting lost.

A good thing, no?

But, as in all things lucky, there is a time when luck ends.

And it was so for Feroz.

You see, this was a time when many of the tribes fought at first shedding of blood. There were no quiet angers or keeping pains heavy in the heart for long years. If you were wronged, you took your grief, and sword, and bow to fix the hurt. And many did this.

Feroz's tribe was no different. But there came a day when they too ran out of luck. He had just enough to be wandering the sands, doing as a young boy often does, only to return to broken bodies, and blood-soaked land. Tents and fallen kites burned.

Orange flame and red smoke. Blood on the ground. And blood on the stones. Shattered shields and wooden poles.

And there was no one left for him to mourn with.

That night, he sobbed. "Make it stop. Make the hurt go away." He held his heart, asking it to have the pain leave him. But while his heart could listen, it had no knowing of how to make this suffering quiet. And it had no one to share this pain with to lessen it.

So he wandered, hoping to put himself far away from his aching heart.

Feroz passed by arched stone and the folded leave-behinds of Alum's touch. And he passed under a sky with moonlight, and sunlight. Soon he found himself walking under a sky of foreign stars and clouds.

A place forever bound to the morning dawn.

She had all the colors of autumn in her skin and hair. Golden touched. That is what the stories say. And she was no human thing.

This was Enshae.

And she told the boy so.

"How did I come here?" asked Feroz.

"Why, through the doorway. Did you not mean to? Have you not come to free me from this place?" Enshae spoke with the patience of someone who had grown used to prison. For that is all she had known for so long a time. Not so long as the beginning of creation, of course. But maybe for most of it.

Yes, I think that is right.

Feroz looked around the woodland realm in which the Shaen woman resided, and she did not look so very much trapped to him. "Free you . . . from what?" he asked of her.

She gestured to their surroundings. "Why, this very forest. It is as much my home now as it is my pen. I am forbidden to leave the edges of this place. Forever cut-lost from my true home. My first home. You have come through the doors, so you have some talent. Can you not help me?"

Feroz thought on this, and he knew he was no hero like in the old stories. He had only ever heard of them. And he did not know of the Shaen but for the fables told to all young children.

"How?"

Enshae stood and summoned Feroz closer. "I will show you. Teach you. And in time, you will learn. Then you can free me. For I cannot act beyond this place."

"What happens if I cannot?" Feroz worried on this, because a part of him was wise enough to know that this was dangerous. And a smart man asks the questions to things he does not know.

She gave him a smile. "Then I suppose you fail. And you fall." Enshae did not tell the boy what this meant, for she did not want to frighten her only chance for survival.

And do you know, I cannot blame her.

So she taught him. Many things, in fact. She told him of the folds of the mind. Enshae showed Feroz the three things every hero needs: candle, cloak, and cane.

If only the once-lucky boy would get the proper use of them.

For under Enshae's tutelage, he grew quick, and clever, and you could almost say he became powerful as well. But he never did grow wise. And cleverness is never the same as wisdom.

Impatient, and wishing to rescue Enshae soon, as many years had now passed with Feroz trapped in the Shaen realm, he set out to leave her forest. He ventured out far into their world, finding plains of ever-evening, and some places caught in always-deepest night.

Spires of woven moonlight and stars, crystal white glass. And the Shaen, who held all that in their own skin. Glimmering things and beings.

Feroz traveled until he reached the court of one of the Shaen lords and introduced himself. "I am Feroz, a traveler who passed through the doors Alum Above hung in the sky."

"A human, here?" said the lord.

"Yes, and I am far from home, unable to return. But I have been promised the way back. For that, I must first free one wrongfully imprisoned."

"Who?" asked the lord.

"Enshae." And at his declaration, the court laughed in open at Feroz. This incensed the young boy, and all young men are quick to anger.

Tst. Tst.

And in his foolishness, Feroz challenged the Shaen lord to a duel.

The lord accepted.

Poor Feroz. He had lost his luck long ago, and in this, he could find no more.

So they fought.

Feroz called the wind and bid it to carry him into flight. From the air he called magics that would shake the sky and earth.

But the Shaen lord had been born to work the bindings. They were in his very breath and blood. He knew magic the way every Shaen knows songs and dance. For they are born to those as well.

And the fight, while terrible to watch, did not last so long.

The Shaen lord struck Feroz down from flight, and the boy, who would have been a hero, fell.

Fell from the doors beyond our skies, hung now in heaven above, burning bright in starlight for his sacrifice.

They say Enshae is still trapped there, tired, and waiting for the next mortal to come. Hopefully less foolish, less clever, and maybe much wiser.

The *Maathi* ended the story and fixed me with a look that spoke of quiet expectation.

I stared, unsure if he wanted a reaction, or had more to say.

"*Zho.* Well, friend, what did you think?"

First, I realized that not everyone had the knack to tell a story the way it was meant to be. I did not share this with the *Maathi,* though. And I appreciated the tale nonetheless. Instead I gave him the gratitude due anyone who shares a gift like that with you. "Thank you for the story, *Maathi.*"

He clapped me on the shoulder hard enough to nearly jostle me out of my saddle. "Ah, well, it is a good story. A good lesson in it. Maybe more than one." He grinned. "But what did you think of the telling?"

I blew out a breath and felt the man deserved the truth. "It was fine, but I liked the one you read before. It flowed better than you telling this from your memory."

He frowned, stroking the underside of his chin. "Mm. Maybe. But that could be you too, no? Sometimes the story is fine the way it is, but it is on the ears of who is listening to see the beauty of its telling as it's told. Stories are pools of water, reflecting us and what we bring into them. Many times a man only hears what he wants in a story, and he is poorer for it, *ayam*? You decide if you wish to hear it true or not. That is all. And that is fine too." The *Maathi* clapped a hand to my shoulder again.

This time I didn't shake in my seat. The man had a point, and I mulled over it. Once I found my tongue, I opened my mouth to speak.

But the sight ahead took all our attention.

Smoke billowed high into the sky. The sign of fire. Only, the color high in the air was the red of blood.

The walls of Iban-Bansuur, tall and holding the gold of sand and sunlight in them, ran red as well. Streaks and tears that trailed slowly into the ground. Fissures ran through the hard stone. Not so deep to threaten bringing the city down, but clear enough that something had tried its hand at breaking those walls.

Surrounding the city's distance were high arches of rock, much like the ones I'd once seen journeying north with Laki. Only these reached a height taller than the highest buildings in the Ashram, or the towers in Mubarath. Each curving band looked as if Brahm himself had traced it into existence out of magic and the sand itself, leaving them to stand so oddly out of place, even in a land as strange as this desert.

"When the chimney smoke goes red as blood." I breathed the words before thinking about it.

"Alum . . ." The *Maathi's* voice barely competed with what wind coursed through the desert. "You cannot do this here. Iban-Bansuur is above this. No man may shed blood here. No man can harm another here. It is . . . *forbidden*." He'd spoken the last word as if the sheer weight of it could make the declaration true.

As I looked at the smoldering city, I didn't think that would be the case.

The whole of the caravan stopped. Swords left sheaths, and bows were nocked.

It was only Arfan that remembered his place and what to do. "No weapons! We will not defile the city any more than it has already been. Not until we find who has done this. Move!" He led the way into Iban-Bansuur, and we followed.

I nudged Anedi ahead of every rider but for Arfan, because I had to be as close to first into the city as possible. I needed to see it for myself.

A foolish thing, of course. I was by no means ready for a confrontation with storybook demons. But I was young, and much like Feroz from the story—unwise.

And I wanted to catch a band of demons.

Because the Ashura had come to Iban-Bansuur.

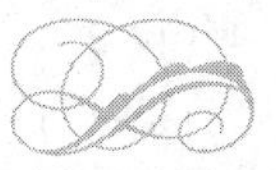

EIGHTY-NINE

The Heart of a Thing

We rode into a city marked by all the signs of demons.

Blood streamed along many of the walls. More than could have ever come from people's bodies. Stone had been cracked throughout Iban-Bansuur.

If it weren't for the red smoke and the heaviness over the place, I'd have given it a better look. As things stood, it reminded me in many ways of Mubarath. Only, Iban-Bansuur was of the size you could lead an army of thousands through its streets . . . and lose them all to its vastness.

It should have been a dream to see in the middle of the desert.

But now? It was a child's nightmare.

And somewhere along it might have been the monsters responsible for it.

The caravan moved slowly through the city as if readying for a funeral. No one spoke. And every hand rested on their nearest weapon, despite Arfan's word not to draw them.

Qimari and Shareem kept close together. Alwi and Baba had returned to the safe confines of the tinker's wagon, and the look of the peddler told me that he wished he'd stuck with another tribe than ours. Both *Maathi*s eyed the walls and passing buildings with the slow measured wariness of men who rarely missed a detail.

One of my hands rested on the black bow. I couldn't be counted on to do much with it, but even a warning shot could be of help. Arfan's word be dammed. I wouldn't risk someone else being hurt by the Ashura.

My other hand brushed along my clothing until it gripped the Arasmus knife, though I didn't draw it.

The sound of a hundred miniature drums, all beating in staccato, sounded from the way ahead.

The caravan halted, and many riders reevaluated Arfan's command. A few swords half left their sheaths, and just a many bows went to hands. No one nocked. And no one brandished their blades.

That spoke to the level of control Arfan held over his tribe.

I spotted the source of the noise.

A rider on a black horse galloped toward us. He wore all red, and the man's face had been washed in blood. Lengths of his long hair were matted to his side, and he rode like someone who'd been run through their gut. He leaned hard at an angle, soon to topple from his saddle.

Arfan nudged his camel faster and I joined him in racing toward the oncoming stranger. "*Maathi!*" Arfan's call came without explanation, but his wizened pathfinder brought his own mount into tow behind us. "The man's hurt. He will need your ministrations."

"Of course, *Mejai* Arfan." The *Maathi* bowed his head as we rushed forward.

The rider's horse came to an abrupt stop, and I feared the man would be thrown clear from it. He remained in place, heaving, and bringing one hand to his ribs. "Help me."

Arfan raised a hand, bidding the man calm. "Easy, friend. What has happened here? Who are you?"

It was only then that I noticed the man's clothing had once been white. Now it shone red as blood.

How much did he have to lose for that to happen? The other option chilled me more. It could have been the blood of everyone else who'd been here, bathing him so deep to have tinged his flesh.

"I am of *Shir* Ahmad's tribe." He blinked and his head lolled, losing what little strength he'd been holding to. ". . . Was of his tribe."

Arfan frowned. "Was?"

"Dead. All dead. I don't know who, if any, are left. Just me. They came so fast. Like a desert storm, only there was no storm. No rain."

That can't be right. I repeated what I knew of the Ashura in my head. The songs I'd heard. If there hadn't been a storm, did it mean that less than their total had come?

It had happened before. At least according to everyone I'd met since who reassured me that they numbered nine, despite the fact I'd only seen eight.

But there were enough signs that *some* of the Ashura had been here. And I hoped they still were. My fingers gripped the bow harder, and I felt its wood give slight flex in my hold. "Who came? How many? The Ashura?" I nearly reached out to steady the man as I spoke, but the *Maathi* had already come to the rider's side, holding him in place.

"Easy, friend. Easy." The *Maathi* looked him over. "He has no wounds? But there is a tightness in his chest, his sides. His heart is thundering. Breathe for me. Breathe."

The man did as instructed, taking a deep lungful of air. He winced as he did so. "Ashura?" The rider blinked several times, repeating the word like it would help him better understand it.

"Ajuura—*bhaalguhl.*" The *Maathi* corrected me and helped steady the man.

The rider exhaled. "I don't know. It happened so fast. My head." He cupped his skull. "It was like drums beating inside me. My heart, it felt as if it would burst.

Everything hurt. The stone of Iban-Bansuur shattered in places. Shattered." The word carried a note of disbelief.

"Wood splintered. What under Alum's sky can do such a thing? Everyone started going mad after a while. Mad." He blinked hard, shutting his eyes both in pain and what I assumed was vain hope at blocking away the memory of what he'd endured. "The horses felt it too. Even the falcons, camels. Everything." He took on the tone of a man speaking more to himself than us.

"*Maathi*, see him fed and looked after. We can speak to him later. He needs rest, *ayam*?"

The *Maathi* nodded and wasted no time, helping lead the rider and his horse back into our caravan.

Arfan looked at me, then behind to *Shir* Sharaam and his *Maathi*. "You heard all of that?"

The three of us nodded.

"Ari, fetch Aisha. You will go with her and others to search the buildings. If there is anyone else, bring them back. I wish to speak to them. If they are hurt, see them tended to. If you find trouble . . ." He frowned, looking away to the sky as if seeking silent guidance. "Alum preserve me." He sighed. "Do what you must. This city has seen blood. Something it should have never seen, and never has under *Shir*s past. I hope god will forgive us if we must spill more to protect it from worse."

I knew enough not to argue with him there, or bring up my own desire to question the rider about the Ashura. Reins in hand, I nudged Anedi back down the way we'd come.

Aisha had been among the few who'd brought out their bows upon hearing the rider. As much as she valued Arfan's commands, the woman was a warrior first. One look at her said as much. And she would not let any harm come to those she protected.

Aisha looked to me, then Arfan. "What happened?"

I filled her in, but made no mention of the Ashura.

The *Al-sayidha* turned her mount around and moved through the rows of people still filtering into the city. She selected another three to join us, passing by Qimari and Shareem as she did. "Your fathers will want you two to be with them."

Qimari and Shareem raised their voices in argument, but Aisha cut them off with a wave of her hand. "*Now.*" The word had the weight of stone behind it and a sharpness to cut through iron.

Both teenagers traded looks before quietly acquiescing to her command.

"Impressive." I watched them leave. "I don't suppose you could teach me that. It'd be nice if I could make people jump to like that." I gave her a little smile.

Aisha rolled her eyes. "It might help if you earned some respect first. Right now, you are the one who helps with chores, and is in debt to *Mejai* Arfan for a box of gold."

I inclined my head. "I suppose I can't argue that."

A hint of a smile touched her lips. "No, you can't. Come on, we should look ahead to make sure as many buildings are clear for us to stay here. The quicker we can get the elderly settled, the better."

And leave us time to find the Ashura. They're still here. I know it.

Aisha led me and three others of the tribe down one street, taking our time to enter every building and ensure they were empty. Some had suffered the same fate as the walls outside. Weeping blood through the pores in the stone and cracks along the surface.

Smoke wafted from the third story of one structure. I raced up the flight of stairs, drawing the Arasmus steel knife as I made it to the top.

A bundle of fabric rested on the ground, still smoldering and sending up plumes of red. The fire still flickered along the lengths of bundled clothing, just enough to bring out another crackle from the material and send up more carmine wisps.

But no one else stood on the rooftop with me. I sighed, sheathing the knife and returning the way I'd come.

"What did you find?" Aisha turned her gaze toward the high billowing smoke.

"Nothing. Just a dying fire. Doesn't make sense, though."

"What doesn't?" Aisha urged her camel back into motion, signaling for me to follow.

I did so, coming up beside her. "They had no furnishings around the fire, so they weren't cooking. And who burns clothes to start a fire?"

"Maybe they had gotten sick of their old ones?" Her lips pulled to one side but couldn't quite manage making the full smile. It faded a second later.

I knew what she was trying to do. Find some humor, even the smallest bit, in hopes of lessening the weight we all felt.

"But you're right. No one would ever light a fire like that. A sign—a message, but what?" The way she said it made it clear she hadn't directed the question to me.

I answered it all the same. "I don't know. But I've seen fires like this before. In my nightmares. Long ago. And . . . some more of late."

The *Al-sayidha* watched me without a word, the set of her jaw hard as she fell into thought.

I left her to it, riding alongside in careful quiet, going over what I could remember.

The Ashura's purpose remained a mystery. And not one tome in the Ashram could explain what it was. They'd burned down my home and killed everyone in it because they'd been telling the wrong stories. And they could pass as other people.

Koli had masqueraded as Vathin, setting out with me from Abhar to Ghal, befriending me in the process.

But why? He'd had the chance to kill me so many times, yet he never did. It almost felt like a game, and that he and the other Ashura derived a twisted pleasure from it.

Strike without warning, and with just as little reason. Then pick up and go. Leaving no clues behind.

"Someone's here!" The voice belonged to one of the other riders Aisha had chosen to come with us. He had to be my senior by ten years, with a lanky build that looked ill at home within his bulky robes. "Wait, don't come out until I tell you to." The rider raised a bow, aiming it at the wooden doorway.

"Alum Above, Marat will kill someone like this. Wait here, Ari." Aisha prodded her camel forward, leaving me just as she'd finished speaking.

Anedi groaned and pulled hard against the reins. I fought him for control. Then he did it again. "No, stop. What's wrong with you?" He snuffed and clopped in place, moving in a half-broken circle. "Brahm's blood, boy, stop."

The camel protested harder and lurched forward a dozen feet before I brought him back under control. Still, the animal shuddered in discomfort.

I patted his side. "*Sshh. Ksthi. Ksthi.* Huh? *Tut. Tut.*" I repeated the reassuring noises several times and eased Anedi into a slow pace. "That's it. You just need to walk it off, huh?" I gave him a pat every few steps, followed by more comforting words. "*Ksthi. Ksthi.*"

He seemed to settle. Just a touch, at least. "Come on, I'll walk you around the next set of buildings and we'll circle back."

Red smoke drifted into the air ahead, thicker than any of the columns I'd seen earlier. Could it be the Ashura had just gone by there? A part of me, fresh-filled with the disappointment of having not found them already, told me that it was nothing more than coincidence. Probably a fire gone unnoticed earlier and nothing more.

Yet my heart leapt into a manic frenzy—driven hard as stone, and cold as deep winter's ice. Would I find them now? What would I do once I had? And would I be any match for them?

One of my hands rested against the hilt of my Arasmus knife, and I wondered if I'd soon put Aisha's teachings to use.

To find the heart of a thing.

One of the Ashura's hearts.

Koli's.

I led Anedi toward the billowing smoke. The camel did not agree with the idea. He bucked, then thrashed his head from side to side.

"Oi. Blood and ashes, boy. Oi!" I used much of my weight to pull and bring him back to some measure of calm.

The creature staggered a bit, and every few steps would try to pull to one side and lead us away from the building.

"We'll be fine. *Tut-tut. Ksthi. Ksthi.*"

Anedi did not share my optimism. A moment later, I knew why.

The cry echoed through the buildings, sharp and high. The sound of someone in pain. Another followed, this the voice of a woman. It rose, and the scream that followed was one of anger. Lastly came the scream of a man who had been killed.

The sounds had come from a street off to the right, leading away from the red smoke. I looked to where the fire burned and perhaps the Ashura could be. Then I turned my attention to where the pained cries had come from.

Someone from the tribe—possibly hurt. A friend? And the distinct possibility crossed my mind that it could be worse than all that: The Ashura could have just struck, and possibly at someone I'd come to know.

Only one way to find out.

"Brahm's blood." I spat and turned Anedi away from the red smoke and down to where people were in trouble. "Come on." I urged him faster, and he obeyed. "Is anyone there?" I cupped a hand to my mouth, hoping it would help my words carry through the streets. "Hello?"

No answer.

I pulled free my staff, tapping it along the doors as we passed them by. It might prompt anyone inside to come out for help. We moved by another building when the broken sound of sobbing drew my ears. The door hung open, giving me a look inside.

The shadows of moving shapes.

I dismounted, keeping my staff in both hands as I approached the door. The butt of the binder's cane pressed against wood and I gently eased the way open. "Alwi, what . . ." The words passed into the air unsaid as I saw the scene.

Baba lay on one side of the room, crumpled in a heap atop Qimari's lap. Blood ran along her hands and down her clothes. Some of it coated the back of Baba's head and just below his right ear.

Alwi's face had twisted into the uncontrollable mask of a child deep in pain and just as much confusion. "It . . ." He choked off whatever was meant to come next. "It happened so fast." The boy sniffled between each word. "I don't know . . ." Alwi gazed to one side and I followed the stare to see what I had overlooked on first entering.

"Brahm's . . . blood."

Shareem lay slumped against the other wall, a pair of goat's shears buried halfway in the center of his chest. His eyes had lost much of their clarity and they flitted over all of us, almost as if he couldn't decide what to focus on. The desert prince's breaths left him in shallow gasps and his chest did not rise much despite the effort. A touch of blood made its way to his lips, spilling over.

I turned to Qimari. "What happened? Are you hurt? Baba . . . ?" My feet moved of their own accord, bringing me a few steps closer to her.

She shook her head. "No, not much. It was Baba. He found the shears, and he was playing with them." She sucked in a breath, fumbling for the next words. "Shareem convinced me to go somewhere private with him. He made an issue of it, so much that I feared what our fathers would think if they heard us. So I did. But I made sure to bring Alwi and Baba just in case."

Of course.

"Shareem tried to get them to leave, but they wouldn't go. He started trying to force Alwi out." Qimari sniffed once.

"He hit me." The young boy turned one side of his face to reveal the reddening skin of a cheek that had been struck. "Baba . . . tried to help me. But the shears. He cut Shareem. It was an accident."

I looked to the *Shir*'s son and the wound he still bled from. It looked a great deal more than just an accident.

Qimari took over finishing the story. "Shareem flew into a rage when Baba nicked him. He grabbed him and started slamming his head into the ground. Then he grabbed the shears." Qimari swallowed the lump that had formed in her throat. "I don't know. It happened fast, like Alwi said." Moisture beaded along her lids before slowly trickling down her cheeks. "He tried to . . . and I tried to stop him. My hands caught his. We struggled and I took the shears. I didn't mean to. I've never . . . not a person, at least. It was practice. Always practice."

Qimari's hands left Baba and began to clench into half fists that never formed. Her fingers moved like they were suspended from strings belonging to a poor puppeteer. Frenzied, spasmodic. Someone in the grips of realizing what they had just done. And it was not an easy thing.

I remembered a young sparrow and the aftermath of three men who died at his hands. Even if they themselves fell off the buildings. It was not an easy place to be, that space of knowing you had just killed someone.

"What do we do, Ari?" Alwi came to my side, clutching my cloak.

I only had eyes for Qimari, though. "It was an accident, like you said."

She shook her head, finding the strength to utter a hushed breath to Baba. The sound of it helped ease the young boy's shakes. "Ari, I stabbed him. This will tear apart everything. My father's dream. *Shir* Sharaam will break the alliance. This will mean war."

I turned back to Shareem. He didn't look to have the strength to staunch his own wound, or to pull the shears free. His hands rested at his sides, palms open. "And if he lives?"

Qimari shook her head. "It doesn't matter. Still war. To blood another tribe's member is to start a feud between your families. To do so to the child of a *Shir*?"

I nodded, understanding. My heart lurched and grew cold. Old bands I'd forgotten the weight of found me next, pulling me into a space cold and deep.

Killing someone is no easy thing. The stories make it seem so. And the hero is never troubled by it. They are always the faceless villains. The monsters. The ones who do terrible things and laugh in the doing so.

But that is not how it happens in the real world. Shareem was no monster. An idiot. Foolish. Selfish. An arrogant child with a temper. That is what he was. And now several inches of cold metal was buried in his chest.

I had killed before. Mithu. Biloo. Askar. Three men who had deserved it. Their deaths had been a necessity, like my adoptive father then had taught me.

Sometimes you do the necessary things. The hard things.

And then there are the moments where it is desire. I had had those moments, the ones where I wanted to kill. Like Nitham, but even then, I could never bring myself to do it. The Black Tower Band thief I'd stabbed. I had come so close to ending him, but I did not.

Now was a moment for the necessary things. Just like before. Once a family of sparrows had been in jeopardy, and if I had not done what I had, then I'd have watched many more die. Now again, my friends were in trouble. If I did not make a decision, they would die.

My hand fell to my waist and I contemplated what it would be like to become again a man I had only ever been but for a moment's time. *Khoonee*. Bloodletter.

To kill someone in self-defense, or to protect your brothers and sisters is a thing that can be forgiven. To murder someone in cold blood is something else.

What does it make you when you choose to preserve the safety and lives of those you love and make yourself the villain?

You see, I had styled myself quite the young hero so far in my own story. But life saw fit to give me a lesson then: that stories seldom take the straightest path, and they will test you. How you answer will determine who you will be. Does the question of why you do the things you do matter?

I certainly hope so. I did then, because I had a choice to make and, Brahm's blood, do I wish I could have had any other. But I didn't know how else to stop a war.

To save Qimari.

So I moved over to Shareem, kneeling by his side. The Arasmus knife left its sheath and I regarded the length of it. Never having done my apprenticeship in the Mendery, I couldn't tell how severe his injury was. But my time with Aisha taught me the basics of how far an arrow had to sink into a man's body to kill him. And where.

Shareem would be spared that sort of death. The kind from when a blade sinks to where your stomach meets the soft flesh beneath your chest. He would live, if left to heal, but be in agony for a time I did not know.

But his survival meant this accident would not remain secret. And the cost would be a war that could see Qimari killed. Unless something happened to change that.

Unless the necessary choice was made.

Shareem's clothes had been the once-white of fresh cream, slowly turning gray. Now they ran red with blood.

"It's all right." Alwi rubbed his face as if to show us nothing was wrong. "I'm not hurt. It just stings. Baba, you're fine too, right?"

The boy sobbed but managed to choke out the words he was named after. "*Bah. Bah.*"

"See, it'll be fine, Qima. I promise." Alwi clasped his hands together in a gesture of almost prayer. "Shareem's fine too. He's not dead yet."

I brushed the desert prince's hair away from his eyes. We locked stares. "Yes, he is."

I used the knife.

I saved my friends.

And I found the heart of a thing.

Just as Aisha had told me to do.

My hands did not shake at all.

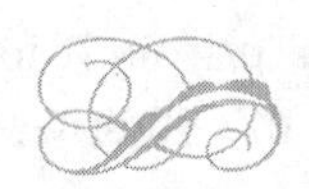

NINETY

Intermission—Things We've Forgotten

My hands clenched around the hilt of a knife that was not there. The memory of what I had done. And now, both of them shook.

Eloine noticed and reached across the table, taking my hands in hers, stilling them. Her thumbs traced slow soft circles along the skin of my palms. "You still blame yourself." She watched me as she spoke, searching for some sign on my face in case I didn't give her an answer.

"How can I not? Shareem was many things, but he was not guilty of what Mithu was. And he hadn't been a threat to anything more than my ego, perhaps. Still, it was my knife that killed him. My hands that drove the blade. I'll remember that."

Her fingers pressed in hard against my flesh, drawing a dull blossom of pain.

"And of the good it did? You said it yourself, had you not done that, Qimari, Alwi, and Baba would have faced fates worse than Shareem's."

I opened my mouth to argue but she dug her nails into my skin, drawing a wince out of me.

"Did they deserve that? Would you consign them to death in his place for your conscience?" She spoke hard and sharp as sword's edge, leaving no room for argument.

I shook my head. "Of course not."

A measure of relief came into her at my admission. "Good. I know you carry that, along with everything else, but some things are meant to be dropped after being carried for so long. Why are you still holding on to it now?"

She had a good point, and a better question. Shame I didn't know how to answer it. So I turned it away with the only thing I could think to. "What good I've done, and for whom, doesn't wash away the bad. That's not how life works. Taking Shareem's life had consequences. Not just for me, but for others as well. Was it my right to put them in that position? To put on them what should have only been meant for me?"

Eloine exhaled and shut her eyes for a moment. The look of a person whose patience had been pushed a hair beyond their limit. "Ari, we all have things we are guilty of, and we have our own burdens. They do not outweigh each other, or another's. That is the nature of guilt. It is meant to be felt, and carried. *Until* it is time to put it down. That is the trick, setting yourself free from it, otherwise it becomes the worst sort of prison. It follows you everywhere you go. It silences your best thoughts and stills your heart from feeling the best of things to be felt."

She was right, but I couldn't bring myself to say anything. That stillness had found me, and the silence.

"You're fond of holding on to your suffering, hm?" A thin and tired smile spread across her face.

I returned the expression. "Well, it's certainly come to make up a good bit of my personality over the years. What would I have if I gave—" A bright line of pain flared through the skin of one palm.

Eloine pulled her hands from mine, miming pinching me in the air.

"And you're rather fond of taking out your frustrations on my body, it seems." I narrowed my eyes.

She had the grace not to grin. Instead, she held all the humor and amusement in her eyes, smiling just as brightly there. "I take pleasure out of setting an ass straight. They're so stubborn, and I've put a good many moments into trying to correct them out of that habit."

I blinked and reached for a piece of crumbling cheese, taking it into my mouth before speaking. "And . . . just to be clear, are we talking about men here, or donkeys?"

She did as I had, breaking off a piece of cheese to savor. "Many times I can't tell the difference, and I did think myself rather experienced on the subject. But I suppose that's unfair. You're certainly not stubborn at all, are you?"

The retort touched the tip of my tongue before I could think, and I almost gave voice to it, but she leaned back in her chair as if expecting that.

Eloine plucked a grape and chewed on it. The edge of a self-satisfied smile played at the corners of her mouth, and her eyes brightened.

I knew enough not to say what I had been about to. Instead, I conceded the point in respectful silence.

"Better." Eloine took the bottle of wine in hand, tipping it back for a sip before passing it to me. "Drink."

I shook my head. "I'm not so sure I should have any more."

"That might be all the more reason to, then. Not because of what the drink can do for you, but to wash away the taste of whatever it is still lingering within you. There's more than guilt there, and it's not just resting in your heart. It touches everything you say right now. Maybe just a note of something else, something brighter, might help you remember there is more to your story, and to you, than just the sorrow you're so keen to keep to." None of the words held any condemnation. Only quiet observation, and the kind-caring of a friend.

I couldn't argue with what she said, and the times I'd tried only left me tied of tongue and just as much in judgment. So I took the bottle and nodded a small thanks.

She'd been right again.

The wine sent the taste of berries and sharp apple to my mouth. An acid bite came under those flavors and only served to brighten the fruity notes from before. In the moment, I thought little of what I had done, and only the pleasure of the drink.

And my company.

Eloine arched a brow. "Well?"

I put the bottle down between us. "I think it might do to listen to you more often."

She gasped, long-drawn and dramatic. Her hands pressed to her breast just above her heart. "Oh, Chaandi, proof you work miracles. I've managed to turn this stubborn man's ear to hear what was always obvious. Though, better now than late, I suppose. Small miracles indeed." She sighed, her lids fluttering.

I gave her a mock scowl. "You're not as funny as you think."

"Which makes me still funnier than you." She didn't miss a beat.

I frowned.

She grinned.

My hands went into the air in a clear sign of resignation. "I know enough to know when I'm beaten."

"Oh, I don't think that's true at all." Eloine watched me over the wine bottle as she brought it to her mouth. "But I'll take it as a mark in your favor you know when to listen to me."

My mind turned to what Eloine had said earlier. "The name you spoke when you were touching the theatrical. Chaandi. What was that?" I'd only first heard the name long ago, and in a story. Why had Eloine called on it then?

Eloine stiffened but for a second and placed the bottle down, never having taken her next sip. "Stories. She's a character I've always tried to understand. Many have forgotten a great deal of truths about her. Some do her great injustice. I suppose I've just always been taken by her."

"You admire her?"

She gave me something of a half nod. "Yes. She's a hero of a different sort that I think the world has forgotten. Much like Etaynia. It seems the way of things. Many men, and the stories, come to forget about the other roles played in the shaping of the world. So many come to forget their own over time. Who they are, and who they've been. The most frightening of those questions, then: Who are we meant to be? And I wish to know what's been forgotten."

A desire I understood very well, and she had the truth of it there. The world *has* forgotten much when it comes to stories. And the vast majority of history has been shaped as much by what is lacking as what has been told to be true. More often than not, the series of lies everyone chooses to be most comfortable with and settles upon.

If I could do something in that regard for Eloine, then I would. I leaned forward and placed my arms on the table. "I know some stories of her. I could tell you one if you'd like?"

Say yes, please. I'd be able to do her just some small measure of kindness for all that she'd done for me.

But of course, as often happens in the stories, this was not the time for us to share another moment in closeness.

A shadow fell upon her face and she looked as if she'd only now become aware of where she was and what she'd said. She pushed away from the table. Not in any rush, but with the slow measure of someone politely excusing themselves. "I've kept you from looking through the library. I'm sorry."

I almost rose with her, but she bid me to stay seated. "No, not at all. What's wrong?"

She flashed a look through the open spaces between the curtains. "Night's waning, and you'll be wanting sleep soon enough. And I still have an appointment before I can rest."

I followed her stare and took in the color of the sky. Another look over my shoulder showed the candle that had been left to burn hours ago in the library. Two-thirds of it had melted away. We'd spoken nearly into the end of last candle, and a new day would be here shortly.

"We still have hours left before . . ." I turned back but Eloine had gone, vanishing as quick and quiet as the moon come morning.

I sighed and eyed our unfinished meal. Perhaps it was a sign.

While I had wanted to search the library for more stories, the night had taken some of my desire and I found myself in no want of any more tales. I left the library and headed to my rooms.

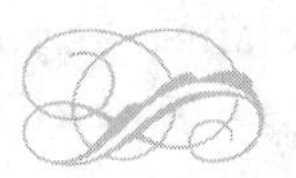

NINETY-ONE

Intentions

Prince-elect Efraine would likely be in bed, preventing an audience. And I had no way of knowing how on guard the man would be after only just so recently killing his brothers. It could be that his own sisters were planning to deal with him in the same manner he'd done the other princes.

Which would save me the trouble of having to do the deed myself.

The Etaynian idea of justice and debts owed was a peculiar one, in that trials had their places, but so did the sharp side of a sword. And if you were to find satisfaction at the end of a blade rather than a jury of peers, so be it. The nature of justice had some fluidity to it, and it rather seemed this malleability was often determined by the gentry. Only the wealthy could get away with serving you at the end of a blade. The poor merely perished for it.

And that in and of itself was a truth I'd found in many countries.

The laws were not made for the benefit of the impoverished, but rather existed to be exercised by the wealthy, when and where they wanted. The legal system was not a shield. It was a cudgel.

I wandered the halls, my footsteps mostly muffled by the thick carmine carpets set over the marble tiles. The walls had been painted the color of bright plum and featured frames set in gold leaf, each containing the portrait of some notable Etaynian. Some I assumed to be members of the long lineage from which Prince-elect Efraine hailed.

A display of wealth, accumulated from all across the world, lay atop the richly polished mahogany tables through the hall.

But something else drew my attention more than the other items on display. First, a domed cap of beaten bronze. It would only come down to just above a man's brow. Most of it had been etched and set with rings of brighter gold against a lacquer of black. A coif of silver-steel chainmail rested within the helm, and a veil of black chiffon hung within that, to better shroud the wearer's face.

The armor itself was much the same. Thin rings interlocked to protect the soldier from slashing wounds, all held tight with riveted straps. A cuirass had been fitted over this, done in the same metal and patterns as the cap.

If you had the patience to give it a longer look, you would notice a section where the chain links had broken. Bent inward to the width of something thin—a hole no larger than a man's eye. And the opening rested above the heart.

The statue held a shield that retained its polish. It stood in heavy contrast to the painted portions of the armor, all of which were the red and gold found in the desert during rare dawns.

But the soldier held no weapons. A spear, broken at its center, rested nearby atop a table. A longer look revealed that it had been blunted in action, and sported a few notches. And the sword next to it told another story.

The scabbard had the slight curve of a knowing smile. Long and set with gold in the rippling Arasmus pattern. A relief had been worked into it of Zibrathi script that I couldn't read in whole. But I recognized the words of "Alum," "glory," and "sovereignty." The hilt held all the green found in faded bloodstones, because it had been set with them. So many so that you could not see the material beneath them. An ornate piece, more ceremonial than for practical use.

But that was a lie.

The blade's edge once held the sharpness to cut clean through flesh, and bone, and sinew. All in a stroke.

Now it rested in a dozen pieces, neatly arranged on a cloth of blood-red. The remains of the saber looked like shattered mirror glass, and they had once been broken as such. I wagered no one remembered how. And no one recalled the name to whom the sword and armor once belonged.

Only me.

I wondered if I would learn the story of how it came to rest in the summer palace of an Etaynian prince. One of my hands reached out for the gem-inlaid hilt.

"A barbarian's tool, from a place far from here." The voice came from down the way behind me, but I didn't turn to face them. "A place close to your land, no?" I recognized the voice as belonging to the pontifex.

Still, I gazed at the pieces of the once-whole sword. Bits of my own face were reflecting in the silver-bright shards, the image just as broken as the blade itself. "Close enough, yes, Your Holiness."

"Mm." He came closer. "Do you know how this sword came to be broken?"

Yes. "No." The lie left me easily enough.

The pontifex now stood a hand's breadth from me. "There was a battle, some time ago. You would have been a child, or perhaps not even born, I think. Far out in a place where there is little water, and Solus is not known. Sand and stone. But there was another place in this place where those things were not true. Clean and clear water as far as you could see along the banks, and trees that offered sweet fruit as much as shade.

"There, the men of the west fought the barbarians, but these devils had a trick. Something that conjured illusions and shadowed visions that stole into the hearts of the western soldiers. And then another army came into the fray. A battle on three fronts, joined by the dead, it is said. But that is a lie that comes into many stories. Only Solus' hand may bring rise to the dead, and those people never walk the world again. They are brought up to his palace in the sky to live among eternal sunshine and his warmth."

None of which explained how the blade had been broken, or why it had ended up here.

The pontifex must have read the thought from my face. "There was a leader among the barbarians who carried this." He nodded toward the sword. "A king, I am told. With his death, their ranks would be broken. It is said he took a wound but did not fall. He sought out the archer on the field and challenged him to single combat where all could see. Their fight would decide much. In the end, his sword met the other man's. You can tell what happened next. His blade broke, and with that, so did his army, and his cause."

True, after a fashion.

"And how did a Zibrathi king's armor come to reside here, Your Holiness?"

The man smiled, showing me a hint of canine teeth. Candlelight washed over his face along with the reflection from the pieces of polished bronze. It brought out the glow in his skin and cast a yellow-gold light across his face and eyes. "A gift. One to make peace and keep our church from bringing word of Solus into their lands by force."

By force, which says nothing of other ways. I did not give voice to that thought. "The soon-to-be king seems to have something of that very sort in mind, however."

The pontifex shrugged. "Who can know the mind of the prince-elect?" There had been no sincere question there. It said that the pontifex knew full well what lingered in Efraine's thoughts, and I had the feeling the pontifex had placed some of those ideas there himself.

"And what will that do to the peace with Zibrath?" I eyed the shattered sword before watching the pontifex.

The slightest quiver of a mouth. Just the edge of a smile, wanting to come, but fell full under the pontifex's control. So it never came. Still, I had spotted it. "I suppose, if Prince-elect Efraine continues on his current course . . . we will have war."

Funny how much that's been happening with men in power of late. "You don't seem concerned by that, Your Holiness."

He pursed his lips as if considering, though the look on his face said this was another practiced performance. "Wars happen, and princes have not stayed in power for long in Etaynia. Who can say what will happen next? Who can say?" The man turned to face me, giving me a smile like a gash in ice. Thin, cold, and hard. "Will you walk with me?"

I inclined my head and moved to the side, gesturing for the pontifex to take the lead. "Of course."

"Do you know the history of Solus and the shaping of the moon, Storyteller?"

I had heard several iterations of the tale over the years, but never the official accounting by the church. "No, Your Holiness."

"Mm." He led me farther down the hall. "It is, I suppose, at first, a story of loneliness. Of Solus, first of all creation, burning bright against blackness and shadow. Against the yawning void of stillness—silence, and nothingness before him. Before life. Before death. And the great sacrifice our lord made in casting off bits of himself, his own light, to hang about the stars we all see.

"But that wasn't enough. Eventually, he came to shape this place, and broke his breath and blood from his body to give us our waters and the air itself. Still, that would not do. For him, or for us, the first peoples." The pontifex placed a hand to his chest, accentuating the claim he'd just made.

I had half a mind to ask him of the first peoples, but even he too only spoke of them in and as stories. Few had figured out who they were by name, only their trade. Singers. Even the Shaen, who walked before all of us, would not discuss the Singers.

"The world held many things we needed to thrive, but in his casting of it, the world was set to turn about. In this turning, we came to have nights so dark that it brought in us a terror deep. And in that depth, monsters and shadows to prey on us. So, Solus shaped the greatest of things after he himself, the sun. And then the moon. She who carries his light when he cannot, and gives it to us in her own way. She lights our night when we need a brightness most. And, sometimes, she gives us her face to let us know she is watching over us."

"You make her sound like a mother—real, and more than just something hanging in the sky." I never knew how much to say to anyone regarding the hidden shape of the world and its mysteries.

Sometimes knowing is its own burden, and in that knowing, you become blind to the things others see as truth. Because you have one all your own.

Truth can be a prison.

The pontifex raised a hand and waggled it. "After a fashion. It is said our

Etaynia, mother of our country, was named after the moon. She was its grace, as well as its strength. Shaped after her in full. Dark, wild, changing, mysterious, and much as strong as the sun itself. After all, the light she carries . . ."

I nodded. "And you believe people can be born of things like that?"

That brought the pontifex to frown and cast his gaze to the ground. "It is in the doctrine of our church." Which didn't answer the question. "As Solus above wills it, so it shall be below. He shaped all things. Why cannot those shapings go on to shape more things?" A better thought, though it didn't tell me what the pontifex believed, just the line of logic he could use *to* believe that, if he wanted to.

"And you, Your Holiness. What is it that *you* believe?"

The edges of his mouth shaped themselves anew—now a thin smile. "I believe in Solus, Storyteller. I would very much like to believe in the shaping of the moon and her kind as well." Was there a silent hope in the way he said it—a need, as much as a want, to believe that? I couldn't tell, but the set of the man's face now told me that was all I'd get from him on the subject.

I thought of what else I could ask. Access to the pontifex was not an easily granted thing. "What are Etaynia's laws concerning foreigners, Your Holiness?"

He eyed me sideways. "Is this concerning the prince-elect's newly voiced intent?"

I shook my head. "Something that happened while I was in Karchetta. It's been on my mind, and has me wondering a great many things. Among them, you seem not so set against me as you were during my trial."

"That was the trial, and we all had our parts to play, Storyteller. To me, you were nothing more than what the prince-elect required you to be. All for the greater good of our country."

"And what exactly is that greater good, Your Holiness? What does it have to do with the clergos arresting people for nothing other than the crime of not being Etaynian?"

He opened his mouth in a silent *ah*. "You are referring to the incident when my clergos were asked by a local innkeeper to remove one of the traveling people from his establishment." His voice remained perfectly neutral and betrayed nothing of a bias against Eloine.

I nodded, but kept what he'd said in mind. He'd called her one of the traveling people. Eloine, from what I could gather, was no tinker. Not by far. Nor was she one of the Ruma, even though she knew of us.

"Her sort have been known to be a disturbance to our people, Storyteller. They bring temptation, falsehoods, and wayward ways to our lands. It is not uncommon to arrest them and ask them to leave."

Only, that wasn't what had happened. "The woman I was with did none of those things, Your Holiness. In fact, she did nothing but share a meal with me. One she never got the pleasure of enjoying or finishing."

He shrugged. "It is not my place to say what disturbs men of the faith. If the innkeeper was bothered by her, he had his reasons."

And those reasons often never amounted to anything more than the shape of someone's face. The shade of their skin. Or the cut of their clothing.

How quick we are to cast out those packaged differently from us, but whose contents are so often the same.

"And how does the church regard those traveling people? What were Solus' words concerning strangers coming to this land for shelter, trade, or work?"

The pontifex stiffened. "Solus has left many words of wisdom for us in our texts. We've recorded and rerecorded them for ages, interpreting their meanings and how best to put them to the good of our people. In guidance, in this life, and the next."

"And how often do people misinterpret those words, Your Holiness? After all, how can man know the mind of a god?"

The pontifex turned to face me in full now. "Careful, Storyteller. The men of the church have dedicated their lives to understanding Solus . . . the *one* true god. Not *a* god."

That told me enough and I nodded in what I hoped came off as sincere apology. "Of course, Your Holiness."

My words looked to placate him and he continued leading me through the hall. "You spoke earlier of a woman whose company you were in. I noticed that you have kept company with a woman during your time in Del Soliel as well. She has been said to have been in the company of some of the *efantes* before Prince-elect Efraine's ascension."

I said nothing, waiting for him to get to the heart of what he wanted.

"Though, I seem to have trouble crossing paths with her when I'd like. All I seem to find is her shadow. And I find her rather curious. So much so I often find myself wondering, *who* is she, Storyteller?"

I've been wondering that myself. Aloud, I gave him a different response. "You would find the best answer to that from her, Your Holiness. I suggest you find her and ask her." My voice wasn't as calm as I'd wished it to be. It held more sharp and biting ice than I should have addressed the pontifex with.

When he faced me, the whole of his face held the bright-cast gold and orange glow of candles. He smiled, bright and wide. "I intend to, Storyteller. I intend to. But it is late, so I wish you a good night. I hope to see you wake so we may continue our conversation."

A threat if I had ever heard one.

The pontifex left and I headed to my room, wondering if he'd try to make good on his words.

NINETY-TWO

INFLUENCE AND OPINIONS

I headed toward the prince-elect Efraine's chambers first thing in the morning, hoping to find him alone and put Aisha's lesson once again to good use.

To find the heart of a thing.

I could risk no less with one of the Tainted in charge of a country.

A pair of guards crossing *lanza*s to bar my way told me that perhaps I should return at another time.

That being when the prince-elect decided, and having nothing to do with my desires whatsoever.

The armed men suggested I take a tour of the gardens to enjoy my morning with some fresh air. I could hardly deny such a pointed recommendation.

The clouds helped bring in a grayer morning than most had been of late. Slate-washed with the promise of an early rain, all giving a comforting coolness to the air. A piece of the moon hung low, set to a half smile, despite it being just after third candle.

The garden had been shaped into rings by stone and fountains, the design further accentuated by the circles of green within them. Shrubbery formed small perimeters in which ferns and grass grew tall, all keeping to their spring-brightness. Some featured low-standing bushes, trimmed to resemble great bulbs, all clumped closely together. These had been decorated in places with streamers of gold and orange, giving them, along with the rings in which they rested, a likeness of the sun.

Other areas had been planted thick with flowers all mirroring the colors found in flame. But then next to one of those, a spot filled with petals of all white, some shadowed gray.

I looked up to find them the same shades as the clouded sky and moon.

"Very beautiful, no?" The voice came from several paces behind me.

I turned to find Lord Emeris Umbrasio approaching, his hands clasped before his waist—his wife was nowhere to be seen.

The man moved with the grace of a shark in water. Slow, each motion sure. And I waited to see just how he would strike.

"The gardens are not to your liking?" he asked.

A court of sparrows had settled along the rim of one of the fountains, trading looks with each other as much as they did fleeting glances with me.

"Just taking them in, Lord Umbrasio. I haven't formed an opinion yet." He and I were the only people here. Not an ideal situation, especially considering the man's disposition toward me. "Should I be concerned about your approach after our . . . history?" I fixed him with a long stare.

He smiled, every bit the predatory fish. "Those feelings haven't left, Storyteller. But most of my ambitions have been met, and the rest remain firmly in Prince-elect Efraine's hands to see delivered. I have every faith they will be." He tilted his head to one side, regarding me anew. "Are you expecting to suffer a similar turn as the former *efantes*? A knife to the throat. Perhaps I'll send one through the small of your back when next you turn around, hm? One sharp twist and it will cut through you, past sinew and the bone. You will die here, under your cloak of red, and alone.

"I wonder"—one his hands went to his chin, stroking it—"will anyone notice the blood under that, or will they simply think you have fallen?"

I shrugged, one of my hands tensing against my staff, though. "I would notice. But if you're telling me this, I wonder if I have anything to fear at all. It wouldn't do you much good to warn me in advance."

He pursed his lips and spread his arms to his side as if in consideration. "True enough, unless . . . I'm merely distracting you for a crossbow bolt to take you in the back."

The thought hadn't occurred to me. It seemed preposterous, and I knew in my gut that Lord Umbrasio had said it to unnerve me. A cruel joke. All the same, I did look out of the corner of my eye to see if it was true.

It wasn't.

My grip softened on my staff and I felt the heavy breath I'd been holding finally leave me.

Lord Umbrasio laughed, rich and rolling through the empty garden. He leaned forward to clap a hand to my shoulder, and I, notably, did not crack my staff over his skull until he bled from his eyes and ears.

A point in my favor, all things considered.

The man's fingers dug in deep against my muscle, but the action of doing so brought him pause. He frowned and the amused light left his eyes as he pulled his hand away. He rubbed his thumb and first two fingers together, looking at where they'd touched my blood-red cloak. "Odd. It felt as if . . ."

I waited for him to go on, but he didn't.

He looked at me again, now with the stare of a man seeing something for the first time, and not so entirely sure whether he stood before a threat or a mirage. Soon, something else took him over. The expression found in a child who thinks they have come across something out of a story. And not the sort to fill them with glee.

But the sort to bring up the old terrors found in darkness. The shadows along the walls that can take the worst of shapes we can conjure.

"I've heard a story or two about something like this." His words had not been meant for me. Lord Umbrasio shook his head as if only just realizing what he'd said, and the old sharklike manner returned. He leaned close again, but now kept his hands to himself. "When I kill you, Storyteller, I will not give you warning, *sieta*?"

I took a breath and brought my mouth closer to his ear, deciding to pay the man back in kind. "And when I kill you, Lord Umbrasio, I promise to make it as much a spectacle as Prince Arturo's death." My smile was all teeth, fit for a wolf and cold enough to drain the blood from a man's face.

A stillness fell between us. It was the unmoving quiet that falls over the world in the deep of winter, when all things are deep in sleep, or long-since dead. The sitting heavy quiet that spreads through a group in mourning as they look over the lifeless form of someone loved. And it was the string-stopped silence of a performance that comes crashing to an end.

The kind that had been built by and between two men, playing melodies of their own, only to have them cross each other. Two men comfortable with killing, having done so before. And who would do so again.

And now they stood in waiting, all to see who would try their hand to break the stillness.

Lord Umbrasio, to his credit, took the threat as calmly as a man used to them would. The edges of his mouth tightened a touch and he moved away from me stiffly. He cracked his neck to one side and pulled the lapels of his coat. "I expect our next meeting to be rather exciting, then."

I held the smile. "May it be our last."

He flashed me a half-lived grin, turning his gaze to the balconies running along the second floor of the gardens. "Shame we're alone. So much empty space. The perfect place for someone to wait in hiding." He bowed his head, just enough to still flash me a look with his eyes. "Storyteller."

I did not return the courtesy.

Lord Emeris Umbrasio turned and walked away. He never once looked over his shoulder to see if I would visit his own threat on him. A knife to the back.

The man had the quiet confidence of a lord, even if I'd shaken him. And he had the reassurances of a king in waiting. Powerful, and ambitious as well.

Which left me wondering if the wrong person had taken my focus. And that maybe there wasn't only one of the Tainted in Etaynia.

Finally alone, I resumed my walk around the gardens, humming a tune only I knew.

"Mm, your singing needs work, Storyteller. Perhaps it's best if you leave that to someone else." Eloine rounded the corner, coming out from behind a row of tall-standing shrubs.

She'd forgone the nobler cut of dress she wore before among the finer company of Del Soliel. The dark of her hair lay covered under a tight-bound wrap the color of shadowed honey. It complemented her skin. A few locks still fell free from the covering, however, drawing attention to her eyes. The memory of redness hung in them, as if she'd been crying and only just wiped the tears free.

One of her hands brushed up a flowing-loose sleeve of fresh white, and she rubbed her forearm in the same manner of a child trying to calm themselves. The rest of her dress followed the same convention, billowing, and kept tight only at her waist with a sash the same shade as her head wrap.

"You're so quiet." Eloine stepped closer to me, then ran a hand along the length of my jaw.

"You're . . . different." I hadn't meant to say it, and it fell far from the more flattering things I could have said.

A light shone in her eyes, but it did not brighten whatever sadness still sat there. "It's custom for a person to change their clothes as the days change, Storyteller." She took my collar in her thumbs, tugging it. "We can't wish away the dirt and grime. We have to wash. You remember that practice, yes?" The touch of amusement again, but as before, it did not last.

I shook my head, tucking my staff under an arm, and took her hands in mine. "That's not what I meant. It's just . . . how you look. You . . ." I trailed off again, unsure of how to say it. It wasn't an obvious thing.

Like the changing of the moon. Though you might only see a sliver of it, it was still and wholly the moon. But you never saw all of her. And sometimes, her new faces could distract you.

"I think . . ." She folded her fingers over mine and pulled them down between our chests. "That you think too much, Ari. You should try to do less of that, and sometimes simply be." Eloine pulled me as she walked backward, leading me away from the fountain.

"Be what?"

Eloine let out a long drawn-out sigh. "Be here, with me." She raised both brows, making it clear it was time not to ask more questions, and simply accept her reasoning.

I could do that much, and I quietly nodded.

"Good. Have you had breakfast yet?"

I shook my head.

She mirrored the gesture. "I should have known as much. You do a terrible job looking after yourself, you know?"

I snorted. "I think I've done well enough all things considered. You've heard how much I've survived."

Eloine pulled one of her hands from mine and reached up to tweak my nose.

"Ow."

She did not grin, and it let me know she had not done that in humor. "Surviving isn't the same as living, Ari. You should consider trying more of the latter than the former."

I arched a brow. "Is that concern I hear?" I pulled my free hand to my heart, pressing it tight there. "I'm so flattered."

She rolled her eyes. "You flatter yourself. My motivations are purely selfish. You see, this man I worry for has promised me a story. But he's done me a terrible turn in teasing me with only parts of it. I haven't heard the whole of it, and I very much would like to. But if he wastes away to man's many foolish behaviors, I'll be left all the poorer without this tale."

I fought to keep from smiling. "And . . . without his company, yes?"

Eloine turned and eyed me askance. "Of course . . . of course. His company. Yes, I would be at a terrible loss without that as well." She kept her voice perfectly measured, without giving the slightest hint by tone of any sarcasm or feeling of genuine loss.

"Well, I'm rather wounded to hear that. I suppose I should go back and find Lord Umbrasio to see if he'll make good on his threat to kill me. You'd be free of my company rather quickly, and I wouldn't have to try to recall all of my story—" I winced as the small bones of my right hand came under hard pressure. Sharper lines of pain lanced across the tops of my knuckles where Eloine's nails dug in.

"He threatened you again? When? Where?" One of her hands brushed along the side of her dress, and I thought I saw a slender shape held firm against her thigh.

Is that a knife?

She didn't give me the time to think, however. "Ari, what happened?"

I told her of my brief meeting with Umbrasio, and the threats we'd both exchanged.

Her eyes flashed and the shade of gray in green gave way to something brighter—darker then. Like a spark of emerald lightning shot through with shadow. "You have a penchant for threatening nobles, no? You should walk more carefully beside them. Or do you mean to kill him like Shareem?" She blinked, realizing what she'd said.

Our hold on one another faltered, and I took my staff back in hand.

"I'm sorry, Ari. I didn't mean—"

"I know. It's all right." I tried to mask my tone, but it left me dry, and hollow.

She caught that. "It obviously isn't. I should have thought about that before saying it." Her hands went back to my collar, fiddling with its edges. "I worry about what you're doing. What you *do*. You're reckless."

"I know, and you're right. I don't fault you for what you said. I did kill Shareem."

The stillness returned, now settling between us, and I wished I knew what to say to break it.

Eloine flashed me a thin and tired smile that faded just as fast. "The necessary thing, as we discussed before." She turned over a hand, palm up. A silent invitation for me to place mine in hers.

I did, and she folded her thumb over my fingers, pulling me along again as she moved. "And you're leading me where?"

Eloine gave me a knowing look.

I sighed. "Right, be here. In the moment with you."

"Mm." Eloine brought me to a circular table fashioned from a white wood that held a grain similar to ivory. The chairs were made of the same. Arched and bent into swooping shapes, like pale-chalk ivy that had been coaxed to grow in that form, rather than made by chisel and plane. "Sit with me?"

I did so, taking the seat directly opposite her. My staff rested against the lip of the table and I waited for her to say what clearly rested on her lips.

"I understand, you know?" Eloine put her hands on the table, her fingers playing with one another as her gaze drifted away from me. "What you did to Shareem, and what it did to you. It's the kind of memory that makes a scar of itself in remembrance.

"And I know what I said earlier, about learning to let it go, is far easier said than done. But at least promise you'll try?" She took one of my hands in hers.

I nodded in weak and silent agreement.

Her posture softened and she let go of me. "Good." She looked around as if expecting someone else to come by before turning her attention back to me. "I'm afraid this won't be as much of a meal as last night." The curve of her mouth took on the shape of something halfway between apology and fatigue.

I gave her a more energetic smile in return. "I'm more than happy just sharing the time with you."

A brighter look fell upon her, but once again, it lasted all too shortly. "You're sweet."

I wanted to ask what had happened. What had prompted her to give up dressing as a noble, and brought about such tiredness in her, but a longer look told me they would be unwelcome questions. So I swallowed the mounting sigh and resigned myself to muted curiosity.

A change of subject would do us better. "Is there anything you'd like? I don't have the influence I'd say you do here among the nobility, but I'm sure I can request something."

She shook her head. "Not right now, and I believe whatever influence I've had is all but gone now. Prince-elect Efraine and I do not . . ." She bit her lip and let the words die off. "His pontifex, I mean . . ." Once again the words fell to nothingness.

Ah. His pontifex. Relations between the two men seemed stronger than any noble's and their churchly leader's I'd seen before. Though I wasn't quite sure who belonged to whom in their situation. And the pontifex's disposition the previous night gave me the inkling that it might very well be him in charge of things, regardless of what Efraine believed.

Or had been led to.

Perhaps the pontifex was playing a better game of Talluv than what Efraine had treated me to. And a prince-elect was nothing more than a piece to move along a board. Which left me wondering, what were the stories told in that game? What were the lies?

"Besides, I have an appetite for something else altogether, Storyteller." More of a true smile touched her face, though it still didn't reach her eyes. "What happened next?"

I licked my lips, bringing up the memory. "I'd just killed Shareem, and only three other people besides me knew it. I was young, and unsure of what to do. With the deaths of Mithu, Askar, and Biloo, the streets of Abhar did what they would. Which is to say, moved on. It was a city with no time to spare for the dead.

"The desert was not such a place. So I had to deal with things the only way I knew how. A child's way, because despite all things I'd been called by then, I was still nothing more than a boy. And there were consequences to be faced for the death of a desert prince, who may not have been one in title, but certainly was in all other ways."

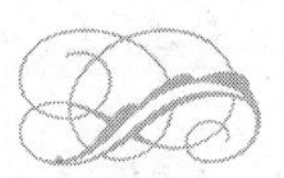

NINETY-THREE

Blood and Tears

Red.

The color washed through his clothes like a drop of ink in water. But the warmth hadn't left his skin as I pressed one of my hands to the side of his throat.

Shareem, son of Sharaam, desert prince and husband-to-be of Qimari, lay dead.

Alwi's chest rose so fast I didn't know if he'd be able to draw breath. Baba's mouth worked in silence, trying and failing to utter any sound at all.

Last there was Qimari. She watched me with the stillness of someone who had just watched their entire world fall apart. And the quiet knowing that nothing would ever be the same again. The weight of the questions, heavy upon her: What did we do now? What happens next? And what consequences would fall upon us?

I had no answers for many of those. At least ones she would have wanted to hear. Instead, I only had a sparrow's solutions.

I could spend time settling Qimari and the others, but every moment I tarried meant the possibility of discovery. First, I would have to hide Shareem's body. Somewhere it couldn't be easily found. That meant moving it, and all without being seen in the act.

No easy task.

Then there remained the fact that Aisha would look for me soon enough. She had given me an order, and she would have questions as to where I'd vanished. The last and eventual problem rested with people realizing Qimari's whereabouts. People had seen Shareem leave with Qimari, even if they hadn't a clue he'd ventured off with her to explore empty parts of the city. They would ask her in hopes of finding him.

Suspicion could quickly fall on her then.

Especially once everyone realized that he had disappeared.

I wouldn't let that happen. Cold practicality and old responsibility fell on me. "Alwi, Baba, help me." My voice had the weight of ice and stone as I ordered the boys out of their stupor. "Find me something to wrap him in. I don't care what it is so long as there is lots of it. Do you understand? Carpet, sheets, blankets. Anything."

The boys looked at me, trading a glance between themselves. Each stayed fixed in place, however.

"*Move.*" I hadn't raised my voice, but it fell on them with the authority I once had as a king of sparrows.

The two boys snapped into motion. They raced up the first flight of stairs and vanished around the turn.

Qimari finally found her voice in the aftermath of their leaving. "What are you going to do, Ari? We killed him. His father . . ."

I shook my head. "*We* didn't do anything. *I* killed him. Shareem would have survived his wound, and then only Brahm knows what would have happened. Maybe you had the right of it, and it would have been war between the tribes. If that was to be, then I'm not so sure I should have let that happen. How many more would die then?" The words came to me from a place I didn't know.

No logic drove them, or experience. Perhaps just a boy trying to find a way to make killing sit easier with himself. And provide what little comfort he could to a friend.

Qimari licked her lips and took a breath. "Then what are you going to do right now?"

I didn't answer her immediately, instead focusing on the floor and our surroundings. Little of his blood had spilled onto the ground, and what bits had were behind me. Likely from when Qimari drove the shears into his chest. Not so much that it would be a problem to hide, or lead to any trouble for us should people come looking.

Alwi and Baba's steps sounded their return.

I looked over to see them carrying a rolled carpet and several folded sheets thrown on top of it.

"This is what we found." Alwi led Baba and the bundle to the center of the room and dropped it to the ground.

The length of each piece happened to be longer than Shareem's full height, but not by much. A small miracle, and I thanked them for finding what they had. "Spread them open, will you?" I didn't wait to see if they did as I asked. My hands went to Shareem's ankles and I dragged his body toward the boys.

They understood my intent and held the carpet firm as the dead prince's body slid over it until it came to rest in the middle. We worked in silence as we lay the other sheets over him.

"Help me roll this." I took one side of the carpet in hand, leaning forward as I applied pressure and began to tuck it into itself. The two boys fell to the task, and soon we had Shareem neatly hidden within the rolls. "There's twine on Anedi's packs. Bring me some. Cut it free if you need to." I took my Arasmus knife, hand shaking now, and passed it toward Alwi.

The boy looked at the red-tinged blade, the blood on my hands, and then to the carpet in which Shareem lay. His throat formed a lump, and it sat there, no sign of it vanishing any time soon. He wouldn't be able to touch the knife, not after what he'd just seen.

And I couldn't blame him for it.

I looked to Baba, and the child turned away from my stare as well.

Qimari came over to me and placed a hand on mine, gently easing the knife from my hold. "I'll do it. It's the least . . ." She took a breath. "It's the least I can do."

I nodded, taking one of her arms in my grip and giving her a tight and reassuring squeeze.

She accepted it with a look that could have been a silent thank-you, but I wouldn't know. Then she left the house and went to bring me the rope.

All of us remained in that silence as we wound cord over carpet, tying it tight to ensure nothing would come undone and reveal Shareem's body. Once done, the obvious and eventual question came to everyone's mind, but Qimari found the tongue to voice it first.

"What now? We can't just leave him like this. Someone might find him."

"I know. Help me get him onto Anedi." I took one end of the carpet. Everyone pitched in and we soon brought it onto the streets and over to my camel.

It took little to bid the usually stubborn camel to kneel so we could pull Shareem's body onto the beast's back and fasten him in place. That done, I mounted Anedi and brought him back to his feet. "Are there other ways out of the city, Qimari? Paths that won't be watched right now?"

Mercifully, there were. And Qimari told me the way.

I nodded. "If Aisha asks about me, tell her . . ." What could I ask her to say? What possible reason could I have for vanishing? A piece of the truth, I supposed. "Tell her I saw something I needed to investigate. A fresh fire, or so it looked. That's close enough to what brought me down this way before I heard you."

I didn't wait to see if she would agree, or if she had anything to say. My boots clapped to Anedi's sides in a gentle tap, urging him to break into motion. We did, and the two of us rode in silence.

Him, in the quiet comfort of a camel doing nothing more than going for a walk. He had no care for where or why.

Me, under the silent weight of what I'd done, and what would happen to my friends if anything went wrong between now and what I had to do next.

I might have terribly envied the life of a camel then.

Anedi eventually brought me to the gate Qimari had told me of, and we rode longer still through it and across the sands. Far, far from the walls of Iban-Bansuur.

Until I reached a set of dunes that made the city look like a child's toy of one, rather than tall buildings that cast taller shadows still.

Then, I cut Shareem's body free from my mount and began to dig. I hadn't been given a spade on my journey with Arfan. There had been no need for one of my own, not with my tents and most things being set up for me.

The small privilege of being in his service. My time had been more valuably spent on doing what he wanted.

I mention this because I don't know if you've ever had to dig a grave by hand, but it is no painless thing. You might think that sand is soft, so it is easy to do this.

You're right in part. But sand is light, and has a want of its own, mostly to settle where it's already come to lay. So for every handful I scooped, a passing bit of wind would push it back. The weight of the world told it to sink down again.

And sand has little teeth of its own. Sharp grains hidden in the softer pieces. Broken shells of creatures I couldn't imagine, and just so of how they came to be there. Old stone that hadn't been smoothed in all its time below the surface, and instead still kept its sharper edges.

Every rake of my hands exposed my fingers to a heat that had nothing to do with the sunbaked warmth of the sands. I dug until night came over the desert. And I kept at it long after the moon had reached her full height.

Eventually, Shareem lay in his grave and I piled the sands back over him.

Then I curled over his resting place, and I wept where no one could see me.

NINETY-FOUR

Sleepless

I returned to Iban-Bansuur before the sun rose the next morning. The shadow of night gave the city a different look. The sandstone walls held a cold grayness, dark and almost warning me to stay away. Things bled of all color.

The intricate latticework along some of the balconies did not seem inviting or made to offer a beautiful view to those behind them. Now they resembled crossing ivy, almost as if meant to bar my sight of what lay inside.

A different sort of prison.

I made my way through the gate and wandered back the way I'd come, taking twice as long to traverse the streets. My stomach knotted and it had nothing to do with hunger, though I told myself that was the cause.

"Ari?" The call of my name sent a new wave of coldness through my heart and spine. Aisha's voice. She'd found me.

I turned to watch her coming down a street parallel to the one I rode on. She'd left her mount behind and traveled on foot. Though I noticed her bow rested in her hand. "Aisha."

Her face betrayed little, but her mouth held the makings of a frown to come. "Where have you been? I told you to wait. We've been looking for you and the others for more than two candlemarks."

I blinked. "The others?" Surely Qimari and the two boys hadn't kept themselves away for that long.

"It took us until late night to find Qima. We still haven't found Shareem. I had thought . . . They were together before we broke apart at *Mejai* Arfan's command." The unspoken question hung clear in her face.

I had no answer for her, though. "Who else is missing?" Turning the matter away would be for the best, and I had hoped it would lighten the weight on her mind.

"Hm? Oh, the two younger boys with Qima. We found them shortly after her. They'd gone off exploring the city." She shook her head. "Boys." The word left her half a curse and just as much light amusement. "Only a man would go looking for trouble in a city that had just seen its share of it."

Her words reminded me of what had happened before we parted ways. "What happened in the building earlier? The sounds, the stranger."

She took a deep breath. "The man is mad. Far gone in the head. He tried attacking us. Screamed about red smoke and dancing shadows. Blood everywhere, and his own hands were covered in it. The bodies we found inside the place . . ." She brought a hand to her mouth, stole another breath, then stilled herself.

"It's bad. Not one of them died a kind death."

I wondered if there was any such thing, but said nothing.

"I've never seen a thing like this, and for a long while, we were all thinking he had done it. But no. I think seeing it done is what broke him. He sees demons in every corner, and *Maathi* had to give him medicine to make him sleep, and even that took a great deal. His heart beat harder than any man's I've seen. Hard, Ari, like a drummer that cannot stop. I was sure it would burst soon enough."

Demons. He'd seen the Ashura. The problem of Shareem had almost made me forget. I nearly leapt from Anedi's back and had the full urge to demand her to lead me to the maddened man. But I reined in the impulse and remembered myself.

"Do you think I'd be able to speak with him, Aisha?"

She fixed me with a long and searching look. "Why?"

I exhaled and knew I couldn't tell her everything, but after what we had seen here, I could share enough. "The things that happened here, Aisha . . . they happened once in another place far away. My home."

Her eyes widened, but she said nothing.

"My family died like this, and I still don't know everything about how or why. I just have ideas, and I think this man might know something that could help me. Please?"

She pursed her lips and I could see the decisions running through her mind. "I will talk with *Mejai* Arfan. He wishes to speak to the man himself . . . after *Maathi*'s ministrations. *Shir* Sharaam's *Maathi* wishes to speak with the man as well. You may have to wait."

"I can't." The words left me before I'd realized. My fists were balled, and my teeth grated. I couldn't risk losing them, coming in so late behind them like in Ampur. Not again.

"It's not for you to decide, Ari." If she'd taken umbrage at what I'd said, she didn't show it. Aisha's face kept to the same expression as before, saying something without giving it voice.

"There's more, isn't there?"

She nodded. "We have found another as well. He is locked in a cell and refuses to speak. No words. Just silence. He is . . . odd. But no threat. He just sits, waiting, watching, and silent. We found him jailed already, and we do not know why, or if he knows what happened. Or . . . how long he has been there. He is being given food and water as we can spare it, but I do not know how much longer the *Shir*s will do that much for him."

Another person who might have been here during the Ashura's attack. Perhaps I'd be able to see him as well. Did he play a part in the chaos?

Aisha must have gleaned my desires from my face. "You wish to visit the man. I can ask, though I do not think it will be worth your time. As I've said, he does not speak." She took another deep breath and let it out. "Maybe you will fare better than we have. Come." She turned a half step and nodded down the way she'd come. "*Mejai* Arfan will want to speak to you before you are allowed to have the day to yourself." An undercurrent of *if* ran through those words.

If I'd be allowed to have any time for myself at all, she'd meant.

I followed behind her in silence, though, not wanting to upset the calm of the moment. She'd found me coming into the city long after I should have already been back by her side. The last thing I needed was Aisha's trust in me broken so soon again after we'd patched things up over Qimari. Especially now that I had to hide Shareem's death.

She led me through the streets until we came to a building close to the center of the city. Inside, we found Arfan sitting on a pile of cushions atop a thick rug.

A steaming beverage had been poured into several cups, and he was in conversation with several of the men I'd seen him with back in his old tent. This included *Shir* Sharaam. Arfan's *Maathi,* however, was nowhere to be seen.

They all turned to regard me as I entered.

The merchant king beckoned me with a wave of his hand, and I approached. "Where were you?"

Straight to it then. I took a breath and told him most of the truth, leaving out the events with Qimari.

He frowned and rubbed his chin. "I heard of some of those fires. Fresh, by the sound of them. My riders found little in them, though. Old, and only kicked up anew by the wind. What did you find in yours?"

I swallowed, not knowing what to say, as I hadn't investigated the flame and smoke as I'd wished. "Nothing, but I thought—hoped I'd see something."

Arfan nodded, more to himself than me. "Because of what happened to your family." He'd already known, and likely from more than one source. I hadn't kept it wholly secret from the people I'd grown close to in his service.

I bowed my head. "Yes."

Shir Sharaam watched me with more attention than Arfan. "At the mention of family, I am very much wondering where mine happens to be. Have you seen my son?"

"I saw him earlier when we first rode into the city, *Shir* Sharaam. I believe he ventured off at some point after that." *Close enough to what happened, at any rate.*

The *Shir* stared long over the rim of his cup, searching me like he could see through me. Eventually he let out a breath and set the drink down. "It is like him. Reckless, doing as he will. He has likely taken to seeing more of the city. He has never been able to search all of it." *Shir* Sharaam then turned his attention on Arfan, and something hardened in his gaze.

"*But* . . . blood has already been spilled in Iban-Bansuur, and I do not wish to see my son's in that."

Arfan raised a hand for calm. "It will not come to that. Our children are as clever as they are capable. They will be safe. You jump too quick to danger, *Shir*."

Sharaam scowled. "There is *kirtaaf* between our blood. Your grandfathers long ago spurned mine—broke their word, and let their honor hold no water."

Arfan stiffened. "And yours took that water from my family . . . from their blood."

The air was sharp strings, and the sharper edge of knives, all ringing that metal-threat sound found in battle.

No one spoke for some time. Only eyes watching. Only waiting.

Then Sharaam scowled. "We bind our families to move past old wounds. But those wounds are still remembered. By me. And by you."

Arfan nodded.

"It would not be beyond someone to shed blood where it was already spilled. Do you understand what I am saying, *Shir*?" Sharaam narrowed his eyes at the merchant king. "Words and vows have been broken before."

Arfan remained cool and impassive as he spoke. "And *should* something happen to Shareem?" The question hung in the air, and unseen knives grew sharper still. Their edges now could be felt along the throats of all in attendance.

And I thought back to the man of shadows who'd been in my room. The question I'd asked Aisha: if she and Arfan had a plan for dealing with *Shir* Sharaam.

But Sharaam spoke then. "Should something happen to me or mine, this will not be all the blood the city sees, do you understand? I will not let the old ways hold sway now when others have already done away with them and defiled this place. Should I not see my son soon enough . . ." *Shir* Sharaam did not finish speaking, leaving the threat unsaid, but as clear as could be.

Arfan's hand gripped hard enough to his cup that I almost thought it would crack under his grip. "You threaten a dangerous thing. Iban-Bansuur is sacred.

It has been done a great evil by what has happened, and it is not our place, or *yours,* to promise more. But I will meet you should you make that choice, Sharaam." He didn't bother with the honorific, and I felt that made the weight of the situation clear enough for all.

"But we will do it outside the walls of the city—in the desert. As it should be. Do you understand? I am not asking if you agree, but if you understand me, my *friend.* Because you are not being given the choice of how and where it will happen. It will not stand, and I will see you named and called before all *Shir*s for betraying the sanctity of this place. You can then choose how your honor holds after that."

No one spoke. And everyone stared at the two leaders.

Shir Sharaam gave way first, shying from Arfan's gaze and getting to his feet. "I wish you a good and safe rest, *Shir.* May you wake to another morning of warmth and find shade when you seek it." The man stood straighter than before, one of his hands going to the curved knife under the sash along his waist. His fingers brushed the hilt but did not rest on the weapon proper. "I will be looking for my son, and I hope for all our sakes I find him. When your *Maathi* is done speaking to the madman, I will be sending mine to speak with him as well."

Arfan bowed his head in quiet acceptance.

Shareem's father left, but the threats that had been shared still hung between us all. The promise of war.

Brahm's blood, what had I done? Even trying to spare Qimari and the boys could lead us to the same place. I had felt as if I'd had no other choice—leaving Shareem alive would have indicted Qimari, and led to her death. Silencing him seemed the best course to avoid that. And now . . . ? A dark part of me wanted to let out a loud and sickly laugh over the realization. But I kept it deep down inside of me, held and buried.

Like Shareem.

I supposed that if things continued as they were, I might soon join him.

Aisha seized the silence to bring up what I had been keeping to myself. "Ari wishes to see the man in the cell, and he asked permission to speak to the madman after *Shir* Sharaam and the *Maathi*s are done."

Arfan took a breath, bringing the cup back to his mouth, finally taking the sip he'd been denied earlier. "Bring him to the man later. Now, all are in need of sleep, for I don't think any took rest through the night. After that, you will return to the work I set you to when first coming to me. Someone knows what has happened here, Ari. And many have seen more than they might realize. You will listen, you will learn, and you will report to me." He tipped the cup back again. "Then you will help look for Shareem."

I nodded, not trusting myself to speak.

He dismissed me with a wave of his hand. "Find a place to sleep for what remains of the night. I do not wish to see anyone now." The words had the intended effect, and everyone in attendance rose to leave.

Aisha gripped me by the arm and led me outside. "You should put your questions with the man in the cell away. At least for now. If Shareem isn't found . . ." She blew out a breath and shut her eyes for a moment. "Have you ever been in a battle, Ari? And not the skirmish we saw in the sands."

I shook my head.

"Let us hope you don't have to. They are not easy things." One of her hands flexed several times and her jaw visibly clenched.

When she said nothing further, I took the chance to ask her what she'd meant. "What about them exactly?"

Aisha licked her lips and motioned for me to follow as she walked on. "What you will be asked to do in them. What you will see and have to remember. You do not have choices in many of those things. They will change you . . . and not for the better, I am afraid."

"Have they changed you?" I hadn't intended the question to be prying, or accusatory. It was born of simply wanting to better understand someone I'd come to care about.

Her lips went thin and the look she gave me had a tired patience hanging in it. "All war asks a price of people. And if someone returns saying it hasn't, they are either lying, or they paid that cost long before." She didn't elaborate, and I followed her until she brought me to another building.

Low, squat, and sporting a domed roof that could have once been glazed and painted bright, though now carried the peeling black of something deeply burned. Even the stone bore the same charred coloring and marks.

"I've set up here, and there is a place for a fire if you wish to set one." Aisha didn't wait for me to agree, entering the space.

I went inside after her. The place resembled where we'd found Arfan. A thick rug and a half dozen plump cushions. One table remained, cracked and furrowed.

The walls were much the same. Stone, laced with spider-webbing lines that revealed their damaged condition. And the smears of now pale red that hadn't quite gone away even under the work of water and rag.

Someone had at least tried to scrub the place clean.

Aisha caught my stare. "I chose it before setting out in search of Qimari and the others. It's small, so it will be easier to hear if someone moves through it. The roof is tight and low and metal-lined, so sound echoes well inside. No one will be able to sneak up on us if there are some still in Iban-Bansuur who mean us harm." That is when she realized I hadn't wondered about her choice of building as much as what had happened to the bloody walls.

"I did what I could to clean it away, as much to sleep easier as to keep this place close to what it was."

"And what was it?"

Aisha lowered her bow and stripped out of her outer layer of clothing. "It's a story for another time, Ari. A long one. You should get some sleep, and let me change in privacy."

I did as she asked, but I found little sleep in what remained of the night.

NINETY-FIVE

COSTS

The morning saw me set immediately to work. The only way I'd be able to speak to those who'd been in the city during the Ashura attack. And that became my principle drive to get as much of what I could done to placate Arfan, and as soon as possible.

I rushed through the city, setting to any odd job that needed a pair of hands. Though it was my eyes and ears really doing the work. The work of plucking gossip.

And all conversation turned up rumors.

What had happened in the city? Ajuura—*bhaalghul*. One suggested that two tribes had gone to war, betraying the sacred promise kept within the city, and fleeing once one tribe fell. Where was Shareem? Still exploring—lost. Some said he'd run away after seeing the bloodied city, a coward. A few felt it to be a ploy for a devious plot not yet revealed. Some whispered *murdered*.

My stomach knotted at mention of that. The world began to look a great deal like a work of woven string. And those strings were quickly fraying.

Exhausting every possible avenue for rumor-mongering, I headed back to Arfan by fourth candlemark's beginning.

He sat alone, holding a vial of milky white fluid that I had long since come to despise. A few drops fell on each of his eyes and the merchant king blinked hard several times. One trail streamed down the side of his check. "Ari?"

I nodded, then realized his vision might be clouded by the use of white-joy, so I answered him instead. "Yes."

He grunted and I took it to mean he wanted me to tell him what I'd learned.

So I did. "People think *Shir* Sharaam's tribe is responsible for this. And the same for Shareem's disappearance. It gives him the pretense for war, and if you would like my personal opinion . . ." I *had* overheard someone else mutter that rumor. It just so happened to be a convenient one that moved suspicion away from me.

He waved a hand, telling me to continue.

"He did seem to offer the ultimatum rather quickly, *Shir.* It felt practiced, almost. Perhaps he has always been looking for a reason?"

Never mind the fact this is your fault. The thought sent cold bands through my gut. I couldn't have known, of course, but then, I did it to spare someone I cared about. To stop a war.

And it looked to be inevitable regardless.

Arfan blew out a long breath, eyelids fluttering. "I have thought on this a long time since we last spoke, Ari. I believe it is possible. Sharaam has always been quick to war, and it has done his tribe good before. And it has earned him enemies. Do you know why I have remained in power as I have, and no tribe has taken my life yet?"

"No."

"The same things I trapped you with. Secrets. I know them for every man I set my eyes upon, and I am willing to sell them. Not just for wealth, but another sort of power. A falcon left as soon as sunup this morning with *Shir* Sharaam's words, all recorded as truth, signed by me and the other men who'd heard. Marked with our blood." He held up a thumb that bore the mark of being pricked.

"My word is above question, as are my men's—well known and regarded through many tribes. And should we be proven to be lying . . ." He brought that same thumb to his throat, dragging a curved line along it.

"They will know Sharaam threatened the laws of this place—its respect. It will not end kindly for him should things go as he wishes—war." When Arfan looked at me, the brown of his eyes had paled a touch, and the whites were far brighter than before. "Do you understand?"

I nodded, but in truth, I didn't. "Do . . . you think it will come to that, *Shir,* war?"

He shrugged. "I cannot see that."

See? I looked down at the vial still in his hands, then his eyes. "What do you mean by that?"

He grinned, and it was a thing like I had seen in him a few times before. A fox's cunning. "Do you know what this can do to a man?" Arfan shook the vial.

I stiffened and bit my tongue, deciding this was a moment to find better words than the immediate truth. "I have . . . had experiences, *Shir.* I have an understanding of white-joy."

"Mm. I'm sure you have and do, Ari. Do you know it has a history among the seers, the wise men, the ones who can see more than there is to see, to glean the truth of things?"

I frowned. "What truth is that?"

He only smiled wider. "Things in motion. Things to be wary of. Things to be." Arfan took a deep breath. "That is for those with the strength of mind to endure the drug's . . . other effects."

I thought of the men who'd once tried to grab me in an alley, and the man who came offering a vial of the liquid, all to pacify them. They would have stripped me and sold whatever pieces of me they could for another drop of joy. I remembered then how it had turned the man I'd taken to be my adoptive father into someone who thought he could fly.

And in his haste to show me he could, he only proved that he was no sparrow.

But worst of all, I remembered a young boy, much like me in appearance, who had been given too much of the drug. His half-sensible words muttered in fever dreams that soon turned to full gibberish. I remembered little else, but I kept in heart his name.

Taki. My brother.

And I remembered holding him until he died.

I said none of these things to the merchant king, however.

"This bothers you." He knew that before he'd asked.

I nodded.

"I understand. I know much of what I have been doing of late has led my people to worry—to wonder, but they cannot see what I see. Know what I do."

Something inside me twisted—turned cold at that. Was this the reason behind Arfan's actions, then? Not the wisdom of his *Maathi,* or some other knowings earned over a life of cleverness and hard living. But now following the lead of a drug that addled the minds and visions of all those who took it.

If Arfan had truly gone the way of becoming a cotton eyes, then he would lead more than himself into danger. He would jeopardize the whole tribe. Qimari, Aisha, and countless others. And none would be able to stop him, because the weight of his own mantle kept him safe from reproach, and reprisals.

I wanted to ask him what he had seen in these visions, but I didn't get the chance.

A man burst into the meeting, breathing hard. "*Mejai* Arfan. My *Shir.*"

The merchant king whirled in place, his face breaking into a storm to strike hard on the man for his interruption. "What?"

"They have found Shareem's horse but no Shareem. There is nothing, no one. And the beast is angry—scared. Something has happened to him, I fear. His father . . . the *Shir* Sharaam, I mean . . ."

Arfan bolted to his feet, the vial of joy falling to the carpeted floor. "Take me to them. *Now.*"

The man bobbed his head and led the way.

I fell into step behind Arfan, hand tight on my staff, my other brushing the hilt of my Arasmus knife.

We were brought to a street nearby. Shareem's horse bucked the hold of two men trying to calm it. *Shir* Sharaam stood there, looking the beast over. His *Maathi,* however, could not be seen.

Voices, loud and carrying hard through the air, told me that the group had been arguing long. A mix of both tribes.

Shareem's father spotted us coming and left the horse's side, storming over to us. "You see! My son's horse. But where is he? Where is my son?" The question echoed with the weight of thunder through the streets of Iban-Bansuur. "I name you bloodletter, Arfan. You or yours have done this thing. My son would never leave his horse behind. Not a gift of this bloodline, of Alum's first wind himself. Purebred, and long has this line been in my family.

"A line that has won the *Il-Faragh* many times. Many times." Fists clenching, jaw flexing visibly as he ground his teeth. His chest rose hard and a thick vein grew noticeable upon the man's throat. "There is no answer for this. Tell me, Arfan. Do you have one? Do you!"

The merchant king looked around, first to his men, then those belonging to Sharaam. He finally shook his head. "I do not."

Shir Sharaam took the stillness then of a world waiting to break into a storm. Silent. Unmoving, even in breath. Finally, he exhaled. "You wish for Iban-Bansuur to see no more blood? I cannot give you this. I will send for the rest of my tribe, and if you and yours are still here when they arrive, we will leave these walls red for a thousand years with your blood. If you leave, I will hunt you, and I will spill so much of your blood along the sands the sun will rise to cry the same color every day until all memories of you are gone.

"Or, you can give me the ones responsible for this, and I will treat them with the old laws. If you do this, I will spare you the pains of war. But, I tell you this now in truth, do not do this, because I do not want to give you that kindness in return. I will kill you. You, your *Maathi,* and your daughter."

Arfan brushed me hard aside, reaching out to take the other *Shir* by his collar. He pulled him close and dropped his voice to a hard and glass-edged whisper. "You will not touch my daughter. You threaten her again—"

Sharaam broke his grip. "Then you shouldn't have touched my son. You will learn the weight of what losing a child means."

Qimari peered from behind the crowd, and I caught her eyes. Wide. Filled with fear. Both for herself, and her people.

Blood and ashes. Brahm, if you're really real, look out for me in what I'm about to do. Once again, the necessary things. I sighed and stepped as close between both men as I could. Because if I didn't, Shareem's death would have been for nothing. And Qimari could soon join him. That, I could not allow. "Wait."

Arfan rounded on me.

Sharaam raised the back of his hand as if ready to cuff me for interrupting.

"If you find out what happened to your son, and who did it, will it spare *Shir* Arfan's people from war?"

Shir Sharaam's eyes narrowed, and he answered me. "I will see them dealt the same fate as my son's, all by the old laws. They will not live but for the grace of Alum sparing them. And I will pray every hour that He Above offers them no such thing. Only suffering. But, should I be granted what I ask, I will reconsider the promise of war."

A way to stop this. To save everyone.

I took another breath and I watched Qimari shove her way past the gathering crowd. Her eyes met mine again, and I saw her silent plea. The request for help, and just as much for me not to do what I was about to.

I looked *Shir* Sharaam directly in the eyes when I spoke. "Your son is dead. I killed him."

Just keep her safe, I thought.

Qimari screamed something, but I didn't hear it.

The *Shir*'s hands came to my throat. A dozen more joined him.

My body crashed to the ground. The world spun and blackness lanced my vision. A moment of white, clarity, and it was ripped away from me again. I remember the distinctive weight of a boot slamming hard against my head.

Then I lost sight of everything but the darkness.

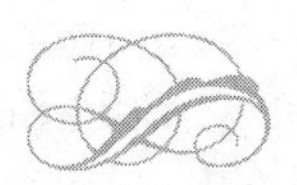

NINETY-SIX

The Fairness of Things

When I dreamed, the world held all the darkness of a night sky lacking stars and moon. I floated on a sea of ceaseless black wherewith I had no way of moving. It carried me until a brightness struck me blind.

Violent bands of brilliant blue—the lance of lightning raking all I could see. It closed on me, threatening to take me whole. A shape hung within it, almost wearing the lightning as wings. It raced toward me with the silent promise of swallowing me in the space of itself.

A bird?

The shape struck me—

—and I woke.

My head felt as if rough sand had been placed between my ears, and it slid to one side as I rose. Each thought felt no more than a sifting grain, giving me no chance to pick one to focus on. My palms pressed against the ground, and a cool smoothness greeted my touch. I blinked until I could see clearly.

The floor had been set with tiles the color of sun-bleached cobalt. Each had patterns of seafoam white. Some were flowers, the rest were the shapes of stars. Things far more intricate and costly than what I'd seen in the parts of the city I'd been able to explore. A door barred my way—fashioned from a wood of dark umber that had lost some of its luster to time and light. Thick plates of metal with heavy rivets had been fixed in place to give it more weight, or to likely keep it from being battered down.

Not a cell. I'd been placed in a room somewhere in the city that had been repurposed to keep me trapped. My head still throbbed like a brass bell struck by a hammer. One of my hands went to my temple in an attempt to assuage the ache.

It did not help.

"Come to, have you?"

The voice sent my heart thundering and I scrabbled in place, reorienting myself until I faced the speaker.

They sat at the far corner of the room, hidden somewhat by the pale wash of light filtering through the latticework that served as a window. My eyes struggled to adjust and take in their form. Then I decided I hadn't quite recovered from the beating I'd received, as the figure's robes were a white that made mine look closer to an old traveler's gray, marred in dust and all roads' grime.

The outfit did not take the shape of any traditional cloak either. It hung around them like a breath of fog made fabric and held heavy around their collar like a mantle. The white of true moonlight, strung and pulled thin into a cloth that held a deeper glow all its own. The shimmerant set of tiny gems—diamonds—flashing along its length. It was a thing that burned with brightness that made me wince to look upon it.

I shut my eyes hard, waiting until water ran along my lids and I could blink it away. When I looked again, I realized the severity of my injury. The world now cleared and I saw the figure's odd garment for what it was.

Just white, threaded with beautiful golden thread along the hem in a script I couldn't understand. But nothing more. Their face, however, remained behind a mask that belonged on stage, and not out in the world.

Near-perfect round as a thing could be, sporting two holes for the speaker's eyes. They had been ringed in a dark paint to draw your attention, and a longer stare made me think of the mask as a bird's face if pressed flat. A hawk, an owl, or perhaps an eagle?

Their drawn hood betrayed nothing within but for the mask. Not even a chance peek at their hair.

I finally found my tongue to ask the obvious question. "Who are you?"

They lifted the mask to reveal their face for a moment shorter than one could blink, but I caught enough. Something about the blow I'd taken had left me out of sorts. But in that distant clouded space, I saw better than before.

I remembered his eyes, and the white of his teeth that had been set in something close to a smile, but not truly that thing.

"My name is Nassih, and I am a prisoner, like you. Though, I have been here longer than you have, boy. Longer than the ones you came with."

I repeated his name inside my head, and it struck me with familiarity. I had known it, but I couldn't say how or why. The sensation quickly fell under the weight of realization.

He had been here before we'd arrived. Before the Ashura! This must have been the man Aisha spoke of.

Questions screamed their way through me, each fighting to make their way to my tongue first. "What happened to the city? Did you see anything? The Ashura! Did you see the Ashura?"

Nassih raised both his hands to calm me. "Easy, Ari. Easy. So fast with the questions, ah? So quick to speak, but never first to Listen." Something in how he'd said that placed emphasis on "listen." "You should take time to hear more, otherwise you'll miss a world of importance."

I opened my mouth to ask what he meant, but I decided to take the advice and stopped myself.

"Ah, look at that, he *can* listen." Nassih clapped his hands together. "You had the right of it before when you asked my name. You meet a man and the first thing you do is ask him why he's locked away instead of how he is, or his story. The who he is and where he comes from. These are important steps to knowing things, you know? The most important. If you want to know how a man's come to be where he is, you should first learn to ask where he's come from. The things that have shaped him.

"Not jumping into other things—other questions. Otherwise you risk yourself running blindly through life. And you'll never know where you're headed." Nassih tilted his head then, regarding me through that mask much like an owl seeing something peculiar.

"Mm. Though, I suppose you're already set to doing that, aren't you?"

I frowned, dredging up a reply, then thought against it.

Nassih watched me for a moment longer and I imagined him smiling from behind his mask. He pressed one hand to his chest, making a show of the motion. "My name has meaning, it means to hear. To listen. Listener. To lend an ear, and that is something I feel everyone should do to another's story. In full."

I nodded. "You're right, I'm sorry for not asking those things, or even how you were."

Nassih nodded. "Good. And I am fine enough as far as things can be. I've been given water and food. There's not much more a man can ask for in a place like this."

I thought about that, then looked around again. The room in many ways reminded me of the one I'd spent years in as a sparrow, albeit with a nicer floor. There hadn't been much to occupy my free time with in there, though.

"I suppose some way to pass the candlemarks wouldn't be so bad."

Again, Nassih fixed me with a slow stare that made me feel like he looked more into me than at me. "Oh, I'm in no need for entertainment, boy. I have stories to keep me busy—so many in mind, and I'm Listening to a new one right now."

I furrowed my brows at that. "What do you mean? What story?"

He sighed and shook his head. "Still the wrong questions. But you could do with an answer. I'm hearing the quiet sounds of a story still in the making, of a brightling flame to be, just a spark, hoping to catch and kindle into something bigger—brighter. Or, maybe it will burn itself out before it can be anything more. Who knows? That's the interesting part of this."

Just then, he caught my eyes, and when I looked in return, I almost saw that same fire he spoke of in his look. His irises burned with a light of freshly lit candles—of binder's lamps, and morning sun. But it passed as quickly as it had come, and now the wash of sun's rays coming through the window only revealed a tired brown in his stare.

"I'm sure you've picked up some stories of your own, haven't you? You've been riding with some interesting men."

I blinked and thought of when I'd told him any of that, then remembered I hadn't. Aisha had mentioned that she and others had tried to speak to Nassih, but he had given them nothing. So how had he learned about us?

"Ah, now he's getting it, huh? Listening. And what have you heard, Ari? What have you caught?"

One of my hands came to my chin and I cradled it as I thought. "That you must be a very good listener, Nassih, to know things about how I've come here. I certainly didn't tell you."

He nodded. "I am. One of the best. It's who I am—what I do. If you get good enough at it, you can come to hear the secret shape of things. The gentle flow of them, where to go, and how to be where you need to be. To follow the unsaid things of the world. And, of course, to your interest, to find the stories you're looking for."

I sat straighter. "Stories . . . of the Ashura?"

This time, he didn't fix me with a look of reproach. "Stories like this, yes. And the others a young man such as yourself might be seeking, and the ones he doesn't know he needs to find."

"You could always just tell me if you know." I gave him what I hope came off as an inviting smile.

Nassih said nothing.

Perhaps my smile needed more work.

After a moment, he let out a heavy breath and rested his chin on steepled fingers. "Do you know the men you've come here with?"

I thought about the question, then turned to the obvious response. "*Shir*s Arfan and Sharaam?"

Nassih clicked his tongue. "*T'cha*. Each man certainly styles himself a *Shir*, no? Though, I suppose they've cut themselves in that cloth and color, though neither is much of a see-er as far as I can see or hear. Titles, far from the things themselves, wouldn't you say?"

I didn't have a clue, honestly, and I told him so. But something in how he'd said "a *Shir*"—almost one word, struck me. Nassih didn't give me the chance to ponder it, however.

"They've come a long way from their paths and purpose, though Arfan might be getting a sense of what to do. The man is going about it the wrong way." Nassih mimed squeezing something over his eyes, and I understood the gesture to mean the white-joy Arfan subjected himself to. But the stranger in the cell should not have been able to know that.

Nassih craned his head toward the lattice window, ignoring me completely. "Ah, do you hear it?"

I shook my head, then got to my feet and made my way over to the opening. The sunlight concentrated hard over it, so I couldn't get a proper look through the woven covering, but I could hear something.

Voices. Low, but they carried up from the streets below.

Below. We're on the third story. No, lower than that.

"Listening does wonders, ah? You can tell a lot with just your ears, if you know how to use them. And just as much your eyes. Imagine the marvels you'll find when you learn to make them all work together, boy. You have no idea the secrets people spill when they talk to you, or around you."

It fell together then. Aisha and others had come to question Nassih, and they must have let some details slip. But it didn't explain everything else he knew. I couldn't believe someone had brought up Arfan's use of the drug around him.

More of my fog began to clear, and I pressed him for what I wanted to know. "Nassih, I once met someone like you. His name was Maathi, and he told me about the power of stories—their importance. He knew things. Important things."

Nassih nodded as if he understood. "Seems like a smart man, and with a name like Maathi, he just might be. Do you know the meaning?"

I didn't, but I had learned what it had come to mean among Arfan's tribe, and the role they played as well. I shared this with him.

"Maybe the role and the name are not so different, hm?" Which was all he offered on the matter before changing the topic. The one I'd wanted with the fervor of a starveling sparrow. "You're catching on, and I cannot complain about that. Now, you still wish to know what you first asked about. This mentioning Maathi was nothing more than leading me down that path, yes?"

I bowed my head, half ashamed, and half in answer to his question.

"Yes. The accursed came here. And, yes, I too was here when they struck. As you can see, things did not go the way I would have wanted." He raised his hands to his side in a hapless shrug. "But most of them are gone now, and you will have an easier time catching lightning or shaping wind than finding them."

The accursed? I latched on to what else he had said. "Most of them? There are still some here? Where?"

Nassih sighed. "There you go again, not listening to the important things. But, yes, I have a feeling some of the accursed haven't left. After all, there is something they wanted here—or someone. But who knows what odd games they play? And they are very keen on keeping their secrets close to heart." He fixed me with a long stare that hit me with the weight of everything I had ever endured.

It was falling stone and burning smoke, choking the breath out of me. It was hard hands striking my soft flesh, and the pummeling of two boys who'd found a lean strip of a child on the streets. It was terror that touched me cold and deep to my marrow. A look that promised to tear its way through me, and I will not hide the fact I had to shy away from it.

When it finally broke, relief flooded me as I regained the ability to breathe again. I took hard and ragged gasps. The only person who'd ever been able to fix me with a look like that had been Rishi Ibrahm.

"You're dead set on chasing them, aren't you, boy? And I do mean *dead* set."

I didn't turn from his stare this time. "Yes." The word was hard and sharp as Arasmus steel.

He tilted his head farther to one side than before, then the other way. It reminded me very much of an owl, curious as to what it was looking at. "You really would go that far, wouldn't you? Yes." Nassih sighed and let his head slump back against the wall. "Stubborn thing. Well, if you're so keen on running after monsters in the night, you'll need something to light your way. Remember that. Every hero needs three things, like the stories."

I rattled them off before he could finish. "Candle, cloak, and cane!"

"That's right. And you've got the cloak, and cane"—Nassih gestured to the wall behind me—"hopefully you'll come across the right candle flame. You'll need it."

I followed where he'd pointed to and found my cane resting on the ground. It must have been tossed in alongside me after I'd been knocked unconscious. That prompted me to search myself to see what else remained. A quick pat-down showed me that my Arasmus knife still rested where I'd fastened it.

It made sense. I sat behind solid walls, with no way out but for a door too thick for my knife to cut. But my staff . . .

They hadn't known about the minor bindings I'd worked into it. I had broken doors with it before, and maybe I could again.

But then what? Strike with thunderous noise and alert everyone? Have both tribes set after me and run me down on the streets? Worse, it would only lead back to war.

"Not so easy, is it? Being trapped behind stone, left to the silence and stillness of yourself and your thoughts. A terrible prison. The worst sort. It can kill a man. And it can quiet the best of his abilities."

I said nothing, knowing him to be right after a fashion. Right then I felt myself slip into a place that held all the unknowing fear of things to come. It kept me falling through all the possibilities of what could happen, and none of them had a happy outcome for me, or the ones I cared about.

I then tried to find some clarity—to reach for the candle and the flame, but it did not come to me. I tried again, but found only the maddening and uncountable thoughts plaguing me. Something built in my heart and chest, battling in an attempt to get out. A scream—a flame, kindling brighter and promising to burn me if I didn't share it.

So I did.

I screamed for Qimari, forced into a situation she had never asked for, and then coming so close to a thing that would have scarred her forever. The death of Shareem. I screamed at the bastard for pushing her the way he did, and leaving me no choice but to kill him. The noise still needed to settle, and I howled again for the simple unfairness of a boy so close to finding what he had wished for, who now found himself locked away before reaching it.

Left likely to die.

And all for trying to do the right thing.

You might think that there is no fairness in the world, and that I should have already known this. After all, storybook demons killed my family for the simple crime of discussing a play about them. Koli had taken Nisha away from me, then masqueraded as a friend, probably laughing all the while.

There was no fairness, and I knew this. But even still, I was a boy, and I confess that I terribly wished for some just then. Even a bit. Anything I could cling to.

Because, behind the screams and anger, I was afraid.

What else could I be?

"Ah, boy. It's not an easy thing. I know." Nassih's voice edged close to grandfatherly. "And, I am sorry to say, your path likely won't get any easier, either. It is the nature of things. But we are all the makers of our own stories, and it is not too late to change yours. Though, I do not think you wish to do such a thing—walk away and—" He stopped, and I took several breaths to steady myself before I looked at him.

Nassih tapped a finger to his ears and I took his cue.

Footsteps padded along the floor outside, growing closer—faster. Someone running.

The door opened and Aisha, Arfan, and Qimari filtered inside. I caught sight of at least three more men behind them—members of the merchant king's tribe.

Shir Arfan looked at me with the expression of someone who had just been bitten by a long-trusted dog. A measure of pain, disgust, and anger. "What have you done, Ari?" He took several steps closer to me, a hand reaching for the blade at his side. The sword he'd once threatened to take my head with. "What have you done?" His voice echoed through the room, and I wagered well outside it.

He drew the weapon, and for a moment, its sliding free was the only sound to fill the space. Like metal strings strumming sharply then come to still, and that quiet came with one last word before it fell: *death*.

A promise.

"Do you know what you have ruined for me? For Qimari? How hard I have worked at this, huh? I should have left you to collect taxes to pay your debt. I should have sent you to sea. I should have killed you then and never should have thought you clever! You only lived to see a cell so Sharaam can take justice from you. But you have been valuable to me, and I had hoped for more from you, little sparrow. So I shall spare you the death at his hands, for one at mine—a mercy." The sword raised and the promise now looked more certain than before.

I shut my eyes.

"No, Father! Stop!" Qimari's voice held less fear than strength—harder than the edge of Arfan's blade, and just as sharp. "It wasn't his fault."

I waited, but the sword never fell, and I was quite sure my head remained attached to my shoulders. Even so, I might have opened my eyes and pressed my hands to my neck to check.

Qimari had stayed her father's hand, gripping tight to him with both of hers. "No. No. He did it to help me. He did it to protect me, Father. It was my fault."

Arfan's struggles stopped and he looked at her as if he hadn't realized she'd been with him all this time.

Qimari let go of him, arms hanging limp at her sides as the strength bled from her. "Shareem and I . . . fought. He tried to attack me, and it was an accident. I didn't mean for . . ." She took a breath and began again. "There were shears, and I didn't think. I stabbed him with them—here." She pressed her fingers to a space above her stomach. "I thought he would die, but I knew what would happen if he lived." She swallowed and I watched Arfan's face go through more expressions than most men were capable of.

The sword shook in his grip, and I could still picture it falling soon. "Oh, Qima." He barely managed to breathe the words out—the slightest of broken whispers. "What have you done to us?"

That sparked something in me that I thought I had let free—the flame that had come as a scream. I crossed the distance between the merchant king and myself. "She did what she had to, and so did I. She didn't kill him, but she knew what would happen if he should live. I put the knife in him, and I did it for all of you. I know it doesn't change anything, but you can't blame her for this. If you want to blame someone, then choose Shareem." My chest heaved and my breath came hot and sharp, straining my throat.

"But since you can't, I suppose you'll have to blame me."

Arfan looked me over again, and Aisha watched with grim patience. The merchant king's hand tightened on the sword and he brought it up again. "I do blame you."

The sword fell . . .

. . . and slipped slowly back into its sheath. "And so does *Shir* Sharaam, Ari. Make your peace in the days you have. He will put you to death in the old ways, outside the city walls. He has that much honor at least, it seems."

Arfan turned and left, Qimari following shortly after, giving me the look of a dog that had just been kicked. Aisha's lips had gone thin and tight, and I saw her swallow what moisture she could. In the end, she offered me a quick nod, one that almost spoke of understanding.

But I couldn't know, because she left as soon as that, never saying a word.

The door shut, and I decided that Nassih had the right of things.

So I found a corner of the cell and slumped against it.

NINETY-SEVEN

Stones, Stories, and Secrets

At least a candlemark passed with Nassih and I keeping to the silence of strangers. I spent the time staring through the lattice window, watching out past the buildings to the desert itself. Some of the tribe had taken a morning ride along the dunes, and others had set up practice for the day. Shots arced through the air, sinking into the ground far ahead. Some had bothered to line up targets and took them in the chest, head, and a few had the precision to strike the heart.

Every arrow moved with a slowness that shouldn't have been possible, and I figured it to be nothing more than a trick of the mind when turned to boredom. Part of me imagined them as falling stones being thrown by a madman's hand. It was easier that way, and I eventually made a game out of it.

My mind could not reach the candle and the flame, or the folds. But then, I didn't have to stop the falling arrows. Just track them. So I did. Soon enough I could imagine the points in space they would pass through, and shortly after that, I could predict exactly where they would land. I kept to it for what felt like another candlemark.

A sharpness struck the side of my head. I blinked and placed a hand to where I felt the mote of pain. Something *clicked* against the ground, drawing my attention. A pebble lay there. I looked at it, unsure of where it could have come from.

Motion caught my attention and I turned in time to see another chip, just as small, hurtle my way. One of my hands moved and I batted the stone away.

Nassih sat across from me, still staring from behind the odd owlish mask. "Many things on your mind?"

I nodded. "How can there not be? I'm going to be executed in a day or two."

"You seem more busy in thought than afraid, my boy. They are not the same thing. So, I ask you, are you not afraid to die?"

"Isn't everyone? I've come close enough many times, but I wasn't able to give it any consideration then. But now? I'm just waiting, and that feels worse. I know it doesn't make much sense."

Nassih bowed his head as if he understood. "The mind has many ways to spare itself the worst kinds of fears, and death is certainly among those. Waiting for death, however, just might be one of the few things worse than the thing itself. It is a prison of stillness that holds the mind and heart." Nassih bounced another stone in the palm of his hand before snapping his wrist.

It sailed toward me, but I still kept something close to the awareness I'd had in watching the arrows. One simple half step and the rock passed me by.

"Perhaps we can find other things to help you pass the time."

I glowered at him. "And do you have something in mind that resembles throwing stones at me?"

"Those were to get your attention. I was thinking more we do the only thing we can: tell stories. I'm sure you've heard some in your time, maybe been a part of a tale or two. How about it? What better to do while we wait?" He had a point, and I would always be in the mood for a story.

The door shuddered with the sound of a heavy fist banging against it. "*Zho! Zho.* Ari, are you awake?" Another pair of thumps punctuated the question. "Open the door, you blind lump, can you not see I am trying to reach the boy?

Zho! Quickly." Whomever the *Maathi* had yelled at did as he'd instructed, and the way opened. "Ah, good-good." The *Maathi* walked into the room, giving Nassih a long measured look as he did.

Then the guide and wise man turned his attention on me. "Good *Mejai* Arfan has told me what has happened, and, erhm, what you have done." He took a heavy breath, then let it loose. "Terrible things. I am sorry, my friend." The *Maathi* sounded as if he truly meant it, and on reflection, I supposed he did. "I wanted to show you, well, that is see you. The thing we have been waiting for, the meeting of the sun and the moon will be on us tomorrow, and I wished for you to know. Perhaps you will have a chance to catch the shadow of it?" He bowed his head toward the lattice-covered window and moved toward it.

The *Maathi* looked through the opening, saying nothing. Another sigh left him, one born of resignation. "It is a sad thing. You and I were to be doing much exploring and finding many more treasures. I spoke to the *Shir* on your behalf, but he was not hearing me. Too angry and saddened is he. And I understand. *Shir* Sharaam will want blood for blood, and yours might stop a war from coming, Ari. As much as both are in their fury and pain for this, you mustn't think they are only thinking with that, ah?"

I clenched my jaw and found plenty of heated words to say on the matter. Then I thought again. Whatever I may have felt, those thoughts were reserved for the *Shirs*, not my friend the *Maathi*.

He rubbed a hand against his face and breathed into the cup of his palms. "Ah, it is their duty and their displeasure in this, Ari. Mm, perhaps not *Shir* Sharaam. He will relish this thing, and he has always been a man quick to heat in his blood, and his want to spill as much. A troubled man."

"Do you think my death will stop Sharaam from wanting war?"

"For now, it is all that keeps them from shedding blood here—within these walls. That would be too terrible a thing to think on, Ari." The *Maathi* then came to my side and knelt, reaching out to me.

It took me a moment to realize what he wanted. I placed my hands inside his and he squeezed tight, like a friend—a father. Strong and reassuring.

"I cannot unmake what has happened, and for that, I am truly sorry, my friend. I am hoping, and wishing." He shut his eyes. "Alum Above, if you hear me, find a way to spare my friend. We have many more adventures to take and wonders to uncover, ah? And I will dedicate each to you and your glory, god above." He exhaled and looked at me. "They will take your life the old way, do you understand?"

I shook my head.

One of his hands came up to cradle the side of my head. "*Zho,* then listen. You will be put out on the sands, and be given whatever you wish to make a fair stand. You will be permitted to speak, and then *Shir* Sharaam, or a champion of his, will shoot you like you are a hare. If somehow his aim is untrue, he will try again, and again, until you rest under the sands."

I swallowed and thought of Aisha sinking arrow after arrow into the heart of a target. Never missing. "And how true . . . is *Shir* Sharaam or his champion's aim?"

The *Maathi* looked away from me and licked his lips. "Ah, do not dwell on this." He shook my head with fatherly affection. "You needed to know, and now you do. But do not think too much on it. You think on this: If he cannot fell you, you are given, by Alum Above's good grace, the chance to give him back in kind. You understand?"

Realization crashed into me as well as hope. "You're saying I can fight back? I can bring a bow and challenge the champion or *Shir* Sharaam in return!"

He raised both hands to stay me and my excitement. "*Zho, zho,* Ari. Yes, I am saying this, but you musn't take the wrong idea of it." The *Maathi* stroked his chin. "You must wait until you are fired on. Only after the arrow finds your body or the sand may you try your hand."

Ah. That was certainly different from knowing I could make a fair fight of it. At least, as fair as someone with my limited training could do against a person who'd likely been riding and shooting most of their life.

But still, it was a chance. And I did nothing so well as taking one of those.

"Thank you, *Maathi,* for everything. What you've told me, and . . . everything else. Thank you. I just wish I knew your name so I could say it one time before . . ." I swallowed and forced a smile on my face.

He returned the gesture, though in more earnest. "Ah, for you, my friend, I can do that." He leaned in close and shared it with me. "I am Khalil." But what I heard was: *I am your friend.*

"Thank you, Khalil."

We shook hands, and the man ruffled my hair one last time before turning to leave. He reached the door and looked over his shoulder to Nassih, frowned, then shut the door behind him.

Nassih waited until there could be no hope of the *Maathi,* Khalil, still lingering beyond the door. "He is a good man. Chasing many things that should be left alone, but a good man. You did well in making a friend with him."

I blinked. "What?"

Nassih waved me off. "Nothing. Just a tired man's ramblings. So, Ari, stories. Tell me one of yourself, will you? You do this, and I will tell you the bones of one that will keep you up for many nights pondering it."

"That's easy enough. I don't have many nights left, Nassih."

He ignored the comment. "There are stories I'm sure you wish to know about, Ari, even if you are, as you say, not long for many more nights."

And what else did I have to do?

So I relented and began telling him of how I came to be here, and for the first time in sharing my story, I shared the whole truth of the night that changed my life forever.

I told him of the Ashura.

"And then what?" Nassih had listened with all the attentiveness any storyteller could have hoped for, and I was far from one of those yet.

"I don't know. I just remembered everything Vithum had taught me and I went through the motions. I didn't think—I just did. Mithu and the others hit the ground and everyone left the bodies there for days. I felt sick and worried and too scared to leave the house of sparrows."

Nassih bowed his head in understanding. "It's a hard thing, killing. But you weren't given much choice. What happened next?"

I shared the following years with him. First of burning Koli's joy house, and what had happened there.

Nassih said nothing during this.

Then I spoke of the sparrows' games and selling secrets, and how it eventually led me to robbing Arfan. I told him the truth of this, and Nassih only laughed.

"He is cleverer than you by a good measure, boy. You shouldn't run through life thinking you're the smartest person in the room. You'll live longer that way."

I gave him a weak grin. "I'll remember that for the next life, I suppose."

He spread his hands wide at that. "Ah, well, some of us aren't so lucky as that. We're only given the one."

I frowned and almost explained the joke but decided against it. The owlish mask weighed on me with a look that made me think it would be better to continue my story. So I did.

We reached the part where I'd come to the Ashram and was nearly turned away. Eventually I arrived in Ampur and chased the Ashura, much like I had hoped to do here. Only, I'd found the Nagh-lokh, and in the end, buried the village.

"Fortune favored you there, boy. Or . . . maybe something else. Your Radi seems like a great friend to have by your side, though I daresay you might be dragging him through one too many adventures for his liking."

I gave a more honest grin at that. "He's the best. I couldn't ask for better." While I could never be sure what expression was hidden behind the mask, I had a feeling Nassih was pleased by what I'd said.

My tale continued through the first binding, and my near expulsion from the Ashram. We reached the following season and everything that had led to The Ghost of Ghal. That drew a deep laugh out of Nassih, and he asked me if I still clung to the identity, or if I had gone back to being Ari.

I told him I hadn't quite decided yet, and that maybe it would be the ghost, with all his legend and powers intact, who would show up to be executed.

He told me that might be wise, and when I had finished, he thanked me for my tale, and started the story he'd promised to share.

A tale of a wise man, and the secrets of three things he shaped and carried.

A story of Brahm the Wanderer.

This is a simple tale, I'm afraid, and it is not one of daring and adventure, my friend. You'll find no battles of grand magic, or monsters felled. Just the beginnings of a new journey for a man, more than a man, who decided to make himself something else. Something new.

This is the story of Brahm, freshly thrown down by his own hand to walk our world as a mortal.

He had no bearings in this new place, walking it closer to us now than what he had been before. So he sat, and he Listened to all things. "Tell me, making mine, what do I need? What should I know before I set out to learn all about this world I've made?"

It took a day, then many more. But eventually, he was answered. So first of all things after the stillness and silence of the void, he reached out to the nearest trees and spoke to them. He asked them their names, and the stories they'd come to have over all the time they'd grown before he'd cast himself down.

Once he'd learned this, he asked for one more thing. "Would you be kind enough to your own flesh lend? To give me your wood and limbs to shape and bend."

And the trees of the woodland agreed.

For you see, Brahm never sought to take and twist the world without its consent. Even then, so fresh and new to it all as a man, he knew enough to Listen, and ask things for their aid. For their secrets.

So he was given what he needed, and he came to shape the binder's cane. A walking stick that would be more than that. The tool with which he could journey far and ease his body's aches, but also cast as a weapon when needed. Or to lengthen the reach of his arm when he felt lazy.

Nassih leaned in close and tapped a finger to his mask's nose. I imagined him grinning under the covering.

Now, Brahm had taken to wandering far, and seeing the sights of this world. A time, though, when the *Behel-shehen* had already vanished behind curtains and folds of their own making, hidden behind the Doors of Midnight. So he had the world of men to himself now, and the other things lurking in between.

He traveled and spoke to the first wanderers—singers and dancers, who plied their trade best at night when the weary needed reprieve from a long day's work.

And then he visited the Ruma, the people who took after the first—travelers too, but set to seeking answers to questions for all things. And in that, led to learning all the stories the world could have, and when that was not enough, they made their own to share.

Brahm found joy, and he found wisdom in the very people he created. But he also saw the hardships of their travels and what it did to them. And he decided he must ask a question of his own. "What would you need to keep yourselves safe from the sun and roads? From the biting things in the world, and those that would hurt you?"

The Ruma man to whom Brahm spoke told him then, "Better clothes, my friend. Something light but strong. A thing that would cover all of me, though I worry more for my son and wife. To shield them with ease, but be just as easy to remove. Something I could tuck away, or roll into a pillow for the night. Shaped as a second blanket. Keep the rain from me. Is there such a wondrous thing in this world? I've not yet seen it."

And so Brahm listened to this man, and thought then of what to do. "You need a piece of the world to keep you safe from the world itself. That, I can do." He set out then on a longer journey than before to shape the next piece of what all binders and heroes must have.

The cloak.

Brahm first returned to the trees, and from them, he asked for their leaves. And they granted them to him. But this was not enough.

So, soon, he sought aid from the flowers. First he thought to make a dye from their petals, but then when he spoke to them, he learned that their beauty was best kept in their true form.

"Do not twist and shape us into color, oh Brahm, lord above. But instead make a cloak from our very selves instead," they said to him.

And so he took their words to heart.

In this way Brahm traveled wide and collected a piece of all things to shape the patchwork cloak. Something that held all the colors of the world within, and with which he could turn away all things of the world as well. Harm, rain, dust, and more. Its colors would let him choose which to burnish bright but with a thought and shine with better light. With a shaping and then piece of will, Brahm could use those shifting colors to hide from even the most Tainted-keen of sight.

And you would never be able to find him.

He showed this making to the Ruma man, and gave this first cloak as a gift to him. For he could always make another.

In return, the Ruma gave him a gift that Brahm had only ever seen from afar, and held in his own heart and flesh. But never had he touched a piece of man's making of it.

"It is called fire. For as long as you walk this world, friend, if you ever come across any of the Ruma, you give them my name and tell them you are welcome for the night. It will be so. And they will share a piece of their fire with you. Warmth and hot food. A safe place to sleep at night, and all the stories you could imagine."

Brahm watched the fire the men had kindled, burning brighter as they fed it. "I would very much like that." And so he spent the night with the Ruma man, and learned all the stories he could. And through it, he came to learn the story of fire—its secrets.

"I hunger for more than wood and air. I wish too to travel, Brahm, lord of all things," spoke the flame.

And Brahm heard it. But he did not know how now to carry a piece of fire with him. Not in man's flesh and form. So he set out to answer this new question.

He asked the birds and the beasts. But Brahm found the answer when he came across a dying hart. He knelt and placed a hand on its body. "Oh, you poor thing. What can I do for you? I can mend your body and spare you from crossing through the Doors of Death."

But the deer did not want this. "No, Lord Brahm, for I know who you are, even if the world of men doesn't. All I ask is you take away my pain, and then put my body to use. Grant me this peace. Do not let me go to waste. I have seen what happens to my kind when we pass. Something else will take my flesh, and my bones will rot. Do something with just a piece of me, Brahm, and I will pass content."

"So shall it be." And Brahm laid his hands on the hart and took away its pain the only way he knew. In the end, the beast lay still as dead, because it was. Brahm laid over its body for a long while.

And Brahm cried for the first life he had to take.

But he kept to his word, and he brought back its body to the Ruma camp. There he sat and Listened once again to the world itself, and to the men and women of wise counsel around him.

And it was one of these women who gave to him the last piece of what he would need. She asked for some of the beast's fat to render down into tallow. "I keep these in little blocks like this to use again later for cooking. See how it keeps its shape? You can do many things with this."

Brahm watched these makings of his go on to make small miracles of their own, and he thanked her for what she'd shown him. Later, he sat with what remained of the hart's body and shaped something new.

He shaped fat to tallow, and then from there, bound it with his own hair and the beast's own fur to make the first candle. But this was not enough. He put its bones to use to make the holder, and learned soon enough his wick would not burn clean. And so he shaped the thing of twine.

And when he was done, he brought this new making to the fire that the Ruma had set. "I see you, friend, and I will grant you your wish. You will live and travel with me. Together, we will light the way, and you will share your glow and your warmth with me, and everything else we come across."

The fire thanked him for this, and for his kindness, it granted Brahm the deepest secret it held.

The key to ever-burning flame.

For as long as Brahm had a candle, he would never be without fire.

Nassih finished the tale and gave me a long look. "I might be one of the only Ruma without a knack for telling stories, but I think the bones of it were right. What did you think?"

I thought it certainly lacked the depth and level of performance Maathi put into his tales, but I would always appreciate any shared story. I told him this.

"Mm. Then remember this last thing, Ari. There are always secrets to be gleaned in stories. Always. A wise person learns to find and pluck those free, and then act on them."

I had heard that before, but before I could ask him what those secrets were, the odd-cloaked man rolled to his side and decided he would appreciate a good rest.

I couldn't blame him, and I felt I should do the same.

After all, it might be my last.

Best to make it a long one.

NINETY-EIGHT

UNSTRUCK. UNHARMED. UNFALLEN.

A series of knocks roused me from sleep.

"Wake up, Ari." The voice belonged to Aisha. "We need to talk."

I groaned. "I don't suppose if we postpone our conversation that the same can be done for my execution?"

The door opened and Aisha walked inside.

That's a no.

She hadn't changed much apart from her hair, which she had bound into a single tight braid, then coiled at the back of her head and pinned in place. "*Mejai* Arfan sent me to ask for your considerations."

I arched a brow, then remembered what the *Maathi*—Khalil—had told me. "Oh, I'm allowed a few things before they stick me with enough arrows that a hedgehog would want to tup me, right?"

Her lips pressed against each other. The joke went unappreciated, though I had hoped it would at least lighten her mood. "This isn't funny, Ari. You're going to be brought outside the city in under a candlemark. And then they'll . . ." She took a breath and started again. "They're going to kill you."

I inclined my head. "I know, Aisha. I'm sorry. I was just trying to—"

She waved me off. "Make it less heavy . . . for all of us. I know what happened. Qima told me all of it. I suppose we've both been trying to keep her safe, and now this." Aisha closed the distance between us and fell to one knee. "You didn't have to tell the *Shir,* you know. You could have kept it quiet, and then you wouldn't be in this position." She searched my face with a look, and I said nothing in return.

"Why didn't you?"

I frowned and thought on it. "It was the right thing." Nothing else came to mind, and I still don't know what made me say that, of all things I could have. But I did.

After a moment, Aisha took a heavy breath. "I suppose it was. You put the tribe and our well-being over your own. That says something in your favor, Ari. And if . . . should somehow you . . ." Aisha shook her head. "There is a chance for people to survive these things, you know? Alum Above is the judge of all, and he will be watching. If you live, there will be a different place for you here." Her mouth went tight then.

"What is it?"

She took a breath. "I'm afraid *Shir* Sharaam will want for war no matter the outcome, but for now, there is the air of peace. And we have time." Aisha didn't elaborate, but I picked up on the meaning.

Time enough to gather themselves should a battle break out regardless. My execution is just a way to stall for that. My next thought died as Aisha wrapped her arms around me tight and squeezed. The hug ended before I realized it'd begun.

"Thank you for what you did for Qima, most of all."

I opened my mouth to ask precisely what she meant, but Aisha placed a hand over my lips.

"Not for sparing her her father's wrath, though a bit of that too. For what you did with Shareem. She should never have to carry something like that." Aisha's eyes met mine, then looked away, but in the moment our gazes touched, I saw and heard what had gone unsaid.

Qimari should never have to carry the things we did. The burden of taking a life, and in that manner. Aisha too had a story of her own that held that weight within. But it wasn't my place to ask her for it. Not now.

"Tell me what you need, Ari, and I'll see it brought to you. I can do that much for you."

I thanked Aisha and told her what I wished for. "First, make sure Shola is taken care of, please?"

She nodded.

"Right." I took a series of short breaths, using the time to steady my thoughts and my heart. "The bow I've been practicing with, and some arrows to start." I gestured to my binder's cane. "And will I be able to bring it?"

Aisha inclined her head again.

That took care of that. All that remained then was a piece of luck. I thought of everything I owned, but nothing else would help me in what I had to face. But the answer came to me. "Am I allowed my travel sack?"

She frowned. "What's inside it?"

I told her.

Aisha exhaled and nodded. "You can have it by your side if that's what you wish. No one will begrudge you for wanting to die with your possessions. Why do you want the candles removed, though?"

All I could offer her was a sharp and clever smile. "Maybe I'd like to die with a secret."

Aisha watched me for another moment, then resigned herself to being answerless. "Well enough, then." She leaned in close, cupping one side of my face with a hand while bringing her lips to my other cheek. "I'll pray for you. May Alum Above grant you peace in passing, Ari. And if there is mercy to be found for you, may he give you that and spare your life." She said nothing further, rising and leaving the room.

Two-thirds of a candlemark passed before the door opened again. Three men from Arfan's tribe arrived with what I had asked for, though they did not put any of the items in my hand but for one of the candles.

The one dyed a soft blue with the imprint of a bird's head.

Nassih looked up at this, stirring for the first time. He eyed the candle, then me, never saying a word.

Just the stare.

I met it and somehow figured the man to be wearing a knowing smile behind his mask. But I never got the chance to ask what for.

The men put their hands on me and led me out of the cell. Out of the building. And out of the city of Iban-Bansuur.

To the desert.

To die.

The sun stood at its zenith, its usual orange bled clean to hold the violent red I'd seen staining Shareem's clothes. A strawberry sun I'd heard some call it.

To me, the name rang false. This sun was drenched the color of blood, and it spilled into the sky, tingeing it with a thin wash of rose over the softer lavender streaks.

As pretty a sight for a man to die under.

Tall arching stones stood around us. Almost like the remnants of broken rings—the humps of rock arced along the desertscape. What had Laki once called them? Fhaalds, she had said. Places in the world where Brahm had put the bends in his shaping.

The men led me, firmly held in hand, to a flat field of sand before a series of dunes hundreds of paces away. A line of figures waited there atop their horses, and I didn't need more than a single guess to know who they were.

Shir Sharaam and his men.

The merchant king and his coterie waited on a crest an equal distance to my right. A quick gaze showed me that Aisha and Qimari were among them. The familiar sight of a lone wagon home, resting comfortably by itself to one corner of the field, brought a smile to me.

Shola would be safe and spared the sight of this, even if Gushvin, Alwi, and Baba watched on.

The men holding me released their grips and one of them dropped my travel sack a dozen feet from where I stood. Another handed me the black bow along with five arrows. No quiver, and no explanation as to why that number.

I decided I wouldn't really need a reason in a few more moments. The heat of the day finally touched me, working its way to my collar and the base of my neck. Sweat beaded along the space but I ignored it. The air in the distance shifted and almost took a form I could see.

A haze or a film that hung behind the figures on the dunes. The longer I stared at it, the more I could see the faint ripples in its form. It was as if the wind itself came to light and bent along the horizon.

I saw the gentle flow of the desert. Not in some vague metaphorical way as it had been described to me. But the truth of it.

Every grain that managed to kick up under the light breath of passing wind. The stirring of cloaks and the rippling ends of robes. In the distance, some of the sand gave way as the head of a desert shrew broke free to check its surroundings. Then, upon seeing the gathered masses, decided that perhaps its noon was better spent under the safety of the dunes.

I saw all these things and more with a new sight that felt wider than anything I'd experienced before. Deeper. Like truly being able to see for the first time.

I took a breath and stilled myself, turning my mind to the candle and the flame. It pulled the fear from me, the wonderings of what would happen, and all other thought. All that remained was the desert, and myself. One of my hands gripped my staff, the other held tightly to the black bow.

There was nothing for it now but to wait. At least I would die with the three things all binders must have: candle, cloak, and cane.

I expected some sort of proclamation. *Shir* Sharaam screaming my sins for all to hear and then drawing his arrow to put me down. But no.

Their way went without ceremony. A silent thing, like the desert at times. A man on horseback raised a bow. I saw the subtle and familiar motions of nocking, then drawing to fire. His finger had pointed up into the sky in my direction but for the briefest of moments, but I caught it.

Just like Aisha taught me.

The first shot arced into the air—a thin trace of black that I nearly lost. But I knew the space in which it would pass. Partway into its flight it no longer held the shape of an arrow—no. It became a stone.

I smiled at it like watching an old friend return to embrace me. The memories of Mahrab trying to ring my skull with tossed stones, then to Rishi Ibrahm who did the same. I planted my staff in the ground and held out a hand as if to catch the arrow, forgetting for the moment that it would very likely take my heart.

It reached the peak of its flight, arcing down to fall.

I envisioned where the stone would pass through, bringing up the folds of my mind to contest its path. Just like the games.

Two at first. They showed the arrow sailing harmlessly to my side. Then four.

The arrow, no longer one, but a rock, came closer.

Still, I saw it fall to the side. Six folds now. Then eight.

As above. So below. The thought came to me, and I kept it quiet in mind. Ten folds. Soon to twelve.

I believed and knew in the whole of me that it would not strike me. My Athir was as firm as any of the mountains in Ghal. As sturdy as the base of the Water Tree we had found not so long ago. And as sharp as a blade of Arasmus steel.

"As above. So below. I bind you stone, Tak, and Roh." And then I felt it. The weight of an arrow in flight striking hard against the space I held in my mind. It was if it had been caught both in hand as much as by my very breath, blown wide and with strings still tethered to me.

It resonated in my grip as much as my lungs.

And the arrow crashed home—

—harmlessly to the ground beside me. Where I had bid it to.

For a moment, nothing happened. The desert returned to stillness, and everything in it. All but my mind, which still raced with the binding, and the sight of the hazy light in the distance.

A piece of me remembered what Khalil had told me. I could raise my bow and return a shot of my own, but I remained caught in the grip of the gentle flow of the desert.

The archer nocked, and they fired again.

I hadn't left the folds, still fresh in my mind and picturing so perfectly the flight of the next stone to take to air. This time I grabbed my staff, then my travel sack, slinging it over my shoulder. I walked toward the men on the dune and gave no sign of stopping.

As above. So below. The words returned to me. *Tak.* I envisioned the arrow and its eventual path, now to fall again by my side. *Roh.*

The archer had aimed their shot well. It should have struck me clear through the throat. But it would not be so.

The arrow landed, and I remained unstruck.

Someone shouted something among Sharaam's people, and three archers drew and loosed.

I did not care. Swept now into the game of falling stones and the lessons of my teachers. I pivoted, raising the head of my staff in their direction as much in rebuke as challenge.

Three arrows sailed toward me. But I saw only the stones, where they would pass, and the harm they wished upon me.

"Tak. And. Roh!" The words broke across the still-silent sands like the first clap of a desert storm that had been long-waiting to come.

The arrows drew close and then struck their marks.

The ones I had decided.

And I remained unharmed.

I moved closer, never giving the black bow the chance to live up to its nature. Instead, I remained deep in the folds and the candle and the flame.

Shir Sharaam's horse turned to one side and the man fought him back under control. He shouted something, but I did not have the ears for it. Every rider who could then drew and fired. And then again before the first volley reached its height. Then still again. Three storms of arrows—no, just stones, took to flight.

I counted them all and had to fight from laughing. Each stone passed high above and touched the point in space I knew they would. From there, I imagined their eventual paths, and then set them to what I wanted them to be. They would fall where I wished, and I would stand firm before them all.

I walked onward and the weight of the arrows fell like a wave against the shore of my folds. My mind. But I had been ready, and I remembered the trouncing I'd once received against Rishi Ibrahm. My vision held, as did my Athir—the pillars of my faith. I believed I could not be struck. I could not be harmed by them. I would not fall.

And so it was.

Ikthab, they had said. So it was written. So it would be.

And so it would be in the world around me.

The arrows fell, but I did not fall with them.

I remained standing—unfallen.

Shaft after shaft struck the ground, none peppering me as I walked onward. To onlookers, it must have seemed as if the arrows themselves bent away from me, choosing to hit anything but my form. Or that the aim of every man in the tribe had been untrue. Somehow, I doubted they would believe such a thing.

No, they saw me, clad in my shining white cloak under the sun, drawing closer to the men on the hill. And they would believe that it was me that had avoided their true-shot arrows.

Shir Sharaam raised a hand, staying his tribesmen.

The desert returned to the stillness of a moment just waiting to be broken. Even the wind granted us this moment of peace. Nothing stirred upon the sands. No movement. No sounds.

After a while longer, I decided I would be the one to break the quiet. I came to a stop at the foot of the dune they stood along and planted my staff again. "As Alum Above is the witness of all things here, you cannot kill me." My heart hammered, though you would be mistaken to consider it the grip of fear.

No. This was something else. Wherever I had gone in my mind after the candle and the flame and the folds held sway over me. Somewhere deep. Far inside myself, to a place few ever come to learn about themselves. And it is from this well I drew the words I spoke.

Maybe just the actor I never had the chance to be.

It gave voice now to something reserved for the old dramas—the moments the hero defies death by all odds, and I leaned into the performance, perhaps going as far as to borrow lines and tones I'd once heard my family speak.

Perhaps . . .

After all, among all things, I was also a thief.

"Here I stand, before your judgment, and your arrows. Unstruck. Unharmed. Unfallen." My hand tightened against the black bow and I very terribly thought of drawing it to loose the thing Aisha had taught me. A single perfect shot.

But that wouldn't solve the problem before me. In fact, it would likely incense them all into trying their hands again.

I had something in mind for that, however. Aside from being a thief, I had learned how to be a marvelous liar, and to play circumstances to my favor. Especially the odd ones.

Like taking the credit for toppling a mountain on a village.

Or something else.

What had the *Maathi* told me about today? Soon enough the sun and moon would meet in embrace.

I smiled and knew what I had to do. "You cannot strike me. You cannot harm me. And you cannot fell me. Alum Above has protected my path, and he himself will prove me beyond your reach."

No one said a word.

Good. The stage is still mine. Now to feed them the biggest lie of all and hope they're willing to swallow it before realizing it's piss and not vinegar.

I pointed the head of my staff to the sun and let my voice echo through the desert. "And beware the day where the moon and sun meet in embrace. Beware the fhaalds on a moon-full sunny night!" I uttered the lines I'd once heard from Vathin—Koli—drawing on them for their dramatic nature.

"Alum Above shall cast his hand through the sky, darken the world and eclipse the sun to prove myself beyond your reach!" My words thundered through the desert.

And they fell on deaf ears.

Nothing happened, and the sky continued to be as bright as it had been before.

Everyone waited, eyeing the horizon for any sign of truth to what I'd said.

My heart screamed and I began to lose my grip on the folds.

Moments passed, and still, the sun remained in place, and there was no sight of the moon.

The sweat from earlier built heavier along my collar.

One of the archers decided that he'd waited long enough and raised his bow. He drew in one smooth motion.

I raised my staff, but the folds would not be enough. Not so close to them now.

And the world fell into shadow as the moon slid before the sun to swallow all the light.

The bowman faltered, and the arrow left his hold. It shot forward.

But still I remained: unstruck, unharmed, unfallen.

And it was because he'd missed. *Merciful Brahm, Alum Above, whomever—thank you.* I stood there, unfazed on the surface, letting the scene add to the myth I was untouchable.

Then the world moved to prove it so. The legend of Ari grew as all eyes turned back to the sky and watched in silence as a crown of fire burned from behind the shadowed shape of the moon.

Darkness.

But for the pillar of light that radiated down from the center of the two heavenly bodies. It was as if they had begun to bleed fire in their union. The shaft of hellish flame continued to drip its way down.

In the distance I could hear a specific cry of triumph. A voice belonging to none other than the *Maathi* of Arfan's tribe.

But above, all I could see was the shape within the darkness. A lance of brighter light than I had ever seen split the blackened moon's shadow. Within that stood another shape.

A figure.

It called to me.

And I answered.

NINETY-NINE

THE DOORS OF MIDNIGHT

A creature unlike any I'd seen before graced our sight from within the burning eye of heaven.

She stood there, hung between the shadowed lens of the eclipse. A world within the two bodies above. Tall, with skin the ashen blue of evening dusk—the gray-dark hue of twilight-touched. Hair, long—the silver-white color of bright and boldly glowing moonlight.

And she spoke.

No human tongue. It didn't touch your ears so much as it struck the heart of you, sending your blood to ripple as much as boil.

Every person along the dunes stood mute and still, fixed on the sight above, and the corridor of flames leading the way.

The black bow slipped from my grasp and I took a step toward the eclipse. What had Taki once said, long lost in that fever dream? He'd called this event something.

The Doors of Midnight. And he'd seen me walking through them.

The creature's voice beat against me still—words I had no hope of translating, but I didn't need to. They came like music. Like the strings of an old friend's mandolin. Fluting pipes I'd once heard in another world within a world—below the Ashram. A place called Stones. And the music seemed to be saying: *invitation. Wonder.* And, of course, *welcome.*

I took more steps toward the figure in the sky.

"Ari!" The voice belonged to the *Maathi.* He broke into a run behind me, snatching up my travel sack. The only one among either tribe who'd managed to not be wholly transfixed on the goings-on above. "Ari!"

At the sound of my name again, the figure amidst the doors looked at me. It was no human look. The weight of it collared me with iron and ice despite what I'd heard to be an invitation. It rooted me in place, but still I fought to move.

"Ari, you cannot go alone! Wait!" The *Maathi,* Khalil, ran harder.

I took a step, then another. Now I stood between *Shir* Sharaam and his tribe. If they still had the will to cut me down, now came their chance.

But even they were transfixed on the figure in the sky, and they had no mind for me. Rooted—slack-jawed—in wonder as much as fresh terror. So I passed them by.

I walked. Closer and closer to the pillar of fire touching the ground. Nearer to the base of the eclipse that had turned our sunny noon into a false night. I moved in on the Doors of Midnight.

"*Ari?*" The question came in Trader's Tongue from the woman in the sky. Hearing my name come from her felt like someone had taken my heart in hand and pressed freshly fallen snow against it. Sharply cold, it pulled the breath from me.

This was no warm and inviting thing.

"*Ari?*" The voice called again, and then again still.

I went toward it.

"Stop him—no, no! My *Shir*!" Khalil's voice echoed through the desert, and some men snapped to enough attention to set after him. Some stayed on their camels, one of the riders on horseback from Sharaam's tribe joined in. All raced toward me.

But they were too late.

I reached the burning column and heard its fire speaking to me as clear as a friend's mandolin.

Invitation. Welcome. Answers.

What had the maiden of the Water Tree told me? I'd find answers through the Doors of Midnight.

The Ashura.

I closed my eyes and stepped into the light.

ONE HUNDRED

Enshae

My skin felt like I'd been left to sleep by a warm hearth, the gentle heat touching every piece of me. The insides of my eyes flashed the soft red of blood under light as I kept them shut against the brightness of the corridor of fire. The colors of flame gave way to an intensity only found in the purest of burning whiteness that crashed against me.

And then it ended.

I opened my eyes and found myself, not in the plains of golden-dusted dunes and grains, but in a place out of Shaen stories. The sky was painted the purple of lilac and lavender, strobed in places with the blues of darkened cobalt and faded sapphires. All this strung along the greater canvas of velvet black.

The stars here shone just as bright as the ones I'd seen in the desert, only, I didn't recognize their shapes.

And through it all, cracks in the veneer—the subtle shine of brassen foil bleeding through the darkness.

Trees surrounded me, but they were not the ones you would ever hope to find in Zibrath or anywhere along the sands. Dark, each had bark the color of crushed coal, and canopies the red of rose. Some were dotted with the white of fresh clotted cream. Others had leaves pulled from a painter's palette—too colorful, in combinations that shouldn't have been possible.

Like the Water Tree.

The world around me had been cast into the deepest of midnight—a darkness out of dream. Though it was not without its light. Both the stars, and the door behind me, still held both the moon's full glow, as well as the full-burning crown of the sun's flame.

I can go back. Just a few steps and I can go back. To people who want me dead.

"*Ari.*" The voice came at me again, now with a smoothness of a freshly blown breath and all its lightness. It pulled at me, heart and ears and mind.

I went toward it, and found it familiar. *Where have I heard it before?* My feet felt the rushing coolness of moving water, and I looked down to see I'd stepped into a stream. Formations of arcing stones, no higher than my knees, dotted its length.

More fhaalds?

The voice beckoned once more and I heeded it, moving toward the source. A shadow, shrouded in smoke that seemed to come from their own form.

I approached, and all my wits told me to raise my staff in case I had need of it. But I paid little heed to that part of my mind.

"Alum Above, Ari! *Zho!* Answer me, boy!" Khalil's cries struck me, and whatever reverie I had been in now lost its hold.

I blinked several times. "What?"

The *Maathi* ran over to me, my travel sack in hand. His free hand went to his heart before touching the hollow of his throat. A soft-spoken prayer, in Zibrathi, left his mouth. It translated to: *Keep me safe, oh good God Above, as I walk through places unseen, in shadow, and away from your light. Please.*

Another look at our surroundings told me that Khalil might have had the right idea.

"*Zho,* boy, you have just come to a place of stories. But do not think to walk blindly, ah?" He rapped his knuckles on my head several times. "There are things we do not know, and while I am hungry to fix this unknowing, we must be careful." One of his hands went to my shoulders and gave me a hard squeeze.

"Maathi, speaker, pathfinder—dreamer, and glory seeker. What treasures do you seek? What knowledge would you have of me?" The air between myself and the speaker grew heavy. It was as if the woman in the smoke spoke without edge. Smooth and lilting, like the words were written with the wind, and the breath pressed from a place past her breast.

Only one other person had ever sounded the same to me before. Shandi.

Khalil nudged me forward. "Together, ah? We will uncover this mystery together, and then we can say we have done another thing men have only dreamed of. *Zho, zho!*" He pushed me again and we talked toward the woman in the mist.

The sounds of hooves stomped behind us and I turned to find two riders on camels had come through the Doors of Midnight, and another on horseback. Their mounts bucked in unison, harder than I had ever seen. The men atop were thrown clear to the ground as the beasts fled, but not back through the way they'd come. They ran off into the nearby trees.

I lost sight of them as soon as they passed the first trunks—a darkness thicker than could ever have been natural obscured their forms.

The fallen riders came to their feet and muttered curses in Zibrathi.

The *Maathi* called them to our side, and the looks on their faces said they knew it to be a very good idea. The comfort of numbers went a long way in a strange land. Especially when they had come here through a doorway in the sky.

Hands went to hips to pull knives, and one of the riders drew a curved sword as long as my arm.

The woman in the fog spoke again. "*Come and tell me what you wish to know. Tell me of all the secrets whose answers you still seek. Come to me one, and come to me all. Share these things. Speak. Speak.*" The words were song now. The soft thrumming strings of a box harp.

I drew closer, Khalil keeping a firm grip on me as I did.

"Together, boy." He spoke in a whisper.

I nodded and moved closer still.

We came on a low rise of stone shrouded in the smoke. As I reached the shadow within, the obscuring gray mist parted, and the air in my lungs left in suit.

Her eyes were the color of my nightmares. The color of storybook demons and wolves. They were the bright and burnished color of gold.

"*Hello, Ari. I am Enshae.*"

We had found the Shaen of story.

And she had designs for us.

The *Maathi* breathed out a word that died before taking any proper shape, and so it was lost to us. His mouth worked soundlessly. Then he found what he had been looking for. "Alum Above, the Shaen. You are one of them—*the* Enshae."

The Shaen woman smiled. She lay there on the rock dressed in garb of pale fog, stretched tight to skin, and just as much woven from starlight. Though no one had eyes for that in the moment.

All of us held her gaze exactly. And none could look away.

"*I am, pathfinder. Long have you sought me and this place. Now that you are here, what will you do, I wonder? What would you ask of me?*" She beckoned him closer with a hand, and my friend, Khalil, did as she asked.

He leaned in close and she brushed her fingers against his cheek. She met him in kind and blew a breath against his ear. And then she whispered something for only him to hear. "I am wanting a great many things. Secrets, yes. I wish to know—" Khalil never finished speaking.

His eyes widened as smoke wafted from her mouth. It billowed and intensified until we lost sight of him. When it cleared, we found a dog in his place.

Small, closer to a fox in height and build, complete with the pointed ears and long snout. Its fur held the same color as Khalil's skin, and the eyes burned with the same brightness and curiosity as my friend's. The animal tilted its head to regard Enshae, then me—confusion writ clear on its face.

I stared into its eyes and the longer I looked, the more I heard something that did not reach my ears, but struck at a place inside me.

Pain. Surprise. Curiosity. And a name, a role. *Maathi.*

I opened my mouth but no sound left me.

Enshae stroked the dog's snout, the curve of a smile breaking along her face. She brought her ears close to the creature again. "*Go now. Run, hound, and follow that nose and curiosity of yours. See if you can find the secrets you seek.*" She gave *Maathi* a gentle shove and the dog that had been my friend took off into the woods.

The tribesman with the sword needed to see no more. He let loose a snarl and raised the weapon over his head. Its silver edge gleamed—the intent clear. It arced downward, but Enshae had risen to her feet and sang. Hard, bright, flowing. A tongue I couldn't understand but for a word caught within the lines. Then another. "*Ahn. Ahl.*" They struck the air as command. And as hammer on ice.

The sword hit the space just before her . . . and shattered like it had been made from glass. The man behind the weapon stared at the hilt, all that remained in hand, and then at Enshae.

The Shaen woman leaned close to him and asked him the same questions she had *Maathi.*

I could not hear what the man said in return, only what Enshae whispered back.

"*Then fly free. Go, and look for her then. Let no man or his mantle stop you from doing as you wish for once. Go.*" She touched him the same way she had the *Maathi.* The same smoke slowly enveloped him, and when it left, a falcon took to the sky. Then Enshae turned her attention to the remaining men.

They had more sense than the rest of us. Each turned and ran in different directions, breaking into the woods, and far from our sight.

All of which left Enshae with just one person to focus the whole of herself on.

Me.

She regarded me, the same crescent-moon smile wide on her face. Her eyes burned with a look of mischief and curiosity. Not a combination I wanted to see in anyone, but especially her at the moment. She stepped closer, and I took one back in perfect measure. Then again, and we repeated the small motions, almost like an awkward dance. For every advance, I retreated.

I thought then to a story I'd once heard. Of a sailor, a warrior, and a man heading home long after war. He and his sailors came upon the hidden home of an enchantress—a goddess—who ensorcelled men, and shaped those who earned her displeasure into animals.

Eventually I remembered the staff in my hand. I leveled its tip at her. When I had fought Askar and Biloo, my hands had remained steady. When I had found Shareem's heart, and then took his life, my hands did not shake.

Now, as I stood there with a creature out of stories, the staff trembled in my grip. "Stay back."

She tilted her head, the smile still wide and now touching her eyes—bringing a better brightness to their gold. The look said: *amusement.* "*Why?*" With that, she brushed my staff aside, never fearing that I would use it to hurt her.

A piece of my mind screamed to trigger the minor bindings. Just enough to send her sprawling to the ground. Something to give me the chance to run after *Maathi,* Khalil, and find my friend.

She moved closer, hand trailing the length of my staff. Enshae cared little for it and came close enough that her breath touched my skin. "*What is it you wish for?*" She regarded me the same way you would a new puzzle. "*What burns inside you, castaway flame, brightling—lost thing?*" Enshae looked me over again, and when I met her eyes, I felt the sudden weight of the ocean swell. Wave upon wave, throwing me back under every time I tried to break through the surface.

Her gaze tore through my white cloak, then every layer beneath, and she saw straight into the heart of me. And whatever she found brought her smile to deepen further still.

"*What is it you yearn for?*"

What did I tell her? What did the others say that had them turned into animals? I thought of what I had always wanted to know. What I had asked the Water Tree, and answers received in riddles.

Enshae took one more step and our mouths nearly met. "*Tell me what it is that you burn for.*"

I swallowed, and felt a new weight push against me. I had come under this before. The familiar pressure of someone pushing against my mind. *The folds!* Someone contesting my very thoughts, trying to force a belief against mine. But I hadn't been holding mine still, had I?

I then remembered that I had never dropped the candle and the flame, and though I had channeled the binding to stop the arrows, I hadn't let go of the folds. What I had done had vastly differed from the time I had bound fire. Those weapons were not living things, and so there was nothing to fight against my mind and self when I had bound them.

So I hadn't fallen free of the clear and focused state of mind it took to hold them. And that might have been the only thing keeping Enshae from subduing my will with but a breath.

"*Tell me.*" The words came now the echo of a thousand times, each repetition a whisper ending just as the next one began. They pounded against me until I gritted my teeth and my eyes watered from the effort to resist.

I held to the candle and the flame and spoke two words in return. "The Ashura."

The pressure died and she stepped away from me, moving with all the grace of smoke in gentle wind. "*What?*"

I repeated myself.

Enshae no longer smiled. "*You should be wiser with what you ask for, little pretender.*"

I frowned at that. "What am I pretending to be?"

She still looked at me like something she could not quite understand. "*You do not know, but you wear the shape of one?*"

I hadn't a clue what she meant, but I did notice she did not turn me into a pig, or whatever else she might have had in mind. So I paid her back in kind: a question for a question. "What are you pretending to be?"

That might have been the wrong thing to ask, in retrospect.

Her eyes went wide and mouth hung aslack as if I'd smacked her. Then she straightened, looking taller and down her nose at me as if I didn't have the better height between the two of us. "*I am Enshae. And I will be that long after you are dust, castaway flame. I was there at the first shaping of all things on this world, and before the folding of it and the Shaen realm. I pretend at nothing. I. Am.*" She retraced her steps and brought herself back before me.

"*And what will you be when we are done speaking, I wonder? A moth, a wolf, a bird? What shape shall I cast you in?*"

I tried to remember what stage training I'd gleaned watching my family rehearse. An old and easy smile came to my face, and I hoped it looked as convincing as I needed it to be. "The shape of me, myself, as I am. Man-shape, that is. Why, what about you? What shape will you be in when we're done?"

Enshae blinked, caught off guard once again. "*I ask you questions and you turn them back on me?*"

Anything to keep myself from being turned into a damnable frog like in the stories. "Aren't you asking me questions back for every one I ask you?" I kept up the stage smile, wondering if I could make my way back to the doors I'd come through. A fleeting glance over my shoulder showed me that the phenomenon had ended.

The way had shut.

And I remained trapped with a creature from stories.

"*Do you think these games will keep you safe, little one?*"

I took a step away from her and she matched me in kind. "What *would* keep me safe? I'd make a terrible moth, and I've already been a bird. I've even been a ghost, believe it or not."

Enshae tilted her head the other way, regarding me. "*I do not.*"

"Oh, well, that's disappointing. I thought I'd done a rather good job convincing others of that fact." Another pair of steps took me away from her—or they would have if she did not follow me.

"*I think you are but a fool, and I am curious as to what way I will bend you.*" Something in her voice then told me she was beginning to find me tedious.

I knew what question would stay her hand at least a moment more. "How old are you, Enshae? How long have you been around?"

"*I have been Enshae since the first shaping of all things.*"

Since the first shaping of all things. Older than anyone could possibly measure. It wasn't a stretch to believe a mind could go mad over that long a time, or become bored. Perhaps one had led to the other. And I wasn't sure if I wanted to know in which order they'd happened.

"And have you been here for all that time?" I gestured to our surroundings.

"*What?*" She sounded as if I'd struck a blow to her gut, driving the breath from her. Something whisper soft and just as airy.

"*N-no.*" She faltered, just for a moment, but it had been there. "*Once I walked the free spaces of the world, before the folding. Then, I have been here, in my garden.*" The word "garden" left her with a touch of sourness that nearly brought my own mouth to purse at the sound of it. "*I have been tending my grounds since the Behel-shehen came to this place.*"

Shehen. The true sound of their name, in their tongue.

"And you've never left?"

Her shoulders rounded and her posture became that of one who'd had their strings cut. "*Never.*"

I looked past her to the endless expanse of sky behind her forested garden. It begged the obvious question: "Why?"

Enshae licked her lips and, for the first time, shied away from *my* stare. "*No one has asked me that before.*" Then her gaze fell on me again, and all the light I'd seen in the eclipse now burned inside her eyes. "*And I do not think I will tell you the story of why and how. The time for talking is past, and I think you will make a fine kitten. Curious, and not one to listen. You can explore my garden to your desire and see if you can find the answers to your many questions in it.*"

I thought of what I could do to stop her from carrying out her threat, then recalled what I had been told many times. The idea of trading a story for a story, and through it, the secrets I could learn.

And the ones I could share in return. Something Enshae might have want of.

"Wait." I raised both hands in the hope she'd pause. "You must have questions about the world outside yours. What would you like to know?"

"*There is nothing you have I wish to know of, brightling castaway.*" She raised one of her hands and I knew I had but seconds before becoming a kitten.

"I suppose you'll never know for certain, will you? You've missed the very changing of the world you left behind. Stories of things you couldn't possibly believe." I didn't know the limits of imagination a creature out of Shaen stories possessed, but there had to be something that would catch her fancy.

"*What stories do you think I could not know of?*"

And I knew I had her.

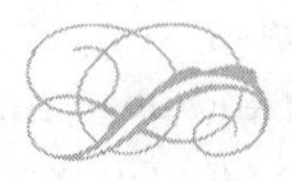

ONE HUNDRED ONE

CANDLE FLAME, SMOKE, AND SHADOW

I rushed to where Khalil had dropped my travel sack. A quick rummage inside and I found Rishi Saira's old tome of tales. I pulled it free as Enshae returned to the flat canted stone she'd been resting on earlier.

"*And how long should I give you, wayward flame, to see if your knowings are worth my listening?*"

I swallowed. I hadn't thought of that. One of my hands brushed against my sides, touching a long lumpen shape that rested within the folds of my cloak. *The candle.* I pulled free the sky-blue length of wax I'd been given as a gift before leaving Ghal, raising it for Enshae to see. "Until the candle burns out?"

That would hopefully buy me the time to think of something equally as clever to secure my survival.

"*Very well.*"

I opened the tome and felt it best to start from the beginning. As most stories should be told.

Enshae motioned at the candle still held in my other hand, and a sound like snapping twigs filled my ears. A gossamer-thin band of smoke rose from the wick as a bulb of flame kindled to life.

"Wait, I don't have anywhere to put this!" I fumbled, trying to keep a hold of the book as well as the candle, lest its freshly spun fire fade from existence.

"*Then hold tightly to it, and let us see if you are a seer or not.*" The smile she showed me was no warm and welcoming thing.

I sucked a breath through my teeth and looked down at the first page. At the story of: the Crown of Flames.

"This is of the weaving of fire, and how a humble man later learned to pull at the ring of fire deep inside him. The flames around his heart."

Enshae's smile widened. "*And you think this is a story I do not know?*"

I hadn't a clue, but I did know a few things: One, I was a marvelous liar. Two, few things are as maddening as an unfinished story. And I could give Enshae both of those things at once.

So I told her of a peasant farmer, born in the land now known as the Mutri Empire, a place she did not know of, nor the name it had once held, and how this man had come to be chosen by Brahm.

She recognized that name at least.

The man was Athwun, and he had lived his life long and toiling hard under the sun. Tilling fields with ox and plow in morning, and sowing seeds by noon. Everything changed the day an old wanderer came across his path, road-weary and travel-torn from all the things you can imagine toll upon a man set to walking the wide ways of the world.

Athwun rescued the collapsed stranger from where he fell and brought him to his home. He offered him shade, water, and when the man grew strong enough, Athwun offered him food as well. But something bothered Athwun about this stranger.

His cloak never seemed to remain the shade it had been before. One instant it was the bright orange of flames themselves. Then, something softer. Soon, it gave way to a touch of yellow that Athwun could swear it had always been. This continued until the cloak looked to be as blue as fresh spring sky, and it had done so after so recently being the dark of sapphire. But to Athwun, it had always held that color.

Hadn't it?

A patchwork cloak of all colors.

Then came the man's walking cane. No ordinary thing. Made from a wood that seemed shadow shaped real, clotted midnight darkness held full in form and in hand.

At first, Athwun was scared to ask the man of the oddities he carried, but when he made the man dinner that first night, he found himself sneaking glances at them. Then again come sunrise when he offered the man morning meal and fresh milk. Eventually, the stranger caught him stealing looks and voiced what Athwun could not.

"Something troubles you, and it is not the stranger who's come to your home, but what I have with me, is it not?"

Athwun nodded and told him it was true. Then he asked what he had been wanting to all this time. "What are they, *sahm*? I've never seen the like."

The stranger smiled. "My cloak of everything imaginable, with which I may travel safely and hide myself should I need to. And of course my staff of endless shadow, pulled and formed from the night sky itself. The black staff grants me many powers, and . . . its protection, of course."

The smell from the candle now filled Enshae's midnight garden. It brought us the scent of a freshly fed fireplace, the soft notes of cedarwood, and the brightest sparks of lemon. The perfect things to grace your senses when taking in a story.

Athwun asked to take each of these things in hand, and the stranger granted him this favor as thanks. Then offered one more. "I have traveled long, and lived twice as hard in this world of yours. Through it, I have come to hear and learn the stories of all things. Man, and those that are more than man. I have seen your hurts, and heard your hopes. I have seen the shadows that walk this world and the shadows in men's hearts. The things that take them, twist them, and taint them. And I am tired. What can I do?"

Athwun had no answer, but asked something else of the stranger. "Who are you at all to do anything? Who am I? Just a farmer, *sahm*. I do not have the mind for these sorts of riddles. I till my field, and reap what I can."

The man nodded. "A farmer, but who says that is all you are made for? Who says that anyone is only their trade, what they set themselves to in order to feed and shelter themselves? What if I told you you were more? That every person is and can be? As thanks for what you have done for me, I can show you. Would you like that?"

"Who are you to teach me these things?" asked Athwun.

And the man revealed himself in a pillar of light—sun-cast gold and morning bright. Atop his brow rested a wreath of fire—the crown of flames. His eyes burned like evening stars, and his touch held all the warmth of a hearth. "I am Brahm, lord of all—"

"*What?*" Enshae rose, propped up on one arm, to look at me. She gave me a laugh light and full of breath-blown air. "*Brahm never walked the world man-shaped, much less to visit some farmer. You tell me a lie and call it a story.*"

I glowered at her, threatening to shut the book. "I suppose you wouldn't know? Were you there? I promised to tell you of things you had missed in the world, and so I am. Will you let me finish or . . . ?" A piece of my anger had come from the first drop of wax that dripped down the candle's length. It fell upon the soft skin of my palm, bringing its heat with it.

If I hadn't been subjected to that prick of pain, I never would have turned my heated look on a creature such as Enshae. But as it was, I had, and she showed me the first hint of weakness then.

She shied away from my stare but for a moment, before returning to face me with one as sharp and hot as I'd given her. "*So you can fan your flame greater when you wish. I felt a touch of it then. Is that how you've been shaping your folds all this time, hm?*"

I frowned. "What do you mean?"

Enshae waggled a finger at me in admonishment. "*No, little one. You will not ask me questions now. Now, you will continue your story and leave me to decide what will happen to you at the end of things.*"

The hanging threat did not frighten me. Not at all. The sweat that had broken out around my collar came from the candle's warmth, and nothing else.

And in that moment, I noticed the candle and the flame played a game of their own. The fire seemed to burn slower, melting away less wax than on any normal candle. Dumb luck? Was I wrong in what I saw? Or was this a measure of hope?

Regardless, I clung to it, and returned to the tale.

And so Brahm revealed himself to Athwun, and he wept upon looking on the lord's beauty, brilliant-bright. Athwun knelt at Brahm's feet and agreed to be his student. "Yes," he said. "I will learn whatever it is you wish to teach me. I will do as you ask."

When Brahm bent to help his first student rise, he imparted on him his own gift of flame, giving birth to the first mortal with his fire. A prince of sunlight.

"Look to your fire, Athwun, and sit with me. As I learned its story, so too shall you. And in knowing this, I will teach you to draw on the crown of flames within all lives, and then you will never be without fire." And so they sat, and they watched. All the while Brahm talked to Athwun of the things he'd seen on his journeys.

The shadows in men's hearts, and what happened when they took root in others. The terrible taint they brought to all places they went, and the darkness in their wakes.

"Will you be my champion against this encroaching shadow? Will you carry my light to whomever is lost in the darkness?"

"Yes, Lord Brahm, I will," said Athwun. And with time, he too learned the story of fire, and learned to pull on the ring of fire inside of him. But this moment of learning and peace would not last, because the shadow in waiting had come to Athwun's home and threatened to swallow its bright lands in a night that would never end.

I shut the book with a heavy clap, letting the jarring noise resound through the air and shake Enshae from the reverie she'd fallen into.

She stirred and her eyes went wide before narrowing into bands of burning gold. The heat of them could have scalded skin at just a look. "*What? Why did you stop?*"

Another bead of wax touched my palm, followed quickly by a second. This time I did not wince. "I thought you said you knew of this story?" I feigned a yawn and placed the book on the ground. "I'm sure it was boring you, wasn't it?"

Enshae rose halfway, sitting cross-legged. "*You won't finish?*" The tone she took belonged to someone long accustomed to having things their own way. There didn't exist a world where someone did not do as Enshae expected or demanded of them.

I shrugged. "Would you like me to?"

She nodded.

I turned my head away from the Shaen woman, eyeing her askance as I did. "Well"—I drew the word out—"I can do that, but someone once told me that a good story is worth payment. Would you be willing to tell me one? As much as I've told you for the price of me finishing. You tell me a story, and I'll end this one."

Her eyes narrowed again. She had to have known the trick I was playing. Then her gaze flicked to the candle, and a slow smile spread across her face. "*Very well. I will share a story with you. But what, I wonder, to tell?*"

The candle continued to burn, not quite so fast as a normal one would, but all the same . . . time would run out.

Eventually.

Enshae made a show of touching her lips. They were wide, and full, and the color of pressed lavender and plums. "*Mm, but what to tell. Shall I tell you of Brahm, the first shaping of things, and the world in which I walked before? Or perhaps the Asir?*"

I straightened at that. Just a piece away from the Ashura. Asking her of them had brought her to threaten me, but the Asir? Maybe I could learn something to help me in my search. And Enshae spotted my interest.

Her eyes widened and a new and hungry light burned in them. "*Ah. Now we know what you wish for—oh, how badly so, castaway?*"

So badly. Those were the words I wished to say to her. I *burned* for those answers. Ashura and Asir. The two were tied together. And a story about either would bring me closer to what I wanted.

I could have asked it of her, but I knew the story would eventually end, and nothing would change. I would have to finish mine, and then Enshae would have her way with me.

Temptation is the great puppeteer, dancing our heart along its strings, and wanting us to sacrifice what's best for us for a moment's wants.

So I did the hard thing. The necessary thing, and it brought me a pain like hot embers placed in heart. All I could do was cry in silence. "No." I shook my head. "I want to know the story of you. Tell me about Enshae. The beginning of you."

She opened her mouth. "*Very well, the Asir . . .*" Enshae blinked as she realized what I had asked—not what she had expected. "*Me?*"

I nodded.

For a moment, the candle burned in silence. The whole of her midnight garden sat still. No movement. And no sounds. Just the flame bobbing between us. When she finally spoke, a sharpness filled the breathless softness of her voice. A crack. "*No one has asked this of me.*"

"I am. Will you tell me?"

Enshae's lips pressed together and she looked away from me. Then she answered. "*Yes.*" The Shaen woman from story leaned forward and blew out my candle. "*Now is not the time for your stories, forgotten flame. Now it is time for mine.*"

And so it was.

Enshae leaned forward, bringing her mouth close enough to me that the warmth of her breath pressed against my cheek. When she spoke, it was edgeless whisper and spring wind. Soft and cool against my skin.

"*Listen carefully, I will only tell this once. This is how I came to be shaped, and how I came to be immured in gardens of forever night.*"

"*First, there was only the blackness—still, and silent—there before the first of all Singers in creation. And then came Brahm, the beginning of all things after the dark itself. He brought smokeless flame from within his own seat and soul, blew it wide, and shaped the first light in this space of darkness. But what good is light without any to share its warmth with?*

"*So this lonely Brahm shaped the stars and all things to come. The children of himself, the Sirathrae, the moon, but not yet her lover, the sun. Then of course came the first shapings on the old world itself, before she was folded in three. And earliest among those beginning shapings was one who came prized before all else.*

"*Me.*"

Enshae arched her back and sat noticeably straighter. The line of her smile was proud, and the look in her eyes was that of fond memory.

"*Brahm himself breathed me to life from strands of woven moonlight, shadow-*

smoked flame made cold and hard, but ever soft and smooth." Enshae reached out, taking my hand in hers, and bringing it to the skin of her arm. There, she pulled my touch along the length of her limb so I could feel and know she'd spoken truly.

"*Of then-clean smoke and still warm ash left over from the creation of the first things. I alone existed on the plane of three names—the three lands over which I walked as I saw fit. There were birds and beasts for me to pass the time with. Gardens and wild things to tend to. But little else for me to do until Brahm had finished making the rest of the Shehen.*

"*But the world was made, and we were left with nothing for ourselves but ourselves. To sit and idle, until I watched and Listened for something beyond what we had been given. And in this I heard the first songs, the things all shaping comes from.*"

I opened my mouth, knowing in part that the disturbance would be unwelcome, but I had to ask. "But I thought the bindings were how the world was shaped? That's how we still—"

"*Quiet.*" Enshae hadn't raised her voice. But the word washed over me colder than ice. It stilled my tongue as much as it sent a deeper chill to my lungs as if to warn me from speaking further.

I inclined my head in a manner that served both to acknowledge what she had said, and to offer silent apology.

Enshae mirrored the gesture, content. "*I don't know these bindings you speak of. There were only ever the songs, and these I learned. With them, I shaped things mine own. Oh.*" She pressed a hand to her chest and let out a soft breath. The look in her eyes grew to distant fondness. "*I remember.*"

I leaned close. "What did you make?"

Enshae gestured to our surroundings.

I stared.

"*The garden.*" One of her fingers pointed to the sky, then down to the ground. "*All things; as above, so below. I shaped them in this space, and this space would become my home—my prison.*"

"Why?"

Enshae's chest rose, and the motion brought her moonlight gown to rise with it. It shimmered and held my eyes in the moment it took her to speak again. "*Because creation inspires jealousy, castaway flame. As you should well know. And the winds of time blow again as they always have. And so my creation inflamed the others who had come to live in Brahm's world as it had been left to us. They felt me overstepping—too bold, and turning against our maker like had been done before.*"

I thought on the stories I'd heard till then, and realized she might have been speaking of Saithaan going against his father, Brahm.

"*But for a time, there was still peace. It broke with the making of the mortal singers. They who'd been given the full breath and talent of Brahm to see and shape as they saw fit, but lacking our grace and long-lived-ness. This sparked the flames of anger between my people and heaven above. Some saw the right in what I did—my makings, and sought then to try their hand as well. Soon, we shaped kingdoms our own, silver resplendent and shining.*

"*Some Shehen did not like us for this, however. And the war broke out between us, folding the world over and over as we saw fit and had need of it. Eventually, we left such scars upon the lands that all Shehen agreed to fold the world one last time, and in doing so, leave to one of our own making. In this, I was betrayed. They feared my power and my knowings, telling others that I would turn my hand to shaping this new place for us into something else. And we would have another war still.*

"*So the lords of Shalsmi cast me here, in the first place of my making, where I can still see and feel the stars and moon in night, but never know the touch of sunlight.*" Her eyes shone, and twin beads of moisture formed at their corners. They caught the barest touch of starlight-glint before rolling down her cheeks.

I came in close without thinking, touching my hands to her face and wiping the tears away with my thumbs. "They trapped you here . . . for that? For making this?" My voice nearly echoed hers. Pressed hard, breathless, from deep inside my chest. Part in marvel at what she had created, and just as much in disbelief for what the other Shaen had done to her.

"It's . . . I can't imagine anyone having the ability to do something like this. I've never dreamed of bindings this powerful."

Her mouth broke from the smile I'd seen into something close to pitying and sympathetic. "*Oh, you know so little. There are none of them lesser or greater than another. It is in how you make your shapings and put them out into the world.*" Enshae took my hands in hers, then eased them away from her face. She leaned close to me and I saw her lips make a shape I'd grown familiar with of late.

I made mine to match as she pulled me close, and her mouth brushed against my forehead in the kiss a mother might give a child.

It is not a stretch to think I might have felt quite the fool then.

The touch of her mouth brought both the warmth of fresh ashes from a dying fire and the lingering coolness of ice touched to skin and pulled away just as fast. When she moved away from me, a grin hung in her eyes, but her lips gave away nothing in expression. "*You are but a boy, but you are sweet. I will let you be this night. And tomorrow, we will try again to find out what you wish for, and see if I can grant it.*"

The grin vanished, replaced by something else. The old cunning I had seen before, and the intent to make good on that threat.

But behind it, I had seen someone who had been hurt so terribly by those that had been her family. A pain I could understand. She was, in many ways, an orphan like me. Like the sparrows, Shola, and the little crow back in Ghal.

And I have always had a soft spot in my heart for orphans.

I resolved to understand Enshae and, if possible, give her something new to pass her time with.

I couldn't have known what I had been setting myself up for.

How could I?

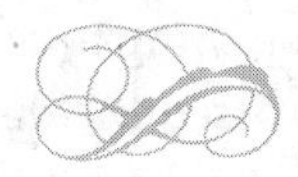

ONE HUNDRED TWO

Fairly Traded

I woke in the patch of moss in which I'd settled before passing out. It had served as a much nicer bed than many I'd had on my travels with Arfan.

Enshae was already up when I turned to look at her. Still clad in her sheer gown of shimmerant light, she stretched to the full arch her body would allow before letting out a yawn. Then her golden eyes fixed on me. They said: *humor, curiosity, pleasure.*

"It has been a long time since any mortal has woken to the next morning in my garden. Ilah, and consider yourself twice fortunate, brightling bold."

I arched a brow. "Twice? What was the first?"

She smiled and pressed a hand to the space above her breast, just below her throat. "*You have seen and talked with Enshae. To have walked through the Doors of Midnight unbidden and without key, that is no simple thing.*"

I thought what it had been like to step into the pillar and the doors. "It didn't seem complicated?" I frowned the longer I fixated on what had happened. "I walked up to it and put my hand to it. I felt the warmth, and then . . ." What had happened? I couldn't remember anything but the enveloping heat and light. Then I found myself in Enshae's nightly garden.

"You found the way through it even if you did so unaware, but a piece of your mind has already been opened to the listening of things. It was this that led you through the doors to me, and left the path behind for those to follow."

Brahm's tits. The ones who'd come with me. The *Maathi*—Khalil—and the tribesmen. She'd turned them into beasts and set them loose in her garden. They were still here. I had to find them.

I jumped to my feet, searching for my staff, but it no longer rested where I'd laid it. "Where's my binder's cane?"

She smiled, but said nothing.

"Enshae, where is my staff?" I hadn't quite raised my voice, remembering enough of myself and, more importantly, to whom I spoke.

Her eyes burned brighter, and for an instant, I found myself reminded more of an old demon than a woman out of dreams and Shaen stories. "*Ilah, you do not need it, do you?*"

I stared, hard as stone, cold and sharp as glacier ice. "It was not yours to do away with."

That might have been the wrong thing to say.

I never saw her move as she crossed the distance between us faster than an arrowshot. Her breath pressed hard against me, just as hot as before, leaving my skin twice as cool in its passing. "*This is my home as much as my prison, brightling. Remember this while you still draw breath. It is exactly and only for me to do with things as I so desire. So too with you.*" She touched a finger to my temple, and in doing so, sent a lance of lightning through my mind.

I winced.

"*With your mind.*" She pressed the finger to the hollow of my throat. "*Your voice.*"

The air in my lungs froze. My chest tightened, and I could no more draw a breath than I could let one out. My insides were wrung tight and beaten hard by fists I could not see, and soon, I shuddered.

Enshae's fingers undid the tie holding my cloak fastened about me, and then did the same to my shirt, exposing my bare chest. She leaned close and pressed her lips to the space above my heart. "*Your body.*"

At her words the world nearly blackened, and I felt as if someone had taken a hammer to my heart. I hadn't noticed the tears running down my face, caught in the greater pains wracking my body. My legs felt as if all strings connecting them to my mind had been cut away. Were it not for Enshae taking me into her hold, I would have fallen, and quite possibly never come to again.

"*And should I want, little one, your spirit. Pray to Brahm or whatever you hold dearest in your heart that I do not set my desires on that piece of yourself, or you will find yourself broken beyond repair.*" Enshae pulled away from me and the rush of feeling that struck me left my vision lanced by whiteness.

I reeled, taking in breath as if it were the first I'd ever drawn. Sharp, cool, and aching. My tongue felt leaden in my mouth and working it again left me making odd shapes with my lips. And my heart now beat as if I'd been running all morning without stop.

You would think the lesson would have cowed me from saying anything on the matter again. But as I've said before: I can be stubborn.

Especially where my friends are concerned.

I found my voice a moment later and did my best to keep it measured and calm. "I just wanted it in case something happened to me while I went looking for the *Maathi.*"

Enshae stepped barefoot through one of the small running streams, eventually making her way to a patch of low-cut grass. She lay in it, regarding me. "*Who?*"

"You turned him into a dog."

She frowned. "*Ilah! Yes, that one. Just moments ago.*"

I had no way of knowing exactly how long I'd slept, but a day had certainly passed at the least.

I remembered the story she'd told me, and how she had been the first thing shaped by Brahm himself on this world.

Old. Older than anyone could ever hope to conceive of. Before mortals had decided to keep and track time. What was a day to something like that, or even the span of a mortal life?

Like mine . . .

"*And what do you fear would happen to you if you went looking for your friend?*"

I gave her a brittle smile. "I don't know. That's part of why I wanted it—to protect myself."

She waved a hand as if to dismiss my concern. "*There's nothing to fear in my garden.*"

Except you. I kept that thought firmly shut and sewn between my lips.

"*Ilah. Your friend is fine. He is doing what any of his kind do. Sticking his nose and other bits wherever he can.*"

". . . Do you mean as a dog? My friend is a *man.*" I stressed the last word.

Enshae's brow furrowed and she pursed her lip. "*I don't understand the difference.*" She said it without malice or humor.

Which told me all I needed to know about how she viewed mortals.

Or it could have only been men.

Who could know with a creature like her?

"*Is that how you wish to spend what time you have left to yourself? Searching for beasts all too content with their newly given lives, as yours hangs on a thread shortly to be cut?*"

I showed no fear at that, but will confess the reminder of my fate chilled me a touch . . .

. . . a touch.

So I returned to cleverness. "I suppose there are other things I would like to know." I turned halfway from her, eyeing her sideways.

She moved. Just a shade, but enough to notice. Enshae leaned closer and curiosity filled her stare. "*What?*"

"Oh, nothing, really. Just a small question. You wouldn't find it interesting." I played a dangerous game now, and I knew it.

But Enshae had a want for knowing things. I understood that, and I appreciated it. I wasn't much different in that regard.

Big questions or small.

And this could be one that could slowly change the nature of things between us.

"*What do you wish to ask?*"

I shrugged with an uncaring grace Shola would have been proud of. I went to my travel sack, rummaging through it until I found one of the other candles I'd brought.

Long, unused, and the plainest of white, it would serve for what I had planned. I made a great show of looking it over in frustration, and muttered words under my breath that I knew would do nothing but irritate her, or draw her curiosity more than before.

"*What was that?*"

"Nothing." I tossed the candle to the ground. "Sorry, I'm just frustrated. I can't find the trick of it."

Enshae looked at me, then the candle. She retrieved and cradled it between her hands. "*What trick is that?*"

I gestured to the wick. "That. What you did the last time. You kindled it without a fire. I'm trying to figure out how."

She adopted the thin bemused smile a mother might make when watching a child struggle with a rather simple task. "*This is what you have to ask? Small secrets?*" A thin breath left her lips. "*Come.*" She took the candle back to the stone she'd rested on when we first came into her realm.

I sat before the stone, looking up at her as she adopted the same cross-legged posture as before.

"*See and attend me, castaway, and listen just as much.*" Once again, she broke into a low and rhythmic song, the words unlike any I had ever heard. Fluting, with the hollow-soft echo of wind through stone. Lilting, and lingering long after she had finished singing. A single note through it all touched my memory: "*Ahn.*" She held the white candle in the seat of her palm with perfect balance.

No, not balance, I realized. She'd bound it in place.

Enshae brought her free hand to the space above her heart and breathed. "*Ahl.*" She pulled away from the spot and touched her hand to the candlewick. A trail of orange light spread from her breast to the candle's head and she sang again.

A flickering first. Then the full spark of light as fire fanned to life.

And all without a source to draw on.

I looked at her, then the burning candle. "How?"

She blinked several times then inclined her head to the dancing bulb of orange. "*Did you not see?*"

"I did, but watching it is like looking at the sun trying to understand how it rises every time. You see the thing, but it doesn't make you any better at understanding it."

Enshae leaned forward and extended her free hand. "*Give me yours.*"

I mirrored the gesture, knowing better than to argue with her. Her thumb touched the inside of my palm and she traced a small circle there before moving her hand with the candle closer to me. The head of the waxen pillar tipped forward and a few beads of wax struck my skin. I winced, but they cooled quick enough to spare me anything more than a moment's discomfort. Then Enshae sang a line, removed the candle from where it rested, and pressed it to the cooling wax in my hand.

I arched a brow, but said nothing, hoping she would explain.

"*Sit, watch, and listen. I will speak. Ilah.*" Enshae licked the tip of an index finger and touched it to the flame, only, she held it there until long after the moisture could have protected her from the heat. "*Fire is old, and it is the first thing in creation after the still and silent dark. First with and from Brahm's own birth. And though this may not be the same flame as that, it is of that fire. Do not doubt this. Fire has memory. It has desire—it is desire. Do you understand?*"

I did, at least in part. Part of what she'd said struck at the memory of when I'd first bound fire. What it had felt like to be so bonded to the flames, and hear their desires almost as if they were my own.

"*It wants to live. How could it not? And so it finds many ways to take shape while waiting to be drawn on, given breath, and kindled. Watch the flame!*"

"I am!"

She glowered at me, and the look held a greater intensity and promise of bite than anything the fire in my hand could do. "*No, you are staring at my eyes.*" She watched me for a moment longer. "*Why?*"

I kept my gaze on the fire this time as I answered her. "They just remind me of someone is all."

She inched closer. "*Who?*"

Here lay someone who could answer all my questions. Someone old enough to have seen the shaping of the world and all things after her, which happened to be everything that existed. At least until she'd been bound behind the Doors of Midnight in the Shaen realm. But her original threat lingered in my mind.

Should I ask of the Ashura, she might grow wrathful, or bored, and I'd become a kitten.

Instead, I focused on the flame, watching its subtle movements until I knew I could shut my eyes and play out the fire's shape perfectly in my mind.

Just like an old exercise I'd been taught so long ago.

"*Who?*" came again the question.

I watched the fire, but finally answered her. "His name is Koli, and he killed my family." In the midst of the tonal oranges and yellows, I saw his face. It danced. It smiled. And for just a moment, its eyes glowed golden bright, just like the lightest color found in the flame. Just like Enshae's.

I told her of him, all without mentioning the Ashura. What he had done to me that night, and then the night I burned down his joy house. And how he'd hid among the rishis of the Ashram for so long a time that none were able to spot him. That he could wear the face of another man if he so wished.

"*Ah.*" She drew the word out. "*He has the bright and burning eye. I might have known. We will speak on this if you survive me another night.*"

More drops of wax bled and dribbled to the cup of my palm, slowly adhering the candle to my skin. The flame burned itself into my mind while I remained wide-eyed, watching. A faint ghostly imprint left dancing in my thoughts.

Enshae turned the conversation away from Koli and back to the flame itself. "*And what do you know of this?*" She waited for me to answer.

And I did, sharing with her all my experience of the first binding I'd performed, and all my teachings under Mahrab.

"*That one had more understanding than many who play at being shapers and folders, but still far from a Singer. But he taught you the beginnings of things. Now, let me show you what is possible.*" She leaned close, shut her eyes, and blew.

Only the breath did not wink the candle flame out of existence. Instead, the bulb roared into a thin and screaming pillar of sunfire. It stretched to a length matching my forearm, and the candle suffered for it.

Wax fell like rain, burning hot as it slid down the shape of the candle to settle into my palm. I winced through it, betraying no sound of pain, nor shying away from the small tower of flame. I watched it, unable to glean anything from it other than the shock and pain.

Still, I refused to turn my eyes away. Part to keep from showing Enshae any weakness, and part due to finding myself falling into something of a trance with the fire. The more I stared, the more I felt like I'd been watching a play, long in making and just as long in performance. It had a familiarity to me, and I felt I could sit there and stare at the shapes within the fire forever.

But Enshae had more to say. She breathed again and spoke, bidding the length of flame low as it had been before. "*Ilah. Fire is strong, alive, and it has wants. Though few ever think to ask a thing about itself, what it desires. They think only of themselves and how to bend something to their will. You do not shape the fire, you shape with it. And with its consent. Watch, and we will talk of things.*"

That set the tone of our first real day together.

"*You have promised to trade me stories, castaway, and there is a price for being given one. So too with knowledge—power. So for every gift I give you in teaching, you shall tell me of yourself, and what you have learned of shaping.*"

And so I did, but she never let me know whether my knowledge was right, however. It quickly became another careful game. Not giving away too much as I saw the cunning behind her eyes as she stored all this information away. I daresay we both became quite good at trading just the barest shape of secrets we could get away with.

My thirst finally deepened to a level I could not ignore, and I broke from our conversation to tell her of it.

She merely walked to the nearest stream, cupped water in hand, and returned. Enshae pressed it to my lips, giving me the silent command to drink.

I did, and nearly spat it back into her face in surprise. It sparked against my tongue, not in coolness, though it had that as well. But it carried a bright sweetness found in some wines and fruits. Whatever fatigue had settled on me washed away.

Something much like what I'd tasted at the Water Tree.

Though I didn't get to ponder this long.

And Enshae's game of prodding me for tales and information continued until the candle nearly burned away. By this time, a pool of wax had bled onto my hand and cooled in place, shielding me from any more drops of the hot beads falling onto the skin.

Eventually the candle sank to nothingness, leaving only a film of white behind. I flexed my fingers and broke up the film clinging to my hand, letting it fall to the ground.

I swallowed and wondered what this meant for our bargain.

Enshae rose and walked over to one of the many trees in her garden, plucking leaves until she had more than enough to fill her hands. She crumbled them between her palms until she'd ground them to fine slivers. Another breath—a whisper of power, and the leaves burst into flame.

"*Here.*" She passed the burning ball to me.

I recoiled. "What? How am I supposed to . . ." I trailed off as I saw her hands.

She'd been holding the fire without anything to protect her. Yet not a lick of flame marred her smooth skin. It remained the soft ashen gray and dusted cobalt blue in places. "*Take it.*"

I held out my hands, but I did shut my eyes as she placed the fire in my palms. I thought of when I had bound the fire at the Ashram, and how quickly I'd called on the folds.

I did so again. First with two, both reflecting the perfect imagery of my skin unburned as I cradled the small flame in hand. Then again to four. Soon six. But that much became an effort when I infused it with the true belief that I would remain unharmed.

It was fire, after all. To burn was its nature.

But I had just seen Enshae hold it as easily as she had held the water. So why not? I kept to the belief as the fire touched my hands. And I spoke. "Whent. Ern."

It did not burn me.

I sucked in a breath, but remembered to keep to the folds and the Athir. My belief had less to do with the understanding of fire and more the idea that it was in fact possible to hold it. That it couldn't burn me. Not the same thing, but it seemed to work.

The fire rested there in the cup of my palms and burned the leaves for fuel, but that was all.

I sat there, half my mind gone into the flames, and the rest remaining within the folds and image of my unburned skin. "I'm doing it!" My eyes went wide and I allowed myself a smile over the small triumph.

She laughed. It was low and throaty. Enshae didn't mock me, but merely took delight in my little joy.

I admit I felt a touch embarrassed by being so happy at something that came as natural as breathing to her. Though it could just as much have been the layer of freshly melted wax protecting my skin from burning.

The full weight of Enshae's concentration fell against me then. Mahrab's pressure had been measured, though strong. The consistent push of strong winds, or a steady current going against you. Rishi Ibrahm's had been the strength of a mountain, set to topple on you with thousands of years of old stone and their grudges.

But Enshae?

She struck me with the fury of a typhoon. So fast and hard a thing that I fell to the full force of its storm before realizing what had happened. Too many stinging beads of rain to count, not washing away my Athir and the folds, but shattering them as if she were a hailstorm and my mind a thin pane of glass. Hurricane winds that blew apart any image I might have tried to hold within. And in the end, nothing remained but me.

I screamed as the fire touched my skin. The ball bounced from palm to palm as I juggled it, finally finding the mind to let it go instead. It fell to the ground and burned until the leaves sustaining it were gone.

My fingers shook and I blew cool air onto them, trying to alleviate the pain. But it did little to assuage the burns. "Why did you do that?" I hadn't quite growled the words.

Enshae rose and smoothed her dress. Well, that wasn't quite what happened. The material bent perfectly with every motion of her body, but never held any hint of crease or imperfection, always returning to its proper shape. "*Do you expect to always shape without another contending your will?*" She motioned for me to follow as she turned around. "*Come.*"

It was not a request, but a command, and little could I do but obey. I gritted through my pain and followed her to a pool of water the color of sapphires and amethysts. A brightness hung in the shades I couldn't understand, almost as if lit from within the water itself.

Enshae slipped out of the gown, leaving me with another part of my body feeling a warmth that had nothing to do with the fire I'd been holding.

It turns out that a young boy cannot, in fact, die from having all of the available blood in his body rush to his cheeks.

She slipped into the pool and watched me—waiting. "*Remove your clothes. I do not want you sullying this place with them.*"

I did as asked, moving with care as to cause my hands as little pain as possible as I went. You might find it odd, but despite the invitation to enter a pool with a Shaen woman out of stories, I didn't want to give up my clothing. At least not my cloak. I felt twice as naked without it, and not for the obvious reason that I in fact was.

No, the truth of it lay in that my cloak was something more than just a covering. It had come to hold a piece of magic to me. Not just that found in the story of how it came to me, and its making. But the cloak had saved me from a knife, and had warded off arrows. Slowly, it had built up a myth of its own, and in that, it made me feel safe.

Now, in a place as foreign as this, giving it up left me feeling more vulnerable than ever before.

I looked down to my hands and realized that perhaps I wouldn't be in any more danger without it than I was with it. At least in the company of Enshae. She could kill me as easy as an outward breath, white-scale cloak be dammed.

So I slipped out of it, even more self-conscious than I had been the night with Qimari, and slid into the pool.

Enshae crossed the small distance between us. Her palms slid down my sides and took my hands in hers. "*Watch.*" She brought some water onto my palms before submerging them into the pool. Once again she broke into low song, and then came the words I'd grown familiar with. And what I had heard Immi say before.

"*Whent. Ern.*"

I felt her will press against me, and I offered no resistance to it. The coolness of the water bled into my hands and she rubbed her thumbs where I'd been burned.

Had been. As soon as her touch passed, the reddened skin looked as if I'd never held the flame. The pain vanished.

I stared at her, unable to speak for a moment. "I've seen someone do a binding like that before, but why the water?"

She tilted her head. "*What are you if not mostly water?*"

"First you call me flame, and now I'm water?" I gave a small smile at that. "Which is it?"

Enshae moved with preternatural speed, taking one of my wrists in a grip of iron. Though she could have crushed the small bones in the joint, she never moved with the intention of doing so. Instead, she straightened my arm, then moved again. Her fingernail carved a long and shallow furrow into the flesh of my limb.

I yelped, but she held me firm.

"*Look at it. What you are of body is not what you are in here.*" She touched her other hand to where my heart lay. Then she repeated her earlier words, rubbing her hand against my wound after bringing it back into the water.

And just like before, the injury vanished as if it had never been there at all.

Enshae motioned to the water, dragging a hand through its surface in a slow manner to accentuate the motion. "*Watch and listen.*" She gently pushed herself away from me and spun once in the water. "*We are apart now, but still connected.*" Her hand traced a path from herself to me through the pool. "*There is a space we all share.*" She moved closer until her body touched mine again. "*I, mine. You, yours. But in closeness, the spaces envelop one another and we begin to share. But even so, there are other ways to share the spaces between two bodies.*" She drifted away again.

The atham. She spoke of the atham. I moved closer to her, but she stayed me with a hand. Despite my want to be nearer so I would not miss a thing she said, I obeyed. But excitement surged through me at realizing with certainty Enshae now spoke of the bindings. At least in a manner I understood.

"*Here this is a knowing between the water and our bodies. We share another space greater than ourselves, but which touches the both of us. And there is a knowing between the water and the water inside of us. Here, we are more. Can do more. Do you understand?*"

I did, at least in part. A sort of similarity. A likeness. And that somehow created a bridge between us, or our athams.

That fundamentally changed my understanding of the bindings. If there were ways to change the spacing between people, then it completely altered the way binders could contend with one another, especially given their environments. Though, I had no idea to what extent this stretched.

Then, I was excited by something else—the bindings. Rishi Ibrahm had been a poor teacher in that regard, but Enshae? She knew them in a manner unlike anything else. And she could teach me more than the Ashram could. With that, I could survive my test upon returning to the school.

If I survived my time with Enshae first . . .

"*Set your will, castaway, and show me.*"

"Show you what? What am I supposed—" I had no warning as the weight of Enshae's mind pressed against mine. I scrambled to pull up the folds, throwing myself quickly into the candle and the flame. It became my center. My compass. And all other thoughts and doubts bled into it, feeding the fire with which to fan myself into resolution and focus.

The folds appeared in my mind, and now the image I held was that of unyielding stone before the storm. Myself, the rock. Enshae, the full fury of the sea. Water washed against me, but none threatened to take me. Not one grain of myself would fall against the constant battering.

I brought myself to hold twenty of these. An auspicious number, given that I had once impressed Mahrab with this, and it had been enough to stave off Rishi Ibrahm's earlier attempts.

Enshae was neither of these men, and they had shown but a whisper of her strength.

There was no battle. And no point in steeling myself against such an assault. Her thoughts crashed against mine, shattering my stone-set self.

No.

Shattering implies breaking with a force that leaves discernible chunks and pieces behind. You can tell what once was with just a look. Enshae turned the wall of my mind into dust in ocean storm, quickly swept away in seafoam never to be seen again. Not even in memory.

Just nothingness.

It was only then I realized what had actually happened.

I lay on the soft grass outside the pool, hair hanging limp and wet from my head. The ground around me had been drenched in water. She had summoned a wave that struck me with such force I'd been flung free into the air until I landed hard.

I blinked, torn between the effort of thinking, and remembering how to breathe. The latter won out as my body decided that the necessity of breathing ranked higher than any thought.

Who knew?

I sucked in a ragged gasp, choking on air. My lungs burned.

Enshae came to stand over me. She knelt and pressed her lips to mine. This was no kiss, though it had all the makings of one. A rush of air pushed its way into my chest, pushing away all the ache and lack of breath I held within. Her lips left mine and she merely watched me before speaking. "*You know enough to begin your shapings, but you have no strength in them.*"

No. Strength.

I had bound fire and stopped a flight of arrows.

That said all that could be said on the matter of Enshae and her ability.

But if anyone *could* teach me how to grow in power, it would be her.

And I resolved to learn.

Because if Enshae didn't kill me, the Ashram would.

ONE HUNDRED THREE
The True Nature of Things

Days passed, at least by my best guess based on how many times I'd slept, and by my count of tales as we returned to our fair trade: I read her a new story, leaving it unfinished till the next time, as by design, and she kept from turning me into an animal.

It would be wrong to say a friendship formed between us, but some of the earlier burrs were certainly filed away. Nothing made this more obvious than when she returned my staff.

She knelt and laid it before me with both hands, the action almost reminiscent of a bow. Except for the fact I would never mistake Enshae showing deference or subservience to another being.

I took my staff from her, looking it over as if I hadn't seen it before. It felt so long ago that I had been relieved of it. The script along the metal bands, and the wood remained perfectly intact. When I extended a hint of my will into it, the cane reverberated with a thrum of subtle power, letting me know it still held a good store of force.

Not that it would be of any help here.

"*You have put small workings into it? Shaped a little song into being along this.*" She reached out and trailed her fingers down the length of the staff. "*But why? You could shape without this toy.*"

I looked away from her then, not wanting to admit that I could not channel a binding like that. But I found a way to explain it to her while also salvaging my pride. "There is a place that teaches the bindings, and many find other ways to first practice shaping with tools like these." I shrugged.

The answer seemed to suffice for her, but I could tell she didn't think highly of my work. She gave the staff another look, and it clearly spoke her opinion: *wasteful*. Enshae then tilted her head, an expression as regal and imperious as could be. "*Then you will learn in my company. For as long as you remain a boy, and not a kitten.*"

I tried not to let the disdain for my cane, and the obvious threat, get to me. Instead, I saw it as salvation—the possibility to learn what I hadn't been able to at the Ashram.

Eventually, at any rate. Enshae had her way of doing things, and one could not move her on that matter. I knew that after trying to contest her will and being trounced.

Setting my staff aside, I went with her to one of the small running streams and filled a bowl of water as Enshae returned with that morning's meal. Red meat that looked like it had been carved from the leg of an animal.

She tore a thin strip free and took it into her mouth. Then offered me a slip.

I stared. I knew better than to openly refuse, but wasn't quite sure how to mention that I preferred my food cooked.

"*What is wrong?*" Enshae took the piece she'd presented to me and ate it. She came to the answer herself a moment later. "*Ilah, of course.*" She fetched tinder for a fire and got one going with a binding. Still without a source of flame to draw on.

I tried to spot the trick of it but failed. Then I looked at the red meat. "What is it?"

"*A lamb.*"

But where did she get it from? My stomach knotted as I considered the possibilities. "How many people have you turned to animals here?"

She blinked several times, looking at me as if she didn't understand the nature of the question. "*How many turnings of the moon have I been here? How many people have passed through? Few are permitted to leave. If not by my touch, then the Shalsmi lords, who do far worse than I. Few have died under my touch, but the lords and their kin?*"

I swallowed the lump in my throat and watched as she chewed another strip of meat.

Enshae noticed my look and broke into a delighted peal of laughter, which made her seem more like a little girl than a woman thousands of years old. "*No, sweet child. This was not once a man. It is and always was nothing more than a lamb.*"

The smell of cooked meat touched my nose. I hadn't noticed that she'd been searing a strip while speaking to me.

She raised it to my mouth and blew. "*Eat.*"

I did, and after a few bites, I finally worked up the nerve to ask her where the lamb had come from.

She laughed again. "*When we shaped this place away from others, we brought with us animals of our own. They have lived here and prospered as many others have.*"

"Ah." We finished our meal, and I turned to watch the fire until it burned out. "Enshae . . ."

She had knelt by one of the streams, washing her hands in the water. "*Hm?*"

"I've been wondering . . . why have you been calling me a castaway flame—brightling? Is that something normal for Shaen to say to humans?"

"*You mean you do not know?*"

I shook my head.

"*It is your nature. Have you not seen the making of your own story?*" When I said nothing again, she motioned me to follow as she rose. She led me for a time I lost track of, passing through tightly growing trees, flat and open fields, and a narrow strip of winding grass that ran through endless pools of water. Once, we passed through an expanse made entirely of flowers.

Every color that had ever been fathomed could be found among those blooms. And every shape as well. I reached out to touch one, but Enshae moved to my side faster than I could blink.

Her hand blurred and struck my finger with the force to bruise. "*No. Watch.*" She raised her own finger to her mouth, baring her teeth to reveal incisors sharper and longer than any mortal's would be. She bit into the flesh of her index finger, letting it hang over the pure white flower I had almost touched.

A drop of blood fell onto the blossom. The folds of the plant rippled as if alive . . . and the red bead vanished, pulled into the color of the flower until it held a light shade of pink. That is when I noticed what had happened truly.

The flower's head had folded in on itself, almost like a mouth pulling something inside. A hungry mouth.

"*The Last Breath is a ravenous thing, and should even a piece of your skin come to touch its petals, it will pull the blood from you. Tread carefully.*"

I watched the flower, a chill spreading through me. When I looked back, I realized just how much of this particular flower Enshae had carefully guided me past without my notice. I returned my gaze to the flower, which had now returned to its original color as if it hadn't just fed on blood. "How much will it take from a person?"

She gave me another patient smile. "*It is called the Last Breath. I leave you to your own reasoning from there, little flame. Ilah. Follow, and step twice as carefully.*"

I nodded and did as she'd suggested lest I come across a flower named: Eats Young Mortals Whole for Nothing but Looking at Them.

The sky slowly lost some of its darkness as we went on, brightening to something closer to evening twilight, now the color of plum and crushed sapphires in place of the heavy black it'd held before.

"The sky's changed." I pointed up at it to bring it to her attention.

Enshae gave me the same smile as earlier. "*Yes. Yes, it has.*" The way she said it made me feel very much like a boy who had mentioned that water was in fact wet.

I flushed. "Why?"

"*We draw closer to the sunset side of things, and a brightening comes on the sky the farther we continue toward where the Shalsmi reside.*"

I frowned. "If that's where the sun sets, shouldn't it get darker?"

She shook her head. "*No, it is where the sun is set—hung immoving. Bound far from the moon and the dark and wild side of things. They cannot be together but for once in many turns of time. As you have seen.*"

"The sun and moon are kept apart from each other here?" That explained why Enshae's garden woodland remained forever in night.

She nodded. "*This place has been folded and shaped away from things—between them, and in this space things do not move as they do in the old world Brahm made.*"

I said nothing else, letting that sink in as we continued our journey.

Eventually we came to a field of pure moss, shrouded in fog. No trees grew here—nothing at all but for the soft bed of green beneath our feet. I followed her to a lone pool, pale gray in color that reminded me of old metal and icy water.

She motioned to it.

I arched a brow. ". . . What do you want me to do?"

Enshae knelt, running her fingers along the surface of the water, yet it never rippled under her touch. "*Look and see the truth of things. Some waters are the mark between places. A space between the being of things, and in those places, more is possible. To see—to glean.*"

"That's it?" I approached the pool and bent over to gaze into its depths. I saw only my reflection. A growth of dark hair had just started taking shape along my face. My hair fell to my shoulders in waves and loose curls, but my time with Enshae had left them looking windblown and close to wild.

Slowly, the image shifted. An eagle screamed, lightning in its wake—the water rippled and the scene faded like fog in the wind. A lion danced where it had been, hurt and bleeding from wounds along its side. It moved through fire and roared in defiance as much as pain. The beast bled away just as the bird had done.

"I don't understand, En—" A hand crashed into my back, sending me into the pool.

Cold. The grip of ice stronger than any I have ever felt takes me now. It holds me in the promise of never letting go.

It hurts. It takes the breath from me and I cannot move to free myself.

Words hammer me in hateful whispers. "Breaker. Collared. Bloodletter. Bound and born again.

"Thief!"

I try to scream but the noise will not build within nor leave my throat. The world is nothing but grayness.

Cold. It threatens to take a deeper part of me, first biting my skin, and then to sinew. It says it will reach the bones of me, then my marrow. And at last, my heart.

The whispers are screams now. Hard as iron, hateful-sharp as ice again. This time I do not have ears for them, fixed on watching the scenes shape themselves before me in the gray water.

I see myself, hands spread, blood raining from my palms, promising to flood the world. The puddle at my knees becomes a pool, and it is not stopping. It grows until I am deep to waist. And it is not stopping. It touches my chest and makes clear it will swallow me whole. And it is not stopping.

The image fades and I am astride the wind itself, violent light of brightest blue in my wake. Anger. A burning filling my chest with a hatred I have only ever known for one man.

Koli.

I scream a scream that echoes a thousand times through time itself. It is the echo of pains once before now come again. It is memory, and it is a promise for the future.

It hurts.

I sit inside a fire that is growing, and it speaks to me. It tells me the story of itself, and the story it wishes to see come true. It grows larger still. And it swallows me. But the flame shows no sign of stopping.

It burns and burns until there is nothing left to see.

The moon hangs overhead and the sun follows behind, but it cannot meet her. She moves, free, dark, and wild, left to choose her own path. The sun bound in place to follow where Brahm has put it. Only a ribbon of red between them.

And the scene is gone again.

I am left weeping on a courtyard of white stone, now touched the color of blood. And I am found weeping in a tower of beaten silver and moonbeams.

The icy touch now moves to fulfill its promise—long since come to kiss my bones, now it comes for the heart of me.

I move, and something pulls me from the pool.

My muscles twitched and spasmed, and I gasped. Water filled my lungs and left me as I turned to retch.

"*Careful.*"

I wanted to shout at her. The nerve to tell me to be careful after shoving me into that nightmare. But I didn't have the strength. Instead, I merely shook.

More water and bile left me as I spat. "What . . ." I couldn't finish the question, gagging and taking more breaths. "What was that?"

"*The pool shows the shape of things inside you. Not truths, but the shape, and those are mutable—set to changing. And they are more than they seem. What did you see?*"

I told her.

"*Do you know what a name is?*"

I shared with her what Rishi Ibrahm had once told me.

"*Wise. Yes. They are pieces of stories, songs that sing inside of us. Potential, meaning. Memory. The thoughts and wishes of those who gave us them. Or not for those things nameless, and the lack of hopes and wishes for them then. So what then does yours mean?*"

I frowned. "Ari? I never thought on it. I didn't know my parents." I thought harder on the question. "It depends on the language?" My words came stilted and through shaking lips. "To break, to shatter. To saw . . . or a saw?" My frown deepened. "It means 'sin' in another tongue, I think? And 'brave' in another. In Brahmthi it means 'sword.' Sometimes to cut—sever?"

Enshae touched a hand to my cheek, and her skin held the gentle warmth of a fire. "*It means many things, and you have not found the many meanings it can have, though you have been shown the shape of it. It is a name of the world, one of the few with a story from everywhere in it, and a story for everywhere to give in return. In the oldest of tongues, it means 'like the sun' as well. But you are no sun. Just a little flame. A brightling spark of fire—thrown to the wayside. A castaway.*" She patted the side of my face and radiated a heat that dried my body to a point like I had never been wet at all. "*And now you know why I call you this.*"

And the pool had called me other things, things I did not wish to speak of. Not yet.

"So the pool shows us ourselves?"

She shook her head. "*No, brightling. It shows you the true nature of things. You saw the makings of your name, I think. And what it can come to be. A story. You will decide what you shall live up to, what you shall not. And what you shall break. But nature is mutable, and changing. Never forget this, castaway flame.*

"*Look to your fires, and then the wind. The ground, and the moving water. None are ever stuck in shape or form. Flames grow and dwindle. They move—dance. So too does the wind. And sometimes it is so still a thing you cannot help but wonder if it is there at all, or if it will ever return. The ground is always changing. Mountains rise, and they fall. Stone crumbles and is born anew. Mortal and Shehen alike shape it as desired. And water? Well, it is all things, and in every thing. It changes most of all.*

"*As is its nature. The nature of all things. To change.*" Enshae sat beside me and motioned to the space between us. "*Sit with me and we will think. We will talk. And I will teach you.*"

We did, and as the candlemarks passed, I felt more like I was discussing philosophy with Rishi Vruk than on a mossy plain with a Shaen woman.

In the end, I suppose you could say I gained a better appreciation for how complex the elements truly were. I still remained far from understanding them. But I grew closer, and that would lead me to what I needed to do.

And maybe what I never should have.

But the next step of my journey in understanding the bindings began there. In Enshae's near-endless garden, a place hung between the sun and the moon—ever darkened, and kept in eternal midnight.

ONE HUNDRED FOUR

The Wolf Who Cried Moon

As time passed, I thought of my dwindling timeline to return to the Ashram and prove I could control the bindings . . . or die as a consequence.

Enshae inquired about the place I'd mentioned before, and I told her its teachings, eventually explaining the use of the minor bindings throughout the Mutri Empire and the greater world.

She couldn't fathom a populace that had little to no command of shaping the world as needed or one saw fit. And proudly exclaimed she could do better, after all, she was Enshae.

This led to lessons of the sort that you would expect from her, but certainly not from a Shaen tale.

Boys who fell into the Shaen realm were seduced by beautiful beings of myth, and returned embettered in grace and skill than they were before. They learned of magics and workings of the world no other could have come by but for having studied at the Shaen's feet. They left with swords of moonlight that could strike clean through any armor. Or boots that made you light as feather—able to walk days without rest, and leap tall walls in a single bound.

In reality, lessons with Enshae went nothing like that. Instead, they remarkably resembled holding a ball of burning tinder and trying not to get burned. This resulted in my hands growing rather used to the touch of fire, and gaining a familiarity with a certain kind of pain that I did not wish to become so acquainted with.

"Brahm's ashes!" I hissed and shook my hands as my latest attempt failed. "I'm not going to get any better with my hands charred, you know?"

Enshae smiled and touched her fingers to my aching palms. "*But you certainly won't worsen any further, brightling.*" She let out a little laugh before healing my wounds as she'd done before. "*Again. Remember, the flame is a living thing. You are not holding a stone. You are holding a child. It breathes, it moves, and it wants—for many things. Do not wrestle with it, cradle it.*"

I steeled myself and tried again as Enshae handed me another kindled bundle. The folds dominated my mind, and I saw nothing but the ever-moving flame in my palms. I kept to the will that it would not harm me. It could not.

After all, hadn't I only too recently bound a flight of arrows? Walked unstruck, unharmed, unfallen?

What was a fist-sized orb of fire to that?

Alive, for one.

Fire is not something to take for granted. It is one of life's most powerful forces. Both of creation, and destruction. We forget this too often. And for that, fire will consume everything we hold dear, and if we are not careful, ourselves in the process.

But for all that, there is a tenderness in the flames. They give warmth, if you are wise enough to respect their boundaries, and know how close to keep yourself. They cook our food, and give us light when there are no others in the dark. Fire, in many ways, is not so different than a person. It pays you back in the same kindness that you give it.

So treat it wisely.

This, I tried to do.

By the end of that day, I grew closer to holding the fire. My hands still suffered for it, but I had enjoyed more successes than failures.

A good sign.

And that night, I made good on my promise to Enshae. So, like the flame, she paid me back in kind.

"—And so Tarun Twice Born set out in pursuit of his friend Hahnbadh, and his chase of the demon who brought rot and ruin to wood and stone—among the oldest of things shaped by Brahm. Now he stepped more lightly than ever, and tired less than before with his newly made boots of thrice-taken step. For every foot a normal man would walk, he could cover three times that, and three times again, before feeling the effort of one.

"This, and his now gifted shadow-shaped bow, gave him all he needed to bring those demons to justice. But, alas—" I yawned and shut the book, exaggerating the motion.

Enshae blinked and woke from the reverie she'd been in while listening to the tale. "*What? What happened next?*"

I shrugged and placed the book down. "I don't know. I've never heard that story myself. I've just been reading them to you from this." I rapped my knuckles on the leather cover.

Enshae stiffened and moved forward on all fours, carrying the stiff back and animal grace of a creature that hadn't quite decided if it would attack me or not. "*So open it again . . . and. Read. Mmmore.*" This was not a suggestion, but rather informed me that my continuing good health would benefit greatly from doing as she said.

But she and I had done this dance enough for me to feel comfortable denying her. "I'm tired. We've spent most of our time finding new and interesting ways to torture me. Drowning in nightmare pools, burning my hands, and trying to contend with your will until you trounce me."

A faint smile touched her lips. "*It is not my fault if you are inadequate in shapings.*"

Ouch.

"Be that as it may, I've been telling you stories every day. It's only fair for you to tell me one back. Maybe a story only the Shaen would know?"

I desired to know, what did they consider to be wondrous and wild? What made their myths and kept them enraptured? Enshae herself nothing more than a story to mortals.

And if she was real, then maybe whatever the Shaen kept in tales was true as well.

"You have to know one."

Enshae pursed her lips and eyed me, suspicion clear on her face. She knew what I was doing, but at the same time she'd gone lost in thought, wondering if there was in fact a story worth telling.

"*There is one . . .*"

I moved closer. "A good one? I mean, those are the only kind worth telling." I returned the dubious look she'd given me. What I said wasn't wholly true.

All stories are worth listening to, and everyone has one. And it is worth your time to learn them, if you wish to understand the person you're speaking to. But I needed Enshae to feel just enough pressure to want to prove me wrong.

She frowned, and the look on her face came more cutting than if she'd raked my skin with her nails again. "*It is a good story. Those are the only kind I could ever tell.*" She arched her back and straightened. "*Now listen, and attend me. I will tell you of the boy who would become a wolf, and set to chase a thing he could never have. Though he still hunts her shadow to this day. A lonely boy, a cowardly boy, and a boy who cowered at the sky's cry.*"

Neither here, nor there, but long ago . . . in a time well before the folding of our realm away from yours, there was a boy. He, like all the nightly walkers and first made, had the bright and burning eye. Enshae pointed to her face and the twin pools of molten gold that shone there.

His name was Akela, and it means lonely. And he was.

It means only. And he was. For this boy had lost his family long ago, and was taken in by the others of his kind instead. But they did not treat him as their own.

It means uninhabitable. And he was, in heart, and the space it held for love. For there was no love for this boy, and none given to him by those that would shelter him, and nurture him. And so he had no love for others.

Many days were nothing but toil for Akela and filled with the hardships some children know. The cruelties done and dealt by other younglings. They beat him, and often left him weeping, and no one heard his cries.

Except one night for a group of wolves.

For every howl of pain Akela cried out, the wolves cried back in harmony. They said they heard him. That he was not alone. And that so long as he cried out, they would cry with him.

Soon, Akela set out in search of those that would share his pain. And he would find them.

The largest of the wolves, a great dark beast with fur black as night, approached him. "Who are you," he asked the boy in the silent tongue of the world. This was a time when those who Listened truly could hear the things said unsaid aloud by beasts and all other shapings.

A gift later passed to the Singers—Maghani, and the Ruma.

Akela looked to the wolf and answered. "I am lonely."

The wolf snuffled and shook his head before baring his teeth. "I ask you who you are and you tell me what you are? Go on, two-leg's cub—begone."

"It is my name, Akela. It means the lonely one."

The leader of the wolves asked the boy what he wished of them.

"To be with you. To be one of you."

While the Shehen had the gift of changing shape and face, Akela was but a boy. He had no talent in this direction, and he had no knowing of the dangers this could pose to him. But all the same, he persisted.

But the wolves welcomed the two-legged cub into their pack, and soon he began to act as they did. For now he had found a new family. One that may not have shared his blood, or the shape of him, but they had his eyes, and they had his heart.

They sheltered him from the cruelty of men and other Shehen. And they steeled his heart against the terrors of the sky. Crack came the thunder and lightning that scared the lonely boy.

"Do not fret, cubling. It is not but the sky's own howl. See?" And the wolves howled and gave back a cry their own. "We have one as well. Show it. Howl with us."

And so the boy learned.

But even still, he feared the crack of lightning and the anger of the sky in storm.

And every night when the clouds gave way to rains and thunder, the lonely, scared boy let loose with cries of his own. Some in answer, some in fear. And who can say with this boy who would be wolf, that both his cries were not in fact one and the same. Perhaps all he learned to do was howl, not in love for his family, or the sky above, but only ever in fear. And in his screaming, hoped to convince others that he was not afraid.

But that is not how fear works. And this lonely wolf did not know this, much less know courage.

Then one day Akela lay in sulking.

"What is bothering you, young cub?" asked the dark wolf who had taken in the boy. The wolf's name is lost to us, but is known as Shadow, for he was as black as such, and moved in silence.

"Nothing," said the boy Akela.

"Something troubles you. I can smell it in you, and see it in your eyes."

The boy sighed. "I thought I would be happier now. I have you, my family, but I still feel an emptiness in my heart."

Shadow the wolf thought on this and then shared with him an old wisdom, something from the law of wolves. "My son, that emptiness is not one that can be filled by something or someone else. It can only be filled by you. Once you have done that, the space grows, and finds room to house another."

Akela thought on Shadow's words, but they did not sit right with him. Perhaps he needed to be more like his family. And so he set himself to shaping his thoughts and form to be like that of wolves.

Soon enough, he had their smile. He had their hunger. Had their voice, and their calls. And of course, he had their eyes.

On a night the clouds were not so thick, Akela saw something he had ignored for so long. The moon, in the fullness of her glory—her brightness, and her shine. He did not see her as mortal things do, simply a shape of white hung high above.

He saw her true, and then, like all the other wolves, he called to her. He sang, low and long. He howled, bright and clear. He cried, sorrowful and heavyhearted.

But the moon did not hear him.

This did not dissuade Akela. Instead he turned to his father. "How do I get her to hear me?"

The wolf smiled. "What makes you think she does not? But just because she hears you, it does not mean you are owed an answer, cubling. Ask yourself: What are you giving her that she hasn't heard a thousand-thousand times before? Give her a reason, and she might answer the call."

And so Akela thought on this, and he listened every night to the calls of other wolves. He watched from afar into the world of men and Shehen, hearing what they had to say to the moon. Few took note of her, fewer still made calls to her. But a small number, the Singers, still remembered her in their hearts.

And they sang to her with silver voices bright as her own shine.
Akela listened. And he learned.
He gave her new calls then.
But the moon did not hear him.
So he followed the Singers and the moon's turn, as long as he could, learning still.
And he sang to her again.
But still, she did not hear him.
Finally, he sang to her the broken song from his broken heart.

"Oh, moon, ever-high in waiting,
full-brightly-shaped,
and in best aspect glowing,
will you not come and see me,
and spare me my lonely fate?

I watch your turning,
finding you perfection,
I wish to see you for myself,
whole in hand and in hold,
and know you are as beautiful,
as is told.

I will sing to you through storm,
I will sing to you in shine.

I ask, I ask,
but one thing to be true,
will you, will you,
be but mine?"

And the boy, Akela—lonely—sang on. He sang as a wolf. Low and long. Bright and shining as the moon. He howled. And he cried like a cubling boy. He offered his tears. He gave her his love, as much as a young boy turned wolf could know of love.

He was far from the truth of this thing, more kept in the shadow of love than love itself.

But in the end, the moon heard him. She listened. And she came to him.

She appeared, bright-beaming and silver-shining resplendent. "I have heard you singing, little one. And I have watched you long—seeing the tears fall from your cheeks." She reached out to brush Akela's face, rubbing away the moisture there. "You've called to me for a very long time, haven't you?"

"Yes," said Akela. "I've followed you ever since I first caught sight of you, hoping you would hear me. I've learned how to sing like a wolf, like a man, and like the Shehen. It was never enough. So I took the songs sung by Singers, and here you are."

She smiled, but it was a pitying thing, because he had not learned the songs as others had. "Here I am. There is blood on your hands, and just as much in your teeth."

"All things have blood on their hands and teeth. It is the way of things," said the lonely boy.

And the moon cradled his face. "You were born with the bright and burning eye of Brahm's first makings, but now when I look into you, I see the eyes of a wolf. You have lived with them long enough that you are now one in heart as much as in face."

This was true. Akela had learned how to shape himself anew after so long a time running with the wolves. And from there, he would leave to walk among men and Shehen, freely, taking whatever face he wished. And in so doing, he walked away from the words Shadow had once told him. He never learned to make a new family, or new friends.

So he grew lonelier still and, over time, hungrier. And that is not a hunger easily filled.

It changed Lonely, and he soon became not the lonely boy, but the lonely wolf, in face, in form, and in heart.

And she saw this in him. but even still, she was the kind and ever-patient moon. "And what is it you wish from me, little wolf?"

"You," answered Akela. "You are the first thing to look at me not in strangeness or hatred. You are the light in the dark. I think I love you, and I know with you that I will never be alone again."

"Oh, child. How can you love something that you have not come to know? You have had the love of others, but it has not been enough for you. You have had the love of those you learned from, but you spurned them because you have been spurned. And when they would not give you what you sought, you took it by force. I think you are lonely because you have not learned how to let yourself be loved, little one. And you do not know the shape of the word itself.

"Just because you love a thing, lonely one, does not mean it loves you back. Or that it will. To know love means to understand this. And you can love a thing from afar and have your love be true and good, but you can never demand for it to love you back. Love is a choice. And to love means knowing this."

This was not what Akela wanted to hear. For never having known love, he had come to know other things instead. He knew that when he was hungry, he had to eat. And that he must get food whatever it took. And the lesson was the same when in the company of wolves. They hunted, and they took what they needed.

When he knew he was tired, he slept. And when he knew he was in danger, Akela fought. His time with the wolves had taught him to take what he wanted.

And now he wanted the moon.

But listen to me now, castaway—Ari. The moon is a dark and wild woman. Understand those words truly. To be dark is not to be bad.

The moon exists herself in the absence of light—whole and wholly unto herself. When she does cast back the sun's own light, it is her choice—her gift. To be dark is to be misunderstood by many, confused and hated.

But she is always herself in the darkness. You do not shine a light on her dark. You sit with her in it, and you share it with her. You seek to understand her in the dark, and her darkness. Know this.

And then there is the wild side of the moon. To be wild is a thing men, Shehen or mortal, will have you think is wrong. It is because they cannot tame a wild thing. And it is not meant to be so. The wild things thrive as themselves, where they are—as who they are.

Know this too, and never try to bend the will of a wild thing.

This is what Akela forgot in his loneliness, and he never learned to respect the wills of others.

Only his wants. And he wanted a great, terrible many more things than just the moon's love.

But he would not have them.

And he would not have her.

"I am sorry, wolf cub, but I cannot be yours, any more than I can be anything other than who and what I am. I made my choice in love long ago, but I can offer you a different kindness." She stroked his cheek and gave him a gift. A gift of three. She gave him then three strands of hair, shining silver-bright. Wound them fast and wound them tight—to then later bind in full and pale moonlight. With that, the moon drew this shaping thin and drew it long. She formed a sword needle-fine, tapered to the sharpest point, but without edge.

"And I give you this. A sword with which to protect yourself from any and all that would harm you, sweet wolfling cub."

But Akela was not happy with this, and the hole in his heart was as deep a thing as could be. Only Tainted-shadow filled it—emptiness. "But that's not what I want. I want you." He reached for her then, hoping that with his strength he could keep her.

But the moon is not a thing to be held. She comes to you in her own time, and you can love her then, as she's meant to be, until it is her time to leave again.

She fought with him, but Akela had grown strong with the wolves, and stronger still when he walked again among men and Shehen. He took their words, and their shapes, and lastly, he took their talents, and their strengths.

In their struggle, Akela took the offered sword and wounded the moon's face, scarring her. And she ran away from him, returning to the sky, hiding behind clouds and storms.

And Akela was alone once again.

Bereft, he returned to his pack of wolves, and when Shadow learned what the cub had done, he flew into fury.

"You hurt the moon! She is our shepherd, and our guide. Why do you think we sing to her each night? How could you be so selfish—so foolish!" And with that, he cursed the boy.

And the curse of wolves is no small thing.

Especially when he was cursed already, unknowing, by the moon.

And now Akela lost the one thing he had fought so hard to have—her love. All the while never having realized the value of his family.

Alone, thrown from the wolves, and forever banished from the sight of the moon. For now when she shone along the sky, she would turn away from Akela's face and his watchful eye.

All he would know is what he feared: the rain and thunder, and the stormy-vengeful sky.

Enshae came closer to me, reaching out to cradle my face in her hands. "*And that is the memory of the wolf who cried moon. The memory of a broken love, one never meant to be. And a story I am certain you have never heard.*"

"It's a very good story." Then I frowned, realizing what she had said. "Wait, what do you mean by 'memory'?"

She pulled my head close and kissed my forehead, much like the moon had done in the story. "*What is a story if not memory? And memory if not a story?*"

I blinked. "Some stories are true, though, but not all?"

Enshae let go of me. "*All stories are true one way or another, even if not for you and your memory. And not all memories are true. They too are like the foundations of a thing: flame and stone, wind and water—mutable. But this is a true thing—a happening that I myself know of. And every story has secrets inside, little one, if you have the wisdom to glean them.*"

And what's the secret there, I wonder? I did not voice that however.

Instead, I thought about what she'd said just before, then things I'd heard from Rishi Saira. "Some memories are recorded, and so are stories. Sometimes they come from the same place."

Enshae nodded. "*And some are locked away, left until needed to be recalled later. And some are left locked forever. It is better that way.*"

"You can't lock a story or memory away"—then I remembered where I was—"can you?"

Her lips tightened, and their corners turned downward just a shade. "*It is a sad thing to do, and it can break a mind to do it—strip one of all they are. But it can be done. Any tale can be locked away, and at great cost to the one it is done to.*"

Any tale can be locked away, she had said. But could any story be reopened? My mind went back to the book Mahrab had gifted me so long ago, which currently rested in my travel sack.

"*I can glean what you are thinking, castaway flame. Right now your mind is on the story in your possession, bound shut by shapings. It was sealed, and not by your hand. But you are a curious thing, and it eats at you. You wish its secret spilled, do you not?*"

I didn't answer at first, part in shock that she had known exactly what was on my mind, and part for not wanting to admit she'd been right. So I settled for asking a question. "How did you know? Can you—"

She laughed. "*Read your mind? No, castaway. Not as you are thinking.*" Her laugh deepened. "*But I can see the shape of your thoughts on your face, and it is an easy thing for me to read. And I can feel the pull it has on you. You burn for it—the answers. You wish for me to open it.*" That was not a question.

I nodded. "Yes."

"*Would you lift a stone in a forest, unaware of what lay underneath?*"

"Is . . . it an interesting stone?" I gave her a smile and hoped she'd recognize the little joke.

She did not. "*Ilah. Curious kittens oft find themselves in the wolf's jaws, and then their stories end quite poorly, forgotten flame. You would lift up the stone not knowing a viper slept beneath it, then find yourself struck and dying. Curiosity, kitten, is not always worth its price to pay.*" She ruffled my head as if I were nothing more than a child.

Then, as far as she was concerned, I suppose I was.

"Depends on the curiosity you wish to sate, doesn't it? And cats certainly seem to have enough lives to chance it." I thought of Shola.

Enshae's smile deepened. "*Oh, but you are a bold one, and perhaps a touch mad. Yes, you would think you could chance escape from the Doors of Death.*"

"What?"

She patted my cheek and motioned to my bag. "*That is enough for now. I give you answers, and you throw two questions more at me. Fetch your candles. We are done with stories for a time. Now we will work your shapings again, and you will learn.*" The gold in her eyes brightened further then. "*Or you will not.*"

I licked my lips before speaking. "And if I don't?"

"*It will hurt.*"

She wasn't wrong.

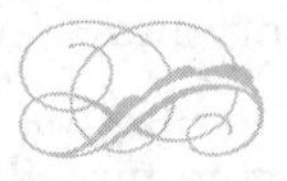

ONE HUNDRED FIVE

Walking Fire. Shaping Stories.

"*Ilah, brightling. Slower.*"

"I am going slow." I kept the harshness out of my voice, showing more grit and gravel instead. The candle I held had burned to its last third, leaving a splotch of drying wax along my palm. The pain of it had stopped bothering me a long time ago, and now I simply kept my focus on the folds, imagining the ability to reshape the flame's movements as I moved. Along with that came the task of keeping it alight as I walked.

Every step threatened to wink the flame out of existence. And if that were not enough, Enshae occasionally pressed a palm to her lips and blew a breath across it. The result came as a current of low wind that tried to snuff my flame out, and all done in the manner of a young girl sending a lover a faraway kiss.

I scowled at her.

She smiled. "*Careful, it is a near thing now.*"

I looked to find her words true. The flame shuddered and nearly flashed out of existence. I sucked in a breath and cupped around the fire, shielding it from anything that might take its life.

This exercise mostly led to an increase of pressure at the center of my forehead, and spotting dancing motes of flame long after we'd stopped for the day. But Enshae among all things was a dutiful teacher, and she believed in practice. Well, as far as mortals went.

For her, the bindings came as natural as breathing.

If only . . .

By what I gathered to be midday we turned to a different fire-walking practice. She set ablaze a new ball of flame and placed it in my hands. Then I walked the path she'd directed me to.

The goal? To keep my hands from being burned to bone.

Enshae did not believe in easy lessons, and did firmly hold to the merits of painful truths. So, I suppose she and Rishi Ibrahm corresponded with one another on occasion. . . .

I had grown more comfortable in holding the bindings and folds to keep from burning my hands, but still nothing close to what Enshae would consider consequential.

Still, some progress was better than none. It was odd, though, that I hadn't been able to perform major bindings aside from the two times I had before. But I could work something to protect my own skin. I didn't understand it. The principles were the same, so if I could employ two bindings like that, shouldn't I have been able to do something more with them?

Enshae had the answer. "*No, that is the wrong understanding. Like with the pool, brightling, you have an understanding of yourself.*" She touched my chest with two fingers. "*In doing this, you are not manipulating the flame as you think. You are simply showing it your boundaries, and asking it to respect them. There are other shapings to keep yourself free from harm. Here you are affecting the shape of space around you.*"

The atham. The space we all occupy outside ourselves. So, I wasn't really even shielding my skin from the flame. What happened between the flame and my hands was this: I employed a binding that created the thinnest of spaces between my skin and the flame—this area being something within my atham. When it failed, I would truly be touching the fire, and it would do as it would . . .

. . . burn me.

This became the pattern. Walk, hold the fire, burn, and be healed. Just like before.

But the memory of the pain remained, and eventually, I would run out of patience to endure any more. And I started to understand what frequent pains, even when washed away, could do to a mind.

Brahm's ashes, Immi, is this what broke you? The thought became common enough to me in that place. But Enshae never let me dwell on it.

One day after practice she beckoned me.

I did as instructed, rubbing my hands in an effort to forget my all-too-recent burns.

"*Once we spoke of stories, and their shapes.*"

I nodded, but said nothing, eager to see if she would change her mind on what I had wanted—asked for.

"*Now you must learn another lesson about their makings, and how they can be shaped by others.*"

"What do you mean?"

"*A story is more than words we tell, and they are not only the memory of a thing. They are your memory of a thing, more so when it is your story. Long ago some learned to change the shapes of their stories, and in doing so, the nature of them. It is one thing to have a story change face the way so many do. Little lies and gossips that all children tell. This is normal.*

"*But to truly change the shape of a story, and tell it time and time again—so often so that the world begins to believe it . . . that is a terrible thing. Belief is a power. It is the foundation of things. And when the world comes to believe a story, the story itself can come to take on a life its own. The story is given life, and kept alive. And when the story of a man changes so much and he comes to believe it, he becomes the story he believes himself to be.*

"This has been done by some through time, and they are now kept alive by all the twisting truths they've told. Horrible things. Hated things. Turned and twisted into all the lies they've shared. But this is a curse in two ways, brightling. For these things cannot die no matter how much they might wish for it, so long as their stories are told, because no thing dies so long as it is remembered. But if it is remembered falsely so, it lives on as that shadow of itself. And that is the other curse, to be shaped by your own making into less than what you are. What you wish to be. And what you need to be.

"And so you must kill your stories and all memory of them if you wish to be set free."

"You mean die?" The words left me before I realized I'd spoken. Her choice of words had been set free, but the implication was clearly death. And who would want to die like that instead of having their stories remembered? The answer came to me the next instant.

"The Ashura."

"Quiet!" Her voice left her still as whisper-wind as always, but for the first time holding the firmest and most noticeable edge. Stone shuddered beneath her, and a single furrow raced along its surface as the hardened rock cracked.

Actually cracked from the sound of her voice.

That alone should tell you the shape of her anger.

And how quickly my heart beat. I froze, going as far as to hold my breath lest my tongue buy me further trouble.

"Do not speak of the accursed unless you wish to bring them on your head, castaway. And you are not so ready as to dance with even one of them, much less all the nine."

The nine. Once again that number. Enshae was the oldest of all things between the realms . . . if she was to be believed. If anyone knew the truth of them, it would be her.

Her tone settled the matter and I decided to move around the question to something else. "How does it work?"

She tilted her head, lips pursed. *"Ilah? How does what work?"*

"Killing a story and a memory so something dies."

"It is not so easy as that, and that in itself is no easy thing. But when you kill a story, you kill the thing within it." She said it so simply as if it were obvious—something anyone old enough to have their teeth ought know.

Evidently that wasn't the case.

When she saw I didn't understand, she elaborated. She sang, same as before, and I only caught the whispers of words I believed to be the bindings within the larger shape of all she said. Her fingers moved, and at their ends trailed motes of silver-white light. Every wave of her hand bled lines of starlight, and the look in her eyes told me to pay careful attention.

"*A story is a thread.*" The previous arcing bands faded, leaving only one that flowed from an index finger. She traced it through the air, letting me follow it with my gaze. "*But that is only the beginning.*" She moved it again, and the line split in two. Then again. It continued breaking apart, and now all her fingers became part of the dancing light show. "*They fray, spread, some are taken off to new paths, others break and are born anew and again. Together they make something larger, more complex than anything you can ever know.*"

I finally realized what her movements reminded me of.

Weaving. Enshae wove a picture out of starlight.

"*The simplest of stories is a tapestry with so many threads, all tied tight together so that you cannot hope to make them all out at first look. Even with a thousand times your attention given to one piece, you would not find them all. And so, even the humblest of things has this in them, and then again—ten thousand times more. So how can anyone come to understand a thing at first chance of seeing its face?*"

I thought of a little girl and the game she'd taught me. And all the times I'd come to use it since.

"*So, you see, it is not so easy to kill such a thing.*" She waved a hand and the lines of light faded like motes of shimmering diamond dust blown by the wind.

I noticed that in her demonstration, she artfully evaded telling me *how* a story is killed. Just that it was possible. But I would take whatever small answer I could get.

For now.

She set to weaving again, and now another tapestry hung before me. But then her hands twisted, and the strings within followed suit. The image that had been forming inside warped, no longer discernible. "*A story's threads can be pulled on, brightling. Twisted, maligned, Tainted. When that is done, many have a hard time understanding what they are looking at, and they fear these stories, revile and misunderstand them, and when it is the story of a person, how can that person not come to hate and revile themselves? Misunderstand themselves? It can rob a thing of truth and its own power. But there are reasons this is done.*"

I did know the answer to that, however. "Because if you twist a thing's story—pervert it, the truth of how to kill it can be lost? If that's hidden inside it, I mean."

She nodded, and whatever small joy she held in her face at teaching me now faded for the somber, flat look of stone. "*Yes, and it is a dangerous thing to misshape a story, but some have done it before.*" Enshae flashed me a knowing look, and I took her meaning.

The Ashura. She wouldn't have said it aloud, but there could be no mistaking the hardness and hate in her eyes. The same she'd shown when I'd asked about them.

So their stories—their truths had traveled far and been twisted along the Golden Road over that time. Even their names had changed shape based on the country and language they were spoken in. Ashura, Ajuura, *bhaalghul*—but the same thing to me.

And the story Khalim had been working on must have held some truth in it. Something enough to warrant murdering my whole family. But what?

"And how do I find that truth within, Enshae?"

She eyed me sideways. "*Clever, and I know why you ask this.*" The Shaen woman sighed and shook her head. "*You learn to see, and listen—better than you have been doing, brightling. You find the threads.*"

Not the answer I wanted. But if Enshae knew I was using this to learn more about the Ashura, there would be no asking her for more. So I thought of something else then. "And if you lock a story away instead? What happens then?"

She frowned. "*Ilah. You do not ask small questions, do you?*"

I grinned. "Not really."

She flashed me another patient and tired smile. "*It is like killing a story, only what is locked can be unlocked—set free. But until that time, what remains in the world of flesh will be but a shadow of itself, and easier to twist, break, and fall apart. The strength of it will be gone. It will be hidden from most who seek to find its truths, and the one within.*"

Had the Ashura done that along with perverting their tales? Had they somehow sealed their stories to bury their truths? No. I realized how wrong I was as soon as I'd thought it through.

Koli had been no mere shadow of power. Mahrab had failed to kill him with the full weight of a toppled building. And then at the Ashram, I had let loose all the fury of an angry child, full in hold over fire itself, and Koli had batted me aside with contemptuous ease.

I did not voice this thought to Enshae, however. But it meant Koli had his own stories out there in the world. Separate from the collective tales about the Ashura as a whole. And in them, a secret truth that could be his undoing. All I had to do was find those tales, and begin pulling on those threads.

Just like Enshae had said. Slowly, I was getting more here in her garden than back at the Ashram. As much as there was the risk in staying, there was just as much potential for knowledge. For power.

A dangerous thing. A tempting one. And Enshae knew how to tempt men with their curiosities until it cost them. But could I find a way to tease more out of her, all while playing another game—keeping from being turned into a cat?

I suppose I'd find out.

And she continued without noticing my reverie. "*This is what makes the stories of creatures and men tricky things. First looks and lies shape others as much as they do themselves. Some will only ever come to see the first of countless layers and decide it is the thing itself whole and full. So they miss the truths of things, and are never able to shape them. To listen to them.*"

Or kill them, I thought.

"*And it is this way with fire, brightling. Which is why we practice. You only understand the barest shape of fire—all it is, all it has been. But that is still more than many. So we will continue until you learn not to burn your hands shaping it.*"

The words were as good as promise, and she made good on it.

The lesson on stories ended, and we returned to my practice with fire.

My hands, unfortunately, did not remain unburned.

Though I confess my mind wandered during my training. To thoughts of the Ashura. To their stories. How I might find the secrets within about the storybook demons.

And how I'd use those to kill them.

ONE HUNDRED SIX

THE TOWERS OF THE MOON

One morning Enshae left early after waking, telling me she needed to journey to the northernmost ends of her garden prison.

When I asked her why, she didn't tell me. Only making it clear she had need to be alone, and to contemplate something. As well as to bring something back.

I didn't push the point for obvious reasons. My first moment of being left unattended, which meant opportunity. A specific one, and a name that came with it: *Maathi*.

I had to find my friend, and now there was no dangerous Shaen to stop me.

So, staff in hand, cloak drawn tight, I prepared to leave. I made sure to bring the blue candle I had been gifted by the beggar girl back in Ghal. Despite using it several times since meeting the Shaen woman, it had barely lost an inch in height, whereas other candles would have long since dwindled to half. Its shaping reminded me of what a tinker had once told me—about certain candles made in a fashion that kept them burning long and true.

That, and the pressed emblem of the owl in its shape made me think of the thing as lucky. Besides, any binder worth a damn knew you must always carry three things: candle, cloak, and cane.

I had mine, and set the candle alight from our fire before venturing westward into the woods.

You cannot describe the depth of darkness in a place like that, already kept under a sky of eternal midnight. The canopy above so thick a shroud that little moonlight or starry glow shone through. All I had was the candlecast glow of orange resting atop my palm. And it would have to be enough.

The shadows within this place had shades their own—deep and lively, moving as much as I seemed to. Any child who's ever spent a night watching shapes cast along their walls knows what went through my mind. And now in a place out of Shaen stories, a piece of me kept in mind that the horrors of my imagination may very well have been more than just figments.

My hand clenched tighter to my staff as I wandered, and I remembered the Arasmus knife resting against my hip. I passed by trees whose bark held the color of washed ivory, others as black as coal, appearing all the darker in the night. Some trees had leaves thin as strands of hair, and shaped of translucent glass and amethyst by the look of them. One tree had flowers with petals the color and shape of drops of blood.

And it wept. Each tear sent a liquid petal crashing to the ground before it burst, only for a new petal to bleed into existence in its wake.

Shaen stories indeed.

I tried to recall what else I knew about them . . . mostly the nightmares that lingered in the tales. As I ventured farther into the nighttime forest, I decided that my heart and sanity would fare better if I did not dwell on such things.

While my candle offered me light, the fact it burned so slowly meant I could not use its length to accurately gauge how much time had gone by. My legs did not burn with fatigue, but that had long since stopped being a measure of distance. The travels from Ghal to Mubarath, then in Arfan's service, had conditioned my body to the rigors of the road.

I walked until I could no longer tell which direction I'd come from, and which I faced. Until I passed too many new sights to be able to take them all in—overwhelmed by things that could have only existed in dreams, and nightmares. And I walked until I finally saw something shining through the thick trees.

Pale. Glowing. Tall.

A pillar of light bled through the tree line, and I wondered if it marked the end of the forest, or something else imprisoned within it. Something that could have easily been a danger, knowing this place.

Possibly more dangerous than Enshae.

I crept closer, brushing aside hanging branches and leaves with the head of my staff.

The soft glow grew brighter the closer I moved. Eventually I reached the line of trees where the forest ended, and peering through them revealed the truth of what lay ahead.

Two spires, each reaching high enough into the sky that they dwarfed any mountain found in Ghal. Their construction? Shaped from seamless stone as white and pale as moonlight—silver shining magnificent. Starlight gems studded their lengths to give extra sparkle to their already shimmerant forms. Between them stood a wall made of the same material, and nearly as tall.

The moon hung and shone full high above.

Voices filtered into the air, carrying an oddly resonant and echoing tune. Something I'd heard before.

In Enshae's songs.

"Al-hisania, o'way
Ihn ah-mur, dharan-dhey
Fahruud amar, sathan-dhey
Ibhan dhir, aman-sey

Alune. Alune.
Alune. Alune."

The voices carried the notes high and bright as the towers ahead. As sharp and ringing as silver-struck bells. It caught me, and it pulled at me until I looked for the source.

A procession of men and women walked along the ground in front of the wall. No, not men and women.

Shaen.

They wore clothes fashioned from the same threads as Enshae's. Thin and light. Flowing free. Some sheer and showing the skin beneath, and they all held the fair smoothness of soft ash and gentle smoke. But one of them above all held the whole of my attention.

The one at the head of the procession.

She had the full breadth of starry nights in her. Softest washed pewter and powdered gray all bleeding through a film of freshly born smoke. Her hair was the perfect contrast to the dark of her skin. Pale shining white, the very color of the moon.

Bands of brass bound strands of her hair, the length of which was threaded with blue flowers. Her dress—a thing of starlight sequins held together by I know not what. And her eyes were like Enshae's, burnished rings of deepest gold.

Something inside me stirred at seeing her. I knew her, somehow. When I looked at her, I saw a familiar face. I cannot tell you how or why I had that feeling. I just did.

The same as when I looked upon the Nagh-lokh and heard the silent plea and apology in its unspoken voice.

They walked until stopping before a particular section of the wall. A brighter light shone from it, bisecting the structure as it opened to admit them inside.

I watched, mouth agape, never having imagined something like this to exist. Not only the Shaen realm, but what looked like a place made out of moonbeams and powdered diamonds. Spires, of beaten foiled silver and wreathed in shapened fog, that reached high enough into the sky to touch heaven itself.

I slunk back into the thicket, moving along so I could get a better look at what lay behind.

If Enshae knew of the Ashura but couldn't speak on the matter, perhaps these Shaen would.

I made my way through the brush, no longer needing my candle for its light. Eventually I came to a point where the forest thinned and fell far short of reaching the nearest tower. The only way to get a better view now rested in leaving the safety of the trees and crossing into the open.

Into the wide fields of pale grass. I reached out to pluck one of the blades, running my thumb along its length. It had the texture of polished steel or glazed ceramic. A touch of my fingers, and it snapped like glass.

A crystalline chime rang through the immediate area, then spread through the field as if I'd struck a bell in an empty stone temple.

I bit back a curse and returned to the safety of the trees, praying that no one had heard the sound. A foolish hope in all honesty. The noise had gone clear and echoing across the field, and likely well past it and the moonlight walls.

I had made it a dozen feet back into the better safety of the forest when something moved through the blackness. A ripple, like velvet shadow in the wind. I gripped my staff and pointed it toward the spot. "Who's there?" I kept my voice low, but sharp.

No answer.

Another swath of darkness moved by the corner of my vision.

I turned.

Then turned again as the nightly shapes continued to move at the edge of my periphery.

I whirled, just in time to catch sight of a length of silver come to rest below my chin.

Something sharp enough in look to promise cutting from a distance, whether or not it touched your skin in truth.

. . . Perhaps I'd made a mistake in leaving Enshae's garden prison.

The wielder stood the very antithesis to the bright and shining blade. Shrouded in shadow, and not by any poetic measure. I saw nothing of their face or features. They stood within a robe of black perfectly matched to the darkness of the forest. I could only see them because their clothing looked to move in a wind that wasn't there.

Then I realized the figure had not come alone. Two more lurked just behind them, still and silent as blackened stone.

"*A mortal.*" The voice had hints of Enshae in it, only more weight—a stress and edge she did not hold. But it still clung to an undertone of song notes in its words.

I said nothing, and I did not nod. The latter proved to be difficult anyhow owing to the sword resting against my throat.

"*How came you here, and from where?*"

My gaze flitted down to the sword, then back up to the hood obscuring the speaker's face. I saw nothing within it, though, only shadow-swallowed darkness within.

The sword lowered from my throat, but still remained steady-held before my face. I had no doubt the robed figure could take my head from my shoulders with a quick cast of the weapon. A single perfect slash.

I had no desire to give them reason to. "I walked through the woods. I don't know for how long. Eventually I came here." It was the truth to a point, leaving out how I came through the Doors of Midnight and into Enshae's realm.

If she truly was a prisoner, it may not have been the best idea to tell them that I had interacted with her.

"*How did you come into the Shehen lands, mortal? The dominion of the Chandni Court.*"

I tried to translate a piece of what he'd said. Chandni. I had heard that before, or something close to it. Silver? No, moon silver? Moonly? The Moonly Court came as close as I could to an accurate translation, and I knew I'd still missed something by half.

"*And leave nothing out, mortal, or I can just as easily leave you as a corpse to feed the forest grounds.*"

I swallowed at that and went into the story of how I came there. "I was in the service of a merchant king of Zibrath, out along the desert. Then one day the sun and moon met in embrace, and a shaft of light touched the ground. Then I walked through it."

The sword remained before my face, but the speaker's head turned to the others for a brief moment. "*These are the woman's woods—he could be one of her strays.*"

Another of the figures in the back spoke up. "*She plays with all mortals who come to her prison, and this one is no pet or beast. Perhaps he did not step into her garden.*"

And that confirmed whether or not I should speak of Enshae.

The Shaen closest to my side turned their attention back to me. "*Why were you lingering at the edge of the forest—skulking about?*"

This time I spoke the truth. "At first, because I didn't know what was ahead. Then I saw the walls"—I motioned ahead—"and the towers. I've never seen anything like them before."

"*And you won't ever again,*" said the sword-wielding Shaen. "*What should we do with him?*"

"*Killing him seems best. He could leave the garden and present a problem.*" The suggestion came from one of the pair at the back, but I couldn't identify which one.

The one holding the sword toward me had a different opinion, thank Brahm. "*He doesn't look like much to worry over, though this is a curious thing.*" They reached out with their free hand to pinch the end of my cloak.

I almost moved, clenching harder to my staff instead. Though the urge to bat the figure's hand away had almost taken me. And I'm sure it would have been met with the instant removal of my head. Instead, I kept still, hoping that their curiosity would settle upon examination of my cloak.

"*White scale and skin. Ah, shaped from one of the worms.*"

The two robed Shaen in the back leaned closer for a better look.

"*I thought the last of them died in Uppar Radesh?*" said one of the pair.

The one holding the sword and a piece of my cloak gave the fabric a little tug. "*How came you by this?*"

I told them the truth. "It was a gift, made for me from the body of one that died in Ampur."

"*I do not recall any such place by that name in the mortal.*" The Shaen speaking to me turned halfway to regard the duo behind them, clearly looking for help on the matter. They let go of my cloak and tilted their heads to regard me. And while I couldn't see beneath their hoods, the motion and set of their heads reminded me terribly of Enshae. "*Ampur? And how did the beast come to fall?*"

I described the village and its location, along with its history in relation to the

Mutri Empire. Then I told them of the incident with the Nagh-lokh, and how the mountain came to fall on it.

But the other two merely shook their heads.

"It's part of Sathvan."

The sword shook, but only for a moment, in the Shaen's grip. "*What did you say?*"

I repeated myself, unsure what had bothered them.

The Shaen closest to me traded another hooded look with those behind them. "*The shape of the mortal has changed a great deal since we last walked it. And what of you, what do you seek?*"

I swallowed, thinking of everything I had just said. It brought back thoughts of home. The Ashram. My one year of time to save my neck. I thought of the friends I'd left behind, and how very long it had been since I'd been in their company.

I missed them. And what I would have given to hear Radi make just one more joke, or pluck his mandolin, or hear Aram reprimand me—rightly so—for doing something rather reckless.

The Crow—Sham. What was he up to now? Was he safe, keeping up his language lessons?

I missed my brother.

And then there were the friends and folks I'd grown close to in Mubarath and Arfan's company. The Hundred Thieves, Qimari, Aisha, and of course the closest one of all.

Shola.

Were they safe? I had left the tribes close to war when I vanished. Had things changed?

I missed them.

And I wanted sorely to return home, and I told them this. "I'd like to find a way back to where I came from. To trouble you no longer."

The sword still remained in place, barring me from leaving, or doing anything other than taking the shallowest of breaths lest my chest touch its point. "*A fair desire, but one I do not think it possible for me to grant.*"

A coldness spread through my stomach, reaching up to tie icy bands to my heart. I didn't trust myself to speak.

"*He may not have crossed paths with the temptress, but are you willing to risk him venturing through the garden again? What if he comes across her then?*" said one of the pair at the back.

"*Then he meets the same fate as any other man to face her. A suckling pig, a hound, or perhaps he ventures as far as he can the other way into the fields of morning, and there is turned to stone. It does not matter.*

"Enshae is only our problem so far as something of hers tries to come into our kingdom, touched by her influence. Beyond that, she is the responsibility of the Shalsmi Court. Their burden, their prisoner." The Shaen in front of me finally lowered their sword.

"She dishonored us all with what she did, and you are too charitable toward her. You always have been, Tharam," said one of the others.

The one who'd sheathed their sword, Tharam, I guessed, turned away to face the pair. *"She did no more than what many of us thought of in heart and mind. It is not our place to judge her, or keep and tend to her. Only our own borders. As for you"*—Tharam turned halfway toward me—*"follow your path back to wherever you came from. I cannot promise you safe return to the mortal plains, nor can I promise you will survive the garden. But you will survive us. If . . . you can run fast enough."*

My gaze flickered to one side—back to the walls of shaped moonlight and towers reaching up to touch the sky. And then there was the question burning inside me: What lay beyond? What stories hidden inside, and of course, what magic?

And what cost? The answer: the Ashura. I'd missed them at Iban-Bansuur. I wouldn't let that happen again.

I nodded at Tharam.

"Good. Now run. Run and pray that you find your home not so long-gone past in time that you do not recognize its shape anymore. For a moment here can be the turning of days in the mortal, and sometimes quite the opposite. Run. And. Pray. Mortal.

"Run."

The trio shoved me hard . . . and then brightness gleamed from where their mouths would be. Sharp teeth—fangs. And I would quickly learn why they smiled.

But what had Tharam let slip?

Time moved differently here, and who knew how much had passed back home.

I turned and did exactly as he said.

I ran.

The Shaen chased me.

And I prayed.

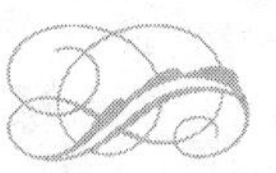

ONE HUNDRED SEVEN

Tolls of Time and Truth

The forest passed in a blur of darkness and branches. Where once I'd picked my way through this place with the greatest care, now I tore through, and was in turn torn. Slender tree limbs bent and snapped against me, finding the soft places beneath my cloak. My hands stung and bore more welts and cuts the longer I ran. A razor's line had lanced along one of my cheeks, burning once in fresh pain, then twice again as sweat touched the open wound.

Strands of my hair caught and snarled along the brush as I moved, yanking free in bright spots of momentary anguish.

And Shaen laughter echoed behind me. Howling—rolling, echoing like the cries of monsters from stories.

As I ran, I felt less like Ari who'd stopped a flight of arrows, walked through the Doors of Midnight, and met the fabled Enshae. Now I remembered Ari who'd lost everything years ago. Before I'd even been a sparrow. Just scared.

Just running.

And just hoping I could find something to hold to, and somewhere to call home, because mine was gone, and so very, very far away.

The staff in my hand was no longer a binder's cane. Now, it was a cudgel, and I used it to bash my way through the foliage I'd nimbly moved through before.

How long *had* passed since I'd come through the doors? Had it been months? Years back home?

I only had one year to prove myself to the masters of the Ashram, and most of that time had gone by in traveling to Mubarath, and then in Arfan's service. Not long remained.

If I return in time at all.

Brahm's blood. What had happened to all those I loved? What would I return to find—*who*? My stomach now burned along with my heart in another kind of pain. The pain of loss.

And still, scything swords cut through brush at the edges of my vision—mocking laughter trailing me.

Hunted by the Shaen. Though, surely they could have caught me if they so desired?

As I ran, the forest took its toll in torn flesh, blood, and my tears.

But, eventually, the laughter stopped, and I reached Enshae's garden.

Had they been merely toying with me at my body's expense?

A cruel joke?

Enshae had returned in the time I'd been gone, and rested on a length of moss near one of the narrow streams coursing through her domain. The Shaen woman noticed me. "*What happened to you? Where did you go?*"

My heart hadn't settled, neither from the exertion, nor from what I had learned. My staff fell from my hands as I crossed the distance between us. "I went into the forest and came to . . ." I detailed the walls I had seen, and then the meeting with Tharam and the others.

"*You found the Behel-shehen and their court.*" It wasn't spoken as a question. "*Did you try to leave the boundary of my woods?*"

I waggled my hand. "There was this . . . grass, but it wasn't—"

She understood before I could finish and explained. "*Yes, a shaping meant to alert their wardens should someone try to leave my grounds.*"

She grabbed my wrist with a strength that could break it should she wish. "*Fetch your toy—your things. We are leaving. Now.*" Her eyes were bright-kindled fury—molten gold flooded with fire.

I did not argue. I did not question . . . for once. She released me from her grip and I did as she'd bade, returning quickly after.

"Where are we going? What happens to those that try to leave your garden?"

Enshae gave me a smile as brittle and sharp as broken glass. "*Those who venture farther than you do not have the chance to share their stories. Especially if they travel toward the fields of Shalsmi. That court would bind you with blood and brass and stone . . . if they did not kill you outright. My brothers and sisters of the Behel are more understanding, but that does not mean forgiving. Do you understand?*"

I did, and I nodded.

"*Good. And the Behel are fond of their games.*"

Don't I know it. I did not say this to her, of course.

"*One is being played now. You were allowed to escape, to see what you would do. You came to me.*"

"Oh . . . Brahm's blood." I'd proven that I'd been in Enshae's garden.

"*They will resume the chase, and you cannot be found in my company, and I cannot trust you to wander alone.*" Enshae took me in her hold, and we ran.

I cannot explain to you what it is like keeping up with a Shaen, but for all my hard travel, and endurance I'd thought I'd built . . . I was quickly humbled.

And shown just how much fire could build on one's legs, and in their lungs.

Far behind us, maddened cackling filled the air again.

The Shaen had come for me.

We did not rest until my body demanded, finally pushed to the point I could not move. I collapsed in Enshae's arms, and she bore me to the ground like I were nothing but a starveling kitten. And she watched me as if I were a broken, helpless thing.

I suppose to something like her, I was.

I had so many things I could have said to her. Among them, an apology for what I'd done. But I hadn't forgotten what Tharam had said, and once I found the strength to speak, I asked her of it. "Why didn't you tell me how time moved here?" The question echoed through the field we lay in. It shattered the quiet peace that had hung through this place, and showed me the first sign of unease in Enshae that I had seen in a long while.

I may as well have slapped her.

Her eyes widened, and for a moment, I thought I had erred greatly. Instead, she let out a heavy breath and turned away from my gaze. "*I did not think it mattered.*"

Some of my anger cooled in place of curiosity. "How could it not?"

"*I have forgotten its passage since my imprisonment here. Every moment is fleeting and eternity at once. Each time in waking, and in bedding. Every visitor—the same result, until you. And now there is something different, something new. Others would see dreams and desires in me and this realm. They would ask, greed in heart and glory in eyes. You asked of me. Not selfish desires, but kindly curiosity.*" Her voice held old weariness, and pain.

But I'd heard another note in there as well.

Loneliness.

Someone who had been alone for so long that she craved companionship. Not in the sense found in some of the old stories. You know the sort: A young man travels into a world of myth and is seduced by a creature of immense beauty. Or the ones of a sailor encountering the witch queen's lost island and taking her attention along with her love. Demigods seduced by dancing celestial maidens above the skies or of the waters.

Those stories.

Enshae wanted someone who intrigued her, challenged her, and perhaps offered her something as close to friendship as she could understand. And in all her time imprisoned, she had only ever known people seeking glory, like my friend the *Maathi*, or those who offered her nothing of interest.

But in our time together, we had developed a relationship somewhere nearing friendship, as well as one close to being teacher and student. How could I fault her for wanting someone like that in all the time unimaginable she'd been locked away?

Especially when I myself had done things for similar reasons. My time with the sparrows had been as much out of necessity as it had been want for family. Same with Sham, and The Hundred Thieves.

Loneliness is a sort of poverty of the heart and soul. Many people confuse this with solitude. They are not one and the same. One is chosen, and in that space of aloneness, one can flourish, and one can heal. The other is a space shaped from the things lacking, and in that lack you are locked away to suffer—alone. That is the truth.

Enshae had not asked to be locked away in this garden. It had been done to her, and in doing so, she'd been stripped of love, companionship, and herself.

And stories were created to help fill that space of stillness, silence, and lonely lack.

The stories she and I had been sharing.

What remained of my anger bled from me and I hung my head. "I'm sorry. I didn't know. I didn't think to—"

Enshae cupped a hand to my cheek. "*I understand your anger, castaway. It was not a thing I thought of. There was no malice in it. You fear for the shape of the world you left behind. You do not know what you could return to find, if you return at all.*"

"Will I return?" I fixed her with a knowing look.

Enshae held my stare, and I wanted to bow away from her unblinking golden eyes. "*You wonder if I will let you. If I am holding you here.*"

"Are you?" A dangerous thing to accuse her of, but at this point, what else could it be?

"*You are not locked beside me here. Is that what you fear?*" A fair response, but she avoided my question.

"Yes, but are you *keeping* me here?"

She blinked—just for a moment, but it was there. "*Yes . . . and no. The doors have closed, so there is no walking away for you. But I could open a new doorway, with time.*" Her tone was that of someone who very much did not want to let something go. Or someone.

"*You have already shown progress—carrying the flame. If you stay, I can teach you shapings no mortal has seen since the first folding of the Shaen realm from yours. Shapings lost to time and mortal memory.*"

Bindings.

She could teach me bindings that would have me follow in the footsteps of Brahm the Wanderer. Tarun Twice Born. Abrahm. Legends and heroes all. Most of all, she could give me the tools to finally handle the Ashura, even if she wouldn't speak of them.

All it would cost me was time. An uncertain amount of time, and all the while, the world and those I loved would change behind me.

But what was all of that for the chance to get what I wanted? Just one word, a simple "yes," and I could have the magic out of stories. Why bother returning to the Ashram at all, then? I could remain here, free from punishment, and to grow in power.

True. Power.

And leave Qimari and Aisha to suffer a war I started. A war Shola, Baba, and Alwi would be caught up in as well.

It meant breaking my word to Sham as well, my brother. I'd promised I'd return. And I meant to keep my word.

I took a breath and took just as long in letting it out. "I don't want to leave. Not with what you're offering to teach me."

Enshae watched me in silence.

"But I can't stay. I don't know what's changed without me, and I have to go back to make sure the people I love are safe. I did things, and there will be consequences. I can't leave other people to face them for me."

"And what do I receive in return? What is there for Enshae when you leave?"

I'd been thinking as she asked that, and I had an answer for her. "Memory, stories, and . . . a promise."

She looked up at me. *"Promise?"*

I nodded and took her hands in mine. My fingers still burned from where they'd been scratched through the forest run, but I ignored the pain, falling into the candle and the flame as my mind calmed. "Memory of our time together, and the stories we've shared." I gave her a little squeeze.

"And the stories?"

I smiled, hoping she'd ask about that. "I've told you stories about the world—the mortal side of things, but when I return, I will tell them stories about you. Enshae the shaper, the teacher, the one falsely imprisoned. I will tell them of the magic you hold in hand, and all the stories you have shared with me. They will remember you better—truer for it, and you will live a different kind of life among the mortal then." I squeezed her hands again.

Something kindled behind her eyes. A spark. A brightness. She stood straighter then, and I knew the idea appealed to her. The idea of rewriting her story for the truth.

She had been nothing but, well, a Shaen tale. Something shared to encourage the imagination of children, and sometimes that especially of a young man. She was a temptress, seducer, and the idle fantasy of many. When to be believed in at all.

In truth? Enshae was a prisoner, and for nothing more than trying her hand at the gift of magic given to her. And now she lingered in a place between her kind without ever seeing them—the only faces for her being mortals too young to appreciate what she knew, and to see her for anything more than a legend.

But she was more than that. And she was less than that. She simply was herself. That made her real in a way you cannot glean from stories alone, only from seeing her in front of yourself.

And she deserved the justice of truth in her story. We all do.

"And the promise?"

"I promise that, if you let me go, I'll find a way to return to you. And, I promise that somehow, some day, I'll find a way to help you be free of this place." And I squeezed her hands again—the third time, making an extra silent promise in doing so.

She returned the gesture with enough enthusiasm that I worried for the safety of the small bones in my hands. "*Ilah. It is done then. A promise made. Come.*" Enshae pulled me to my feet.

"Where are we going?" I could barely walk. But I learned the answer to my question moments later.

Rolling laughter echoed across the land, and I could not spot the source, but I knew to whom it belonged.

"*We . . . are running, castaway. Find your legs, or my brethren just might find your throat.*" Enshae led the way.

And despite a fatigue that touched me to my bones, I found my legs and followed her. Because nothing motivates a man like the promise of death.

So we ran, and the laughter followed us.

"Brahm's tits, Enshae, can we—"

She clamped a hand over my mouth, pulling me into a thicket of trees I didn't remember seeing before. We hid under cover of their shadows and blackened bodies. Slowly, painfully, she forced me to creep deeper still into the dark.

"*Now, tell me more of what happened. Leave nothing unsaid.*"

I struggled to catch my breath, whispering the details of my conversation with Tharam, and the procession of singing Shaen.

"*Alune?*"

I blinked at her confusion, then clarified.

Enshae frowned in thought. "*There is no one among the Shehen named that. You must have Listened and gleaned a shadow of her name—something similar, but not whole-true. One in mortal tongues—your kind have so many. And Tharam is one caught between duty and desire, as well.*" She smiled at that, and then it faded. "*He is well?*"

"I couldn't see his face from inside the hood. It was like the insides were actually filled with darkness."

Enshae nodded. "*A small shaping, but powerful to those without the eyes to see past it. It is maya, the art of illusion. To make things be seen and seem as something else. There are many things to take into account with them, brightling. Listening, Seeing, and Seeming.*" She speared the air with a single finger, wanting my attention.

I gave it to her, waiting for her answer.

But her eyes widened and she placed her hand to my mouth again, silencing any protest I might make. "*Silence.*"

Something rippled in the darkness of the forest. A sinuous black with undulating, serpentine grace. Silver brightness arced through the air, shining despite the all-encompassing black of the space. An echoing whistling filled the air—nightmare wind chimes made of coldest metal. Branches and brush fell to every masterful stroke of the Shaen swords.

Enshae moved her hand to cover my nose as well, holding me until my lungs promised to give way, and my heart would burst in strain.

The world dimmed, and I couldn't tell if the blackness grew closer, or I began to slip from consciousness. Probably both in this damnable place.

Mercifully, Enshae finally let go, leaving me to suck down ragged breaths.

A time uncounted passed before I could speak again. "I could barely see them."

She nodded. "*Their cloaks. As I was saying before. First in Listening is the understanding of a thing. True and whole to its nature, now and what it has been through time. To Listen, truly listen, to a thing's unspoken story and shape takes practice. It takes a cleanness of mind and heart to hear without the prejudice of men. Seeing is a sister to this—held hand-in-hand. To be a seer is to glean a thing's nature with your eyes. To see through the many masks all things wear. Some are crafted from necessity to survive, others to allure and blend, and lastly there are the masks to deceive.*

"*Some to trick others, and the rest to trick ourselves. They are both dangerous, castaway.*"

I nodded, understanding some of what she said. The storyteller Maathi had said something of the same once, as had Rishi Ibrahm. But Enshae had mentioned something else along with those things. "And seeming?"

She smiled. "*And Seeming is the art of two parts. It is first the belief one has when looking at another thing and believing it to be something other than it is. The seeming that comes without knowing. When you saw Tharam in his cloak of woven shadows and darkness, it and he Seemed to be made of those things to you. A shaper's mind is a powerful tool, and can hold the mind in thrall. So, those false thoughts of yours seemed real. To you, the cloak seemed all the more shadow-shaped.*

"*But there is another Seeming that can be done. The shaping of making things seem. It is not the same as a true shaping—know this. But an illusion—maya? With it, a cloak of simple black may look to be one shaped from the night sky itself. And one of shadow true can be made to look as nothing more than tattered cloth of faded gray. Seemings are meant to deceive, and it takes a keen Listener and seer to glean past them.*"

I thought back to the moment when I had seen Rishi Vruk's face fade away to reveal Koli's. The question came naturally then. "And . . . can someone with the right skill make their face, their whole selves, *seem* as another person?"

Enshae turned and gave me a sideways look. "*I understand the shape of your question, castaway. Do not think I cannot see what you are asking.*"

I swallowed, but said nothing.

She sighed. "*You would have made a fine cat—curious and clever. Yes, one can shape a Seeming to hide their face. It is simpler than changing the story of oneself, but not apart from it. For if you go too long looking at a stranger's face in every pool, and acting in their manner, how long before you begin to see yourself as only what you seem to be?*"

Chilled, I thought of the students locked away in the Crow's Nest. Of Krisham. A young man who believed himself to be heroes of the past, all depending on the time and thoughts he happened to be in. A man caught between identities, and all because of the very power of the Athir he had cultivated and shaped upon himself.

And then the art of Seeming Enshae spoke of. Something held within the bindings as well. Each carried consequences, and it seemed they all had the capacity to shape you back as much as you shaped them.

I shuddered at the thought of what could go wrong if I attempted something like that and lost control. Worse, if I succeeded.

"*It is this that the accursed have done, all to better hide themselves among the mortal side of things. One could stand before you and you would never know lest their signs betray them. Is that what you wish to know?*"

I nodded.

"*Good, because I will not waste breath on them again. We are being pursued by the Chandni Court, and should they hear the pair of us discussing the accursed, it will go very poorly for you.*"

That stopped any more talk of the Ashura, but not my curiosity. "Enshae, what exactly is the Chandni Court?"

If I had any sense of wisdom I would never have asked that.

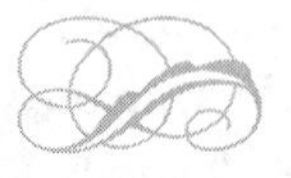

ONE HUNDRED EIGHT

MOON AND MORNING

We walked far, always keeping an eye over our shoulders for any sign of the Shaen. Eventually, Enshae brought me back to the pool she'd thrown me into earlier. She picked up a small stone, turning it in her grip before it vanished from sight.

"*This is not a small story, little castaway. It is the knowing of night and day. Of moon-shadow and morning light. Of songs by dark and firesides kindled by man's hand. And the tale of happenings between them all. This is a story of when we folded away from one another. Not first from the mortal, but Shehen from Shehen."*

"A war?"

She shook her head. "*War is too big a word for what happened, though do not mistake it for a small thing, castaway. This would sow the seeds for what hurts would blossom between the Shehen in times to come. First there was the shaping of the moon—dark and whole, held in the comfort of itself and Brahm's light. The world below knew only deep shadow, and the soft glow given by the moon. And it was enough.*

"*We lived under it, knowing its pale light and its beauty, and that of the stars. With it, we saw the truth of all things, and shaped from those. Starlight and shadow, moonlight and dark stone. Then came those that sang songs as if born to. Better even than my kind—Ilah, and that was to the ache of many. That would birth the hollow hurt found in the hearts of many of us.*"

"Jealousy?"

She tilted her head, looking unsure whether to be offended or sad. "*Ilah, brightling, all things have the wish to be loved as they are, and not for what they could wish to be. To be loved for what they have, and not put aside for what they lack. And in the shaping of those that sang, many Shehen came to feel this way.*"

I thought of the story of Brahm that I had told Nisha. Of Saithaan's hurt and his jealousy, and how it had twisted him—tainted his heart. Then I remembered something else. "Wait, I thought the Shaen folded themselves away *before* Brahm made the first people."

"*Our leaving the mortal happened after the Singers and the Ruma came to being. But we began to shape before the first mortals' coming. First, small things. Seemings, children's playthings to fool one another and make merry. Then we used them to tell tales and dance and sing stories of our own. When that was not enough, we began to make places of our own—things of our own. Then the Singers came, and we saw Brahm's love and attention go to them.*

"*And soon came the second, the Ruma. They shaped differently than us. Not with songs, but stories, things to be broken and retold by others until they lost all meaning.*"

I bristled at that. "Stories have meaning."

She gave me a sympathetic smile. "*Of course, brightling. But a story is a song without melody. You cannot break a piece of music and expect it to remain whole. But stories can be broken—parts remembered, and still carry enough to have life of their own, and then that life begins something new in a new shape. Not so with song. You keep it whole, or you keep none of it.*"

I didn't believe that to be true whatsoever, but I'd interrupted her enough. So I adopted the silence she wanted.

"*With the Ruma came mortal shaping, as they too had a touch of the gift in their blood. They kindled fire anew. They did not borrow or pull its light from pale-star glow. And with that, everything changed. Ilah.*" She sighed and looked down into the pool. "*Brahm saw what the mortals had given birth to and then shaped the sun itself. He hung it apart from the moon, tethered them tight, but never let them share the closeness all lovers yearn for. Still, they remain connected—strung together by the thread of blood-red. But with that shaping came the morning. And soon some of the Shehen were no longer night walkers, and came to rejoice in the mortal way of things and their time of day. They changed. First in face, then full in form.*"

That didn't seem so bad a thing, but one look at Enshae's face told me that it was.

She stared now as if watching pure memory—a painful one—reflected in the pool's surface. Face tight, and eyes distant. "*Shehen broke bread with mortals and shared our ways with them. For a time, things were well. But, Ilah. Soon, the Shehen split in truth, and a court arose for each side. Those who clung to night and our first ways, and those who kept to the mortal and spent their lives amidst the brighter day. This too changed how we shaped, and in turn what would shape us.*"

"You had a philosophical disagreement?" I thought back to what she had first said about when she tried her hand at binding, and how it had led to her imprisonment.

"*We wished to shape in peace so that we would not harm or change the mortal in ways to stop your kind from flourishing. They wished to shape with your kind in hand, though they did not see the peril this could bring. We look alike at first glance.*" Enshae held up her hand, splaying her fingers wide.

I realized she was waiting for me to match the gesture. So I crossed the space between us and pressed my hand to hers.

She pushed against my touch, then pulled back, lacing our fingers together. "*We have the same limbs, and same shape to us. Our lips may press to frown, in anger, or to kiss. Our hearts know pain, and they know bliss. We are quite similar in this. But we are not the same here*"—she brought our joint hands to her chest, just above her heart, then pressed our shared grip to her forehead—"*or here.*

"*Our understandings of the world are different. How we shape it is different. And this I and the moonly court—Behel-shehen—wished to spare your kind. For a world we shaped beside yours would be cruel to you.*"

I thought of the flowers that pulled the blood from a person with but a touch, then the pool I had nearly drowned in. Enshae might have had a point.

What would mortal kind have lived to see should we have shared a place with the Shaen? Would we have lived long at all?

"*And so Enshae thought to spare you this and began to shape a world away from yours. First but a pocket for Shehen-kind to dwell within and try our hand at greater makings. Then our creations flourished and others came to cast workings of their own. But for every one we performed, the Shalsmi lords matched us in kind. This changed the shape of the world and the mortals, as I feared, were not ready for this. Many died. New things walked the world, and you suffered for it. Monsters and creatures twisted—tainted, and most foul.*" She broke our shared hold and turned away from me, her arms wrapping around herself in a tight hug.

I reached out to brush her shoulder in comfort, but stopped short. Something about the set of her spoke quietly, and it was not in invitation. She needed the moment to herself—both for the memory she lingered in, and whatever it roused in her.

"I'm sorry. I . . . I've seen monsters before, and I've never forgotten what it was like. I can't imagine what it was like for you, and all while watching your people split apart."

A ghost of a smile touched her face, and just like one, it faded on another look. "*Ilah. You are a sweet thing, but you do not know monsters. And may you never come to.*"

I had seen the Ashura. I had spoken to Koli, burning bright with golden eyes as he stood above the bloody and broken bodies of my family, his mocking laugh echoing in my thoughts. I had watched the shadows play along the walls as they wept tears of red. I had witnessed the wreckage of Ampur in their aftermath, and I had traveled to the sacred city of Iban-Bansuur, ravaged by their passing.

I *knew* monsters. And I knew them to be real. Enshae would not speak of them at length, which said something. So what, then, did it take to be considered a true monster to her?

I decided that whatever it was, it might not be best to dwell on it.

"*Mortal man and our kind came to odds, and your fury at the things you do not know or understand is a terrible thing. Soon you loosed it on us, be we shadow-kept and in the night, or creatures lived in Brahm's own morning light.*"

Another truth I've learned long over my life. Few things are more frightening than a mob caught in fear. One person, afraid and alone, will act to save themselves. Many will balk and then bark long before they will fight. It is our nature. But together? A group of scared people will quickly turn to anger, and in that anger they will find their teeth and quickly turn to bite.

And what do we fear more than that which is different to us? Unknown to us and in the dark. The Shaen were both of those things, and as Enshae had said, we might look the same, but we are very much not alike.

"*So the court of moon and night came to me for guidance, and what could I do but spare the mortal a conflict worse to come? I reached for greater shapings then and shaped something new. I folded a piece of time and space far away from any mortal place.*" She gestured to our surroundings. "*And I tended my garden well and gave open invitation to any Shehen looking for a new home. And they came. They lent me their faith, and their strength, as I shaped the beginnings of this land. Soon, others took root and grew it as well. But the Shalsmi lords were not pleased with this.*

"*They came to this space and then we shaped against each other. Tearing and making a world within a world anew until no dream of peace was in sight. So what could the courts of morning and of night do to end this never-ending fight? They blamed me, the first to shape, to seek to shape further still. Temptress, deceiver, and ruiner, they called me. A bargain was struck, and for the peace of morning my brothers and sisters confined me here, and the lords of light became my stewards, and my jailers.*

"*You see, in their eyes, I am to blame for losing Brahm's favors. For the split between our family, never mind that the Shalsmi court could not see how they would imperil your lives with their shaping by your side. We were not meant to share the same place, so how could we not come to craft and crave our very own space?*"

She had a point. Even without the dangers of sharing a world with Shaen who could reshape it at their whim, there is a certain nature to all things to want their own private space. Be it a spot under a stage, a small space in a house of sparrows, or a room high above in a tower among mountains of snow.

A space like she had now.

And it had only cost her everything and everyone she'd ever known.

"You were locked away . . . for saving us."

Another short-lived smile. Another low-cast look. And another tight grip on herself.

This time I reached out to her, and she came into my arms. I hugged her, and held her, unsure of what to say.

Sometimes there are moments when words are not enough, and times when they are not needed. This was one of those. So I gave her the quiet comfort one body can give another. It said enough without saying:

I'm sorry. You were wronged. I'm sorry. And maybe, the quiet unspoken promise of a child who had never quite liked those who would take something away from someone else. The silent reminder of a promise: *I will come back. And one day, I will free you.*

Time would prove if I could keep my word.

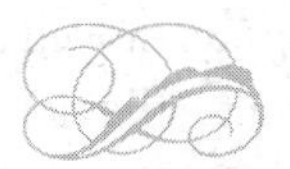

ONE HUNDRED NINE

Small Shapings

A piercing cry filled the air, and a songlike voice followed. "*There's no such treat, quite as sweet . . . as fresh mortal meat!*"

My eyes widened and I turned to Enshae. "Please tell me he's kidding. I thought you were supposed to teach me the bindings—something to protect myself with?"

She knelt and picked up a curious stone, speaking to me without looking my way. "*Can you shape while tired? While your legs hold a deeper fire than any I might give to you in hand? Can your mind keep from breaking while you are hunted, hungry, and in want of rest? I will teach you, brightling. And I hope you are as strong as I might think.*"

"And if I'm not?"

Once again, Shaen voices echoed around us.

Enshae smiled, and it was all teeth. "*Then they will find us, and you will die.*"

I suppose I didn't have a choice.

It had been one thing to train with fire in the safety of Enshae's garden. It was another to do so while on the run.

The fire rested in the cup of my hands. And twice that burned in my body as I ran, trying to keep the wind from stifling the flame. Burning to keep my mind fixed on the candle and the flame—on where I was going, and the threat of the Shaen somewhere out there, wanting to kill me.

My hands would burn, and Enshae would keep me from crying out. Flesh would be mended with her touch, and her words. And we would begin again.

I would cradle the flame and move until I knew only three things: movement, pain, and the sight of fire. My mind ached in new ways, never having been forced to juggle the amount of strain I now found myself under. This continued until I asked Enshae if she had any other ways of keeping me safe.

She, of course, had the answer. And it began with my cloak.

"My cloak?" I slipped out of the folds and the ball of flame I'd been cupping touched my skin. This time, my hands moved away before it burned me much. I hissed and shook my hands, trying to alleviate the minor pains.

"*Ilah, yes. I do not know how long we have lost them for. Do not waste this time.*" She reached out for it as if already expecting me to comply.

I frowned, but undid its clasp. The touch of the white scales filled me with regret as I passed the cloak to her. A second's hesitation in which I wondered if I should be letting go.

It didn't matter as Enshae pulled it from me with a gentle strength well beyond my own. "*Ilah.*" She turned it over in her grip, eyeing it. One of her fingers traced its folds, stopping to touch some of the scales. "*You've been careless with this.*" She tapped one of the spots where the scale had broken free from the skin beneath. "*And here.*" Enshae's fingernail scratched the space chipped away when I'd been struck by an arrow atop Mubarath's roofs.

"*So reckless for one playing at being an Asir, and you are no seer, brightling. Not yet.*" She smiled the smile one makes when amused at a joke only they are aware of.

I didn't quite see the humor, or understand what she meant. But she had spoken of something I did want to know about. "Enshae . . ."

"*Hm.*" She didn't look up as she fingered other parts of my cloak, giving it a thorough examination.

"You said you wouldn't speak on the accursed." I licked my lips, hoping my question wouldn't draw her ire. "But what of the Asir?"

"*You would wish to know of them, wouldn't you?*" She sighed. "*Ilah. Have you not learned enough by playing with fire what can happen to your hands?*"

I fidgeted, not wanting to drop the subject.

"*Very well. The Asir began as tools—shaped to serve a purpose.*"

"What purpose?"

Enshae narrowed her eyes at my interruption, the look turning them into copper-gilded knives. "*To help mortal kind. At first they were set to be your shield, then your sword. Against tainted shadow and the darker things of the world. The monsters that came from the shapings between Shehen and mortal.*" She must have meant from the time she'd told me of when the moon and morning court split from our world.

"*Then their purpose turned toward hunting the accursed, those they were shaped to hound, challenge, and confound.*"

Which implied the Ashura had a purpose too. But what was it? I knew I wouldn't get an answer from Enshae, so I thought on it myself. All it did was lead me to a more terrifying question: Who shaped the Ashura? My only recourse came in the form of asking Enshae the opposite of that.

"Who made the Asir?"

She flashed me the same look from earlier, though lacking in its full intensity. "*Another shaper. Some brightling.*"

No real answer, and I had been about to ask another question when I finally caught notice of what rested between the pinched grip of Enshae's forefinger and thumb. A slender piece of silver that I hadn't seen her pull out.

Besides, where had she gotten it from? Her clothing had no pockets.

No, not silver, I realized. *Moonlight.* Enshae had plucked a sliver of pure moonlight out of its reflection found on an errant dewdrop. A smooth disc the same color hung in her grip—one end diffusing into thin air like a drop of blood in water. She kneaded it into my cloak, little care for the toughness of the scales.

Enshae caught me staring and only gave me a smile. One filled with knowing, secrets, and maybe a good deal of self-satisfaction over the fact she could work a magic I could only dream of. Not only did she wash my cloak in the moon's reflection, casting it abright with newfound glow, but she reformed its scales—threaded new lining into place!

"*The first Asir vanished long ago, and another piece of flame became their steward, though I do not know who. Those who follow now must be new shapings, but whether they hold a candle to the flames of old . . .*" She held up her other hand, open and palm upturned. "*Ilah, who can say?*"

Enshae then wound the cord of starlight around her thumb, bringing the trailing end to her teeth, where she snapped it loose. The remnant strand flitted through the air but for a moment before crumbling into fine grains of crystalline sand. Then it faded from sight altogether. She pressed her thumb to one of the scales of my cloak and ground down on it, then repeated the motion to another piece. Then again.

She rose and began walking again, never breaking her stride, or her attention on mending my cloak.

I followed her and watched as a light of moon-glow, diamond, and crushed pearls seemed to shimmer along the scales. Vanishing, only to come back as quick in shimmerant sparkle.

It was the same shine I'd seen along the sands of the desert at times. A dazzling white, like glass in sunlight.

"*A small shaping, surely, but a fitting gift for leaving my company, no? I have fixed the damage done and placed a Seeming along its length. Maya. Now it will shine better bright, be it day or under dark moonlight.*" She held the cloak up for me to see, and she had spoken truly.

Where before the scales had shone under certain light, it hadn't been due to any magic. Now? I could scarcely count the glinting beads of light coming off each scale as the whole of it shone.

We'd now come to a worn bed of dark stone. A shallow pool of water rested in its hollow.

"And should you be still set on seeking the accursed—"

"I am. I will *never* stop looking for the Ashura." Beaten iron flooded my voice, quickly chased by fire. My hand clenched, and a trace of the pain from when I'd earlier touched the fire returned.

Enshae dipped my cloak into the moon-brightened water, washing the garment in the glow. *"Ilah. So keen on wanting his own flame blown out. I cannot protect you once you leave my garden, but I can give you the means to better protect yourself."* She stood and held the cloak wide and open between her grip. *"Now, when you wear this, men will think twice before causing you harm. You are a curious one—a storyteller—a castaway flame and light.*

"You should have something fitting. They will look on this and have questions. They will think of stories and you will give them that. You will tell them of the worm you felled and Enshae whose hands shaped this better. And they will wonder, and they will fear. I will show you its workings so that you may enbrighten it as you wish, and temper its touch."

"Its touch?"

Enshae smiled and ran a hand along the length of the cloak. It straightened—looked to harden as if it had been made from stone and not skin. *"It will not turn away all who seek to harm you, but it is stronger than before."* At another touch the cloak returned to hanging as softly as it had before. *"And a more fitting gift for you, brightling. With this cloak now you shall find the touch of fire to be turned away and be spurned. You will walk through its grasp, untouched, unharmed, and unburned. But in battle long I would not dwell, for even with this gift, you can still be felled."*

I thought back to when I had been sentenced to die out on the sands of the desert and the binding I had performed. A smile crept along my face.

"And finally there is one last working hidden still. Should you be caught along the accursed's path, this cloak will shine brighter then to warn you of their coming." And true to her word, all the shimmering died, but the cloak did not dim. It burned with the bright solid light of the moon full in glow. It thrummed. It sang a song, silent but striking the heart of me.

Silver strings quivering—their vibrations felt along my skin even though I stood feet away. I reached out to touch it, but the light faded, and soon my cloak looked no different than it had all along.

Enshae passed it to me. *"It is a fresh seeming. It cannot burn so long and bright. It will need more time under sun and long starlight."*

I blinked at that. "It needs . . . both kinds of light sources to shine?"

She looked at me as if it should have been obvious.

Then it struck me. The binding she had performed, even if through a manner and skill I couldn't understand, resembled very much the principle in which the binder's lights back at the Ashram worked. Only, Enshae's results were much more efficient, and prettier.

Not to mention the obvious use I could get out of them. She had been right, you see. I *was* a storyteller. Not by trade yet, but certainly by action. I had crafted all manner of them about myself since my time in Keshum, and never bothered to stop the ones that sprouted up about me.

I had kept to it at my time in the Ashram, and then again in Mubarath. What stories could I spread once leaving Enshae's company? Stories about her, and my time in the Shaen lands.

And what stories were they telling back home, after having watched me survive a storm of arrows only to vanish through the Doors of Midnight?

I smiled at the thought.

I slipped into the cloak, feeling its weight settle back around me almost like a hug from an old friend. I welcomed it. "Thank you, Enshae. I don't know what to say. Thank you." I reached out, the gesture awkward as I started to place my hand on her shoulder, then moved to offer her a hug. But I had no idea what the Shaen woman would have wanted.

She told me the moment she wrapped her arms around me and held me tight. "*You are a foolish thing, and reckless. Too curious and clever for your own good, and I know this thing, because Enshae was this herself. But you are a sweet thing, and no brightling past has ever asked to hear my story, or promised to return. And none has ever wanted to free me from this place.*" She kissed my forehead then.

"*Come, let us give you another lesson then.*" And with that, Enshae set to teaching me how to manipulate the new and improved piece of clothing.

In some ways I felt the same as when I had begun my studies with Mahrab. A return to the folds and conjuring the imagery of what I wished to see. The cloak shimmered in my mind as bright as it had in Enshae's touch, and soon, when I had impressed enough folds upon the matter, it came to be true. A day of practice soon enabled me to take the cloak from shining starlight to the color of freshly driven snow.

Pure white, but nothing remarkable about it. This would allow me to make the material pass as mundane to most eyes. The principle of changing its rigidity was much the same. A return to the folds without needing to force a binding over the material. It was as if the cloak shared a bond with my thoughts, and the simple act of focus allowed me to change it to my needs. I could shape its weight to be light as gauze, catching the faintest breeze to whip behind me. Or, I could sew it with unseen lead, leaving it to sit around me like a shroud of stone.

Not much use to many, but the dramatic effect of that could not be understated. And I just so happened to be a dramatic story in the making. What better tool for me?

It would need it sooner than I realized.

ONE HUNDRED TEN

ONE HUNDRED AND ONE NIGHTS

Enshae and I remained on the move, an act requiring me to push my body to the fullest, as well as my mind. And she continued to pluck odd stones along the way.

All shape of my senses blurred until I had only the focus for the candle and the flame. My pains—distant. All questions, buried. For a time I lost track of, I'm not sure I could have considered myself human. There was only the flame in hand, the one in heart and mind, and I fed everything into them.

But eventually, we would stop, and I was given the chance to remember what it was like to be a boy.

We traded four more stories. Four more nights. One hundred and one tales in all.

I told her of the young pirate prince, Sakhan, and his hunting of mythical beings shaped from wind, water, and mortal women's flesh—freely given. Some called them the Sithre of the seas.

I told her of mythical dragon turtles threatening to sink his fleet—each beast pretending to be an island offering his weary crew respite.

Countless treasures have been lost to these monsters. Or so it's been said.

Then there were Makara, the great oceanic serpents like the Nagh-lokh. Sea dragons in the truest sense of the word. Long enough that a single angry thrash of their tails could kick up tsunamis to swallow islands whole. Their breaths summoned hurricanes, and angered the god of storms, incurring his wrath. Creatures so big only three of them could exist at any one time in the world.

All the while, the last of my gifted blue candle burned away to nothingness, marking the end of our game. And it was time to leave her midnight garden for home.

Enshae eventually led us back to the spot in her garden where I'd first met her, assuring me by now Tharam would have grown bored. She'd continued collecting the stones I'd seen before along the way. Finally, I asked her what she'd been up to.

She opened her palm, revealing a ring of pebbles joined by an unseen force.

Each stone was different from the next. They had been shaped small and perfectly smooth. If they hadn't been formed into a perfect circle, but rather half-

Not to mention the obvious use I could get out of them. She had been right, you see. I *was* a storyteller. Not by trade yet, but certainly by action. I had crafted all manner of them about myself since my time in Keshum, and never bothered to stop the ones that sprouted up about me.

I had kept to it at my time in the Ashram, and then again in Mubarath. What stories could I spread once leaving Enshae's company? Stories about her, and my time in the Shaen lands.

And what stories were they telling back home, after having watched me survive a storm of arrows only to vanish through the Doors of Midnight?

I smiled at the thought.

I slipped into the cloak, feeling its weight settle back around me almost like a hug from an old friend. I welcomed it. "Thank you, Enshae. I don't know what to say. Thank you." I reached out, the gesture awkward as I started to place my hand on her shoulder, then moved to offer her a hug. But I had no idea what the Shaen woman would have wanted.

She told me the moment she wrapped her arms around me and held me tight. "*You are a foolish thing, and reckless. Too curious and clever for your own good, and I know this thing, because Enshae was this herself. But you are a sweet thing, and no brightling past has ever asked to hear my story, or promised to return. And none has ever wanted to free me from this place.*" She kissed my forehead then.

"*Come, let us give you another lesson then.*" And with that, Enshae set to teaching me how to manipulate the new and improved piece of clothing.

In some ways I felt the same as when I had begun my studies with Mahrab. A return to the folds and conjuring the imagery of what I wished to see. The cloak shimmered in my mind as bright as it had in Enshae's touch, and soon, when I had impressed enough folds upon the matter, it came to be true. A day of practice soon enabled me to take the cloak from shining starlight to the color of freshly driven snow.

Pure white, but nothing remarkable about it. This would allow me to make the material pass as mundane to most eyes. The principle of changing its rigidity was much the same. A return to the folds without needing to force a binding over the material. It was as if the cloak shared a bond with my thoughts, and the simple act of focus allowed me to change it to my needs. I could shape its weight to be light as gauze, catching the faintest breeze to whip behind me. Or, I could sew it with unseen lead, leaving it to sit around me like a shroud of stone.

Not much use to many, but the dramatic effect of that could not be understated. And I just so happened to be a dramatic story in the making. What better tool for me?

It would need it sooner than I realized.

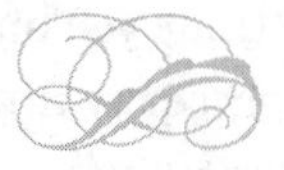

ONE HUNDRED TEN

One Hundred and One Nights

Enshae and I remained on the move, an act requiring me to push my body to the fullest, as well as my mind. And she continued to pluck odd stones along the way.

All shape of my senses blurred until I had only the focus for the candle and the flame. My pains—distant. All questions, buried. For a time I lost track of, I'm not sure I could have considered myself human. There was only the flame in hand, the one in heart and mind, and I fed everything into them.

But eventually, we would stop, and I was given the chance to remember what it was like to be a boy.

We traded four more stories. Four more nights. One hundred and one tales in all.

I told her of the young pirate prince, Sakhan, and his hunting of mythical beings shaped from wind, water, and mortal women's flesh—freely given. Some called them the Sithre of the seas.

I told her of mythical dragon turtles threatening to sink his fleet—each beast pretending to be an island offering his weary crew respite.

Countless treasures have been lost to these monsters. Or so it's been said.

Then there were Makara, the great oceanic serpents like the Nagh-lokh. Sea dragons in the truest sense of the word. Long enough that a single angry thrash of their tails could kick up tsunamis to swallow islands whole. Their breaths summoned hurricanes, and angered the god of storms, incurring his wrath. Creatures so big only three of them could exist at any one time in the world.

All the while, the last of my gifted blue candle burned away to nothingness, marking the end of our game. And it was time to leave her midnight garden for home.

Enshae eventually led us back to the spot in her garden where I'd first met her, assuring me by now Tharam would have grown bored. She'd continued collecting the stones I'd seen before along the way. Finally, I asked her what she'd been up to.

She opened her palm, revealing a ring of pebbles joined by an unseen force.

Each stone was different from the next. They had been shaped small and perfectly smooth. If they hadn't been formed into a perfect circle, but rather halfway into arches, they would have resembled the fhaald stones I'd seen across the world. Though these were smaller than those by far.

Enshae fastened a cord of leather through a band at the top of the piece. "*For you.*" She pressed it toward me.

I didn't take it right away, eyeing it, then her.

"*It is not a trick, castaway. Simply a working over fhaald stones. There are not so many in my garden that I have my choice of which to use and shape, but there are enough for this.*" Enshae gave me a small smile before she pushed the stones into my hand.

Each piece of the pendant had the smoothness of polished pearls instead of stone. "It's pretty." I raised it to slip the piece over my head, but Enshae stayed one of my hands.

"*It is a gift to help you fulfill your promise. Should you wish to return to the Shehen realm, simply shed a drop of your blood on these stones and shape your will to reflect the place you wish to be. These will lead you to greater fhaalds, and there the doors will open, and you will walk into the Shehen.*"

My eyes widened and I traced my thumbs over the stones. A way to open a door straight into the Shaen realm, and only at the cost of a drop of blood. I thought of the people who would have loved to have something like this.

A piece of true storybook magic.

Something my friend the *Maathi*—Khalil could appreciate. That snapped me out of my lesson. "My friend! When I leave, would you be kind enough to let me go with the man I came with?" I reminded her that she had turned him into a dog.

Enshae exhaled. "*Yes, castaway. I will return him to as he was before.*"

"Thank you, Enshae." I let out a breath of relief.

She smiled, then took my hands in hers, guiding me toward a mossy patch of ground to rest. Its softness was welcome, and seemed to pull the aches from me.

Enshae sank to the ground beside me. "*We will share one last story before you . . .*" She stopped and licked her lips. Her gaze trailed away from mine, turning to focus on a distant spot in the forest that I could not find. Eventually, her attention returned to me and she gave me a thin grin, like a gash in a sheet of ice. Cold and brittle. Something close to breaking.

She collected herself, chest rising as she inhaled. "*One last story. Ilah. One last telling between Enshae and a lost flame.*"

I made myself comfortable, wrapping the ends of my cloak around myself almost like a blanket.

"*This is a story of a mortal hero and the Shehen princess he'd come to love. This was long ago, flame, in a place not quite this place, and certainly not unlike it either. Something and somewhere between, when the world was one and unfolded as it has since come to be. He, a soldier, shaper, wanderer, and a poet.*"

Enshae sang and formed flat-floating shapes of light that resembled the outline of a man. It walked through the air in accordance with the movement of her fingers. She pinched one end of the creation and soon it had a cloak, silver bright. But before long, Enshae's own form changed.

No trick of light. At least, I couldn't see how. But where two arms had been, now moved four—the second pair being fixed just below the ones of old. And they moved with perfect autonomy—long-practiced, and as if she had always had them. Light trailed between her many fingers now.

Not to speak of her face—faces. Each a different mask in expression. One, somber-kept and hurt in heart. The next, mischief-made, eyes-a-merry, with secrets deep. The third . . . cannot be spoken of. But it was shrouded in mystery, deceit, and lies.

And haunts me still.

Was this maya? The illusion and Seeming art she spoke of? Or . . . had she always been this way, and all I'd seen before nothing more than the mask she wore?

What else had I overlooked in the world? What else hid behind an illusion?

"*She, a princess, and Shehen. What more need be said? She was above all things. Perfect. As all Shehen are said to be.*" Then she shaped the Shaen woman, making sure to keep the princess in her other hand and away from the mortal.

I might have taken a touch of umbrage at her comment, as I had certainly seen the aspects in which they were less than perfect. But it would have been a terrible shame, and rather quick an ending to my story, to infuriate Enshae on our last night together. So I kept still. And I kept silent.

"*This was when the morning and moonly courts had grown at odds, and the mortals began to take their sides as well. Between them all there were two who would shape the world to come. Their lives, their love, and what they lost.*

"*She was of the Behel court, and he a man who had journeyed the world, chasing the thing all mortal men fall prey to: glory. And in his wanderings he came to see our princess from afar, and she him. They heard stories of one another and eventually came to meet in flesh. But, Ilah.*" She sighed. Her hands spread apart, parting the two figures of moonlight even farther. Their heads looked downward, as if hung in sadness.

"*For you see, brightling, the man had been pressed into the service of those who stood against the princess and her family. And so they could not be together, never mind that he was mortal, and she Shehen. It could never stand, and were it to happen, there would be another war with which to contend.*

"*But this mortal was not so weak as to bow to the whims of others, be they Shehen, king, or demon. Skilled with both sword, and use of bow, he plied his trade in the world, finding fortune and more glory still. With this he made his way into the Shehen courts and his sweet moon's company.*" The figure of light danced through the air, swinging a sliver of moonbeam like a sword, then pulled on it, bending it into the familiar curve of a bow. The puppet launched arrows that faded into sparkling dust.

"*They would meet in the mornings under cover of shade, and they would meet in the nights, among moonlit glade. And their love grew.*" Now Enshae brought the glowing shapings closer together. He leaned forward, the princess' head came toward his, and they met. They kissed. And for a moment, they stayed there in the quiet embrace.

While Enshae didn't have Maathi's flair for storytelling, her workings with the light puppetry enraptured me once again. I hadn't seen someone tell a tale quite like that. Her use of images and motions to narrate dazzled me, and they made an impression I would never forget.

Just as I smiled at the kissing pair, Enshae ripped them apart. The man and Shaen princess raised their heads as if moaning in despair. Their hands reached out for one another, but nothing could be done. The space between them was too great, and I stopped smiling.

"*But it would not be. Ilah.*" Enshae sighed. "*For his mortal king had need of him and did not want him distracted by his love for this Shehen. And her father's needs were just as dire, to wed her off for heirs to sire. But still, love is not so easy a thing to quell. And our lovers staged an escape, but there were others clever and so watchful, waiting to intervene and subvert their fate.*"

Enshae formed strings of new light that fell into shape as faceless men and women. Some with the features of anyone you'd find along the Golden Road. Others had the clear marks of Shaen.

"*He stole into the palace and when stealth was not enough, he turned to strength of arm and his sword.*" The figure lunged, cutting down Shaen and man alike with his curving blade. The weapon changed—now a bow, sending free arrows to lance more targets still.

I gasped.

One of the arrows struck a Shaen woman amidst the group. The shaft penetrated just beneath her breast, to the heart of her.

One perfect shot.

Only, it wasn't one of the Shaen who'd been attacking the hero.

It was the princess.

"*Ilah.*" The beginnings of tears glistened within her eyes, but they didn't fall yet. "*And thus it came to be, that their time together had now passed. Their love was not to be, or meant to last.*" Beads of moisture cascaded down Enshae's cheeks, hanging at her jaw, almost as if teasing their desire to fall fully free.

I took her face in my hands and brushed away the tears with my thumbs.

We locked eyes, and in the moment, I came to see another side of her. Enshae was many things. Old and powerful. Wise as she was cunning. Proud and temperamental, enough so that no cat could ever hope to come close. Patient, prudent, as well as tricky. A marvelous actor in a way I could only dream to be. The Shaen were not made like us—no. They were creatures of smoke-cast flame and ash. Moonlight and stardust. You saw it in their shape and color, most obviously.

But also in their mannerisms. They did not think like us. They did not hold our ideas of right or wrong.

However, they shared our knowing of some things. Like love.

I saw it then in Enshae. Not for me, but a love long-lost. She'd known it once, so long ago I could only believe it had been before the folding away of the Shaen realms. But she had never forgotten the shape of it, and she held in its place the memory of what it had been. It had shown in her story as much as it had sung in her voice then. And at last, it left her in her tears.

That is how I would like to remember Enshae. The Shaen woman who was not afraid to share her tears with me. That is how I would like to remember our last moment of sharing stories together.

Just us. The tale of a love lost. And the quiet tears shed in the aftermath.

ONE HUNDRED ELEVEN

Intermission—the Lies Men Tell

Eloine leaned back in her seat, frowning.

"What's wrong?"

She didn't meet my eyes when she spoke. "Nothing. It's just that . . . Enshae . . . she's not what I expected from the stories, or you and your time with her."

My mouth parted in silent understanding. I knew what sort of thing she had expected to hear. "You thought it would be a story of the young hero seducing the Shaen woman thousands upon thousands of years old?" I gave her a thin and crooked smile. "I'm charming, when I have a mind to be, but I'm not so sure I am *that* convincing. No. Enshae had no want for any of that, at least with me. And I didn't with her. What we had was the fondness of a student and a teacher, and, maybe, close friends."

Eloine said nothing and nodded, but the set of her face told me she didn't understand the discrepancy between my story and all she had heard.

"I know the stories men tell about her. The stories everyone expects to hear.

Yes, Enshae was beautiful in a way that mortal men and women could not hope to understand, or ever stand beside."

Eloine raised a brow at that, the motion cool, collected, and controlled. And it carried all the subtlety of someone sharpening a knife while holding your gaze.

I did not miss the gesture, or the undertone. "Present company excluded, of course."

"Of course."

I continued as if that had not just happened. "Enshae's reputation has suffered in the same way as my own, and that is through the countless lies all men tell. Any man granted escape or with the wits to turn back through the Doors of Midnight before their closing has had something to say about her. And they are all wrong. They speak of frolicking and cavorting under star-studded skies like a fantasy from young men's dreams. And why wouldn't they? How many of them could admit the terrible truth that there was not one whit of something special in them for Enshae to care for?

"It is where I learned another truth of the world: The lives and legends of many a man are emboldened by the lies they tell at women's expense. Enshae was no different.

"If they didn't spend their time in the shape of an animal, lost to thoughts and reasoning, then they were cowards who ran. So what else could they do but tell lies? And what lie is sweeter than the painting of your own triumphs, especially when and where you had none? And that is how they saw her, something to triumph over—a conquest."

Eloine gave me a hooded look, with just the hint of shadow along her eyes. "It sounds a great deal like how many men view a great many things."

I couldn't argue that, so I didn't. Instead, I returned to Enshae. "She was a dream, Eloine, and like many men's dreams, she was their vanity laid plain. And that is the story they shared with all. Not the truth of her. Not the good, and certainly not the rest." *The things she hid from all, even me,* I thought.

For a moment, nothing lingered between Eloine and I but for the silence that comes in a story's aftermath. But I couldn't bear to let it settle between us, so I broke it. "I couldn't tell properly, but for a spell there, I swore you were a mite jealous of Enshae." I didn't smile, as my goal was not to antagonize Eloine. But I knew a shadow of that had made its way into my expression when I looked at her.

She rolled her eyes and turned her gaze away from me, but her hands fidgeted. Eloine's shoulders squared, just a bit, and her posture straightened.

Agitated. Her body spoke so clearly about how she felt, and I decided it best not to try my tongue at any more lighthearted quips.

"I suppose I sympathize with Enshae. We both know what it is like to have others write our stories for us." That brought Eloine back around.

She eyed me sideways, but without any heat or judgment. "Some would say that you wrote your story more than any other hand."

That was true to an extent, but it would be a lie to ignore how many others had had their fun with the stories about me. And I told Eloine this.

She bowed her head, gaze sinking deep into the table as if she could stare through it. Her arms crossed over her chest and she held herself. "I know what that's like too."

I hadn't expected to hear that from her, though I should have guessed. After the scene back at the inn with the clergos, it had been abundantly clear that Eloine was no stranger to others deciding who and what she was, never mind the truth of things.

And I wanted then to ask her what her truths were. To know what few people likely ever got to hear. The things I know many would have loved to ask, but never had the chance. And now I did.

"Would you—"

Eloine placed a hand on mine. The action stopped me from speaking and I looked down at her touch, then back to her eyes. "Was it worth leaving her?"

The question drove the previous thoughts from my mind. "What?"

"Enshae. She offered you all the things you wanted to know. Learning the bindings, the history of things that no one else has, and the magic out of stories."

"Everything but revenge on the Ashura. She wouldn't speak of them, no matter how I tried to coax it out of her."

"But you did learn something of them?" she said. "And you learned something before, something you didn't tell me back when we were translating the *Tales of the Nine*."

I swallowed, then inclined my head. "Yes."

She watched me, saying nothing, but the question remained.

"Something I'd forgotten—lost to memory, now I recall in telling you this. Enshae taught me that the Ashura had obscured their tales, and with that, the truths within. But chasing stories isn't enough, because how do you know what story is the right one without the right name to go along with it?"

Eloine understood where I was going with this. "The book brought up their names."

I nodded. "I had never considered which name went with what story as I'd known Koli as Vathin once. Who's to say either of those were his real name, and so, any stories I might have heard about them with those names might be untrue. Meant to mislead the listener. But finding their first names would let me know which stories just might be true, and in them, a way to destroy them."

"Much like what's happened to your name, Ari—your stories?"

"I've spent so long chasing the tales, never thinking to connect the right names to the right stories. Just sifting through the mass of them. What I learned from that tome, and recall from Enshae, changes a great deal."

"And now that you know?" She arched a brow, and I gave her a knowing look.

Eloine bit her lip, now regarding me as one might a dog with its hackles up. Then she squeezed my hand, bleeding some of the tension out of me that I hadn't been aware of. Not so hard as to cause pain, just to draw my attention. "You didn't answer my earlier question about leaving Enshae."

"I don't know." I mirrored Eloine's earlier look down at the table. "I thought it the right thing then, and that's all I know. I couldn't have known what would happen after leaving, and all that I'd go on to do. I suppose the world would be in a better shape had I never left her garden at all."

Her hand broke the hold on mine and pulled away. "And you still feel you're responsible for so much suffering?"

I blinked and met her eyes. "How can I not be?"

She shrugged. "I don't know, but I do know this: You're a man. Just one man, aren't you?"

I gave a ghost of a smile. "The stories say otherwise." The look Eloine flashed me then told me I might have done better to have traded the smile for something more serious. So I bowed my head and relented. "Yes, I'm just one man."

"And for all that, you think you can be responsible for a world breaking into war? That is arrogant, even for you."

I opened my mouth to protest, but any hope of that died well before the air left my lungs. Instead, I turned away from her and stared at the sealed book resting atop the bed, losing myself in the silence and the stillness of what I stared at.

"Ari." Eloine's touch met me again—fingers brushing along the back of my hand. "Nothing I've heard puts the sorry state of things on your shoulders."

When I spoke, I kept my attention to the spot I'd chosen to stare into. "What do you know?" I'd said the words without any malice—edgeless, only with the resignation of someone very much in need of rest.

"Only what you tell me."

I adopted a grin best fit for a dying man. "And I haven't told you all there is to my story, so believe me when I say that I am responsible for the worsening shape of the world. Do you want me to skip to that point? To tell you plain what I've done and why—" I winced and looked to where Eloine had flicked my hand.

"Don't be an ass." Her eyes had hardened, now storm clouds brewing behind a thin veneer of jade. "I want you to stop reopening the same guilty wounds. Fine, blame yourself all you want, but you don't need to cut yourself every time you do. Or there'll be nothing left." When she spoke, it wasn't the hard-sharp edge of anger filling her voice. Nor was it painful pleading. It was something else.

This was the tiredness of someone who couldn't bear to watch a close one go through any more of the same old pains. And it was the weariness of someone who knew all those motions all too well.

Her, too, of course. I sighed. "I'm sorry, Eloine. I didn't mean—"

"I know what you meant, and what you didn't. And you understand what I did?"

I nodded.

"Good." Eloine licked her lips, the sign of another question to come. "You mentioned something Enshae had said about stories. That people can change theirs, and they can lock them away."

I said nothing, waiting for her to ask what she truly wanted.

"Do you think it's true?" One of Eloine's hands fidgeted, as if writing a script only she could see. When she realized what she was doing, she stopped.

I knew then what she wanted to hear—what she perhaps needed. But sometimes the things we want, and what we believe we need, are not what will be best for us. Sometimes they are the things that will cause us the greatest harm.

I kept this in mind when I answered her. "Enshae believed it was true." Then I met Eloine's eyes, making mine hard and full of all the knowing I had. "And she believed it was a dangerous thing to do."

Eloine blew out a light breath. "Yes. But do you believe it?"

I exhaled, rubbing a palm against one of my eyes. "I believe it's true. Both things." When I stared at her then, Eloine let her gaze drift back down onto the table. The quiet look of someone lost deep in contemplation. I left her there for the moment, seeing the signs of someone who wanted to be in that place as they thought. And she needed no input from me.

"What happens when someone's story is locked away?" She spoke the words so low and whisper soft that I knew they hadn't been meant for my ears. All the same, I caught them. And I answered.

"They die."

My words snapped her out of the reverie and she stared at me, wide-eyed, mouth open. "What?"

"Stories are how we keep things alive. To do the opposite is to bury them—kill them in a way. But few have ever had their stories truly shut away. Some that do eventually realize how bad of an idea it is after having done it. Then all they can do is try to set free what they've locked away."

Eloine frowned and her gaze almost returned to that half-lost place. Almost. "What happens then?"

I shrugged. "Some try to do the only thing they can: to keep the stories alive themselves. They end up retelling their own, but it's difficult to recall what's been shut away. You end up with something half-remembered, wrong. But if there's enough of the truth in it, what can be remembered at any rate, then it will live. And so too the person who sealed their tale."

"You just no longer belong to your name, or your story." *And everything else that goes with those things leaves you behind.*

"Like a ghost?"

I gave a smile fit for one. "Yes, like a ghost. One of your own making."

Eloine fidgeted with her hands again, picking at her fingernails. "Why would anyone do something like that?"

"It's hard to track a myth, especially when it's half lies, and the truth is mostly buried." *Or so I thought.* "And it's nearly impossible to understand the real story of something when all you have is everything but the truth." *Sadly, that's all so many of us ever find in our searches: the lies.*

"You mean the Ashura?"

I opened my mouth but stopped myself, realizing I had almost given her a different answer. So I buried what I had wanted to say, then began again. "Yes. But with things like them, people have kept their stories alive long enough that they have no hope of hiding every piece found along the world."

"So they change them?" Eloine leaned forward. Not much, but just enough to make her hunger clear.

I nodded again. "Or they let them be changed. Sometimes it's the same thing. Other times it's not. It's complicated. Truly rewriting your story is not . . ." I stopped and thought of a young man so long ago who'd done something similar. And the results were exactly as Enshae had said: dangerous.

"Ari?"

I blinked and returned my attention to Eloine. "Sorry, I drifted off."

She watched me with all the careful consideration of a cat. "You were saying?"

I found a hint of old humor to draw on, more for my sake than hers, and I let it bleed into me. "Was I?" I grinned.

The sharp-slit stare of earlier returned and she gave me the full of it. "You know, I can't for the life of me understand how all those women in your story ever found you quite so charming."

My smile widened and I touched both index fingers to my cheeks. "I am in possession of the most marvelous dimples, Eloine."

She opened her mouth to retort, likely, then reached out with one hand. She moved with slow patience and I let her touch her fingers to the spot I'd been gesturing at just moments ago. Eloine stroked my cheek, then introduced me to a sharpness I hadn't expected.

"Ow." I flashed her own glare back at her as I rubbed the spot she'd pinched me. "You know . . . I don't know how so many men I've seen you in the company of find you so charming."

She flashed my own grin back at me, all before touching her fingers to her face as I had. "I am in possession of the most marvelous dimples, Ari." The smile widened, and on her, I could not say that it didn't wash a touch of my pain away. Nor that it didn't cause my heart to miss a step.

But only the one.

I wish that moment between us could have lasted longer, but it did not.

The smiles faded, and Eloine bit her lip before speaking. "Can I ask you something else?"

"You must already know the answer to that."

A touch of warm light filled her eyes, but like the grin, it didn't last. "I suppose I do." She took a breath, then began again. "How does someone free a story that's been shut away?"

By remembering, I thought. "You don't." The words left me harder than I'd intended and Eloine's sudden stiffness told me that more than hearing myself. I apologized soon after.

It wasn't the answer she'd been looking for, but she didn't voice any displeasure over it. Instead, she ran her hands against the fabric of her dress, occasionally pulling at the material.

Nervous? No. Distracted? Something else held her thoughts, and it wasn't me. But what? I had a mind to ask, but she stopped me before I could.

"Do you mean you can't, or . . . ?" She left the unfinished question hanging in the air.

It wasn't one that I had been hoping to be asked, much less answer.

Her eyes then held a depth I don't quite think I'd appreciated before. This wasn't hunger, and it wasn't something poets wax on about. Just the look of someone who wanted to know something, painfully so, and it was a look I knew all too well. I'd worn it myself many times.

So I swallowed, and I told her what I could. "Eloine, people who lock their stories away usually do so first believing it's for a good reason. Even if they believe otherwise later. They can be dangerous."

A hint of the old fire returned to her, but not in anger, just in how she pressed. "The stories . . . or the people?"

The shape of my mouth turned crooked. "Both. There are always secrets in stories that can lead you to trouble as much as they can to treasure."

"You're still not answering me, Ari." Eloine took one of my hands in hers again and I flinched. She arched a brow at that, eyeing me. "Worried?"

"Depends . . . are you going to pinch me again?"

Her eyes glittered, though the rest of her face remained perfectly neutral. "Depends . . . are you finally going to give me a clear answer?"

I have known enough people in my life to know when someone will not leave something well enough alone. Eloine happened to be one of those people, and this happened to be one of those subjects. So I sighed, and I relented. "You free a story by remembering it. All of it. The greatest moments—triumphs and painful truths. You wash away the lies, and lay everything bare before yourself and others. That is the way. The only way."

Eloine's mouth worked in silence as she thought on what I'd told her. Then she rose, motioning with a slight turn of her wrist. "Walk with me?"

She wouldn't see my smile as I rose to follow, but I gave her one nonetheless. "You need to ask?" And while I didn't catch her face, I had a feeling she matched my expression.

"Mm. If only you were so quick to answer when I ask you other sorts of questions." She took an extra step just as I tried to come to her side, keeping ahead of me by a pace.

"I wouldn't be any fun if I jumped to every thing you suggested, would I?"

"Hm, *fun*." She sounded the word out as if it were her first time hearing it. "Is that Brahmthi for 'donkey'?"

I blinked, at a loss. "What?"

"No, that's *gadha,* isn't it? My mistake. I think I was close, though." She tapped a finger to her lips. "It's close to 'ass,' isn't it?"

I saw where she was going, and decided I'd be better served with silence.

"It's just some men seem to get the two confused, and it makes it ever so hard for me to tell the difference when they think they're being fun, or asinine. Do you know the difference?" She turned halfway to regard me, a brow arched. "Could you educate me?"

I opened my mouth, then shut it.

Eloine continued leading the way through the garden.

We passed a standing fountain that had attracted a single bird to its edge. A firecrest. So named for the sharp plume of sun-shaded yellow running along the top of its head, accentuated by the black stripes beneath it. The bird could have easily been swallowed by the cup of my hand.

It watched Eloine and me as we moved by, tilting its head to regard us curiously.

"No answer?" Eloine eyed me sideways.

"Sometimes silence is the answer."

This time I caught the upward turn of her lips. Not quite a smile, but close. "Sometimes it is."

Ask her. The prompt came to me unbidden and I almost acted on it. "Eloine, I was wondering . . ."

"Hm?" She didn't face me, still leading me through the garden. One of her hands gently brushed along the petals of a flower I didn't recognize. Bright and white as fresh cream, or the moon in full glow. Its size surpassed the full spread of my own hand. She had touched it absently, but an air of familiarity hung in the movement.

"I've shared a piece of my story with you, and you've mentioned—"

"She's nearly all gone." Eloine's attention had turned to the sky.

"Huh?" I stopped short and followed her eyes, trying to spot whatever she focused on. There wasn't much to see, however. Morning clouds and the pale half-faded shape of the moon, quickly vanishing at that. All that remained of it amounted to less than a third, and even that could have been lost soon enough should the sky change.

"Lady Etiana?" The voice pulled me from my thoughts. A man, slim and wearing the clothing of the porters I'd seen. Most of his hair had left him prematurely, and he had compensated for this by styling a thin and dark mustache, trimmed to points. It made him look like a villain out of the old plays, in truth.

Eloine's posture straightened, an invisible rod going through her back. Her shoulders pulled tight and her chest rose. Not fear, or stiffness. This was practiced regality. An act. And she did it well. "Yes?"

"I've been asked to escort you to your luncheon with the some of the *burgesa*."

She inclined her head, all while managing to keep the face of someone looking down her nose. Not an imperious stare, or something to belittle the porter. Simply the look of someone used to being treated with that measure of respect. "Storyteller." Eloine gave me the practiced curtsey of the gentry. Straight back, no bend in the waist, only the knees.

I knew dismissal when I heard it. *Exit stage left, Eloine. Depart in silence, Storyteller, right.* My own smile came stiffer than it should have, experience or not. But I managed it and the following bow. "Lady Etiana. Till the next time I can enjoy your company."

She didn't return the smile, nor give me a last look as the porter ushered her away.

I watched her go, and the clouds overhead moved to blot out everything but the sun.

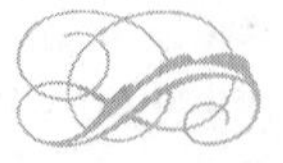

ONE HUNDRED TWELVE

GAMES

It would be an exaggeration to say that I stormed through the halls in irritation. I stalked, and was closer to dour than visibly angry. A subtle difference, but a difference nonetheless.

My soured mood must have caught the attention of a serving boy. He stopped for me, but kept his legs moving in place as if afraid should he stop, he would remain stuck there. "My lord . . . ?"

I shook my head. "Not a lord. Nothing like that at all."

The boy frowned and his eyes darted ahead, then back to me. The fleeting look of someone wondering how far they could risk offending me by returning to their task. He looked me over again, then his eyes widened. "The red cloak, *sengero.*"

I didn't smile, but my lips twitched, and I waited.

"It's like the one Amarias had."

I must have worn my confusion on my face, because the boy explained.

"He was a knight, *sengero.* Don't you know? A famous one." Childlike enthusiasm kindled behind his eyes. "He was a foreigner, bathed again in Solus' light. They say he converted after hearing the voice of God himself. He fought for us out in the sands against the savages, and he saved a convent of the church. His cloak was red from all the foreign blood he spilled. Just like your cloak. But some say it was red as his lady's heart, because she blessed him with it."

"Is that so?"

He nodded. "*Sieta, sengero.* It is a good cloak."

I grinned. "It is. Would you like to touch it?"

He balanced a tray in one hand, reaching out to pinch the edge of my cloak. "It hasn't rained, *sengero . . .*"

But . . .

The boy frowned. "It's wet. It's like blood." He pulled his hand back, gasping and looking at his fingers. Only, they didn't run red as he'd thought they would. His face became a mask of concentration, trying to work out the silent puzzle.

He wouldn't understand it, and even if I told him, he wouldn't believe it.

A man will always go more easily to bed with comfortable lies than hard truths.

So I gave him what would put him at ease, and spark a child's delight. The comfortable lie. And all before he had the wit to ask me for the truth. "It's just a little trick. . . ." I let the words hang, hoping he would get his cue to introduce himself.

"Pachecho, if it please you, *sengero.*"

I placed a hand on his shoulder. "Pachecho, do you know where I might find Prince-elect Efraine?"

"*Sieta, sengero.* He is in the audience chamber speaking with some of the *burgesa.* They bring him things now that . . ." He trailed off, looking away from me.

Ah. So the boy heard what had happened. I suppose there was no way he wouldn't have. And news of that nature could do all sorts of things to a young person's mind. Like make them afraid of following in the footsteps of those nobles now since gone. After all, when princes begin to fall, the pawns quickly follow.

I gave the boy's shoulder a reassuring squeeze. "I understand. Look at me for a moment, will you?"

He did, meeting my eyes, unblinking. Though the tray shook in his grip. Just a touch, but enough that I could hear the faint rattling of the cover's lip against the metal base.

"You're scared about what happened."

He nodded.

I gave him a gentle jostle, as what a father might do to settle a nervous son. "If it ever gets to be too much, you come and find me, *sieta*?"

Pachecho eyed me. "What will you do?" An edge bled into his voice, then he remembered himself. "*Sengero!* I mean . . ." The boy stopped short, aware of his social blunder.

I laughed, more practiced than true, but I knew it'd set him back at ease. "It's fine. And I'll keep you safe. That is what I'll do." I saw the doubts and questions form along his face. But I cut him off before he could voice them. "Do you believe in magic?"

Pachecho rolled his eyes, but said nothing. A boy caught between the truth in his heart, a silent-hopeful yes, and the no he knew any rational person would say.

So I didn't let him answer. I dropped my voice to a conspiratorial whisper, leaning in close with one hand cupped to the side of my face. A clear sign that we were sharing a secret. The boy leaned in, and all I had to do was play my part. "Watch this." I held my other hand open, concentrating. Surely I could manage another small performance? That was all this would be.

No great working. Nothing serious.

Just a storyteller's trick. That's all. And that's all I am anymore, aren't I?

I envisioned a cloud of breath, deep inside my lungs, and let it fill the folds of my mind. Two, then quickly to four. I shouldn't need more than that for something so small. But I brought the total to eight regardless. Just in case. A sliver of doubt bled into me, and my heart shook as much as the folds.

None of that now. The boy needs to see this. That resolved me. Much like another young boy, far from this place, and so long ago, who needed a sight of magic to help him truly believe.

And I blew, pushing the breath out of me and into my palm with only a word. "Ahl." It flowed like an unseen ribbon, coursing over the soft skin of my open hand. Though its current could not be caught proper by the human eye, the small particulates in the air that followed in its wake stood out. They held errant bits of light as much as they did Pachecho's eyes.

He said nothing, but I could tell I had the whole of his attention.

Now for the hard part. I reached down into the heart of me. A place old, and a place tired. Hard and hot—holding to pain and memory, bright and burning.

Like fire. A crown of flames held there that had never lost its fire. My chest ached, but I brought up the folds again.

This time I buoyed a new image—a whisper-thin band of flame passing through my lips—the fire threaded along the current of air and to be held fixed along its shape. "Whent. Ern." And so it was. It bled out from me, Pachecho's eyes widened farther, and his breath caught in his throat.

The burning tendril wrapped itself around the coil of air and took shape. It welled and blossomed into a bulb-burning-bright, holding all the boy's attention in its firelight.

A whisper nearly left his lips, but he caught himself. Pachecho dared not let a careless breath leave him lest he snuff out the ball of flame sitting in my hand.

"Magic." The word left him with all the reverence a young child could muster—so low a thing you could barely hear it, but all aquiver with excitement. I watched the light of the flames dance in his eyes. He twitched, and I knew the urge he had. The want to touch the flame.

I warned him off that. For while I managed to carry the current of fire comfortably, it was still flame. And its nature was to burn that which did not respect it.

I thought back to all the times I'd learned a piece of fire—its story. The folds wavered, and suddenly, a new flower of doubt bloomed to life inside me. I fought back a sigh, and the urge to curse. Instead, I slowly banished the folds of my mind until the flame dwindled in kind—then faded altogether. The breath of air I'd bound above my palm scattered, its only visible trace the dust it sent skittering along with it.

Pachecho exhaled. "Wow." He reached out to the now empty space above my hand. His fingers raked the air, then pinched, almost as if searching for some remnant of the bindings to still be there. But they were not.

"Just a small trick, Pachecho. A little magic. But if you should feel scared, know that I'll work a bigger one to protect you. *Sieta?*"

He nodded, eyes still owlish over what he'd seen. "*Sieta, sengero. Sieta!*" Then he blinked and looked down the hall. "*Ayo diavello.* I'm late. I'm sorry, I have to . . ." He sped off without another word.

I watched him go, hoping he wouldn't earn any trouble on my behalf. Once he vanished, I made my way toward the audience chamber.

Its entry consisted of a pair of doors cut to form a perfect arch. Few precious spaces of the wood remained untouched by man's hands—shaped in intricate carvings to display a scene out of the old stories. A man, painted in cherry red and resplendent gold, shone bright as the sun. He stood tall, shoulders broad, back straight and held proud. Not the simple farmer you would expect him to be, but a soldier.

A crown of fire burned above his head, and one above his breast. In his hand, a sword bright as sunlight. In the other, a shield of pale moon's glow. But as with every light, there must be shadow. And a number hung behind him.

A number of ten.

Each shade held a distinct shape, all without betraying any identifying features beyond their form. They loomed over the figure in red and gold—watching him from aback, as much separate entities as they could have been as his own shadow cast wide into many. Another row of figures hung beneath the darkened ten as if marionettes from unseen strings. Their forms, however, were not washed in blackness and were designed to be obscured. They had been raked with a carpenter's sharp tools until little of their original selves remained.

A sign.

A rebuke.

And all clearly sending the image that these ten were not intended to be seen, or recorded.

But one of the characters had survived the shaper's scorn, and they remained. So I took them in.

One a man with the head of a wolf, the head of a boy, and the head of a man with a hood in which there was nothing. Nothing but two pools of burning gold from within a field of deepest dark. The man who was no man held out both his hands and in the curve of their cup rested something bright as a pearl with all the shine of a diamond. But this was not the tender touch of someone trying to carry something needing the care of water. No.

This was the covetous hold of greed found only in the most lacking of men. The ones who would grip so tightly to a thing that they would risk killing it rather than chance letting it go. And in doing so, they would bring their fear to life.

I stared at the figure, ignoring the image of Antoine, burning as bright as a prince of sunlight could. But then I noticed the last space on the doors. The space carved in the shape of a figure that was meant to be, but who never came. The hollow space among the nine, perfectly in line with the ten shadows above. The empty space. The waiting space. Only, it had been washed in a single color.

The color found in all men's hearts. The shade found when you make a single perfect shot. And the color of devils.

My cloak felt heavier upon my shoulders and tighter around my throat. I reached up to loosen it and found myself breathing easier.

Footsteps sounded behind the doorway, and voices followed. The majority of words filtered through in Etaynian, but the occasional slip of Trader's Tongue arose when a speaker faltered on a word, or had given in to frustration.

The blessing and curse of the multilingual.

I moved aside just as the doors opened and several of the *burgesa* approached.

The three moved in perfect synchrony—at each other's sides with near-choreographed steps. They were dressed in the soft yellow found in sunflowers.

The cut of their coats, and the sole woman's gown, had been styled in the fashion popular with the gentry. But I paid them no mind. Well, almost no mind.

"—barbarians along the steppes," said one of the men with a voice that sounded as if it had come more from his nose than his throat.

The woman nodded as if agreeing. "But bringing them to Solus *will* bring rewards."

"Easier than if we have to deal with them by force," added the third member.

A few of the household guard trailed the group, paying me as little attention as I had the trio. Once they left, I entered through the doors, taking the initiative to shut them behind me.

The audience chamber could have been pulled straight from Etaynian stories of old. Floors of cold gray stone that had received the brightening treatment only noble westerners would touch upon it to lighten the space. Lavish rugs, made in the east, and dyed the most garish of colors. The only windows in the room were along the back wall, filtering in the morning sun through panes of glass that looked to be fractured. Golden vines raced through their shape, segmenting little pieces, all of which had been stained different colors.

They brought a soft, subtle beauty to the room that compensated for what the carpets took away.

My hope had the new ruler alone. Rather a shame then that several clergos, and a few Alabrose, stood at attention throughout the room. To kill a member of the nobility was one thing, and no easy task. To assassinate a king-in-waiting in front of many armed guards was another matter entirely.

Prince-elect Efraine sat at the end of the chamber, resting atop a wide chair padded with cushioning in the colors of the royal family.

"—and I believe we can avoid that route altogether, Prince-elect. Converting the steppes to Solus *before* any attempts to reconcile Rokash and Arokash. It will ensure war, and we only need—"

Prince-elect Efraine dismissed the man with a motion. "Yes-yes. Speak to His Holiness about it. He will see you provisioned, and send priests as well as clergos, *sieta*?"

"*Sieta, efante-ecantio.*" The man bowed, turned on a heel, and left in the march of a seasoned military man.

The prince-elect's gaze fell on me with the lazy attention of a lion taking note of something mildly curious. "Not a subtle man, Storyteller."

I looked down to my cloak. "I suppose not."

Efraine's mouth quirked to one side. "I meant *Ambassadario* Marelle. He has designs for the nomads of the east, you see."

"I heard."

"Mm. You are familiar with Rokash and the now Arokash." It was not a question.

I nodded again, refusing to share anything more lest I give away something better kept secret. Or bring up memories best left buried. "I have passed through that part of the world once when there was less to pass through. And then again when there was twice as much to see."

Prince-elect Efraine frowned. "You have an interesting way of saying so much while saying little at all, Storyteller. Do you know this?"

I grinned. "Yes."

He returned it. "Ah, there it is again. It's a particularly irritating thing." The prince-elect took a sip from the goblet resting at his side. "His Holiness tried in the past to spread the good word of Solus to the people of the steppes. They have not always warmed to our ways."

People seldom do when you offer them a choice of salvation in one hand and a knife in the other.

"But now there is civil war. One group wishes to retain sovereignty over both countries, the other wishes freedom of self from the other, or if it cannot be, to be the one to then claim dominion over the other."

I saw where this would go. "And the ambassador wishes to use the fissure between warring Qaghans to, what, find grounds to spread the word of Solus?"

He shrugged, the gesture all practiced nonchalance. But the spark in his eyes betrayed the truth. I had struck close, but still not hit the mark. "Something of the sort, yes."

I thought back to our game of Talluv, and the manner in which he'd played. "You seek to convert one of the Qaghans, and in doing so, you will have an ally who shares the same god as you. Etaynia enters the war, and helps the converted Qaghan win. Trade reopens and is all the more welcome among the steppes, and Etaynia has better inroads through the east."

No. I realized then what else I had missed.

But Prince-elect Efraine did not wait for me to sort my thoughts. "Something to that effect, yes. However, it is a bit too early for us to decide where we will intervene."

Unless your ambassador manages to sway one of the Qaghans sooner than later.

The prince-elect must have gleaned my thoughts from the set of my face. He leaned forward, resting his chin on a balled fist. "You don't believe me?" His voice held no hint of judgment, merely curiosity. Then he opened his mouth, a silent *ah* escaping him in realization. "You have another theory?"

I sighed and told him the truth. "I think one of the Qaghans is already predisposed to accept your offer . . . and Solus, of course—"

Prince-elect Efraine smiled and leaned farther forward in his seat. "Of course."

I went on as if he hadn't interrupted me. "And I think that the real benefit

here is that one of the Qaghans has no desire to expand beyond their domain, while the other does. That would lead to an instability your country could not tolerate so far at the end of the Golden Road." *And my own.*

"You'd be hard-pressed to trade into Laxina with the roads through the steppes barred to you."

"Assuming the wrong Qaghan wins." Prince-elect Efraine's eyes glimmered, but the rest of his face gave away little. Save for a twitch at one corner of his mouth.

I inclined my head to cede the point.

"And you disagree with this plan?" Prince-elect Efraine arched a brow.

"I'm not fond of any man being brought to religion at sword-point, especially under false pretenses."

If I had offended Efraine, he didn't show it. Instead, he maintained the calm and collected composure of a prince still playing the Game of Families. "False? You don't think we mean to bring them salvation?"

I gave him a thin smile. "I think the pontifex might believe that, but that whether or not the Qaghan in question accepts Solus, they will take an ally. And that you will benefit greatly from a strictly isolationist and unified Rokash—god or not."

Prince-elect Efraine leaned back in the chair and matched my smile. We stared at one another, unblinking, now giving away as little as we could in the exchange. Neither moved, and neither shied away.

But Efraine relented first, and I found my breath leave me in relief.

The prince-elect bowed his head in acknowledgment of my point. "Not so far from the truth. Yes, Storyteller, that is certainly my hope." He turned up both his palms. "Can you blame me for thinking this way?"

The horrible truth of the matter was that I could not. For a man in his position, what more could he do than ensure the prosperity of his people? Something any good man would want, but then, Prince-elect Efraine wasn't a good man. Not anymore. Not if he'd been taken and tainted.

Somewhere at the heart of him, he no longer saw true and straight. The man might have believed he could tell right from wrong, but his perceptions were warped. And soon with the power of a king . . . ?

What kind of harm could a man like that do?

I thought back to what he had said during the trial, while the table ran red with the blood of his brothers. "No, I can't, Prince-elect. But what of your words among the gentry—the *burgesa*? Do you really believe that?"

To his credit, the prince-elect remained perfectly aware of the clergos in the room. The religious knights who would accept nothing less than his dedication to the promise he'd made—to bring Solus and his light to all barbarians as they saw them. The knights of the Etaynian church had showed their true loyalty when they'd butchered the other princes. They served the pontifex and his agenda. And it seemed that man's motives might not align with the king-in-waiting's.

If that was the case, then the game for power might not have concluded, even if Efraine thought himself to have won. The only question that remained was: Would the pontifex and the king play with wits and wiles, or knives in the dark?

And where would I be left in all of this?

Prince-elect Efraine's gaze flickered toward the churchly knights, but never gave any sign that he turned his head to look at them. A careful, fleeting glance to remind himself of their presence before he spoke.

And it told me enough. The man did have a game all his own, and his ran in line with the pontifex's only so long as it was mutually beneficial.

"I wouldn't do anything less, being a devoted servant to Solus. I rule by his grace and good fortune. But, one cannot expect every barbarian to see the light, much less to welcome it into their hearts and their lives."

A convenient excuse before the swords come out and arrows leave their quivers. But I kept that to myself. I'd antagonized the man enough, and I wouldn't be able to get what I wanted if I pushed him further.

"Did you come here to argue foreign policy with me, Storyteller, or . . . ?" He left the question dangling in the air, and I wished he hadn't. It would have been easier to find an answer if he had left me a choice. Instead, it fell on me to come up with a reason for my visit. Especially since I couldn't corner him alone here.

I tipped my head in what could have been an apology. "Forgive me, Prince-elect Efraine. Yes, I had come here hoping to ask for a private audience. My research with your brother . . ." I gave the appropriate pause. "It remains unfinished. I would not only like your leave to continue that with access to your family's library, but perhaps discuss it with you and hear your own theories."

Efraine pursed his lips. The unsaid question of *why* hung in the expression.

I had an answer for him. "And I would hope to continue my service to your family with perhaps another performance or two. I'm certain the *burgesa* wouldn't mind some stories to take their minds from how short-lived a noble's ambition might be within the walls of Del Soliel."

The laws of the land may have allowed him to get away with murder during the game, but he knew he'd soured the gentry's disposition. Rousing speech or not, anyone who valued their own life now harbored doubts about their safety under him. He would need to quell those fears. Likely how his days would now be spent in his audience hall.

But another option remained to him: distraction.

I could offer that. And Efraine knew it.

We exchanged another knowing stare—one full of things better said and understood without words. Then he inclined his head, making a motion of both acceptance and dismissal.

I bowed in return, having gotten what I wanted. All it would cost me was a performance, some lies, and some cleverness. Things I could manage. And then I would be able to get the prince alone.

So I could begin to right all the many wrongs I'd set upon the world.

ONE HUNDRED THIRTEEN

Quick to Blame

I left the audience chamber and headed toward the royal library. But I didn't get far.

"Storyteller!" The word struck me through the hall, carrying all the edge of freshly honed steel, and all the coldness of snow-capped stone.

I turned halfway to regard the speaker.

A thin man with all the severity of a knife in face and form. His clothes were fitted to his frame, and this did him no favors. Today he wore a coat the color of powdered indigo, and the pants to match. A sash of carmine ran over one shoulder and across his torso. At first I thought it symbolized something, only then I realized it existed solely for the purpose of fashion.

Something that has eluded me all my life, despite having spent considerable time among the *better class* of folk.

His hair had been slicked back and carried the slight sheen of oil. And he seemed to have applied the same to his thin mustache, making it look even narrower. The man had all the sharp-hollow gauntness in his face to remind me of an underfed dog.

And I had seen him before. Back when he was threatening older men who hadn't seen the light in a very long time, and when he was promising to kill me.

A quick look down the hall showed me that the two of us stood alone. How fortunate for him. He might very well be able to make good on his desire.

I shifted my body to position my staff arm between us. Should he make any sudden moves, I could use the binder's cane to keep him at a distance. "You visited me in the dungeon."

The man brushed aside his coat, and I tightened my grip on my staff. His motion revealed a hilt of polished bright wood. Some of his clothing obscured the sheath, but I saw enough to make out the certain curve of a *taldero,* the Etaynian short knife used by the gentry to obtain satisfaction.

Not much for reach, but easy to conceal. And easier still to use in busy halls and tight spaces to find the heart of a man.

"Ernesto Vengenza, wasn't it?"

He squared his shoulders, but they quickly lost their stiffness. His knees showed the slightest hint of bend—betraying his softened stance. The man had dueled before, and now rested with the comfortable spring-in-step that could see him lunging a short distance.

Small luck I just so happened to linger outside that reach, but that could change. And he could be quicker than I gave him credit for.

"Yes." The word left him like a string freshly plucked. Quivering, though not from any fear, but the voice of a man holding back old anger.

"You still blame me for Prince Arturo's death."

Ernesto's face flickered through a series of expressions. All too quickly to be taken in, but enough to let me know he harbored conflict. Something had changed since last we met, and he might not have blamed me in full as before. Though I stood before him now, and anger is a funny thing—a dangerous one. It often seeks the quickest way. And in that, it often leads you to miss your true mark.

Before, Ernesto Vengenza wanted the easy satisfaction. He wanted to give in to anger. Now, he wanted something else, though the old anger still blossomed. But what the man really desired was vengeance. And that is a different thing altogether.

"Who else can I blame?" Each word came with acid enough to scour rust from steel. He stood now so close to the edge that the merest thing could set him off, which would bring about consequences neither of us would enjoy.

I let out a soft breath and then took a chance. "You can blame the men who really sent your prince to an early grave."

The blade left the sheath, its edge looking every bit as sharp as Ernesto's hatred. But it shook in his hand, and the man's eyes had lost some of their hardness. "What do you mean?"

"Who was it that set your prince up in the Game of Families? You witnessed the trial?"

The man nodded.

"And you know how it ended."

His jaw went hard. "I do."

"The clergos don't answer to any prince. And Prince-elect Efraine came out of the trial the only surviving male heir. Neatly done, wouldn't you say? Bit odd to have a trial for a foreigner accused of killing an *efante*. A lot of effort went into that sort of thing, and I can't imagine what benefit it served anyone except for—"

"Getting all of the *efantes* into one room." The next breath that left Ernesto

Vengenza was that of a man who had realized the long-hidden truth before him, and how easily he had been fooled.

As a rule, people do not like being made to look like idiots.

"*Diavello pinchero.*" My Etaynian was nowhere near Eloine's skill, but it sounded like Ernesto had just said, "Devil prick me." The *taldero* remained in his hand, however, and his face gave away nothing of his intention.

I waited, my staff held firmly between us.

"And what would you have me do about this, Storyteller, hm?" The man's mustache twitched. "You want me to seek satisfaction against a *Reyole*?"

I smiled. "Prince-elect Efraine is no king. Not yet."

It was as easy as that.

Ernesto Vengenza sheathed the knife and invited me to take a meal with him.

And we left together to plot how best to kill a prince of Etaynia.

ONE HUNDRED FOURTEEN

How Honor Holds

Ernesto Vengenza led me to a veranda looking out over one of the other many gardens Del Soliel had to offer. We were alone, far from prying eyes, and in the most perfect of places should he have a change of heart and feel his knife would be better buried in mine.

Conveniences. They do add little pleasures to life.

We had been brought toast browned well, and daubed with salted butter. One plate had been layered with slender silver fish, fanned out for our taking. Each was no larger than my smallest finger. *Baquerene,* the common snack for Etaynians at lunch. A jug of what looked to be pomegranate juice followed, as well as flat pieces of bread that reminded me of *fahaan* but which had been coated in melted cheese.

I did not take any of the food, nor the drink. Consider it appropriate caution. I had seen what happened to those careless with their drink in Etaynia.

Ernesto must have guessed what went through my mind. "Ah, no, Storyteller. If I wanted to kill you, rest assured"—he brushed aside his coat and revealed his dagger—"I would give you the satisfaction of making it an honorable death. A clean one."

Ernesto Vengenza and I had different ideas on what would bring me satisfaction. But it wouldn't serve either of us for me to discuss that. Instead I turned to the other word he'd chosen: honorable. I decided to begin our conversation with that.

"And what exactly is an Etaynian's honor worth, Ernesto?"

The man paused as he tipped the jug of pomegranate juice over his tin cup. He'd managed to pour in enough of the drink to nearly fill the goblet before I brought him to a stop. He arched one eyebrow and set the jug back down. "A complicated question, and quite possibly an insulting one, Storyteller." Ernesto Vengenza fixed me with a knowing look, and one of his fingers traced along the curve of the dagger's sheath.

A warning? A message? Quite possibly both. But I decided to wait and let the man make his intentions clear.

"Ah, *Geuma des Familiya.* What you saw during the game is how you see us." Ernesto nodded as if he had expected as much from me. "It is true, to a point. The game . . . allows for certain liberties with and around our honor. It is an old thing, a time from when Antoine had only just saved us, and Solus had come to bless us with his light."

A time right after shadows took shape as well as took the hearts and minds of men. Shadows that took their tongues so that they may only spout lies. And twisted their sight so that they could not trust their very own eyes. I could see how a game like that would spring up in the aftermath of such a time.

Sometimes tradition isn't the act of keeping something valuable alive. Sometimes it is the fear of removing old shackles because we have worn them so long we do not know what it is like to be free of them. And so better to keep the fears we know than to walk a life unknown, new, and with all the terrors unmet for us to face.

"To play the game is to accept many things, and sometimes . . . yes, it can lead one to death." Ernesto's grip tightened around the goblet, and the soft tin gave way. Not much, just enough to bring smooth folds into the metal's previously perfect lip. "But to kill an *efante*?" He gave me a look that made it clear the game did not usually go that far.

I reached out to finally fill my own cup, and take some of the bread. The *baquerene* followed. I ate with the slow patience of someone listening to a story, never turning my eyes and ears away from Ernesto.

"What Prince-elect Efraine has done goes well past the game's allowance, but . . ." Ernesto trailed off, availing himself of more juice. Though the shape of his face suggested the man would have very much preferred something stronger to drink in the moment.

I finished chewing the bread and fish, washing it down with a sip of my own juice. "What about was done outside of the game?"

Ernesto frowned as he brought a piece of the thin cheese-covered dish to his mouth. "How do you mean?"

"After I was given the blame for your prince's passing, the game was declared suspended, yes?"

Ernesto nodded.

"The murder of his family took place during my trial." That was all I needed to say.

The man who had once wanted to kill me now tore a chunk of flatbread and chewed hard enough that he risked cracking a tooth. His eyes narrowed and shot a look sharper than his blade's edge. Though it wasn't meant for me. "This is true, Storyteller."

"It is, which raises the question: How does Etaynian honor hold when someone commits such an act outside the one thing that permits it? How do you deal with a man who has killed his entire brotherhood for the throne outside of the game?"

Ernesto took a deep breath and set his food down. His tongue ran against the front of his teeth and I could see all the subtle motions in his face, and his hands, that betrayed a man fighting to control his emotions. And what he wished to say next. Because he had so many things in his heart, and on his mind.

I knew that the two did not share equal desires.

The man before me sawed through a piece of bread topped with fish with the savagery I imagined he would have liked to turn on Prince Efraine. Or, barring that, me at some point. He chewed, then washed it down with cold efficiency. The fork came to rest on the plate, but his knife remained tight in hand. His knuckles whitened, which told me enough.

"You understand I am not one of the *burgesa, sieta*? I am not one of those soft and comfortable lordlings born into position because my fathers happened to do the right thing at the right time . . . or wrong time, depending on your view. I dress the part, and I play the game well enough. But I am a second. I *serve.* For me to take satisfaction on an *efante* . . ."

He made his point clearly enough. Ernesto Vengenza could not act against someone so high of station. At least, not publicly.

"Besides, with the support of His Holiness, Prince-elect Efraine has the support of the gentry and church. What can we do?"

We. And like that, the man had decided that he and I did share common thinking, even if on this small and singular matter. Prince-elect Efraine was a problem for the both of us.

"He killed your prince, or had him done in—all the same—during the game."

"So you say." Ernesto leveled the bread knife in my direction, but the gesture held little malice. "I did not see what happened."

I met him point for point and with the same quickness. "You're right. You did not. Lord Emeris Umbrasio poisoned his tea. In all your searching of my things, did you find anything indicating I could have done so? In what you know of my reputation, is there anything to suggest I'd kill a lord?"

My heart panged and my stomach knotted at that, but as far as this man was concerned, I *was* the Storyteller. Not Ari. And in this moment, I needed to be the former and forget the latter. To bury him, as time and stories had done.

Ernesto's lips went thin in pondering, and he took another sip of juice while he reflected. "True enough. But it is your word against Lord Umbrasio's."

"True, except if I were truly guilty . . ." I didn't need to explain, only give him a knowing look.

"Yes. You would be sharing a fate with the other *efante,* Solus grant their souls the warmth their bodies now lack." The man touched an open hand to his heart, then brought those fingertips to his lips to kiss. Finally, he gestured to the sun.

"I think it is fair to say that neither of us will see true justice here. But the man killed your prince, and he killed the remainder of the family I assume you held *some* loyalty to, if not love."

Ernesto inclined his head.

"And there is the matter of the prince killed before I even arrived."

He repeated the gesture, another conciliation to my point. "Something you argued well at your trial."

"So, with all of that, how does Etaynian law suggest you satisfy your honor? And, more than that, your late *efante*'s?" Those were the questions that hooked Ernesto Vengenza's heart, and brought mine to a cold shame.

Vengeance is many things, but it is rarely clean. And though my desire to see Prince-elect Efraine dead came from other reasons, I'm not so sure they were any nobler. Much like Shareem's death, I could justify it in many ways.

The necessary things. One of the Tainted.

Brahm's blood, I didn't want to think on it. And I did not wish to dwell on what I had just done either.

Manipulate a man, and his sense of honor, to kill another. Even if he wanted it himself, a part of him had held to reason. Otherwise he would already have acted. But I had pushed him against his better reason. To vengeance.

Because vengeance, and the heart, often have no room for reason. They are wild things. And the heart is quick to take slight, quick to anger, and quickest still to act on those things.

And we can so rarely take back what we do when urged by our angry heart.

Ernesto Vengenza sat for a long time with the stillness of old-forgotten stone. And he held all the silence of a man contemplating his next words as if they would be his last. Finally, he took a deep breath, and he spoke. "Prince Arturo took me in many years ago, you know?"

He sipped his juice and placed the empty cup down. His hand moved, a callous action, and he knocked the goblet over. A color just shy of freshly spilled blood ran over the table, pooling against the white cloth. "He gave me a life when I had none. Purpose where there was none. And a future when there wasn't one for someone like me."

I almost opened my mouth to ask what his life had been—what his story was, but Ernesto Vengenza was as sharp a man as he was hard. And he caught the question in my eyes.

"No, I will not tell you more than this thing. It is mine and mine alone. And once was my prince's."

I nodded.

"I owe him everything, and I would give him everything if it could bring him back. But it cannot. But I can still give something to see his memory honored, and his desire for this country. Prince-elect Efraine is not a man who shows any love to his brother's dreams. That is clear. Now, let us talk of things that would see the both of us dead. Let us talk of things that only dying men feel free to share, because they know where they are headed, and that leaves them without care."

I leaned closer.

Ernesto matched me. "How good are you with a bow?"

The guise of the Storyteller left me in that moment, and I thought back to a time when a black wooden bow fit so comfortably in my hand. A time when its curve had almost been made for my hold. I didn't answer him, but I did smile.

"Good. So, let me tell you, Storyteller, how we kill the last prince of Etaynia."

And so he did.

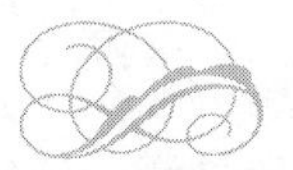

ONE HUNDRED FIFTEEN

DIFFERENCES

Ernesto Vengenza and I planned well into the night until I finally left him to stew on his anger. And on how best to kill a prince.

This left me free to finally ponder something else of import in my rooms. A book I'd been gifted by the late Prince Artenyo.

Tuecanti des Nuevellos. Tales of the Nine. A book in which I'd found one useful thing about the Ashura. Eloine had been set to help me translate the work, but our efforts had been interrupted well before completion.

A knock at the door pulled me from my notes.

Eloine lingered in the opening, watching me. She'd changed her clothes for what you would expect Etaynian nobility to wear to bed. A shift the color of washed carnations, adorned with lace along the neck and lines at her waist in a pattern of flowers. But I saw no trace of any of the jewelry I'd so often seen her wear.

No earrings. No bangles.

Her hair hung loose and framed her face in thick and curling waves. The dark of them should have complemented the brightness of her eyes, but those had now lost their intensity. They were the color of old sage shrouded in fog—the weakest of green amidst just as faded gray.

I rose to my feet and almost moved to embrace her, but the hung-tired look in her eyes told me it wouldn't have been welcome. "I didn't expect to see you tonight. Not after you left for . . . whatever your business was."

She gave me a smile and it only served to illustrate her fatigue. "Draining is what it was. And night is the best time for me to find you."

I blew out a breath. "Hardly. I'm not exactly inconspicuous." I turned my attention to the red cloak around me, then to my staff. "I'm sure you'd have no trouble finding me wherever and whenever you wished."

Her mouth made the shape again—a wan smile that never reached her eyes. She crossed the distance between us and laid a hand on my arm. I had opened my mouth to say something, but she spoke before I could. "Still thinking on them?"

I blinked, then followed her stare to the book we'd once pored over. "I suppose it's only natural. After all, we didn't get a chance to finish our research."

She arched an eyebrow, and a touch of her old self and warmth flooded the expression. "Oh, is that what we were doing?" A hint of a more honest smile returned to her then.

"What else could it have been?"

She rolled her eyes. "My mistake. I thought we were only using that as an excuse for the real dance the pair of us have been doing. You remember the one? The piece in which we finally shared the stage together and you kissed me? I thought all this was merely a clever ploy to continue that performance." She took the book from my hand, closed it, then rolled her wrist in a gesture someone might make when wanting the story to move along.

"Last I remembered, it was you who kissed me. You had just finished a lovely song and taken my face in your hands, and before I knew it, the lady had her mouth on mine and had stolen a kiss from me." I pressed a hand to my chest, playing up the theatricality.

Eloine pursed her lips and eyed me askance. "Mm. Is that how you remember it?"

"It is."

"Odd, I don't recall it the same way." One side of her mouth quirked.

"Funny, isn't it, how events get twisted and misremembered as time goes by, or by who is doing the recollecting?" I matched her expression, falling short of flashing a smile.

Eloine's hand crashed into my chest, sending me onto the bed. "Then do me a favor?"

I looked up at her from where I lay on my back. "Anything."

She fell beside me, propping herself up by her elbows. Her proximity gave me a better view of the subtle things I'd missed before. Faded shadows hung under her eyes and some of the gold in her skin seemed paler now. Her fingers rubbed together, and in doing so, brought my attention to the smear of red along the skin there and just under her nails. Eloine caught me staring, but said nothing.

The look in her eyes was unspoken invitation. *Ask me,* it said. *Care,* it pleaded. *See that I am not fine,* it asked of me.

So I did. My fingers brushed against hers, and despite the look, she pulled away. I did not reach for her again. Instead, I addressed what I had seen. The color of dried blood, and the question of how it had come to be there.

"What happened?"

To Eloine's credit, she didn't bother denying what I had spotted. "It isn't mine."

"I'm not sure if that's supposed to make me feel better, or worry me more. Buy yourself some more trouble?" I gave a little laugh, hoping it would set her at ease.

She let out a breath through her nose that came as close to amusement as she could manage in that moment.

I took some comfort in that, at least.

"It was a small problem, and I handled it. Besides, everyone needs their secrets, don't they?" Eloine reached out, tapping me on my chin before trailing a finger down my throat to my cloak's tie. She pulled on it, bringing my face closer to hers.

And in that moment I believed I would be given a reminder of what we'd shared at the conclusion of our performance. A thing come from soft and pliant lips—warm breath, and warmer passion still. Her eyes touched mine, and it seemed the right time for it. Only, it never came. Her finger let go its hold and she finally gave me the best smile she could. And it was a weak and tired thing.

Eloine pulled her hand away from me, but I took hold of it, wrapping her fingers in a tender grip.

"Not everything needs to be kept secret. I've been sharing mine, haven't I? All of mine." I stopped at that, as those words weren't wholly true. And Eloine had the wit to know as much.

She eased her hand out of mine and slid away from me. Nothing so much as a foot, closer to a hand's breadth, but the action was enough. "*All* of yours?" Her tone held a note of accusation, and the curve of her brow accentuated the point.

"*Most* of them, at least."

Her eyes gleamed. "*Most.* But not all." She drummed her fingers against the bed. "Though I suppose it's a fair request, given how much you've shared with me." Eloine exhaled and curled her fingers tight, perhaps just in frustration, or maybe to hide the blood-stained skin.

Possibly both.

"It was an accident, and someone ended up hurt by my carelessness. It's still too soon to talk about it at length. I'm sure you understand what that feels like."

And I did. We both knew the pains of bringing hurt to others.

It is no easy thing, especially in the freshness of it. And, if you live long enough, it is an ache every person comes to feel. Because to live is to at some point wound another, even if you never mean to. Even if it is the last thing you could ever wish for. We are human, and we hurt as easily as we love.

She looked back up at me then, another plea in her eyes. One just as silent as the one before, but I heard it all the same: *Wait for me.*

I hoped my eyes spoke my answer as loud as could be. And I hoped she heard it: *always.*

Aloud, however, she said something else. "Give me time?"

I understood that need all too well. "Of course."

Eloine took my hands in hers now. "In the meantime, would you still tell me more of yours? I understand if you wouldn't—not after all I've kept from you. I know you have questions. And I haven't been—"

I squeezed her with all the care I could give. "It's fine. I'm just glad you're not hurt. And I know all about how the heart and mind need time to heal from the things that hurt us." I exhaled and glanced to the book we had been translating, then flashed her a look best fit for a fox. Cunning and sharp-eyed enough that she could not help but catch it.

"I'll happily tell you more of my story, and all the secrets within it. . . ."

"I'm sensing a 'but,' my Storyteller."

"*But* . . . will you promise to spend more time with me?" I broke my hold on her hands, tapping the book to draw her attention to it. "To translate the book, of course, because we haven't finished."

Eloine's hand blurred, and my shoulder ached. She raised her palm, making it clear she had no problem swatting me again should I get too clever for my own good. But she shook her head the next moment and lowered her hand. "Oh, the shadow of love." It was said only for her ears, but I'd heard it all the same.

I blinked. "Huh?"

"Oh, nothing. Just something a clever man once said. I had hoped it had fallen on the ears of a man equally as sharp." She gave me a sideways and knowing look. "But sometimes I'm still left to wonder." Eloine didn't bother explaining, of course.

Sometimes I felt that she took pleasure in leaving me dangling—hooked and waiting for the next word in hopes that it would bring me some measure of clarity. Then again, I did much the same as the Storyteller.

Were we really that different, then?

One of her fingers tapped the side of my lips, drawing me out of my reverie. "Oh, you've gone all pensive again. Lost in thoughts, were we?" She didn't give me a chance to answer as she looked me over. "You already know."

I had forgotten what I had been about to say. "What?"

"The answer to your question: If I will spend more time with you? You already know the answer, and the best way to ensure that."

I fought to keep myself from laughing. "I suppose I do. All right, then. Story for story." I rapped my knuckles against the cover of the *Tuecanti des Nuevellos.*

Eloine reached out and placed a hand over mine. "I can live with that."

Our fingers twined and I broke back into the story I'd left unfinished. "Enshae and I had just spent our last night together, and in the morning, I would leave. We had shared some of our pains, stories, and, maybe, something close to friendship. A sort of companionship over loneliness, if you will. And in that, I had learned more than I realized about the story of fire. But that will come later. Then, it was time to leave the Shaen realm. To head back through the Doors of Midnight."

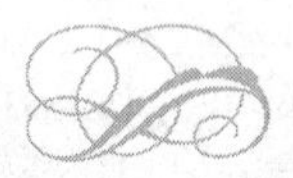

ONE HUNDRED SIXTEEN

LEAVETAKINGS

I gathered all I owned in my travel sack. Enshae watched me with the cool, collected patience of someone used to waiting for all time, and its passing never bothered her. Though, I knew now, in this moment, that it did.

You could see it in her stare—a long and distant thing. Something caught halfway between the memory of the time we'd spent together, and just as much a space only she could see. Perhaps wondering if and when I'd return to fulfill my promise, or maybe simply seeing a dream in which I didn't leave at all.

Who could say? The minds of most people were beyond me then. So what hope did I have at gleaning the thoughts of a Shaen, especially one older than recorded time?

I made sure to watch Enshae out of the corner of my eye, not wanting to give away that I might have caught more than what she wished to show. My hands brushed against the cover of a book and I paused. The tome Rishi Saira had given me that contained all of the stories I'd been sharing with Enshae.

Part to entertain her, and part to keep myself from being turned into whatever animal she thought best at any given time.

I had teased her each night, withholding their endings until the next night, only to begin a new one to leave unfinished once again. And the cycle had continued. But now . . . well, I knew what it was like to want to know all of a story, and have pieces kept from you.

Like those belonging to the Ashura.

I looked up at her and she caught my eye.

"*Brightling?*"

I made my way over to her. "Everyone should get to hear the whole of a story. Here." My hands shook as I passed the tome over to her. "I'm sorry for keeping them from you, but now . . ." I trailed off, unable to properly say the part we both knew was coming. The word: goodbye.

I seemed to struggle with farewells.

She smiled. Sweet, and with all the brilliant curve and brightness of the moon. "*Thank you, brightling.*" Enshae took the book from my hands and motioned to one side of the forest around us.

I tracked the gesture and saw a dog lingering within the treeline. It watched us with a mixture of curiosity and healthy reservation.

My friend, the *Maathi*—Khalil.

"*Ksthi-bhaag. Ksthi-bhaag.*" Enshae clicked her tongue with each call, beckoning the dog that was also my friend. The hound sniffed the ground twice in consideration, then plodded over to Enshae. She extended an open hand, running it along his snout before cradling one side of his head. Enshae's fingers scratched his ears and she leaned close. Her mouth moved, though I couldn't make out a whisper of what she sang.

The world around the pair was shrouded in smoke the color of night, threaded with silver and violent red. Quick as that, the obscuring veil vanished and I saw my friend, whole as could be, standing before Enshae.

Khalil blinked several times, staring at the Shaen woman. His eyes widened in realization and he took two steps back, nearly tumbling. "Alum Above. Most Merciful High." The man's hands blurred in gestures I guessed to be half-motioned prayers.

"It's all right, Khalil." I raised my own hands, signaling for calm and hoping he'd take my urgings. "It's fine. Enshae won't hurt you." I shot her a look, asking the question in silence . . . just to be sure.

You never knew with one of the Shaen, after all.

Enshae, for her part, spread her mouth into a wide grin. It was not a smile to set you at ease.

And Khalil knew as much. He recoiled, waving his hands as if that could ward Enshae off.

She threw her head back and let out a laugh much musical touched with a smoky undertone.

I couldn't help it. Her amusement set me off, and the pair of us enjoyed my friend's unease. "She's just joking, Khalil. I swear."

"Swear it on Alum Above. Most Merciful High." He kicked against the ground, putting more distance between himself and the Shaen woman and making his way over to me. "Truly, Ari? She's not going to do anything else . . . unnatural to me?"

I clapped a hand to my friend's shoulder and helped him to his feet. "No, Khalil. I promise."

The man held on to me in the grip of true fear.

"*Zho.* Then you will excuse me"—Khalil made a curt bow in Enshae's direction—"if I stand a good bit away from you two until we leave, yes?" He didn't wait for an answer before bustling away from us.

She watched him go, smile still wide on her face. "*For all his cleverness and curiosity, he is a wiser man than most.*"

"Because he's quick to get away from you?"

Her smile didn't falter, but her eyes betrayed a hint of hurt at the comment. Perhaps because it was just another reminder—a barb—that I was about to leave as well. "*Because he does not linger where it is dangerous. He knows enough to see what all mortals should fear.*" Enshae stood, tall and proper—back straight, shoulders squared. And though she stood no higher than me, in that moment, she towered.

Proud and with all the strength only the oldest of the Shaen could show. "*You, my brightling and little castaway, do not. And it will lead you to ruin if you do not temper your cleverness and curiosity . . . and your anger.*" The smile changed, and now became something close to pity.

No, I realized. *Sorrow?* The look of someone deep in resignation over something that could not be avoided. But Enshae never bothered to explain what was on her mind, and I didn't have the skill to glean it from her expression.

Instead, she reached out and took me in her embrace, holding me there as if I would be lost to her forever should she let go. But, eventually, she did. "*I have given you gifts to survive the mortal fold. One a cloak, brilliant bright, woven strong of star's own glow, and silver moonlight. Two, a tool to find me still, would you have the wish, and the will. And now there is a final gift for you to see. To pay back in kind what you have given me.*"

At that, Enshae reached out to pinch a piece of the very air before the long flat stone she often rested upon. She pulled, and a part of the world before us blurred, then moved, as if it had all been a painted canvas hung in front of me.

The scene behind was much the same. The stone from earlier, only something stood atop it that I hadn't seen.

A candle.

No, it would be wrong to simply call it that. It looked like one much the way some stars resemble gems at great distance. But it was something shaped by more than just wax and twine.

It resembled the candle I had been given, true. But its color had been pulled from the night sky itself. A black so deep and dark that I could almost lose sight of the thing should I turn my eye from it. Closer inspection revealed the hidden shades of twilight blue that swirled and faded as if alive—moving into and out of clarity by the moment. Flecks of light sparkled within the body of the candle, and I realized them to be the light of crushed diamonds.

Enshae must have read my mind, because she explained what I had gotten wrong. "*A piece of starlight, caught and shaped, broken and placed.*"

A piece of a star . . . and she had taken it and wrought it into new form, simply for its beauty, with all the ease of a child shaping clay.

"This is for me?" One of my hands flexed, and I resisted the urge to reach out in rudeness and take it before her confirmation.

She nodded. "*Ilah. This is my last gift to you. A candle to light your way in the darkest of times. So you should always have a fire to call upon as any shaper must who walks in the path of Brahm, and all the ones before you. Especially for a castaway brightling. Take it.*"

I did, cradling it in both hands as if it were a weight of gold and I was but a sparrow all over again.

"*And now for the final piece.*" She tapped the head of the candle, and I realized it had been fashioned without a wick. But before I could open my mouth to comment, Enshae plucked a strand of her fine silver hair free. Then another. Then again. Three strands that she held before me. She twined them then, shaping them into a single piece.

"*Now to complete this working.*" She kissed the end of the newly twisted lengths of wick, then ran a pinched grip along its length. When she finished, the piece hung as something solid—no longer three distinct strands of hair. She pressed one end to the tip of the candle and sang—her voice just as it had been all the times before.

Resonant. Ringing. Silver bells, pounding at the heart of me as much my ears.

And no sooner than that, the new wick sat within its shape as if it had been there all along.

"*When you need of it, simply touch your flesh to its head, castaway. Think of the flame you have held here. Think of me. Bid it burn. And it will.*"

"But I can't kindle fire, Enshae. Not without a source already. I can't bind like—"

She pressed two fingers to my lips, stopping me. And when I tried to protest, she pressed her lips to the back of her touch, just shy of my actual mouth. The gesture said enough, and I remained quiet. "*Ilah. The flame can learn. I am not asking what you can and cannot do. I am telling you what you must do, understand?*"

I nodded.

"*Good. Ilah. Then lastly there is one final thing. The one outside the giving of three. The freely given gift.*" Enshae unfurled a clenched hand.

What sat within looked a pale trinket compared to what she'd gifted me before. At least at first look. A small disc, much like one I'd purchased the previous year during a winter festival of fire and light, and held the same promise in its glass form. However, those had been nothing but cheap keepsakes. This?

A longer look showed me that it carried all the proper brightness of a piece of star plucked free and pressed flat. A working of distant light made hard. Something far beyond any small working in Ghal. A true treasure. And the perfect gift for someone who'd once asked for something similar.

Its touch filled me with a soft and subtle warmth I nearly missed, almost as if the now-light hadn't forgotten the fire of a star.

Enshae didn't quite smile, but her mouth twitched at the corners, and the glow of her eyes deepened. "*I, too, once received a gift of star-made glass, pressed into my hands by a mortal. And now I give one to you. This is memory. And it is a piece of story, something you should appreciate, brightling. The half-heard cry and memory of a nearly forgotten flame. Pulled from one of the first shapings before there were worlds at all. A when before there even was an Enshae.*" She said this in a way to make sure I knew the significance of a time marked by such a way. "*This is to remember not a promise, but to remember me.*"

It could have been a trick of light, or perhaps the oddity of all things in that realm. After all, I *was* in the Shaen, and nothing was quite what it seemed. But Enshae's face bore all the signs of a mask made of glass, soon to crack, and quicker still to break in full. All only held together by her own strength of will. And that was fading. The longer we stayed in this awkward lingering, the closer she came to shattering.

There are few things harder than leaving. Sometimes it's best done quick and distant, all to spare your heart the breaking. This I know.

And I have done.

So too did Enshae. She gestured behind me and I turned to see what she motioned at.

Brilliant sunlight cast around a solid circle of shadow. A pillar of burning fire at its base that vanished far below out of sight.

The doorway home.

Back to the desert.

Back to Qimari, and her father.

Back to a war that I had failed to stop, and which may have already been over.

What would I find?

I turned back to Enshae, and saw her watching me. I may not have known what lay ahead, but I knew what would await me should I stay.

Safety. A temptation of another kind.

Freedom from consequences. The temptation grew.

The ability to grow in my learnings and hear things no man ever had. And the temptation told me then I would never leave again, nor would I want to.

For that is how temptation works. It's not done with body and smooth skin. It is quiet whispers and promises of power. The gentle seduction that makes you betray your truest self. And your deepest wants.

I broke the hold Enshae's eyes had on mine, and mine hers, and turned to walk toward the doorway.

The *Maathi* rushed toward me and grabbed my arm. "*Zho. Zho.* Let us be away from this place, Ari."

"Yes, let's." The words left me with all the dryness of old roads, long traveled and weary-worn. And the words broke in my throat as soon as I spoke them.

So did I.

We reached the burning way, and I looked over my shoulder one last time to catch sight of Enshae.

But she wasn't there.

I stepped through the Doors of Midnight once again, and back toward all that I had left behind.

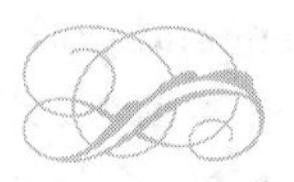

ONE HUNDRED SEVENTEEN

The Truth of Things

Blinding light swallowed me and drove needles of flame through my whole body. And as quick as that, it all faded.

I opened my eyes to be greeted by low rising dunes and loose grains of sand sent skittering in the afternoon breeze.

The *Maathi* let out a heavy breath followed by a string of curses in too many tongues for me to track. "Most Merciful High, Ari. The Shaen. The Doors of Midnight! She turned me into . . ." He trailed off, looking over his shoulder at his backside. Then he turned again, running his hands down against himself. "*Zho.* She made me an animal. What about you?"

I opened my mouth, then paused, realizing both the opportunity before myself and the necessity for the truth. Something Enshae had long been denied when it came to the stories about her.

So I told my friend what happened with the oldest of the Shaen, mistress of midnight and her garden prison.

"*Zho.*" Khalil waved a dismissive hand. "You tell me lies. She is a Shaen. They are . . ." He frowned, cradling his chin with a thumb and forefinger. "She is . . ."

"She is lonely, Khalil. She has been for thousands of years. But if you want to know how I survived her, I'll tell you." A smile made its way across my face. "Mind you, she did want to turn me into a kitten. She wanted to kill me. She wanted to do all the things you can imagine and then some."

The *Maathi*'s eyes widened as we walked. "How?"

I gave him my story of how I'd tricked her, night by night, with never-ending stories. All for one hundred and one nights. Through our days, we warmed to one another, and eventually, she taught me the subtle workings of magic in ways I had never considered before.

I told him of our duel, an exchange of violent and powerful magics. Though in truth, things hadn't exactly happened that way. She had thoroughly trounced me in a display of bindings I couldn't manage even in my dreams. But I'd added a nice touch to the story, and every tale needs something like that woven through. Otherwise it's terribly hard to believe them.

The thing with stories is . . . we value true-seeming more than truth. The truth is hard to swallow—thick and often bitter. True-seeming is far easier to take in hand, and in mind. And no one likes to admit it, but most already have their truths decided, and firmly set. This was as true of Khalil as it was of so many others.

I watched him carefully as I told him the story of my time with Enshae. And I made out the subtle changes in his face when I edged too far into the world of his disbelief. So I would have to change the tale to be more of what he could believe.

It was too far out of the realm of possibility for him to ever see Enshae as a sympathetic figure. Though that might have had something to do with the fact that she had turned him into an animal. Nevertheless, he had to believe that she and I fought. That there had been grim contention between the two of us, and that I had only survived through the best of cleverness, and no small amount of charm.

That may have been true, but the saddest truth of all rested in the fact that I survived because Enshae wanted me to. Because she was alone. And in need of a friend who would listen to her story, whole as it was, and without judgment.

A truth the world wasn't ready for. One they wouldn't want to believe. Starting with Khalil.

So as we walked across the desert, and light gave way to darkest night, we spoke of Enshae, and the story that would come to be remembered about us. Something so very far from the truth of things.

But I never lied about her nature. And I made sure to preserve the truth of why she was banished.

I will not have it said that I denied her that kindness.

"We should stop for the night." I opened my travel sack, then stopped as I remembered I didn't have any of the tools to set camp with.

The *Maathi* shook his head before gesturing to the sky. "*Zho. Zho.*" He pointed to a shaping of stars he'd once shown me before. "Look. The way to Iban-Bansuur."

Small fortune that we had come out of the Doors of Midnight so close to where we'd entered them. By that I mean an extra day's walk away. Not so great a distance that we were in any danger of wandering the desert for long, but certainly an inconvenience. Never mind the fact neither of us had any idea how much time had passed in the mortal realm while we'd been trapped in Enshae's garden.

Would anyone still be in the old sandstone city? I gave voice to the question before realizing I'd even spoken.

Khalil's lips pursed and he looked down as we walked onward. "I do not know, but there is something to be said for hope, ah? If we think there is no point, then we would still go to Iban-Bansuur. Khalil and Ari will still need warm fires, and the safety of walls. Otherwise, we will be lost here. I would not like that."

Neither would I.

"So we march to the city and pray to Most Merciful High that good *Shir* Arfan is still there." His voice shook near the end, and I heard the words that never came. *And we pray that too much time hasn't passed. Is the world still the one we left behind?*

I decided that sometimes it isn't wise for a man to hold on to questions like that. Sometimes we should trade our thoughts, no matter how sensible they might seem, for something better like hope. After all, no one clings to anything harder than hope in the darkest of moments. And there is a reason for that.

But it would take a wiser man than me to ever be able to explain it.

And as I've often said, I am no wise man.

So we held to hope and followed the stars, secret prayers in heart as we walked to the city of sandstone. The place where so many things had gone so very wrong. Where I had broken the sacred rule—and spilled blood within its walls. Where I had murdered an innocent young man, and buried his body in the sands.

Where I'd started a war.

Merciful Brahm, what were we about to walk into?

ONE HUNDRED EIGHTEEN

PIECES ALL

The sun had risen and painted the old stone of Iban-Bansuur in a light of gilded copper. For the first time, I found myself truly able to appreciate the place's beauty.

When we'd originally come to the city, it had suffered an attack from the Ashura. Red smoke and smoldering flames. Blood along the walls. A place of only fear. Just horror.

Its walls had since been cleaned, whether by man's hand, or wind and the brush of sand, I didn't know. But now it no longer bore the marks of nightmares and demons. And so its golden stone shimmered, and I noticed the beaten copper roofs, domed and patinated the green of old emeralds. Something I never noticed under the smoke. Some towers had been set with turquoise and gemstones that made it look as if parts of the sea had come to rest along their shapes.

How could I have ever missed all of that?

"See. See! *Zho,* Ari, we have some fortune. Alum Above, blessed be his name." Khalil placed his hands together, then kissed the tops of his fingers before raising them to the sky as if passing on the gesture to god himself.

We made all haste to the golden city and reached the heavy doors soon enough.

"Oh-ho! Good *Shir* Arfan, your *Maathi* has returned, and I have many things to tell you. Great wonders and things you need to hear!" He banged his fists against the doors.

"*Ai-ye,* you keep that up, and I'll have you skewered where you stand. Alum Above as my witness . . . wait, *Maathi*?" The speaker's tone changed to surprise and recognition. The doors shuddered, and I heard the sounds of heavy bolts being thrown free.

The way opened and we found ourselves staring at a group of heavily armed men. Curved swords—scimitars—flew free of their scabbards. A look past the assembly showed me more of the tribe upon the balconies of the nearest buildings. They had leveled their bows at us—arrows nocked.

The men were on alert. How close were we to war?

The one who'd spoken regarded Khalil with wide eyes. "Most Merciful High. It *is* you. How . . . we saw you . . ."

Khalil didn't miss a beat. "*Zho!* A story it is, and what a one. And I will tell you, but it is all thanks to this one here!" He clapped a hand so hard to my back that I staggered forward and all but forgot how to breathe. Most of the air left my lungs, and whatever thoughts I'd had were thrown clear by the impact.

So I stood, dumbfounded and just as mute, letting the *Maathi* do the talking. He regaled them with most of the story I'd told him, and when he couldn't quite remember the truth of things, he decided to do what many storytellers do: He lied, and filled in the pieces with what sounded best.

Soon, the men stood slack-jawed. But through the conversation, we'd learned only two sets had passed since I vanished beyond the Doors of Midnight. Any longer and I would have risked being unable to return home.

My trial at the Ashram!

I still had time to make it back. Just enough, at least.

Would what I had learned at Enshae's feet be enough? I certainly hoped so. All I had to do was survive a war, continue to practice, and return with the skills to avoid imprisonment.

Or death.

I'd suffered close to both of those already, and had no desire for more.

I was given little time with my thoughts as we were rushed to Arfan. The merchant king occupied a building in the heart of the city. Several of the men I'd seen before—his council—were with him, all resting atop cushions. As were Qimari and Aisha. The two women almost ran to meet me, but stopped short as they cast sidelong looks to the merchant king.

We'd interrupted a war council, and what I heard did not bode well.

Shir Sharaam had taken my display of the bindings as cheating of a sort. Despite the fact my survival was surely a sign from Alum Above that I'd been spared, the desert king felt cheated out of justice for the death of his son.

I couldn't blame him.

War was coming, but not to Iban-Bansuur. The fact blood had already been spilled inside the city had spread far, mostly due to the word Arfan had sent through falcons, informing the various other *Shir*s. Should *Shir* Sharaam try to bring his vengeance within the walls of the hallowed city, the fury of every other desert king would fall on him. And the odds of war would tilt too heavily against him to ever dream of winning.

So he would come for *Shir* Arfan, and for me. He would bring the battle to the desert ahead of us, or at our backs. But so long as we waited in the city, we were safe. Until Sharaam came to box us in. Rather than wait for the other man to dictate the terms of war, Arfan had sent for more of his tribe while I'd been playing student beyond the Doors of Midnight.

We would march soon ahead into the desert and wait. Train. And when the day came, we would fight. And if Alum Above, Most Merciful High, saw it fit, we would live.

Or not . . .

I've often found the judgment of gods to be mercurial at best.

And what was my role in all this to be? Well, that was obvious, wasn't it? Look at it from the perspective of those sitting around me. When last they saw me, I had walked through a storm of arrows, untouched by any. Unstruck. And unharmed.

I'd confronted *Shir* Sharaam face-to-face, and been declared free from judgment by God Himself. No sooner than that had the world fallen into a false midnight—reddened skies washed with violet all behind a darkened eye above us all. The moon and sun had met in embrace, and the Doors of Midnight appeared for all to see. And they watched as I walked through them, only now to return, safely sound, and with stories of Enshae.

If that hadn't been enough, I caught more than a few eyes lingering on my newly improved cloak. Enshae had worked it to be truly a thing out of the old stories. Even if you glanced at it out of the edges of your vision, you couldn't help but wonder if the cloak had more behind it than clever workings and good materials.

It *was* a thing of starlight and diamond dust. Moonlight and crushed pearls. As far as the tales were concerned, and I had no inclination to correct people. Let them assume. After all, the best stories are sometimes the ones we tell ourselves. Never mind the truth.

So I let people stare and whisper soft gossips to each other, and all the while Arfan detailed his plans for the war to come. His eyes never left me as he spoke, and though he never said it, I knew all the things he wished to tell me.

This is your fault. I have many regrets, and welcoming you into my fold is chiefest among them. Should you die in the battle to come, I will find relief.

I didn't voice the thought that should *he* die in battle, he might find some relief that way as well. Instead, I let him continue talking at us, and then the *Maathi* filled him in on what had happened beyond the Doors of Midnight, as best he could remember the story I'd told him.

And what he decided to cobble up to plug the gaps.

Eventually, we'd exhausted all listeners, and Arfan dismissed everyone but me.

Qimari and Aisha gave me long sympathetic stares as they left the room.

Arfan exhaled and reached into the folds of a sleeve to retrieve something. The thin glass vial of white-joy I had seen before. He unstoppered it to drop a bead of liquid onto each eye. The merchant king blinked several times, one tear rolling down the side of his face.

The man blinked again, this time tilting his head back. The color of his eyes clouded, taking on the tinge I'd seen so often in some of the most dangerous men and women on the streets of Keshum.

The Cotton Eyes.

"Tell me what has happened, Ari." His voice held little emotion, giving me no clue as to what hid behind the simple question.

So I did, leaving nothing hidden from him as I had with the *Maathi.*

Arfan listened with the stoic silence only a Cotton Eyes could offer when in the depth of the drug's hold. He watched me like I was half mirage—not really there at all—and half a specter, truly occupying the space before him, but only a shadow of a man once living. Something that had survived after my body failed to return through the Doors of Midnight.

Perhaps he believed no one could have walked back out from that place. Occasionally, he rolled his eyes at something I said, but then they would catch on the edges of my cloak. And I could see him begin to wonder: What if he's actually telling the truth?

By the end, Arfan knew it all. How much he believed? I couldn't say. And he wouldn't tell me. Instead, he asked me a question. The only one that probably mattered in the moment.

"You said she offered you a chance to remain with her. Teach you magics no man could hope to know of."

I nodded.

"What made you come back?"

"What I did here. I couldn't leave you to face the consequences of my actions. And a responsibility back at the Ashram." I met his eyes then, and he held mine. I can't tell you what he saw in me then, but I can share what I gleaned of Arfan.

He was a man of hardness, from a harder life still, and it had taught him early on about the necessary things. How to do them, and how to live with them afterward. I knew a bit of that myself, but still fell far short of this man. And in all that, Arfan saw the world as a game to be played. Every piece had its uses, but some had their perfect uses. The moments to be played—and the times to be sacrificed.

And it is this he wavered over now. My piece. My timing. To be played on the field, or to be sacrificed. The choice to do so would not break him, and he would lose no sleep over my finding a more permanent rest.

But I saw something else behind that. Arfan understood me. He not only knew why I had done what I had to Shareem, but he respected it, even if he couldn't condone it. The weight of his responsibility to his people, and his love for them, could not be ignored. But neither could the other love he held. The one for his daughter. And in doing what I did, I had saved her. He couldn't forget that, and he wouldn't.

That knowing blurred the line between what he knew was best for the tribe, and what he wished in his heart. To preserve the lives of the many by spending just one life—mine. Or to keep the affections of his daughter—ones he'd already strained.

Not an easy choice.

The man finally smiled—all sharp guile and cleverness. "I can respect that, Ari. Admire it, even. Many men do not have that sense of conviction to their beliefs. You could have been free of me—of your debt."

I kept my gaze locked on his. "Maybe, but the sparrows wouldn't be, would they?"

He didn't answer, but the smile deepened. *Shir* Arfan, the merchant king, had gotten to where he had by playing this game of people for many years. And he'd told me as much a time ago. Now he played it again, with my life, and he wasn't a man to lose.

I just had to find a way where we both won.

Because if I didn't, I had no illusions whether my piece would be played . . .

. . . or spent.

"I wish you a good night, Ari. May you wake to find warm sun on your face."

ONE HUNDRED NINETEEN

NAKED TRUTHS

I left Arfan's company and stepped onto the street.

Aisha and Qimari waited for me, along with one more familiar face.

"Shola!" I nearly crossed the distance between us in a full run.

At mention of his name, the cat roused from his deep sleep, quick to fix a look of narrow-eyed displeasure at whomever had the audacity to wake him. He saw me, then decided that I of all people wasn't quite deserving of that level of disdain. So he settled for glowering at me instead. Probably for having left him without my attention for two sets.

I extended my hands and he wriggled free of Qimari's hold to leap into mine. "Thank you for caring for him." Shola added his own appreciation in the form of a low purr against my chest. I stroked his head, helping lull him back to sleep as Aisha reached out to scratch the cat's ears.

"It wasn't any trouble. He was a little prince, weren't you?" She scratched him under his chin, and Shola's face broke into a self-satisfied smile.

"Don't say things like that where he can hear them." I mimed covering his ears with a hand. "It'll go to his head, and then he'll be impossible to be deal with."

Qimari rolled her eyes. "That'll still make him half as much trouble as dealing with any other man."

Aisha laughed.

Shola and I must not have gotten the joke, as neither of us found anything remotely funny about it at all.

Once their laughter subsided, Qimari moved over to me and wrapped me in a tight hug. "We were worried when you . . ." She licked her lips then began again. "Disappeared."

"Through a tear of darkness in the sky, no less." Aisha crossed her arms under her chest, looking me over as if half expecting me to vanish again.

I grinned at that. "I did. And I came back out the same way, after spending one hundred and one nights with Enshae." That might have been the wrong thing to say.

Both women narrowed their eyes at me, and I felt very much like a piece of hide ready to be freshly skinned and tanned to leather. "We heard the *Maathi* tell the story, Ari." Qimari's tone had all the roughness to scour old stone smooth.

If you have ever had the feeling along the nape of your neck that sends your flesh prickling and brings you to the knowing that you are in very real danger, then you'll understand how I felt in that moment. Every animal instinct I'd carried on the streets of Keshum told me that it would be best to change the subject.

So I did.

"What kind of reinforcements are we waiting for? What about *Shir* Sharaam's forces?"

Qimari exhaled, then looked to Aisha.

The warrior reiterated what Arfan had: that Sharaam had decided my survival wasn't the will of god, but devilry of my own doing.

There was truth to that.

And so there would be war. Sharaam's tribe had set hard pace out of the city, heading for one of their smaller, closer camps, only to be on their way back now. They would have added sixty or more to their number—all soldiers.

The figure chilled my blood, as Arfan's company had certainly edged toward that same number of travelers, but they were not all trained to fight. We had the small mercy of remaining in the city, where Sharaam would not attack. But that could only last so long, and the longer we delayed, the greater the chance of being trapped within. A death sentence of another sort. It was a race to leave, to find safety, and get reinforcements first.

My expression must have given away my thoughts, for Qimari placed a hand on my shoulder in comfort. "Father sent for help before *Shir* Sharaam even left. They'll be here any day now."

I arched a brow. "And then what?"

Aisha already had the answer. "Then we go to war, and we pray Alum Above favors us more than *Shir* Sharaam."

A sobering thought.

And it was one that kept us occupied for most of the afternoon as we walked and shared the quiet comfort of each other's company. Shola decided to wriggle free of my hold and saunter behind us at his own pace. The two women eventually led me to a well at the center of the city. It had been fashioned from enameled stone, painted the colors you'd find in a full spring sky or summer seas.

Qimari motioned toward my travel sack and I unslung it. She reached into the bag and found my waterskin, giving it a little shake. "You're lucky you didn't reappear too far away. Another day, even, and you'd have been left without a drop." She worked the pulley and brought up a clay vessel with water. She filled the drinking skin before tossing it back to me.

I thanked her and took a swig. It tasted smoother—cooler than I'd have imagined, and I caught a note of something that edged on citrus. "That's good."

Shola, upon hearing my declaration, decided to leap up to the lip of the well and try to get his own taste in.

Qimari smiled, stopping the cat from falling in, but it was Aisha who moved to take the clay container in hand and explain the story behind the well. "Neither here, nor there, and sometime quite long ago, but not nearly as long as you might think, there was a city." Aisha reached into the vessel with a pair of cupped hands, lifting free some water. She sipped it, slow, drawing out the act of it. Then she offered some to Shola, who lapped it with more enthusiasm than I'd seen him show for a treat of something sweet.

Aisha waited for him to finish before she resumed the story. "And they say the Idhan-barahni had water flowing all across it. Cities of all make and shape floated atop these bright and clean waters, but something happened—a disaster. Alum Above, in his wrath, birthed the sun and it boiled everything away until there was only sand. Only stone. And the memory of salt.

"They say Iban-Bansuur was built in the aftermath of what once was. Something new and fitting for this place of sand and stone, but still, when the first people here dug, they found a promise of what once was. The cleanest of water that all life once rested on. That is why the water here tastes so clean—so cool. And that is why this place is special to us."

At first, I'd been paying too much attention to the story to realize what Aisha had really shared with me. All stories are important, and in all stories lie some truths.

If you know how and where to look.

What she told me then wasn't about the water, or the history of the place. Not in all. What really happened was Aisha choosing to tell me something special that belonged to her tribe. This knowing.

It was not a thing freely told to outsiders.

What it really meant was: Welcome to the tribe.

Aisha clarified why she'd shared that with me a moment later. "You came back." A shadow of doubt bled into her tone.

"You didn't think I would?"

Aisha shrugged and busied herself with lowering the clay vessel into the well. "We didn't even know if you *could* come back. No one would have faulted you if you never returned. You accepted your fate before two *Shir*s and everyone else. I saw you walk past arrow after arrow meant to fell you. And I know some of those archers, Ari. *Shir* Sharaam's warriors are not lax in their practice. Any number of those should have struck you."

But they didn't. I said nothing, however, choosing only to give both women a sliver of a smile. It was something that Shola could have appreciated. Self-satisfied without edging on smug, and utterly belonging to a cat all too content with itself.

She told me how people whispered in the aftermath of my leaving. The stories they turned to—the growing superstition. Mutri devil—demon. A boy meddling with things best left unlearned. Was he even a boy at all?

And then I'd vanished, clean and clear—far from reprisal, and responsibility. And having left others to face the consequences. But then, I returned, knowing what *Shir* Sharaam would do after being denied my death. And now we stood, unsure of when war would come.

Today? Tomorrow? A set from now?

"That is why I told you, Ari. Because you made the choice to act as one of the tribe—maybe more than many ever really do, more than even some born to the tribe. It's not for me to say on them, but I saw you, Ari. I see you now, and you are here, with us." Aisha reached out to grab the collar of my cloak, giving it a firm tug.

"For what you did for Qima as well."

The younger woman shuffled in place almost as if embarrassed, then I realized it for what it was. Qimari met my eyes, and I saw in her the same unease she'd had when facing the reality of what to do about Shareem.

"You could have let her take the blame for Sharaam's shit of a son. You could have done anything, including nothing. But you did not. You took the blame."

"That wasn't too hard. I *did* kill him." I held Qimari's stare, hoping the iron in my voice reminded her that Shareem's death had been my fault. I held the knife, and I had used it, sparing her that.

I hoped.

"And you did it for her. You did what was necessary, no matter how hard."

The necessary thing again. It made me wonder: How often do we do the *necessary* things, time and time again, unaware at the time of doing so? Each time it is in the moment. The new and necessary thing. How long of doing it before it becomes as natural to us as breathing? And where does it lead us then?

I had one answer in my life, and it was not one I liked.

But Aisha didn't let me linger in the thoughts, and in truth, I owed her thanks for that. "For Qima, thank you." She wrapped me tight in a hug before letting go just as quick. "Whatever happens in the days to follow, you are one of us, Ari. I wanted you to know it. And I have."

I thanked her with just a whisper, not able to find the full strength to voice my words.

Qimari moved, then stopped as if self-conscious now that she'd done so. She turned and quietly moved away from us.

I almost spoke, hoping to say something that would keep her there, but she vanished down a street before I could think of anything.

Aisha watched me stare, then sighed. "In some ways she is still raw from everything."

I arched a brow, waiting for her to explain.

She moved to sit on the edge of the well, crossing one of her legs over the other. Shola came to Aisha's side and she reached out to scratch his head idly. "The night with you." Aisha eyed me sideways, but the look held no recrimination in it. "Then what happened the night of the *Saraansar*—our kiss."

"You kissed me."

Aisha's mouth went tight, but a hint of a smile shone through the expression. "I did. And I would again. You know why I did it, but still . . . Qimari, like you, is young. Even if she knows I did it for her good, it will still bother her at times."

I hadn't expected that answer. "She knows?"

Aisha looked at me as if I were every inch the young and clueless boy.

And to be fair, I was exactly that.

"Qima's not an idiot, and she knew what would have happened if she gave you her favor that night. It could have torn the marriage pact apart."

I sat next to Aisha on the well, Shola between us. The cat seemed to get the better end of the deal, reveling in both our affections as we petted him. "Well, I managed to ruin that for everyone anyway."

She exhaled. "Yes, you did. But Qima didn't need to be doing that that night before everyone watching. She has forgiven me, somewhat." Aisha's gaze sank to the ground, and I recognized the look of someone wondering if they were telling themselves a lie.

So I gave Aisha the lie she needed then. One of my hands fell on her shoulder, and I gave her a reassuring squeeze. "I'm sure she has. If anything, she probably hasn't forgiven me for some things . . . though I'll need her help to figure out what those might be."

Aisha threw back her head and laughed. Three full, hearty cries that came right from her belly. Each note was bright, imperfect, and for that, held honest music in it. She covered her mouth in an effort to stop herself, but she failed.

I didn't think what I had said was that funny, but when I gave her a long and searching look, she only fell further into giggling behind her hands.

Finally, she took a breath and sighed. "Oh, perhaps it's better if she doesn't. If she does, then you will have a different problem on your hands. A larger one. If it isn't something she feels is worth mentioning, then consider it something not worth your worry. Most of it, at least."

I opened my mouth, then frowned instead. That didn't make much sense to me, but I got the sense asking further after it wouldn't yield me much of an answer. So I returned to the heart of the matter I'd been getting at before. "I just thought things were getting better between us. I got to see the real her, naked behind the mask, and I thought—"

Aisha let loose a single rolling laugh. "Why? Because you have seen her without her clothes? You think a person's mask falls after their clothes do? Tell me, Ari. What could ever break her heart, truly? What does she yearn for beyond anything else? Tell me the songs she sings when she thinks no one is listening—the ones that bring her to tears. Tell me her favorite story, Ari. The one that her mother told her, and her mother before her. The secret things kept in her heart and between her lips." Aisha smiled, and it was a patient, sympathetic thing.

"Ari, you have seen her without her clothes. And you have touched her then and there. True intimacy is not nakedness of the body, but of the heart. You know as much of her as you do a book you have never opened." She sighed and returned the reassuring gesture I'd given her moments before. A gentle shake of the shoulder. "Perhaps you will get the chance to learn her, though . . . should what happens next go our way. Alum Above, Most Merciful High, I beg you, make it so."

I swallowed what moisture I had in my throat, leaving me hoarse when I spoke. "And what happens next?"

Aisha walked away from the well. "Make sure your arrows are sharp, Ari. You will need them. Make sure your aim is true. You will need it. And make sure you remain: unstruck, unharmed, unfallen. You will be tested."

She was not wrong.

ONE HUNDRED TWENTY

DWELLINGS

Aisha left me, and I returned to my old rooms in the city with Shola in tow. That evening ended in early sleep, by which I mean I got very little. I tossed, I turned—occupied by the distant dream of Enshae and all she'd shared with me.

My restlessness brought me to rummage through my travel sack, pulling free the candle she'd given me. I did not dare light it, but looking at its shape reminded me of something special. A piece of magic out of the old stories—a candle shaped from midnight skies, stardust, and moonlight.

What more could a young boy who dreamed of heroic tales ask for? This was how it worked, you see. The hero always went into a strange land, or crossed into another world, and then came away with the story of the time, but few ever believed him, of course.

That is, until they saw what he returned with. Some object of wonder, usually. A magical cloak. Perhaps a sword, enchanted to cut through anything. Some left with compasses that pointed not to true north, but rather to your heart's desire. Items that could only have been found and made in a world so very much unlike ours.

And my candle was one of these things. I stared at it, wondering just how it would burn when the time came to use it. The thoughts filled me until I finally fell asleep.

When I dreamed, my mind went to different kinds of stories. The ones that had entertained me a great deal when I was younger—and more foolish. The stories of war.

If I'd known then what I would soon come to, I never would have dreamed of them.

"Wake up, Ari." Aisha roused me early the next morning. "We train."

There was little else to be said. *Shir* Sharaam could arrive any moment, so any moment not spent with the bow was one wasted.

Shola followed me as we made our way out onto the dunes. Some of the tribe had been out for over a full candlemark already, already long at practice. Arrow shafts protruded from wooden beams, and where they didn't use those, they had other targets—the bodies of hares and desert rodents hanging from a line between the posts.

Even from a distance, I could tell they'd already been butchered for their meat, but enough remained within their shapes to offer targets, especially to the more skilled archers.

I looked at Aisha, and she caught the meaning behind my stare.

"'Waste not, for the land I have given to you is bountiful for those who know where and how to look. Blessed will be those that reap the full harvest of this place.' Alum, Most Merciful High, left those words, among many others when he gave this place to us."

I arched a brow. "Us?"

Aisha gestured to the tribe. "The first people of Zibrath were not born down south behind sandstone walls, Ari. They were shaped here: from his blood, his breath, and the sand in our skins—our flesh, our color. The night sky in our hair." She pulled her hair, which had been tied into a long braid with red strips of leather. "And this place's warmth—its fire—in our hearts. To live here is no easy thing, but all things are given to those who wish to make this place home. If you want for the same, Ari, you'll have to learn that." She smacked the back of a hand against my chest.

Aisha led me all the way to where the other tribe members were loosing. Once there, she passed me something familiar. A thing made from shadow-dappled shade. Dark. With all the color of blackest sky in its shape.

The black bow.

"You dropped it before passing through the doors in the sky, Ari." Aisha gave the weapon a little waggle. "Remember how to use it? The pointy part goes into your target, not you or me."

I ran my thumb down the length of the bow as Aisha stuck a row of arrows into the sand. Before I could take one, though, she settled into place by my side. The archeress then sent shaft after shaft into targets in a display that could have left any marksman speechless, and someone like me slack-jawed.

She caught my look and explained. "It isn't practice if you're not challenging yourself. You're just going through motions."

I frowned as I pulled one of my own arrows free from the sand. "But that's all you've had me do." My thumb and forefinger pressed against the butt of the shaft as I nocked.

"*I* need the challenge to grow. *You* are sticking to the motions until I am certain you won't turn someone's ass into a porcupine's backside. Namely, mine."

A hint of young man's hubris, as well as opportunity, flooded me then. "I suppose I could always just use some of my dark and terrible magics to do the fighting for me."

That had been the wrong thing to say.

Aisha blinked then turned to face the other archers. "*Qalf!*" The word cracked through the air like thunder striking an old tree—shattering the quiet that had persisted through the desert. Everyone stopped, and all eyes attended Aisha.

"What's wrong?" I half lowered the weapon, releasing some of the pressure I had just begun to apply to the arrow.

Aisha marched over to the target directly in front of me and raised her own weapon. "Shoot me."

"What?" I barely managed to get the word out as I caught myself between sputtering and choking.

"Shoot me." Aisha raised her bow, setting an arrow—her intent clear.

I scrambled, nocking my own, but I couldn't bring myself to draw. "Aisha . . . I can't."

"Do it!" She loosed. The arrow shot toward me with a speed I could not track.

It sailed close by before I had the wits to move out of the way. The kiss of wind in its wake brushed by one of my ears, but it passed me harmlessly by in the end.

"Shoot!"

I fumbled and drew. All of Aisha's training knotted in my mind. My eyes trained on her, and it would have been so simple a thing to release. But my fingers tensed, and the small muscles in my hand trembled.

"Ari, if you do not shoot me, I will shoot you!" To make good on her threat, she pulled free another arrow, nocking it. I knew Aisha to be a woman of her word.

I loosed the arrow, but I didn't have to try to miss her. I could tell you that the shock of her request had ripped my aim to tatters and turned my muscles into water. It was the truth. Part of it, at least. It could have just as easily been the fact that I couldn't bring myself to shoot at her. One, for our friendship. Two, for the role she'd played as my teacher.

And I valued her twice over for each of those things.

I suppose the real truth of the matter was all of those things. And so the shot went free and wild far to one side.

Aisha's . . . did not.

The shaft soared toward me, too quick for me to do anything but watch as it struck me just above the shoulder. The head of the arrow hit the folded material of my cloak, making a sound like stone against glass. I staggered more in shock than from the impact, and watched as the arrow fell away, having done nothing but crack one of the scales. Were the shot an inch more to the right, it would have struck the meat of the muscle that connected my shoulder to my neck. Any closer than that, and it would have cut me along my throat.

For anyone else, that would have been an imperfect shot. But I had seen Aisha strike targets anyone else would struggle to, with all the ease and familiarity of someone walking a well-trodden path. This was a perfect shot. One meant to get my attention, and make a point.

"Again!"

I faltered, bending halfway to pull another arrow, bringing it up just as Aisha had loosed.

This one zipped past on my right, nearly nicking my elbow. I lurched to one side in panic. In doing so, the arrow I'd drawn left the bow, and all with the lame aim and strength to do nothing but arc forward and fall uselessly between the two of us.

Aisha's next shot, as could be expected, tore through the air and nicked the side of my hood.

I moved again, once more too late. My hand went to the right side of my face, mostly in slow reaction to the thought that her shot could have cut my ear had but a gust of wind blown the arrow any closer.

"Hit me, Ari." With that, Aisha took several steps closer to me, bow still raised. Another arrow fell into place, and I didn't need to guess what would happen next. The arrow left faster than I could register.

Whatever understanding I thought I'd achieved of the arrow fled me in the moment. No longer did I have the frame of mind to think about binding the shaft in flight and forcing it aside.

Something batted against my leg and my heart lurched in realization. Shola stood there, idly pawing at me to get my attention. He'd been bathing in the desert sun for most of the exchange between Aisha and me, now choosing to inform me that he was done for the day.

I knelt in the cold grip of fear for my cat's safety, ushering him away with a hand.

The arrow sailed overhead.

"Shola, move. Get out of here!" I gave him a shove that I hoped would send him away. Instead, he decided that I had chosen to play with him, and leapt against my leg, batting at it several times.

Brahm's tits, cat. I swear. The bow left my grip and fell to the ground. I scooped Shola up to hold him to my breast, turning my back to Aisha as I did.

"Hit me, Ari."

Holding Shola finally helped me find the voice I'd buried, and I brought it back to the surface with all the heat of the sands below me. "No." I turned to face her, still cradling Shola in my arms.

Aisha closed the distance, arrow still drawn and leveled to the space above my heart. The perfect shot . . . should she choose to take it.

I took a step of my own and moved to meet her.

"I could shoot you right now and your pretty cloak wouldn't save you, Ari."

I nodded. "You could. And no, it wouldn't. But why?" Shola stirred in my hold and, in doing so, positioned himself before the head of the arrow. The fire of fresh-birthed sun flooded me then, making its way into my stare. I could have turned skin and sinew to ash, sending it sloughing clean from bone with my look, and I knew it.

To her credit, Aisha managed to hold my gaze for several long moments before finally shying away. But her grip never faltered on her weapon, and the arrow never shook—staying steady-still over my heart—over Shola.

"Because of what you said—what you think. It's foolish—dismissive. Look at yourself."

I did, and I couldn't see what it was that she did. Only myself. Only my cat—my friend. Someone I'd rescued from a life all too close to the one I'd once lived. Starving and orphaned. Pariah wherever I went within the city of my own birth.

"What do you think the point of this is?" She nodded at her bow.

I sighed. "Whatever it is, it's not what I said, clearly. I was wrong, Aisha. I'm sorry."

"This is a tool. To survive, to shape our world around us, Ari. And us to it. This is meant to protect, even in war. Not your magics. Not unpredictable things. Something learned—practiced, and that comes with responsibility! What happens if I shoot you right now?"

I tensed and thought of Shola. I am not proud to admit that a flush of renewed fire burned its way through me. Acid seared me, bone and sinew and marrow, bringing a sharpness to my words. "I'll do something worse than I've done to those who've tried to hurt me before, especially the ones I loved."

Her eyes widened at that and, for the first time, the bow shook in her grip. Then I saw it. The thought running through her mind. What Ari was she looking at in the moment? The one behind the rumors all the way from Ghal? Ghost. The one who'd taken root in Mubarath? The one who couldn't be stabbed or pierced. The young boy who'd walked through a storm of arrows and bid them turn aside with but his will and want.

That boy was unnatural. And quite possibly a monster.

But Aisha knew me better than that, and she regained her composure at the same time I realized what I had said.

My mind went to the candle and the flame for the first time since returning to the mortal world. Taciturn coolness took the place of the old kindled fury, and I waited in the calmness of it. "I'm sorry, Aisha." I blew out a breath before answering her question again. "If you shoot, you'll . . . kill my cat. And I don't think that's something you want to do."

She finally lowered the bow. "Yes. And what do you think would happen in a battle, Ari? Do you think you will always find your mark? That you will have the time for one perfect shot? Or rely on magics?"

I shook my head, knowing well enough not to speak.

"I am not training you to be a master marksman in this short time. I am teaching you to be careful and only hit what you set your eyes on so you have less a chance of hurting someone! Hurting one of them." She gestured with a hand to the tribe members watching us.

Remembering that we were not alone, a heat that had nothing to do with the sun filled my cheeks. And if I could have shrunk several sizes to hide within my cloak, I would have.

Aisha had been right to chastise me.

"In the middle of a fight, Ari, you cannot always hope to have true aim. To hit what you wish to, and so it is important you know when and why to shoot. And where *not* to shoot. You cannot afford to be careless with this." She nudged the fallen black bow with one of her feet. "You. Are. Reckless, Ari. If you cannot control this, how can I trust you to control your black magics? How do I know I will be safe near you in battle?"

That particularly stung because I knew it to be true. I could say my quickness to leap into action came from good intentions, and few would be able to deny that, but all the same, those intentions had gotten me into trouble before. And brought others along.

I thought back to how a simple job to steal some gold should have freed the sparrows from a life of theft and allowed me to go on to the Ashram. And I thought of how it had turned out. An unseen noose around the necks of every member of my adopted family, and a golden collar around my own throat. Press-ganged into Arfan's service, which now saw me in the desert. Awaiting a battle that was my fault.

And what it would cost me back at the Ashram. Expulsion . . . or worse.

"I know, Aisha. You're right. And I am sorry, really."

She looked me over, eyeing me with more care than I'd seen her give to her weapons, or any shot she'd taken of late. But whatever she noticed on my face seemed to be enough. She nodded to herself and let out a heavy breath. "I believe you." Then she turned to face the others. "Take practice somewhere else. Leave me with him."

When the *Al-sayidha* of the tribe spoke, everyone listened. Soon, the desert emptied save for Aisha and me. Shola had chosen to be as opportunistic as any clever cat could be and cozied up to another of the tribe members heading back to the city. He hitched a ride in their arms back to the shade and safety of Iban-Bansuur, leaving me to swelter in the heat. Alone.

Little ingrate.

But I didn't have long to dwell on the matter. Aisha promised to work me until I dreamt of clean shots in my sleep, and my muscles only knew the movements of the bow and arrow. Until my arms and back burned hotter than the sands, and begged for relief.

She lived up to her promise.

ONE HUNDRED TWENTY-ONE

TRUST AND JUDGMENTS

Arfan's reinforcements arrived in the days that followed. Some on camels, and at least two dozen with horses. While the former were better suited to the desert climate and offered a higher perch from which to see, if the battle came fast and hard, it wasn't difficult to see the horse would be the better option. And the horses bred by *Shirs* were said to be of a fabled bloodline. Old, and brought to life by Alum himself.

If you believed their stories.

I caught sight of one of them as the men and women filtered into the city. They had coats of oiled shadow—dark as a thing could be, but with a slight shine along their hair. But we were given little time to welcome the arrivals, as Arfan set us to packing as soon as they appeared. Now we left Iban-Bansuur. Its safety, and its holy grounds where blood could not be spilled.

Gushvin the tinker did a brisk business dickering with the newcomers for anything they might need, trading trinkets for coins as fast as a man could think. Alwi and Baba helped him unload various goods to their new owners before retreating into the traveling tradesman's wagon home.

The tinker informed me he had no intention of following us into war. He, and the two children, would stay far clear of it, doing what he did best—collecting things to sell. Stories in this case. And stories of war sold well in the tinker's trade.

My wanderings soon brought me to who I searched for. The merchant king moved through the streets of Iban-Bansuur, inspecting every camel and their packs.

Arfan looked over hooves and pads from camel to horse, and gave orders to make sure each beast received its rest and feed before we set out together. He asked one man to hand him a scimitar broader than any I'd seen before, with all the curve of a broad leaf in its shape. Arfan held the blade out into the sun, looking along its edge, then the dull barrier on the backside of the weapon. Content, he rolled his wrist and sent the sword through a single tumble before passing it back to the man he'd taken it from.

Arfan finally noticed me watching, gave me a grunt of acknowledgment, and never broke his stride.

I waited in silence as he went about his business.

"Horses are strong things, but they can be stubborn. Camels will let you know when something is wrong, but horses will go until they die. They are a gift, and a maddening confusion from Alum Above." Arfan spoke as if the words were for himself, but I couldn't help but think it was his way of having a conversation without directly addressing me.

"They were born of the wind—the first breath Alum Above blew into being before shaping man. For that, they are dark and wild things. Free things. He then wrapped them in shadow, skin and coat"—Arfan patted the side of a horse as dark as what he'd said—"to keep them safe from the worst of the sun. But for all that, some of the horses carry a southern wind within them. It makes them thick-headed." Arfan looked at me out of the corner of his vision, and it carried an unspoken message behind it.

One I recognized was comparing me to those rather stubborn horses. And I couldn't exactly argue the point.

"Their skin gets too hot for them to bear if their rider is careless and doesn't find them good shade to rest under. It's worse if the skin is too cold, though. Their blood loses its quickness, and the horse begins to die. It is a bad thing to see in something so beautiful." He gave the horse an affectionate rub along its snout. Then he patted its backside to gently urge it onward.

"If you survive what is to come, you might look to understand one of these someday." Arfan nodded toward the horse that had just departed. "You might have need of one in future service to me."

I'd wondered about that in my time with Arfan. How long would he keep me in my position, stuck trying to outearn a king's fortune? The answer: as long as he saw fit.

One of my hands balled into a fist, but I released it as quick as that. If the merchant king spotted the gesture, he said nothing about it.

"So, what is it you wish of me, hm?" asked Arfan.

I cleared my throat. "Back when you had me locked away, there was another man in the room with me."

Arfan nodded, but said nothing.

I told him of what I'd heard about the prisoner. That no one could get any information from him. I, however, had managed to trade stories with him.

Arfan perked up at this.

I gave him just the barest shape of the truth. That I'd told the prisoner the story of my life, leaving out the details of the Ashura—of Koli. And Arfan took away the real reason I brought this conversation up. My desire to speak to the prisoner again.

Arfan exhaled, then nodded more to himself than me. "I see. And you wish to know if he is still here?" He didn't wait for my reaction. "Yes, he has remained in the city. And the madman has even kept to his cell. When we leave Iban-Bansuur, he will be given food and water enough to make his way somewhere reasonable. Rhabia, or back to Zibrath. I care not."

I arched a brow at that.

"You've heard the stories of this place by now, and its meaning—the promise to shelter all men. *All.* I hold to that promise. But war is coming, and I will not tarry any longer to see us trapped within. So if you wish to speak to this man, you should do so before the day ends. Because when it does, you are mine again, and we leave to find *Shir* Sharaam, and see whose swords are sharper—and arrows quicker."

There wasn't much to say to something as grim as that, so I left to find Nassih.

The stranger in the white cloak and robes remained exactly where I'd left him, resting against one of the walls of his cell.

He raised his head and looked at me, but I still saw nothing within the raised hood he wore. "You've returned."

I set my staff against the door and sank to my haunches to at least regard the man at eye level. "I have."

"Mm. And where did you go, if I can ask?" I couldn't quite make it out, but his tone hinted he already knew the answer to his question.

All the same, I gave him the truth. "You won't believe me but—"

Nassih laughed, and it was a thing full, rich, and rolling. "You'll find I can believe a great many things, Ari. Go on, tell me."

Then it drubbed me with the weight of stone and force of thunder. "You said my name the last time we were together."

Nassih's head tilted to one side, but he remained silent.

"I never told you my name."

If I could have seen inside that hood of his, I imagined I'd find him smiling. "No, you didn't. But you wouldn't have had to for me to glean it." He raised a hand and reached inside the hood to tap it against his masked face, probably at his nose.

This is what Maathi had done when I first met him, and then something similar had happened to me in Ampur with the Nagh-lokh. An ability to somehow take in information—knowings—never shared aloud. Being able to understand parts of something's story, and sometimes all of it.

"I see your cloak has a brighter shine to it. A man might wonder what brought that about." Once again, he'd said the words as if he already knew what had happened.

And once again I told him the truth anyways. "The sun and moon met in the sky at the same time." I watched Nassih for his reaction, but he gave me none, so I continued. "A doorway opened in the heavens and I . . . walked through it." Still, Nassih gave no sign of disbelief or awe. "I met Enshae and—"

The silent man stirred. Nothing dramatic, just a visible straightening of his posture. His shoulders squared, and for a man who wouldn't show his face, he made the tenseness in it plain for me to see. Hood or no.

"She turned some of my company into animals, including Arfan's *Maathi.*"

"But you survived, clearly."

I pinched a piece of my cloak and pulled it for him to better see. "I did, and I walked away with my cloak touched by her hand, and her magic." This did not impress Nassih, nor get the reaction I had been hoping for.

I heard him swallow and his head lowered, gaze perhaps shifting to his own white cloak. "What did you have to give her for it? How long did you speak with her?"

"Nothing. Well, no, that's not true."

"What did you give her, Ari?" Nassih stood. He actually stood, and in doing so, I realized how the man would tower over me even if I got to my own feet.

"Stories. I traded her stories. One for each night she didn't turn me into something. I never told her their endings, though. That's how I kept the game going."

Nassih exhaled and sank back against the wall as if the act of suddenly standing took the last of his strength away. "Clever." The word left him with the weak air of a man who'd run too hard. "How long passed in her domain?"

"One hundred and one nights."

"A long time. Long enough for her to tell you many things."

I nodded. "And teach me. Or, well, try to, at any rate. She didn't know of the bindings, at least by that name. She talked of shapings, and songs."

"No, she wouldn't have." He didn't bother to elaborate. "She's an old thing. A clever one."

"She told me about her history, and how she'd been wrongfully imprisoned. I think in the end we almost became friends."

Nassih tilted his head. "Be very careful, Ari, when making judgments about those locked away and the 'why's behind them. There are reasons for such things, and be doubly careful about believing what you hear from those behind those doors."

I bristled at that. Enshae had been a damn sight clearer with me than Nassih had, and both happened to be locked away. "What about you, then? You ended up in this room, unable to leave. Should I trust you?"

Nassih stared at me, and a stillness grew between us. But as he continued watching me, something cold and prickling took over my body. Something I hadn't felt since being orphaned on the streets of Keshum.

The fear that turns your joints hard and blood to snow-cooled slurry. A look of chilled lightning and old fire. I became painfully aware of my own heartbeat, even up to my ears where it drummed. An animal instinct rose in me that told me to run from Nassih. To be anywhere other than in this closed room with him.

But the look abated, and with it, the maddening craze that had taken me over.

I exhaled, feeling as if I could finally breathe after being drowned in emotion.

"I suppose I have earned that comment. I haven't answered many of your questions, have I?"

I shook my head.

"You asked about the Ashura before."

I nodded.

"Then let me give you this piece of advice. When I leave, Ari, come with me. If you stay with Arfan, you will surely meet the Ashura again, and that is not something you are ready for."

To a young man, quick to anger, and quicker still to set after vengeance, he couldn't have set me on their heels any better than if he had pointed a finger where to go.

"Where? When? How?" The words left me faster than an arrow in flight. "What do you know about them, Nassih?"

He sighed. "Leave Arfan. Come back with me."

"Come back with you where?"

Nassih rose again and looked out through the barred window. "To somewhere you can learn to use your talents properly. And maybe learn to cool that hot head of yours."

An option to leave, but once again it came at the promise of a stranger. Enshae had made me an offer to stay, and it would have given me everything I wanted. In theory, anyways. And now Nassih gave me a competing one. To go with him.

Traveling with Nassih meant forgoing my trial at the Ashram. And so, I would never be allowed back there again.

It seemed no matter the choice I was offered, I would lose the Ashram as a result.

And leave the merchant king to do battle for something that was my fault. It would also leave the sparrows at Arfan's mercy.

I couldn't walk away from people again. I had done enough of that in my life. So I shook my head, not trusting myself to speak.

Nassih let out another breath of resignation. "I thought as much. Then take another piece of advice before we part ways.

"One day, if you come across them, remember this old rhyme, hm?

> *"When come they demons—ash and ember*
> *On clouds of reddest smoke*
> *With cries of rain*

And sounds of thunder
Two things man must remember
White Hokh's sacrifice,
must burn fast and quick,
to cast Ashura asunder."

Something in how he said it brought me to pause. The word "oak." He'd stumbled over it and spoken it softer than he should have, and all with an emphasis that made it sound more like "hokh." I corrected him on it.

"It's oak . . . the children's rhyme uses the word 'oak.'"

He gave a short and mirthless laugh. "Does it now?"

I inclined my head.

"Well, I suppose stories and rhymes change over time. All the same, do yourself, and me, a favor and remember it the way I told you as well, hm?"

I made the same silent gesture again, letting him know that I would.

"Good. Now you should leave. We both have preparations to make, and our own paths to walk. Yours will see you your way, and mine, mine."

I almost thought to ask him where exactly his path lay, but something about the way Nassih's head hung low told me that the question better remained shut behind my teeth. And so it was.

I left the odd white-cloaked man alone in his prison, and set about packing my belongings for the trip back out into the desert.

And toward *Shir* Sharaam's waiting forces.

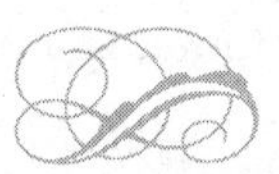

ONE HUNDRED TWENTY-TWO

SANDS AND PRAYERS

We wasted little time setting out into the desert. Evening hadn't quite set in, so what remained of the sun brought the candlecast glow of orange and bronze to the roofs of the city. A parting beauty, and I found myself missing it until we set up camp for that night.

"Black sands! Black sands!" came the cry.

Everyone moved with age-old fluency, quickly uprooting camp. No one rested near any patch of black sands, for what you saw on the surface was ever only the slightest hint of what hid beneath. And all it took was the thrown embers from a pipe, or newly lit fire, to set the sands ablaze. Once that happened, there was no telling how far the inferno would spread.

Or how long it would burn.

We journeyed onward till we were certain we'd found sands clear of the dangerous substance. Camp set again, I left Shola to rest before restlessly wandering the grounds until I came to a tent I'd grown familiar with.

Arfan's.

The flickering of candlelight, and stooped shadow in motion, told me that the merchant king found sleep as easily as myself. Which is to say not at all.

I parted the flap and entered.

The smell struck me first. The scent of warm wood with a hint of floral notes. The slightest promise of spice, and just a touch of musk. I caught sight of the source as wisps of smoke curled out from a stone bowl. A pile of stones, all the soft washed pink found in lotus flowers, burned in that container. A longer look revealed that they were not small rocks, but pieces of resin. Incense.

Three candles shone on a stand, dripping wax onto brass holders. Arfan sat on his knees, facing the long tapered pieces of wax and burning incense. A plush rug was his only cushion. His eyes were closed and hands joined. I couldn't hear the words on his lips, but his mouth moved as if whispering to himself.

"It's rude to disturb a man at prayer, Ari."

I froze, fumbling for words. My time in Mubarath had led me to cross paths with people in prayer before, but I had paid them little mind. I myself have never been religious, though I can afford people respect for theirs. And I've certainly found myself performing the desperate man's last-moment prayers before.

I watched the merchant king, noting how his rug had been set at an odd angle, pointing toward the corner of his tent. Then I realized the direction in which he faced.

Iban-Bansuur. The city we'd left behind. There must have been a reason for it, though I knew there were better times to ask why than in the midst of a man's prayer. So I waited for Arfan to finish.

The *Shir* pressed his palms to his breast, holding them against his heart, all while muttering something too low for me to hear. Then he brought the tips of his fingers to his lips, kissed his flesh, and raised them overhead as if for god to see. "I thank you for not interrupting me, Ari." His eyes remained shut, and he didn't turn to face me as he spoke.

"I didn't know you were . . ."

"Devout?"

I shook my head. I had known that much about Arfan, but not that he regularly engaged in prayer. Most of our conversations had happened outside the times he must have chosen to have his moment with Alum.

Arfan sighed and turned on the carpet to face me, finally opening his eyes to meet mine. "Every man needs a guide, Ari. More so with a life like this." He gestured to the tent and all inside it.

"I thought you had the stars for that." I had spoken literally, but I knew that was not what Arfan referred to.

He inclined his head. "We do have those for guides. But they only guide us to our destination."

"Isn't that what matters? Getting to where you want to be? If the stars do that much for you, what need is there for anything else?"

"Like God?" Arfan arched a brow.

Or a god. But I kept that thought to myself.

"Do you think it is the destination that always matters? That there is any destination on this plane of life that matters at all?"

I opened my mouth, then stopped short.

Arfan continued at my lack of reply. "A man has need of a guide that has nothing to do with where to go in life, but rather *how* to get there. And I do not mean the paths on which he walks. It is in the manner in which he carries himself on the journey. Do you understand?"

I did, and nodded to let him know.

"It is my faith in Alum, and his teachings, that better me as a man. A leader. I cannot bring my people—my family—to the best of what life offers us without Alum. Without that guidance. I can lead them to water, yes. But how does one know who should share in that water? What of the laws of the desert? They have their ways, but Alum shaped it all. Do I live only by the rule of the desert—the strongest survives? Or do I follow the path Alum has left for me, that every man under my care is mine to shepherd. More so the nonbelievers who come into my care." He gave me a knowing look.

"If I were to live my life the way many do, I would be racing to a destination I could not find. And in doing so, I would never savor the pleasures of moments meant to be lived. I wouldn't know *how* to live them. Alum has given me that. I know *why* I do what I do as a *Shir*, as a father, and as a man. Do you?"

I didn't have a response to that.

Arfan searched me with his stare and must have come to some conclusion because he nodded. Though, whatever it was he saw in me, he kept it to himself. "Do you wish to know what I prayed for?"

I felt it polite to play along. "Yes."

Arfan rose and went over to the candles. He licked a thumb and forefinger and pinched one of the wicks to stifle its flame. "I prayed that Alum grant us his watchful eye and protection in the battle to come. That should any of mine fall, they fall in glory, and that they know peace. Both in dying, and in the life to come after death. I asked for our aim to be true, and our cause truer still. And I asked for my daughter to be safe." He gave me a sideways look. Another bulb of flame winked out of existence.

"I hope she stays safe too." It was all I could bring myself to say, but it was the truth. It is a hard thing to hope for in battle, but easy enough to ask for. And all men will have something they wish for on the eve of battle.

Arfan looked back at me as he brought his fingers to his mouth. He licked them again, but did not put the last candle out. "Tell me, Ari, do you pray?"

"Sometimes, when I'm desperate enough." I smiled.

"But you've had moments you wished someone would hear you, even if your wishes were kept silent at heart? You've hoped for help." The last one was not a question.

I nodded.

"We're heading toward war, Ari. So I suggest you find someone to pray to. And if you cannot do that, then at least find something to pray for. Most people decide too late to ask for help. A wise man asks for help before the moment arrives when he needs it most. And if you are wrong, then you have lost nothing but some words said to empty space and skies. But if you are right . . ." He didn't finish, and he didn't need to. The message was abundantly clear.

"Find something to pray for, Ari. *Before* you find yourself facing another storm of arrows." Arfan touched the last candle, and its flame winked out.

I returned to my bed too late into the dark to do anything but fall unconscious. But I managed to fight off the call of sleep just a bit longer to tend to something else I had been thinking of. I pulled out the candle gifted to me by Enshae and touched my fingers to the wick. I entered the folds of my mind, though I knew there was no cause to.

It simply felt right.

I envisioned a flame springing to life, then mirrored the image again. The world inside my mind glowed bright with candle flame, quickly shown through four folds. Soon enough, eight.

Heat blossomed between my fingers and I released my hold on the candlewick. But my mind remained seated in the folds, slowly easing its way out of each one until only emptiness remained. When I opened my eyes, the candle burned a color that made me wish I'd remained in the darkness after the folds.

The color was the red of fresh spilled blood. The shade of my nightmares, and odd smoke filtering from a burning building.

My throat tightened, but I remembered why I had lit the thing in the first place. Arfan's words echoed through me, and I thought then of who to call to.

Alum Above? I supposed it could be said that he had spared me my fate at Sharaam's judgment. But that wasn't wholly true. I had done that. With Brahm's bindings, of course.

So then did I ask Brahm for his help?

What did I value and wish for?

The answer came with my next breath. Stories, and more importantly, the heroes within them. The ones I wished to be like, all so I could have the power to do what they did: protect the ones I cared for, and to stop the monsters of the world.

So I prayed to them: Tarun Twice Born, Brahm the Wanderer, Sakhan the Pirate Prince. I prayed to Naathiya, the one shepherding miscreants like myself, who oversaw the Asir.

I prayed for the power to end the battle, however that might be, and the wiles to survive it. To see my friends safely through it, and Arfan sated by its conclusion. And perhaps I had a prayer all for myself. I prayed for glory.

Foolish thing to pray for.

But as I have learned, a fool's prayers are often answered.

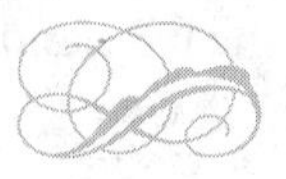

ONE HUNDRED TWENTY-THREE

DRUMS, FIRE, THUNDER

We set out hard the next morning after packing camp. I would like to tell you that we sang songs and traded light gossip. But no such thing happened.

The mood had all the somberness of darkening storm clouds, and I supposed it would, because we all knew where we were riding. And it was toward no pleasant thing.

Talk of battle was on every pair of lips. All eyes scanned the horizon with a tiring wariness—the thoughts of ambush, riders over the dunes.

A surprise patch of black sands forced us into detour once again, drawing tired grumbles from our numbers. But it led me to wonder just how much of the viscous substance lay under these grounds. How much black danger did these golden grains hide?

And could every night I lay my head down to sleep be my last, resting above something as volatile as a barrel of white-joy?

The silence eventually reached the point of being unbearable. At least for me. I could think of no greater curse than to be beset with the utter stillness of the desert, and the quiet that came with it. So I sought to break it.

I nudged Anedi ahead until I reached Arfan. The merchant king noticed me, giving me a look that invited the question he knew I must have had.

And so I asked. At first, where we were heading.

He told me, "Ahead."

I asked him our plan to confront *Shir* Sharaam. The when and how of it.

He gave me an answer as cryptic and simple as before.

Strangling a man is a terrible thing, and it's rather a difficult one at that when they're taller than you and atop a camel. That being said, I will not hide the fact that all my training of imagination and folds suddenly turned to the task of visualizing that very scene. And I figured it would look a lot like this: myself, arm locked around Arfan's neck, all while several dozen of the best archers in the world decided to take their practice for the day in a target that shockingly resembled my backside.

Arfan sighed and rubbed a folded cloth along his brow. Then he told me the terrible truth of our situation. He had no idea where *Shir* Sharaam would be, only that it was an inevitability to come across him. But we had to leave the city; if we did not, we'd be forced to fight with it at our back. And that was a terrible situation to be in. Worse if we were driven to retreat into it. To hide within the sacred city then was to mark us as cowards. A look at Arfan told me then he would have rather died than be labeled as such.

All I was left with was the heaviest question in my heart. So I asked it. "Do you think we will win?"

And he gave me the answer I feared. "Only Alum Above knows. It is by his will."

"Black sands!" The cry came from ahead of us, and a chorus of groans echoed at our backs. We would have to take another detour, and we had already been in our saddles long enough today that my ass had flattened into near nonexistence.

How much of this damnable stuff is out there?

Arfan displayed no outward discontent at the delay. Instead, he told me of the other considerations for our battle, and how *Shir* Sharaam had lost favor with the other *Shir*s for his actions and words.

More to the point, they were out there, somewhere unseen, marching with their men. You see, the other *Shir*s would not let our battle happen unwatched. They planned to be present, to ensure no one violated the laws of Alum Above—whatever those happened to be.

It wasn't unheard of for one *Shir* to come to the aid of another during battle. But I only heard the uncertainty of what could happen if they chose to side with Sharaam. Would we be swept away under the tide of trampling horses and desert warriors? Our blood nothing but a morning's veneer of red over bronze sands until it was swept away by time and the wind.

Nothing would be left of us. Not even memory.

Arfan wiped more sweat from his brow. "But we will meet them regardless. Many things can be said about me, Ari. My daughter has said them, my tribe has, as you have told me. But it will never be said that I am a godless man. That I have strayed from Alum Above, Most Merciful High. Whatever I do, however others see it, never let it be said my hand and heart are not led by God Himself." With those words, Arfan told me more about himself than anything he'd ever said before.

I had watched him, cold and calculating. Exacting a razor's edge of cunning and maneuvering with my own life, as well as the lives of others. Ruthless. And yet, he managed to justify this in service of his god. The greater good, as far as he saw it.

But how did one square that kind of behavior with being so devout? Could you?

And it was that which prompted me to ask my next question. "Couldn't you send the man you sent after me to deal with *Shir* Sharaam?"

Arfan clicked his tongue. "Ah, Azrim. No, Ari. I would not use a Rashin for this purpose. They are talented men and women, but to send one to *deal* with another *Shir* is *dighar*." His brow furrowed and he thought for a moment before giving me another look. "There is no clean word for that in Trader's Tongue. But it is ungodly." Arfan made it clear the definition still fell far short of the depth of wrongness in such an act.

But I took enough of the meaning from it. "It's fine to send this sort of person after me, though?"

Arfan barked out a short laugh. "Ari, you owe me a debt that most men could never even dream to pay back. Yes. I will see that repaid from you, one way or another. And you are no *Shir*. You have no blood to speak of. No title. No power. Do not act as if you do." The words were not meant to cut me, nor insult me. When Arfan spoke, he did so from a place of having all the things he pointed out I lacked.

"And you are clever, I have seen this myself. And you are dangerous. A clever, dangerous man is not one to take lightly. So, yes, I sent a shadow to you to make my position clear. My power. I wanted to see how you reacted to his provocations. I did. And I learned." Again that cunning smile took his face.

I opened my mouth to speak, but a rider on horseback came in at speed, slowing as they approached.

"*Shir* Arfan." They placed a hand over their heart, then the hollow of their throat.

The merchant king's mouth drew a thin line and he turned away from me. "What is it?"

"*Shir* Sharaam's men have been seen. Over a day's ride from here, but we will be on them soon enough. We could cross them in the night." Each word came labored, though I couldn't tell if it was from exertion or fear.

Arfan stroked his chin, looking toward the horizon. The clouds seemed to blacken as the merchant king looked on them. Not a sign of anything other than we would in fact see a storm. "We will be riding the long way around. Black sands."

The horse rider nodded then motioned in the direction they'd come. "If we travel around the ridge"—they gestured to where they meant—"we can come back onto the path to *Shir* Sharaam's men, Most High willing."

Arfan nodded. "Ride out and see the others return, then join us as well. We stay together now, and we meet them together. I will call for *kurtif* when we cross paths. Then we will decide what happens next."

The rider urged their horse to backpedal a few steps as they bowed. Then they turned their mount and rode back off they way they'd come.

"Well, it seems you have your answers, Ari. We will see them soon enough. And I hope you have learned as much from Aisha of the bow as you have your strange teachings at the Ashram. Because we will have need of both those things soon."

So do I.

So. Do. I.

Arfan led the caravan to where we would settle for the night, and eventually, where the fate of the tribe would come to be decided.

❧

Evening passed us by with an early setting of the sun, and it did not leave without a sign. Its color had lost much of its copper warm brightness and bled into the color of a child's hot anger. A red deep as freshly spilled blood. As far as omens went, it was all rather storybook.

Night soon came. We had no fires this evening, keeping ourselves to the shadowed company of the dark itself. And in it, I confess I found some safety—a comfort. After all, a thief is never more at home than in the dark.

Aisha joined me, sitting in silence as she sharpened her knife. After a few more passes along her blade, she turned to her bow. Her mouth pressed together before she reached to one side and retrieved another of the same weapon.

Only the color of this bow could have taken in all the shades of the night in its making. So black a thing it defied description. To fully appreciate the depth, simply imagine the deepest color you can think of. Something so far gone into blackness that no other color could ever hope to shine against it. Then you will have some understanding of the thing.

Aisha turned it over in her grip before passing it over to me. "Sleep with it tonight. Tomorrow, you will likely need it."

I said nothing, accepting the weapon with a polite bow of my head.

Aisha exhaled. "A rider in the night. *Shir* Sharaam's forces are a short march from here. Too close to take them any longer than a morning's ride to reach us. *Mejai* Arfan has sent a rider to ask for *kurtif,* and the *Shir* must at least send reply. He can deny the meeting, but it would not look well when the other *Shir*s learn of this." Aisha ran a hand along the length of her bow, giving it a longer look.

"We will be riding to see them shortly. Are you ready?"

I blinked, and nearly let go of the black bow. "*We?*"

Aisha pointed to her chest. "Me"—she jabbed a finger my way—"you, Qimari, and the *Maathi,* and *Mejai* Arfan. *We* will be present at the *kurtif* between them. Witnesses."

I didn't linger with Aisha long after that, making my way back to my tent and packing some of my things for the ride. Low prowling thunder made itself known through the camp, and I looked to the sky, only to find it had come from much closer to the ground.

Drums. They beat slow and steady, all to a meter I couldn't make sense of. The sounds loudened by the moment, almost falling in tandem with every step I took. It quickened my blood, both in fear and excitement, and I understood the nature of the drumming then.

This was for every person who could not find sleep this night. This was to set them to the edge most needed before they went to battle. And as simple a thing as it was, it worked.

I stood straighter and felt my heart join the thunderous tempo as I retrieved my staff and fastened the Arasmus knife to my side.

I saddled Anedi and rode out to where Aisha had made camp. She'd been waiting for me and led the way to join Arfan and Qimari. Unlike us, the merchant king had chosen a horse for his mount. He looked at us, then to the other side at a rider closing in.

The man waved from atop his camel. "*Zho!* Good *Mejai* Arfan, are you sure this is the right idea?"

Arfan spat to one side. "Do I think it is a wise thing? I am not sure. Is it the right thing?" He sighed. "Under Alum Above's laws, yes. I think that."

The *Maathi* pursed his lips, then nodded in silence.

And that set the tone for our ride. The world around us adopted a somber silence.

No grains of sand stirred, and the wind settled itself. The desert was motionless. Almost. A lone candle bulb flickered to life behind us every time I turned to look.

Just a lone flame held in the grip of someone needing its light. And I only had eyes for that fire.

I found comfort in the sight. I saw the shape of the flame whose image I'd first learned to hold in my mind under Mahrab. I saw the warm hearth of The Fireside back in Ghal. A night of celebration with my friends after being promoted in the Ashram. And I saw the brazier from which I had first bound fire.

The last images of flames soon took root in my mind, and I gave them the space for it. I fell into the folds as we journeyed to the meeting between *Shirs*. No bindings came to me in that time, of course. That hadn't been the point. I simply felt the fire calling to me—a comfort, and I welcomed it.

So, first two folds. Then four. The usual image exercise until I had worked my way to the old twenty I had once been so proud of.

We reached a large lone tent lit by a pair of burning braziers, dismounted our camels, and tied them to nearby posts set for that purpose.

Arfan gave us a long measuring look before heading toward the tent. One of his hands fell to the hilt of his sword, and for a moment, I thought he would draw it before entering.

How would that have played out? I saw the merchant king, in a fit of fury, realize that this was the cleanest way to end all this, and rush into the tent to take matters into his own hands. And the head of *Shir* Sharaam.

But his touch left the weapon as he parted the opening to the tent.

Qimari and Aisha followed close behind with the *Maathi* stopping to gesture for me to go ahead. I shook my head, wanting a moment to myself. Khalil understood and went inside. My chest tightened and my pulse quickened.

A thousand thoughts went through me, most of them worries. You can likely imagine them given what I had done.

So I took a breath and stilled myself. Soon after, I found my heart, and entered the tent.

All the while I hoped no one else would try to find mine.

The interior was furnished simply. A large rug, the color of dark wine and ruby, had been set out. Piles of cushions littered the place. Three oil lamps burned, casting their soft orange glow on the already red-touched room. A silver bowl had been placed between where we stood and the party that was already seated. It was filled with an assortment of slivered almonds and pistachios atop a bed of dried fruits. A heaping dollop of thick goat's cream rested over that, and it was crowned in a syrup made from what looked like palm sugar.

My tongue may have begun working against the back of my teeth at this point.

Shir Sharaam rose to his feet. He wore a long robe of purest white that hung to his ankles. No adornments, his hair let loose. The set of his mouth matched his jaw, thin and severe as a blade.

His own *Al-Sayidha* sat to one side, his *Maathi* on the other. Both men however had dressed much as they had when our parties had traveled together.

Shir Sharaam took each of Arfan's party in. His eyes went to Qimari, but quickly passed her by. He dismissed Khalil just as easily, giving the longest of the looks to Aisha. The stare spoke of respect as well as consideration of threat. Both things said something for her.

But I had been wrong on who would receive the longest look from *Shir* Sharaam.

Me.

Whatever passed behind his eyes when regarding Aisha left to be replaced by something singular: hatred.

A kind of heat I have only ever felt once, and it threatened to take me from the inside. The bone-bitter and biting fury of a child who had watched his cat be thrown to the fire, just after having his binder's cane broken.

The *Shir*'s anger could have cut me less were it knives. So heavy a hate did he have for me. I felt it more than the lingering warmth of the braziers we'd passed. It threatened to blister my skin.

But it passed as *Shir* Sharaam returned his attention to Arfan. "There are many things that should be different tonight. You bring your daughter here." The man's eyes darted to an empty spot beside his group. "My son should be here as well. This should not be a *kurtif*, but a wedding."

Arfan said nothing.

"But that you would bring *him* here." Sharaam's eyes flicked to me.

I stiffened, and Aisha's hand quickly found mine, taking it in a tight hold. I understood her concern, and her want for me to remain still. So I did.

"You do not come to talk in good faith. You come to spit, and to reopen wounds. You bring him here to see me angry?" *Shir* Sharaam took a step toward us, his feet coming to the side of the silver bowl.

"My *Shir*"—his *Maathi* stood—". . . you almost knocked over the *rathif*." The man gestured toward the mountain of sweets.

I didn't know the significance of the meal during this meeting, but the way the *Maathi* spoke made me think his comment had been more a mask while trying to draw *Shir* Sharaam's attention.

The *Shir* composed himself and flashed me another look. Short, but just as sharp as the one before. Then he motioned for us to sit.

We did, Aisha still keeping her hold on my wrist.

The *Shir*'s hand fell to the hilt of a curved dagger fastened to his hip, and I wondered if he were as devout a man as Arfan.

A tension hung between our groups, too thin to see, like fine-drawn wire. But the weight of it touched our chests, and pulled every person forward, leaning close as if all ready to get to our feet at the first sign of trouble. Arfan broke the unease by reaching toward the silver bowl, never once looking up to see if someone would use that moment to strike at him.

He either had that much confidence in himself, or believed *Shir* Sharaam would honor whatever rules the *kurtif* asked of those in attendance.

The merchant king took what looked like a dried apricot, making sure to get some of the sugar drizzle, and plopped it into his mouth. He chewed, drawing out the action as if trying to irritate the other party. "I hoped you would be willing to talk, *Shir*." Arfan's voice held only sincerity for the man threatening him with war.

"You asked for a *kurtif*, and I have given you one. If you wished to talk, you should not have brought my son's murderer." Another quick look my way. Another motion of the hand that brought it to the dagger on his waist. And another sharp sliver of hatred. Though this one went unsaid, I heard it all the same: *If I could kill you now, I would.*

I almost wondered why the man didn't. *Unless Arfan's presence keeps you safe.*

Arfan reached out and this time took hold of a single pistachio, rolling it between his fingers before eating it. "You were there, as were your most trusted. You saw what we did, did you not? Ari met your judgment before all eyes. And you could not strike him down, Alum Above his witness. The Most Merciful High spared him."

Shir Sharaam wracked his throat, building up the moisture that made it clear he would spit. But one look at his *Maathi*, and he reconsidered it. "Alum Above isn't the one who lost his son. What do you want, *Shir* Arfan?"

The merchant scooped up a palm's worth of the sweets, passing them to Qimari. His daughter shook her head, then accepted after her father eyed her. "I wish to speak, to stop something that will bring both our tribes pain that can be avoided."

Shir Sharaam opened his mouth, and I saw the muscles in his neck pulsate. His hands flexed, and I knew what he would say before he spoke. Only, he never got the chance. His own *Maathi* held him by the wrist and decided to take control of the conversation.

"My *Shir* understands the importance of a *kurtif* and will respect it. But you can understand what it is to lose a child." The man's eyes fell on Qimari, and for a moment, the firelight burned brighter in the brown of them. It made them a color closer to gold, though with all the warmth from the carpets and lamps, the same shade shone in his skin as well. "It is not an easy thing to bear, and my *Shir* is well within the law to take what he feels owed by the sword. He cannot pass judgment again on this one"—the *Maathi*'s stare fell on me—"but he can seek it from your tribe."

The *Maathi* reached out and took some of the fruits himself, taking the time to chew through each piece before continuing. "All of your tribe, *Shir* Arfan. And this blood feud is long and old enough that none of the other *Shir*s will think much of it."

Arfan grunted. "I remember our history well. Do not lecture me on things that my father's father told me himself." The merchant king turned his attention back to his counterpart and the other *Shir*. "What would it take for you to stop this? We had a chance for something beyond ourselves—something better for our children."

This appeal had been a mistake. *Shir* Sharaam lunged and struck the bowl, upending its contents onto the rug. "*Our* children are no longer a future for me to think on. Only my son's blood debt. You want to know what you can give me?" His eyes fell on me then, and my stomach sank far below the surface of the sands.

Arfan gave me a stare just as long and heavy as *Shir* Sharaam's. "And if I give you him?"

I turned to face him. "What?"

Qimari got to her knees and rounded on the merchant king. "Father!"

Aisha, however, remained the dutiful *Al-sayidha*, though her hands betrayed her. One clenched hard against the fabric of her pants, and I could see the effort going into keeping her mouth a perfect and neutral mask.

Arfan held up his hand for silence. "What happens after I give you the boy? Do you stop with him?" He shook his head. "I have known you a long time. The boy's death would only quiet your anger for a short passing. Then you would be out for my blood again, *Shir* Sharaam. I gave you the boy before, and he walked away without a scratch. That was by God's will. If you wish for a second chance, then you will have to take him." Arfan did not add gravel or stone to his voice. There was no false showing of strength or intimidation.

No. When the merchant king spoke, he did so as if stating well-known fact. As if saying the sun would rise tomorrow. He meant for the other *Shir* to try his hand in taking me by force, and Arfan would meet him on the field over it.

"I had hoped I could offer something that would help even someone like you find some measure of peace, Sharaam." The lack of honorific in Arfan's words didn't go unnoticed.

Shir Sharaam's *Maathi* leaned forward, but the *Shir* held him back. "I will see you tomorrow, then. I wish you good rest, and pray that you wake to warm sands, and to find yourself still living." He rose and inclined his head.

Arfan mirrored the gesture. Qimari and Aisha followed suit. Khalil and I managed to trail just behind in what I hoped did not come off as rude lateness. "I wish you the same." Arfan turned and left the tent. Everyone else followed, but when I made my move to leave, a hand fell on my wrist.

It gripped me tight and whirled me back around. I stood face to face with *Shir* Sharaam.

"I will look for you on the sands, boy. If you are lucky, maybe Alum Above will preserve you." *Shir* Sharaam gave me a smile that made it clear he hoped I would be anything but lucky.

I have an aversion to many things, but bullying is among my greatest. I cannot abide those with power who leverage it against those smaller than them. The less fortunate. The weak. Perhaps it stems from my upbringing as one of the Sullied. Maybe it has to do with my time as a sparrow.

Or perhaps it's simpler than that. I have known what it is like to be helpless and alone, and I know what it is like to be able to help people. I have done my best to do the latter. I have failed at times, but never let it be said I haven't tried.

So I gripped the *Shir*'s wrist back in kind. A mad thing to do, really, but I have been mad before.

I looked him in the eye with the heat to make all the red and fires in the room seem weak in comparison. "He already has. Or have you forgotten? You tried to kill me, and I turned your arrows away. But I'll give you some advice, *Shir.* If you come looking for me on the field, you'll find me. But you will wish you hadn't." I broke free from his grip.

But his *Maathi* gave me a stare that drove all of my newfound bravado from me. It was a golden-shone smile all held in the eyes. Bright as polished copper, and speaking of danger. The look of a wolf come across an easy meal.

I shook it from my head as I turned and left.

Arfan asked me what had happened, and I told him most of the truth. Just that I had been threatened. He had expected as much. And he told me to sleep well when we returned to our tents, for we would wake to ride into battle.

Thunder rumbled overhead, signaling a storm to come.

It broke out as we reached our camp.

An ill omen.

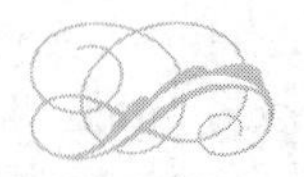

ONE HUNDRED TWENTY-FOUR

The Gates of Hell

I found little sleep that night and turned back to the candle gifted to me by Enshae. It sparked to life with ease, and I watched its fire. My mind went first to the candle and the flame. The old exercise helped me clear my thoughts before I turned to the folds. A piece of me returned to the Ashram then—the memory of what awaited me. My trial, my chance to prove myself. Or find myself banished from the place that held the secrets of the ten bindings all men must know.

Shola stirred in his sleep, casting a look toward the entrance of my tent. His chest shook and he let loose a low and undulating *mrowl.* A sound of clear discontent.

That pulled me out of my focused state. "What is it?"

Shola rose to his feet, back arching and the noise in his throat deepening.

"Stay here, not that you'll listen." I grabbed the candle by its body, accidently knocking over its base. *Brahm's tits.* I didn't bother collecting the metal rest, choosing to grip the wax pillar the same way I had when training with Enshae.

I found my knife and fastened it to my hip. Next, I grabbed the black bow that Aisha had left with me as well as the quiver of arrows, fastening both things to hang from my back. By no means was I anything close to a marksman, but I could land a shot when I needed to. Lastly came my staff, resting comfortably in my grip. So with candle, cloak, and cane, I headed outside.

The camp remained as still and silent as you could imagine in the dead of night. Not a person stirred, and even the wind felt compelled to respect that. No breeze. No movement.

The moon shone full overhead. Bright as polished pearl and without a stroke of cloud to obscure her shape.

I walked from my tent toward the next one, moving with care as not to upset the balance of the candle resting on my open palm. A line of pressure, all with the sensation of fine sand along skin, ran down the nape of my neck. Familiar, and the old wary sign of someone following me.

Now I returned to being a sparrow. Fear-driven awareness took me and I turned in time to catch the figure stalking me through the shadows.

They wore clothes well-suited for the dark. Black robes that seemed to turn away even the blood-tinged light of my candle. Their face remained shrouded behind a veil the same color as their outfit, leaving only their eyes to meet mine. A length of silver sat in their right hand.

A *fulifquar*—forked blade. Curved much like a scimitar, its tip had been split down the middle to give the head of the weapon two points. I never understood the practical purpose of it, and still don't to this day. But it certainly made the sword appear all the more foreign to me, and for that, twice as frightening.

My staff fell to the ground and the Arasmus knife came to my hand. It rested there as a comfort, though I knew in truth it offered me little. What training I'd had so long ago had been for swords, not daggers. And while my weapon might have been the better fashioned, the stranger had the advantage in reach, and likely training.

"It would have been better were you found sleeping. A quiet death. The rest of you will meet Alum Above peacefully. I will give you that much." The man lunged, weapon blurring in an overhead arc.

I don't know what possessed me to move as I did, but I pivoted, positioning the candle between the attacker and myself.

They paused, regarding the odd pillar of dark wax. The bulb of bright red flame gave off smoke the same color, and for a moment, the man's eyes widened. I realized then what he must have been thinking.

The Ashura, Ajuura—*bhaalghul*. Different by name in these parts, but the stories were the same. And they raised the same fears. Had he heard of what happened to the city of Iban-Bansuur? Bleeding stone and not a sane soul left to tell the tale? The marks of fire, and red smoke in the sky?

But the moment was all I needed.

I moved, hoping that surprise would serve me best.

The man's body snapped back as if he'd been struck. He arched, then staggered to one side in an effort to turn. It mattered little, however. The head of an arrow protruded from his breast, and a second soon followed, coming to rest so close to the first that no man could survive such a thing. He fell to the ground an instant later and proved me right.

Aisha stood several dozen feet behind the corpse, bow drawn. She hadn't bothered donning the heavier clothing worn by tribe members during the day. Instead, she wore pajamas of loose cotton, and a shirt much the same. Her quiver hung from her hip, not her back, and she'd fastened both a knife and a sword to her other side. "Rashin?"

She crossed the distance between us then brought the tip of her boot against the body, turning it over. "No. One of *Shir* Sharaam's tribe." Her mouth worked into a snarl and she spat to one side. "To attack a tribe at night . . . in our sleep? It's . . . it's not done. It is *dighar*."

A heat took her and manifested in her eyes—their browns smoldering like coals. "Wake everyone. This is no small, quiet thing. This was the first move of battle!" Aisha didn't wait for me to follow her instructions, taking to crying the warning herself. Some roused, shambling from tents in confusion. Others remained fast asleep. One of her hands crashed into my chest, nearly toppling the candle from my hand. "Move, Ari! Wake anyone who isn't already on their feet with a bow in hand."

I blinked, working my way out of the stupor. "Right. What do I do after that?"

Aisha waved a hand back toward my tent. "Stay safe and don't draw any attention to yourself. Leave this to those who can fight." An arrow came into her hand with the speed and smoothness of magic, resting nocked in place. But she hadn't drawn.

I bristled and my hand gripped tighter to the Arasmus knife. "I can fight. You've seen me."

Aisha nodded to the ground and I followed her stare to see my staff. "You dropped that and pulled your knife in panic. You traded a longer weapon for a shorter. You were scared, and you were not thinking properly. You're not ready for this. Go back."

I opened my mouth to protest but Aisha had no ears for me. She turned and continued shouting to rouse the tribe.

More men and women bled into the camp, and they moved with blades drawn. Some with arrows pulled fast to be loosed. The enemy had come in full.

I had no intention of hiding in my tent while others paid the price for my actions. So I sheathed the knife, retrieved my staff, and added a cry of my own to the night. My voice echoed as I screamed for people to wake and fight. And my feet carried me until the ground gave way beneath me.

I sank for a step and quickly pulled my foot free, staring at the sands below. A small crater in the grains continued to deepen, and something seeped out from below. Something black as pitch.

Brahm's blood. Black sands. The rains earlier must have washed them deeper below the surface until all the moisture had been absorbed. Now that it had, the viscous substance rose back toward the surface and threatened to break through.

The very flammable viscous surface.

More of the tribe had come to their senses and taken arms. Sword met sword, and riders on horseback aimed their bows. Arrows lanced the air as much as screams. Silver flashed, and orange sparked.

All the while everyone stood atop something as volatile as a keg of white-joy . . . waiting to burst at the first hint of flame. The whole camp, friend and enemy alike, would be nothing but dying embers within a candlemark should the sands catch fire.

Candle. The thought roused me and brought my attention to the mote of reddened flame from Enshae's gift. "Brahm's tits." I nearly dropped my staff in fumbling to put out the candle.

"Ari!" The cry stopped me in my motions and I turned toward the source.

Qimari raised her bow my way, and I opened my mouth to scream in protest. An arrow shot forth.

I whirled in panic only to see the arrow sail harmlessly by toward an oncoming horse. The rider of said mount had their blade raised, and bore down on me with a speed that signaled one thing. They would use that momentum to send their scimitar through my neck.

And should that happen, my body would tumble to the ground, my candle along with it. The same sands that currently hid the blackened danger beneath. Thus everyone would share a cremation.

"Black sands!" I let the words carry far into the night, drowning out any of the sounds of battle. The butt of my staff jabbed the ground where I had seen some of the dark substance pooling. I hoped the motion would draw the rider's attention and signal the danger.

It worked . . . in part.

They reined their horse to slow, and the animal faltered, stepping from side to side in confusion as their rider fought to retain control.

I seized the opportunity and lunged forward. My staff arced through the air, and I wondered for a moment just how much momentum it had stored over all this time. My mind triggered of the minor bindings I'd inscribed so long ago, releasing a fraction of the energy within the binder's cane.

The rider flew from his horse. The sounds from the blow and his body told me that he had cracked several limbs. He didn't have the strength to writhe, and I imagined the air had been driven from his lungs.

I took a step forward, reaching out toward the horse with the head of my staff. It rested against the creature's face and I leaned in. "*Ksthi-bhaag. Ksthi-bhaag. Ch-ch.* Hey, now." The horse calmed itself and snuffed the air in what could have been frustration or disdain.

"It's all right. You're all right." I moved to the creature's flank, tapping it with my staff, and urged it to leave. "Go on. Get out of here. *Bhaag. Bhaag.*" I can't say how I knew this, but when the horse traded looks with me, I had the feeling that it understood me perfectly. Not my tone, nor my simple motions telling it to flee.

No, it had taken my full meaning to heart. All my fears and want for it to leave. And it heeded them. The horse turned, nearly bowling me over with its bulk before breaking into the best run it could manage over the sands.

Qimari opened her mouth to speak, but her eyes widened and she nocked another arrow. She drew. And released.

It lanced the man who I'd knocked down moments earlier, driving the last of his breath from him. He had been struggling to his knees, to quite possibly use what strength he had left to try one last time to end me.

"Ari, what's wrong with you?" Qimari closed the distance and one of her hands tensed, betraying the desire to slap me, perhaps. She instead reached out and clenched the collar of my cloak tight. "You're going to get yourself killed. Pay attention!" The flat of her hand bounced off my head, trying to jar some sense into me.

I shook that off and motioned instead to where I had been before. "Black sands."

She shook her head. "You can curse later. Come with me."

"No, Qimari, look!" I moved past her to raise my candle above the ground I'd stepped on. The red glow managed to bring to light the darkened mass forming in the sands below.

A quiet string of prayer left Qimari's mouth. "Most Merciful . . . How much is there? How far does it go?"

"Is there such a thing as just one patch of black sands?"

She gave me a look that implied the question had been idiotic.

I swallowed. "Then I guess there's enough of it for it to be a problem."

Qimari shoved me aside, and it took all my effort not to lose hold of my candle. She blurred, letting loose another arrow. Its shaft sank into a rider on camelback. "Put out that damn thing before you cook us all, then."

More riders poured into the camp, and some of Arfan's tribe rode out to meet them. Bodies clashed as much as weapons as some were dismounted. People wrestled—tangled limbs vying for control before sheathing a blade in someone's flesh. Arrows arced and whistled through the air.

Qimari slapped my side. "Tell everyone about the sands, maybe we can still stop this. If not . . . may the Most Merciful preserve us." She rushed away from me to join the fray.

Someone screamed and I rounded about to find a trio of swordsmen storming the tents nearest me.

I echoed a cry of my own and moved to meet them.

One of them turned, bringing their sword around. The attacker sent the blade through a whirling flourish likely meant to disorient me, but I remembered something from long ago, and a man who moved with a dancer's grace.

Don't keep your eyes on the sword, but the arm. Vithum, the old choreographer from the theater, brought his words to life through my mind. And I heeded them.

The black-clad tribesman moved forward, a shadow in night—silver flashing out.

My staff met the blade and I triggered the binding, this time releasing all of the stored force. The sword bit into the wood, but the force within passed into the blade. A sound like stone striking old glass filled the air. The weapon did not bow or bend. It shattered, the hilt tearing free of the assailant's hold just as the same momentum carried through my staff, threatening to do the same.

My arm ached from the effort to keep hold of my cane, but I did. Another swing sent the head of the instrument crashing into the tribesman's skull. A second followed for good measure. And since all folktales speak of the magic of threes, I struck them again.

They crumbled to the ground and the pair who had been with them now gave me looks weighed with more caution than before.

I could see the thoughts running behind their eyes. The stories they must have heard through *Shir* Sharaam's camp. The boy with the cloak of pearled moonlight. The child who'd stopped a storm of arrows with his hand and but a few words from his lips. The one who'd vanished through a doorway in the sky. Someone who could shatter a sword with but a strike.

One of them turned a fleeting look to the candle in my hand. Some of its wax had melted and trickled to solidify along the base. A touch more had gone as far as settling against my palm, almost fixing the pillar crafted of Shaen magic to my skin. But it was the light and smoke that held the attacker's eyes.

The shadow of a monstrous smile showed on my face, and a terrible thought came with it. "When the candle smoke goes all red, and stone weeps the blood of the dead."

Both of the attackers stiffened. One took a step back.

I moved forward in tandem, extending the hand with the candle flame. "Ashura-Ajuura."

The pair exchanged a look with one another, and then they made the best decision they possibly could have. They turned and ran from the demon out of story.

I exhaled, taking a moment to catch my breath and still my quickening heart. My mind fell into the candle and the flame—a wakeful version of the exercise lest I lose myself and sooner still lose my head to a passing swordsman on horseback.

A coolness filled me that certainly shouldn't have in the midst of battle, and I leaned into it, using the clarity to refocus myself.

The battle was now told to the song of singing steel and crying arrows. Bodies collided, some fell. And through it all, the ground ran as red as my candle flame and smoke.

I swallowed, remembering the fire. The black sands. The cry took me again and I shared it for all to hear. "Black sands! Brahm's tits and ashes. Black sands!" But no one had the ears to hear me.

Khalil, the *Maathi* of Arfan's tribe, ran through the mess to my side. "*Zho,* boy. *Zho!* Away! What is wrong with you, ah?" He took hold of my staff arm, but didn't pull. "You are no warrior. Come with me, Ari. This is madness."

"Will you promise me something?"

Khalil frowned but bobbed his head. "Yes, anything, my friend. What is it? *Zho,* and tell me quick!"

"Go to my tent, take my sack and Shola. I don't care about anything else. Just take them and go!"

Khalil met my stare, and I knew then that I had the weight of stone in my look, for he shied away and muttered something under his breath. But he left, and he rushed to do as I asked.

And then the world around me took on the faint glow of distant flashing stars. The shimmerant color of brightest pearlent shine found in the better white of my cloak. The working Enshae had laid within the garment. A warning.

A sign of the Ashura.

Another rider came into view, and I recognized him. The *Maathi* of *Shir* Sharaam's tribe. The man had drawn a sword unlike those around him. A blade I had seen before. One burned into my memories.

Something shaped from finest steel to a tapered point, silver bright, and with the shine of pale moonlight. An edgeless needle—impractical—yet it could run a man through with the ease of great blades from stories. And it proved this a moment later.

One of Arfan's men charged the opposing *Maathi* on foot, brandishing their curved blade. They leapt. Brilliant silver danced—it arced. There was a song. And it was cut short as the needle sword plunged deep into the man's chest to pierce through his other side. The *Maathi* ripped the blade free, casting its point back in a quick slash along the man's throat. Flecks of red took to the air.

I watched the motions in silence, remembering such movement from a time years ago. And when I finally found the courage to look at the man's face, it too came from old memory.

But the worst of it lay in the man's eyes. They shone a color found in the treasure of kings. They burned bright. And they held the burnished light of gold.

Thunder rumbled despite no sign of storm or darkened clouds. Then they came overhead in a blackened rush, and the moon slowly slipped from view.

The *Maathi*—Koli—met my stare with the smile of a wolf finding a wounded hart. "Little sparrow to desert hare now, hm?" He nudged his horse into a slow walk toward me.

The ground sank under the beast's hooves with every step, protesting its weight.

Or something else. The truth of the situation struck me then. But a coldness unknown to me for years seized me. It was a hand with all the ice of Ampur, gripping my heart tight. It threatened to squeeze the breath from me, and turn my blood to stone. It promised to root me in place until Koli crossed the distance and showed me just how sharp that needle of his truly was.

I don't know where the words came from, but the question left me regardless. "What are you doing here?" A whisper, something so soft it could not hope to be heard by anything other than a storybook demon.

"Me? I am playing a game, little one. A most dangerous game. The longest kind. Playing with a story, and a puppet on strings. And you? You have been chasing me a long time." Koli snapped his teeth in the air. "Biting at my heels. And now you have found me. What now, little one? What now, little binder?"

At those words something else flickered to life inside me. The memories of Brahm. Brahm the Wanderer. The one who'd birthed fire and passed it to man. The one who'd given us the ten bindings all men must know. Fire.

Fire. The word blossomed in me as if it were the only one I knew.

"Do you mean to kill me?" The words left Koli as if he wasn't sure whether to laugh, or wonder over the madness of attempting such a thing.

"Yes." All I could say, but it was enough. Every piece of desert grit and grain filled my voice. Every portion of unbearable heat the sun above had to offer our days. And every bit of hatred a young man could carry within.

My staff fell to my side and I drew the Arasmus knife.

"And what will you do with that, ah?" Koli came closer. All the while the battle worsened. Men and women moved now like wraiths—shadow-hamed and cast dark across the campsite. And the tide spoke one message most clear: We were losing.

"I'll kill you."

Koli threw back his head and laughed. When he looked at me next, the fire in his eyes brightened, and they burned a better gold than ever before. Thunder cracked again, and lightning followed in its wake. Then came the storm.

And I found the one hidden deep inside me.

The flame from stories. The fires kept to memory and old heartache. Every piece of burning light I'd laid my eyes upon, both in truth, and in the lessons from Rishi Ibrahm.

The fires of an imprisoned Shaen woman. The flames of Enshae's teachings.

All the quiet contemplation of candle flame and oil lamps. The wrath of a young boy before a burning brazier, just about to lose his kitten.

I called on all of it. My mind tipped into the folds, and the most horrible of thoughts I could dare to dream found me. A promise followed it, and it was one I had held deep in my heart for the longest of times.

I would end Koli, and I would do so following in the footsteps of Brahm. The candle in my hand weighed heavier, and the bright red flame sang to me then. And I heard its story.

I Listened. And I gave into it.

The flame spread through my mind, every fold quickly overtaken by the hellish brightness of orange and tonal reds. I screamed a word for all to hear. "Whent!" I thought of the sands where Koli walked, and what lay beneath them. Under us all. "I'll kill you. I'll make you burn." And I spoke the last word of the binding then. "Go to hell—ern!"

The candlelight flickered as if dying out. The glow dimmed.

But the fire had taken root somewhere else. Somewhere deep within me. And it flickered bright. It screamed. And it burst back to life, larger than before. A pillar of flame screamed from the head of the candle and moved to my will.

A lance of brilliant light raced from Enshae's gift and struck the ground.

The black sands.

And the desert burst into flames.

Torrents of waves, brilliant-bright—incarnadine—leapt from the earth, twisting along unseen paths wherever buried pools of black sands hid. Tents fell under the fresh wash of fire. Broad swathes threatened to overtake Koli, but the Ashura remained unperturbed.

Fresh rain hammered the ground, but it would not stem what I had birthed.

And the fire grew. And with it, its will.

My cloak blazed in a whiteness unmatched.

I burned, the whole fire of a fresh-forged star laid low upon the ground. The silver bright of best-white starlight. My cloak and I shone unmatched, carrying all the magic of a Shaen story. A lone candle in the dark, against the monsters of the night. A white flame in rebuke of the Ashura, thrumming in incandescent fury—the burning eye within the greater inferno around me.

Fire takes me in its hold—whole-tight as once before. But I remember, and this time, I welcome it. It fills me with a heat that sears me blood and bone. Flesh and sinew. It touches the heart of me, and my marrow. It brings to breath a scream I cannot let loose and so it stays in the core of me, building, fanning greater to billow a flame that will take me should I not find release.

I hold it still, letting it grow to flood the folds of my mind until there is but one color for the whole canvas. The color of nightmares. The shades of hate given full-form and lighting the desert aflame.

But the fire wishes for more than what I can give. It takes and takes and takes. First tents known to me, then soon the bodies of invaders come into the camp. It takes their clothes. Then their flesh. It takes their screams, and soon their breath. But it has one thing to give. And it gives them this then.

It gives them death.

But when that is not enough, it takes more from them still. It comes for their blood, breath, and their bones. There will be nothing left of them but ash, and in the morning it too will be gone. The fire will take them all, even the memories of them.

It is hungry, and there is no amount of giving that will sate it.

The storm deepens and strikes the sky and ground with the sound of thunder. But it beats twice as loud inside me. I let loose the scream built large and share it for all to hear.

"I'll kill you!" The folds of my mind find new shape, and it is that of Koli come under waves of fire.

And the fire obeys.

But it asks a toll. One I cannot pay. And if I try, it will take me as it has taken those already turning to smoke and burning shadow. And I hear the echoed words of another, and they are a warning, and they are a lesson.

Rishi Ibrahm's words from the last time the fire threatened to take me so.

I remember them, and I enact them. I Listen.

The folds of my mind showed me the walls of flame within me, but I willed them smaller. Wished them to dwindle as if they no longer had the will to burn in full. They shrank—grew further from me, and so from my heart. No more did the intense heat race through me and threaten to take my body, and my mind.

The fire dimmed until it resembled the small bulb of candle flame. But it was enough. And I held to that. The ties to the inferno around me died, and I freed myself from their fury.

But the fire I'd kindled in the black sands still raged, and they took the camp. And the ground. There was no respite from their touch. No span of land spared their hate. And no flesh granted safety from their hunger.

A body burst through a row of hellish orange. They screamed. They flailed—then quickly fell to spasming. And then they did not move any longer.

But it was not the body I had wished to see burning.

A touch of lucidity returned to me and I whipped around to search for Koli. The storm continued to hammer down, but it could not quiet the enflamed black sands, so hot did they burn.

"Koli!" My cry carried far, but no one paid it any mind.

"Black sands!" Someone finally managed to give voice to my warning from earlier.

Another took it up. "Black sands! Run!"

Someone screamed for Alum. Others followed. Tribes didn't matter, only survival.

I moved through weaving bands of flame, still deep in the folds of my mind, though no longer trying to contend with the will of fire. Instead, I'd turned to something else.

I hadn't meant to, but I had fallen into the exercise Enshae had drilled into me for most of our one hundred and one nights together. The outermost edges of the flames called to me. They pressed against the very edge of my atham, the space I occupied outside my physical self. And I felt their weight and desire against my Athir—my binder's faith.

I welcomed them in part, but I refused to let them cross that space. Only ever to brush against it much like the gentle touch of a friend. And I walked through the fires.

I picked my way through milder fires, brushed aside by my cloak and my Athir. It was as if the flames themselves guided me through these gentler paths.

An unseen current leading me.

A gentle flow of all things.

I moved unburned, watching as shadows grew streaked with bands of light only to die out.

But no sign of Koli.

I screamed for him again. "Koli!" But nothing. The candle continued to burn. My source of light. And my link to the fires around me. The seat of my binding.

The knife grew heavy in my hand and so I sheathed it. A figure raced ahead on horseback, their arm working to send something scything through the air. Its shape remained obscured through the smoke and storm as much as the fires. It took me a longer moment to realize the movements as those of a sword in action. Some of the blackened clouds thinned and I caught sight of who rode ahead of me.

Shir Sharaam.

My hands moved and the candle finally left my palm, bits of wax peeling away from my skin as the crafted gift fell. I had no eyes for it as it struck the sand. The black bow had already come off my shoulder and now rested in my grip.

Had the rain slickened the string so much that I wouldn't be able to manage a decent shot? Or had the heat of the flames spared it that fate? I didn't know, and couldn't until I took the risk to shoot.

An arrow came to hand, quick as thought, and I found myself pointing with an index finger as I nocked. A simple motion and the shaft had been drawn. I could end all of this with just a single arrow.

The one to find the heart of man.

I loosed, and the arrow took flight.

And an arrow struck home.

One. Perfect. Shot.

Shir Sharaam was taken in his side, the shaft piercing his ribs deep into his heart. The tribal leader had just enough time to turn in my direction and focus his eyes on the person who'd sent the arrow. His look fell on me and we held each other's stares before he tumbled from his horse.

The rain hadn't dimmed the fires, but it had cut through some of the smoke. Enough that the remaining members of both tribes could see what had happened, and who had fallen.

Screams broke out through the burning campgrounds. Some for victory, and just as many in despair.

But the fires screamed loudest still. And everyone continued to run.

I shouldered my bow, turning to look to my side at the one who'd made the perfect shot.

Aisha ran toward me, her chest rising from the effort she put herself through, and doubly so with the hot acrid air around us. "Ari." She raised a thin scarf over her mouth before coughing into it. "What is wrong with you? Why are you lingering . . ." She trailed off and noticed what lay at my feet.

I followed her stare to the candle lingering there. Its head still clung to the once kindled flame. I knelt, retrieving it and holding it in one hand as before.

"The fires . . . did you . . . ?" She didn't finish her question.

But I answered all the same. "A binding. I'm still in it, I think." The words left me like an echo—distant, hollow. I remained deep in my folds and continued to walk while Aisha tried to force me into running. "Where is their *Maathi*?"

"What?" She looked at me as if I'd lost my senses. "What are you on about? Ari, we need to leave, now! The battle is done, and we need to get to the other *Shirs*. They are probably watching close by. They can offer us aid until we can get back to Iban-Bansuur." She placed a hand on my collar, trying to tug me along.

But I slipped free of her hold. "Where is Sharaam's *Maathi*? I need to find him."

"He's gone, Ari. If he has any sense to him, he is gone." She pulled again and I found myself slowly moving in her wake.

Gone? Had the torrent of fire taken him? No. Of course not. I had tried something like that before and Koli had survived. But I hadn't seen him after the wave had washed over him, had I?

Could even an Ashura survive a binding of fire such as that?

I'd finally found Koli after so long, and once again, he'd slipped out of my clutches. I'd summoned a storm of fire, tried to burn him whole—and now he was gone without a sign.

Again.

It brought a needle's point to my gut, my mind, and my heart. Piercing bright pain that manifested soon as grinding teeth. A new ache, and a new fury. Enshae had warned me. Nassih had offered me new teachings. And I'd ignored them both.

As a result, Koli bested me.

The realization threatened to silence my connection to the folds—still my mind, and whatever power I'd brought to bear.

"Come. On." Aisha smacked the side of my head, nearly snapping me from the folds altogether. "Help me find a way out."

Her urgings drove me deeper into the space of my mind and I returned to the exercise I'd been taught. I wasn't holding the fire in a space above me so much as a space around me. My atham thrummed against the flames and I just knew where they would be.

I moved accordingly, leading Aisha through their shifting paths until we came to the end of the battleground.

Other members of both tribes limped and lurched out to safety, leaving all of their anger and blood feuds back in the only place that had the space for them. The burning sands.

All eyes turned to the inferno, and then they turned to me.

The boy who still held a candle of burning red in his hand. With smoke billowing from its head the same shade. The color of nightmares. The color of demons.

Of the Ashura.

And the firelight was not the only glow that night. My cloak shone as bright as fresh moonbeams and polished pearls.

Mouths moved and they made familiar shapes. I could guess what some of them were saying, but soon, I didn't need to.

"I saw him. He called the fire," said one.

Another pointed to the flames we'd left behind. "I saw him, and he didn't call a thing. He opened a door. The ground itself opened and hell came through those doors. He opened the gates to hell."

Another voice uttered a prayer. "Alum Above, preserve. Oh, God. Most Merciful. Most High." Others followed through.

Someone stumbled through the inferno, kicking off one of their boots now wreathed in flames. They stamped it clean and gave it a long look before noticing the crowd ahead of them. "*Shir* Sharaam is dead!" Their voice carried over the desert and through the storm.

Someone pointed my way. "It was him. I saw him walking through the flames, not a one touching him. And I saw him make the shot at the *Shir*!" Another looked at the fire, then agreed with the speaker. Several voices followed.

And after all, why not? They had witnessed me perform a binding. A spark, really, but a flicker of fire is enough to call up a storm to swallow the desert whole. At least when you happen to be standing atop a large pool of extremely flammable substance, that is. But it didn't matter. They had witnessed me make the binding, and then control a piece of that fire for just long enough.

I opened my mouth to speak the truth of the shot, however. But my mind grew heavy, and the folds required more of me than what I had left to give. So I shut them down, one by one, until only darkness remained.

And then that too took me.

ONE HUNDRED TWENTY-FIVE

SCAPEGOAT

"Leave him be. Who knows what devilry he might bring about if he wakes." A man's voice. Then the sound of rustling clothing, then flesh striking flesh. Someone fought to restrain another by what I heard. "I said leave him be." The speaker wracked his throat and spat.

"I saw it myself. Alum Above as my witness. I was there. The boy walked through a storm of arrows we'd shot at him. Not a one touched him!" This woman's voice carried as much ash in its grit as it did smoke. Likely all from the fire.

"Alum spared him twice. I saw him over a candlemark ago in the fires. He called Saithaan himself. I heard him. The boy conjured a devil in the sands and opened the gates of hell. Why else would those fires still be burning?" Another man now, all with the same fire-touched voice as the one before.

Another man coughed and added his own piece to the story. "Glass. I saw it.

Some of the sands turned to glass before my feet. Smooth and hard. What kind of fire burns that hot?"

Black sands. I smiled at the realization.

"None of the fires touched him. He walked through them. I saw it. Alum Above, I saw it. Him and that candle of his. He held it in his hand and walked. Through. The fires—*unburned*!"

My smile widened. *Like Tarun Twice Born.* Then I sank back into much needed sleep.

Somewhere between the darkness of nearly dying, and close to proper wakefulness, my mind floated on a sea of placid black. With it came thoughts I wished hadn't at all.

Memory of the night before. Of fires burning deep and bright—blood-tinged smoke like when a theater burned so long ago. A sword of needle-sharp—woven-moonlit promise. And the demon amidst it all.

Koli.

He had survived somehow. I knew it in my bones the way animals know when the sky will break into storm. What had he said? He was playing a long and dangerous game. And I'd been chasing him all the while—all without a clue. But I'd learned many things.

Enshae had been right, as had Nassih. I wasn't ready to fight the Ashura. A cold and sobering lesson that drove all remaining fire out of me, and left me feeling like a young boy whose home had just burned down.

I had thought myself strong enough. Cleverer by far.

And I had been wrong.

But the next time I faced Koli, I'd be ready.

I remembered what Enshae had taught me: The Ashura had been changing their stories over time and distance. Hiding their truths. And I, being the reckless one I was, had been chasing all the wrong sorts of tales. The whispers—gossip-mongering, and what had been recorded wrongly for who knows how long. But somewhere out there were the true stories of the Ashura. Their first. And what could be found could be locked away, according to Enshae.

So there *was* a way to stop the Ashura.

To kill them.

To kill Koli.

"*Zho! Zho.* Ari, you have me thinking you are going to be sleeping until the next doors in the sky, ah? Wake." The words were punctuated by a pair of hands shaking me by the shoulders harder than any man should ever have the right to do to another. Especially when they are well within the depths of their own sleep.

Men have been killed for less. . . .

I groaned and blinked my eyes open. A lance of golden brightness drew a pained gasp from me as I shut them again. "Brahm's blood and tits, what time is it?"

"Alum Above knows, my friend. No one is keeping candles or count now, ah? Not after yesterday." The voice sobered, and I realized who'd been speaking.

"Khalil?"

"*Zho!* But of course. You did not think me foolish enough to be dying in that mess, ah?" A finger and thumb reached out to take hold of one of my earlobes and tugged.

"Ow." I shook free of his touch and rose halfway.

The ground beneath me slowly slid away from the sledge on which I lay. It had been fastened with thick ropes to a familiar wagon home I hadn't seen since departing Iban-Bansuur.

"Gushvin?"

My friend the *Maathi* placed a hand on my forehead and nodded. "*Ayam*. The good tinker came with the other *Shir*s." Khalil leaned close and dropped his voice to a conspiratorial whisper. "Though I am much thinking that the tinker was given a good offer, ah? The goodest kind that is at the end of a sharp sword. The *Shir*s must have promised him a longer life for bringing his wagon here, and his goods. There is much need for a tinker's many trinkets on the sands. *Zho,* this is true."

I snorted, then regretted the action. My nostrils felt as if they'd been rubbed down with rough sand, then spent a night inhaling smoke. I suppose that was close enough to what had actually happened. My throat ached and I wondered if its lining had cracked from the strain.

The *Maathi* had anticipated my struggles and fetched a skin, giving it a vigorous shake. He unstoppered it and brought its mouth to mine. "*Zho.* Drink, and slowly, friend. Too much and you will drown on your own thirst, *ayam*?"

I moved to take a sip before the smell of the drink struck me. "What is it?" I coughed, wishing I hadn't. My throat burned.

"Mostly water."

"Mostly" is what I'm worried about.

"It is palm sugar, and its water too. Pinch of pink salt, good for the dryness. This I know and promise." He pressed it to my lips again and I drank. "Oh, and there is some camel urine, of course. Very good for the—"

My throat seized and I tried to spit out the vile concoction, but the *Maathi* burst into laughter and pressed me back into my litter. "A joke! Ha! And good *Shir* Arfan is only thinking I am good for this, ah?" He tapped a finger to his temple. "But I am twice as good with the humor." He patted his generous belly.

I swallowed the drink and narrowed my eyes at him. "Khalil, wit and wisdom come from the same place." I touched my head much as he had.

He motioned me off with his hand, making it clear he disagreed. "No-no. Laughter comes from here." He pressed back against his stomach and let out a rolling laugh, drawing attention to how his belly moved as he did. "See? Never forget this. Laughter is buried deep here, and that is why you must let it out, or it gets too big—too heavy, if it sits too long in a man. Then he forgets how to free it. And he can only ever know sadness. That is not a good thing. Too many men die from such a thing, Ari." He gave me a reassuring pat.

I knew enough not to argue with him and changed the subject. "Khalil . . ."

"Mm?"

"Earlier I heard people speaking about things"—I took a breath—"about me."

He opened his mouth as if he'd expected the question. "*Ayam*. Yes, many men and women. From both tribes, you see. They are all talking of the night. You did many wonders, my friend." He dropped his voice back to his earlier hushed tone. "And many horrors. You must remember, everyone is still in remembering you killed Shareem. You defied *Shir* Sharaam's judgment, and survived the Doors of Midnight, friend. They are very much thinking you to be a monster." He gave me a thin smile, but it was what hid behind Khalil's eyes then that I listened to.

The unspoken fear my friend shared as well. And it said: *I am not sure if they are wrong. I am not sure that you aren't a monster, Ari.* But he didn't speak it aloud, and because of that, I suppose it did not hurt as much as it could have.

All the same. I heard it. And I remembered.

I only had the strength to nod.

He must have picked up on my discomfort for he gave me a solid slap against the shoulder. "*Zho!* It is not good to be thinking too much on these things, ah? We have lived another day, and the battle is done. Good things. And the *Shir*s saw what happened. They came to our aid after, and they and theirs are taking us back to Iban-Bansuur. What *Shir* Sharaam did, coming in the night like that . . ." He trailed off, shaking his head.

"It was no good thing. Alum Above, Most Merciful, is not happy. It is a thing most *dighar*. He has broken the laws of God Above. And he will suffer for it." Khalil shook his head, as if both lamenting the dead man's fate, and expressing his shame over what had happened.

The small doors at the back of Gushvin's wagon creaked open, and a familiar face burst through it. "*Arrey,* Ari!" Alwi beamed and waved a hand that looked caked in plum-colored syrup.

"Oi!" The cry came from the tinker. "What's that you've got on your grubby paws, ah? If you touch anything of mine with them, I swear I'll have you dragged behind the other one!" Gushvin must have been referring to me with that. "And you won't be getting a sledge. You mark me on that. I'll have the sands scrub you so clean there won't be a hair left on your dented ass. You hear me?"

Alwi shrank and cast a wary-eyed look back over his shoulder. "S'nothin' on my hands. Promise to Alum Above!" The boy quickly rubbed the offending limb against the back of Gushvin's home and business, smearing the wood and canvas with the sticky juices.

Brahm's blood, tits, and ashes, the boy had a remarkable disregard for good sense and his own life. If I could have laughed, I would have.

Another head came to rest near Alwi's crossed arms, though it didn't belong to his counterpart, Baba. No. This one had all the color of fire in its fur, and a pair of eyes the shade of powdered emeralds.

"Shola." I smiled and propped myself up higher.

The cat perched on the lip of the wagon's window, leapt onto the end of the sledge, and sauntered over to me before resting his full weight against my chest.

A rush of air left me as he fell with more force than needed. I told myself he'd done it out of love, though it could have equally been an innocent-looking attempt to murder me by taking the last of my breath.

Either way, I raised a hand and brought it to him, holding my cat close to my heart.

But the moment was not meant to be enjoyed as a shadow fell over me. Arfan rode at my side, having traded his horse for a camel. The merchant king looked me over with an eye that weighed me as easily as a man did an ounce of saffron.

"You survived."

I inclined my head.

Something in the way he'd said it left me uncertain whether the merchant king found my survival a good thing . . . or a problem. "And you called more of your foreign *jadhu*. Those bindings." Again, it wasn't a question.

And again I gave him the same answer.

"The other *Shir*s watched from a good distance in the night. They saw Sharaam's attack, and what happened after." I noted the lack of honorific on the former tribal leader. Perhaps now stripped due to his actions, or because he was dead. I didn't know, and Arfan did not see reason to explain it. "They watched him and almost rode to intervene." He wore his fox's smile with all the cunning that came with it. "That would have been something."

I cleared my throat and met his stare. "Then why didn't they?"

He gave me a knowing look. "By the time they had rallied their men . . . the camp had burst into flames." Arfan raised a brow. "And soon enough, a young man in my service killed another *Shir*. So what need had they then to ride to our aid?" The merchant king gave a tilt of his head that invited reply, but I didn't have one ready.

I took a long moment to think before I finally spoke. "I didn't kill *Shir* Sharaam."

Arfan's eyes narrowed, and it could have passed for a look of anger, but I realized it for what it truly was. A shrewd and calculating gaze. And it told me he had known the truth already. "Ah, but you have, Ari. The *Al-sayidha*'s life is not one always meant for glory. It is one of duty. I do not know if Aisha has told you this."

She had, in fact.

"And sometimes the best duty an *Al-sayidha* can do for their *Shir* is knowing when not to take credit for work well done. A foreigner comes into my tribe and service. One clever enough to steal secrets and profit from them, then rob me clean of my gold." The makings of a smile showed on his lips. "Then he comes here after banding together The Hundred Thieves, and survives his own hanging. He defies a *Shir* and a thousand arrows."

. . . There had certainly not been anywhere close to that many shots aimed at me, but it made for a good story, of course. And Arfan knew that.

Oh, merciful Brahm. I realized what had gone through the merchant king's mind, and the better game he'd been playing.

"And then he calls a storm of fire to defeat my enemies and kills their *Shir* before witnesses. That is the story that will be told, and that is the story I will allow to spread."

"You . . . mean for everyone to believe that. To think that I did all that for you in your service."

His smile finally showed, and it had all the bright-gleam sharpness of a wolf's in moonlight. "But of course. I told you once I could hang you with your reputation, and that I would use it. I plan to. Never forget, Ari, you owe me. And your debt is still not paid, and I will see it taken out of you in full . . . whichever way I must. So it is for this reason we ride back to Iban-Bansuur."

The thought of the old city conjured memory of another. One I had to return to, or lose hope of the one place remaining to me that could teach me the ten bindings. The Ashram, and my test. Because months remained, and the journey to return would surely consume them all.

I reminded Arfan of my other debt of a sort. I'd be little use to the man if I couldn't return to master the arts I'd called on the night before. Besides, all stories need time to breathe, and if he hoped to prosper further from mine, he needed me out of the way to keep from being the focus instead of the tales themselves. After all, a lie travels best when left alone. The truth becomes nothing more than a burden.

And he knew this.

The merchant king rubbed his chin as he mused on my want for home. Then, he agreed. "You will learn more of your *jadhu,* and I will see your reputation grow. I will let your frightful tales fester among the tribes who wish to give me problems in the future. And I will see those tribes as mine—one day. I will have them—have them all, and bring them under one family, as is my destiny.

"Besides, Ari, you have killed a *Shir.* I agree that it would be the best for you to leave for a time. Sharaam's tribe will come under mine after his defeat, and with no heir. His people will swallow their anger over it. But for you, a stranger . . . ?"

He grinned, and it was wide enough to be no human thing. "They will keep their arrows sharp, and their memories long and clear. One night, Ari, you might find yourself to bed only to never wake again. That would see us both the poorer. I would not have that. I like my investments to mature. I would see you live, long and prosperous, so that I may get my full value from you. Do you understand?"

I swallowed and nodded. He had effectively made me a devil—a nightmare for his people. Used as a threat to keep them all in line lest the monstrous child be let loose against them. And he had made me a scapegoat for the passing of another *Shir.* Masterfully done, in fact. If I countered his claim, I would cut my own reputation down in a way, and likely still be a target for all I'd done that led to the battle. But by leaving the lie intact, I gained the notoriety of killing a tribal leader with a perfect shot. Something that would also lend me a measure of protection.

How dangerous was a young boy that could swallow the sands in a fire hot enough to turn them to glass, then best a *Shir* with a bow?

The best I could make out of the situation, I supposed. Neither of us wholly got what we wanted, which, after all, is the sign of a good compromise. But we left with enough.

But what Khalil had said still echoed through my mind, raking my gut with an iron-cold razor. *Monster,* he'd said.

That word was reserved for the Ashura, and I was certainly different from them.

Wasn't I?

That flooded me with a coldness unfelt in the desert.

"Good." The word passed through Arfan's lips with a weight that ended all conversation. "Now rest. The ride will take some time, and you will find little rest back at the city. You will be sent home, and I hope to not see you for some time, Ari. When you dream, dream clever dreams. Dream of how you will pay me back, of what tricks you will bring to me in the future. And dream still of what I can do to you and your sparrows should you decide to ever try that cleverness against me." He did not need to say anything else.

Silence fell between us as we rode back to Iban-Bansuur.

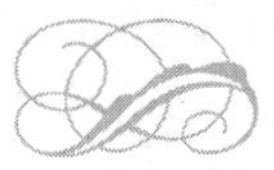

ONE HUNDRED TWENTY-SIX

NORTH BY EAST

I'd been forbidden from seeking out Qimari, by Arfan's direct command. But he'd said nothing about Aisha. And I'd regret finding her soon enough.

"You set the desert aflame, Ari." Her tone was near breathless, talking of the act as if it were the highest sacrilege.

"This is our home, given to us by Alum Above. I feared you were reckless. Your quickness with your magics, leaping before thinking. And I was right in my fear." Each word was a hammer on a heart turned to brittle stone. "I should have never put a bow in your hand."

I'd asked about that very weapon in fact, and Aisha had told me the black bow had been recovered in the aftermath of the battle and safely sequestered away.

"I need time to think on what I saw of you there, what you did. I know you did it for our good, and you saved lives, but you took them as well. Just as a careless shot can take an ally's heart, you did that with your fire. You burned men, Ari."

The desert grew colder, though the sun remained high above, filling the world with a heat I too should have felt. But ice water filled me instead.

Aisha's face then twisted, and while she didn't say it, I heard the *Maathi*'s words once again. *You're a monster.*

I may have started to believe it.

"I can't look at you right now, Ari." The last words she said to me, and I had none for her but a quiet bow of the head.

You see, I lingered in a state of pariah after what happened, and how Arfan spun my story. A hero, as well as a devil.

As I've said, stories are what we make of them. And mine had become the perfect tool to be shaped as needed among the tribe. The only thing that could ruin it would be my continuing presence.

Thus I'd been made to leave before I could say anything to change the tribe's mind.

So I made no true farewells, or traded any last remembrance with those I'd come to know. It would have only led to trouble, and I had caused more than enough of that.

A reminder of an old lesson, then.

Sometimes the best thing we can do for those we love is to leave. And that is an old pain I am well familiar with. I suppose it could be said that the longest friendship I have ever had has been with pain.

It has never once lied to me all that while.

It promises to hurt.

And it has always kept that promise.

Arfan saw me off from the city of Iban-Bansuur, well-provisioned, and with a parting gift: a trio of metal discs. "I am not in the business of giving away coin, though I seem to be breaking many of my rules when it comes to you. You have done me three services, and it will never be said I do not pay a debt." He flashed me a piece that looked like flattened pearl. A white radham, also called white gold, or a poor man's gold coin.

"First for bringing me my own hundred thieves." He pushed the middling coin into my open palm. A silver dhiran followed. "For your assisting my *Maathi* and leading us to the Water Tree." Then he waved the final coin before me. A full golden Zibrathi rayhal. "And the last is for bringing me Sharaam's tribe. Perhaps under different circumstances than I had wanted, but now they are mine all the same." He pressed the last piece into my hand, folding my fingers over the coins. "This is what I leave you with, and my favor. It will see you home."

That it did.

Gushvin, the tinker, served as my ride back to Mubarath, having decided that he'd had enough of *Shir*s and their tribal feuds.

I couldn't blame him.

Our road to the Zibrathi city had been blissfully uneventful, minus the gossip-mongering of the two extra bits of cargo we brought along. By that I mean Alwi and Baba, both of whom returned with us.

In truth, I had heard that the pair of young boys had considerably exhausted the patience of many members of the tribe. I suppose I couldn't judge them for that. Like minds, after all.

They spent the ride jabbering away about every odd story they'd heard about me over the course of our time together, as well as getting very wrong the things they'd managed to see with their own eyes.

How's that possible, you ask? Well, consider this. They were both of them young boys, and boys of any age are prone to the occasional bit of exaggeration. More so those who haven't quite matured. So great deeds done by me became grander still. There was no harm in it, of course. They were only trading these back and forth.

That is . . . until we reached Mubarath.

Once inside the familiar sandstone city, the two boys quickly left the care of the tinker, flagging down a group of urchins who looked to have just come away with a fresh clutch.

And I heard whispers of a new band of outlaws, quickly growing to notoriety within the city. Their name?

The Hundred Thieves.

While I couldn't tarry within the city, I might have spread some gossip of my own. Of the ghost in white who'd cobbled the new group of pickpockets together. The one they'd tried to hang, and who'd walked away clean from the gallows' rope.

Gushvin went about business, bartering goods with whomever he could. But the best of what he had to offer came in the form of stories.

Rumors. The kind people could take back to their favorite tavern by evening to trade over drinks, maybe use to capture a slice of time for themselves. After all, stories do not only let us live out a piece of fantasy, or remember a time once ago, they give us the ability to capture a piece of time in the here and now. For those brief moments we are sharing a tale, true or not, we are creating a new kind of story.

A tale of and for that moment there. And the people we are with. Memories. And what are stories if not memories? Even the fictional ones.

Sometimes . . . especially the fictional ones.

Because no story is ever wholly untrue. At least not in my experience. The trick simply lies in finding the space between the truths and taller tales told within.

And the ones Gushvin had to tell happened to revolve around a boy come from far off. One of those who practiced magic and wore a cloak of woven moonlight. Every rumor and truth of mine fell on eager ears.

I listened to the tinker enrapture every passerby with stories of my time out in the desert, and heard how quickly they changed their shape as they passed from one set of lips to another pair of ears. It was a sort of magic in and of itself.

Stories took a life of their own, each new telling taking a bit of the heart and touch of the one who spoke them last. What piece of past did they value most? What did they love out of the old heroes? And what bits of bias did they always share? All of those things, and none of those things, filtered into the stories of me.

And they followed the tinker and me as we left Mubarath. As we broke back out onto the Golden Road, and we traveled back to the east. And the north.

Toward home.

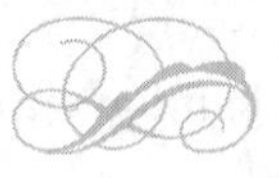

ONE HUNDRED TWENTY-SEVEN

Time to Tell

We made all haste toward Ghal and the Ashram, joining a caravan full of traders. As you can imagine, Gushvin used the crowd to peddle further rumors about me.

When the crowd fell into wary suspicion of the tinker's many claims, he prodded me mercilessly until I relented and brought out the shaping Enshae had gifted me. The candle forged from darkness and stars, which burned a red bright as blood. So too its smoke.

Everyone knew the stories, of course. And mouths moved without word, all to say, "Ashura. Ajuura."

Demons, demons.

We only had to bring out the candle once. And it served its purpose. After that, everyone gave me a bit more room to myself on the journey, and a warier eye anytime someone turned to look at me.

The price of fame, I suppose.

But I heard other whispers along their lips. *Was he one of them? Was this small boy an Ashura as well?*

The distance between me and others grew over the trip. A small coincidence, I'm sure . . .

All the same, I ruminated on what had happened, and was beginning to see how a story could be more than a shield. It could just as easily be a millstone around your neck. Some of the joy of what I'd been building for my reputation now soured, and I wondered what stories would reach the Ashram.

And would Ari be a hero, or a monster?

I'd find out soon enough as we made all haste back to the Ashram, hopefully just back in time.

Because my sentence had not been forgotten, nor my grievances forgiven. So I had something left to prove, or I would very quickly find out if the legend of unstruck, unharmed, unfallen would remain true.

As far as ill omens came, we could find no worse than reaching Ghal just as winter deepened. Sheets of snowfall caked the roads, leaving Gushvin to devolve into a stream of profanity that you would never think to hear from a tinker's mouth. He had profited tidily along our journey, and had let slip that the travel had done him a better turn in coin than he had imagined. So much so that he almost felt bad about wanting to charge me for his service bringing me home.

. . . Almost.

But I had learned enough of the tinkers by now to know that they truly love their trade, and quite literally at that. So I bartered for my passage with a few more stories I knew the tinker would want to pass along.

In the end, Gushvin and I parted ways on rather good terms. He'd made his coin, and I arrived with just enough time remaining in the season to see to the most pressing of my concerns: proving to the masters that I had gained some level of control over the bindings. At least enough to show I wasn't a danger.

And it weighed on my mind all the while. Because the desert had shown me that I was most certainly a danger, which meant I'd have to be quick and clever in telling a carefully constructed story to the masters.

Or lose my neck.

So I rushed up the Ashram's many stairs, deciding that Gushvin had the right of it earlier with his cursing. I may have taken a page—or several—out of his book, drumming up a storm of muttered foulness as I stomped my way to the top. Shola found nothing about the weather the least bit problematic. This owed mostly to the fact that he rested well within the confines of my cloak and robes, kept warm and snuggled tight against my chest.

When I reached the courtyard, I headed straight for my rooms in the Rookery to settle Shola and my belongings. That done, I raced to the courtyard, hoping to find my friends crossing the ground.

A passing monk paused when he recognized me. "Ari?" He blinked twice then remembered himself. "Kaethar Ari?"

I nodded, unsure whether to speak or not. The monk's surprise caught me unaware, and I didn't know the reason for his reaction.

"I thought . . ." He trailed off.

"You thought what?"

He shrugged, not bothering to face me. "You left the Ashram. Some said you were expelled. Others said you ran away. I heard a rumor that you had died out on the sands somewhere. Someone else said . . ." He finally glanced over his shoulder, his eyes falling on my cloak. He said nothing else, but he didn't need to.

I knew what went through his mind. Everyone had heard the stories of The Ghost of Ghal before my leaving, and they'd only grown after I'd left. Spreading along the Golden Road as a ghost in white leapt over roofs in Mubarath. But I did wonder just *what* the monk had heard about me, and how much those stories had grown in his mind.

But sometimes, the best way to let a secret spread is to keep your own mouth shut. Others are eager enough to spill them, so let them do it for you. They'll do a better job than you, and you might find your reputation growing in ways you couldn't have imagined.

This I did.

So I smiled at him and figured it best to let him decide, was I a legend? Or was I a monster?

He eventually left, never telling me what he decided about me, and I returned to scouring the courtyard in hopes of finding my friends. Instead I found someone else.

"*Arrey,* look what mischief managed to come back to the Ashram!" Rishi Ibrahm joined his hands together in what could have passed for prayer. "Oh, good Lord Brahm, I thought you would spare me this suffering. Have I not been a good and devout—*hrmph!*" Rishi Ibrahm blinked and worked his mouth to free it of freshly lodged snow. "Ari . . . do you know what the grievance for striking a master with a snowball is?"

Truthfully? I had no idea. But I figured it couldn't be as bad what they'd already levied against me. Besides, what harm has a little snow ever done?

Rishi Ibrahm wasted no time in setting this grievance right. Notably . . . in his own manner. I didn't hear the words that passed his lips, but I saw their result when snow piled high enough to form a boulder well capable of trouncing my ass. And it sailed forward with the promise to do just that.

The snow struck me full in the chest, and like I had thought, flattened me to the ground. I saw twice as many clouds in the sky until my head cleared.

Rishi Ibrahm stood over me, offering a hand to help me to my feet. I took it, and he laughed. "Good gods, Ari, it does seem your travels have made you a bit bolder than before, ah?" He smiled and touched a finger to the side of his nose. "Get it . . . bolder?" He nodded then to the ground where the monstrous snowball he'd fashioned had broken apart.

There are always jokes that will fall flat in the world. Sad truth that it is. Then there are the few, most commonly shared by men who reach the age of fatherhood, that prompt others to contemplate murder. So bad are these japes.

But, being a respectable and even-tempered student of the Ashram, I of course reined in my cruder impulses and instead settled for a deadpan stare aimed at Master Binder.

Once he helped me upright, he dusted off some of the snow that had touched my cloak. Then he frowned, and a moment later his eyes widened with a gleam I had long since taken to viewing with healthy suspicion. He pinched my cloak between his fingers. "Oh, interesting." He flicked a fingernail against a scale, then winced and bit off a stream of curses.

"Thought as much. A Seeming. Haven't worked a binding of your own on this, not that you'd need to. Nagh scales are tough as diamonds and bright as moonbeams. But something's embrightened your cloak, and it wasn't you."

I gave him a look full of storybook cunning. "How do you know that?"

He rolled his eyes. "It takes a patient mind, and subtle skill to work something like this. Neither subtle or patient describe you, Ari."

I stared.

Rishi Ibrahm was unperturbed by the look. "I've been hearing stories about you. Things from far off. I heard that you once again earned the name Unburned." He looked me over slowly. "Was it a clever trick, or a true binding?"

I grinned. "I can tell you all about it."

Rishi Ibrahm matched my expression and led me to the amphitheater he'd taught classes in. Mercifully, no one else occupied it, and he shut the doors behind us to keep it that way. With privacy granted, I fell into the whole tale of my adventure.

I spoke of my time in Mubarath, and my tinkering with the minor bindings to help me deal with the Black Tower Band. My idle time watching kites and falling stones on the roof with Baba. Then to my travels with Arfan and his company. I told him of archery practice, the Water Tree, and of course, I told him of Enshae.

If Rishi Ibrahm doubted me, he kept it to himself with all the careful control of a master performer. Not one curve of mouth or movement of eye to betray the fact he might have found parts of my tale rather tall indeed. No. He listened with full attentiveness, and in the end, he weighed in on my adventures.

He laughed and rubbed a hand against his mouth. "What did I tell you about moon-full sunny nights?"

Only then did the odd phrase finally strike me in realization. "You knew?"

He looked at me as if I were particularly thick. "I had an inkling. You aren't the first to have gone through the Doors of Midnight, Ari. And I wager you certainly won't be the last person with stories in their head in place of common sense to go looking for them. But you're focusing on the wrong part of your story."

"I am?"

He nodded, some of the mischief and madness bleeding away from his voice and his gaze. "At the end of it all, in the desert, you say you bound fire once again."

I inclined my head.

"But what you did after it is more impressive."

I frowned and thought back. "What . . . did I do?"

"You didn't let go of the binding, but you shifted your folds. You redirected your mental energy and focus, your Athir, toward a different binding. A subtler one."

I thought back and struggled to recall it properly. All I had been focused on was preventing the black sands and fires from turning me into ashes.

Master Binder must have seen the confusion on my face, for he clarified. "Back when you first bound the arrows as you did. A part of you learned more of Tak and Roh than you realized. You did so by watching things in motion. Things falling. You understood the bindings involved, even if only a piece of them."

I almost opened my mouth to mention that this had little to do with my binding of fire, but Rishi Ibrahm was deep in thought now, and any interruption on my part would be an unwelcome thing.

"Think back to your time with Enshae. The practice with holding fire in your hands."

I did, and then made the connection I'd thought little of. "I treated the fire like I had when handling the flames in Enshae's garden. I manipulated the space around the flames? I just tried to feel them and keep from being burned."

Rishi Ibrahm snapped his fingers. "That's it exactly! Same binding, after a fashion. Whent and Ern allow you to manipulate the space within your atham. But you went from trying to force your will on living fire, to instead feeling what was already there, and enacting a boundary. Something you asked the fire to respect, even if you didn't understand all of what you were doing. A part of you did. And it likely came from all the time practicing with Enshae. A good sign."

I pursed my lips and furrowed my brow as I thought on that. "Is it?"

"Of course it is." His hand struck my back with nearly enough force to drive the air out of me. It had likely been meant to be a reassuring clap, but as with all things Rishi Ibrahm . . . the reality was a bit different from whatever he intended. "Ari, you performed a subtle binding. Something of finesse, and control. And you did so after practice. You are in fact, to my great surprise, teachable! It means we don't have to string you up by your ears until you—" Master Binder crossed his eyes and stuck his tongue out.

The expression didn't require much translation.

And it didn't exactly fill me with confidence despite what he had said.

But I had left something out of my story: the truth of what happened on the sands outside Zibrath. That binding had not been something of control.

But wrath. *And what if you lose control again during your test?* I swallowed and said nothing.

"Cheer up, Ari. As far as I'm concerned, you've shown enough potential to warrant some extra practice before the season ends. Just because you did it before doesn't mean you can do it again. So let's see if you can reconnect with fire, *ji-ah*?"

I smiled. "*Ji.*"

ONE HUNDRED TWENTY-EIGHT

Reconnections

I went looking for my friends after my conversation with Rishi Ibrahm, but I couldn't find Radi in Clanks or the Scriptory. Which only left one place.

Stones.

I made my way down the broken tower's stairs and entered the cavern below. My friend sat on one of the naturally formed benches of cold black stone. He fiddled with the pegs of his mandolin, deep in thought, muttering to himself. A part of me wanted to rouse him out of the focused state, and hopefully brighten his mood. But something about his posture told me it better to wait.

Eventually, he pulled his hands away from the instrument as if burned. Resignation and frustration shaped the set of his mouth and of his eyes. "Brahm's tits. I swear . . ."

"Are you swearing on his tits . . . or for them? I can't ever tell with you." I tried to keep my voice as neutral as possible.

Radi looked up as if stung and searched for the source. He locked eyes on me and his mouth worked through several expressions, all of them failing him. "You bastard!" His mandolin came to rest gently where he'd sat, and he rushed over to me. I noted that his hands remained tightly clenched.

Then he swung.

Both arms wrapped around me in hard embrace. "Brahm's blood and ashes, Ari. A whole year. Where have you been?"

I didn't break his hold, but did signal for him to ease off a touch. "*Almost* a year."

He rolled his eyes and moved his fingers, then realized that he didn't have his mandolin in hand. "All that time and still a pedant, Ari. Girls don't like pedantic men."

I arched a brow and said nothing.

Radi took in my reaction. His mouth twitched, his eyes sparkled. Finally, he broke into the laughter he'd been holding back, and I joined him.

Gods, it was a good sound to hear after so long a time away from home. Every now and again during our talk, I would cast a long look at the wall of solid black in Stones. The place where the very air seemed to press around me, stifle all my folds, and flood me with an uneasy stillness and silence. I wondered what binding lay over that place, and of course, how to break it.

Radi demanded to know what had happened, and I told him. For more than a candlemark, we sat and traded stories.

I asked after Aram, but he frowned and told me to leave off the subject. She had been called back home to Abhar to deal with family matters. In the middle of the season no less. She had only recently returned. It had left her in a foul mood, and whatever happened with her family had only worsened her demeanor. Radi had gleaned her family had begun pressuring her to begin considering future marriage prospects.

The Mutri Empire is home to many things, but among them, parental pressures and expectations rank highly. A shame the empire never learned how to package, trade, and export that. We have an overabundance of it.

Our conversation soon returned to my many adventures, and most especially of binding the arrows, then walking through the Doors of Midnight. Enshae, as you would imagine, held all of Radi's interest. And it wasn't long before his mind, and his fingers, soon set to working a song of my wanderings.

He promised to play it for me in a set's time. And, dutiful friend that I was, promised to be there to hear him sing it.

Soon after that I headed to the Crow's Nest to see someone I'd been meaning to. I just needed to get past one obstacle.

The doors opened and I entered to find Krisham scouring the many shelves behind the desk he often sat at. I almost called to him, then realized something had changed.

His hair had been short-cropped for as long as I'd known him. Only now it fell to his shoulders, in thick and waving locks that couldn't have grown out in the time I'd been gone.

The former student moved with the frenzied motions of someone caught in panic, or perhaps a fit of mania. He brushed books aside, and looked close to ripping the wooden shelves from the walls in his fury. I finally decided to interrupt him when I realized the Crow's Nest wouldn't endure his flailing any longer, especially if he lost control of himself and resorted to any of the major bindings.

I cleared my throat in hopes of getting his attention. "Krisham?"

He whirled about, long hair whipping across his face. "Don't move, Ari!"

At least he remembered my name this time. . . .

I raised my hands in a gesture of placation. "I won't. What's wrong?"

His lips pulled into a tight frown. "You just moved. And something terrible has happened, Ari. Truly devious and monstrous. You wouldn't believe it." His eyes widened, and his mouth followed, the makings of true distress. That brought my heart to quicken. If something had unnerved someone who walked the line of madness, it must have been worth considerable fear.

"What happened? What can I do?" One of my hands went to the Arasmus steel knife still resting against my hip.

"Oh, Brahm's blood." Krisham's face contorted into a mask I had seen a few times in my life, and I hoped to keep it to that low number. The expression of someone who has lost someone held deep in their heart and in love. It's an anguish like no other.

I took a step forward, reaching out with a hand. "Krisham . . . what happened?"

He clamped both hands to the top of his head. "I've lost my hat! It's been taken from me. Thieves, scoundrels, ne'er-do-wells!"

All of the blood left my heart and face, quickly finding space in my fists. Both of which clenched hard, and I began to wonder what Krisham's already changed appearance would look like after considerable adjustments made by my fists.

I took a breath, and might have asked for Brahm's endless patience in that moment before addressing Krisham. "Where did you last see it?"

He looked at me as if I had said the dumbest thing he had ever heard. "Ari, if I knew that, I wouldn't be without it, would I? Honestly!"

I found a point of sharp pressure building within my forehead and decided to assuage it. My palm ground against the space as I tried to think of how to bring Krisham back to reality. "Krisham . . . where did you go where you could have lost it?"

That made him pause his rummaging. He frowned and brought a finger to his lips. "Not quite so far as Myrath, but I did do a good bit of sailing. Oh, no, wait. I got terribly into my cups with a band of *kiraysh* out on the untread paths of jungles beyond the Mutri, but before you get to Laxina. You know?"

I, as a matter of fact, did not know. But I let him work through his many lies and tall tales, knowing it would calm him down. Eventually, I was proved right, and some semblance of the odd old student returned.

"What are you doing here by the way? I haven't seen you for most of the year. Honestly, I thought you'd died."

I grinned. "It turns out I'm rather hard to kill."

That didn't get the response I'd hoped for. Instead, Krisham's frown deepened and he looked down at the ground. "Be careful with what you think, Ari. If you go on like that, you might live up to those words. And that's a terrible kind of life to live."

I wanted to ask him what he meant, but his hand snapped into motion, striking hard against the desk.

A drum of thunder rang out from the impact and Krisham slammed a balled fist into the open palm of his other hand. "Oh, of course! I left my hat on a ship." The moment of certainty faded, soon replaced by the previous consternation. "I think . . ."

I decided to press my luck, otherwise risk being trapped there forever. "Can I see Immi? It's been so long, and I've been thinking about her."

That brought him back. He blinked several times then smacked the side of one of his legs. "Oh, of course. That's probably why you've come, isn't it?"

I had the dignity not to reply to that.

Krisham led me to Immi's room, and shut the door behind us.

My friend rested on her knees, facing the nearest padded wall. She remained much the same as when I'd last seen her. Only the white soft surfaces of her room should have been unmarred. They carried smears of a color both Immi and I were well acquainted with. Her fingers twitched, and I watched her bite her lip as if trying to resist an urge.

Twitch. Twitch.

Her fingers moved—jerked, and I could see the dried residue along her fingernails. Her eyelids twitched. A minute motion that would have gone unnoticed by many. But I watched Immi with all the careful consideration I could manage. One of her hands rose and her fingertips brushed against the padded wall.

But she didn't scratch at it. Instead, she pulled away with a measure of resigned control.

That was enough for me. I worked to keep my voice low and gentle—the reassuring tone a friend takes when offering comfort. "Immi? It's Ari." I patted my hand against the nearest portion of the wall. A soft noise, like someone striking a pillow, filled the space between us.

Immi whirled, halfway getting to her feet. Her chest rose and her eyes had the full wideness of a hart ready to flee. "Ari!" She took a few steps toward me, then stopped. Her gaze flickered to the reddened wall. "You've been gone a long time."

I took a step closer to her, still keeping my voice gentle. "I have. I'm sorry." I offered her what I hoped was both an apologetic and inviting smile. "I've missed you."

Her lips pressed together but for a moment before she nodded. "I missed you too. I thought you would be back sooner."

I had hoped that as well, but I kept my mouth shut, unsure what to say.

"Did you not want to come back?"

That question drove whatever reticence I'd been holding to out of me. "What? Of course I wanted to come back, Immi."

"But you waited so long. Was . . . is it because of me?" Her eyes flickered to the mess she'd made along the walls. Her fingers twitched again, but she was aware of the motion. One of her hands clamped tight to the other as if to rein in the impulse. "I'm sorry, Ari. I tried. I really did for so long. I didn't mean to be bad and—"

Those words turned my heart into glass in ice, and a memory followed. I once knew of another young girl who never wished to be bad, but certainly thought herself to be at times. Even though it had never been any fault of hers. Seeing Immi there, frightened, and quivering over something similar brought the hammer to my already brittle chest.

I forgot whatever I had been meaning to say and crossed the distance between us. Then I pulled her into the tightest and most reassuring hug I could. "Blood and ashes, Immi. No, no. Nothing's your fault. Don't ever think that." I didn't let her go, hoping the closeness would keep her focused only on me. Only my words. "I am so sorry for taking so long, truly. Believe me, I would have liked to have come home far sooner than I have. Remember, my neck's on the line." I finally broke our hold, then flashed her a crooked smile as I drew a long line across my throat.

That pulled a little snort out of her. "S'true. You made so much trouble last year. Did . . . you make any more troubles out there?"

My smile widened. "Oh, did I ever." I took her hands in mine.

Her eyes brightened, and a touch of a smile found her face as well. "Will you tell me about it? I promise I'll behave and—"

I gave her a light squeeze and hushed her. "Of course. Let's see . . ."

That was all I had to say, and Immi's hands found each other, held clasped and tight. All of which meant she wouldn't hurt herself anymore.

I fell into the story of stories, a better performance than many I'd given before. After all, I'd learned new tricks along the way, and I put them to use. It would be wrong to think that I was any good at them, but I was young, and I was excited. That often makes up for a great deal in beginning something.

So I made crude shapes with my hands to cast odder-looking shadows along the wall. But they served their purpose. And I told Immi all of what happened as we reconnected. In the end, I gave her something to remind her that I hadn't forgotten about her at all.

Or the promise I'd once made her.

A shaping. A making touched with something more. A Seeming. And all in the shape of a white star, though at first glance to many, it would look like nothing more than something fashioned from brightest clean glass. But a longer look would show you the truth.

I pressed Enshae's token into her hands. Her fingers shook, but her eyes held a sharper light than any I'd seen in her before. But it was her smile that blossomed full on her face, and fuller still in my heart on seeing it.

Immi softly folded her hands over the token, bringing it close to her breast and holding it there. "Oh." The word left her in a soft hush, equal parts quiet wonder and just as much reverence. "Ari, it's beautiful. It's . . . warm. I can feel it buzzing against me."

I had known of the gentle heat that radiated from the token, but most of that had faded over my time carrying it from Enshae's domain.

"There's a fire inside of this, Ari. A nice, quiet fire. Did you listen to it?"

I shook my head, marveling that Immi had picked up on the nature of the shaping. "No, I'm still not quite sure how."

She beamed. "I can teach you. And you've gotten closer than before. Like you told me about the fire, and the Shaen lady." Immi had taken my whole story in stride, not once betraying a hint of suspicion or doubt. It all seemed perfectly normal to her, and I appreciated her all the more for it.

"Here, take my hand." Immi's fingers folded over mine and she pressed my touch to the white shaped star. We sat there together, reconnecting over more of my story, and that of the fire within Enshae's making.

I would like to say that it came to me as easily as the binding back in the desert. But that would be another lie. Instead, let us simply say that I most certainly tried my best. And at the end of our time together, I may have felt a little flicker of warmth. Maybe I heard something as well.

Maybe.

Time would tell.

ONE HUNDRED TWENTY-NINE

Crow and Concerns

The days wound down toward the end of the season, and with them, my deadline for proving to the Ashram's masters that I was, in fact, not a walking disaster.

One year of traveling evidence to the contrary . . .

Merciful gods that the masters hadn't heard the truth of what happened in the desert yet. Only my accounting of things. The truth would have ensured a quick death or being locked away in the Crow's Nest.

So, I used what free time I had to tend to the important things: practice, my friends, and those I cared for.

But there was someone else I'd been ignoring since coming home. So I saw to him first.

I moved through Ghal's collection of bubbles until I reached a door crudely set in place within the stone of a mountain.

Only, the door now sat perfectly, almost as if it had been reset. I leaned closer and saw that was the truth. And the old rags that had been stuffed along its edges to keep out the cold were now gone. A molding of some sort had been shaped to the design of the door and fitted around it. Something that would have cost an amount of coin Sham hadn't had in his possession when I'd left him.

I smiled and knocked on the door.

Silence. No response.

I frowned and knocked again.

Footsteps echoed soon enough back down the tunnel and through the entryway. I stood—patiently.

The peephole opened. "Brahm's tits 'n' salted ass. It's 'n' . . ." The voice stopped short, but I had heard enough to know who it belonged to.

A crooked smile took over my face. He'd been neglecting his language lessons.

. . . Again.

Sham cleared his throat and started over. "Ari!" The door opened in a peculiar silence. He'd oiled the hinges, then.

It seemed The Crow had taken better care of himself than I could have hoped for.

The boy who'd once needed a good amount of filling out looked like he'd done just that. Nothing drastic, but a noticeable weight in his cheeks, and he'd found someone to cut his hair into something almost tidy, and not a tangled, knotted mess. That, and he might have grown an inch or two.

And he was dressed in a fine black cloak, having all the bearing of a clever, roguish bird.

Sham beamed, showing me a mouth full of as much mischief and chagrin as it was lacking teeth. He must have noticed my stare for what it was because he hooked a finger to his upper lip and pulled it away. "No worries, Ari. Lost them from falling out. Baby ones, you know? Means I'm a comin' to bein' a man, now." His eyes widened as he realized he'd slipped back into his old cant.

"Sorry."

I smiled and clapped him on the shoulder. "Nothing to apologize for. So . . ." I leaned to one side to look past him. "Are you going to invite me in, or leave me out in the cold?"

Sham wasted no time, snaking a hand to my wrist and yanking me along.

Soon enough he brought me into the cavern home that he'd claimed so long ago. Nearly a dozen children filtered through the space. And every single one of them wore the black cloaks I'd once paid a tinker for. Sham had been busy, building a family of his own in my absence.

Much like I had tried. Once with the sparrows, only to have to leave them. Then with The Hundred Thieves, all for them to betray me. But one family had grown, and remained close.

And all under the careful, kind shaping of Sham. He'd done as I'd hoped, and now he wouldn't be alone ever again.

I couldn't help it, I took Sham into my arms and just held him there.

"Ugh. Ari, not when people are watching. What if some of the girls see?"

I snorted and let him go, ruffling his hair. "What do you know about girls, huh? Still the same as before?"

Sham muttered something utterly ungodly under his breath, and I pretended not to hear it. Instead, Sham's eyes widened as he realized something. "Where's Appi?" Some of the other children turned their heads to help him search. "Stop him from going out." At that, someone shambled into the main cavern room.

They wore a cloak fashioned from rags, much like what Sham had once worn. However, all of their clothing matched the various shades of white found in mountain snow. Some the better bright of fresh-fallen frost, other patches closer to the worn color found in ice after it has sat for a set or more. The perfect colors to be lost in a snowstorm.

All the colors of a ghost, perhaps.

I arched a brow as the figure shuffled about, trying to move properly in an outfit just a touch too big for them. "Do I want to know?"

Sham gave me a smile that had been made to mask obvious embarrassment and anxiety. "Um, I'cun 'splain it, promise."

"I do love a good story."

And so Sham told me what he and his care of orphans had been up to.

Oh how he'd grown. The Crow, my little brother, had taken to passing my lessons on to others. But they had lacked one thing. A protector in case any ear or eyes turned too eagerly toward the little band of miscreants.

So they turned to a myth to save them.

The Ghost of Ghal.

Only, the real ghost had gone west for a time being. So what was Sham to do?

Well, he'd decided to do what I had, and cobble a ghost of his own.

And so he'd told the orphans to find whatever scrap of snow-white they could to create my doppelgänger, then set him loose through the streets and atop the roofs. At first, he'd confined his activities to nights touched with fresh frost-fall, all to keep himself better obscured. Good logic, and over time, the stories I'd left behind had come to grow due to their diligent care.

A terribly reckless thing to do. Though, I suppose I'd showed them much worse through my actions. It could be said I am a terrible influence. . . .

In the end, I couldn't fault them when I heard the unsaid part of Sham's story.

This had been a way for him to keep more than the story of the ghost close at hand. It was a way to remember. After all, what are stories if not memory? Of course, many are tall tales at best, but even then, who's to truly say they never happened? Stories are tricky things, and we all think we know the truth of them.

And in listening to Sham's, I understood the silent prayer The Crow had been holding on to. The hope that I would come back, and two brothers could be whole again. Knowing that, how could I be angry?

And over that time, Ghal had become the city of two roguish legends. The White Ghost of Ghal, righting wrongs, and giving coin to the poor. And the little King of Crows. Sneakthief, shadow-clad, and quick to pluck a rich man's purse, or their secrets.

Sham and I spent the afternoon together, discussing how to continue building his reputation.

And maybe I decided to give him another lesson in plying the miscreant's arts.

Because a thief's work is never truly done.

My time with Sham ran long, leaving me to rush back to the Ashram and make it to Mines before the masters decided to carry out my sentencing without a word from me.

I entered the imposing chamber of dark stone.

All of the masters were seated in their usual positions behind the long desk. All except Master Binder, who hadn't bothered to show for my review, despite being my mentor and the only opinion keeping me from a severed head.

. . . Typical.

Master Spiritualist, the Ashram's headmaster, looked around, likely for the same reason: searching for Rishi Ibrahm. After a few moments, he cast a long-suffering glance up at the ceiling and sighed. Master Spiritualist rested his chin atop folded hands. "We're here to consider Kaethar Ari's readmittance to the Ashram and render judgment for his grievance of channeling a dangerous binding the previous year. His year of supervision was to be overseen by Rishi Ibrahm, Master Binder, who—"

"Is here!" The doors to Mines flung open as from the force of a crashing wave. But Rishi Ibrahm's hands remained at his sides.

Was it a binding?

The man strode into the room, clad in his traditional sleeveless robe. Though it looked more like a shoddy patchwork cloak than the garb befitting a master of the Ashram. "And no thanks to the lot of you. Honestly, you couldn't even send me a runner to tell me you had changed the time." He crossed his arms and managed to flash each of the other masters a glare that took them all in whole, and at the same time seemed to be made for each of them separately. The Master Binder crossed the distance between the others and took his place, kicking his feet up and onto the table.

That earned him a series of sideways glances, but no one said anything further.

Master Spiritualist's eyelids fluttered and his gaze returned to the top of

Mines. His mouth moved, and while I hadn't become an expert in reading lips, I swore he'd mouthed the words *Brahm's tits.* Not exactly proper behavior for the Ashram's headmaster, and the chief among spiritual studies.

I tried not to grin.

I failed.

Rishi Ibrahm flashed me a wink.

If our exchange had been caught by the headmaster, he chose to ignore it. "As I was saying, this session will be used to judge Kaethar Ari's competency in the major bindings, as well as his hopeful growth in control . . . and better judgment."

I may have squirmed at the last part. While it was true that my control had grown, to some degree, my judgment remained in question.

Even by me.

Master Spiritualist turned his head to regard Master Binder. "Well, you've been working with the boy. Has he shown you any of the promise we'd been hoping for?" The headmaster didn't bother waiting for Rishi Ibrahm's answer before turning to me. "And you, Ari, how have you fared in your own estimation?"

Two options lay before me: the truth, and then my experiences, whole and laid bare as they were. I'm not sure if binding a storm of arrows at my own execution for murder would have counted as sound judgment. But it did prove I had some semblance of control. And then kindling a still-burning inferno over black sands didn't say much in my favor either.

Fortunately, I was spared having to answer.

Rishi Ibrahm fumbled with his robes, pulling out a long chime candle—the sort used to mark time. "Let's find out together, shall we?" He gave me a smile that should have been reassuring, except the old manic light shone in his eyes. "Could be the boy surprises you all." Rishi Ibrahm then frowned. "Could be he burns us all to smithereens. Who knows?"

The masters flicked narrowed eyes toward him.

I suddenly developed the intense desire to shrink into my clothing until nothing but empty robes remained.

"Hold out your hands, Ari." Rishi Ibrahm gave me a knowing look as I approached the desk.

I did as instructed, holding out both of my palms, pressed together to form a crude cup.

Master Binder pressed the naked butt of the candle into place and then murmured something too low for me to catch, despite being so close to him. He released his hold and the candle remained firm in place as if it had been fastened there. His eyes danced as if lit with a flame itself and his smile grew further crazed. "Ready, Ari?"

I didn't know what he had in mind. The knot in my throat grew, and I swallowed it before nodding.

"Good." He shut his eyes and moved his mouth. "Start with whent. Then go to ern." *Tsst.* First a sound like dead leaves trailing along a sandy road, then a wisp of smoke before the full flame bloomed to life. A crown of flames that had sprung from nowhere—no source.

Enshae did that, but she's no mortal. How did Rishi Ibrahm—but the flame's motions pulled me from my thoughts.

It flickered, reminding me of the first time I'd practiced with a candle and learned to keep its shape in my mind.

Old memories, and I smiled at them.

The fire could have been said to look at me then, and I did much the same, as if regarding a friend I hadn't seen in ages. It bobbed, and I could tell the next movement it would make before the fire did as much. It flickered, then swayed, almost dancing.

"Now, Ari, little tip, *ji.* Focus on this flame as it is—this size." Rishi Ibrahm's eyes held more of the firelight than before. Then he spoke again. The minute bulb burst into a screaming pillar, long as my arm. Wax melted, now raining down in thick rivulets to rest on the tender skin of my palm. I winced and pushed it from my mind, focusing on the flame instead.

My mind tipped into the folds. He had said to keep the image of what the fire had been before. So I did as instructed. But I did more than that.

I returned to the first candle I'd held. The one with Mahrab. Then cast that wide into countless folds. A single repeated image formed fresh and anew into dozens.

So I held to that and believed with every ounce of heart and mind that the flame before me held the same shape and form as the ones inside my mind.

"Start with whent." I kept to the belief I'd just formed, and had chosen to repeat the binding as Rishi Ibrahm had spoken. There wasn't any special magic to doing it like that, but in a way, there was. I had seen it work for the Master Binder, and because of that, I believed in it. That belief helped pave the way for what happened next. "Then go to ern."

Stinging beads of wax pooled against what bits of my skin remained free from its hot touch. The rest puddled atop the already building pile.

Unseen threads brushed against the edges of my mind—a gentle weight like the reassuring touch of a friend. Warm, and welcoming. I extended my will toward it like trailing fingers along a surface to inspect it.

I remembered all my quiet contemplation of firesides, from hearths, to the fire that kept me warm in Ampur after we toppled a mountain and an old god. I remembered my lessons under Enshae, and her brilliant golden eyes.

And at that, the eyes in memory became someone else's. Equal in shape and shade. But full of cunning and hate. A wolf's eyes of hunger, and the fire in me changed as well.

I remembered the night of broken bodies and reddened smoke. A fire to take stone and wood and home from me. The hateful hue found in a brazier that promised me power, and a fire to turn a once teacher, and a spoiled noble, to ash and cinder.

It took me, and my control. It promised me that I would fail.

My heart quickened, and I felt a new heat that left all my control in question. And my judgment far from sound.

I could burn it all. The Ashram. The doubt. Stone and flesh and sinew alike. Every bit of anger ever kept in the hollow places of me, along with the buried hurts, could be free with just the right thoughts. The proper will.

I would fail my test. And it would not matter. There would be nothing left to condemn. The fire would take me from the seat of my very soul, to full in form.

You cannot kill that which is dead.

The fire offered me that freedom. And it begged me to take it.

I would fail.

The thought and threat loudened, now giving voice to the fire in a tone I'd rarely heard. The sharp wailing keen of monsters from stories.

"Ari." Rishi Ibrahm's voice was not a thunderous thing. It was a gentle breath against my atham, and my Athir.

The fire raged, and I did not dare look upon it or the candle. Instead, I went back to Enshae. The shared stillness and silence we traded over stories and through the lessons. I slowed, and I remembered my desire. The promises I'd made, and the strength of will I'd committed to seeing them fulfilled.

To stand before the thousand arrows of Alum Above, and cast aside his judgment. The will to return from Enshae, and to trick her. The courage to walk into war, and walk my friend through the walls of fire I had summoned along the desert night.

And the candle followed that will.

I hoped . . .

The flame no longer burned—body or mind. It simply brought itself against my atham and Athir. I felt it flicker and bob, nothing so much like the howling pillar Rishi Ibrahm had shaped it into.

One of the masters sucked in a breath, finally forcing me to open my eyes. I couldn't help but smile on seeing what lay before me.

The flame danced on a stump of a candle. Most of the wax had solidified against my hand, but the fire hadn't gone out. Now it burned as gentle as any candle flame should have.

Just like the one in my folds.

Rishi Ibrahm wore the widest grin of all the masters, which wasn't saying much considering few smiled. Though I counted no frowns or the makings of anger along any of their faces. Most had taken to parting their mouths in silent surprise.

"No, no. Wait for it." Rishi Ibrahm waggled his fingers in a gesture that could have been described as vaguely magical. Something better suited to storybook magic than anything actually used by someone in possession of wizardly talent. His lips moved and I couldn't make out what he'd said, but I imagined him to be working another binding.

I prepared my Athir, wondering what he could be planning.

"Remember your time trying to keep your hands unburned?"

I blinked, then nodded.

"Good." Master Binder's smile touched his eyes. "Think fast, Ari." At that, the remaining candle turned to a puddle of wax, but the flame did not die.

I gasped, but didn't lose my hold on the bindings.

"Ha!" Rishi Ibrahm leaned to one side, clapping a hard hand to Rishi Bearu's back.

The muscular rishi—Master Conditioner—turned halfway in his seat to regard Rishi Ibrahm with a stare that could have cracked stone.

Even the crazed teacher knew enough to look down at the desk and avoid eye contact. "Heh. Sorry about that. But look at the boy now, *ji-ah*?"

We all glanced down at my palms, and the bobbing flame that rested perfectly in the cup of my hands. And I remained—unburned.

I couldn't help it. I laughed.

Rishi Ibrahm joined me, and soon, smiles came to the rest of the masters' faces.

"That settles that." The headmaster looked to the others, taking silent consideration from them. "Kaethar Ari has demonstrated enough control and responsibility in channeling one of the major composite bindings. This combined with Master Binder vouching for him is enough in my mind to reinstate him as a student of the Ashram." He looked around again, asking for the others to weigh in with just a look.

Every hand went up.

But it was Rishi Saira, Master Lorist, who had one last question. "I've heard you managed to go on quite the adventure in the time you spent away from the Ashram, Kaethar Ari?"

I nodded.

She leaned closer, a dangerous light in her eyes. "I seem to remember leaving a book in your care. Do you remember?"

The fire may have been resting comfortably in my hands, but now I felt it more along the collar of my neck. I nodded again.

"It hasn't been returned, according to several lorists in training. So, what, may I ask, happened to the book?"

Rishi Ibrahm let out a long, low whistle that did not help my situation in the slightest.

"Well . . . Rishi Saira, it's a long and funny story."

That didn't deter her. "Tell me."

So I did, with all the masters listening.

ONE HUNDRED THIRTY

CELEBRATIONS

Night found me in the broken tower near the backmost parts of the Ashram grounds. I made my way down the stairs into Stones, finding Radi and Aram already there and waiting. My recent readmittance back into the Ashram warranted a celebration party, you see. Several other students, noticeably plucked from Rishi Ibrahm's more advanced binding class, were there as well. A few of the musicians I had seen before soon filtered in, and a larger throng of students followed after.

I moved over to Radi and nudged him with an elbow. "How did you manage to drag this many people out?"

He shied away from my look, turning to Aram in silence for help.

Aram first embraced me as if I hadn't been an absent friend for a year, both literally and figuratively. And I loved her even more for it. But a weariness hung in her eyes, and it was a look that clearly spoke of wanting no questions. So, to preserve our friendship, I swallowed my curiosity, and my care, pretending nothing was wrong. "Radi might have led with the fact that he has a new song to play, and that this is more of an end-of-season celebration. You just happen to be here too."

I looked at Radi, but my friend had suddenly taken a great interest in the geological construction of the cave around us.

I couldn't wholly blame him. I suppose I had made it hard to convince students to come out solely for me rather than for a fun night of music and dancing. A shared celebration worked just as well. After all, I have always loved a crowd.

Soon enough, I was given the very thing.

Radi, always the performer, had the gift of perfect timing burned into his heart, and saw what I had. No better moment existed to take everyone's attention than the one before us now. And Radi moved to do just that.

More students filed into Stones, a few carrying tin cups, and it didn't take much guesswork to know what they drank. Not this late into the day and after classes. Some moved with the bleary-eyed expressions you expected of those just short of full inebriation.

But sometimes that's the best audience you could ask for.

And Radi knew this. He stood atop one of the flattened protrusions from the cavern floor, letting his fingers move along the mandolin's strings. Slowly, smoothly, he coaxed the first threads of music out from the instrument. Low and lilting—a thing to catch at the edge of your hearing and turn yours ears toward him. And it worked.

Soon, most of the crowd had stopped their private mutterings and gave Radi their full attention.

Artist that he was, Radi was not one to be satisfied with just their stares and ears. He wanted them, hearts and minds. To have them held wholly on the end of every note he played, waiting for whatever breath came next—whatever sound plucked free from the mandolin. And he would have to earn that. So he set to it.

Radi had turned the story of my new travels into a song. One meant to bolster his name as much as mine, and in a fairer world, men and women would remember his name all the greater. They'd be speaking of him over mugs tall with beer rather than whispering misheard rumors about me.

But the world is not a fair place, and it has no use for memory or for the stories of singers. Only a fascination with monsters. It would be better were it the other way around.

So Radi sang. First nothing but a whisper—words meant only to be heard by the closest around him. It brought smiles to some faces, but the rest crowded closer. Motes of light warmed the place with their pale orange glow as some students brought long candles to life. A few had managed to smuggle binder's lamps into Stones, bathing the place in a cleaner white than what the flame offered.

The notes loudened, and the expression of self-satisfaction faded from Radi's face. Now his brows furrowed and he pulled the song out of the mandolin as much as himself. You've probably heard the like, but I'll do my best to describe it. It was soft wind over warm sands, bright and clear and as teasing as a lover's whisper against your ear. This wasn't a song to strike you. It flowed through you. It kissed along your skin, and you leaned into it—in for it, hoping as you did, you would take away more of it. And Radi's voice was the same.

Low and long, it was a honey-hummed echo through Stones. He spoke of bandits across the sands, and The Hundred Thieves who made those dunes their homes. A band unseen in the night who moved across the desert gold and over stone homes far out in Zibrath. They would steal your coin as much as your secrets. He sang still of tribal nomads, fighting on horseback and camel's hump, launching arrows as quickly as rain in storm. And of course of the young man come so recently into their company. One who killed a desert prince, in a duel, because how else would you kill someone of that sort?

Somber then, downward the song and Radi's tone went. Darker. To what followed in the aftermath of Shareem's death. The judgment passed and a hail of arrows meant to leave only the memory of me upon the sands. A memory made and left in red.

But it would not be, and Radi sang it so, of the binding and what happened next. How I passed through the Doors of Midnight—the passage of stories and into a world of fantasy. This set some of the students gossiping, most discounting it, of course. But they had been drinking, and a few thought back over the lines, then stared at me, and my brilliant white cloak of starry threads and moonlight bright.

Then. Then they wondered. They frowned. And I could see the beginnings of the question behind their eyes: What if? What if in fact I had done those very things? What if they were true?

And that is all the song needed. All I did.

For true to Radi's hopes, everyone now hung on the end of his every breath—waiting . . . waiting for more. And he gave it to them.

The crowd closed in tighter around him and Radi leaned into the performance. To say his voice became golden-burnished-bright would dull just how much shine can fit in someone's words, and their heart. Radi gave it all to us by the end.

Smoother, quicker, shifting into the weight and drumming thunder that comes with a gathering storm, much like the ones that had broken out over the desert.

In the end, every chest rose in tandem with his. Every breath caught the edge of his, and for a moment, we all shared that singular act. Breathing together in the aftermath of the performance. Some voices carried the ends of the dying tune, humming it long after Radi's own words had faded.

Several students came even closer than before, offering to help him down from a place he needed no aid in leaving, but all the same. He'd been a tiny king for those moments, and now his subjects wanted to have their time with him.

He caught my eye, and I his—we traded smiles, and I let my friend get the best of the attention that night. He deserved it.

Aram found me in the throng of people, taking hold of my arm at the elbow. She fixed me with a stare.

I frowned. "What's wrong?"

She didn't say anything, motioning with a slight tilt of her head and arching of brows.

I turned to find Nitham mingling with some of the crowd closer to the back. He wore his better robes, those the blood-red of beets, the color of his house. But it was one of the other people in the group who took my full attention.

Her hair hung in a loose braid—threads of ivory white, touched with the soft-flowered blue of spring afternoons. And she wore the same warm-flowing robes as any other student in the winter.

Nitham reached out to her with a hand, but she moved just out of reach, leaving his fingers to brush through empty air.

I took a step forward before fingers dug hard into the flesh of my arm.

Aram held me, and once I would have bristled at her attempt to stop me.

But a great deal had happened in my time away from the Ashram. And I supposed it could be said that I had grown.

. . . Somewhat.

Then, I didn't see Nitham, the spoiled child of princely means. I saw Shareem. And I remembered not so long ago when his clothes spread with the color of blood. So I stayed in place, and for once, exhibited the sort of control the masters of the Ashram so desperately wanted of me.

The same could not be said of Nitham.

Nitham finally turned enough to catch my eye and flashed me a hateful glare he seemed to have been keeping in his heart all season for only me. Then he broke from his group and came toward me with all the speed of someone who knew I'd torched his home.

But he found a thread of restraint just before reaching me. "I was hoping I wouldn't have to see you this season, or the next."

"Funny thing. I was hoping the same." I matched his tone. "But here you are."

Nitham's hands pumped several times before finally forming fists. "You burned down my rooms, didn't you, you filthy Sullied trash." He leaned closer, dropping his voice to a whisper. "Didn't you?"

I leaned in and brought my mouth close to one of his ears. "Last I heard, all people saw was red smoke, and a ghost atop the roofs. Must have been the Ashura." I pulled away and swallowed all my temptation to smile. "You should consider yourself lucky. What if they come back? What if next time the fire starts while you're soundly asleep?"

Nitham's eyes widened before going thin as razor slits. "Careful, Sullied, that almost sounded like a threat."

I kept my face a mask of stone. "Just a question."

He took a step toward me, our foreheads meeting as his nose touched mine. I leaned in as well, my breath quickening. Is this how it would play out? Who'd make the first move? Would we fall into a tangle of thrashing limbs as a crowd of students looked on?

Not what I needed right now. Especially considering I'd only just been given a second chance by the masters. So I did one of the hardest things imaginable for a boy still fresh in his impressionable and . . . impassioned youth.

I swallowed my pride and pulled myself away.

Nitham's lips twitched, and just the hint of a smile graced the corners of his mouth. He'd won a small victory, and he knew it. "That's right, Sullied, walk away or you'll get the thrashing you know I'll give you."

I gritted my teeth, and one of my hands pumped into a fist. And the memory of another time came to me. A fist closed in anger at another young man. A hand tight around the hilt of a blade, and what it had led to. So I exhaled and relaxed my fingers.

Nitham saw that as a moment of weakness, but someone else decided to seize the chance to break the tension. Shandi brushed past the students, the flowers threaded through her hair shaking as she placed herself between Nitham and me. Her arms crossed and she gave us a look that could cow a stampeding horse.

Nitham shied away from the stare, but I met Shandi's gaze straight on. In her eyes, I caught all of the palest bright of the nearby binder's lamp. It brought a color close to citrine out of their light brown. A color touching gold. The look cooled and the shine faded as she gave me something just short of a smile. Perhaps a patient quirk of the lips at best.

I supposed I had earned that much, being a touch stubborn. "Sorry."

Her mouth twitched, almost betraying a grin. "*And here I thought you were only hotheaded.*" The words came from her as if pressed from her breast, and not her throat. Low, the very wind within her voice.

Nitham placed a hand on Shandi's shoulder and forced her to turn to regard him. A mistake on his part. Certainly not his first, and assuredly not his last.

She rounded on him and brushed his touch aside. "Don't *ever* . . . Nitham." Her words did not give voice to the anger made plain in the tenseness of her neck and shoulders. No. But it was there, clear as could be for all of us to see.

"Shandi, I just—"

She turned again, this time crossing the distance between us and taking my hand in hers. A few voices raised and the crowd fell into all the sorts of talk you could imagine of young students. Gossip, arguments, and my friends falling into bickering with Nitham and his crowd. But it didn't matter to me because Shandi had me in her hold, and she'd made it quite clear she had no desire to let go.

She led me out of Stones and up the stairs of the broken tower until we came out on the rear grounds of the Ashram. "I swear, one of these days he's going to say something that'll finally make me slap him."

I snorted. "Now I wish he had. I'd pay to see that."

Shandi laughed, then caught herself in the act. She soon sobered and her eyes turned to the ground. "He brings out the worst in people."

Immi had said something similar. And I made sure to add this to the long list of grievances I could tally against Nitham.

One of Shandi's hands folded over the other, and she went through all the little motions I knew came with nervousness.

I reached out with one of my own, not touching her until I saw the silent invitation clear in her eyes. Once I had that, I pressed one of my palms against her hands and hoped it offered at least a small comfort.

"Oh, I'm well aware of what Nitham brings out in people," I said.

She pursed her lips before speaking. "I suppose so. He's been pushing at you ever since you came here, *ji-ah*?"

I nodded, not bothering to speak.

Shandi led me away from the main courtyard, closer to the large patch of empty frozen land beyond the Crow's Nest. A piece of flat mountaintop that overlooked Ghal and gave us an unimpeded view of the night sky. Her gaze turned toward the stars and she let out a light breath. "Do you ever wonder about them?"

I followed her stare, but didn't have the faintest idea as to what she meant.

She thrust her chin upward. "The stars. What they've seen, what they talk about, what they remember? They say Brahm shaped them before everything else. First of his fires. They've been there longer than anything in creation. And they've watched it all take shape beneath them."

I shook my head. "No. At least not as much as I should have."

Shandi gave me a sidelong look, asking the question in silence.

"I spent most of the year away from the Ashram—"

"Yes. I missed you."

Four words, and they certainly were not responsible for the sudden flushing of my cheeks. That had most assuredly come from our leaving the warmth of Stones, with all the burning fires, for the cold mountaintop where we now stood.

Shandi must have noticed my reaction, and of course taken the wrong assumption. "It was nice when we danced. And you're one of the few people who hasn't chased me around the Ashram. You're not like Nitham and his friends."

The winter air had gotten to my throat, or perhaps I had been humming along to Radi's song, all without knowing, and that had taken its toll.

Whatever the reason, I found the stars slightly less alluring, and all questions about them gone from my mind.

But they hadn't left Shandi's. More's the pity.

"What made you think you should have paid them more mind, Ari?" Her eyes remained on the stars.

I told her then of my journey across the desert—time kept in the *Maathi*'s company and our mapping the skies. How he told me of the stars and how they served as our guides. I almost spoke of my time with Enshae, and her shapings. The piece she'd made that I'd given to Immi especially came to mind. But I didn't think that bit of Shaen story would help me have that sweet moment there with her, so I left it out.

Shandi pointed to one star in particular and opened her mouth to speak.

"Shyla." We both turned toward the voice. Rishi Ibrahm stood several feet behind us, staring exactly at the star Shandi had gestured to. "That's her name, Shyla. It means 'little dove.'" He frowned. "Or is it white dove?" Master Binder touched his thumbs together, spreading his fingers into a crude imitation of wings. He flapped them several times.

It was then that both Shandi and I noticed what Rishi Ibrahm was wearing. Or rather, what he had forgotten to wear. The Master Binder of the Ashram stood there, in the winter snow of Ghal, without any socks or boots. The hem of his patchwork robe hung to just under his knees, and the way it rested betrayed an utter lack of undergarments.

A theory I did not want to confirm.

Shandi, a braver soul than me, however, decided to find the answer for us. "Um, Rishi Ibrahm . . ."

Master Binder stopped his flapping and turned his attention on her. "Hm?"

"Aren't you cold?" Her gaze fell to Rishi Ibrahm's exposed legs before inching up to where a hint of bare chest showed through his robes. "It doesn't look like you're wearing . . . much."

He blinked at her as if he couldn't comprehend what she'd said. Then, looking down, he finally noticed what we had. "Oh. Too many clothes don't let you feel the winter the way you're supposed to. Makes it difficult, you know, to understand the cold."

I finally found my tongue. "I don't think we're supposed to understand it, Rishi Ibrahm."

The Master Binder turned his attention to me. "Part of your problem, Ari, is that you think too much. You'll think yourself into circles when you're better off shutting up and just doing, hm?" He opened his mouth as if to chastise me further, then stopped upon looking at Shandi. "Oh, Shandi." One of Rishi Ibrahm's hands pressed to his chest and he gave her a formal bow.

My friend stared back at him for a moment before inclining her head ever so slightly. "Master Binder."

I had the good sense to remain respectfully silent, though that had less to do with respect itself than the fact I had no clue what in Brahm's name had just happened. And so the silence persisted awhile longer before Rishi Ibrahm returned to his usual form.

"It's a good night for stargazing. You can learn a lot watching them, you know? They're old. And they've seen the turning of things for a time uncounted."

"And they have stories all their own." The words might have come from my mouth, but certainly not from any place I'd known of.

Rishi Ibrahm turned slowly to face me. "Yes . . . yes, they do, Ari. Maybe you don't have as much snow between your ears as I thought. Good. But . . . we could always fix that." He smiled and wiggled his fingers.

"Huh?"

"Think fast. Ahn. Ahl." Rishi Ibrahm gestured in my direction and the weight of powdered frost struck me.

I hit the ground—hard. Snow slipped in through my robes and, if he had had any doubt about the quantity of snow between my ears, he could now rest assured that they were thoroughly filled.

When I came out from under the ice, he had left.

The night quickly drew itself to a close after that. But it had left me in the company of Shandi, who had decided to take me to my rooms to see me warmed and out of the cold.

We traded talk all while Shola watched us, eyes fluttering with the weight of sleep soon to come on the little flame. I told Shandi the most believable parts of my journey, going so far as to bring up the Doors of Midnight.

But I might have left out the parts with Enshae.

She resumed our conversation of the stars, and eventually, we returned to a subject we both had a great deal of passion for.

Nitham.

I learned everything he'd been up to over my absence, and that in my time away, he had been left unchallenged in the kite festival. He'd only entered because I hadn't been around, which gave me the perfect idea of how to spike his wheel the following year.

When Shandi left, I dreamed of kites, and my entry in the next festival.

And perhaps of Nitham's face when I trounced him again.

I was in a good mood. And you can hardly blame a young man for such thoughts that bring him pleasure.

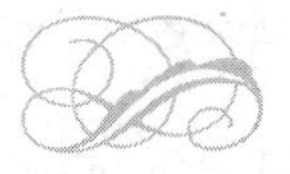

ONE HUNDRED THIRTY-ONE

The Last Page

One last piece of work remained that season, and I didn't look forward to it. I had amends to make to Rishi Saira for gifting her book of stories to Enshae. My punishment? To carefully transcribe a new copy.

So I headed down into Ghal and found where I'd be paying my debt.

The Last Page.

I'd been told it had begun as an independent dealer of books in the city, but was eventually co-opted by the Ashram to recondition tomes that could not be fixed in the Scriptory. In addition, it acted as private storage for overflow, and a seller of transcribed copies of works out of the fabled academy. For every coin that came into them, some went back to the Financiary.

The building resembled many others in Ghal in most regards. But the differences were not subtle, and they made it stand out amidst the other shops. Round and rising upward for four stories, it ended in a domed cap with a spire protruding from its top. The roof had been set in beaten golden foil. This drew all the brightness of any light to The Last Page, only for that glow to be lost in the black of its stone walls. So dark a color that I had rarely seen its like save for in the woodwork of a bow I had trained with on the sands of Zibrath.

On closer inspection, I noted a flowing script carved along the stone. Minor bindings, though I couldn't make out their function. A longer look revealed that the magical writing ran across the place's entirety, including the gilded roof.

I made my way inside to find a place that looked as if it had been plucked out of the Scriptory and set here. The interior was nearly identical in every way save for having less room to operate in.

A woman shuffled into view, carrying a load of books that she set down on the other end of a counter. Her complexion held more dark bronze than I'd seen in most people native to Ghal. She could have been somewhere in her forties, though her hair had reached the gray of steel rather early. But it suited her. Heart-shaped in face with bright eyes full of matronly kindness.

"Ah, you're him, *ji-ah*?" Her voice had a dryness that made it seem like she'd gone days without water.

"Sorry?"

She pursed her lips and tapped the spine of a book she'd placed on the wooden surface. "A sweet little owl told me a troublesome young boy would be coming here. She lent him a book, and the dung-for-brains happened to lose it. Now he'll be here to scribe a new copy."

I thought on what she'd said, then blinked. "Rishi Saira sent me here to do something like that, yes."

The woman brushed her hands down her robes and fixed me with a smile. "Yes, my owl sent you. She's too busy with her nose and specs stuck in books to help me bind the things for storing and selling." She formed circles with her hands and mimed a pair of optics over her own eyes. "Come on, we'll get you to work."

I followed as directed. "How do you know Rishi Saira?"

The woman, who I learned was the proprietor, smiled at the question. "Oh, about the same way as any woman knows her lover. That's why I also know it is a good thing that it is me looking after you today and not her. She'd have welted your rump red enough that no amount of snow would cool its sting. But, she's also one of short mind when it comes to this sort of thing." The owner of The Last

Page sighed. "She's quick to return to her work and the questions. Always the questions. 'Who? Who? Who?'"

I tried not to laugh at one of the Ashram's masters being so easily mocked. And I failed, breaking into a low chuckle that I quickly swallowed.

"If you are ever lucky enough to find someone to give your heart to, boy, you'll learn to find the humor in the things that come to bother you about your love as well. Here." She gestured to a room ahead of us.

A table stood there with a graphter and a stack of fresh parchment. Only, it looked like I would be sharing the table.

Shandi sat there, poring over a tome. She wore the inner robes that students kept to during warmer months of the year, and that's when the temperature of the room struck me.

Despite having no visible fires, the place felt as comfortable to the skin as the hearth of an inn.

Perhaps the bindings scrawled along the building's surface? But I had no time to ponder it as Shandi caught my eye.

"Ari." She smiled, brushing a few strands of hair out of her eyes.

"Remember"—the owner of the shop placed a hand on my collar—"you are to return every day until you complete the work, *ji-ah*?" The tone brooked no argument.

"*Ji.*" I nodded.

"Good." The elderly woman waved a hand to Shandi. "Would you be kind enough to get him a copy of *Sashra ta-tathan kahniye*? We have one for transcription purposes."

Shandi bobbed her head and left, returning quickly with the book in question. She set it down on the table and I moved to join her.

The owner left us in privacy and I set to my task.

I would say I suffered the sort of tedium you'd expect from that sort of work, only that wouldn't be true. It offered me another chance to dive into my love of stories, and keep company with Shandi.

Certainly no chore.

We talked of tales, she told me of songs, and we would have our first argument. Though certainly not our last.

I'd just finished inking the first of many stories when Shandi finished speaking.

"What do you mean?" I looked up from the page and met her stare.

"Songs are older than stories. Before people wrote words to tell tales, they sang." She touched her finger to a passage in the book she'd been reading.

I leaned over to get a better look at it, then frowned. "People told stories by firelight before we could record them in writing. It's one of the oldest traditions in the world."

"So is singing. What's a story but a song without music? The rhythm? A song is a story that can only be sung. It doesn't need thousands of pages to make you feel what it means to. It just does."

I snorted. "A song is nothing more than a story strung along to music to make up for what it lacks."

She closed the book and stared—a fresh-kindled flame of anger bringing out the brightness of her eyes. More the yellow-gold of fire than their usual sun-touched brown. "Tell that to Radi the next time he sings something of your madness when you're gallivanting about." Her words were hot enough to set our papers aflame.

"Shandi, I'm sorry." I raised both my hands in apology, hoping that would mollify her.

To a degree, it did. She exhaled and thumbed the book back open. "They're a touchy subject for me. A lot of my studies and projects are fixed on songs. And they're not something catered to by the Ashram. At least not much."

"I understand. It's sort of the same way with me and stories. I've . . . I'm looking for a certain one. But I haven't been able to find it." I thought of the Ashura, the Asir, and Brahm.

Shandi reached out and gave my hand a squeeze. "Maybe we could help each other." And when she smiled, it came as white and bright as freshly fallen snow.

How could I do anything but grin back and accept the offer? "I'd like that."

So we set to it together. She would help me transcribe the stories, quickening the process, and thus give us the free time to peruse the other books within The Last Page.

And we may have participated in some mischief in this time of togetherness.

After all, Rishi Saira had tasked me with copying over the lost stories into a new volume, but she hadn't made a single mention about those being the only tales I could include. I had certainly had my share of those of late. So the two of us may have begun the process of adding another character into the book of legends and folklore.

His name was Ari.

You might have heard of him.

He battled a serpent of white iron scales atop a mountain of ice and snow. And but with a word and a cry, he brought down the mountain low. He robbed a merchant king and was a demon in the night along the streets of Abhar. He'd bound fire, and then again out across the desert. Opening the very doors to hell. Flames so hot that they fused the sands to glass.

Some say those fires still burn today.

And he walked through the Doors of Midnight and lived to return.

We thought it rather funny. Besides, what harm have a few stories ever done?

It turns out, more than I could ever have imagined.

But let us leave this story there for now. Home again at the Ashram, in good company, and closer to performing the ten bindings all men must know.

Things were well, for once.

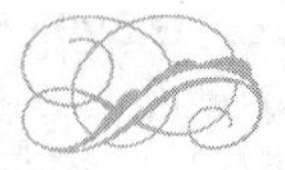

ONE HUNDRED THIRTY-TWO

TALK OF STORIES

Eloine took my hand in hers, stroking her thumb along the soft flesh between my thumb and forefinger. "So you finally started thinking of the Ashram as your home, hm?" No smile, but the soft light in her eyes served as the same thing. "A place worth staying for, and a family being built?"

I waggled my free hand. "After a fashion. It had become a place of familiarity for me. One could say it was almost safe—*almost*. Certainly for others, but I had the uncanny knack of stirring up trouble as much as I did getting myself out of it. Some on account of great luck, the rest through just as much in cleverness."

"Mm." A candle's glow of amusement danced in Eloine's eyes, but she said nothing further. Though she didn't have to. Her light and mocking judgment shone clear through in her stare. "Your cleverness certainly seems to be a sword to cut both ways. Even in your home." The gleam in her look left her then—a somberness falling quick over her face.

She picked at one of her fingernails before playing with her dress. Signs of minor discomfort? Perhaps agitation. I couldn't tell. Eloine met my eyes again. "I like the sound of a place like that, the Ashram—sometimes, at least. My people are wanderers. We're not ones for roots, be they trees or mountain schools. We are bound everywhere—welcome, and settling, nowhere."

I gave her a gentle squeeze back. "My people are the same. Though I didn't know it at the time. But I suppose the blood was always in me, and that left me a restless soul, especially at the Ashram. I was never one to sit still or linger long. Maybe things would be different if I had." I gave Eloine a thin and short-lasting smile.

She gestured to the ceiling, making it clear she meant to reach for something far above it. "It can be a good life for my people. So long as we have the moon above us, and the stars, we're never really lost. We're never alone. And we are always home. There's some comfort in that." In the moment, Eloine looked very much as if she wanted to believe her own words, but could not. And just as much wished for a moment to have that thing she spoke of.

Comfort.

And I wanted to do everything I could to give her even a second's worth.

But I didn't know how. All I had were my words—what I always had, then. So I gave them to her, first hoping to craft a bridge to her melancholy. Something along which she could walk away on, leaving those thoughts behind.

"For my people it's the sun. We walk under its light and warmth—all roads open to us during its brightness. We find busy taverns in need of performers for their afternoon crowds. And then again at night. All we need is a piece of the sun for ourselves. A piece of fire. With that in hand, we're never too far from its light, and our homes. A Ruma is never more at peace than by the side of candlelight and a good story for the night." The trick worked, and Eloine caught on to the seed I'd planted within my words.

Curiosity flooded her, knitting her brows close together. Her lips pursed, and soon the words I knew would come left her mouth. "I've heard tell that you've taken a piece of that for yourself. Some say you stole a sliver of the sun itself. Others claim it was but a piece of its breath. An ever-burning fire. That's what they say."

I said nothing, this time keeping the smile on my face through sheer will and practiced memory of the old actor's craft. No sincerity. And certainly no honest joy in it. "I've heard people say the same." I gave her a little laugh. The kind any performer would know was fake upon first hearing it. "But as you've seen for yourself, you can't go believing every story you've heard about me." My heart couldn't find its way into the words, however. Instead, it brought to life an old ache, and a pain that burned as bright as any freshly fed flame.

If Eloine noticed this, she said nothing. The songstress turned her gaze to one of the candles burning on the mantelpiece. She stared at it as if trying to lose herself in its light. "But you grew closer to it. The fire, I mean. Back in the desert . . . with one of the Ashura—"

"Koli." The name left my lips half in curse, and all in shadowed whisper. So low and harsh a thing I didn't know if she'd heard me speak at all.

Eloine turned back to me. "What did he want? Why was he out there? What do you think his game was?"

I licked my lips, thinking back to the moment we crossed paths on the sands. To how I'd gone wrong in chasing the wrong kinds of stories. But first I remembered the needle-thin sword. A thing edgeless and drawn to a point so sharp it promised to cut even the air before it. And I remembered its length run red with blood. Finally, I returned to what he'd once said to me.

I exhaled and forced myself to speak. "He was playing the most dangerous sort of game. The slow kind. The patient sort. The one long in waiting and planned from the very beginning. A trick as much as a trap. For a clever bird, not at all wise, to fall into that trap." I thought to my time with the prince-elect earlier.

"Have you ever played Talluv, Eloine?"

She nodded, and her mouth twitched at one corner. If it had moved in full, I'm sure I would have been treated to a crooked smile. The one tricksters and con men wear most well. And I knew her to be at the very least as clever as those. I remembered the night my purse went missing, then decided that Eloine might just be a shade more cunning than me. "I'm familiar with the game, Storyteller."

"Then you have some understanding of how a game can be more than just the pieces on the board. It is a thing of lies, all hidden within truths. And picking falsehoods free from facts is no easy thing. They get tangled together—mixed, and you often find yourself tearing it apart entirely rather than getting the bits you need. You can be misled until you end up right where the enemy wants you.

"On the journey back to the Ashram, I thought often about what had brought the Ashura to the desert. Was Nassih right? Had they come hearing the stories about themselves? A truth amidst the lies they'd been so careful to cultivate? If that was the case, I never got to find that story as no one but Nassih survived. So all I had were the truths told to me, and there is no clean way to know if what we are told by others is the truth they claim it to be."

Eloine's eyes fell on my mouth before she touched a finger to the very place, tracing it along the shape of my lips. "You've gone dour again, and I fear that Koli's left a different sort of wound in you than the one on the night you learned he was an Ashura."

I frowned, not sure what she meant.

"See, there it is." Eloine moved her finger again, now bringing it around the lines of my more somber expression. "He's left a hole in you that makes it hard for you to trust." She pursed her lips and looked down to the space between us. "I wonder if you even trust me?" The question came with the breath of whispered air and all the sorrow of broken-edged stone.

I touched two fingers to Eloine's closest wrist, running them up along her arm until they rested under her chin. More liberty than I'd taken with her before, but I wanted to look her in the eyes when I spoke. So I applied as gentle a pressure as I could to raising her head to stare at me. "I've trusted you with my story so far. All the truths of who I am. The good . . . and the bad. All my flaws and crimes laid bare." I swallowed a touch of moisture that had formed in my throat. "I'm trusting you with what I've entrusted to no one else." More words wanted to follow.

They told me to give voice to the unspoken truth deep in my heart. That I had trusted Eloine with more than she had me. My secrets were shared. Hers still kept in keeping-deep in heart. But I knew that would only drive her from me. It would be easier to catch the moon in hand than wheedle something out of Eloine she did not wish to share. So I left it alone, and swallowed all the burning curiosity that had driven me through most of my life.

"And I thank you for it, Ari." Few things sound as sweet as your own name from the mouth of someone you have come to care for so deeply as I had Eloine. When she'd said it, it carried all the comfort and invitation of a cool breeze on a warm summer's day. "I know it hasn't been easy for you. I know that *I* haven't made it easy for you."

I opened my mouth to protest, but knew a glimmer of the truth shone across my face.

Eloine never gave me the chance, in any case. She seized the open moment, and open mouth, to steal any and all objections I might have given voice to. The scent of her graced me first, and it was a thing of warm wood and the faintest promise of citrus. An undercurrent of lavender came through before I lost all track of whatever else may have been there as her lips pressed against mine.

Any questions I might have had died far at the back of my mind, and whatever lingering doubts my heart held found themselves cast far below to a place I would not retrieve them from for quite some time.

A kiss is a simple thing. Often an overlooked thing. But there is a reason the word shares the same number of letters as two other important words. Love. And. Time. They can be one and the same, depending on the circumstance. And in that moment with Eloine, I found them to be that.

All the same.

I lost track of time in the depth of the kiss, and if I could, I'd have felt every second ten times as long. In the heat of it, I came to remember the first sparks of what I had come to believe was love—a time so long ago. And another person. A warmth and promise pressed firm against my own skin.

Sometimes it is the simplest things that are the most special. The most memorable. And those come to be anything but simple.

When she pulled away, the awareness of all other things crashed into me with the ferocity of the sea in storm. I opened my eyes to find her already standing, the copy of *Tuecanti des Nuevellos* in her hand. "I believe we promised each other story for story, yes?"

I grinned. "Yes."

She lived up to her promise.

We traded away the hours deep in conversation as we pored over the book. Most of it, to my dismay, provided as much as most stories of the Ashura ever had.

Which is to say . . . nothing.

Eloine touched a finger to a page, running it along a line of words. "What's this?"

I leaned over, peering at the Etaynian script, unable to parse it.

"It speaks of the one in red, wayward facing his shadow. The first and greatest of the *Nuevellos*. Red the color of his misdeeds. Red the sign of his crimes. Red the shade of blood he's spilled." As she spoke, I watched her eyes slowly turn from the pages of the book to my cloak. They worked their way up along its length until her gaze rested on my face.

I let out a light breath through my nose. "Abrahm."

Eloine's lips pressed tight together. "You never mentioned him apart from the stories."

My voice grew leaden, hollow, and distant as an echo close to dying. "No."

A moment passed in silence. Then another. But before it grew to be too long, Eloine took it upon herself to break it. "Perhaps it's best if we talk of different stories then, hm?"

I arched a brow, waiting for her to explain.

"How about . . . rumors?" A fire kindled in her eyes, and it carried the invitation to ask a question.

So I obliged. "Oh, and what rumors would those be?"

Eloine moved just an inch from me, eyeing me sideways. "The sort that say our Storyteller is putting on a performance. Something in the king's garden grounds outside. A story to celebrate Prince-elect Efraine's coming into the crown."

"Ah." I drew the word out, then permitted myself a smile. "I had heard something about that. And your interest in this is . . . ?"

She wore a look of mock offense. "You should know very well, being a fellow performer at that."

I rose, but she took a step away from me for every one I made toward her. "I've offended you. You feel, what, left out because I decided to take all the attention for myself for one night?"

She sniffed and turned away from me, but I could feel the edge of her gaze still upon my face.

I tried not to smile.

"After our last moment in the light together, I thought we had made a rather special item. Perhaps I was wrong." Each word could have cut another man's heart, but I heard the thrumming strings of humor under them. A laugh not quite coloring her voice, but there all the same.

"*Well . . .*"

Eloine turned back to me. She said nothing, but her expression spoke for her. It said: *Curiosity. Anticipation. Asking invitation.* And, of course, a very silent, hopeful *yes*?

"Well . . ." I drew the word out once again, letting it be as teasing as a thing possibly could be. "I *did* need an assistant—" The book Eloine had been holding sailed through the air and I rushed forward to catch it between both my hands. "What are you—" My question died in my throat as Eloine closed the distance and reminded me of a lesson in time, simplicity, and perhaps several other things.

When she had finished, I had quite forgotten what I had been meaning to say. I only had space for the lingering taste of her mouth.

"I would love nothing more than to be your partner, Ari. We could put on a performance that these Etaynians would remember for a long time."

I thought of what Ernesto and I had spoken of earlier. *They'll never forget it. I promise you that.* Aloud, I gave voice to something else entirely. "Of course, I meant partner. Isn't that what I said?" I gave her a roguish grin and leapt to one side as her hand blurred.

Her lighthearted swat passed through empty air. "Ass."

"*Yee-haw.*" I did my best to make the sound carry the full harshness of a donkey's bray.

Eloine stiffened and her eyes narrowed into slits. "Ari . . . for someone who has come so perilously close to death many times . . . you do like flirting with it, don't you?"

My grin widened. "Oh, is that what I was flirting with? I thought it was something else entirel—ow!" I grimaced and fell onto the bed, grabbing hold of where Eloine had stomped my foot. The blow hadn't landed with enough force to bruise, but I'd feel the mark for at least an hour. Maybe two.

"That was very un-partner-like."

The heat in her look promised to intensify, but it doused itself as she broke into laughter.

I joined her.

The two of us lingered in that space of shared amusement that we very much needed before sobriety took us in its hands.

"And will my partner be telling me what we are to perform?" Eloine didn't join me on the bed, instead moving closer to the door.

I didn't miss the action as her silently making to leave. But I didn't rise from the bed, nor make a move to stop her. I'd learned by then that no one could keep her where she didn't want to be, nor did they have any right to. "It's a story about the sun and moon. About the eternal dance they've been put in—only able to come in reach of arms and lips so rarely in time. It's as much a dance as it is a story. But it's a different sort than most are used to. This one is special because it is a silent story."

Eloine's eyes held a shine that made the heavenly bodies I'd just mentioned pale in comparison. "I'm familiar with that one. And I know such a lovely song for the two. I suppose I'll practice before we perform. I'll need a new dress, and we'll need masks. You know how the Etaynians are. They love their masks."

We all do, and some of us grow too accustomed to their fit. And in doing so, we forget the face beneath, or how to ever remove the masks we've come to wear. I did not share this thought with Eloine. I gave her the answer she sought instead. "I'll give word to see them catered to."

The glow in her eyes intensified. "Maybe I'll be the one to do so."

I finally moved, wanting to at least stand in the closeness of her before she left. One last time.

But it wasn't to be. She waved her fingers at me and slid through the open doorway, shutting it behind her.

I could say that in her absence I turned to the book on the Ashura. That I thumbed through it and tried to translate it alone. Or that I thought to brush up on the story I was to perform. But no. Those would be lies.

In truth, I thought of only one thing.

I thought of a scene. How to set it.

And how best to kill a prince.

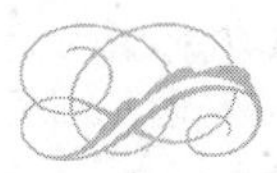

ONE HUNDRED THIRTY-THREE

A Silent Story

What time I had before we were to perform did not pass easily. I took a meal in my room, and received no invitation to speak with any of the nobility within Del Soliel.

Fitting, I supposed. The game had concluded, and while I may have been proven innocent of killing a prince, the trial had soured many against me. So I kept to myself, studying a story I knew as well as my own name.

And how well do you really know that? I banished the voice of doubt, turning instead to my travel sack. A book rested within that I decided to give my full attention, lest my wandering mind find something else depressing to fixate on.

The book was not unlike the one Mahrab had given me so long ago, though it held a different secret inside. Another story. One just as locked away.

My fingers brushed against the grain of its leather and I paused upon touching one of its corners. No amount of wrenching on it would free the pages. All the same, I did just that, knowing the futility of the action.

Some stories cannot be forced. They can only be remembered. This was one of those, and no one could get through to its secrets until they were ready.

But still, I tried. My mind went to the folds, and I envisioned the pages freeing themselves at my next touch. Then again. Twice more. Then three times more still. I went until I'd held twenty. An old and important number for me.

"Open, *please*." I pulled. And pulled. And I pulled.

The book would not open. The story would not be freed. And I would not remember its secrets.

So it remained shut. And with it, the truth of a character from story. All the best of what he'd been, and the worst. His power scattered. His truths mislaid. His name . . . barely remembered true.

Resigned, I stored the book and turned my thoughts to something else. A performance, and where exactly to position the most important player.

Prince-elect Efraine.

The right placement, at the right time. An invitation he could not refuse, and with that, the prince-elect would be the star of the show. And he would make the most unforgettable scene.

Of that, I'd make certain.

When I finished reading, I did the only thing left to me.

I waited.

Because one could not rush killing a prince of Etaynia.

A knock sounded at my door.

I opened it to find the same porter who'd first tended to me on coming to Del Soliel. "Yes?"

The man held a folded robe, done in all the colors of the sun itself. Atop it rested a mask of beaten copper-gilded gold. Spiked rays sprouted from its top, matching the bright heavenly body after which it had been made. The piece would only cover the upper half of my face, but that would be more than enough for the performance. "The Lady Etiana said that Prince-elect Efraine directed her to tell me to—"

I waved him off, keeping the gesture as polite as possible. "These are for my story tonight."

The man nodded, pressing them toward me.

I took the mask, giving the robes another look. "I won't be needing the robes. My own clothing will suffice." I gestured to the blood-red cloak, though I knew what I wore beneath hardly lived up to the splendor that Etaynian nobles chose to prance about in.

"But *sengero*—"

I shut the door, letting the porter know he'd been dismissed.

His footsteps sounded, and they grew more distant by the passing second.

Small relief.

My gaze lingered on the mask, and my thoughts on all the stories of the sun

I'd collected over my life. So many alike, and so very different at the same time. But like all stories, they have a thread that connects them to the ones before them. Even if unseen. A truth many wish to deny when it comes to telling tales.

We are all originals, or so we like to think. But in truth, we are retreading old paths walked before us. We just move a bit differently from the ones who walked them first. We leave different sized footprints in different taken steps.

And we are all the products of the stories that come before us. Whether we like to admit it . . . or not.

I brushed my fingers over the mask, noting that despite never being made for me, its shape seemed perfectly fit to the lines of my face. But we would find out its true fit when it came to the performance, and the finale. The best masks betray nothing but what they are meant to, and I would need mine to show a performer so caught in his role that the sudden break in the story was as much a shock to him as others.

Staff now in hand, I put on the mask over the one I already wore, and I left my room.

It was time to grant Ernesto Vengenza what he wanted most.

Vengeance.

❧

The king's gardens spoke of all the lavish expenditure you expected from a royal family.

Pillars of white stone, clearly from Zibrath, lined the walking paths. Bands of ivy raced along them, further accentuated by paintings of the same vines but in blue. Glass lamps hung from cords strung overhead to cast the place in a muted glow of firelight.

Tables had been set heavy with food and drink of every manner, and seating had been arranged for close to fifty people at best guess. So the performance would not be witnessed by all within Del Soliel. Likely only the most favored of the gentry, or the ones closest to Prince-elect Efraine.

Fair enough. Small crowds work just as well as large. And sometimes, better.

I made my way toward a stone dais at the head of the garden. It would be the perfect place to draw all eyes to me tonight. And in doing so, hopefully away from the walls and who skulked along them.

My eyes flitted to the balconies that provided the best view of where I would be standing. The perfect place for someone to put an arrow through my heart.

At least if Azrim decided to wait no longer to seek his satisfaction. Not a bolstering thought before I was to perform.

The evening darkened.

Some of the nobility had already gathered, lingering near the seats close to where I would stand. They kept close enough to trade the idle gossip the men and women of their station chose to, but as I passed them by, their eyes turned to me.

I ignored them and stepped onto the dais.

"And after all that work I went through to find you those robes—*tsk.*"

I turned to face Eloine.

If my mask had been well-suited to the shape of my face, hers, as well as her dress, had been thought of for only her. Half her visage remained obscured behind a crescent moon covering. It looked a thing drawn of pure silver-fine light-made metal, set with sequins like crushed diamonds, and pressed-flattened stars. The same color had been used to paint her lips and dot the lines of her brows, all serving to better draw out the green of her eyes.

The dress could have been made from polished mirror glass, and the trailing cape that fell off a shoulder looked made from nightly clouds.

Next to her, I was very much the poor sun—a child's crude painting next to the true moon resplendent.

"No clever response?" She arched a brow, the line of her mouth curving.

"Wow."

Her smile widened. "I'll take that as a 'no.'"

"I'm not wholly sure if there's a need for me to be here at all. Not if you plan to sing and outshine me." I pressed a hand to my heart, bowing slightly.

Eloine's mouth twitched, and a brighter light kindled in her eyes. "Flattery, before we're supposed to work? How unprofessional."

"It seemed the better option than asking how much work you actually put into finding me those robes." I turned, eyeing her askance as I did.

"I'll have you know that I spent the better part of an hour waiting for someone to come along and take my suggestions."

I mouthed the word *suggestions.*

Eloine had the grace to no longer meet my eye, turning instead to stare into the growing crowd of nobility. "Fine. My request to find a piece that may or may not have already been close to what we required. It still needed some work—"

"That you did?" I kept my voice neutral as I asked.

"That I oversaw."

I pressed my lips tight, trying not to laugh. "Mhm."

"If I could swat you right now and get away with it, I would." Her tone held no malice, though.

"What fun is it if you can get away with it? Sometimes getting into trouble is the best part."

Eloine took a step closer to me and leaned in. One of her hands cupped her mouth and she spoke in a stage whisper. "And is that what I'm here for? To get into trouble with you?"

"What's better than getting into trouble with someone you know?" My attention was not all on her, though. I searched the balconies as I spoke, never once moving my head to give away my intent. No sign of anyone perched along them, which was a good thing for the moment.

Or a bad one if he's changed his mind. A thread of worry bled through me.

"The crowd's nearly settled." Eloine kept her voice just low enough for me to hear now. "Are you ready?" She moved close enough to nudge my ribs with an elbow, and all under the careful cover of her half cape.

"Of course." I thumped the butt of my staff against the stone dais, drawing the attention of the closest nobles.

They turned to face me.

Just a small binding. This is an act, and that much the Storyteller can always do. The staff became an extension of my will as well as my atham. I brought up the folds, knowing I would need few to influence the world around me for the performance. My voice left me as silver burning threads, wrapping their way around the length of my tool. I saw them spreading and flashing as poor lightning against the ground, and each clap rang with the weight of thunder.

"Start with whent." My voice would echo across the gardens as if borne by drumbeats and brass horns. I believed this as truth. "Then go to ern." Those words, however, were not spoken as such. They left me as the sort of whisper meant to be heard by no one but myself.

I banged my staff against the stone dais once again. A clap of thunder, and the nobles fell into the stillness I wanted. Then I spoke as if mine were the only voice for the whole world to hear. "Lords and ladies! Noble blood and landed gentry. Esteemed company of Etaynia's best!"

The flattery worked to draw the slightest of smiles from the crowd. Some took the cue to find their seats while the rest remained standing, taking drinks in hand from servants. A few had the gall to return to their soft whispers.

The butt of my staff met stone again—this time it drew the full drumming weight of thunder to sound throughout the garden. Every noble stiffened and gave me their attention.

Good.

"Tonight we celebrate an end to *Geuma des Familiya*—the Game of Families. To mark Prince-elect Efraine's victory, and soon his taking of the throne of Etaynia."

The brought about a small chorus of applause, but many of the audience cast wary looks around the gardens.

I couldn't blame them. Not with how Efraine had handled himself during the game. How many other nobles would now try to be so bold after seeing what he was capable of? He'd shown them as much strength—after a fashion—as he gave them reasons to fear him.

"To begin, I offer you a story of the beginning of things. Of before Solus took shape as a man and walked your lands. I give you a tale of a man chosen by heaven above to find and settle this place, making it your own. Of a sailor, who had as much the sea in his blood as he did a love for the sun above. Someone who came from unseen waters and just as much a place far off the map, and brought the first of your folk here—to home. And the sacrifice he made under the watchful eye of the sun and moon themselves, those that shepherded his journey across seas, and over the grounds of what would one day become Etaynia."

I needed no further words. The crowd knows the cue and takes their seats—silent, still, waiting for a story to begin. One that will flatter all they hold in best regard about themselves, and their history.

Some only want this flattery—their vanity laid plain in a tale. Some want to see themselves a hero, simple and nothing more. Some more simply want for a safe place to explore their many curiosities left unfulfilled in their real lives. But the underlying truth of all the best stories?

They give you the chance to escape. To another place. Another time. And other people. For those moments, you are safe—free, and you are in a world that can only be found in stories.

A magic of a different sort. An old one. The most powerful one.

Eloine takes her place and we begin the dance. Slow at first, moving counter to one another as if on trailing strings that have locked us in position.

Another binding then. I ease out of the folds and let go the imagery of the booming voice and thunder. This is a time for softer things, and not all stories need a voice to tell them. I think back to shadows shaped along a wall, and to the one who made them. Then to dancing puppets formed of light—a trick and making I have only seen once.

My cloak grows tighter around my throat at the thought, but I pay it little mind. There is a world of tiny dancing flames around me, and I turn my heart and mind toward them. Candlelight and soft lamp glow give me all I need. The folds return and I imagine them as strings of brightened orange that I can pull on, and I do so.

"Tak. Roh." Each band leaps toward the space I envision, the soft cup of my hands. I remember another time now—a lesson, and the one who gave it to me. "Whent. Ern." The space is now to my desire and my making, and so I shape it still to nurse the flames in my keeping and save my skin from their touch.

For a moment, there is no light but for that in my hold. All eyes rest on the flames in my hand, and their glow washes a better brightness out of my mask and Eloine's. There are only two figures worthy of holding the whole of your attention. Her, and myself. The moon, and the ever-burning sun.

We resume the dance and I turn the folds of mind again, now imagining the flame as living clay. My fingers knead and pinch bits of fire free from the larger mass. They come to shape under my touch, and soon hangs a ship of tonal oranges.

Eloine sucks in a breath but never breaks her stride.

I smile, keeping the dance going as I craft more flame-born figures. Soon there is a man atop the ship and I carry him through the air until he reaches his destination. A country now fills the sky, no larger than my fist, but its shape unforgettable. Its lines are those every Etaynian would know had they ever looked at a map.

Home.

Our hero leaves his ship but there is no rest nor solace for the weary sailor. For he and his are set upon the moment of their arrival. Flames turn to arrows—others, lances—and strike down men I weave from dancing shadows.

Eloine watches, never saying a word, but the shape of her mouth tells me something brews behind it. She wishes to speak. Has something to say—perhaps sing.

I leave the flames hanging where they are and take a step from her, breaking our harmony.

She does the same, and in doing so, we grow further distant.

But there is a tug—an unseen pull between the two of us, an unseen binding, like once-red thread, and it lures us back but for a step. The dance resumes. Slower now. We watch the scene between us—shaped flames and the men who've fallen. Grief strikes Eloine's face, and it is for those under the moon's watchful eye that have fallen.

Eloine comes closer then.

And she breaks the silence between us.

"So long in wandering,
have you been.
Set far to traveling,
far from this watchful gaze,
seeking that I do not know of,
farther still from my love.

Chased by shadowed hunger,
and its wolfish grin.
I've set to trailing in your wake,
hoping to catch you still,
and have your heart in mine to take.

There is a hole in this heart seeking after mine,
of empty call and mournful pine,
a thing so broken,
lonely made,
with nothing left to fill its need,

left now only,
in the hold of shadowed greed."

I want to listen longer, but the song is not for this story. My look makes this clear, and I nearly falter in my confusion. But Eloine smiles still, uncaring for the measure of the tale. Hers is a different story now, and she tells it to me still.

I return to shaping the flame, bringing out the scenes of war that follow. Still quiet now, and taking our sailor strong against the tide of those that held these lands before. His arm moves, familiar patterns once burned clear into me by a man more a dancer than a swordsman.

Faceless forms fall before him with ease, but like many a hero's story, this is a tragedy in the making. And so too he must face that reality.

It draws nearer now.

The sun and moon come closer, watching over the one they've chosen to carve out a kingdom of their own.

Eloine breaks from me again.

"A sun born of itself,
and cast free-flickering,
now left in wandering,
its flame eclipsed,
all thoughts lost,
but for remembering."

I falter once again. Not for the interruption, but what she said.

"But the moon is all things,
and memory,
she remembers still,
and keeps your secrets,
close to heart,
and safe // ly

a reminder to this errant son,
that your secrets are still safe with me

but she asks one thing in return,
for this son of suns to dig deep,
into stories lost,

and kept tight in old,
me // mo // ry

all so he can,
remember,
remember me."

I stop, but the practiced story of old carries me on in motions unforgotten. The tale reaches its height, and I am in need of a volunteer now.

My eyes scan the balconies and I find them absent of the thing promised to be there. A man in want of vengeance, and his promise to help me right a wrong.

Thunder takes my heart and threatens to hold it till it can no longer keep to the beating tempo.

Am I betrayed? Has the plan been discovered? Or both, and I have set the stage for myself to be taken.

Even still, I cannot break the performance, and keep to the artist's hope that somehow the story will resolve as I dream.

I catch sight of a shadow pressed hard against the balcony wall. Its shape is one known to me, as is that of its heart.

So easy a thing to have a change of that now and end a different man's story tonight.

Mine.

Because hearts are fickle things—prone to changing. They do not bow or bend to man's logic. Theirs is their own, and they do not move to rhyme or reason, but to a music sung silent all for them. Songs all their own.

I stretch out a hand—an invitation. "And now for the hero of the story to come join us. To receive the blessing of the sun and moon as a brave sailor did so long ago before laying down his life to shape Carmeaum, long before it was ever to become Etaynia. The man who would spread word of Solus far across its plains, and the man who wishes to still hold to this faith and mission today."

It could be no one else, and I spot Prince-elect Efraine recognize the call. He rises, chest held high with pride.

And that can be quite the dangerous thing.

He marches onto the dais, smiling and waving to fresh applause. The man is dressed in the royal red and golden bright of noblest blood.

The dance resumes and we circle him now.

The hero of the story makes flourishes of his own, swatting at the flaming enemies and brandishing his muscles. Small signs. But the crowd takes it in delight.

A shadow grows bolder along the balcony.

And the story has come to its conclusion.

I reach back into the folds and pull on the fiery figures, drawing a row of arrows from them. They rain down on the burning bright hero, but he remains unstruck. But it does not matter, because there are always more of those—unseen, all ready to strike a man's heart.

And so it is tonight.

I mime a bow of my own as a shaping of fire does so too. We loose. Mine, empty air. The fire's takes the hero of flame I'd conjured, straight through the chest.

But there is the third arrow still.

And it sails down from up on high.

I move, flourishing my cloak. My will bleeds into the fabric blood-red all. Its length trails longer then. It is a streamer cast wide before the prince-elect's body, and sweeps to swallow the flames I'd once cast.

The scene is darkness now as Prince-elect Efraine collapses, hands pressed to the arrow that has found his heart.

One. Perfect. Shot.

Eloine does not see it in the happening at first. She moves close to me and comes to take her bow. I join her just as the crowd breaks into soft applause, for they know this is not a story for loud celebration now.

But their expressions are all that of joy and of equal measured pride.

Until the length of my cloak moves away. And I break my folds to release the fires to where they'd once been.

Light.

The pontifex is the first to see it, eyes wide in realization. His mouth moves in the silence after the applause fades. Then the screaming begins.

My head does not move, but I cast my eyes to the balcony and the figure still lingering there.

Move, fool. What are you doing?

He draws closer now, coming into what light there is. The man looks as if he'd been underfed his whole life, though the cut of his cloth could match any noble's. Sharp, in all detail, as much as wit and temper. Though it is by his anger I know him best. His hatred. His vengeance.

Brahm's blood, man. Run!

He throws his crossbow over the balcony for all to see. Eyes turn to him now, and men with swords are already in motion.

"My name is Ernesto Vengenza, and you killed my prince. My *efante*." No more venom could be found in the world than what his words held. No Arasmus knife had an edge quite as keen or promised sharp. Ernesto Vengenza glares down at the body of Prince-elect Efraine.

The spell is broken, and the story is ended.

I looked down at the king-to-be. His chest moved in the shallow motions of someone well close to death. The shaft rested in his heart, and he would not be long for this world.

Ernesto would not find peace in that knowledge, however. "Prince Arturo was a good man. A just and kind man. He was an *efante* of Etaynia, and would have been a great king. He would have been *my* king. You killed him, and I cannot give him justice. So I give him vengeance." He spat over the balcony. "And I am satisfied."

Prince-elect Efraine's breath grew shallower, and the light of his eyes slowly dimmed, but that is not what held my attention. I had sheltered him but for a moment behind a piece of my cloak, red as blood. But that leaving Efraine came a different color altogether.

His blood ran black as night. The color of shadows. The hateful hue found in the Tainted.

A prince of Etaynia was dead.

And I had killed him.

Long live Etaynia.

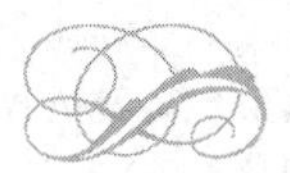

ONE HUNDRED THIRTY-FOUR

A Victory in Stillness

The king's garden sat in stillness.

A silence.

The restless quietude which yearned to be broken, but the weight of what transpired had laid leaden all tongues, bidding them to preserve the shrouding hush that had fallen over the audience.

Hands pressed to mouths, keeping them shut in the quiet of secrets best left unsaid. The sort of held-breath silence that threatened to swallow all other noises, for the scene unfolding demanded that unspoken watchfulness from all in attendance. This was the unmoving horror held hard in witnessing the death of a prince, and the quieter-still question making all wonder who would be next.

The emptiness in heart that had dared dream of better days—now left the sullen hollowness that could not hope to be filled.

This was the smothered, silent noiselessness of a kingdom that had died.

. . . And become ripe for the taking.

It was the stillness of a holy man, with all the waiting-patience of the watchful wolf in face. The quiet cunning of a man whose eyes carried the gold-orange light of candle flame, and the curve of whose mouth said one thing: *victory*.

This was the careful, measured quiet of a man who had been playing a long and dangerous game.

And who had just won.

Because I had just given him the victory he so sorely sought.

The silence hung through the grounds, and it brought about all the stillness of one last breath from a world before the storm. And all the quiet of the hangman's wind—the empty breath to leave ships in doldrums, and their crews to die.

Someone screamed.

And the stillness gave way, like it had done once before.

So long ago. And by my own hand.

The crowd surged; most broke back toward Del Soliel, but some rushed toward the fallen *efante*'s body.

I watched as the pontifex stared back at me, then the fallen prince, and we both wondered the same question in our silence. In our shared stillness.

Who now would come into power?

Who would rule Etaynia?

I had a feeling, as much a fear, that we had both come to the same conclusion. And it had been done by my hand. My misstep.

With the throne and church better allied under Efraine's proclamation, what could stop the pontifex from making a claim to the crown?

Brahm's blood, what have I done?

"The prince-elect is dead!" came a voice.

A prince of Etaynia lay dead.

The second the stories will say I've killed.

We are all legends in the making. Stories. Breathed to life and given form. Yours is no less exceptional than any other. Your story is your own. Find it. Pursue it. Passionately. Chase it off the corners of your map, and then some. You will come to make your personal legend true.

This, I did.
—Tarun Tharambadh

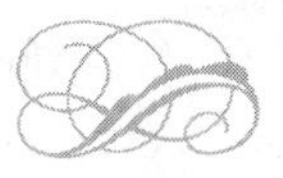

Acknowledgments

To Katie Norris for too many reasons to list, but certainly being an angel, and very patient during a lot. Stone Sanchez for being a textbook definition of great friend. Yudhanjaya Wijeratne for nearly a decade of brotherhood. Nancy Greene for being wonderfully kind, supporting, and openhearted. Michael Mammay for no end of support, kindness, good advice, and going above and beyond the call of friendship. He knows what I mean.

This book might not be dedicated to Jim Butcher, but I will never miss a chance to thank him for being a great human being, and always being there for people. In a world that can get pretty dark, Jim's one of the brightest lights.

And, LJ Hachmeister. The world lost one of those best and brightest lights this year when you left us. You were a special kind of candle flame in this life. You made this place better.

I'll miss you.

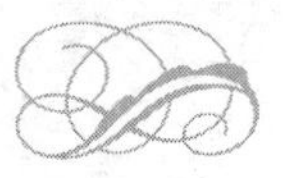

About the Author

R.R. Virdi is a two-time Dragon Award finalist, Nebula Award finalist, and *USA Today* bestselling author. He is the author of two urban fantasy series, the Grave Report and the Books of Winter, as well as the epic fantasy novel *The First Binding.*

He was born and raised in Northern Virginia and is a first-generation Indian American, with all the baggage that comes with. He's offended a long list of incalculable ancestors by choosing to drop out of college and not pursue one of three predestined careers: lawyer, doctor, or engineer. Instead, he decided to chase his dream of being an author. His family is still coping with this decision a decade later. He expects them to come around in another fifteen to twenty years.

rrvirdi.com